Cowboy Dreamin'

Make Mine a Cowboy
Healing a Cowboy's Heart
For the Love of a Cowboy
Tempted by the Cowboy
Forever Kind of Cowboy
Kiss Me, Cowboy
A Cowboy and a Country Song
A Cowboy of My Own
A Cowboy's Promise

Erotic Romance

Sandy Sullivan

Dedication

For the cowboy lover is all of us!

MAKE MINE A COWBOY
Cowboy Dreamin' 1
Sandy Sullivan

Chapter One

"No, no, no, no!" Mesa Arraguso banged on the steering wheel of her rental car with both fists. The gas gauge read *E*. "I can't be out of gas! I'm in the middle of fucking nowhere." The sting of heat from the leather burned her fingertips. The stifling warmth rose exponentially inside the car without the air conditioning running. It was, after all, the middle of May in Bandera, Texas.

A rumble of thunder broke the stillness as she contemplated what to do. She'd taken a drive to clear her head and jumpstart her muse for her next book, not end up on the side of the road, out of gas, with no houses within several miles.

This was cowboy country. Hill Country in Texas boasted some of the biggest longhorn cattle spreads in the state. Several cattle mooed in the distance but she couldn't tell how close a house might be. At least cattle meant humans…somewhere.

Large banks of dark clouds continued to roll across the sky. Several huge raindrops hit her windshield with a loud *splat* before the sky opened up in a torrential downpour.

"Just fucking great. Now fate is going to throw me into a huge thunderstorm. Why? Because I was stupid enough to go for a drive by myself during a writer's conference in San Antonio and I ended up out here in the middle of the country. Now, I'm stuck on the side of some dirt road, out of gas, and God only knows how far from the nearest house."

Lightning flashed, followed shortly by a loud crash of thunder. Mesa jumped. A shiver raced through her body as her heart clenched in fear. She hated thunderstorms.

Her cell phone beeped—the ominous sound of no cell phone coverage. *Great!*

She glanced out the window and saw water rushing under her car along a gulley she didn't realize she'd straddled when she stopped. "Shit. Flash flooding? I'm so screwed."

As the water began rising rapidly, she realized she needed to get the hell out of her car before it was washed away. In the distance she could make out several larger rocks. "If I can get on top of them, I should be safe from the rush. Of course, that means I'll be out in the rain getting soaked." Fear rose, threatening to choke her with the lump in her throat. She rubbed her arms trying to calm the chills while deciding what to do. She really didn't have much choice. Water ran in rivulets down the windshield. Lightning continued to flash and thunder rolled over the area. She sucked in a large breath as she bit her lip.

A moment later a *tap, tap, tap* on her window startled her out of her thoughts. She jumped and screamed as a face appeared near her door. Blue eyes with long lashes stared back beneath a black cowboy hat. Black hair ruffled slightly with the wind.

"Ma'am? Are you all right?"

"I'm fine."

"You need to get this car out of the water. You'll be washed away. It's rising fast."

"I can't. I'm out of gas."

"Open the door."

"Hell, no. Do I look crazy to you?" she asked, her voice shrill with terror.

"Trust me. If I were a serial killer, I wouldn't be out in this shit trying to find women to abduct. I'm going to help you, but you need to get out of the car first before we're both swept away."

Mesa bit her lip. Should she trust him?

"Ma'am?"

"All right." She eased open the door to find the water almost reached the bottom of the car. The cowboy pulled the door the rest of the way as she grabbed her purse.

"We have to hurry," he said, offering her a hand to help her from the car. "Let me help you. This water is rushing pretty fast."

A red horse stood patiently several feet away with its head down, riding out the storm the only way horses knew how. *A cowboy on a real horse out here in the middle of nowhere? Surely, it's safe. I mean serial killers don't ride horses, right?*

Her tennis shoes were soaked the moment she stepped into the rushing stream, chilling her feet even though the temperature outside today was a balmy ninety degrees. She shivered as the man pulled her from the car, but chalked it up to her cold toes rather than the broad chest, wide shoulders and trim hips of the cowboy in front of her.

Oompf!

"Sorry, ma'am," he said, setting her back from where she landed against his chest. "Let's get out of this downpour." He slammed the car door before he pulled her toward his horse. "You'll have to ride behind me."

"No problem."

His ass looked fabulous swinging up into the saddle. *What the hell? I'm checking him out like a piece of meat and the man is here saving my butt from drowning.*

"Ma'am?" he asked, holding out his hand so he could help her behind the saddle.

"Oh, yeah right. Thanks." She swung up behind him and grabbed his waist like a drowning victim in the middle of a raging surf. "Sorry."

"No problem. You need to hang on. I don't want to dump you off the back."

"I'm sorry you're getting wet because of me."

"I was wet before I found you. I've been ridin' fences in between the downpours."

The horse sidestepped to the right. A squeal broke from her lips. "Sorry."

"You don't have to apologize, ma'am. I shoulda asked if you were okay on horseback."

As the horse continued forward she caught the rhythm of its walk and relaxed into the gait. "My name is Mesa."

"Excuse me?"

"Mesa is my name. I feel like some fifty-year-old woman with you calling me ma'am."

"Sorry. Habit."

"I can imagine."

"It's nice to meet you, Mesa. I'm Joel."

"Hi, Joel. Do you live around here?" she asked, liking the feel of his firm chest beneath her fingertips until she let them slip down to wrap around his waist. The urge to run her hands along the ridges under his wet shirt overwhelmed her, sending tingles up her arms. She could feel the ripped abdomen beneath her palms.

"A few miles up the road. My family owns a ranch on the ridge."

The man knew his way around horses from the way he sat comfortably in the saddle riding the animal's gait like he was born to it.

Well duh, Mesa.

The rain had moved off, only pelting them now and then with big, fat drops. The smell of wet leather reached her nose and she wrinkled the bridge at the stench. Another smell permeated her senses. Cologne? She slowly inhaled, taking in the scent from his shirt. *Damn, he smells good.*

"What are you doin' out here on this back road?"

"I took a drive. I've been in San Antonio at a conference and I needed to clear my head."

He chuckled, a low, dry reverberation that made her sit up and take notice. Her nipples pebbled at the sound, sending frustration down her back. Could he feel the hard nubs rubbing against his solid back? *Probably, you dummy.* It had been way too long since she'd been with a man if just sitting close to one made her horny. The rear end of a horse wasn't the place to get hot and bothered.

The material of her shirt caught against her breasts. The rough fabric of her jeans chafed the inside of her thighs. The seam of her pants rubbed against her clit, turning her insides to mush. Never mind the clean, musky scent of the man squashed against her boobs.

"What kind of conference were you at?"

"A romance writer's conference."

"Romance writer?"

"Yes. I'm an author. I write romance novels."

"Oh."

She waited for him to ask what type of romance novels she wrote, but he didn't. Wasn't he interested? Maybe not. Really, how could she tell him she wrote about guys like him? Westerns. Cowboys. Riding off into the sunset with some hunky cowboy on horseback. It would be totally embarrassing to tell him, so maybe it would be a good thing he didn't ask. "Where are we headed, by the way?"

"My parents' place." He chuckled again. "We'll get you some warm, dry clothes to change into. If the car didn't get washed away, we'll get you some gas so you can make it back to San Antonio."

"Thank you. You don't know how much I appreciate you coming to my rescue."

"It's what cowboys do."

Oh, hell yeah, they do. Especially in my dreams.

They continued chatting about mundane things as they plodded along. The constant shift of the horse's rump made her realize how long it had been since she'd ridden. *How far was this place anyway?* "Joel?"

"Yeah."

"How much farther?"

"A mile or so."

"Hell."

"Somethin' wrong?"

"I'm gonna feel every step this horse took tomorrow."

A deep laugh started beneath her fingers and rumbled up his chest until it burst from his lips. "You are too much, Mesa."

"I'm glad I could make your day," she grumbled, a little put out by his laughter. "I haven't been on horseback in ages. My thighs are already screaming mercy." She felt his body quiver from laughter again. "How do you ride all day without dying?"

"I'm used to it. I ride all day everyday so it doesn't bother me."

"You live on a working ranch?"

"Yep. Longhorns and city folk."

"Huh?"

"We have what most folks call a dude ranch. We let people come and stay on the ranch. Do ranch work, ride horses…you know, play at bein' a cowboy for a while."

"Really? That sounds like fun."

"How long are you in town for?"

"The conference is over in a couple of days."

"So you're flyin' or drivin' home afterward?"

"Flying, yes."

He got quiet for several minutes as the horse continued to walk along under his expert guiding hand. "What kind of books do you write?"

There it was. "Westerns."

"Oh yeah? Like cowboys and Indians? Louie L'Amour type stuff?"

She shook her head and almost unseated herself from the back of the horse. A fistful of his shirt kept her in place. "No. Like cowboys and the love of their lives. I write erotic modern westerns."

"Interestin'."

The house came into view and she sighed in relief. She'd be able to get off the back of the horse shortly, but it also meant giving up sitting behind Joel and removing her hands from his magnificent chest.

As they rode into the yard, she could see what appeared to be a main house and several smaller cabins of some sort. She assumed this is where the guests stayed. A large corral sat in the back of the biggest building where several horses stood. A handful of cowboys hung around the front of the tack room.

One guy stepped forward, taking the reins of the horse as she slid off the left side. "Hey, Joel. Where'd you pick up a rider?"

"Behave yourselves," Joel answered, swinging down from his saddle. "This is a lady whose car stalled out near the north pasture line. Mesa, these are some of my brothers, Joseph, Jackson and Josh. Guys, this is Mesa."

"Howdy, ma'am," Joseph said, tipping his hat.

Wow, twins? "Do you all always call every woman ma'am?"

"Yes, ma'am," Jackson replied. "Our mama would skin our hides if we didn't."

"Well, call me Mesa, please. I feel old when you call me ma'am."

"So." Josh moved closer, taking her hand and slipping it through the crook in his elbow. "How did a beauty like you get stuck with Joel?"

"Uh…" she stammered slightly as she blushed from the attention.

"Enough, Joshua. I'm taking her into the house so Mom can help her into some dry clothes," Joel said, taking her hand from his brother and capturing it within the warmth of his own. Tingles started in her fingers and worked their way up her arm. She frowned at the sensation. Surely she wasn't attracted to Joel other than being grateful for his rescue? *Why the hell not? I fantasize about cowboys all the time. He's the finest specimen of a cowboy I've ever seen.*

"Don't mind them, Mesa. They're all bachelors. When a pretty woman gets within fifty feet of them, they can't help but drool and act like idiots."

He thinks I'm pretty? "Thank you for the compliment."

"It's true. Anyway, let's get you inside and dry."

"You don't have to do that. My clothes are almost dry now from the heat."

"I'm sure you could use something to drink and to at least dry your shoes. I can hear 'em squishing from here."

"True." She laughed as she wiggled her wet shoe. "I would be nice to put them in a dryer along with my socks. I'll probably get blisters."

"Mom will try to feed you too since it's almost supper time around here."

"I hope I'm not taking you from your chores. You said you were checking fences when you found me."

"It'll be fine," he said as they walked toward the large, house-like structure. "We don't work on any time schedule."

Built out of what appeared to be logs and flagstone, the house boasted three huge dormers, a porch the size of a football field stretching across its front, and huge, wooden doors on the side they were headed toward. Joel held the door as she made her way into the dining room. Several picnic tables lined the huge room. Each one gleamed from the sunlight now pouring in through the big windows. Rough wood paneling lined the walls with a brand burned into several boards—TR with a circle around it. Huh. Interesting. *I wonder what it stands for?*

"Thunder Ridge."

He read my mind?

"It's the brand our cattle wear too."

"It's really cool you have it burned into the wood on the walls."

The smell of cooking food floated to her nose. Her stomach growled impatiently when she realized she hadn't eaten since breakfast. Joel grinned and her heart flipped over in her chest. *Damn, he has a sexy smile.* He could probably melt butter with that grin.

With her hands still encased in the warmth of his, he tugged her along toward a room in the back. "Come on. We'll get you something dry to wear, put your shoes in the dryer, and get you some food." As they approached the back of the dining hall, she noticed a small office built into the back of the huge room. The woman taping away at the computer screen seemed oblivious to their presence until Joel said, "Mom?" Mesa could see where Joel got his black hair. The cascading length only added to the woman's stunning beauty.

"Hey baby." She glanced up with the same blue eyes that Joel had and stared. "What'cha got there?"

"I found her out on the road with her car stalled."

Indignation ruffled her ego, causing her back stiffened. They were making her sound like some lost puppy or something.

"Well, welcome to Thunder Ridge. I'm Nina Young. This here is my son, or one of them anyway." She held out her hand and when Mesa took it, she pumped it several times.

"Mesa Arraguso. I'm sorry to intrude. I don't want to make you feel like you're taking in a lost stray."

"Nonsense. No intrusion. We love company. It's why we run a dude ranch." Nina looked at her clothes and said, "Oh my. You're soaked, honey. Let's get you something dry to put on. You look about my size. I'm sure I have something that will fit." Nina shuffled her out of the office leaving Joel standing in the doorway. "Come with me."

Nina walked her through another huge room with an enormous fireplace standing from floor to ceiling and almost wall-to-wall. Large leather couches invited people to sit in front of a roaring fire, should there be one blazing away. Not today, though.

Mesa followed Nina toward the back of the room and down another long hallway with a door marked private. *Must be the family's quarters.*

"What on Earth were you doing out on a back road like ours?"

"Running out of gas."

"Oh my, really?"

"Yes. I took a drive and my GPS got lost. Did you know some of these roads aren't on the thing?"

Nina laughed. "Oh yes. Our road doesn't exist on most of them because it's on our land. We maintain it ourselves." Mesa continued to follow Nina toward a set of double doors at the end of the hall. "We should be able to find you something to wear. Would you like jeans or a dress?"

"Anything is fine. I really appreciate this."

The room looked rustic with its wood walls, large bed, and wooden dresser along the left wall. Paintings depicted different flower arrangements of pinks and purples, matching the floral comforter on the bed. A couple of good sized windows overlooked what appeared to be a garden with roses, lilacs, and several other species of flowers she didn't recognize.

"We'll get you something." Nina opened a door to the right, exposing a huge walk-in closet with rows of clothes hanging on each side. Everything was color coded with yellows together, blues together, and so on.

"Damn."

"I have a thing for clothes. My husband calls it an obsession." She shrugged. "What can I say, I love to shop, although most of this never gets worn since we live out here on the ranch. I'm usually in jeans." Nina grabbed a red sundress off the rack. "This should fit you. Plus, red would look fabulous on you with your black hair." With a tilt of her head, she looked Mesa over from head to toe. "Do you have Native American blood?"

"Yes. Somewhere in my past, anyway. I'm not sure how far back."

"Ah." Nina handed her the dress before she walked to the window to look out. "You're lucky to have received the thick, dark hair of your heritage like some of my sons did from me. I am a quarter Choctaw."

"I have no idea how much or what tribe my ancestors were. It's not talked about much in my family."

Nine turned back to face her with a stern look in her blue eyes. "You should be proud of your heritage no matter how little Indian blood runs through your veins. We are a proud people. I try to bestow on my sons the love of the tribal people."

"How many sons do you have? I've met four so far."

"I have nine. My wishes for a daughter were never answered, although I hope to have beautiful daughter-in-laws and lots of granddaughters when the time comes. I have one grandson already, from my oldest son's failed marriage, whom I adore, but it's not the same as having a granddaughter to spoil." Nina took her hands and spread them wide. "You would make a beautiful daughter-in-law."

"Wait a minute. I don't even live near here. I live in California."

"I'm joking, Mesa, although you are a beautiful young woman and any one of my sons would be proud to call you wife."

"I'm only here for a few days. No matchmaking while I'm here."

Nina laughed and tipped her chin toward the floor. "No matchmaking." She walked toward the door. "I'll leave you to change. If you bring your wet clothes and shoes down the hall, we'll get them washed and dried for you. The supper bell will be ringing soon. You will join us for dinner, won't you?"

"I would love to, Nina. Thank you for all you've done for me. You have a beautiful home. I wish I could stay longer to explore. It would make a great backdrop for one of my books."

"You're a writer?"

"Yes, ma'am." Mesa blushed, dropping her gaze to the dress in her hands.

"You must tell me all about it at dinner. I can't wait to hear what you write about." She opened the door. "I'll see you in a few minutes. Take your time. There are sandals at the bottom of the closet that might fit you temporarily until your shoes dry."

With a soft snick of the door, she was gone, leaving Mesa in the middle of the huge bedroom to contemplate the turn of events her day had taken. First she ran out of gas, and then was rescued by a handsome, melt your panties cowboy, and now she stood in the middle of a magnificent bedroom borrowing clothing from a woman so gorgeous she could stop traffic. Wow, what a day this turned out to be. She surely didn't think things like this happened to ordinary women like her. Adventures didn't come her way on a routine basis. She could count on one hand how many men she'd been out with her in lifetime. Slept with? That would only take a few fingers.

After she quickly slipped off her wet clothes and put on the red sundress, she smoothed the material over her hips. The dress fit perfectly. A pair of leather beaded sandals sat inside the closet. They looked like they would fit. Slipping her feet into the cool leather, she wasn't surprised to realize they too fit perfectly. Weird. Joel's mother wore the same sizes she did?

Not wanting to be late for dinner as she heard the clang of the dinner bell, she grabbed the clothes from the floor and opened the bedroom door.

Joel stood on the other side with a wide grin, propped against the wall with his arms over his chest.

"Well now. Don't you look pretty?"

"Thank you, sir." She dipped a small curtsey.

"I'm here to show you where the washer and dryer are, and then escort you to supper since the crowd is already gathering."

"I'd appreciate it, since I don't know my way around the house."

He took the clothes from her arms before he grabbed her hand with his warm one. "This way."

Within moments, they had her clothes washing as her stomach growled again because of the mouthwatering smells coming from the dining room.

"Let's get you some food before you waste away to nothing," he said with a large grin. They headed back down the hall in the direction of the clanking utensils.

"Oh please. I'm plenty plump that I could miss a few meals."

"You are not plump. Rounded in all the right places, I'd say."

"Flatterer."

He stopped and glanced down at her with a serious look on his face. "Don't let my brothers ride roughshod over you, because they will. They're a bunch of men, after all."

"I think I can handle it."

"Don't be too sure. I'll jump in to protect you."

"Aw, thank you, Joel." She skimmed her free hand down his chest. "What a gentleman." *What the hell made me do that?*

Her reflex was to pull her hand back, but Joel grabbed it in his before she could. "You're a beautiful woman. Other than guests, which are normally families with young kids, we don't get a lot like you around here. Prepare to be overwhelmed."

He kissed her fingers before he let his grip slacken on her hand so she could pull it free. The zing that raced up her arm bothered her. Those things only happened in her novels, not in real life. "Um, okay."

As they rounded the doorway, the volume of noise increased tenfold. Several people either sat at the picnic tables chatting away or they were lined up at the serving area with plates in hand. One long table she hadn't noticed before took up an entire wall. When she did a double take she noticed nine people, eight men and Joel's mother, who sat there chatting while they waited for the others to be served. *Holy shit! How many freakin' brothers does he have again?*

"Eight. There are nine of us boys."

"Stop reading my mind."

"Sorry. I can tell by the look in your eyes what is running through your head. You have very expressive brown eyes." Joel tugged her hand and brought her to the spot where there were two empty seats. "Hey, ya'll. This is Mesa." A chorus of hellos echoed through the room, shushing the rest of the conversations going on around them. Joel quickly introduced the brothers around the table and that's when she noticed two more who looked like…ohmigod. *There are three of him?* Yes, you could tell they all were brothers by the similar features, but…

"We're triplets," he whispered next to her ear with a chuckle.

Ah, hell! One gorgeous hunk to tantalize my senses is enough, but nine of them? And two who look just like him? I'm so screwed!

Chapter Two

Joel thought she looked cute with her eyes wide. Most people were surprised when they realized he, Jason, and Joshua were identical triplets. "Let's get our plates," he said, as the group of men took their places at the serving line. "We all wait until the guests have been served before we get ours. Mom's orders."

"She's a wise woman."

"Yes, she is."

"She must be tough as nails to raise nine boys, especially with three of them all the same age."

"I'm sure it hasn't been easy, but Dad is a strong man too. Never took any guff from any of us boys."

"Where is your father?" she asked.

"He's in the barn I imagine. One of the mares is foaling. He likes to be there in case there are any problems."

"Now, that I would love to see."

He shook his head and laughed. For a woman who wrote about cowboys and ranch life, she sure didn't seem to have much hands-on-experience with it. "We'll head out to the barn after supper to see how it's coming. Maybe you'll get lucky."

"Thank you. This is sure turning into an interesting day. I can't believe my luck. At first I thought I had about run out of any kind of luck when my car ran out of gas, but you showed up and rescued me."

"Oh, by the way, Jeff and Jeremiah brought your car to the ranch while you changed clothes. You left your keys in the ignition so they gassed it up before they drove it back here."

The server slid a hamburger bun with a large burger patty on her plate. "Wow. You guys eat hearty around here."

"Wait until you taste it. Even though I live here, I never get tired of the food. They always seem to get just the right taste on everything."

Next came the condiments, a bag of chips, and pink lemonade. The perfect picnic type supper. He led Mesa back to two chairs at the family table, hoping his brothers would behave. She seemed like a lady…a beautiful one at that. Sure, he'd been with lots of beautiful women before. After all, the reputation around San Antonio, and Bandera especially, had the Young brothers as catchable material for the mothers of the town. They had land—a worthy commodity in the hill country. Sure they had the reputation of being playboys, but it made them all the more chaseable to women.

"What were you doing out in this neck of the woods, Mesa?" Joshua asked.

"Running out of gas in the middle of nowhere."

They all laughed as she blushed a pretty shade of pink. "Actually, I've been searching for inspiration."

"For?" Jeff questioned. As the oldest of the brothers, he always had a suspicious mind about strangers hanging around the area. There were too many accidents happening lately, accidents involving their cattle. They had to be careful. Too many of the neighboring ranches were being bought out by big corporations wanting the land for housing developments.

"Inspiration for my books. I'm a writer."

"What do you write?" Nina asked.

"Romance novels."

"Really? How very cool. I'm an avid reader of romance myself. Are you published?"

"Yes, ma'am. I have a pen name, though."

"Why don't you write under your own name? Mesa is a beautiful name and very different. I would think it would be a great pen name."

"I love my first name. My mother wanted something special for me when I was born. My father is Italian and my mother said she is Mexican with a little Indian blood. I write under Mesa West."

"You have the beautiful dark hair and sharp facial features of your ancestors, Mesa. Do not be ashamed of it."

"Thank you, Nina. You've made me very welcome in your home."

"You are welcome anytime. I hope you come and visit another time when you can stay longer."

"Actually, I'm in the area because of a writer's conference in San Antonio. If you have room here at the ranch, I'd love to stay a few days?"

"Of course we do. I have a special room in the main house you can have all to yourself."

"Which room, Mom? I'll make sure it's ready for her. I imagine she'll need to go back to town to get her clothes."

"Yes, I will. Thank you, Joel. You've been more than kind."

"So what kind of books do you write?" Jacob asked.

Mesa pressed her lips together as a deep blush stained her cheeks. Apparently, she thought it embarrassing to tell a bunch of cowboys she writes about them with sexy heroines. He would have to learn more about her writing while she stayed at the ranch. Having never read a romance novel, he really had no idea what they had in them.

"She writes about cowboys," Joel said, earning himself raised eyebrows from his brothers. He shrugged his shoulders as he put a potato chip in his mouth. "What? I already asked her."

"It's true. I write about cowboys in modern day and historical settings."

"How hot?" Nina questioned, sitting forward in her chair. "I love the erotic stories."

"Very hot," Mesa answered.

"If you have some with you, make sure to bring them back. I would love to read some of yours. Cowboys are right up my alley."

The boys laughed as the subject changed to other topics including the buyouts of the other ranches.

"The Mitchells are selling," his father said as he approached the table with a plate in hand.

"Mesa, this is my father, James Young. Dad, this is Mesa."

"It's nice to meet you, Mesa."

"You too, sir."

"Shit, seriously? They're selling?" Jeff cursed. "Excuse my language, Mom. Mesa. How many more are we gonna lose to these sharks?"

"I don't know, Jeff. They seem to be buying up the ranches who have been hit the hardest by the beef prices. The drought hasn't helped either. Feed is scarce in this country half the time anyway, but when it doesn't rain, it's worse."

"We've managed to stay ahead by doing the dude ranch thing, right, Dad?" Jonathan added to the conversation.

"So far, yes. We've had a great clientele of guests to keep things going, but the prices are hurting even us."

Joel knew their whole lives depended on this ranch. They couldn't lose it. But the developers driving the local ranchers out only spelled harder times for everyone. The hill country was home, had been since before he could walk. The five thousand acres encompassing Thunder Ridge Ranch would be their legacy. Each of them. They all had a stake in the place and as far as he knew, they all planned to stay and ranch their own small section deeded to each brother when they turned eighteen.

His parents bought the ranch when his mom had been carrying his younger brother, Jonathan. Little did she know there would be a total of nine before she finished. Now, she wanted daughter-in-laws.

He chuckled under his breath. Little did his mother know, none of them had any aspirations of a bride at the moment. She wouldn't care, though. Fixing them up with decent women had become her pastime these days.

The rest of the conversation around the table went back and forth between who might be going out tonight to the rain pushing through the area earlier. Even though flash flooding could be a constant worry, they needed the life-giving essence of the rain. The ground right now needed it badly.

"If you want to head back into town after supper to get your things, I'll make sure your room is ready."

"Thank you, Joel."

"If you're back in time, we're having a bonfire later out near the pit. Most of the guests will be there."

"Sounds like fun. I haven't been to a bonfire in ages."

"We'll get you countrified while you're here if it kills us, city girl."

Mesa laughed. The sound sent chills down his back as goose bumps spread across his arms. The soft tinkle of her laughter reverberated along his nerves before settling in his groin. Not good. Getting mixed up with a guest on the ranch always came back to bite a guy in the ass He'd caved into the urge once or twice, much to his regret and his brothers' enjoyment. Not to say he didn't get his shots in when they decided to play. "I can show you more of the ranch tomorrow so you can get some ideas of the life."

The fork disappeared between her plump lips. *God, I never thought watching someone eat was sexy before.* Her brown eyes sparkled in the overhead lighting of the dining hall. He shook his head. Thoughts of her in any kind of romantic situation would just lead to trouble.

"I would appreciate it. I have a vivid imagination but to have firsthand knowledge is priceless. Makes it much easier to describe scenes when you have information."

"Do you know horses?" he asked, pushing his empty plate back.

"A few. I don't have any of my own, but I've ridden before."

"We can do some ranch work tomorrow if you like. Ride fences and the like."

Her smile lit up the room like a beacon for wayward ships at sea.

"Awesome. I haven't been on a real working ranch before so this will be the best experience I could ask for."

"Joel, you've got roundup tomorrow," his dad interjected.

"Do you think it would be okay for Mesa to go with us?"

"If she doesn't mind watching you and your brothers branding. Castration might be a bit much for her to watch."

"Oh no, Mr. Young. I would love to watch!"

"Please, call me James."

"Very well, James. I think it would be a great experience for me to watch everything." Her excitement almost bubbled over like a boiling pot.

"It's smelly, dirty, nasty work. The boys can tell you."

The group murmured their agreement, but she wasn't to be dissuaded. If she wanted to watch branding, she'd watch branding, he decided. He was going to give her the full experience for the time she would be in his care.

Most of the guests had finished their meal and put their plates in the tub for the dirty dishes so the group of men picked up their plates too. Mesa followed with her own until she spied the chocolate mousse cake sitting on the side cupboard for the guests. "May I?"

"Of course. It's dessert for everyone. You'll really like it if you are a chocolate person. It's very rich, though." He grabbed two cups and headed back to the table. "These are my favorite."

As she spooned a little bite into her mouth, her eyes closed and she groaned. It was the sexiest thing he'd ever seen. His cock jumped to attention behind the fly of his jeans. *Fuck!* She looked like she might orgasm at any moment and he wanted nothing more than to see the same look on her face as he drove into her hot pussy.

He cleared his throat and swallowed hard past the lump. Her tongue slid over the surface of her lips, swiping at the bit of chocolate clinging to her bottom lip. He wanted to suck her tongue into his mouth and taste the decedent chocolate mixture on her lips for himself. The groan rumbling in his chest stopped at his lips. If he let it out, she'd know how much her little display turned him on. *I'm so screwed.*

"You okay, buddy?" Joshua slapped him on the back and grinned.

"Yeah. I'm fine."

She opened her eyes and he noticed they twinkled with mirth. Of course she knew what she did to him. Didn't every woman have the ability engrained in her psyche to torture a man until his balls turned blue?

"This is fabulous, Joel. I'm glad you suggested it. I've never tasted anything this good."

"Glad you like it," he squeaked. He cleared his throat as he blushed. His brothers laughed, as they filtered out of the room joking around and punching each other. *Damn them all.*

The dining room slowly cleared of guests, leaving her and Joel alone at the table.

"I guess I should get going so it doesn't take me long to get back. I hate driving in the dark on roads I don't know."

"Would you like me to go with you?"

"Would you?"

"Sure. You know, so you don't get lost coming back."

"True. I probably will. Of course, you'd have to come rescue me again."

"I'd rescue you anytime, darlin'."

She blushed and dropped her gaze to the table. Surely, she wasn't embarrassed by his attention? Women like her should be showered with it. Curvy, cute, and sexy, with a rack big enough to bury himself in, would get her lots of interest around these parts, especially from his brothers. They all liked curvy women.

"Is that a southern boy endearment you all use to get in women's pants?"

"Huh?"

"Darlin'."

"I use it for anyone I like, so it doesn't apply to just getting into a woman's jeans."

She took his hand between hers, stroking her finger over his knuckles. The sensation reminded him of what she could do to his cock if he could get far enough with her. She'd only be there a few days. Maybe she'd be interested in some wild sex.

"Sorry. I didn't mean to insult you. I use it a lot for my characters. I'm curious if I'm doing it right is all."

"It is an endearment southern men commonly use, I guess. I never noticed before."

"Do you mind if I write all this down? It's great to have someone I can base characters off of now that I've met a real cowboy."

"You never met a real cowboy before?"

"Well some, yes, but not one who works on a ranch or lives the life every day. This is great!" She scrambled to her feet dragging him up with her. "We should go if we're going to get back."

"I need to let my parents know I'm leaving with you."

"All right. I'll meet you outside by the car. Jeremiah slipped me the keys at dinner."

As she headed down the middle of the room toward the door, he couldn't help but notice her cute little ass. His mother's sundress molded to her like a second skin, emphasizing the round curve of her backside. Her long legs would look good wrapped around his hips.

"Damn, I need to get my head out of the gutter. She's a guest. We don't fuck guests." He shook his head to clear the lingering thoughts as he headed to the ranch office.

"Mom, I'm going to town with Mesa to get her stuff."

"How sweet of you, Joel. I'm sure she'll appreciate the company. It is a forty-five minute drive back to San Antonio."

"I'm afraid she'd get lost coming back."

His mom looked at him with an arched eyebrow. "Are you sure it's not just to spend more time with her? She's an interesting young woman."

"She's a guest, Mom."

"I know. You boys don't mess with guests, no matter how beautiful they are."

"That's right. It's your rule." *Never mind the two times before. Mom would kill me if she knew.*

"It hasn't been a problem for you…until now."

"No problem."

"Are you sure? I think you're trying to convince yourself more than me." She stood up and wrapped her arms around his shoulders. "Son, if you're interested in Mesa, go after her. There is nothing wrong with finding the right woman in a strange circumstance. God has a way of bringing us together with our soul mate."

"Soul mate? Mom, I'm only thinking of fucking her for a few days, not marrying her."

"You never know. She might get under your skin so fast you won't know what hit you. Love works in mysterious ways sometimes."

"Stop trying to get us married off so you can have daughter-in-laws. I'm only twenty-eight."

"Plenty old enough to have a family of your own. You're all stubborn mules when it comes to women."

"No, none of us have found the one. I personally won't settle for anything less."

"Good for you, Joel. I don't want any of my sons to settle for less. Y'all need to hurry the hell up with this woman thing though."

Joel rolled his eyes. After a big hug, he stepped back and kissed her on the cheek. "I love you, Mom, but I'll find the right girl someday. Don't rush me."

"Rush you, hell! It's time all of you settle down. Especially, Jeff, Jackson, and Jacob. They're all in their thirties."

"Then go bug them. I know Jacob had a hot date with a girl from town last night. He didn't get home until early this morning."

"I'm worried about him. He's been drinking a lot lately."

"I know. I've tried talking to him about it, but he just tells me to butt out. He doesn't think he has a problem." The sadness on his mom's face hurt his heart. He knew she wanted the best for all of them. "It'll work itself out."

"He needs to get his ass kicked. Maybe that'll straighten him out."

"I don't know. Only if it's by a woman. I better go. Mesa is waiting by the car. We'll be back in a couple of hours."

"No problem. We're doing the bonfire tonight."

"I know. I already told Mesa about it. She's excited. She wants to see the foal being born, too, but I'm not sure of the mother's timeframe. I don't know whether she'd want me to wake her up in the middle of the night."

"She probably would want you to, but you need to get going. Don't keep the lady waiting." Nina grinned like she had a secret. His mother was playing matchmaker again, and this time he was the target.

Chapter Three

Mesa stood near the car waiting for Joel to emerge from the house. The whole ranch was beautiful. She couldn't seem to look quick enough to take it all in. The house, the barn, the cabins, the cowboys…Good Lord, the whole thing overloaded her cowboy sucking brain.

She frowned. That wasn't a good comparison for this particular situation. Not like she had an aversion to sucking anyone, especially if it included Joel. Her whole chest expanded with a deep sigh. Getting involved with anyone right now wouldn't be good. Her life included her apartment in Los Angeles, her cat, Tigger, and no boyfriend in sight. Even if she only wanted a quick fling, he wouldn't be the right guy to do it with. His charming good looks, cowboy manners, gentlemanly behavior, and nice ass in those jeans made him hard to resist, though.

Joel stepped out the door of the main house and headed in her direction. The wide chest, bulging biceps, and trim hips made her panties wet. She could easily fashion one of her characters to look like him. The dark hair curling slightly by his ears and around his neck, the sparkling blue eyes, the trim, sensuous lips she wanted to kiss with everything inside her. All of it made her body sit up and take notice of the hot man coming closer.

"Ready?"

"Yep," she said, opening her door. "You know, you don't have to go with me. I think I can find my way back by myself."

"I doubt it with these roads at night. Besides, you can tell me more about your writing while you drive."

She slid behind the wheel before she buckled her seatbelt. "You don't want to hear about my writing do you?" The car turned over with a twist of the key.

"Sure," he said, buckling his own seatbelt. "It sounds interesting."

As she backed out of the spot, she replied, "It's not very interesting, really."

"Why don't you let me be the judge of that? I've never met an author before." He pushed the seat back to accommodate his long legs. "So, explain to me what you write."

"I told you. I write cowboys."

"I got that part, but you said they weren't like westerns, really."

Heat crawled up her neck, splashing red across her cheeks.

"Are you blushing, Mesa?"

"Yes. You're teasing me, Joel." Her hands gripped the steering wheel tighter.

"No, I'm not. I really want to know what you write."

She inhaled through her nose, blowing it out through her mouth in a rush. "All right. I write erotic cowboy stories."

"Erotic?"

"Romance. The guy and the girl meet, they have some kind of conflict, they split up, and then they resolve things to get back together. In between, there is lots and lots of hot sex."

"Oh. Sounds fun."

"They think so, I'm sure. They certainly don't argue with me when I'm writing it."

"These people talk to you?"

"Of course they do. They tell me their story. I just write it down." She glanced at Joel. "I'm not crazy."

"Okay."

"You don't understand. The characters are like voices in my head."

"Okay."

"Stop it."

"No, really. It's fine. Just let me out here. I'll get a ride back to the house." He laughed at the sour look on her face as she scrunched up her nose. "I'm kidding, Mesa. I think it's good you write books."

"You don't think I'm nuts?"

"No. We all have our little quirks."

Quirks? "Authors are a bit over the top sometimes."

"I wouldn't know. You're the first one I've met, but if they are all pretty like you, then I don't mind."

"I'm not pretty."

"Sure you are. I like my women curvy, and you have just the right amount of curves."

"I'm not your woman." With a flip of her hair over her shoulder, she concentrated on the road in front of the car. Texas junipers sped by the windows in the fading daylight. More longhorn cattle dotted the landscape. Blacktop stretched in front of the car for miles. She knew she'd been driving away from the main road for a while before she'd run out of gas.

"Don't get testy. It's a compliment."

He shifted in the seat, bringing her awareness of him into sharp view. *Damn.*

"Do you not get complimented often? You should, you know."

"Not much, I guess." She shrugged. The sunlight had begun to wane, creating long shadows in the scenery. Rocks of all shapes and sizes sprouted from hard ground. She'd have to ask Joel what kind they were so she could be accurate in her description, should she use it in a book. Inspiration flowed, abound in her imagination since she met him. The surroundings of the ranch, his brothers, him, all of them sparked something in her she'd been afraid had died over the last year. Her writing had suffered—badly. Yes, she had a few best sellers, but her last book flopped. The next one needed to be stellar to bring back her fans.

The breakup with her longtime boyfriend, Kurt, hadn't helped matters, but she couldn't fault him. The decision to call off their relationship came from her. He hadn't liked it, but they parted on friendly terms. Their sex life fizzled out some time ago with her need to explore. She wanted more and Kurt had been satisfied with missionary position. No fun. No excitement. Nothing. What would sex with Joel be like?

"Do you write full time?"

His question brought her mind back to their conversation. Thinking about sex with Joel wasn't where she needed to be. Well maybe it was, but she couldn't act on it even though it had been a while since she'd been between the sheets with anyone. "Yes. It keeps me plenty busy."

"I imagine it kind of makes you a hermit, though. Sitting in front of your desk all the time."

"I guess. I don't go out much."

"Where do you live when you aren't going to these conferences?"

"Los Angeles."

"In L.A. itself, or one of the suburbs?"

There he went, stretching out his long legs again. *Damn, the man looks good in a pair of jeans.* "A suburb. I have a small apartment with my cat."

"Ah. A catlady."

Her head whipped around as her gaze locked with his. Those intense blue eyes stared back until she focused on the road again. "I only have one. I don't consider myself a catlady."

"Boy, you're testy. I didn't mean anything by it. I like cats."

"Do you have pets, other than your horse?"

"A horse isn't a pet. It's a working animal. Something required for my job."

She raised a hand and said, "Sorry. I think of horses as pets. They can be big babies."

"Ours aren't pets."

"But you love him, don't you?"

"Yeah. He's my buddy."

"Then he's your pet."

Joel laughed. "All right. I'll give you that. He's my pet. I've had him since I was young. My parents got him for me on my thirteenth birthday."

"Did your brothers get one, too?"

"Yeah. We all three got our own. Before, we would ride one of the stable horses. Jet is my horse."

"Jet? But he's red."

"I know. He fit the name 'cause he's quick. He's a cutting horse."

"You don't mind if I pick your brain while I stay with your family, do you? I'm realizing even though I write about cowboys, horses, bullriders, and all things western, I don't know everything I should to make my books authentic."

"Sure. I don't mind."

She glanced his way and smiled. "Have you ever ridden a bull?"

"A few times, yes. In high school, mostly. We all did those crazy-ass things during our younger years."

"You make yourself out to be this old man. What are you? Twenty-five?"

"Twenty-eight, but when you're doing rodeo for a livin', it makes you old fast. Ever realize there aren't a lot of old rodeo guys? It's a hard life."

"Any of your brothers do professional rodeo?"

"Nah. We have too much work to do around the ranch."

"Oh."

"Ranchin' is a hard life too. Don't get me wrong." He wiped his palms on his pant legs. "We get up before dawn most days and don't get to bed until late."

"I'm sure you all have a normal party life though, right? I mean, all work and no play makes Joel a dull boy."

"We get around," he said with a crooked little grin on his lips.

She wanted to kiss it right off his mouth.

The lights of San Antonio came into view as more businesses sprouted up along the sides of the road.

"What hotel are you staying at?"

"The Marriott near the airport. The conference is being held there in the business suites and ballroom."

"How's the conference been?"

"Pretty boring, actually. I was hoping for more reader interaction, but it's been mostly panels and such. There is a book signing tomorrow, but I think I'll skip it for the research the ranch offers me." She pulled down the road toward the hotel. The Marriott stood five stories high and encompassed the whole block. Concrete walls and steel framed windows, painted a bright yellow with white trim, outlined the hotel. Native bushes lined the walkways. She pulled into a space and shut off the car. "Do you want to wait here? I don't have much to repack."

"I can help you bring the stuff down if you like."

Hmm...a sexy man in a hotel room with a bed? So not a good idea. "Why don't you wait in the car? It'll only take me a minute."

"Okay. If you're sure. I came to help, you know."

"Yeah, but you don't need to see all my underwear and stuff strung all over the room."

He laughed a deep, throaty laugh that made her toes curl. "Fine. I'll stay in the car."

"Great. Be right back."

After she slipped out of the car, she shut the door and hurried toward the side door of the hotel. Luckily, her room was on the second floor, so it wouldn't take much to get her big suitcase and her computer bag down to the car. She really didn't want Joel seeing all her makeup, toiletries, and personal unmentionables. It seemed weird to have a guy in her room, especially since she'd only known him a few hours.

The door lock beeped open as she slid the keycard into the slot. When she pushed the door, the darkness of the room surrounded her for a few moments until she flicked the lights on with a press of the button on the wall. She grabbed her suitcase from the closet and quickly folded her clothes to pack back in the bag. *Shampoo, conditioner, makeup bag. I think I got it all.*

She grabbed her computer and slid it into the case. *That didn't take long.* She glanced around the room to make sure she had everything as she pulled up the roller bar on the suitcase. The conference had included her hotel room so she would be losing the money there, but the chance for front row seats to a real ranch setting would be worth it in the long run. Her book would be authentic and her hero would be to die for!

* * * *

Joel checked the reflection in the side mirror of the car. He could clearly see the door Mesa disappeared through in the glass. *What to make of her?* When he'd found her stranded in her car, he wasn't sure she had a brain cell in her pretty head. Who would take a drive out into the middle of nowhere without enough gas to get back? But while he chatted with her, he realized she actually was a very intelligent woman with a big heart. *She sure is beautiful with all of her long, dark hair and brown eyes.*

He checked his watch. She'd been in there for several minutes. *What the hell is taking so long?*

Tap, tap, tap.

Joel turned his head to see a security guard tapping on the window with his flashlight.

"Can I help you?" he said, after he rolled the window down.

"Can I ask what you're doing sitting in this car?"

"I'm waiting for a friend to come out. She's getting her stuff."

"She's checking out?"

"Yes."

"Why didn't you go in and help her?"

"She asked me not to. Come on, man. I'm just sitting here."

"In a guarded parking lot of a nice hotel. How do I know you aren't casing cars to break into?"

"Do I look like a thief? I'm sitting here in muddy jeans, cowboy boots, and a T-shirt."

"Step out of the car please."

"Are you a cop?"

"Yeah, I am."

Joel glanced at the man's shirt and noticed the San Antonio police badge. *Shit.* This is all he needed. Trouble with a capital T. He pushed open the car door and stepped out. His six-foot-four frame towered over the cop, but he didn't try to intimidate the guy. *Be nice to the policeman, Joel.* He heard his mother's voice in his head as clearly as if she were standing next to him. After all, the man had a gun.

"What's going on here?"

Mesa skidded to haul next to him with her suitcase dragging behind her.

"Our friend here thinks I'm casing cars."

"He is not, officer." She tapped her chest with her finger. "He's with me. I came to check out and get my things before I headed back to his house."

"His house?" the cop asked with a raised eyebrow.

Great. Now the guy thinks I'm soliciting or something. Shit. He stuffed his hands in the front pocket of his jeans. "It's not like that, officer. My family owns a dude ranch out in Bandera. She's a guest. I came with her to get her things so she wouldn't get lost driving back out there since it's dark now."

"Do you have your check out paperwork?"

"Not yet. I brought my suitcase out here first to put into the car before I walked back into the front desk."

"Put your things in the car then and we can all walk in together."

"Seriously? This is ridiculous," she snapped, hitting the trunk latch on her key fob. She slid the suitcase in the back before she slammed the hatch with a loud bang.

Joel walked behind her with the cop beside him. He couldn't help but notice how her ass jiggled a little as she stomped her feet. The girl had a temper, it seemed. He liked girls with enough gumption to stand up for themselves.

They walked in through the sliding doors. The desk stood off to the left with large plants flanking either side. Mesa had her dander up now. She slapped her hand down on the counter and snapped, "Tell this idiot I am a guest at this hotel and I don't appreciate my *guest* being harassed in your parking lot."

"And you are?"

"Mesa Arraguso. I'm here with the writer's conference and I'm checking out." She slid her keycard across the counter. "My room is 2103."

"Of course, ma'am." The guy tapped on a few keys of the computer. "You do realize there won't be any refund on your hotel stay because of the special rate and…"

"Yes, I know. Just check me out while I deal with this idiot." She stomped back to where he and the cop were standing. "Now do you believe us? We weren't giving you a line of shit, officer. What we told you was the truth."

"I'm sorry, ma'am, but we've had a rash of car break-ins around the area and your friend here looked suspicious when he kept checking the doors."

"I kept looking for her. Nothing more."

"I'm sorry but you have to understand, we are only protecting the hotel guests." At least the man looked sheepish. "I didn't mean to harass you."

"Then I suggest you go out there and find whoever is really breaking into these cars. It's not my friend."

"No harm done, Mesa. Really. He's doing his job."

"Believe me, I know how these guys work. I deal with the same crap in Los Angeles with the police out there. Everyone is guilty until proven innocent, not the other way around." The cop tipped his hat before he walked out the doors. Mesa huffed out a sigh. "Really, he should have been more apologetic. I hate being harassed like I'm some kind of criminal."

"It's fine. I get into trouble with the police sometimes in Bandera. Luckily, they all know us. They don't here in San Antonio." He shrugged. "I didn't give him my name or he might have recognized me. I don't like throwing names around, you know?"

"Yeah. I appreciate you standing up to him, though."

"I didn't do anything."

"Ms. Arraguso? Here is your receipt. Thank you for staying with us."

"I appreciate it. I'll keep this hotel in mind should I have need for a room in San Antonio again. Thank you."

Joel grabbed her hand as they walked outside. Knowing there were people out casing the cars in the lot didn't sit well with him. He had a permit to carry a gun, which he did in his truck, but not in someone else's car. Bandera didn't have these kinds of problems. The small town kept to themselves most of the time. To each his own. They took care of each other with their small police force and didn't have much trouble in the way of things in San Antonio. The bigger city had a lot more issues.

"Are you okay?"

"Yeah, why?"

"You're squeezing my hand kind of tight," she said, tugging on her limb although he didn't release her.

He kind of liked how her hand felt in his so he pulled her in tighter. "Sorry, darlin'. Knowing there are people possibly hanging out in the parking lot for nefarious reasons makes me nervous for you."

"Aw, how sweet. I'm fine though. I can take care of myself."

"Maybe, but as the man, I'm supposed to take care of you."

"Very chivalrous of you."

"It's the way my mom raised us. The men take care of the ladies." They'd reached the side of her car. Once she unlocked it, he opened the door for her, and then shut it behind her before going around to the passenger side.

"Do you always open doors?" she asked after he'd settled himself in the seat again.

"Yep."

"I didn't think men did those kinds of things anymore."

"Southern gentlemen do, but I don't know any other way to be, so there you have it."

"It's nice." She smiled and he relaxed.

"I'm just a simple, country boy."

"Perfect for what I'm needin'."

"And what might that be?"

Chapter Four

"Inspiration, Joel. For my next book."

"Ah." He quirked an eyebrow at her as she flushed in embarrassment from the little smile on his lips.

"Men," she whispered under her breath.

"What did you say?"

"Nothing."

They headed out of San Antonio on their way back to the ranch. Quiet surrounded them, so she flipped on the radio to a country music station and sat back in the seat, prepared for the long drive.

"Have you ever been married?" he asked, breaking into the low radio hum of the song playing. His voice reminded her of a sexy growl. She totally needed to use that in a book.

"What brought that on?"

"Just making conversation."

"No. I had a long-term boyfriend up until about six months ago."

"What happened?"

"We just grew apart, I guess. We'd been dating about three years." She glanced across the car, then back to the road. "What about you?"

"Nope. I haven't found the right girl yet. Of course, if Mom had her way, all of us boys would be married already and have a dozen kids each."

She laughed. It felt good with everything her life had turned into lately. Her career had gone into the toilet after her last book. Her love life sucked. "Why am I not surprised? Nina reminds me of my mother. She's trying to marry me off, too. She was pretty upset about my breakup. More so than I was, I think."

"Only one of our family has been married before. Jeff. It broke up a few years ago."

"What happened?"

"Misha was a total ho bag. She tried getting half of us in bed with her. When she couldn't accomplish that, she went after the sheriff. She succeeded there." Joel rubbed his eyes with forefinger and thumb like he had a headache.

"I bet it's a bit awkward for Jeff then if he ever gets stopped by the guy."

"The two of them keep clear of each other. Jeff caught them in bed together. The guy was lucky Jeff wasn't armed at the time. Jeff just beat the shit out of the guy."

"He didn't press charges, did he?" she asked, her voice a slight pitch higher with worry. She liked his family even though she'd only met them a short time ago. They seemed close, like families should be. She loved her own parents, but they constantly seemed to be on her tail about one thing or another. When was she going to marry? What about children? Even though she was only twenty-five, shouldn't she be thinking about her future? Did she plan on writing novels for the rest of her life? She needed a day job to pay her bills. She'd been lucky. Her first novel took off three years ago and hit the NY Times Bestseller list, as did her second. Her third flopped…badly.

"No. Art knew better, even though he could have." He sighed and shifted in the seat. "Jeff loved her."

"I'm sorry for him then. It's not fair to put someone through the heartbreak. Just leave if you don't want to be married to them."

"She did want to be. She wanted the money and land she thought went with the Young name, she didn't want Jeff or their son."

"They managed to have a child? We wasn't at dinner."

"Yeah, purely by accident, I think. She hated being pregnant. Hated Jeff during the whole pregnancy. They fought constantly. She made everyone miserable while they were married. We were all thrilled when it broke up."

"No one noticed any of this before they got married?"

He shook his head. "You couldn't have told Jeff anything anyway. He never thought badly of her, even when the rest of us could totally see her flirting. He kept telling everyone she was being friendly."

Silence enveloped them for a minute as she contemplated how she would have felt had one of her brothers gone through the same thing with a spouse. She probably would have kicked the woman's ass for hurting her sibling. "I'm sorry for his pain."

"We all were. I hated seeing him hurting, but I'm glad he saw her for what she truly was. Unfortunately, because they have a child together, he still has to see her on occasion."

"Does he have custody?"

"Yeah. Mom and Dad made sure she didn't take off with their grandson. He's a cute three year old and gets into everything."

"I bet he's a total cowboy, like his uncles and dad."

"Yep. He has a set of boots, a cowboy hat, and the whole nine yards."

"I need to get a picture of him. I bet he's a doll."

"Looks like his dad." He cleared his throat. "Do you want to be there when the foal is born?"

"I'd love to."

"Even if it's in the middle of the night? It's very possible it'll come sometime tonight when you're asleep."

"I don't mind. Wake me up no matter what time it is. I've always wanted to see a foal come into the world."

"We can check out her progress when we get back to the ranch."

The time had flown. Before she knew it, they were pulling back up to the gate of the ranch. "See? I could have made it back without your directions."

"I see, but it does help having a GPS telling you where to go. They do get lost out here on the back roads."

"True." She laughed. "But I memorized some landmarks as we were headed into San Antonio so I'd be able to find most of the way back."

"I'm glad I went. It was great to sit and talk to you. You're an interesting woman, Mesa."

"Thank you." She scrunched up her nose as they pulled up in front of the hitching post. "I think."

He laughed and leaned over to kiss her cheek. Goose bumps rose on her arms when the smell of his cologne reached her nose. Of course, he had to wear her favorite scent, damn him.

"It was a compliment. We'll have to talk more tomorrow, but for now, let's get you settled in your room. Hopefully, you can get a few hours of sleep before the foal is born." She bit her lip. "What?"

"Can you get into the kitchen?"

"Sure. Why?"

"I'd love another one of those dessert things we had at dinner." She smiled hoping she could persuade him to sneak into the kitchen to swipe one of the decadent chocolates for her sweet tooth. She had a terrible one, especially right before bed. Ice cream usually calmed her cravings at home, but here, she needed to improvise, if only she could get Joel to go along.

The warm chuckle coming from his mouth made her smile. She liked his laugh. Hell, who was she kidding, she liked everything about him from the top of his sexy cowboy hat to the tip of his cowboy boots—the man had it all. Those lips made her want to kiss him into tomorrow. His chest made her want to bury herself against those muscles. She wondered what he'd look like without a shirt. Did he have chest hair? A lot? A little? She knew he had a six-pack. No cowboy who looked as good as he did, didn't have a six-pack, or sex-pack, as she liked to think about it. He had some of the prettiest blue eyes she'd ever seen on a man, along with eyelashes any woman would kill for. What would his hands feel like stroking her skin? Did he have a sexy happy trail? *God, I want to find out.* A heavy sigh escaped her lips.

"What?"

"Nothing. I just had a thought."

"Anything you'd like to share?"

"Really? I shouldn't because it would totally embarrass me."

"About me?"

Heat crawled up her neck as she blushed.

"Ah. It *was* about me."

"Totally."

"Share."

"Nope."

"Why not?"

"Because you don't need your ego stroked, I'm sure."

"Sure I do. Stroke me, baby."

She rolled her eyes and smiled. *I know he doesn't need a bigger head.* "All right. I totally pictured you without a shirt and I wanted to know if you had a little happy trail like most men with dark hair like yours do."

"Oh, you kinky girl, you."

He laughed. The rich, deep sound sent shivers down her back. *Damn, the man could turn me inside out and upside down.* She hadn't even known him very long. This wasn't good. How would she feel after being around him for several days? She hadn't quite decided how long she planned to stay at the ranch, but she knew it would be more than a day or two. The opportunity to have firsthand knowledge of cowboys, how they work, etc. wasn't something she wanted to pass up. "So?" she asked, her bravery waning now they were back at the ranch.

"Happy trail, huh? I've never heard anything referred to as that before. Explain what you mean."

"You know. The trail of hair usually linking chest hair to pubic hair." Her face flamed with heat. How did one discuss this kind of thing with a man?

"Oh that!" He laughed again. *The bastard.* "Yes, I have one. Wanna see?" He started unbuttoning his belt buckle as she shrieked.

"No! I mean not here."

"I'll show it to you any time you want."

"You're just teasing me now, Joel. It's not funny."

"I'm not teasing. I'm sure you've seen pictures of men nude before or in only underwear, right?"

"Well yes. Some have them and some don't. I'm curious about you since the hero in my head is turning out to look a lot like you."

"Aw, how sweet. I'm the hero in your next book?"

"It all depends on how the days I'm here at the ranch turn out."

"How do you want them to turn out?" He waggled his eyebrows and grinned.

"You're an impossible flirt."

"Yep."

"I bet every mama in this town turns their daughters' head away from you and your brothers when you hit Main Street. The whole lot of you are like this, aren't you?"

"Definitely, but the mamas are after every one of us to marry their daughters."

"Really?" His eyes crinkled at the corner as he glanced out the window.

"It looks like Dad is headed to the barn. Let's go see what's up."

"Oh. Great!"

She met him around the front of the car seconds later. He grabbed her hand again to help guide her to the barn he said, since darkness had fallen in an inky black curtain on the ranch. Soft country music wafted from the speakers next to the bonfire where several people sat around the crackling light. They would go there after the barn, she hoped. She hadn't been to a bonfire since summer camp approximately fifteen years before. S'mores? Hmm. She'd have to ask Joel if they had chocolate, marshmallows, and graham crackers, but then again, if she had her choice, she'd take the chocolate dessert they had at dinner. The smooth chocolate and whipped cream mixture was what chocolate dreams were made of.

"Careful. It's so dark you can hardly see your hand in front of your face. Without a flashlight, you could twist an ankle or something."

"But look at all the stars." She stopped so she could look up at the night sky. Billions of stars winked off and on lighting up the sky. "Look! A shooting star." She closed her eyes to make a wish though she couldn't believe she wished for a kiss.

"What did you wish for?"

"I can't tell you or it won't come true."

"Sure you can. I won't tell a soul. I promise."

"All right. I wished you would kiss me."

She could see the white of his teeth as he smiled. "Is that all?"

"Yes." The word came out in a soft whisper.

He stepped in front of her and slipped his hand along her cheek to bury his fingers in her hair. *God, it felt wonderful.* The slight tug on her scalp set her heart to racing a hundred miles a minute. A flutter started in her belly, spreading lower until she felt on fire from his touch. She closed her eyes as his warm breath spread across her lips. Her lips parted on a sigh, accepting the warmth of his mouth. His lips were soft, yet strangely unyielding, like he wanted to absorb her strength through her mouth. One of his hands rested on her hip, pulling her into the curve of his body. His chest felt hard beneath her hands. The soft brush of his tongue on her lips parted them to his invasion. She wanted this, needed to feel alive, needed to be a woman again.

A soft moan escaped her as he took the kiss deeper, bringing both of his hands up to cup her face.

The sound of wolf whistles brought her back to the present as she heard the catcalls from his brothers near the fire. Joel stepped back, breaking the kiss.

"Sorry."

"I'm not. It was totally worth it."

He laughed and grabbed her hand again as they continued on their way to check on the foal.

The barn came into view when they rounded the corner of the house. The large, two story structure with wide doors stood outlined by the moon in the background. A single, bare light bulb in the middle of the row of stalls reflected the black, wrought iron parts of the upper doors where the horses could stick their heads through. The barn was pretty fancy from what she knew about barns. Wood surrounded the bottoms of the stalls and each one had a sliding door. One off to the right stood open. She could see Joel's dad crouched on the floor next to the mare's head.

"How is she, Dad?"

"She's laboring pretty hard, son. I hope she foals soon." His big hands ran down the heaving sides of the mare. "I think the foal is pretty big for her, but she could drop it shortly."

"Do you mind if I stay and watch?" she asked.

"Oh, hi. I didn't see you there." He glanced back down to the mare. "You can stay as long as you like but it might be a while yet."

"I don't mind." She took out the ever-present notebook from her purse and jotted down information. She wanted to get the whole thing on paper for her next book. There's nothing like having a cowboy helping with a laboring horse to make the cowboy image stick in the reader's mind. She wrote more details, the position of the horse, the coloring of her coat, the rapid breaths, the concentration on Joel's father's face, the worry line along his forehead like laugh lines around his eyes and mouth. It mesmerized her how he ran his hands on the mare's stomach, calming her in the process. She could see the horse physically relax as he worked them down her side. She would have to ask more questions when all was said and done. Details like the gestation period for a horse, whether they could be ridden during pregnancy, how big a normal size foal is. All of this important information she needed...eventually. For now, the process looked worrisome for the two men.

Joel crouched down next to his father, balancing on the balls of his feet. "Want me to check her?"

"Sure. Maybe you can tell if things are progressing. I haven't checked her in a bit."

Joel stood and grabbed a long, plastic sleeve from the shelf outside the stall. Once he had it slipped on, covering his shirt to his armpit, he kneeled near the horse's rump and moved her tail out of the way. A lump formed in her throat as he slid his hand into the back of the horse.

"Appears it's in the right position," he said. "I can feel the hooves and they seem to be right side up. Its nose is right there, too. I think she'll deliver soon." He peeled off the sleeve and tossed it into a bucket in the corner.

"We'll just watch and wait then."

"Do horses normally deliver without complications?" she asked with her pen posed to write down his answer in detail.

"Yes," the older man answered. "The horse does all the work most of the time, although we do have to step in occasionally. There are times where they come nose first or with their hooves upside down, which can be a problem. With something like that, we call the vet."

"Fascinating." The horse grunted as her legs flailed for a few seconds. Mesa could see her side ripple with a contraction. Moments later, two tiny hooves appeared.

"Looks like it's time," Joel said, moving away from the horse.

With a gush of fluid, the foal made his entrance into the world. Slimy mucus hung from its body. The mare struggled to her feet, and then began licking the foal clean.

"Oh, it's beautiful!" Tears stung her eyes. She'd never witnessed anything so precious in her life. "Will it start nursing right away?"

"Usually within a couple of hours. The mother will clean it up first."

The baby stood on wobbly legs for a few seconds before it nuzzled against its mother seeking out her nipple. "Oh look! It's already trying to walk and feed. This has been fabulous. Thank you."

"We didn't do anything." Joel's father chuckled. "The horse did all the work."

"But you allowed me to witness this. I've got some great notes for my next book. I can't thank you enough."

"Our pleasure." Joel moved closer to her and slipped his arm around her shoulders. "I'm glad you got to watch the birth. She's the only one we have close to delivery."

She smiled, snuggling into his side to absorb his warmth. The wind seemed to have kicked up a bit, cooling down the heat of the day.

"How about we head to the fire so you can get your fill of that, too?"

"I'd love to."

"I'll check on her later, Dad, if you want me to."

"Thanks, Joel. I'll stay with her for a bit to make sure the foal is nursing. If you want to check her before you head to bed, I would appreciate it."

"Sure."

"Have fun by the fire. The weather seems to be cooling down with the wind kicking up."

"Yeah, you never know about Texas weather in April and May. It can be unpredictable."

Joel spun her around and headed toward the barn doors with his arm still around her shoulders. The weather had indeed cooled down, and goose bumps rose on her arms—though she wasn't sure if they were from the wind chill or the sexy cowboy next to her.

The flames rose into the night sky, stretching like fingers toward the inky blackness. Several people surrounded the warmth, absorbing the heat into their fingers by holding their hands or feet out toward the fire. Joel found them a carved out seat made from an old log. The bottom had been smoothed out of the cut log to make a great chair.

"Would you like a couple of marshmallows to roast?"

"Sure."

"I'll be right back." A large picnic table sat nearby with chocolate, marshmallows, and graham crackers for S'mores. "Do you want the whole fixin's?"

"No. Just the marshmallow is fine. If I try to make S'mores, they'll make me sick with all the sweetness. I love chocolate but too much doesn't like me, since I had the chocolate dessert earlier."

The rich sound of his laughter sent chills down her spine.

"A woman who can't handle chocolate. That's a first for me."

Heat rose up her neck in embarrassment. It was hard not being able to tolerate chocolate too much. She usually had to have a white cake with whipped cream frosting as a child because her stomach couldn't handle too much.

Joel returned to her side with a straight wire holder containing two prongs. With a marshmallow stuck on both ends, it would serve as their roasting stick. "Do like them barely roasted or black?"

"Sort of dark, but not too burnt."

He shook his head and handed her the stick. "Why don't you roast them and I'll eat whatever you fix? I don't care how they are roasted. I just like the sticky sweetness in my mouth."

Laughing, she shook her head. So much for being the difficult cowboy. He seemed almost too sweet to be true. She needed him to be a little more arrogant and self-centered to be the hero of her novel. Oh well. She could always tweak his personality a bit to make him difficult for the heroine to deal with. Ah, the job of a romance writer.

Within moments, the marshmallows caught fire and she lifted them toward her mouth to blow out the flames. Just right. Squishy but not burnt. "One for you and one for me," she said, holding out the stick so Joel could slide one of the fluffy things off the end of the metal contraption.

"Perfect." He stuck one between his full lips, grinning like a kid on Christmas.

Her body tingled in all the important places as he licked the sticky substance off his fingers. She wanted to lick him all right. Everywhere.

"Aren't you going to eat yours?" he asked, winking.

I'd like to eat something. "I'm letting it cool a bit."

The grin grew wider like he knew exactly what she had on her mind. *I wanted him a little more arrogant. I got it.*

"Have you always been such a ladies' man?"

"I've had my share of women."

"I bet you have."

"Jealous?"

She shrugged, trying to be nonchalant about the whole thing. "Nah. Just not surprised, is all. I bet all of your brothers are the same way. The women of Bandera and San Antonio better watch out when you all are on the prowl."

"When I find the one, I won't be prowling anymore."

The marshmallow melted on her tongue as she slid it between her lips. Joel's lips parted as one eyebrow arched over his left eye. Damn, he looked sexy as hell with the little smirk of a smile on his mouth. She wanted to kiss him again. Wanted to do other things with him. *Not a good idea.*

"Good?"

"Yes," she whispered, wondering whether she meant him or the marshmallow. The sticky sweetness on her fingers had her licking it off as she watched his eyes dilate in the firelight. He sure seemed like he might be a little into her. The whole thing seemed weird, though. Surely a guy like him wasn't attracted to a girl like her. She knew her hips were too wide and her butt seemed a bit too big for her liking. Getting guys like him to notice her didn't come with instructions. Popular wasn't an affliction she had growing up. She was the quiet, shy girl. Something she had to get over rather quickly as a writer, since she was in front of dozens of people at times, but she never quite managed to be outgoing with men.

Jason sauntered over. "Hey you two."

"Jason."

"Would you like more marshmallows, Mesa? You seemed to be enjoying them."

"Sure. Thanks."

Jason took her stick from her hand and headed back to the table.

"Don't get too close to him." The serious tone of Joel's voice had her on edge.

"Close?"

"I mean be careful."

"Why? He seems like a nice guy. You wouldn't warn me away from one of your own brothers, would you?"

"He's my brother, yes, and I love him but he likes to play with women."

"I don't understand," she said, sitting forward on her seat to hear him better.

Joel grasped her hand in his. "If you want the bad boy for your novel, he's your man. He's more into one-night stands than any of my other brothers. Women are like playthings for him. He doesn't get serious about women at all."

"You know, he does sound like the bad boy of the group."

"Well, we all are to some extent, but he seems like the worst. I don't know if he'll ever settle down."

"Why don't you tell me about each one in turn? Give me details of their lives, their personalities. You know. Those kinds of things. I can morph all of your personality traits into one kick-ass hero."

Jason returned with her marshmallow stick. "Here you go."

"Thanks."

"Don't listen to Joel about me. He's a bit biased because he's not as attractive as I am."

She laughed at his words. They were identical in most ways, especially looks. "You two are terrible to tease me like that."

The two men laughed. Jason sauntered back to his spot, flashing her a wicked grin and a wink from his seat several feet away.

"Okay. You want to know more about each of us. I'll start with Jeff. He's the eldest at thirty-four. I already told you he'd been married once before."

"Yes." She pulled her pen and paper out to jot down some notes.

"Jeff is Mom and Dad's pride and joy. The prodigal older son. He helps Dad run things around here. He's kind of bossy, but he's a good guy. We all hated when his marriage broke up because he really loved her. On the other hand, we were glad because she wasn't the right woman for him. I hated to see him so heartbroken. He's very adamant about running this place as a working cattle ranch. He didn't like when we went to accepting guests here to supplement the income. Sometimes I think he was born in the wrong time. He's cowboy to the bone. I hate to see the woman he really falls hard for because she better be country through and through to win his heart. He won't settle for some high rise, corporate type."

Mesa quickly wrote down Joel's description of his older brother along with a few notes on the woman who would turn out to be someone he could live the rest of his life with. As a romance author, she grinned. The hero didn't always fall in love with the woman he thought he would. She giggled a little.

"Jackson is the second eldest. He does what he has to do around here, but sometimes I think he hates playing the cowboy. He rides a motorcycle more than he does a horse. He has several tattoos, gets a bit rowdy when he drinks, but overall he's a great guy and good friend. He's saved my ass more than once in a bar fight."

"Do you fight often?"

"No. I try to be the peacekeeper more than anything. Jackson likes the ladies, too."

"Don't you all?"

Joel grinned. "Yeah, I guess so. The women seem really attracted to his bad boy persona, though. I think it's the tats."

"Could be."

"He's really a big teddy bear, though. I think he got more of Dad's personality whereas some of the rest of us are more like Mom. Jacob is third. He's thirty this year and is feeling every bit of it, I think. He's been drinking a lot lately. I'm not sure if he's debating his life—. Not that he would ever hurt himself or anything, but I wonder sometimes if he knows where his life is going. He's kind of quiet. More so than the rest of us. He just does his work around here and spends a lot of time in his room. Doing what, I'm not sure. He didn't do sports in school like most of us did. He's more the creative, artsy type."

"He sounds sweet."

Joel smile and shrugged. "Fourth is us triplets. Me, Jason, and Josh. You know about me. Josh, we're a little worried about. He's been drinking a lot lately, too I think he got his heart broken recently. He won't talk about it though. I've tried. We are very similar in looks, but our personalities are very different. At least to me, they are."

"Josh is a ladies' man, definitely."

"Yeah, but he's been down in the dumps lately. I hope whoever broke his heart was worth the pain he's going through now. I hate to see him like this. He's trying, but you can see the pain in his eyes if you look hard enough."

"It's never easy breaking up with someone you've been with for a long time even if it's a mutual breakup."

"True. I haven't been in a long-term relationship really, so I wouldn't know that kind of pain. I hope I never do."

She dropped her gaze to her paper for a moment and let his words sink in. Why didn't she feel pain over her breakup with her ex? She loved him, didn't she? Maybe not like she should have. The pain didn't seem to be there.

"And then there is Jason."

"You almost sound exasperated by him."

"He's an exasperating individual."

"How so?"

"He likes the ladies. Definitely. I think he's got several women on the string at the moment and I'm just waiting for the bubble to burst. If they found out about each other, it could sure make for some interesting fireworks in the neighborhood."

"Ah."

Joel scraped the toe of his boot in the dirt, digging up a small rock in the process. "This isn't the first time he's done this type of thing either. He's been caught before and almost got himself shot by one girl's father. He found Jason's ass hanging out the window of the daughter's room a few years ago. His truck still bears the bullet hole."

"Wow."

"I think my parents wish he would go in the military or something to straighten his ass out, but then they'd be totally worried he'd be in some combat zone and get his butt killed or something."

"I think your parents could handle it."

"I think my dad could, but I'm not sure about Mom. She loves having her sons around here."

"I'm sure she does. She's a very strong lady, though." Mesa tucked a stray piece of hair behind her ear.

"Yes, she is. I doubt Jason will do anything of the sort. Military lifestyle doesn't suit him, I don't think. He likes sleeping late, getting into trouble, and staying out all hours of the night. The discipline would do him good, but I doubt he'd do it."

"Trouble with a capital T."

Joel chuckled. "The fifth of us is Jonathan. He tries to be the cowboy Dad wanted in all of us, but he's not so much cut out for the life. He rides, but he's not as comfortable on a horse as the rest of us. He's more at home in front of a computer. He's a gamer."

"Nothing wrong with that. Computer programmers make good money."

"Yeah, but he doesn't get to do it much. I think Dad should let him take over the website and marketing for the ranch, but he hires out to someone else. Dad doesn't see the potential in Jonathan doing it. I do. I think he'd been great at it. If they send Jonathan to school so he could get some formal training, he'd be kick-ass at it. I don't think Jonathan has ever had a girlfriend. He's really shy."

She laughed. "I didn't think any of you were shy."

Joel grinned. "He really isn't when you get to know him. I think he feeds off the rest of us with our personalities. He kind of goes along with the bunch."

"I bet he's got a deeper personality than you give him credit for."

"Maybe." He lifted his gaze and glanced across the fire to where Jeremiah sat talking with a couple of the young women who were guests. "Jeremiah is the sixth in the bunch." Joel shrugged as he shifted on the seat. "How do I describe him? Hmm. He tends bar at the local club when he's not working the ranch. I don't think he cares so much for the ranch work. He likes doing financial stuff. He plays the stock market a lot. He's a very personable guy and gets along with just about everyone. See how he's talking to those girls?"

"Yeah."

"Most would think he's flirt. Trying to get one of them in bed with him, but he's not."

"No?"

"Nope. He just likes to talk to people. The numbers thing is really what he likes. I constantly see him with his nose buried in the newspaper or on the computer. Someday I expect him to be rich beyond all of us the way he plays with numbers. I'm not sure why he's here at the ranch except that he doesn't want to leave Mom and Dad. He'd be better off in New York or somewhere."

"Wow. Such a diverse group you have here." The notes on the group were getting longer and longer. How much more could she possibly need to develop the hero in her book? Maybe there needed to be an entire family.

"Then there is Joey or Joe. He's the baby of the family and boy do we all know it. He gets away with murder. I swear. Mom and Dad think he can do no wrong. Well, it looks like it from the rest of us boys' perspective anyway. He's the one in charge of the horses. He helps Dad buy and sell those for the Remuda and keeps us in a good supply of gentle to a little more rowdy for the experienced riders. We have a wide range of horses we keep on the property. Joe breaks most of the newer horses and he competes in bronc riding at the rodeo. I think he does some bull riding on the side, too although he doesn't want Mom to know about it and it's not professionally. One of these days, he's gonna break his neck, but it's what he loves. He's got the adrenaline junkie personality. Definitely attracts the buckle bunnies with his happy-go-lucky attitude. Woman in every town."

"Wow. You've got such a wide variety of personalities in your brothers. I've got five pages of notes on them."

"Good. I hope you get some great information while you're here."

"This is going to be awesome, Joel. Thank you for giving me the lowdown on everyone." She reached over and kissed him on the cheek.

"Would you like to go for a walk?"

"In the dark?"

"I grabbed a small flashlight while we were in the barn."

"Okay," she said, sliding her pen and notebook into her purse. She wasn't sure how much they could see in the dark, but she didn't want to call it a night quite yet. Being close to Joel ramped up the heat between them. Her body felt on fire as she shivered in the night air. It wasn't from being cold.

As they stood to make their way into the blackness surrounding the bonfire, one of his brothers called out, "Behave yourself, Joel. She's a guest."

"What's that all about?"

A shrug lifted both his shoulders as he laid his hand on the small of her back guiding her around the boulders and path rocks blocking their way. "Nothing really. We just have a don't mess with the guests policy."

"Oh?"

"Yeah. It's really to keep my brothers from coming onto some of the single women we get staying here, which doesn't happen a lot. We tend to meet more women in town. The ranch is packed most of the time with families."

"Does the no messing with the guests policy include me since you kissed me?" she asked, cuddling closer to his side. She really hoped the policy didn't apply to her. She wanted Joel to kiss her again.

Chapter Five

He stopped and looked down at her. "Technically, yes. I shouldn't have kissed you earlier. I'm sorry."

"Don't be. I wished for it. Remember?"

"Yeah, but…"

She pressed two fingers to his lips. "I wanted you to. It's not your fault. If your mother says anything, it was me, not you."

The warmth of his lips under her fingertips sent chills down her arms. He kissed her fingers, then her palm. Shivers raced down her back. Her heart sped up, threatening to jump from her chest.

Moonlight lit the path now that they were away from the fire. It also reflected the white of his teeth as he smiled. The wink he gave her did nothing to calm her out of control libido.

"I'll blame it all on you then."

"Great." He grabbed her hand to lead her down the path headed for the front of the house. Clouds raced across the face of the moon blocking the light at times, but giving everything an slight eerie silver glow.

He led her to the front of the main house where several rocking chairs and other assorted benches lined the porch in front of the windows. Light from the main room of the lodge spilled out onto the front lawn, but did nothing to cut the darkness beyond fifty feet. Joel took her shoulders in both of his hands as he pushed her down on one of the rockers. "I thought you might like to sit here for a bit and watch the clouds drift across the moon. It always seems kind of strange to me to watch with the outline of the trees beyond the light from the house."

"It is spooky out here."

The front door of the ranch house creaked open, but no one came out. She glanced at Joel, but he didn't seem to notice. *It was probably someone from inside who opened the door, and then changed their mind about coming outside.* She glanced through the window, but didn't see anyone near the door. *Okay, that's weird.*

"How long have you lived in Los Angeles?"

"All my life. My parents moved there before I was born."

"Do they still live there?"

"Sort of. They spend part of the year in Arizona." His profile intrigued her. The slope of his nose looked regal, except for the small bump near the bridge indicating he'd broken it at least once. His lashes were long, dark spikes any woman would give her eyeteeth to have. The black Stetson sat back on his head, framing the black curtain of his hair. He wore it longer than most guys, she noticed, almost to his shoulders.

"What?"

"Nothing, why?"

"You're staring at me." He smiled and winked.

"Sorry. I didn't mean to. I'm admiring your profile."

"Why?"

"I'm committing it to memory for a book cover. I want to take your picture before I leave." *Yeah, sounded like a good excuse to me. I certainly can't tell him I think he's hotter than Hades.*

"Oh?"

"Yeah. Preferably with your shirt off."

He laughed. The rich, deep sound made her pussy weep with need. *God, I want this man to make love to me. Make love, hell! I want him to fuck me six ways to Sunday.*

With a quick glance at his watch, he said, "How would you like to go into town? The bar there should be just starting to swing right about now."

"Sure. I haven't been out to a bar in quite a while."

"No?" He stood and held out a hand to help her to her feet.

"Nope."

"Well then you need to loosen up a bit. Have a few drinks. Dance."

"I can't dance."

He tucked her hand into the crook of his elbow as they walked back toward the parked cars behind the main house.

"Sure you can. Everyone can dance."

"I have two left feet. Trust me."

"Have you ever tried to two-step?"

"No."

"I'll teach you. It's easy. I'll lead, you follow. You'll have the hang of it in no time."

"I'll probably bruise your feet stepping on them."

"You can't be any worse than Willa Miller."

"Who?" She giggled as he opened the door to the biggest truck she'd seen in her life. White and huge with big mud tires.

"Willa Miller. She's been hanging out at the bars since she turned twenty-one. She's now fifty something, I think." Once he got around the front of the truck, he hopped inside and closed his own door. "She's got to be the worst dancer I've ever seen. Most of the guys tolerate her because she so sweet, but man she's hard on the toes." Her laugh turned into a snort. Joel roared with laughter as he turned over the engine. "You snort when you laugh."

"Only when I'm laughing really hard." She placed her hand over her nose and mouth trying to hide the sound. "It's not funny, Joel."

"Sure it is. I think it's cute." He grabbed her hand to lace their fingers together.

"You would." *What to make of this enigma named Joel?* He acted like he was attracted to her, but she didn't know whether to take him seriously or not. Could they have a fling for a few days while she stayed on the ranch? She could. Would he be willing? The attraction was definitely there on her part. She slowly pulled her hand out of his grasp to wrap her arms around herself. What to do?

"Are you cold? I can turn on the heater if you want."

"No. I'm fine. I got the shivers for a minute, is all." She rubbed her arms to calm the chills.

Within moments they pulled into a bustling bar in the center of Bandera. Tons of trucks sat in the parking lot, but very few cars. *Figures. Everyone drives a truck in cowboy country.*

Joel walked around the front of the truck to open her door. Such a gentleman, but then again, his mama raised him to be like that, especially around women. He opened the door and held out his hand to help her down from the twenty feet off the ground his truck stood—okay, maybe not that high.

"I should have dressed up more."

"You look great, Mesa. Besides, most of the women in here wear jeans and T-shirts."

"Maybe I'm overdressed then."

"I like you just the way you are."

"Thanks."

The doors to The Dusty Boot opened and closed several times as they made their way closer. She could hear the music playing loudly every time they opened. Several cowboys stood on the porch and called to Joel when they reached the doors. He waved back, but didn't stop to chat.

They walked inside only to be immediately swallowed up in the crowd of cowboy hats and rhinestones. A band played from a small stage near the back of the bar. A loud cowbell clanged causing her to jump. Joel put his lips near her ear. "The mechanical bull. They ring the bell when someone rides for eight seconds."

"Are you going on it?" she asked, breathing in his cologne. All man, cowboy, and musk. *God, he smells good.*

"If you will."

"Me?"

"Yep. I want to see those sexy hips swing with the back end of the bull."

Heat crept up her neck as she bit her lip to hide her smile. Sexy hips, huh. She almost felt giddy. He thought she had sexy hips. "Okay. I'll give it a go."

The smile he gave her could have set her panties on fire. She sniffed hoping she didn't smell smoke, because damn, he probably would melt the silk of her underwear.

"Hey baby." A beautiful blonde scooted close and pressed her size double D breasts against Joel side. "I've missed you. You haven't been around here much, Joel."

"No, I haven't."

"Wanna hang out? I'm free tonight and all yours."

"I'm with someone, Brandy."

"Oh yeah?"

"Yes. Brandy this is Mesa. Mesa, Brandy."

"Nice to meet you," Mesa said, glancing at the woman hoping she could hide her disdain. The blonde didn't even acknowledge her. *Well, so much for pleasantries.*

"I'll see you around, Brandy."

"Sure, cowboy. Call me."

"Uh, yeah."

Joel took Mesa's hand and wormed his way through the crowd toward the back of the bar. A large mechanical bull sat in the middle of a padded ring. Several people stood around the outside of the ring, laughing whenever someone climbed on and was tossed off on their ass.

Great. He wants me to get on that thing?

"Yes, I do," Joel said. "Climb on. You can do it."

Joel went back to pay the operator as she sucked in a ragged breath. *I can do this. With Joel watching, it'll be much more fun.* She grinned as she realized she could totally tease Joel at the same time. With a sexy swing of her hips, she approached the steel beast. She stuck her foot into the metal stirrup and swung her leg over the back of the bull. Adjusting herself toward the handhold, she tucked her dress between her thighs so she could save what little modesty she possessed, and then grinned like an idiot. Centered on the bull, she flung her left arm out and nodded to the operator to start the ride. Once the bull started bucking, she shifted her body in the sexiest motion she could as she glanced at Joel standing off to the side. He wolf-whistled, bringing a smile to her lips.

The music seemed to roll along her spine with each swing of the bull. Her left arm snapped back and forth as she rode for the full eight seconds and earned herself the cowbell ring. When she jumped off the back of the bull, Joel met her in the middle of the padded ring, swept her up in his arms, and planted a fat, juicy kiss on her mouth.

She lost the ability to think beyond his mouth on hers. Their tongues entwined, battling from her mouth to his and back. He lifted her up in his arms, holding her against his chest as she wrapped her arms around his neck.

Moments later, someone slapped him on the back and they broke apart as the guy jokingly told him to take it somewhere else.

She was so embarrassed she hid her face in his chest while he escorted her outside the ring. What had gotten into her? She wasn't the type to be affectionate in public with anyone. Her ex-boyfriend even mentioned it several times, but here she stood making out with a guy she barely knew in a bar in his hometown. *Good gravy.* She'd turned into a regular slut in this small cowboy town.

"Don't be embarrassed."

"I don't do these sort of things, Joel."

"It's okay. Nobody even noticed."

She lifted her face from his chest and caught the dirty looks from the women as well as the thumbs up from several of the men surrounding them.

"Okay. So a few noticed."

"A few? If looks could kill, I'd be dead from the dirty looks the women are giving me, especially Brandy."

"Don't worry about it. Come on. Let's dance." He led her out onto the dance floor, put her hand on his shoulder, and took her other hand in his. "Now, relax. The step is called a two-step. You step once, shuffle twice and step again."

She took a deep breath, trying to concentrate on his words as he slowly led her around the dance floor.

"You're doin' great." He touched a finger under her chin to make her lift her gaze to his. "See? It's not so hard."

She stepped on his toe. "God, I'm sorry."

"It's okay. It's happened before. You aren't the first lady to step on my toes."

"I'm not supposed to, though. You're such a patient teacher." His gaze pulled her in as the music faded out of her conscious thought. She'd never seen eyes the color of his. Blue like a glacier, or maybe a swimming pool. She could so drown in his stare. The five o'clock shadow of a beard on his face made him sexier. Rugged. So fucking hot.

The music changed to something slow. A song she recognized. Dustin Lynch's *Cowboys and Angels*. *Damn. This is my favorite song.* Why does Joel have to be so gorgeous? Why can't he be some scraggly old codger who would be willing to tell her all his cowboy secrets over a cup of coffee? *And holy hell, there are three of him! Fuckin' A.*

"You slow dance well," he whispered, nuzzling her ear.

"There isn't much to it, really. You just shuffle back and forth. I probably won't bruise your toes on this one."

"We could always try a faster song. I can swing dance, too." He laughed at the shocked look on her face.

"Oh, hell no. I got your feet with the simple two-step. I'd probably break something swing dancing."

"I like this better anyway. I can hold you closer."

"You were holding me pretty close with the two-step."

"Not close enough." He pulled her in tighter. Her breasts brushed against the front of his western shirt, making them peak like mountaintops reaching for the warmth of the sky. *Damn, traitorous nipples.* "Are you excited, Mesa?"

"Excited?"

"Are your panties wet?" he whispered, brushing those full lips over her ear.

"A bit bold, aren't you?"

"I know when a woman is excited."

"Not this woman."

"Really?" he asked with a raised eyebrow over those damn sexy eyes. "Your nipples are poking me in the chest. Cold?"

"Why yes, I am."

"Liar." His lips brush her neck.

Her eyes drifted closed as goose bumps danced down her arms. His hands settled on her hips, slowly dragging her into the warmth of his embrace. *God, the man was sex on a stick.* Did he think she was some loser in the bedroom that he could drag into his web with eyes blue enough to drown in, lips full enough to lose her mind, and a body to stop traffic at a green light?

Of course he did.

She stepped out of his embrace. "I need a drink." She blew the hair off her forehead with a frustrated breath.

"I thought you were cold?" he asked with a smirk.

"Smartass."

"But yours is cute enough to eat whipped cream off of."

Fuck! She was so screwed. *If he wants to get me into the sack, he's doing a damn good job of it, even if I want it too.* "I thought you weren't supposed to seduce the guests?"

"Seduce? Who me?" He grinned as he wrapped his arm around her waist to escort her to the bar. "Beer?"

"Sure."

"Two Buds in the bottle please," he said, signaling the bartender who responded with a nod.

"Someone you know?"

"I know everyone in here, pretty much. We also know the judge, the sheriff, the lawyers, the schoolteachers, the principal, and everyone else. Most all of those you see in here now are guys and gals I went to high school with." He reached up to wave to someone nearby.

"I don't know what it's like to be surrounded by people I've grown up with."

"No?"

"Nope. I went to a high school where my graduating class had three thousand kids in it."

"Holy shit! Mine had one hundred fifty and I thought it was huge. It took three hours to read all the names off."

He paid the bartender before he handed her the bottle, then tipped his to his sensuous lips. *Lordy, the man could kiss.* The slow glide of his mouth over hers earlier in the dark, had been enough to curl her toes, but the lip smacking, tongue tangling kiss he'd laid on her after her bull ride still had her panting for air. She tentatively sipped at her beer, hoping it would wash away the taste of the kiss. No luck. She could still feel his mouth on hers. The slide of his tongue. *Damn.*

"Mine had to be split into two days. A through L one day and M through Z the next day. It sucks living in such a large place sometimes. I like having things to do all the time like shopping and stuff, but it's crazy not knowing who your neighbors are."

"I don't think I could live somewhere like that. I'm so used to living here. I couldn't be comfortable in a place where I didn't know the guy living above me. Concrete jungle comes to mind."

"Yeah. Now that you mention it, I don't care for it much either."

"Why do you stay then?"

"Because it's home. My parents are there. My siblings are nearby. I've lived in the same neighborhood for five years. I know where everything is."

He wrapped his arm around her waist to tuck her in close to his side. "Haven't you ever wanted to move to a place you didn't know anyone? Learn a new town, a new city?"

"You're one to talk, Joel. You've lived in Bandera all your life."

"True and I love it here. I love the area. I love my neighbors. I love working the ranch with my brothers and I hope someday the woman I marry with learn to love it like I do."

"Tall order."

"Not really."

"I guess not if you plan to marry someone who is already from here. They'd fit right in." He bent down and kissed her. "What was that for?" she asked, bewildered by his behavior.

"Just to let you know I'm thinking of you right at the moment. Not someone else."

"Thanks…I think." She wrinkled her nose. He laughed.

"It's a compliment, Mesa. You're a beautiful woman. I'm glad I'm here with you."

"You confuse me, Joel."

"Why?"

"Because one minute you kiss me and tell me I'm beautiful. The next I'm not sure if you're talking about me or someone else you've been with recently."

His mouth pulled down at the corners when he frowned. "What gave you the idea I was talking about anyone but you?"

"Just…oh never mind."

"I'm with you tonight. I think it's rude to talk about other women when you're with one."

She shrugged. "But we aren't together. We're here as friends."

"Still."

"Let's just have a good time. Forget about the rest for now."

"Sounds good to me. Are you finished with your beer? I want to dance with you again."

"And have me stepping on your feet more?"

"You're so cute when you're joking," he said, tweaking her nose, and then brushing his mouth against hers.

What the hell was she going to do about these feelings? She wanted to jump him and ride his hips into tomorrow like some rodeo bronc rider, but on the other hand, getting involved with a guy like him in a situation like this was a sure way to feel like shit when she went back to L.A.

He swept her up in his arms the minute they hit the dance floor again, doing a quick two-step. The dance brought her close enough to smell him. She wanted to taste him. Find out if his skin tasted salty under her tongue. Did he have a little sweat she could lick off?

"What are you thinking about?'

'Nothin', why?"

"You've got a guilty little smirk on your lips."

She captured her lips between her teeth.

"Ah, somethin' dirty?"

"Maybe, but I won't tell."

"How about if I tickle you until you tell me?"

"You wouldn't." His hand curled into her side and she giggled like a schoolgirl. "That's not fair!"

"Sure it is. You're keeping secrets."

"I'm a woman. We have secrets."

"Tell me." He tickled her again.

"Stop!"

"Not until you tell me."

"Okay, okay!" She gasped for breath as he led them to an empty table toward the back of the bar in a secluded corner. How this particular table became available, she would never know, but here she sat with one the most gorgeous men she'd ever seen in a darkened corner.

"Spill it."

"I was thinking about you."

"Me?"

"Yeah."

"And?"

She forced a ragged breath between her lips. Surely he didn't really expect her to tell him she wanted to lick the sweat from his body after he fucked her like a couple of bunny rabbits? "Nothing, really." He reached over and tickled her side. "All right!" She sighed. "You are rotten, you know?"

He touched her side again, making her jump.

"I was thinking about you being sweaty."

"Like after working outside?"

"Yeah."

"Why would you be thinking about me being sweaty?"

"Like licking you after sex." Heat crawled up her neck as she dropped her gaze to the table. "I'm so embarrassed."

"Why?"

"Seriously? We've only known each other like not even twenty-four hours."

"So? I think you're beautiful, sexy, interesting, and a great dancer. There's nothing wrong with being attracted to each other." He reached over and slid his hand along the side of her face. "I want to kiss you."

"You've kissed me before," she whispered, drowning in his eyes.

"I want to do it again."

His breath flittered across her lips. She wanted his mouth. She wanted his tongue. God, she wanted all of him touching her, holding her, making love to her.

"We should go."

"No. Not until I've tasted you again."

"Hey, Joel. Mesa," Josh said, sliding into the booth on the other side of her.

"Josh. What are you doing here?"

"I saw your two leave and figured you might be headed here."

Shit. Now I'm sandwiched between two good-looking men. Threesome? No, no, no.

"Yeah, we did. We've been dancing."

"I rode the bull," she said, moving a little further away from Joel. She needed the breathing room. Being close to him did all kinds of funny things to her insides.

"You did? Wow. Great job!" Josh exclaimed. "Did Joel?"

"No."

"Chicken, brother?"

"No. I got busy congratulating Mesa and forgot."

"Uh-huh."

The look on Joshua's didn't face bode well for their continued anonymity. She really didn't want his family knowing about their shared kisses or the fact of her wanting to get him in bed. She needed to forget about that part. He really should be beyond her reach. Girls like her didn't get guys like him. Women like Brandy roped in guys like the triplets, with their penetrating blue gazes, rock hard bodies, and kissable, full lips. *Damn.*

"Dance with me, Mesa," Joshua said, holding out his hand. "Please?"

"I'll warn you, I step on toes."

"No, she doesn't," Joel added. "She just learned to two-step though, so take it easy on her."

"Of course, brother."

She scooted out of the booth, allowing Joshua to take her hand and lead her to the dance floor. The whole time, she felt Joel's gaze on her back. The moment they reached the wood flooring, Joshua swept her up in his arms, bringing her in close…too close. She pushed on his chest to put more space between them. "Ease up on the hold buddy, or you're gonna lose something precious to you."

"Come on. You like Joel. I can see it in your eyes. We're identical."

"In looks maybe. But you need to think about what you're doing here." She pushed again.

"What? I'm dancing with a pretty woman."

"Who happens to be here with your brother."

"So?"

"You don't get it, do you? Do you guys always fight over women?"

'No." He grinned and winked. "I usually win."

"Why? Because you're an ass if you ask me."

He put one hand on his chest. "I'm hurt, Mesa. I thought you were a nice girl."

"I am, but I don't put up with bullshit like what you're trying to pull. Let me go."

"I could make it good for you. Joel won't go against the wishes of our mother and I think you want a good, hard lay."

She pushed out of his arms, pulled back her arm and slapped him as hard as she could. "How dare you! Someday you're going to find a woman who will put you in your place, Josh, and I'm going to laugh my ass off when I see it. Joel is twice the man you are."

"What's going on?" Joel asked, sliding to a stop between her and Josh.

"Nothing. Josh was just leaving."

"No I'm not."

"Yeah, you are brother. You've obviously insulted my lady friend and I won't put up with it. Go home before I kick your ass."

"You can try."

"Take it outside boys," the bartender hollered from behind the bar. "No fighting in here. You know the rules."

"Fine. Outside?" Josh asked, egging on his brother by smiling at Mesa.

"Bring it on, bro. I can kick your ass anytime."

"Stop this!" she shouted, pulling on Joel's arm. "Don't do this. Don't fight over nothing."

"It's not nothin', darlin'. He insulted you or you wouldn't have slapped him."

Joel followed Josh to the door with Mesa following close on their heels. A crowd of people trailed behind her. Surely it wasn't anything unusual for the Young brothers to fight? With nine of them, it couldn't be that big of a deal, right?

"Joel, please."

"No, Mesa. He's been asking for this since he came onto you at the barn this afternoon. He thinks he can do whatever he pleases and there aren't any consequences. Well there will be tonight."

The moment they cleared the parking lot, Joshua spun around to rush Joel, pushing him up against the side of someone's pickup.

"Fucker!"

"Kiss my ass, brother, and leave my girl alone."

"She ain't your girl, dumbass. You've known her what, six hours?"

Joel pushed Joshua back and swung, connecting with his jaw. Mesa flinched at the bone jarring sound, not sure if it was Joel's knuckles or Joshua's jaw. Josh took a swing, splitting Joel's lip. Blood spurted everywhere.

"You'll pay for that." Joel jabbed Josh in the ribs, doubling him over as he grunted in pain. "I told you I could take you down, asshole. Just go home."

"I'm gonna kick your ass," Joshua wheezed, rolling over onto his side.

"You can't even get up, Josh. Just stay down."

"Fucker!"

"It's not worth it. Go home."

"I'll go when I'm damned good and ready!" Josh rolled to his stomach and pulled his knees under him as he attempted to stand. One hand braced his ribs. "You fuckin' broke my ribs!"

"You asked for it by being a jerk to Mesa."

"She's just a piece of ass, Joel."

Joel swung again, connecting with Joshua's jaw. The blow took Josh flat on his back and out cold.

"He's unconscious!"

"Good. At least he won't get up again."

"You can't leave him like this." Mesa dropped down on the ground near Joshua's head. Josh moaned but didn't open his eyes.

"The hell I can't!"

"At least call one of your other brothers to come, Joel. He's your brother."

"He deserved it." Joel wiped at the blood on his lip with the back of his hand, smearing it across his chin.

"I know he did, but please?"

"Fine." Joe grabbed his brother's arm and hoisted him over his shoulder. "He's ridin' in the back."

"All right."

"Get in. I guess our night is over." He sounded disappointed.

Within moments, they were speeding down the road back toward the ranch with Joshua in the bed of the truck. He'd regained consciousness from what she could tell by looking out the window, but he didn't sit up or anything, just stared at the stars.

"He'll be fine. Mom will take care of him when we get home."

"I'm sorry," she murmured, feeling like shit for causing Joel and Joshua to fight. Of course, she'd never had two men fight over her before, much less two who looked like they did.

"For what?" He glanced her way, then out the windshield of his truck.

"For causing you two to fight."

"He asked for it, Mesa. Besides, it's not like it's the first time we've fought. We've done it for years off and on. It's what brothers do." He banged his hand on the steering wheel. "You didn't do anythin'. He treated you like shit and I won't have it. He can be a nice guy when he's not drinking, but get a little alcohol in him and he turns into a jerk." He glanced her way again. "Why are you being so nice to him? He called you a piece of ass."

"I'm not going to let it bother me, Joel. He's a guy. It's what guys do. Since I know it's not true, it doesn't matter to me."

"But what about all the people at the bar? They probably think we're having sex."

"What do I care? I'll probably never see them again. You and I know we aren't." She placed her hand on his thigh. "They are people. Nothing more."

"You're a better person than I am then. I don't like worrying about what other people think but it's in my nature, I guess. I've always had to fight to be an individual since I'm a triplet. It's hard to make people realize you are who you are rather than just one of the Young boys and a troublemaker."

"I suppose you got into trouble a lot as a kid?"

"Sometimes. I'm the middle of us triplets so it was pretty rough."

"I'm sorry."

"Nothin' to be sorry for. It's how it was."

They pulled up to the gate of the ranch, the headlights reflecting off the wrought iron fence. Joel punched in the code and the bulky piece of metal slowly slid open.

"Where are we?" Josh asked from the back while they bumped along the road toward the house.

Joel slid the window on the back open. "Home, you jackass," Joel called from inside the cab. "You'd better apologize to Mesa. What you said was totally inappropriate."

"Sorry, Mesa."

"I accept your apology. You know, if you act this juvenile when you drink, maybe you shouldn't drink."

"Wait a damned minute. I don't act like a kid."

She raised an eyebrow and smirked. "Are you sure?"

"All right maybe a little, but it's only in fun."

"It's not fun when someone's feelings get hurt."

"Did I hurt your feelings, Mesa?"

"It's not important."

"Yes, it is. If Mom found out you acted like an idiot, she'd tan your hide," Joel answered even though the question wasn't directed toward him.

"I'm too old for a whuppin'."

"Not from Mom. You know how she is about disrespecting women." Joel stopped the truck before he went around to open her door.

"Thank you."

"For what?"

"Opening my door."

"Sorry. I don't think about it. It's been ingrained in us since we were old enough to know manners."

"It's still a nice gesture and I appreciate it."

"You're welcome."

"I'm headed to my place. If Mom sees me, she really will tan my hide." Josh touched his chin. "Damn, dude! Did you have to hit me so fuckin' hard?"

"Don't think I'm not tellin' her what you did and yes I did. You were an ass."

"I already apologized, Joel. Let it go."

She placed her hand on Joel's arm to get his attention. "It's fine. He did apologize."

Joshua kissed her cheek before he headed off toward what she assumed to be his house. She could see a small, cabin like structure outlined in the distance. She'd have to check it out in the daylight although she didn't want to encourage Joshua, only Joel. "Let me clean up the cut on your lip."

He touched it and winced. "You don't have to. It'll be okay."

"You were gallant in standing up for me the way you did. It's the least I could do." They walked toward the main lodge in companionable silence. She really wasn't sure what to think with Joel. He acted like he was attracted to her, but then he wouldn't go against the rules of the ranch it seemed. They could be friends only, she supposed, although she wanted him hot between the sheets.

As they walked in the side doorway, she caught a glimpse of a cowboy walking out through the front door and wondered who he was. She thought she'd met all of those working the ranch during dinner. "Do you have someone not in the family working as a wrangler at the ranch?"

"No. Why?"

"I thought I saw someone I didn't recognize walk outside."

Joel shrugged. "It was probably one of my brothers."

"Maybe. He looked older."

"My dad?"

"Could have been I guess."

"Let me grab your key from the office. Your room is upstairs."

"Sure," she answered although he'd already walked away. A chill raced down her back and she rubbed her arms. *Weird.* It's still like seventy degrees outside even though her watch read eleven when she glanced at the dial.

Joel came back with a grin on his face but frowned the moment his lip started to bleed again. "Damn Josh. My lip hurts."

"Poor baby. You'll be fine. He got the worst part of the deal, I think." She grabbed his hand and said, "Lead the way."

They walked toward the wooden staircase at the back of the room hand in hand, but she stopped to look behind her for a moment.

"Something wrong?"

"I thought…" She shook her head and started walking again. "Never mind."

He led her up the first flight of stairs to the door in front of them and handed her the old fashioned key on a tag. "Wow. I haven't seen one of these in a long time. I didn't think anyone used these anymore."

"We do. We don't have the fancy credit card sliders like most other hotels and motels. This is a small, family run dude ranch."

"I wasn't critizing, Joel. I think it's cool you guys are regular country people." She slipped the key into the lock and opened the door. Mesa walked over to turn on the lamp on the bedside table, bathing the room in soft, muted light. Dominating the smaller room stood a double bed with a beautiful wedding ring comforter. Her clean clothes sat in a nice neat pile by the pillows. A wooden dresser sat at the end of the bed and to the right. The single large window overlooked the garden behind the house. Something she would have to explore tomorrow. She loved gardens. Right now, it looked spooky bathed in moonlight but romantic at the same time.

"The garden is my mother's favorite place to hang out. She's got lots of flowers back there, a sitting bench, a swing, and a barbeque. We throw parties out there during the cooler months."

"Texas does get warm in the summer."

"It's been pretty here this week. Not too hot and not too cold."

"Just for me."

He laughed. "Maybe."

"Except for the rain shower today."

"Those are normal for this time of year too."

"Just my luck."

"If you give me the keys to your car, I'll grab your suitcase and bring it up."

"All right." She handed him the keys. "On one condition. You let me wash the cut on your lip."

"Yes, nurse."

She startled a little, and then smiled.

"What?"

"I always wanted to be a nurse."

"Then why didn't you?" He held up his hand. "Wait to answer that until I get back." A moment later, he closed the door behind him, disappearing from sight.

Mute voices drifted through the wall. *Must be some other guests in the room next door.* The man's voice rose in anger. She cringed knowing where those tones usually led. She heard a slap, and then muffled crying a moment later. The sound died away after a few seconds as if it had never been there in the first place.

Mesa frowned, rubbing her arms as the room dropped in temperature like the air conditioner kicked on, but it hadn't. She shook her head and went to the connecting bathroom to fetch a warm washcloth to clean Joel's lip. The bathroom was decorated in the typical old-fashioned way with wood accents. A claw foot tub with a shower curtain to one end, and a large showerhead reminded her of the rain showerhead she had at home. Maybe tomorrow night she would take a long soak in the huge tub. A soft knock on the door brought her out of her musings.

She quickly grabbed a washcloth from those hanging on the rack, stuck it under some hot water and went to answer the door. She opened it to find no one on the other side. After she leaned out, she glanced down the hallway to both the left and right without seeing anyone nearby. "All right, Joel. That's not funny. You're scaring me."

"What are you talking about, Mesa?" he asked, coming up the stairs in front of her. "Who are you talking to?"

"Uh. No one, I guess."

"I've got your suitcase."

She stepped aside to allow him into the room. "Just set it on the bed and I'll unpack it in a minute." She told him to sit on the edge of the bed as she took a spot between his spread thighs. She exhaled forcibly through her lips so she could focus on the task at hand and not his hard thighs now encasing her lower half. The cut on his lip didn't look too deep. With her finger inside the cloth, she dabbed at the cut.

"Ouch."

"Sorry."

"It's okay. I know you didn't mean to hurt me."

He winced as she dabbed again. It had to hurt, she knew but all she could think about was kissing those full lips. She wanted to see his eyes dark with desire. Feel his hands on her bare flesh. Have those lips on other places of her body like her breasts, her nipples, or her clit.

"You okay?" he whispered, glancing up through those impossibly long eyelashes.

"Yeah." Her heart pounded behind her ribcage.

"Your pulse is fluttering."

"I know."

"Why?" His voice continued in a soft, coaxing tone reminding her of how he spoke to the horse while she gave birth to her foal.

"It's nothing, Joel."

"Do you want me to kiss you?"

She closed her eyes and licked her lips. *God, do I ever want you to kiss me. More than my next breath. More than a winning lottery ticket. More than...*

The next thing she knew, he had twisted her around so she lay flat on the bed with him hovering over her. He bent down and brushed his lips against hers so softly she wasn't sure if he'd actually kissed her.

"You shouldn't be doing this."

"I know."

He kissed her again, this time with his tongue softly brushing her lips as if to ask for permission to deepen it. Her lips parted of their own accord without her even thinking beyond how his lips felt against hers. The dip of his tongue tore a moan from her mouth. She tangled her hands in the front of his western shirt, wanting nothing more than to remove the barrier between his skin and hers.

The fire burning in her gut prompted her to return kiss for kiss, touch for touch. The caress of his fingers against the side of her breast brought her straight up on the bed, breaking the kiss.

"What's wrong?"

"I…uh. We shouldn't do this. Remember your mother's rule."

"I know, but I can't help but want to touch you. Kiss you." He ran his fingers down her cheek. "You're a beautiful woman, Mesa. I'm not sorry."

She touched her fingers to her lips as he turned to go.

"Goodnight, Mesa."

"Goodnight, Joel."

Chapter Six

"Stupid, Joel. Really, really stupid!" He threw the horse's bridle across the tack room before he raked his fingers through his hair, knocking his Stetson from his head.

"Whoa. What's got your panties in a twist?" Jacob asked, putting one of the saddles back on the rack. "You aren't usually this strung up."

"Nothin'."

"It doesn't sound like nothin' to me. Throwing tack usually means you're pissed."

"Fine. I'm pissed."

Jacob removed his hat and tossed it on the desk in the corner. "About?"

"A woman."

"So?"

"It's Mesa." He paced from one side of the tack room to the other with agitated steps. The thing with Mesa had him wound up tighter than a string of barbwire.

"Ah."

"I kissed her."

"Yeah, we all saw it out by the bonfire."

"No, after that. More than once."

"I still don't understand what the big deal is."

"I can't get involved with someone who is only going to be here for a few days. It's crazy."

"So you have a quick fling. What's the problem?"

He stopped and turned to face his brother. "The big deal is she's not the kind of girl you have a quick fling with, Jacob. She's a nice girl. The kind of girl you settle down with."

"Seriously, Joel. Settle down?"

"I'm not thinkin' of settlin' down, idiot, but she's not the barfly type."

"Maybe she is. You never know." He picked up the bridle and hung it on the rack. "Maybe you should ask her?"

"Ask her? Really? What do I say? How about a quick fuck, Mesa?"

"Sure. Why not?"

Joel picked up his Stetson and put it back on his head. "Maybe. I mean she's attracted to me from what I can tell. She definitely got into the kiss we shared."

"Just fuck her already, would ya," Jason added, coming in from the corral. "I'll take her off your hands if you want. Not like she could tell the difference between us anyway."

"I bet she could."

"I bet she couldn't."

Joel stuck out his hand. "How much?"

"A hundred bucks," Jason answered.

"You're on."

"Fine. After dinner, I'll take her up to her room and turn on the charm. I bet she kisses me and lets me feel her up."

Joel squinted and snapped, "I bet she calls a halt to everything after the first kiss if not before."

"You know very few people outside of the family can tell the difference between us, Joel. I bet she can't."

"I think she's more into me and will be able to tell right away." Joel kicked a rock near the toe of his boot back out into the corral. He sounded confident to his brother, but he wasn't so sure. What if Mesa couldn't tell the difference? What if she liked Jason better than him? *No, this is nuts. I know what our kiss was like. We could set the sheets on fire if I could get her between them.* "I know what I felt when we kissed."

"She's just a woman, Joel. Nothin' special."

"You're wrong there, Jason. She is special."

* * * *

The dinner bell clanged and Mesa frowned. She hadn't seen Joel all day. Was he avoiding her? Probably. Men didn't take well to being put off when they had sex on the brain. Stopping their kiss the night before wasn't a bad idea, but maybe he felt like there wasn't anything to gain now by hanging out with her.

As Mesa made her way down the stairs to the dining room, the sound of voices got louder. A bus full of tourist had arrived earlier in the day, making the whole place buzz like a swarm of bees. Many of them went riding earlier, leaving her the run of the ranch house to herself. She'd taken her laptop into the main hall, set it up on one of the tables and managed to type out the beginning of a new novel called Mission: Cowboy. She cringed. She wasn't sure she liked it, but she figured a new title would come to her when the characters started adding their voices to the storyline. She wasn't a plotter when it came to her stories so everything depended on what they said.

Stopping on the stairs, she looked over the group. All the tourists were back and the place was packed to the gills. The family waited at their table for the group to be served while they chatted about their day. Joel sat at the end of the table next to an empty chair she hoped might be for her. Or was it Joshua? Maybe Jason? *Damn.* From this distance she wasn't sure which one was which? *Damn it.*

"Mesa, come sit by me, darlin'." One of the three waved from the end of the table.

She chewed on her lips a moment and then started down the stairs. *Okay. Joel? Shit. I'm not sure.* She took the seat he held out for her, dropping into it with little grace. *Nice, Mesa.*

"How was your day?"

"Great. I got a lot of writing done in the main lodge."

"Awesome."

The rest of the group had been served, so the family got up to get their own plates, which included her. Joel or whichever one of them this was standing next to her, grinned and motioned for her to take the spot in front of him. His cologne drifted to her nose. It seemed different somehow. She looked closer. No, she couldn't really tell if it was Joel, Jason, or Joshua. Well, yes she could because Joshua had a small cut near his chin and Joel had a small abrasion near his bottom lip from their fight at the bar last night. This must be Jason. But what was he up to? Was he deliberately playing like she didn't know the difference? Surely they didn't think she was that stupid.

"I enjoyed our kiss last night," he whispered near her ear.

Okay, she didn't like this game. What the hell was going on? "Really? I'm glad."

"Me too. I want to take you out in the moonlight tonight after dinner. You game?"

"Okay." She frowned. *Really?* She grabbed a plate in order to get her dinner as the conversation lagged. Discussing this in front of his family wasn't a great idea. She glanced around looking for Joel. He stood at the back of the line frowning. What kind of game were they playing?

She returned to her place at the table, setting her plate down first before she retrieved a glass of lemonade and a dessert. Jason slid his hand along her shoulder as he took the seat next to her. Now she knew why the cologne was different, he wasn't Joel. Why was Joel giving her the cold shoulder? What did they plan?

The conversation around the table focused on the day's labors. They'd moved cattle from the south pasture to the north pasture. Several of the cattle had dropped their calves already making everyone worry it might be too late in the season and they would suffer without extra feed. She could hear many of the tourists talking about their ride on the horses that day and she mentally planned to do some riding of her own tomorrow. Horseback riding was one of her favorite past times. She wanted to explore the ranch more with Joel, though. Not on a strict trail ride.

"Would you like to go riding tomorrow?" Jason asked.

"Um, yes I would."

"Great. I'll saddle a couple of horses. I can meet you at the stable around nine in the morning."

"Okay." *What the hell? This whole thing stinks.*

They finished dinner in silence while the rest of the family talked about different topics. The moment she finished, Jason grabbed her plate to deposit it into the dirty dish bin.

"Walk with me."

"All right," she answered, deciding to see where this whole thing might be leading. Did Joel push her off on his brother because he didn't want to hurt her feelings by saying he wasn't attracted to her? Did Jason think she wanted him?

She let Jason take her hand and walk her out the front door of the main lodge to the chairs lining the porch. Even though the full moon happened the night before, it still shone bright enough to see the walkway.

"You look beautiful in the moonlight."

"Thank you."

"You know, the kiss we shared last night blew my socks off. I wish you hadn't made me leave."

Frowning, she opened her mouth to tell him she knew he wasn't Joel, but he bent his head and kissed her full on the mouth. She quickly stepped back and smacked him across the face. "How dare you."

"What?"

"Do you think I'm stupid? Do both of you think I wouldn't know the difference between you, Jason?"

"You knew I wasn't Joel?"

"Hell yes! Even if I hadn't figured it out at dinner, I would have known from the kiss."

"Most people can't tell the difference between us."

"Joel has an abrasion near the left side of his mouth from where he got in a fight with Joshua at the bar last night."

"Damn."

"What the hell is going on here? Why the ruse?"

"I'll tell you, Mesa," Joel said, coming around the side of the house. "I was pissed off at myself this morning because of what happened last night. Our kiss, I mean."

"Well you know what? Fuck both of you! You want to play these sillyassed games, you can play them on some other unsuspecting woman. I'm not doin' it."

"Mesa, listen," Joel implored, holding out his hand to touch her arm.

She jerked back and slapped at him. "No. This is childish. I can't believe you two! I thought I might have meant a little more to you than this, Joel, but apparently not. What we shared last night was special to me, but not to you. I'm just another girl to you."

"No, you're not, Mesa."

"Yeah, whatever." She spun around to head back into the house. Maybe it was time to go. Head back to Los Angeles and lick her wounds.

"Mesa, please."

"What Joel?" She turned back around.

"Let's talk about this."

"What the hell is there to talk about? You and your brother were playing me for the fool. How many times have you three switched places on a girl, huh? I bet a lot."

"No."

"Yes." During her discussion with Joel, Jason had disappeared either back into the house or whatever. At this point, she really didn't care. He probably slinked back into his hidy hole. Man, if she ever became a permanent part of this family, she'd…what? *Those are crazy thoughts.*

Joel slipped his hand along the side of her face before burying his hand in her hair. He dragged her in closer with a fistful of her hair at the back of her neck. "I want you."

"You made a fool of me."

"No, I wanted to make sure it was me you wanted." His lips whispered over hers. The softness skimmed across her cheek to her ear. "I need you."

"Need is a powerful word."

"It's totally what I'm feeling, but I can't promise you anything beyond tonight."

"I don't need anything more."

"Are you sure?" he asked, listing his head to look into her eyes. The blue glistened in the moonlight like a beacon for her lost soul.

"Yes. I need you. I need this."

"Your room or my place?"

"You have somewhere we can go?"

"Yeah. I have my own cabin a few miles up the road."

"Make love to me, Joel. Fuck me."

He pulled her head back as he raked his teeth along her neck. Shivers raced down her arms as a soft moan escaped her mouth. "Come home with me."

"Yes, please."

He looked deep into her eyes for a moment as if judging whether she was serious or not. Little did he know, she'd wanted this from the first time he'd kissed her or maybe it was when she had her breasts squished to his back as they rode in the rain back to the house? Who cared?

"Let's go," he said, grabbing her hand and half dragging her to where his truck stood in the parking lot behind the main lodge.

"A little horny are we?"

"Hell yeah. A lot horny. You've had me wound up tighter than a damned spring from the moment you climbed up behind me to rest those gorgeous breasts against my back." He opened the door on the driver's side of his truck, practically shoving her inside the cab by the seat of her pants. "Sorry, baby."

Oh I love the little endearments coming from his mouth now that we're going to have sex. "You can call me all the little pet names you want."

He grinned as he turned over the truck and shot gravel behind it as he tore out of the drive. "You have no idea how much I want this."

"If I'm judging your craving to mine, I bet I do."

"How long has it been since you've had sex?"

"Several months. You?"

"Me too."

"You do have condoms, right?"

"Yeah. A few." He grinned.

"I hope you plan on using several tonight."

"Oh, no problem there, babe."

Damn, he almost sounds cocky. Well, why wouldn't he be? He could probably have any woman he wants. She frowned, feeling a bit self-conscious at her rounded little stomach and even rounder hips. She wasn't a skinny woman by any means.

"Why the frown?"

"Nothing."

"No, baby. Tell me. No secrets tonight."

She bit her lip.

"Come on."

"I'm just not the skinny little cowgirls you're used to."

"I'm not into skinny."

"Younger?"

"I'm not into jailbait either, Mesa. I like you the way you are. Rounded curves and enough softness for me to sink myself into. I don't plan on coming out until tomorrow mornin'. You okay with that?"

"Are you sure?"

"Positive, babe." He grabbed her hand to place it on his groin.

The hardness behind his fly let her know he wanted her…needed her. *God, he's huge!*

"I hope you plan on goin' easy on me."

"Why?"

"Like I said, I haven't had sex in a bit and you aren't exactly small."

"I'll take care of you."

Within moments, they pulled up to a small cabin with a porch around the front. It wasn't anything huge by any means. Just small enough for a single man, or a couple maybe. *Get those thoughts out of your head. You're only here for a few days.*

"Nice place."

"Thanks. It's not much, but it's got a king sized bed."

"That'll do for tonight then." *King sized bed and Joel for the night? Hell yeah!*

No lights shone from the windows. White curtains blew in the breeze of the one open to the left front corner. The house wasn't decorated at all. No woman's touch anywhere.

"Sorry. It's kind of a mess."

"A bachelor lives here. I wouldn't expect anything else." Dishes were piled in the small sink to her right as they walked through the door. He had a stove, refrigerator and a few cabinets to hold dishes, she assumed. The couch in front of the fireplace would make for great cozy nights. She shook her head. She didn't need to go there.

"This way." He took her hand and led her back down the hall to the first door on the right. "There's a bathroom to your left if you need it."

"Thanks," she said, walking through the small doorway and shutting it behind her. The florescent lighting over the mirror showed her wild hair from Joel running his hands through it. Her eyes were bright. The pupils dilated. Her lips were puffy from his kiss. All in all, she looked like a slut. "Great." She ran her fingers through her hair to try and straighten it out a little before she went back out there. "Okay, really Mesa. I don't think he cares what your hair looks like except if it's the hair between your legs."

Oh, crap! I didn't shave my legs this morning. What if they are stubbly? I didn't shave my bikini line lately either. Shit!

"Mesa? Are you okay, babe?"

"I'm fine, Joel. I'll be out in a second."

"I've got some wine. We can sit and relax for a bit. No hurry on this." It sounded like he ran his knuckles on the door. "I mean, we can talk a while or whatever."

"Okay." Could he tell her nerves were shot? Probably. He definitely was trying to soothe them. She used the restroom, washed her hands, and then opened the door. Joel stood on the other side with a little smile lifting the corners of his mouth.

"Better?"

"Yeah. Thanks."

"Come with me," he said, taking her hand. With his hat now gone the light reflected in a blue-black sheen on his curls. "We can watch television, talk or whatever you want to do. We don't even have to have sex if you've changed your mind."

"I haven't. Have you?" she asked, taking a seat next to him on the couch.

"No, but I don't want you to think I'm some kind of caveman. You're comfort means everything to me."

She wiped her sweaty palms along the thighs of her jeans.

"Are you nervous?"

"Yeah, a little," she said with a shrug. "I've never had casual sex before."

He ran his fingers along her jaw. "I've never been in a relationship, so I guess it makes us even."

"Never?"

"Well, nothin' serious anyway. I've dated a couple of women for a period of time, but it never got serious on my part."

She frowned. He smoothed his thumb between her eyes.

"What's the frown for?"

"I was thinking about my ex."

"A hint here, Mesa. Guys don't want to hear you're thinking about your ex when they're about to have sex with you."

She turned to face him as she placed her hand on his chest. "No, nothing like that. I wasn't comparing you by any means. There's nothing to compare with. I mean, you're lean, muscular and drop dead gorgeous. Those eyes could melt chocolate and you know how much women love chocolate. He didn't have any of those things."

"What were you comparing then?"

"I wasn't comparing anything. I had a thought about how my relationship with him seems so different than this with you. When I went out with him, things moved very slowly. We didn't have sex for six months after we met. Even then, it wasn't anything to write home about." With a giggle, she covered her mouth. "Not like I would write my mother about my sex life, but you know what I mean."

He laughed. "Yeah, I do. There've been a few women I wouldn't make love to twice."

"Really? I thought all guys were just in it for the end result. You know, gettin' their rocks off."

"Not if they are any good, they aren't. It's more fun for me to make sure the woman has several orgasms when I'm with her."

The lump in her throat almost choked her. "Several?"

He leaned in and ran his tongue along her jawline until he reached her ear. "Yeah, several."

Holy shit, he's got one sexy voice. The lower rumble of his voice threw her heart into overdrive. The slow seep of moisture between her thighs surprised her. She never got this wet with her ex. Not from only a whisper in her ear. Those were things she wrote about in her novels, not something she experienced for herself. She swallowed *hard.*

"Um, Joel?"

"Yeah?" he asked, sliding his tongue around her earlobe.

"Damn, you're good."

He chuckled softly as he nipped the fleshy part of her ear between his teeth. She closed her eyes, letting the feelings overwhelm her. Hooking up with him probably wasn't a good idea, but every time he got close to her, she couldn't think of anything except getting him between the sheets to see how good he really was.

One hand slipped up her stomach to cup her breast. Two of his fingers plucked at her nipple through her bra and her whole world tilted on its axis. She'd always known her nipples were sensitive, but the slight pain of his pinch sent her body into a spiral of need.

His hand disappeared, reappearing under her shirt, pushing her bra out of the way. The warmth of his hand on her breast brought a moan to her lips.

Seconds later, her shirt found its way over her head to leave her sitting on his lap in just her bra and jeans.

"God, you're gorgeous. All curves."

"You mean fat."

"No, curves. I love curves on a woman. I'm not into skinny like a rail. I want something to hold onto when I'm pounding my cock into your sweet heat."

"I want you to."

"Shall we head into the other room where it's more comfortable? Not that I wouldn't love to make you come a dozen times right here on the couch first."

"A dozen?" She gulped a lungful of air as shivers raked her body.

"Oh yeah."

He stood with her in his arms and headed down the small hall toward the bedroom. She hadn't got a good look at the bedroom when they came down here before, but she did now. He didn't have a lot of furniture. Just a bed, a small nightstand, and a dresser. The deep blue comforter on the bed seemed typical guy décor. A shade on the window gave him privacy, but did nothing to soften the room. No curtains hung there. Nothing to indicate a woman had ever called this space home. Someday, one would, though. When, she didn't know and didn't want to think about right now, but yeah, someday he would bring a wife here until they could build a bigger home for children.

"You're thinking too much," he whispered, from behind her as he wrapped his arms around her.

"Yeah, probably."

He cupped her breasts in both hands and tugged her back against his chest. "Your skin is so soft. I could eat you up."

"I hope you do."

"Oh, I plan on it, baby. I'm gonna eat you until you scream my name."

"I don't think it'll take much."

"Good." He licked the side of her neck before he nipped at her collarbone. "I can't wait to feel you ripple around me."

He skimmed one hand down her abdomen, flicking open the button at her waist on his way to pulling her zipper down. The moment he had her pants parted, he slipped one hand under the waistband of her underwear to push a finger deep inside her pussy. "You're wet, darlin'."

"You've made me wet, Joel, with your sexy voice, wicked tongue, and demanding nips."

"You'll be wetter before I'm done with you."

"Promises, promises."

"Oh yeah."

She widened her stance to allow him better access as he ran his wet finger over her clit. Her whole body shook. The man was wicked. Sex on a stick.

The elastic of her bra gave way to his insistent fingers, loosening around her breasts until it barely hung on her body. She drew the cups down over her breasts, letting it slide completely off to the floor at her feet. "You need to be undressed, too."

"I will. For now, I'm enjoying your beautiful breasts. I love your nipples. Rosy, hard, and standing straight out. I wish I had a set of nipple clamps for them."

"Nipple clamps?"

"Have you ever had them on?"

"No, but I've heard of them."

"Yours are perfect for a set."

"Thanks."

He pinched her nipples, causing her to close her eyes and moan from deep in her chest. The next thing she felt was his hands on her hips, pushing her pants to the floor. "Step out."

Doing what he told her felt natural, but a little scary. She wasn't one to take orders very well normally. She started to turn around until he held her in place.

"Uh-uh." He pulled her arms behind her, binding her wrist with his hands. "I like my sex a little rough. How about you?"

"What do you mean by rough?"

"Spankings, hard sex. Fuck me like you mean it."

"Spankings? I've never liked those."

"Ever had an erotic spanking?"

"Can't say I have." She shivered as he ran his hands from her breasts to her hips, and then smacked her on the right butt cheek. The groan escaping her mouth surprised her. Maybe she did like erotic spankings after all or spankings in general.

He chuckled as he did it again. "Sounds to me like you enjoy a little pain with your sex."

"Maybe. I've never had anyone do the things you're doing to me before."

"It'll be a brand new experience for you then."

She rubbed her burning butt cheeks against the roughness of his denim jeans. She wondered what it would feel like if he really got going?

"Another time."

Damn the man! Why does it seem like he knows what I'm thinkin'?

"Your eyes are very expressive. I can usually tell what you're thinking by seeing your eyes. Right now, you're turned on by what I did." He pushed his fingers into her pussy. "You can't hide your body's response."

"How can you see my eyes? You're behind me."

"Look toward the dresser."

She hadn't noticed it before but a large mirror reflected their bodies in the most erotic way she'd ever seen. She frowned as she saw the pooch of her stomach and the roundness of her hips.

His handed landed a blow to her thigh. "Ouch."

"That wasn't meant to turn you on. Punishment comes in different forms. You won't frown at this body when you look in the mirror. It's mine for now and I love how it looks."

"But…"

He smacked her thigh again. "Mine. Do you hear me?"

"Yes."

"Now look at it as I see it. Beautiful, high breasts." He cupped her breasts, lifting them. "Gorgeous rosy nipples." He pinched her nipples between his thumb and first finger. "Mine."

"Yours."

His hands skimmed down her abdomen before resting on her hips. "These hips are curvy with just the right amount of padding. I won't have to worry about breaking something if I fuck you hard from behind."

She tried to see herself from his point of view. Her breasts were pretty, still pert with dusky, pink nipples. Her hips were rounded, but those were supposed to be good for child birthing. Long legs. She'd heard men liked long legs. She wasn't fat, really but maybe a little plump.

"You're a beautiful woman, Mesa."

He stood behind her. A head taller than her five foot eight inches making him over six feet. His dark hair curled slightly at the end resting near the nape of his neck. Glacier blue eyes stared back at her in the mirror, dilated widely, and burning hot with lust. They reminded her of a blue flame. The calluses on his hands abrading her skin felt luscious on her body. His five o'clock shadow scraped her shoulders as he rubbed his chin along the slope.

"Cold?" he whispered, running his tongue down her neck.

"No. Excited would be a better word."

"Good. I want you excited." He stepped around her and took her hand, drawing her closer to the big bed in the corner.

With a little tug, he sat her on the edge. Now, he stood directly in front of her, his belt buckle even with her face. Should she touch him? Help him undress? She wasn't sure of the next move.

"Only do as I tell you. I'll make sure you know exactly what to do."

"Okay."

"Unbuckle my belt."

She reached for the large buckle at his waist, slipping the belt through the loops until it had been pulled complete free of his pants. The leather was soft and worn under her touch. *What would it feel like to have him use it on my ass?* She bit her lips in concentration. Should she undo his jeans?

"Some other time we'll play with the belt. I don't want to overload you." He ran the tip of his finger over her bottom lip. "Open my pants."

A soft sigh escaped her lips as he stuck his thumb between her teeth, forcing her mouth open slightly.

"You're gonna suck me. I want to feel those plump lips wrapped around my cock."

Once she got his pants open, she tugged the jeans and his boxers down around his hips so his cock sprang free.

"I don't think I can take all of you."

"You'll do fine, darlin'. I believe in you."

"Can we turn off the lights?"

"No. I want to see you goin' down on me. There's nothin' sexier than a woman's mouth wrapped around my cock."

The heat rising from her chest to splash across her cheeks burned her skin. She wasn't used to being so open with a bed partner. Hell, sex with her ex consisted of lights off and strictly missionary. This was totally different. Sexy. Spontaneous. Hot.

"Take me in your hand. Cup my balls with the other one."

She wrapped her hand around the base of his cock and cupped her hand around the slightly furred sacks below. "Like this?"

"Have you ever given a blow job before, Mesa?"

"Yes, but I want to do this right."

"Do what you want. I'll guide you. You'll be able to tell what feels good for me by the sounds."

She took just the head of his cock between her lips. His hips surged toward her, shoving it a little farther inside her mouth.

"Oh yeah. That's good."

Giving into the notion he enjoyed what she did, she sucked lightly on the head, bringing him more into her mouth. She gagged slightly as he pushed past her palate and hit the back of her throat.

"Breathe through your nose. The gagging will pass."

She backed off in depth and sucked air in through her nose. Her gag reflex had always been very sensitive.

"If you can't go very deep, it's okay. Use your hand to give me the pressure from the bottom and your mouth to counter it. Roll my balls between your fingers."

She pushed him back slightly and dropped to hers knees so she could get better leverage on what she was doing. The little whimpers, groans and other sounds coming from his mouth as she pleasured him, drove her own desire higher. Wetness coated her pussy. She wished she had a hand free to touch herself. The pressure building between her thighs drove her crazy.

"You're doin' great, darlin'." He pushed his hips toward her face. "A little more suction. Oh yeah. Perfect." She bobbed her head, running her tongue around the tip of his cock as she drove his pleasure higher. "That's it. Okay stop or I'm gonna blow in your mouth and I don't want to. I want to be inside you when I come."

He helped her stand before pushing her back onto the bed and quickly removed the rest of his clothing. The gorgeous body standing in front of her blew her mind. His cock stood long and thick against his abdomen and she wondered again how it would ever fit inside her without tearing her apart.

"I love your breasts. They are fucking gorgeous." He cupped them in both hands, lightly sucking the right and then the left nipple. After he feasted on her breasts for a couple of minutes, he worked his way down her abdomen until he knelt on the floor between her thighs.

"Wait."

"What?"

"What are you gonna do?"

"I want to lick you clean and make you come so hard you see stars."

"But..." He licked the inside of her thigh, stopping with a little nip to the skin. "Ouch."

"This body is mine tonight. No more talking."

He spread her thighs further apart and settled himself *down there.* Embarrassment flushed her cheeks. Her ex had never done this before, which may be part of the reason their love life sucked so badly. Now she knew the difference and...*oh.*

His wet tongue skimmed her outer pussy lips. The rough texture felt heavenly on her pussy as she relaxed into the comforter and let Joel do what he wanted. Fire built her in pelvis. Need scorched her body, flushing her skin to a pale pink. Blood pounded in her ears. The wet slide reached her clit and her hips lifted off the bed. His hand pushed her back down as he flicked his tongue over the hard nub.

"Oh God."

"Come for me, Mesa."

Heat crawled up her legs. Her pelvis burned. Blood rushed in her veins to the one spot he continued to lick. The moment he sucked her clit between his lips, she exploded, screaming his name in the heat of passion she'd never felt before.

"Very nice, baby." Two of his fingers pushed into her pussy. "You're beautiful when you come. Shall we try for another?"

"Another?" she squeaked, exhausted from the first one.

"You can do it again. I know you can."

The two dangerous digits in her pussy felt like heaven and hell at the same time. He shoved them in and out in a slow, taunting rhythm that she found had her blood pounding again in a few short minutes. Surely she couldn't come again so soon?

His tongue returned to her clit doing quick figure eights. His fingers continued their movement and the next thing she knew, she exploded again without much warning this time. No heat in her legs, no tingling in her pussy, nothing to warn her of the impending blast.

"Oh God!" she screamed. "Joel!"

As she slowly returned to awareness, she realized he'd moved from between her thighs to hover over her. His latex covered cock nudged at her opening.

"Are you ready for me?"

"You're so big."

"It'll fit, darlin'. You are so wet, it'll slide right in. Open for me."

She pulled her thighs further apart, tensing as he pushed the head of his cock inside.

"Relax. I won't hurt you."

The slow glide of his cock felt amazing. Her muscles relaxed as he slowly stretched her to take him. "Holy shit, you feel fantastic. More."

"Your wish is my command."

Within moments, he had fully filled her and she had her legs wrapped around his hips. "I need more, Joel."

He chuckled. "There isn't any more, Mesa. You've got all of me, darlin'."

"No. I mean you need to move more." She raised her hips to take him deeper.

"Ah. That I can do, babe." He shifted his hips, dragging his cock from her pussy and then snapping his hips to slam his cock into her.

"Yes, ah God, yes. Do that again." She fisted the comforter beneath her in her hands. Lord, she needed this. Every slide, every movement, every touch brought her higher and higher. He bent over to take her nipple into his mouth. The moan escaping from her lips sounded primal. He growled low in his throat as he continued to pump into her, practically scooting her across the bed. His fingers dug into the fleshy part of her hips. She'd probably have bruises there in the morning but she didn't care. She wanted this with him so badly.

She could taste him on her tongue.

She struggled into a sitting position so she could be closer.

"You okay?"

"Fantastic. Don't stop. I just want to taste your skin." She ran her tongue over the ridges of his chest. His right nipple tempted her so she tongued it and then sucked it between her lips.

He continued to pound into her flesh. The pretzel maneuver felt like wave after wave of sensation breaking over her. Her climax hovered on the edges of her consciousness. She reached for the stars as the final moment crested her mind, throwing her into a spiral of sensation as he groaned her name.

"God, Mesa." He panted. "That was…"

"Awesome?"

"Stupendous. I've never come so hard in my life. I think I lost consciousness there for a second."

"I'm glad."

"Nothin' like makin' an impression, babe."

"And take a little piece of your heart with me?"

Chapter Seven

Her stomach felt like she swallowed a rock. *Not a good thing to say right after sex.* "I'm kidding!"

"Don't do that! You scared the hell out of me." He slowly eased from inside her before he went to dispose of the condom in the bathroom. "Do you need to wash up?"

"Yeah. I'm kind of sticky." She sat up and brushed the hair back from her forehead. Watching him walk away was almost better than watching him walk toward her. The man had a body like a Greek god. He even had a real six-pack!

"Want me to bring you a washcloth or do you want to use the restroom?"

"I better use the bathroom."

"It's all yours," he said with a sweep of his hand.

Even flaccid, his cock seemed huge. *Damn!*

"Do you want to stay here tonight or do you want to go back to the lodge?"

"Either is fine with me. I don't want to crowd you. I know how guys get."

He stopped her at the bathroom door with a hand on her bare shoulder. She felt a little self-conscious standing in front of him completely naked, even though they'd just had mind-blowing sex. "Mesa, I know this is supposed to be casual and all, but I would love for you to stay here and sleep in my arms."

She tossed back her hair and replied, "Then I will. I would love to sleep snuggled up to you."

"Good. Would you like something to drink? I have soda, milk, water, beer…just name it."

"A diet soda would be good if you have one. If not, regular is fine."

"One soda, coming right up." He raised an eyebrow and glanced down at her. "I imagine you didn't bring anything to sleep in so you can use one of my shirts if you like."

"Thanks."

He grabbed a T-shirt from the drawer and handed it to her. "No underwear."

"Huh? Why not?"

"I might want to ravish you again before mornin'."

"Oh. Well then. I'm game." She reached up and kissed him on the lips. "I've gotta get it while the gettin' is good, ya know."

He frowned slightly before he spun on his heels and disappeared down the hallway. His nice, rounded tush caught her attention. He didn't even bother to put anything on before he went into the other room for something to drink. *Now there is a man who is comfortable in his own skin.* She went inside and shut the door to get cleaned up. She definitely wasn't comfortable with her body even if he said he liked it. The mirror showed high color on her cheeks, full lips, red from the pressure of his, whisker burn on her chest and neck from his five o'clock shadow, and a sparkle in her eyes she hadn't seen there in a long time. Joel was good for her. Too bad it wasn't a permanent thing.

She found a washcloth on the counter to clean away the stickiness between her thighs.

"I don't keep a lot of food around here since we take meals at the lodge house," he shouted from the kitchen.

"It's fine. I'm not really hungry anyway," she said, coming out the door of the bathroom.

"I have some snack stuff, if you'd like. Chips, pretzels, popcorn."

"Nah, I'm good." Now, she pulled the comforter down to the end of the bed and crawled beneath the sheet. She frowned. She hadn't thought about what side of the bed he slept on. Would it make a difference? The only man she'd ever slept with on a regular basis was her ex.

"Here," he said, stopping by her side to hand her the soda can.

"I'm okay here, right?"

"You're perfect." He leaned down and kissed her. "Don't be surprised if you end up in the middle. I usually do."

"Are you a snuggler?"

"I guess. I don't have women here very often."

"Really? I'm surprised."

"Why?" he asked, going around to the other side and sliding under the sheet.

"I would think you would have a lot of women. That's all." She sipped from the can before she set it on the nightstand.

"Not really."

"Well, I'm a snuggler, so for tonight, you get to snuggle."

He smiled and wrapped his arm around her shoulders as she settled down along his left side. Her head rested nicely against his chest. His heart pounded in her ear. The hair on his chest tickled her chin, making her giggle.

"What's so funny?"

"Your hair is tickling me."

"You are ticklish?" He slid his hand up her side and curled his fingers into her ribs.

Giggling, she squirmed against him. "Shit. No! Don't tickle me, please? I'm terribly ticklish. Remember at the bar?"

"I'll quit if you give me a kiss."

"All right! No…tickling." She quickly pecked him on the mouth.

"Not good enough." He tickled her again as she squealed.

"Okay!" She grabbed his face on both sides and lip locked his mouth. She pushed her tongue between his lips, tangling with his own. The moan escaping him did nothing to cool the kiss she took deeper still, pressing her breasts against his chest. He never got redressed after the bout of lovemaking earlier, leaving her the ability to graze his body with her fingertips. The muscles beneath her hands drove her desire higher. She wanted to feel him over her, in her, surrounding her until they both came apart at the seams.

Mesa pushed him down on his back and crawled over him, wanting to take in every inch of his body on her way down. Sex wasn't something she enjoyed much with her ex. Moderation and tolerance had become her mantra with him, but she knew with Joel, there would be no tolerating. She needed to be involved in having sex with him. She ran her tongue along his jaw to his ear, nibbling it between her teeth for a moment.

"You're so fucking hot, Mesa," he whispered between panting breaths. Goose bumps rose on his skin following the trail of her fingers.

"You're pretty hot yourself, cowboy. I wanna lick you all over." She ran her tongue across his chest, stopping to nip at the tips of his nipples. Were his sensitive, too? She whipped the T-shirt over her head and tossed it to the side of the bed.

"God, you're drivin' me nuts."

"Good. I don't want to be horny all by myself."

His cock lay hard between them against her stomach, pulsating with life, just waiting to bring her to ecstasy again.

"Oh, hell no." He surged up and flipped her onto her back.

He tasted her breasts, licked at her stomach and then positioned himself between her thighs, spreading her to accommodate the breadth of his shoulders. He dove in, taking no prisoners on his way to bringing her to orgasm within a matter of moments. Her ears burned as the blood rushed to her head before it quickly centered in her pelvis. Her clit throbbed with every beat of her heart, but wasn't letting up. He licked and sucked until she screamed his name on a hoarse cry of delight.

He kissed his way back up her body until he reached her mouth. "I love to make you come."

"I was supposed to be seducing you. Not the other way around."

"I wanna fuck you."

"Good. I want you to."

He hopped down from the bed after a quick kiss to her lips. A frown wrinkled the skin between her eyes as she watched him retrieve his belt. *Holy shit!*

"Ever been tied up?"

"Can't say that I have. What are you gonna do with the belt?"

"No beating you with it, although welts on your ass would turn me inside out." He looped the belt around her wrists and secured them loosely to the headboard. "Roll over onto your stomach and get up on your knees. I'm gonna fuck you hard from behind." He grinned rolling the condom he retrieved from the nightstand drawer over his rigid cock. "Ever had a man in your ass?"

She swallowed the lump clogging her throat and shook her head, unable to speak through the fear making her heart pound in her chest. Her ex tried it once and the pain had almost killed her. Terror made her shudder uncontrollably.

"What's wrong, darlin'? I won't do anything you don't want, but you look terrified."

"I can't," she whispered.

"Can't?"

"I won't, I mean. You won't do that will you?"

"Take your ass, you mean?"

She nodded furiously.

"Honey, I can see the thought scares you to death. I wouldn't do anything to hurt you. If you don't want to try it, then we won't. Obviously you've had a bad experience with it or something to make you so afraid." He skimmed his hand over her breasts bringing the peaks to hard little points. "You like a little pain with your sex, but I won't do anything beyond what you can handle."

"Thank you."

"Relax, darlin'." He helped her roll over, rubbing her shoulders turning them to mush in the process. He kissed her butt cheeks before he smacked each one in turn just enough to make her wet. His fingers probed at her pussy, driving two in deep as he finger fucked her for several minutes. She moaned as she closed her eyes. Her thighs spread of their own accord. She had no will to do anything but let him to whatever he wanted to her.

He helped her rise up on her knees, bracing herself on her folded arms. "Fuck me, Joel."

"Oh I intend to, darlin'."

She felt his cock nudge at her pussy and groaned as he sank balls deep inside her.

"God, you're tight, babe."

"You feel amazing."

"Hold on, honey. I'm gonna fuck you hard."

He set up a steady, ass thumping rhythm, throwing her head over heels into a screaming orgasm almost immediately, but he didn't stop. He continued to pound into her, shaking the mattress on the frame and banging the headboard against the wall.

"Ah God, Joel!"

"You can come again. I know you can. Squeeze me with that hot pussy of yours."

The second she exploded into another orgasm, she heard him lose control. He growled low in his throat and lost the rhythmic pounding of his hips to a completely uncoordinated cadence as he shot his sperm into the condom.

"You're gonna be the death of me."

"Nah, you're a man. You can handle it." She giggled as she smacked him on the butt cheek the moment he let her out of her bindings.

"Hey. I'm supposed to do the ass warmin'."

"What you aren't a switch?"

He withdrew from her and sat up on the side of the bed with a puzzled look on his gorgeous face. "What do you know about being a switch?"

"Not a lot. I've read some romances with BDSM in it. I don't know how much of it is true, but it interests me."

"Does it, now. Hmm. Maybe we need to explore a bit more while you're here."

"So much for not ravishing the guests."

He frowned and reached for his pants. "Don't get me wrong, we have to be careful, but there's a lot of fun to be had. We just can't let anyone know what's happening between us."

"We have to keep this a secret? Seriously?" she asked, pulling the sheet up to cover her breasts.

"We had some good sex, Mesa. Nothin' more. If we tell anyone in my family, especially my mother, she'll have us married and havin' kids before the end of the week," he said from the bathroom. "Besides, the fuck was almost the best I've ever had."

"Almost?" she snapped, fury rushing through her at his offhanded compliment, then slamming her back down with it being almost the best he's ever had. *God, I'm such an idiot!*

"Easy, Mesa. I didn't mean anythin' by it," he replied, coming out with his pants on but not buttoned.

"Yeah. Tonight was a test. Just a quick fuck, with the potential for more during my stay. I get it, Joel." She grabbed her clothes from the floor, struggling to snap herself back into her bra with about as much grace as an octopus.

"What are you doin', darlin'?" He touched her shoulder but she shrugged him off.

"Don't darlin' me. I want you to take me back to the lodge or I'll walk."

"No you won't."

"Yes, I will. Don't tell me what to do. You might be able to dominate me in bed, but I'm my own person and I don't take kindly to men telling me what to do. I have a mind of my own. I can make my own decisions." She flipped her hair out of the collar of her shirt as she slipped her tennis shoes on her feet. "Are you gonna take me back?"

"Fine," he growled, tugging the T-shirt she'd been wearing on.

His magnificent chest disappeared from view. She bit her lips to keep from moaning at the loss. "Fine."

He slid on a pair of flip-flops, then stood there impatiently tapping his foot. Without another word, she headed for the door with him on her heels. So much for a great evening spent in the arms of a hot cowboy. Yeah, they'd had great sex but the minute things got a little testy, they were at each other's throats. He wouldn't tell his family they were sleeping together because he didn't want his mother playing matchmaker. Well, she didn't want that either. He didn't have to make it sound like a huge mistake for them to make love. Now she felt used and cheap.

Several moments later, they pulled up in front of the lodge. She didn't even wait for him to come around and open the door. She just hopped out on her own, slammed the truck door and headed for the house. Joel sprayed gravel as he backed out and then sped off down the driveway.

Tears rolled down her cheeks. *God, I've been such an idiot where he's concerned. Good lookin' cowboy is all it takes. I'm all over it and him.*

"Great job, Mesa. Sleep with the man. What a fuckin' waste of time."

The door to the lodge opened in front of her, and then closed as a cowboy she didn't recognize came out.

"Ma'am." He tipped his hat and walked down the stairs. She shook her head as she turned to see where he was going, but he'd disappeared.

"All right. I'm gonna have to ask someone. This is getting too weird for me. Doors open and close without anyone around, voices and knocks on my door when there is no one there, people disappearing without a trace."

She opened the door and walked inside. The house was quiet. No one stirred. She headed across the dining room toward the stairs to go to her room when goose bumps started to rise on her arms. The air turned colder. She glanced back at the door she'd just come through in time to see it open, and then closed on its own.

Just a little freaked out, she ran up the stairs. She fumbled with the key to her room for a moment before sprinting through the door and slamming it sharply behind her.

* * * *

Joel stepped through the door of his cabin, flinging the keys to his truck against the wall. Frustration, anger and just a little bit of fear raced through him. *How could things have gotten so screwed up? What the hell did I say to piss her off so badly?*

"I said it was good sex. What the hell more does she want? I certainly can't let my family know we slept together. Mom would have a coronary or have us in front of a preacher as soon as she could arrange it." He tossed off his flip-flops and dropped onto the sofa. His cell phone jingled in his pocket. "Yeah," he answered after he'd pulled it out.

"What's up, bro?"

"What do you want, Jacob?"

"I thought I'd check in with you. I thought I saw you drop Mesa off at the lodge."

"I did."

"And?"

"What? She's majorly fuckin' pissed at me for some damn reason."

"What the hell did you do?"

"I don't fuckin' know. That's just it." He raked his fingers through his hair. "I mean we had great sex. I thought everythin' was great. She got a burr under her blanket and insisted I take her back."

"Tell me what you said."

"I told her we couldn't let anyone know what's happened between us."

"She said, we have to keep this a secret and I said yes. We had some good sex, Mesa. Nothin' more. If we tell anyone in my family, especially my mother, she'll have us married and havin' kids before the end of the week. Then I said, besides, the fuck was almost the best I've ever had."

"Holy shit! Are you fuckin' dense man?"

"What?"

"You told her she was *almost* the best. You might as well tell her she's okay in the sack. You never tell a woman they are almost the best you ever had. Then you told her you couldn't tell anyone you'd been together."

"Well, we can't. Mom would have a cow. You know she would."

"Seriously, Joel. Don't you think the rest of us have fucked a guest before?"

"You have?"

"Hell yeah. Remember the set of twins who visited last year in late summer. Blonde, big boobs?"

"Tiffany and Trena?"

"Yeah, I guess. Hell, I don't even remember their names, but I had both of them. At once."

"What? Are you fuckin' kiddin' me?"

"No and Mom knows. The girls weren't quiet about it the next day. They were discussing it in the dining room. Of course, they couldn't tell any of us apart so I doubt they could even say which one of us fucked them."

"I know it wasn't me."

"I know who it was, dipwad. I might have been a little drunk, but I sure remember fuckin' both of them."

"I've never had two at once."

"It's an experience." He coughed in the phone. "I assume you enjoyed yourself with Mesa."

"Hell yeah. She was fantastic, but I doubt she'll even talk to me the rest of the time she's here."

"I don't think she'll hold a grudge."

"Why?"

"Because she's hung up on you, dude."

"I've only known her a couple of days."

"Yeah, but it doesn't mean shit when a heart gets involved. I've seen the way she looks at you."

"We'll see tomorrow, I guess."

Their conversation wrapped up a few minutes later when he clicked off the phone. *Did I really screw things up so bad with Mesa that she won't talk to me again? I hope not. I really like her a lot and in bed? Holy fuck!*

He grabbed a beer from the refrigerator before he walked into his room and stripped off his clothes. The sheets felt cool to his heated skin as he slid beneath them. The light slipped off with a twist of his fingers.

Moonlight streamed in through the open window as a cool breeze tickled across his skin. The scent of Mesa drifted to him on the air so he rolled over and pulled the pillow her head had been on, to his face. He couldn't quite place the flowery scent, but he knew it belonged uniquely to her. He'd smelled it on her hair when he'd been buried deep inside her pussy. His cock hardened at the mere thought of her wrapped around him. He groaned, fisting his cock in his hand. There would be no getting any sleep tonight with his raging hard-on. It had been a long time since he'd been this turned on by a woman…any woman. He pumped his fist several times while he imagined Mesa's hot pussy surrounding him, scalding him with her heat.

In no time at all, he felt the pull of his balls to his groin and the tingling sensation signaling the inevitable release. Cum shot out the end of his dick, splashing the white substance across his stomach. He moaned and slumped against the pillows. *Damn.* He swung his legs over the side of the bed as he let his head drop in exhaustion. For several moments he sat there inhaling lungsful of air, trying to calm his racing heart. Getting himself off like that after already coming with Mesa, almost hurt, but it was better than trying to sleep hard as a damn rock. He stumbled to the bathroom to wash the cum from his abdomen before he succumbed to sleep.

Now he might be able to actually sleep, although he feared dreams of her would bother him through the night whether he wanted them to or not.

Chapter Eight

She needed to talk to Joel or Nina or Joel's dad. The noises of the couple arguing again woke her at two in the morning. The knock sounded on her door shortly afterward but she feared opening it to find no one on the other side. Things seemed too strange and she needed to find out what was going on.

A light misty rain fell from the gray skies. *It gets cloudy in Texas?* Thunder rumbled in the distance. Goose bumps rose on her arms. Thunderstorms bothered her some, but there was electricity in the air trying to fight for substance like nothing she'd ever felt before.

The breakfast bell clanged downstairs signaling the return of the crowd staying at the ranch for the next meal. She dreaded facing Joel or his family after the night before. Sure, they'd had sex. At least for her it had been phenomenal sex. Apparently for him, it was just okay. She should have known. A guy like him didn't usually have anything to do with women like her. The plain, a little plump, and the nothing-to-write-home-to-mom-about type girl didn't get the gorgeous, hunky cowboy. It just didn't happen except in her novels.

After she slipped on her shoes, she grabbed her small backpack and locked the door. She glanced down the hall to the left and right almost expecting to see someone there. Nothing.

The aroma of bacon and eggs drifted to her nose. Her stomach rumbled in protest. She took the stairs begrudgingly as she prepared herself for the inevitable rush she felt every time she saw Joel.

The entire family sat at their usual table waiting for the guests to get their plates. She glanced down the long expanse to notice one empty chair. Joel wasn't there.

Where was he? Surely he didn't feel guilty about the way they fought last night?

She got into the line for her food and chatted with an older woman about the weather.

"Too bad it's raining today. We wanted to go riding."

"You can still ride even in the wet weather, although it's not as comfortable."

"We are city slickers. We don't do wet leather or wet jeans," the woman answered with a smile. "We're living out our fantasies of cowboys with all these hunky men around, but I think today will just be a sit-around-and-drool day."

"Anyone special you are drooling over?"

"Well the triplets are just awesome. Can you imagine having the attention of all three at once?"

"I don't think I could handle all three at once."

"I'd sure give it a try," the woman replied, giggling under her breath as she glanced at the table.

The door burst open with a gust of wind. Mesa gasped as she glanced at the door and the silhouette of the man outlined. The width of his shoulders. The breadth of his chest. The ruffle of hair at his neck. The black Stetson shading his face. Even though she couldn't see his face, she knew him. She knew his body like she knew her own…by the touch of her hands.

Joel.

He pulled the door shut behind him, blocking the gust of wind whipping through and blowing rain in from outside. His eyes never left hers as he walked up to her and smiled before moving down to the table where the coffee sat.

"Interesting." The woman she'd been talking to moved away.

Mesa's gaze never left Joel.

Once he had his coffee, he turned toward her, sipped the dark brew, and gave her a sexy wink.

Well, apparently he thinks I'm not pissed at him anymore. She didn't respond except for a frown as she grabbed her plate.

Instead of sitting in her normal spot next to him at the family table, she chose a table with a bunch of women. "Mind if I sit with you ladies?"

"Of course not. Please," a large, older woman replied. "There's always room for one more."

"Are you ladies here for a few days?"

"Yes. We love the ranch life and wanted to experience it for ourselves. You know instead of always reading about it, we wanted to see it."

"Oh? You ladies read?"

"Of course we do," a petite blonde answered. "We are a book club."

"Wonderful! What do you ladies like to read?"

A redhead to her left giggled. "Romance, of course. Hot cowboys." She glanced at the family table with wide eyes. "You know. Like they are."

"I know exactly what you mean." She took several bites. "Who are your favorite authors?"

The ladies glanced at each other and said in unison, "Mesa West."

"Really?"

The lady to her right clapped and said, "We heard you were here visiting when you posted on your Facebook status. We would love for you to sign some of our books we brought."

"Of course!"

"Many of us live in San Antonio and were disappointed you weren't at the book signing yesterday, so we drove out here to have some one on one time with you if you don't mind."

"Of course I don't mind. You ladies have made my day. I would love to sit and chat with you for a while about books."

"Is Troy going to get his own story?" a brunette asked from the end of the table as she clapped excitedly. "I absolutely loved him in Trouble in Cowboy Boots."

"I did too, and yes, he's definitely getting his own story."

"When?"

"Soon, I hope. I'm here trying to get some inspiration for a new series."

"Wow! Really?"

She nodded as she glanced at Joel from the corner of her eye. One eyebrow went up above his left eye. *Damn the man.*

Excited chatter enveloped her while the women shot her question after question about her characters, stories, and inspiration. Where did she come up with her stories? Were there real men who inspired her cowboys? The more questions, the more she lost herself in the enthusiasm of her readers.

The crowd came and went from the dining room while they continued to talk. Several moments ago, Joel had walked by, brushing her shoulders with his fingers in a gesture mistaken for innocence, but she knew different. He was ramping up her need for him with the simple touch.

"Are you seeing the cute one who just walked by?" the redhead asked as Joel walked out the door, taking his scent with him.

"Seeing? No. He's just been helping me with research about ranch life and cowboying while I'm here. We've only known each other a couple of days."

"He seems taken with you."

"Me?" She laughed ruefully knowing there wouldn't ever be anything more than a quick tumble between the sheets with Joel. "Yeah, no. His kind doesn't get taken with women like me."

"You're a beautiful girl. I don't know why you say such things. We love you."

"Aw, thank you, ladies." The kitchen workers eyed them. "I think we should clean up our dishes and maybe move into the main lodge to continue our discussions. They want to get things ready for lunch in a few hours."

The group picked up their dishes and deposited them in the washbasin before they retreated to the main lodge area where the fireplace and large bookcases where located. There were several couches all arranged in a semi-circle in front of the cold fireplace where everyone could chat without bothering anyone else. Mesa took a chair at the center of the group, fielding the rapid-fire questions the women threw at her. She loved chatting with readers and being the only author in the room, she could let their enthusiasm surround her, lift her spirits, and give her muse a quick kick in the butt.

The women spent the next couple of hours pounding her with questions, laughing at some of her responses, and just generally having a good time.

"I totally appreciate you ladies making the trip out here just to see me. I'm thrilled you came. You've all made my day."

"Thank you for spending a few hours out of your busy schedule to chat with us, Mesa. It's been fantastic and I'm sure we'll all be buying your next book the moment it hits the shelves."

"I hope you get some great inspiration from your cowboy friend."

"Yeah, me too. He's been fabulous so far, but now I need to track him down and ask him a few questions so if you ladies will excuse me."

"Of course. Thank you again and we'll see you at the next conference. You'll be at the one in Dallas, right?"

"Yes, ma'am. The one in a couple of months is my next stop."

"Awesome." The ladies waved goodbye as they made their way back toward the main lodge door, leaving her in silence.

Nina came out of her office with a big smile on her face. "You made their day."

"Thanks but it was more like the other way around. They made mine. I really needed the boost to my morale."

"Oh?" she asked, taking one of the empty seats.

"I've just been really down in the dumps lately, questioning my writing."

"You're a fabulous writer, Mesa. I don't see why you're questioning yourself. I got two of your books yesterday after you were here and I haven't been able to put them down since I started reading them. My husband finally forced me to turn off the lights last night at four in the morning."

Mesa laughed. "Thank you. That's the best compliment a writer can get."

"You're welcome."

She looked at Nina with a frown. "Can I ask you a couple of questions about the ranch? You know, from a woman's perceptive?"

"Certainly."

For the next hour, Mesa picked Nina's brain for information on the ranch life, raising nine boys and life in general with a bunch of men.

"I need to ask you a couple more questions about the ranch."

"All right."

"First of all, do you believe in ghosts?"

"Yes, I do. We have a few on the ranch."

"Really?"

"Yes. The main lodge used to be a bordello. That's the reason for its size. It's been added onto over the years, but it used to be a bar and whore house. The upstairs bedrooms were where the women took their men." She laughed. "Of course, we've cleaned them up since then."

"Wow."

"It has a very interesting history."

"What kinds of ghosts are here?"

"A cowboy. A couple who visit upstairs. A saloon girl and a few kids who run the ranch. You can hear them giggling outside sometimes."

"You have so many!"

"It's been a lively place for a long time." She tilted her head to the side. "Why so many questions? Have you seen them?"

"I think so." She took a deep breath and let it out slowly. "A cowboy at least. Someone has knocked on my door twice now in the middle of the night. I've also heard arguing in the next room."

"The cowboy you've seen is a regular around here. The best we can figure is he used to work the ranch many years ago as a wrangler and never left. We haven't been able to pinpoint his identity exactly."

"And the fighting couple?"

"Probably one of the cowboys and his girl fighting in the room up there."

"It sounds like he slaps her."

"Yep. That's them. They get kind of noisy sometimes. If you bang on the wall and tell them to knock it off, it goes away. Don't worry about the knocking. If there were an emergency, we would shout through the door. We haven't been able to figure it out yet, but it happens frequently."

"Kind of creepy, don't you think?"

"If it bothers you, I can move you to one of the outside cabins. They aren't haunted."

"I'm okay, but don't be surprised if your ghosts end up in one of my books."

Nina laughed. "I would love it. They are characters for sure. Have you seen the saloon girl?"

"No. Just the cowboy. Last night when I came back from Joel's, he…" *Oh shit.*

Nina patted her hand and said, "Don't worry about it, Mesa. I heard you come in last night and the roar of Joel's truck out in the yard. I looked out the window as he tore out of here. His truck has a distinctive sound."

Mesa felt the heat of a blush rushing into her cheeks. Her heart pounded in her ears as she sought to apologize for breaking the rules. "I'm sorry, Nina. I know you have a strict rule about the guys and guests, but…"

"It's fine, honey. If you and Joel are attracted to each other, it's okay. I just don't want the boy's going through guests on a regular basis, like water down the stream. You know how men are."

"Yes, I do."

"Did y'all have a fight last night? I thought I heard the truck door slam."

"A little bit."

"Would you like to talk about it?"

She blew out a breath. Talking to his mother about problems with Joel didn't seem like a good idea, but she really needed someone to talk to. She wasn't really close to her siblings or her mother, but Nina seemed to understand these kinds of things. It didn't take long at all for the entire story to spill from her lips. Nina murmured between her sentences in a soothing voice meant to calm her. "It'll be all right, honey. He's a man. Men tend to get pigheaded sometimes and trust me, I've seen it more than I care to with my boys. They take after their father that way."

Mesa laughed. She could totally see the stubbornness in Nina too, but she didn't want to insult her hostess. "Thank you for talking with me."

"Let me give you a little piece of advice. Avoid Joel for the day. You're going to be here for a few more days. You'll have plenty of time to talk to him. Go for a walk. Write. Read for your own pleasure for a change. I bet you don't read very often without worrying about your own books."

"True."

"I saw the way he touched you on his way out the door. He's a very possessive guy when it comes to women. It was his way of marking you, to let his brothers know you're taken."

"Seriously?"

"Yes, ma'am." Nina nodded with a smile. "Y'all are cute together. I haven't seen him act this way toward a woman before."

"I'm so not his type though."

"Sure you are! He's never been into skinny women. You're just his type." She patted Mesa's hand and then stood. "I've got some work to do. You enjoy your day and don't worry about Joel. He'll come find you either later tonight after supper or tomorrow."

"Thank you, Nina. You've been a huge help."

"You're welcome, honey. I've enjoyed having you here."

"Oh. I'll get your dress and shoes back to you later this afternoon. Would it be okay if I did some laundry? I didn't bring very many clothes with me on this trip and I'm about out of clean underwear."

"Of course. You know where the laundry facilities are. Use whatever you need. There is soap and dryer sheets on the shelf."

"You've been such a great hostess. You can bet I'll be singing your praises and those of the ranch on every social network I'm on when I get home."

"Word of mouth is the best advertising we can ask for. Thank you." She nodded again before she headed back for her office, leaving Mesa to sit alone in front of the fireplace contemplating her thoughts.

Maybe Nina is right. I should avoid Joel until he comes looking for me. She bit her lip as trepidation rush through her. *But what if he doesn't come looking? I'll feel like a total fool.*

The smile he gave her earlier brought back memories of their night together. His hands on her flesh. His lips taking what he wanted. His body covering hers as he took her to heights of ecstasy she'd never felt before. Did he do the same thing with every woman he made love to? She shook her head. Surely it was that way with any man who knew how to make love to a woman, right?

Remember your ex, her head said before she could think any further. He couldn't fuck if he tried. All he knew how to do was stick it in, pump a few times and flop down on top of her. Then he actually had the nerve to ask if it was good for her. Well nope, it wasn't. It sucked!

Now with Joel, wow!

"Okay, enough thoughts of Joel. I've got some writing to do."

* * * *

Joel wound his horse around a boulder keeping an eye out for snakes as he checked the fence for breaks and the cattle for strays. His thoughts weren't on his job though. He wanted to see Mesa. He knew he'd pissed her off last night with his casual remark about their lovemaking, but he really didn't want to give her the impression it might turn into something more than a quick fuck. Hell, she didn't even live in Texas!

"Yo, Joel!"

He pulled on Jet's reins as Jeremiah rode up on his horse.

"What are you doing out here?"

"I came to find you. Mom was looking for you earlier."

"Oh great."

"Yeah. I'm sure it's something about you coming home with Mesa last night."

"What the fuck? Does everyone know?"

"Of course they do, dumbass. One, you brought her home in your truck with its loud-assed muffler and two, she's staying in the main lodge. Everyone in the place probably heard you bring her home."

Joel tipped his head back on his shoulders and sighed. *Great.* Everyone in the family knew they'd been together without him or her saying a damned word. His mom probably wanted to kill him. "I guess I better go find her."

"Yeah, I would say so. You know how she is. Mom's gonna rip you a new asshole, buddy."

"Great. Thanks for the support, Jeremiah."

"You're welcome, bro."

"Asswipe."

Joel kicked his horse into a slow gallop headed for the barn. Despite the probable indigestion, he wanted this confrontation with his mother over with before supper. *Maybe I can find Mesa while I'm at the house.*

Several minutes later, he rounded the barn for the corral as Jeff came out of the tack room. "Joel? What are you doin' back from ridin' fences?"

"Mom wanted to talk to me if it's any of your business."

"Everything on this ranch is my business. The horses, the cattle, where the hands are…everything."

"I'm not your damned employee, Jeff. What I do is none of your concern no matter whether you think you're in charge or not." He swung down from the saddle, and then began unbuckling the straps. "Besides, what the hell are you doin' in the barn this time of day? Don't you have somethin' to keep you busy besides the barn?"

"I'm checking the feed stock, fucktard."

"Well get busy then, asshole. I've got my own worries."

"Oh? Like fuckin' one of the guests?"

"Blow it out your ass, brother. What I do is none of your damned business. How many times do I have to tell you?"

"One day Dad won't be here and everything will fall on me. I'm not doing anythin' more than what will be expected of me when the time comes."

"Dad isn't going anywhere for a long time, Jeff, so back off. I'll talk to Mom about me and Mesa."

"Keep your hands off the guests."

He pushed against Jeff's chest. "Make me. I can fuck whomever I want to and you can't say a damned thing."

"The hell I can't."

"Enough you two!" shouted his father. "Jeff back off."

"What?"

"I said back off. What happens on this ranch is mine and your mother's concern. We will deal with your brothers. Not you."

"But Dad…"

"But nothing. This is between me, your mother, and Joel."

Joel smirked, earning a growl from his brother as he balled his fists at his sides. He could tell Jeff wanted to kick his ass. Let him try. Jeff might be about the same size as him, but he had a little more bulk to his frame, whereas his brother wasn't quite so muscular.

"In the house, Joel."

"I'm not done with you, Joel," Jeff snarled.

"Fuck you."

"I said in the house," his father snapped, pointing to the main lodge.

As Joel's steps took him toward the lodge, he whistled knowing his father stayed back for a moment to reprimand his eldest brother. Jeff really needed to get laid or something. The guy had a serious stick up his ass the size of a fence post.

He walked inside, relishing the cool interior. The rain hadn't let up all day and he was soaked to the bone. A nice dry change of clothes would be good but he'd have to make a trip back to his place to get them.

"Joel?"

"Yeah, Ma."

"I'm in the office."

"Be right there."

He dragged his feet as he released a heavy sigh. Twenty eight years old, and that tone still sent chills down his spine. With a heavy sigh, he shuffled his feet toward his mother's domain.

"Have a seat," she said the minute he stood in the doorway. "We need to talk."

"Are you gonna wait for Dad?" he asked, sliding into the chair across from her desk. He hadn't felt so put on the spot like this in several years. Not since she'd found out he'd been visiting their neighbor's daughter.

"Your father will be along shortly, I'm sure. But we've already discussed this at length before I went looking for you earlier."

"So what's up?"

"It's you and Mesa, son."

"What about us?"

"So there is an us?"

"Well…"

"No hemhawin' about it. I know you were together last night. I saw her come in and heard you peel out of the driveway, digging up about three quarters of the gravel we laid this summer."

"Sorry, Ma."

"Joel, honey. I'm not mad at you. I like Mesa. I think she's a wonderful girl. The reason for this talk isn't to chew you out for bein' with her. It's so you don't hurt her."

"I don't plan to hurt her, Ma. We're just havin' a bit of fun while she's here."

"That's exactly why I made the rule of you boys not pursing guests." She stood up and paced the room like a cage animal. "I don't want this place getting a reputation for the wild Young boys taking all the single guests to bed."

"It's not like that. Mesa understands."

"Does she? I think she's a nice girl who's been swept off her feet by a handsome cowboy. She doesn't come across as a worldly type woman. She's not one for casual relationships, Joel. What if she does develop feelings for you?"

"Aren't you the least bit worried about me?"

"You're a lover, son, not a fighter although you wouldn't believe it the way you and Jeff were ready to go toe to toe in the barn a few moments ago," his father said, coming into the room.

"And the way you and Joshua went at it the night before last."

"It doesn't matter. Aren't we here to discuss me and Mesa?"

"Yes we are. I want to you stay away from her, Joel," his mother said. "I'm afraid she's gonna get hurt."

"I don't want to hurt her, Ma. She's a friend."

"A friend with benefits?" his dad asked.

Joel pulled off his Stetson, raking his fingers through his hair. "Hell, I don't know what she is. We had fun together. Where it goes from here, I'm not sure. She doesn't even live here. She lives in Los Angeles, for God's sake!"

"What if she moved here?"

"She's not moving here."

"What if she did?"

Joel got up and paced the room now. "I don't know, Ma. I like her a lot. We have a lot in common and she's a wildcat between the sheets, but is there something else there? I don't know."

"Do you want to find out?"

"Sure I would."

"Then ask her to stay."

"What? You can't be serious. She doesn't live here. I told you, she lives in California."

"I understand she lives somewhere else, but she's also a writer who has the ability to be wherever she wants because she's self-employed."

"You've done your homework, Ma."

"Thank you, Joel. I like to know about our guests. We had a nice conversation earlier today."

"You did?"

"Yeah and I think, for the record, she likes you a lot, but she's confused by your actions. You marked her earlier."

He hoped his mother and father understood the confused looked on his face because he didn't have a clue what she meant. "Marked?"

"You ran your fingers along her shoulder on your way out of the lodge this morning. You marked her in front of your brothers, the other males in the room, as your own."

"You've read too much Native American History, Ma."

"So what if I have?" She stopped in front of him. "Honey, I want you happy. If Mesa makes you happy then be my guest, but I like her too and if you hurt that girl, I'm going to kick your ass."

Chapter Nine

The window she stared out of overlooked the back of the lodge house. Her laptop sat in front of her, the cursor blinking mockingly. She had been at it for hours now, the story flowing so rapidly, she could hardly type fast enough. Now, she looked out the window, her mind almost blank.

She could see the comings and goings of several of the boys from her window, but she never saw Joel. With her state of mind, it might be a good thing she didn't. She wanted to get some words on virtual paper before supper.

After several hours of typing, she went back to read what she wrote, realizing the entire book was her trip to the ranch, meeting Joel, and their subsequent love making the night before. Reading it on the screen made her realize how hot the whole night had been and how much she wanted it to happen again.

A heavy sigh rushed from between her lips as she tipped her head back on her shoulders. The cowboy in her book even sounded like Joel.

Joel.

What the hell was she going to do about him? His mother said to avoid him today, which she'd done with regret. She needed to talk to him. Wanted to see him. Would die to taste him.

"Enough. We need to write."

She glanced at the screen, realizing the story stood where her own life stopped at the moment. *What to do from here?*

The supper bell clanged downstairs. She stood, stretching her back until it popped, relieving some of the pressure at her spine from sitting without moving in the hardback chair. Her stomach rumbled reminding her she'd missed lunch. Even though she'd heard the bell earlier, the book wouldn't release her long enough to go eat. Now, she regretted not going even though it would have meant seeing Joel.

Ah, the life of a writer. Caffeine and snacks at the desk. She couldn't remember how many times those things had been her sustenance for days on end while she fought to finish a book before the deadline.

The rumbled of voices downstairs reminded her of supper.

"Well, I can't avoid him for the meal unless I sit somewhere else."

She grabbed her key, opened the door, and shut it before heading down the stairs to join everyone for the evening meal.

Laughter met her ears as she reached the bottom stair and looked out into the expanse of the dining room. The rain had stopped, finally allowing the sun to come out later in the afternoon, lightening everyone's mood.

Several women sat at one table laughing and passing around a bottle of wine. They didn't serve liquor at the ranch, but you were welcome to bring your own.

The family sat at their regular table and several of them called out when they noticed her standing in the entryway. She waved before she got in line to get her dinner plate.

Where to sit. Where to sit. She glanced around hoping to find the women from earlier in the group, but no one looked familiar. The book club must have left right after her chat with them. Too bad. She would have enjoyed talking books with them a little longer.

Warm breath tickled her ear, sending goose bumps down her arms. Joel. "No escape, little bird. You've been avoiding me."

"No I haven't. I've been writing." Well, both were the truth. She had been writing, but also avoiding him like his mother suggested.

"Good. I'm glad you've been busy. I've missed you today. It was kind of lonely riding by myself. I thought you were going to ride with me."

She swallowed hard. "I have to strike while the iron is hot."

"Oh, the iron is hot, mi'lady."

"I thought you didn't want to see me."

"I never said I didn't want to see you and now that my whole family knows about us, we don't have to keep it a secret."

"Your whole damned family!" Everyone turned to look at them as embarrassment flushed her cheeks with heat. "Great. Just fucking fabulous," she grumbled under her breath.

"Sorry, darlin', but apparently they all heard you come in last night and me peel out of the driveway."

The young woman dishing up the roast beef winked as she placed the meat on her plate. The next woman smiled while she put mashed potatoes next to the meat. *Just fucking great. Everyone does know about Joel bringing me back to the ranch. They couldn't know we slept together, but they are all assuming as much from their behavior.*

"I don't want to talk about it."

"We need to, Mesa. It's important."

"Leave me alone, Joel. I'm here for research and to write, not hook up with a hot-ass cowboy for a few nights."

"Hot-ass?"

She exhaled sharply, rolled her eyes and headed toward the opposite end of the dining room. One of the tables near the door was empty so she took it. She didn't want company tonight anyway. The moment she sat down, the bench across from her scraped the floor as Joel took the seat on the other side.

"Why aren't you eating at the family table?"

"Because I want to talk to you."

"I thought we'd said everything there needed saying. You didn't want your family to know about us. Well, we apparently took care of that last night. There isn't any need to further our association. You got what you wanted. A lonely, plump, not so attractive woman to fall into bed with you. You've marked your bedpost, I'm sure. One more in the sack for Joel. Great. Good for you. You can chalk it up to experience because I'm done."

"Why are you so upset?"

"Because I don't like being used, Joel, and I feel like you did nothing more than use me."

"Didn't you use me a little, too? I mean, we had a good time last night. Obviously, you needed me and I needed you. We both got what we wanted."

"We both got…you seriously think that?"

"Yeah."

Anger rushed through her so fast her head began to feel funny. Like she'd been swimming and stayed under too long. Her ears burned as she glanced down at the plate in front of her. Not wanting to ruin her own dinner, she grabbed the edge of his plate and unceremoniously dumped the contents of his dinner into his lap.

She grabbed her own plate and walked over to a table where a couple sat alone talking quietly. *Let him stew.*

Watching from the corner of her eye, she saw him slowly scrap the roast beef, gravy and mashed potatoes from his lap back on to the plate. Once his lap was sufficiently cleaned off, he dumped it into the washbasin where the dirty plates go, and stomped out of the lodge, slamming the door behind him.

That should teach him not to mess with me.

Mesa slowly put the spoon in her mouth, avoiding eye contact with any of his family. The whole dining room finally resumed talking after the blow up, but they seemed quiet and subdued. Well, it didn't matter whether their whole affair made the rounds of the entire ranch. She wasn't staying there much longer anyway. Soon she would be home, in her own bed, curled with up her cat and her half-gallon of chocolate chip ice cream eating her cares away. The situation would be a distant memory just like them making love. Would she forget? She hoped, in time.

Several minutes later, Joel returned in clean clothes but he didn't get another plate of food. He walked straight up behind her, grabbed her hand, and forced her to her feet.

"What the hell are you doing?"

"We're having this out, right now."

"I'm not going anywhere with you."

"Yes, you are."

He tugged her along, practically dragging her up the stairs to her room. "Key." She stubbornly narrowed her eyes. "Give me the key, Mesa, or I'll strip you bare until I find it, right here in the hall."

"Fine," she growled, pulling it from her front jean pocket and handing it to him. "I don't want you in my room."

"Too fuckin' bad, baby doll, because I intend to make you listen to me."

He opened the door and literally pushed her inside before he slammed it closed. "Strip."

"Excuse me?"

"I said strip. Do it now."

"I'm not taking my clothes—"

He grabbed her T-shirt and pulled it over her head. "I'll do it for you then."

"What the hell, Joel!"

"Take it off."

"No."

"Fine." He grabbed her pants, popped the button and shoved them down around her ankles so fast, she didn't know what hit her.

Within seconds, she stood in nothing but her bra and panties. Desire pooled in her belly. *How fucking sick is that!* "All right. You have me in nothing but my bra and underwear. I'm not stripping down to nothing. Take it or leave it."

"All right. You can keep them unless you start arguing with me again. If you do, I'm taking those too."

"Fuck you."

"Only if you ask nicely."

"You son of a bitch. Why can't you just leave me alone? I don't want anything more to do with you. You're a user, Joel, and I don't want to be part of your game anymore."

"Stop. Just stop, Mesa. Listen to yourself? Do you hear what you're saying?"

Tears rolled down her cheeks unchecked. She didn't want to cry but she didn't have a choice. His cavalier attitude hurt her heart. When did she start caring about this rotten asshole? "I hate you."

"No you don't," he whispered, stopping in front of her to wipe the tears from her cheeks. "That's our problem. Neither of us hates the other, but we don't know what else to call it." He kissed her cheeks before he brushed his lips against hers. "God, you taste like Heaven and Hell wrapped up in a single package. What am I gonna do with you, darlin'?"

He kissed her again, pushing his tongue into her mouth tentatively like he was waiting for her to give into her feelings and return the kiss. *Why am I giving into this, him? God, I hate myself for wanting him.*

She grabbed fistfuls of the front of his shirt and pulled the edges apart, buttons pinged off each surface they touched in their flight across the room. He lifted his head, staring down into her eyes, his crystal clear blue eyes bright with lust.

"That's it, Mesa. Take what you want." He pulled at his belt buckle, unhooking it from the loops as she worked his shirt from the waistband of his jeans.

His jeans and boxers hit the floor while he toed out of his boots. She worked frantically at the clasp of her bra until it came free. The next second her panties hit the floor at their feet and he grabbed her around the waist to fling her onto the bed.

"I'm gonna fuck you hard."

"Too much talking." She pressed her mouth against his as she ground her pelvis against his hard flesh. "Tell me you brought a condom."

"In my wallet. Let me get it."

He left her side for a moment, taking his heat with him while he searched his wallet for the protection they both needed.

"How long has that one been in there?"

"Quite a while actually," he said sliding the latex over his engorged cock.

"I wanted to taste you."

"Later. I need to be inside you."

She closed her eyes and sighed a happy sigh when he positioned his cock at her opening and slowly slid deep into her pussy.

"Fuck, you feel fantastic."

"Deeper, Joel. Please."

She pulled her legs up to her chest, opening herself for his deep thrust. He didn't disappoint as he slammed his pelvis against hers, pushing everything he had inside her much deeper than he'd been before. Each thrust pushed her across the bed until he grabbed her hips and held her still.

"Come for me, Mesa. Squeeze me until I explode. I wanna feel your heat."

With a small thought in her brain, she grabbed the pillow from the bed and put it over her face as she screamed his name at the top of her lungs.

Within seconds, he growled her name while he shot every bit of his cum into the end of the condom.

He laid his head on her chest as the air sawed in and out of his lungs in a deep pant.

"Was that makeup sex?" she asked with a giggle.

He chuckled a dry laugh before he peeked up at her through his gorgeous lashes. "I guess you could call it makeup sex. After all, we were having a pretty big fight." He kissed her quickly. "I'm sorry."

"Me too."

He slipped out of her and disposed of the condom in the small trashcan near the bathroom door. "I hope everyone in the dining room didn't hear us."

"I tried to be quiet but it's kind of hard with you."

He grinned a silly grin. "I'm glad I make you lose all control."

"Yes, you do cowboy." She frowned.

"What's the frown for?"

"What are we gonna do, Joel? This can't possibly work into anything beyond a few fun-filled days before I go back to California."

"Let's take it slow. Okay? I don't know what's goin' on here either, but I like you a lot, Mesa, and I don't like fighting with you. We have a good time together."

"All right. Slow. Got it."

"Would you show me what you've written today?"

"No!"

"Why not?"

She chewed her lip. There wasn't any way she could show Joel her new book since it paralleled what had happened to her on the ranch. "I never let anyone but my editor read my stuff until it's been published."

"But I want to read it."

"Not until it's done. I don't know what the ending is going to be yet and I don't want to spoil it until I get there. I only wrote about five thousand words today so the whole plot has a long way to go development-wise before it's done. I never know how they are going to turn out until I'm finished. And even then there's times when I change my mind about parts."

"All right, all right. I won't look then."

She crawled up on the bed to lay her head on the pillow. He took the spot next to her and gathered her into his arms. He kissed her hair while his hand did a slow crawl from her shoulder to her wrist.

"I love holding you like this."

"You just want me naked next to you."

His cock stirred, taking on a life of its own. "Well, yes. I love you naked any way I can get you."

"Typical man."

A knock sounded on the door. "Are you two okay in there?"

"Yeah, Ma. There's no blood. We're fine."

"Good. I'll see you in the morning."

"Night, Ma."

"Night, Nina." She snuggled down closer to his chest. "Kind of awkward, don't you think?"

"Nah. I think my mom was trying to get us together like this."

"Why? She knows I don't live here. It's not like this could possibly develop into a relationship."

"It can't?"

"No. I have my life in Los Angeles. You have your life here. We are two very different people, Joel."

"She's playing matchmaker again. She told me to stay away from you earlier."

Mesa laughed. "She told me the same thing this morning. I should avoid you today."

"Sneaky woman, my mother."

"Yep. She knew by telling us to stay away from each other, it would force a blowup and eventually we would have to talk. Thus, leading to this."

"Well, she might not have thought it through to this end, but she definitely had it right about staying away from each other. I can't."

She rubbed her face against his chest, loving the feel of the springy hair beneath her cheek. "Me either. You're like a drug. I can't get enough."

"I say we let it go where it may. If this is supposed to be something besides a short term thing, it will work itself out."

She pressed her lips together, thinking about the situation. Could she walk away after her week here was over without regrets? Probably not, but she had to. Her life in Los Angeles came first. She was a writer after all. A semi-famous author who had a full, rewarding life in the big city. She liked having stores around the corner. She enjoyed having the nightlife and clubs to visit if she so chose to, not that she was much of a nightlife person, but the option was there.

Here you would have the abundance of ranch life to jumpstart your muse. You would have the quiet, the horses, the cowboys, and the little bar in Bandera where you could dance the night away in the arms of one hot cowboy.

But what if things with Joel didn't work out? What if she gave up her life in Los Angeles, moved here to be with him, and they broke up after a time?

I could always move back to Los Angeles at any time.

"You aren't helping."

"Huh?" he asked sleepily when she glanced up at his face. His eyes were closed and his breathing had slowed into slumber. "Did you say something?"

"No. Go to sleep, big guy."

Soft snores reached her ears moments later as she snuggled back against his chest. There wouldn't be any use trying to make a decision like this on a whim. Like he said, let's take it slow and see where things go. If it's meant to be, it's meant to be. She should be able to make a decision by the time her week at the ranch went by.

Now, if she could just keep her heart from being the deciding factor in the whole thing, she might be able to make an intelligent decision.

Chapter Ten

Sunlight streamed through the window, dragging her from her dreams. Dreams of Joel danced behind her eyelids, keeping her from fully awakening to the birds chirping outside and the low bawl of cattle in the distance. She could get used to these sounds. The quiet country sounds instead of the blare of car horns, the chatter of people below her window, the bark of neighborhood dogs and the hustle of everyone in the city. No one slowed down to appreciate the things in life.

She reached to the side of the bed expecting to find Joel's warm body next to her only to find cold sheets. She sat up, pushing the hair from her eyes and looked around the room. His clothes were gone.

"Well duh, Mesa. He works on a cattle ranch. He has to be up with the chickens."

The clock on the table read seven-thirty. She jumped out of the bed, grabbed some clean clothes, and headed for the shower. Breakfast would be served in thirty minutes and she still had to be presentable. She wasn't sure why she cared so much since it was a cattle ranch. They lived with dirt and mud every day, so what difference did it make?

She lifted her arm and sniffed. "Okay. I do need a shower."

Several moments later, she stood beneath the warm spray of the water and drifted into a little daydream. Joel's lips on hers, firmly taking what he wanted. His hands, slick with soap, drifting down over her breasts and pinching her nipples between his fingers. The feel of his lips on the tight nubs, pulling and sucking them between his lips, drove her desire higher. Her hand drifted down between her thighs to touch her clit. A soft moan escaped on a sigh.

"Are you touching what's mine?"

Now her fantasy had a voice.

"I want you."

"Open your eyes."

She opened her eyes to find him standing at the bathroom door, leaning against the frame with a wicked grin on his lips.

The screech she released made him laugh. "What the hell? How did you get in here?"

"Master key."

"I thought you were working. I was trying to get cleaned up for breakfast."

"You looked like you were enjoying yourself a bit. Mind if I join you? I could use a shower, too."

"Somehow I don't think we'll be doing a lot of showering."

"I hope not. Watching you touch yourself was so fuckin' hot, I almost came in my jeans." He quickly stripped off his clothes and climbed into the shower with her. "Much better." He grabbed the soap and lathered up his hands until they were slick. "Now I can touch you like I wanted to this morning before I left your bed."

"Why didn't you?" she asked, whispering along his throat. "I would have loved to wake up like that."

He ran his hands over her breasts. "Because I didn't want to wake you. You were sleeping so peacefully with a beautiful smile on your lips."

"I was dreaming of you like this."

He laughed as he pinched her nipples, drawing them to little points of pleasure. "In the shower? I thought that dream came when you were touching yourself."

"Well yes, but I dreamt of you just the same, touching me, loving me. I can't get enough."

He slanted his mouth over hers, driving his tongue between her lips in the erotic dance only two lovers know. His hands skimmed down her abdomen and around to her hips to draw her closer to his body. His rock-hard erection pressed into her stomach. "Do you want me?" she asked, pulling away from his kiss to lick his throat.

"Oh, hell yeah. I snuck away from my chores to have you."

"So romantic, you are." She released a throaty laugh as she nipped at his skin. She wanted to bite him, eat him up until he couldn't escape her feast on his flesh.

One of his hands slid around to the front of her body to dive between her thighs. "God, you're wet."

"I'm in the shower," she said with a laugh before it turned to a moan the minute he thrust two fingers inside her pussy. "Okay, that's not because of the shower."

"Let me grab a condom."

She glanced into his eyes. "I don't want a barrier between us."

"What are you saying, Mesa?"

"I'm clean and I'm on birth control. Are you?"

"Clean, yes."

"Then fuck me, Joel."

He put both hands under her buttocks. "Wrap your legs around me."

"You can't li—"

"I wrestle cows for a livin', darlin'. I can handle a little thing like you."

He lifted her in his arms and she wrapped both legs around his waist. With her back against the cold tile, he slid home, filling her to the brim with his hard flesh. Her satisfied moan echoed off the tile enclosure.

"God, you feel good, baby."

"Move, Joel. I need you."

He rocked his hips back and forth, sliding his scalding length deep inside her. His groan matched hers. Ecstasy fogged her brain. Water beat down upon them in a cascade, pounding in a solid stream between them as he continued to rock his hips.

"Damn, I'm not gonna last like this. The sensation is killing me."

"Make me come."

He shifted his stance. The slide of his cock hit her G spot in exactly the right place to shoot her desire to explosive. She exploded on a cry, his name a mantra from her lips. Stars burst behind her eyelids, blinding her to anything but the feeling of him deep inside her.

His own climax echoed hers until she felt the stickiness of their mingled cum sliding down her leg.

She rested her head on his chest, dragging air into her starved lungs until her head cleared and she could think straight again.

"I like it much better without the barrier between us."

"Me too, but I didn't want to push."

The breakfast bell clanged, startling them both. He pulled out of her and grabbed the soap to finish washing her. "We need to hurry or we're gonna miss breakfast."

"We can always hit the diner in town."

"Don't you have work to do?"

"Yeah, but I'll already be in hot water for skipping out this morning."

"I don't want you to be in trouble."

"It's okay. Josh covered for me."

"He knew you were coming up here to seduce me?"

"I didn't tell him if that's what you mean. I think he might have assumed so from the silly grin on my face." He washed himself, and then waited for her.

She quickly washed her hair and rinsed in the warm water that seemed to be turning colder by the second. "I think we're about to run out of hot water."

"Yeah, I think so too. Hurry."

"I am." Within minutes, she'd washed every bit of soap off and grabbed one of the fluffy, white towels hanging on the wall to dry herself with as Joel rinsed.

He shut the water off then pulled the other towel down.

"What time did you wake up this morning?" she asked, heading back into the bedroom with the pile of her clean clothes.

"I'm always up when the sun comes up. We have to feed and water the animals before we take them out for the day."

"I know the bed was already cold by the time I woke."

"Yeah, I'd already been up for a couple of hours by then."

"Wow."

"Do you want to go to town?"

"Sure."

They dressed in a rush in between kissing and touching. His lips found her throat as he nibbled from her earlobe to her collarbone. "If you don't stop, we'll never get out of here. Food calls," she said in between moans of ecstasy and trying to button his shirt.

"Maybe I want something else to eat."

Her pussy creamed at the thought, soaking her panties. She loved when he ate her out. "Later, cowboy. My stomach needs sustenance."

"Party pooper," he replied, pressing his forehead against hers. "Promise?"

"Oh yeah."

"Okay, let's get food then." He stepped into his boots as she tied her tennis shoes. "Did you bring boots?"

"I hadn't planned on being on a ranch. I really should go buy some, I guess."

"Yes, you should, especially if you plan on ridin' with me."

"Riding you?"

"With me, Mesa, but I'll take the other, too."

"I bet you would, cowboy."

About fifteen minutes later, they pulled up to the front of a quaint little diner situated near the light in the middle of Bandera.

"Does everyone come here?"

"A lot of the older crowd comes for coffee early and so do many of the wranglers. They shoot the shit during the morning before they head out for the day's work."

"This place sounds so fun." She took out the pen and paper she always kept in her purse to jot down some notes on the diner. A waitress showed them to a booth near the window. Joel took one side and she took the other. She set the book aside to glance at the menu. A ham and cheese omelet sounded good to her.

"What are you havin'?"

"Omelet. You?"

"Bacon and eggs."

The waitress appeared at their table, barely glancing at Mesa, but focusing entirely on Joel. "Hey, Joel."

"Hey, Marie. Coffee, Mesa?"

"Yes please."

He looked up at the waitress and said, "Two coffees. I'll have bacon and eggs over medium with hash browns and my lady friend will have?"

"Ham and cheese omelet."

"Got that?"

"Yeah," she said, simpering over him and batting her eyes. "Are you busy tonight?"

"Yes, I am actually."

"What about tomorrow night?"

"Sorry, Marie. I'm not interested in dating you. We've already had this discussion before. You're a sweet girl, but you aren't my type."

"And she is? Look at her!"

"What's between me and Mesa is none of your business. I'll thank you to remember that and please call us another waitress."

"But I…"

"Ann?"

"Yeah, Joel?" an older woman called from behind the counter.

"Can you come here and take our order please."

"Be right there." She grabbed a coffee pot and two cups before she headed over toward their table. "I got this, Marie."

Marie huffed off toward the kitchen, glancing behind her several times.

"Sorry about her, Joel. You know she's had the hots for you for a long time. She just doesn't know when to quit."

"It's fine. I just didn't want to subject my friend here to her."

Ann poured them two cups of coffee, smiling at Mesa and whole time. "You ain't from around here."

"No, I'm staying at the ranch for a few days."

"Ann Quimby, this is Mesa Arraguso. She's from L.A."

"Nice to meet you, Ann," Mesa replied, taking her hand in a firm shake.

"You too, Mesa. I ain't sure how you corralled this youngin', but hang on tight. You're in for the ride of your life, honey."

Mesa blushed to the roots of her hair. Was it so obvious they were sleeping together that the whole town could tell by looking at them? "Thanks for the advice."

"No problem, darlin'. What are you two eatin'?"

Joel repeated the order to Ann then she took off toward the kitchen to get their order up. Mesa bit her lip and sipped her coffee. Joel watched her over the rim of his cup, his eyebrow raised over his left eye. "What?"

"You're blushin'."

"I didn't think it was so obvious we're lovers, but apparently it is."

"Are you ashamed, because I'm not."

"No. I really didn't think it was written on my forehead though." She tapped the spot between her brows. "You know. Joel's slut."

"You aren't a slut, Mesa, for God's sake. There's a big difference between someone who goes around sleeping with everyone and anyone and someone who hooks up with one person for a short term fling."

"Did you just hear yourself? It means the same thing, Joel."

"No, it doesn't." He lowered his voice. "Sluts sleep with everyone or anyone. You are only sleepin' with me. Of course, we aren't doin' much sleepin'."

"Shush. I don't want everyone hearing you."

"It's none of their business what we do, Mesa."

"I still don't need everyone hearing you talk about our sex life."

"What does it matter? After you leave, you won't ever see them again."

"What if I come back?"

"Are you?"

"Am I what?"

"Coming back after you leave."

"I don't know, Joel. It all depends on what happens between us. I mean, maybe we could just have a fling every year around the same time." She sipped her coffee before setting the cup back down. "Isn't there a movie with the same storyline? I know." She snapped her fingers. "It's called Same Time Next Year. We could do that."

He drank a little of his coffee. "I don't want to think about when you're goin' home."

"I don't either, but it's reality. I have a life back in Los Angeles. Your life is here."

"You're becoming a very important part of my life, Mesa."

"Here you go, folks. Omelet for the lady. Bacon and eggs for you, Joel. More coffee?"

"No, I think we're good, Ann. Thank you."

They ate in silence while the thoughts of going home soured her stomach. She didn't want to go back to Los Angeles. She didn't care about her life there anymore, but Joel didn't want to talk about her leaving either.

After they finished their breakfast and quietly sipped their coffee, Joel asked, "Are you finished? We can hit the small western wear store for a pair of boots before we go back to the ranch."

"Yes, I'm done."

She grabbed her wallet to pay for her breakfast, but he beat her to the tab, thrusting twenty dollars into Ann's hands as she brought the bill. "Keep the change."

"Thanks, doll. See you around?"

"Of course, darlin'. You know I can't stay away from you."

He kissed her on the cheek and jealousy rushed through Mesa. *What the hell? She's old enough to be his mother.*

"Tell my sister hello for me when you get back to the ranch."

"I will. Ma needs to come in here once in a while to get away from the house. She spends too much time on the books."

Her sister? Nina is Ann's sister? Well that explains the familiarity of Joel with Ann. She's his aunt!

"Are reservations up this year?"

"Yeah, business is doin' good. Now, if the damned housin' development people would back the hell off and quit buyin' up the properties, we'd be fine."

"Are they buyin' up more?"

"Yeah. One of our neighbors sold out."

"Y'all have enough land to keep them from bein' too close to you."

"True, but it cuts down on the range land overall, which makes it difficult for the wildlife."

"True, baby doll." She patted his cheek before she hugged him. "Kiss your mama."

"Sure. Love you."

"Love you too, honey. Take care of that girl. She's good for you, Joel."

Color spread across his cheeks as he blushed a deep red. "I will."

The warmth of his hand at the small of her back made her feel cared for. She wasn't sure why having him show his possession of her on such a visceral level brought her spirits up, even when it wasn't what it seemed.

Next they hit the western store for boots. He helped her pick out a nice part of Ariat boots with soft rawhide. The pair hugged her feet, molding to the shape of her foot so well, she felt like she was walking in slippers. "These are fabulous, Joel. Thank you for helping me pick them out."

"You're welcome, darlin'. I have a pair similar in my closet I wear out dancing because they are so comfortable."

"Do you go to the club a lot?"

"I wouldn't say a lot. I don't go every weekend or anything."

"What else do you like to do?"

"Huntin', fishin', four-wheelin', muddin'. You know, outdoorsy things."

"What's muddin'?"

"You've never been muddin'?"

She laughed and punched his arm. "If I had, I wouldn't have asked you what it is, now would I?"

"Well hell, darlin'. We'll get the boys together after work this evenin' and show you what a good time muddin' is! We usually do it on the weekend when we don't have so much work, but it's fun in the dark, too. We get the big ass lights on the back of the truck, turn them on and have a great time."

"So what is it?"

"We get our trucks out in the big mud bog down near the fishin' hole and race around in it. It's a blast! You get mud in places you never thought you'd see mud."

"Sounds like fun."

"Let's head back to the ranch. I need to do a little work today if we are gonna get everyone to cut out early tonight. Mom and Dad will probably go, too. Hell, they might even invite all the guests. We sometimes get people settin' up their lawn chairs out there just to watch. Some of the guys from town come out too if they know we are doin' it, just to join in." Joel helped her into his truck before he went around to the driver's side. "This is gonna be fun. We haven't been muddin' in several weeks. It's been too busy at the ranch."

"Are you sure it'll be okay?"

"It'll be great. It's been kind of slow at the ranch this week so Mom and Dad shouldn't have a problem with it."

He started the truck and backed out of the spot at the western wear store.

Several minutes later, he punched the code into the gate at the front of the ranch. "Why do you lock the gate?"

"Mostly to keep unwanted visitors out. We have a pool and some of the local kids want to come by and swim. We don't have a lifeguard, so for liability issues, we keep the place locked. It also keeps out the people wandering around looking for ranches to check out. We've had people poach our cattle before."

"Wow, really?"

"Yeah. We have the longhorns who roam the ranch, but we also have the beef cattle we use to sell for meat."

They pulled up in the front of the main lodge as Nina stepped outside. She waved and started for the truck. "I'm going to the barn," he said once they stood in front of it.

"Chicken."

"Yep. I don't want another lecture from my mother about our love life." He reached over and kissed her. "I'll see you after while. I'll get the guys set up for muddin' later. You just wear somethin' you won't mind gettin' all dirty in."

"Yes, Sir."

His left eyebrow rose. "I like when you say that. We'll work on it more later." He kissed her again just as Nina reached the truck. "Later, Mom."

"Where are you goin'?"

"To work."

"You haven't done anything all morning, young man. What's makin' you start now?"

He grinned and started to whistle as he made his way toward the barn without answering her.

"Where'd you two go? I didn't see you at breakfast."

"We went to the diner in town since we were late getting up."

Nina grinned. "I'm glad you two are gettin' along much better."

"Not that you had anything to do with us not talking to each other yesterday and then getting into a big fight so we would make up."

"Me?"

"Playing matchmaker, Nina?"

"I just want my son to be happy. You make him happy." She shrugged. "I haven't seen him in such a good mood in a long time."

"We've come to a mutual agreement."

"Oh?"

"Yes. We aren't going to talk about anything past this week."

"What happens after this week?"

"We don't know at this point. We're playing it by ear, so to speak."

Nina tilted her head, giving Mesa a look like her mother would. "What do you want to happen?"

"I have a life in Los Angeles, Nina. Joel is a great guy and we get along fine, but I don't think there is anything beyond this week for us."

"I'm sorry to hear you say that, Mesa. I think you two are fabulous together, but I understand where you are coming from. Moving all the way here would be a huge mistake on your part. I mean what happens if things don't work out between you and Joel?"

"I've been telling myself the same thing for the last couple of days. I'm glad you understand."

"I really do, but let me tell you a story."

"Okay." Mesa took a seat on the picnic bench as Nina sat across from her.

"I wasn't born and raised here."

"But you're Native American."

"Yes, I am, but Texas is not where I came from. I met the boys' father when I traveled with my own father to Washington on a business trip. He was high counsel in our tribe. The trip was to try to talk the government into giving us more money for schools and medicine. We didn't have access to a clinic for the young girls to go for birth control and my father wanted me to talk to them as a teenager on the verge of womanhood with all the sexual urges of a budding young lady."

"Wow."

"Yep."

"Did you meet Mr. Young there?"

"No. He worked for the government agency and was sent to the area to do a report on our needs after my father gave them his plea. He was a suit and a half when he walked into our home to talk to my father. I'd never seen such a man before except for those in Washington. The only people I'd seen were those of our hometown in New Mexico."

"You two were so drawn to each other, he moved out here, bought the ranch, and moved you to it to raise your family."

Nina laughed. "Oh, if only it were so romantic. No. I hated him on sight. He was arrogant and self-righteous. But he kept coming back. We saw him several times over a two-year period. I came to realize he wanted to do what was best for us no matter what the government said we needed. He helped us in ways no one knew. I turned eighteen the last summer he came. We got to talking one day out by my parents barn. He reached over and kissed me. Shocked me somethin' fierce. I didn't know what to make of it. You see, I'd never been kissed before. I held onto my virginity like a sacred vow to the gods and I wasn't going to give it up to just anyone. James swept me off my feet, but then he didn't come back. I didn't see him again for five years. He went back to Washington and left me in New Mexico without a word. He never wrote, never called, nothing."

"I'm sorry."

"It was for the best. I wasn't ready to be anything but a young girl when he was there during that summer, but when he returned I knew what I wanted. I wanted him and I wasn't going to take no for an answer. I knew he liked me or he wouldn't have kissed me." She laughed. "I made him work for it though. No, I wasn't easy to catch when he returned the bit older man. You see, he's ten years my senior so at eighteen, I wasn't old enough for him, but at twenty five, I knew what I wanted." Nina took Mesa's hand in hers. "All I'm saying is if you want Joel, don't let him go. He might not be there when you're ready for him." Nina patted her hand and climbed to her feet. "I have a feeling there is more between you than either of you is willing to admit. Just don't let it be too late. I got lucky."

Nina moved off toward the house leaving Mesa to think things through on her own. Thinking wasn't part of the plan though. Thinking meant she had to feel and she wasn't sure she wanted to let her heart do the talking.

Chapter Eleven

The roar of the trucks sent tingles down her arms as they sat on the edge of the mud pit waiting for the signal. Joel sat in the driver's seat with her buckled into the passenger seat. Her heart raced in excitement. She had her hair pulled back in a ponytail and wondered if she really would get as muddy as Joel suggested. She kind of hoped so. This would be one hell of an experience to add to the authenticity of her cowboy romances.

"Ready?" he asked, flashing her a wide grin. His eyes sparkled like blue topaz in the dim light of the truck cab.

She could tell he was totally in his element here amongst his brothers and friends with their beer, trucks, mud to their elbows, and country music turned up so loud she could hardly understand the words.

"Yeah." She gripped the *oh shit* handle so tight, her knuckles turned white.

The girl holding the flags on the other side of the pit threw her arms ups and they were off. Mud sprayed the sides of the trucks practically obliterating the view out the windows. They slipped and slid around in circles. Mesa laughed as Joel kept the truck upright. She never had so much fun in her life.

After they had their turn at the pit, they drank beer, roasted hot dogs and marshmallows over the open bonfire, told stories, and laughed until their stomachs hurt. Some of the trucks from town even came out when they heard the Young family was havin' a muddin' party.

Mesa had mud in her pants from when Joel tossed her in before diving in after her. Not to mention the muck in her hair, down her shirt and everywhere in between but she hated to see it end.

The mud had begun to dry on her skin, pulling it tight. She couldn't wait to get back to her room and into a nice, warm shower. Her eyes began to droop as she snuggled up into the curve of Joel's arms. He'd sat on the ground with his back against a rock, drawing her into the cocoon of his embrace.

"Ready for bed?"

"Hmm. Yeah, if you're in it."

"I hoped to be. I need a shower first though."

"Me too."

"How about we head back to my place, shower, make love, and sleep until noon tomorrow?"

"Yeah, right. You'll be up with the chickens."

"True, but one can dream, right? I wanna hold you tonight."

"I need to stop by my room and get clean clothes then."

"Okay." He stood up, drawing her up with him. "We're headin' back to the house. See y'all in the mornin'."

The good-natured ribbing brought a smile to her face. Not like anyone in the group knew for sure, but they had an idea what would happen when they made it to a bed.

"You got condoms, brother? I think you're gonna need a few."

"Don't worry about me, Jeremiah. I'm prepared. Trust me."

The group laughed as she blushed to the roots of her hair. Good thing they couldn't see her face in the dark.

"We're going to get the interior of your truck dirty."

"It washes. I got leather interior for a reason. This is what we do around the Hill Country."

"Tonight blew my mind, Joel. You guys were great. I can see why you love it here so much."

"I do. It's where I was born and raised. I can see bringing up my kids here."

"You want kids?"

"Someday, yeah. A couple. Nothing like my parents. Wow. I couldn't handle nine boys, I don't think. I don't know how they did it."

"I can't imagine it either. I mean I have a couple of siblings, but nine…"

They pulled up in front of the house. "I'll just be a minute if you want to wait here."

"I'll walk with you. I've been walking this ground my whole life. I know every pot hole, rock, and nook in this yard, but there are still dangers of walking out here at night and I have a flashlight on my key ring for just this purpose."

"Always prepared, huh?"

"I try to be, but you've thrown me for a loop more times than I can count."

"Me?"

"Yes, ma'am. I wish I knew what to do with you."

"Just love me."

He tripped over a rock and she laughed.

"So much for knowin' every rock."

He grinned as he swatted her butt.

She took off at a run up the steps of the house and through the doorway. They laughed as he chased her up the stairs to her door. With a hand on either side of her head, he trapped her against the door.

"Now you're mine."

Her lips parted on a sigh. "I've been yours from the moment I rode behind you on your horse."

"Are you, because I need to know."

"Yes."

He bent his head to take her lips in a soul-searing kiss meant to curl her toes, which it did. She tangled her fingers in the hair at the nape of his neck. His tongue tangled with hers, spreading warmth from her mouth to every part of her body. Her belly clenched in need. She needed this man with every breath in her body.

When he lifted his head, his eyes were darker blue and burning with lust. "We can shower here."

"Let me get the door."

"I want you, Mesa," he whispered against her ear when she turned around to unlock the door. Shivers rolled down her back as goose bumps flittered across her arms.

They stumbled through the doorway.

"What the hell?" they said in unison.

Every drawer on all the furniture was open although nothing seemed disturbed in the drawers. She looked around the room, but nothing was missing.

"It had to be the ghosts."

"Ghosts?"

"Yeah, they've been bugging me since I got here. Knocking on my door when there is no one there, voices, arguing, the cowboy who disappeared."

"Oh."

"Yeah, oh. You know about them, right?"

"Yes. They don't usually bug people or do this kind of stuff though. They get a little noisy sometimes, but I've never had them open drawers like this."

"Well, it doesn't matter. You're here. He won't bug me tonight."

"He?"

"Yeah, the cowboy or the guy who argues with the women next door. I think it's her knocking on my door sometimes, but I'm not sure. There isn't anyone there when I answer."

"You're okay with all this?"

She shrugged as she removed his cowboy hat and threw it on the bed. "I have to be, Joel. They are part of this house. If they leave me alone, I'm fine with sharing their space."

"You're an amazing woman, Mesa."

"Thank you, now get naked."

"Yes, ma'am." He grinned, unzipping and stepping out of his jeans after he pushed them to the floor.

His full length made her mouth water to taste, but she burst out laughing.

* * * *

"What the hell is so funny?" he asked indignation rushing through him while he watched Mesa double over in a fit of giggles.

"You…mud…on…your…"

He smiled when he looked down and saw mud caked on his cock. Well, it wasn't a good muddin' trip if there wasn't mud everywhere. "Shower now, woman."

She continued to laugh as she removed her clothes and left them in a pile on the wood floor so they wouldn't get the carpet dirty with the mud. Too late. It seemed to be everywhere.

He followed her into the bathroom and began rubbing his hard cock between her butt cheeks while she adjusted the temperature on the shower until the water seemed warm enough. "Easy, big boy."

"Hell no. I'm fuckin' you in the shower against the tile wall."

"Oh yeah?"

"Yep."

"Let's get the mud and crud out of my hair before we do the nasty."

"The nasty, huh?"

"Of course. Haven't you heard the term before?"

He laughed. "Not put like that, I haven't." Her butt looked delectable when she turned around to wash her face. He squeezed a cheek as a moan escaped his mouth. What he wouldn't give to bury his cock in between those hot little cheeks. *Would she let him eventually? Interesting thought.*

After she spun around to wash her hair, he grabbed the soap to lather up her breasts. *Man, she has pretty tits, too.* "I love your tits."

"Breasts, Joel," she said rising her hair while he enjoyed himself with the soap. "Women don't like them called tits. It's vulgar."

"What about this?" he asked, sliding his hand down between her legs.

"Pussy is fine by me, but I don't like cunt."

"Fine. I want your pussy squeezing me."

"I want that too."

"Are you wet for me?"

"Fuck yes." She moaned, tossing her head back as he worked her pussy with his fingers.

Her hard little clit poked out for his touch. He wanted to eat her until she creamed all over his face, but for now, he was going to fuck her against the wall.

He twirled her around so he could wash himself real quick. He wanted to get down to the good stuff in short order. She laughed when he washed his hair and body in record time.

"Anxious are we?"

"Horny would be a better word for it," he said, rinsing the last of the soap from his chest. He leaned down and kissed her as he wrapped her in his arms. *God, I love kissing her, touching her…loving her. Where the hell did that thought come from? I don't love her. I can't. She's leaving in a couple of days.*

"What's wrong?" she asked when he cut the kiss short.

Joel shook his head and leaned back down to kiss her again as he whispered, "Nothin'." He slid his tongue past her lips to tangle with hers. With his fingers, he pinched her nipples into hard little points like he knew she enjoyed. His little city girl liked a little pain with her sex. A soft moan escaped her mouth around their kiss. He lifted her with both hands on her butt cheeks until she wrapped her legs around his hips and pushed her against the wall of the shower. "Give me everythin', darlin'."

"You have everything, Joel."

I want your heart.

He nudged his cock against her opening and slowly slid as deep as he could possibly get. "Aw, fuck."

"Do it. Fuck me."

He braced his feet wide apart so they didn't slip in the shower and fucked her until she screamed his name on a prayer.

His balls drew up against his groin and he knew he wouldn't last much longer. She needed to come again before he let go.

"Play with your clit."

"What?" she asked in a panting whisper.

"Play with your clit. Make yourself come again."

"But…"

"Do it now."

She snaked her hand down between their joined bodies until she reached her clit. With her head back against the shower stall, she completely lost herself in the pleasure she built with her fingers while he slowly guided his cock in and out. *God, she's beautiful.* "Come for me, darlin'."

A high scream echoed off the stall doors when she climaxed the second time, drawing his own from deep inside his body to explode inside her with gushing spurts. His legs shook as he tried desperately to draw air into his starving lungs.

"Oh my God."

"Yeah, you can say that again." He slowly let her legs down and helped her stand on her own two feet. "You're fabulous."

"You are pretty good yourself."

They quickly washed the cum from their bodies before they climbed out and dried off. "Do you want to stay here instead of going to your place?"

"I can make you scream more at my place. No neighbors."

"True. I'm not quite done with you yet, cowboy."

"Good. I ain't nearly done with you yet, city girl."

They got dressed and then snuck down the stairs, listening for any noise from the family to know whether they'd come back from the muddin' party. She giggled like a child as they sprinted toward the door on tiptoes, trying to be quiet even though he didn't think anyone had come home yet.

He pulled the door open to come face to face with Jeff.

"Where the hell are you goin'?"

"Back to my place. Later, brother."

Jeff just shook his head as they went around him laughing as they took off running hand in hand toward his truck.

"We can't take this, Joel. It's full of mud on the seats."

"Let's take your car then."

"Let's just stay here."

"Fine by me, babe. I just didn't think you wanted everyone in the house to know how loud you get when you come."

"Let's take my car." She pulled the keys from her purse and unlocked her car that sat two spots down from his truck.

It only took a few minutes for them to reach his cabin, get inside and strip down to skin. He loved having her close. *There's that word again. I am not in love with Mesa.*

"What's wrong?"

"Nothin', why?"

"You're frowning as you look at me. It's kind of hard on the ego, you know."

"Sorry. I just had a thought."

"What?"

"It's nothin', really. I'm sad you're leavin' in a couple of days."

"Yeah. I know."

"Let's not think about it right now. Okay? I wanna love you all night long."

"An all-nighter, huh?"

"Oh yeah." He drew her down in front of the fireplace.

"Too bad it's too warm for a fire. I've always wanted to make love in front of a fire."

He held up one finger. "Wait right there." He walked to the thermostat and cranked up the air conditioning. "Now, it'll get cold in here so we can have a fire." The fireplace was gas logs so he just hit the switch and ignited the thing. "How's that?" he asked, snuggling down on the rug and pulling her into the crook of his arm. Nothing like a willing female to appreciate in front of a roaring fire.

"Perfect. Thank you. You don't know how much this means to me."

"Me too. I love the way the firelight bounces color off your skin."

"My pale skin, you mean."

"No." He kissed her shoulder and run his tongue along the curve until he reached her neck. "You have fabulous skin. All soft beneath my tongue. I love your taste."

"I didn't realize I had a taste."

"You do. Sweet with a little tang. It's addicting."

"Is it?"

"Yep."

She turned around in his arms until she rose up on her knees between his legs. "I like your taste, too." Her tongue danced along his jaw until she reached his ear. "I could fall in love with you so easily."

He pushed her back and looked into her eyes. Sincerity and insecurity shone bright in her gaze. Did she really mean what she said? Was she in love with him? What about his feelings for her? Did he feel love for this enigma of a woman who'd turned his life upside down since he found her on the side of the road?

"Don't freak, Joel. I just meant if we had more time."

He exhaled on a rush.

"Make love to me."

He pushed her back on the rug and kissed her from the tip of her nose, over her shoulder, across her breasts, down her abdomen, settling between her legs. "I'm gonna eat you until you cream for me."

She moaned softly and closed her eyes.

Her pussy glistened with her juices in the firelight as he looked at all the pink flesh. She wasn't a waxer, but she obviously kept it well clipped. No stray hairs anywhere. Funny he hadn't really noticed before.

"What are you doing?"

"Lookin' my fill. You are so gorgeous, you take my breath away."

"It's bit disconcerting to have a man between your legs just so he can look."

"We like to look." He licked from pussy to clit in one long stroke.

Her head fell back on the carpeted floor as she growled deep in her throat.

He loved the way she tasted, too. He loved everything about her. *God, I'm so screwed.*

Not willing to give into the feelings surging through him at the moment, he loved her until she came twice by his tongue and his fingers. He moved up between her thighs. With one skillful snap of his hips, he buried his cock so deep inside her, he knew he'd come home.

* * * *

Two days later Mesa stood at the side of her car as Joel loaded her suitcases. Nina hugged her with tears in her eyes. "You know you can come back anytime, honey. You'll always be welcome."

"Thanks, Nina, but I'm not sure I can."

"He loves you, you know."

"No, I don't think so."

"He's just bein' stubborn. He's a man after all."

"I know, but I don't think things would work out between us even if I were here permanently. We're too different."

"Wait and see."

"Everythin' is in the trunk, Mesa."

"Thanks, Joel."

"I'll leave you two to your goodbyes. You take care, honey. Call and let us know you got home all right. I'll worry until you do."

Nina hugged her again. "Thank you for everything," she whispered in the older woman's ear.

"You're welcome."

Joel stood off to the side with his hands in his pockets until his mother walked back to the house. "Come 'ere."

Tears spilled down her cheeks as she hugged him close to her heart. She loved him. She knew she did, but she couldn't give up her life in Los Angeles to move to a small town in Texas and she couldn't ask him to leave the only life he knew to do what? He would be so out of place in Los Angeles, it would be comical.

He moved back and wiped the tears from her cheeks. "Don't cry, darlin'."

"I'm gonna miss you."

"I'm gonna miss you too." He glanced at his watch. "You better get goin' or you'll miss your flight."

She closed her eyes and sniffed, holding back the tears without success. "Bye, Joel."

"Bye, darlin'."

Chapter Twelve

"You're being an asshole, Joel. Go fuckin' get laid or something!" Jonathan yelled as the two of them stood toe-to-toe in the barn.

He knew his brother was right. He'd been a total dick the last few weeks, but he didn't know what to do to fix it. "Fuck you."

"Go find some chick to fuck and get it over with. Mesa left. You didn't stop her. It's your own damn fault you let her get away and now you're miserable. You're totally in love with her."

"I'm not in love with her, damn it!"

"The hell you aren't. Look at yourself. You barely eat, you aren't sleepin', and I bet you haven't been able to fuck another woman since she left."

"What difference does that make?"

"You couldn't could you? You tried and you couldn't get it up."

"Get the hell away from me before I kick your ass."

"Try it!" Jonathan put up his fists and backed up. "I'm waiting."

"You aren't worth the bruise on my knuckles." He stomped off, heading for the peace and quiet of the main lodge. Guests were few this week, so he should be able to sulk in private. He hoped.

A few moments later, he stood by the window of the main lodge looking out over the front of the house. He hadn't talked to Mesa in a month, not since she walked out of his life. Miserable would describe his state of mind since she left. His life had come down to this, up at dawn, ride the fences, help his brother break horses, feed the animals, and mope the evening away with a bottle of beer and his television. He couldn't eat, couldn't sleep and certainly couldn't even think about being with another woman. He'd tried that. The weekend after she left, he'd gotten drunk at the bar in town, took someone home and then couldn't preform. The woman had left pissed.

"Son, why don't you call her?"

"Because I can't, Ma. She doesn't love me."

"I think you're wrong."

"Why wouldn't she say it then?" he asked, turning to face her.

"She's just as stubborn as you are." Nina jammed her hands on her hips to take up her I'm-the-mother-so-listen-to-what-I'm-telling-you look. "Did you tell her you love her?"

"No."

"Then why would she say it first? Why do you think it's up to her to tell you, but you couldn't tell her?"

"I'm not in love with her, Ma."

"You really believe that, son? You've been miserable since she left. I've seen the way you mope around here like someone killed your dog. Give it up. I don't know if you think to convince me or yourself with that statement, but it won't work on me." She hugged him and stepped back. "You love her, Joel. It's written all over your face. You were happy when she was here. Go after her. Convince her you love her and bring her back home where she belongs. If you don't, you'll regret it for the rest of your life." She placed her hand on his cheek. "I love you, son, but you're drivin' us all nuts with this."

* * * *

Four weeks. It had been four damned weeks since she left Bandera and Joel. Mesa buried her faced in the pillow on her couch. She hadn't been able to eat, couldn't sleep, didn't want to do anything but dream of Joel where he visited every night. She was miserable. "This is fuckin' crazy!"

Her phone rang, but she didn't feel like answering it. Every time it rang the one person she wanted to talk to wasn't there. She'd made sure he had her phone number when she left, but so far, he hadn't used it. Obviously, he'd moved on without her. She needed to do the same. She just couldn't seem to breathe without thinking about him.

Her answering machine picked up and she heard the voice of her agent. "Mesa, darling. I need to talk to you about this book you sent me. Please pick up."

"All right, Mesa. I hate to say this, honey, but we can't publish this. We write romance. This doesn't have a happily ever after, honey. The heroine is miserable and we can't sell this to anyone. You are a talented woman beyond words, but this won't sell. You need to rewrite the ending. I'll call you this afternoon."

"I wish I fucking could!" she screamed at the answering machine, bursting into tears. "God, I wish it had a happy ending. I want my happy ending."

"Never mind. I'm at your door. We need to talk now."

The phone clicked indicating the woman had hung up just as the doorbell rang.

"Just fucking great." She buried her head in the pillow. "Maybe if I don't answer it, she'll leave."

"I know you're in there, Mesa. Your car is in the driveway. Open the door, honey."

Mesa sighed and climbed to her feet. She was just going to have to get this meeting over with so she could wallow in peace. "I'm coming!" she yelled as the doorbell rang again. "What do you want, Madeline?"

"You look like shit, darling. What the hell happened to you?"

"Nothing."

"Oh, something definitely. I've never seen you like this," Madeline said, shoving past her to enter her hallway. "Like I said on the phone, we can't sell this piece with this ending, Mesa. It won't do."

"I'm sorry, but it is what it is."

"You need to rewrite it. The hero and heroine have to come together somehow. Make him show up on her doorstep begging for her forgiveness and confessing his love. It's romantic. It's fun. It's what it needs."

Mesa closed her eyes as she exhaled a deep sigh. "I just can't right now, Madeline. Maybe in a few weeks I'll get over this melancholy me and be able to give them their happy ending."

"Honey, what happened in Texas?"

"Nothing."

"You look like someone died, darling."

"No. No one died. I'll get over it. I'll be back on track in no time. You'll see."

"A man?"

Her eyes widened. Surely Madeline couldn't tell she had a man on the brain, could she?

"I'm fine really. Thanks for stopping by." She pushed Madeline toward the door. "I'll call you next week. We can do lunch."

"All right. If you're sure."

"I'm sure. Thank you for being worried about me."

"Call me if you need anything. All right?"

"I will." She shut the door behind her agent and pressed her back against the wood panel. She really needed to get over Joel, now. "Enough. I can't keep doing this." She swiped at the tears rolling down her cheeks. "He obviously didn't love me. It was nothing more than a quick fling like he said from the beginning. I should never have let my heart get involved. Big mistake from the get go."

The doorbell rang, echoing the sound throughout her apartment until she wanted to scream. *Bong. Bong.* Whoever was out there wasn't going away until she answered the damn door.

"What?" she yelled as she opened the door to find a deliveryman.

"Ms. Arraguso?"

"Yes?"

He handed her the clipboard. "Sign here."

She signed her name and he handed her a single red rose. "That's it?"

"Yes, ma'am."

He walked away while she looked at the flower. *How weird.* Maybe it's from a fan. She closed the door and walked into her kitchen to set the beautiful blood red bud down. She needed a drink. Something strong. Lots of alcohol to drown her breaking heart in.

She poured whiskey straight from the bottle into a glass and then looked at the flower again. Something odd caught her attention, and she frowned as peered closer at the flower. "What the hell? There's writing on the petals."

She slowly peeled the silky layers back.

I can't eat.

I can't sleep.

I miss you.

I'm miserable without you.

The last one said…*I love you.*

A soft knock sounded on the front door as she stood there in shocked silence. Not even aware of what she was doing, she moved to the door and opened it to find Joel standing there in all his cowboy glory with eleven more blood red roses clutched in his hands. She let her gaze roam over him from the top of his black Stetson to the tips of the dirty cowboy boots. He looked good enough to eat.

"Do the tears mean you missed me, too?" he asked, his blue eyes hopeful.

"God, did I miss you!" She threw her arms around his neck and kissed him with all the pent up passion and love she held in her heart for this crazy man. "I love you. I love you. I love you." She punctuated each phrase with a kiss.

She heard the rest of the bouquet crunch to the carpet as he pulled her arms from around his neck and dropped to one knee. "Mesa, baby. Will you marry me?"

Mesa covered her mouth as more tears streamed down her cheeks. "Yes. I'll marry you. When? Where? Right now? Let's go to Vegas. We can be married today. It's only a four hour drive."

"Slow down, baby. I'd marry you today, but my family would kill me."

She stuck out her lip in a small pout, hoping he would give in. They could be married before the end of the day.

"I love you, Mesa."

"I love you too, Joel."

"We have to wait."

"Why?"

"Because, I want to marry you in front of everyone. All my brothers, your family. Everyone." He grinned his heart-stopping grin. "But we can start the honeymoon now."

"Really?"

"Oh hell yeah!"

He swept her up in his arms before he kicked the door shut with his boot. "Where's your bedroom?"

"Down the hall, cowboy."

"I'm gonna make you scream, city girl."

"Promise?"

"Promise with all my heart and soul."

Epilogue

The fire in the fireplace hissed from the gas logs. Rain pounded on the roof outside but Mesa didn't care. She sat wrapped safe and warm in her husband's arms while they lounged on the rug in front of the fireplace in nothing but bare skin. She had her very own happily ever after with her cowboy. Soft country music played over the stereo system. A little George Strait always put her in the mood for lovin'. Tonight was no exception. Of course, it was their wedding night. The honeymoon would commence the next day with a trip to Jamaica, but they'd decided to spend the night in their cabin.

After he'd shone up on her doorstep in Los Angeles, they'd spent the day and night making up for lost time. It only took one I love you to tell her she belonged with this man back in Texas. He went home after a week, leaving her there to settle her life, give up her apartment and pack a truck. He then flew back to ride from L.A. to Bandera with her. Their wedding took only three months to plan. She couldn't have waited much longer even though they loved the nights away in their little spot of heaven beneath the wide Texas night sky.

Noise coming from outside startled her out of her musings until she snuggled back down against him.

"Don't worry, darlin'." His kissed the top of her head. "It's just my brothers causing a ruckus."

"What are they up to?" She sat up and turned around in his arms. "They aren't like painting your truck with shaving cream or something, are they?"

"I don't know, but I'd expect them to tie cans to the back bumper. I ain't the first to get married since Jeff did it before me, but I'm the first to have my wife snuggled up next to me on our weddin' night here in my cabin. Jeff spent his wedding night alone."

"Seriously? What the hell?"

"I told you she was a bitch. She went out after the wedding with her friends, passed out on someone's floor and didn't come home until two days later."

"Wow." She glanced down at her wedding rings with a smile. "I can't believe we're married." A not so quick kiss to his lips forestalled her next words for several minutes. She loved kissing Joel, anytime, anywhere. They usually made the family uncomfortable with their show of affection. "It was a beautiful ceremony even though it rained."

"But it was great to have it in front of the fireplace in the main lodge."
He pushed a piece of hair behind her ear before he trailed his fingertips along
her jaw. "You looked beautiful in your dress. Did I tell you that?"

"You have now. You looked pretty handsome in your cowboy finery."
She kissed his neck. "Did I ever tell you I have a thing for cowboys?"

"No really? I would never have guessed." He laughed.

She punched him in the side.

"Ow!"

"Oh, I did not hurt you."

He gave her a wounded look with a little pouty lip. Unable to resist, she
leaned in and sucked his bottom lip between her teeth before she took a nip
of it. A soft moan escaped his mouth as he grabbed her head, slanting it just
so for a deeper kiss. Their tongues tangled for a good while before he lifted
his head and looked into her soul with those beautiful blue eyes.

"I love you Mrs. Young."

"I love you too, Mr. Young. So much. More than anything in this life."
Tears formed, spilling down her cheeks.

"Hey! Why the tears?"

"Happy tears. I'm so glad you came to L.A."

"You've already thanked my mother for her intervention on your behalf
like a thousand times."

He tucked her in next to his side, holding her close. Her head rested on
his broad chest. "I wouldn't know what to do if you hadn't."

"I'm beyond thrilled we don't have to find out. Now, hush. I have a wife
to love."

"Hmm," she hummed in between kisses. "I like your thinking, Sir."

"Good. Kiss me, woman."

"Where, Sir?"

"Anywhere you want."

THE END

HEALING A COWBOY'S HEART
Cowboy Dreamin' 2
Sandy Sullivan

Chapter One

"What the hell?" Jeffery Young slammed on the brakes and pulled his beat up Chevy truck over to the side of the road.

"Where we goin', Daddy?"

"To the south pasture, but I need to figure out what these people are doin' on our land, buddy. You stay here." He hopped out of the truck but left it running to keep it cool in the interior for his son. Three-year-old Ben loved to go with his dad on ranch business. Even though summer had officially come to an end, the days still got hot in Bandera, Texas. Today they'd planned to check on the water trough in the south pasture. He needed to patch it before winter set in.

"Okay," Ben said, swinging his small booted feet.

Jeff hopped out of the truck, slamming the door behind him. "Who the hell are you? What are you doin' on Thunder Ridge land?"

A petite blonde stood next to a larger guy he recognized from the land surveyors office in town. He noticed right away how her hair caught the sunlight, bouncing it off the curls when she turned to face him. Green eyes the color of spring grass gazed at him behind the small round glasses perched on her nose.

"Excuse me?"

"What are you doin' on my land?"

"Surveying. What does it look like?"

The woman sounded way too damned perky for his taste. "Who are you?" He turned to face the man from town. "George, what's goin' on here?"

"We're doin' a land survey, Jeff." George motioned to the woman next to him. "This here is Terri Kennedy."

"Nice to meet you." She held out her hand, but he ignored it with a scowl.

"No one ordered a survey of our land. You don't need to be on our property."

"It's not for Thunder Ridge. It's for the new development." George looked uncomfortable as he shifted back and forth on his feet.

"Get the hell off my property," Jeff snarled. "We ain't supportin' the developers takin' over the ranch land out here."

"We have a right to use this road to survey the property boundaries. It's a county road."

"Not as long as you're off the blacktop, it ain't. It's Young property."

"Is he correct, Mr. Scott? Is this private property beyond the blacktop?"

"Yes, ma'am."

"Well then, we shall move to the blacktop area." She stomped her booted feet as she moved twenty feet up the road. Her curvy little ass bounced with each step, emphasizing the cute roundness much to his chagrin. "Now, we can continue where we left off. I'm sure you can make the adjustments to the measurements."

"Yes, ma'am."

The little smirk on her kissable lips drove his anger higher. He didn't want to notice anything about the woman, but here he stood watching everything about her. "Fuck."

"Did you say something?"

"No, ma'am. Get your business done and get off this road."

"You know you don't have to be so surly. I'm not doing anything wrong. I'm here as the architect for Meyer, Jessup and Cole."

Jeff moved closer. Something about her pissed him off. Was it the development or her in general? He didn't care. She needed to leave and leave fast. "Whoever they are."

"They are the firm handling the land development in this area."

"We don't want a damn development here. We have plenty of problems with not enough open land for the wildlife around here. Having houses will take away the natural habitat."

"I'm sorry, sir, but there isn't anything I can do about it. I'm only here to make sure the surrounding property the developers bought will be able to handle the architecture they are planning to build."

"Just get done and get out of here. If you ain't gone before I get back, I'll have you arrested for trespassin'."

"Try it, buddy! We aren't on your property now."

"You *were* lady," he growled, spinning on his booted heel and heading back to his truck. "Damn infuriatin' woman. Who the hell does she think she is? This is our property. She doesn't belong out here in her fancy shit-kickers, her designer jeans or her fancy western shirt. Like her outfit would make her fit in. Ha!"

"Daddy?"

"Yeah, buddy?" he asked, trying to calm his temper. The last thing he wanted was Ben thinking he'd gotten pissed off at him. His mother did enough damage when she had him to last a fucking lifetime.

"How come we missed the cake at Grandma's? I wanted cake."

"We'll get some when we get back, okay? I didn't think a wedding reception was a good place for you." It wasn't the whole truth and he knew it. He'd taken the easy way out of watching Joel and Mesa cut their cake. The wedding was beautiful, but he just didn't want to see his brother happily simpering over his new bride when his bitch of an ex-wife didn't even spend their wedding night with him. She went off with her friends, got drunk and disappeared for two days while he frantically tried to find her. He should have known from day one what kind of life they would have, but he didn't want to realize she wanted only his family's name and the prestige of the ranchland they owned. "Grandma will save you some, I'm sure."

"Okay."

He glanced at his pride and joy. Even if he hated his ex, at least she'd given him Ben. He loved the kid with everything in his heart. His boy was turning into a miniature of himself from the tip of his straw cowboy hat to the belt buckle he insisted on wearing. The kid was cowboy to the bone. No doubt about it. Not like he had much choice since all eight of his uncles were cowboys and so was his granddad. They ran Thunder Ridge Cattle Ranch including the small dude ranch they'd turned the place into to supplement their income.

He took his job of feeding his pony to heart too. Every morning they went out to the corral behind the main house, fed and watered the small horse before any other chores were done.

"Let's get this done then so we can go back for the cake."

"Yep."

Jeff glanced in the rearview mirror only to catch the woman watching him pull on down the road.

* * * *

Terri shielded her eyes from the glaring sun as she watched the man slowly pull down the road. She noticed his long, lean frame when he'd climbed out of the cab of his dirty, old truck. He definitely had cowboy down to an art from the top of his cowboy hat to the tip of his dirty boots. She could tell he was the real deal unlike the men she knew in Houston. Even though Houston was smack dab in the middle of cowboy country, most men she dated weren't cowboys. They were strictly corporate types—suits, ties and penny loafers.

Too bad she couldn't see his eyes. You could tell a lot about a man by his eyes.

Oh well, he'd been so pissed off at her being there, it's not like he would have looked twice at her anyway. She glanced down at her outfit. The new jeans, western shirt and pointed toe cowboy boots looked cute this morning when she'd put them on, but up against his tattered jeans, plain blue T-shirt and worn boots, she looked like a city slicker. Not something she wanted. She needed to fit in according to her clients. She had to rethink her clothing choices apparently.

Getting in with the locals was a priority. She needed information on the water levels, plants, wildlife and other pieces of the puzzle to be able to put together the plans for the housing development, and who better to get it from than one of the local cowboys.

She looked at George wondering whether she could get the information from him. Nah, he seemed like a nice enough guy, but he wouldn't have the ins and outs knowledge of a cowboy. Hmm. Maybe she could stay at one of the local dude ranches and pick the brains of the wranglers. Yeah. Sounded like a good idea to her.

"Hey, George. I know there are several dude ranches around here. Which one do you think is the best?"

"Thunder Ridge."

"Like the one that belongs to the cowboy who just chased us off his land?"

"Yep." George spit tobacco juice several feet away.

Totally gross!

"It's the nicest in the area. They have a great main lodge, meals are included, swimmin' pool. You name it. They got it. The small little guest cabins are the best, although I hear there are ghosts in the main lodge."

"Really?"

"Yep." He scratched his chin. "One of the boys just got married this weekend to a city gal from Los Angeles."

"Boys?"

"There's nine of them out there, including Jeff who you just sort of met. He's kind of testy, that one. Doesn't take kindly to strangers on their property. He's been very vocal about hatin' the land developers buyin' up the property out here."

"I gathered that."

"He's got a real piss pour attitude about him these days. 'Course with his ex bein' such a bitch, I can certainly see why."

"Hmm."

"You could do worse than goin' out there for a few days if you're thinkin' along them lines."

"I was, yes. I need more information."

"Get in good with one of them boys and you'll have everythin' you need. The family has been here for a long time. Those boys grew up here. No one knows the land like they do."

"Thank you for the information, George. You've been a big help." She glanced at the sun making a slow decent into the evening sky. "Are we about done here?"

"Yes, ma'am. Just figuring up the last of it. I'll get the stakes posted tomorrow so you all know where to cut the parcels."

"Thank you. You've been a huge help."

"You're welcome, ma'am."

George packed up his gear a few moments later before they headed to where his survey truck sat on the side of the road.

Oops. They hadn't moved the truck. It still sat on Young property. She snerked. *I should have George put one of the survey stakes right there since it's on the dirt road. Really piss off Mr. Jeff Young, the jerk.*

She could see dust billowing in the distance. "We'd better get out of here. I think our non-hospitable company is coming back. I don't know about you, but I don't want to end up in jail."

"Jeff is a lot of talk. He wouldn't call the cops since he doesn't want to have to deal with the sheriff."

"Oh?"

"Yeah. The sheriff is who his ex cheated on him with. They don't have much to do with each other if they can avoid it."

"Oh. I can see why he wouldn't."

"Yep, but we should be goin' anyway. You don't want to rile the Young family. You could use them on your side if you're set on puttin' in them houses you're plannin'."

"Thanks. Let's get out of here, then."

George started the truck just as Jeff pulled alongside his vehicle, slowing down to glare at them from inside his own.

Damn, the man is a jerk! What an ass!

George rolled down the window when Jeff rolled down the passenger window of his. "We was just leavin', Jeff."

"See that you do, George. I don't wanna see her back out here."

Terri saw a cute little boy wave from the passenger seat and she waved back. "Cute boy."

Jeff glared before gunning his truck, fishtailing slightly until the truck found pavement.

"Is he always so personable?"

George chuckled. "Yep. Wait until you get to know him a little better. It's even worse when you're close to him. He's always gettin' into fights with his brothers over somethin'."

"Sounds like a charming family."

"Oh, they're nice enough, especially Nina. She's his momma. Nice lady. Her sister works at the diner in town. Ann. She's sweet too. They just don't want to roll with the times. I'm surprised the ranch started takin' guests."

"Why's that?"

"They run cattle. Longhorns and beef cattle. Angus, I think. They're kind of stuck in the past, but I think they are working towards keepin' things more modern even though Jeff would live on the cattle alone. Unfortunately, beef prices have fallen on tough times over the last several years."

"I wouldn't see how beef cattle could survive out here. Or any cattle for that matter."

"Where'd you say you were from?"

"Houston."

"Well then you should know the story of the longhorns. They are a hearty bunch. I swear, they can live off nothin' for a hell of a long time. The Youngs have some great pasture land they cultivated over the years to be able to run the cattle on."

"Interesting."

"If you want to know ranch life, go stay out at their place."

"I think I will."

"Stay away from Jeff though. Talk to the other boys. They love the women, they do."

"Great. A bunch of bachelors, huh?"

"Yep, except for the one now. But a pretty woman like you should be able to get information out of them easy enough."

"Thank you for the compliment, George."

George shrugged and grinned a wide tobacco stuffed grin. "Just sayin'."

They pulled into the parking lot in front of the surveyor's office. George came around to open her door as she grabbed her briefcase and purse from the floor. "Thank you."

"You're very welcome, ma'am. I'll get things together and have the report for you by five tomorrow evenin' if that works for you."

"Perfect. I'm going to check out Thunder Ridge on the computer in my hotel room. I'll probably be stayin' out there by tomorrow evening so if you could, call my cell and leave me a message when it's ready."

"Sure." He tipped his hat. "Talk to you tomorrow then."

After a quick nod to George, she walked to her car and hit the key fob in her hand to open the back. She slipped her things into the trunk, then slammed the lid closed.

"Now for some dinner." The diner sat across the street from the surveyor's office. "Great. Maybe I can find out some information from the waitress at the diner. They usually love to talk and if she's relation to the owner's wife, she'd probably be more than willing to chat with me if I tell her I'm thinking of stay out there."

The bell over the door tinkled as she pushed it open. The place seemed quiet. *Great. Much easier to talk.*

"Take a seat anywhere."

"Thank you."

She found a booth near the back.

"What can I get you to drink?"

"Um, how about a Coke?"

"Sure. The menu is by the napkins there. We have meatloaf on special today with mashed potatoes, green beans and fresh bread."

"Oh, that sounds wonderful. I'll take it."

"I'll be right back with your drink." The waitress walked away as Terri studied her. Dark hair pulled back in a tight bun at the back of her head made her features sharp. Long straight nose and high cheekbones spoke of a Native American heritage somewhere down the lineage. The woman was stunning.

When she returned a few moments later with her drink, Terri asked, "Might you be Ann?"

"Yes'm. What can I do for you?"

"My name is Terri Kennedy and I'd like to know about Thunder Ridge Guest Ranch. Can you help me?"

"Certainly, sweetie. My sister and her husband own the place. You won't find a better time if you're lookin' for some real cowboyin' and ranch life."

"Great."

"You ain't from around here, huh?"

"How can you tell?"

"The clothes for one. You dress like a city girl, but you have a Texas accent."

"You caught me. I'm from Houston. I'm here on a little business, but I wanted some authentic cowboy exposure."

"You ain't gettin' it in Houston?"

"I live in the city. There are a few ranches around, but I wanted to see what the Hill Country cowboy ranches are like."

"You'll get in out there for sure."

"Sounds like a great recommendation."

The bell dinged behind the counter. "Be right back. Your dinner is ready."

Terri sipped on her Coke while she waited for Ann to bring back her plate. There were a few other patrons in the place, but they all looked like they belonged there. Wow, did she feel out of place.

"Here ya go."

"Looks fabulous, Ann. Thank you. Do you run this place all by yourself?"

"For the most part. I have a couple of girls who help during the rushes and the cook, but otherwise, it's mostly me. I worked the late shift today so I could be at my nephew's weddin' this afternoon."

"Oh, yes. George told me one of the boys out there got married today."

"George?"

Shit. I need to keep my big mouth shut if I plan to pass this off as a simple trip and not arouse suspicion. "Yes."

"Scott? The land guy?"

"He helped me out on the back road. I got stuck. He must have been out there doing some surveying or something."

"Seems we've had quite of bit of city folk gettin' stuck out on the back roads. Runnin' out of gas and such." Ann's eyes narrowed and her lips firmed into a straight line.

"Oh?" She needed to be careful or her cover would be blown before she got started.

"Yeah. It's how Joel met his bride. She ran out of gas back there near their ranch."

"How utterly romantic. The cowboy rides away with the girl on the back of his horse."

"Hey, Annie? Can we get some more coffee?"

"Hold your drawers on, Mick. I'll be right there." She glanced down at Terri with a smile. "Enjoy your dinner. I'll check on you in a bit. Holler if you need anything."

"Thank you."

"You're welcome."

The meatloaf melted on her tongue. She'd never tasted anything so good in her entire life. Within minutes, she's wolfed down her entire dinner and licked the fork clean.

"You must have been hungry," Ann said, bringing her another Coke.

"Apparently. You'd think I was starving or something, but you made the best meatloaf I've ever tasted."

"Thank you. My cook does most of the meal prep, but I still do a few things myself. The meatloaf is one of them."

"It's fabulous."

"I love someone who appreciates good food."

"My stomach loves you." She grabbed her wallet. "Here's a twenty. Keep the change for such fantastic service and food." With her purse in hand, she scooted out of the booth. "I've got a reservation to make for the ranch tomorrow night." She hugged Ann. "Thank you again. You've been great."

"You're very welcome. I hope you come by again before you head for home."

"Definitely! I wouldn't miss it."

Terri pushed open the door, catching the fragrance of lilies hanging in the baskets near the front of the diner. A cool evening breeze had worked its way up, bringing the temperature of the day to a tolerable level. Rain clouds threatened and she knew enough about the weather to know it would storm soon. She loved thunderstorms but getting caught in one in the middle of Texas Hill Country wasn't a great idea. Flash floods happened regularly although she doubted they had them in town. It was the outlying areas that had to worry more.

She drove her car to the small motel, which wasn't much, but it was clean and homey. She liked the room with its wrought iron bed, homemade quilt and fantastic lacy curtains. It reminded her of her grandmother.

As she opened the door, the cooler air of the room hit her in the face. Now, the temperature seemed almost cold. She quickly turned the thermostat down. *A bath would be nice.* Her suitcase lay open on the bed with all of the clothing she'd brought for her two week stay in Bandera. She might have to check out the western wear store in town to see if she could find something not so citified. They had faded jeans these days. Maybe she wouldn't stick out so much. She glanced at her boots. She needed to go walk in some mud with them or something. Scuff them up a bit so they didn't look so new.

Jeff's boots looked well worn.

"What the hell made me think of him? He's difficult, cranky, egotistical, and he's going to be a pain in my ass. I just know it."

She grabbed her pajamas before she headed toward the bathroom for a nice long soak. She'd even found some bubble bath in the bathroom when she's checked in so she could have bubbles, hot water…ah. Relaxing. She needed it after her week at work, the long trip from Houston to San Antonio in her car and being threatened with jail because of where she stood.

"Enough! I don't need to think of him. I'm sure I'll be dealing with him soon enough when I show up at his family's place. My stay should be interesting."

Chapter Two

The next morning Terri packed her suitcase, stuffed it into the trunk and headed back out to where she'd been the day before with George. The country was beautiful in the bright sunlight of the fall. Texas junipers dotted the landscape along with a multitude of rocks, brush and flowers. They sure had a different type of shrubbery than she had in Houston.

City blocks with its skyscrapers reaching for the heavens from every angle, left something to be desired most of the time.

She'd grown up in a small suburb of Houston and enjoyed the camaraderie of knowing her neighbors. Her high school had a small class and when she'd gone away to college in Houston, it had been a culture shock. The classes were huge. Teachers didn't know the students names and the campus stretched for miles.

The many years she'd spent studying for her architecture degree stretched on and on. Oh, she'd made friends, but it wasn't the same. She really wished some days, she had a close friend to just talk with, call on the phone or have lunch with.

She'd been working freelance for herself since she left her first job out of college two years ago. It was great working for herself, especially when she had a multi-million dollar account hanging in the balance like this one for the developers, but lately her existence seemed lonely, even to her.

At thirty years old, she really needed to quit jumping around so much. Her parents wanted her to settle down and raise a family, but she hadn't found the guy she wanted to settle down with yet.

She'd had a couple of boyfriends over the years too, but nothing serious. No one could live up to what she had in mind for her forever love. The man she had in mind had dark hair, pretty blue or gray eyes, a kick-ass smile and a killer body. He needed to be the same age as her or a little older. He'd have a great job. Some money saved. Maybe even a retirement plan.

A giggle escaped her mouth. Didn't she just have it all planned out even though she had no prospects of a boyfriend, much less someone to settle down with.

The gate to Thunder Ridge came into view. She hit the buzzer on the com when she drove up to the stone pillar.

"Can I help you?"

"Terri Kennedy. I'm a guest."

"Thank you."

The wrought iron bars slowly slid open. *Interesting.*

Several longhorn cattle grazed in the distance. A large home could be seen behind the trees as she drove up the long driveway. Several smaller cabins stood to the right when she pulled up in front of a three foot wall that separated the drive from the walkways. "What a cool set of buildings." A huge barn stood off to the back and she could see several cowboys walking around the corral. It looked like they were about to take a group of guests out on a ride. She'd have to take one while she stayed here. It'd been years since she'd been on a horse.

"Ma'am?"

A gorgeous looking cowboy stopped at her door. Dark hair framed his face and he had the most amazing blue eyes she'd ever seen. They reminded her of crystal blue water like you see in the pictures of the Caribbean. She opened her door. "Hello."

"Can I help you with your luggage?"

"I only have one suitcase, but if you'd like to grab it out of the back, I'll get my computer case. Thank you."

"My pleasure, ma'am."

"And you are?"

"Joshua, ma'am."

"Damn you make me feel old with the ma'am stuff."

He tipped his hat. "Sorry. It's part of how I was raised, ma'am."

"Thank God for cowboys," she murmured.

"Ma'am?"

"Oh, nothing." Joshua put her suitcase near the door of the car as she grabbed her briefcase and computer bag from the backseat. "Can you tell me where to check-in?"

"Yes, ma'am. I'll take you in there."

"Thank you."

She followed the gorgeous cowboy up the walkway to the side door made of wood. The damn thing must weigh a ton. He pushed it open and preceded her inside. "Follow me." They walked through what appeared to be a huge dining room with several wooden picnic type tables and one huge table at the front of the room. A staircase sat to the back leading up to what she assumed would be the guestrooms in the main lodge. *This is where George said they had ghosts.* She looked around quickly, but didn't see anything. *Stupid. Like they show themselves in the daytime!*

"Ma?" Joshua yelled. "I have a guest with me."

"I'm in the office."

"Follow me, please." He led her around the coffee station, through a large archway and into the hallway where she could see an office to the back of the room. "Here you go."

"Thank you, Joshua. I think I can handle it from here."

"All right. This is my mother, Nina. She handles the guest registration." Joshua set her suitcase against the wall.

"Terri Kennedy," she said, holding out her hand to shake Nina's.

"It's nice to meet you, Terri. Welcome to Thunder Ridge." Nina glanced at the card on her desk. "I have you in one of the outside guest cabins for a two week stay. Correct?"

"Yes."

"Great. I just need your credit card and we'll get your key." Nina glanced at Josh. "You can go back to work now, son. I can show Terri where she'll be stayin'."

"Uh, sure." Josh looked back as he walked down the hall and ran into the doorframe.

She giggled as he turned beet red.

"He's a good man. You seemed to have turned his head."

"Apparently."

"What are you hoping to accomplish while you stay here, Terri?"

Shit! Did she somehow find out about what I'm really doing here? "Just some hometown cowboying and ranch life."

"You have a Texas accent. Where are you from?"

"Houston."

"They don't have dude ranches there?"

"Well yes, but I wanted to come out to Hill Country and snoop around a bit. I'd love to talk to some of your sons about the cowboy way of life. I hear you have nine?"

"Ah yes, my sons. I'm sure they'd love to spend time with you. A pretty woman always gets their attention. They enjoy talkin' about ranch life."

"Perfect. I need to make some notes on different things about the ranch too. The soil, the water, the plants…you know."

"Really?"

"Yes. Um, I'm a conservationist."

"We have some very interestin' things on our land. I'm sure you'd love to explore. I could probably even convince one of the boys to take you out ridin' if you like to ride, so they could show you around the property."

"Absolutely, Nina. Thank you."

"We'll let you get settled in your room. Lunch is at twelve-thirty and dinner is at six. We ring the dinner bell outside and inside so you should hear it anywhere you are." Nina handed her the copy of her receipt and her key. "Follow me. I'll show you where your room is."

She followed Nina out the main doors and to the left. Two small cabins set off a little ways from the main lodge, each with two doors on them.

"Each cabin has two separate rooms that are connected by a door, but it will be locked between you and any other guests who might rent the room across from you. It's empty at the moment." They reached the door to the cabin. "I hope you'll be comfortable."

"I'm sure I will. Thank you."

"You're welcome. See you at lunch."

Terri opened the door so she could wheel her suitcase inside. Glad she packed light, she hoped they had laundry facilities or she'd be without clean clothes within a few days. The double-sized bed took up most of the middle of the room with its wooden headboard. The patchwork quilt was beautiful. Small bedside tables graced each side of the bed and a small doorway to the left looked like the bathroom. She'd have to check it out in a minute. Against the wall sat a small couch which looked like it might pull out into a bed too. The whole room would probably sleep four adults comfortably. A small window looked out over the front yard of the main lodge and the swimming pool. If the pool was heated, she might partake of the water. She'd have to ask.

The clouds overhead promised cooler weather than the day before. Fall in the Hill Country could be unpredictable with rain or cold temperatures. The high today called for the seventies, which suited her just fine.

She quickly put her clothes in the wooden dresser against the wall, noting which ones needed washing. The more casual clothes she's brought would probably suit out here better than anything else she had. She might get away with not being called a city girl.

The lunch bell clanged in the distance, calling her to the main lodge. She sucked in a ragged breath and blew it out on a sigh. It was now or never.

She crossed the yard with slow, deliberate steps. Would he be in there eating? She didn't know whether the family ate with the guests or not. She hoped he wouldn't be because he would totally blow her cover if he saw her.

When she opened the door, she was met with utter chaos or what looked to be a chaotic area. A bunch of guests had gathered in the room formerly empty. Probably thirty people stood in line to get their lunch from the five people serving over the hot plates. She swallowed hard looking toward the gathering of people as she slowly made her way toward the back of the line.

"I just love it here, don't you?" an older woman asked her friend standing in front of Terri.

"Oh yes. It's fabulous! Everyone is so nice. The cowboys are sweet as can be, but then again, it could be because we're old ladies. They were definitely taught their manners by their momma."

"She's a doll too."

"I think it's sweet how they all wait for the guests to get their plates before they get their own. It's nice that they have their own table, too, although I think it would be great if the cowboys ate with us."

The first lady giggled. "You just want one of those hunky youngsters to simper all over you, Marg."

"You're damn tootin', Liz. I may be old, but I ain't dead!" They both laughed as they approached the serving tables.

"Brisket, ladies?"

"Yes, please."

They went through the line chitchatting away like two little chickadees roosting on their nests. The two of them were too cute.

Terri looked down the long room and noticed the table with Nina sitting with a group of men. Younger men, except one older gentleman Terri assumed was probably her husband. The rest looked a lot like Joshua with one of them looking identical. Twins? *Wow.* She glanced around hoping to see Jeff so she could avoid him, but he didn't appear to be present. Had she gotten a reprieve? She hoped so. Now if she could avoid him for her whole two week visit, she would be thrilled. Somehow she didn't think she'd get so lucky.

The little boy who'd been in his truck sat next to Nina. He really was a cute kid. *Jeff's? Hmm.*

One thing she had noticed yesterday when they'd run into the infuriating man, he hadn't been wearing a wedding ring. George had mentioned an ex-wife who was a bitch, but he hadn't remarried or anything? Why she'd noticed was beyond her, but she had. Surely, she wasn't attracted to him?

Well maybe she was, but it wouldn't do any good. They were definitely on opposite sides of the spectrum. Her an architect with a firm trying to take the rangeland and turn it into housing developments and him a cowboy trying desperately to hold onto his way of life. She really couldn't blame him, but she was just doing her job, the one she'd trained for all through college.

The door creaked open at the end of the dining room. Terri glanced behind her to see Jeff come waltzing through the door looking like a cowboy of old. Dusty cowboy hat perched on his dark hair, western style shirt molded to his broad chest, dark worn jeans encasing his legs and dirty cowboy boots on his feet.

She quickly hid her face, turning toward the serving girl as she approached the hot tables. Jeff walked right past her without paying any attention to the people around him, although his cologne lingered.

The two older women sighed. "He's so standoffish. What do you think is his story?"

"I'm not sure. He's friendly enough when you talk to him, but he sure doesn't give anything besides polite conversation."

"He's the eldest you know." She waved her hand. "Of all the boys."

Terri continued to listen to their conversation as they made their way to the refreshment table to get coffee, milk or lemonade.

"He runs pretty much everything around here, but I think he tries too hard."

"The little boy is his from his marriage."

"He's a cutie."

"Yes he is, but the father? Sad case of being burned by a woman."

The women wandered off to a place to sit, while Terri kept her head down and moved as far away from the family table as she could to avoid Jeff. She'd eat and hole up in her room. Maybe she could find Joshua to ask about the things she needed to know or one of the other brothers although she didn't know their names.

Hopefully he would be working most of the time so she could get her research done. She bit her lip. She really needed to find out the answers to her questions. Unfortunately, he seemed to be the best one to ask being the eldest.

She ate her brisket while she kept a keen eye on him. Not that he was such a hardship to look at. He did have the cowboy thing down pat.

He touched Ben's head and smiled at him before he leaned over and kissed the boy on the head. Apparently, he cared a lot for his child.

Her heart skipped a beat. The man had a great smile, but obviously didn't seem to do it a lot. The family continued to chat amongst themselves.

She hoped Nina or Joshua wouldn't mention her.

She finished her food and pushed her plate away. If she got up to put her plate in the dirty dish bin now, he might see her. Maybe she'd wait until other guests were going up there. *Damn, avoiding him might be harder than I thought.*

Several other people went up to put their dishes in the bin so she took the chance and followed. She managed to put her plate in the tub, but when she turned to head back to the door to make her escape, her heart stopped when she heard Jeff raise his voice over the crowd.

"What the hell are you doin' here?"

* * * *

The last fucking person Jeff wanted to deal with tonight was his ex. He'd had a shitty ass day working in the south pasture on the water trough. Damn thing had sprung another leak after he'd fix the one yesterday. "What are you doin' here, Misha? I told you never to come out here without callin' first."

She pushed forward, headed for the door, past a blonde woman. "I need to talk to you."

"There's nothin' you need to say to me in front of my family and our son."

"Please, Jeff. It's important."

"Everything is important," he snapped, grabbing her arm to drag her into the main lodge area. Whatever she had to say, he didn't want said in front of the guests or his family. "What the hell is this all about?"

"I need a thousand dollars."

"What? Are you fuckin' crazy! I ain't givin' you any money."

"You will or I'll take custody of our son."

"Bullshit! We've been through this, Misha. We've already been to court and they gave me full custody. You have visitation. Nothin' more."

She yanked her arm out of his grasp. "I'll lie or whatever I have to do to take him from you."

"You bitch!"

"That's right. I'm a bitch. The same bitch you fucked, got pregnant, and then dumped the minute your dick didn't get what you wanted."

"I'll see you in hell before you get my son or any money from me. Now get the hell off my property before I have you thrown out of here on your ass."

"Is there a problem here, brother?" Jeremiah asked, standing close enough to Misha to intimate her from the shifting of her stance.

His entire family surrounded Misha and him. "I can handle her."

"You don't have to alone, Jeffery," Nina said, wrapping her arm around his waist. "You'll leave now, Misha, and don't bother threatening Jeff or Ben again. I'll mortgage this entire property to keep him from your clutches."

"We'll see about that!"

Misha pushed her way through the throng of people his family made up, stomping her way toward the door. She didn't even stop when Ben called, "Mama?"

Jeff hurried to Ben's side and picked him up. "It's okay, buddy. Mama had somewhere to be."

"She didn't even stop, Daddy."

"I know. I'm sorry." He hugged Ben tight as tears gathered in his eyes. *What the hell did I ever see in her?*

"Don't worry, son. We won't let her take Ben," James said, patting Ben on the head as he stuck his thumb in his mouth and laid his head on Jeff's shoulder.

God, I wouldn't know what to do if anything happened to Ben. The kid was his life. He was sorry every day for the hell Misha had put him through, but he wasn't sorry she'd given him Ben.

Maybe someday soon he'd find a woman he could tolerate long enough to get laid, but he sure wouldn't be able to handle one as a permanent fixture in his life. They are all too bitchy, self-centered, whorish, and didn't give a shit about the man or what his needs were. A man had the need to feel loved too. Not just used for the pleasure he could give a woman even though doing those things were pretty cool, they weren't everything.

"Why don't you take Ben in the kitchen for some ice cream?" Nina said, pushing him and Ben toward the double swinging doors. "I'm sure there are even some sprinkles in there."

"But, Ma?"

"Nonsense. He needs some Daddy time right now, Jeff. Go on."

"Thanks."

"You're welcome, son. Don't worry about her. She's all talk."

"I hope you're right."

He took Ben into the kitchen, found the scoop and the five gallon bucket of ice cream.

"Want some ice cream, buddy?"

Ben nodded before he wiggled to get down. "I love you, Daddy."

"I love you too, Ben."

After about an hour, they finished eating their ice cream, cleaned up the kitchen and he took Ben out to his truck to head for home. He hoped he didn't run into any guests. He didn't want to have to play nicey-nice with anyone tonight. If they could just run cattle on the place, he'd be a happy man. His parents didn't see it the way he did though.

As he walked out toward his truck, he noticed a blonde woman standing on the porch of one of the cabins the guests stayed in. From a distance, she looked familiar, but he couldn't quit place her. He shrugged. Didn't matter. He didn't mix with guests. He avoided them more times than not, unlike his brothers who liked schmoozing with them. His job was to take care of the cattle and keep the ranch running smoothly. Keep the stock fed. Keep everything from falling apart on the cattle side of the operation. If he did that, the rest of them could run the guest ranch into the ground for all he cared. He didn't like having people on the ranch playing cowboy, but he supposed the investment kept things in the black.

The woman backed away into the shadow of the porch. Odd. He shrugged.

"Let's get you to bed, buddy. It's past your bedtime."

"I don't wanna go to bed."

"Sorry. It's bedtime. We have to be up early to feed the horses."

"Okay."

Jeff opened the passenger side door on his truck and put Ben in his seat before he belted the boy in. When he went around to the driver's side, he glanced over his shoulder to see the woman again on the porch. He wondered for a moment why she seemed to be watching him, but he blew it off as a curious guest.

He drove up to his cabin a few minutes later. The place was home even though it didn't have a woman's touch. He didn't need it anyway. He liked his place just like it was. Roughhewn logs with a porch going around the front of the house. Two small windows overlooked the front yard he had fenced off for Ben to play in. He loved the small living room with the large fireplace gracing one wall and the kitchen where he had hoped one day a woman would love to cook for him and their children. "Bah! Women. They aren't worth the trouble."

He got a sleepy Ben out of his car seat and carried him inside. Within minutes, he had the boy stripped down to his Spiderman underwear, into his pajamas, and between the sheets on his bed. Ben snuggled down beneath his blankets.

"Night, Daddy."

"Night, buddy." Jeff turned off the lamp, but didn't leave the room right away.

Moonlight played on Ben's face coming through the window over his bed. His little boy. The tyke carried his dark hair and gray eyes, thank goodness. He was glad he couldn't see much of Misha in the child, but he knew she was his mother all the same and that chafed his hide.

If he would have listened to his brothers, he probably wouldn't have married her in the first place, but he hadn't. He'd loved her with all his heart.

They'd told him she flirted and propositioned them for months before the wedding. Then when she'd disappeared right after the ceremony with her friends and didn't come home for two days, he should have realized what a mistake he'd made. Stubborn fool.

"I'm sorry, buddy. God, I wish your mama was someone else."

Jeff wandered out to the refrigerator and grabbed a beer. Damn, he needed to unwind before he tried to sleep. Dealing with his ex always soured his mood.

He tipped the bottle to his lips before he studied the clear bottle in his hands. The light reflecting off the golden liquid swirling around in the bottle reminded him of the woman he'd met yesterday. *Terri Kennedy. The sunlight reflecting off her hair looked like the beer in the bottle.*

"What the fuck? Where did that come from and why the hell am I thinking about her?"

He took another swig. *Her eyes were green like new grass in the pasture.*

"Huh."

He laid his head on the back of the couch as he remembered the woman standing next to George in her citified outfit. She was kind of pretty with her hair back in a ponytail and those wire rimmed glasses perched on the edge of her nose. He laughed a dry, not so funny chuckle as he rolled the cold bottle over his forehead. "I've been too damned long without a woman if I'm thinkin' about her." He took another long draw from the cold liquid. "She works for those fuckin' developers who are tryin' to take over all the property out here to make housin' developments out of them. Bring all those city folks out here to take over the land."

Grabbing the remote for the television from the coffee table, he flipped on the news just for some background noise. He didn't like the way his thoughts were roaming tonight. Women were the bane of his existence. Thinking about them just brought about heartache on his part. Look where Misha had gotten him. Miserable, that's where.

Terri didn't do anything to you.

"Terri? Why do I have to think about her?" He finished his beer. "She's out to destroy the whole damned place!"

"In more news. The firm working on the land developments in Bandera have hired Terri Kennedy, architect, to work on the particulars concerning environmental aspects of changing the landscape."

Jeff sat forward as the woman he'd seen out on their land came into focus on the television.

"Ms. Kennedy, can you tell us what plans you are working on at the moment?"

"We are studying the impact the development will have on the surrounding community, but rest assured we are planning to make the smallest changes possible and still get the housing project done. We don't want to affect the landscape at all if we can help it."

"Yeah right. They'll be fuckin' digging up trees, moving rocks and disturbing the wildlife the minute they fuck with anything."

"It's imperative that I talk to the local people to find out more about the area. I'm looking to get immediate feedback from the cowboys foremost since they work with this every day."

"Not from me, sister."

"How are you planning to get your information?"

"I'm staying at one of the local guest ranches in hopes of talking with the family and wranglers for my research."

"Which one?"

"I'd rather not say. My sources will be kept confidential except for in my report."

"There you have it, folks. Straight from the mouth of the firm's representative. It's a very controversial topic amongst the locals in Bandera since many would be affected directly by these housing developments. Several of the local ranches in the area don't want the development in, but there are a few selling out to them in hopes of a better life elsewhere. The weather has been particularly brutal this year with the lack of rain, making grazing especially hard. Many of the ranchers have given up. We haven't been able to get any of them to talk to us here at Channel Four News, but we'll bring you continued coverage as the story develops. Back to you in the studio, Marie."

"Thank you, Ashley."

Jeff flipped off the television before he set the remote back on the coffee table. Seeing the woman's face on the screen brought back the rush of anger he'd felt after meeting her the other day, but also something else. He remembered the slope of her neck, the curve of her shoulder and the shape of her hips. Why, he wasn't sure. She wasn't particularly pretty. Not a beauty in the model sense of the word, but she had something about her, a confidence maybe, that drew him to her.

"Doesn't matter." He stood to head into the bedroom. A nice warm shower would do him good before he tried to sleep.

With a touch of his hand, the light in the bathroom flipped on. One thing he did enjoy in life was a hot shower. Tonight he certainly needed it. He wrenched his shoulder this morning fighting with a particularly ornery calf who didn't want to come out of the brush even when its mama called to it. Some days he really hated his job, but most of the time he loved being a cowboy. Not like he'd known anything else in his life. Cowboying was in his DNA. He couldn't see his life any other way.

He quickly stripped out of his clothes and turned on the hot water. One thing he'd insisted on when his parents helped him build his house was a top of the line bathroom. The shower had tile from top to bottom along with a large rain showerhead.

With a weary sigh, he climbed in and shut the door. Hot water streamed down on his head as he closed his eyes. *God, that feels good.* He worked his shoulder under the heat of the water to try to loosen it up. He hoped it didn't stiffen up tonight while he slept, but he figured it would. *Some liniment might help.*

While he washed the dirt of the day from his body, his mind wandered to baser thoughts. It'd been several months since he'd been with a woman and even though he didn't need the headaches of a female in his life, he still had the needs of a man.

Maybe it's time to hook up with someone. I could do a bar run into San Antonio and probably pick up some chick there who wouldn't know who I am.

Terri Kennedy's green eyes popped into his head. She did have pretty eyes behind those wire rimmed glasses from what he could see.

He rubbed the soap over his cock and balls, losing himself in the feel of his hand over his flesh.

Would she be good in bed? How would she look with all of her blonde hair spilling over his abdomen while she sucked him off?

His eyes popped open. "Wow. Her?"

What the hell. He shrugged and closed his eyes again. *She's pretty enough.*

With his cock wrapped in his fist, he imagined her sucking the whole shaft between her lips. Each suck, each lick brought his desire higher. Her beautiful green eyes sparkled with lust as she sat between his thighs bringing him the best pleasure he'd had in a hell of a long time. Moments later, cum sprayed over his hand as he came so hard, he saw stars.

He slumped against the wall of the shower as he tried to catch his breath. It'd been a long damned time since he'd exploded like a sixteen-year-old kid with his first fuck. After he shook his head to clear his thoughts, he stood back under the water to wash the cum from his body. *Wow. That was pretty intense.*

Once he finished his shower, he shut the water off and grabbed a towel from the rack. He dried off before he wrapped the towel around his hips so he could head into his bedroom. Warm night breezes blew through the open window, sending goose bumps along his arms. Sleeping with the window open at night was one of his favorite things to do, along with hearing a women's sigh of completion. He rolled his eyes and shook his head. A woman was the last damned thing he needed.

Chapter Three

Sunlight filtered in through the window over Terri's head, bringing her out of her dreams gradually even though she didn't want to wake up. The gorgeous hunk of a man slowly licking her from head to toe had her desire at a peak. The moment she slowly came awake though, he disappeared like a wisp on the wind. She didn't even know who he was. His face had been shadowed in the dream. His dark black hair the only feature she'd been privy to see with any clarity.

Her whole body hummed with sexual tension. *God, I need to come.* It had been way too long since she'd had sexual gratification with anything other than her vibrator, but without a man in sight, she'd have to do this herself…again or do without…again. The clang of the breakfast bell echoed in the distance as she rolled over and looked at the clock. *Damn it! I over slept.*

She rushed to get dressed and pull her hair back out of her eyes with a ponytail holder. She didn't have time for makeup or anything else. *Not like I'm going to meet Mr. Tall Dark and Handsome at the breakfast table.* After she quickly slid her feet into her flip flops, she rushed out the door and ran smack into a broad chest.

Oomph.

"I'm sorry. I didn't see you."

"My fault, ma'am."

She glanced up into gorgeous blue eyes. "Joshua?"

"Jason, ma'am. Josh, Joel, and I are triplets."

"Ah. I can see the similarity, although I don't think I've met Joel."

"No, ma'am. He's off on his honeymoon with his new wife, Mesa."

"How great. I love weddings."

"Are you headed to breakfast?"

"Yes."

"May I escort you?" he asked, holding out his elbow. "I wouldn't want you to run into anyone else this morning on your way to get food."

"Well, thank you, kind sir."

"You're more than welcome, ma'am."

"Call me, Terri."

"Nice to meet you, Terri." They walked along the path headed for the main lodge. "I guess you're stayin' in one of the cabins?"

"Yes, for a couple of weeks. I'm doing some research."

"Research for what may I ask?"

"Rocks, brush, trees, animals of your native area for a uh…paper I'm doing."

"Interestin'. If you need some help, please feel free to find me. I'm usually around doin' one thing or another. Maybe I could take you ridin' so you can check out stuff."

"Good idea! Thank you. I'll see if I can find you after breakfast."

They started through the doors only to be almost run over by a racing three-year-old. "Whoa there, little man."

"I'm hungry, Uncle Jason."

"You shouldn't be runnin'. You know what Gran and your dad say. Besides, you about ran over one of our guests."

"Sorry." Ben dropped his head so she couldn't see his face. All she could see was the bent head with his little cowboy hat on.

Damn, if he wasn't the cutest little thing in his hat, jeans and boots. "It's okay."

"No. I'm not supposed to run in the house. I'm sorry."

"You're forgiven."

"Thanks." The kid spun around and rushed off toward the huge table at the end of the room where several more family members seemed to have gathered.

"Would you like to sit with the family?"

"Uh." She withdrew her hand from his arm. "No thank you. I don't want to intrude."

"No intrusion. We have special guests sit with us all the time."

She backed up a couple of steps. "No. Really. I see a couple of ladies I know. I'll sit with them."

"All right, then. Find me later and I'll hook you up with a horse."

"Thank you, Jason."

"You're welcome, Terri." He tipped his hat before he walked away.

Air rushed from between her lips in a heavy sigh. *Damn, these folks sure made a bunch of handsome cowboys.*

"He sure is a pretty one," one of the ladies from the day before said as they came up behind her in line. "What a nice smile too."

"Yeah, he really is." Terri couldn't help but agree.

"He's one of the triplets," the other lady added. "Can you imagine?"

"No," Terri replied. "I think one of those would be enough for me on even a fantastic day."

"I'd sure like to give it a whirl," the first woman replied. "I'm Marg, by the way. We didn't introduce ourselves to you yesterday at dinner. We're staying in the Annie Oakley room." She waved toward her friend. "This is Liz."

"Nice to meet you ladies. I'm Terri."

"Are you here for relaxation, Terri, or just to get away?"

"I'm actually doing some research on the area. I thought this would be the best way to get it."

"Great idea," Liz said. "I hope you get to spend some time out with one of those boys getting your research done."

The two women giggled as Terri frowned. She wasn't sure, but she thought she'd just been set up by the two older women who now seemed to be playing matchmaker with her. Yes, the men on the ranch were gorgeous from what she could tell. Each one had their own look about them, even the triplets. They were identical, but there were subtle differences between the two she'd seen. It made her wonder about the third, who wasn't there at the moment.

When she'd literally ran into Jason this morning, at first she'd thought he was Josh, but when she looked closer, she could definitely tell the difference. Joshua wasn't quite as broad across the shoulders as Jason. All the yummy hardness of both men made it difficult to decide which one was the cutest. She'd only observed the others from a distance except Jeff. The thought of that man made her frown as she glanced over the shoulder of the person in front of her to see him talking with Nina. His dark hair glinted in the lighting of the dining room, a blue-black color. Thick and straight to barely above his collar, she wanted to run her fingers through those silky looking strands.

Seconds later, he lifted his head and made immediate eye contact with her. A frown marred his features as his eyes narrowed.

Oh shit.

She dropped her gaze, moving behind the front person hoping he wouldn't confront her here in front of the other guests.

Cowboy boots appeared in her line of vision. *Damn it!*

"What the hell are you doin' here?"

"Excuse me?" she asked, lifting her head to stare into the stormy gray eyes of Jeff Young.

"You heard me. What are you doin' here on my family's ranch?"

Nina appeared at his side. "Jeff this is one of our guests. What's the problem?"

"She needs to leave."

"I'm not leaving. I'm a paid guest."

"Guest my ass. She's a damned spy," he snarled, his lips curling back in a ferocious look. He kind of reminded her of a pit bull with a bone protecting it from intruders.

Nina stepped between them and got in her son's face. "Enough, Jeff. Terri is a guest on our property no matter her reason for being here."

"I'm sure she'll report back to the developers on everything we do so they can undermine us or somethin'."

"Jeffery. I'll have no more talk like this. Go back to your seat."

"But, Ma…"

"But nothin'. Go on. We'll talk about this later."

His gaze snapped fire at her as he glared again before turning on his boots heels to head back to the table.

"I'm sorry, Terri."

"It's fine, Nina. Nothing to be sorry for. He doesn't like me at all."

"He sure does react to you rather oddly." Nina stared for a moment. "I'm sorry. Get your breakfast and I'll handle my eldest son at least until the meal is over. After that, I'm not sure what he'll do. He does have a temper."

"I can handle him."

Nina cocked her head. "You know. I think you can." She patted Terri on the shoulder before she returned to the family table.

"Wow. Interesting," Liz said, as they finally got to the serving table and grabbed their plates.

Terri smiled. She really didn't need the two older ladies getting in her business or being in the middle of what might become a knock down drag out with the eldest son of Thunder Ridge Guest Ranch.

* * * *

Jeff got his breakfast, all the while keeping a keen eye on the intruder. The spy. He knew she had to be up to no good if she decided to become a guest on his ranch. Something was up. He just knew it. He'd have to keep a close eye on her to make sure she didn't get information she could use against them with the land developers. *Damn it! I certainly don't need her snooping around right now.*

He returned to his place at the table with his and Ben's plate. "Here you go, buddy."

"What was that all about, Jeff?" Jeremiah asked, taking his chair.

"Nothin'."

"It didn't look like nothin' to me. You were all up in the woman's face."

"I said, it's nothin'."

"Fine, but as the financial planner of this ranch, if there somethin' goin' on that affects the financial stability, I need to know about it."

"You keep your nose in the books and leave the ranchin' to me."

"Kiss my ass, brother. Remember who controls the paychecks around here."

"Fuck you."

"What's with you lately?" Jackson asked, lifting the fork to his mouth. "You need a woman or somethin'?"

"The last fuckin' thing I need is a woman."

"Watch your mouth," Nina snapped. "We have guests present."

"Sorry, Ma."

"You shouldn't be cussin' around Ben anyway. He hears enough from you when you're out with the cattle, I'm sure."

"I think he needs to get laid," Jackson added with a grin. "It usually helps my mood."

"Your answer to everything is being between a woman's thighs."

"Why the heck not?" Jackson winked. "Sounds like a perfect place to me."

"Why were you in her face, Jeff?" Jason jumped in the middle of the conversation.

"What the hell do you care, Jason?"

Jason took a drink of his coffee. "I walked her to breakfast. She seems like a nice girl to me. Kinda pretty too."

"Just say away from her. She's trouble."

"What kinda trouble?" James asked, as Jeff finished his breakfast.

"Ma won't let me discuss it here. Let's just say, she needs to be off our property immediately."

"She's a paid guest, Jeff. I won't have you kickin' guests off the ranch. We need them to keep this place runnin'. She's paid up for two weeks."

"Two weeks?" Jeff growled. "What is she gonna do here for two weeks?"

"I didn't ask her when she paid up. What doesn't it matter anyway?"

"Just keep her away from me."

"You're the foreman on this ranch, Jeff," James said. "Your job is to keep everything runnin' smoothly. You'll be bound to run into her sometimes. We can't keep you two completely apart."

Jeff rolled his eyes. *Ah hell! This is gonna be the most miserable two weeks of my life if I have to constantly be nice to her.*

He glanced down at the end of the room to see Terri look his way. She was kind of pretty in a nerdy sort of way with her glasses, her hair back in a ponytail and those jeans. He frowned. At least she seemed to have gotten some jeans that didn't look like they just came off the rack at the western wear store or might leave a blue streak should she fall down snow skiing. The thought brought a smile to his lips. Imagining her with her butt in the middle of a snow bank while her new jeans bled into the snow almost made him laugh.

Skiing was one of his favorite pastimes and he hadn't had a chance to go in forever or at least since Ben had been born. Maybe this winter he'd be able to convince his mom to watch Ben and he could take off for a weekend by himself.

He shook his head. Getting involved with a guest was against the rules anyway you sliced it, even if he wanted to. Terri was trouble with a capital T.

A heavy sigh left his lips. He had work to do. "You stay with Grandma, Ben. I'm headed to the barn, Ma. I need to inventory the feed and see what we need to order."

"Go head, Jeff." She grabbed Ben in a big hug and set him on her hip. "We got this covered, right, Ben?"

"Yep. You go on, Daddy."

Jeff rolled his eyes and laughed. His kid was growing up way too fast.

He walked outside glancing around for what he wasn't sure. *Liar. You're lookin' for Terri.* He didn't want to care about what she might be doing right now, but he did. After he told himself he needed to keep an eye out for her to make sure she wasn't doing something she shouldn't, he felt like kicking his own ass for being stupid.

Why he kept her real purpose for being in Bandera a secret from his family, he wasn't sure. Maybe he wanted to give her the benefit of the doubt. *Why? I know she works for the developers. She told me she did.* "She's up to no good. I know she is."

He headed to the barn with a sharp stomp to his step. His anger bubbled inside him making him all the more pissy as he grabbed the clipboard from the doorway on his way inside. *Damn meddling woman. She needs to go, but how do I get her to leave?*

"Maybe if I make her time here miserable, she'll leave on her own?"

"Jeff?" Joey called coming into the barn.

"In the back, Joe."

"I've got a horse I want to go look at over at the Marshall place."

"So? Why are you tellin' me?"

"So you can watch the horses."

"Where is Jacob or Jonathan?"

"Hell if I know. It's not my job to keep track of the rest of the bunch. I'm just tellin' you where I'm going so you can watch them. There's a group out now with Jackson on the trail. They just left and won't be back for an hour."

"Great. Just great. I have my own work to do and now I have to do yours?"

Joey grinned. "You can clean some tack while I'm gone."

"Fuck you, Joe. Cleanin' the tack is your damned job."

"Yeah and so is breakin' the horses so they don't throw the guests, but I don't see you helpin' with that either, big man."

"I ain't got time to do everyone's fuckin' job along with my own."

"You wanted the foreman job, buddy. You got it." Joey waved and headed off toward where the cars were parked. "I'll be back in a couple of hours."

"The Marshall property is five goddamn minutes from here."

"Yes it is, but I still need to check the stock. See ya!"

"Fuckin' son of a bitch." He threw the clipboard across the barn.

He headed for the tack room so he could keep an eye on the horses in the corral. Why, he wasn't sure. It wasn't like they were going anywhere, but a guest might have questions so he needed to be there. He could clean tack. *Fuck that!*

A soft voice came from the doorway. "Jeff?"

Great. Terri. "What do you want?" he asked with a snarl. He wasn't about to make it easy on her.

She twisted the end of her T-shirt between her fingers. He obviously made her a little nervous. "I'm sorry things have gotten off on the wrong foot between us."

"We aren't on any damned foot, lady. You're here under false pretenses and I don't like it."

"I'm not here to spy. I need to ask questions and the best people to ask are the locals. I figured cowboys knew the lay of the land the best."

"Why us?"

"Because your land is adjacent to the land the developers purchased for their housing development. Your land is very similar to the land over there."

"I'm not helpin' you."

"Fine. I'll ask one of your brothers. Two of the triplets have been nice enough to me. I'm sure I can get one of them to talk."

"Leave my brothers out of this. This is between you and me."

"There's nothing between you and me, Mr. Young. You're a self-centered bully who thinks he can intimidate me because I'm a woman. Well forget it. You won't drive me away from doing my job. It's all I'm trying to do and—"

Jeff stepped closer, wrapped his hand around the back of her head, and slammed his mouth against hers.

She pulled back. "What the hell?"

He did it again, but this time her lips softened under his, molding themselves to the curve of his mouth. His hand tangled in her ponytail, pulling her head back slightly so he could deepen the kiss. With the tip of his tongue tracing the seam of her lips, he asked for her to open for him. Her lips parted on a moan. He pulled her hair harder. Her moan deepened into a low growl in her throat. Their tongues danced, tangling together from her mouth to his and back. His hand left her hair to trace the curve of her neck.

Thinking beyond how her mouth felt under his left his brain in a fog.

Her hands fisted in his shirt, pulling him closer still.

The clink of a horses bridle brought him out of the mist with a startled step back. "I'm sorry. I…"

"You what?"

"I shouldn't have lost control. You're a guest."

"So?"

"We don't mess with guests."

"Well apparently some of you do if your brother married a woman who was a guest here at one time."

"That's different."

"Different how? You're the one who kissed me."

"Just go back to your cottage and leave me the hell alone, would you please?"

She fisted her hands on her hips. "No. I need your expertise to answer some questions."

"I'm not telling you anythin'."

"We can go round and round about this for days, Jeff. If you help me, I'll be gone sooner."

"Sooner?"

She nodded as she swept her hair back and fixed her ponytail where he'd almost pulled it out of its confinement. "Yes. I won't stay the entire two weeks if I get the information I need."

Maybe helping her would help him. Surely she didn't need personal information about the ranch, just general stuff. "What kind of information do you need?"

"How many cattle do you run?" she asked, pulling out a pen and small pad of paper from her pocket.

"I can't tell you that."

Air rush from between her lips in a heavy sigh as she tipped her head back on her shoulders. "What are the native trees to the area?"

"Texas Junipers and several other types of brush. I can't name them all, but you could get samples I guess."

"Rock types?"

He told her what he knew.

"Do you have to supplement your cattle with feed often?" she asked, biting her lip.

Damn, she was turning him inside out with her innocent gesture. "During dry summers, yes."

"How did the rainfall go this year in comparison to years previously?"

Their conversation went on this way for over an hour while he sat with her in the tack room. The guests who'd been out with one of his brothers on a run had come and gone, but still she asked more questions than he could give her answers for and some he wasn't willing to. If it meant she'd go away, then so be it. He could get on with his life if she wasn't nearby.

Damn. Why did I kiss her?

He shook his head as he remembered his dream from the night before. After she'd given him a blowjob, he'd fucked her senseless in his bed. Now she stood in front of him with her lips still red and swollen from his kiss. A kiss he shouldn't have given her on a good day, much less how they'd started off.

"Hello?"

"Sorry. My mind wandered. What did you ask?"

"How many guests do you all have in a good year?"

"I'm not tellin' you that either." He stood up from his spot on the edge of the metal desk. "Look. You should have all the information you need. You can go now."

"No, I need to ride out to the property line between your ranch and the development so I can see what types of rocks and plant life are there. Will you take me?" she asked, chewing her lips again.

"You can't be serious."

"Of course I am. George got the measurements he needed for the survey, but I need a more up close look at the landscape."

"No, I meant you can't be serious about me taking you out there." He folded his arms over his chest. "Darlin', I already helped you more than I should with what you are tryin' to do to this countryside."

"Darlin'?"

"Never mind. We're done here."

"Please, Jeff?" She placed her hand on his arm. He didn't like the warmth spreading up the appendage. Usually that kind of reaction meant trouble, especially when she stepped close enough he could smell her shampoo. Vanilla. Damn, he loved the smell of vanilla. "It won't take long."

"Fine. When Joey gets back from…"

A honk sounded outside as Joey pulled up the ranch truck in front of the tack barn.

"I take it that's Joey?"

"Sorry. I hadn't realized you didn't already know all of my brothers."

Joey stepped out of the truck and slammed the door. "Howdy, ma'am."

"Hi."

"Joey, this is Terri. Terri Kennedy, this is the youngest of the group, Joey."

"Nice to meet you, ma'am." He tipped his hat.

"You, too." She nodded to the trailer. "What do you have in there?"

"A new mare for the brood. Want to take a look?"

"Sure. I love horses."

"She's a filly so I need to train her, but she's a beauty. Black as the midnight sky with a pretty blaze on her nose." Joey popped open the trailer's back door and slid inside to unhook the horse's lead rope. "Such a pretty girl." The filly's ears flicked back and forth to the sound of his voice. There was a good reason Joey took care of the animals. He had a way with the ladies especially.

"Oh my! She's beautiful."

"She'll make some pretty colts, I bet," Joey said, stroking her as he backed her out of the trailer. "Easy now." The horse's withers shook as she stepped out onto the solid ground.

"You did good, Joe." His compliment earned him a scowl. Surely he hadn't been so hard on his brothers lately they all hated him.

"Thanks, Jeff." Joey glanced between him and Terri with a raised eyebrow. "I'm gonna take her into the barn. Since I'm back, you can go about doin' whatever you needed to do earlier, Jeff."

"Actually, I'm goin' to take Terri out to one of the pastures. She needs to check some things out over there."

"Really?" she asked, surprise written all over her face.

"Yeah."

"Well, the group is back, aren't they?"

"Yeah."

"You can take any of the horses then."

"I'll get her set up."

"See you two later." Joey led the new filly toward the barn.

"How much ridin' have you done?"

"Some, but not recently. I mean I can stay on one and make them go where I want them to. I don't consider myself an expert by any means."

"Most of our horses are very tame. We have a lot of beginner riders but I don't want to give you one who won't do anything either."

"Mediocre then?"

He chuckled, startling himself and Terri. It had been a long damn time since anyone made him smile, much less laugh.

"You have a nice laugh."

A sobering thought ripped across his mind. He didn't have anything to be happy about. His life sucked right now. Unfortunately, he didn't see it getting better anytime soon.

"I didn't mean to upset you."

"You didn't. I have a lot on my mind is all." He headed back into the tack room to grab his saddle while she followed on his heels. Why in the hell had he agreed to take her out to the property line anyway? The last thing he needed was to encourage her into thinking he might be okay with this damned crap with the developers when he wasn't. "Let's get this over with."

"I'm sure I could get one of your brothers to take me, if you would rather not."

"I'll do it. Besides, I want to keep an eye on you."

"I'm not trying to do anything illegal, Jeff. I need to see a few things."

"We've had this discussion, Terri. I don't want you on our property. The sooner you leave the better for everyone, especially me."

"Why especially you?"

"I don't like you."

She stepped forward and ran her fingernail down his chest. "Your problem is I think you like me a little too much."

With her fingers in his fist, he snapped, "No, I don't."

"Then why'd you kiss me?" she asked, glancing up through her lashes with those incredibly green eyes.

"Hell if I know, but it won't happen again." He started to push past her, but she stopped him dead in his tracks with her words.

"What if I want it to?"

A lump formed in his throat and he swallowed hard to push his words past it. "Well, it won't. I don't need a woman in my life. I don't need you."

"Not even for a little bit of quick fun?"

His cock hardened behind the fly of his pants at the sultry sound of her whispered words. His dream came back to haunt him in the flesh as she stood there promising him sweet release if he'd only give into the desires blazing between them. "What'd you have in mind?"

"You seem like you could use a good romp in the hay. I'm just thinking we could help each other out a little. It's been a bit for me and from the conversations around the ranch, it sounds like it has for you too."

"Let's get this ride over with."

"And then we'll talk more?"

"Maybe."

She smiled with a sexy little tip of her lips that drove desire straight to his balls. *I'm so fuckin' screwed.*

Chapter Four

They rode along with the sun beating down on their shoulders. Sweat trickled down her back between her shoulder blades. She wiped at the moisture on her forehead wishing she would have thought to bring water.

Jeff reached into his saddle bag and brought out a water bottle. He handed it over as she sighed in relief.

"Thank you."

"You're welcome, city girl."

"I'm not a city girl."

"Could have fooled me. Who rides out here without bringin' water?"

"I didn't think…"

"Yeah, I know. Good thing I did, huh?"

"Ass-wipe," she grumbled under her breath.

"What did you say?" he asked with a grin.

"Nothing." She really did like his smile even though right at the moment she'd like to wipe it off his lips with her fist or a kiss. She wasn't sure which one and it bothered her.

How far it would be until they reached the property line, she wasn't sure.

Several types of plant life made it into jotted notes of her book while the rode along. Rocks and animal life got noted too. The more information she had, the better her report to the developers would be. This job meant a lot of money to her fledgling company so she had to do her best.

"What are they plannin' on doin'?"

"Dividing up the property into five acres parcels, building a few houses on them to get started and then selling off the plots so people can build their own."

"Wonderful. Just fuckin' wonderful," he snapped.

She reached over to lay her hand on his arm. For some reason his misery at the prospects bothered her. "I'm sorry, Jeff. I know you don't want to be a part of this, but its progress. You have to look at it in the sense where it's going to be good for the community to have the additional population here. It will help the local stores, restaurants, bars, and your family's ranch."

"How in the hell will it help us?"

"Think of it this way. People will come to visit family and friends who live in the new development. If they don't have a place to stay, they'll stay at Thunder Ridge. You have a great set up! You can teach them about cowboying and how to live life with the cattle as part of your life verses the citified people coming out here to mess up the land."

"Maybe."

"It's true."

"I have to have somethin' to leave my son when he's grown." He shook his head, glancing at her even though she couldn't see those arresting gray eyes beneath his sunglasses. "We won't sell off any of our property to them. They have to know that."

"You'll have the land to give Ben. The developers aren't looking for more at the moment." The horse shifted under her as she grabbed the pommel in a death grip. It really had been a long time since she'd been on a horse, but it came back like riding a bike.

"Right now, they ain't, but what if they do in five years or even ten?"

"If you aren't selling, what difference does it make which way they expand?"

"More and more people tearing up the roads, using up the land, dammin' up the water for their own use. All of those things take away from what we've built here."

"You can't keep living in the past, Jeff."

"I don't want things to change."

"Change is good."

"Not always."

She continued to mull over what he said. True, change wasn't always for the best, but in this case it had to be. Her life and her job depended on it being the right thing to do.

They came around a large boulder to see a barbed wire fence stretching far into the distance in both directions.

"This is the property line." He leaned over the pommel of his saddle, resting his forearms across the padded leather in a relaxed, totally cowboy state. "Do what you need to do."

She swung her leg over the back of the horse and dropped her booted feet into the loose gravel. She grabbed the binoculars from around her neck and scanned the area. Several birds flew out of a nearby bush into the afternoon sky. With a note in her book, she described the birds in as much details as she could. Their species might be important in the long run.

"I'll hold her while you look around," Jeff said, swinging down from his own horse. "There's a small spring over here to the right. I'll water them."

"Okay." She sighed as she took her pen and paper in her hand to make some notes. After several minutes, she glanced off to the right where she heard the spring tinkling down over the rocks. Instead of making the notes she needed to make and the drawings of the area, she found herself wandering to where Jeff said he was going. *Surely they had the same rocks and bushes over there, right?*

"Jeff?"

"Over here." She followed his voice until she saw him crouched down near a pool.

"How pretty."

"It's one of the natural springs we have running through our property. This one has a great little swimmin' area right here." He pointed to the two boulders on the other side with a sweep of his hand. "It's not terribly deep but you can swim in it. I bet it would feel good right now."

"Can we put our feet in?"

"Sure."

She giggled as she quickly stripped off her boots and socks before she rolled up her pant legs. The water felt cold on her feet when she dipped them in, but after the heat of the day during their ride, it felt like heaven. "Lordy, that's great!"

Jeff took the rock next to her and dipped his feet in too. "We used to come up here swimmin' when we were kids much to my mother's disappointment. Came home wet all the time."

"I can totally see you and your brothers getting into trouble with your mom. She's a strong lady."

"Yes, she is. She's the glue holdin' this whole ranch together. God forbid somethin' happen to her, none of us would know what to do."

They sat in silence for several minutes while she contemplated the man near her. He really didn't seem so grouchy while he sat with her dipping their feet in the cool water. She wondered more about him. How had he grown up? He seemed like such a strong man, but around Ben he buckled under to be the dad the boy needed in his life. He ran the ranch with an iron fist, but seeing how he handled his younger brothers, she thought he needed to let up on them some.

"What are you thinkin' about?"

"You."

"Me? Why me?"

"I'm wondering about you is all. You've had it pretty rough from what I've heard."

"Not really. I've had a great life livin' out here on the place I grew up. I love runnin' the ranch, doin' the chores, workin' with the animals. You know, ranch stuff."

"I can see that."

"What do you do when you aren't out in a place like this? You seem like a city girl to me."

"I live in Houston. I have my own architecture firm."

"Definitely a city girl." He laughed when she frowned.

"I'm not either."

"What do you call those clothes you were wearin' yesterday with your fancy boots and designer jeans?"

"All right. I don't have worn boots like yours or ripped jeans, but I'm not a city girl like New York or Los Angeles. Houston isn't the city."

"Sure it is."

"No, it's not." She cupped her hand in the water before she tossed the small trickle onto him.

"Hey!" He threw some back at her.

Within minutes, she stood halfway in the middle of the pond to her waist, soaking wet while they laughed like children as they splashed each other. Jeff stood at the edge with the water to his calves, but his jeans and T-shirt were soaked too. She bit her lip while she stared at the material clinging to his chest. The muscles rippled beneath the material when he moved. *Damn, he's got a magnificent chest and abs.*

He quickly flung off his hat and rushed into the water as she squealed and tried to get away. "No! Wait," she shouted right before he pushed her under. She came up sputtering with her hair partially in her face. "You've done it now, cowboy."

"Come after me, babe! You don't have what it takes."

"Oh no?" She rushed him, jumping full into his chest and taking them both down into the water. They broke the surface together laughing while she clung to his shoulders. A moment later, she realized how close their mouths were as she looked up into his gray eyes that turned to molten silver with lust.

His cock hard between their straining bodies kicked up her desire to raging. She could feel every inch of him against her stomach. Water clung to his lashes, making them looked like diamonds in the sunlight. The man was beautiful.

Silence stretched between them. She wasn't sure what to do. She wanted to feel his mouth against her again, feel the heat raging between them. "Kiss me."

"I shouldn't."

"But you want to."

"Yeah, I do."

"Then do it." She sucked in a ragged breath, blowing it out on a sigh. "Afraid?"

He dragged her closer still. "I'm not afraid of you."

The hard plains of his chest brushed against her peaked nipples. Her whole body ached from wanting to be closer, needing to be closer. "You're afraid of what you want to do to me. You think because we're supposed to be enemies, you shouldn't want to fuck me."

"I don't want to fuck you."

She tossed back her hair and laughed. "Have you got a salami in your pocket then?"

"Fine," he growled. "I want to fuck you until the sun drops in the western sky. I want to bury myself in your sweet heat and let you scald me until this need for you burns out like a blue flame."

"Then do it cowboy. Right here, right now."

He picked her up by the waist and she wrapped her legs around his middle. She wanted this, needed this more than her next breath. Ever since she'd first run into this tortured, lonely man, she'd wanted to hold him, comfort him and fuck him into tomorrow.

The fine gravel lining the edges of the pond bit into her back when he laid her down. His fingers made quick work of the front of her shirt, parting it to reveal her water soaked bra to his gaze. "Beautiful."

He took her nipple into his mouth, sucking it through the sheer fabric of her bra. Her whole body hummed as he bit the flesh. "Ah, God." Within seconds, he had her bra open and her breasts revealed to his scorching gaze.

The warmth of the sun quickly dried the water on her skin as he peeled open her jeans. The wet fabric clung to her, making it difficult for him to work his hand into the parted material. A brush of his fingers over her throbbing nub shot her straight into mega arousal. "Please, Jeff."

"You're so slick."

"I want you inside me." He worked his fingers into her grasping pussy while his thumb worked her clit.

"I want you to come for me."

"Now? But…"

"You can do it. I feel your body vibrating around my fingers."

He stroked her clit quickly. Her body shot straight through the buildup to orgasm in seconds flat. Her scream of his name bounced off the rocks around them, drifting off on the wind as she slowly came back down, blinking in surprise at the intensity of her orgasm.

"You're beautiful when you come."

"Thanks." She frowned. "I think."

"Jeff?" someone shouted from their left.

"Oh hell!" Terri quickly scrambled out from under him, trying desperately to right her clothing.

"Stay where you are, Jackson."

"I ain't movin'. I'll stay right here and enjoy the scenery."

The sound came from the rocks not very far away. "He can't see me, can he?" she asked, putting the finishing touches on her clothing. *Shit. His brother probably heard me scream out my orgasm. How embarrassing.*

"I'm not sure where he's sittin', but I doubt he missed your scream."

"Thanks, Jeff."

"You're welcome, darlin'."

He grinned like a Cheshire cat, the jerk. At least his brother didn't catch them in the middle of having sex. *He probably would have if he'd waited a few more minutes to make his presence known.*

"What are you doin' out here, Jackson?"

"Lookin' for you. Joey said you were comin' out here to the property line. I came to tell you the feed store brought the load."

"You couldn't have waited until I got back?"

"You're always bitchin' when we don't tell you the load is here."

Jeff didn't respond to that.

"Took a swim, did ya?"

"Give the lady some privacy, will ya?"

"I ain't lookin'. I heard the splashin' from a mile away."

Which means he heard me scream. Just fucking great. "Jackson, you can come down now."

"Thank you, ma'am." He appeared moments later around the crop of rocks not a hundred yards away. "I don't think we've met," he said, holding out his hand. "Jackson, ma'am. I'm the second eldest behind Jeff."

She blushed to the roots of her hair as his laughing gaze trailed down her body. "Terri Kennedy. It's nice to meet you."

"Enjoy your swim?"

"Yes, actually. It was very refreshing."

"Sounded like it."

The small smirk on Jackson's face made her want to slap it right off his lips. "I believe we're done here, right Jeff?"

"Yeah. We were about to head back anyway. You can go on home, Jackson."

Jackson swung up onto the back of his horse and tipped his hat as he kicked the gelding into a canter, riding off into the brush.

"I'm so embarrassed."

"Don't be."

"Why the hell not? He probably heard me scream your name as I came all over your fingers!"

"True, but it ain't like he hasn't heard it before," Jeff replied, earning himself her ire.

"You bring a lot of women out here and fuck their brains out?"

"I didn't fuck your brains out, Terri. If you remember correctly, I didn't get to come…yet."

"So sorry. Should I take care of it for you before we head back?" Her sarcasm seemed lost on him.

"Not necessary right at the moment, darlin', but I wouldn't mind visitin' you later in your cabin."

"I thought there was some kind of rule about you guys and the guests?"

"Who told you?"

She shrugged as she examined her fingernails on her left hand. "You told me in the tack room, remember? You do have a little gaggle of geese who love to follow you around with their gaze just like the rest of your brothers."

He scuffed his boot in the dirt. "We do have the rule."

"Well I guess you already broke it since you fingered me to orgasm a few minutes ago." She picked at her wet clothes hoping they didn't chafe her thighs on the ride back to the ranch. "I guess you could come by my cabin after supper." The thought sent a thrill through her belly. The thought of actually making love with this man brought another rush of heat to her cheeks. Yeah, she'd gotten off with a pretty terrific orgasm, but he hadn't. Riding back to the ranch with a hard-on probably wouldn't be the most comfortable thing to do. Oh well, it couldn't be helped. He really did need to get back if Jackson's conversation meant anything.

"Listen, Terri. Maybe this isn't such good idea."

"What?"

"Us."

"I didn't think there really was an us, but why not?"

"Well there is sort of. I just think with our differences of opinion on the land development, your involvement in it, and how I feel about it, we shouldn't be doin' anythin' together."

"We're fucking, Jeff. Nothing more. It's a little release from the pressures of everyday life. Don't read more into it than there is."

"I'm not. I don't need a woman in my life. In fact, it's the last damned thing I need."

"Maybe if you did have a woman, you wouldn't be to fucking up tight!"

"Uptight? I'm not uptight!"

"Bullshit! You're wound so damned tight, I'm surprised your dick even works!" She climbed back into the saddle as she watched the magnificent butt of the man next to her, do the same thing.

"I'll show you how well my dick works, baby. Just spread them thighs, this dick will make your pussy weep."

"Only because I haven't had any dick in two years." She turned her horse back toward the house. "Any dick would do."

"You want dick, honey, you come lookin' for me. You'll stay away from my brothers."

"I'll fuck whomever I want."

"No, you will not!"

His face looked thunderous so she backed off. She didn't know the exact details of his past relationships, but obviously there was something there she didn't want to go into. It wasn't like she wanted any of his brothers anyway. She wanted him. Pain in the ass and all.

Chapter Five

The supper bell clanged as Jeff stood in the doorway of the barn watching the guests wander toward the main lodge. Should he join the family for supper or not? He really wasn't sure. If he did, would it give Terri the impression he would join her afterward? Maybe. Should he? He didn't know. He wanted to. God, did he want to.

Everything about her turned him inside out. He wanted to see her blonde curls spread out over the pillow as he pounded into her hot flesh or tickling his abdomen while she sucked his cock until he squirted cum down her throat.

He'd never wanted a woman so badly before. The thought drove him nuts.

"Are you going in?" Joey asked, coming from the stable to the left of the barn.

"Yeah, I'll be there in a second. I need to check on something."

Joey shrugged and walked toward the house. "Hey, Ms. Terri." He waved as he caught Terri walking up the concrete path toward the house.

Jeff watched from the barn doors while Joey caught up with her and walked her into supper. Jealousy surged through him, catching him unaware. Jealousy? Why should he be jealous? He didn't care a whit about her. Well, maybe a little, but he couldn't get caught up in her at all.

Hurting her didn't fit with his plans either. He didn't want to hurt her. He hoped she wasn't thinking anything between them could go on and turn into anything permanent. He didn't do permanent. Not anymore.

Ben came running from the swing set they'd put up for him in the side garden. "Come on, Daddy. It's supper time."

"I'm comin', son."

Jeff followed Ben's little body to the house. Smiling, he ran up behind him, grabbed him and swung him up on his shoulders, much to the gleeful squeals of his son.

When they walked inside the building, he caught Terri's gaze from her spot to his right. She sat with a group of women chattering away, but she remained silent as she watched him set Ben down. *Damn, she's pretty.* She didn't wear a lot of makeup. Her clean complexion glowed with healthy vibrance as her gorgeous green eyes sparkled with something he wasn't sure he wanted to name. He tipped his hat, catching her little half smile when he walked by her table.

The ladies twittered around her, but he kept walking. He didn't want anyone to get the idea there was anything going on between them. *Jackson better keep his big mouth shut.*

As he approached the family table and his assigned chair, the family got quiet. "What?"

"How did the ride go?" his mother asked, tilting her head to the side as she grinned.

"What ride?"

"Jackson went out to find you and Terri, right?"

He glared at his brother who just laughed. "Yeah, he did. The ride went fine. I showed her where the property lines are so she could get some samples and take some notes. The quicker she's gone, the better for all of us."

"Better for you?"

"Yes. I don't want her here."

"It didn't sound that way to me," Jackson said with a laugh.

"Shut up."

"She's really not causing any harm, Jeff. I'd rather she be here so we can keep an eye on what she's doing, which by the way, you haven't explained to the rest of us."

"I'll handle her, Ma."

"I think you already did," Jackson added.

"I told you to shut the fuck up."

"Jeffery!"

"Sorry, but he's crossin' the line."

"You'll not talk like that at the dinner table with the guests here. I've discussed this with you before."

"I said I'm sorry."

"Fine." She glanced at Jackson. "Apparently you have a secret between you and your brother. I would appreciate it if you would keep it to yourself. There is no need to discuss it in front of family or guests."

"Sorry, Ma."

"You should be. Whatever is part of Jeffery's private life is private. Keep it that way."

"Yes, ma'am," Jackson replied although Jeff could see the twinkle of mischief in his eyes. It wasn't over by a long shot.

Once supper was over, he needed to get someone to watch Ben for a few hours and needed to figure out a way to be able to get into Terri's cabin without being seen. Not like he planned to stay the night or anything, but he couldn't leave his son alone in their home without someone to keep an eye on him. He debated on whether to ask Jackson since he already knew about Jeff and Terri's rendezvous by the pond, but he also debated on whether to ask his mother. What would she think? *She'd be jumping my shit for fuckin' a guest.* "Of course, she was all over gettin' Joel and Mesa together."

The guests cleared the dining room leaving the family to finish up their own supper.

"Mom, can you watch Ben for a couple of hours?"

"Of course, Jeff. Do you have plans?"

"Yeah. I need to go into town for a bit."

"I know it's been a long time since you've been around a female, son." She patted his hand. "I'll watch Ben."

Jeff glanced at the ceiling as he sighed. *Great. Mom thinks I'm headed out to find a woman.* "Thanks, Mom."

She winked.

I obviously didn't fool her one bit.

Jeff cleared his and Ben's plates before he hustled his son back outside with the intention of getting him home and in bed before his mother came over to watch him. He hoped his mom didn't know who he planned to fuck tonight, but at this moment, he didn't care.

Remember when you gave Joel shit for fuckin' Mesa?

He really should apologize to his brother when the two of them got back from their honeymoon. He did come down pretty hard on Joel for sleeping with a guest when here he was about to do the same thing and enjoy every damned minute of it if this afternoon had been any indicator. Terri was hotter than a firecracker on the Fourth of July. She's been spectacular when she'd come apart in his arms by the pond. He'd never seen a woman look so beautiful when she came. He hoped to fuck her face to face so he could see it again.

Hell, who was he kidding? He wanted her any way he could get her. In her hot pussy, up her delicious looking ass, in her mouth. He didn't care.

"Daddy?"

"Yes, Ben," he replied as they walked through the front door of their cabin.

"How come Mommy doesn't come over anymore?"

He took Ben's hand and headed into the bathroom to get his bath ready. "I don't know, son. I guess she's busy."

"I want to stay at her house."

Jeff got worried. Ben never said he wanted to stay at Misha's. Whenever he did go over there, by the time she brought him back, he was difficult to deal with for a few days afterward. Sometimes, it was like there wasn't any discipline at her house, which he figured was the case. "Why?"

Ben took off his clothes and climbed into the warm water Jeff had run into the tub. "She lets me eat chocolate ice cream and watch Dora."

"You do those things here too."

"How come Mommy doesn't love me?" Ben asked, playing with his truck absently in the bubbles.

"I'm sure she does in her own way, Ben."

"She never says it like you do. You always say you love me."

"Because I do, Ben. I love you very much."

"I love you too, Daddy."

The conversation drifted off into other topics, like his horse, when Grandma was coming over and did he really have to go to bed. The normal things they talked about almost every night.

"Will you read me a story, Daddy?"

"Of course, son. We're still reading the Tommy the Train book, right?"

"Yes," Ben answered, climbing into the bed.

Jeff tucked the covers around his shoulders. The book they'd be reading sat on the nightstand next to the bed. Jeff read five pages before he glanced at his son to find him sound asleep. He put the book back on the stand, turned off the light and closed the door as he walked out.

He found his mother on the couch with her knitting.

"I didn't hear you come in."

"I know. You were tucking Ben in. I heard you reading."

"Thanks for coming over, Mom."

"You're welcome, honey. I know you need some time out. You need adult company. It's normal for a man your age."

"It's not a big deal."

"Sure it is. I understand men's needs. Just remember, we women have them too. Take your time tonight. No hurry to be home. I'll stay until the morning if you want."

"Not necessary. I'll only be gone a couple of hours."

"Whatever you want, Jeff."

He grabbed his keys off the hook next to the door where he always kept them, put on his cowboy hat and opened the door.

"Tell Terri hello for me."

"Mom?"

"Yes, dear."

He shook his head. He knew better than to question how his mother knew things. "Never mind. Thanks."

"You're welcome." She blew him a kiss as he shut the door behind him.

Darkness surrounded him. Stars winked overhead. No moon tonight to light the way but he knew the land like the back of his hand. He hopped in his truck and drove the two minutes it took to get from his cabin back to the main lodge area. He wasn't sure which cabin Terri was even in so he hoped she waited for him on the porch.

He pulled down the driveway and stopped near the parking area for the guests. Terri sat in a rocking chair on the porch of her cabin, directly in front of where he parked. He took a deep breath, checked his wallet for condoms and then stepped out.

"Hey."

"Hi. I wasn't sure if you were going to show up or not."

"Why wouldn't I? The promise of great sex is a promise I don't want to pass up."

"Yeah, but I wasn't sure you'd have someone to watch Ben tonight or a hundred other reasons why you might have changed your mind." She tucked a piece of hair behind her ear as she rocked in the chair.

Her hair lay on her shoulders caressing them like a lover's hand. He wanted to run his fingers through the silky strands. Her green eyes sparkled behind her glasses when she raked her gaze down his frame. It set him on fire to see the lust in her eyes.

He held out his hand, waiting for her to take it into her grasp so he could pull her into his arms. The porch light on her cabin outlined them for anyone to see, but tonight, he didn't care. Let them talk.

"You look so pretty sitting there."

She took his hand and stood.

"Thank you. You look pretty handsome yourself you know."

"Shall we go inside?"

"Sure."

He opened her cabin door, tugging her along behind him. Being with Terri made him feel like a sixteen-year-old kid with his first fuck, and he wasn't sure why. Yes, she was a beautiful woman, but he almost felt like he might get caught by her parents or his. Hell, at thirty-four years old, he should be over this feeling by now. *It must be the anticipation.*

"I'm nervous."

"Why?" he asked.

"I'm not sure. It's not like we haven't been together before, but I guess not like this."

He raised her hand as he entwined their fingers. "We don't have to do this if you don't want to."

"But I do," she whispered.

He slid his right hand along her jawline and then into her hair. "You have beautiful hair. It's so soft."

"Thanks."

Her lips called to him to taste. He slowly drew her closer, watching as her lips parted in anticipation. The need to feel her mouth under his drove everything out of his mind.

"Can you see at all without these?"

"Close up, yes."

He took off her glasses and set them on the nightstand. "You have beautiful eyes."

"You talk too much, Jeff. Kiss me."

He slipped both hands along her jaw and into her hair, pulling her closer as his mouth brushed hers. The softness enveloped him. He needed to bring her closer still. The feel of her lips under his drove his desire higher and made his cock swell behind the fly of his jeans. The need to be inside her overwhelmed him. He'd never gotten this hard this fast with any other woman. Not even Misha and he thought he loved her.

Lust, old man. Just lust.

She took two fistfuls of his shirt and popped the snaps in one swift tug. The moment, she tore her mouth from his, she said, "Damn, you have a nice chest. And look at those abs? A real six-pack."

Her lips did a little dance along his neck until she reached his ear. Her teeth nipped at his earlobe.

Damn, the woman took over like a Domme. He wondered if she might be into a little rough sex. Not like he would give up control, but he kind of liked her taking over their love making a little bit.

"Let me please you."

Her mouth trailed down his chest, biting at his nipples with her teeth, drawing on them with the tip of her tongue. His flesh erupted in a huge mass of goose bumps. She followed the line of hair down his chest, across his abdomen to the waistband of his jeans. Her tiny hands worked the belt buckle loose and drew the zipper down before she tugged his jeans and briefs down around his thighs. The moment she took him into her mouth, he almost exploded.

The feeling of her sucking on his cock, her mouth doing sensational things to him had him shaking so hard he could barely stand. "Terri, wait." He tried to pull her up but she refused to let go of his cock. She sucked harder, drawing his climax to the breaking point. He lost control and came deep in her throat in an explosion of cum he could barely handle. "Oh God!" She licked and sucked until he felt drained. "You didn't have to do that."

She glanced up through her lashes. "I know, but I wanted to. You took my anxiety level down a notch earlier by the pond. I figured it would help keep the second time from being a five minute race to see who came first."

"Smart woman."

She smiled before she enveloped him in her warm mouth again.

"Easy lady. You're gonna be the death of me."

A giggle escaped her mouth as he drew her up to her feet and kissed her. The taste of his cum on her lips felt almost weird, but gave him a sense of completeness with her. She took care of him in a way no woman had done before. "Your turn, darlin'."

He drew her tank top over her head, leaving her completely bare from the waist up. "You are so beautiful, you take my breath away."

"You're just saying that."

"No. It's true."

"I'm sure you've been with woman far prettier than I am."

"Maybe so, but they didn't have the inner beauty you have. The love of life. The light shining from your soul. You're a truly beautiful woman."

"Thank you, but you don't have to say that to get laid. You're already gonna get laid."

He grinned and raised an eyebrow. "Good, because I can't wait to be inside you."

With a slight push, she sprawled out on the bed in a heap of glorious hair and lusty green eyes. He unsnapped her jeans and drew them off her hips. Her painted toes peeked out of the hem of her jeans in all their pink glory. *Such a girlie girl. She'd never fit on the ranch in any capacity with her city girl ways, pink toenails and designer jeans.*

He got her jeans and underpants off in one fell swoop, and then divested himself of the rest of his clothing so he could concentrate on pleasuring her. She never moved from her spot on the bed.

Her glistening pussy called to him to taste, to explore. He swiped one finger over her pussy, across her clit and skimmed her puffy little lips hiding the rest of her from his gaze.

"Touch me more."

"I'm going to. I'm gonna make you cream for me."

"Like earlier?"

"Even more so."

He crouched on the floor between her legs and pulled her so her pussy was right on the edge of the bed. One swipe of his tongue on her clit had her moaning her need. Good. He wanted her to come apart under his mouth. He needed her to lose control with him. It had been too long since he'd had a woman in his arms.

She groaned softly, her head swinging back and forth on the comforter. Both her fists grasped the bedding beneath her as he worked his mouth on her pussy. He licked, sucked, fingered and sucked more on the tasty flesh beneath his mouth. With two fingers deep inside her, he could feel her coming unraveled. Her cries of ecstasy sounded raw and emotional to his ears, like it had been a very long time since she'd had a climax so strong. He couldn't wait to be inside her when she came apart again. He grabbed his pants, fished out a condom and rolled it on his aching flesh.

The high bed frame put her in perfect line with his cock when he stood and eased his cock inside her hot pussy. "You're incredible."

"Fuck me, Jeff. Hard. Give it to me hard. Please. God, I need you."

The sensation in his balls made him ache to slam into her with enough force to scoot her across the bed. "I might hurt you."

"You can't hurt me. I need it. Harder, please."

He slammed his groin against hers in a desperate attempt to get closer. He needed to be closer. Pelvis to groin, cock to pussy, eating her up with everything inside him. They rocked the bedframe as he fucked her with every fiber of his being until he got so close to coming he thought he would combust into a ball of flames. "Come with me, Terri."

"Rub my clit. I need the friction to come again."

He shook his head not only to clear his thoughts, but to take control. "You do it. Make yourself come."

Her hand snuck down between their bodies as she rubbed her clit with her finger until he felt her vibrate around his cock.

"Oh God."

He picked up the pace of his thrusts. She wanted rough, he'd give it to her rough. "Fuck yes. Perfect."

Seconds later, she squeezed his dick so hard he thought he'd lose it for sure. His balls drew up against his groin. Sweat popped out on his forehead. Surely his head would explode from the sheer force of his climax.

"Fuck!" Cum shot from the end of his cock into the latex condom. His whole body shook. He grasped her hips with his hands, knowing he'd leave bruises to mark her come morning, but he couldn't quite work up the ability to care beyond the satisfaction he'd marked her. *Mine.*

He shook his head as he slowly withdrew from her sweet warmth to dispose of the condom in the waste can next to the bed. *Where the hell did that thought come from? I sure in hell don't need a woman.*

Possessiveness whipped through him. She was his. At least until she left. He tapped her clit causing her to moan. "This is mine until you leave. Are we clear?"

"Yours?" The look of incredibleness flashing in her eyes made him feel even more possessive.

He wanted her, needed her with a fierceness he didn't know he possessed. "Yes, mine."

"Does that mean you're mine too, until I leave?" She stroked her hand down his chest. "It's only fair, yes?"

"All right. I'm yours until you leave, but don't think there will be anythin' beyond the time you're here. I don't want a woman in my life on any kind of permanent basis."

"I know, Jeff. You've made it abundantly clear." She scooted up to lean against the headboard on the bed. "Join me?"

"For a little bit. I can't stay. Mom is watching Ben and I told her I wouldn't be gone more than a couple of hours."

"Fuck and run, huh?"

"It's not like that, Terri. I don't want you to think I don't want to be here with you because I do, but my son comes before anyone."

"I know, Jeff. I appreciate the way you handle your son. It's endearing." She looked down at her body before she pulled the sheet up to cover herself. "I saw the blowup you had with your ex the other day. Kind of rough dealing with her, huh?"

"You have no idea." The bed dipped from his weight when he sat next to her. "I should have listened to my brothers when they tried to tell me she wasn't good for me."

"Hindsight is twenty-twenty."

"I know, but it doesn't make it any easier. Since we have Ben together, I have to deal with her for the rest of my life."

She stroked her hand down his arm. "I'm sorry."

"Somehow I get the feeling you wouldn't treat anyone badly. You seem like such a nice person."

Her nose wrinkled as she scrunched up her face. "I don't want to be nice. I want to be sexy, bold, and more woman than you can handle."

He laughed. The sound seemed raw and unused even to him. He didn't know how long it had been since he'd really laughed out loud. He always seemed to be in a bad mood except around Ben. Taking out his frustrations on his son wasn't an option so he kept his temper in check, but it took its toll. *Maybe I do need more adult company in my life other than my brothers and my parents.*

She sat forward, running her hand down his chest. "Stay a little while?"

"For another hour or so."

"I'm good with whatever time you can give me. Really."

He slipped beneath the sheet, curled his arm around her shoulder and tugged her in so her breasts pressed against his side. *Damn, she's got fabulous tits.*

Her arm snaked across his stomach to pull him closer to her side. "There. Better."

"Thanks for this, Terri."

"Thanks?"

"Yeah. I didn't realize how much I'd been missin' bein' with a woman until tonight. You've made me feel alive again, even if it's only for a little while."

"You need contact like this occasionally, Jeff." Her hand drifted down his abdomen. "You can't totally cut yourself off from being with a woman. It's a fundamental need for a man."

He kissed the top of her head. "Where'd you get so smart?"

"I'm a college graduate." A giggle escaped her lips as she brushed them across his chest. She tongued his right nipple, humming her appreciation when it hardened beneath her mouth. "I hope you brought more than one condom."

"I didn't want to be presumptuous."

"Presume all you want, cowboy. I need some lovin'."

With a quick flip, he had her on her back with her hands above her head. "Leave them there or I'll tie them."

Her eyes dilated. Her lips tilted up in a little smirk. "Yes, Sir."

"Good girl. I don't want to have to discipline you."

"But what if I want you to? I can be very bad."

Wow, he sure hadn't expected her to get into D/s play, but she jumped right into the role like she was made for it. "Spankin's can be arrange."

"Please."

"When I say so."

"Damn."

Her breasts tempted him to suck and nip. He wanted to drown in her smell, live in her eyes, and be a small part of her until their short time ended.

Chapter Six

The sun rose outside her cabin, pulling her from one of the best night's sleep she'd had in ages. She rolled over and propped herself up on her elbow to look at the sleeping man beside her. *So much for only a couple of hours.* The tattoo on his back left shoulder blade tempted her to touch while he lay sprawled on his stomach across her mattress. The dragon with the wide wingspan looked majestic and proud like the man it marked.

He wouldn't be happy about staying the entire night, but she didn't have the heart to wake him when he'd dozed off in the wee hours of the morning after they'd made love for the third time.

The warmth of the skin beneath the tattoo made her fingertips tingle and her pussy damp. How could she want him again? He must've turned her into some kind of slut or something if she wanted him again so soon.

"What?" Jeff shot up in the bed and looked around with a dazed expression. "What time is it?"

She glanced at the clock on the nightstand. "Six-thirty."

"Shit. I stayed all night? Why didn't you wake me?" He jumped out of the bed to grab his pants. "I need to get home. I need to get out of here before my brothers see me leavin' your place."

"Are you ashamed to have made love with me?" she asked, sitting up on the bed with the sheet clutched to her chest.

"No, darlin'. Not at all. I can't keep them from fuckin' around with the guests if I'm doin' it, now can I?"

"This isn't over is it?"

"Not by a long shot, but we need to keep it on the down-low. My mother will know since she stayed with Ben all night. I need to keep the others from findin' out."

"How do you plan to do that when I'm sure someone is probably up already?"

"I don't know." He raked his fingers through his hair. "Just pretend nothin' happened for now."

"I'm not going to hide the fact of our sleeping together, Jeff. There's nothing wrong with it."

"I didn't say there was."

She stood, bringing the sheet with her to hide her nakedness. "You're confusing me. You either don't care if your family knows or you do, which is it?"

"I don't want them to know because then all of my brothers will think it's open season on the single, beautiful women on the ranch."

"Then you don't want them to know. Fine. Don't let the door hit you on the ass on the way out."

"But Terri…"

"Don't but Terri me, mister. Get out!"

He threw his T-shirt over his head before he tugged on his boots.

Pain in the ass man!

When he pulled open the door, he glanced over his shoulder at her. "And don't bother comin' back, cowboy."

"You're mine."

"Bullshit, mister. You can't have it both ways. Either you want me or you don't. Either you do care if your family knows about us or you don't."

He returned to her side, wrapped his hand in her hair and slammed his mouth against hers. The kiss took her breath away, leaving her shaking and warm when he stepped back.

"This isn't over by a long shot, woman. I'll be back."

He shut the door quietly behind him, leaving her standing in the middle of the room with the sheet clutched to her chest and her head spinning from his kiss. She wiped at her mouth trying to erase the kiss, knowing full well she'd feel it for a long time to come.

"The gall of that man!"

Her cell phone rang on the nightstand bringing her out of her wandering thoughts of the disturbing cowboy who'd just left. "Hello?"

"Hi Terri. It's Bob Cole."

"Hi, Mr. Cole. How are you?"

"I'm fine. I'm just checking in with you to see how the information gathering is going."

"Great. I should have all the information you all need by the end of next week."

"Hmm. The end of next week?"

"Yes, sir."

"We need it sooner, Terri. We want to break ground on the new development by the beginning of next month. I need the information by the end of this week."

"But it's already Wednesday. I can't have it done before Friday."

"The contract depends on it being done before the end of this week."

She exhaled on a rush. "I'll do my best, sir, but I'm not promising everything by Friday."

"You'll have to or we'll have someone else finish the job. We like you, Terri, but we hired you to do a job and we expect it done satisfactorily on our time frame or no deal."

"But sir…"

"It's imperative we have the information. We hear some of the townspeople aren't happy about us coming in there so we need to get ground broke before they can organize a formal petition to stop us."

"I hadn't heard anything of the sort and I'm staying on one of the ranches out here to gather the details you need."

"Which ranch?"

"Thunder Ridge."

"Really. Interesting. One of their family members is rallying the townspeople to fight us on this. A," she heard paper shuffle before he came back, "Jeffery Young."

"Jeff?"

"You know him personally?"

Yeah, you could say a little personally. "Sort of. I've met him."

"What a great thing! Get close to him, Terri. We'll give you the extra time you need if you can find out a weakness with this guy. Something has to rub him the wrong way so we can stop his petition with the courts. The last thing we want is for him to manage to convince someone we are doing something wrong."

"You aren't, right? Everything is on the up and up?"

"Of course, it is Terri. We aren't doing anything illegal. Everything is above board."

She sighed. How in the hell would she be able to see Jeff and spy on him or give them something they could use against him? "Fine. I'll do what I can, but I can't promise anything."

"I'm sure you'll be able to find out something. He's got to have a weakness."

Yeah, his family.

"Remember, Terri. This could mean a lot of money for your business. The reputation of being involved in this project alone will help you become one of the big leaguers in Houston."

"I'll remember, Mr. Cole." The clock read seven. It would be breakfast soon. "I have to go. It's breakfast time."

"I'll call you again in a couple of days. You'll have the full two weeks you need so long as you help us with this little problem."

"I understand."

"Good. Talk to you soon."

"Bye." She flipped the phone shut with a decisive click. This wasn't going to be easy. Jeff already didn't trust a lot of people. If he found out she tricked him into divulging information to help his enemies, he would shut her out completely. "What to do. What to do." She tapped the phone against her lips. "Well, first I need a shower. I certainly can't go to breakfast looking like I just crawled out of bed." She glanced at her reflection in the mirror over the dresser. Well loved. Those were the words she'd use to describe her look. Her lips were slightly puffy from Jeff's passionate kiss before he left, her hair curled around her head in a wild disarray and her neck showed signs of whisker burn. She smiled. The look did wonders for her self-esteem. *A drop dead gorgeous cowboy fucked me five ways to Sunday. And I liked it!*

'Mine.' The growl of his words came back to make her blush. Did he really think of her as belonging to him? How should she feel about it? The thought brought goose bumps to her flesh. The sparkle in her eyes wasn't there before either. *Apparently, I really like the idea.*

With a smile on her lips, she grabbed clean clothes so she could take a nice shower before the breakfast bell clanged calling the guests to the main lodge. The non-descriptive bathroom in the guest cabins didn't have anything to write home about, but they were functional all the same. The white walls, white tile, white tub and white shower curtain left something to be desired. She leaned over the tub to turn on the water and let out a scream loud enough to wake the dead.

* * * *

Jeff had just returned from his cabin with Ben in tow as they were getting ready for the breakfast bell to be rung soon.

The blood curdling scream coming from Terri's cabin sent chills down his back. "Come on, Ben. Let's see what's up." The next scream brought him up on the porch at a dead run with Ben on his hip. "Terri?"

She screamed again.

"Terri, open the door."

"Jeff?"

"Open the door."

"It's open. Get in here!"

"What is it? What's wrong?"

"There's a big hairy bug in the tub."

"A what?"

"A big hairy bug. Get it out!"

He almost burst out laughing when he found her standing on the toilet lid with the sheet wrapped around her. "Ben. Stay out here by the bed. Okay, buddy?"

"Yes, Daddy."

"Where is it?"

"In the tub."

He held his chuckle in as he grabbed some toilet paper, pulled back the shower curtain and squashed the spider she called a big hairy bug. "There. It's gone."

"You're laughing at me."

"No, I'm not." He smiled. He couldn't help it. She looked so cute standing on the toilet shaking like a leaf in a wind storm. "It's all gone. You can take your shower now."

She slowly climbed down with the help from his hand. "Thank you. I hate bugs."

"You live in Texas and you hate bugs?"

A shiver rolled over her frame. "Yes."

She glanced through her lashes at him, making him want to kiss the daylights out of her. "We'll go now so you can shower."

He took Ben's hand before he headed for the door.

"Jeff?"

"Yeah?"

"Thank you."

"I'll slay your bugs any day, darlin'." He glanced over his shoulder, wishing he hadn't when his cock jumped to attention. Seeing her outlined by nothing but the sheet made him wish he hadn't left this morning. "See you at breakfast."

"She's purdy, Daddy."

"She sure is, buddy."

"Can she be my mama?"

"What makes you ask somethin' like that Ben? What about your real mama?"

"I don't think she loves me. I want a new mama."

Jeff squatted down in front of his son. "Buddy, you can't trade in your mama no matter how much you don't like what she does."

"But you don't like her anymore."

Jeff tipped his head back on his shoulders. How do you explain dealing with a bitter ex because you love your kid to a three-year-old? "Sometimes parents don't get along anymore and can't live together. It's not that I don't like her, we just can't be together anymore."

"I still like the purdy lady in the cabin."

"Me too, buddy. Me too." He stood and took Ben's hand again to head toward the main lodge. "Let's get some breakfast, huh? I think Grandma will be wondering where we are if we don't hurry up."

"The bell hasn't rung yet though."

"Well it will soon. We can get our juice earlier than everyone else."

"Yay!" Ben jumped as Jeff swung him up into his arms.

"Hey, bro!" Jackson came walking from the barn. "We missed you at the bonfire last night. Where did you run off to?"

"None of your business."

"Ah. A little more fun with Ms. Terri."

Jeff stopped at face his brother. "What I do on my private time is none of your damned business, Jackson. Back off."

"Easy, brother. I, for one, am thrilled you've found a nice lady. Terri seems to be a keeper."

"No one is a keeper for me. I'm done with women." Jeff glanced at Ben. "Buddy, go on into the house, okay?"

"All right, Daddy."

The minute Ben disappeared into the house, Jeff rounded on Jackson. "Back the fuck off."

"Sounded like you and Terri were havin' a good time by the pond. What happened?"

"One more word and I'll deck your ass."

Jackson put up his hands. "Whoa. I didn't mean nothin', Jeff. I hope you find a nice girl is all. The way Misha has run you through the ringer has us all worried about you. I think you'd do well to find a nice woman."

"I don't need a fuckin' woman. A quick lay is all I'm interested in. Gettin' tied up with a woman is the last thing I need. My son and my job are enough to satisfy me."

Jackson glanced over Jeff's shoulder as he tipped his hat. "Mornin', Ms. Terri."

"Morning, Jackson."

Terri walked around the two of them, but he grabbed her arm when she tried to scoot by. "Terri, wait."

"For what? You certainly don't give a shit about me or my feelings, Jeffery Young." She tried to yank her arm out of his grasp. "Let go."

"No." He dragged her around the corner of the building and pushed her against the wall of the house.

"You can't treat me like this."

"Listen to me."

"No. I'm done listening to your shit, Jeff. I get it. You don't want a woman in your life. You've told me enough damned times, I've memorized even the fluctuation of your words when you say it. A quick fuck. I got that part too." She pushed against his chest. "I don't need you either."

"It's not what it sounded like."

"The hell it wasn't!"

"Terri, please listen to me." He brushed his fingers against her cheek. "I didn't lie to you. My life hasn't been great and my ex is a bitch. I've been burned, darlin'. I don't have a heart left to give anyone even if I wanted to. All I have left, I give to my son. I live for him and only him."

"I know, Jeff." Tears streaked down her cheeks. "I never asked for your heart."

"I don't want you to be misled. I want us to be honest with each other from the start. What I told Jackson is the truth, but you knew everything from the beginning. Do I want you? Hell yes, baby. I want you more than my next breath, but I can't let another woman in only to be dragged through the mud again. I won't do it." He brushed his lips against her cheek, tasting her tears. "But if you want me to leave you alone, I will."

"No."

"No?" he asked, staring down into her beautiful green eyes as he cupped her face.

"I don't want you to leave me alone. I need you. God knows why I'm putting myself through this with you, but I want you too."

"Good." He stepped back after a quick peck on her lips. "I've decided I don't care whether anyone on the ranch knows we are together."

"You don't?"

"No. Hell, half of my brothers probably saw me leave this morning since most of the time they're up and in the barn by daybreak to get chores started." He wiped the remaining tears from her cheeks. "I won't put you in front of Ben though. I hope you understand."

"Of course, I do. He's your son."

"He's my life." He took her hand, threading his fingers with hers and headed for the door just as the breakfast bell clanged. "You can sit with the family today if you want or you can sit with your friends, but I want everyone to know about you. I don't want to sneak around anymore."

"You don't have to do that, Jeff. I know how much your privacy means to you."

"Yeah, but if you're with me, my brothers won't hit on you either."

She punched him in the arm. "Brat!"

He grabbed her and kissed her hard. "You'll pay for that later."

When they walked into the main lodge with the rest of the crowd of people, he waited for her to decide where she wanted to sit. He watched as she squared her shoulders and indicated with a tilt of her head she would sit with him at the family table. As they approached hand in hand, he garnered some weird looks from his family. "Everyone, this is Terri." He named off all of his siblings and his parents. "Joel and Mesa aren't here. They're still on their honeymoon until the end of the week."

"How fun."

"Welcome to the family table, Terri. You can sit next to Jeff and Ben at the end," Nina said with a twinkle in her eye.

"Thank you."

"Aren't you one of the guests?" Jacob asked, his eyes bloodshot from a probable hangover.

Jeff needed to talk to his brother to find out what the problem was now. It seemed Jacob was drinking more and more.

"Never mind, Jacob."

"But we ain't supposed to mess with the guests."

"Terri is here gathering information so she isn't really a guest," he answered his brother, hoping it would cut off the questions before Terri got uncomfortable or he had to tell the family her real purpose for being nearby.

"It doesn't matter. Welcome, Terri," Jeremiah said, taking her hand and kissing the back. "Let me know if you'd like to see more of the area while you're here. I'd be glad to take you around."

Jealousy reared its ugly head, making Jeff frown. He had no right to be jealous. "I've already taken her out, Jeremiah."

"Well, I'm sure there is *something* she hasn't seen."

"Back off," he growled, earning a huge grin from Jeremiah and the rest of his brothers too.

"Actually, can you show me the barn after breakfast?" she asked, looking between him and Jeremiah.

"What do you want to see the barn for?"

"I'd like to see the entire operation if I can."

His eyes narrowed on her. "I'm sure I can find something to interest you." *What the hell is she up to?*

"I'm sure you can." One eyebrow arched over her beautiful green eyes.

Did she have an ulterior motive for wanting to see the barn? Maybe she wants a roll in the hay. "All right."

"Great." She glanced down the table. "So who does what for the ranch?"

The table exploded into a beehive of conversation as everyone tried to talk at once. Terri laughed causing his balls to ache with want. He wanted nothing more than to take her back to her cabin and bounce the headboard against the wall some more.

They all managed to get their plates and sit back down before the talk started again. She got an earful of what everyone did on the ranch.

Jeff glanced at Jacob who seemed to be almost falling asleep in his breakfast. Had he been out all night drinking again? His brother seemed to have some issue. It was up to him as the eldest to find out what seemed to be the problem.

Jacob glanced up with a frown. "What?"

"You okay?"

"Yeah. Got in late."

"On a work day?"

"Back off, Jeff. I'm a big boy. I can handle a few late nights and some beers."

"I'm worried about you."

"I said back off!"

The entire group grew quiet.

"We can talk about this later."

"It's none of your damned business what I do on my off time. As long as I get the shit done around here, I can do whatever the hell I please." Jacob jammed his hat on his head and stomped out of the dining room.

"Well that went well," Nina said.

"Sorry, Ma. I'm worried about him." His gaze followed his brother's departure.

"We all are, Jeff, but bringing it up at the breakfast table wasn't a great idea."

"I didn't plan to. I just asked if he was okay. He exploded in the fiery temper he's known for." Jeff glanced at Terri concerned the ruckus might have given her the wrong idea of his family. She reached over to lay her hand on his thigh. A squeeze of reassurance let him know she didn't mind what happened. His heart flipped at the encouraging touch. No one had ever felt the need to do that kind of thing for him before. He held her hand in his for a brief moment before he released it to eat.

Breakfast ended without further incident, but he kept a leery eye on the female next to him.

"Finished?" she asked, getting to her feet.

"Yes."

"Let me grab the plates then. Did you want another cup of coffee before we head out?"

"Sure. Thank you." He glanced her way, determined to figure out this enigma of a woman who'd blown into his life like a tornado sure to destroy everything in her path.

"Black or cream and sugar?"

"Black is fine."

"Be right back," she said, her eyes twinkling with laughter. "Did you want more juice, Ben."

"Yes, ma'am."

"Please."

"Yes, ma'am, please," Ben repeated.

Terri smiled and bent to give him a hug before she picked up the plates. When she finished depositing the dishes into the dirty dish pan, she got him a cup of coffee and Ben more juice. "Here you go."

"You didn't want more?"

"I'm headed back to get me another cup right now."

Suspicion raced through his mind. Hadn't Misha started out sweet to everyone in her path too? He'd blown off her flirting with his brothers as her being nice rather than what it really was. She would have slept with any of them to become part of the family. She just happened to sucker him in with her dark hair and caramel eyes. Man, she'd done a number on him and still was if her threats yesterday meant anything. The bitch. If she tried to take Ben away, he'd kill her himself.

"What's got you looking so serious, cowboy?"

"Nothin'."

"Nothin', huh? It didn't look like nothin' to me. You looked ready to shoot someone."

"If I could, I would. My ex."

"Oh. Let's not talk about her, okay?"

"Good. I don't want to anyway."

The rest of the family had cleared out from the dining room, leaving the two of them and Ben finishing up.

"Can I go out and play, Daddy?"

"Wait until Grandma can go out with you. I have to get my chores done."

"Okay."

"I'll take him in a minute, Jeff. Let me finish up these bills first," his mother called from her office.

"Sure, Ma. We'll take him to the barn with us until you're ready." He finished his cup as Terri was finishing hers. "Ready?"

"Yes. I can't wait to see everything. I'm so excited!"

He laughed. Surely a bunch of cattle, hay, horses and animal droppings didn't seem so exciting, but then again, she lived in Houston where they had things like this, but you didn't see it much. "This stuff ain't that exciting."

"Sure it is, Jeff." She bounced on her toes like a little kid waiting for candy.

"All right. Off to the barn then." He helped Ben off the chair. "Come on, buddy."

"Can I hold your hand, Ms. Terri?"

"Oh, Ben. Of course you can, pumpkin."

Ben grinned from ear to ear as he took one adult hand in each of his. They headed out to the barn like a happy little family.

Oh fuck!

Chapter Seven

The barn smelled of hay, horse manure and leather. Smells she didn't like before, but she seemed to inhale them now with a new sense of worth or purpose, she wasn't sure which. Deceiving Jeff like this didn't sit well with her. Unfortunately, she had to with the hope things would work out for the best.

"What do you want to see?"

"Everything."

"Well, the horses are stabled here at night and in bad weather. Each has their own stall where we feed them and water them. We have a feed room and a tack room where we keep various things like grain or hay. The tack room is where we keep all the riding paraphernalia for the horses. You've already seen it."

"Yes. The lovely smell of leather."

"Daddy, can I show Ms. Terri my horse?"

"Sure, buddy."

Ben pulled her along to the small stall at the end. Inside, there was a beautiful palomino gelding. "Wow, he's gorgeous, Ben."

"I know. He's gold."

"What's his name?"

"Blackie."

She smiled when all she wanted to do was laugh. "Why did you call him Blackie when he's gold?"

"'Cause Daddy's horse is Blackie and I wanted to be like Daddy."

"Oh, I see."

"We call him Blackie and my horse Black Jack so we can tell them apart," Jeff said with a proud grin.

They two of them were so cute together, she couldn't help but smile.

"Will you be my new mama, Ms. Terri?"

"Ben, we already discussed this."

"I know, Daddy, but I thought I'd ask Ms. Terri for you."

"Sorry," he mouthed.

What do I say a three-year-old? "Honey, you have a mama already."

"I know, but I don't want her to be my mama anymore. I want you to be."

"Ben, listen. I can't be your mama. I don't live here with you and your new mama should live here so she can love you all the time."

"Okay."

The disappointment on the little boys face broke her heart.

"But we can be friends while I'm here."

"Yay!" Ben bounced in front of her on his little feet until she picked him up in her arms.

A quick kiss to her cheek almost made her cry. *What a great little boy.*

"Can we go for a ride, Daddy?"

"Not now, buddy. I have some work to get done. I need to organize the feed room." He glanced at Terri. "Would you mind keepin' an eye on him until my mom can take him back to the house?"

"Sure." She glanced at Ben. "How about we go dig in the dirt for a while?"

"Can I get my trucks, Daddy?"

"Of course you can, Ben."

"You have dump trucks?"

Ben nodded quickly.

"Awesome. I love playing with dump trucks."

"I have lots of different ones too." He squirmed to get down.

"He keeps them in the feed room," Jeff said, following the running little boy down the dirt aisle of the barn.

Two cowboys in their finery. Ben had his little hat, tiny jeans and miniature cowboy boots where Jeff had the mighty fine grownup version. The man looked delicious. His ass looked tight in the Wranglers. *Damn.*

"You comin'?"

"I wish," she mumbled, following the man as she admired his backside.

Ben grabbed the box with his trucks in it, struggling to hold all of them. "Let me help."

"Okay."

She took the box out of his arms. "Will you hold my hand and show me where you play?"

"Yes, ma'am."

With a quick glance at his beaming father, she winked and said, "After you, sir."

Ben led her back down the aisle of the barn, around the outside and to a small dirt mound next to the wall. Shaded by a large tree she wasn't familiar with, she made a mental note to include it in her findings for the development company although she wasn't sure she'd get a lot accomplished on her mission by playing trucks with a three-year-old. Today, she didn't care. Today was about playing and having fun. Later, she'd worry about details like how much feed they went through, where they bought their stock and how many guests they had in a month. She didn't know how that would help the land developers, but she figured the more information she had on Thunder Ridge Guest Ranch, the better.

For the next hour, she played alongside the little boy in the dirt pile, until his grandmother came outside.

"What are you two doin' over there?" Nina asked, coming to a stop next to them.

"We are building houses, Gram."

"Are you now? Is Ms. Terri helping you build those houses?"

"Yes, ma'am. She draws them on paper and then the constuction man put them together."

"Oh?"

Shit. "I'm an architect by trade."

"Really? We've thought about adding on to the main lodge at times, maybe you can talk to me about square footage, building plans and permits one of these days before you leave."

"I would love to."

"Pick up your trucks, Ben. It's time to wash up."

"Aw, Gram."

"Come on, little man. You need to come inside so Ms. Terri can talk to your daddy. I believe she has some questions for him."

The twinkle in Nina's eye didn't go unnoticed. What was the woman up to? Playing matchmaker? Surely, she didn't think anything could come of her short stay here at the ranch? "Thanks, Nina. I do need to talk to him about some things."

Nina patted her on the hand. "There ya go. I knew you two needed some alone time."

Terri shook her head in denial. "It's not like that. I need to make some notes on a project I'm working on."

"Of course you do, honey."

Terri rolled her eyes. Apparently, Nina wanted her son hooked up with someone hopefully better than his ex. *You're spying on him. Does that make you better?* She bit her lip to keep from blurting out her purpose. She didn't like lying to these people.

"Come on, Ben. Let's go inside."

Nina walked away with Ben in tow, leaving Terri with the box of trucks at her feet. She grabbed it in her arms and headed back inside the barn to find Jeff. He stood inside the feed room with a clipboard in his hands as he scratched his head in apparent frustration.

"What's wrong?"

"Huh? Oh, hi." He pushed his hat back down on his forehead, and then jotted down some numbers. "I can't figure out where all the feed is going. We seem to be going through a lot more than normal this month."

"I wonder why."

"Well it could be because it's been rather dry so far. I'll have to ask Joey if he's been doubling up on feed or something for some reason."

"How much do you go through a month normally?"

He narrowed his eyes as he looked at her for a moment. It took him a second to answer and she hoped he wouldn't get suspicious about her questions. "Several tons of both hay and grain."

"How many animals do you have?"

"We have fifty horses and thousands of head of cattle. We don't feed the cattle much out of the stores unless the grazing is bad. They have round bales of hay we feed them to supplement their grazing."

"Sounds like a huge operation."

"It is. With the guests and running the cattle operation, it's a big job."

"I can't imagine."

"What are you getting at, Terri."

"Me? Nothing, why?"

"Why all the questions? I thought you had everything you needed when I took you out to the property lines."

"I did. I mean, I do. I want to spend some time myself learning about the operation though for my own information. It has nothing to do with the developers, Jeff." She cringed. Lying to him put a bad taste in her mouth.

"Why don't I necessarily believe you?"

"I don't know. I haven't given you a reason to distrust me."

"I distrust all women so it's not just you."

"I wish you didn't have such a terrible view of women. You've been hurt. I get it, but you know not all women are like your ex. You should think hard on that before you mistrust everyone."

He put the clipboard down on the bale of hay and pulled her close. "True." He brushed her lips with his. "I want you. Right now."

"Now?"

"Yeah. We can lock the door. Ever fucked in a tack room on a bale of hay?"

"Can't say that I have."

"This can be your first," he said, trailing his lips down her neck.

"You're very persuasive, you know." Shivers raced down her arms as she grabbed a fistful of his shirt. The snaps gave way with a forceful tug of her hands. "I love your chest."

He lifted her shirt over her head before he unsnapped her bra and drew it down her arms. "I love your tits."

She rolled her eyes.

"What?"

"Women don't like the word tits. It's vulgar."

"What do you call them?"

"Breasts or boobs."

He cupped her bare breasts in his palms, thumbing her nipples to hard little points. "I like your boobs, then."

"Men."

"They fit perfectly in my palms."

"They're too small."

"No they aren't. They're perfect."

He ran his tongue over one nipple, pulling a gasp from her lips. She hadn't realized her nipples were so sensitive to his touch. "Mmm."

"Like that?"

"Oh, hell yeah."

He worked the button at her waist loose while he continued to bite at her nipple. Her jeans fell to a puddle at her feet.

"My shoes."

"Up on the bale and I'll pull them off. I want to eat you anyway."

Her pussy clenched as desire raced through her.

"Let me grab a blanket. It might be a bit itchy." An older horse blanket lay in the corner. He grabbed it and spread it on the hay bale. "This would be better in your bed or mine, but I'm so damned hard for you, I can't wait."

"Just fuck me, Jeff. No prelims, just raw sex."

He grabbed a condom from his wallet, unbuckled his pants, shoving them to the floor in his haste and then rolled the condom down his impressive cock. "Are you wet?"

"Damn right, I'm wet. I've been dripping since you walked down the aisle after Ben with your tight ass in those jeans. You are one impressive cowboy, cowboy."

The head of his cock bumped at her opening.

"Sweet Baby Jesus." He slowly pushed his cock inside her pussy, dragging out every inch in sweet agony. His thumb found her clit, pulling a moan from between her lips. It felt wonderful, magnificent. She lost the ability to think as he moved in and out of her pussy.

"God, you feel like heaven."

"Harder, Jeff."

His pace increased. Heat crawled up from her toes. She was going come and come hard. "Kiss me."

He pulled her in for the most devastating kiss she'd ever had in her life, just in time for her body to explode in a climax big enough to curl her toes where they rested around his hips.

The kiss broke as he panted her name over and over until he climaxed in a rush.

"Jeff?"

"Shit!"

"Seriously? Who the hell is calling you now?"

"Jonathan."

"Fuck." Jeff scrambled to ditch the condom and right his jeans so he could answer his brother while she quickly grabbed hers from the pile to slip on. They were going to be caught red-handed fucking in the stock room.

"Hang on, Jonathan. I'll be right out."

"Are you in the tack room?"

"Stay where you are," Jeff growled as he tucked his shirt into his pants. "You dressed?" he whispered glancing her way while she struggled to get her bra back on.

"Does it fucking look like it?"

"I'll meet him out there so you have time to finish."

"Thanks." Hell, she still needed to get her pants back up. Guys had it so much easier. Whip it out, fuck like bunnies and stuff it back in.

Jeff closed the door behind him, but she could still hear the voices.

"What's up?"

"I needed to ask you something about the program to keep track of the feed so you aren't doing it all by paper anymore."

"Okay, what?"

"Can we go into the tack room? I need to see how big the sacks of grain are so I can—"

"No."

"Why the hell not?"

"It's a mess."

"What? Seriously? Who the fuck cares if it's a mess?"

"I do. I've got shit all over in there. I don't want you messing with my system."

"System? You don't have a damned system, Jeff. I need to see the sacks."

The next thing she knew, the door flew open and she came face to face with Jonathan.

"Oh."

"Hi."

"Hello." His face turned bright red as he dropped his gaze to the hay covered floor. "Sorry. I didn't mean to interrupt."

"You didn't," she said, holding back laughter as she put her shoes back on her feet.

"I'll uh…get those later, Jeff."

"You do that, Jonathan."

Jonathan took off at a dead run out of the barn, his face still bright red even from where she sat on the hay bale.

"Sorry. I guess I should have hid or something."

"No, it's fine. It's not like he's a virgin or somethin'. He's kind of shy, is all. He takes care of our website and computer stuff around here. He's building me a program to keep track of all of this without having to do it on paper."

"Sounds interesting." She stood in front of him now, wishing they'd had more time. It had been so great having him sleep beside her all night, but she knew it wouldn't happen again anytime soon. Ben took priority over everything he did, as it should be for a father. It just made her realize with kids, personal time took a backseat to the needs of the child. "What else can you tell me about the operation?"

"We have six guest rooms outside of the man lodge house. Ten more rooms upstairs from the family quarters where my parents sleep."

"Sounds like you can take a lot of guests."

"Yeah. We have a few double rooms upstairs where families can have two rooms or two of the cabins have connecting doors for families too."

"Have you ever been in a lawsuit for an accident on the ranch?"

He frowned. "What kind of question is that?"

"Just curious is all."

"Well, not that it's any of your business, but no, we haven't. Keeping our guests safe is a huge priority for us. We make sure everyone who rides is given instructions beforehand. They are screened to make sure their riding ability is good before they ever get on a horse. If they've never been on one before, they are given their own riding lessons."

"I didn't mean anything by it, Jeff. I would think this would be a high risk operation for liability purposes is all. I'm thinking of you."

"An accident could shut us down."

"I'm sure."

Her cell phone jingled in her pocket, but she planned to ignore it. She knew who it was without looking since she'd assigned a specific ringtone to the developers. The last thing she needed to do was answer it in front of Jeff.

"Aren't you gonna get that?" he asked, propping himself up against the doorframe with his arms over his chest, looking all the more enticing with his clothes back in place.

"I know who it is. It's my mother. I'll call her back in a bit." She stepped forward and ran a fingernail down his chest. "Is there another time we can get together, maybe?"

"I don't know."

"What about at your place?"

"I have Ben."

She fiddled with the buttons on his shirt as she glanced up through her lashes. "I know, Jeff. I wouldn't ask you to put anyone in front of his needs. He's your son."

Her cell phone jingled again.

"Sounds important. Maybe you should answer it."

"I guess so." She glanced at the screen. Yep, the developers. "It's almost lunch time anyway so I'm going to head back to my room to freshen up. I'll see you in the main lodge."

"Okay." He kissed her quickly on the lips.

A simple brush of his mouth against hers, but her panties felt drenched from the small touch.

The smile she gave him was genuine. She really liked him. Probably a little too much.

Chapter Eight

Terri took the phone from her pocket as she opened the door to her cabin, to call the developers back. Annoyance rushed through her. She had a job to do, but they certainly didn't seem to want to let her do it.

The phone redialed with a push of her finger.

After the receptionist rattled off her greeting, Terri asked to speak to one of the partners. Mr. Cole picked up the line. "Terri, we need an update."

"I don't have an update for you. I haven't learned anything really. It hasn't even been half a day."

"My source on the counsel has informed me the committee has all but agreed with the idiots at Thunder Ridge to postpone the land development until they can do more research on land impact. I need something right now. What about the operation itself? Surely you've been able to find out some information on their financial situation?"

"I know they haven't had any lawsuits." She frowned. What did all of this have to do with the development and building houses on their property? It almost sounded like they wanted to put Thunder Ridge out of business if they could.

"Well maybe we'll need to work on that then."

"What do you mean? These are nice people."

"Don't get attached, Terri. We're in business to make money. We need more property to make more money. It's as simple as that."

"It's just a family run guest ranch with some cattle on it. They are no threat to you."

"Everyone in the area is a threat to us."

"Why?"

"We need more land. We don't care how we get it."

"I don't understand?"

"Just get the information we need or you won't have a job when this is through. Maybe not even a company to go back to." *Click.*

What the fuck?

"He didn't seriously just threaten me, did he?"

"My guess is, yes, he did."

She spun around to find Jeff at her open door.

"You left your underwear in the feed room. I thought I'd bring them back before someone else found them."

The concern in his eyes had feelings blooming that shouldn't be there. Feelings for him would complicate things. "It's not what it sounds like."

He moved inside the room and shut the door. "Explain it to me then. Is someone threatening you?"

"I…"

"If there is something I can do, tell me. I don't like the thought of someone hurting you for any reason."

"Why?"

"I've grown kind of attached to you while you've been here. If someone is hurting you and I can help, then let me."

"It's nothing, Jeff. Really. I can handle it."

"Are you sure?"

"Yeah." She took the underwear from his hand. "Thanks for bringing these back." She tossed them on the bed. "Going commando isn't what it's cracked up to be."

"No, it's not. I've done it a time or two myself."

"Have you now."

"Yep."

She glanced down at the straining material of his jeans. "Like now?"

"No, but somethin' is wantin' to come out and play." He glanced at his watch. "We have about fifteen minutes."

"I think we should wait."

"Why?" he asked, his eyes wide with confusion.

"You might be able to get off in fifteen minutes, but we women like to take it a little slower sometimes. The quick fuck in the feed room should have satisfied you for a little bit, cowboy."

"All right."

The little pout on his mouth made her smile. A quick nibble on his lips brought the reaction she wanted as he moaned softly and took the kiss to explosive in record time. When they finally came up for air, he groaned as he pressed his forehead against hers.

"Tonight. My place."

"I thought you didn't want to do anything with Ben there?"

"He'll be asleep by seven. We can have the whole night. Bring your car so you can leave whenever you want. You can follow me home after supper tonight." He grasped her butt to pull her closer. "Ever had a man in your ass, honey?"

"Nope."

"Want to?"

Her butt cheeks clenched at the thought. She'd always wanted to try, but she hadn't had the nerve or the trust in someone to allow them to go that far. "Maybe."

"Don't worry. You'll love it and if you don't we don't have to pursue it any further."

The rock hard chest beneath her breasts made her nipples ache for friction. She wanted to run them all over the front of his shirt.

"Quit lookin' at me like that."

"Like what?"

"Like you'd strip me to bare skin and ride my hips into tomorrow if we had time."

"I do?"

"Yep."

"Sounds good to me." The lunch bell clanged. "Well damn." He laughed, rich and deep. *Damn, I like his laugh.* "You should laugh more often."

"You know, darlin', I've laughed and smiled more since I met you than I have in several years."

"I'm glad I could help."

"You've done wonders for me." He hugged her, and then opened the door. "I love you."

What the hell? She stumbled over her feet before she glanced up into his eyes.

"I didn't mean that how it sounded. "I meant I love bein' around you. You've brought a lot of joy into my life I haven't had for a long time."

He took her hand as he shut the door behind them.

"Good. You had me scared there for a minute."

"I'm glad I let you in, Terri. I'll just be sorry when it has to end."

"Yeah, me too, Jeff. Me too.

* * * *

He mentally kicked himself in the ass as they walked to the main lodge for lunch. *What the fuck was I thinking? That had to be the stupidest thing I've ever said in my life, well maybe except for when I talk to Misha.*

Luckily, Terri seemed to go with his explanation because he sure as hell didn't have anything else to say. *I love you. Stupid, man. Really stupid.*

They walked through the doors into the chaos of the noonday meal. Several new guests had come in during the morning hours it appeared. "Do you want to eat with us at the family table again?"

"Of course," she gushed and he frowned.

God, I hope she isn't taking this too seriously. Maybe they needed to slow this shit down. Hell, he wasn't sure anymore himself. He seemed to by flying by the seat of his pants and the fuckers were on fire for this woman.

They greeted everyone at the table with hello. His brothers seemed to be keeping a secret with all the smiles and looks their way. Hopefully, they didn't think there was something else going on between him and Terri. He'd have to straighten them out before too long. His mother played matchmaker all the damned time with her sons, but he wasn't gonna to fall for the whole lot of them trying to hook him up. He didn't need their help. He was gettin' laid on a semi-regular basis while Terri hung around and that suited him just fine, thank you very much.

"Why is everyone grinnin'?" she asked quietly.

"This is the second meal you've shared at the family table. They're probably gonna be askin' about church bells soon."

"Hell no," she hissed.

"My thoughts exactly."

"Should I tell them?"

"No, let them wonder. It's a game. Think of it that way."

Her green eyes twinkled with mirth. "Oh, I like pulling the wool over their eyes. I think it'll be fun."

"Yep."

The guests were served so everyone at the family table got up to get their food. "Can I get you some coffee or lemonade?" he asked.

"Sure. Lemonade sounds great."

When they returned to the table and sat down to eat, conversation sped around the table in varying degrees, everything from problems on the ranch to issues with the cattle from the morning rounds.

"Jeff, I found a couple of cattle down in the south pasture. The water trough was empty again."

"What? I fixed it two days ago."

"There's a big hole. Looks like a bullet hole to me."

"Do we have to start patrolling the fence line again? Jesus."

"Jeffery."

"Sorry, Ma, but this is nuts. You'd think we were livin' in the frickin' eighteen hundreds. Worryin' about cattle rustlers is crazy."

"We'll deal with it, son," James added before he took a bite of his food.

"We don't have the man power to have to patrol the fence twenty-four/seven, Dad."

"I know we don't, but we'll figure somethin' out. First thing, move the water trough to behind a rock so it's not visible from the fence line. At least it will make it more difficult for someone to take potshots at it."

"I'll take care of it, Dad," Joshua said.

"Thanks, Josh. I've got some things to work on in the barn this afternoon," Jeff answered.

"Yeah, we know," Jonathan added with a smirk and a look at Terri.

Great. I hope the whole damned bunch doesn't know about our tryst. "Jonathan," he growled, hoping his brother would take the hint.

"There must have been possum in the feed room earlier. Did ya get it?"

Jeff wanted to punch his brother. "Yeah, I got it."

The whole table erupted in laughter.

"What did I miss?" Terri asked, apparently not getting the joke.

"Never mind, darlin'. I'll explain later. Just ignore shithead over there."

"It's kind of hard to ignore being the butt of a joke, Jeff."

He leaned over and whispered, "Apparently, Jonathan has informed the whole family of what happened in the barn between us earlier."

She bit her lips as her eyes closed. Red swept up her neck, splashing across her face in a bright hue as everyone laughed.

"Enough!" James shouted. "You boys should be ashamed to treat a guest this way."

"Sorry, Terri. I didn't mean to embarrass you." Jonathan sounded trite, but Jeff wasn't sure it was genuine. Either way, he planned to kick his brother's ass for him after lunch.

She opened her eyes and smiled. "It's fine."

Wow. She's a better person than I am.

They finished the rest of the meal without any more hassles from his family. Jeff picked up their plates when they finished, taking them to the dirty dish pan. He grabbed three desserts on his way to returning to the table. The rest of the family cleared out leaving him alone with Terri and Ben. They seemed to be doing that a lot since she'd arrived.

"Do you have somethin' you can do this afternoon? I've got work to get done." The spoon disappeared between her tempting lips, making him want to stick something else between those plump lips. Maybe tonight he could get her to suck him. Just for a minute. He'd probably explode the minute she took him in her mouth. He shook his head to clear the erotic thoughts. The last thing he needed was a raging hard-on to work with this afternoon. Of course, throwing some hay bales would quickly deflate it.

"Sure. If you don't mind, I'd like to talk to some of your brothers about some of the other stuff they do around the ranch."

"Why's that?" he asked, suspicion crowding his thoughts. She did work for the developers trying to take over everything around Bandera.

She shrugged as she took another bite. "I'm curious. I've never been on a working cattle ranch. I'd like to know more about each man's job on the ranch."

Her thigh plastered against his waylaid his thoughts again. *Damn.* He needed to get his mind out of bed with Terri and back on work. "There is a hay ride this evening if you'd like to go. Dad does a great informational thing on the longhorn cattle we have."

"Great! I'd love it. He seems like an interesting person."

"He's been doin' this a long time."

After she finished her dessert, she pushed the small cup away as she licked her lips. He so wanted to taste the chocolate confection on her mouth. He leaned in ready to do exactly what he thought until Ben squeezed between them. "Hey, buddy."

"Can Ms. Terri come over our house tonight?"

"What for?"

"I wanna show her my room."

Jeff raised an eyebrow in a questioning look trying to convey to her this would give them a perfect opportunity for a night of lovemaking at his place.

"Sure, Ben," she answered. "I'd love to see your room."

"Okay. Off with Gram, Ben. I've got work to do and so does Ms. Terri." He stood and helped Terri to her feet. "I'll walk you back to your cabin."

"You don't have to do that. How about if I get with Jonathan and Jeremiah so I can get the business side of things?"

"There's an office by the check-in office where Jeremiah works on the books. I'll take you there before I head to the barn."

"Thanks."

They rounded the corner of the main lodge just in time for the front door to open and close by itself. He rolled his eyes. He hoped she didn't have a problem with ghosts since they had a few of them running around the ranch, especially in the main lodge since it used to be a brothel. They didn't have a lot of problems in the cabins, but the main house had its share. The local cowboy who haunted the place kept things lively, but the real draw for a lot of folks was the noisy couple upstairs. Even Mesa had a run in with them when she stayed there.

"Did that door just open and close by itself?"

"It's ghost," Ben whispered in a loud voice.

"Ghost?" she asked, her eyes wide with wonder.

"It's nothin'. Probably the wind," Jeff answered before Ben could go further. "Off to see Gram, Ben."

"Okay, Daddy." Ben scrambled into Nina's office as he rounded the corner to show Terri where Jeremiah's office was.

"Here you go." He knocked on the door and heard a muffled greeting. He opened it to find Jeremiah bent over his desk with papers scattered everywhere. The office looked like a bomb had gone off in there. "Damn, Jeremiah. I don't see how you can get anythin' done with this mess."

"I know exactly where everything is so just back off."

He held up his hands. "I brought Terri in to talk to you. She has some questions."

"Sure. Come on in, Terri. There's a chair there in the corner if you'd like to sit."

"Thank you," Terri answered, grabbing the wooden chair from its spot to drag it closer to the desk.

"I'll leave you two alone then. I'll see you at supper, Terri."

"Of course."

"Have fun and behave yourself, Jeremiah."

"Always, brother."

He closed the door, but stopped with his hand on the doorknob. *Why was she so interested in the financial aspect of the ranch? Things weren't quite addin' up with Terri Kennedy. Maybe if I get to know her better, she'll tell me what she's up to.*

Jeff shook his head as he walked out the doors headed for the barn. What to do with her, he wasn't sure, but keeping an eye on her seemed to be a priority now. Her inquiries into things going on at the ranch worried him. A talk between him and Jeremiah would be in order after work had been completed for the day. He hoped she wasn't up to no good. Trust came hard for him and he'd begun to trust her. He just hoped it wasn't misplaced.

Jacob came out of the tack room, stumbling slightly.

"Are you okay?"

"I'm fine."

The smell of alcohol coming from his brother's breath almost knocked Jeff down.

"Jacob, are you drunk?"

"No. I wish to hell I was."

Jeff grabbed his brother's arm and hauled him into the tack room. "What the fuck is goin' on with you? You've been drinking in here?"

"Fine. Yeah, I've been drinkin'. It's none of your fuckin' business what I do." Jacob shoved Jeff back, yanking his arm out of his brother's grasp. Without the added support, he stumbled again.

"We're here for you, Jacob. But, listen, man. This has to stop."

"Just leave me the fuck alone." Jacob tumbled backward into a chair sitting near the desk they used to do some of the tack repairs on.

"Tell me."

"You don't fuckin' care about any of us! Why the hell should I tell you anything."

"Because you're drinkin' way too much. Here it is the middle of the damned day on a weekday and you're drunk off your ass. Were you drunk at breakfast too?"

"Yeah, I was!" Jacob straightened himself in the chair and he tried to rise. Jeff slammed him back down with a hand on his shoulder.

"Jacob, what's gotten into you? You didn't used to drink like this."

"It doesn't matter. I ain't tellin' you anything so back the fuck off, Jeff. What I do isn't your business."

"Everythin' at this ranch is my business. Get it through your head brother and we'll be fine. The drinkin' has to stop. I mean now, Jacob."

"Fuck you." Jacob stumbled to his feet as he pushed his way past Jeff.

Jeff grabbed his arm, but Jacob yanked it back. "Come on, Jacob. Talk to me."

"Leave me alone, Jeff. The problems I have are none of your business."

"I want to help you."

"You're too wrapped up in your latest woman to care about me or anyone else on this ranch."

"Don't bring Terri into this. She ain't got nothin' to do with you or me."

"Why the hell not? She's another slut…"

Jeff pulled back his fist and hit Jacob on the chin, laying him flat out on the floor of the tack room. "Terri is a good woman. She's not a money-hungry female after this ranch or what money she can get from me. She has her own business and is working an important job. Keep your filthy opinions to yourself."

"What's goin' on here," their father said, stopping in the doorway.

"Jacob is drunk again. He's been drinkin' on the job. He's probably got some booze hidden in here somewhere so he can sneak a drink whenever he comes in."

"Is this true, Jacob?"

Jacob tried to sit up. "I was drunk last night. Today, I'm hung over. That's all, Dad."

"You can smell the alcohol on his breath."

Their father held out his hand to help Jacob to his feet. Jeff wasn't fooled. He knew his father planned to smell Jacob's breath for himself.

"Jacob, go to your place. You need to sleep off whatever you've been drinking."

"But, Dad?"

"But nothin'. I don't want to hear another word from you."

"I'm thirty years old. If I want to get plastered, I can."

"Not while you're workin' this ranch, son." Their father turned him toward the door. "Go on. We'll talk later about this."

Jacob stumbled out the door, almost falling on his face as Jeff and their father stood by to watch.

"What are we gonna do with him, Dad?"

"I'm not sure, Jeff. I wish I knew what caused him to start drinkin'."

"I don't know either."

"Have you heard of woman problems or anythin' with him?"

"No. I know he had a girlfriend not too long ago, but I thought their split was a mutual thing." Jeff shook his head. "Maybe he took it harder than I thought."

"Maybe, but I don't think Jacob was in love with her. Do you?"

"He might have been, Dad. I know he never brought her around here. I saw her with him a couple of times at the bar. They seemed chummy, but he sure didn't act like he was in love." He stepped back inside the tack room when Jacob went inside his trailer. His wasn't far from the house to the back of the garden area. "I sure ain't an expert on the subject though."

James laughed, and then sobered. "Sorry, son. I didn't mean to make fun of you, but you sure aren't an expert with your track record."

"Misha was a huge mistake even though she gave me Ben."

"He's the light of our lives, Jeff. You know that, right?"

"Yeah, Dad, I do. He's my pride and joy. I love him with all my heart."

James took a seat on the edge of the desk. "What's going on between you and Terri Kennedy?"

"Nothin', why?"

"You seem pretty familiar with each other for nothin' goin' on," his father said, folding his arms over his chest.

"She's a great gal. We're havin' a little fun together until she leaves."

"Yeah, Joel said the same thing until Mesa left to go back to Los Angeles."

"Joel fell in love with her in like a week, Dad. That's not normal."

"When love finds you, son, you don't have a choice in the matter. Not if it's real love."

"Well, I don't plan to fall in love with anyone. Women are more of a pain in the ass than their worth."

One eyebrow rose over James' left eye. "True, but the love you get in return more than makes up for the hassle you go through."

"I don't think so."

"With the right woman, it is."

"Hmm." Jeff took a bridle down from the wall and fiddled with the bit. "Did I tell you I had to save Terri from a bug in her tub this mornin'?"

"No." James laughed. "I thought she was from Houston. Surely she knows about the bugs in Texas."

"I woulda thought so but she apparently doesn't do bugs." Jeff laughed too. It had been rather funny to see her standing on the toilet wrapped in a sheet.

"I haven't seen you laugh in a long time, son. I think she's good for you."

"Don't get your hopes up. It's nothin' permanent."

"What's she doin' here anyway? I think there is more to her visit than meets the eye. She's interested in things most normal guests aren't."

"I'm keepin' an eye on her."

"Why?"

"Don't judge her, okay? I don't think she means harm, but I can't be sure." Jeff laid the bridle on the desk. "She's an architect for the development firm who bought the land next to ours. They plan on putting a housing project in there. She's doing some research on the area to get an idea of what types of houses she'll be designing for them to build."

"That's serious stuff."

"I know."

"She's in talkin' to Jeremiah." James rapped his knuckles on the desktop. "I don't like her knowing our financial situation, Jeff."

"I don't think Jeremiah is stupid enough to tell her anything pertinent. I hope she's gettin' general information is all."

"I'll talk to Jeremiah after she leaves to find out what exactly he told her," his father said.

"Those money-hungry land barons could be trying to put us out of business."

"Yeah, and she'd be helping them."

"I don't see how gathering information to figure out what kind of houses to design would be helping to put us out of business."

"Why else would she need financial information or anything along those lines?"

"I don't know."

"Why don't you ask her?"

"How the hell do I do that, Dad? In between orgasms I say, *tell me what you're up to, Terri. I need to know if you're trying to ruin my family.* Somehow it doesn't come across to me as pillow talk."

"You'll know what to do, son. You always do."

Chapter Nine

Terri watched Jeff eat each morsel with finesse. She wasn't sure how he made eating look sexy, but he sure did. The tines of the fork slipped between his full lips, tempting her to want to taste him or have him taste her. He'd been quiet since they'd met up for dinner. Conversation flowed around them from all of his brothers, but he didn't seem interested in talk this evening. Ben kept up a lively conversation with his grandmother about their activities for the day. Terri smiled while she listened to him.

Jeff finally broke the silence between them as he leaned over and whispered, "Are we still going to meet later?"

"I hope so."

"Do you want to?"

"Yes."

When she glanced up, she met the narrowed gaze of James. Why she earned the distrust of the monarch of the family, she wasn't sure. She didn't like it though. She hated having anyone mistrust her or question her motives. *Why shouldn't they? I've been mysterious the whole time I've been here, gathering information on them that really isn't any of my business. By passing this along, will it hurt this family in the long run? I don't know.*

"You okay?" Jeff asked.

"Yes, why?"

"You looked concerned."

"Your father seems to dislike me for some reason."

"He doesn't dislike you. He doesn't know you, how could he dislike you?"

"I don't know." She glanced at Jeff. "Did you tell him why I'm here?"

Jeff blushed and dropped his gaze to his plate.

"You did. No wonder he doesn't trust me," she whispered out the side of her mouth. "What did you tell him?"

"Your reason for being here was to collect data for the developers."

"True. What else?"

"Nothin'." He finished his plate and pushed it away. "We'll talk more about this later."

"Fine."

"Ben, are you done, buddy?"

"Yes, Daddy."

"I'll get your dessert."

She looked up to see him staring at her.

"Would you like something?"

"The apple crisp looks good."

"I'll grab one for you while I'm up."

"Thanks." When she glanced across the table to Jeff's dad, the older man smiled. She hoped that meant he'd give her a chance to explain. Of course, explaining might mean telling him what she really had up her sleeve.

"Here you go," Jeff said, sitting the small cup down in front of her.

The apples, cinnamon and crispy granola melted on her tongue with each bite she took. They had the best desserts at this ranch. If she lived here all the time, she'd weight a lot more than she did now. Not that she was a skinny person by any means. Her hips were too big, she had a bit of a stomach roll and her boobs were too small for her. Jeff didn't seem to mind though, which was a good thing.

"We can watch a movie with Ben until he falls asleep which is usually within the first hour or so."

"Sounds good."

Terri glanced around the table, meeting several of his brother's gazes. She didn't like the looks they were giving her. *Had they somehow heard about her real job?*

"You didn't tell your brothers, right?"

"No, just my father, but you have to admit your behavior has been rather suspicious."

"Suspicious how?"

"Most guests don't want to talk to the financial planner of our group. I don't know if Jeremiah might have told them what things you were asking him. What did you ask, by the way?"

"Nothing much."

"I don't want to discuss this in front of the family."

Her dessert was already gone.

"Shall we go?"

"Uh, sure." *Does Jeff suspect something? I don't like the way he seems to hint at a conversation concerning my information gathering and then goes off on another topic. Should I tell him what I'm doing? Think Terri, think.* "Is everything okay, Jeff?"

"We'll discuss it at my place."

Oh, I hate when people do that! It drove her nuts to be put off. "Are you sure you don't want to discuss it now?"

"Not in front of my family."

"Oh."

They put their dishes in the dirty dish pan, took Ben's hands and walked out of the door toward his truck. "Let me grab my keys and purse from my cabin."

"Good idea."

She turned left to take the path to her door, unlocked the cabin and walked inside. She debated on whether to change into something sexy. At least sexy underwear? No, she really didn't have time. He wouldn't wait forever and she already planned on having sex with him tonight. Before or after their talk, she wasn't sure. *Maybe before. If he gets wind of what I'm really up to, there may not be any sex.*

Putting off their *talk* sounded like a good idea.

With her purse and keys in hand, she shut the door to her cabin before she checked the lock to make sure it was secure. Jeff stood by his truck's passenger door buckling Ben into his car seat. The way Jeff treated Ben said a lot about the man. He cared. He might not care for her, at least not in any meaningful way, but in his own way, he cared. She'd seen it when he asked about her phone call and someone threatening her.

"Ready?" he called as she approached her car.

"Yeah."

"Good. Follow me. I'll be slow so I don't lose you."

"Is it far?"

"Nope. Just over the ridge on the other side of the main road."

"Great." She slipped inside her car, started it and then waited for Jeff to back up so she could follow him. Her stomach twisted into one big knot. Did she really plan on spending the entire night in his home with him? How did she really feel about it? Nervous, that's how.

Her palms were slick with sweat. It had been a long time since she'd spent an entire night with a man except for Jeff. The one night he'd slept in at her cabin really didn't count or did it? Once he found out her real purpose for being here, he'd cut all ties.

His trust would be gone.

She frowned. Trust. A tricky emotion. One she hoped she didn't lose with this family, but it seemed inevitable.

They turned down a gravel road to the left outside of the main gate of Thunder Ridge. A couple of turns later revealed a beautiful little cabin set back against the hillside. The roughhewn outside reminded her of the rustic cabins of old. You could find them in the mountains of the eastern states and sometimes on the western plains. She loved it on sight. Two windows graced the front. A small porch lined the face of the house, holding two rocking chairs waiting for someone to enjoy the evening while they sipped sweet tea. Maybe someday she'd enjoy the sight with him.

Get those thoughts right out of your head!

"I don't need to be thinking of anything permanent here. He's made it clear he doesn't do long term and I'm not inclined to either."

Seconds later, Ben struggled to open the door of her car for her. So sweet.

Jeff laughed and opened the door for him. "Come on, Ms. Terri. I want to show you my room."

"All right, little man. One second. Let me grab my things." She picked up her purse from the seat and stepped out of the car. Ben grabbed her hand and pulled her toward the door.

"Easy, sport. You don't want to hurt her by pullin' too hard."

"Sorry, Ms. Terri."

"It's fine, Ben. You didn't hurt me." She winked at Jeff, earning herself a genuine smile. She liked his smile. He had the hint of a dimple in his left cheek she hadn't noticed before.

They reached the front porch as Jeff opened the door. "My lady."

"What a grand invitation, sir."

"I hope you enjoy your stay."

"I'm sure I will." The inside of the cabin took her breath away. The rusticity of the furnishings appealed to her primitive side, bringing to life the old west along with a little bit of Indian culture as well. "Jeff, it's gorgeous."

"Thanks."

"Did your ex have anything to do with the décor?"

"Misha? Hell no. She hated this place."

"I'm glad because I love it. It's very much you."

"Come on, Ms. Terri."

Ben pulled her along down the hall. His bedroom had the rustic feel too, but still showed the little boy with his Toy Story bed, a hand carved toy box in the corner and a quilt, obviously made with love by his grandmother.

"Did your mom make the quilt?"

"Yeah." Jeff stuffed his hands in his pockets. "She was so thrilled when we found out Ben was a boy, although she wanted a granddaughter. She didn't really care as long as the child came out healthy. He did at nine pounds and ten ounces."

"What a big boy."

Ben mimicked his dad's stance by shoving his hands in the front pockets of his jeans too. "I have a big boy bed."

"You sure do, pumpkin."

"And I wear big boy panties."

"Great job!" She smiled at Jeff. "I bet he's a handful sometimes."

"Oh yeah. You can say that again."

"See my toys?" Ben pointed to the toy box before he rushed over to lift the lid. "I like Toy Story."

"I can see that." She got down on the floor in front of the toy box. "Who is your favorite?"

"Woody. He's a cowboy like me."

"He sure is." Terri felt her heart overflow with love for this little boy. He had a great dad, awesome grandparents and the affection of his uncles, but he didn't have the love of his mother. It didn't seem fair to her.

"Let's watch a movie," Jeff said, taking her hand and helping her to her feet.

"Yay! Toy Story!"

She laughed as she shuffled out of the room behind Ben and Jeff. "Why am I not surprised."

"Did you think it would be anything else?"

"No, not really once I saw his bedroom. It's okay. I like Toy Story."

"One, two or three?"

"Wow, I didn't realize there was more than one."

"You are so behind the times, lady."

"Apparently. All I can say for myself is I haven't been around kids very much."

"Hang around for a while. We'll teach you, huh Ben?"

"Yes, Daddy."

"Do you want me to?"

"To what?"

"Stick around?"

Both of his shoulders lifted in a shrug. He wouldn't meet her gaze. "I don't know. I mean, we have fun together. I wouldn't mind getting to know you a little better."

"I thought you didn't do relationships?"

"I don't. It wouldn't have to be a relationship. We could just…"

"What? Sleep together?" She didn't like the way this conversation seemed to be headed. *Friends with benefits?*

"We can talk about this after Ben goes to bed."

Ben pushed the movie into the disc player as he flipped on the remote for the television. *Damn, the kid was smart enough to know how to put his own movies on? Apparently.* He plopped down on the soft right in the middle.

The moment he gave her those puppy dog eyes, she couldn't resist. Each of them took a spot on the couch, one on either side of the little boy.

She'd seen the movie before, but low and behold within thirty minutes Ben was asleep leaning against her side. "He's asleep."

"I told you he'd be out inside of a half an hour." Jeff stood and pick up Ben in his arms. "I'll be right back."

Trepidation twisted her guts. They'd talk now and she wasn't sure she was ready for *the talk.* Maybe she could convince him to have sex first. She unbuttoned her blouse. A glimpse of skin should do it. Jeff was a sexual man. She didn't know how he went as long as he did without sex. The moment they'd been together, the whole room threatened to combust.

"Terri?"

"Yeah?" she called back.

"Can you come in a kiss Ben goodnight? He won't go back to sleep until you do."

"Sure. Be right there." *Damn it.* She rebuttoned her blouse, but left it untucked from her jeans. When she walked into the room, the small beside lamp next to the bed was on. Ben had crawled beneath the sheet. "Hey, buddy."

"Can I have a hug and a kiss goodnight?" He raised his arms for her.

"Sure, Ben." She leaned over and his little arms wrapped around her neck. "Night." She kissed him on the forehead, holding back tears his trust and unconditional love toward her brought. *Leave it to a little boy to bring out the feelings the dad is fostering.* "Sleep well."

"Will you be here tomorrow mornin'?"

"I don't know, Ben. I might be back at my cabin near the main lodge, but I'll see you at breakfast if nothing else."

"Okay. I love you, Ms. Terri."

"I love you too, buddy."

Ben rolled over as she wiped her eyes and stood. He needed the love of a mother so much, it hurt her heart.

Jeff took her hand and let her back out to the couch. They sat down side by side. "Thank you for being there for Ben, but I wish you hadn't lied to him."

"I didn't lie to him."

"You said you loved him when I know you don't."

She spun to face him. "How do you know what's in my heart? I do love that little boy. He's a treasure and I wish I was going to be around to see him grow into a man someday. If he's treated right by the women in his life, he'll grow into a special person."

"All right, I don't know how you feel about him, but I don't want him led on either. You know you aren't a permanent part of his life."

"I know that too, Jeff, but I can't help but love him. He's a special little boy."

Jeff ran his hands over his eyes in a weary motion, shoving his hat from his head to let it drop on the arm of the couch. She didn't know how to help him.

Comforting him seemed natural to her. She brought him down so his head lay on her lap. "You've done a great job with him," she said, running her fingers through his hair. "He's a great kid."

"Thanks. I wish his mother loved him as much as I do or you." He glanced up as she pushed his hair off his forehead. "I don't deserve you."

"Sure you do."

"No, I don't. You've been everything a man could want in a woman."

"But?"

"I can't give you my heart like you deserve. I have nothing left to give."

"It doesn't matter, Jeff. We'll go with what we have. Great sex, a kind of friendship or at least that's what I hope we have."

"Yeah."

He grabbed the back of her head and pulled her down to meet his lips. The kiss took her breath away. Everything about the sexy man had her body standing at attention and her panties wet.

"I want you," he whispered against her lips.

"Good. I want you too."

He sat up and spun around. Quick as lightning, he had her on her back as he hovered over her.

"Here?"

"Why not?"

"What about Ben?"

"He won't wake up."

"I'd rather not be caught with my pants down around my ankles by your three-year-old son."

He kissed her, leaving her panting for more. "Let's go into the bedroom. I wanna fuck you hard."

"Oh yeah."

He helped her to her feet, and then lifted her into his arms to carry her down the hall to his bedroom. "You're going to hurt your back, doing this."

"Please. I wrestle cattle, throw hay bales and lifted fifty pound feed sacks two at a time all day long. I can lift one little hundred and twenty pound woman like you."

"God, I wish I weighed a hundred and twenty pounds."

He laughed. "I'm not gonna ask how much you really weigh then."

"A hundred and fifty."

"Wow. Those thirty pounds will kill me!"

He acted like he stumbled under her weight. The jerk. The minute he dropped her in the middle of his bed, she scrambled up to a sitting position. He shut the door and locked it. "Come here."

"No."

"I said, come here."

"I said, no."

He growled low in his throat. The deep rumbling sound sent shivers down her back. Her panties were soaked from his manhandling.

"You're gonna pay for that."

"Oh?"

"I'm gonna have to punish you."

"Say what?"

"Ever been spanked before?" he asked, stalking toward her like a cat on the prowl and she was the prey.

"You aren't going to spank me like a child." Her pussy clenched at the thought. *What the hell? I want him to spank me?*

He quickly flipped her over onto her stomach, dragged her across his legs and proceeded to spank her ass. She screamed.

"*Shh.* You'll do what I tell you while you're with me."

His hand came down hard on her left cheek, then her right.

"If I want you to suck my cock, you will without question." *Smack.* "If I tell you to take your clothes off, you'll do it immediately." *Smack.*

"All right. I will." She sniffed back tears she hadn't realized she'd been shedding.

He rubbed her sore cheeks, until she realized the fire in her butt had spread heat to her pussy.

"I must be crazy to want this, but it's making me hot."

"Ever heard of BDSM?" he asked, helping her to a sitting position.

"Some. I've read some books with it in it."

"I'm not full into it, but I do like to be in control."

"Obviously." She rubbed her butt now that he let her sit up.

"Take your clothes off. Your answer?"

"Yes, Sir?"

"Good girl. You'll learn my wants and needs aren't very particular. I'm not into whips, floggers and the like, but I might want to tie you up sometimes."

"And do what exactly?"

"Eat you out until you are so wet I could ride your ass with just the juices from your pussy."

She'd never had a man there, but she like the sound of having him eat her out. She liked when a man did some of those things to her. Not that she'd had a lot of men in her past, but it sounded good. The few romance novels she'd read with BDSM in turned her inside out. She just wished she knew where this was going. They couldn't have much of a relationship with her living in Houston and his life being all about the ranch. It's a drivable distance, but not convenient for last minute sex.

"I said take off your clothes."

She stood, unbuttoned her shirt and let it fall to the floor behind her. The bra came next. She wanted to be sexy for him, but she felt inadequate and fat. After she unhooked her bra, she let the straps slid down her arms, but held it to her breasts.

"I want to see."

"But I have stretch marks."

"Why?"

"I weighed a lot more a few years ago. I topped the scale at over two hundred pounds. My skin stretched to accommodate."

"I love how you look. I'm not into skinny woman. You've got curves. I love curves on my women."

"Am I your woman?"

"For now, yes."

"I guess it's all I can hope for, huh?"

"You know where I stand on this, Terri. We've talked about it."

"I know. A girl can wish, right?"

"Don't fall in love with me. I don't want to break your heart."

Too late. She sniffed back the burning of tears. *I already do.*

Chapter Ten

The moment she stood naked in front of him, she heard him take in a ragged breath.

"Damn, you're beautiful."

"Thanks."

"I mean it." He stood so he could move closer. With his palms, he cupped both of her breasts in his hands as if he wanted to cherish them. He stepped closer and took one turgid nipple into his mouth.

A soft moan broke from her mouth at the suction of his lips. *God, I love when he sucks my nipples.* She threaded her fingers into his hair, pulling his mouth closer still. His fingers rolled her other nipple while he sucked the first one until her clit throbbed with the beat of her heart. When his hand left her breast to trail down her stomach, she brought her bottom lip between her teeth and bit down to keep from screaming *touch me.* She spread her thighs. His fingers slipped over her mound and between her legs. She whimpered in need.

The tip of his finger grazed over her clit, tearing a tortured groan from her lips. "Yes."

"On your back on the bed."

Her legs wobbled as she moved to comply. She wanted this…wanted him. "You do have condoms, right?"

"As in more than one, yep."

"Thank God." She lay full out on the bed with her head near the top. She didn't bother to remove the covers.

He laughed. "Greedy wench."

"You bet when it comes to you."

"I'm glad. I'm feelin' kind of greedy myself tonight."

"Can I suck you?"

"Not now. We need to take the edge off first. I'm about to blow. I probably will the moment I get inside your hot little pussy."

"I need you, Jeff. Please."

"I need to do somethin' first, darlin'. I want to taste you."

She spread her thighs as he moved to settle himself between them. The first swipe of his tongue had her hips coming up off the bed.

"Easy, darlin'."

"God, Jeff."

Her pussy felt on fire. She wanted him to hurry, but on the other hand, she needed him to take his time. She wanted to come. Not too fast, not too slow. It was torture, pure unadulterated torture.

Within seconds, she felt heat crawl up her legs and explode in her pelvis, tearing a muffled scream from her throat.

"Nice save, babe."

Sweat beaded on her upper lip. *Yeah, that's sexy.*

He moved over her and took her mouth with his in a deep, penetrating kiss.

"You still have your clothes on," she murmured when they broke apart for air.

"I sure do. Now I want you to undress me."

"Can I lick and touch?"

"All you want, darlin'." He stood up in the middle of the room with his hands at his sides, just waiting.

She got to her feet and stopped in front of him to admire the view. His wide chest tapered to trim hips. He always seemed so cleaned and pressed when she saw him. With all of the work he did on the ranch, he never seemed to have a hair out of place. She wanted to ruffle him up.

She let her lips skim over his jawline as her hands unbuttoned each button on the front of his shirt, very slowly. When she reached the bottom, she pulled the material from the waistband of his jeans, letting it flutter to a rest at his waist. "I love how you taste."

He groaned and she smiled against his skin. Torture would be sweet tonight.

The five o'clock shadow of a beard on his jaw tickled her tongue as she ran it over his skin.

He lifted his hands to touch her, but she swatted them away. "No touching. It's my turn." They dropped back to his sides, but he clenched his hands into fists.

With the shirt loose, she pushed it off his shoulders to reveal the breadth of his chest. No doubt about it, the man was built. Hefting hay all day sure built muscles upon muscles on his gorgeous chest. His arms bulged when she ran her hands down his biceps to push the shirt to the floor. "I love your chest."

She reached for his belt buckle, fully aware of the ridged cock beneath her fingers. She ran her fingernail down the outside of his jeans over his cock, dragging another groan from his lips.

"You're gonna pay for torturing me, darlin'."

She loved when he called her that. It made her feel special…his.

"Oh, I think you love it, cowboy."

"I do, but you're killin' me."

When she had his pants undone, she pushed them as well as his boxer briefs to the floor at his feet. He'd kicked off his boots while they'd watched the movie with Ben, so they didn't have those to deter them now.

He stepped out of his clothes, pushing them to the side with his foot. She loved him with her hands and her mouth, licking, sucking and trailing her lips from his ear, over his collarbone to his nipples. The ridged tips called to her. She flicked them with her tongue, bringing them to hard points of flesh.

Her next move was to drop to her knees and run her tongue from his balls to the tip of his cock.

"Just your mouth. No hands."

She put her hands behind her back, determined to suck him until he exploded in her mouth. The head of his cock was soft. The whole thing was soft skin over hardened steel. She couldn't believe he'd had the entire length inside her more than once. The man wasn't small by any means.

With as much finesse as she could without the use of her hands, she ran her tongue around the head, up and down his shaft, licked his balls and literally made love to his cock with her mouth.

"Enough."

She shook her head as she sucked hard.

"I'm gonna come in your mouth then."

She nodded quickly running her tongue around the head again before she sucked the majority of his length into her mouth.

"Fuck!"

The warm, salty taste of his cum wasn't unpleasant as it shot to the back of her throat. She swallowed every bit until his legs wobbled and he pulled himself from her mouth to collapse on the bed.

"You didn't have to do that, darlin'."

"I wanted to."

"Thank you," he said, taking her face between his hands and kissing her. "Give me a minute to recuperate and I'll take care of you again."

"Take care of both of us."

"Yeah."

She sat next to him on the bed before she scooted up to rest against the headboard. He followed her up to sit next to her, pulling her against his chest. He kissed her on the forehead much like she'd done with Ben.

Did he care for her at all? She wasn't sure. Sometimes he seemed to let her in and then he'd shut himself off from her like he was afraid to care. He said he didn't have a heart left to give anyone. He was wrong. She just knew he had it in him to love someone, she wasn't sure it would be her though, especially when he found out what she'd done after she talked to Jeremiah.

* * * *

It didn't take any time at all for him to be hard again. He had it so bad for her. Sex though, it was only sex. He couldn't think of anything else. Going beyond that wasn't an option. Not now, not ever.

"Ready so fast, cowboy?"

"You bet, city girl."

"I told you, I'm not a city girl."

"Honey, from the minute I saw you, your clothes screamed city girl from the tips of your brand new boots to those designer jeans."

She laughed. "I was tryin' to blend in."

"Not like that you weren't."

"Not so much, eh?"

"Do you even own any other boots?"

"No."

"You would have blended in better if you would have worn your power suit."

"Power suit?"

"I assume you own one." He glanced down at her confused face. "You know, tight skirt, white silk blouse, blazer jacket, and fuck me pumps."

She sputtered in indignation.

"You do have one."

"Of course, I do, but I don't call it my power suit."

"I'd like to see you in only those shoes." He moved sideways and slid down in the bed, taking her with him. "I want to be inside you."

"You need a condom first."

"No problem, darlin'." He reached over to the nightstand, grabbed a condom and rolled it on in two seconds flat. "Ready for me?"

"More than ready."

He moved between her legs, rubbing the head of his cock on her clit.

"Wait."

"Wait? Why?"

"I want to do something." He moved off her and stood on the side of the bed. "Come with me." He held out his hand until she got to her feet. Once she was standing beside him, he lifted her so she had to wrap her legs around his hips. With his cock poised at her pussy, he waited for the perfect moment to slide home. He moved so her back was against the wall. "Now, this is fuckin' awesome."

"Oh shit," she growled low in her throat as he pushed his cock into her hot pussy. "Oh, God!"

He pulled her legs up so they lay across his forearms, giving him more leverage and deeper penetration. It was his turn for his eyes to roll in the back of his head. The heat of her pussy beckoned with each thrust. He could feel each scrape of her G spot along the head of his cock, dragging every moan from his mouth. He wouldn't last long like this. Each stroke of his cock threatened to end their erotic dance too quickly. He wanted this to last, wanted to bring her along for the ride.

"You need to come, darlin'."

"I can't. I need a little more…" Her words trailed off into a moan.

He pistoned his hips in sharp, jabbing thrusts, bringing them both to the brink in seconds. "Come with me."

Her high scream was smothered by his mouth as they both came apart together.

His legs wobbled, unable to hold them. He released her legs, pulled out his cock, and let her slide down his body so they could both catch their breath without falling down into a heap of melted bone and muscle on the floor. He'd never come so hard in his life.

They stumbled back to the bed, collapsing on the coverlet in a heap. "Wow."

"Yeah, you can say that again."

"Wow."

She laughed and shook her head. "You're impossible."

"But, wow."

"I get it."

They laughed together for a moment before he disposed of the condom in a trashcan near the bed. "Do you want to watch a movie for a while?"

"Sure. What kind of movies do you have besides Toy Story?"

"Some action flicks and maybe a few chick flicks too."

"Can I pick?"

He pulled her down on the bed with him. "Sure, but let's lie here for a bit before we rush off to watch a movie." He ran his fingers down her arm. "I kind of like having you here next to me."

"Do you want me to stay until morning?"

"If you want to. I won't push, but I enjoyed waking up next to you the other day even if it wasn't planned."

"As you exploded in a panic that your family would find out about us sleeping together and have a cow."

"You don't understand. We have a rule about sleeping with the guests. I can't very well enforce it if I'm doin' it."

"I think it's a silly rule."

"You would." He wet his finger before rubbing it around her nipple.

Goose bumps rose on her chest as her nipple hardened into a small nub. "You keep that up and we won't be watching any movie, at least not for a little while yet."

He palmed her breast. "Fine by me. I like fuckin' you."

"I got that impression, yes, which is a good thing since I like it too."

Concern crossed his mind. He needed to ask her some questions. Her information digging had both him and his dad troubled. "We need to talk."

The look on her face told him she was confused again. "Uh-oh. About what?"

"Why are you askin' so many questions about the ranch?"

"I told you. I'm curious."

"Curious doesn't explain wanting to know the financial stuff. Curious might describe wanting to know what kind of horses we have."

"It's nothing, Jeff."

"I don't know whether to trust you or not."

She bit her lip. A sure sign of nervousness. "You're sleeping with me, but you don't trust me?"

"You do work for the enemy."

"Only in the sense that I'm gathering information for them on the area."

"Are you sure you aren't giving them any other information on us?" She glanced away. "Terri?"

"I haven't told them anything."

"Why does it sound like there's a *but* in there?"

"No but." She rolled away from him and sat up on the side of the bed. "I thought we were going to watch a movie."

"I thought we were gonna make love…I mean have sex again?" *Great, dumbass! What a stupid thing to say.*

Fluffing her hair with her fingers gave away more of her nervousness. Why did she seem upset by the questioning? *Damn it. I should never have started this.*

He rolled off the side of the bed and grabbed his pants. One foot in, then the other. He needed to keep his mind off where his thoughts were headed right now. Trust came hard for him and right now she wasn't doing anything to cement his trust in her. "Terri?"

"I can't talk about it, Jeff. Please don't ask me to."

"You've told me you were gathering information on the area. Like what?" he asked, sitting down on the side of the bed next to her.

One of his old T-shirts now graced her shoulders, covering up her tempting body. Her scent drifted to his nose from her hair. *Damn, she smells good.*

"Information on the soil, water, those kinds of things. Nothing special."

"What does our financial stuff have to do with that?"

She jumped to her feet. "Nothing. All right. I was curious. That's it!"

"I don't believe you."

"No shit!"

She threw off his T-shirt and pulled her clothes on.

"Where are you goin'?"

"Back to my cabin. Obviously you don't trust me and you don't believe me. I can't be with a man who thinks I'm totally up to no good."

"If you aren't up to something, why are you so defensive?" he asked, coming to his feet too. Something wasn't right here.

"Fine. I'm telling them every fucking thing I can find out about your family. Your financial situation, everything!"

"Why?"

"Because they want to buy you out!" She pushed her fingers through her hair. "Hell if I know, Jeff. I'm an architect. I'm not a damn financial wizard. They want information on you. I've been gathering it, but I'm not sure I'm giving it to them."

"You're plannin' on betraying my family?"

"I'm not planning anything. Some of the things I've found on the area lead me to believe things aren't as they seem."

Anger zipped through him. "I think you need to leave."

"I am!" She shoved her feet back into the shoes she'd worn to the house.

"Leave my family alone. I want you off the ranch tomorrow morning."

"I'll leave when I'm damned good and ready."

"You aren't welcome here anymore."

"I have a job to do."

"Do it from someone else's ranch."

"Fuck you! I'll do what I need to do. Plus, I've paid for the time to stay here. If you don't like it, too bad. Talk to your mother."

"I will!"

She stomped out to the living room, grabbing her purse from the couch on her way by.

The door slammed on her way out and he raked his fingers through his hair. *What the hell just happened?*

His cell phone jingled on the counter where he'd left his keys. "What?"

"Tell your family their done in the Hill Country."

The phone clicked in his ear.

"Great. Now I'm getting threatening phone calls too? Jesus."

He grabbed a beer from the refrigerator and down half of it in several long gulps. Trust. *Damn, it's a two edge sword.* He learned not to trust a woman when Misha stabbed him in the back. Now Terri. He'd really begun to think she was different than any other woman he'd known, but apparently not. She used him to get close to his family, just like Misha.

What the fuck? Why do I keep running into these bitches out to use the hell out of me?

Chapter Eleven

Terri walked into the diner in town through the tinkling glass door. The '50s décor was a welcome change after everything cowboy the last few days. The checkered tablecloths gracing each of the tables with vinyl and metal chairs at each one seemed almost quaint.

After she'd left Jeff the night before, she'd received a phone call from the partners demanding to meet her today. Up until now, she hadn't decided whether she was going to give them the information she'd gathered or not.

She took a seat in one of the booths. The vinyl seat felt cool against her back and legs.

"Hi there, sweetie. What can I get you to drink?"

"Coffee, please, Ann."

"Coming right up." Ann stayed for a minute as she tilted her head to the side. "Where's Jeff?"

Terri frowned. "Working I guess. I really don't know."

"Oh, I'm sorry. I thought you two were friends from what Nina told me."

"We were, but things have changed a bit with our friendship. He doesn't want to see me anymore."

"Now, that seems just like Jeffery. Stupid cuss."

"Can I get that coffee, please?"

"Oh sure, honey. Sorry." Ann shuffled off but came back a moment later with the coffee pot and a mug. "Do ya need cream?"

"Yes, please."

"What would you like to eat?"

"Just coffee for now. I'm meeting someone."

Ann nodded. "Okay. Just holler when you're ready."

"Thank you."

When Ann had walked away, Terri looked at the door to the diner with trepidation. She didn't want to do this anymore. Betraying Jeff and his family left a bad taste in her mouth, but what else was she supposed to do? If she told the developers the truth, they'd try to buy out the entire Hill Country. The information she gleaned from her research told her the piece of property next to Thunder Ridge would make a fine development property but if they tried to put in a golf course or something along those lines, they would have to divert a lot of the natural springs to keep the thing watered. She knew a course was part of the developers plan for their property.

One more thing she'd learned. Jeff's family had never had their property tested for oil. The soil samples she'd taken initially told her there was a possibility. She wanted to tell Jeff. She wanted his family to drill and see if there might be a rich oil deposit on their property, but he wouldn't talk to her now. Not after their blowup the night before.

"Terri?"

"Yes? Hi, Mr. Cole."

He held out his hand for her to shake.

"Hello," she said taking his hand. The sweaty palm grossed her out, making her shiver in revulsion.

"May I?"

"Of course."

Ann appeared seconds later. "Coffee?"

"Yes, please."

As soon as Ann departed again, she turned to the gentleman at the table with her. "I don't know why you wanted to meet this morning."

"We need a report."

"There's nothing to tell you other than the information I have on the area with the soil, water, etcetera."

"What about information on the family?"

"I don't have anything."

"Nothing? Surely you gleaned something from your time spent with the eldest son?"

"No."

"You mean you were fuck buddies with him and didn't learn anything?"

"Excuse me?"

"We know you've been getting cozy with Jeffery Young. Surely you gained some kind of information we can use?"

"The Young family is a stable part of this community. Leave them alone."

"We want that property, Terri, and you're going to help us get it."

"I'm not doing any such thing."

He tapped the spoon on the edge of the cup, grating on her nerves like fingernails on a chalkboard.

"Then the loan you took out to open your business comes due immediately."

"You can't do that! That's a quarter of a million dollar loan. I don't have that kind of money."

"I'm sorry, but it's your choice. Tell me what you know or the loan comes due today."

"There's nothing to tell."

"I find that hard to believe, my dear."

She shivered. The blackness of the man's eyes made her think of the devil, all he needed was a couple horns sprouting from his forehead. These men were cutthroat and now she was in their sights.

"I don't know anything. They've been very closed mouth about their family and their business. They haven't told me a single thing that would be helpful to you."

"Let us be the judge of that."

She inhaled sharply. What the hell could she tell him to get him to leave her and Jeff's family alone? "They are very stable financially. They haven't been sued for any accidents or anything on their property. The cattle and the guests keep them in a good position." She bit her lips. "There is something."

"What?"

"Some information I found out about the property itself. You can't build on it."

"What?" He slapped his hand down on the table, making her jump. "That's crazy. We've got plans. We've got investors. You're wrong!"

"I'm not wrong. Water rights are held by the Young family for the property you want to build on. All of the natural springs run through their property."

"We'll ruin them so they'll have to sell."

Think quickly.

"I've also checked with the local zoning codes. The area isn't zoned for a development."

"We've already talked to the zoning committee about changing the zoning."

His self-righteous smirk made her want to slap it off his lips.

Her cell phone buzzed. "I need to check this." The report she'd been waiting for popped up on her screen. *Thank you God!* "I just received a report I've been waiting for. You can't build on the property you already own because it's a natural habitat for a rare bird. It's now been classified as a wildlife refuge."

"No fucking way."

"Yes, way." She turned the cell around so he could see it. "I spotted the bird when I was out riding with my 'fuck buddy' as you called him. I wasn't sure until now."

"We'll move the damned bird."

"You can't. The paperwork is being processed as we speak to reclassify the property. There's nothing you can do to stop it."

He jumped to his feet, pointing one finger at her. "You've done this!"

She raised an eyebrow, but managed not to grin.

"You're going to be ruined. I'll see to it myself."

"Do your best. I didn't do anything wrong. I'm just doing my job, but you know what? If it means keeping you from ruining a nice family's livelihood and kicking them off property that has been in their family for a long time, then so be it."

Ann stepped to the side of the table. "You need to leave, sir. Your coffee is on the house."

"You can't kick me out of this establishment."

"Oh, yes I can. I own this diner and I don't want your kind here. Good day, sir."

Mr. Cole sputtered a few obscenities under his breath, grabbed his briefcase from the bench and then stomped like a two year old throwing a tantrum as he left the diner.

"Thank you, Ann."

"You're welcome, honey." She slid into the booth seat. "Tell me what's going on between you and my nephew?"

"Nothing really."

"I think there is."

She ran her finger around the rim of her coffee cup as she stared at the brown liquid hoping for some answers. "It doesn't matter."

Ann patted her hand. "What you've done for the family matters. You can bet Nina and James will hear of this because I'll be sure to tell them."

She focused on the friendly face of the waitress across from her. "Please don't. I didn't do anything."

"Yes, you did. You saved their place from those vultures. They have the money and the resources to close Thunder Ridge should they decide to."

Her heart rate slowed now since Mr. Cole had left, leaving her feeling relieved but anxious at the same time. Would he come back? Would they be able to change the mind of the wildlife committee with enough money greasing palms? She hoped not, but this might not be over yet. "Luck was on their side. If I hadn't spotted the bird, things would have not gone as well."

"I heard what you said to him. You were trying to stall hoping for this news from the wildlife people, weren't you?"

"Yes. I tried everything I could come up with to make him think they wouldn't be able to build on the property. I knew the report would come through this morning, but I didn't know when."

"God watches out for us in mysterious ways at times."

"Yes, he does."

Ann's gaze narrowed. "What did you and Jeffery fight over?"

"All of this." She waved her hand indicating the entire situation. "He knew I worked for the developers and that I was asking a lot of questions. I needed the information from his family. Originally, the developers wanted me to find out something to ruin them, but I couldn't do it. Never mind my feelings for Jeff. I just couldn't see doing anything to hurt such nice people." She took a sip of her coffee, now gone cold. "I hate cold coffee."

"Let me warm it up for you." Ann took the cup and returned a moment later with a fresh one.

"Thank you."

"Now, go on."

"Nina, James…everyone has been so nice to me. Even Jeremiah gave me the information I needed to be able to bluff Mr. Cole with until the report came through, but I couldn't tell Jeff what I was up to. He thinks I got the information to give to the developers."

"Which he was correct in a way."

"True, but I couldn't tell him the real reason behind my need for the information. I wasn't sure the wildlife committee would come through."

"So tell him now."

"He won't talk to me." She sipped her coffee. "Besides, he doesn't trust me now."

"His ex-wife took care of the trust thing."

"Yes, she did."

Ann tapped her fingers on her lips. "I think he'll come around when he finds out what you've done."

"It doesn't matter. I'm going home to Houston today. My work here is done. I have to make sure Mr. Cole's threat is nothing more than a threat. He could kill my business if he forces those I borrowed the funds to start my business from into making my loan come due. I don't have a quarter of a million dollars to pay them off."

"Don't worry, honey. Everythin' will work itself out."

She squeezed Ann's hand. "Thank you for listening. I think I'll take breakfast now."

"Good. What can I get you?"

After she ordered a ham and cheese omelet, she sat back in the booth with a satisfied smile on her face. She'd done a good deed. It felt wonderful to her heart even as the organ broke inside her chest. Somehow during the time on the ranch, she'd come to care for the enigma of a man who wouldn't open his heart to her no matter how much she tried or what she said. He wouldn't trust her now because of her deceit.

As the bell dinged over the door, she glanced up. Nina Young strolled in and took a seat across from her.

"What's this I hear you're leaving for home today? You still have a good few days left at the ranch."

"Hello to you too, Nina." She laughed.

"I'm not into niceties when my eldest son's heart is involved."

Terri shook her head and glanced over at Ann. "She works fast."

"Yes, she does. Good thing I was already in town at the bank and courthouse dealing with Jeff's ex this morning when she called."

Ann placed a cup of coffee in front of Nina and Terri's plate in front of her. The food look fabulous as her stomach rumbled in earnest.

"Go ahead and eat while we talk."

"You mean while you talk?"

"Yes." Nina smiled. "I like you, Terri. I like what you do for Jeff. He needs someone like you in his life."

"He doesn't want me in his life. He's told me as much."

"He doesn't know what he needs or wants."

"And you do?"

"Yes. Ann told me what you did for us. I want to tell Jeff."

"Please don't."

"He needs to know he can trust you. You saved our ranch."

"He can't trust me. He knew all along what I was doing and he chose to believe the worst in me…in all women."

"Damn his ex-wife."

"She did a number on him, yes, but it doesn't explain everything."

"You've heard she left him on their wedding night to party with her friends and didn't return for two days?"

Terri nodded as she took another bite of her omelet.

"Well the part most people don't know except me and his father is that he found her with another man."

"Seriously?"

"Two days into their marriage, she cheated on him. In fact, at first we didn't know whether Ben was Jeff's or someone else's. Why he didn't leave her ass the minute he caught her cheating, I don't know except he was in love with her."

"He's a lot more patient and loving than any man I've known."

"You know he loves you, right?"

Her stomach flipped over. "No he doesn't."

"He's been nothing but a bear this morning. Slamming things. Cussing up a storm. When I asked him what was wrong, he told me you were gone and you weren't coming back." She shook her head. "The sadness in his eyes tore at my heart. Yes, he's angry because he feels like you betrayed him and us, but we both know you didn't. He needs to know the details of what happened so he can realize his feelings for you are genuine."

"I don't want him to know."

"You don't care about him?"

"I care too much for him."

"I don't think anyone can care too much."

Terri shook her head and glanced down at her plate. "Please, Nina. Let it go."

"All right. I will because you've asked me to, but I think you're making a big mistake."

"It wouldn't be the first time." She finished her meal and pushed the plate out of the way. "I'll be leaving for home in a couple of hours. I'll be back to the ranch to get my stuff."

"I wish you would talk to Jeff."

"I know, but it's not meant to be."

The bell tinkled as another couple came in. "Hey, Ma!"

"Oh my. I didn't realize you two were coming back today!" Nina stood and hugged them both before she turned around to face Terri again. "Terri, this is my son Joel and his new bride Mesa. They just returned from their honeymoon."

"It's nice to meet you." She noticed immediately the blue eyes and identical features to Jason and Joshua. "So you're the third in the triplets."

"Yeah." Joel laughed before he put his arm around the cute woman next to him. The love they shared shone bright in both their gazes.

"I've met everyone on the ranch but you."

"You're staying on the ranch?"

"Only until this afternoon. I'm headed home to Houston."

"Too bad. I would have like to get to know you," Mesa added.

Ann walked up and kissed both of them on the cheek. "Aren't they so cute together?"

"Stop, Ann." The crimson coloring staining Joel's cheeks made Terri laugh.

"I'm trying to convince her to stay longer. She's been seeing Jeff."

"What?" Joel's face registered his shock with wide eyes and an open mouth. "Jeff? I didn't think he liked women anymore."

"Well he likes Terri or did until last night. They had a fight."

"It wasn't really a fight, Nina."

"A misunderstanding then."

"You should stick around and try to work things out," Mesa said. "He's really not a bad guy once you get to know him."

"I think she knows him pretty well."

"Ah." Mesa smiled a knowing little grin.

Heat rose in Terri's cheeks.

"Well, we're heading home." Joel took Mesa's hand. "We just happened to see the ranch truck here on our way back from the airport."

"I'll see you at home then." Nina stood and grabbed Terri's check as Mesa and Joel waved goodbye. "Breakfast is on me."

"No, it's not. I've got it."

"Nonsense. I ruined your breakfast with talk so I'll pay for it. Ann, is that her total?" She shoved a twenty dollar bill at Ann along with the ticket.

"Thank you. You really didn't have to buy my meal."

"It's the least I can do. I'll see you back at the ranch too." She hugged Terri. "Think about what I said, honey. He does love you and I think you love him too, but you two have some talking to do."

"I will."

Nina left with a wave of her hand as the bell tinkled on the door.

Terri felt lost. She'd become such a part of the family and life on the ranch in the several days she'd spent there, she didn't want to leave. She finished her coffee and stood. No time like the present. Getting her stuff and hitting the road sounded like a great idea, although the possibility of running into Jeff soured her stomach. She didn't want to deal with him and the hateful looks he'd be giving her, but it wasn't to be helped. Hopefully he'd be busy and wouldn't even know she'd been there and gone.

"Thanks for everything, Ann. You've been a great help."

"You're welcome, sweetie. I hope you and Jeff work things out."

"I don't think we will, but thank you for the sentiment."

Terri grabbed her purse and headed for the door. *Might as well get this over with.*

Chapter Twelve

Terri inhaled on a sigh as she drove through the gate of the ranch. Longhorns grazed in the distance to the left in the open area. Birds flocked from one of the juniper trees as she drove by, clouding the sky with their mass. Gravel crunched under the tires of her car. The sunlight filtered through the puffy white clouds overhead. The main lodge house came into view along with the small cabins to the right, which included hers. Her little home away from home. She closed her eyes for a moment hoping the burn of tears would go away before she had to face packing her stuff for the trip back to Houston. The big city didn't feel like home anymore. The slow pace of life here on the ranch felt more like family than anything she'd ever experienced.

When she opened her eyes she caught movement by the barn. A cowboy stood leaning against the doorframe with his arms crossed over his chest and a black cowboy hat shading his eyes. Jeff. *Damn.* She'd really hoped she wouldn't see him, but it was almost as if he'd been waiting for her to show up, watching for her car or something.

The ache in her chest made her rub the spot over her sternum. She hoped she wasn't having a heart attack or something. *Yeah, more like heartache.*

He didn't move. Just stood there watching with lips firmed in a straight line. She couldn't see his eyes, but the slash of his lips told her he wasn't happy.

She stepped from her car, slamming the door behind her firmly. This wouldn't take long, she hoped, and she'd be on her way back to her life.

With her back ramrod straight, she headed for the front of the cabin, keeping an eye on the man in her peripheral vision. He never moved. She couldn't even tell if he blinked. The concentration on his face never changed.

She opened the door to her cabin to glance inside. Nothing had changed. Her clothes still hung in the small closet. Her suitcase still sat open on the dresser waiting for her to put her clothes in it. Her computer sat on the desk right where she'd left it when she'd sent the report off to the wildlife committee the day before.

Jeff had changed her life irrevocably, but still life went on. How she would move on without him, she wasn't sure, but she had to. He didn't want her. The trust was gone and if she learned one thing about Jeffery Young, when you lost his trust, you lost everything.

She exhaled sharply as she shut the door. Tears formed, burning her eyelids as they trickled down her face. She would miss this place. Maybe someday she would come back for a visit, but then again no. Seeing him again would tear out her heart.

A knock sounded on the door. Did she dare answer it? Jeff? She hoped not. She didn't think she could face him right now. She bit her lip as the knock sounded again.

"I know you're in there, Terri. Open the door."

It was him.

"Leave me alone, Jeff. Haven't you done enough?"

"I want to talk to you."

"You made it perfectly clear we were done last night."

"Open the door or I'll bust it down."

"Fine." She grumbled under her breath about stubborn-ass men as she opened the door. *Damn it.* He looked almost good enough to eat in his cowboy finery. He made even dirty boots and jeans look damn good. "What do you want?"

He pushed his way inside the room and closed the door. "You're leaving?"

She looked at him like he'd lost his mind. "Of course, I'm leaving. You told me to. My work here is done. The developers got their report."

"And?"

"And what?"

"What are they planning to do with it?"

Apparently Nina hadn't told him…yet. Terri paced the room, hoping for something, but she didn't know what. Did he want her to stay? Did he really love her like Nina suggested? His words sounded clipped and fraught with anger. "I don't know. They weren't happy with my results. I'm sure they plan on getting another opinion, but it won't matter. Things won't change."

"What did you tell them?"

"I can't divulge my findings."

"So this is it?"

"This is what, Jeff? What are you asking me? Last night you said you wanted me gone. I'm going. What else is there?"

"Nothin' I guess."

"Exactly. There's nothing between us. There's nothing left to say."

"I guess this is goodbye then."

"Yeah." She wiped her face, not realizing tears still streaked her cheeks until his eyes narrowed. "Tell Ben goodbye for me."

"I will."

"He's a great kid, Jeff. Take care of him."

"I will."

"I hope things work out with Misha. It would be great if she would disappear from his life, but I have a feeling you'll be dealing with her for the rest of yours."

"You didn't hear?"

"Hear what?"

"The paramedics found her dead in her house this morning. The initial diagnosis was cardiac arrest from overdose."

"Wow, really?"

"Yeah. I haven't told Ben yet. I'm not sure how to tell him."

"Just be up front with him. I'm sure he'll miss her."

"Yeah. I never wished her dead even though she was a pain in my ass."

Terri stepped toward him and wrapped her arms around his neck. She needed to feel his heat one more time before she walked out of his life forever. Jeff returned the hug. They stood that way for several minutes as she fought the return of her tears. "Give him a hug for me," she whispered.

"I will."

She closed her eyes and inhaled his scent. Musk, man and horse. She'd never be able to be around livestock again without thinking of him. "I guess this is goodbye."

"Yeah, I guess so."

She stepped out of his arms and said, "Thanks for everything and I hope things work out for the best with the land next door."

"I hope so too."

"Just know I did my best."

He tilted his head to the side with a look of confusion clouding his eyes, but he didn't linger. His boots sounded hollow on the tile floor beneath his feet as he approached the door. With a quick look behind him, he returned the sunglasses to his eyes and disappeared with a soft click of the panel behind him.

* * * *

Jeff watched from the barn as Terri loaded her suitcase into the car. He wouldn't ask her to stay. He couldn't. His trust in her had been broken by the secrets and lies she'd told even though his heart said they didn't matter.

"You're an idiot, son."

"Thanks, Mom."

Nina stood next to him watching Terri slide into her car and shut the door. The car started a few minutes before she backed out and slowly disappeared down the gravel drive. They continued to watch together until her car disappeared from sight.

"Have you told Ben about Misha yet?"

"No. I need to, but I'm not sure how."

"Just tell him the truth, Jeff."

"What is the truth, Mom? She didn't love him. Not like a mother should."

"I wouldn't tell him she overdosed on drugs since we don't exactly know what the cause of death is."

"There's no denying it from what I heard from the paramedics. They found Meth crystals and needles at her apartment. I'm sorry I didn't notice track marks before or the fact that she seemed wired every time I saw her."

"It explains her manic behavior when she showed up here earlier and her demand for money."

"Yeah, it does."

"Jeffery?"

"Yeah, Mom?"

"Why did you let Terri leave?"

"What do you mean?"

"You're in love with her, aren't you?"

He pushed his hat back on his head. "No."

"Yes you are, son. I can see it in your eyes."

"Even through the sunglasses?"

"Jeffery."

"It doesn't matter, Mom. I can't trust her and without trust, there's nothin'."

"Why do you say that?"

"Hello?" He looked at his mom like she had two heads. "How can you ask something like that? After what Misha pulled and knowing Terri was working for the developers while they tried to put us out of business?"

"But in the long run, she didn't, right?"

"I don't know, Mom. We don't know what they're gonna do. They might still succeed with their plans. Terri wouldn't tell me what she told them in her report. It was like she didn't trust me."

"Now there's a turn of the cards. A woman not trust you?"

"You aren't funny."

His mom brushed her fingers from his cheek to his ear like she used to do when he was little. The soothing motion calmed his heart some. He knew he would always have the love of his family to fall back on and now he didn't have to worry about Misha trying to take their son from him ever again. Was it wrong to be glad she was dead? Maybe. He'd have to have a chat with God tonight on his knees to beg for forgiveness.

"Honey, you're in love with her. Why don't you admit it?"

"In love with who?"

"Terri."

"Because it doesn't matter what I feel for her. She betrayed me."

She exhaled through her mouth in a heavy sigh. "I wish I knew what to say to make you see she's the right girl for you."

"She might have been, but we'll never know now." He pulled his hat from his head and raked his fingers through his hair. "I guess I'm destined to live alone."

The lunch bell clanged calling them inside. "We need to talk more after lunch. I have something to tell you I think might make a difference and maybe even make you go after her."

He frowned wondering what his mother might have to tell him. What could possibly change his mind concerning Terri? "Why don't you tell me now?"

Nina patted his cheek with her hand. "Because I want to give the girl a head start and give you the time to come to the same conclusion the rest of the family already has. You're very much in love with her, but you can't see past the hurt in your heart to see the wonderful woman she truly is."

His mother turned to head for the main lodge with him bringing up the rear with slow, steady footsteps. *What am I supposed to think? Obviously Mom knows something Terri's done that might redeem her in my eyes, but I can't possibly think what.*

Lunch would be a noisy affair. The ranch was busy this week with guests. Every cabin had a family or a group in it. *All but Terri's now.*

Jeff detoured toward her cabin. The door was unlocked so he slowly pushed it open. The room smelled like her. Her soft scent enveloped him bringing his thoughts back to the night they'd made love in this room. She'd given herself to him without reservation. Took everything he'd dished out with a relish few women he'd known could. It felt right. She felt right.

His heart lay tattered in pieces in his chest. She'd come and gone taking it with her as she drove down the driveway on her way back to Houston. Did she feel anything for him? He didn't know. Could she? Possibly. She cared for Ben. He was certain of that fact.

Would she give him another chance if he asked? Could he put his heart out there like that again hoping she wouldn't betray him like Misha?

What he wanted from Terri went beyond what he thought he'd felt for Misha. He'd never loved Misha like this.

Terri had his heart in the palm of her hand.

I love her.

The thought brought a smile to his mouth. He loved her. His heart felt lighter than it had in three years.

He spun around and headed for the main lodge. Going after her would be the right thing to do. He would convince her he loved her and wanted her to come back to Thunder Ridge with him if it was the last thing he ever did.

The big heavy door on the side of the building gave way to his insistent push. The crowd grew quiet as he walked toward the family table. An expectancy hung in the air.

"I love her!"

"It's about damned time you figured it out," Jeremiah said with a laugh.

The whole room erupted into cheers.

"I'm glad you understand now, son," Nina said, patting the chair next to her for him to sit. "Eat lunch and then go after her. Bring her back here where she belongs."

Soon the crowd of guests had their fill of food and the family took their places to pile their own plates. Jeff sat down with his and Ben's.

"Daddy, did you ask Terri to be my new mom yet?"

"Not yet, buddy, but soon."

"But she left and didn't say goodbye."

"She told me to kiss you." He leaned over and kissed Ben's head. "And tell you she loved you, but she'd see you again soon."

"Yay!" Ben clapped his hands. "When?"

"Hopefully before the weekend, son."

"I'm glad you've come to your senses, Jeff," James added to the conversation.

"What did you want to tell me, Mom?"

"Terri saved the ranch."

"Huh?"

"She had a meeting with one of developers this morning. Because of the information she gathered, they won't be able to build on their land. It's now a wildlife refuge because of a rare bird she spotted. It's useless to them now."

"She what? Really?"

"Yeah. They won't bother us anymore."

"Why didn't she tell me?"

"Because she didn't want your love based on something she did to save the ranch, I imagine. You needed to come to the conclusion you loved her for herself. If you couldn't, then you didn't love her enough."

He turned to face his mother. He needed to understand some things about women and how they thought. Of course, it was probably too late for that. "So why tell me now?"

"You said you loved her. You've moved past the hurt Misha caused and found love again with someone who will love you with all of her heart."

"What if she doesn't love me? What if I drive all the way to Houston and she slams the door in my face?"

"Do you think that's the truth?"

"I'm not sure. She never said she loved me."

Nina patted his hand. "Son, until you confess your love for her, she'll hold her love inside her heart and only bring it out when she's alone and can cry without worrying about someone wondering what's wrong. Women do those kinds of things."

"I need to go now." He jumped to his feet. "I have to catch her before she gets home."

"Sit down and eat, Jeff. She doesn't have much of a head start on you. Besides," Nina's eyebrow rose over her left eye, "you'll need her address to get to her home, wrap her in your arms and never let her go."

Mom is probably right. She's been right about everything so far. He nodded at his mother, who gave him a sly grin. *I knew I should have paid more attention to her when I had the chance.*

Lunch couldn't be eaten fast enough for him while he contemplated what he would say to Terri when he caught her. Catch her he would whether it be somewhere along the way or once she got home. She'd have a good hour head start on him, but he'd catch her one way or another.

The moment he finished eating, he grabbed his plate and set it in the dirty dish bin. "I'm going now."

"Go get 'er Jeff," Joel said from his spot next to Mesa. "I can vouch for the bein' in love thing."

"Shut up, Joel," Jonathan replied. "You're sappy in love."

"Just wait until he comes back with her. He'll be the same way."

"God, I hope not. Y'all are makin' me ill."

"You'll get your turn, Jonathan. Just wait."

"I need the address."

"Wait a second. I'll be right back." His mom disappeared for a minute before returning with a sticky note. "Here. Be careful."

"Watch Ben, please," Jeff asked his mom.

"Of course, son. We'll see you in a couple of days."

Jeff hurried out the door to the cheers of the crowd in the dining room. The smile spreading across his lips almost made his face hurt, but he was happy. For the first time in a long time, he was happy.

After jumping in his truck and turning the key for the third time, he knew he had a problem. It wouldn't start. His old reliable Chevy wouldn't start. *Fuck!* He banged his hand on the steering wheel before he pushed open the door and then slammed it shut again.

He raced for the lodge to borrow his parents' truck. *Damn it. I'm not letting her get away.*

When he hit the door, he almost ran into his mother coming out. "Problem?"

"I can't get my truck to start."

She pulled the keys to theirs from her pocket. "Go!"

"Thanks, Mom." He kissed her on the cheek before rushing around the edge of the building to where their truck sat.

Within seconds he tore down the gravel driveway silently asking for forgiveness at tearing up the rocks on his way out. He hit the gate opener on the visor above his head, early enough to watch the wrought iron metal swing just wide enough for the truck to get through.

The ride to Houston would take three plus hours. He had a lot of time on his hands to think about what he would say to her besides I love you. What did you say to a woman who thought you didn't trust her? I'm sorry would be a good starter, he figured. Then I love you. He shook his head. He needed to beg for her forgiveness. Tell her he trusted her and loved her with all his heart.

"Damn, this is getting sappier by the minute."

Flowers. Good idea.

He'd stop somewhere along the way to get a dozen roses. *Hell.* He didn't even know what flowers she liked, what her favorite color was or anything. What about her family? Did she have siblings? Were her parents still alive?

Doubts began to surface. How could he love someone he knew so little about? Yeah, they were good in bed together and they could learn more about each other over time, but what really did they have to build a relationship on?

"She loves Ben. There's a start. It's a hell of a lot more than Misha had and she gave birth to him." He sighed. "I'll learn about her. We can spend the next two days talkin'."

Yeah right.

"Okay, makin' love and then talkin'."

Before he knew it he was on the interstate headed for Houston singing along with the radio. His fingers tapped along with the beat while he wondered if she might have the radio on in her car. What if he called the station and dedicated a song to her? Would she hear it? Would she care?

He grabbed his cell phone from the clip on his belt and dialed. Luck seemed to be on his side when the DJ picked up.

"KJ Country what can I do for you?"

"Listen, man. I need a huge favor. I'm chasin' a girl down to tell her I love her and I want to see if you'll play a song in case she's listenin'."

"Sure, man. How about I record you and we'll get it over the airwaves in the next fifteen minutes."

"You are fantastic." He breathed in through his nose and out through his mouth. "Okay. I'm ready."

"I'll do a little intro and then I'll have you come on. What's your name, dude?"

"Jeff Young."

"All righty, Jeff. Ready?"

"Yeah."

"Well folks, we have a brokenhearted cowboy on the line wanting to dedicate a song to one special lady friend. Are ya there, Jeff?"

"Yes, sir."

"Go ahead, man."

"I want to send Cowboys and Angels out to Terri Kennedy. We had a bit of a misunderstanding and she's headed back home to Houston right now. Terri, baby, I love you and I don't care if I have to chase you across the map. I'm gonna find you and tell you in person how much I love you."

"Cool man. I hope you catch her."

"Thanks, bro. You're the best."

They clicked off the recording and the DJ came back on the line. "Thanks, Jeff. I hope you catch your lady friend."

"Oh, I will sooner or later, but thanks for running the song for me. She's my angel and I can't wait to hold her again."

"Good luck."

"Thanks."

Jeff clicked off the phone and waited during the longest fifteen minutes of his life for the song to come on. *Then what?*

When the DJ came on, he heard his voice as he held his breath.

Chapter Thirteen

Tears had long ago dried on her face during the drive toward home. She wouldn't cry anymore for him. *Damn him!* Falling in love with him was the stupidest thing she could have done, but alas, it happened and she would have to deal with it for the rest of her life. Maybe someday she would find someone to take his place. Somehow she wasn't so sure.

She inhaled a sharp, weary sigh and reached over to turn on the radio. Maybe a little music would help. "I hope they don't play a bunch of sappy love songs. I sure don't need those right now."

A few songs later she found herself tapping her fingers on the steering wheel in rhythm to Save a Horse, Ride a Cowboy. It wasn't a sappy song, but it still reminded her of Jeff.

Will everything remind me of him?

"Probably for a hell of a long time to come."

"Hey, folks. I have a special request from a lonely cowboy. He's got a plea for a special lady. Take a listen and I hope she hears this. We recorded this a few minutes ago."

Terri half listened as the DJ's recording came on.

"Well, folks, we have a brokenhearted cowboy on the line wanting to dedicate a song to one special lady friend. Are ya there, Jeff?"

"Yes, sir."

"Go ahead, man."

"I want to send Cowboys and Angels out to Terri Kennedy. We had a bit of a misunderstanding and she's headed back home to Houston right now. Terri, baby, I love you and I don't care if I have to chase you across the map. I'm gonna find you and tell you in person how much I love you."

"Cool man. I hope you catch her."

"Thanks, bro. You're the best."

Her heart pounded in her ears. Did she just hear what she thought she heard? Jeff on the radio saying he loved her?

She fumbled with her purse, trying to grab her cell phone without crashing her car. When she checked her phonebook, she cussed under her breath. She didn't have his number!

The DJ came back on. "Terri if you're listenin', darlin', give me a call here at the station. I want to find out what happens between you and Jeff. Of course, you can wait until you actually hook up with him somewhere along the highway." The guy rattled off the number as he laughed and then moved onto something else.

Her hands shook. She wasn't sure what to do as she continued to drive along at seventy miles an hour toward home. She couldn't call him. She could call the ranch and ask for his number. *Hmm.* What should she do? Call the station and hope he was still listening on his end of the radio dial? Should she wait until she got home? No, she couldn't do that. It would drive her nuts to wait that long.

She quickly dialed the radio station.

"KJ Country."

"I'm Terri Kennedy."

"Well hello, Terri Kennedy."

"Is this the DJ who talked to Jeff?"

"Yes, ma'am."

"I can't call him. I don't have his number."

"Where are you, darlin'?"

"On the interstate about an hour out of San Antonio. Can you do me a favor?"

"Sure, honey."

She glanced at the roadside sign as a plan formed in her head. "Get on the radio and tell Jeff to meet me in the parking lot of the Quickie Mart off the highway." She rattled off the exit number to the DJ, thanked him and hung up, then waited for him to come on the radio.

The exit came into view and she pulled her car off the highway to wait. *God, this wait is gonna kill me for sure.* If he just left San Antonio, it would be probably forty-five minutes before he would get off the exit and they would know whether what he said came from the heart or not.

The DJ came on the radio again and put her message out there for all of San Antonio to hear. She hoped Jeff heard it. *What if he didn't? What if he thought when I didn't call that I don't love him too or I don't care if he loves me? What about the trust thing? He probably still thinks I'm working for the developers and out to ruin him and his family. The financial information seemed to be a stickler for him, but all I wanted was information to make sure they were secure enough financially to fight the developers in court if need be.*

Terri sat in her car watching the off ramp for his beat up Chevy truck. The minutes ticked off slower than molasses in June. Every few minutes, she cursed the slow time.

Several cars, trucks, and big rigs got off the exit, but no Jeff.

"What the hell? Shouldn't he be here by now?"

A black dully pickup was the next one off the exit, coming at her like a bat out of hell. It drove straight for her car, almost looking like the driver didn't plan to stop until he ran over the hood of her car.

The driver stopped at her front bumper, but didn't exit the truck.

Terri held her breath. *Jeff doesn't drive a black truck.*

Her heart pounded in her ears as she waited.

The door opened and a guy in a black Stetson stepped out.

Her mouth went dry.

Jeff.

She opened her door and rushed around the doorframe straight into his arms.

The minute their lips met in a heart-melting kiss, a huge roar of applause erupted around them.

They broke apart long enough to see a hundred people surrounding them clapping and cheering.

Heat crawled up her neck and splashed across her cheeks in embarrassment. Apparently, all these people heard them on the radio as they hollered congratulations.

"Come back to the ranch with me."

"But…"

"But what? I'm guessin' you heard me on the radio."

"I did, but I want to hear it from you."

"I love you, Terri. You own my heart." He cupped her face. "We can work out the rest later."

"The rest?"

"Do you love me?" he asked, fear clear in his gray eyes.

She threw her arms around his neck and held on tight. "Yes. God, yes. I love you with all my heart."

"Good. Everything will work itself out then."

"I'm not sure I know what you mean."

He kissed her eyes, both cheeks and then pressed a quick one to her lips. "A few facts I realized I don't know about you is all, darlin'. I know enough to know I love you and want you in my life."

"And Ben?"

"He loves you. He already asked me when I was gonna ask you to be his new momma."

"I would love to be his new momma."

"We'll plan the rest later. Right now we need to find somewhere so I can love you like I want to."

"Why don't we wait until we get to my place? I have a great bed."

"You'll move home with me?"

Trepidation rushed through her. What if he still didn't trust her? "What about the trust thing?"

"Mom told me what you did for me…for the family. I still don't understand why you needed the financial information, but finding the rare bird was priceless. I would have loved to seen the developer's face when you told him his land was worthless to build on."

"I wanted to make sure your family was financially secure enough to fight them in court if need be. It could still go to court, Jeff, but the wildlife resource committee is on your side. The last thing they want is to have to try to relocate a rare bird's nesting ground for some home developers. The judge they got to sign the order declaring it a wildlife refuge is fully onboard with the whole thing. He knows the drill.”

“All thanks to you.”

“There are a few more things we need to talk about with your family’s property, Jeff. I found a few other things that might be of interest.”

He pressed his fingers to her lips. “Later, darlin’. Right now I want nothin’ more than to sink into your sweet heat and never come out, but we certainly can’t do that here in the parking lot of the Quickie Mart.”

A giggle left her lips. “You’re right, but how am I supposed to drive home knowing you’re behind me all hard and waiting?” She shifted her hips, brushing her pelvis against his erection. “All for me?”

He hissed as a low growl left his lips. “You’ll pay for torturing me.”

“Oh, I certainly hope so.”

* * * *

Terri groaned as she rolled over and opened her eyes. Sunlight poured through the blinds on her window. Jeff lay on his stomach next to her with his head buried in the pillow, snoring softly. They didn’t go to sleep for a long time after they reached her apartment. Loving a cowboy definitely had its perks.

The tattoo on his shoulder blade caught her attention. She’d seen it before, but the night he’d slept in her cabin, he’d been in such a rush to get out before anyone saw him, she hadn’t had a chance to examine it closely.

The dragon started on his shoulder blade and ended with its tail wrapped around his upper arm like a tribal tattoo. It suited him to a T. Ben’s name graced the arch of the dragon’s back. A tribute to the love this man had for his son. She slowly traced the nose of the dragon with her finger, loving the feel of his skin under her touch.

“You’re gonna make me hard again, you know,” he said, without opening his eyes.

The little quirk of his lips made her heart race. “I hope so.” She leaned over to kiss the tattoo. “I love how you have Ben’s name on your back.”

“He’s my life.” He rolled over and pulled her into his arms so her head rested on his chest. “Now, you’re my life too.”

“I know, Jeff.”

He kissed the top of her head as he trailed a fingertip down her arm. “You know. I don’t know much about you at all. Family? Where do your parents live?”

“South of Houston. Santa Fe actually.”

“Siblings?”

“One brother.”

“Will it be strange for you to be a part of such a big family?”

She laughed, propping herself up on her elbow to look into his eyes. "Are you kidding me? I've always wanted to have more brothers or sisters, but my mom got cervical cancer and had to have a complete hysterectomy."

"I hope she's okay now."

"She is. She's been cancer free for ten years. I count every day with her as a blessing."

"I bet."

She laid her head back on his chest.

"Where were you born?"

"Houston. I've lived there all my life. Santa Fe is just south of Houston."

"What's your favorite color?"

"Blue. What about you?"

"Green."

"You aren't saying that because my eyes are green, are you?"

"They are? I hadn't noticed."

She punched him in the side before he rolled her over onto her back and straddled her hips. She didn't even have time to blink. The scruff on his cheeks deliciously abraded her skin as he kissed her neck, across her shoulder and then scooted down to nuzzle her breast.

"I want your ass, Terri."

His lips on her nipple made her shiver. Goose bumps flittered across her body in a wave, from the top of her head to the tips of her toes. "Like smacking it or what?"

"No, I wanna fuck it." His words sounded muffled against the skin of her breast.

Her nipple hardened under the rough slide of his tongue. "Did you say you want to fuck it?"

He lifted his head as his eyes seemed to dance with the flame of need. "Yeah. Will you let me?"

"If you promise to make sure things are well lubed. I've never had a man there before."

"Sure, baby. I would never do anything to hurt you. I'll make sure you're so excited, you'll beg me."

She giggled. "Beg, huh?" Nerves wracked her body, but she trusted Jeff. She loved him so if he wanted to do her ass, she'd work with it.

"Oh yeah."

His hand slipped down her abdomen to play in the curls at the juncture of her thighs. "Open for me."

She spread her legs as she sighed her pleasure when his fingers pushed inside her pussy. *God, I love this man more than life itself.* "Please."

"Please what?"

"More."

He quickly spun around into a sixty-nine position before he slid his lips down her body, stopping momentarily to flick his tongue around her belly button before continuing down to bury his face between her thighs. She cupped his balls, rolling the hard little nuggets between her fingers. He moaned deep in his throat. The sound reverberated against her skin.

The rough pad of his tongue felt like heaven on her swollen, heated tissues. At the rate he was eating her out, she wouldn't last long before she came undone in a high scream loud enough to wake the neighbors. "God, Jeff."

He shoved two fingers deep inside her and pumped the digits until she felt her pussy clamp down on them. Her wail of ecstasy sounded primal with need. Never mind she'd already had this man twice the night before.

One finger spread the juices from her pussy to her ass. She shivered as he slowly pushed one finger past the ring of muscles. The intrusion burned slightly, but wasn't completely unpleasant. His tongue made a return trip to her clit, flicking the distended button back and forth until she felt on fire again.

"Easy, baby."

"Feels weird."

"Weird good or weird bad?"

"Good."

He pushed two fingers inside her ass as she hissed at the burn.

"You okay?"

"Yeah. Burns a little."

The slow crawl of his fingers soothed the ache, but also brought it higher at the same time. A different need took its place.

"Do you happen to have some lube around?"

"Yeah, in my nightstand. I needed it sometimes before. I kind of get dry."

"You ain't dry with me, sweetheart." He spread more of her juices around her clit. "You're soaking wet."

"Because you wind me up so much, I can't wait to get you inside me."

He removed his fingers and turned so he was positioned between her legs. She tensed up. "Easy, darlin'. We won't do anything without lube." He grabbed the tube from her drawer and placed it on the bed beside them. "I'm gonna fuck your pussy a little before we move on. I love to feel you squeeze me."

"Oh yeah." Her words came out in a soft purr as he pushed his length inside her. No condom. "Uh, Jeff?"

"Yeah, babe?"

"Did you forget a condom?"

"Do we need one?"

"I'm not on birth control. I haven't been active with anyone in a long time so I didn't need it. What if we get pregnant?"

"Do you want to?"

She smoothed his hair back from his forehead. "I've love to have a baby with you, but we haven't really talked about the future of this relationship yet."

"I want you with me."

"I know you do. I love you and I really believe you love me too, but what happens next?"

He shifted his hips. "Can we talk about this after we're done?"

"No." She moved so his cock wasn't penetrating her anymore. "We need to talk about this now."

"Fuck."

"Do you love me?"

"Yes."

"Say it."

"I love you, Terri. I told you that before."

"So what are your plans for our future?"

"I don't know. I thought you'd move back to the ranch with me. We can be a family."

"Do you ever plan to marry me?"

"Marriage? Wait a minute."

"That's what I thought." She pushed against his chest until she could slide out from under him. "I think you need to leave."

"Leave? I'm not leaving."

"Yes, you are. Go back to the ranch or whatever. I don't care."

"I thought you said you loved me?"

"I do, Jeff. I love you with all my heart, but I'm not shacking up with you until hell freezes over because you're scared to get married again or live in a long term relationship with the intention of marriage at some point."

He jumped to his feet, grabbed his pants and then shoved his legs into them. "So this is all to get a marriage proposal out of me?"

"Fuck off!"

His chest rose and fell with his rapid breaths. A sheen of sweat coated his upper lip. The man was in full panic attack mode at just the thought of getting married. "I ain't leavin' until we talk about this."

"There's nothing to talk about."

"Come on, Terri. I love you. Isn't that enough?"

"No, it's not, Jeff. I'm sorry, but it's not. I want to get married someday. Have a family. Raise my kids with the man who helped me produce them. I'm not going anywhere. You don't trust me."

"Yes, I do."

"No, not really. You say you love me, but the trust isn't there."

"What can I do to change your mind about this?"

"Ask me to marry you."

"I can't." He threw up his hands and let them fall. Dejection clouded his eyes.

"I know," she whispered in a tearful voice. *Am I doing the right thing? What if he walks away and never comes back? What if I never see him again?* A twenty pound lump clogged her throat. She slipped on her bathrobe, uncomfortable now with her nakedness in front of him.

He raked his fingers through his hair. "This isn't over."

She glanced at the ceiling as she pressed her lips together to keep from telling him it didn't matter, when in truth it mattered a great deal.

Chapter Fourteen

Jeff pulled his parent's truck into the driveway of the ranch, hit the gate button on the visor and sighed. What the hell went wrong? He loved Terri, but here he was returning to the ranch without her. This whole thing seemed totally fucked up.

"Daddy!" Ben raced from the door of the main house toward the truck as Jeff put it into park.

Nina followed closely on his heels, but her lips turned down in a frown when she saw the passenger side of the truck was empty. "Is Terri following you in her car?" she asked as he stepped out and shut the door.

"No, Mom."

"What happened?"

"I can't talk about it right now."

"Yes, you can and you will." She hollered toward the barn for his father who poked his head out of the double doors. "Can you take Ben please? I need to have a chat with our son."

"Uh-oh. You in trouble, Daddy?"

"I guess so, buddy. Go on with Granddad."

Ben raced across the yard as fast as his little legs would carry him.

"Come with me."

Apparently he was in for the talking to of his life with his mom and he couldn't bring up the feelings to care. He'd left his heart in Houston, but he wasn't sure what the hell to do about it. Marry Terri? His stomach rolled at the thought. Not that he didn't want to be with her. He did. More than anything, but marriage? Tied down to her for the rest of his life? What if she turned out to be like Misha? What if she cheated on him?

"Now," his mother said, pointing to the chair in her office for him to sit. "What is this all about?"

"Terri told me to leave."

"Well you spent the night with her last night, right?"

"Yeah." He raked his fingers through his hair, knocking off his hat in the process. "I don't get her, Ma."

"You love her, right?"

"Yeah and she said she loves me."

"Then what is the problem here?"

"She wants a marriage proposal."

"And?" His mother had a look of *are you stupid or what* on her face.

"I can't do it, Ma. I won't. What if somethin' happens again?"

"So what. Jeffery," she clasped his hands between hers, "honey, you're in love with her. She's in love with you. Marriage is the next logical step. You can't live your life worrying about if it's going to fall apart, sweetheart. You'll be miserable for the rest of your life if you do. Do you seriously want to let the hell Misha put you through ruin your future?"

"No."

"You have to move on. Terri is your future. The future for you and Ben." She ran one hand down his cheek and came away with wet fingers. "You'll be miserable without her. Don't you trust her?"

"I'm not sure."

"Why are you crying?"

"Because I miss her. I need her with me."

"You'll have to get over this fear you have then. I don't think she's going to settle for anything besides a marriage proposal from you." She patted his hand. "Take a few days to think about it, son. I think you'll come to the same conclusion I have."

She walked out leaving him with his thoughts. Everything seemed jumbled and out of focus. His life was up in the air all of the sudden. Yes, he still had his job on the ranch. The future of the ranch appeared secure thanks to Terri. His heart would never be the same without her in his life.

He sighed and let his head fall back against the wall behind him. What to do? What did he want from Terri? A friends with benefits situation? No. That didn't seem right either. He loved her. He knew he did, but could he get past his fear of marriage and a committed relationship to secure the future with her she wanted?

"Daddy?" Ben put his hand on his leg. "Did you ask Ms. Terri to be my new momma?"

"No, Ben, I didn't."

"Why not? I want her to come live with us."

"I want her to live with us too, buddy."

"Then why isn't she here?"

"It's complicated."

"You love her?"

"Yeah."

"Then it's not comli…whatever you said. You just bring her back here."

Jeff laughed. Oh to have the simplicity of life of a three-year-old. *Just bring her back here.* Could he? Would it be as easy as that?

A plan began to form in his head. He needed some help from one of his brothers, but he needed to think about what his future held without her before he planned a future with her in it. The bleakness without her choked the life from his heart.

"Let's go home, buddy."

"Okay." Ben rushed out toward the front room but stopped short.

"What's wrong?"

"The ghost man is sitting in the chair over there, Daddy."

Sure enough, Jeff could see the figure of an older gentleman in cowboy clothes sitting on the leather couch near the fireplace. He tipped his hat and faded away. Shivers raced down his back. He'd never get used to seeing the ghosts around the house no matter how many times he ran into them.

Jeff took Ben's hand as they walked through the dining room headed back outside. He had some thinking to do and some plans to make. Within minutes they were pulling up to the front of his small cabin. He knew no one waited for him to come home. The house needed a woman's touch. Even when he'd been married to Misha, she'd never done anything to make it a home. The small things counted like flowers in window boxes, fluffy white curtains blowing in the breeze at the kitchen window, and a pretty comforter on the bed, even pillow shams would make it more homey. What would Terri do to the place should he get her to come home with him? Would she want to make it hers like he hoped or would she turn into a shrew like Misha who didn't want his home, his child or his family?

Terri wasn't like that.

He opened the door to help Ben out of his car seat and get him down. His son ran for the front door, pushing it open in a rush. Since they didn't have anyone to come home to, the house looked forlorn.

"Bath time, Ben," Jeff called to his retreating son.

"No."

"Yes."

"No."

Jeff sighed. Times like this, he wanted someone in his life more than anything, someone to take over mommy duties so he didn't have to fight with the kid every night.

Ben ran past him, but Jeff grabbed him up in a bear hug and headed for the bathroom with the wiggling, giggling child in his arms. He got Ben into the bathroom and stripped off his clothes before he turned on the water. The bathroom looked like a typical kid's bathroom with thousands of toys in the tub. The naked kid tried to dash out the door, but Jeff got it shut with his boot before Ben escaped in a naked streak down the hall.

As he plopped the kid in the water, a knock sounded on the door. *Who the hell could that be?*

"I'll be right there!" He looked at Ben. What the hell to do? He only had two hands and a wet, wiggling child took precedence over whoever was at the door. No way would he leave Ben alone in the bathtub.

He shut the water off, wrapped Ben in a towel and propped him on his hip. This is just what he needed.

Opening the door with a sharp snap, he asked, "Yeah?"

The last person he thought he'd see standing on his doorstep spun around on her heels.

"Terri?"

"Hi." She pressed her lips together. "Can I come in?"

"Uh, sure." He stepped back.

"Hi, Ms. Terri!"

"Hiya, Ben. Bath time?"

"No."

"Yes," Jeff said with a laugh. "I was just getting him into the tub."

"I can wait until you're done." She laid her purse on the end table next to the couch.

His gaze slide down her frame, taking in the tank top curving around her breasts as it clung to every inch of her delicious body.

"Go take care of your son. I'll be right here."

Jeff disappeared down the hall with the squirming Ben in his arms. Tonight would be the fastest bath in history of bathing a child, he vowed. He put Ben in the tub, quickly washed his hair and body before he took the handheld showerhead down off the wall and rinsed him off. "Okay, Ben, out we go."

"I wanna play."

"Nope. Not tonight, buddy. Bedtime for you."

"But I wanna play."

Jeff sighed. The kid was going to drive him nuts before he reached his fifth birthday. He had other things to do tonight. Terri was here and he'd be damned if he let her go again.

* * * *

Terri smiled at the splashing sounds coming from the bathroom as she waited for Jeff to finish bathing Ben. She hadn't really thought this trip through when she'd gotten into her car to drive back out to the ranch to confront Jeff. She'd come to some conclusions after he'd given up and walked out of her life earlier in the day. It hadn't taken her more than an hour of soul searching to realize giving him the ultimatum of a marriage proposal or nothing wasn't right on her part. The gun-shy guy she loved didn't do well with choices like that.

What the hell am I gonna do if he doesn't want me here? "Surely if he didn't, he wouldn't have let me in the door."

She glanced around the living room realizing she hadn't had time to check out the home she hoped to share with the amazing man in the other room. The dark décor and lack of feminine touches didn't surprise her. His ex-wife didn't come across as a very family oriented woman from what she knew of her, although granted that wasn't much. Terri started picturing the little things she'd do to the house to make it more of a home. Some flowers outside. Curtains on the windows. A nice comforter on the bed. Toy Story curtains on Ben's window. It was obvious Jeff didn't bother with anything except the bare necessities.

Realizing the sounds coming from the bathroom had quieted, her stomach knotted in anticipation. She stood and moved toward the fireplace. She put one elbow up on the mantle, and took it down. Then twisted her fingers into a ball of knotted flesh. *Damn, I'm nervous*. Her stomach rolled, making her nauseous. It wouldn't bode well if she puked up her dinner before she even had a chance to talk to him.

She exhaled on a sigh to try to calm her stomach. It didn't work very well. Her heart thumped against her ribs like a terrified bird in a cage.

The sound of his boot steps coming down the hall didn't help her nervousness, but the time had come to answer some questions.

He stopped in the doorway and took in her entire body as a small smile played on those oh-so-kissable lips. *God, is it bad I want to curl myself around him and stay there forever?*

A nervous wipe of his hands down his thighs gave away his true feelings about her being there too as he walked into the living room. "Why don't you have a seat?"

"I would, but I'm nervous."

"Why?" he asked, taking a seat on the couch.

"Because I didn't know whether you'd hear me out. I rehearsed this whole long speech on the way here, but seeing you made every bit of it slip straight out of my head."

"Is that a good thing?"

She smiled and shrugged, taking a seat on the other side of the couch. "Maybe."

The silence stretched between them for several minutes while she tried to think of what to say since her speech didn't mean anything now. "I'm sorry. I guess I should start with that."

"Sorry for what?"

"Pressuring you. That wasn't fair to you. I know how hard it is for you to trust and we really haven't known each other very long." She twisted the ring on her right hand. It was one her mother gave her on her sixteenth birthday and she never took it off.

"No, we haven't." He seemed relaxed now as he stretched his arm across the back of the sofa.

"Are you sure you love me?" she asked, hoping he hadn't changed his mind.

"Yeah, but it's gonna take some time for me to get to the marriage part. I ain't sayin' I'll never get there, Terri."

"I guess it's all I'll get for now, huh?"

"No. I want you to be part of my life. I want you to move in here with me and Ben."

"Are you sure? I mean, isn't it kind of a big move?"

"Not as big as marriage."

"True."

"We'll keep everythin' separate. You can come and go like you want. I won't expect you to take over the house like you're my wife or anythin' if you don't want to."

"What if I want to?"

"Then you can. I want us to be more than just roommates with benefits." He smiled. "I like the benefits parts though."

"Can I do some decorating here? Nothing major. Curtains, flowers…things like that."

"Sure you can, darlin'."

Her heart tripped over itself when she heard his endearment. He hadn't given up on her completely, but she'd earn his trust and his long term love. If he never asked her to marry him, it was really okay. She'd have him in her life and that was the most important part of the whole thing.

"Come 'ere."

She launched herself into his arms, kissing all over his face in a rush to reach his lips. The softness of his mouth against hers brought tears to her eyes. "I love you."

"I love you too, Terri. Don't ever forget that no matter what, okay? I want you in my life."

"I want to be there too."

"Good. When can you move your stuff in?"

"I'll have to pack up my apartment, but I brought enough with me to stay for a while."

"Awful confident weren't you?" he asked, pushing his fingers into her hair.

"Hell no. I planned on staying in one of the cabins at the ranch until you said you loved me again."

He kissed her quickly, a little smooch that left her wanting a lot more. "I never stopped, baby. I just can't commit to marriage right now."

She ran her tongue across his jaw, enjoying the stubble of the unshaven line. "I know and I'm sorry I pushed you. It wasn't fair to you."

"Will you stay with me tonight?"

"If you want me to."

"Yeah, I do. The thought of not havin' you in my bed tonight had me goin' crazy." His gray eyes reflected the love he felt for her.

After all, a ring didn't mean anything. The feelings between two people resided in their hearts. "You can have me every night in your bed with no strings. I promise not to pressure you anymore about a ring."

"I hope you know how much I love you."

"You mean everything to me, Jeff. I've never felt this way about anyone before and I don't plan on feeling this way about anyone ever again. You're it for me."

He pushed her back, forcing her to stand. "Come on. I've got a woman to love on for the next hundred years."

"Only a hundred?" she asked with a giggle as he swept her up into his arms and headed for his bedroom.

"We'll start there."

"I can do a hundred or a thousand. As long as I'm with you, it doesn't matter how many years go by. We'll be together."

"In this house, in this bed. Together. Just the two of us."

"Or three depending on how many times Ben ends up in bed with us."

"Oh, he might too. He does tend to crawl into bed with me when he has a nightmare or something. Since he has a new momma, he might tend to be there more than we want him to be."

"I'm sure he'll get over it soon enough," she said as he gently laid her down on the comforter.

He stripped off his shirt, revealing the smattering of chest hair to her gaze. She loved running her fingers through the springy curls. The belt buckle and jeans came next, leaving her to take in his hard cock as he pushed everything to the floor. She loved having all that hard flesh inside her. Would he want her ass this time since they'd been interrupted before? She kind of hoped so. She wanted to feel everything with him.

"Take off your clothes."

She sat up on the bed on her knees and pulled the tank top over her head. The softness in his eyes as he took in her body told her more than anything how much he loved her. She laid back down to remove her shorts in one swoop. Luckily, she left her sandals in the living room when she'd taken a seat on the couch.

"God, you're beautiful."

"You aren't so bad yourself, cowboy."

His cock bobbed against his stomach, begging for her touch or her mouth in a little dance she wasn't sure he didn't orchestrate just to torment her. She wanted both. With her hand wrapped around his length, she took him between her lips and sucked the head.

A soft moan broke from his mouth. "I love when you suck me."

She took him deeper, swallowing as much of his length as she could. He wasn't a small man by any means.

His hips shifted, pushing more of him into her mouth. He wrapped his hands in her hair, pulling slightly. The sting of his tug made her weak and wet. She didn't realize how much rough sex turned her on, until Jeff came along.

He reached over to land a heavy smack on her ass cheek. The pain of his heavy hand had juices dripping down the inside of her leg.

"Enough." He pulled her back by her hair until she released his cock. "I don't want to come in your mouth. I want so much more from you."

"Like what, cowboy?"

"Your pussy, your ass. Can we make it a triple penetration night?"

"Maybe. Goin' for the trifecta huh?"

"You bet. Spread them legs for me, babe." His cock pushed against her opening. "You okay with no condom?"

"Yes. I trust you, but I'll see about birth control in the next few weeks."

"Do you want a baby with me?"

"Of course, I do. I love you, but I think we should wait a bit."

"Then let's use the condom until you're on something to keep it from happenin' until we're ready."

He grabbed one from the nightstand drawer and rolled it on. "It's not foolproof, but it's better than nothin'."

"If it happens, it happens, Jeff. It's God's will if we make a baby even using a condom."

The slow penetration of his cock drove her wild. She loved having him inside her. Her swollen tissues stretched to accommodate his size as her pussy dampened even more.

"I love bein' inside you."

"I like it too. Fuck me, Jeff. Give it to me hard. I need this more than you know."

He shoved inside her in one thrust, tearing a groan from deep in her chest. The rapid push of his thrusts had her on edge in seconds. "Yes," she whispered in a rapid mantra to the rhythm of his pace. Heat crawled up her legs in a rush to reach her pelvis. The burst of sensation ripped a moan from her lips as she came in a heated gush.

"Now, I want your ass," he said, as she slowly came down from her orgasm.

"Lube."

"Got it." He grabbed a tube from the nightstand drawer and set it on the bed next to her.

"Tell me what to do."

"Roll over onto your stomach."

When he had her positioned how he wanted, she heard the squirt of lubrication and felt the liquid on her ass. "Damn, that's cold."

"Sorry, I should have warmed it up a little."

"It's okay." He spread the wet slickness around her anus before he shoved a finger past the ring of muscles. The burn felt odd, but not too bad this time.

"Ready for two?"

"Okay." Her ass contracted around his fingers when he stick two inside and scissored them to stretch her hole.

"Are you all right?"

"Yeah." She pushed back against the invasion, wanting more. "I need more."

More lube ran down the crack of her ass as he spread it inside. "Ready for me?"

"I guess. Just go slowly."

"Sure, babe. You can drive this train."

The feel of having his cock bumped at her ass and then slowly push inside felt like hell. *The burn!* "Wait."

He stopped pushing.

She breathed through the pain. "Okay."

He moved a little more. "Okay?"

"Yeah. I want to push back against you."

"Good. That's what you're supposed to feel. Do what you want. I'm almost all the way inside."

"Really? Wow."

She pushed back taking the rest of him inside until she felt the hair at his groin touch her butt. "Oh my God!"

"Pretty intense, huh?"

"Oh, hell yeah." She wiggled her butt.

"You're gonna kill me woman. I can't hold still much longer."

"I don't want you too. Fuck me, Jeff."

He slowly drew his cock out, and then just as slowly pushed back in. The sensation was something she couldn't even describe. The burn had disappeared with the deliberate slide of his cock in and out of her ass.

"Faster."

"You sure?"

"Yeah, please."

He increased the pace of his thrust, pulling a tortured moan from her mouth. The gritty sound torn from her lips felt foreign, but good. It felt incredible to share this with him. Something she'd never given to another man in her entire life, only to give it to the man she loved with her whole heart.

One of his hands snaked around her hip to run a finger over her clit. Her whole body vibrated with need. She had to come soon or the top of her head would explode into a splattering mess all over his bed.

"Come for me, darlin'."

Stars exploded in her head as her body detonated into a thousand tiny particles of sensation. Every nerve ending in her body prickled like tiny electrical charges on her skin.

Jeff moaned softly as his hips pistoned at an uncoordinated rhythm meant to bring him to satisfaction. She wanted it, needed to feel him come hard and enjoy the fulfilling intimacy they'd just shared.

"Oh God," he whispered as his body shivered against her backside and then collapsed along her back, driving them both to the bed in a heap.

"Good for you?" she asked with a laugh.

"Hell yeah."

"I thought so."

"Did you like it? I mean if you didn't we don't have to do it again, but I thought…"

"I loved it, Jeff. You made it special. It wasn't something I'd been able to trust anyone with before now, but you are the man I love. I want to experience everything with you."

"I love you, Terri."

"Good. Now, I think you need to clean up and I know I do. All this cum and goo between my legs is sticky."

"Shower?"

"Hmm. That would be great especially if you'll join me."

"I wouldn't miss it."

He pulled his cock from her ass and stood, then helped her stand too. "First one in gets to adjust the temperature," he said, racing for the bathroom.

"Women first, mister!"

The laughter ringing through the house brought goose bumps to her body. She'd found the man she could love for the rest of her life. She sent up a silent thank you to God for helping her see the error of pushing him too far too fast. He would come around in time, but for now, loving him and Ben, building a family with them would take up all the time she had.

Epilogue

Christmas was a time for family. The family she'd built with Jeff and Ben meant everything to her. She'd moved her business to Bandera and had to finally take time off from work to spend the season with them.

The four-year-old child of her heart sat by the Christmas tree bouncing on his butt waiting for his father to say he could open the mountain of presents.

"Now, Daddy?"

"Nope. Wait just a minute." Jeff crawled on the floor toward the tree and sat down next to the boxes. "Okay now I'll give you one at a time to open."

She smiled. The amount of presents under there probably set her back a pretty penny, but she didn't care. This was their first Christmas as a family.

"This is from, Grandma and Granddad."

The brightly wrapped box became a shred of paper within seconds and he squealed in delight at his present. "More?"

"Slow down, buddy, or you'll have them all opened so fast, it'll be over."

Ben frowned. The next present was opened a little piece of paper at a time. Another squeal at the train set she'd bought with Jeff brought a smile to her lips. He still loved Toy Story, but Thomas the Train was quickly becoming his new favorite thing. Kids.

She had a special surprise for Jeff, but it would have to wait until Ben went to bed.

Within thirty minutes, all the presents under the tree were opened. Ben jumped up and hugged Terri, bringing tears to her eyes. "Thank you, Momma. Thank you, Daddy."

"You're welcome, honey," she said, hugging him right back. Her love for this little boy grew every day.

"Time for bed."

"No."

"Yes," Jeff said. "Santa won't come if you don't go to bed."

Ben looked at her with wide eyes. "Off to bed with you, Ben."

"All right."

Jeff laughed and she smiled. They went through this ritual almost every night. Jeff would tell him to do something, but as soon as Terri told him to do it, he'd automatically say yes and off he'd go.

"I'll be right back." Jeff grabbed Ben, tossed him over his shoulder to the gleeful squeals of the boy and off to bed they went.

Nervousness gripped her stomach. How would he feel when she gave him his present?

Within moments, he returned to take the seat next to her on the couch and wrap her in his arms. He winced a little, drawing her concern. "Are you okay?"

"Yeah, why?"

"You're acting like you're in pain."

"Well, it's a surprise."

"Really? What kind of surprise?"

"First I need to give you your gift." He grabbed a small box from the end table, she hadn't noticed before. "Open it."

Anticipation coiled her nerves. It looked like a jewelry box of some sort. *Dare I hope?*

The blue velvet box shook in her hands as she slowly slid open the top. A gorgeous diamond necklace winked back at her with two hearts entwined.

"Oh my."

"Do you like it? I thought it signified what we have at least for now. I love you so much, I wish I could express it more."

"Baby, you do every day in how you treat me and love me. It's beautiful. It's perfect. Will you put it on?"

She spun around to let him clasp the necklace behind her neck. When she turned back, she saw tears in his eyes.

"There's one more thing. I hope it means as much to you as it does to me." He pulled his T-shirt over his head and turned around. There on his tattoo was her name next to Ben's, the skin still raw and red from application.

"Oh Jeff." To have him ink her name on his body meant the world to her. It wasn't an engagement ring, but it almost meant more. He'd accepted her as a permanent part of his life just as he accepted the permanent ink on his body. "Thank you."

He spun around and kissed her. Her world tipped on its axis as he stuck his tongue into her mouth and dueled with hers. A moan escaped her lips, but she couldn't get caught up in his kiss just yet.

She pushed him away and smiled at the exasperated look on his face. "You already opened your gift from me."

"And I love the new belt buckle with our names engraved on it. It's great."

"Thanks, but there is one more thing and I hope you're okay with it."

"I'll love anything you have to give me, baby. I hope you know that."

"What about a baby?" she asked as she bit her lip.

"A baby?"

"Yeah. I know we didn't plan this, but I'm pregnant."

"Seriously? Wow."

A slow smile spread across his lips, bringing down her anxiety to a tolerable level. "You're okay with this?"

"I would love to have a baby with you, Terri. I'll love any child we have between us whether it be another ornery little boy like Ben or a beautiful little girl who looks just like her mother." He pulled her onto his lap. "When did you find out?"

"A couple of days ago."

"When will he or she be born?"

"I don't have an actual due date yet since I haven't been to the doctor, but sometime late summer."

He kissed her in a slow, loving kiss of two hearts beating as one.

The End

FOR THE LOVE OF A COWBOY
Cowboy Dreamin' 3

Sandy Sullivan

Chapter One

The music coming through the bar doors as they swung open, had Paige Tyler tapping her boot clad feet to the beat as she pulled her Harley to the curb. A knowing smile flirted at her lips when she heard low whistles and cat calls from a group of men nearby. No doubt they were liking how the soft leather bustier she wore pushed her breast up in an enticing display. The matching pants that went with it, hugged her ass just right and showed off how long her legs were. The whole outfit–she knew–virtually gave the impression that she could give any man she wanted the vision of a good time.

Her daddy would kill her if he saw her, but what the hell. This is why she came to Bandera to do her barhopping. No one here knew her, or her father in this small town bar that cater to the local cowboys. She glanced up at the huge neon sign of a boot with a spur hanging off its back.

Over the past few months, she'd become a regular here at The Dusty Boot. The faded wood exterior reminded her of an old western saloon with a hitching post and everything. They even had sawdust on the floor.

Her father didn't know where she went on her little excursions. He thought she spent her evenings reading to the poor little old ladies at the local nursing home, but she always took her car to the storage building where she kept her bike and clothes. After she switched out, she'd put on her helmet and hit the highway.

Another round of wolf whistles had her turning her head in the direction of a pickup truck as she removed her helmet. Damn, if she had one weakness it was a man in tight Wrangler's and dusty boots. She blew him a kiss.

"Oh, honey, come on. I'm sure you got more than that."

She cocked an eyebrow. "We'll see, cowboy." With a toss of her brown curls, she waltzed through the double doors and straight up to the bar. "Hold this back there for me, please."

"You be careful, Paige," Dan said, taking the helmet. "We got a rowdy crowd tonight."

"I'm always prepared."

"I know, honey, but I don't want to see you get hurt." He shook his finger at her, making her laugh. She loved the big, burly guy even though she hadn't known him long. He reminded her of an ex-marine with his shaved head and multiple tattoos. "Stay outta trouble, you hear me?" He'd taken it upon himself to treat her like a daughter he'd never had.

She blew him a kiss and a wink that probably drove the man crazy, but he just smiled and shook his head with a mumble of words she couldn't hear.

Thanks to all her years of Tae-Kwon-Do, she'd earned her black belt and knew how to take care of herself in any situation. She didn't use it for anything except defense, but sometimes it took a little persuasion on her part when a man got randy on her.

A crowd of dancers twirled and whirled around the dance floor in a flash of sequins and denim. She took a chair at the opposite end of the bar from the door. It helped to keep everyone in sight in case things got out of hand.

"What are ya drinkin', Paige," Peyton asked her when she approached her end of the bar.

"Hey, Peyton. Coke, please."

Peyton shook her head and laughed. "You're the only woman I know who comes to a bar dressed like that and drinks Coke."

She smiled. She sure was an enigma to most, pre-school teacher, preacher's daughter who wore leather, rode a Harley, and hung out in bars on the weekends. "I have to keep my wits about me. I just want to be around the crowd and music. I don't need the alcohol if I'm ridin'."

The woman set the glass down in front of her. Paige lifted it to her lips and took a slow sip from the straw as she turned around to take in the scenery. Several people had already paired off for the night, but there were still a few cowboys hanging around who didn't seem to be with anyone special. It didn't bother her. She wasn't here necessarily to pick anyone up. If it happened, then she'd go with the flow.

A few cowboys played pool at one of the tables set toward the back of the room while others moved in and out from the dance floor with each switch of the music. Rows and rows of tables with wooden chairs sat all over the place in various configurations depending on who moved the tables around to accommodate their group. Neon signs covered most of the walls. Everything from Bud Light to Captain Morgan lined the panels from the back of the bar to the door.

A sea of cowboy hats and rhinestones encompassed the crowd, everything from tight Wranglers to sundresses and cowboy boots. The wide variety of dress seemed funny to Paige, but she couldn't say much as she sat there in her leather.

Lots of groups laughed as they pushed each other in a joke or two. The ages ranged from early twenties to fifties. There were a few couples who seemed like then been together a long time and others who were hooking up for the night.

The normal loneliness she felt when she realized she didn't have a lot of friends, overwhelmed her for a minute. *To hell with friends. I don't need them.* The few people she still hung out with a time or two thought of her as

Paige Tyler, the preacher's daughter wearing the paisley dress on Sunday with her Bible in hand, listening to the sermon like the good little girl she was supposed to be. If they saw her dressed in the leather wear she had on tonight, they'd have a frickin' heart attack.

A couple of cowboys pushed one guy back. "You're fuckin' drunk again, Jacob. Why don't you go home and sleep it off until next time."

"Leave me the fuck alone."

"You ain't worth shit anymore, man."

"Just play. I've got twenty bucks says I can beat your ass."

"I ain't takin' your money. You couldn't shoot pool right now if you tried."

"Yes, I can."

The man called Jacob got right up in the other guy's face and spit. *Oh shit.*

"You did not just fuckin' spit in my face, man."

"Yeah, I did. What are you gonna do about it?"

The bigger man pulled back his fist and hit Jacob in the stomach, doubling him over with a groan. The smaller man flew across the bar floor, sliding on his butt until he hit the wall. Paige got to her feet, moving with the crowd toward the fight. If she had to get involved, she would. Even though the one called Jacob deserved to get his ass kicked, she wouldn't allow the bigger man to beat the shit out of him especially if it got to be two against one. As he shook his head to clear it, two guys picked him up and the third punched him in the stomach.

Oh hell no.

"Paige?" the bartender pulled her back by the arm as she surged forward. "Leave them alone."

"It's three against one, Dan. I can't have that." She pushed through the crowd. "Hey, asswipe!"

The bigger guy turned around, squinting as he looked through the crowd. He was huge. His biceps bulged as he clamped his hand into a fist. Blond hair peeked out from beneath a straw cowboy hat. His blue eyes narrowed into slits. "Who said that?"

"Me, fucktard."

The man looked straight at her and laughed a gut rolling belly laugh. "You? Baby, step aside and let the men handle this."

That kind of reaction usually pissed her off, but not tonight. Dumbass didn't know what he had on his plate now that she'd decided to step in between him and drunk he wanted to beat the shit out of. "Not three on one, you aren't."

"And what the hell are you gonna do about it, baby doll?" His gaze slid over her attire as he grinned wide enough she caught a glimpse of the gold teeth in his mouth. "Your leather outfit is hot, I'll give ya that, but leave this to us men." He spun around to face his two friends.

"Bring it on, big man." She needed the man to make the first swing. It went against her grain to hit someone first. She motioned with her hands to bait him.

He laughed as he stepped closer. "I don't hit women."

"Come on, goliath. You too much of a pussy?"

"What did you call me?"

"Pussy."

The laughter from the crowd had the man's face turning purple. Their amusement died when he took a swing at her. Her first pass of her boot caught the man in the chin, splitting his lip open in a gush of blood. The next kick swiped his feet out from under him, laying him out cold on the floor.

The other two men dropped the drunk guy on the floor before backing away. "We don't want no trouble."

"You got trouble when you ganged up on one man," she said stepping in front of the man they'd called Jacob. "You okay?" she asked him without taking her eyes off the other three.

"I think I'm gonna be sick." He rolled over and pushed to his feet. The crowd parted like the Red Sea as he rushed for the bathroom, almost losing his footing a couple of time.

She cringed when she heard him puke in the hallway.

"I suggest you three take it somewhere else."

Dan pushed through the throng and appeared at her side "Yeah. Out you two. I don't want any more trouble." He motioned to the man on the floor. "Take your buddy and go."

"You ain't kickin' her and Jacob out?"

"She didn't do nothin' but stand up to you three bullies. You knew Jacob was messed up as usual, but you took advantage of him anyway."

She rolled her eyes as she heard the man heave again. She'd seen him here before, but he'd always been the quiet drunk in the corner. Yeah, she'd noticed him, all six-feet-plus of him, dark hair, built like a man who did a lot of physical labor. He'd never bothered her or anyone else, just drank his beer until he got wasted enough someone who knew him took him home or wherever. She hoped the man didn't drive like that. There'd been a time or two she'd thought about approaching him for a one night stand, but she'd always changed her mind at the last minute, unsure of whether he might be a mean drunk or just a quiet one.

He pushed his way back to the edge of the crowd as he wiped the puke from his face. "Thanks."

She winced as she glanced at the front of his shirt. "No thanks needed."

With his hat in his hand, he nodded to her and headed for the door.

Oh hell no, he isn't drivin' like this. "Where ya goin', cowboy?" she asked walking up behind him to tap him on the shoulder.

"Home," he mumbled as he pushed his hat on his head with one hand while reaching for his keys with the other.

"You ain't drivin'." She snatched the keys from him and spun out of reach. She wasn't a small woman by any means, but the man still had her by several inches.

"Yeah, I am. I'm fine." He reached for the keys, but she stuck them in her front jeans pocket.

"Buddy, you're so drunk you can't see straight."

He laughed. "I ain't that drunk. I only see two of you, not three this time." The laughter burbling from his lips sounded strained, like he hadn't laughed in a long time.

"What kind of vehicle do you drive?" she asked, sliding underneath his arm to wrap it around her shoulder. *Why the fuck do I get myself into these messes?* They walked into the cooler air of the early spring evening.

"Black Ford truck, why?" he asked, stumbling beside her.

"'Cause I'm takin' your ass somewhere so you can sleep off this drunk before you drive and I can't put your ass on my bike." She glanced across the street to the small motel. Originally, the thought of getting him home consumed her, but after she thought about it, settling him in a room would be a better idea. "Come on, cowboy, let's get you settled for the night."

"Are you takin' me home 'cause I don't think I'm up to doin' anything tonight." He stumbled beside her again and she barely caught him. They almost tumbled into the street in a tangled heap. "I really need to brush my teeth."

"I bet you do." She put her arm around his waist as they walked across the street to try to steady him a bit more. Getting to the motel without laying both of them out flat on the pavement would just make her night.

"You're pretty," he said as he looked at her profile, his puke-ladened breath wafting across her nose.

She fought the bile in her throat. God, she hated when people got puking drunk. "Thanks."

"I like the tits. Are you a biker chick?"

"Sort of."

"Where ya takin' me?"

"To this motel so you can sleep off whatever the hell you drank."

"Oh good. I can't go home like this. My parents would kill me. They don't like me drinkin' so much, but I can't help it. My life is totally fucked up."

"Sorry, dude, but I'm not psychotherapist."

"I could probably use one."

"I'm sure you could." They walked in through the glass doors of the motel. She noticed a long counter to check-in and several cheap plastic chairs along the wall. *Huh, maybe they charge by the hour.* She rang the bell when no one came out to greet them for several moments. She glanced at the open doorway where a television blared in the back. "Hey! Can I get some help here?"

A large, portly man came through the doorway scratching his crotch. "What do you want?"

"A room would be great." She grimaced and rolled her eyes.

He chewed on the cigar in his mouth as he grabbed some paperwork for her to fill out from the slots in the wall. She put Jacob in one of the chairs next to the desk so she could write. His head dropped to his chest while he mumbled to himself about something or another. Once she had the forms completed, she handed the man her credit card.

When he handed her the keys, she helped Jacob to his feet with an arm around his waist, and they stumbled outside to find the room. One-twelve, one-thirteen, one-fourteen. There it was. One-fifteen. She pushed opened the door and managed to get out of the way just in time for Jacob to hit the bed in a tumble of arms and legs.

Soft snoring met her ear.

Oh hell! The man was sleeping already and he wasn't even on the bed right. She stood with her hands on her hips deciding what to do with him. She could leave him just like he was or she could at least take off his boots to make him a little more comfortable. His feet hung off the bed so her estimate of his height seemed true although she didn't know why it made an impression on her.

She pulled off his boots and placed them near the end of the bed so he could find them in the morning. After several minutes, she decided to try to straighten him out so he could at least sleep comfortably and hopefully not vomit in his sleep. She pushed and shoved on his big body until she got him into a semi-comfortable position. "It'll have to do."

Grabbing the key to the room, she pulled the door shut behind her as she pointed herself in the direction of the bar to retrieve her bike. When she walked inside, Dan waved her over to where he stood behind the bar pouring beers. "How's Jacob?"

"Sleepin' like a baby."

"What'd you do with him?

"I left him lying on a threadbare comforter in room one-fifteen."

"You took him to the motel?"

"Yeah. He was too drunk to tell me where he lived, so I figured it would be better if he sleeps off his drunk over there. I wasn't about to let him drive home. He would have killed someone. If he does this often, I'm surprised he hasn't already."

Dan poured a beer for the waitress. "I know. I usually cut him off before he gets too drunk, but we have a new waitress tonight and she kept serving him."

"Does he do this often?"

"Too often, yeah." Dan wiped at some imaginary spot on the bar while he talked.

"Man's got a drinkin' problem then."

"I'm sure there would be some who would agree with you." He shrugged. "What are you gonna do now? You drivin' home?"

"I guess. My night is kind of ruined. Hell, I might even have to find somewhere else to hang out now that the whole bar knows I can fight."

Dan leaned toward her with his hands on the bar. "Maybe, but I think you'll be fine. Besides, I'm sure Jacob will want to tell you thank you for savin' his ass."

"I doubt he'll even remember me."

"I bet he does."

She gave him a one shoulder shrug as she glanced around the room. "Whatever, Dan. Anyway, thanks for the Coke. I'll see you next week, maybe."

He handed her the helmet from under the bar as she pulled her Harley keys out of her pocket.

With a quick wave, she disappeared back outside. A shiver rolled down her arms from the night air. It sure got cold in early spring. She straddled her bike, hit the ignition and then slipped on her helmet. She needed to go back over to the room and maybe leave the cowboy a note or something so he knew his keys were on the table. Hopefully, he would figure out where he was in the morning so he could drive home. She shook her head. Leave it to her to get in a bar fight on a Friday night in a bar forty-five minutes from home when she wasn't supposed to be doing anything like this. Preacher's daughters didn't go to bars, didn't get into bar fights, and didn't save drunk cowboys from getting their ass kicked. Only Paige Tyler would.

* * * *

Jacob Young rolled over onto his back, groaning when his head felt like it was going to split in half. Sunlight poured through the dingy drapes on the cloudy windows as he peeled his grainy eyelids open far enough to see where he was. He recognized the motel. He'd spent enough weekend nights here to know the inside of this disgusting place from corner to corner.

What the hell happened? He didn't remember much. He drank way too many beers the night before and then started to play pool with some guys he knew he shouldn't have. He didn't remember much after that. How did he get to the motel, pay for a room, and get himself to bed?

He sat up and grabbed his head as it pounded out the rhythm of a set of drums. Bongo drums if he thought about it, but that hurt too. *God, I feel like shit.*

As he squinted trying to bring the room into focus, a piece of paper on the grimy table caught his attention. He blinked several times as he leaned over to grab it.

Jacob –

Who the hell is Angel?

He didn't remember last night at all. Maybe the bartender could tell him. He glanced at the clock. *Fuck.* The red digits read nine. Jeff would kick his ass when he got home. It was bad enough his brother thought he drank too much, but now he had proof if he wanted it. Somebody saved his ass last night, paid for a motel and kept him from driving drunk.

Jacob looked down at himself. *What the fuck?* He picked at the dried substance and slapped his hand over his mouth before he lost what little was left in his stomach. Apparently, at some point, he'd thrown up because the stuff covered the front of his shirt.

He unbuttoned the shirt and took it off. Luckily, he was wearing a T-shirt under it. Spring usually meant colder weather, even in Bandera, Texas.

Once he found his keys and his boots, he got to his feet and headed for the bathroom. He needed to wash out his mouth. Unfortunately, this Podunk motel didn't have toothbrushes or toothpaste for their patrons. Hell, they barely had a bed.

After he took a piss and rinsed out his mouth, he pulled on his boots and stumbled into the sunny morning.

Getting home had to be the priority right now. He was actually surprised no one had called his cell phone looking for him. *Maybe they don't care anymore. This behavior has been goin' on for some time. They must realize I'll make it home eventually, right?*

He pulled the phone from his pocket and glanced at the screen. His battery was dead. No wonder no one had called him.

His truck sat in the parking lot across the street all by itself, the rest of the patrons long gone home the night before. He squinted against the sunlight as he slowly made his way to his vehicle.

The door opened with a tug of his fingers. He crawled inside and shut it behind him. The engine turned over with a twist of the key as he took a deep breath and put the truck into drive. Hangovers sucked, but he'd have to deal with it today. Hopefully, Jeff or his parents wouldn't be around to harp on him coming in late.

Saturdays should be their day off anyway. Even if Jeff worked himself until he dropped from exhaustion, it didn't mean the rest of them had to.

"Maybe since he hooked up with Terri, even big brother wouldn't come in early."

Several minutes later, he pulled up the gate of Thunder Ridge Ranch, his family's home and business. They raised cattle on the multi-thousand acre ranch they owned, but they also had opened it to guests.

He punched in the code and watched the gate slide open all the way to allow him entrance. Yeah, sitting there was a stall. But he knew he'd be in trouble, even if he had turned thirty-one not long ago. His parents still treated him like a kid, damn it!

Not stopping at the main lodge house, he drove around between the guest houses and the stable until he reached his trailer at the back of the garden. It wasn't much, but then again, he didn't want much. He didn't have a woman to come home to, so it didn't matter. A small bachelor pad was enough for him. When or if he ever found someone to settle down with, he'd ask his parents to help him build a home like Joel or Jeff had. He didn't care enough to maintain anything yet.

He pulled up in front of his place, threw the truck into park and then stepped out.

"Where the hell have you been? We've been worried sick. You didn't answer your phone or anything," his mother snapped as she rounded the back of his truck.

"Sorry, Ma."

"Where were you, Jacob?"

"I spent the night in town."

"Again? Son, what's gotten into you?"

"Nothin'."

"Honey, please talk to me. I'm worried sick about you."

She rubbed his arm. The obvious worry on her face bothered him. The last thing he wanted in this world was to hurt his parents, but things for him weren't in a good place at the moment. "It's nothin', Ma. Can't a man have a few beers without his family goin' all ape shit?"

"Jacob, please."

"I said it's nothin'."

"Fine. I'll send your father to talk to you then."

"No. I don't want to talk to him either."

She sighed as she hugged him. "I love you, Jacob."

"I know. I love you too, Ma, but really, it's nothin' you can help me with." He pushed her back by the shoulders so he could look into her eyes.

"If you would just talk about it…"

"I can't. This is something I need to deal with on my own. It's not somethin' you, Dad, Jeff or anyone else would be able to fix. I have to do it on my own."

"You're drinkin' way too much."

"I know. I'll slow down. I promise."

He could feel her gaze on his back as he headed for his single wide mobile home, opened the door and walked in. Right now his priorities were food, shower, and to brush his teeth. The grit clinging to the enamel made him want to barf again even though he had nothing in his stomach. He toed off his boots and left them in the living room while he headed to the bathroom, dropping his hat and other clothes in the hall on his way.

His stomach rolled from too much alcohol. *I need to get a grip. This shit is for the birds. I hate being sick to my stomach.*

The mirror reflected the hell he put his body through in the last several months. His dark hair lay stuck to his skull in a matted disarray of curls. Blood shot eyes reflected the hard life he'd taken up lately. His arms and chest showed the physical labor he usually performed in his everyday life, but the sallow skin told a different story. Too much alcohol had taken its toll. He hadn't been holding up his part of the ranch. He knew it deep in his soul, but the question was how to get out of the hell he was living now. He wasn't sure if he possessed the strength to face life anymore or the miserable existence his had become.

His parents were worried. He knew the whole family was concerned about him, but he couldn't seem to dig his way out.

With a turn of the handle, the shower sprayed hot water into the corner stall of his small bathroom. Once he stepped inside, he sighed with a deep, bone weary groan. Water cascaded over his head and down his chest as he leaned against the plastic wall absorbing the heat from the water.

When had everything spiraled out of control? He wasn't sure anymore. It had started out so simple.

He shook his head to erase the disturbing memories. Thinking about them right now would make him want to drink again and he couldn't—he wouldn't—not today. Maybe this would be the first day without alcohol in a long time. Today would be the turning point in his life. Today, he would be able to move on and forget the hard decision forced on him, but he would never forget. Never in a million years.

Flashes of memory pounded his skull, bombarding him with pain like he'd never felt before. It almost brought him to his knees. A brown-headed woman in a leather bustier and skin tight leather pants flew before his closed eyelids. *What the hell?* Green eyes the color of emeralds glinted dangerously as she glanced over her shoulder at him.

He massaged his head trying to bring the memory into clarity.

Booze. Lots of booze.

Pool tables.

The Dusty Boot.

It all came back with a sharp stab to his head.

The woman jumped into the fight of three on one to save his ass. The big guy had punched him in the stomach, pushing him halfway across the bar on his butt. She'd taunted the guy while Jacob sat there on the floor like a pussy. He *was* the pussy like she'd called him, not the big guy. He'd let a woman defend him. How could he do that?

His life had come full circle. Jacob Young used to be someone to fear in a bar fight. Now, a woman took care of him.

Oh God! He remembered where the puke on his shirt came from. After the punch to the stomach, he'd rush for the bathroom only to make it to the door before he threw up all the alcohol in his system as well as the nachos he'd eaten for dinner.

How humiliating.

Jacob turned off the water and wiped his face off. *What the hell have I done? I've resorted to a woman havin' to defend me in a fight when I should have been defendin' her.* "I need to find out who she is and at least apologize."

He'd never seen her before though. Who was she? Did the bartender know her? Maybe he could help him or maybe he would run into her again, but that meant going into the bar. The one place he needed to avoid.

Chapter Two

Another Friday night found Paige putting on her satin and leather to see what the bar held. Did she dare go back to The Dusty Boot to try her luck? What if she ran into the drunk? Jacob. His name was Jacob. Not that she'd forgotten really. Who was she kidding? She hadn't forgotten him all damned week. His brown eyes had haunted her from the time she'd pulled into the storage shed to deposit her bike before she went home until now.

She wanted to know how he'd faired.

The look he'd given her as she helped him across the street haunted her. He looked so lost, she wanted to take care of him.

"Bullshit on that noise." The cracked mirror inside the shed reflected her bright green eyes, red lips and high cheekbones. No one she knew would recognize her in this getup, at least no one from church or Heaven forbid, her father.

Once she walked the bike out of the shed, she slid on her helmet, hit the ignition on her Harley and slowly pulled out onto the street. Should she go to The Dusty Boot or try a different bar?

Forty minutes later, she found herself parking at the curb outside the same establishment, as music ebbed with the opening and closing of the doors. What did she hope to accomplish other than no one recognizing her from the week before? She exhaled sharply as she set the kickstand down.

"Hey baby. Weren't you here last week on this nice lookin' machine?"

"Maybe."

"I saw you pull up. Can I buy you a beer?"

"No thanks."

"Aw, come on, darlin'." The man grabbed her hand as she stepped away from the bike. "Just one. You and me can get better acquainted and maybe have us a little fun."

"I said no thanks, buddy. Let go before you lose the limb."

"Tough girl, eh?"

"More than you know. I won't tell you again to let go of my hand before I break your arm."

"Fine, fine. It ain't worth the hassle." The guy backed away with his hands in the air.

Her boots clicked as she walked toward the door ignoring the man as his cronies laughed at his expense when he joined them. It didn't matter, but she'd keep an eye on him just in case. She didn't want trouble, but it seemed to find her.

She walked to the bar to set her helmet down as she said, "Hey, Dan."

"Paige, honey. I'm glad you came back."

"Why's that."

"Jacob has been asking about you."

"Oh?"

"Yeah. Seems he remembers you to some degree and wanted to know your name. I told him I didn't know, but he's been in here every night looking for you."

"Great, just fucking dandy."

"If you don't want nothin' to do with him, just let me know. I'll take care of him."

"No, it's fine, Dan. Maybe he just wants to say thank you and it'll be the end of it."

"I hope so."

Dan stored her helmet beneath the bar as she walked to the end and found her favorite spot open.

Peyton was tending her end of the long mahogany. "What are you drinkin', Paige, or do I have to ask."

"You don't have to ask, do you?"

Peyton laughed as she slid a tall Coke toward Paige. "No." Moving closer, she stuck two cherries in the glass. "Dan tell you Jacob has been here lookin' for you?"

"Yeah."

"He's sittin' in the corner near the back." Peyton glanced over Paige's shoulder. "I think he spotted you."

"Let's get it over with, I'd say." She spun around only to come face to chest. She glanced up at the face she couldn't forget. "Hello." Tall. Six-foot-four, at least, of pure muscle stared back. Dark hair peeked out from beneath his straw cowboy hat and the deepest brown eyes she'd ever seen on a man looked right into hers. She cocked her head to the side when she noted no alcohol coming from his breath, just a clean, refreshing minty smell. *Interesting.*

"Hi. I'm Jacob Young."

"Nice to meet you, Jacob Young."

"And you are Angel?"

She grinned thinking about the name she'd put on the note she'd left on the nightstand at the motel. "Angel is a nickname. My real name is Paige."

"Nice name. It fits you."

"Thanks. My dad thought so I guess."

Taking off his hat, he twisted the brim in his fingers. "I hoped I'd see you again. I needed to say thank you."

"For what?"

The girl sitting on the stool next to her left, so he took the seat as she spun around to face him. "Savin' my ass last week."

"I didn't do anything." She sipped her soda.

"Yeah, you did. My memory is kind of cloudy about the particulars, but you kept those guys from killin' me and then took me to the motel across the street to keep me from drivin'."

"You remember quite a bit then, Jacob."

"Where did you learn to fight?"

"Tae-Kwon-Do lessons for way too many years."

"Ah." He glanced at her glass as she drained it, then signaled for the bartender. "Another of whatever the lady is drinkin' and Coke for me."

"Two Cokes, comin' up."

"You aren't drinking tonight, Jacob?"

He dropped his gaze to his hands, slipped his hat back on his head and then looked at her. "No. Funny really. After the trouble last week, I haven't had a drop since. I have you to thank for that too, I guess."

"Listen. I'm not sure what got you drinking so heavy in the first place and I hope what happened last week opened your eyes, but I didn't do anything."

"Yeah, you did. You showed me how destructive my life had become over something I really didn't have a lot of control over." He reached over to squeeze her fingers.

Goose bumps rose on her arm, making her frown. She'd never had a reaction like that over a man's touch before. Calluses scraped against her skin. He worked for a living apparently.

"Sorry. I didn't mean to be forward."

"It's okay." She sipped her drink. "What got the fight started last week anyway, if I might ask?"

"Somethin' stupid, really. I challenged them to some pool for money thinkin' I could win back what I'd lost at darts, but I was too drunk to even shoot the cue."

She thought about the puke on his shirt and grimaced. "Yeah, you were pretty drunk."

"Unfortunately, I've been more or less in the same condition for the last several months."

"Too bad."

"Yeah, but I think things are turnin' around. Like I said, I haven't had a drink in a week."

"Great. I'm glad."

"The best thing is, I don't want one. I've been in this bar every night since last week waitin' for you to show up and it hasn't bothered me not to drink. I've watched others actin' really stupid and I realize now how senseless the whole ritual is." He drank half his drink and then set the glass back down. "You don't drink when you come in here?"

"No. I lost my mother to a drunk driver several years ago so I refuse to drink and drive. If I drink, I bring a driver with me, but since I'm on a bike, it's hard to bring someone who can ride."

"What kind of bike?"

"Harley Softail."

Jacob whistled through his teeth. "Wow. Nice bike."

"You know Harleys?"

"Yeah. I don't own one, but I've had my eye on one for a long time. Money has been an issue."

"I know the feeling. They aren't cheap toys."

"No, no they aren't."

The band struck up a haunting melody in a little two-step rhythm. "Would you like to dance?"

She tipped her head to the side and smiled. He really seemed like a nice guy when he wasn't sloshed off his ass. "Sure."

He took her hand sending goose bumps racing up her arm again. Her whole body exploded in the annoying little bumps. The feeling seemed weird, but nice. Maybe it wasn't a bad thing after all. She wouldn't mind gettin' down and dirty with a nice lookin' cowboy.

Paige wasn't small by any means at five foot eleven, but this devastatingly gorgeous cowboy even towered over her.

When they reached the dance floor, he turned around to face her with a saucy little grin on his lips. He swept her into his arms as he began to two-step her around the dance floor.

"I guess I should have asked if you know how to two-step."

"Yeah, I do," she said, getting into the rhythm he created with the shuffle of his feet. The man was good. Solid muscle bunched and rolled beneath her fingers resting on his right shoulder. His hand clasped hers in his left as they scooted around the wooden floor.

"Do you come here often?"

"I have recently. I just found this place a few months ago."

"You aren't from Bandera, are you? I would remember if I'd see you around."

"No. I live in San Antonio."

"Why Bandera to come to a bar then? Surely there are a few honky-tonks in San Antonio."

The devilish grin returned. What did she say to that? She sure couldn't tell him the truth. *I'm a preacher's daughter and I can't be seen anywhere in San Antonio without my dad hearing about it. He'd have a stroke if he saw me dressed like this.* "I don't like the bars there. I found this one on one of my rides. It's quaint."

"Quaint, huh?"

She nodded as she realized he was backing her into a corner with all this talk, feeling her up for information on a personal level. "What about you? Do you frequent The Dusty Boot a lot?"

"I have in the past, but I won't be anymore."

"You're givin' it up?"

"Yes. I need to get my life together. I've taken the first step by quitting drinking."

"That's a great thing, Jacob. I'm glad you've seen the destructive power of drinking. You had me worried last week when you wanted to drive."

"I'm sorry. I should never have put you in a position to have to take care of me."

"I would have done it for anyone."

"Really?"

"Yeah. I tend to take care of people."

The music changed into a slow song, but he didn't release her. In fact, he pulled her closer and slowed their steps. "I'm glad you did it for me. Maybe I can return the favor some time."

"Maybe."

"Would you like to get a cup of coffee?"

"Are you asking me on a date, cowboy?"

He grinned. "Maybe."

"In that case, no."

"No?"

"I don't date my rescued victims."

"Okay. One friend to another then?"

"How about a Coke and a piece of pie?"

"Sounds like a date to me."

"No. No dates remember?"

"All right. Two friends havin' a piece of pie and somethin' to drink."

She stepped out of his arms, but frowned at the loss of his heat. "I'll go for that."

"What's wrong?"

"Nothin'. Why?"

"You were frownin'."

"I thought of somethin'."

"What?"

"I don't know you very well. Should I really be havin' coffee and pie with you?" she asked, coming up with something fast as an excuse rather than telling him she frowned because she didn't want to leave his arms.

"I'll be a perfect gentleman. I swear." He took her hand again. "I'd like to get to know you a little, Paige. You saved my life."

"I wouldn't go so far as to say that."

"I would. I might have killed someone if you hadn't kept me from drivin' home."

"You'd been lucky up until then."

"I know. I'd done a lot of things in the last few months I haven't been proud of." He tucked her hand in the crook of his arm to escort her to the door. "We can have pie at the diner two doors down."

"Are they open?"

"Yeah, for a little bit yet." He winked. "I know the owner." They chatted about Bandera as he told her he'd lived there most of his life. "My parents moved here when I was little."

"They live around here?"

"Yeah. We own a cattle ranch and guest place outside of town."

"Nice. Do you have siblings?"

"Yep. Eight brothers, one sister-in-law and one live-in partner for my eldest brother."

"Live-in partner? Like is he gay or somethin'?"

Jacob laughed. The sound sent chills down her back. The low, intense chuckle sounded rough like he hadn't done it in a while. "No. He just settled down with a great girl, but they aren't married or anything. They're livin' together with his son and she found out she's pregnant right around Christmas."

"Congratulations to them."

"They are pretty excited about it. My parents are too. They'll have another grandchild to love."

"Sounds like a great group."

"It's interesting livin' out there."

"Do you all live together?"

"Sort of. We all have our own places if we want or we can stay in the main house where my parents have their place. We all got deeded a piece of the home place when we turned eighteen."

"How generous of your family."

"For now, we all work together and split the profits as well as the bills."

They reached the diner and he pulled open the door.

"Hey you."

"Hey, Ann."

"What are you doin' around here this late?"

"I have a lady friend I met at The Dusty Boot and we were going to see if we could sneak a piece of your great pie and some coffee."

"Sure, honey. Have a seat anywhere. I was just cleanin' things up to close."

"Oh, don't bother on our part," Paige said. "If you're gettin' ready to close, we can go somewhere else."

Ann chuckled as she waved them into a booth. "Honey, there ain't nothin' else open this time of night in Bandera except the bar and my little diner."

"I don't want to put you out or anything."

"It's no bother. I have a fresh pot of coffee I just made and the pie only takes a minute to dish up. What kind can I get you?"

"Paige?"

"Cherry or apple with a little ice cream if you have it."

"'Course, honey. Jacob?"

"Same for me."

"Comin' right up."

They took a seat across from each other as she glanced around the diner. The décor was simple but homey with the stools sitting along the counter and the booths with their gleaming tables. "This is a cute place."

"I'll pass it along to my aunt."

"She's your aunt?"

"Yeah, my mom's sister. She never had kids of her own so she adopted all of us."

"That's right. You have a huge family."

"What about you?"

"Just me and my dad."

"I bet it was interesting growing up an only child."

"Just like I bet it was interesting growing up with eight brothers."

"Touché."

Ann brought two cups of coffee along with some cream and the pieces of pie piled high with ice cream. "Good Lord, I'll never eat all of that."

"Oh sure you will. Little thing like you—"

Paige laughed out loud. "Little? I haven't been called little since I was twelve with my height."

"You ain't that tall to me, honey. Nina and I are pretty tall too and all the boys are six foot or better."

"Six four," Jacob said, with a grin. "I like my women tall."

Her heart tripped over itself in a funny beat as she raised one eyebrow. "I ain't your woman, cowboy."

He shrugged with a grin. "Okay. I like my dance partners tall."

"Ya got me there."

They continued talking about little things. Bandera and how the town had changed in the years he'd grown up there. San Antonio's differences as well.

"Did you grow up in San Antonio?" he asked as the fork disappeared between his full lips.

Why was she thinking about what it might feel like to have those tempting, kissable lips on hers? She didn't need his kind of trouble and trouble he would be from what she'd seen of him. "No. My dad is a pre—" *Shit.*

"A what?"

She bit her lip, debating on whether to tell him the truth or not. Surely he wouldn't know her daddy, would he? "He's a preacher." A roar of laughter erupted from his mouth as he almost choked on his pie. "I didn't think it was that funny."

"Oh my God. That's priceless!"

"Jacob," she growled in warning. A warning he didn't heed.

"He's a preacher? I bet he doesn't know his little girl dresses in a leather outfit and rides a Harley either."

"No he doesn't. He would have a stroke if he knew, so just hush about it."

Jacob coughed several times to clear his throat. "Where does he think you go on the weekends?" He raised his hand to stop her words. "Wait. Let me guess. The hospital?"

She sighed in a rush. "A nursing home to read to the older ladies."

"My, my. The preacher's daughter is a little liar."

"Do you really think I could tell my father I want to ride a motorcycle, dress in leather and have sex with random men?"

"You do?"

"Sometimes, yeah, but I sure as hell can't tell him what I do on my weekends."

"How do you get away with it? He doesn't know you own the bike, *huh*."

"No. I keep it and my clothes in a storage shed." She scooted out of the booth. "Forget it. Why I'm even telling you this is beyond me. Just forget I ever told you anything. You don't know me. I don't know you." She headed for the door. "Think of it this way, Jacob. We never met." She pushed open the door and headed back down the sidewalk to retrieve her helmet. This whole night was a mistake. She should never have helped him. She should have let him get his ass kicked and drive home drunk. *And if he would have killed someone or himself, I would have felt like shit.*

"Paige, wait!" He caught up with her as she pulled open the door to the bar. "Come on, Paige. I'm sorry. It's not funny. I'm sure you have your reasons for doing what you do. You aren't really any different than me."

"I'm a lot different than you, Jacob. I don't get drunk to drown my sorrows and forget about things or whatever the hell the reason you were drinkin' like a damned fish for. I face my problems."

"Face them? You call hiding yourself from your father facing your problems?"

"Don't judge me, mister."

He grabbed her arm. "I'm not, Paige. I'm trying to understand."

"What the fuck do you care?" She yanked her arm out of his grasp. "You've got your own issues."

"Yeah, I do and I'm learning to face them."

"By drinkin' yourself into stupor?"

"I'm sorry you had to see me like that."

"It doesn't matter." She shoved her way into the building and headed for the bar. "Can I have my helmet, please?"

"Don't go, Paige."

"We're done, Jacob."

"I'm afraid if you leave, I'll never see you again."

"What part of we're done don't you get?"

Chapter Three

Paige. Paige *what*? He didn't know and it was pissing him off. Jacob tossed a bale of hay from the door of the loft into the stack near the wall, one right after the other until sweat poured down his back.

She'd hopped on her bike and tore out of the parking lot of the bar like her ass was on fire and he wished he'd followed her or knew her last name for God's sake! Maybe he could find out from the bartender. The guy seemed to be friendly with her.

He wiped the sweat from his forehead with the back of his shirt sleeve before settling his straw cowboy hat back on his head. He was tired and he wanted a drink, but he wouldn't. Drinking was a thing of the past for him. It sure as hell didn't solve anything in his life so he figured it wouldn't do him any good now. Didn't mean he didn't want one though.

"Jacob, you up there?"

"Yeah, Dad."

"Can you come down here a minute? I need to ask you something."

"Sure. I'll be right down." He slipped off his work gloves and laid them on the next hay bale ready to be moved. The ladder to the bottom of the barn stood back to his right, outlined by the hole in the floor leading down. When he reached it, he hopped down the rungs, taking one at a time until he reached the floor beneath. "What's up?"

"I just wanted to talk to you about your drinking."

"I've given it up, Dad."

"I know you have, son, and I wanted to say how proud I am of you. You've taken steps to change your behavior. It's commendable." His dad dropped his hand onto Jacob's shoulder.

It had been a long time since he thought his father might be proud of him. Being the third eldest of nine boys, he sometimes felt like he got lost in the shuffle of not being the oldest.

"I don't know what made you start in the first place, but I'm glad you found something to help you stop."

"A woman, both times, Dad."

"I'm sorry to hear that, but I'm glad whoever helped you quit was there. Is it someone we might meet someday?"

"I doubt it. I've only met her twice myself."

"I see."

"No, you probably don't, Dad. You see a couple of weeks ago, I almost got my ass kicked in a bar fight over a game of pool. A tall, slender woman jumped into help me, taking the biggest of the guys down with a couple well placed kicks. His friends bailed the minute they saw what she could do, I guess." He shrugged and then readjusted his hat. "I made a fool of myself in front of her and several other people by throwing up everything I had in my stomach outside the bathroom door at The Dusty Boot. Instead of leaving me there to wallow in puke or drive myself home drunk off my ass, she paid for a motel room."

"Wow."

"Yeah."

"Do you know who she is?"

"Sort of. I spent last week at the bar hoping she'd show up so I could tell her thank you. Funny thing was, I saw how stupid people were acting with alcohol in their system and I realized I'd been acting the same way. I haven't had a drink since the night she helped me."

"Interesting way to quit drinking."

"Yeah. I'm not sure why it made such an impression on me, but it did."

"Did you find out who she is?"

"Yeah. I met her two nights ago again. We had coffee and pie with Ann at the diner. When we got to talkin', I found out she's a preacher's daughter."

"And she's hanging out at bars?"

"Yep."

"Interesting."

"I know."

"So what's her name?" his dad asked, propping himself against the stall door like he didn't plan to go anywhere anytime soon.

"Paige, but I don't know her last name. All I know is her father is a preacher in San Antonio, but there are thousands of churches there." He wiped the sweat from his neck, realizing his T-shirt was stuck to his back. Didn't matter. Work needed to be done. Sweat came with the job of handling cattle or running a ranch. "I'm hoping to talk to the bartender to see if he knows her last name, of course he wouldn't even tell me he knew her when I asked him the first time. I think he's protecting her a bit."

"How are you gonna find her?"

Jacob crossed his arms over his chest. "I don't know, Dad, but I have to. I need to see her again."

"It sounds like you're a bit intrigued by this girl."

"Yeah, sort of. I'm not sure what it is about her."

"Whatever it is, I'm glad for it."

"Me too. But I really don't want to get involved with another woman right now."

"Want to talk about it?"

"I can't. It's a situation forced on me a while back and it's somethin' I'm gonna have to live with for the rest of my life."

"I hope you know me and your mother are always here for you, Jacob."

Jacob wrapped his dad in a hug before he stepped back. "I know, Dad, but this is somethin' I don't think you or Mom would ever forgive me for."

"We would forgive you anything, son."

"This wouldn't be easy for either of you."

"Try us."

"I can't right now, Dad. Maybe someday I can come to grips with what I've done, but for now I'm strugglin' with it every day."

"Well, I hope you find your lady friend."

"I hope so too. I'm not goin' back to the bar until this weekend. Hopefully, she'll show up, but I'm not holdin' my breath. She was pretty mad at me."

"I think she'll be over it and be willin' to talk to you. You're a handsome fellow."

"Looks don't always make it easier."

"You'll do fine, son."

"I hope so. I really want to get to know her a little better, you know, as a friend. I think she'd be a great person to be friends with."

"Friends, *huh*?" The grin on his dad's face told Jacob he didn't buy that explanation at all.

Jacob smiled. "Well, maybe friends with benefits."

"I bet." His dad clapped him on the back. "I'll see you at dinner."

"Thanks for the talk."

"You're welcome, Jacob. Anytime."

Jacob climbed the ladder into the loft to get back to work. The hay wouldn't stack itself. He could have left it for Jeff or Joey, but he wanted the physical labor to keep him sane. Hard work never hurt anyone.

A low, masculine laugh followed by a high pitched giggle, made him pause. Joel and Mesa or Jeff and Terri?

In the tack room.

Jeff and Terri.

"Hard, baby?"

"Like a damned rock. It sucks we have to sneak into the barn to have a little alone time."

"Ben has been hard to deal with lately."

"And your pregnancy isn't makin' this any easier."

"Aw, poor baby. You'll live."

The soft feminine laugh made him smile. Jacob took a seat on the hay bale, not wanting to disturb his brother and his girl if they were going to have a little fun. Maybe someday he'd find a woman to have a serious relationship with, but he wasn't sure. The situation with Veronica soured him on relationships. Her situation and the subsequent decision they made together didn't make him want a connection on a serious level with any woman. The minute everything had taken a turn, she'd basically bailed on him and found someone else.

Funny thing? Most of the women in Bandera were trying to get their claws into any of the Young brothers, but Veronica didn't want to turn her relationship into marriage with him. He'd asked. She'd turned him down flat.

His thoughts turned to Paige. *What would she be like in the sack*? She seemed rough around the edges. Her personality was a little persnickety. He wanted to get to know her better, he knew that much, but how much better? *Huh*. He wasn't sure.

Her emerald green eyes were gorgeous. Her tall, slender body could melt chocolate on a winter's day. The way she handled herself with men left a little to be desired. She said she was into random sex though. There might be something there. He could use a good lay. It had been a long time since he'd had meaningless sex with someone. Paige might be up for something along those lines if he could ever figure out her last name or get a phone number.

Damn.

Well, nothing he could do about it right at the moment.

He'd heard the door to the tack room close and lock a few minutes ago, so he figured it would be safe enough to go back to work even though he could still hear his brother's sighs and Terri's groans. Listening to someone else have sex wasn't good for his libido. He wanted that. He wanted a warm pussy around his cock. Just the thought of licking juices from Paige, made him hard as a brick.

Maybe he'd take a trip into town tonight to see if he could find a random woman. No, the thought soured his stomach. He wanted Paige in a leather bustier, little leather G-string and those fuck me boots she wore the other night. *Oh yeah*. He could do her in a minute. Was she into rough sex? He sure hoped he could find out and soon. Tonight, it would be a cold shower and his slicked up hand. By this weekend, he'd know her name and where to find her or he'd damn sure die trying.

* * * *

Paige smoothed the paisley dress down as she took her place in the pew for her father's Saturday evening service. *Just a little longer and I can make my getaway.*

After spending time with Jacob last week, she'd been restless. She smoothed the material around her thighs again as her toes tapped out an unheard rhythm inside her short-heeled pumps. No fuck me boots this evening. She sighed. This service couldn't be over fast enough for her. She needed to feel the wind on her face.

"And God said…"

Oh, Lord help me.

Her father droned on and on. Most of his sermon seemed lost on her as her thoughts drifted to last week.

She really shouldn't have taken off like she did, but Jacob's words hit too close to home. Was she really running from her problems with her father like he suggested?

Nah.

Well, maybe.

Okay, yes, but that didn't mean he knew anything about her or her father. Their relationship was a strained one on a good day. If he knew about her bike and her weekend trips, he'd disown her. She couldn't have that now could she? He was all she had these days with her mother resting beneath the big oak tree in the church cemetery. God, she missed her some days. What would her mother think of her riding a Harley and dressing in leather? Maybe she needed to spend a little time out there tomorrow after church.

Tonight she needed something.

Jacob.

Why?

She wished she knew. What was it about the troubled cowboy that drew her to him like a moth to flame?

The Dusty Boot would be her destination. In one way, she hoped Jacob was there to greet her. In another, she hoped he wasn't. Maybe some random guy would work better. No, she wanted Jacob.

Mrs. Robertson patted her hand and smiled. "He does drone on, doesn't he?"

"Sometimes."

"I'm not sure how you do it, child."

She smiled and shook her head. "I don't know either most days."

"God love the man."

"I'm sure he does."

"Visited your momma lately?"

"No, I was just thinking about goin' out there tomorrow after services."

"Good idea. You look like you need a good mother daughter talk."

"And Jesus rose up…"

"Oh brother," Mrs. Robertson said as Paige giggled under her breath earning a stern look from her father.

"Let us pray."

"Thank goodness," Mrs. Robertson added.

Paige smothered another laugh with a cough.

The moment services let out, she headed next door to the church where she and her father lived. The quaint little white house had been home for several years now with the swing on the front porch and the flowerbeds she loved to tend. White curtains adorned the two front windows, now closed against the winter winds. Early spring in San Antonio could still be rather cold in the evenings even being in south Texas. The days were mild with temperatures in the fifties or sixties, but nights grew cold when the sun went down.

"Paige?" her father called several minutes later.

"Yes, Papa?"

"There you are." He patted her shoulder as he headed for the kitchen. He usually took a nip before bed from the whiskey bottle he kept in the cupboard above the refrigerator. She pretended not to notice. "Are you headed to Sunnyside?"

"Yes."

"I'm sure the ladies love havin' you there to read to them every weekend. You're such a good child."

If you only knew. "I'll be home late. Don't wait up." She knew he wouldn't. His nip of whiskey usually meant half the bottle and resounding snores by the time she came home.

"Be careful."

"I will." She grabbed her purse, the keys to her small sedan and a jacket to ward off the chill of the coming night until she reached the storage shed where her bike sat. Good thing the place gave the tenants the code to get into the gates. She could come and go as she pleased.

Several minutes later, she punched in the code and watched as the gate swung open. One-forty-two. There it was. Her lifeline to the outside. Her private domain for her *other* personality. Will the real Paige Tyler come on down!

She shut off the engine of her car and stepped out. The wind chilled her arms, but she didn't care. The wind would feel good on her face. There wouldn't be a leather bustier tonight, but her leather jacket would cut the chill in the air as she rode.

The lock gave way under her fingers. She lifted the roll door of the shed and then flipped on the bare light bulb in the center of the room. The Harley Softail sitting in the center of the storage unit made her smile. *All mine.* Every inch of the gleaming bike belonged to her and she loved it like a child. "Aw, baby. I'm sorry I haven't been here in a few days, but we'll be ridin' the wind shortly."

The door rolled back down with a push of her hand until it banged against the concrete floor. Goose bumps pebbled her flesh as she stepped out of her dress to reveal her lacy strapless bra and G-string underwear. She loved sexy underwear and the men she ended up with usually liked them too. She giggled. Would Jacob? She hoped he was at the bar tonight. She needed his hunky self to scratch the incredible itch she'd developed since she met him.

She pulled on the white tank top from the dresser and her skin tight leather pants. Her fuck me boots sat in the corner waiting for her to slip them on. What about fucking with just the boots on? *Wow. That would be really hot.*

She lifted the door on the storage shed again before she straddled her bike and slipped on her helmet. Once she pushed it out into the open, she tapped the ignition to start the bike.

The distinctive Harley growl made her smile. Lord, she loved that sound. She could almost come from the rumbled of the bike between her legs.

Once she was outside the door, she stored her purse and keys in the saddle bags and then locked the storage shed with a snick of the lock. Her car would be safe until she returned.

The tires hummed under the machine as she headed down Interstate 10. Cars zipped past her, but she didn't pay any attention to them. The destination she had in mind took up her entire thought process or more like the man she hoped to find there invaded her thoughts to overwhelming. Why was she so stuck on him? What made him so special? Was it the sadness in his eyes or the overwhelming need to take care of him she felt every time she got near him?

She wasn't sure. Maybe fucking him once would take care of those thoughts.

It wouldn't hurt anyway.

Before she knew it, she was pulling down the side street in Bandera where The Dusty Boot parking lot took up one whole block. The music could be heard with each swing of the doors.

The parking lot overflowed with trucks and cars of every shape and size. She couldn't tell if Jacob was there or not since there were several trucks matching the description of his.

I hope he's here.

Once she got inside the bar, she found Dan behind the mahogany expanse and waved. "Hey, Dan."

"Hey, Paige. I didn't think you'd be here this weekend after the way you left last Saturday."

"I know, but I couldn't stay away from your handsome face."

"Yeah, right. Mimi would believe that like she would believe one of these hot young cowboys was comin' onto her."

Paige laughed. Mimi was Dan's wife, stood about four foot nothing and weighed in at about two hundred pounds. Don't piss the woman off though or she'd take out your knees before you could blink. She took no shit off anyone, especially her husband, the big tough biker dude.

Dan put her helmet beneath the bar before he wiped down an imaginary wet spot with the towel in his hand. "He's here you know."

"He?" she asked, pretending to be nonchalant about what she wanted.

"Jacob." Dan cocked his head to the side, indicating the back corner of the bar to his right.

"Why would you think I'm lookin' for him?" Paige picked at the imaginary lint on her top, leaving the zipper open on the front of her jacket.

"I saw you two last week. You can't put anything over on this old fella, Paige. You two are hot for each other. I saw the way you was dancin'."

"It's nothin', Dan. Just gratitude on his part."

"I don't believe a word you is sayin', darlin'."

Paige took the Coke Dan set out and moved down to the other end of the bar to her normal spot. Amazing, it always seemed to be open when she got there. With her back to where Jacob sat, she concentrated on the music, letting it surround her with the beat.

The band they had in here every Saturday night actually sounded pretty good. Maybe someday they'd make it big in Nashville. She hoped so. The members were nice people.

She waited knowing sooner or later Jacob would approach her.

Her skin tingled from the heat of his gaze.

She wondered if he'd started drinking again. She knew how hard it was to give up a habit.

Several minutes later, the warmth of his breath on the back of her neck told her he stood near. "Paige."

Goose bumps flittered across her arms at the sound of his voice. She closed her eyes to absorb his heat before she turned to face him. Her whole body exploded in sensation the moment she met his gaze. "Jacob."

He leaned in to talk in her ear. "I'm glad you're here."

"Are you?" she asked, fighting the urge to rub herself all over him.

"Yeah. I prayed I'd see you again."

"Why?"

"I wanted to apologize for my behavior last week."

So it's all about his behavior and not really his need to see her again. Disappointment surrounded her heart. She'd really hoped he wanted to see her for other reasons. "Apology accepted." She spun back around to face the bar.

"I'm not done."

"I am." She shot over her shoulder. *Why am I doin' this? If he's sincere in his apology, which I think he is, why am I givin' him such a hard time?*

He took her arm and spun her back around on the bar stool. The next thing she knew his mouth slammed down on hers in a desperate kiss that pushed her back against the bar. Even though the kiss was harsh and demanding, she dove into it with all the pent up desire in her body for this man. Her hands found the front of his shirt as she grasped the material in her fists to pull him closer. She spread her thighs to take him between them as he deepened the kiss to volatile.

She didn't taste alcohol on his tongue, just man and desire.

He pushed his hands into her hair, fisting the strands at the back of her head. God, she loved a man to take control.

When he finally pulled back, she could see the need in his eyes as he stared down at her.

"Wow."

"Pretty good for a cowboy."

"You ain't seen nothin' yet, darlin'." He glanced around them for a minute. "Care to get out of here?"

"What are you askin'?"

"I'd like to take our kiss a bit further if you're game."

"Oh, I'm game all right."

"We can go back to my place. It's not far. About ten minutes."

Did she really want to get personal with this man on the level of seeing his bachelor pad or would it be better to get a motel in town. She cringed at the thought of the seedy place across the street. She wanted a little more pampering from this man for the hell he'd put her through the last couple of weeks. He'd better live up to the desire she saw in his eyes. "Sure."

"You can either follow me back to the ranch or you can ride with me."

"I'll follow you." She hopped off the stool and followed him toward the door. Dan already had her helmet out sitting on the edge of the bar as she rounded the end. He smiled and winked. "I don't want to hear anything out of you."

"I didn't say a word."

"Good." She tucked her helmet under her arm. Letting Jacob chase after her, she pushed open the door and headed for her bike.

Minutes later she found herself tooling along a dirt road behind a black truck. The gate to the ranch came into view to the right. Jacob pulled up and punched in a code allowing the gate to swing open.

She followed him down the long driveway. Several double cabins stood off to the right and a huge main house stood silhouetted in the moonlight to their left. She couldn't see a lot of the place because of the darkness, but it reminded her of a typical cattle ranch. The sound of cattle mooing in the distance brought a smile to her lips. Definitely a cowboy, her Jacob. *My Jacob? What the hell?*

They continued to follow the dirt road between the cabins, past the big barn to a single wide mobile home near the back of the main lodge. It wasn't much, but what did she know. Really, she barely knew the guy. *What am I thinking?*

He stopped his truck near the small steps leading inside as she pulled up next to him. She really hoped the loud bike hadn't awakened anyone on the ranch. It wasn't every day someone on a Harley drove onto a cattle ranch.

She shut the bike off and pushed down the kickstand, letting it lean to the left.

"Someday you'll have to take me on your bike," he said, stopping next to her as she pulled off her helmet.

"Maybe."

"You can leave your stuff out here. No one will mess with it."

"Okay." She draped the helmet over the backseat rest. "Do you have a lot of guests?"

"Not this time of year. Most people come in the summer when it's nice and warm." He took her hand in the warmth of his own as he walked toward his home. "It isn't much."

"You're a bachelor. I wouldn't expect much."

"It's better than a dingy motel room though."

He opened the door and she got her first look at Jacob's personal space when he flipped on the light switch. A couch sat to the left, a big screen television sat to the right and a recliner took up the space next to the couch. A kitchen sat behind the living room with an open space between them. The kitchen was small, but had all the amenities from what she could tell. Not much decorated the walls, but then again she wouldn't think a single guy would have a lot of flowery pictures or anything. She did see a few photographs in frames sitting on the end tables.

"Your family?"

"Yeah. The one on the wall is all of us."

"Big family."

"Yep."

She looked closer. "Triplets?"

"Yeah. Joel, Jason and Joshua are identical triplets. Joel got married recently."

"I bet that was fun growing up."

"They were a handful as kids."

"You're the third oldest you said."

He nodded. "Jeff is the oldest."

"Wow. Nine boys. I bet your mom is completely gray."

"Actually, no. She's got beautiful long black hair."

"Do you have Native American blood?"

He pointed to the large picture on the wall. "Some, yes. You can see it more in my mother than any of us boys, although most of us have the dark hair. The triplets have blue eyes. Jeff's are grey and mine are brown like my mother's. The rest of the boys are a grouping of those three."

"What a combination."

"You could say that, yeah. It's an interesting family dynamic."

"You all seem to be close though?"

"Not always. Typical boys, you know."

She bit her lip and dropped her gaze to her feet. "Jacob, why were you drinkin' so heavily?"

He moved away from her to drop his keys and hat on the coffee table. "I don't want to talk about it."

"It would help if you did."

"No it won't. I'm past it. I'm not drinkin' anymore."

"I can see the sadness in your eyes."

"It's over. There's nothin' I can do to change what happened so I'm moving on." He stopped in front of her. "Wanna get nekkid?"

"That's what we came here for, isn't it?"

"Yeah, but all this serious talk, I thought you might have changed your mind."

"No. I want to help you for some ungodly reason."

"Nothin' to help, darlin'. It's done." He shoved his hands into her hair to tip her head back with a sharp tug on her scalp. "I'm gonna lick you all over."

"Promises, promises," she whispered as his lips did a slow crawl along her jaw to her ear.

"Not a promise, honey. It's a fact."

She found his firm chest beneath the shirt encasing it. One thing she'd noticed about him from the get-go was how toned his body was. He must do a lot of physical labor on the ranch to keep his muscles in such good shape.

"Touch me."

"Oh, I plan to, honey."

His hand encircled her breast, palming her flesh until his fingers found her nipple under her tank top. She moaned as he pinched it between his thumb and first finger. Pain along with pleasure. She couldn't get enough. Would he go for a little forceful fucking? She hoped so.

He stepped back to slowly push her jacket from her shoulders, letting it fall in a heap to the floor. "Nice. You have beautiful breasts."

"Thanks."

"Just the right size for my hands."

She placed her palm flat against his. "I like your hands. Long lean fingers. Strong. Callused."

"They might be a little rough on your skin."

"I like rough," she said, watching his eyes.

"Good. So do I."

"Make me yours for the night, Jacob."

"You got it, babe." He scooped her up in his arms before she could utter a squeak and then strolled down the hallway toward the back of the trailer.

His room wasn't much, a huge bed, a long dresser, a couple of nightstands, and nothing more. He dropped her on the mattress and covered her mouth in a desperate kiss.

"God, I want you."

"Me too."

He stood. "Undress me. Slowly."

She crawled up on her knees so she could reach the snaps on the front of his western shirt. Her fingertips tingled touching the hair roughed skin after she parted the material to reveal his chest. *Wow.* Dark, dusky nipples tempted her with their pebbled hard tips. "I want to taste you."

"Go ahead."

She skimmed her lips from the center of his chest to the right nipple, encircling it with her tongue until he moaned low in his throat. Unable to resist, she nipped it with her teeth.

"Naughty girl."

"*Mmmm.*"

As she nipped and sucked on the tip, she worked the belt buckle at his waist loose before she parted the denim material to reveal his incredible length to her touch. The man had an impressive cock although she really didn't have a lot to judge by. She talked the talk, but she hadn't really walked the walk as much as she made it sound. Her experience in the bedroom department lacked something like numbers. Oh, she wasn't a virgin by any stretch of the imagination, but she'd only been with two other men in her lifetime. Luckily, they'd both taught her something about pleasing men.

She licked her way down his washboard abs as she pushed his boxers and his jeans to the floor. "Step out."

He quickly toed off his boots and stepped out of his clothes, leaving them in a heap near the window.

"Wow. A little horny are we?"

"A lot horny, darlin'."

"God, I love when you call me that."

"What else do you like?"

"Lots of things," she said, as he stalked closer in an unhurried gate meant to tantalize her into wanting him. He didn't need to do anything of the sort. Her pussy already wept with need for this cowboy. "I wanna suck you."

"No."

"No?"

"Later, maybe." He held out his hand and she slipped her palm into his as she stood. "I'm going to undress you now."

"Okay."

He slipped the tank top over her head, leaving her standing bare from the waist up. "I love these. They're perfect."

"One is a little bigger than the other."

"Such pretty, rosy nipples."

He encircled one with his tongue like she'd done to him. Shivers skittered along her arms at the feeling of his mouth. He flicked the tip with his tongue, bringing her up on her toes. Her nipples were one of the most sensitive parts of her body. She could almost come from nipple stimulation.

"I want to put clamps on these."

"Clamps?"

"Yeah, nipple clamps with a cute little weight hanging between them. Have you ever had those on your breasts?"

"No."

"Wait here." He moved to his dresser and opened one of the drawers. A moment later, he returned with something in his hands. "I haven't used these on anyone before, just so you know."

He held up a small chain with a pinchers on each end and a small sliding ball in the middle of the chain. "You keep nipple clamps in your drawer?"

"I bought them a while back. I hadn't had anyone special I wanted to use them on, but your nipples are just right for clamps." He sucked one of her nipples hard between his lips until it stood up pointed and stiff. "Perfect." The clamp slid on with a slight twinge of pain. He tightened the end down until the pain brought tears to her eyes. "A little too much?"

"Yeah."

He loosened it slightly and then did the same to the other nipple. When he stepped back to admire his handy work, the weight hanging on the chain between her breasts pulled the clamps on her nipples until they stung.

"Okay?"

She took a deep breath and nodded.

"Good." His eyes glittered with lust. "They look fabulous on you."

"Thank you."

"Now, for the pants." He worked her belt loose before pushing her leather pants to the floor and indicating she should toe off her boots. "Are you wet?"

"God, yes."

He skimmed his hand down her abdomen, pushing his fingers between her thighs. "Soaked. You like a bit of pain with your sex, *eh*?"

"I guess. I think so. I like the way it feels when you pull my hair and take what you want."

He looked surprised. "You've been with men before, right?"

"I'm not a virgin, Jacob, although I'm not terribly experienced either."

"How many guys have you been with?"

"Two besides you."

He shoved his fingers through his hair, leaving it sticking up in several directions. "Shit."

"What?"

"I thought you had been with several guys." He moved to take the clamps off her nipples.

"No, leave them."

"They shouldn't stay on more than a few minutes especially since you've never had your nipples in clamps before. Brace yourself. This is gonna hurt."

He removed one and as the blood rushed back into the tortured tip, she hissed with the pain. He soothed it with his tongue until it no longer hurt.

"That wasn't so bad."

"I hate to be the bearer of bad news, darlin', but last time I checked, you have two of those."

"Aw, fuck!"

When he removed the second one, she cried, "Owie, owie." Again, he soothed it with his tongue, but this time her clit throbbed with the beat of her heart in the tip of her breast.

"I'm sorry."

"Don't be. I liked the way they felt while they were on."

"You do like a little pain then."

"Yeah, I guess I do." He pulled back his hand and smacked her bare ass. "What the hell was that for?"

"To see how much pain you like."

"I've never been spanked before in my life. That hurt."

"Your mom and dad never spanked you?"

"No." She rubbed the sore spot with the palm of her hand. "I was the perfect preacher's daughter, remember?"

"Ah yes. Daddy's little angel in leather."

"Don't make fun of me."

He held up his hands in a defensive posture as he backed up a little. "I'm not, honey. I think it's great how you are the little angel with a crooked halo being held up by devil's horns." He put his hands down and crooked his finger. "Come 'ere."

She tipped her chin down as one eyebrow shot up. "Why?"

"Because I wanna fuck you until the sun comes up."

She sauntered closer. "Good because I want it too."

He grabbed her around the waist and hoisted her up so she could wrap her legs around him. His cock stood hard between them.

"Condom?"

"Crap. Let me grab one out of the drawer." He set her down and walked to the nightstand drawer. After rummaging around, he cussed a blue streak.

"What's wrong?"

"I'm out apparently."

"You can't be serious."

"Dead serious."

"All wet and nowhere to go."

He held up a finger. "Let me throw some clothes on. I'll be back in a minute."

"You aren't drivin' to town to get some, are you?"

"Honey, I have eight brothers. Don't you think one of them will have a condom they can spare?"

"You are really goin' to go around to your brothers asking for a condom?"

"Do we have a choice?"

"Well yeah, I guess we do." She bit her lip. "I'm on birth control. Have you been tested lately?"

"Yeah, after my last girlfriend."

"Me too. I mean after the last guy I slept with even though he used a condom every time we were together."

"What are you sayin', darlin'?"

"I'm sayin' do you think we can skip the condom this time?"

* * * *

Should he trust her? Did he have a reason not to? She is a preacher's daughter, right?

"What's wrong?"

"I'm not sure if I should trust you."

"Seriously, Jacob?" She jammed her fists on her hips. "I can show you my birth control pills if you want. They are in my purse in my saddle bags on the bike."

"All right. I guess I don't have a reason not to trust you."

"Do you want to get laid tonight or not, big boy?"

Shivers raced down his back. "Oh, hell yeah."

"Then I guess you'll have to trust me. I mean, really. Do I have a reason to distrust you? No."

He grabbed her around the waist and tossed her on the bed. "Prepared to be fucked."

"Come and get it, handsome."

God. He loved her mouth, her tits, her ass and he was about to really love her pussy.

She scooted up on the bed until her head lay on his pillow. Her brown hair lay in a halo around her head, giving her an ethereal look. He brushed the hair off her forehead. "You're so beautiful," he whispered, in awe that such a gorgeous woman would want to go to bed with him.

"You're pretty gorgeous yourself, cowboy. I could eat you up."

"I'm gonna eat you until you scream my name."

"What was your name again?"

"You're gonna pay for that." He ran his tongue from her lips to her ear, down her neck and across her collarbone. He left a little love bite on her shoulder.

"You bit me!"

"Just a little one."

"I hope it can't be seen. My father will have a cow."

"Not unless you're naked in front of him."

"Never."

"Then you're fine. I like marking my women."

"I'm not your woman, Jacob. We've had this talk."

He kissed her quickly. "You are for tonight, honey." He continued his journey down her chest, stopping to lick and nibble on her breasts for several minutes as she moaned under him. The little sounds she made with her arousal were music to his ears. Speaking of arousal, he could smell her sweet scent, letting it wrap around his senses.

Her abdomen quivered under his licking assault.

The thatch of hair at her pussy tickled his chin as he made his way to the treasure he sought. Eating out a woman was the best. There wasn't anything better than sweet cum on his tongue as she came undone beneath him.

She spread her thighs, begging on whimpers for the touch of his tongue on her clit.

"Please, Jacob."

"Please what, darlin'?"

"I want your tongue."

"Where?" he asked, pressing his nose to the curls guarding her sweetness from his mouth.

"On my clit. God, please. I need you."

The first swipe of his tongue had her hips coming off the bed. Moans escaped her lips as she tossed her head on his pillow. With both hands on her hips to keep her in place, he continued his assault on her clit, bringing her to a screeching orgasm within seconds. Her screams probably told the entire ranch he had a woman in here, but he didn't care. Her satisfaction meant everything.

He continued to softly lick her clit while she came down from her high, giving her a minute to recover before he took her to the heights of ecstasy again.

"Again?"

"Oh yeah."

Her clit hardened under his tongue, waiting for the touch, friction or whatever you wanted to call it. Her pussy glistened with her cum, so he licked until every drop had disappeared. The moan that spilled from her lips made him smile. He loved taking a woman to the highs of good sex.

It took a bit longer this time and a bit more stimulation to get her there, but he managed to bring her to another orgasm with his tongue and fingers. Her pussy was so tight. He could almost believe she was a virgin. He frowned. Maybe she lied about it. Maybe she really hadn't been with anyone before. Of course, she knew a little by her actions earlier, but her hesitation with it all seemed almost virgin like.

Quit second-guessing her.

He moved so his cock was nestled in the v of her spread thighs. The sight of her pussy lured him in. He needed to feel her warmth more than he needed his next breath. Going bare with her scared him a little, but he trusted her. He didn't know why, but he did.

He sank into her warmth with a sigh. "God, you feel amazing."

"Fuck me, Jacob. I need it hard."

"Give me a minute, darlin' or this will be over before we get started."

"We can do it again. Just fuck me."

"Such dirty language from such a good girl."

She wrapped her legs around him and dug her heels into his butt, urging him on as he sank farther into her slick pussy. Her muscles quivered around him. He hit her G-spot with each slow thrust, driving her crazy with need. Her eyes were wild with desire. Her fingernails dug into his biceps as he increased the pace of his thrusts. He couldn't stop. Within what seemed like seconds, his balls drew up, signaling his imminent release. Paige screamed his name as she came apart in his arms.

"Oh God," he murmured, losing his own tempestuous hold on his desire.

Cum squirted out the end of his dick, coating both of them with his seed. It had been a long time since he'd went without a condom. He'd forgotten how awesome it felt.

"You okay?" she asked in a whisper as she reached up and kissed his chest.

"Yeah."

"That was pretty awesome, cowboy."

"You can say that again."

"That was pretty awesome, cowboy."

They laughed together, but it turned into a mutual moan as he slowly pulled out of her warm body.

"Give me a minute to recover and we can do it again."

"You're serious?"

"Of course, I am. I told you I wanted to fuck you until the sun came up. I wasn't jokin'."

"Well, you know I'd love to stay, but I really should be gettin' home. I can't stay all night, Jacob."

"I know, Paige. Your daddy would have a fit if you stayed out past midnight."

"That is the understatement of the century."

She rolled off the bed and headed for the small bathroom off to the right of his bedroom. A minute later, he heard the toilet flush and the water run in the sink while he laid there on the bed with a stupid grin on his face. Paige was the first woman he'd slept with since Veronica. He'd done pretty damned good, he thought. He could sure get used to Paige being around a little more often. Maybe they could even be exclusive fuck buddies or something. He certainly thought she was beautiful and sexy enough.

He propped himself up on an elbow watching Paige as she came out of the bathroom and gathered up her clothes. "When can we get together again?"

"Again?"

"Yeah. I mean I thought we were pretty spectacular together tonight."

"Uh. I don't know, Jacob. I mean with you livin' way out here and me in San Antonio, it might be kinda hard to get together again."

"Are you sayin' you don't want to see me after tonight?"

"No. Not really. I mean, it was good, but I can't keep coming out here indefinitely. My father is goin' to get suspicious if I keep coming home so late every weekend."

He rolled out of the bed and stalked toward her as she fastened the last button on her pants. "You're makin' excuses, Paige."

"No, really I'm—"

He wrapped his hand behind her head and crushed his mouth against hers. At first her lips were hard beneath his, but they soon softened and she opened her mouth to accept his tongue. Kissing her was like eating his favorite dessert. He wanted more, so much more. When he finally lifted his head, he whispered against her mouth, "Say I can see you again. I'm not done with this mouth."

"When?"

"I don't care. Tonight. Tomorrow. Next week. I'll take anything you'll give me."

Her fingers were splayed on his chest. The touch almost brought him to his knees. *God, I want her again.*

"I'll make something work."

"Promise?"

"Yes."

"Good girl." He swatted her butt for good measure. He loved her little squeak, which did nothing for his quickly hardening cock. She had to go. He knew that. It didn't make it any easier to watch her leave.

"Do you have a cell?"

"Of course."

"Does your dad see it?"

"No. Never."

"What's the number?"

She rattled off her cell number and he quickly memorized it to add it to his contact list. "Expect a call or text from me."

"Do I get yours?" she asked, stepping back out of his reach to slip on her boots.

"You'll have mine as soon as I send you a message." He shoved his legs into the jeans he picked up off the floor.

"True." She stood as she pressed her lips together in a firm line.

He didn't like the look at all.

"I guess I'll see you around."

"Soon."

"Yeah, soon."

She headed down the hall to the living room to retrieve her coat. "Thanks for a good time."

"You're welcome. I enjoyed myself immensely."

"Me too."

"Good."

"Good night then."

"Paige?"

"Yeah?" she asked as she turned around with her hand on the doorknob.

"Be careful going home."

Chapter Four

Paige grabbed the dandelions with her ungloved hand, yanking them from the ground surrounding the flowers in her small garden. She loved how the blooms smelled when they reached for the sun to warm their petals on this warmer than normal March afternoon. The soil between her fingers calmed her restless heart in a way she couldn't quite understand. Several flecks of dirt clung to her fingertips, coloring her pale skin to a muddy brown. The earthy smell surrounded her as the sun beat down on her bare shoulders, tingeing her fair skin to a pink, freckled slope.

A heavy sigh escaped her lips as she brushed the dirt from her hands onto her jean clad legs, smearing it along her thighs. Why couldn't she be happy with her life? Why did she have to find ways to escape her humdrum life as a preacher's daughter? The pressures of taking over the duties her mother normally would have lay heavily on her shoulders. She didn't want to be the designated woman to handle the woman's auxiliary duties or the other hundred things required of her. She wanted to be the young, careful woman of twenty-seven, live her life the way she wanted to and not have all the responsibilities of caring for the church activities.

This whole thing began after her mother was killed by a drunk driver when she was twelve. Being raised by a devote Christian preacher as a single parent left something to be desired. He'd been strict, but loving in most things, except she'd never had the love of a woman to guide her in her teen years. Now she struggled with being a woman hell-bent on proving herself as a woman. Did she pretend to be so wild so men would be attracted to her? Men liked wild women, didn't they? She wiped the sweat from her forehead smearing dirt across the bridge of her nose in the process. *Wonderful. I need a shower.*

The whole drinking until you were stinking drunk pissed her off. If the man who'd killed her mother hadn't been driving, she never would have been killed on her way home from the grocery store. Paige didn't understand how people could act so irresponsible especially at the detriment of someone else's life. She rarely drank, not liking the taste of alcohol very much and she thought people acted really stupid when they were drunk.

Her thoughts turned to Jacob as she stared at the mulch in the flower bed, spreading it with her hands to even out the lumps. She picked up a small clump, not really seeing it in her hand as she contemplated the developments between them. What the hell was she going to do with him? He seemed attracted to her at least on a physical level. They were good together in bed. She frowned. Good together in bed sounded so trite. She didn't want just a physical relationship with anyone. She wanted to get married someday, have children and build a life with a man, but then again, the physical was pretty damned good with the cowboy.

Blood hummed in her veins at the thought of the things Jacob had done to her. She'd never been so turned on in her life as she was the night they'd made love. No, had sex. Heart stopping, body humming, sex. What he'd done to her body she'd never experienced before with any man. It scared her spitless. The last thing she needed right now was another man to take care of.

She had enough troubles keeping her personal life out of her father's line of sight. Good grief! If he ever found out about where she really went on weekend nights, the poor man would probably have a heart attack or something.

Her mama would have understood.

A tear slipped down her cheek to land on the back of her hand. She quickly swiped at it with the tips of her fingers only to find more replacing them faster than she could wipe them away. Why she was crying, she wasn't sure. Just missing her mother? Maybe, but why now? Her mother had been gone over fifteen years.

"Daughter?"

"Yes, Daddy?" A very stern looking older gentleman walked down the tree-lined path toward her as she struggled to her feet, wiping at the wetness on her face and hoping he wouldn't see.

At just about six feet in height, he didn't tower over her like he used to. His green eyes were clouded with worry today as he stared down into her face. "What's wrong?"

Damn. "Nothing."

"Why are your eyes red?"

"Allergies."

"Ah."

He nodded, dismissing her emotional distress as he usually did, with the normal brush-off she found upsetting at times. Today, it didn't matter. She didn't want to explain her tears to anyone.

"Well, the ladies of the auxiliary would like to talk to you about the bake sale at the spring dance we're having as a church social."

She sighed, hating the fact that she had to take over the duties normally associated with the preacher's wife. "Yes, Daddy."

"Thank you, Paige. I know you don't always like doing these duties."

"It's not that. I just don't feel comfortable with the older ladies. There isn't anyone my age involved in these things."

"We should work on getting the younger crowd involved in the church socials. You and I should talk more about it."

"Of course."

"Wonderful. Now off you go." He kissed her on the cheek. "I'll see you at lunch."

"I love you, Daddy."

"I love you too, sweetheart."

She headed for the house to change her clothing before she went to the church. No use showing up in dirty jeans and a tank top. It wouldn't go over very well with the elderly women of the church. They already weren't too happy with the way she handled things as the daughter of the preacher.

Well too bad. She grinned as she turned on her heels to walk toward the side door of the church. It was about time they saw the true Paige.

The ladies were chattering like squirrels on the hunt for nuts. None paid much attention to Paige as she came to stand behind them.

"Really. She's such a nice girl, but she just doesn't have it in her to be a preacher's daughter."

Oh hell no!

One of the ladies looked past Mrs. Johnson and swallowed visibly. Paige shook her head as she pressed her fingers to her lips.

Another of the threesome said, "And the Preacher Tyler is such a great man. He's so personable and handsome. Oh, lordy is he handsome."

Paige almost giggled. Obviously the widow Martin had the hots for her father.

"Well of course he is, but he's still very distraught over his wife's death."

"But she died over fifteen years ago."

"Apparently he isn't ready to move on."

"I think I might invite him and Paige over for Sunday dinner this week. You know, to be neighborly and all."

"Of course."

"Where is that girl anyway?" Mrs. Johnson spun around. "Paige?"

"Mrs. Johnson. Widow Martin. Mrs. Williams. Nice to see you ladies."

All three women took in her attire and frowned. "Gardening?" Mrs. Johnson asked.

"Yes, I was. It's a beautiful spring day out there. The sun is just warm enough and the flowers are blooming. My daffodils are budding and they look so pretty next to the ground cover blooms that are starting to come up as well. My Agarita are out now too."

"You have a beautiful garden, Paige," Mrs. Williams choked out, obviously embarrassed by the talk going on around her while Paige listened.

"Thank you. I do love gardening." She stuffed her hands in her pockets. "Shall we get down to business so I can get back to it?"

"Certainly."

For the next hour the four women chatted, drank tea and made notes about the spring social event the church was planning. They were going to have a carnival type atmosphere with a dance later in the evening to bring in the local younger crowd.

"And with the dance, we should be able to draw some of the locals in, I would think," Widow Martin said.

"What kind of music are they listenin' to these days, Paige?"

"This area would be great for a country music type dance I would think. Maybe bring in a local band. I know someone—"

"Oh no." Mrs. Johnson shook her head with enough force her glasses tilted. "We couldn't have a band."

"Why not? I think it's a great idea."

"Bands tend to bring in the drinkers. You know. The kind of people who hang out in those seedy bars."

Seedy bars? The Dusty Boot wasn't a seedy bar. The ladies would fall over dead if they saw her in her leather gear or saw the tall drink of water wrapped up in the package of Jacob Young.

Her nipples pebbled at the mere thought of the man.

"Cold dear?" Widow Martin asked with a raised eyebrow and a glance at her chest.

"Uh, yeah."

"You should have worn a sweater. It's not quite warm enough for those skimpy tops you young girl's wear these days."

"I'm fine." She crossed her arms over her chest and scowled. "Back to the band? If we want to draw in the younger crowd, we need to have something they'll like in order to get them into the festivities. Punch and cookies aren't going to do it. I'm not suggesting alcohol be served, but a band would be great."

"Well I think it's a good idea."

The deep voice behind her made her jump as she swung around. "I thought you were leaving this to us women, Daddy?"

"I was." He nodded to the other women as he placed a hand on her shoulder. "I thought I would put in my two cents. I think having a band come and play during the party is a grand idea." He tipped his head to the side as heat crawled up her neck. "How on earth do you know anyone in a band, Paige?"

"I, *uh…*"

"Never mind. I'm sure it's one of your friends who mentioned it or something. If you know someone who might be interested in playing, by all means, talk to them."

"Are you sure?"

"Of course. Maybe we should have this over the Memorial Day holiday? Wouldn't it be grand to have a barbeque picnic type thing with a band, fireworks, and games?"

"What a wonderful idea, Reverend Tyler," Widow Martin interjected. "You come up with such fantastic ideas."

The older woman batted her eyelashes as Paige shook her head and rolled her eyes.

"Thank you. Anyway, I'll let you ladies work out the details. We have a few months to plan this if we are doing it over Memorial Day weekend. You'll need to work on this to get it planned." He rubbed his hands together.

"This will be wonderful to bring in the local community as well as some of the younger crowd."

Her father smiled as he walked toward the back of the church with a new spring in his step. Paige hadn't seen him this excited about something in a long time. Maybe this would be good for all of them.

Talk switched to the Memorial Day celebration as they were now calling it. Paige took over the job of booking a band. She had the perfect one in mind if they would do it, the band from The Dusty Boot. Of course, it depended on whether they were available or not. If not, they might know someone who would fit the bill.

She tapped her fingers against her lips. Would some of the families from Bandera come? What about inviting Jacob and his family? They probably didn't go to church in San Antonio, but it might be a chance to see him outside of their once a week hookup from The Dusty Boot.

"Paige?"

"Oh. Sorry. My mind wandered there for a minute. Did you have a question?"

"You never did answer us or your father. Where do you know a country music band from?" Mrs. Johnson asked.

"Oh around. I have a couple of friends who sing in a band."

"Not the type of people I would think a preacher's daughter should be hanging around with," the widow said with a frown.

"Sorry, ladies. It's time for me to leave. I must get lunch on the table for my father." She stood. "We'll talk again soon. In the meantime, I'll be looking into the band." Paige quickly dismissed herself from the company of the women to avoid talking about her personal life. They didn't need to know anything about her, the busybodies. Her life was her own to live and damn it, live it she would.

The cooler interior of the small house she and her father shared greeted her with warmth. She loved living there even though it held some hard memories of her mother. The church had welcomed them into the family many years ago, but it was time for them to let her lead her life in whatever manner she chose.

"Daddy?"

"In here, sweetheart," her father called from the small den.

She headed down the little hall until she approached the doorway leading into her father's office. "Are you ready for lunch?"

"Sure, honey." He never glanced up from his laptop.

She sighed in disappointment. On one hand she wished he would take more of an interest in what her life held, but on the other hand she hoped he'd never know about the more intimate details.

After a moment, she turned and headed to the kitchen. Sandwiches and chips would have to do. She hadn't been to the grocery for their weekly staples. She quickly made their lunch and delivered it to her father's desk, knowing he wouldn't join her at the table. The solitary life they led drove her crazy. She needed to be around people on a regular basis. *Might as well do the grocery shopping now.*

She finished her lunch and went to her room to change her clothes. Even though she didn't mind being seen with dirty jeans and a smudge of mud across her nose, her father would be appalled if she went out in public in her gardening attire. With a bright sundress hugging her curves, she slipped on a pair of sandals and grabbed her purse. She stopped at the mirror in the hall to wipe the dirt from her nose as she called, "I'm going to the store, Daddy. I'll be back in a little while."

He still never looked up as she glanced through the doorway. "Be careful, sweetheart."

"I will."

"Don't forget to stop at the liquor store. My bottle is empty."

It had been half full last week. "Of course." At least he only drank at home.

Once outside the house, she slid into her car and shut the door. This little excursion would give her some time away. She loved her father, but he did get on her nerves once in a while. Probably more often than she cared to admit sometimes. "Maybe if he started dating again, he wouldn't be so worried about my life."

The grocery store came into a view a few minutes later. It really was more of a large food outlet than a grocery store, but when she did their major shopping, she liked the warehouse bargains of the store.

The place was mobbed. Why there were so many people there was beyond her. *Oh yeah, it's Saturday. Oh hell.* She found a parking spot next to a large, crew cab truck and stepped out. The swarm of people heading for the doors felt almost suffocating, but she managed to go with the flow and reach the front.

One cart left. She grabbed it, flashed her card at the door attendant and went inside. The cooler air of the store felt good on her skin. With the list in her hand she'd grabbed from the refrigerator door at home, she moved down the first aisle. Laundry soap, dryer sheets, starch for her father's collars. Slowly her cart filled until she reached the meat section. She found the steaks, chicken and ribs she'd been looking for until a beautiful dark haired woman next to her glanced over. The woman had the most beautiful dark brown eyes she'd ever seen.

"Those ribs looks fantastic, don't they?" the woman said as she grabbed a package to put in her cart.

"I love the meat here. They always have such a wonderful selection and quality. Do you shop here all the time?"

"Yes. We have a lot of people we cook for." Paige glanced at the woman's cart piled high with meat. "This will only last us about a week."

"Wow."

"We run a guest ranch so we have to feed a lot of people."

"Oh, how fun. I bet you have a great place."

"We try. We run cattle too, but it's mostly the guests these days and my boys. They'll eat me out of this food quickly enough."

Boys?

"I have nine of them and two wonderful new daughters-in-law. Oh, and a wonderful grandson and another on the way."

"I love big families."

"We definitely have one of those."

As she looked down at the package of meat in her hands, Paige blanched as a deep voice penetrated her conscious thought. "Well hi, Paige."

Oh shit. It can't be! She turned to her left only to look up into the brown-eyed gaze of Jacob.

* * * *

The last person he expected to see at the store when his mother suggested he accompany her was Paige. Not that he hadn't thought a lot about her over the last several weeks. If truth be told, he'd thought of little else except her pebbled nipples in those clamps or of her pussy slick with juice and ready for him as he slid home.

"What are you doin' here?"

"Shopping."

"I see. Oh, Mom this is Paige. Paige this is my mother, Nina."

"It's nice to meet you, Paige. How do you know Jacob?"

"We met a few weeks ago," she said in a choked up voice as she threw the meat in her cart.

"At The Dusty Boot," Jacob added.

Nina's eyebrows rose as she did a double take at Paige. "I see."

"No, really you don't. I don't frequent bars." Paige started to breathe faster, her chest rising and falling rapidly. Panic flashed in her eyes.

"It's fine. I understand perfectly."

"I, *uh,* have to go."

"Wait."

"No. I really need to go. My father is waiting for me in another aisle."

"Great. I'd love to meet him."

"No!" She grabbed her cart and disappeared around the edge of the aisle.

"Paige!" Jacob rounded the corner, walking quickly to catch up with her. "Wait."

"Leave me alone, Jacob."

"Why?" He grabbed her arm, pulling her to a stop. "What's wrong?" He glanced around, but there weren't any other patrons in the paper goods aisle. Surrounded by toilet paper, paper towels and napkins, he tried to soothe her with a calming hand on her arm.

"I don't want to get involved with you on a personal level, Jacob. We had sex. That's it." The alarm in her gaze hadn't dissipated.

Disappointment rushed through him. He wanted more from her although he wasn't sure how much more. *Keep it simple.* "But you never answered my text or my calls."

"Maybe I needed some room to breathe."

"I don't want you to feel suffocated. I'm sorry if bein' with me does that to you."

"It's not that." She shook off his hold. "I need some space. Meeting your family is too much."

"I'm sorry. It just happened. Not that I could have controlled when you met my family by running into us at the store."

She swallowed visibly as she pressed her hand to her chest. "I'm sorry for losing it. I just never expected to see you anywhere other than the bar, I guess."

"I like the dress."

"Thanks."

"You look beautiful."

"Stop, Jacob. Just stop, okay?"

"What am I doin' wrong here, Paige? I thought women liked bein' complimented on their looks."

She took a step back. "I need to go."

"Can we get together again this weekend?"

"I don't know. Don't press me."

"All right fine." He pushed his fingers through his hair. *Women!* "How about you call me when you want a little action since bein' nice doesn't seem to get through to you. If you want rough and tumble, baby, you got it." He grabbed the back of her head so he could press his mouth against hers. The pressure of his kiss didn't lessen even when her lips softened under his. When he finally let her go, her lips were swollen and red. "See you around, darlin'."

Chapter Five

Memorial Day weekend. Paige shuddered with concern, she didn't want this weekend to happen at all, but here it was. She dreaded the days with every passing month since March, since the last time she'd seen Jacob. He hadn't called. No text. Nothing. Her dreams were haunted with his touch. She woke many a morning trembling with need and hungry for his kiss, but she refused to reach out to him.

"Are you sure everything is ready, Paige."

"Yes, Daddy. It'll be a great party. The band is set to be here by seven and will play until ten. All the games are ready. The fireworks will be handled by the pyrotechnic company. Don't worry."

"I want this to be a wholesome celebration to bring the younger crowd to our church."

"Do you have your sermon ready?"

"Yes."

"Can I read it?"

"Of course."

He handed her the paper. She scanned the wording, cringing at a few lines here and there, but overall, it wasn't bad. "I think it's fine. You are planning on having the sermon this morning at eleven and then the barbeque will start, correct?"

"Yes. Our regular church members will be there, I'm sure. I'm hoping new members will come for church services before the barbeque starts."

Paige glanced down at her sundress. The bright red complimented her skin without making it too sallow like it usually did. Of course, it helped that she'd been gardening a lot the last several weeks while she avoided indulging in her secret life. Her restless soul screamed for release from her humdrum existence, but she refused to give in for fear of seeing Jacob. She didn't know whether she could handle being close to him without dropping to her knees so he would fuck her silly.

The weather had warmed up considerably for the end of May as it was prone to do in Texas. The sun beat down relentlessly as she set up the table for the punch. Luckily, most of the food and drinks were under tents the church had rented, although the sermon would be outside. She hoped the temperature wouldn't climb too high today.

The church bell clanged signaling the beginning of festivities as people began pouring onto the grounds behind the church. She smiled as the crowd grew with young and old. Hope sprang in her heart for some younger members who would be willing to start attending their church, for her father's sake, of course. It would be nice to have a few others to hang with and talk to during bible studies.

She glanced across the lawn in time to see a large family group walking toward one of the big trees. All of the men wore cowboy hats and the three women with them wore shorts or sundresses. Her heart skipped a beat when she noticed one of the women was extremely pregnant and another had beautiful long, black hair tied back in a braid. A small boy ran around in circles until one of the cowboys picked him up to swing him up on his shoulders.

It couldn't be.

One tall cowboy peeled away from the group once they were all settled and headed toward her. *Shit. No, no, no.* She quickly looked to her left and right trying to figure out where to hide. The last thing she wanted at this party was to run into him. *What the hell is he doin' here.* She spun to her right and disappeared out of the tent headed for the house. Surely he wouldn't follow her there.

Wrong.

The moment she opened the door, she heard the clomp of his boots on the wooden porch of the house.

"Paige."

"Jacob." Her breath came in shallow gulps of air as she tried to get her rapid heart under control.

"Why are you runnin', darlin'?"

"What are you doing here?"

"My family heard about the party for the weekend and thought it would be a great way to get to know some people in San Antonio. Besides, it has been awhile. I thought you might've been a little lonely."

She turned to face him. "You knew this was my father's church?"

"I had your phone number, remember? It's not hard to get information once you have that."

"You asswipe!"

"Tsk, tsk. Such language from a daughter of God."

She pulled back her hand, landing a stinging slap to his left cheek. "Fuck you, Jacob! How dare you use this as an opportunity to corner me." When she moved to do it again, he grabbed her hand and slowly reeled her in like a fish on a hook.

"You got one. Don't push it." He walked her backward into the house and slammed the door behind them. "Miss me?"

"Not in this lifetime." The warmth of his breath on her mouth had her lips tingling for the touch of his. Had she missed him? Damn right, she had. More than she'd ever let onto him. To hell with him! He hadn't called or anything, the bastard. *Not like I tried to call him either.*

"Oh, I bet you did, baby." He nibbled at the corners of her mouth. "I missed you."

The slow glide of the tip of his tongue over her bottom lip had her trapping a moan in her throat as her eyes drifted shut. Her lips parted as she swiped her tongue over her lips hoping to brush it with his.

The palm of his hand abraded her nipple through her dress, forcing the groan to the surface of her mouth.

His mouth slid along her jaw to her ear, the scrape of his whiskers sending her body into an overdrive of sensation. Goose bumps skittered across the flesh of her arms when his breath tickled the whorl. He nipped at her earlobe as she tipped her head to the side asking, no begging for more.

"Paige?"

"Shit. It's my father coming in the back door," she growled, pushing against his chest with her hands. "Let go!"

Jacob stepped back as she smoothed her dress down and turned to face her father as he came in through the doorway from the kitchen into the living room. "In here, Daddy. I was checking to make sure I didn't forget anything."

"Oh. Well, hello there." He held out his hand. "I'm Paige's father, Reverend Tyler."

"It's nice to meet you, sir." Jacob shook her father's hand. "I'm Jacob Young. My family is here for the picnic. We have a place out in Bandera."

"Wonderful! I'm thrilled to see some young people here." He turned to face her. "Isn't this wonderful, Paige? It's what we hoped for."

Jacob faced her as well and she wanted to punch the smug look off his face. "Yes, Daddy. It's great. I'm sure it'll be lots of fun."

"How do you two know each other? I'm surprised I haven't met you before, young man."

"We met at—"

"The nursing home, Daddy. He has a family member who is a resident there."

Jacob's eyebrow rose as a smirk settled on his mouth. "That's right. At the nursing home."

"Do you volunteer there as well?"

"Not as much as I used to, sir. I don't get there very often these days."

"That's too bad."

"Yes, yes it is, but I'm a better person now and I felt my time there needed to be more limited so I could spend it helping my family at home on our ranch."

"You own a ranch?"

"My family does, yes. It's a guest ranch, but we also run cattle."

"How fascinating. A real cowboy."

"To the bone, sir."

"I think we have everything. Why don't we head back out to greet our guests, Daddy? I'm sure everyone will be wondering where we are." She glanced at her watch. "It's about time for the games to begin anyway."

"Of course, Paige." He hugged her to his side as a wide grin spread across his mouth. "I'm so proud of you for organizing this."

"You organized the party? Wow."

"Not all of it. I was on the committee."

"We're having a live band later."

"Awesome. Save me a dance?" Jacob asked with the same silly smirk on his face. The bastard. He knew she wouldn't say no in front of her father.

"Of course, Jacob, but I think it's time to join the others." She peeled herself away from her father and headed for the door. The only way she was going to get them back outside as they stood there chatting, was to push them out.

The two men followed her back outside into the bright sunshine toward the food tent. She wanted to check on things again, plus she needed to put some distance between her and Jacob. It drove her nuts to think of how easily she succumbed to his advances in the house. She'd practically melted into a puddle of goo at his feet from merely the brush of his mouth on her skin. That wouldn't do. Never mind how his hand felt on her breast, kneading the globe with his palm and pinching her nipple between his fingers hard enough to remind her of the nipple clamps.

"Would you like something to drink, Jacob?" she asked, politeness dripping from her words like honey from the comb.

"I would love some, but let me check on the family to see if they need anything." He disappeared back toward the group by the tree as her father watched him walk away.

"What a nice young man."

"*Uh*, yeah."

"Now, he's the kind of man you should be looking for, Paige. Charming, well-mannered, and I bet he's a good Christian man."

Paige spit the water she'd just taken into her mouth out, in a spray of liquid. Luckily, she didn't get anyone with it. "Don't get ahead of yourself, Daddy. I haven't known Jacob that long. We only met a few months ago."

"Well, your mother and I didn't know each other long either before I knew she was the love of my life."

"I know you loved Mom with your whole heart, but you probably should think about dating again."

"Pah! I don't need to date. I have you to do the duties for me so why should I look for another woman?"

"Someday, I'll move out and have a family of my own. I won't be here to do everything like I am now."

"I know, Paige, but it'll be a few years yet I'm hoping. Besides, the woman's auxiliary can handle most of those things with or without you."

"Then why do you insist I do them? I could be out with my friends, finding a husband, raising a family." She stomped her foot. "I hate doing all of these things."

"Paige." He glanced around them noting the few stares she was sure were aimed their way now. "We can discuss this another time."

"Fine," she grumbled. "This conversation isn't over by a long shot."

She whirled around and almost ran nose first into Jacob's chin. "Let's walk, shall we," he said, taking her arm in his firm grasp.

"Fine."

He tucked her hand into the crook of his arm and headed down the knoll toward the cemetery. "Is your Mom here?"

"Yes." They ducked under a tree branch. "To the back on the left."

They wandered in that direction, stopping to note some of the smaller stones as she often wondered what the story was of the souls lost so long ago. The church had been there for over a hundred years and there were several families buried in the cemetery, some from the late 1800's.

Tears gathered in her eyes as she got closer and closer to her mother's headstone. She silently wiped at the tears with her fingertips, hoping Jacob wouldn't see.

"Sshh." He turned her in his arms and held her to his chest.

Broken sobs tore at her throat as she cried into his neck, soaking his shirt. He never asked any questions, just held her tight, all the time sweeping his hand over her braid.

After several minutes she stepped back. He wiped the remaining tears from her cheeks with his thumbs.

"Seems you've needed a good cry for a while."

"I guess I did. Thank you."

"No thanks needed, darlin'."

She swallowed hard. The endearment from his lips almost made her forget the animosity between them. She wanted to forget the loneliness of the last two months without him. "Just hold me."

"My pleasure, baby."

They stood in the silence of the grounds with the laughter of the fair atmosphere in the distance, for some time. The warmth emanating from his skin as he rubbed his hands up and down her back, made her want to sink into him and never come out. "I suppose we should get back. Your family will be worried about you."

"It's fine. Mom knew I was headed your direction."

"Well my father will be worried. I was supposed to announce the games."

"I think Charlie from the band took over for you. I hear his deep baritone announcing away." They turned to walk back toward the crowd with their arms around each other.

"You didn't want to participate?"

"Only if there are three legged races and you are my partner." He stopped to kiss her nose. "Are you okay?"

"Yeah, I'm fine. Again, thank you for the shoulder."

"I have some pretty broad ones so anytime you need one, you holler."

"I could do that." She reached up and kissed the corner of his mouth. With his hand in hers, they walked back into the refreshment tent so she could take over some of the duties from the other ladies of the auxiliary.

Jacob smiled for a minute, tipped his hat and wandered back to his family.

His family. Next he would want to introduce her to everyone. She wasn't sure she was ready for that kind of familiarity. Well hell, he'd met her father even though it wasn't planned on her part. *I guess it wouldn't hurt to meet his family.*

She could pretend it was on the pretense of inviting them all to the potato sack races going on in a few minutes. *Sure, what a plan!* She shook her head as she told one of the teenage girls helping her she would be right back.

The entire clan size overwhelmed her a little when she made her way closer, but the warmth in Jacob's eyes as she walked toward him, dissipated all the butterflies in her stomach.

"Well hello. Paige, isn't it?" Nina asked when she stopped next to the group.

They all looked her way as she blushed bright red. "Yes, ma'am. It's nice to see you again."

"You too."

"I wanted to invite everyone to enjoy the games we are having. I believe the potato sack races are next."

Jacob touched her elbow, drawing her attention back to his family. "Let me introduce you to the group, Paige. These are my parents. You know Nina, my mother and sitting next to her is James, my father."

"Ma'am."

"Nice to meet you."

"These are my brothers, Jeff and his girl Terri." He indicated with a nod to one couple next to the tree in the shade.

"Nice to meet you."

"My other brothers, Jason, Joshua, Jackson, Joey, Jeremiah and Jonathan." He pointed to another couple to the right of the huge blanket. "And over there is Joel and Mesa."

"Wow, what a group."

All of the men tipped their hats and grinned while the women smiled and waved. "The little rascal running around is Jeff's son Ben."

The announcer shouted about the potato sack races as four of the brothers jumped to their feet.

"Can I get anyone anything to drink? There is soda, water, coffee and ice tea at the refreshment tent. From the smells coming from the barbeque area I would say the food will be ready soon."

"Great! I'm starved," Joshua said, whisking by her on his way to grab a sack.

She watched him as she laughed at the exuberance of the group. Typical men.

Jacob's hand dropped to her hip in an almost possessive way, which she found kind of endearing around his brothers. Did he want to stake a claim on her around his bachelor brothers? She put her hand on top of his to remove it, but he held firm. He wasn't budging as his fingers dug into her hip.

"I think we're fine, Paige, but thank you," Nina said. "Unless Terri or Mesa need something?"

"I'm fine, Mom," Mesa said as she jumped to her feet. "I'm going to go beat the pants off these Young brothers in the potato sack races."

"Terri," Jeff asked, smoothing his hand over her protruding belly. "Do you need somethin', honey?"

"I'm fine too. I have my water."

"Just don't overdo. Let me know when you want to go home."

"Yes, Dad." She kissed him on the mouth. "I'm fine. Stop worrying."

Paige thought it was cute how the men took care of their women. She wanted that someday, but could Jacob be man enough to treat her like something precious in his life? Maybe. She didn't want to be treated like an antique piece of furniture to be admired, but never handled. She needed a man's touch, his touch.

He'd been so loving out at the cemetery when she'd busted out in blubbering tears all over his shirt. She really began to wonder if the Jacob who had been seemed cut off from everything two months ago, really existed.

"Well, it was great meeting you all. Let me know if you need anything. Enjoy the festivities."

"It was great meeting you, Paige. Come back and visit when you have a moment," Nina said with a smile.

"I will." She turned out of Jacob's hold. "I have to get back."

"I'll walk back with you."

"It's okay."

"I want to."

She sighed as she rolled her eyes.

"I saw that."

A giggle escaped her lips the minute he spun her around to face him and pressed his lips to hers.

Her hands pressed against his chest as he lifted his mouth. The deep brown of his eyes twinkled in the sunlight, letting her know he'd kissed her on purpose to let everyone in the area know they were a couple. *But we aren't, are we?*

"Yes, we are," he said, pecking her on the lips again before he wrapped an arm around her waist to escort her to the tent.

"Did I say that out loud?"

"Yeah, you did and I did it for that reason. Everyone around now knows we are together."

Chapter Six

The afternoon had been wonderful. Jacob was attentive and sweet. They'd even won the three-legged race by him practically carrying her down the race course. But when they'd fallen at the end, she'd ended up on top of him. Her body went haywire as his scent and touch surrounded her. Every muscle bunched beneath her, reminding her of how he'd fucked her senseless. She wanted that again more than anything in this world.

Now she stood wrapped in his arms as the band played a slow song. They swayed to the music as if they were meant to dance together for a lifetime. It scared the shit out of her.

"I shouldn't be dancing with you."

"Why not," he whispered, his lips pressed to her ear.

"Because I'm hosting this shindig. I should be working."

"You can have fun too."

"I shouldn't be."

"Yes you should. You did a fabulous job with this party. Tons of people came. Your father's little church is on the map now."

"I wonder how many people will come to services."

"I think a lot will. I overheard several people talking about how personable your father is and how they would love to attend his sermons."

"What about the younger people? We need a new crowd to keep the church going."

"My family has been looking for a church to attend. The one they were going to before, the pastor left. They don't like the new one."

"I'm sure with a prominent family like yours attending, we'll get a great turn out."

"You might have to build a bigger church."

She glanced up as surprise raced through her. "We love this little church. It's been here for over a hundred years. We don't want a bigger, fancier one."

"What if the congregation grows so big, you can't handle it in this church? I mean a big wedding would be hard pressed to attend in there. It's quaint, yes, but it's very small."

"But it's beautiful. My mother used to sing in the choir in there. My father has been preaching there for over fifteen years. They can't want a bigger church."

"Easy, darlin'. It's just a thought."

"Well, get that thought right out of your head, Jacob. I won't have them tearing down my church."

"No one said anything about tearing it down."

"But they would have to so they could build a bigger one. Bigger isn't always better."

"Honey, calm down."

"I won't! No one is tearing down this church."

Jacob pressed his lips to hers as she twisted in his arms. How could he want to kiss her while she was so upset?

Her mind sidetracked to the feel of his lips on hers. She loved to have him kiss her. Her mouth opened to the touch of his tongue as she wrapped her arms around his neck.

A moment later, a throat clearing penetrated her foggy brain. She glanced over Jacob's shoulder to see the frown on her father's face. *Oops.*

"Hi."

"Can I speak to you a minute, Paige?"

"Sure." She gave Jacob a peck on the mouth figuring she was already in deep shit, what did one more kiss hurt. She followed her father into the shadows, prepared for the reprimand coming.

"Paige, is it necessary to be kissing the man like that in front of everyone? Where are your morals, young lady?"

"Right where they should be, Daddy."

"I find your behavior offensive and I won't have you pawing at him in front of parishioners. You're acting like some loose woman."

"Maybe I am. There is nothing wrong with me."

"I didn't say there was, Paige, but this behavior isn't becoming of you in the least. You don't act like this. What would your mother think?"

"I have to believe mother would be happy for me." She closed her eyes for a moment, but when she reopened them, the disappointment in his eyes still hurt her heart. "I'm sorry you are upset with me over this, but I like Jacob. A lot. You said yourself he seemed like a nice Christian man when you met him earlier."

"That was before I saw him seducing my daughter in front of the churchgoers."

"He wasn't seducing me. He kissed me. Nothing more."

"With tongues!"

"Like you never kissed mother with your tongue."

"We were married."

"So maybe I'm marrying Jacob!"

"Whoa." Jacob stepped into the shadows. "We aren't gettin' married."

"I know that!"

"Then don't say we are."

"Just stop, all right. It's nothing, Father. We weren't having sex in the middle of the dance floor."

"You might as well have been."

"Really? What we were doing wasn't even close to what sex was like between us."

"Paige!" Both her father and Jacob yelled at the same time.

"What? It's wasn't and you know it to be true, Jacob. What happened between us was a lot more explosive than merely kissing out there."

"You've had sex with him?" Her father whipped his finger between the two of them. "The two of you had sex?"

"Yes, Daddy we did. Not that big of a deal."

"Oh my." Her father stepped aside, sinking onto a chair sitting near the empty refreshment tent flap. "Heavenly Father, please help this wayward child come back to your loving presence. Show her that premarital sex isn't the right thing to do and that you forgive her for her sins."

"I'm sorry, but I don't think there is anything wrong with it."

"Now Paige," Jacob added.

"Don't now Paige me, buddy." She pressed her finger into the middle of his chest. "You were there too so you've done your sinly duties in this mess too."

"Ask for forgiveness, Paige, and the Lord will see you've repented."

"I'm not, Daddy. What I had with Jacob was wonderful and I'm not sorry."

"Go to the house then."

"No."

"Paige—"

"I'm not twelve anymore, Father. So stop treating me like I am. I'm a grown woman. If I want to have sex with Jacob, I will. If I want to stay out late, I will. If I don't want to go the nursing home anymore, I will." She dropped to her knees in front of him as she took his hands in hers. "I'm twenty-seven years old, Daddy. I can make my own decisions."

He swept her bangs away from her face. "When did you grow up?"

"A long time ago."

"I never saw it coming. I want my little girl back."

"She's still inside me, Daddy, but she only comes out to enjoy sunshine picnics, swing sets and daydreams." She kissed his cheek. "I have my own life to lead now. I can't be what you want me to be." She stood and walked into Jacob's arms. "Let's go watch the fireworks."

Her father stayed on the chair as she led Jacob down to the knoll where they could see the fireworks better.

"You didn't have to do that, you know."

"Yes, I did. I needed him to see me for the real me instead of the child he remembers me as."

"You broke his heart."

"I don't think so, but I do wish my mother were here. She would understand and help him understand." Jacob sat on the grass and pulled her between his legs so her buttocks rested against his crotch. "Happy to see me, big boy?"

"Always, baby. It's been a while."

"For you too? I wondered."

"I haven't been with anyone since we were together, Paige."

"Why?"

"Because I wanted you."

"Sounds like a serious ailment."

"It is. It's been torture the last two months. I haven't masturbated that many times since I turned fifteen."

The band quit playing as the fireworks started exploding over their heads with the appropriate *ohs* and *ahs* from the crowd with each burst of color. Jacob's hands did a slow crawl up and down her arms as she snuggled against his chest with her back.

"You look beautiful today."

"Thank you."

"It's kind of strange seeing you without your leather."

"You saw me at the store without it."

"Yeah, but I was surprised." He played with her braid. "I like your hair loose better so I can run my fingers through the strands."

"I didn't want it loose so it was in the food or anything."

"It's soft." He tickled her cheek with the end of her braid. "I love it wrapped around my fist as I fuck you senseless."

"Charmer."

"I can't wait to get you alone."

"It might be a bit. I have to clean up."

"I'll help." He wrapped his arms around her waist as she settled hers on top of his. "I love holding you like this."

"We didn't do any snuggling really, when we were together before."

"We haven't done a lot of things dating couples do."

"Are we dating?"

"What do you think?"

She sighed.

"That didn't sound very happy."

"I am. I'm just upset with my father. The conversation didn't go well."

"Let's get this talk about us out of the way first and then we'll worry about your father. Okay?"

"Sure. What do you want to talk about?"

"We're dating, right?"

"I guess. I mean you haven't really asked me out or anything. You just show up here, bully-kiss me and then expect to be welcomed with open arms."

"Yep. That's about it."

"Typical man."

"No. A man who knows what he wants and got tired of waiting for the woman to figure it out. You didn't call me."

"No, I didn't." She plucked at the hair on his arm, pulling slightly. "Not that I didn't think about you, *a hell of a lot.*"

"I'm glad I wasn't alone then, because I thought about you a lot too."

"You don't know how many times I pick up the phone to call, but lost my nerve."

"Why?" he asked, concern in his voice.

"I wasn't sure what to say to you," she whispered, unsure of confessing all her secrets to him would be a wise decision.

"How about I want to see you?"

She shook her head. "Too easy. I knew I wanted to see you, but it would have meant an apology for my erratic behavior at the store."

"Why did you freak?"

She shifted so she could look into his eyes. "We'd slept together once, Jacob, and there you were introducing me to your mother."

"It wasn't a big deal, Paige. It was only a coincidence thing. Not something I planned. It wasn't like a big family to-do where you came over to the house so everyone could meet you because we were getting married or something."

"I know, but meeting the family seems too permanent to me."

"You met everyone today."

"Yeah, but you realize it was after you met my father."

"Which we hadn't planned either." He stroked a finger down her cheek. "He wasn't at the store was he?"

"No. It was an excuse to leave."

"I figured as much."

"I'm sorry I lied."

"Don't lie to me again or I'll punish you."

"Punish me?"

"Remember your spanking before?"

"Yeah and I didn't like it."

"You wouldn't like it if I gave you another one, would you?"

"No." She bit her lip for a moment. "I thought there was more to doing kinky things than smacking on a person."

"Oh, there is and smacking on a person isn't the same."

"I won't allow you to beat on me."

"I don't beat on women."

"What do you call the spanking then?"

"I wasn't beating on you. I was letting you know who is in charge of this relationship."

"We aren't in a relationship and we certainly weren't then."

"What would you call this then?"

"I don't know."

"Dating is a sort of relationship."

"I guess so."

"You don't want a relationship with me?"

"It's not that. I didn't think you wanted anything permanent. Eventually, I want a husband, family, two point five kids, and a white picket fence. You don't seem into those things."

"Maybe not right now, but I might be in the future."

"Are you helping us clean up, Paige?" Mrs. Johnson asked, stopping next to where they sat on the ground.

"Yes, ma'am. We'll be right there."

Mrs. Johnson walked toward the refreshment tent as Paige climbed to her feet. She held out her hand to help Jacob up, which he kissed her palm, ran his tongue around her first finger, and then jumped to his feet.

"Come on, doll. Let's get this cleaned up so we can get some alone time."

"Such a charmer you are, Mr. Young."

"I aim to please, darlin'." He tucked his arm around her waist and escorted her to the refreshment tent.

Several minutes later, his entire family arrived to help clean up as well.

"We're here to help," Jeremiah said, standing next to the table. "Tell us what you want us to do."

As she directed everyone, she smiled. Why wasn't she surprised that his family would jump in and help with the cleanup even though it was getting late in the evening.

"Paige, it was nice to meet you. We would stay to help, but I need to get Terri and Ben home," Jeff said, holding out his hand.

"Oh, it's fine. Thank you for coming. We hope to see you all in church someday soon."

"We will. Give us a couple of weeks. Terri is about to pop and I don't want her to be doing too much right now."

"Oh stop it, Jeff. I'm not the first woman to have a baby. Besides, we still have a few months to go."

"But you are havin' my baby, honey. I take care of you."

"Yes you do and I love you for it." She kissed him on the lips as she snuggled closer to his side. "Thank you for inviting us to the barbeque. It was fabulous."

"You're very welcome."

"Jacob, Mom. We'll see y'all at home."

"Be careful driving home, Jeff."

"We will. Night all."

She watched Jeff, Terri and a sleepy Ben walk toward the parked cars hoping someday to have what they had. The next thing to catch her eye was Joel and Mesa. They stacked chairs together in one corner as he snuck a kiss with each chair they put on the stack. *Wow. They seem so in love.*

"What's the sigh for, darlin'?"

"I love watching your family. Those paired off seem like they love each other so much."

He slipped his arm around her waist as he brushed a warm kiss across her cheek. "Yeah, they do. I'm glad my brothers found it in each of the women they have. I wondered about Jeff for a long time. He had it pretty rough with Ben's momma."

"Oh?"

"Yeah. I won't bore you with the details right now, but lucky for him she's no longer in the picture."

"I can't imagine anyone leaving their child."

"She overdosed late last year on meth."

"Wow."

"Things were pretty messed up with her. I'll tell you about it some other time. We're almost done with this clean up so we can get out of here."

"I think we're done. The tent guys will be here tomorrow to tear down the tents. We just need to move the chairs to the back so they'll be able to load them easier, fold up the tables, and put the coolers with the leftover drinks at the rear of the church."

Jacob whistled to get his brothers attention. Once he gave them all directions on what needed to be done and moved, things went smoothly until all was accomplished.

"Nice to have such wonderful help," Mrs. Johnson said stopping near where they stood.

"Yes, it is." Paige surveyed the area to make sure everything was in its place.

"How do you know them?"

"Paige and I are dating," Jacob replied, kissing her on the cheek.

"I didn't know you had a boyfriend, Paige." She leaned in to whisper, "He's quite handsome too."

"I think so."

Jacob threw back his head and roared with laughter. "I think I like her."

Mrs. Johnson blushed as she excused herself, grabbed her purse, and headed for her car.

Once the crowd had dispersed, she grabbed the front of Jacob's shirt to pull him in for a kiss. Shadows surrounded them, shifting with each movement of the trees overhead. Moonlight bled through the leaves, scattering silver beams across the ground. She didn't see her father standing in the shadows until he cleared his throat in the midst of their kiss.

A sigh escaped her lips as she turned to face her father. "Daddy."

"Paige, can we talk?" he asked in a timid voice, one she'd never heard him use before.

Not wanting to give up her time with Jacob, she said, "Not now. We're done cleaning up, but I'm going out with Jacob for a while. Don't wait up."

"But—"

"I'm sorry, Daddy. We'll talk tomorrow."

"All right." She heard the disappointment as he disappeared into the shadows surrounding the side of the church.

Several moments later, she heard the door to their little house close.

"You really should have talked to him."

"I can't. Not tonight. I'm still upset with him and his irrational behavior."

"He wasn't being irrational, Paige. He's trying to protect you."

"I don't need protecting, remember?"

"I know you can take care of yourself physically in a fight, but darlin', he is your father. He wants what is best for you."

She brushed her lips against his. "Can we not talk about this right now?" She plucked at the buttons on the front of his shirt. "I want you nekkid."

"Do ya now?" he asked, laughter tingeing his words. His hands did a slow crawl up and down her arms.

Goose bumps skittered across her torso, before settling low in her belly. Wetness coated her panties. She wished she hadn't worn any.

God, she loved his touch. "Oh hell, yeah."

His mother approached, breaking the two of them apart with guilty smiles on their faces. "We're headed home, Jacob."

"Okay, Mom. I'm going to stay with Paige for a while."

Nina grinned as she hugged him. "I thought as much."

"See you tomorrow?"

"Yes. We have guests coming in during the early hours of the morning so we'll all need to be onboard for a bit anyway. There are never ending chores on a ranch."

"Love you, Mom."

"I love you too, Jacob. Goodnight, Paige."

"Goodnight, Mrs. Young."

"Nina, honey. Call me Nina."

"All right. Goodnight, Nina."

Nina waved as she disappeared into the darkness. A few moments later, she heard several trucks start and then roll out of the parking lot, leaving her and Jacob standing in the deserted tent alone.

"What shall we do now?" Paige asked, looking around. "Everything is cleaned up."

"I thought you wanted me nekkid?"

"I do, but I think we should take it slow."

"Why?"

"Would you like to dance?" she asked, looking up into his expressive eyes. Lust sparkled in their depths. Lust she could handle.

"There's no music."

She stepped into his arms, placing one on his shoulder and cupping his left hand with her right. They slowly swayed. "Sure there is. Listen to the frogs, the crickets and the owls." She stepped closer so her breasts brushed the front of his shirt. Her nipples pebbled into hard peaks at the friction.

"Paige," he whispered, bending his head.

The slow slide of his lips glided across her skin until he reached the crook of her neck. "Jacob." The nibble of his teeth on her flesh drove her desire to explosive. Stickiness coated her thighs. She wanted him. No doubt about that.

"Where do you want to go?"

"Back to my place?"

"Okay."

"You'll ride with me."

She liked that idea. A smile crossed her lips as a plan began to form in her mind of how she could torture him all the way there and make him want her more than any woman he'd ever been with. "Okay. Just let me grab my purse." She disappeared around the back of the tent where she'd hidden her purse, stripped off her panties and stuffed them inside the receptacle. *Let's see what he thinks of this.*

Several minutes later, he opened the door to his truck and helped her inside with a hand against her behind.

"You are goin' commando?"

She giggled as she glanced over her shoulder. "I thought it would spice things up a bit."

His cock strained against the front of his pants already. What would be do when she unzipped his jeans and engulfed him with her mouth?

"Thinkin' about you with no panties on all the way home is gonna drive me crazy."

"Oh good. How about when I suck your cock while you're driving?"

"Holy shit, woman. How do you expect me to drive with you doin' somethin' so scandalous?"

His eyes glittered in the moonlight with desire. She knew the look. It said he wanted her. Good, she knew how to please him.

"Oh, I'm sure you'll manage, cowboy."

He gave her a long, slow, melt your panties kiss as his hand slid up under her dress. Two fingers pushed into her pussy as she groaned her need.

"You're wet, darlin'."

Her thighs spread of their own accord. "Hell yeah, I'm wet. You make me that way." He kept pumping his fingers slowly in and out. "You're tryin' to make me come."

"Are you going to or do you need a little more friction?" His thumb glanced off her clit.

"Damn, Jacob. I was supposed to be teasing you."

"You do, honey, with every breath you take you tease me unmercifully."

Her pussy quivered around his fingers. He never hurried the pace, just kept up the slow glide of his hand. "I feel you. You're right there." He pulled out his hand as he smoothed down her dress. She noticed his hand shook, bringing a smile to her lips. He wasn't so unaffected after all.

"So not nice."

"Anticipation, darlin'. It'll be better later when you come apart in my arms."

He stepped back, shutting the door to the truck. She watched as he went around the front of the vehicle to the driver's side, sighing in appreciation. *Damn, the man is gorgeous.* She wanted to trace every ridge of his amazing body with her tongue. Maybe he'd let her tonight. She hoped so. God, she needed him, but she wanted a little slow lovin' tonight. Maybe fast after that.

"What's the sassy little grin for?" he asked, as he slid into the cab and pushed the key into the ignition.

Chapter Seven

"Just thinking."

"About?" he asked, as he pulled out into the street and headed for his place.

The forty five minutes it would take to get there would be a very long ride. "You and me."

"What about us?"

"How I want to do this." She unhooked her seatbelt before slowly sliding across the seat toward him.

"You shouldn't be out of your seatbelt." His grip tightened on the steering wheel.

She worked his belt buckle lose, pushing it aside. Waiting for a moment to see if he would stop her, she grinned as she kept going with the button at the top of his jeans and then the zipper.

"Commando, huh? And you were giving me shit about it."

"I was hoping for a little action tonight although I hadn't anticipated it in the front of my truck while I drove."

"But, baby, it's gonna be so much fun suckin' you while you drive."

"You tryin' to kill me, darlin'?"

"Nah, just love on you a little." She freed his cock from his jeans as they pulled to a stop light. "Lift up." He jerked up his hips while she tugged his jeans down around his thighs. "Oh yeah." He hissed between his teeth as she slowly licked him from base to tip. "So soft." She circled the head with her tongue. "Salty."

The tires squealed as his foot shoved down the gas pedal.

"Easy up on the gas, cowboy. You'll get us busted."

He slowed as she took the head of his cock between her lips.

"Ah, fuck."

"Mmm." She hummed as he canted his hips toward her face. "Concentrate." She glanced up to see the strain on his face. "You can do it, cowboy. I have faith in you."

"You'll pay for this when we get back to my place."

"I'm sure I will."

A little bit of suction made him moan so she did it again. Lick. Suck. Slide. *God, I love his cock.*

"Eyes open, cowboy."

"I am!" He groaned. "I'm gonna blow."

"Good. Explode for me."

He pulled over on the shoulder of the interstate and slammed the truck into park as cum shot down her throat.

"Oh God, oh God."

"Praise be the Lord." She laughed as she took her time licking him clean.

Satisfied with her work, she started backing away when blue lights flashed in their rearview mirror.

"Shit." Jacob scrambled to pull his jeans up and button them before the cop climbed out of his car.

She burst out laughing as she slid back into her seat so she could buckle her seatbelt. A moment later, a cop tapped on the driver's side window, then motioned for Jacob to roll it down.

"Can I help you?"

"Just checking on you since you're pulled over on the side of the road. Problem?"

"No sir. I thought I might have had a flat, but it'll be fine until I get home."

"You haven't been drinkin', have you, sir?"

"No, sir. You can test me if you like."

As the cop peered inside, she waved to him. "I don't think that'll be necessary since I don't smell alcohol on you. Be careful drivin' and safe travels home."

"Thank you, officer," Paige hollered from her side of the truck.

The cop tipped his hat before he headed back to his patrol car.

"You are definitely gonna pay for that, darlin'."

Jacob pulled back out onto the highway keeping a close eye on her. She gave him a cheeky grin every time he glanced her way.

"Come 'ere."

"Where?"

"To the center. There's a seatbelt. Buckle yourself in."

"What are you going to do?"

"Tease the piss out of you until we get back to my place."

"Oh?"

"Do it now."

"Yes, sir." She loved when he went all commanding on her. "Whatever you say, Jacob." She unbuckled her seatbelt, slid over into the center and refastened the belt around her waist.

"Lift your dress."

She pulled the skirt up and secured it in the waistband by tucking it in, revealing her thighs to his gaze.

"More. I wanna see your pussy."

Inching the remaining material above her hips, she laid everything bare for his gaze.

"You're gorgeous. You shaved?"

"I thought of you while I did it."

"Sexy." His knuckles turned white on the steering wheel where he gripped it hard enough to strangle the thing. "Spread your thighs."

She placed one foot on the floorboard behind his leg and one on the other side of the gearshift. "Like this?"

"Fuck. You are so hot."

Her thighs were sticky from her arousal. She wanted him. Maybe she could convince him to pull off one of the side exits so they could get in a quick fuck to tie her over. Sweat beaded on his forehead when she glanced at him. "Maybe we could stop on the way home."

"Nope."

"But—"

"I want you to make yourself come."

"Here?"

"Yeah. I'm gonna watch you finger yourself to orgasm."

It sounded arousing even to her.

"Lick your fingers. Get them good and wet. Then circle your clit real slow."

She stuck her fingers into her mouth, making the digits almost dripping wet. "Like this?" she asked, sliding her fingers around the hard nub. *God, I'm so horny.*

"Oh yeah." His breathing sped up. "Now, dip your fingers into your pussy. Feel those muscles gripping your fingers? That's how it feels when I finger fuck you."

She growled deep in her throat.

"Circle your clit again." The instructions coming from his mouth had blood rushing in her ears. Her heart throbbed in a rapid pulse. Her breath came out in little pants. "Rub it hard. Faster now."

The nub hardened more. If he kept this up, she would indeed come all over his leather seats.

"This is so fuckin' hot. You have no idea." The panting of their breathing drowned out the hum of his tires on the pavement.

She continued to rub her clit in a slow, tantalizing motion. Eventually, she would come, but she could do this for a while before she did.

"Faster. I wanna see you squirt before we reach Bandera."

"Squirt?"

"You've never squirted before?"

"No."

"It's when you come so hard, cum literally squirts out of you."

"But, I don't want to do that all over the interior of your truck."

"Baby, it washes. It's leather. Now, make yourself come and if you don't squirt, we'll have to start all over."

She sped up the friction on her clit, driving her desire up so high, she thought she might lose control of her bladder. Stars flashed behind her squeezed eyelids. Heat crawled up her thighs before it centered low in her belly. She felt like she would explode from the inside out. "Oh, God!"

"That's it, baby. Come for me."

She moaned as she felt herself lose control. Cum spilled from her pussy to coat her thighs and buttocks as well as his leather seat.

"Fuck yeah. Gorgeous." The friction on her clit grew stronger as he switched her fingers to his. "Come some more."

She lost herself in the sensation of his fingers on her clit. When he pushed two inside her pussy, she shouted his name as she exploded again.

As she slowly came down from her high, she realized he still continued to slowly finger her clit until she felt it getting hard again.

"Think you can come again before we reach the house?" he asked with a grin.

"No." She sat up when she found herself slumped almost horizontal on the seat. "Do you have napkins in here? I have cum all over my thighs."

"Good." He leisurely removed his fingers and licked them as they drove up to the gate of Thunder Ridge. "Leave it. I wanna lick all that sweetness off when we get inside."

"But it's sticky."

"We can always fuck in the shower."

"Such an inventive guy, you are."

The crooked grin on his face made her smile. Tonight would be off the charts on the sex scale, she could tell. He said he hadn't been with anyone since the last time they'd fucked, but could she trust him? What difference does it make whether he was with someone else or not? It didn't, she supposed, but it would be nice to know he'd suffered while she'd been thinking of him the whole time.

They pulled up to his trailer moments later.

Lights shone from the main lodge windows as she glanced out the front windshield of his truck. One of these days, she would have to get a good look at the ranch. Since she'd only ever been there at night, she hadn't seen much.

"Let me get the door," he said, popping out his side of the truck and shutting the door behind him.

With her dress up around her waist, she tugged it back down to make herself at least a little presentable as he went around to her side of the truck. Paige frowned as she heard the giggle of children's laughter.

When Jacob opened her door, she asked, "Are there children staying on the ranch?"

"Not that I know of," he replied as she slid out and he shut the door behind her.

"Didn't you hear the children laughing?" Although, she didn't hear it now. Not a sound. No rustle of wind or anything. The night was completely still, almost eerily so.

"No."

"Huh. I could have sworn I heard children when you opened your door to come around this side."

"It's probably the ghosts."

"Ghosts? You have ghosts on the property?"

"Yeah, a few."

"Wow. How cool is that!" She took his hand as he led the way toward the door of his home. "Who are they?"

"We aren't sure. We have an old cowboy who hangs out in the main lodge, a couple who argues upstairs and a mother and her children who play in the yard sometimes." He shoved the key in the lock. "The main lodge used to be a brothel."

"Cool." The chilly air of his home hit her in the face like a frigid blast. "It's freezing in here, Jacob."

"Let me kick on the heat. I turned it off this morning before we left for the barbeque." With a whoosh, the air in the room started to thaw. "It'll be warm in a minute." He rubbed her arms. "Should have brought a jacket."

"I didn't think it would be this cold. It's warmer outside than it is in here."

"I'll have you hot in a hurry." His mouth descended, taking hers in a surprisingly fierce way.

Her body warmed from her toes up as he took possession of her. It wasn't a soft, lingering kiss, it was a set-your-panties on fire kiss meant to jack up the heat in her body to inferno within seconds. His lips moved from her mouth to her jaw as she tilted her head to the side with a groan. God, the man could kiss. "Jacob."

"Hmm?" His lips vibrated against her flesh. Next stop, her earlobe with his teeth.

After several seconds, he lifted his head to stare down into her eyes. The dark brown pools sparkled with desire. "I want you naked in my arms in five seconds flat."

His cock strained the front of his Wranglers, tenting the material with his size so she could feel every inch against her abdomen.

She reached for the bottom of her sundress and whipped it over her head.

His eyebrow shot up. "Good girl."

When she moved to take off her sandals, he pushed her into the recliner and knelt at her feet. "I love a man at my feet."

Once her left shoe was removed, he kissed the arch of her foot before working his way up her calf with his tongue. Never in a million years would she thought of her leg being an erogenous zone, but he sure had her toes curling in response to the scrape of his whiskered cheeks and the softness of his lips on her calf.

"You're making me shiver."

"Good." He did the same thing to her right foot. "Spread your thighs. I'm gonna lick you clean."

Her body exploded in goose bumps as her stomach flipped over.

He kissed his way up the inside of her thighs as she watched mesmerized. Her lips parted on a sigh. *Damn the man.* He certainly knew what to do to get her horny, not that she wasn't before this, but what he was doing to her was downright sinful.

His palms slid under her buttocks, dragging her forward in the chair until her pussy was even with his mouth.

"Hold on."

She grabbed his shoulders, digging her fingernails into his impressive width as he swiped his tongue along her slit in one long lick. The moan that broke free from her lips sounded almost primal.

He growled his appreciation as he ate at her pussy like a starving man. At this rate, he would have her coming within seconds.

"Come for me, Paige," he said as he shoved two fingers into her empty center.

Heat exploded through her pelvis in a long, rolling wave of warmth as she groaned his name through clenched teeth. He'd made her come so hard and so fast, her brain went numb.

He lapped at her juices, bringing her down from her climax slowly with long licks until she pushed his head away, not able to handle the stimulation any more. His chin glistened as he grinned like a man who'd just won a gold medal as he sat back on his heels. "Better?"

"I really need a shower now."

"Great." He got to his feet, pulled off his shirt and then toed off his boots. "I'd love to fuck you in there."

"Are you sure there is room? Trailers like this usually have small showers."

"There'll be plenty of room." He swept her up in his arms and carried her down the hall.

She giggled as she wrapped her arms around his neck and buried her nose in the crook of his shoulder. "Mmm. You smell good."

With a flick of his fingers, he caught the light switch, illuminating the bathroom to her gaze. She hadn't noticed the shower stall when she'd been here before, but there wasn't any way they'd both fit in there much less have the room to fuck like bunnies. "We aren't going to fit in there, Jacob."

"You'll be ridin' my hips, babe. We'll fit." He flipped on the water and pulled the curtain. A moment later, his cock sprang free from the confines of his jeans as he pushed them to the floor.

Her mouth watered to taste the pre-cum glistened on the tip.

"*Uh-uh*. In the shower."

She frowned until he swatted her butt. "Ouch."

"In the shower, I said."

"Yes, Sir." She climbed in with him right behind her. The stall was so small the tips of her breasts brushed the expanse of his chest. "This isn't gonna work."

She squeaked in surprise as he grabbed her butt and lifted her.

"Sure, it will."

The minute she had her legs wrapped around his waist he positioned his cock at her entrance. Snapping his hips, he buried his full length inside her, earning him a steady groan.

"Oh, hell yeah." He leaned her back against the wall behind her and began to piston his hips. "God, you feel like heaven and hell wrapped in one tempting package."

"I'm your angel, remember?" She nipped him with her teeth to drive him crazy while he pounded into her flesh.

His feet began to slip on the slick bottom of the shower stall. "Hold on." He pulled out of her, letting her legs slid down until she was standing on the bottom with him. "This isn't gonna work. I can't get leverage in here. Let's take this into the bedroom, babe." He shut off the water and grabbed a towel to dry her with.

"I told you it wouldn't work."

He swatted her on the butt with his wet hand. "No back talk outta you."

The minute she was dried off, he herded her quickly into the bedroom with a palm to her butt. The slow massage of his hand there made her belly dip as he settled her on the bed on her knees. She'd heard about anal sex, but she'd never tried it. The thought intrigued her though. Jacob wasn't a small man by any means.

"Ever had a man in your ass?"

"No."

"One of these days, I'm going to take you there."

She closed her eyes and shivered.

"But not now. This minute, I want to feel your pussy grip me like a vice."

"God, you make me so hot."

"I'm gonna take you from behind. Fast and hard."

"Do it." He positioned her so her knees were barely on the bed, her ass was high and he had the perfect view of everything. "*Uh*, now Jacob." His hand came down hard on her right butt cheek. Unlike before, heat spread from where his hand landed all the way to her clit. "Do it again." For six swats, he switched back and forth between the left and right, making her ass hotter than anything she ever felt before. It stung, yeah, but the pain turned to pleasure the second he stopped.

"Lordy, that's the prettiest ass I've ever seen."

His cock bumped at her opening before he slowly pushed inside.

The low growl coming from him had her pussy quivering for more until he was balls deep inside her. "Fuck me hard, Jacob."

"Love to, babe."

He grabbed her hips in both of his hands and did just that. The slam of his pelvis against her ass almost shoved her across the bed, but she braced herself with her hands wide and her back bowed to take everything he wanted to give her.

The rough sex felt fantastic. She needs this, wanted this with him unlike any man she'd ever been with before. They treated her like a princess, but she didn't want to be treated like a fragile flower. She wanted to be treated like an equal.

His right hand snaked around her hip to find her clit. "I know you can come again."

"I don't think so."

"Oh, yes you can."

His finger worked her clit until she held onto the precipice of the abyss by her fingernails. "Ah, God."

"See. Come for me, Paige."

"Fuck yeah."

The sucking sound their bodies made as he brought her to the best climax of her life, made her realize she'd never had sex like this before. With Jacob it was different, he was different. What they had between them could be classified as meaningless sex, but she didn't think so. Their connection went beyond that.

To what?

Chapter Eight

The horse Jacob rode plodded along at a slow clip. It moved beneath him as he shifted his weight with each step, steadily descending the rocking path they always took the guests on.

The scenery was beautiful even to eyes that had seen it way too many times over the years. Junipers clung to the hillside. Wildflowers bloomed in varying shades of blues, yellows and purples including the native bluebonnets of the area. He could see several of their neighbors' places in the distance from up here. The beginning of the tourist season was upon them and he'd been the unlucky bastard to take the group out riding this morning on the ranch. At least the heat wasn't too bad yet. It would be worse later in the day while he was doing some other mundane task on the ranch like shoveling horse shit or stacking hay.

He wanted to kick the horse's sides and feel the wind rustle his hair, like the way Paige ran her fingers through it. Even though the length wasn't too long she did seem to enjoy fingering it.

Paige. Hmmm. What to do about her?

He'd driven her home early this morning after they'd had a couple bouts of explosive sex. With a kiss goodnight and a promise to call, she'd disappeared behind the door of the little house she shared with her father, leaving the scent of wildflowers behind her. He'd stood like an idiot on her steps, until the light had come on upstairs in what he assumed to be her room. The outline of her form reflected against the drapes had the blood rushing to his groin. The ride home hadn't been a pleasant one while he fondly remembered eating her pussy until she'd screamed his name in ecstasy. *God, my name on her lips is a turn-on.*

He frowned, shifting in the saddle to relieve the sudden presser against the fly of his jeans. Yeah, he wanted her, but what about the future? What about where they went from here?

Let's face it, he was terrified of getting involved on a permanent basis.

After the break up with Veronica, he'd sworn off women until his balls ached and his dick threatened to fall off if he didn't get some sex. His hand could only do so much. Sooner or later a man needed a woman. Enter Paige. She'd certainly brought his blue balls down to a tolerable level, to the point he hadn't thought about another woman in months.

His mind wandered to the last time he'd seen Veronica as she dropped the bombshell on his heart.

It had been over a year, his child would have been born by now. His gut ached with the knowledge he would never hold that baby in his arms, carry them around, feed them, change them or anything else. Yes, they'd made the decision together to abort the pregnancy, but really she hadn't given him much choice in the matter.

"It doesn't make sense, Jacob," Veronica said. "I don't want a baby and neither do you."

"But, I do."

"No you don't. You live in a single-wide trailer on your parent's property, work on their ranch and live on what little income you get from doing whatever it is you do around there. I want more. I want a man who is going places. You know, someone who lives in a big house, has a nice car, and can afford to raise a child. I don't want to live in a trailer. I've done that my entire life."

"In other words, I was good enough to fuck, but not good enough to be the permanent man in your life."

"I like you, Jacob. I really do, but yeah. Besides, I sure don't want a baby right now."

"How can you think of abortion? You'd kill our child?"

"I don't think of it like that. It's my body and I can do what I think is best for me. Marrying you and raising a baby isn't it. I have plans...big plans."

Without his knowing, she'd made an appointment and aborted the child. She'd called him two days after to tell him it was done.

That's when the drinking started. At first it was to drown the sorrow he felt for the loss of his child, but it became a way to deal with the guilt of not stopping her. Of not doing what he could to keep her from going through with it. When he'd see a baby in a carriage, his heart would break. The sounds of a child's cry almost brought him to tears. Someday he would have a child of his own. Someday he would find the woman he could spend the rest of his life with, raise a family, build a house, and see their children grow into adults.

It bothered him to watch Jeff and Terri as she continued to get bigger with her pregnancy. He'd wanted to be able to touch his woman's belly and feel their child kick. Funny thing was, Veronica's face wasn't the one he saw these days when he thought about having a child with someone, it was Paige.

The heat from the sun pounded down on his shoulders as he wiped the sweat from his forehead with the back of his hand. Soon, they would head back to the house and he could get a cold glass of the lemonade they always kept available in the main lodge. The tangy, tart taste would be heaven right now.

"Hey, mister?"

"Yeah," he answered the twelve-year-old kid riding on one of the gentler mares behind him.

"You been a cowboy all your life?"

"Yep. My parents bought this place when I was little."

"Wow."

Silence for about ten seconds.

"Hey, mister."

"Yeah."

"You married?"

"Nope."

"Gotta girlfriend?"

"Sort of."

"Is she purdy?"

"Yep. Real pretty."

"What's she look like?"

"She has long brown hair, big green eyes and she's a..." *Well shit*. He didn't know what she did for a job outside of helping her father at the church. "Her father is a preacher in San Antonio."

"Oh. So she's a good girl."

Jacob almost choked on his spit with that one. Wouldn't Paige think it hilarious to be labeled a good girl? "Yeah, she is."

"Do ya like her?"

"Yeah. A lot."

"You gonna marry her?"

He pushed his fingers through his hair before readjusting his hat on his head. Kind of a weird conversation to be having with this kid, but what the hell he guessed. "I don't know. I haven't known her long enough to tell."

Jacob heard the kid's mom scold him from behind. "Eric, don't bother the wrangler like that. He's busy making sure we get back to the ranch in one piece."

"It's okay, ma'am. I don't mind."

"You have lots of brothers, huh?" The kid started again and Jacob smiled.

"Yep. Eight brothers."

"Wow. I bet it was fun growing up with a big family."

"Sometimes. Other times I didn't like 'em so much. Do you have brothers and sisters?"

"Yeah, a sister. She's back at the cabin with my dad. He doesn't do horses."

"Too bad. Horses are pretty neat."

"I like horses. What's this one's name again?"

"Whiskey."

"I like him. He's a good horse." The kid patted the neck of the animal.

"Did you check out the pool already?"

"Yeah. I was in there this morning and I want to go swimming again when we get back. This cowboy stuff is kinda hard work."

"It sure is."

"What else do you do?"

"Clean stalls, pile hay, break horses, you know. Cowboy stuff."

"Did you always wanna be a cowboy?"

"Sure did." Jacob smiled again. "What do you want to be when you grow up?"

"I dunno. Maybe an astronaut."

"Sounds cool."

"Yeah, but I don't like to fly."

Jacob swallowed a laugh. "Could be a problem then."

"Yeah. Maybe a scuba diver. I like to swim."

"Good idea then."

"But I don't like sharks."

"They can be kind of mean sometimes."

"Hmm. I guess I have some thinkin' to do."

"Sounds like it, but you have time, buddy. You are what, twelve?"

"Thirteen. I'm a teenager."

Oh shit. Poor parents. "Sorry. You have lots of time to figure out what you want to do with your life."

"How old are you?"

"Thirty one."

"Wow. You're kinda old for a cowboy, ain't ya?"

Jacob did laugh at that one. "No. My dad is a cowboy and he's in his sixties."

"Has he always been a cowboy too?"

"Most of his life, yeah."

"I didn't think you could be a cowboy for a long time like that." A hawk flew overhead. "Those guys who ride bulls ain't very old."

"No, they aren't. Bull ridin' is a hard profession to be in for a long time."

"I think those guys are crazy."

"Me too," his mother added for emphasis. "What did you say your name was again?"

"Jacob, ma'am."

Another woman giggled from behind Eric's mother. He'd seen her when she'd mounted up. Nice looking woman with blonde hair, big blue eyes, and nice tits. She was visiting the ranch with a couple of friends and they had all been eyeing the Young brothers since they had driven in.

Monica. That's what she introduced herself as. They'd been there a couple of days already and if he remembered right, his mother mentioned they were there for two weeks. He rolled his eyes behind his sun glasses.

They came down the final path to the back of the corral and he sighed. Thank goodness the ride was over. As he led them into the fenced in area where the horses were kept, Joey met them. He normally took care of the horses, broke the new mares, and tended to the tack. He'd hurt his leg breaking one of the horses the week before so he was tending to the stock on the ground instead of riding out with the visitors.

"Hey, Joe."

"How'd the ride go?"

"Good. Got a talkative kid, but other than that, nothin' big."

"Great. Ma wants to see you in the lodge." He took the reins to Jacob's horse. "I'll get your gear off."

"Thanks." He swept his hat off his head and wiped the sweat from his forehead again. *Damn, it is getting hot.* "Any idea what she wants?"

"Nope."

He noticed Jason eyeing the blonde woman as he helped her down from her horse. Leave it to Jason to swoop in on a woman ripe for the picking. Jacob shrugged. He didn't care. They could do what they wanted, he supposed. Jeff was the stickler for not messing with the guests, although he couldn't say much now since Terri had been a guest before they got together.

After he helped a couple of guests dismount, he headed for the main lodge to see what his mother wanted. He needed something to drink anyway. The heat had begun to rise outside and more work waited in the wings of a working cattle ranch.

The cooler air of the main lodge hit him in the face as he pushed open the door. He exhaled as he waited for the sweat running down his back to dry before he went to find his mother.

He grabbed a glass of lemonade before he yelled, "Ma?"

"In the office."

He moved around the wooden posts strategically placed throughout the building to hold up the massive structure, and then through the doorway to where the office stood near the back of the huge main room. "You wanted to see me?"

She glanced up at him through the small glasses perched on her nose. His mother was still a stunning woman even in her mid-sixties. A few strands of grey streaked her black tresses, but it only made her look more beautiful. "Yes. I needed to ask you about the hay supply. Did you stack it yesterday?"

"No. I was doing it this afternoon. I had to take a group out. We rode back in a minute ago."

"Good. Let me know when you're done what we have and what we'll need for next week's delivery, okay?"

"Sure."

"How did the ride go?"

"Good. I had a pretty talkative kid on the ride."

"Kids are so cute. I definitely want more grandkids."

"Well Jeff and Joel will have taken care of that in the coming weeks."

"Jacob, sit down for a minute."

He frowned. "Okay."

"Why didn't you tell me and your dad about Veronica and the baby?"

He tipped his head back against the wall behind him and sighed. "How'd you find out?"

"I ran into her mother in town not long after she aborted it."

"You've known all this time and you didn't say anything?"

"I kept waiting for you to tell us. I didn't feel it was our place to bring it up. Is that why you started drinkin' so heavy?"

"Part of it, yeah. I still feel really guilty about not stoppin' her."

She reached over and grabbed his hand. "Honey, it was her decision."

"No, it was our decision, but I should have been able to talk her out of it or somethin'. Ma, it was my child and I let her kill it."

"But, baby, you couldn't really stop her if it was her choice to do it. It's her body. If she didn't want to carry the pregnancy, there wasn't much you could do."

"I guess, but I'll never forget and I certainly don't think I'll ever forgive her for goin' through with it. You know she didn't tell me she was havin' it done until two days after she did it?"

"She probably knew you'd try to stop her."

"I would've."

Nina stood, pulled Jacob to his feet and wrapped her arms around him. "It's okay to grieve, Jacob. I'm glad you've slowed down on the alcohol though. You had me worried."

"I know, Ma. I've stopped all together."

"Good for you. I'm glad to hear it. What made you stop?"

"A woman."

"Paige?"

"Yeah. She kept me from gettin' my ass kicked in a bar."

Nina tilted her head to the side. "She hangs out in bars? A preacher's daughter?"

"Yeah, but don't you say anything to her dad."

"He doesn't know, I take it."

"No."

"What a tangled web we weave."

"I know. I wish she wouldn't keep it a secret from him. He's bound to find out sooner or later. I don't think it'll be a pretty blow up either."

"You really like her, huh?"

"Yeah, I do."

"I'm glad. You need a good woman in your life."

He smiled and kissed her on the cheek. "Don't be plannin' weddin' bells just yet."

She brushed some hay from the front of his shirt. "I'm not."

"Enjoy Mesa and Terri for a while yet, Ma. I don't want you to get your hopes up on me and Paige."

"She's a nice girl though."

"Yeah, she is, but we are gettin' to know each other right now. Takin' it slow, you know?"

"All right, baby. I'll lavish my attention on Mesa and Terri for now."

"Thank you. I love you, Mom."

"I love you too, Jacob. Now, back to work with you."

He kissed her on the cheek again before he disappeared out the office door. A quick glance at the leather sofa's in front of the huge fireplace in the main room revealed a cowboy sitting on one of the couches. The man tipped his dusty cowboy hat and disappeared. Man, he'd never get used to seeing the ghosts who inhabited Thunder Ridge ranch. The lonesome cowboy was the one they saw most often especially in the main lodge.

The lunch bell clanged signaling it was time to eat.

The noise level rose exponentially as the crowd poured in from outside for the noon meal. The tang of grilled hamburgers and hot dogs made his stomach rumble. He'd missed breakfast this morning taking Paige back to town.

The blonde, brunette and two redheads from the group on the ride this morning came in to get in line for lunch. Monica glanced his way with a smile. How could a woman look good after a sweaty morning ride without smelling like horses? She wasn't bad looking. A little on the plump side, but he wasn't one for skinny women anyway. Her friends were kind of pretty too. The brunette caught his attention, curvy with nice round high breasts, slim waist, and nice ass. Her shape reminded him of Paige. One of the redheads smiled and waved. Her eyes were a very pretty green, kind of like new spring grass. Paige's were emerald green and sparkled like the stone itself.

Wow. He was really messed up if everyone reminded him of Paige in one way or another.

When the guests had all been served, the family rose as a group to get their lunch. The rules according to his mother, to make their guests feel welcome. He smiled. She had a lot of rules. No messing with the guests. No eating before the guests. Treat them with respect, but flirting wasn't out of the question. Make them feel welcome. *Sheesh.* Of course, they had one of the most guest friendly ranches in the area and it showed especially during the summer when they were full all the time.

After they'd all been served and the family sat back down, talk around the table settled into what they had to do this afternoon. He knew he had to stack and count the hay bales for his mom to tally the feed needed for the rest of the week. Stalls needed cleaning too.

Sighing, he longed for a nice cool shower already.

"Are you okay, Jacob?" Jackson asked from his seat across the table.

"Yeah, why?"

"You seemed tired. Late night?" Jackson grinned as he bit into his hamburger.

Jacob knew something was up if his brother had that sparkle of mischievousness in his eyes. "Kind of."

"The pretty green eyed girl from the barbeque yesterday sure had eyes for you this morning when you took her home."

Shit. "Mind your own business Jackson." He should have known. They left early enough, but his brothers were usually up before the sun doing chores.

"I was, but it's hard to miss your laugh and her giggle at six in the mornin'."

"I didn't realize Paige was here last night, Jacob." His mother smiled too as he narrowed his eyes.

She would really push the matchmaking now that she knew things were a little more serious between him and Paige than she'd first thought. *Getting a little sex doesn't mean things are serious.* "Butt out, Ma."

His brothers all glanced his way. He couldn't blame them. He'd never brought a girl back to his place before. Paige had been there twice.

"You brought a girl home?" Jeremiah asked, leaning forward in his chair. "You never bring women back here."

"Let it go. It's nothin'."

"It is something, Jacob," Jeff said. "At least she's not a guest."

"You're one to talk, Jeff. Terri was a guest when you were—"

"Jacob," his father growled in warning. "That's enough."

"And Mesa was a guest too."

"Leave Mesa and Terri out of this," Joel warned as Mesa blushed a deep red. Terri wasn't at the table this morning for some reason.

"Sorry, Mesa. I'm a little touchy this mornin'."

"Apparently."

"That's enough, boys," his father said, taking the tension down a notch. "This conversation isn't appropriate with guests in the room. Let's move onto something else. Joey, how are the new mares working out?"

"Good. Jacob took two of them on the morning run with guests. Jacob?"

"No problems." He shoveled some potato salad into his mouth. At least if he was chewing he wouldn't have to talk. His disposition seemed to be getting sourer by the moment with all the talk of Paige. Things were going good between them. If his brothers started in, she might bolt like a skittish foal. He wondered if her father managed to corral her this morning for a talk. He'd have to call her later.

He frowned. Since when did he really care about how things were going in her personal life? *Since you fucked her brains out last night after a very family oriented day with her.*

"Mom, I'm going to be updating the website this afternoon so the reservations system will be down for a couple of hours," Jonathan said as he shoved his plate aside.

"All right. Thanks for the warning."

Jacob wanted to escape. Even throwing hay would be better than sitting here listening to the mundane conversation around the table with his family. "I'm headin' to the barn."

"Are you all right, Jacob?" his mother asked, glancing up at him as he stood ready to bolt.

"Yeah. I'm fine. I need some breathin' room is all." He jammed his fingers through his hair before he adjusted his hat on his head. "See y'all at dinner."

He tossed his plate into the dirty dish bin as he tuned out the laughter and conversation of the guests around him. The barn would be quiet except for the occasional shuffle of horse hooves, the meow of the barn cat or the rustle of wind through the rafters. Peace. Right now he needed the atmosphere of the barn to think.

The heat of the day would be almost oppressive in there, but he needed to work off some of this nervous energy. His muscles twitched and bunched as he walked with a purposeful stride toward the large structure at the back of the property. The main compound consisted of the large lodge and several guest cabins. Each cabin had two sides connected with a door between them so they could be opened up for a larger group. There were four of these double cabins as well as rooms in the main lodge where guests stayed.

Right now he wanted to be away from everyone.

He stepped into the shadowed doorway of the barn inhaling the scent of hay, manure, and leather, letting it calm his restless soul. Dust danced in the sunlight coming through the rafters above his head, illuminating pieces of hay on the ground at his feet. Horses shifted in their stalls. The scurry of mice along the rafters reached his ears. The barn cats had their work cut out for them. A couple of kittens wrapped themselves around his boots so he leaned down and picked one up to scratch it between the ears. The little grey striped one was his favorite.

"I'm such a sucker for kittens and babies, but you're a cutie, aren't you?" He ran his hands over the little furry body a couple of times before he set it on its feet and headed for the loft.

Leather work gloves sat on the pile of hay to his right. He shoved his hands into the soft kidskin to shield his skin from the rough bailing string around each bale. They went through a lot of hay and feed this time of year.

As he began to stack the bales in the corner, he let his mind wander to what he was going to do about Paige. Everything seemed to be going okay for now, but he wasn't sure where it might be headed in the future. Was there a future for them?

He didn't even know what she did for money to live on. Something he would have to correct. She knew more about him than he knew about her. What was her favorite color? Her favorite flower? Did she like certain perfumes over others? She definitely had a different personality, kind of an enigma so to speak. She rode a Harley, dressed in leather, but didn't drink alcohol. She also had the sweet, innocent, church girl thing down pat from what he saw at the barbeque yesterday. It fit her too.

He grinned as he threw a bale into the corner stack. He sure would enjoy unwrapping all the layers of Paige Tyler.

Chapter Nine

"I don't know what you're thinking anymore, Paige." Her father raked his hands through his greying hair.

When had the grey started to come in? She hadn't really noticed before, but she did now. He seemed to be growing older by the day. It worried her. He probably needed a doctor's visit. He hadn't been to one in years. "Daddy, I just—"

"Honey, what's going on? You're a totally different girl these days. Is it that young man I saw you with so much yesterday? Is he causing this change in you?"

"No. I've been like this for a while."

"Wild?"

She bowed her head. "I'm not wild."

"Yes, you are. You haven't known him long and here you are staying out all hours of the night with him. You came home early this morning. I heard you come in."

"I'm a grown woman, Daddy."

"Really? You sure aren't acting like a mature, young woman doing all these crazy things."

"You have no idea," she whispered under her breath.

"What did you say?"

"Nothing. I'm sorry. I'll try to behave more appropriately for a preacher's daughter."

"You should. This behavior isn't becoming of you. You can't attract a nice Christian man like this."

"Maybe I don't want a nice Christian man."

"Paige." His exasperated voice raised the hackles on her arms.

"I'm sorry, Daddy. I can't be the girl you think I should be. I have to be me."

"And exactly what does that mean?"

"What would you say if I went to bars on the weekends?"

"Instead of going to the nursing home?"

"Yes."

"You lied to me?"

"In a sense, yes."

"Is that how you knew the band members who played yesterday? You met them at a bar?"

"Yes. I don't drink though. I go to listen to the music and dance."

"Dancing too?"

Oh Lord what would he think if he knew I dressed in leather and rode a motorcycle? Confession time I think. "Yes, dancing too. I need to tell you something. I've been going to bars for a few months now. It's how I met Jacob. I saved him from a bar fight."

Sweat popped out on his forehead as he took a seat at the kitchen table with her.

"Are you all right?"

"I'm fine. I have a little nausea at the moment. Breakfast must have upset my stomach this morning."

"You don't look very well, Daddy. I should call the doctor."

"I'm fine." He pressed the heel of his hand to his chest.

"Are you having chest pain?"

"A bit of pressure. Nothing serious." He wiped the sweat from his forehead with a handkerchief he'd pulled from his back pocket. "Back to you. Why do you feel the need to hang out in bars and why did you lie to me?"

"You wouldn't understand."

"Try me."

She clasped her hands together, putting them on the table in front of her as she tried to explain this need to her father. "I need to be around people my own age. Dancing is fun. Hanging out with people is fun."

"Do you really enjoy these things?"

"Yes, I do. I can't always be the preacher's girl. I need to do things people my own age enjoy. I don't want to hang out with the ladies from the auxiliary. The guys in the band are my friends. Jacob is my friend."

"You're sleeping with him, true?"

"I have, yes."

"Premarital sex, Paige?"

"It's common these days, Daddy."

"I never thought my daughter would engage in those sorts of things. What would your mother say if she were here?"

"I'd hope she'd understand as I hope you'll understand." He leaned over and put his head on his folded hands. "I'm calling an ambulance."

"I'm fine," he mumbled right before he slid from the chair onto the floor.

"Daddy!"

He didn't respond.

"Shit." She grabbed the phone from the wall, dialing nine-one-one.

"What's your emergency?"

"My father. He was complaining of nausea, pain in his chest and sweating profusely. Now he's on the floor."

"Is he breathing?"

"Yes."

"I'm sending an ambulance. You'll need to meet them outside."

She rattled off the address, stretching the phone cord far enough she could reach his side and still be on the phone.

"Keep talking to me," the dispatcher said. "If he stops breathing or his heart stops, you'll need to do CPR until they get there."

"No, he's still breathing, but he hasn't regained consciousness." Sirens wailed in the distance. "I hear the ambulance."

"Okay. Hang up with me and go meet them. They'll need to know where to go."

"Thank you."

"You're welcome."

She needed something, someone. She wrung her hands together as she headed for the front door. "This way," she said as the paramedics stepped onto the porch.

"What happened," the dark-haired paramedic asked.

"We were talking and he just collapsed from the seat onto the floor. He's been out for several minutes."

"Any symptoms before that?"

"Sweating, nausea, chest pain, I think. He wouldn't really tell me, but that's what it seemed like."

The paramedics cut his shirt and pasted on plastic sticky things to his chest. His heartbeat blipped over the screen on their machine. They quickly stuck a needle in his arm for fluids. She'd seen enough trauma in the ER to know a few things. It sounded like he had some kind of heart attack. *Great. Tell him about your secret life and send your father into a heart attack. Brilliant.* "Do you know what's wrong?"

"I'm not sure, but we are going to treat him as if it's cardiac related by the symptoms you told us."

"What's going on?" her father asked, his eyes now open. "Paige?"

"You're on your way to the hospital, Daddy."

"But why?" He started to sit up.

"Lie back, sir. We've got you hooked up to some machines to monitor your heart and we're giving you fluids. We'll be transporting you to the hospital in a moment."

"I'm fine."

"No you aren't. You need to go," she said, holding him down by the shoulder.

"All right. I guess it wouldn't hurt to have a doctor look at me."

"How long were you having chest pain before you passed out, sir?"

"I've had discomfort in my chest all morning and a little last night."

Great. After the barbeque I pushed his need to talk out of the way for Jacob. He was probably having a heart attack last night. "You'll be fine, Daddy. I'll be right beside you."

"Thank you, Paige."

The paramedics lifted the gurney they'd put him on and locked it in place. With all the monitors beeping and dinging, they wheeled him out through the living room and out the front door to the ambulance.

"What's going on?" Mrs. Johnson asked, coming from around the side of the church. "I saw the ambulance."

"It'll be fine. We'll let you know when we know something."

"Is he going to be all right?"

"I'm sure he'll be fine, Mrs. Johnson." Paige had already grabbed her keys and her purse off the side table before the ambulance crew had him through the doorway outside. "I'll follow you to the hospital."

Within moments, she was following behind the screaming ambulance toward the hospital, thoughts of losing her dad rushing through her mind. She couldn't lose him too. *I need Jacob.* She grabbed her cell phone, scrolled through the numbers and hit talk.

"Paige?"

"Hi. Listen. I'm on the way to the hospital with my father. I think he might have had a heart attack."

"Which one?"

"University Hospital."

"I'll be right there."

"Are you sure? You don't have other things you need to be doing?"

"Honey, if you didn't need me, you wouldn't have called. I'll be there in forty-five minutes."

"Thanks."

"You're welcome. Be tough. It'll be okay."

"I feel terrible, Jacob. I think I brought it on."

"Why?"

She could hear the jangle of keys and an engine start on his truck. "I told him about my weekends. I lied to him."

"Babe, it'll be okay. He's a tough guy."

"But the stress brought this on. I know it did." Tears began to roll down her cheeks. With her hand on the phone and one on the wheel, she couldn't brush them away.

"Calm down, Paige. You're drivin', right?"

"Yeah."

"Be careful, darlin'. You can't help your father if you're in the bed next to him and if you do that, I'll have to kick your butt."

She laughed through her tears. Leave it to Jacob to make her feel better. This is why she loved him. *What the hell?* She sniffed. "It'll be fine, I hope. Thank you for making me laugh. I needed to talk to you. I really need you to hold me."

"I'll be there soon."

She pulled into the parking lot of the hospital behind the ambulance. "I'm at the hospital. Meet me in the emergency room waiting room when you get here. I'm sure they won't let me back there until they know something anyway."

"Okay. Be strong. It'll be okay."

"Thank you."

"You're welcome. See you soon."

I love you was on the tip of her tongue, but she held it in. This was a new feeling for her and she wasn't sure what to do about it. She really didn't know him well enough to say I love you, did she? The phone clicked in her ear, signaling Jacob had hung up. She bit her lip and slowly laid the phone on the seat next to her purse. *Do I really love him? Wow.* This wasn't something she'd expected to be racing through her heart. *What the hell do I do now?*

* * * *

Jacob raced through the streets on San Antonio, tapping his fingers on the steering wheel of his truck. Paige needed him. It felt good. He liked the thought of her needing him a little too much. What did it mean for their relationship? He wasn't sure, but it was a step in the right direction.

The hospital parking lot came into view. He found the emergency room entrance as he pulled into a parking spot big enough for his truck. His heart thumped in his chest. She needed him. The thought brought a smile to his face even in the wake of this tragedy with her father. He liked being needed, he found. With her being such a strong woman, admitting she needed him had to be tough on her as well.

He jumped out of his truck, locked the doors and headed for the entrance. The double glass doors slid open when he stepped in front of them, revealing the stark whiteness of the room. Even the curtains on the windows were white. Double doors to what he assumed led to the back of the emergency room, sat back against the walls.

Paige stood off to his right, rubbing her arms as she paced in front of the chairs. "Paige?"

"Jacob." She flew into his arms like a bird coming home to roost.

Her tear stained cheeks broke his heart. "How are you holdin' up, babe?"

"Not good." She rubbed her face on his shirt. "You smell good."

"I'm sure I smell like sweat, hay, and horse shit. I was throwin' hay when you called."

"I like it. It's you." She stepped back, but not completely out of his arms. "Thank you for coming."

"You needed me."

"Still. You didn't have to come, but you did. It says a lot about you."

Her green eyes glistened with unshed tears as he wiped the remaining wetness from her cheeks with his thumb. "He'll be okay, darlin'. Was he talkin' when they brought him in?"

"Yes, but he'd lost consciousness at home. I'm scared."

"I know."

"Paige Tyler?" a nurse called from the doorway.

"Yes?"

"Your father wants to see you now."

"Can my, *uh*, friend come back with me?"

"Sure, but you two can't stay long. We're still running tests."

"Thank you."

They followed the purple clad nurse back through the doors, down a long hall to a curtain off area to the left. "In here."

"Do they have any idea what happened?"

"I'll let the doctor talk to you both. He'll be in momentarily." She pushed the curtain aside to reveal her father's pale face lying on the gurney with his eyes closed.

"Daddy?"

He opened his eyes and frowned. "What is he doing here?"

"He came because I called him. Be nice."

"He's the one who led you down the road to Hell, Paige. How can you expect me to be nice? You need to find a Christian man to be with, not some hoodlum who hangs out in bars." He coughed several times, making his heart rate increase enough to set off the dinging bells on the monitor.

"You need to calm down, Daddy."

"I won't calm down. Get him out of here."

"I won't. I need him here."

"Then you need to leave too."

"Daddy!"

"What's going on in here?" the doctor asked, pushing through the split in the curtain. "You need to slow your heart rate down, Mr. Tyler."

"It's Reverend Tyler and I want these two to leave my bedside. Tell my daughter I'm fine so she can leave."

"I can't say that, Reverend. I don't know what's wrong with you yet. Are you sure you don't want her here?"

"I'll go wait outside, Paige. It's obvious he doesn't want me here." He rubbed her arm before he turned to go. "I'll be in the waiting room."

"I'm sorry."

"No need." He leaned down to kiss her quickly on the forehead, not wanting to disturb her father any more than necessary.

The man started coughing heavily again as Jacob disappeared around the curtains and back down the hall. *Well, that went fabulously. What the hell? Does he really think I'm the reason Paige went to bars? What did she tell him was going on between us?*

He pushed through the doors to find the cafeteria. Coffee sounded mighty good right about now.

"You look lost, cowboy," the receptionist said from behind her little desk. "Can I help you find something?"

"The cafeteria? I could use a cup of coffee."

"Down the hall to your left. It's at the end. You can't miss it."

"Thank you."

"No problem."

The woman seemed nice even as she eyed him with a blatantly appreciative stare, but he couldn't really revel in the look when Paige's father might be fighting for his life right at this moment. Not that he'd looked at many women since she'd come into his life. He found he compared everyone to her these days.

The click of his booted heels down the long corridor sounded ominous even to him. He really didn't like hospitals all that much. They reminded him of sterile, stark environments meant to keep people from interacting with each other. He liked to touch, to hold, or to kiss. Maybe that made him kind of touchy feely, which didn't seem natural for a guy, but it was for him. He liked the feeling of skin beneath his fingertips.

He poured a cup of coffee and dumped in some sugar and cream before heading for the checkout. Once he paid for his cup, he went straight back toward the waiting room. He was there for Paige and he'd be there until she didn't need him anymore.

His cell jingled in his pocket. "Hello?"

"Hey, son. Where'd you run off to?"

"Sorry, Ma. I didn't get a chance to tell you. Paige called. Her dad is at the hospital in San Antonio. We don't know what's going on yet."

"I'm sorry to hear he's feeling poorly."

"I planned to call you in a little bit when I knew more so I could tell you how long I'd be gone, but he kind of chased me out of his room."

"Oh?"

"Yeah. I'm not sure what's going on yet, but I didn't want to upset him further."

"That doesn't sound very good."

"It's not. I'm in the waiting room for when Paige comes back out. I'm here for her anyway, not so much for him."

"If you get a chance, tell him we're thinking of him and praying everything is okay. He seemed like a nice man when we met at the barbeque."

"I'll tell him. I'm sure prayers wouldn't hurt right now."

"Will do. We'll see you when you get home or give us a call later to update us when you know something."

"Sure. Thanks."

"Be careful, Jacob. There's a storm moving in from the west. Sounds like we might get hit pretty hard with rain and wind later."

"I will. Bye, Mom."

"Bye, sweetie."

The long line of empty chairs along the back walls looked like a good place to rest his butt so he slid into a seat with a weary sigh. This wasn't the way he wanted to get out of back breaking, grueling work this afternoon, but he'd take any break he could.

As he sipped the hot liquid in his cup, his thoughts rushed backed to what Reverend Tyler said about him. He definitely needed to talk to Paige and find out exactly what she'd told her father. How could that man think he was the reason behind Paige's apparent spiraling into the depths of Hell? Or something along those lines.

Paige came through the double doors, spotted him sitting in the chairs and headed in his direction. "I'm really sorry about that."

"It's okay. We'll talk about it later. What did the doctor say?"

"They aren't sure if it's his heart or something else. He hasn't had any changes in his EKG so they don't think it's a heart attack, but they are doing chest x-rays, blood tests, CAT scans and other stuff to try to figure it out."

"Well at least he didn't have a heart attack."

"True." She sighed as she sat back in the chair. "I hate this not knowing."

"About what he said in there."

She looked down at her hands before looking back up at him. "Don't listen to him."

"Why does he think I'm to blame?"

Her gaze beseeched him to believe her and understand, but he wasn't sure he could. How could he deal with her not telling her father the entire truth? This could be detrimental to their relationship. What if she couldn't deal with telling her father?

"For some reason he has it in his head, I didn't start going to the bars until you and I met. Not that we met at the bar because I was already there."

"You haven't told him about checking out places like The Dusty Boot, riding your motorcycle or dressing in leather, have you?"

"No. He knows I don't go to the nursing home. I told him I'd been going out to spend time with people my own age. You know, dancing and stuff."

"You didn't correct him about our meeting, did you?"

She grasped his free hand, holding it between her own cold ones. "No. Not yet, but I promise I will, Jacob. I'm not hiding how we met necessarily. I just didn't want to upset him anymore."

"When, Paige?"

"Soon."

He sipped his coffee until he got to the bottom of the cup. Extra sweetness hit his tongue with the last dregs. He grimaced at the taste as he set the cup on the table to his left. "I don't like this. Not at all."

"I know. I really didn't mean to keep it from him. When he started having pain at the house, I panicked. I let you take the blame and I'm sorry."

"But you haven't corrected his misunderstanding."

"I will. As soon as they tell us what's wrong and I know he won't have a heart attack because he finally knows his precious little preacher's girl isn't the sweet, innocent twelve year old he remembers. I know we had the discussion about the fact that we've already had sex, but I don't want to make things worse."

"I know he wasn't thrilled when he found out either."

"He knows I didn't come home until this morning. He figured out we spent the night together again. He's not happy about it either."

"Well there is at least that much. Of course, I'm sure he blames me for that too." He jumped to his feet. "I don't like this, Paige. I don't want your father to think I'm Satan's son come to defile his precious daughter. We're in this together. This is a relationship. How are things supposed to work if he thinks I'm corrupting you?"

"Do you think of it as a relationship, Jacob? I thought we were just having a good time."

"I'm in this for more than that. What about you?"

She climbed to her feet and faced the window as she rubbed her arms.

"Paige?"

"I don't know what you want me to say."

He put his hands on her shoulders as she leaned back against his chest. With his lips to her ear, he whispered, "I want you to say this means more to you than casual sex." The reflection of her face in the glass revealed her slowly closing her eyes, almost like she didn't want to face the reality of their relationship. "I guess you really don't need me after all."

"I do."

"No, I don't think you do or you don't want to face the fact of our relationship moving onto something more permanent. You care more than you want to. I know I do." He dropped his hands to his sides so he could step back. The realization hit him like a sledge hammer to the chest. "I'm going to go now."

"Please stay."

"I think you need some time to think. I'm not doin' anything here, but waitin'. Your daddy needs you and he doesn't need my presence causing more harm than good."

"I need you, Jacob."

"For what exactly?"

"Support?" A tear slipped down her cheek as her breath caught in her throat. "Don't leave, please."

"All right. I'll stay for a while." He wrapped his arms around her, pulling her into his embrace. He loved touching her, holding her, but she really needed to give him some idea if his growing feelings were returned. Right now, he felt like someone had stomped on his heart before they shoved it back in his chest. He didn't like the feeling at all.

Chapter Ten

Paige realized with the look on Jacob's face she was royally screwing this up. "I'm sorry. I'll tell him right now." She pulled out of his arms to head for the door.

"Wait, Paige. It's probably not a good time. Not until they find out what's wrong with him."

"But he needs to know you aren't the devil incarnate come to drag me off to the depths of Hell."

"We'll tell him eventually."

The same nurse stuck her head out of the door. "Ms. Tyler?"

"Yes?"

"The doctor wants to talk to you and your father together."

"I'll be right there." She turned to face Jacob. "Come with me. We'll talk to him together."

"Honey, that's not a good idea. Getting him worked up and upset could make things worse than they already are."

"Are you sure?"

"Yeah. Just come back out after you talk to the doctor. Then we'll face him together once they get him comfortable in a room or whatever they're gonna do."

"I love you."

Jacob's eyes darkened to an almost black as a startled look crossed his face. "What did you say?"

"I love you. I wanted you to know that before I talked to my father because you mean everything to me. Whatever happens won't have anything to do with us. We are who we are and when we're together, it's right. That's all we need to know." She kissed him quickly on the lips. "I'll be right back."

She disappeared behind the doors only to lean back against them once they closed to catch her breath. She certainly hadn't expected to blurt out I love you in the middle of a hospital as they waited for news on her father's health. *Brilliant.* "Oh well." She pushed off the wooden panels to walk down the aisle to her father's bedside. The doctor met her outside the curtained area.

"Let's go in, shall we?"

"Of course."

The color had returned to her father's cheeks as he rested against the pillows. He opened his eyes as she took his hand in hers. A cough raked his body for a moment until he caught his breath again. "What's the verdict?"

"You have pneumonia. You probably passed out earlier at home because of the lack of oxygen in your blood. Your saturations were low when you came in. Now that you've had some oxygen, your color is much better as are your saturations."

"Does he get to go home?"

"No. We'll need to keep him a few days for observation and medication. He needs some strong antibiotics to combat the problem. He would be much better staying here so we can watch him. Monitoring is the best thing for him right now."

"Wonderful, doctor. Thank you."

"So it wasn't my heart?"

"No, sir. Your heart seems pretty healthy. Overall, you seem to be in pretty good health besides the pneumonia."

"Thank God."

"He's watching out for me. Always has, Paige."

"I know, Daddy." He kissed his cheek as she pushed his thinning hair back from his forehead. He looked so much older to her than his sixty years as he laid there against the white bedding.

"We'll get him moved to a room within the next hour."

"Thank you, doctor."

"You're welcome. Rest, Reverend Tyler. It's the best thing for you. No excitement. If you have a coughing attack, your oxygen saturations drop."

"You got it, doctor."

The man disappeared behind the curtain as Paige took the chair next to her father's bed. "They'll have you in a room soon, I'm sure. You'll have to rest and not get too excited."

"I won't." He patted her hand as he asked, "Did that young man go home?"

"No. He's in the waiting room."

He frowned as he pursed his lips in the way she knew meant he was about to lecture her on something.

"You aren't supposed to get excited so stop right there."

"You aren't to see him anymore."

"But Dad—"

"I'll hear no more about it. I don't want you associating with him."

"I'm an adult. I can make my own decisions." Her father closed his eyes in dismissal, refusing to engage in the discussion again. "I'll be back in a bit."

"Fine," he said, not even opening his eyes.

Dread crawled down her spine. She needed to talk to Jacob, but how was she supposed to turn her back on the man she loved?

She reluctantly walked back down the aisle and through the double doors. He waited in the same spot he'd left him.

"What's the decision?"

"He has pneumonia. They'll be keeping him for a few days for treatment."

"I'm glad it's not his heart."

"Me too. I've already sent up a dozen prayers for a good outcome today." She wrapped her arms around his waist as she leaned into his chest. "They'll be moving him to a room soon and then I can go home. There won't be any reason for me to stay any longer."

He kissed her head as he pulled her in tighter. "I told you he'd be okay."

"Thank you for being here."

"Anything for you."

They stood wrapped in each other's arms for several moments while she absorbed his strength.

"Would you like something from the cafeteria while we wait for them to get him a room?"

"No, thank you, but you can get something else if you want."

"I'm fine. The coffee wasn't bad, but I've had better."

He pushed her back a little to look into her eyes. She wasn't sure she liked the look on his face. "About what you said before you went back there."

"Forget it, Jacob. I didn't mean it like it came out."

"Are you sure, because I'm not sure I'm ready to say it back to you and I don't want it to get awkward between us."

Her heart turned into a blob resting in her stomach. He didn't love her in return. She should have known as much. Really, they didn't know each other that well. She didn't know much about him at all. "It's fine. I meant like a friend, you know."

"Friends with benefits?"

"Maybe, but I don't want things to get weird."

"Okay. We'll leave it be for now."

"Good."

The nurse poked her head out of the door. "Ms. Tyler, they are moving your father up to a room now."

"Thank you." She pulled out of his arms, missing the warmth and security she felt having them around her. "I should see him up to his room."

"Do you want me to come back there with you?"

"No!" She swallowed hard. "I mean, it's okay. I'll be back shortly. There's no reason for you to go up there. I don't want him upset any more than he already is."

"Are you okay?"

"Yes."

"Why do I get the feeling there is more to this than you're letting on, Paige."

"It's nothing, really. He was so upset before he had a coughing fit which drops his saturations. They don't want him excited."

He shoved his hands into the front pockets of his jeans as he rocked back on his heels. "All right. I'll wait here. After you get him settled, we should go have some dinner. It's getting late."

"You don't have to stay, Jacob. I can get home. I have my car here since I followed the ambulance to the hospital."

"I want to hold you tonight. Is that all right with you? I mean, I don't want to put you out or anything."

She hugged him again, kissing his cheek. "I'm sorry. I'm making a big mess of this whole thing. I would love for you to stay if you want to. I just don't think it's a good idea for my father to see you with how upset he got earlier."

"Can I stay at your place?"

She bit her lip. "I guess so."

He stepped back. "Don't bother. It sounds like you don't really want me around so I'll go. Get your father settled and go home. You probably could use the night alone."

"But, Jacob…"

"It's fine, Paige." He kissed her on the lips. "Take a bubble bath or something. You've earned it with this stress." He turned on his heel and disappeared through the sliding glass doors.

As she watched him walk away, she felt as if her whole world had just walked out the door.

* * * *

Jacob slammed his hand down on the steering wheel of his truck as he drove out of San Antonio headed for home. "Why didn't I say it back? I mean, I care about her a lot, but in love with her?" He shrugged. "Yeah, I guess so." *I've never been in love before. Is this how it feels?*

The long drive back would give him time to think. Something wasn't jiving with her keeping him from seeing her father. *Yeah, he'd been upset because he thought I was the one dragging Paige to bars, but she'd told him the truth, right?*

"What if she didn't tell him? What if she's still keeping our real relationship a secret?"

His head began to hurt with all the strangulated thoughts tangling up in his brain. He didn't want to question her motives, but she sure gave him reason to when she acted so strangely. What a difference a few hours makes. Thinking about last night, reminded him of the feel of her lips under his. Her nipples were hard little knots of flesh beneath his tongue when he flicked them. Her taste was addicting. She felt like heaven wrapped around his dick. Her pussy milked him dry when she'd come apart in his arms with a cry of his name, which he loved to hear on her lips.

His cock pressed against the fly of his jeans, making it uncomfortable to sit.

Before he realized, he'd pulled up to the gates of Thunder Ridge. Home.

Maybe he'd talk to his mom about Paige. She might be able to give him some insight to women. Yeah, couldn't hurt to try.

The main lodge house came into view with its three big dormer windows in the front, long porch with the rocking chairs waiting for guests to enjoy the sunset or sunrise from the wide expanse and the donkeys hanging around waiting for handouts or petting. He smiled. This place really was home to him.

He parked around back by his trailer and stepped out. His mom would be in her office for another few minutes tonight even though dinner had already been served to the guests. The smell of dinner still lingered in the air. He'd have to raid the kitchen later.

"Ma?"

"In the back, Jacob."

He found her right where he thought he would. "Can I talk to you?"

"Sure, baby. What's up?" she asked, turning to face him.

He grabbed a chair and spun it around to sit down. "It's about Paige."

"Go on."

"Her father has pneumonia, by the way. Sorry I didn't call from the hospital, but we kinda had a little spat so I came home."

"I'm sorry to hear that. I hope he's feeling better soon."

"I'm sure he will. They're keeping him a couple of days at the hospital for treatment."

"Good. That's the best place for him." She patted his hand. "What did you two fight over?"

"Well, apparently her father thinks I'm the reason she's been going to bars, which isn't true. We met at The Dusty Boot, but she'd been comin' there off and on for several weeks. I vaguely remember seein' her there before she saved my ass."

"She didn't correct his misguided notion?"

"No."

"Hmm."

"I thought maybe you could give me some insight to how women think."

She laughed as she leaned back in her office chair. He didn't think the subject was that funny, but apparently she did as she rolled with laughter. "I truly wish I could help you, honey, but I don't know what to tell you."

"I wish I knew what was going through her mind." He sighed as he thought about how much he wanted a drink right now. "She told me she loved me at the hospital."

"How fantastic! Another daughter-in-law."

"Don't rush things, Ma. I didn't say it back."

"Do you love her?"

"I'm not sure. That's why I wanted to talk to you."

"What do you think?"

"I think about her all the time." He leaned forward in the chair, dangling his hands between his legs. "I want her with me every waking moment of every day. I haven't really looked at another woman without thinking about Paige and wondering how she compares. She doesn't. She beats any woman I looked at, hands down. Being with her makes me happy beyond my wildest dreams."

"Sounds like love to me."

"Really? Because I'm not so sure."

"Why don't you think you're in love with her?"

"Because I've never been in love before. I don't know if this is how it feels or not."

She put her hand on his cheek. "Honey, if you can't imagine the rest of your life without her in it, it's love."

"Then I guess I'm in love with her."

"I bet she'd love to hear you say it in person."

"Should I drive back to town to tell her? She probably needs tonight to herself. It's been a hard day with her dad."

"I'm sure a night alone would probably do her good, besides, she's not going anywhere."

"Thanks, Mom. I love you."

"I love you too, Jacob. I'll be happy to have another daughter to love on." She brought him to his feet and hugged him. "Grandkids. I want more grandkids. You aren't gettin' any younger, mister."

"I know, Mom. Trust me. I know." He kissed her cheek. "I'll be sure to bring her home for the whole family to get to know better soon."

"You do that."

He walked out into the main lodge room as he pulled his cell phone from his pocket. Should be call her? No, he didn't want to say I love you on the phone. He wanted to do it all special like with flowers, maybe a bubble bath for two. He snapped his fingers. He'd rent a luxury hotel room in town, wine and dine her before he told her he loved her. Women loved that kind of thing.

Would Paige like livin' on the ranch?

Was he really thinking along permanent relationship lines with her? *Yeah, I guess I am.* He could see his life with her, raising babics in their own little house way back off the beaten path of the rest of the ranch. His own little piece of Heaven. She'd sit on the porch, her belly round with their child and rock the other small one in her arms until they fell asleep. They'd have lots of babies. Maybe enough for a baseball team like his parents. Nine of them.

He grinned. Of course, he'd have to convince her of that, but he was sure he could.

* * * *

Paige tucked the sheets around her father as he got comfortable in the regular room.

"This is much better than the gurney they had me on."

"I'm sure it is."

"Not as good as my bed at home though."

"Stop complaining. You'll be fine here for a couple of days."

"Are you sure you'll be all right at home without me there?"

"I'm going on thirty years old soon. I think I can handle a couple of days alone. Besides, I have to work the next two days."

"I'm sure the kids will be glad you're back to work from your few days off."

"I hope so. I love them a whole lot."

"You'll have to give me grandchildren soon, Paige. I'm not getting any younger."

"Oh pish posh. You're still a young man and there is plenty of time for grandchildren."

"I want a lot you know. You're my only child so you must give me several."

She sat on the chair next to the bed. "I'm sure my husband will have something to say about how many there are."

The frown crossing his face worried her. She'd hope to avoid any more confrontational discussions about Jacob.

"Did you tell that young man you couldn't see him again?"

"Well, I..."

"You didn't, do you?"

"No."

"I forbade you from seeing him anymore, Paige. You are my daughter and you'll do as I say."

"I'm sorry, Daddy, but I'm old enough to make my own decisions regarding who I will and won't see. I like Jacob."

"He's bad for you."

"No, he's not."

"I've spoken so I'll hear no more about it." He leaned back in the bed and closed his eyes, signaling to her the discussion was over as far as he was concerned.

She sighed as she grabbed her purse and her keys. "Goodnight, Daddy. I'll see you tomorrow sometime. Rest." She leaned over to kiss his forehead, noting the coolness of his skin beneath her lips.

"Goodnight, Paige."

As she walked out, letting the door close softly behind her, she wondered what the hell she was going to do about her father and Jacob. She loved them both, but could she risk hurting her father over Jacob? Maybe she could keep them apart until her father came around? It was worth a try. She certainly didn't want to tell Jacob she couldn't see him anymore, but she couldn't defy her father either.

Her stomach grumbled and she realized she hadn't eaten since this morning with everything that had gone on. She figured she'd grab a bite on the way home and take Jacob's suggestion. A nice bubble bath would be just the thing she needed to relax. She may even read a book in there while she soaked. She glanced at her phone only to see no missed calls. She'd hoped Jacob would have called her by now to make up after their fight. *I could always call him.*

She scrolled through the numbers on the phone until she found his name. Her thumb hovered over the talk button for several minutes before she shut the phone off and stuck it back in her purse. Maybe it was a good thing not to talk to him tonight. They probably needed some time apart after her bumbling attempt to tell him she loved him. *Really stupid thing to do. He's probably not ready for love with me. I mean, we really haven't known each other very long.*

"Keep telling your heart that, Paige," she said out loud as she walked to her car. "Love doesn't care whether you're ready or not."

Several moments later, she pulled into the local burger house for some dinner. "Cheeseburger, fries and a strawberry milkshake, please."

"Seven-eighty-two at the window, please."

Once she had her food, she sucked some of the milkshake through the straw, sighing as the cold liquid went down her throat until a racy thought crossed her mind. What would it be like to eat ice cream off of Jacob's chest? Hmm. Sounds like an interesting concept. Too bad he's at home.

She glanced at her purse thinking about calling him again, but decided against it. Tonight was for her and her alone. She didn't have to worry about her father, she didn't have to worry about Jacob, and she didn't have anywhere to be except at home in a warm bath with a glass of wine. Oh, that sounded heavenly to her as she remembered a bottle of Pinot she had hidden in the cupboard above the sink.

The church and her little house came into view. She hadn't left the light on when they'd took off for the hospital, so the front of the house was dark and spooky with only the large floodlight behind the church to guide her steps.

She pulled out her keys, juggling them in her hand to find the front door key without dropping her food on the ground when someone came rushing around the corner of the house, barreling into her.

Chapter Eleven

Paige spun around, holding onto her sack of food like a shield as the big ball of fur almost tripped her. "What the hell?"

Ruff. Ruff.

A large yellow dog plopped his butt on the ground as he stared at her with his big brown eyes. His tongue lolled out of his mouth and she could have sworn he grinned. He looked kind of skinny though and wasn't wearing a collar.

"It's mine, dog. Back off."

He barked again before he lay down on his belly with his paws sticking out in front of him.

"Well, crap."

The dog whined and Paige knew she was a goner.

"Where is your home, buddy?"

He rolled over onto his back wanting her to pet his stomach.

She unlocked the door as the dog jumped back up onto his feet, wagging its tail hard enough his whole butt moved. "Well come on in. I'm sure I can find something for you to eat." The dog obediently followed her into the house, staying right on her heels the entire way into the kitchen. "You can't have my hamburger, but I think there is left over spaghetti in here you can have."

Ruff.

"Yeah, I know. You're too cute to be mad at, but you can't stay here, buddy."

Ruff.

She grabbed the spaghetti out of the refrigerator and set it on the floor. The dog didn't move. "Don't you want it? I thought you were hungry?"

The dog sat on his haunches.

She tapped her hand on her leg. "Come here. You can have it."

The dog launched itself toward the plate, eating so fast she thought he would choke on the food. "Oh, you have manners, do you? Wouldn't eat until I told you it was okay."

When it was finished, he licked his mouth, walked to the rug by the sink and laid down.

"Oh no you don't. I'm going to eat my dinner and you need to go back outside so you can find your way home." She pulled her food out of the bag and then spread it out on the kitchen table. When she looked back at the dog, he'd closed his eyes, resting peacefully as if he belonged there. She sighed as she drank some of her milkshake. "What am I going to do with you?"

With a shake of her head, she ate her dinner, glancing every few minutes at her new friend while he slumbered peacefully on the rug.

As she finished chewing her food, she wadded up the wrapper and tossed it in the trashcan sitting at the end of the counter.

The dog never moved.

She rolled her eyes as she got up and headed toward the stairs to take her bath. When she looked behind her, the dog was right on her heels. "So you're going with me, *huh*?"

Ruff.

The dog lumbered up the stairs, slowly following until they both reached the landing at the top.

She shrugged and headed for the bathroom to run the water before she went into her room to get her nightgown.

The dog lay down on the rug next to the tub, staring at her with expectant eyes.

After she grabbed her night clothes, she returned to the bathroom, stripped down and slid beneath the water with an audible sigh.

"Damn. I forgot the wine." She struggled to her feet, wrapped a towel around her wet body and started for the stairs.

The rattling of the front door knob brought her up short. Was something there? She thought she heard hushed voices. She glanced down only to see the dog at her side, hair standing up on end as his ears perched forward. Had he heard something too?

"Shut up you idiot or she'll hear us."

Laughter radiated through the front hallway as the door knob rattled again.

"This isn't such a good idea, you guys. We could really get into trouble."

"It's fine. He'll love it when he finds her in his bed."

The dog growled as Paige backed toward her bedroom for at least a robe. Maybe she could put clothes on before the apparently drunk hoodlums ended up on the floor in her front hall. She didn't care if she kicked their asses buck naked, but they might.

The door creaked open as the bumbling idiots laughed again.

Of course, she might be able to reach her father's room where he kept the shotgun too.

Footsteps echoed on the hardwood floor of the entry way as the men slowly walked inside.

"Damn it. Where the hell is she?"

"Upstairs maybe. I saw a light on in the window around the side of the house."

The dog growled.

"Fuck. She has a dog?"

"We need to leave now, Jason, before we get into trouble."

"Quit whinnin', Joey."

"I have to drive your drunk asses home so I can whine as much as I want to."

Joey? Jason? Why do those names sound familiar?

"This was your idea, Joshua. What if Jacob is pissed off at us for doin' this? He ain't gonna like it, I'm tellin' you."

Jacob's brothers?

"He was in the barn bitchin' like an old woman about bein' alone tonight. He wants Paige. I heard him say so. He's our brother so we're gonna help him out."

"By kidnappin' his woman?"

"I'm tellin' you, they'll both think it's funny as hell," Joshua said, giggling like a school girl with a crush.

Paige rolled her eyes as she slipped on a T-shirt and jogging shorts. They apparently hadn't heard about how she'd saved Jacob's ass in a bar fight.

The dog growled again in warning even though he'd followed her into her room.

Of course, it wouldn't be much work kickin' their asses if they were as drunk as they sounded. Just for fun, she grabbed the shotgun.

She stopped at the top of the stairs and cocked the gun. "Who's there?"

"Uh. Fuck. She's got a gun, you guys."

"Paige?"

"Yeah, who's there I said. Speak up before I blow a hole the size of Texas through your gut and don't think I don't know how to use this thing."

"It's Joshua, Jason, and Joey, Jacob's brothers."

"What the hell are you doing in my house at this time of night?"

All of them laughed as she stepped down a couple of stairs to see the three of them. "We thought it would be funny to kidnap you and take you back to the ranch tonight. Jacob is missin' you real bad," Joshua said with a hand on his chest over his heart. "He was in the barn cussin' and a raisin' hell because he left you here after you fought earlier."

"Is that so?"

"Yeah."

"You three think you can take me?"

"Well sure. You're a girl."

"I'm assuming Jacob didn't tell you how we met?"

Joey squinted like he was trying to bring her into focus. "How's that?"

"I saved him from getting his ass kicked by three guys at The Dusty Boot."

All three men snickered as the covered their mouths. "That right," Jason said.

"Yeah."

"How'd you kick their asses?"

"I have a black belt."

"No shit," Joey whispered. "Can I see it?"

"Some other time. You boys need to get on home, but I think all of you are too drunk to drive."

"Yeah, probably so," Jason said as he swayed on his feet. "But we'll be fine."

She walked down the rest of the stairs to stand in front of the three big men who stood in her front hallway clinging onto each other. "No you won't. I'll drive your asses home so you don't kill someone on the way."

Joey pushed Jason's shoulder. "See! We didn't even have to kidnap her. She's gonna take us home 'cause we's too drunk to drive."

"And I'm going to tell your mother what you planned."

"Aw, shit. Don't do that. She'll kick our asses."

"As she should. Kidnapping innocent women from their home in the middle of the night."

Joey looked at his watch. "It ain't the middle of the night. It's only ten."

The dog stopped next to her eyeing the strangers as if to ask her whether he could chew them up and spit them out or not. "Easy, boy."

"Is he mean?"

"I don't know. He followed me home tonight. He's not my dog."

"He's awful protective."

The dog growled as she put her hand on his head to calm him.

"Let me grab my stuff and I'll take you boys home. Hand over the keys to whatever you're drivin'."

Joshua pulled the keys out of his front pocket and handed them to her. "Yes, ma'am."

"You boys probably won't remember anything about tonight."

"Sure we will. We ain't that drunk," Joshua added as she took the keys from his hand. "We were trying to make Jacob's night better. That's all."

"He loves you, ya know," Joey replied, bringing her to a dead stop.

"What did you say?"

"He loves you. I heard him talkin' to hisself in the barn." The words came out slurred from Joey's mouth, but her heart heard every word.

"Really?"

"Yeah."

She sighed as she reached for her keys and purse. Her slip-on sandals were conveniently located next to the table. She jammed her feet into the soft leather. "Let's go."

The three cowboys stumbled out the door behind her. "You go on home, boy, good dog." She watched him walk around the house. "Okay, where's your ride?" Joshua pointed to where he'd parked the truck. A big white pickup with an extended cab sat in the gravel, parked sideways in front of the church. Great. The damned thing appeared jacked up high enough she'd have to step up to get in. *What is it about cowboys and their big ass trucks?*

The three of them started to pile into the cab as she struggled to get into the driver's seat.

"Sorry." Joshua came around her side and placed his hand on her butt.

She squeaked as he propelled her into the truck with one push.

"Just helpin' out."

"Jacob ain't gonna like you havin' your hand on her ass, Joshua." A high girlish giggle escaped Jason's lips as he laughed like something caught him funny.

Paige smiled. They were all kind of cute when they were drunk. "Y'all are hilarious."

"I didn't do nothin'. I was helpin' her in to the truck."

"You coulda put your hands on her waist, man. Not on her ass." Joey smacked Joshua in the back of the head when he returned to the passenger side of the vehicle.

"Hey!"

A scuffle ensued and Paige had to roll her eyes. Was it like this every day with nine boys? She could only imagine. "Enough you three. It's a forty-five minute drive back to your ranch. I won't have you rustling around while I'm trying to drive this big ass truck." What would it be like raising that many children? A shiver of fear ran through her at the thought.

The men settled down as she drove them home. In fact, the two in the back started snoring almost the minute they'd left San Antonio. Only Joshua remained awake.

"Do you love him?"

"Who?"

"Jacob, of course."

"I don't think that's any of your business."

"He's my brother. Of course, it's my business."

She let silence envelope them for several minutes before she answered. "I care a lot about him, yes. Love? I think that's between me and him, but right now there are things beyond our control causing issues."

"He's a good guy even though he was drinkin' a lot."

"I know all about his drinking and yes, he's a great guy."

"You could do worse."

"I sure could." She glanced across the cab as he leaned back in the seat with his hat over his eyes. "Do you have a girlfriend?"

"Nope. Don't want one neither."

"Don't you want to get married some day?"

"Maybe, but I ain't in no hurry."

"What happens when you meet the right girl?"

"Then I'll see if it's meant to be."

He sounded pretty sober to her with his talk of meant-to-bes. He really was a nice guy. All of Jacob's brothers were even if they each had their own issues. She hoped someday they would all fall in love with a woman strong enough to corral the rowdy brothers. Those women sure had their work cut out for them.

The ranch gate came into view as she pulled up. "Code?"

He rattled it off as he sat up in the seat. "It's on the box."

"Oh yeah. I didn't see it." She punched in the code and watched as the wrought iron gate swung wide. Darkness settled outside the headlights of the vehicle making the surrounding scenery almost spooky. She remembered the laughing children she'd heard before and wondered if they would make a reappearance tonight. She didn't really believe in ghosts, but she didn't have an explanation for the sounds she'd heard either.

"I love this place."

"Did you all grow up on the ranch?"

"For the most part. Jacob and Jeff were little when my parents bought the place. The rest of us were born and raised here. It's home."

"I kind of think of the house my dad and I live in as home. We've been there a number of years."

"What happened to your mom?"

"She was killed by a drunk driver several years ago."

"I'm sorry."

"Thank you. I wish more people would find a designated driver when they've been drinking."

"Now, I'm really sorry we showed up at your house. Thanks for bringing us home. You were right. None of us should have been drivin'."

"No, you shouldn't have and you're welcome."

They drove up to the low wall surrounding the front of the main lodge house. Beams of light reflected out the three dormer windows in the front, illuminating the front yard with a soft glow. One of the rockers moved slowly as if someone sat in it, pushing it with their foot in a rhythmic rocking motion. *Weird.*

The two cowboys in the backseat sat up with a snoring snort. "Are we home?"

"Yes."

The three men tumbled out, almost falling on their faces in the gravel driveway. "I hope you three are headed to bed to sleep it off."

A tall, broad shouldered silhouette came out of the barn, heading straight for them.

"Paige?"

"Look, Jacob! We brought her home for you." It was Jason's turn to laugh hysterically at their situation.

"Looks like she brought you home, not the other way around." He pushed his hat back on his head. "What the hell is going on here?"

"We was gonna kidnap her for you," Joey replied, swaying slightly on his feet.

"Paige?"

She dropped the keys to Joshua's truck in his hand. "They showed up at my house, drunk off their asses saying they were going to kidnap me and bring me back here for you since you were so upset about our fight earlier that you were cussin' and raisin' hell in the barn."

"You three were out drivin' like this?"

"Yep. Sorry," Joshua answered. "Good thing Paige brought us home."

"Damn right. You coulda killed someone, you idiots."

"Hey! You're one to talk. You were drinkin' pretty heavy up until a few months ago. You drove drunk several times if I remember right."

"Yeah, I did, but I've learned my lesson. I sure don't do it anymore."

"It was a mistake, Jacob. We didn't mean nothin'." Joey sat down on the low rock wall, leaning back into the grass behind him.

"I hope you three don't ever do this again. It was a really stupid move."

"Sorry," the three of them mumbled in unison.

"I planned on letting your mother know about this little incident, but I think they've been chastised enough."

"Thanks for bringing them home. Do you want me to give you a ride back to town?"

She stepped close enough she could smell the hint of leather, hay, and man. *God, I love that smell on him.* "Do you want me to leave?"

"Hell no, woman. Are you crazy?"

"Shall we discuss this further at your place?"

Jacob grabbed her hand and literally dragged her across the yard, around the back of the main lodge and up the stairs of his trailer. "Does this answer your question?" His mouth dove for hers, trapping her lips in a demanding kiss meant to melt her panties.

When they came up for air, she noticed her heart pounding in her ears as excitement thrummed in her veins. In the heat of the kiss, she'd grabbed his T-shirt, holding him close with a fist of material in her hand.

"I ain't goin' nowhere, darlin'," he said, backing her into the front room and slamming the door behind them.

"Good." She licked his neck from the edge of his T-shirt to his ear. "I love the way you smell."

"I've been workin' in the barn all evenin'."

"It's sexy." She worked her hands into the waistband of his jeans. "I love this butt."

"Do ya now?"

"Oh, hell yeah."

"I'm glad because I love yours too." He grabbed her ass with both hands, pulling her up on her tiptoes. "I want this ass."

A shiver rolled down her spine. Did he mean what she thought he meant? He wanted to fuck her there? She'd read up on it a bit after his last mention of the topic and it sounded kind of kinky and hot at the same time. She wanted to give it a shot, but her ass squeezed together with a little fear of the unknown.

He reached for the bottom of her top and pulled it over her head in one fell swoop, exposing her nakedness to his gaze. "I love your boobs. They fit perfectly in my hands. So round. Nice perky nipples pulled into tight little points." He rubbed one with his thumb. "Horny, baby?"

"I'm always horny around you, Jacob." She pushed his hat off his head, letting it fall to the floor.

"Good because I'm hard as a damned boulder for you."

He pushed one hand down the front of her jogging shorts. One finger glanced off her clit, bringing her up on her toes in a rush of sensation. Her pussy flooded as he slid further down to scoop up some of her cream and spread it around her clit.

"You *are* wet."

"Fuck me, Jacob."

"Oh, I plan to." He removed his hand, lifted her into his arms and headed down the hall to his bedroom. "I'm gonna fuck you six ways to Sunday, baby. I hope you don't have anywhere else to be."

She nipped at his neck, earning herself a soft groan from his lips. "Only right here with you."

When he reached his room, he dropped her legs so she could stand in front of him. "Get them shorts off, darlin'."

She'd lost her sandals in the living room somewhere, so it was easy to drop the shorts in one fell swoop.

"God, you're gorgeous." He traced a finger from her jawline, across her shoulder, down her chest until he reached her nipple. "You got a little sun the other day at the barbeque. You're pink."

"My skin is pretty fair."

"You need sunblock."

"I was wearing sunblock." She leaned into his touch. "Kiss me."

"I plan to kiss you, lick you and eat you all over."

She pushed her fingers into his hair so she could drag his head to her straining nipple. "Go for it, cowboy." When his mouth closed over the protruding point, she came up on her toes to push it further into his mouth. "So good." He flicked the opposite one with his fingernail, earning himself a hearty groan from her. The rough calluses on his hands abraded her skin as he slid it down her abdomen to the curls between her thighs. *Touch me.*

He backed her against the bed, releasing her nipple long enough to push her down on the comforter. "Spread your thighs for me."

When she opened her legs, he dove for her pussy with a deep growl. She giggled at the primitive sound escaping his lips. He sounded animalistic in his need for her. Did he feel as overwhelmed by their connection as she did? She hoped so.

His tongue danced over her clit, down to her slit, and back up. He moaned his delight in her taste. "This pussy is all mine."

"Yours." Her body felt like a guitar string strung too tight. If he plucked it just the right way, she'd break with a sharp twang. "Oh God."

He shoved two fingers into her pussy, stroking it in a slow, torturous rhythm, not fast enough to get her off quickly. He obviously planned to string this out until she snapped.

"Please."

"Please what?"

His tongue did wicked flicks that made her toes curl. "Don't tease me."

"I'm not. Hold off the climax, babe. It'll make it that much better."

"I hate you."

He chuckled as he flattened his tongue and drove it hard against her clit. Heat spiraled through her abdomen.

"I'm gonna come."

His wicked tongue stopped as he kissed the inside of her thigh on both sides. "Easy, girl."

Why did she get the feeling he was calming her like he would a skittish mare? Probably because he was.

She sighed as her body slid into a calm, floating state. Her pussy throbbed for the pressure of his mouth, but he wasn't giving into her whimpers. "Jacob, please make me come."

"In a minute." He leisurely licked her clit, shooting her immediately to incredible need in a second, but not enough to come.

"God, please."

Two fingers drove straight in as he sucked her clit between his lips. She exploded in a spattering of lights and sounds loud enough to deafen her before floating on a cloud of sensation. Her whole pussy quivered, sucking at his fingers when he slowed the rhythmic slide. She wanted more. She needed more.

"I want you inside me."

He quickly stripped out of his shirt, slid those tempting jeans off his hips in one fell motion and kicked them quickly across the room. "I'm comin' home, Paige. Take me inside you."

With the head of his cock at her entrance, she enveloped his hips with her thighs as he slipped his cock in, pushing deep.

Their bodies were meant for each other. There wasn't any way she could ever let this man go.

Chapter Twelve

"You know I planned on a nice romantic way to do this, but you're ruinin' all my plans."

"What's that supposed to mean?"

"I love you. I want you in my life, Paige. You mean everything to me."

"Oh God." She pushed him back so he had to slip out of her. *Now what the hell am I gonna do? What will daddy say?*

"That doesn't sound like you're happy to hear me say I love you."

"It's my father."

"What about him? I know he doesn't like me at the moment because he thinks I'm corrupting his precious daughter, but as soon as you tell him the truth, things will be fine."

She bit her lips before she blurted out, "He forbade me from seeing you, Jacob."

"When the hell did this happen?"

"At the hospital."

He jumped to his feet. "When were you gonna tell me this little piece of news?"

"Soon. I was trying to figure out how to handle this."

"The hell with that. I love you." He shoved his hands through his hair. "We're gonna be together. He'll just have to get over it."

She sighed as she pushed herself up to sit on the bed. "He's a sick man." With her arms wrapped around her knees, she chewed the inside of her mouth as she tried to think of a way out of this mess. "I can't just drop this on his lap."

"He'll be fine, Paige. It's pneumonia, not his heart."

"I know, but pneumonia can still kill a person. What if he gets worse?"

Jacob wrapped her in his arms as she put her head on his chest. "Antibiotics will make him better."

"Let's just keep this between us for now, okay? Let him get over this bout of sickness before we drop this bomb on him."

"I don't want to keep things a secret, Paige. I love you."

"I love you too, but I think this is best. We can still be together here and there."

"Here and there? You sound like you don't have time for me."

"Well I still have to work and do things around the church. I'll be with you as much as I can."

"You know. I don't even know what you do for a livin'."

"I teach pre-school kids."

His fingers did a slow crawl from her elbow to her shoulder, forcing goose bumps along the surface as they moved. "What's your favorite color?"

"Blue."

"Favorite flower?"

"Daisies." She glanced up into his eyes. "Why all the questions?"

"I realized the other day I don't know much about you. You know, those little things one should know about the person they're in love with."

"We have the rest of our lives to learn about each other."

"Yeah, but I've known you for goin' on six months. I should know these things."

"Wow, a whole six month, *huh*?" He rolled her over on her back and startled tickling her sides. She squealed as she laughed hard enough to snort like a pig. "Stop it!"

"No." He tickled her more. "I like when you giggle."

"Jacob! I'm going to kick your ass! Stop!" He pushed her hands up over her head and captured her left nipple between his lips. Her laughter turned to moans. "That's not fair."

His mouth left her breasts with a pop. "Why not? I like the way you taste."

"I thought you wanted my ass."

His eyebrow shot up over his right eye. "Are you going to let me?"

"I want to try it, but you'll have to go slow."

"I will, baby. We'll use lots of lube."

He jumped off the bed heading into the bathroom so fast, her head swam for a minute. *Damn, the man has a nice, tight ass.*

Seconds later, he returned with a white tube. "I'll make sure you are so horny, you'll love this."

Trepidation rolled down her back as she glanced at his ever growing cock. He wasn't a small man by any stretch of the imagination. Would it fit without tearing her apart? He pulled out the nipple clamps she hadn't seen since the first night they were together. "What do you plan to do with those?"

"Put them on your pretty nipples." He leaned over her and captured a nipple again, bringing it to an achy point before he clamped the alligator clip on the protruding point.

"Ouch."

"Too tight?"

"No. I think it's okay."

Nipple number two enjoyed the sensation a little too much, she decided as her body started to hum from the pressure on the hard little nubs.

"We'll leave them on a bit longer this time."

He licked the tips, drawing a deep moan from her. Her clit began to fill with blood. "Fuck."

"I wish I had another one to put on your clit."

"Oh, hell no."

"Hell yeah."

An evil smile spread across his lips as his eyes began to sparkle with a devilish glint. She could almost believe he was the devil incarnate with the look on his face right now. Were those horns she saw? She shook her head to dispel the look. No, this was Jacob. The love of her life.

She spread her thighs when he pushed her knees apart so he could settle there. His tongue began a rapid flicking over her clit, bringing her to the brink of a mind blowing orgasm within seconds. Her nipples throbbed. Her clit throbbed. Everything hummed to the blood rushing in her ears as heat spread from her toes and burst through her belly in an all-consuming orgasm meant to take her breath away. "Ah, God!"

He lapped at her pussy like he never meant to stop.

Once she came down from her high, he rolled over onto her stomach and pulled at her hips until she hung half off the side of the bed. A cold dollop of lube hit her ass, making her hiss at the sensation. "Damn, that's cold."

"It'll warm up real fast once I start fuckin' you there." He pushed a finger into her ass.

She hissed at the burn. How would she be able to take him if one finger hurt? "I don't know about this."

"Relax. You'll do fine." He pushed two fingers in, scissoring them to stretch her hole. "If you want to stop, let me know."

His words helped to relax her into the sensation of having his fingers in her butt. Oddly, it didn't hurt anymore as he spread the lube around and finger fucked her ass for several minutes.

"Ready?"

"Not really, but go ahead."

The hard head of his cock bumped against her ass. The burn made her suck in her breath and hold it. "Breathe, baby. Relax."

"I'm trying, Jacob." She lifted up on her hands and knees when his hand snaked under her to flick her right nipple.

"I know."

He unhooked the nipple clamp, causing the blood to rush back into the tortured tip in a rush. "Fuck!"

His cock pushed into her butt farther as her nipple throbbed from the blood coming back, taking her mind off the pain in her ass. She felt the odd sensation to press back against his groin. "More."

He chuckled as he removed the clamp on the other nipple.

"Damn it!"

"Such language."

"Those fucking hurt, but God I need more."

"I'm in. Oh, Lord, you feel like heaven."

"God, Jacob. Fuck me."

He began moving slowly against her ass. The sensation was something she couldn't describe. She felt full, but empty. She needed more. With a little wiggle, she earned a growl from the man behind her.

"Don't move or I'm gonna blow too fast. I can't handle how you feel."

"It's a weird feeling."

"I can't wait, Paige. You have to come with me."

"I don't know if I—oh." He increased his pace to a jagged thrusting, bringing her to an explosive orgasm as he reached around and pinched her clit.

Jacob groaned behind her, shifting his hips in a slower rhythm now that he'd come. "You're amazing."

He slowly pulled out of her and headed to the bathroom. She collapsed face down on the bed with a moan. A moment later, he rolled her over and cleaned her up with a warm, wet washcloth.

"You didn't have to do that." The washcloth felt soft on her abused tissue.

"But I wanted to. I bet you're kind of sore now, so it's my turn to take care of you."

"You're so sweet."

He leaned over and kissed her abdomen. "And you are fantastic. Thank you."

"For what?"

"Letting me do that. I know it's kind of uncomfortable especially the first time."

"It was pretty awesome. I haven't come so hard in my life."

He chuckled. "I'm glad you enjoy it then. We'll have to do it again some time." He returned the washcloth to the bathroom before snuggling her under the sheet and pulling her into a tight embrace.

Night sounds surrounded them. Crickets echoed in the distance. An owl hooted.

Faint in the distance, she heard children giggling.

"It's the kids. Ignore it."

"It's hard. How do you deal with it all the time?" she asked, running her fingertips through the hair on his chest.

"I don't hear it most days, even when others do. I guess I'm used to it." He laughed. "You should be worn out."

A yawn escaped her mouth. "I am."

"Then drift off and let dreams of us surround you."

"Aren't you the poet these days."

"Love does that to a man."

Within moments, she heard the soft snores of the man beside her and smiled. She really did love him. The question remained, how to get her father to love him too.

* * * *

The next morning, Paige woke up in an empty bed. Birds chirped outside as the sun blazed through the curtains on the windows. She stretched the muscles of her back like a cat in the sun while she wondered where Jacob ran off to. It had to be early yet.

The smiling man of her dreams came through the doorway wearing nothing but a worn pair of sweat pants, and he was still sex on a stick.

"I brought coffee."

"You are my knight in shining armor, sir." She reached for the cup, but he held it away from her.

"Not before I get a kiss."

"Oh, well then." She let the sheet drop as she stood on her knees and pressed her lips to his. She took her time tracing his lips with her tongue before nipping at his bottom lip in order to tangle with his tongue.

He quickly leaned over to set the coffee cup down on the nightstand before he cupped her face with his hands and deepened the kiss to overwhelming. With a giggle, she broke away from him. "Coffee."

"Fine." He handed her the cup. "I guessed cream and sugar, since I didn't know how you took it."

"Good guess." She sipped the hot liquid. "It's perfect. Thank you."

"You're welcome." He stepped back and dropped his pants.

"Now?"

He chuckled. "Insatiable are you?"

Tilting her head, she said, "If you insist."

"Actually, no, babe. I have to get some work done. It's already getting late and everyone will wonder where I am. Breakfast is served in the main lodge in about an hour. You can take a shower and meet me in there if you want."

She frowned at the thought of facing his family after spending the night at his place.

"What's wrong?"

"I don't want your family to think I'm a slut, Jacob. Spending the night with you makes me sound loose."

He smacked her butt. "Stop that, right now. You aren't a slut. We love each other. My family will love having you as a part of it so stop with the self-doubt."

"I'm just not used to being around a big family."

"They loved you at the barbeque."

She pulled her shoulders back and kissed him on the lips. "It'll be fine. You go on and get what you need to get done finished. I'll take a shower and meet you in the main lodge when the bell goes off."

"That's my girl."

He slipped on a pair of jeans and shirt before he kissed her quickly and disappeared out the bedroom door. Paige leaned back against the headboard as she sipped the coffee he'd so thoughtfully brought her. She could do this. Facing his family wouldn't be that difficult, surely. After all, she'd met them all at the barbeque and they seemed like nice people.

But how are they going to feel after you come strolling out of his place wearing the same clothes you did last night?

She glanced at her tattered shorts lying on the floor. Such wonderful attire to be having breakfast with your boyfriend's family in. Maybe she should make an excuse and get him to take her home. She could always return for lunch or dinner and she really did need to check on her father today. *But first a shower.*

Her coffee now gone, she rose from the bed to head for the bathroom. The shower turned on with a flick of her wrist, spraying warm water throughout the shower stall. She stepped inside as memories of the last time they'd been in the shower, swamped her. He'd fucked her hard in here, but they couldn't finish when his feet slipped on the slick floor. She shook her head as a laugh bubbled out.

Shampoo and condition sat in the corner of the stall. She picked up the bottle, sniffed the contents and smiled. *So that's why his hair smells so good.* After she rubbed some of the shampoo in her hair, she scrubbed her scalp and then rinsed. Conditioner came next before the body wash. She giggled. She'd smell like Axe today.

Eyes closed, she enjoyed the warm water splashing her skin until she felt two hands squeeze her breasts. Screaming, she quickly thrust her elbow backward, jabbing the intruder and eliciting a grunt.

"Damn, Paige."

She spun around, slinging water everywhere. "Jacob. God, I'm sorry, but you scared the hell out of me. Are you okay?"

"Other than a few broken ribs." His breath came out in a wheeze.

"Shit, really? I'm so sorry."

He laughed. "I'm fine. I was kidding. I forgot how touchy you are and quick with your reflexes. I won't startle you again." He grabbed a towel and held it out. "Are you done?"

"Yeah." As she stepped out, he wrapped her in the soft terry cloth. "What are you doin' back here? I thought you had work to do?"

"I do, but I couldn't resist knowing my gorgeous girlfriend was in my trailer in all her naked glory possibly taking a shower without me."

"You need to go back to work."

"I will. Kiss me first."

She leaned up as he pulled her in tighter with the towel. The kiss turned steamy when his tongue dipped into her mouth, tangling with her own.

When she cut him off with a nip to his tongue, he scolded, "Ouch."

"You need to go back to work, but first one thing." She dropped to her knees on the floor, undid the buckle on his pants and shoved them to the ground. "I'm gonna suck you off."

"We don't have time for that. Breakfast will be soon." He moaned as she encircled the head of his cock with her mouth. "Okay, maybe we have time." Another groaned surfaced when she swallowed him deep. "Oh, hell yeah." She sucked and swallowed, massaging his balls until she felt his legs shake. "You're gonna kill me, darlin'."

She sat back on her haunches for a second as she glanced up through her lashes at him and ran her hand along the length of his cock. "You can handle it, big boy." She leaned in to suck his balls into her mouth, loving the feel of the rock hard orbs between her lips.

"I'm gonna blow, babe."

"Let me have it, cowboy." She swallowed his cock head as he squirted cum down her throat in a primitive growl from deep in his chest. She loved to hear that sound from him. It made him seem human when he lost control with her.

His legs almost gave out as he stepped back against the sink. "God, you're fabulous."

"Glad you liked it." She wiped her face discreetly on the towel, hoping he wouldn't notice how she spit out cum on the cloth. She didn't mind the taste so much, but sometimes it gagged her. This was one of those times.

"You okay?"

"Yeah. I just need to wash my mouth out."

"Sorry, babe. If you would have told me you didn't like it, I wouldn't have come in your mouth." He yanked his pants back up and buckled his belt.

"It's fine, Jacob."

He rubbed her back as she rinsed her mouth in the sink. The breakfast bell clanged in the distance. "Breakfast is ready."

"You know. I'm not really hungry."

He frowned. "Are you sure you're okay?"

"I'm fine. I'm just not hungry," she said, heading back into his room to retrieve her shorts.

"Your shirt is out in the livin' room."

"I know." She walked down the hall to get her bra and shirt. "Can you take me home? I really should go see how my dad is fairing at the hospital."

"Sure, if you want me to."

"Yeah." She slipped on her bra and shirt, only to find him standing behind her with a perpetual frown. "Your face is gonna freeze like that."

"I'm just tryin' to figure you out."

"Good luck with that."

"I'm sure." He stepped in front of her and rubbed both of her arms. "If you don't want to eat with my family, that's fine. Just say so. You don't have to make excuses."

"It's not that. I'm feeling kind of frumpy in these clothes. I didn't come here anticipating staying all night with you. I wanted to drop off your brother's and just get you to take me home."

"If you didn't want to stay last night, you should have said so. I would have taken you home then."

This conversation wasn't going well at all. "I wanted to stay. I just didn't plan on it, but I really need to be getting home so I can check on my father."

"All right. Let me grab my keys so I can run you back into San Antonio."

"Thank you." She slipped on her shoes as a knock sounded at the door. "Jacob?"

"It's my mom," he whispered. "Yeah, Mom?"

"Are you all right? I saw you come back to your trailer and you haven't come to breakfast."

"I'm fine."

"Okay. Will we see you and Paige inside?"

"Well shit," Paige grumbled.

Jacob pushed open the door to find his mother standing on the stoop. "No, Mom. I'm taking her back to town."

"How about for dinner tonight?"

"Sure, Mrs. Young."

"It's Nina, honey. You're part of the family now." She waved goodbye as she stepped back and disappeared down the small walkway to the main lodge.

"That went well." Jacob laughed, but she didn't think it was the least bit funny. "I didn't want them to know I was here."

"Well, I'm sure my brothers told her all about it this morning already."

"Great."

"It'll be fine, babe."

He ushered her out the door to where his truck sat parked near the back of his trailer. At least she didn't have to walk past the main house in her sweat shorts.

Within minutes, they were traveling down the road to San Antonio. She felt like shit. She didn't want to make him miss breakfast with his family, but she just didn't feel comfortable being the center of attention as Jacob's fuck buddy. That wasn't true. She wasn't a fuck buddy. They were boyfriend and girlfriend, right? He'd said he loved her and she loved him, so why was she feeling like this?

He put his hand on her knee. "Are you okay? You're awfully quiet."

"I'm fine. Thank you for taking me back to town."

"Of course, babe. I love you. I'm there for you no matter what."

"Thank you." She leaned her head on his shoulder as she stared out the front windshield of his truck. She still had to deal with her father today, which she wasn't looking forward to. Telling him about her and Jacob wouldn't be a pleasant experience, she knew, but it had to be done. They were a couple, right?

"I love you, Paige."

"I know, Jacob. I love you too. Everything will work out."

"Your father isn't going to be happy about us, but we'll get through this."

"I'm sure we will."

Silence enveloped them for the rest of the ride to her house. When they pulled up to the front, the big yellow dog bounded out to meet them. He jumped up on Jacob, taking to him like they were old friends. "Where'd he come from?"

"He's adopted me I guess. He scared the crap out of me last night, but he was ready to protect me from your brothers."

"No collar?"

"Nope."

"Will your dad let you have a dog?"

"I guess we'll find out. For now, he'll just have to hang around the house until things are settled with my father at the hospital."

"I'll leave you so I can get back to work." He kissed her sweetly on the lips. "I'll pick you up later this afternoon, if that's okay?"

"What about around four? That'll give me enough time to see how my father is doing before you get back?"

"That's fine. Dinner is usually served around five-thirty."

"Perfect." Her cell phone jingled in her purse. "I better check this." When she pulled it out, she frowned. "It's a hospital number."

"Do you want me to stay?"

"No, it's fine. I'm sure it's just Daddy wanting to know where I am. I'll call him back in a minute."

She kissed him again before she backed up to unlock the door. She watched as he walked back to his truck and slipped inside. Her phone rang again with the same hospital number. *Damn*. Her father could be so persistent. "Hello?"

"Is this Paige Tyler?"

"Yes. Who is this?"

"I'm your father's nurse here at the hospital. We need you to come in. There's been a change in his condition."

Her heart jumped into her throat. "What happened?"

"I can't talk about it on the phone. You need to get here quickly."

"I'll be right there."

Chapter Thirteen

Paige rushed into the hospital and straight for the elevator without stopping. She had to get upstairs to see what the problem was. *They'd said it wasn't his heart. What could it be now?*

The moment the elevators doors opened, she sped down the hall at almost a dead run toward her father's room.

The doctor stood at her father's bedside when she walked in. "What's going on? I got a frantic phone call from the nurse."

Her father opened his eyes and she could see the facial droop on the right side of his face. His mouth pulled down on that side as well.

"He's had a stroke, Paige. I'm sorry."

"What does that mean?"

"Well there are varying degrees of a stroke. So far his seems to have affected his right side as you can tell by the drop of his eye and lip. He does seem to have some weakness in his hand and foot on that side as well. We won't know the damage for a few days. He'll have to go into rehab."

"What?" She sat on the side of the bed. "How could this happen? He was fine yesterday."

"A stroke is caused by a blood clot traveling to the brain."

"Daddy?"

"I'll be okay, Paige." She understood what he said even though his speech was slightly slurred.

"He won't be able to take care of himself more than likely, but it depends on the damage."

"Thank you, doctor. I'll take care of him, just like he's taken care of me."

The doctor disappeared out the door with a soft click.

"I love you, Paige."

"I love you too, Daddy. We'll get through this." She stroked his hand with her fingers.

"This is going to make me dependent on you, daughter. I won't be able to get around and take care of things for you anymore."

"It's fine, Daddy. I'll be there for you no matter what."

"But this stroke could make things very difficult for you to have a life away from me. I want you to get married and have a family of your own. I want you to give me grandchildren."

"I will, but don't be trying to get rid of me so easily."

"I can hire someone to come in and help me around the house. I think you need to find an apartment or something on your own."

"Are you trying to get rid of me now?"

"No." He weakly lifted his right hand to her cheek. "I need to ask you something."

"What?"

"Do you love that young man?"

"Who?"

"Jacob?"

"Yeah, Daddy, I do."

"Then I won't stand in your way. You need to be with who you love like your mother and I were. I don't like how he has taken you into things that are bad for you, but I'll be there no matter what."

"Daddy, it wasn't Jacob. I went into the bars on my own long before I met him." Tears streaked down her cheeks knowing she was about to break her daddy's heart a little more. "There are a lot of things about me you don't know."

"Like?" he asked, wiping the tear from her face.

"I've been visiting bars for several months. It was my way of rebelling against everything you've been forcing me to do. I don't want to be the preacher's wife and do the duties my mother should have been doing. That's not who I am. I'm me, not Momma."

"I know."

"You do?"

"Yes, Paige. I'm sorry I've forced you to take over those duties. I knew you didn't like them, but you kept doing them anyway so I let you."

"I met Jacob at The Dusty Boot in Bandera. He was drunk off his ass and three men were going to beat the shit out of him. I stopped them."

He laughed, which was a sound she wasn't sure she would hear from her father after everything they'd been through in the last few days. "Leave it to my little girl to save some redneck hell-bent on getting his butt kicked." He coughed several times. "I'm not happy he's a drinker with everything we went through with your mother."

She patted his hand and kissed his fingers. "I know, Daddy, but you've been drinking a lot yourself lately."

"I'm quitting as of two days ago. I won't have another drop."

She smiled as she pressed his hand to her cheek. "Good. Neither is Jacob. He hasn't been drunk for several months now."

"I'm glad to hear that."

"He said after I saved him, it embarrassed him so much that he quit drinking. He used to be such a hell raiser at the bar, he almost couldn't show his face back in there anymore after that." She scooted closer. "You know his family. They are nice people, Daddy."

"I remember them. Big family."

"Yes. There are eight brothers and a couple of wives in there."

"Does he love you?"

"Yeah. He told me he did. Not that he's asked me to marry him or anything, but I think this is the real thing."

"Maybe I've misjudged him."

"I think you did, but it's my fault. I let you believe he was corrupting me when it wasn't the truth. I should have told you from the beginning. I'm sorry."

"Call him."

"What?"

"Bring him to me so we can talk."

"But, Daddy. That's not a good idea. You should be resting. There'll be time for a confrontation between you and Jacob when you're feeling better."

"I want to make sure he's going to take care of my little girl. Call him and bring him here."

"All right. If you insist."

"I do."

She stood and removed her cell phone from the pocket of her purse. Once she scrolled through the numbers, she found Jacob's and hit talk.

"Paige?"

"Hi."

"What's wrong?"

"Are you home?"

"Almost. I'm in Bandera right now."

"Can you turn around and come back. I need you."

"What's happened?"

She moved to stare out the window of her father's room. "Daddy's had a stroke."

"I'll be there in thirty."

She sighed in relief. She hated asking him for anything, but she really needed to feel his arms around her right now. "I love you, Jacob. Be careful. There's nothing that can be done for now, but I need you with me."

"I love you too, darlin'. Hold tight. I'll be right there."

She closed the phone and returned to her father's bedside. "He's on his way back. He was almost home from dropping me off at the house this morning."

"What was he doing dropping you off at home in the morning?"

Oh shit. "Well you see, his brothers thought it would be funny to kidnap me and take me out to their ranch last night, but they were drunk off their asses—oh excuse me—butts, so I drove them home."

"And?"

Heat crawled up her neck. Telling her father about her sex life wasn't the most pleasant thing to do. "Um, I stayed with Jacob instead of coming home right away."

"I'm glad you're in love with him and he loves you, otherwise I would be having a shotgun discussion with a certain young man about how he's treating my daughter."

She laughed as she took the seat she'd vacated to make the phone call.

"I don't think this situation is funny, Paige."

"The reason I laughed was because I had the shotgun out last night when his brothers broke in."

"They broke in?" he asked, his eyes wide with alarm as he fiddled with the blanket beneath his hands.

"Not really. The door wasn't locked yet."

"This family sounds like a pretty rowdy bunch. Are you sure you want to get involved with them?"

"Do I have much choice? I love him."

"I guess I have to deal with a rowdy bunch of rednecks being my in-laws?"

"There's no wedding planning going on yet, Daddy. Besides, you met his mother and father at the barbeque. They weren't a bunch of rowdy rednecks there."

"No, but it was a church picnic. I would hope they were on their best behavior in the house of the Lord."

"I'm sure they were." She stood back up. "I'm going to get some coffee and some breakfast. I'll be back in a bit." She wanted to head Jacob off before her father got ahold of him anyway, so she figured it would be best to hang out down by the front doors.

About thirty minutes later, Jacob came skidding in on his cowboy boots through the front door. "Paige, what's wrong?"

She sat him down on the bench so she could brief him. "Daddy's had a stroke. They called me right after you left me at the house."

"How's he doin'?"

"Okay, but he's got some weakness on the right side. He'll have to go to rehab for a while to regain his strength."

"I'm sorry, darlin'. I wish I could have been there when you got the call."

His arm went around her as she placed her head on his shoulder. "It's okay. We didn't know this would happen. There isn't anything you could have done anyway."

"Except be here for you."

"You're here now. That's what counts."

They sat together for several minutes before he shifted to the side to look into her face. "So why didn't you let me come up to the room?"

"Busted, *huh*?"

"Yeah. I didn't expect you to be down here."

She caught her lip between her teeth for a minute as she sighed. "Daddy knows about us."

"I knew that before. He didn't like me very much."

"No, what I mean is he *knows* about us. I told him the truth about the bar."

"And?"

"He understands, sort of. He also knows I love you and not being with you isn't part of the deal. He'll just have to get over his feelings or whatever is the problem, but I think he's okay with everything."

"Shall we get this over with then?" he asked, getting to his feet and dragging her up with him.

"I guess."

He kissed her quickly on the lips. "It'll be okay, darlin'. I love you. That's all that matters."

With heavy steps, she led Jacob back to her father's room. She wasn't sure how this meeting would progress and she wasn't ready to find out. They reached the door to his room and she hesitated.

"Paige?"

"I don't know if I can do this."

He brought her hand to his lips. "We'll face him together, baby."

A heavy sigh escaped her lips in a rush. "Okay. I can do this."

They walked through the doorway together only to find her father with his eyes closed lying in the bed.

"Daddy?"

Her father didn't move.

She walked closer, picked up his hand and stroked the back with her fingers. His eyes never flickered.

"Daddy?" Her voice trembled as she shook her father's shoulder. When she turned to look at Jacob, the concern in his eyes drove terror through her heart. "Jacob?"

"I'll get the nurse." He grabbed the door as he shouted for a nurse, his voice clear with panic.

"No, Daddy. Don't do this." She shook him harder.

A nurse came rushing through the door calling her father's name. She ran her fingers along his neck to check for a pulse. "You're going to have to move, Ms. Tyler." The nurse hit an alarm on the wall and within seconds, it seemed like a hundred people rushed through the doorway.

One nurse pushed in a cart. A doctor shoved her out of the way as another nurse pushed the bed flat. They lifted him up to stick something beneath him. The moment he was flat again, another nurse started pressing on his chest.

"Jacob?" she asked moving toward him.

"Come here, darlin'. Let them work."

"It would probably be better if you took her out in the hall. This could get messy."

Jacob nodded as he wrapped an arm around her shoulders and pressed her face against his chest.

Noise. Too much noise. The loud beeping, shouting, calling out of things she didn't understand pierced her being with terror. *He's dead. He's dead.*

They took a seat on a small couch down the hall from her father's room. "What's going to happen, Jacob?"

"I don't know, honey. We'll have to wait and see."

"He's dead, isn't he?"

"Baby, I'm not a doctor, but things don't look good. I don't know what happened so I can't guess what's going on in there."

"What'll happen if he is dead? I never got to tell him about other things going on with me. I mean he doesn't know about the motorcycle or the clothes. I told him about the bar, but we didn't really discuss who I really am."

"It's God's will. Whatever happens, it's how things are supposed to be." He ran his fingers up and down her arms.

Hot tears streaked down her face as she tried not to think about what was going on in her father's room. She didn't want to know. How would she deal with not having either parent? What would her life become without her father there to guide her?

"Don't think about it for now."

"I can't help it. What'll I do if he dies?"

"You still have me."

"I know, but how will I cope not having a parent?"

"We'll get through this together."

"Thank you for being here with me."

"I wouldn't be anywhere else."

After what seemed like hours, the nurses and doctors filed out of her father's room. One of the men walked toward her with a solemn look on his face. Her heart plummeted. *No!*

"Ms. Tyler?"

"Yes?" She stood with Jacob's help, clinging onto his arm for dear life.

"I'm sorry, but there isn't anything we could do."

"No!"

"Since he'd had a stroke this morning, we fear another one took his life. I'm so sorry."

She slowly slid to the floor as racking sobs shook her frame. Jacob picked her up like she weighed no more than a child, to cradle her in his arms.

"Where can we go?"

"Follow me. The chapel is down the hall."

Numbness enveloped her in its grasp. She felt nothing, heard nothing. She clung to Jacob's shirt with a death grip. She couldn't let go. *It isn't true. It can't be true.*

Jacob took a seat on the bench with her on his lap. The feeling of his arms around her held her together even though she felt like a piece of glass shattered into a million pieces.

"Take your time. We won't move him until she's ready."

"Thank you."

They sat that way for what seemed like hours. Jacob holding her while she cried into his shirt. The wet material clung to her cheek where she pressed it to her face. She needed his strength. He didn't say anything, just held her.

"I'm sorry. I got you all wet."

"No problem, darlin'. It'll dry in no time."

She sat up, but didn't move off his lap. "We should make arrangements. Tell the church."

"In time. There's no rush."

"I don't even know his wishes. I'm assuming he wants to be buried next to my mother."

"I expect so."

She slowly got to her feet, wobbling slightly as she stood. "I'm okay."

"Are you sure? You don't look okay. You look pale and drawn."

She saw red. "I just lost my father. What the hell do you think I'm going to look like, some fucking fashion model?"

"I know you're upset, darlin', but don't take it out on me."

"You don't understand! I killed him!"

"What? No you didn't. He probably had another stroke. The doctor said so."

"But if I hadn't told him about you and the bars, he might not have had the stroke in the first place."

He cradled her in his arms as the tears came again. "Baby, strokes aren't caused by stress. God called him home."

"I hate God! I hate this whole thing! He took my mother and now he's taken my father. I have no one!"

"You've always got me."

"Do I really or will you leave me too?"

"I'm not going anywhere, darlin'."

"How do I know that? What if you decide you don't love me or you find someone else?"

"I do love you, Paige. I'm not going to find someone else. Stop talkin' crazy."

She stepped back, her heart thumping loudly in her chest. She loved him. He looked hurt and confused. How could she do this to him? "I don't know, Jacob. I need to get things taken care of for my father. Maybe you should go."

"Go where?"

"Home. I'm sure you have work you need to get done on the ranch. I'll be okay."

"I don't want to leave you, baby." He reached for her, but she stepped out of his grasp. He dropped his arms to his side with a dejected sigh. "I'll go because you asked me to, but know this, I love you and I'm not going to stop loving you any time soon." He walked out of the chapel as she sank to her knees and cried.

Chapter Fourteen

The funeral was well attended. Everyone at the church came, even some of the new members including Jacob's family. Jacob arrived with his parents, sitting in the back of the church, but she saw him just the same. Her heart ached for him to hold her, but she sat alone in the front pew dabbing her eyes as a friend of her father's led the service. Several people got up to say a few words about how wonderful he was, how caring he was, and how thoughtful of each of his parishioners he'd been over his time at the church.

Soon afterward, they all filed out to the small cemetery at the back where they laid him to rest beside her mother. Once the service had concluded, the ladies of the church put on a small reception where they fed everyone.

Paige stood alone in the corner hoping no one would approach. She didn't want to talk to anyone. She didn't want to see anyone. She only wanted one person, but he kept his distance even though his gaze never left her. She didn't know what to do anymore. She didn't want to give him the power to hurt her or leave her like her parents had done.

She felt cold, so cold.

"Are you okay?"

She looked up into Jacob's brown eyes. A quick nod was all she could manage.

He stuffed his hands in his pockets like he was afraid to touch her and probably was. The last time he tried, she backed away from him like a frightened child, which is exactly what she felt like these days.

"Thank you for coming."

"You thought I wouldn't be here for you?"

"We didn't part on good terms a few days ago."

"I told you then and I'll tell you again. I love you. I'll always be here for you no matter what, but you'll have to come to terms with the fact that I'm never going away. Yeah, your parents are gone, darlin'. People die. It's the facts of life. I can't promise I'll die after you so you won't be alone, but I'll do my damnedest to make your life the best it can be while we have the next seventy to a hundred years together."

"I don't want to risk it."

"You'd rather be alone than risk lovin' me?"

"Yes."

"Then we have nothin' more to talk about. I guess I'll see you around."

He turned on his heels and walked away.

Paige started to shake. Her whole body vibrated as she ran her hands over her arms trying to calm the chills racing through her. Her teeth even clicked together.

"Are you all right, dear?" Mrs. Johnson asked as she stopped next to her. "You look pale."

"N-no. I need to go home." Black spots appeared before her eyes. Dizziness engulfed her. She slumped against the wall to try to catch her breath, but darkness pulled at her, tempting her to give into it to escape the pain surrounding her.

The next thing she became aware of was the softness of the comforter beneath her on the bed. She didn't want to open her eyes, didn't want to face what life had thrown at her the last couple of days.

A soft voice whispered in her ear as she felt fingers stroking her face. "Paige, baby, wake up."

She slowly opened her eyes to see Jacob's concerned face hovering over her. "What happened?"

"You passed out, I'm guessin'."

"I've never fainted before in my life."

"When did you eat last?"

She glanced at the ceiling as she tried to remember.

"That's what I thought. I'm makin' you somethin' to eat. You stay right there in bed. I'll be right back." He climbed to his feet. "Don't move a muscle."

"Yes, sir."

He actually smiled at that.

A little while later, he returned with a sandwich on a plate and some chips along with a cold glass of milk. "You can't go without eating, Paige. I know you've been under a lot of stress, but it's not good for you."

"I know. It's just been so busy with arranging things for my father and such." She sat up higher in the bed before he placed the plate on her lap. "Thank you for doing this."

"No problem. How are you feeling now?"

"Better. I got dizzy before."

"I'll stay until you feel better."

"I'm fine, Jacob. You can go. I'm sure it was from not eating."

He shoved his hands in his pocket like he was afraid to touch her. Did she want him to? Yes and no. If he did, they'd end up in her bed all meshed in a tangle of arms and legs. If he didn't, he'd walk out of her life again. Right now, she needed him to leave before she threw herself at him and begged him to make love to her.

"I'll go then. You have my number. Call me if you need anything."

"I thought you didn't want to see me again?"

"I can't stop caring in a few days time, Paige. I still care a great deal. When I saw you sliding down the wall in a heap, my heart dropped into my stomach. I didn't know what was wrong. I scooped you up and brought you here."

"Why did your family attend the service? I didn't expect to see you."

"I respected your father and what he stood for. He was a good man. We came to pay our respects like any good Christian would do."

She glanced down at her toes. He'd taken her shoes off so the only thing she could focus on was the pink painted toenails on each foot. He hadn't come for her. She should have known. He wasn't happy when they parted the other day. She couldn't blame him. Pushing him out of her life because of her guilt over her father's death seemed trivial now, but she didn't know what to do. So many things needed to be taken care of. She would have to find a place to live. The church wouldn't allow her to stay in the home they'd lived in for fifteen years if her father wasn't their preacher anymore. The house would have to be cleaned out soon.

He shifted from foot to foot.

"Thank you."

"You're welcome."

He leaned down to gently kiss her on the forehead. The temptation to tilt her head up so she could capture his mouth overwhelmed her before she fought the urge. It would do no good at this point.

"Bye, darlin'."

"Bye, Jacob."

* * * *

Jacob stepped out into the bright sunlight of the summer day. His chest ached for the woman lying in the bed upstairs. He loved her, but she apparently didn't love him enough to try to make a go of this relationship they'd started. Walking away wasn't really an option. Did he have a choice? She didn't want him. It was something he had to face even though it came with difficulty. He'd never been in a position like this before. He knew he'd never loved Veronica. Even though she'd been pregnant with his child, he would have married her to give his child a father and a mother.

His father came around the corner of the church followed by the dog who had friended Paige. "Is everything all right, Jacob? I saw you carry Paige out the door."

"Yeah. I think so anyway. She passed out. I carried her back here. She's awake and eating a sandwich."

"What happened?"

"I think it's because she hasn't eaten in a couple of days. Probably several, but she couldn't remember exactly. Stubborn woman."

James smiled. "She sounds a lot like your mother."

"She is a lot like Ma. That's probably why I love her so much."

"So why are you down here and not up there with her?"

"She's got something going on in her pretty head I'm not sure how to deal with. Guilt is a hard war to wage and she's got it twofold."

"Why is that?"

"She told her father about us right before he died. She's thinking his stroke is her fault because of the stress. I can't convince her otherwise."

"Maybe talking with his doctor would help."

"There's an idea." They started walking back toward the church. The square walking stones guiding their way were worn with use. Flowers bloomed on either side of the path and he wondered absently if Paige took care of them. Gardening seemed like something she would do. Jacob paused, bringing his father to an expectant halt as well. "I'm not sure what to do about her. I love her, Dad, but she's pulling away from me."

"Give her time, son. Time heals wounds no matter how deep. She's lost both parents. It has to be difficult for her."

"But I want to help her. I want to hold her and love her."

"I know you do, Jacob. She seems like she needs the space more than you at the moment."

"How can that be? I need her, but she doesn't need me?"

"She does. She's just so torn right now, she's not sure which way to turn."

"She keeps saying she doesn't want to risk lovin' me and losin' me."

"Give her time."

Jacob sighed as he tipped his head back on his shoulders. "I guess I don't have a choice, do I?"

"Not really."

He walked back with his dad to claim their family so they could head for home. The sun slowly slipped into the afternoon sky, signaling the end of another day. Work beckoned on the ranch. It was never ending even when someone died, someone got married, a child was born, or whatever. Ranch work continued to be the one thing he always had to do even when he didn't want to. Maybe a few chores would take his mind off Paige.

The moment they hit the road to the ranch, his thoughts shifted to what needed to be done. He had more hay to stack and he'd promised Joey he would help break a couple of horses today. There would still be a few hours of daylight left before they'd call it a day.

"Where'd those two new geldings come from?"

"The Circle M."

"How is Jessica?"

Joey blushed. "I wouldn't know. I haven't seen her."

"Then why the hell are you turning red?" Jacob laughed. Joey had liked the youngest Marshall girl for some time, but he'd never made a move on her.

"It's nothin'."

"Nothin' *huh*?"

"She's too young for me anyway. She's only seventeen."

"She won't be some day."

"Don't worry about my love life. You need to figure out what's goin' on with yours."

"I wish I knew, brother. I wish I knew."

"What's goin' on now? I thought you and Paige had worked things out?"

"So did I last week, but this week things have changed again."

"Fickle woman."

Jacob laughed. "A little, yeah."

They pulled up to Jacob's parking spot before they both jumped out.

"You still want to help me break one this afternoon?" Joey asked, coming around the back of the truck.

"Sure. I could use a good kick or two. Maybe one to my head would help."

"I'll meet you back here in ten. I need to change out of these clothes." Joey laughed as he clapped Jacob on the back.

"Sure."

When they met up again a few minutes later, they headed to the barn to get the horse they would break. The palomino gelding stood in the stall happily munching on some hay.

"Come on boy. It's your turn." After grabbing the halter hanging on the nail next to the stall, Jacob slipped it over the gelding's face, hooking it behind his ears. Joey had been working with this particular horse for a bit so he wasn't too terribly gun-shy around equipment. "You've done good with him so far. He's not scared of the halter."

"I got him halter broke last week as well as blanket broke. I got the saddle on him once and he did well with it too. I think he'd ready to be ridden."

"Let's see what he's got then."

"I'll saddle Buster and get him in the round pen if you want to saddle him."

He led the horse out of the stall to the tie down area so he could get the blanket, saddle, and bridle on him without fighting with the animal since he didn't know how he would react. He trusted his brother's judgment, but it never hurt to be cautious around horses when they worked with them. The horse never baulked at the tack. Good. He'd rather save the bucking and kicking for the round pen.

Joey sat ready for him inside the pen when he came out of the barn. "You sure you want to ride him or do you want me to?"

"I'll do it. I need the rush."

Once the gate was closed behind him, he stuck his foot into the stirrup and pulled himself into the saddle. The horse didn't move for several seconds and then all hell broke loose.

The horse went straight up in a four-legged jump meant to jar the rider from his back. It did. Jacob ended up in a heap.

"Well, hell. That's a good start."

Joey laughed as he leaned over the pommel of his own saddle, resting his forearm on the leather knob.

Jacob dusted himself off as he headed for where the horse stood quivering. "Shall we go again, boy?"

The horse snorted as if to say, "Bring it on, cowboy."

Again, the horse went straight up. Jacob held on this time, gently digging his boot heels into the side of the gelding to urge him forward as Joey rode beside him. The horse dropped his head to jump again, but Jacob pulled his head up to prevent the buck. Round and round they went. The horse would throw him off, Jacob would crawl back into the saddle and they would go again.

After two hours, they finally got the horse gentled. He walked the pen circle with the pressure of Jacob's boots in his side while Joey guided the animal with a light tap of a crop to his butt.

"You've done well with him. Thanks for the help."

"No problem, brother. Anytime." As Jacob swung his leg down to dismount, the horse reared. His boot heel caught in the stirrup. Before Joey could calm the horse, Jacob had taken a hoof to the side of his chest and arm. "Fuck!"

Joey got the horse to stop by grabbing the bridle.

Jacob pulled his foot out as he rolled onto his side, grabbing his arm with his hand. "Son of a bitch!"

"You okay?"

"No. I think he broke my arm and a couple of ribs."

Joey let out a shrill whistle they saved to alert the family there'd been an accident. Within minutes, the entire family surrounded the round pen as his father moved inside to help him. "Where are you hurt?"

"My arm and ribs, I think."

"Let's get you to the hospital."

Jacob nodded. *Just fucking great. This is not what I needed.*

His father guided him out of the pen and they headed for the main lodge. A crowd of guests watched from the sidelines, whispering about riding those crazy animals. Those crazy animals are part of the ranch experience for the guests, but being hurt by one came with the job.

"Let's get this splinted so you can get off to the hospital to get some x-rays."

"Yeah. Hurts like a bitch."

Several hours later, he eased his broken body down on the bed in his trailer. The horse had broken his forearm and a couple of ribs when it had kicked him. They'd given him pain medication at the hospital. Grogginess crept into his consciousness, assisting him down into a restless sleep.

* * * *

Two bloody months. Paige hadn't talked to Jacob in two months and it was driving her batshit crazy. She'd moved herself into a small apartment, gave away most of her father's things and started her lonely life on her own. He hadn't called either, but she knew he was waiting for her to come to terms with everything going on and decide whether she wanted to risk loving him or not. She didn't know anymore. Every waking moment revolved around her memories of the time with him. Did she do the right thing? Her heart argued no, her head argued yes. She patted the dog she'd come to love on the head as he sat next to her on the floor.

Her stomach rolled. She'd had this damned flu for a week solid and it didn't seem like it was letting up anytime soon. She awoke every morning with a sour stomach and headache, threw up nothing but stomach acid, ate some toast and went back to bed. The afternoons were fine, although some days she had the icky stomach if she didn't eat something. An ulcer maybe? Who knew. With all the stress she'd been under, it wouldn't surprise her if she did have one.

Maybe it was time to see a doctor? Yeah, probably. Nothing seemed to help. Fatigue ruled her life these days. She always seemed tired and cranky.

She picked up her cell phone to dial her family doctor. *Better get this over with.*

"Doctor Orlio's office. Can I help you?"

"Yes. I need to make an appointment for a routine visit."

"Is there a specific problem you need to see the doctor for?"

"Well, I've been sick with the flu or something for a week now."

"The flu is going around even though it's an odd time of the year for it. We had a cancellation this afternoon if you'd like to come in."

"Fantastic. What time?"

She wrote down the time for her appointment and hung up the phone. Hopefully he would be able to give her some answers quickly so she could get past this and move on with her life.

By three o'clock, she sat in stunned silence in the exam room of the doctor's office. "Pregnant? You can't be serious?"

"I take it this wasn't a planned pregnancy."

"Hell, I mean, heck no! I can't be pregnant. I'm on the pill and I haven't had sex with anyone for two months!"

"Did you miss any doses about that time?"

She glanced down at her hands on her lap. *Shit.* "Yes. I missed three days. My father had a stroke and then died."

"I remember. I was sorry to hear about his death."

"Thank you, but anyway, yes I did miss some."

"There you go then."

A heavy sigh escaped her lips as tears gathered in her eyes. *What the hell is Jacob going to say?*

"Here is a prescription for some prenatal vitamins. I'll need to see you back here in one month for a checkup. You can get dressed now. I'll see you in a month."

"Thank you, doctor."

He patted her hand. "Things will work out, Paige. I'm sure you'll do what needs to be done."

"Can you tell me about abortion?"

"Is that what you're contemplating?"

Her whole body shook from the shock of this new development. *I can't raise a baby alone.* "I don't know at this point in time. I'm not sure what the father is going to think about this. We aren't together anymore and I don't know if I can raise a baby on my own."

"The nurses have some information at the desk. I'll have one of them bring it in here for you, but please don't make any hasty decisions. This isn't a simple thing to decide."

"I know. Thank you."

Several minutes later, she stood dressed and ready to leave when the nurse came in with some pamphlets. "Here is the information you requested."

"Thank you."

"I hope you aren't really thinking abortion is the way to go."

"I don't know. This whole thing is a major shock for me. It wasn't planned."

"As someone who went through this about two years ago with one of the nicest guys in the area, don't do it. I wish I hadn't."

Paige glanced at the nurse's name tag. *Veronica. Hmm.* "Thank you for the advice. I'll take that into consideration."

"You're welcome. I hope to see you in a month."

Paige left the doctor's office in a fog. Pregnant. *Now what am I going to do?* "First things first, I need to tell Jacob. It's his child too."

She glanced at the phone in her hand. Call him? No, this is something she needed to tell him in person. Something they needed to decide together.

She drove back to her apartment to get something to eat. The doctor's orders were to try to eat small meals to curb the empty stomach. She didn't think she could, but right now she felt utterly starved. After she made herself some soup, she sat down on her couch and stared at the black television screen. A baby. She touched her palm to her still flat abdomen. Jacob's baby.

"He's going to be furious." She patted the dog on the head as he pressed himself against her leg. The mutt had adopted her when she moved from the church's house to her apartment and she was lucky to have his companionship these days.

Eyes burning from unshed tears, she let them fall as she sat back against the couch. Another symptom, the doctor said. Great. She hated crying, but right now it seemed the thing to do. "Daddy?" She glanced up. "God, I wish you and Momma were here. You would know what to do."

He would never let me have an abortion. She wiped her tears with the back of her hand, attempting to fortify herself with a deep breath.

After she finished her lukewarm soup, she grabbed her jacket and keys to head to the cemetery. The drive gave her time to think about how she planned to tell Jacob about the baby. Should she just blurt it out, tell him slowly or maybe wait? The pregnancy was still in the early stages so she had time.

Luckily, the sun wouldn't set for awhile so she would have time to be able to sit and talk out her situation while she visited her parents.

She parked next to the church in the spot she used to call her own. The church parking lot was deserted today, thank goodness. The small cemetery looked forlorn in the afternoon light as the sun began its decent into the evening sky.

With a deep breath, she pushed open the door to her car so she could make her way to the spot near the back of this field of stone. Gravel crunched under her tennis shoes as she walked closer and closer to her destination. A huge oak tree shaded the area she sought. The wind picked up with a slight breeze, blowing her hair across her cheek in a caress.

"Momma?" she whispered to the wind without an answer. She rubbed both her arms to calm the chills suddenly springing up. It almost felt as if her parents were there with her.

She sank down on the soft, green grass between the headstones bearing her parent's names. A tear rolled down her cheek. "I miss you. Both of you."

The breeze picked up, rustling the few leaves on the ground.

"Help me." She wasn't sure if she was asking for God's help or her parents', but she needed someone to tell her what to do. "Tell me what I should do about this baby? I can't raise it on my own, but I don't think Jacob wants me anymore. I'm so scared."

The brush of something across her forehead calmed her heart as she heard the whispered words, "Tell him."

"What if he turns his back on me?"

"He loves you," came the reply in her daddy's voice. Should she believe her father wanted her and Jacob to be together?

She brushed some dry grass from the headstone with her mother's name. "Momma, I wish you were here to hold me. I need you so much right now."

"I love you, baby," reached her ear on the breeze. She felt as if her parents held her in a three way hug, assuring her everything would be okay.

She just had to talk to Jacob.

Chapter Fifteen

She pulled up to Jacob's trailer behind his truck and sighed. This wouldn't be easy. He would probably be angry. After all, they hadn't planned this at all. They weren't even dating anymore and here she turns up pregnant.

Her car door was whipped open, startling her into a yelp.

"What are you doin' here, Paige?" Jacob asked, holding the door open as she slipped out.

"I needed to talk to you."

He slammed the door shut behind her. "About what?"

"Can we go inside? It's kind of warm out here." Sweat trickled down between her shoulder blades. "I'm not feeling so hot."

"Sure." He led the way to his trailer, opened the door for her and then stepped back, allowing her to enter in front of him.

The cooler interior of the trailer felt like heaven on her overheated skin. She moved inside to take a seat on the couch. He took the chair opposite her. Great. He didn't even want to sit by her anymore. This wasn't going to be easy.

"Are you okay? You look pale."

"I'm okay. It's just warm."

"I didn't think it was that warm."

"Can I lie down for a minute? I don't feel so good."

"Sure. Leave your purse there and you can lie down on my bed. I'll get you a cool rag for your forehead. Are you sick?"

"A little. I've been sick for about a week. This is the first day I've really been out of the house for any length of time."

"Well whatever we have to talk about could have waited until you felt better," he said, holding her arm as they walked down the hall to his bedroom. Once he had her on the bed, he retrieved a cool cloth from the bathroom and draped it over her eyes. "Better?"

"I've got a splitting headache. Could you grab the Tylenol out of my purse? I should take a couple."

"Of course."

When he didn't come back for several minutes, she began to wonder what the hell was taking him so long. He should have been able to find the Tylenol in her purse easy enough. "Jacob?" she called, removing the washcloth and sitting up only to find him standing in the doorway of his bedroom holding the pamphlets on abortion in his hands.

"You're pregnant?"

"I, *uh*..."

"Answer me!"

"Apparently, yes. I went to the doctor today. I thought it was the flu."

He waved the pamphlets in front of her face. "No abortion, Paige. Don't even think about it. I won't let you."

"But Jacob—"

He began pacing back and forth next to the bed, clenching his fists. "No. I went through this once before and I'm not going through it again. This is the reason I kept drinking myself into a stupor."

"Over someone being pregnant?"

"Yes. I got a girl in town pregnant. We talked about abortion because she didn't want the baby, but I begged her not to. She did it anyway and told me two days later. The guilt drove me to drink. My child would have been born by now."

"God, Jacob. I'm sorry. I didn't know."

He raked his fingers through his hair, dislodging his cowboy hat behind him. "You can't abort it, Paige. Please."

"I wanted us to talk about this. It wasn't planned. Hell, I was on birth control, but I missed a couple of days right around the time we were together last."

"I don't want to talk about it. I love you. I haven't stopped loving you and I'll love a baby we made together no matter what the circumstances." He pulled her to her feet and wrapped his arms around her as he buried his face in her hair. "Baby, please don't abort my child."

"I won't, Jacob. I promise, I won't."

He pushed her back, cupped her face between his hands and said, "Marry me."

"What?"

"Marry me, right now. Today. Whenever. I don't care. I want us to be a family." His eyes brimmed with tears. "I love you."

"Are you serious?"

"Yes I'm serious. What do I have to do to prove it to you? I've been miserable the last two months. Do you have any idea how many times I've picked up the phone to call you before putting it back down?" He placed a small peck of a kiss to her lips before he continued, "A million times, that's how many, but I knew you needed time to get past your doubts."

Tears rolled down her cheeks and he brushed them away with his thumbs. *Damn hormones.* "You still love me?"

"More than anything. Say you'll marry me, please?"

"Yes. Yes, I'll marry you."

"What about all the guilt you've been feeling?"

"I sat down and had a long talk with both my parents at the cemetery this afternoon when I returned from the doctor's office and I realized it wasn't my fault they died. Both instances were controlled by someone much higher than I am. I just hope I can adopt your family. Do you think there is room for one more?"

"Oh, hell yeah! My mom already loves you and I'm sure my dad will become like a second father to you. They'll spoil any baby we have together like they spoil their other grandchildren."

"Terri had her baby?"

"Yeah, another little boy. They have two now."

He leaned in, taking her lips in a panty melting kiss obviously meant to break any resistance she might have had to keeping his baby or marrying him. Not that she planned to resist either situation. She loved him and wanted to be with him always.

As their kiss ended, she stepped back. "I want a wedding."

"Okay." He stepped toward her.

"We can plan something quick. At my father's church." She stepped back again.

He moved forward. "Anything you want, baby."

"A ring."

"We'll go buy one right now. I have money saved up. It might not be huge, but you can pick what you want."

"I don't want a huge ring, Jacob. Whatever you think is appropriate, I'll love." Her knees hit the bed. "Can we make love now?"

"I thought you'd never ask, but I thought you had a headache?"

"I feel a hundred percent better knowing you love me and want this baby."

"More than anything in this world."

"How do you feel about a dog?"

"Dog?"

"The big yellow one. He's part of the bargain."

"I love animals so I don't see why we couldn't use another protective member of the family around here."

Epilogue

Moonlight caressed her skin through the gauzy curtains of the cabana. Jacob slowly slid his fingers from the curve of her hip to the edge of her breast as she sifted the hair on his chest through her fingertips.

"I love you."

"I love you too."

"I wish we could stay like this forever, but unfortunately, we have to go home tomorrow."

"I know," she whispered, her lips caressing his chest.

His cock hardened even though they'd just finished making love. *God, I'm insatiable around her.* Good thing she'd married him a week ago.

The wedding was a small, intimate affair at her father's church with the preacher who'd done her father's eulogy performing the ceremony. Only the church members, her friends from the pre-school and a few dozen family and friends of the Young's were in attendance. It still filled up the little church with the white steeple.

Paige had worn her mother's wedding dress. She looked like a princess in the stark white gown with the beautifully beaded bodice and skirt.

His father had walked her down the aisle after Paige had insisted she needed him to be her fill-in father. They had a great little discussion just the two of them about a father's love. A discussion he wasn't privy to except to know they'd talked. His father had tears in his eyes when he'd handed her over to Jacob at the altar. Jacob knew there would be bond between his wife and his father, from that day forward, no man would ever break and he loved his father even more for becoming that for her.

"What are you thinking about?"

"Our wedding."

"Why?"

"You were beautiful."

"Thank you, but you cut a pretty handsome cowboy in your tux jacket, black jeans and boots. I loved the black Stetson too. Wow."

"Should I fuck you with just my hat on?"

"Would you?"

He roared with laughter. "Anything you want, darlin'."

She crawled on top of him, straddling his hips. "I want you. Like this. Right now."

His cock was at full attention. "I could go for that."

She eased her pussy down his cock a slow inch at a time until he was fully inside her. "God, I love how you feel inside me."

"I love how you surround me with your heat. Ride me, baby."

She lifted her body until only the head of his cock still rested inside her. She made several shallow dips that had him panting his need.

"You're teasing me."

"*Uh-huh.*"

"Wench." He quickly rolled her over onto her back, pushed her legs up until the bend of her knee rested over his forearms and shoved his cock inside her. The heat of her pussy was his undoing. He couldn't keep himself from pushing so deep that she growled low in response. He loved when she did that.

"Please, Jacob."

"Please wait, babe?"

"Oh God, no. Don't wait. Fuck me just like that."

"Your wish is my command." He fucked her so hard she had to brace herself against the headboard. Luckily they were in a small independent cabana where they had no neighbors. They had been kind of loud in their love making over the week they'd been there. If she wasn't already pregnant, he surely would have made her that way this week.

He felt her pussy quiver around his cock. With his thumb against her clit, he drove her into a screaming orgasm as she cried his name out in between panting breaths.

He slowed his thrusts.

"No, God, don't stop. Please."

"More."

"Hell yes. More."

He pulled out much to her whimpers of need, flipped her over so she was on her hands and knees and shoved back inside.

"Yes, yes."

"I don't want to hurt you or the baby."

"You won't. Please, Jacob. God, please."

He reached around to pinch her nipple between his thumb and finger, knowing the pain would send her over the edge again.

"Oh yes."

The sucking sounds their bodies made as he fucked her drove his desire to screaming proportions. He knew he wouldn't last much longer, but he wanted to make her come one more time. "Do you have another one in there for me?"

"I don't think I can."

"Sure you can," he said, dragging his finger through the wetness between her legs to clasp her clit in a heavy pinch.

She exploded again, coating his cock in cum and bringing him to a moaning, thrashing of the hips orgasm and probably killing off a few brain cells in the mix.

His body shook from the force of his release as he eased down beside her and drew her against his side. "You are magnificent."

"You're pretty good yourself there, handsome."

They lay side by side quietly for several minutes before he spoke again. "What do you want the baby to be, a boy or a girl?"

"I don't really care as long as it's healthy."

"You know what I want?"

"What?"

"A beautiful little girl who looks like her mother."

"You're gonna make me cry."

"No crying."

She swiped at the tears rolling down her cheeks. "You know I can't help it, Jacob. I'm such a mess these days with this pregnancy."

He laid his hand on her slightly rounded belly. "Baby, I love you more every day and if that means putting up with a few tears, then so be it."

"I love you with all my heart. I hope you're happy."

"I'm ecstatic! I can't believe how great my life as turned out. I have a beautiful wife, a new baby on the way, a good job, we're working on building our own house on my piece of land, and my investments guided by my brother Jeremiah, are turning into real moneymakers. Who could ask for more?"

"*Um*, Jacob?"

"Yeah, baby."

"How would you feel about twins?

The End

TEMPTED BY THE COWBOY
Cowboy Dreamin' 4

Sandy Sullivan

Chapter One

Peyton Matthews stood at the edge of the crowd watching as the Young brothers did their best to sling mud in every direction. Muddin'. The cowboy way of having fun on a hot early summer evening. A little dirt, a lot of water, some big mud tires on a pickup truck, and you had yourself a grand time in Bandera, Texas.

She wasn't sure why she let Aaron talk her into coming to this tonight. The cowboy way of life came hard for her. With her multiple tattoos, piercings, and loner mentality, she really didn't fit in here. Even as a child, she'd been out of place with her tomboyish attitude. She hadn't grown into her female body until later in high school as she cursed every curve, swell and period from then on. Not that she didn't like being a woman now, but she sure hadn't during puberty. And when the boys started noticing she had boobs? Oh boy! The gloves came off. Several of them got bloody noses from a well-placed fist.

Next up, the infuriating Jason Young, who took his turn at the hole. Mud flew in several directions, coating the crowd watching with the sticky substance. His red truck took the brunt of the splash, slinging the dirt over the entire side.

The grin he flashed from the driver's seat was infectious and she couldn't help but smile in return. He sure did have a pretty smile. Not that she really noticed or anything.

She knew his type. She'd seen it several times over the last several months as he played each female in The Dusty Boot like a fiddle with the strings too tight. A different one each time he came in.

As one of the bartenders who worked the joint, she saw him a lot. More than she wanted to, most of the time. She couldn't help but notice the way he carried himself. Nor, could she take her eyes off the cut of his shirt over the muscles of his chest, the snug way his jeans molded to his nice ass and those lips. God help her, those lips. Dark, thick hair hung to his collar with a slight wave. Her fingers itched to run through those strands.

A slight shift in her stance relieved some of the pressure on her clit, just not enough to satisfy the ache building. Maybe she'd let Aaron have a go tonight. She glanced toward where he sat reclining against a hay bale with a long-neck beer between his fingers in one hand and a cigarette clutched between his teeth. Okay, maybe not. Why she even went out with the guy, she didn't know other than she didn't want to spend another Saturday night off, sitting at home watching reruns of Will and Grace.

She sipped her beer, grimacing at the taste. The malty liquid had the ability to make her stomach lurch. Give her a shot of whiskey and water before the taste of this shit, any day, but it was liquor. Right now she needed the bite of alcohol on her tongue.

Today sucked. The whole thing from morning until now bit the big one. Memories had swamped her most of all, bringing down her mood into the pits of hell.

One year ago today, her mother had passed away from breast cancer. She took another sip from the bottle in her hand. *Yuck!* She tossed it into the trash can to her left before she stuffed her hands into her back pockets.

Jason took another run at the hole as she shook her head. The man knew what to do to make himself visible. Again, he probably had to being one of the Young triplets, identical triplets at that, although she had always been able to tell them apart when she'd had the privilege of gazing into their gorgeous faces. The other two weren't quite as broad across the shoulders as Jason. Something lingered in his gaze too. She wasn't sure what, but it intrigued her. Something wild. Something untamed maybe.

They all had the sweetest dimpled grin, but Jason seemed to have the half crooked tilt to his lips down pat. Boy did it work on the ladies.

She scuffed the toe of her boot in the dirt as she sighed heavily. It wouldn't do a bit of good to get tangled up with the likes of him even if he might be available. He wasn't as far as she knew. She didn't necessarily keep up with his whereabouts or latest fling. Well that's what she told herself anyway even if she noticed every girl he came in with or went home with. *Damn.*

"Hey, babe. Why don't you sit here with me," Aaron said, patting the hay bale next to him.

"No thanks."

"What's wrong?"

"Nothing. Why?"

"You came with me, you know."

"I know I did, Aaron, but don't pull your macho shit with me. I can find another way home. There are plenty of people from town here I could hitch a ride with."

"Like one of the Young boys?" He climbed to his feet, swaying slightly. "Don't think I haven't seen you watchin' several of them tonight."

He grabbed her arm, but she yanked it out of his hold. "Don't manhandle me, jackass."

"Aw, come on, babe. I don't wanna fuss with you. I wanna love on you."

"Yeah, not happenin'."

"Problem?" Jason stepped out of the shadows of the tree line.

Her breath stopped in her throat as it closed off. "No problem." The words came out in a squeak, not at all what she'd hoped to sound like—confident in her ability to take care of herself.

"Back off, Young."

"Fuck you, Scarborough. You don't get rough with a woman while I'm around."

"She ain't your woman."

"She isn't yours either, asshole." He touched her arm where Aaron had grabbed. "Are you okay, Peyton?"

"I'm fine. Thanks." She tipped her head back slightly to look down her nose at the idiot she came with. Big mistake, but one she'd own up to. "I can handle him."

"I'm sure you can, darlin', but you don't have to."

"It's okay."

"If you need a ride back to town later, let me know. As for now, have a good time."

He walked away, taking his scent and the heat of his hand with him. Goose bumps rose on her arms. The urge to calm them with her hands, flittered across her shoulders. She ignored the urge, almost embracing the affect he had on her as desire coiled low in her belly.

Aaron burped loudly. "You aren't his type, you know."

"What are you yammering about now?"

"Jason." He pointed with the bottle in his hand as he took a drag on his cigarette. "You aren't his type. He wants a downhome country girl, not a tattooed up, rough around the edges chick like you."

"I don't care what his *type* is." She shrugged as she glanced down at the nails on her left hand. "I'm not looking to hook up with any of the Young boys."

"Good. Come here then." He jerked her into his arms, effectively caging her in his tight embrace.

The wet slide of his lips along her neck almost made her gag. The inclination doubled as she glanced across the clearing straight into the glittering blue gaze of Jason. The frown pulling down the corners of his mouth made her frown in return. "I don't want this, Aaron."

She pushed him back by the shoulders.

"What the fuck, babe? I know you're horny. I can smell it on you."

"I'm not horny for you."

"Bitch!" He slapped her hard across the cheek, tossing her to the ground at his feet. "You fucking cunt. You aren't good enough for the likes of me. I wouldn't fuck you if you were the last pussy in Bandera."

Within seconds, Jason had him by the front of his shirt as he lifted him until his feet dangled. "I told you, you don't hurt a woman while I'm around." Jason pulled back his fist and proceeded to punch Aaron in the nose. Hard. He landed two more before two of his brothers hauled him off even though he struggled in their hold. "Let go. I'm gonna make sure he never hits a woman again while I mess up his pretty face."

"He's not worth the trouble, bro." Joel held one arm while Jackson had the other.

Jason shook off their hands.

"Fuckin' bastard! You're gonna be sorry you did this," Aaron threatened as he struggled to his feet.

Jason lunged, but his brothers grabbed him before he could do any further damage. "Get the fuck off our property, Scarborough. Don't ever come back or there will be nine of us against one of you."

Aaron held his nose, making his voice come out in a deep nasally sound. "You don't own the God damn county, Young. I can do what I want."

"Not on our property." Jason glanced at her as she struggled to her feet. "You okay?"

"Yeah."

He touched her cheek with his fingertips. "You'll probably have a bruise tomorrow."

She winced from the scrape of his calluses. "I'm sure." She dropped her gaze from connecting with his. She never could handle looking deep into his eyes. The color of a clear lake somewhere in the mountains, she'd always melted into a puddle of goo when they connected. "Thanks for sticking up for me."

"I'd do it for anyone."

Ouch. "Thanks anyway. I appreciate it."

Nina, Jason's mother, came to her side. "Are you all right, Peyton?" She looked at the boys who'd begun to gather. "Get him off the property. I don't care how to you do it, but I want him out of here."

Jeremiah and Jackson grabbed Aaron by the arms none too gently and pushed him toward where his car sat off to the back of the packed group.

"I'm fine, Nina, but thank you."

"Don't thank me, honey. I didn't do anything. You should be more careful who you keep company with."

"I know. Trust me, I won't be keeping company with him again. I won't tolerate a man hitting me. If Jason hadn't stepped in, I would have decked him myself."

Nina laughed. "I get the impression you can take care of yourself most of the time."

Peyton nodded as she touched her fingertips to her cheek. "I can." She sighed when she dropped her hand back to her side. "I guess I should find someone to take me home."

"I will." Jason took out his keys. "Just say when."

"You know, I think I'll stay awhile. I'm not going to let one asshole ruin my afternoon. Let the mud sling, baby!"

Jason laughed. The sound rippled down her back in a slow shiver. He pulled her in for a quick hug.

"I like you, Peyton Matthews. How about you take a run with me through the mud?"

"Run?"

"Yeah. You came to get down and dirty, didn't you?" he asked, his hands on his hips. One eyebrow cocked over his eye right before a panty-melting grin spread across his lips. He dove for her, pressing his shoulder into her abdomen as he lifted her off the ground before he strolled for the mud pit.

She reached down to smack his taut ass, realizing just how tight his butt was. *Holy hell!* Her long hair swung back and forth, blocking her vision as the catcalls flew.

"Get her, Jason."

"Hey, Peyton. Takin' a bath with Jason?"

She felt her face flush hot. "Put me down."

"Nope."

His boots hit the edge of the mud pit, with both feet sliding until they went down into the water. He'd tried to bring her back over his shoulder before they landed, only to hit a dirt mound in the middle. This caused him to lose his grip until she landed directly on top of him, her face to his crotch and her legs cradling his head. The crowd roared. Jason laughed and she couldn't help but laugh too no matter the precarious place her face brushed against.

The shape of his cock stood proud, outlined by the tight wetness of his jeans.

"Havin' a good time down there?"

"What? Shit." She scrambled off him to land butt first in the mud.

The whole crowd got into it by jumping into the pit with them. A huge mud fight ensued with everyone throwing globs of sludge at each other until the entire group stood dripping from head to toe.

The parental unit stood on the sidelines laughing until they bent over at the waist.

Peyton crawled toward the edge, only to be pulled back in by her boot. When she twisted around, Jason was grinning at her like a fool. Dirt smudged his cheeks and dripped from his hair as his shirt lay plastered to his chest.

"Where do you think you're going?"

"Out?"

"Nope." He dragged her back in until they were stuck in the middle of the dirt party again. Someone pushed him from behind, propelling him toward her until she thought he'd land directly on her, drowning her in the process. Right before he landed, he braced himself with his arms so he didn't squash her, but it brought them in close proximity from nose to toes.

She lost herself in his eyes until he slowly bent his head, closing the distance between them for what she really hoped to be a light-me-on-fire kiss.

Right before he brought their mouths together, one of his brothers tackled him, throwing him off of her. *Damn it!* She pushed herself to her elbows, grimacing as the mud squished under the pressure. She laughed as she watched the entire crowd sling mud every which direction at each other.

Two of the Young brothers grabbed their parents to drag them into the fray. Everyone got into it, even the wives or girlfriends of the boys already paired up. Mesa jumped in with both feet, Terri threw a big mud ball at Jeff, and Paige pushed Jacob down even though he took her with him into the mud. They seemed like such a happy family. All of them. Something she wished she'd had growing up.

Her mother had been a single parent from the time of her father took off when she was a child. She'd never had siblings so she didn't know how to act around a lot of people sometimes. She'd always felt it must have been her fault her father left. He didn't love her…didn't want her or something. She'd only been two when he'd taken a business trip and never came back. She didn't want to find him, never wanting to know the truth behind why he took off like he did. Her mother didn't discuss him. There were never any pictures. She didn't even know what he looked like anymore.

Enough feeling sorry for myself. I'm going to enjoy this time with a family even if I'm not part of it.

The party died down as everyone worked their way out of the mud pit and started for their vehicles to head home. The sun started to go down over the horizon, bringing with it the inky blackness of the night way too soon. The Youngs usually had a bonfire with their muddin' parties, but since everyone was head to toe in mud, they decided to forgo it this time and have one at the house should anyone want to clean up before they came by.

"I'll take you home to change if you want to come back for the bonfire."

"I would appreciate the ride, but I don't think I'll come back."

"Why not?" Jason asked, wiping a smear of mud from her cheek.

"Even though it was a lot of fun hanging out with your family, I just don't fit in with the family thing."

"Sure you do. You'd get along great with Mesa and Terri. Isn't Paige one of your friends?"

"Yes."

"Then there you go. You'd fit right in."

She cocked an eyebrow. "Really? I'm not the good little girl, perfect housewife and mother type."

"Good. I kind of like the wild ones."

She braced her hands on her hips. "Are you coming onto me, Jason Young?"

"Is it workin' 'cause I can really turn on the charm if it's not." He grinned as she laughed.

"I'd be obliged if you'd take me home."

"Sure enough, darlin'. Let me change clothes and I'll be happy to take you." They walked to his truck in silence as she took in the mud slung all over the sides.

"How do you keep the mud from getting inside when you're all muddy yourself?"

"I have blankets to put on the seats until I get home, but they are leather so it's a quick wipe off anyway." He grabbed the blanket out from behind the seats to spread it out.

"Good thinking." He helped her into the jacked up truck with a hand on her butt. When she turned around to scold him, he just grinned. She rolled her eyes. Being mad at that handsome face wouldn't go very far so she didn't try.

Once he sat behind the wheel, the engine roared to life with a distinctive growl that settled low in her belly. She loved the rumble of a diesel engine.

They pulled out, bouncing along the rutted road until they made it to one of the ranch gates where he could get out onto the small highway. "We'll head back to my place so I can change."

"Sounds fine." She wasn't sure she could handle being in his house while he changed clothes and not jump him. All the looks he was giving her had her wound tight and ready to bust loose. If she could just get home without him touching her, she could relieve some of the pressure with her friendly battery operated boyfriend until she could possibly scope out someone else. *Why don't I bust this dry spell with him? I'm sure if I propositioned him, he'd be willing. A one night stand with a handsome cowboy wouldn't be so bad, right?*

Within minutes, they were pulling through a side gate of the ranch she hadn't known existed.

"You live out here?"

"Yeah. I built this place over the last couple of years."

They pulled up slowly toward a wood frame, two story log cabin. "Even though you don't have a wife or steady girlfriend?" *Wow. It's beautiful!*

"Yep. I used to stay in one of the bedrooms upstairs in the main lodge, but it got kind of noisy with the tourists, so I got me a log cabin kit. I've been building on it. The outside is finished, but I don't have any landscapin' or anything. It's not finished on the inside yet, although I have my bedroom and bathroom done."

"You're living out here then?"

"Yeah. I'm slowly doing things when I have time away from my duties at the ranch. Do you want to see the inside?"

"No!" She cleared her throat. "I mean, no. I'm head to toe in mud. I don't want to get your floors dirty or anything."

"You could shower here and I could wash your clothes."

Wow, the opportunity to have Jason Young all to herself in his house almost overwhelmed her. No other women around. No one hanging on his every word.

"What do you say? I'll even share the shower with you if you want."

"Oh you are so tempting."

"I only want what is best for both of us, darlin'. When you have clean clothes and showered, we can go back to the bonfire. No hanky panky unless you are feelin' the burn."

"What if I say yes?"

"To what?"

"All of it. I wouldn't mind ridin' you like a wild stallion."

His sexy-ass grin reappeared. "If you are propositioning me, babe, I'm ready, willing and able to take care of your needs all the way around the clock if you want to."

"Let's check out your bathroom then and we'll see where it leads."

The moment the engine cut, he was around the passenger side of the truck, pulling the door open with a yank. He scooped her up from her seat into his arms, hurrying for the cabin. "Uh, you forgot to shut the door."

"Crap." He walked back and used her booted foot to push it closed.

Seconds later, he fumbled with the key to the door lock. "Let me." She took the keys from his hand to open the door. Even though the house wasn't finished, what he had done amazed her. A large stone fireplace encompassed one wall to her left. Although it wasn't lit currently with the warmer temperatures of the early summer months in Bandera, she could see him sitting in front the flames reading a book. Okay, maybe not reading a book, but reclining in his naked glory on a fluffy rug just waiting for a woman to rub him all over.

She blinked as he set her down on her feet.

"Strip it off, babe."

"Right here?" she asked as he plucked a couple of buttons loose down the front of her shirt.

"Yeah. I mean this way we won't carry the mud through the house and I can put your clothes in the washer right now."

Self-consciousness swamped her. This would be the first time he'd see her naked and she wasn't sure what he'd think. She wasn't slender like a lot of women. She had curves, bulges and even some cellulite. What about her tattoos and piercings? Would he find them sexy or disgusting? She covered her breasts with her hands.

"What's wrong?"

"I've never undressed in front of you before."

"I know." He grinned. "I can't wait to see what treasures you're hidin' under there."

"How do you feel about tats?"

"I love them. I have two myself."

"You do?"

"Yeah. I have a band around my left bicep and a tribal swirl around my right shoulder and chest." He pulled his shirt out of the waistband of his jeans, then eased each button down the front from its hole, one by one.

Her breath caught in her throat as the spit in her mouth dried up like the Mohave Desert. She was going to finally see the fine pecs of Jason Young. The man she'd fantasized over for the last several months.

When he pulled the shirt from his shoulders, she caught her bottom lip between her teeth. *Dayum!*

"You like?"

Without realizing it until she touched his chest, she had reached her hand out to trace the swirling black along his pec. "Nice. It suits you."

"Thanks."

She glanced at the band around his bicep, noting the simplistic design of the silver spur brand entwined in the ink. "You have the ranch brand in there."

"Yeah. The ranch means everything to me, probably more than any woman ever will."

"Not makin' points here, cowboy."

"Sorry, but I figured you should know up front, I'm not lookin' for a wife."

"Good. I'm not lookin' for a husband."

He worked the buttons on her shirt until it hung loose at her waist. She'd worn a chemise top underneath with the sleeves cut off and a pair of jeans to the party.

"So where are yours?"

"I have a few."

"Where?"

"My ankle. My shoulder blade. One above my breast for my mother who died of breast cancer last year."

"I'm so sorry," he said in a soft whisper as he brushed his lips against her temple.

No one had ever moved her as deeply as he did with that simple touch. "It's okay. She'd been sick a long time. Even beat it once, but it came back with a vengeance. Brain cancer finally took her life in the end."

He worked the shirt from her arms, dropping it at her feet in a heap. "Toe off your boots so you can shed those jeans."

"I think you're just trying to get me out of my clothes, mister."

"Is it workin'?" he asked with a grin.

"Seems to be," she said, glancing down at her slowly building pile of clothes at their feet.

"Good." He unbuckled her belt and pushed down the zipper until her pants gaped at the waist, then fell to the floor. "Step out."

She complied blindly. Why, she wasn't sure other than she'd had it bad for this man for some time and if it meant taking the bull by the horns this one chance, she'd do it in heartbeat. Before she could change her mind, she lifted her chemise over her head, exposing her complete nakedness to his roaming gaze.

"You're beautiful."

"I bet you say that to every girl you have naked in your house."

"Nope, since you're the only woman who's been naked in this house with me."

"Really?" *He's never had a woman here before?*

"Yes."

"The sexy Jason Young? Hmm."

"Believe it or not, I haven't had a woman here before." He glanced around before his gaze came back to her. "This is my space. My sanctuary so I don't usually bring women here."

"Why me? Why now?"

"You're special and I want to help you. Nothin' says anything has to happen between us unless you want it to. Really, I only brought you here so you could shower and I could wash your clothes. You seemed like you were having a good time at the muddin' and didn't want it to be over. This was a way to keep the night from ending." He slowly traced the heart tattoo on her upper breast. "This is nice. Kind of a tribute."

"Yeah."

He stepped back.

"Aren't you going to strip too?"

"Yep."

"Right here?"

One eyebrow lifted. "Care to watch?"

"Oh hell yeah."

She admired his chest again. He sure was pretty to look at. Next, came the pants. Without preamble, he unbuckled and unzipped his jeans, pushing them to the floor in a whoosh. "Sweet mother of God," she murmured when his cock sprang free.

With a quick spin, he headed down the hall, assuming she would follow blindly. How could she not with his tight ass jiggling slightly as he walked.

"Come on. I'll show you the bathroom before I throw your clothes in the washer."

Even though he said the inside of the house wasn't done, most of his personal space was. They walked by the kitchen with its hickory cabinets and stainless steel appliances, to the next doorway at the end of the hall. It opened to reveal his bedroom. The deep grey on the walls complimented the dark furniture expertly. A burgundy red comforter graced the bed with deep pillow softness she wanted to sink into and never come out.

"The bathroom is through here."

With a flick of the switch, he illuminated the beautiful bathroom. "My God, Jason. This is gorgeous."

Travertine tiles graced the floor, but it was warm to the bottom of her feet.

"Radiant heat."

"Wow."

A huge shower sat in the back corner with a big rain type showerhead, glass walls, and silver accents. "The shower has several jets so you can get water everywhere."

"This is beautiful. You sure went all out."

He shrugged as pink stained his cheeks. *A blush?*

"What can I say, I like my luxury in the bathroom."

Her gaze kept bouncing from one thing to another as she tried to take it all in. "I'd say. I haven't seen a bathroom this nice in a long time. Usually at a high end hotel or something."

He pointed to the floor to ceiling cabinet to their left. "There are towels in the cupboard. Shampoo and soap in the shower. Take your time. I'll find you something to wear until your clothes are washed. It'll take about forty-five minutes in the washer and half an hour in the dryer probably."

She pressed her lips together for a moment. "Thank you. You don't know how much this means to me. I really never thought I'd be here with you like this when this evening started out."

His lips quirked up in a half smile. "You're welcome. Take your time. I'll use the other bathroom."

"What? Wait! No, I'll use the other bathroom. You use yours." She stepped toward him. "I'm not going to take your bathroom from you."

"I insist. Use it. I need to get other things together before I can get in."

She captured her bottom lip between her teeth. "Maybe you'd like to join me?"

Chapter Two

Jason sighed. *I'm actually going to walk away from having sex with one of the hottest women in Bandera. Yeah, damn it!* "You know, darlin', I would love to."

"But?"

"I don't think now is the right time for you and me."

"Why not?"

"It would be just sex."

"Yeah and?"

"I don't want to use you like that."

"Neither of us is looking for a relationship at the moment, right?"

"True."

One sharp fingernail skimmed down his chest. "Then what's wrong chasing away the lonely night with someone we are attracted to?" She glanced down at his erect cock. "I assume you are attracted to me."

His cock bobbed in agreement. "Not just yeah, but hell yeah."

She encircled his left nipple with the sharp end of her nail. His whole body went on high alert as shivers rolled from the top of his head to the tips of his toes.

Hot didn't do her justice. Brown eyes sparkled with mischief as a small smile curved her lips at the corners. Her breasts were high and full, plenty for a man's hand. Long, light brown hair brushed the curve of her waist. A waist that dipped in, not sharply like a stick model thin woman's, but gracefully like she wasn't afraid to eat. He groaned silently at the thought of those willowy legs wrapped around his waist as he sank into her heat.

Getting tangled in the sheets with her sounded like an *awesome* idea. Unfortunately for his willing cock, tonight wasn't the night. For some crazy-ass reason, he wanted to let the sexual tension build like the pressure of a volcano before he let it loose on the beauty standing in front of him.

"Make no mistake, baby. I want you. I want you bad, but I'm not going to take advantage of the situation. When we fuck for the first time, it's gonna be mind-blowing. Tonight ain't the night." His cock ached for the tight wetness he would find between her gorgeous thighs when he stepped back and left the bathroom with a click of the door.

He released a tortured, frustrated sigh as he leaned against the door jam. *Why did I think denying myself the pleasure of her body was a good idea?*

"Because in the end, it'll be worth it."

He dejectedly pulled himself away from the door before heading down the hall toward the other bathroom. After a minute, he reversed direction to grab their clothes from the front hall to throw them in the washer. He hoped she didn't require her unmentionables to be hand washed or anything. Like any typical bachelor, everything went into the washer together after he poured soap in the dispenser. A quick turn on the dial had the washer filling with water. He chuckled. She might end up with pink underwear should he do anything fancy with them.

"Shower." He picked the dried dirt from his hair as he walked back down the hallway to the second bathroom. When he'd finished it, he never really thought he'd be the one using it. Not this soon anyway. The inside of the house had only been done for a few months and he still had a ton to do. Kitchen, two other bedrooms, his game room, and another barn needed to be built to house his animals. Like his father before him, he planned on running cattle on his piece of property as well as breeding bucking bulls. He wasn't so much into the rodeo thing as a rider, but he sure wanted to cash in on the lucrative business of bucking bulls for the Professional Bull Riders Association.

He snapped his fingers. *Damn, the shampoo is all in the master bathroom.* He switched directions again to get some stuff to shower with, hoping the shower stall door would be totally steamed up so he wouldn't have to see the gorgeous woman gracing his shower.

No such luck.

The minute he opened the bathroom door, he was struck by the silhouette of her. Each curve made his mouth water. His fingers itched to touch. He wanted to skim his palm along the slope of her breast.

She tipped her head back to rinse her hair as a delicious sigh escaped her lips, at the same time as his.

He shook his head to clear the erotic vision although it didn't help since his gaze kept going back to her. *God, I want—* He wasn't sure if he could put a name to his want at the moment.

With a deep breath, he moved his feet reluctantly to the cabinet under the sink so he could retrieve shampoo. He quickly escaped back out the door without wanting to return to fuck her against the wall with his aching cock.

The hotter the water, the better. The water sprayed out the head of the smaller shower. Lucky for him, one of his brothers had used the bathroom just a few days before when he'd had an accident out on the range and ended up in the middle of a wrestling match with a cow in the mud. There were still clean towels on the hook.

The water eased the ache between his shoulders as he sank back to let the liquid cascade over his back. Once he'd wet his hair, he quickly scrubbed the mud from the thick strands. After he'd shampooed his hair clean, he went to work on the dirt clinging to his arms and legs, but his sensitive cock wouldn't let the image of Peyton out of his brain. He would have to take care of the problem, otherwise there would be no denying what he wanted in the end.

He soaped up his hand before skimming the slick palm over his cock as he closed his eyes, losing himself in the dream of having her all to himself.

Those chocolate brown eyes of hers sparkled in the light as she swallowed his cock. The rough slide of her tongue along the shaft about drove him up on his toes. Lord, she knew how to give head.

"Close your eyes. Let me suck you off."

His affirmation came out in a high-pitched yes as she took him all the way to the back of her throat.

Oh shit. She has a tongue ring. The scrape of the metal ball on his cock drove him to the brink of exploding. When she cupped his balls in her hand and circled the head with her tongue, rasping the ball around and around, he lost it. Cum squirted out the end of his dick to coat her tongue as she swallowed every drop with reverence.

Jason slumped against the wall of the shower as he tried to catch his breath. He didn't think he'd ever come so hard in his life. *God help me when we finally have sex.*

When he finally was able to stand on legs that felt like noodles, he finished washing his body, then shut the shower off.

She would have to be done by now. He started to get hard again just thinking about her running around his home in nothing but a towel. A wicked little chuckle escaped his lips as he wrapped the towel around his waist before he opened the door.

The first thing he saw when he got to the living room took his breath away. She stood in nothing but one of his shirts. It had to be the sexiest thing he'd ever seen in his life. She had the sleeves rolled up to her elbows and the shirttails hung to mid-thigh. He almost swallowed his tongue.

"I hope you don't mind. I didn't have anything to put on, so I grabbed a shirt from your closest."

After he cleared his throat, he said, "Not at all. I'm glad you found something to wear."

She glanced down as she picked at the hem of the shirt. "It was the first thing I found."

"You couldn't be more sexier right now if you tried, darlin'."

He could tell by the reaction on her face he must have worn a little smirk on his lips. Her perfectly shaped eyebrow shot up over her left eye as her lips twitched when she tried not to smile.

"How long before the clothes are done?"

"Probably another fifteen minutes in the washer and at least thirty minutes in the dryer."

"Hmm." She crossed her arms over her chest, hiking the hem of the shirt up even further. "So what are we going to do while we wait for the clothes?"

"Since we aren't going to have down and dirty sex, how about I show you the rest of the house? But, let me throw some jeans on first."

"Of course."

He disappeared into his room to throw something on to cover his erection even though she would notice right away as it strained against the front of his pants. A groan escaped his lips as he shoved his cock into his jeans before he zipped them up. The scream he trapped in his throat almost escaped as he caught a few hairs in the zipper, ripping them out by the roots. *Holy fuck!*

"Everything okay?"

"Yes." The word came out in a squeak.

"Are you sure? You don't sound very good."

"I'm fine. I'll be out in a second." *Sweet mother of God.* He bit his lip as he shoved the zipper back down. Sweat poured from his temples as he stifled the scream in his throat. *That's what I get for trying to go commando.* "Well sex might not happen tonight." He pushed the jeans off his thighs and feet, grabbed a pair of boxers to slip on before he pulled his jeans back up over his hips. He wiped the sweat from his forehead with the back of his forearm as he blew out a long breath. *Good Lord that hurt.*

When he opened the door to the bedroom, she stood leaning against the opposite wall. "Are you sure you're okay? I thought I heard you scream."

"Nope. I'm fine." He walked out, shutting the door behind him.

"You're walking funny."

"Okay. All right. I caught my pubic hairs in my zipper."

He figured she'd laugh, but the gut rolling belly laughter escaping her mouth as she doubled over at the waist, made him frown. It wasn't that damned funny, was it?

"You…you got…caught in your zipper?"

"Yes."

"Oh God." She exploded in another round of laughter.

"It isn't funny."

"I'm-I'm sorry." She giggled. "Really, I'm sorry. I've caught pubic hair in zippers before, but—She exploded in laughter again as she reached out her hand. "Want me to kiss it and make it better?"

"Don't—don't touch it."

"I don't mean to laugh, but shit, that's funny."

"Are you done?" he asked, crossing his arms over his chest.

She pressed her lips together as her eyes danced with mirth. "Yes."

"Do you want to see the house or not?"

"Yes, I do.

He took her hand and led her back toward the front of the house. "The kitchen will be over there. I've got a few cabinets in, but the rest will be installed in the next coming weeks."

"I like them. Very nice." She stepped closer to the cabinets and ran her hands over the finish. "Did you buy them?"

"No. I made them myself."

"Wow. These are beautiful, Jason."

"Thanks." He pointed to the empty area where the stove stood, the dishwasher would go, and explained how he planned to put in granite countertops on them as soon as he had everything installed.

"Sounds like a beautiful kitchen anyone would be proud to cook in. Do you do a lot of cooking?"

"Actually, yeah. I do a lot of my own. We can eat with the family at the main house, but I spend as much time out here as I can. I like my space. After growing up with nine brothers, I like being alone. With three of them paired up now, there are even more at the table these days."

"I can totally see you standing at the stove making grilled cheese sandwiches for your kids."

"Kids?"

"You want kids someday, don't you? You know." She spun around. "Carry on the Young name."

"Maybe, but I sure ain't ready for kids right now. I still have some oats to sow."

"Oh, I'm sure you do. I've seen the women you come in with or pick up at the bar. I'm not blind."

"You've been watchin'?"

"I watch everything. I see a lot behind that bit of mahogany."

"I bet you do."

She scraped a fingernail down his chest, igniting his libido again even though his cock still ached from his brush with the zipper. "You really should be more careful about who you pick up at the bar."

"Why?"

"You know Tammy Ritz?" she asked, circling his nipple with a fingernail.

"Yeah. I went out with her a few weeks ago."

She shrugged before she walked toward the couch to take a seat. With her feet tucked under her, she said, "She's only after your name."

"How do you know this?"

"I heard her talking to her friends at one of the tables the other night. She thinks she's got you on the tow line, honey, and she plans to rein you in."

"Ain't happenin'." He took a seat on the opposite end of the couch, turning to face her.

"You'd better inform her of that little fact when you see her next."

"Oh I plan to. Thanks for the information."

"You're welcome. We can't have your magnificent body off the market so soon, now can we?"

"You're trying my self-control, lady."

"I hope so."

"Why are you hellfire bent on having me fuck you tonight?"

She turned to face him on the couch as she inched up the hem of the shirt she wore. She had nothing on under it. "I'm horny as hell and I'm sitting with a gorgeous male specimen. Why wouldn't I?"

His body went on high alert. She definitely kept putting that beautiful body out there, he might have to give in. He could only handle so much.

The washer beep as the load finished. Using it as an escape, he jumped to his feet to throw everything in the dryer. Maybe he could convince her to do something else like play pool. While he tossed the clothes in, he said, "How about a game of pool?"

"Sure." The closeness of her voice made him jump. He hadn't heard her come up behind him.

He swallowed hard as her warm breath caressed the back of his neck. She wasn't a small woman by any means if her mouth reached his neck. At over six feet, he liked his women tall. He liked her, everything about her on a physical level anyway. He didn't know much about her on a personal level, but he wasn't too interested in taking things beyond a physical relationship, so what did it matter.

"Great. Let me get these going and we'll go upstairs to what will be my game room. The walls aren't in, but the pool table is available for use." *Oh shit. That didn't come out right.* "I mean for us to play on." *I should just keep my mouth shut before I make this worse.*

"Anything you want, Jason, remember that."

She turned and walked out of the laundry room, giving him a little breathing space. It didn't help as the scent of her skin and his shampoo mixed in an intoxicating mingling of smells meant to drive him insane.

Good God, I need a cold shower now.

He stopped for a minute, bracing his hands on the tumbling dryer, but all it brought to mind was fucking her on the spinning washer.

"Jason? I thought we were going to play?"

"Fuck." He blew out a long breath, hoping it would calm his raging hard-on. It did nothing. "I'll be right there. You go on up." Oh, he wanted to play all right. Play with her gorgeous pussy all night long. He'd gotten a glimpse of the pink flesh when she'd hiked up the shirt, tempting him to throw everything to the wind and fuck her until they both couldn't breathe. Why did he torture himself this way? Why didn't he just give her what she so obviously wanted? He wasn't sure anymore. What difference would it make if he took care of her now or waited?

"Anticipation would make things so much sweeter."

Oh yeah, but...

"Leave it be."

Shit.

He turned to head up to the game room anticipating the torturous evening ahead of him until he could get her back into her clothes and on her way home. Why the hell he ever suggested washing her clothes for her, he wasn't sure. All he managed to do was afflict himself with the worse night in the history of Jason Young's life.

* * * *

Driving Jason insane with lust sounded like a great plan to Peyton. She'd wanted his body for some time and being this close was driving her insane. Her pussy throbbed with need, her clit swelling beyond the size comfortable to walk. She wanted him badly.

"Jason?"

"I'm coming." He cussed a blue streak quietly even though she could still hear him. "I mean I'll be right there."

She smiled to herself. She had him right where she wanted him. In so much pain, he'd give into her sooner or later. A little more teasing wouldn't hurt. She tapped her fingers against her lips. Maybe loosening a few buttons down the front of her shirt would push a few more of his buttons. A wicked giggle escaped from her mouth. *Oh this is fun.*

His steps on the stairs echoed in the empty room where she stood next to the nice sized pool table. *Leave it to a man to not have the walls up, but the pool table in place.*

"Ready?"

"Ready as I'll ever be," she replied, as she glanced down at the crotch of his jeans, noting the tented front. She had him right where she wanted him.

As he grabbed two pool cues from the corner, she unbuttoned two of the small pearl buttons on the front of the shirt she wore.

His eyes narrowed when he turned around and his gaze went to her chest. "Warm?"

"Yeah a little." She didn't think she'd fooled him one bit.

"I'll let you break."

Oh hell yeah. She took the cue as he moved to the table to rack. "I'm not very good at this."

"At what?" he asked, shoving the balls into the plastic triangle on the table.

"Playing pool."

"I'll teach you."

"Aren't you sweet?" The sugar sweetness in her voice didn't have him fooled as his eyes narrowed again while his hands grew still.

"Behave yourself, woman."

"I am. I'm not doing anything."

"I've got your number, darlin'. We already agreed not to have sex tonight."

"We did?"

"Okay, I said we weren't havin' sex tonight. I meant it."

"Of course, Jason." She lowered her gaze before she glanced up at him through her lashes. With a little luck, the coy look would work.

"Stop it, Peyton."

"Stop what?"

"The come-on. I don't want to have sex with you."

She glanced at the front of his jeans. "Are you sure?"

"All right. My cock wants to have sex with you, but my head says no. I'm listening to this," he tapped at his forehead, "head and not the one between my legs."

As she rolled her eyes, she said, "Fine. I'm doing everything in my power to seduce you, but apparently you aren't interested or have this manly sense of right and wrong that seems to be getting in the way. So be it."

"Do you know how to break?"

"Yes." She leaned over the table, giving him ample view of her naked ass. *Take that, stud.*

He groaned.

She smiled as she shoved the stick against the cue ball, shattering the perfect formation he placed at the other end of the table.

"Why do I get the feeling I've been shafted?"

"It was your idea to play." She moved around the table, shooting at intervals as she quickly cleared the table of all the solid colored balls.

The dryer beeped and she heard a long sigh with a *thank God* behind it.

She almost laughed out loud when he ran for the stairs, taking them two at a time down in his rush to get her clothes. Within seconds, he stood in front of her again, holding them out like they were on fire. "Here."

"Thanks." She proceeded to unbutton the shirt ever so slowly, just on the off chance she could tease him a little more before they parted ways for the night. If she had to be ready to explode, she was going to make damned sure he suffered just as much. After all, the man hadn't even kissed her.

"Peyton," he growled.

"Yes?"

"Take the damned clothes." He shoved the clothes at her before he spun on his heels, racing for the stairs again as she laughed behind him.

After several minutes, she shrugged and proceeded to get dressed. There would be another time to torture and fuck the gorgeous Jason Young before the summer concluded. Fuck him she would. Sooner or later, she'd have him in her bed spread eagle so she could ride his hips into tomorrow just to see if he was as good as the rumor mill proclaimed.

Chapter Three

Peyton no sooner got downstairs to find him completely dressed tapping his booted foot in a rapid tempo against the file floor near the front door. "Problem?"

"No. Let's go."

"Where are we going?" she asked, slipping on her muddy boots.

"To the bonfire."

"Why?"

"Because I can't be alone with you anymore tonight without giving into this thing between us."

"Thing?"

"Aren't you just full of questions?" He took her elbow, ushering her out to the truck with a firm hand.

"I didn't realize it was a problem, Jason. I mean, usually you are all over a willing woman, right?"

"Usually, yes, but not tonight."

"What is it? You won't take advantage of me?" She yanked her arm out of his grasp. "I mean really. I am free, white, and over twenty-one. I'm willing. I'm eager to sample what you have to offer. What's the deal?"

"That's right. I'm not taking advantage of you."

"If you don't want to fuck me, then just say it. I can find someone else to ease the ache, cowboy."

He dragged her into his embrace with a hand on both of her upper arms until her breasts were squashed against the hard plains of his chest. "Let's get one thing straight, babe. I'm gonna fuck you sooner or later, but not tonight. It's not the right time for us and that's all I'm sayin'."

As she drew in a breath to tell him where to take his right time, he slammed his mouth down on hers in a lip crushing kiss meant to melt any resistance she might have. Not that she would resist at all. This is what she wanted from the moment she locked gazes with this gorgeous hunk of manflesh.

She softened her lips until they molded to the hard line of his. He growled low in his throat as he wrapped his arms around her back and pulled her in tighter. When she brushed her tongue against the seam of his lips, he lost control, bruising her lips to deepen the kiss even further.

He finally pulled back far enough she could see the glittering of his blue eyes in the moonlight overhead. "Don't push me, babe."

"Why not, stud? I can handle you."

"Right now, you wouldn't be able to. I'm horny enough to break you in half."

"I can take it." The tip of her fingernail skipped over the buttons as she raked it down his chest. "Let's stay here and fuck like bunnies."

"You don't understand."

"I want you."

"I know."

"Then why not?"

"Peyton, please don't push this."

She sighed and stepped out of his embrace. "Fine. Let's go the bonfire."

The physical relaxing of his shoulders told her he was relieved she'd backed off. Oh, she understood all right, probably more than he knew. He didn't want her. That's fine, she guessed, even though disappointment raced through her. She'd never had a man turn her down before. Didn't they all want sex whenever or wherever they could get it? A man like Jason Young didn't turn down anyone she'd ever seen when she'd had the chance to observe him at the bar. He *always* went home with someone. What was it about her that turned him off? The piercings? The tats? Well to hell with him then. She couldn't do anything about those things if they were a problem for him. If he didn't like them, then so be it. They were a part of her, part of her personality. Maybe he didn't like them on his woman even though he had tats himself? She shrugged as she grabbed the door to his truck to open it and haul herself inside. She'd ride this pony as far as it would go, then move on with her life. There were other fish in the sea and plenty of men to choose from.

Without another word between them, they drove back to the main ranch house where she could see the roaring fire licking at the sky with the bright orange flames. Such a cowboy thing, a bonfire. Well maybe not, she did like camping out and sitting by a fire cuddling with some guy. Not that she'd done it in a long time, but it was still nice to sit under the blanket of an inky sky with stars twinkling above. Someday, she'd get the chance to spread out a soft quilt in the back of a pickup, lay her head on a guy's chest and stare at the sky for hours. Why had her daydreams always seemed to revolve around Jason lately, she wasn't sure, but she needed to put it behind her. He apparently wasn't attracted to her that way.

Maybe he liked men?

Nah, that was stupid. His prowess with the women of Bandera bordered on legendary.

So why wasn't he interested in her?

She shrugged. Oh well. Time to move on.

As soon as he parked the truck, she jumped out and slammed the door behind her. No more waiting on or dreaming of Jason Young. He was part of the past now.

"Hey Peyton!" Jonathan shouted, coming to his feet from his spot at the fire. "You got cleaned up easy enough."

"Yeah."

Jonathan glanced at her, then back to Jason. "Oh. I see."

The dejected look on his face gave her an idea. Jonathan seemed like a nice enough guy, maybe a little shy and nerdy, but what the hell. Jason didn't want her. That stung her pride a little. Maybe one of the other Young brothers might quell the itch she had before the night concluded. She moved right to his side and sat down. "Sit with me."

"Uh, okay." He swiped his palms down the leg of his jeans before he took a seat next to her, glancing quickly at his brother.

Jason frowned, but didn't say a word as he took a seat opposite them across the fire.

"So what do you do around the ranch, Jonathan? I don't see you in The Dusty Boot like your brothers very often."

"I'm not much of a drinker."

"You don't have to drink to come to the bar. There are pool tables, dancing, darts, all kinds of things to do not involving alcohol."

"True, but I'm not real comfortable in bars. I like spending time with the website and marketing for the ranch. It keeps me busy most days."

"Do you do the cowboy stuff much?"

"Not really. I leave that to my brothers." He shifted so his hips weren't quite touching hers anymore. "I ride. You can't grow up on a ranch and not ride, but I'm not as comfortable on a horse or herding cattle as my brothers are. I mean look at Jason? He's all about the cowboy stuff. He wants to breed bulls for the PBR."

"PBR?"

"Professional Bull Riders Association." He smiled down at her. "You don't do cowboy much, do you?"

"No." She laughed. "Is it so apparent I'm lacking in the Texas pastime?"

"Yeah, a little. Do you know anything about a cattle ranch?"

"Not really. Why don't you teach me," she said, looping her hand through the crook of his arm. "I'm eager to learn." She glanced across the fire and noticing Jason's eyes narrowed, their gazes locked in a battle of wills.

"Well, we run longhorns on our property. They are one of the original cattle to be raised here in the Texas Hill Country. They are a hearty breed of cattle who do well here where the land isn't so grassy and plentiful. Our ranch is pretty big for one out here where several of the local ranches are selling off to developers. Jeff has been very adamant about us not selling off any of our property to them. Keep everything in the family, you know."

"Is Jeff like the foreman?"

"Yeah, pretty much. He's tight reined on what goes on around here although he's mellowed out a lot since Terri came along."

"Didn't she just have a baby?"

"Yeah, not too long ago." He shifted on his seat. "We also have guests we rent out rooms and cabin space to, especially in the summer months. They come from all over to learn about cattle ranching, I guess. I'm not quite sure what the fascination with it is, but they pay to come. It's a great income for the ranch when selling cattle isn't paying so much."

"How fascinating."

Jonathan's voice faded as he went on to talk about the website building for the ranch. Not like she wasn't interested, but the glare she was receiving from Jason had shivers rolling down her back. *Why does he have to affect me this way? Damn cowboy.*

"So that's what I do all day," Jonathan finished.

"Wow. Sounds like you really stay busy."

"I try. There's a lot to do when you are marketing a guest ranch plus managing the website for both the cattle ranch and the guest ranch. We have two websites. One for buyers of the cattle and one for guests of the ranch."

"Care to take a walk with me?"

"Uh, sure. I can show you the front of the main lodge. It's pretty cool all lit up with the lights."

"Awesome." She rose to her feet, not relinquishing her hold on his arm as they headed for the front part of the ranch. The tingling along her back let her know Jason's gaze followed their every move, making her wonder whether he would come after her.

As they rounded the house toward the front, she caught a glimpse of someone sitting in one of the rocking chairs, but the moment she turned her head to ask Jonathan about the man, the figure on the porch had disappeared. *Weird.*

"We have the rocking chairs out here for people to sit so they can enjoy the sunrise or evening air. It's really cool out here in the early mornings."

"Are you an early riser?"

"Yeah, most of the time I'm out here by myself with a cup of coffee before anyone else is even up. Joey and Jeff are up with the sun most mornings too, dealing with the ranch stuff."

"I bet the cowboy life tends to do that to you. Does Jason get up early too?" *Damn, Peyton! Just shut up about him.* "Never mind. None of my business."

"Are you two having a fight or somethin'."

"No, why?"

"Well, you left with him earlier and came to the bonfire with him." He pulled her hand out from around his arm. "I don't mess with my brother's girl."

"I'm not his girl."

"Then why did you leave with him?"

"He offered to wash my clothes after I got in the mud."

"You were naked at his house?"

Well, fuck a duck. She stepped from his side to take a seat on one of the rockers. "Yeah, I guess you could say that, although I wore one of his shirts the whole time my clothes were in his washer."

"Listen, Peyton. You're a really nice girl and I think you're hot, but I won't come between the two of you."

"There isn't anything between me and Jason, Jonathan. Trust me. He doesn't want me."

"I can't see why not. You're beautiful."

"Thanks, but apparently he doesn't think so. I mean he could have had me any time he wanted me, but he won't. I don't know what to think."

Jason's voice penetrated the darkness as he came around the corner. "Jonathan."

"Jason."

"Peyton."

"Jason. What do you want?"

"Nothin'. I wanted to make sure everything was okay."

"Everything is fine. I'm having a great conversation with your brother."

"It's not what it looks like, Jase."

"It doesn't matter, Jonathan. There isn't anything going on between me and Peyton anyway."

Just as I thought.

"I won't step on toes, Jason, you know that."

"No toes here, buddy." Jason clapped Jonathan on the shoulder. "Go for it."

Bastard. "Thanks for giving him permission to pursue me, you asswipe!"

"What?"

She stood up, bringing her five-foot-nine-inch frame as close to Jason as possible. Intimidation wasn't her strong point, but rage at his audacity washed through her now. "Just because you don't want me, doesn't mean other men don't. I can get a guy if I want one whether you think so or not. I don't need your fucking permission to date someone. There are plenty of men out there."

They stood nose to nose.

"I didn't say you couldn't. I just didn't want there to be any mistake that we were a couple."

"We aren't."

"No, we aren't."

"Then leave me the fuck alone. If I want to date Jonathan, then I will."

"Go ahead."

"Fine!" She turned around only to find Jonathan had melted into the darkness leaving her alone with Jason...again.

* * * *

"What an absolutely infuriating female you are!" He took two steps back and raked his fingers through his hair. He'd never understand women at this rate. "Why can't you leave well enough alone?"

"I wasn't doing a damned thing but talking to your brother."

"He's not your type."

"What the hell do you know!"

"I know you."

"You don't know shit about me."

"You're independent, hard-headed, impossible, stubborn," his voice dropped an octave, "sexy, gorgeous, and hot."

He watched her breath catch in her throat. What the hell was he getting at? He didn't want her, right?

"Leave it be, Jason. You don't want me, remember?"

"I never said that, you did."

"Then why push me away?"

"Because I don't want you…"

"See?"

He grabbed her arm, dragging her back until her breasts brushed his chest. Her nipples puckered at the friction.

"Let me finish." With her lips pressed together, she tempted him beyond reason. He wanted her in the worst way. "I want you between my sheets. Me between your legs eating you until you come all over my face. I want my dick buried so deep in your pussy, you scream my name loud enough to disturb the cattle. My cock aches for the warmth of you wrapped around it."

"Then why?" she asked, her voice barely a whisper.

"You're different."

"Different?"

"I don't know how to explain it. There is something about you. I don't want to just fuck your brains out and walk away the next morning like I've done so many times before. You aren't like all the other women in Bandera. You don't wear cowboy boots. You have a tongue ring, which by the way is hot as hell. You have a tat on your breast." He skimmed his index finger over the swell of her breast where the tattoo sat below her shirt. "I want to explore you way beyond just a quick fuck."

She pushed out of his arms, rubbing her skin like she was cold. "I'm not looking for a relationship, Jason."

"I know you aren't. I don't think I am either, but…"

"But?"

"I wish I knew. I don't want to hurt you, Peyton. I'm afraid if we just fuck, then you'll be hurt by whatever is between us."

"I'm willing to take the chance."

"I'm not sure I am."

"What are you afraid of?"

"You." He'd just bared his soul to the one woman who might be able to crush him and he didn't care. Okay, well a little, but what did it mean? He wasn't supposed to think of any woman as much as he thought about her over the last few months. Every time he'd been at the bar, there she was with her long hair either back in a braid or cascading down her shoulders like it was now. The itch to wrap his hand in those strands and tug overwhelmed him at times. Some other thoughts had him running his fingers through it to feel the silky softness against his palms. She didn't seem to take to one type of man over another. He'd never seen her leave with anyone either. What did she like? What type of man did she go for? His type? He didn't know, but he wanted to find out.

"Why are you so afraid of me? I'm just a woman looking for a good time."

Crack. His resolve split wide open. He had a conversation with his reflection this morning about how he would stop using women for his own pleasure and here this one just threw a noodle into the soup. He exhaled sharply, recalling the conversation he had with his mother about this very thing. Nina was all over him about his playboy ways. *But, I'm only in my twenties. I shouldn't be thinking of settling down with one woman, right?*

Peyton laughed, drawing him out of his reverence. "Don't sound so relieved, Jason. I told you before I'm not in for a relationship right now, just to relieve a little pressure between the thighs if you're willin'."

"I'm willin'."

"Then shall we go back to your place to heat up some sheets?" she asked, running her tongue around the shell of his ear.

His cock jumped behind the fly of his jeans. It seemed like he'd been forever horny around her, but tonight would see the end of his self-induced torture…he hoped.

Chapter Four

The truck no more stopped at the front of the house and they were both out of the vehicle locked in an embrace. They stumbled together toward the front door, his mouth on hers, doing his best to get her clothes off in the process. A shirt here, another there. Nothing mattered but getting him naked and between her thighs.

She ached for this man.

The calluses on his palm abraded her nipple into a tortured point as Jason walked her backward down the hall from the front room to his bedroom. His mouth never left hers. Their tongues tangled as they explored in a way she hadn't before. *I think he plans to devour me.*

He lifted his head when they reached the door to his room and he backed her against the expanse. "I hope you plan on spending the entire night because it's going to take me that long to find all your hot spots."

"If you want me to."

"Oh yeah. I plan on fucking you every which way but up."

"I can't wait."

He turned the knob on the door as his mouth dove for hers again. He flipped the light on only seconds before he scooped her up and deposited her onto the bed, then followed her to the mattress. Somewhere along the path to the bedroom, he'd lost his shirt. The hair on his chest tickled against her breasts as she moaned into his mouth. She wanted him so badly, she could feel the wetness between her legs. This kind of thing didn't happen with a man or hadn't before. It normally took her a bit to get going, but not with Jason. *Figures.*

"I can smell you," he whispered against her neck before raking his teeth along the curve of her throat.

Shivers danced along her arms and legs. The weight of his body on hers felt right, so right. The warmth of his skin singed her body with a delicious heat all its own. She wrapped her jean clad legs around his hips, urging him on with a raise of her pelvis. Need had her in its claws, ripping at her sanity a little at a time.

His lips skimmed over the slope of her shoulder on their journey to her breast. A gasp escaped her mouth the moment he closed over the tip. Desire exploded through her, soaking her panties in preparation for him.

He lifted his head momentarily as the soft whisper of breath pulled the taut bud into an achy point. "Can you come from nipple play?"

"I don't know. "

"Let's try, shall we?"

For a solid ten minutes, he sucked, pulled, pinched, bit and tortured her nipples until she thought she would go mad. They were sensitive, yes, but she'd never had a man focus solely on tormenting them until she thought she would lose her mind. Jason did. Her belly clenched as he nipped at the tip with his teeth. *God, I might actually be able to orgasm from this.*

He released her breast much to her dismay, but when his hands worked at the button near her waist, she lifted her hips so he could get her jeans off. A wicked grin spread across his mouth as he tossed one boot, then the other before he whipped the pants down and off in one tug.

When his lips returned to nip at the achy peak of her left breast, his finger did a slow crawl from her knee, up her thigh, across the mound of pubic hair to glance off her clit. She exploded into a body numbing orgasmic kaleidoscope of colors behind her closed eyelids. "Jason!"

He lifted his head, revealing the smug grin on his face. "There it is. I knew you could do it."

Her breath came out in a halting seesaw of air as she tried to bring her heart rate back to normal. "That was…"

"Awesome?"

"Amazing. Do it again."

One eyebrow rose over his eye like he couldn't believe she asked that. Honestly, she couldn't believe she asked it of him. She wasn't a demanding lover. Normally things were all about pleasing the guy, right? Wasn't it supposed to be all about the guy? Half the time, she'd be lucky to even orgasm once when she had sex. "I mean, if you want to that is."

"Oh, I want and you'll get, babe. No doubt. It turns me on somethin' fierce to watch you come."

"Really?"

"What the hell kind of men have you been with?"

She shrugged as she tried to close her legs, but his body had her trapped open and ready for him. "I don't know. I don't get a lot out of it sometimes."

His hand moved between her legs, scooping up her cum on his fingers before he spread it around her clit. "Not with me, darlin'. I take care of my women."

Women. That's not what I want to hear. "I'm sure you do, cowboy."

"You'll see. You'll be walkin' funny tomorrow if I have anything to say about it and in my house, I do." He slid down her body, kissing his way from her breasts, across her belly, and down between her thighs.

Her breath caught in her throat as his mouth hovered over her pussy. The first swipe of his tongue had her hips coming off the bed as a groan escaped her lips. There wasn't anything better than a starving man feasting on her pussy. Not that she'd had it very often, but she loved it when they did this. "Oh God, please, Jason, don't stop."

"I don't plan to until you come all over my face."

The rough pad of his tongue drove her desire higher. Each swipe and each lick had her hips meeting his face as she lifted her pelvis. He laid one arm across her hips to keep her down. With her fingers tangled in his hair, she rode out the sensations to the peak of fulfillment as she screamed his name again at the top of her lungs.

"We can try for a little louder, darlin'. I don't think they heard you at the main lodge."

"Bastard," she gasped, panting hard. The nerves down there jumped in an erratic rhythm as she came down from her high. "Now you."

"I'm good. I'll be nice and snug in your warm place here in a minute."

"But I should give you head or something."

"You don't have to."

"Seriously? I thought all guys liked getting head?"

"I'm not saying I don't like it or I don't want it, but tonight is about you and your needs. I want to make sure you never forget tonight."

"Oh I won't," she whispered, taking his face between her hands to bring his mouth to hers. "I've been waiting for this for a long time."

He kissed her slow, long and deep, meshing their mouths together like they'd done this a thousand times before. Maybe they had in another life. The thought of it made her mind spin out of control.

"Mmm. Hang on. I need to get a condom out of my wallet."

"Okay."

He moved off her to remove his boot and pants. When his cock sprang free, she sighed in appreciation. He really was built in all the right places, long, heavily muscled legs, trim hips, flat, washboard abs, muscular chest with just a bit of dark chest hair, and kissable lips. When he bent over to retrieve his wallet from the back pocket of his pants, she got a nice view of his taut ass. *Holy shit! No wonder it looks so nice in Wranglers.*

"Appreciatin' the view?"

"Oh yeah. You have a nice ass."

"Why thank you, ma'am."

"Don't call me ma'am. You're older than I am."

"Why? It's a term of endearment."

"For your mother or grandmother maybe."

"No. It's a sign of respect from any cowboy to a woman. Haven't you had anyone call you ma'am before?"

"Yeah, but it's usually at work when they open the door for me."

"Well then, there you go."

"Call me darlin'."

"You like that do you?" he asked, his eyes glittering in the lamplight as he cocked his head to the side.

"Yes. There is somethin' about a cowboy calling me darlin'."

"I'll do it any time you want, darlin'."

She shivered as he rolled the condom over his erection before he slowly came toward her in a deliberate, almost panther like saunter. *Damn, he is what wet dreams are made of, at least mine anyway.* "Fuck me, Jason."

"My pleasure, darlin'."

He moved between her thighs, settling himself in the cradle of her pelvis. The moment he slid his cock slowly between her pussy lips, she thought she'd died and gone to heaven. With his cock slowly being pushed inside her, she gasped at the first moment of penetration. A soft moan escaped with each inch. He fit perfectly.

When he was completely inside her, she sighed with the fullness and rightness of having him there. "You feel good."

"Oh, babe, you have no idea how good you feel. Warm, wet, just right."

As he started to move his hips, she wound her legs around behind him. He slowly moved inside her, driving her mad with want as he painstakingly brought her to the brink of insanity again before he would let her fall over. She'd fool him though. She doubted she could come again after having two orgasms already, but he could try—and lord help her, she wanted him to with everything inside her.

"You'll have another before I'm through."

"I can't."

His hand slid down between them. "You will."

"Jason."

"Peyton."

"Do it hard."

"Oh yeah." With a snap of his hips, he drove his cock deep inside her.

Her stomach clenched as he hit her G spot with each thrust. She didn't think she'd ever had a G spot orgasm, but she just might tonight.

His pace increased until he was slamming his cock inside her so hard, she had to brace herself on his headboard to keep from banging her head. "Yes, yes, yes."

She felt his finger on her clit, rubbing first one side and then the other before he took the wetness seeping between them and spread it around the tip. She thought her head would blow off as her body exploded in a mind-numbing orgasm that left her shaking each time he shoved his cock inside her again.

"Oh God," he whispered as he came to a shuddering halt. "Fuck yeah."

He collapsed on top of her with his face resting in the crook of her neck. She smoothed her hands down his sweaty back as their bodies pulsed and shivered together until their hearts stopped galloping out of their chests. He'd just given her the best sex of her life.

Chapter Five

Her fingertips felt soft against his back as he allowed himself the comfort of her arms. He didn't usually do this, cuddle thing with women after they had sex, but with Peyton, it felt right.

"That was somethin', cowboy."

"I'm glad you enjoyed yourself."

"Oh definitely." She grunted. "But you need to get off my chest so I can breathe. You're kind of heavy."

He laughed as he rolled to her side. "Better?"

She gasped a few breaths. "Yeah."

"Sorry."

"No problem. I'm just not used to a couple hundred pounds of manflesh on my chest."

With his finger, he tucked a strand of stray hair behind her ear before he kissed her nose. "You were fantastic."

"Thanks."

"Are you not used to having orgasms or somethin'?"

"Why do you say that?"

"Because you acted like having three was out of the question."

"I've never had three with a guy before. Half the time, I'm lucky to get one."

"You're with the wrong man then, darlin'."

"Apparently so." She skimmed her hand down his chest. "I think you're the right man."

"For now."

"Yeah, for now."

He swung his legs over the side of the bed and sat up. "Do you want something to drink? I'm kind of parched after all the exercise."

"I could use some water, if you have some."

"Bottled or tap?"

"Either is fine. I'm assuming you are on well water?"

"Yep. Best water in the territory right here on Young property."

She pushed herself up on the bed and shoved a couple of strands of hair off her forehead. "Tap is fine then."

He stopped to stare for a minute thinking she had to be the prettiest thing he'd ever seen in his bed. Of course, he hadn't had anyone in this bed before now, but she was a great first.

"What?"

"Nothing. Why?"

"You're staring." She smiled as her cheeks turned a slight shade of pink.

"You're beautiful."

She crossed her arms over her chest to hide her breasts. "No I'm not."

"Yes, you are." He shook his head to clear his thoughts. "I'll be right back." A pair of old sweat shorts sat on the floor, so he grabbed them, disposed of the condom in the trash before he pulled the pants on and went out the door toward the kitchen. No use getting all gooey over her. She already said she didn't want anything to happen beyond tonight. Things had been hotter than the Fourth of July between them though. He hadn't come so hard in his life until this moment with her. What made her so special? Yeah, she's pretty, got a great set of knockers, killer ass, and lips a man would die to have wrapped around his cock, but other than that?

"Isn't that enough?"

Well maybe, but I don't want anything permanent either.

Once he reached the kitchen, he grabbed a soda from the refrigerator and a glass for some water from the cabinet. As he filled the glass, he glanced out the window. He could see the glow of the lights from the main lodge house in the distance. He loved his family, but he was glad he built his place far enough away so he could have his own privacy. Now if he could just finish the house, he might actually think about settling down. The thought startled him. Never in a million years would the thought cross his mind any other time. Why tonight? Why after he made love to Peyton? He shook his head. No, he fucked her. Plain and simple. He didn't make love to any woman.

"Jason? Everything okay?"

"Yeah. I'll be right there." He shook his head as he headed back into the bedroom. He had a waiting, willing woman in his bed for the night. He would think about the rest later.

When he walked back into the bedroom, he found the most amazing sight. Peyton lay on his pillow with her hair fanned out like a cloud around her head, her legs spread apart and her fingers working her clit.

"I started without you."

"Holy shit, woman, that's hot."

"What? Never seen a woman pleasure herself before?"

"It doesn't matter if I have or not, I've never seen you do it. That is about the sexiest thing I've ever seen."

"I want you again."

"Fuck yeah."

"Are you up for an all-night rodeo, handsome?"

"More than up for it." He watched her gaze drop to the front of his shorts as they tented from his erection standing straight and hard against his abdomen.

"I see." She gave him a come-hither look as she continued to pleasure herself. "If you don't hurry, I might come all by myself."

"I'd like to see that."

"Would you now?"

"Uh-huh."

"Sorry, cowboy. After you made me climax three times, I think it'll take a little more stimulation to get me there again."

"Is that a challenge?"

"Only if you want it to be."

"You're on, babe." He handed her the glass of water and took a sip from the can in his hand. "Drink up. You'll need to stay hydrated if we plan on ridin' until mornin'."

"Will you take me home?"

"What? Now?"

She laughed. "No, in the morning."

"Of course, I will. I never push my women out of my bed until they're ready to leave."

"There it is again." A frown marred her pretty face as her lips thinned into an aggravated line.

"What?"

"Your women. Can we not discuss the women before me? Not that I have any foolhardy notion that there weren't hundreds before me and will be hundreds after me, but I really don't like hearing about them."

"Sorry."

"Thank you." She finished her water before setting the glass on the nightstand. "Now, where were we?" She raked her fingernails down his chest. "Oh yeah, right about here." His shorts dropped to the floor as she took his cock in her palm.

Fuck yeah.

His cock swelled even more when she opened her mouth and took the head between her full lips. *Good God.* He thought he would die right there. His legs shook. His cock ached. His balls felt like they would implode. When she moved one hand down between his legs, he though his head would spin around. "Oh God." The slide of her tongue ring on the underside of his cock drove him wild.

She hummed deep in her throat as she took the rest of his cock into her mouth. His legs almost buckled as his breath lodged in his chest. He cupped her head between his palms, threading his fingers through the thick strands of her gorgeous hair. He wanted to wrap a hand in those brown strands and pull so badly, he ached with it.

"Mmm."

Fuck, he was about to lose it down her throat if she didn't stop and he didn't want to come that way. He wanted the warmth of her pussy around him when he lost his load. "Peyton, stop."

She grabbed his ass cheeks in both hands, scooted closer and held on.

"I can't hold...*fuck!*" He exploded into her mouth, shooting his entire load of cum straight down her throat in a climax so violent, his whole body shook from the force. "Baby, I didn't want to come like that."

She wiped her face with the back of her hand. "I wanted you to. You don't taste half bad. A little salty, but overall, not bad."

After he sank down on the edge of the bed to catch his breath, he turned to smile at her. It had been a long time since a woman had sucked him off. Not as if he didn't like it when they did, but he usually took care of them, not the other way around. "Thank you."

"For what?"

"For sucking me off. You didn't have to."

"I know. I wanted to." She tilted her head to the side. "Don't tell me you've never had a woman suck you off before."

He pushed a strand of hair behind her ear. "That's not it at all, it's just I don't let them do it very often. I'm more interested in taking care of you rather than you take care of me."

With a shrug of her shoulders, she said, "Well I wanted to take care of you for a change. I'll get mine. I'm sure you'll take care of me."

"Most definitely." He reached over to caress her breast with his right hand. The full mound of flesh fit perfectly in his palm. "You have fantastic tits."

She laughed.

"What's so funny? I'm being serious here."

"Tits?"

"Oh. Sorry. Breasts."

"It doesn't bother me, but I think it's kind of funny to have them referred to as tits when you are in the middle of having sex unless it's rough and tumble sex."

"Do you want rough and tumble sex? I can accommodate, I'm sure."

"How about you fuck me against the wall?" she asked, glancing up at him through her lashes.

"I could since this room is about the only one in the house with walls."

"Sounds like fun."

"First you need prepped."

"Prepped?"

"Lie back and spread those gorgeous thighs for me."

"Oh, I can do that."

She leaned back on her elbows on the pillow with her legs open. Her pussy glistened with juices already wetting the pink surface. *Good God, in heaven.* She had a nice pussy, all plump and ready for his mouth. The smell of her arousal tempted him beyond endurance as he situated himself between her legs. His shoulders kept her thighs spread when he rubbed his whiskered cheek over the sensitive area. He swiped one finger down her slit, from her clit to her waiting opening. "You're so sexy."

"Taste me. I want your tongue," she whispered, watching when he inhaled her scent right before he went in for more of her taste.

She relaxed back against the pillows, her gaze never leaving his face. With both hands, she cupped her breasts, pinching the nipples as she rolled them between her fingers. Soft little moans escaped her mouth, fueling his already out of control libido.

Her engorged clit peeked out from beneath its hood, waiting for a nip of his teeth. He didn't disappoint. Her hips surged up as a hearty groan exploded from her mouth.

"Yes. More."

Juices flowed from her, coating his tongue and chin. *Such sweetness from a beautiful woman.*

He continued to lick, suck and nibble at her flesh until everything turned a bright red. She exploded in a bone shaking, body trembling orgasm.

"Fuck," she gasped that desperate, breathless sound only a satisfied woman can make.

"Now I'm going to pound into you so hard and so fast, you'll make those little mewing sounds I love so much."

"I don't mew."

"Wanna bet? You made them when I fucked you last time, but this time, it's going to happen with each thrust." He picked up her boneless body, wrapping her legs around his hips as he slid inside her hot, waiting warmth. With her clasping his cock so tight, he thought she might break it in half, he pushed her against the wall, pulled her legs up over his forearms and slammed into her.

"Ah, God."

"Oh yeah." The little mewling sounds escaped her mouth with each thrust, earning a smile from him. He knew she would. She was as responsive as a woman could get and he loved hearing the sounds coming from her mouth. "That's it, kitten. Come for me."

"I can't." A gasp escaped her lips.

"Yes you can, baby. Yes you can."

"Please."

"Please what, darlin'?"

"Harder. God, please harder."

He spread his legs to give himself a little more leverage. The change in angle had his balls drawing up against his groin in preparation for his own release. If he didn't clamp down on his orgasm, he'd come before her. That wasn't an option in his world.

The *slap, slap, slap* of wet flesh echoed in the room. The smell of sex drove his desire higher.

Her pussy clamped down on his cock as the flesh quivered. She was going to come if he had anything to say about it. If only he could reach her clit. "Reach down and finger yourself."

"What?" Her panting gasps resonated in his ear.

"Finger your clit. Make yourself come."

Her small hand snaked down between them until he could feel her fingers on her clit. Her breathing sped up. Her pussy creamed as she quickly moved her fingers around her clit.

"I'm gonna come."

"Yes."

She screamed his name just as he lost his own battle with holding his orgasm down. He couldn't stop the flow of cum from the end of his dick any more than he could stop the world of spinning. Liquid seeped down between them, coating his thighs.

"Ah fuck!"

* * * *

"What?"

"I forgot the condom." He slowly slid out of her, releasing her legs so she could stand on her own. "God, I'm such a fucking idiot!"

"Easy, slick. It'll be fine."

"No it won't. I never forget a condom unless I've been with a woman a while."

"I'm on birth control. It's fine."

He shoved his hand through his hair in a motion she'd come to realize meant he was agitated. "What about other things? I mean I'm clean."

"Me too." She leaned against the wall for support as her legs still shook from the force of her orgasm. Having so many so close together almost hurt, in a good way. "Not like I fuck around a lot, Jason."

"I didn't think you did, although I really don't know you very well."

"Yet you were willing to fuck my brains out?"

"It's not like that, Peyton. You and me are like two peas in a pod."

"How so?" she asked, moving on shaky legs toward the pile of clothes on the floor. The need to be covered overwhelmed her. Somehow, this wasn't the way she thought their conversation *afterward* should go. Not like she expected professions of love or anything, but she sure didn't think he would go all prude on her.

"We both want the same things. Sex without strings, right?"

"Yep." She slipped her underwear over her feet, and then stood to pull them up.

"What are you doing?"

"Getting dressed."

"Why? I thought you were staying the night?"

"I don't think that is such a good idea."

"I don't understand."

"This is just a fling, Jason, nothing more. I mean, not that I wouldn't mind having sex with you now and again. What happened here tonight proved we're pretty good together. I just don't want anyone to get any ideas we are a couple. If your family sees you taking me home in the morning, they might think there is more to this than there is."

"True."

"Good. Then why don't you put some clothes on so you can run me home." He frowned as he watched her pull her chemise on. "Problem?"

"No. I just like watching you."

"Get dressed?"

"Yeah. It's sexy."

She rolled her eyes as she smiled. Why did she think this guy was the most adorable cowboy she'd ever seen and there had been a few of them in the couple of years she's lived in Bandera. "Put some clothes on, cowboy, so we can go."

"Fine, but don't blame me if we stop somewhere along a back road and fuck again before we get to your place."

"I'm not havin' sex with you in your truck."

"Wanna bet?"

They were both laughing by the time they made it out the door. She really didn't think he'd fuck her on the way home, but sure enough, they stopped at a small gate outside his parents place. "What are you doing?"

"We're gonna fuck again before I get you home."

"Really, Jason. This behavior is so becoming of you. I love it!"

"Good." He pulled through the gate until he found a flat spot near a tree. "I have a couple of sleeping bags behind the seat. Let's fuck under the stars."

The minute he jumped out of the truck, she had to giggle. In all the time she'd been sexually active, she'd never had sex in the back of a pickup under the stars. This would be a first, although she kind of hoped there would be more firsts with him. He kind of turned her upside down and inside out with his kissable lips, luscious body and killer personality. She just hoped she wasn't getting in over her head with him. The last thing she needed to do was fall head over heels in love with a playboy like Jason Young.

Chapter Six

Morning raised its ugly head as Peyton rolled over in her bed. The night before had been what sexy dreams were made of and she didn't want to wake up from that particular dream quite yet. Sunlight poured through the lacy curtains on her window, willing her to open her eyes and face the day, a day without Jason Young next to her. She had the memories though. Those would have to do until the next time she could get him to make love to her like he had last night.

"You are so screwed, Peyton Matthews." She sat up as she pushed the hair out of her face. "The last thing you should be worrying about is getting that man back in your bed. You need to focus on school and work."

She had to work tonight at The Dusty Boot so she rolled back over on her bed and closed her eyes. She'd need the extra sleep if she was going to make it through her two a.m. shift without being tired to the bone.

Her cell jingled on the side of her bed, indicating a text message had come through. *Who could that be? The person obviously doesn't know I don't answer before noon.* She struggled to sit up, realizing again she was completely naked beneath the sheet. When Jason had finally got her home, she'd quickly stripped off her clothes and went to bed since it was three in the morning by then.

After she tucked the sheet around her breasts, she grabbed her phone to check the message.

Hey beautiful. Are you up?

"He seriously thinks he's talking to me at this time of morning?" she grumbled, as she stared at the screen. "He's too damned chipper for nine a.m." She huffed as she tried to decide whether to put the phone back on the nightstand or whether to actually answer his text. After a moment, she decided on the later.

I'm up barely. You're too damned high-spirited for this early. What the hell?

I'm always up early. I'm a cowboy, remember?

Yeah and I'm a bartender who has to work until two in the morning tonight. I planned on sleeping in today.

She laid the phone back on the nightstand before lying back on her soft, comfortable bed, and closing her eyes. Sleep wouldn't come. Flashes of memory bombarded her brain as she relived every touch and every caress from the night before. Her body caught fire. She needed to come…badly, but she couldn't. She hadn't been able to masturbate herself to completion in some time. Not since Charles broke down her self-esteem and made her feel like she wasn't the least bit sexy. Some of the piercings had come from his emotional abuse. She didn't cut, but she felt the need to pierce herself to take care of the heartbreak from him.

"God, I thought I was over this."

Tears burned the back of her eyes as she fought not to cry. Jason thought she was sexy, damn it, so why didn't she believe him. Maybe she needed to talk to him, but how? He didn't want to take this past a physical relationship. Neither did she, right? A man in her life would complicate things. School, life, work. She didn't have time for a man on a regular basis.

"Well sleep is out of the question. Maybe I should take a nice, hot shower and do some house cleaning. That always gets my mind on other things."

School would be starting soon and she needed to focus on that, but for now, she needed to get out of this funky frame of mind so she could start living again. The counselor she saw regularly helped her tremendously and that's why she decided to go into this particular line of work herself. Hopefully someday she would be able to help someone just like her.

She flipped the sheet off before she walked to her dresser to retrieve some clothes. A shower would be a good place to start her day. Maybe taking a nap later so she wouldn't be so damned tired tonight during her shift wouldn't be such a bad idea. "We'll see how things go."

For the next several hours, she cleaned to the tune of country music blaring in her earbuds. She liked different sounds so her music consisted of a wide variety, but today she wanted country and old rock.

Noon rolled around and her stomach reminded her she hadn't eaten.

The doorbell rang, earning a frown from her as she passed the hallway mirror, headed for the door. *Who could that be?*

She opened the door to find a young man smiling sheepishly on her doorstep holding a beautiful bouquet of mixed flowers. "Miss Matthews? Peyton Matthews?"

"Yes."

"These are for you. Sign here, please." He handed her a clipboard for her signature.

"Where did these come from?" she asked as she held it back out for him to take.

After he handed her the vase, he said, "There's a card attached."

The flowers were gorgeous. A huge mixed bouquet with daisies, roses, lilies and flowers she didn't even recognize, spread out in a great arrangement big enough to fill her doorway. "Wow. These are gorgeous. I wonder who they are from." Her hands shook, rattling the flowers in the vase as she moved to set them on the table. She hoped Charles hadn't found her. After she'd run from him a few years ago, she'd done her best to cover her tracks, but there was only so much one woman could do to protect herself.

Peyton now carried a concealed weapon just for that purpose.

Wetness coated her palms as she rubbed them down the thighs of the sweatpants she'd thrown on when she went to clean. Perspiration popped out on her forehead. She didn't want to open the card.

She inhaled sharply. *This is ridiculous. There's no reason to be scared. You've done your best to hide yourself. He would have a hard time finding you in Bandera, Texas.*

Capturing her bottom lip between her teeth, she bit down sharply to bring herself back into focus. The pain helped. She snatched the card from its plastic holder, folded the edge back and yanked it out.

The words blurred a little as she read the sweet card from the man she didn't want to have feelings about, but realized he was getting under her skin a little too quickly.

> *Thanks for last night. You're a sexy, gorgeous woman*
> *and I can't wait to love on you again.*
> *Love Jason*

"How sweet." The swooping in her belly calmed as she read the note again. Jason. She tapped the card against her lips. First the phone call. Then the flowers. What more should she expect from the man?

A smile played on her lips for the rest of the day as she finished cleaning her house, washing her laundry and getting ready for work. She needed to get some food. Her shift started soon. She had to be on top of her game tonight. Saturday's were pretty rowdy at the bar most weekends. Lots of cowboys and cowgirls got a little out of control. Even though it wasn't part of her job to bounce, being a woman, she still needed to know when to call in the troops should someone get too boisterous.

She put on her leather halter top and jeans before she slipped on her cowboy boots. Playing the part of cowgirl wasn't an easy thing for her, but it went with the persona the bar had so she'd do what she needed to. Her breasts were displayed enticingly above the cleavage of her top. The jeans showed off the soft curve of her hips and with the legs tucked into her pink and brown cowboy boots, she figured she played the part well enough.

The clock on the wall chimed eight-thirty, rousing her enough to realize she needed to get moving. The bar waited.

Music blared loudly as she waltzed through the door several minutes later, to find the place in full swing. Cowboy hats and rhinestone jeans took up most of the scenery. Neon lights in every kind of beer graced the wood walls. A band played in one back corner as the dancers two-stepped around the floor. Several people congregated in small groups laughing and having a good time. The place was packed even for a Saturday night.

"There you are. Good thing you're here. It's getting crazy," Dan said, wiping the bar on his end, keeping a close eye on the patrons of his establishment. He owned the bar along with his wife. The big, burly guy was like a father to her and too many of the other women who frequented the place. He seemed to take his job seriously. He didn't like it when some drunk cowboy started coming onto a woman who didn't want the attention.

"I'm on it, Dan." She swung around the bar's long expanse and immediately started working her way down the patrons sitting on her end to see what they needed. Faces blurred as she worked even though her thoughts were never far from the dark-haired cowboy she'd left standing on her porch early this morning.

Time sped by without her even being aware of how fast the clock was ticking until she wiped the sweat from the back of her neck.

"Hey babe."

She glanced up into the green eyes of a man she didn't know. "What can I get you?"

"You."

"Not for sale." She braced her hands on the bar. "What'cha drinkin'?"

"Whiskey straight up."

"Do you want one or two shots?"

"A shot at you."

"Lay off, buddy or I'll cut you off and have you bounced right out of here."

The man rapped his knuckles on the bar. "Fine, give me a shot then."

She poured his drink as she noticed an empty table across the bar the waitress hadn't cleared yet. Figuring she'd clear the glasses so they had more clean ones behind the bar, she wiped her hands and went around the bar's end to head for the table.

The minute she walked near the whiskey guy, he grabbed her around the waist and pulled her into his lap. "I told ya I wanted a shot."

"Let go."

"The lady said let go, mister."

She glanced up into the clear blue gaze of Jason. "I can handle him."

Jason ignored her. "I suggest you let go."

"Or you'll what, cowboy? Me and the lady were gettin' acquainted."

"Jason, I said I can handle this."

"You know him, little lady?"

"Yes, but that's not important. If you don't let me go in five seconds, you're going to lose a couple of teeth."

"I like my women feisty."

The man spun her around in his arms and tried to kiss her. She jammed her hand under his chin, gnashing his teeth together in a grind just as Jason landed a punch to the side. The man let her go as he grabbed his mouth and side simultaneously.

"Fuck!"

She backed up as the man rushed Jason, taking them both to the floor. Fortunately for Jason, the man apparently was already half drunk so he stumbled as they went down with Jason ending up on top. Jason swung, punching the man in the jaw. The man threw a punch, hitting Jason in the eye.

"Stop it!" She pulled on Jason's arm, trying to stop the brawl. "Stop." When they two men continued to throw punches at each other, she hollered for Dan and the bouncer.

The two men pulled Jason and the man apart, allowing them to rise from the floor. "Out. Both of you," Dan told them. "I don't want this kind of shit in my bar."

"But I was helping Peyton," Jason said, wiping the blood from his mouth.

"I can take care of myself, you dumbass."

"You didn't seem to be able to handle him very well, darlin'."

"Don't darlin' me. I had it under control whether you want to believe it or not."

"You needed me. Admit it."

"I didn't need you. I don't need you. Leave me the fuck alone!"

Hurt clouded his eyes, but she didn't care. He needed to know she could take care of herself. She'd made sure of that after the shit went down with Charles. He touched his quickly swelling eye with his fingertips.

"Fine. Call me whenever you get over yourself and realize you want to see me again." He wiped his mouth with the back of his hand before he turned to weave his way through the crowd to the door.

"Fight's over folks. Have a drink, dance, have a good time, but no more fighting," Dan said, pushing her back toward the bar. "You okay?"

"I'm fine."

"What's up between you and Jason Young?"

"Not a thing, why?"

"He seemed awful protective of you for some reason. Not that he wouldn't be around any woman getting manhandled, but I think there's more than meets the eye between you two."

"It's nothing, Dan. He's was being protective. Nothing more."

"Okay, honey, but if you want to talk, let me know. I have a good ear especially where those Young boys come into play. Ask Paige."

"Yeah, see where that got her? She's pregnant by one of them with twins."

He grinned and clamped a hand on her shoulder. "Yeah, but she's happy as a little pig in shit."

Rolling her eyes, Peyton grinned back. She'd give him that. Paige was definitely happy with her Young hunk.

After she took her spot behind the bar, she let her thoughts wander to the triplet who'd taken up residence in her mind for the last several months. *Damn him.* She glanced across the bar only to notice a couple of the other Young boys playing pool. Joshua stood off to one side of the table with the cue in his hands. She couldn't help but notice him since he looked just like Jason. Although she could tell the subtle difference between the two enough to tell them apart even from a distance. Jason carried himself a little differently. More confident? She wasn't sure, but there were definitely differences.

"Hey, can I get a beer?"

She dragged her thoughts back to the job at hand. She still had several hours to go before she could go home and lose herself in her fantasies again.

* * * *

Jason banged his hand on the steering wheel as he drove back toward the ranch. "Son of a bitch!" His hand throbbed from the beating it had taken just a short bit ago. His eye was almost swollen shut after the guy got a good punch off, hitting him in the left eye. He touched the swelling tissue and winced. "Fucker."

A bag of peas from the kitchen freezer would do for the swelling although it wouldn't help his damaged pride.

"What the hell is up with her anyway? I was trying to protect her and she went off on me like I was the one who tried manhandling her."

He didn't get women at all. Here he wanted to be her savior and she chewed him out for it. Didn't women want to be taken care of? Wasn't that what they were all about?

"I might need to talk to Mom on this one. I'm sure she could give me some advice on how to handle Peyton."

He drove through the main gates of the ranch, then up to the house. The light in the office glowed in the darkness so he knew his mother still sat at her desk even though the clock on the dashboard said ten. She really needed to knock off a little earlier, but tonight he needed to ask her advice on the matter of Peyton Matthews.

As he walked up the main lodge door, it opened and closed on its own, earning a frown from him. A chill went through him for a second as he kept walking toward the house. The ghosts around the place kept things lively even though they freaked him out a little sometimes. The cowboy who tended to hang around the main lodge seemed to be the most apparent, but there were others. A faint, distant childish giggle caught his attention for a second before he shook it off and kept moving. He had more important things to do than deal with ghosts tonight.

When he reached the office door, he knocked softly until his mother spun around in her chair. "Oh my. What the heck happened to you, Jason?"

"I got in a fight at the bar trying to protect Peyton."

His mother got up to head for the kitchen with him trailing behind like a lost little boy. "Let's get something to put on that eye before you lose sight in it completely." They moved through the double doors into the kitchen where the long cutting tables sat waiting for the morning meal. Two big walk-in refrigerator/freezers stood off to the left. His mother moved inside one and grabbed a plastic bag of peas. Once she had them wrapped in a cloth, she put it on his eye before she leaned back against the counter waiting for him to talk. "So what happened?"

"Well, I went to the bar after everything was done on the ranch today. I wanted to talk to her."

"You seem pretty friendly with her the other night."

"It's not a big deal, Mom."

"Are you sure?"

"Yeah. We're just having a good time."

"Okay, but I've heard that one before from Joel, Jeff, and most recently Jacob."

"I'm not falling into the trap of a relationship. That's not what this is about. She doesn't want anything and neither do I." He moved the cold sack away from his eye.

She grinned as she crossed her arms over her chest. "If you say so, Jason."

"It's the truth."

"All right, son. I believe you." She pushed his hand back so the frozen peas were on his eye again. "You were watching her while you were at the bar?"

"Well yeah, but just in between pool games with the other guys. Not like I was doing nothing more than watching her as she slung drinks." He shook his hand as his mother glanced at the raw knuckles. "She's really good, you know?"

"I imagine so. She does it for a living, right?"

"Yeah. She works there full time."

"So what happened?"

"Some guy hit on her when she came around the bar. I stepped in because he was all over her. The guy rushed me and we went down on the floor. He got in a couple of good punches before Dan broke it up."

"What did Peyton say about all this?"

"She got pissed off at me! I was trying to help her."

"I get the feeling she's a very independent woman, Jason. She probably thought she could handle the guy."

"That's what she said!" He threw up his hands. "I'll never understand women."

His mother laughed. "Maybe you should be having this conversation with your father."

"But how am I supposed to know how to handle her, Mom?"

"Don't handle her, Jason. She doesn't want you to."

"I don't understand."

"She wants someone to have a good time with. Nothing serious. Am I right?"

"Yeah, that's what she said."

"Then be the guy she wants. Don't force it. If you two are meant to be, then you will be."

"I don't want a permanent relationship, Mom. I'm not ready to settle down."

"Then don't worry about what you and Peyton have. If a good time is all you want, then that's what you should have, but I think there is a little more there than either of you want to admit. It'll happen in time."

He sighed as he put the bag on his eye. "This stuff is so complicated."

"Honey, if it wasn't, everyone would be doing it all the time."

"It was so much easier when I just took my pleasure from the whole thing and moved on. This stuff about giving a shit is for the birds."

"So you do care?"

"Maybe a little. I mean she's a nice girl. She's got her insecurities like any other woman, but I like to see her smile." He shook his head and glanced out the window. "Did you know she has a lot of piercings?"

"Like what?"

"A tongue ring, her ears, and her belly button. She also has a tattoo on her breast for her mother who died of breast cancer."

"Oh?" Nina smiled.

Shit. "I mean I saw it when she had her halter top on tonight at the bar."

She laughed. "Honey, I know you two were together the other night. You couldn't get away from the bonfire fast enough. I think I heard the bedsprings from your house clear over here."

"Sorry."

"Nothing to be sorry for. I'm glad you've found someone you connect with."

"Don't be planning a weddin'." A sneaky little grin spread across her mouth. "And no matchmaker stuff. I've seen your work with my brothers."

"I didn't do anything."

"No, just told Joel to stay away from Mesa, which he turned around to do the opposite. Jeff did the same thing with Terri. I'm sure you had a hand in Paige and Jacob too."

She shook her head innocently. "I didn't have a thing to do with Jacob and Paige. They found their way together without my help."

"But you don't deny interfering in meddling in the other two's relationships."

"Not at all. Those kids were meant to be together. You have to admit, they are much happier now that they've found love."

"True, but I'm not lookin' for love."

"No one is ever looking, Jason. It just finds us when the time is right."

"Well it's not the right time."

She patted his cheek with her hand right before she leaned in and kissed him. "If you say so, son."

Chapter Seven

Peyton sighed as the last of the patrons left the bar at two a.m. It had been a long night and the fight Jason had been in, didn't help. She found herself worrying about it after he'd left. His eye had begun to swell even before he disappeared. The blood on his lips bothered her too. She wanted to hold him, care for him, and the thought drove her nuts. She should call him, but then again she shouldn't. She didn't need him or so she kept telling herself. He could be the hero for some other woman. Not her. She didn't want him to be her hero, right?

"Well, tonight was an interesting night," Dan said, stopping next to where she stood putting clean glasses away.

"It sure was. Same Saturday night we always have, except a few fights tonight."

"One especially."

"Leave it be, Dan."

"He was protecting you, Peyton. Nothing a good man wouldn't do."

"Well I don't need a man to protect me. I take care of myself."

"I know, honey, but guys like Jason need to be the hero sometimes."

"He can be someone else's hero."

"He wants to be yours."

She let out a disgusted sound from deep in her throat, the sound almost like a sigh. She didn't want him to be her hero, right? Well maybe just a little. It was kind of nice to have a guy jump to her defense for a change. Jason didn't need to know that though. He needed to leave her the hell alone to give her some space.

"Think about it, Peyton. He's a good guy."

"I know he is, Dan. I'm not looking for a permanent fixture in my life though. I've got too many things going on to have time for a man."

"You need to make time. Jason isn't the type of man to wait around forever, honey. If you want him, you'd better go after him."

Dan walked back to the other side of the bar to fiddle with the cash register while she contemplated what he said. She knew Jason was a ladies' man. She watched him pick up women every weekend while she worked the bar, not that she was paying attention, mind you, but she'd see the women flock to him. He had a reputation for being good in bed and she could attest to that fact easy enough since he'd rocked her world the night before without much effort at all. Did she want more? She didn't know. The life she'd set up for herself didn't have room for a man in it on a long term basis, but she could do short term fling with him without too much effort on her part, sure enough.

As her cell phone started jingling in her pocket, she wondered who would be calling her this time of night. After she set down the glass rack in her hand, she grabbed it from her pocket and glanced at the screen.

Jason.

"Hey," she said, answering on the third ring. "How is your eye?"

"Fine. Listen I wanted to apologize."

"For what?"

"Trying to take care of your problem for you. I get you're the independent type and I overstepped my boundaries. I'm sorry."

"Did you have a talk with your mother?"

He laughed. "What makes you think so?"

"Because that sounds like something Nina would say. The few times I've had a chance to talk to her, she sounded like a very insightful woman."

"Okay, yeah, but it's true."

"All is forgiven."

"Are you sure? That was too easy."

"What can I say? I don't hold a grudge."

"Thanks." He cleared his throat. "How did work go after I left?"

She continued wiping glasses to put them away as she cradled the phone between her cheek and shoulder. "Smooth as every other Saturday night with a bunch of rowdy cowboys."

"That good, eh?" he asked, laughter in his voice.

"Yep, but at least I didn't get hit on again." She ran the dry towel over the surface of the bar.

"Too bad."

"Why do you say that?"

"I imagine you get hit on a lot."

"Actually, no, I don't. I think a lot of men are put off by my piercings and tats."

"I think they are sexy, especially your tongue ring when you sucked my cock."

"Bad boy."

"You like bad boys, don't you, Peyton?" he asked, his tone now gone serious.

"Yeah, kind of." Shivers rolled down her back as he dropped his voice into a low growl.

"Do you want me to come by your place tonight?"

"I think it's a bit late for any extracurricular activities tonight, don't you think, Jason? It is two in the morning."

"I'm up for it."

"I bet you are, cowboy, but I think I'll pass. I'm really tired since I didn't get to sleep in this morning and I cleaned house all day before I came to work."

"Sorry about the text earlier."

"No problem. It's fine. Oh, thank you for the flowers by the way. They're beautiful."

"It wasn't a big deal."

He almost sounded shy and unsure of himself on the phone. "It was to me. You'll never guess what?"

"What?"

"Those are the first flowers I've ever gotten."

"Really? A beautiful woman like you?"

"I guess I never found the right guy."

"I'm the right guy then."

"I suppose so." Silence stretched for several minutes while she continued to clean and stock before it was time to leave. "You still there?"

"Yeah."

"I better go. I'm almost done here and I need to head home."

"Let me walk you to your car."

She laughed as she blushed. "How? You're at home."

"No, I'm not."

"You're not?"

"I'm outside the bar."

"You've been out there this whole time we've been talking on the phone?" she asked, peeking out the blinds to see his truck sitting near the curb with him leaning on the hood talking on his cell phone.

"Yeah."

"You're a nut."

"Are you going to let me walk you to your car?"

"If you insist."

"I do."

"Let me grab my purse and I'll be right out."

"Okay. See you in a minute."

She clicked the phone shut as she shook her head. "The silly guy is standing outside by the curb talking to me on his cell."

"Sounds like he's smitten," Dan replied, heading toward the back office. "Bitten by the bug."

"I'm headed out."

"Okay. Be careful going home. I'll see you tomorrow."

"Yep. You be careful too. Talk to you then," she said, pushing open the door and locking it behind her with the key Dan had given her. She turned around to face the gorgeous man standing not ten feet from her. He made her breathless just looking at him. The floodlight on the street shadowed his face beneath his cowboy hat so she couldn't see his eyes, but she knew they stared right through her. She could feel the heat of his gaze without seeing his face. "Hi."

"Hi yourself."

"How's your eye?"

"Swollen shut almost."

"I'm sorry. You shouldn't have been hurt defending me."

"I wanted to or I wouldn't have."

"I can take care of myself."

"I know you can, babe, but I wanted to help and you shut me down."

"I don't need a hero."

"Yes you do and I want to be your hero."

"You don't understand. I haven't needed anyone for a long time."

"We all need someone sometimes."

"Not me."

"Yeah, even you." He ran his finger down her cheek. "Even a tough girl like you needs a man once in a while." His hand snaked around the back of her neck, pulling her in close. "I'm going to kiss you now."

"What about your lip?"

"My lip can handle a little lovin' from you."

"I'm glad because I want to kiss you too."

He tilted his head to the side as his lips brushed hers. She wanted more, so much more. The feel of his mouth brought with it the memories from his loving the night before. She found herself pushing her tongue into his mouth, capturing his tortured groan with her own. As they kissed, her world spun out of control. She'd come to need this man more than she ever thought possible in such a short time.

"Come home with me." She gasped as his hand found her breast.

"Are you sure?"

"Yes. I need you." He pushed his palm against the crotch of her jeans, grinding the stiff fabric into the engorged button between her legs. She moaned softly. "Please."

"Anything you want, darlin'."

"I want you."

"Let me walk you to your car and I'll follow you home."

"Okay." The breathless sound of her voice echoed in the dark night surrounding them. *God, I sound desperate, but I don't care.*

Within a few short minutes, they pulled into the driveway at her place as he parked his truck behind her. Was this crazy? She thought so, but really they probably only had tonight. He'd go on his way, find someone else to fuck on a regular basis, and she'd be alone…again.

The moment she stepped out of her car, he swept her up into his arms before he walked toward the front door. She squeaked as he picked her up, but ended up winding her arms around his neck. His scent drew her into his web of seduction as she found the crook of his neck with her nose. "You smell nice."

"Thanks. I showered before I came back to town."

"For me?" she asked when he stepped up on the porch.

"Yep. I needed to get the blood off my face and a shower felt good."

"I'm glad. Freshly washed cock is the best."

"You don't say?"

"Oh yeah." She fumbled with the key from her perch in his arms. He waited patiently as she jammed it into the lock and turned, then opened the door.

"We could always take another shower. I'm kind of partial to freshly washed pussy too."

Once he released her legs, she slid down his body, noting every bulge, muscle and contour of his impressive frame. "Oh, sounds like fun. I need one after the smoke and stink of the bar."

"Then let's share it. I'd like to soap every inch of you."

She took his hand, leading him toward the back where the bathroom stood off her bedroom. The place seemed small, but since it was just her, it didn't matter. Although, being such a big guy, the place felt even smaller. She'd bought the house with the inheritance from her mother when she passed. It was the only thing she owned outright, but it gave her the peace of mind knowing she always had a place to live.

"How long have you lived here?" he asked, following her to the bathroom.

"Not too long. A year or so."

"I thought you'd been in Bandera longer than that."

"A little. A couple of years is all though."

"Where'd you move from?"

"Can we not talk about me?"

"I want to know more about you."

"Why?" She turned on the shower and let the temperature adjust to warm as she stripped off her clothes.

He shrugged as he changed the subject. "I really like that top on you."

"I like it too."

Her clothing quickly found its way to the floor as she glanced at him through her lashes. "Are you going to shower with your clothes on?"

"Nope, but I'm enjoying watching you strip."

"You should have said so. I would have done a little strip tease for you."

"You did fine, darlin'."

Shivers raced down her back. She loved when he called her that. "Do I get to undress you?"

"If you'd like."

She bit her bottom lip as she concentrated on undoing each button down the front of his western shirt, one at a time, very slowly. His chest was such a sculpture of flesh, she wanted to trace every inch of it with her fingertips. With a sharp tug on the tails of his shirt, she released them from the waistband of his jeans. What was it about Wranglers and a cowboy butt? She didn't know, but damn they sure looked good.

His belt came next as she tugged on the buckle to release it from the hole with a clank. "These things are pretty heavy."

"Yeah, but they do a good job of holding up a pair of jeans."

"I don't want it to hold anything up at the moment."

"Neither do I. I can't wait to feel you wrapped around me. It feels like it's been ages."

"It's only been a day."

He skimmed his hands down her arms as she worked on his belt. "I know, but I've been thinking about it all day. My dick has been so hard for you, I almost had to take care of my problem myself. I haven't had to do that for some time."

Once she had the zipper down, she shoved his pants to the floor, releasing the impressive length of his cock to her hand. She loved his cock. The length seemed to fit just right in her palm, her mouth or her pussy. A soft moan escaped his lips as she palmed him.

"Nice. I like when you make those soft little moaning sounds."

"Kind of like when you make the mewing sounds I like so much," he whispered, guiding her hand to the rhythm he liked as she cupped his balls. "Like a little kitten looking for its mother."

"This kitten has claws." She raked her nails down the length of his cock.

"Oh yes, she does."

He shivered, earning a smile from her. She loved torturing him beyond his control, just a little. It made him a man she could do such delicious things with and not feel guilty about her weird sense of need in the bedroom.

When she finally got him fully undressed, she turned toward the shower to step inside. Hot water cascaded down over her head as she dunked herself under the spray. Warm hands covered her breasts, kneading the flesh. He pinched her nipples between his thumb and first finger as she groaned deep in her throat. No mewing sounds when he did that. Those earned a hearty groan of satisfaction.

"Your breasts are very sensitive."

"Yes they are."

"I love them."

"I'm glad." She reached for his cock to palm the long, thick shaft, earning another moan from him. "I like your dick."

"Such a dirty mouth."

"No, I just believe in calling it what it is. It's a dick or cock and I enjoy it very much." A few pumps of her hand had him swelling even further while she managed to massage his balls.

"I love it when you touch my balls."

"Good." She dropped to her knees right before she enveloped his cock in her mouth. The indescribable sounds coming from his mouth made her hotter. She loved giving head to a guy who appreciated the talent a woman had when they sucked them off or just brought them to a higher plane of pleasure. She wouldn't suck him to completion this time. Nope. She wanted all his hard flesh deep inside her pussy when he exploded in rapture, but she'd make sure he was good and hard when that happened.

After several minutes, she stood again, taking his mouth with hers. She wondered if he thought it was sexy to taste himself on her tongue like she did. It made her hotter to taste her essence in his mouth when he went down on her. Too bad he wouldn't be able to do that in the shower. The confined quarters made it impossible.

Their tongues dueled from her mouth to his and back again in the most erotic dance she'd ever witnessed. She loved kissing him so passionately he lost control and ground his mouth against hers. Rough sex turned her on. Forcing a man to lose it while they had sex brought her desire to the peak.

When she finally moved her head to his ear, she growled. "Fuck me hard."

He grabbed her around the waist, lifting her until she could wrap her legs around his hips. His cock slipped into her pussy easily thanks to the cum dripping from her pussy. She wanted him so badly, she ached from it.

With her back braced against the tile wall of the shower, he fucked her so hard she groaned with each thrust of his hips.

"Play with your clit. I love to watch you come."

"It won't take much."

"Good. You come now, then we can fuck again in your bed after we finish the shower."

"I like it."

She reached down between them to finger her clit as he kept them fucking against the wall. The *slap, slap, slap* of wet flesh made her desire soar while she brought herself to brink with her fingertip massaging her clit. The friction was enough to send her over, but when he whispered, "Come for me," in her ear, she lost all control over holding back her orgasm.

She moaned his name in his ear as she spasmed around the thick cock inside her. Fullness stretched every inch of her pussy to accommodate the length and girth of his cock. He wasn't a small man by any means. It felt so good to have him inside her, she didn't want it to end, but end it would as he pumped his hips a few more times and filled her with his cum.

His whole body shook from the extent of his climax as he released her legs so she could stand on her own. "That was…"

"Awesome? Fantastic? Mind blowing?"

"All of the above, but I can't wait to do it again."

She grabbed the soap and began to lather up the hair on his chest. A little hair there just turned her inside out. These guys who waxed did nothing for her. "I love chest hair."

"Good thing I have some then, eh?"

She skimmed her fingernail over his nipples, watching in fascination as they pebble into hard points. Apparently, men had sensitive nipples too. "I like your chest. It's just right. Nice pecs. A little hair. Sensitive nipples. It's perfect."

"Thanks, but I really like yours."

The hair on his chest abraded her nipples deliciously when he leaned in and rubbed it across the tips of her breasts. "Oh. I like it when you do that."

"How about when I do this?" He dipped his hand between her thighs, pulling her pussy lips apart as he drove a finger into her.

Her breath caught in her throat. "Oh yeah."

"Let's take this into your bedroom," he said, slowly removing his finger from inside her.

She rinsed quickly and shut the water off. He grabbed two towels from the rack, handing her one to dry off with before he stepped out onto the bathmat. After he wrapped the towel around his tempting hips, he headed for the door as she quickly wiped the water from her body. She couldn't wait to get him between her thighs again. She had it bad it seemed, for one hunky Young brother.

Lordy, I'm in trouble.

Chapter Eight

Jason sat on his horse's back surveying the surrounding herd of cattle. Today was his turn to bring his family's herd down from the north pasture into the south area for grazing. It was a never ending thing with a cattle farm, but one he enjoyed immensely. He took a lot of pride in his work, but he hoped soon he would be able to leave working for his family and just do his own thing with his cattle and bucking bulls.

"Hey!" Jeff rode up beside him. "Is this all of them?"

"Yeah."

"Huh. Seems short. Did you count them?"

"Of course I counted them, dipshit. I'm not stupid."

"I didn't say you were, Jason. What bit you in the ass to make you so bitchy?"

"Nothing."

Jeff leaned on the pommel of his saddle with a grin across his lips. "A woman?"

Jason pushed his hat back on his head with his finger as he squinted into the afternoon sun. "Hell no."

"I know that voice. It *is* a woman. Let's see if I can guess who." Jeff leaned back and said, "Peyton Matthews?"

"Leave Peyton out of this." Jeff grinned, the silly fool. Just because he was happily encased in a relationship with a nice girl didn't mean the rest of them had to be.

"So it is her." He slapped Jason on the back, earning himself a punch in the arm. "Easy man. There's nothing wrong with being a little woman crazy."

"Speak for yourself."

"Got an itch to be between her pretty thighs, I'm guessing."

"Shut up, Jeff."

"What's wrong with that? We all need a little pussy once in a while, even you."

"I'm warning you. Back off."

"I bet it's been what? About a week since you've been inside her. I know the feeling, buddy. I need it at least a couple of times a week from Terri, otherwise I go batshit crazy."

"I don't need to hear about your sex life, Jeff. Let it be."

"But you're my brother. I'm giving you brotherly advice. Take the afternoon off and go get laid."

"You are letting me blow off work for pussy?"

"If you are as uptight as you sound, yeah. You need it." Jeff pulled his horse around to head back to the house. "Take my advice. Invite her over for dinner, a little wine, some flowers, you know. I'm sure I don't have to tell you how to wine and dine your woman."

"She's not my woman."

"But you want her to be or you wouldn't be all tied up in knots over her."

"No I don't. I don't need a woman."

"Yeah. Okay. Why don't I believe you, brother?" Jeff laughed as he kicked his horse into a gallop and headed back to the house.

"Fucker."

But what Jeff said had a ring of truth to it. He did want Peyton. Badly. It never seemed to get better either. They no sooner made love and he wanted her again. *Whoa!* Where did that come from? Made love? He thought it was simply sex, but the more he thought about it, the more he realize yeah, it hard turned into making love with her, not just sex.

Wow.

He kicked his horse to circle the herd again to double check the count since it was his job to make sure they all made it down from the pasture.

A few minutes later, Joel rode up. *Jesus. What is this, get Jason a girlfriend day?*

"What's up, Joel?"

"Not much. I figured I'd check on you. You seem distracted at breakfast."

"I was. Got a lot on my mind."

"Oh yeah?"

"Yep." Jason leaned into the saddle, resting his forearm across the pommel.

"Like what?"

"Same shit, different day."

"Woman troubles?"

"Why the fuck does everyone think I'm having woman troubles? I'm not. I'm getting laid on a regular basis by a pretty gorgeous woman. We aren't serious so get that thought out of your head. It's just making love!"

One dark eyebrow rose over Joel's left eye. "Making love?"

"Having sex. Same thing."

Joel laughed as he tipped his cowboy hat forward on his head. "No it's not, brother. If you are calling it making love, you're in deeper than you think. Trust me on that one. I thought the same damned thing until Mesa went home and I realized I didn't want to live without her."

"That's you, brother, not me. I don't need a woman and the woman doesn't need me. She's already told me as much."

"Did she?"

"Yeah. The night I got this nice shiner I'm still sporting the remnants of, when I tried to step in and help her at the bar. I don't need a hero, she said."

"Maybe she thinks she doesn't, but she really liked having you there for her."

"Don't get philosophical on me, Joel. It's not like you have a ton of women experience."

"I didn't need any when I found Mesa. I just knew."

"Oh yeah, like a bolt of lightning. You just knew she was the one."

"Well no, but talking to Mom helped. She showed me what I was missing if I walked away from Mesa."

"Mom has already given me the daughter-in-law speech."

"She has? Well then you are one step ahead of where you need to be. Peyton is a nice girl. You could do worse."

"But Peyton doesn't want anything beyond friends with benefits."

"Yeah, I thought that too, before Mesa walked away and I realized I didn't like the thought of her sleeping with anyone else."

Jason frowned as he took off his hat and swiped his fingers through his sweaty hair. It was hot today, even early summer in Bandera tended to be that way. "So what are you doing out here besides lecturing me on women?"

"Jeff asked me to relieve you so you could skip out and get laid."

"He's such a pain in the ass now that he's getting some regular like."

Joel grinned. "He has your best interest at heart and you know if you stay out here, Peyton is gonna find someone else soon enough to fulfill those desires swimming in her veins. She's a feisty one."

"Fuck that! She ain't getting some from anyone but me!"

The ring of Joel's laughter echoed off the rocks as Jason kicked his horse into a full gallop headed back to the main house. He quickly calculated in his brain how long it would take to unsaddle his horse, brush him down, head back to his house, get a shower in, and call Peyton with an invitation for dinner. He had approximately one hour to get everything done before it got too late to invite her.

He hoped she wasn't working the bar tonight. That would throw a whole new wrench in the plans.

When Jason rode into the barn, Jeff stood next to his horse, brushing the gelding down as he glanced over at Jason.

"Don't say a word."

"I wasn't going to."

"No, but I can tell you're thinking about it."

Jeff grinned, continuing to brush his horse down as he whistled softly under his breath.

The minute Jason had his horse's tack off, he quickly brushed the animal down and stabled him. Lucky for him, he hadn't worked the animal very hard today, and damn it, he was in a hurry.

Once he reached his truck, he slid inside, pulled out his cell phone and dialed Peyton's number.

"Hello?"

"Hey, babe."

"Hi Jason. What's up?"

"I thought we could get together tonight for a little dinner at my place."

"Dinner?"

"Yeah. I'll cook. I want to wine and dine you."

"Like a date?"

"Uh, sure. Why not?"

"Well, we really haven't been on a date."

"I know. I thought this was a good place to start."

She sounded unsure when she replied, "Uh, okay, I guess."

His heart plummeted into his belly, forming a knot he didn't like. "If you don't want to, just say so."

"No, I do, it's just…"

"What?"

"I had plans tonight."

"Plans?"

"Yeah."

She had plans. *What the fuck?*

"Like what? To wash your hair?" he growled. Surely she wasn't seeing anyone else, was she?

"I planned to spend the evening with a couple friends watching movies in our PJs, eating popcorn and ice cream, and just having a girl's night, but it's fine. I can cancel."

Relief washed through him. She wasn't seeing anyone else. "No, it's okay. We can do it some other night. I just kind of missed you this past week."

"You did?"

"Yeah."

He almost heard the smile in her voice. "I missed you too."

"Good. I'm glad I'm not alone in this mutual missing thing."

"So you want to date me, huh?"

"Well, yeah. I thought that's what we were doing anyway?"

"No, we've been fucking, Jason. There's a difference between dating and fucking."

"How about we do both?"

"I kind of like that plan. I mean, I miss having you in my bed, but I'd like to get to know you as a person too."

"How about tomorrow night?"

"I have to work the bar. I'm off on Tuesday though."

"Tuesday it is then. Plan on wearin' something sexy."

"Like?"

"A short skirt. A frilly top and no underwear."

"Oh, kinky. I like it."

"Can we meet for lunch or something before Tuesday? It's only Thursday."

"You'll survive without me until Tuesday, cowboy."

A low growl rumbled in his chest. "I don't want to. I'm pretty damned horny right now."

"So am I, but you'll have to have fun without me until then."

"Bullshit on that noise. I'll wait for you. Don't keep me waiting very long. I'm not a patient man when it comes to pussy."

"Damn, I wish I hadn't made plans tonight."

"Me either, babe, me either."

"I guess I'll talk to you later then," she whispered into the phone. "You know I'd kiss you silly right now if I was there. Slide my tongue along your neck, bite you on the shoulder. Fuck, I'm horny."

"Quit teasing me or I'll crash your party no matter who is there."

"Sheila."

"Sheila?"

"Yeah. That's who is coming over for our girl's night. Oh and Mandy. I also invited Paige even though she can't drink. We haven't had a chance to catch up lately."

"What are you going to watch?"

"Probably some chick flick with blubbering, hot men and nakedness."

"Oh?"

"Magic Mike or something."

"Isn't that like a stripper movie?" he asked, gripping the steering wheel. Why all of the sudden did he not like her looking at other men, sleeping with other men or anything else with another man. This was stupid. He didn't need to get involved with her on any regular basis.

Too late.

"I better go. The girl's will be here soon and I have to go to the liquor store for alcohol yet."

"Be good."

"I will. No worries there, cowboy. I kind of like the idea of a steady guy and a steady lay."

"You do? I thought you didn't want a relationship?"

"Who said anything about a relationship? Dating isn't a relationship."

"I'm the only man in your bed though."

"Yes, you are. I don't spread myself thin like that. There is no use sleeping with more than one. It gets kind of messy doing that. You know, keeping names straight and all."

"Peyton," he growled.

She laughed. "Bye, Jason."

The phone clicked in his ear. She had him tied up in knots and she was laughing about it like a schoolgirl. He wasn't sure he liked the way this thing was turning, but he wasn't sure how to stop it spiraling out of control.

* * * *

Peyton hung up the phone and smiled. Why the whole situation seemed to lift her spirits beyond the stars, she wasn't sure. She kind of liked having Jason Young wrapped around her little finger. He wanted her. That much was clear, but how much? A lot apparently.

Her phone rang again. This time Mandy's name came up on the caller ID.

"Are we still on?"

"Yep. There will be four of us."

"Four?"

"I invited Paige to hang out too although she can't drink."

"Okay. Are you going to get booze?"

"Yep. On my way there now."

"Who were you talking to before? Your phone went right to voicemail when I called a few minutes ago."

"Jason."

"Jason Young?"

"Yeah."

"Since when are you dating him? He's like a total playboy."

"Just recently. We've only done a few things together. Nothin' serious."

"A few things like what?"

"The shower. His bed. My bed."

"You fucked him?"

"Hell yeah. Fabulous sex with a hot guy. Are you kidding me?"

"Wow."

She chewed her bottom lip for a minute wondering whether she should ask what was on her mind. *What the hell.* "You haven't done him, have you, Mandy?"

"Hell no. Not that I wouldn't given the chance, but I've never had the occasion to."

Peyton exhaled sharply and answered, "Good."

"You were totally worried, weren't you?"

"Uh, yeah. He's been with a lot of women in this town. I'm just not sure who."

"I don't know if he's done Shelia though. You'll have to ask her."

"I'm not sure if I want to know. I mean, that was before me, right?"

"Sure it was, honey. Sure it was."

She didn't like where her thoughts were headed. "I'm going to go so I can hit the liquor store. See you in about two hours."

"Sure. I'm bringing the popcorn. Sheila has the ice cream. What is Paige bringing?"

"Chips and dip."

"Awesome. Lots of junk food to eat while we watch some chick flicks."

"Talk to you in a bit."

"Sure. Bye."

She hung up the phone and then pressed it to her forehead. Her thoughts went haywire thinking about Jason with another woman even though she knew he'd been with plenty. It didn't mean she had to like it. Nope, not one bit.

When she pulled back into her driveway about an hour later, she noticed Paige sitting on the porch with a bottle of water. "Did I tell you the wrong time?"

"No, I figured I'd come early."

"What's wrong? You look like you've been crying."

"Nothing. I got into a fight with Jacob. That's all."

"Hang on. Let me open the door. We'll get something to drink and you can tell me about it." Peyton opened the front door, bringing the bags of alcohol with her. She'd offer Paige a drink, but she knew that wasn't going to work with her being pregnant and all.

"So what happened?" she asked as she set the bottles on the counter in the kitchen.

She liked her small house on the edge of town. She couldn't have animals or anything there without fencing off part of the yard, but she had a little porch with a couple of rocking chairs on it, a nice living room with leather furniture, a modern kitchen with granite countertops and stainless steel appliances, two bedrooms and two bathrooms. The yard wasn't very big, but she had a garden with some flowers so she was happy.

Paige was quiet for several minutes, but she didn't want to push. Peyton arranged the bottles on the counter to give herself something to do. Being the woman friend felt foreign to her so she wasn't sure how to handle this situation, but when she heard a muffled sob coming from her friend, she turned around to take her in her arms. "It'll be okay."

"I'm not so sure."

"What did you fight over?"

Tears rolled down Paige's face, making Peyton choke up herself, before she blurted out, "He wants two boys!"

Peyton did a double take. "You fought over the sex of the babies?"

"Yes. He insists that it's two boys. I think it's two girls even though I want one of each. We got in a huge fight and he walked out. He left, Peyton. What if he doesn't come back?"

"Honey, listen to yourself. This is silly. He loves you. Besides, what difference does it make whether the babies are boys or girls? You'll love them no matter what sex they are and so will he."

"I'm being silly, huh." Paige sniffed as she wiped the tears on her face.

"Yes you are, but it's hormones, honey. You're full of them right now and everything that man says is either going to piss you off or make you love him all the more."

"You're right. This is silly. I'm going to call him." Paige grabbed her purse and then wiped her face as she pulled out her phone.

Peyton went into the pantry in the corner to get the cups and other things they would need as she listened to the one-sided conversation from Paige to Jacob. "Hi, honey. I'm so sorry I got so upset with you. It's my fault. Peyton says it's the hormones, but I wanted you to know I don't care whether the babies are boys or girls. I love you. I want a family with you."

Apparently Jacob made her cry again as Paige began to sniff back tears.

"I love you too. No, I'm okay. I won't be driving tonight. I'm staying at Peyton's. Okay. I'll see you in the morning."

She heard Paige hang up as she arranged the chips in a bowl and mixed the onion dip into the sour cream. "All better?"

"Yeah. Sorry."

"No problem. That's what friends are for."

"So what is going on between you and Jason?"

"Nothing. Why?"

"I heard you two had raunchy sex at his place last week."

"Where did you hear that?"

"Jacob."

She jammed her hands on her hips. *Men!* "Man, those boys don't know how to keep anything a secret, do they?"

"They're brothers. They talk amongst themselves especially when it has to do with a woman."

"What else did Jacob say?"

"That you two looked cute together." Paige popped a chip into her mouth. "Are you dating?" she asked, in between bites.

"I wouldn't call it that yet."

"So just non-committal sex?" Paige asked, taking another chip and dragging it through the French onion dip.

"Yep," she said as she shooed Paige away so she could set the bowls on the table.

"How is he?"

"Um, fine. Why?"

"I mean is he good in bed?"

"I would say so although I don't have a lot to compare to." She blushed to the roots of her hair at the admission. Why she felt she couldn't just say it without blushing, she wasn't sure. It wasn't something to be ashamed of, right? "Good God! I don't ask you how Jacob is in bed. What's with the questions?"

"I just wondered since he has such a reputation with the women in Bandera."

"Yeah, I know." She slapped the spoon on the table. "I don't need to hear about it."

Paige raised her hands. "Easy girl. I was just askin'."

"Well don't ask. I don't care who he's slept with. He's with me at the moment and that's all that matters."

Paige wrapped her arms around Peyton's shoulders and pulled her in for a hug. "Yes it is."

The doorbell rang and Peyton went to answer it, expecting Sheila and Mandy any minute. The other two ladies were standing together at the door when she opened it up. "Come in."

"Where's the booze?" Sheila asked, making a beeline for the wine bottle on the counter. "I need a drink."

"What's up with her?" Peyton asked Mandy as she shut the door behind them. "It's not like her to jump into the alcohol so fast."

"She's had a rough day. She just found out about you and Jason."

Chapter Nine

Peyton knocked on the bathroom door after Sheila took one of the bottles of wine and locked herself in. "Sheila?"

"Leave me alone, Peyton. I hate you."

"Then why the fuck did you come to my house?"

"Because you're one of my best friends." The sound of a sob broke through the pane of the door.

"I don't get you at all."

"I love Jason Young and you're fucking him."

"Oh please. You do not love him. You went out with him what? Once or twice?" Peyton tapped on the door again. "Come out of there."

"Not until I'm good and drunk so I don't punch you."

Peyton leaned against the wall near the door, sipping a glass of wine she'd poured before she went after Sheila. *This whole thing is stupid.* "Try it, babe. We can go round all night if you want. I'm game. I haven't been in a fight lately."

"You'd hit me?"

"If you hit me first, yes."

"What a bitch."

"You're in my house, drinking my wine, and you're calling me a bitch?"

Silence.

The lock clicked right before the door slowly opened. "I'm being stupid, aren't I?"

"Yes, you are. Besides, there's nothing between me and Jason other than some hot sex." Peyton wasn't sure she wanted to know, but she asked anyway. "Did you fuck him?"

Sheila bit her lip.

"You did." The jealousy Peyton felt surprised her. Surely she wasn't upset that Jason had slept with Sheila, was she? Maybe. But why? They were only having a good time, right?

"Yeah. Twice."

"I'm not sure I want to know."

"Why not? You asked." Sheila walked past her into the living room and then spun around. "You aren't jealous, are you?"

Peyton folded her arms over her chest. The protective stance didn't fool her friends though as Sheila, Mandy and Paige looked on. "No."

"Yes you are! You totally are!" Sheila flopped down on the couch as she brought the wine bottle to her lips. After she swallowed, she said, "You're in love with him."

"No, I'm not. We're fucking. That's it."

"I can see it in your face."

Peyton glanced at Paige who shrugged and Mandy who nodded. "You all are full of shit. I'm not in love with him. We are just two people finding solace in each other's company. That's it."

"Then don't fuck him anymore," Sheila said, taking another swig from the bottle.

"But I don't want to stop making love with him. We're good together. He's the best I've had in a long time."

"Do you hear yourself?" Mandy asked, taking a seat next to Sheila on the couch, reaching for the wine bottle.

"What?"

"You said making love, not having sex, not fucking, making love." She pointed at Peyton with the bottle top before she took a long drink. "You are totally in love with him."

"We aren't discussing this anymore. I'm done. I'm not in love with him. We are fucking, that's it. Nothing more." She glanced at Paige who stood nearby with a little smile playing on her lips. "What?"

"You sound like me before I realized I had it bad for Jacob. Now look at us, expecting twins."

"You totally fell the minute you saw him."

"The minute I saw him, he was drunk off his ass and getting it kicked by three other guys. Then he came back after puking in the hall at the bar, with throw up on his shirt. Not a good first impression, Peyton."

"True, but once you hauled him across the street, paid for his room so he could sober up, you were hooked."

"Yeah, no and stop trying to change the subject of you and Jason. I can attest the Young brothers are definitely worth the trouble, but make sure you don't get hurt. Jason is a player. He always has been."

"I know, Paige. I've watched him enough at the bar to know his game."

"Then make sure you don't fall into it. If he's playing you, then blow him off. Don't get me wrong, I love all of Jacob's brothers, but there are several of them that are into seeing how many women they can fuck in a year." She glanced at Sheila from across the room. "No offense, Sheila, but he used you if you fucked him."

Sheila took another swig from the bottle. "I know."

"Enough of this talk. We were supposed to be having a good time, not talking about who we are fucking this week." Peyton grabbed the bottle of wine, then poured herself more into the glass she held. "What are we eating, ladies? We can call for pizza or go for burgers, although not a good idea since we've been drinking."

"I could drive. I can't drink anyway," Paige said, skimming her hand down her gently rounded stomach.

"You are so cute with your belly," Sheila replied, her words beginning to slur.

"Thanks. I'm glad I didn't have too much morning sickness with this pregnancy. I was afraid of that when I found out it was twins."

"How are you going to handle two babies at once without family help?"

"Nina has already promised to help me a lot with them. She's excited about having more grandbabies."

"Do you know what they are?" Peyton asked, sipping her wine. "I mean the sexes?"

"Not yet. We go for an ultrasound in a couple of weeks."

"What are you hoping for?"

"One of each. I think it would be great to have a boy and a girl. Nina wants girls." Paige laughed. "She already has the boys so she's hoping for at least one girl in the mix. Plus having nine boys, she really wants granddaughters."

"I really like Nina. She's a hoot," Peyton said. "I've had the chance to talk to her some while at the feed store and things. We've even had lunch a couple of times together."

"She's bringing you into the fold," Paige replied.

"What do you mean?" Peyton didn't like the thought of being manipulated.

"She's a sneaky one. I think in her roundabout way, she's setting up women she likes to get her boys married off." Paige shifted in the chair so she faced Peyton. "She was very sweet to me before Jacob and I got together. We kind of found our way together without much help, but as soon as she knew we were seeing each other, she totally jumped onboard with our relationship."

"Oh, she's definitely sneaky."

"She never helped me when I was dating Jason," Sheila whined.

The sound grated on Peyton's nerves. She really didn't want to compare her *relationship* such as it is, with Sheila's. It was bad enough Jason slept with her. This was something Peyton would have to deal with for however long they were together, but she didn't want to be constantly reminded of it. "Maybe she didn't think you were the right person for him?"

"And you are?"

"Hell if I know, Sheila." Peyton shrugged, sipping her wine. Sheila was three sheets to wind or getting close and she didn't really want to get into some kind of a brawl with her friend over a guy. "We are having a good time, nothing more. It's still very early for anything to be even called a relationship."

"How many times have you fucked?"

"Does it matter?"

"Yes it matters, to me."

"I'm not telling you an exact amount. We did it several times at his house."

Sheila jumped to her feet, spilling wine from the bottle on the carpet. "At his house? He took you to his house?"

Okay, this is getting out of control.

"Well, yeah. After I'd been to the muddin' party. He resisted a lot, for some reason I'm not quite sure of even now, but he finally gave in."

"You threw yourself at him? You are a fucking slut!"

"Okay. I'm tired of your mouth, Sheila. What is going on between me and Jason has no reflection on you or what you had. You slept with him. Unfortunately, it's something I have to deal with, but I'm not a slut. I haven't been with a shit ton of guys. Yes, Jason and I fucked. It was good. It was fabulous. The best I've ever had, but it doesn't mean I'm a slut. Take it back!"

"I will not! You went to the muddin' party with Aaron and ended up sleeping with Jason? That's what I call a slut."

"I'm calling you a cab."

"I'm not leaving until we've had this out."

"Girl, there is nothing to have out. Jason didn't want you past however many times you had sex. He still wants me after several times. Get over it!" Peyton set her glass down and stood to retrieve her cell phone. She needed to get Sheila out of her house before something happened to ruin their friendship altogether. With her cell phone in hand, she dialed the local cab company phone. She kept them on her cell phone for patrons at the bar. "Yeah, I need a cab at…" She rattled off her address and closed the phone. "They'll be here in fifteen minutes."

"I told you I'm not leaving." Sheila shoved Peyton, pushing her back a few steps.

"Don't do this, Sheila."

"He's mine."

"No, he's not. For the moment, he's mine." Sheila shoved her again, pushing her into the end table where her glass of wine sat, spilling the contents. "Enough, Sheila. You can get your bag and sit out on the front porch to sober up."

"This is total bullshit." Tears welled up in Sheila's eyes. "I love him."

"No you fucking don't. You went on like two dates. That's it."

"I can fall in love in such a short amount of time."

"I did," Paige answered. "I denied it, but I was totally in love with Jacob very quickly."

"You aren't helping matters here, Paige."

"Sorry."

"See! Paige loved Jacob that quickly. I can totally be in love with him."

"You are not, Sheila. Besides, he doesn't love you."

"You think he's in love with you?"

"There isn't love here. It's mutual sexual satisfaction, nothing more, at least for now. I don't love someone in a few days."

"But he took you home."

The whine coming from her friend made her ball her hand into a fist. She hated whiny people.

A honk sounded outside. "Take the cab and go home. You need to sleep this off."

"Fine, but I'll remember this conversation and we'll be having this out sooner or later, Peyton."

"Whatever, Sheila. It doesn't matter."

Sheila grabbed her purse before she opened the front door. "Yes, it does. He's mine."

Peyton shook her head and rolled her eyes as Sheila shut the door behind her. "Wow."

"Yeah, wow," Mandy said, taking another sip from the bottle Sheila left on the coffee table.

"How about you get a glass?"

"I'm redneckin' it tonight."

"Not in my house." Peyton grabbed a wine glass from the rack in the dining room and handed it to Mandy. "If you're going to drink here, you drink from a glass."

"Sheila wasn't."

"I'm not sure what her deal was, but I'm glad that's over with. It was getting crazy."

"You know you shouldn't have taken her man."

Peyton mopped up the wine from the table with the towel she'd retrieved from the kitchen. "Don't you fucking start or you can leave too."

"I'm just sayin…"

"Well knock it off! I didn't steal her man. Jason wasn't dating her when we started seeing each other, so I didn't take him away from her."

"So you are dating?"

"Fuck if I know what this is. We slept together a couple of times. He wanted to have me come over for dinner tonight at his place, but we already had plans for our girl's night."

"I'd call that a date," Paige said, chomping on some chips sitting on the coffee table.

"I suppose, but it hasn't happened yet."

"I've never heard of him dating anyone for more than a month or so," Mandy added, eating a couple of chips herself.

"It doesn't matter. I'm playing this out for whatever it's worth. I'm not looking for a husband and he's not looking for a wife so we're on the same page there."

"Good for you. I don't think he'd make good husband material from what I know of him," Mandy said. "But I don't know him that well either."

"I don't think any of the Young brothers were looking for wives when they hooked up with their respective mates. I know I wasn't looking for a husband and babies when we got together. It just happened."

Peyton poured herself more wine, emptying the first bottle of many she'd purchased for tonight. Maybe it was a night to get drunk. She might. It had been a while since she'd allowed herself to let loose and hang out with the girls. Of course, this night hadn't started very well with Sheila and her drama.

"If it happens, it happens. I'm not looking for it is all I'm saying."

"So what are we having for dinner?"

"Pizza sounds really good to me, right now," Paige replied. "With ranch dressing."

"Eeewwww!" The other two said in unison as they all laughed together.

An hour later found them watching Magic Mike on television with three pizza boxes between them. Paige had her cheese with ranch dressing, satisfying her pregnancy cravings, as Peyton and Mandy had their own concoction of whatever they wanted on their pizzas. No ranch dressing here. The movie had lost interest for Peyton after the first few minutes. Yes, Channing Tatum is hot, but Jason was homegrown cowboy built without the gym to supplement his muscles. Although, she had seen a weight set sitting in the corner of his bedroom so he apparently did some working out.

She wasn't sure why he held such fascination for her, but he did from the first moment she'd laid eyes on him at The Dusty Boot. The drawl of his words, the way he filled out his T-shirt or western shirt, the size of his arms, the trimness of his waist, the long legs in those boot-cut Wranglers, and oh, his butt was to die for.

"Peyton?"

"Sorry, yeah?"

"Mandy asked you a question. You seemed lost in thought. Aren't you enjoying the movie?" Paige asked, biting into the last piece of pizza on her plate.

"Oh, it's great."

"What was the last thing Channing Tatum said?"

"Uh…"

"You don't even know, do you?"

She blushed as she set her plate on the table. "No."

"It's bad when he can't even hold your attention." Mandy grabbed another slice. "What were you thinking about or should I ask who?"

"Jason."

"Well duh," Paige answered. "I could tell the by the look in your eyes. The faraway gaze gave it away. Nina says I get the same look when I'm thinking about Jacob too."

"Well you should. You're in love with him."

"Are you admitting you're in love with Jason?"

"No. In lust, yes."

Mandy scooted closer to the table, crossing her legs under her as she focused on Peyton. "What is he like?"

"You want me to give you details?"

"Hell yeah, baby. Spill it!"

Could she really give them details of making love, no, having sex with Jason? Maybe. What was it about women wanting to know what it's like between two people? "Details?"

"I'm living vicariously through the two of you. I haven't been with a guy in six months," Mandy shared.

"Six months?"

"Yep and even then, it wasn't great. He was pretty quick and not much into foreplay."

"That sucks," Peyton said.

"Exactly, now spill. I want to know what it's like with those Young boys. Maybe I'll hook up with one just to see."

"There are a couple who aren't tied down yet." Peyton laughed. "Maybe you could hook up with one of them."

"Maybe I just might. You never know." Mandy blushed. "I could do with finding me a good man who knows what the hell he's doing in the sack. I'm tired of this shit with these losers." She pushed against Peyton's shoulder. "So tell me."

"Well, he definitely knows how to eat a girl out."

"Seriously? I've never had a guy do that to me before."

"You're missing out then. I love when a guy goes down on me. His mouth down there licking, sucking, and when he shoves those fingers inside you, holy shit!"

"Yeah?"

Peyton noticed Paige blushing from her seat across the room. "Right, Paige?"

"Yes," she whispered, covering her cheeks. "I can't talk about this stuff."

"And?" Mandy asked. "Do you come?"

"Oh yeah, several times if he's into doing it right."

"Shit, really? Hell, I'm lucky to come once with a guy."

Peyton sat back against the rear of her chair. "You've been dating the wrong guys, then. You need to find one who is into what makes you tick."

"Wow." Mandy's sigh of the word made Peyton smile.

It sure was wow with Jason.

"What about when he actually sticks his cock in there?"

"It's like being filled up to the brim." Peyton shifted on the chair as she remembered the feeling. She'd been horny before, but all this talk wasn't making it any better.

"What's the best position?"

"Against the wall."

"Holy shit! Against the wall?"

"Uh yeah. He gets so deep, it's like amazing."

"What about your G spot? Have you ever had him hit that?" Mandy shook her head. "I think it's hogwash myself. I'm not sure it even exists."

"Oh it does." Peyton knew it was there. Jason has it hit several times during their raunchy sexcapades, but when her back had been against the wall…oh yeah, he'd hit it big time.

"Yeah?"

"Definitely. Trust me, it's there. You just have to have the right angle of penetration."

"Okay, now I want to sleep with Jason," Mandy said with a laugh.

"Not happenin', girlfriend."

"I was kidding, Peyton, but maybe one of his brothers." She glanced at Paige. "Is Jacob good too?"

"He is with me." Paige blushed again. "I mean we are good together, yes, but I don't know if he'd been that way with anyone else. It helps we are in love." She pointed at Peyton. "Not that you can't have good sex without being in love. You know?"

"I don't think you have to be in love to have great sex, but it helps if the guy gives a shit about your pleasure. If he's all about himself, you aren't going to get much out of it. Believe me, I've been with some losers too."

"How do they compare with Jason?"

"They don't. Not even close."

"You know. I think he's totally in love with you," Paige said.

"Why do you say that?" Peyton asked, taken aback by Paige's revelation. Surely it wasn't true.

"Because I've never seen him in this good of a mood. The last couple of days he's been whistling while he works, smiling a lot more and everything."

"It doesn't mean he's in love with me. We've had a discussion, him and I, and neither of us is looking for anything other than a good time."

"Then why are you dating him?"

"To see."

"See what?"

Peyton wasn't sure how to answer Paige's question. What was she looking for in the relationship with Jason? Surely she wasn't looking for love, right?

Well maybe.

"I don't know, really."

"I think you're half in love with him already."

"I can't be, Paige. I've only been seeing him for like a week."

"But you've known him for several months. You've seen him at the bar, how he interacts with his parents and his brothers, how he takes care of others around him and the hot sex is just a bonus." Paige nodded. "Yep, you're in love with him, all right."

"I am not."

"Are you having trouble keeping your mind on things other than him?"

"Sometimes."

"You think about him all the time?"

"Sometimes."

"You can't wait to see him again?"

"Sometimes." Peyton shook her head. "I'm not in love with him."

Paige shrugged and sipped her soda. "If you say so."

They let the movie continue to run as Peyton thought about the conversation. Yeah, she thought about him *a lot*. Yeah, she wanted to be with him night and day. She wanted to find out more about him, his dislikes, his interests, what made him tick, but she wasn't in love with him, right? People didn't fall in love with someone in a week?

Chapter Ten

Tuesday rolled around and Jason was nervous. He wasn't sure how this evening would go with Peyton, but he had high hopes they would end up in his bed. It had been too long without, even though it had only been not quite a week without her hot little pussy around him.

He'd been to the bar each night she worked, just watching. He loved how she interacted with her customers, smiling most of the time. There had been a couple of times he wanted to step in when she had a particularly rowdy patron, but he didn't. He stayed in his spot in the booth near the back, just watching.

She was beautiful no matter what she wore, how she had her hair, how much makeup she had on or whatever. She twisted his guts into knots.

When the doorbell rang, he wiped his sweaty palms on the thighs of his jeans, checked everything was in its place on the table waiting for their intimate dinner to commence and headed for the door.

He knew he had a shit eating grin on his face that slowly slid off when he opened the door.

"Sheila?"

"Can I come in?"

"Uh, sure. I guess. I'm having company soon."

"I know. Peyton is coming over. I wanted to be here when she got here because this is something you should both hear."

"I don't like the sound of this."

"You probably won't when I tell you what's up."

"Why don't you just tell me what's the problem."

"No. Peyton needs to know."

The doorbell rang again as dread now slid through him. He didn't like the way Sheila was looking at him and he sure didn't like the glaze in her eyes. She almost looked like she was high or drunk.

He opened the door to find Peyton on the other side. "Hey." He kissed her quickly on the lips.

"Hey." She stepped inside the house and he shut the door behind her. "Sheila here? I saw her car outside."

"She just got here," he whispered. "I don't know what's up, but she insisted you be here when she told me why she's visiting."

"I can totally hear you."

"Why don't we all take a seat in the living room so you can share with us what your visit is about, Sheila."

"Fine." Sheila took a seat in the chair across from the couch.

He took one of Peyton's hands and led her to the couch so she could sit beside him. Somehow he thought this was going to affect both of them and he wasn't sure he liked the feeling. Right now, he wanted to shove Sheila out the door, lock it behind her and lose himself in Peyton's arms.

"What's this all about?"

"Peyton knows we slept together."

"So? I don't keep things from her, but I don't necessarily enjoy telling her about other women I've been with."

"And you told me you'd slept with him when you were at my house last week."

"That was before I found out something today that has changed everything."

"What?" Jason asked, his gut twisted in a knot.

"I'm pregnant."

"What?" He jumped to his feet. "That's impossible."

"We didn't use a condom, Jason."

He raked his fingers through his hair. This was nuts. She couldn't be pregnant. "You said you were on birth control."

"I wanted you. I would have said anything to get you into bed with me."

He glanced down at Peyton. Her face had turned ashen. "Peyton?"

"I think I'd better go. This is between you two."

With both of her hands in his, he pleaded, "No. Stay, please. I need you here."

"You need to talk and decide what you're going to do about this, Jason. It doesn't concern me."

"Yes, it does. You're part of my life now."

"We're only dating."

"Not to me. I need you here."

Sheila jumped to her feet with her hands on her hips. "This is all so touching, but what the hell are you going to do about me? I don't want to have a baby out of wedlock."

"I'm not marrying you, Sheila, if that's what this is all about."

"I don't want a bastard child."

"If the baby is mine, I'll take care of it, but I'm not marrying you. I don't love you."

"If? You think I was fucking around with more than just you?"

"Hell, I don't know what you've been doing. If you gave it to me so easily, you could have been with a half a dozen guys at the same time."

Sheila's hand snaked out and slapped him across the cheek. "How dare you. I'm not a slut unlike someone else in this room who slept with you after going to a party with another guy."

"Leave Peyton out of this."

"I won't. She's standing between the two of us."

"There is no you and me, Sheila. I won't be blackmailed into marrying you because you *might* be pregnant with my child. As I said, if it turns out to be mine, and yes, I will insist on a paternity test, then we'll deal with it, but I'm not marrying you."

"You haven't heard the last of me." Sheila stomped to the door, whipped it open and left in a huff.

"Are you okay?" Jason asked, taking Peyton in his arms. He wasn't sure how this would affect his budding relationship with the woman in his arms, but he didn't like how quiet she had become or the paleness of her complexion.

"I'm okay."

"I didn't see this coming."

"I know you didn't."

He moved to the front and shut the door. When he returned to her side, he sat them both down on the couch together. "I'm sorry. This is not something you should have to deal with. I need more information from Sheila like how far along she is. It's been a while since we've been together."

"Like how long?"

"A few months anyway." He glanced at the ceiling as he tried to remember. "Three months at least."

"She never mentioned anything to me when she was at my house drinking like a fish last week either and she knew you and I had been together."

"Somehow I think this is a ploy. If she is indeed pregnant, it's probably not mine. She'd have to be several months along for it to be."

"Do you think she's lying?"

"Could be. I mean, she sure jumped on me marrying her. Maybe she thought she'd get a ring from me and then play at a miscarriage. She wouldn't be the first to pull that kind of stunt."

"Why would she want to do that?" Peyton asked, sitting back against the arm of the couch.

"To break us up."

"I thought she was my friend."

"Some women do nasty things when men are involved."

A smile curved her lips as one eyebrow rose over her eye. "And men don't?"

"Maybe."

"I've seen some men do silly things too for a woman they were head over heels for."

"Oh, like what?"

"Cook them dinner."

"That's not a big deal. I'm cooking you dinner tonight," he whispered, sliding his lips along her neck. *Lord, I like to nip at her skin.*

Her breathing hitched. "Fuck them against the wall."

"Really?" he asked, liking where this conversation was headed. Fucking her against the wall sounded like a fantastic idea. He'd sure liked it when they'd done it before. He could hit the exact right spot inside her with that angle. "Wanna fuck?"

"More than anything."

He tugged her tank top over her head, revealing the lacy bra covering her breasts. *She sure has pretty tits.* "I like your boobs."

"Thanks."

He skimmed his mouth down her chest to capture a nipple in his mouth through her bra. "They are magnificent."

"I'm glad you like them."

"They are perfect for me. Just the right size for my hands to cup. Someday I want to fuck you between these gorgeous mounds."

"As I suck the head between my lips."

"Fuck yeah." He pushed one hand down the waistband of her jeans.

"Unbutton them first. It's easier to reach me." The minute he had them unfastened, she shoved them and her panties over her hips, revealing the tuft of hair at the juncture of her thighs. She toed off her boots as she wiggled out of her clothes. "Touch me. I need you."

Her hot pussy almost scalded his fingers as he pushed them inside her. His cock ached to be there. His balls burned for release. He wanted to fuck her on the kitchen counter.

Without breaking he sweat, he picked her up and headed for the kitchen. She squeaked when the cold countertop hit her butt cheeks.

He chuckled as he unbuckled his belt. "I'm going to fuck you hard and fast."

"Good. I'm so horny, I could combust."

"Open for me, babe. I'm comin' home."

He positioned his cock at her entrance and slowly slid the engorged flesh inside of her. The hot, silky feel of her pussy welcomed him like no one else ever had.

"That's it. Fuck me."

He slowly drew his cock out until just the head remained. She whimpered as she grabbed his hips, trying to pull him back inside her. With his hands on her hips, he began a slow, torturous fucking that would leave them both breathless, but wanting more. "Slow."

"No, fast. Hard."

"Nope. I'm controlling this."

The soft mewling sounds she made ramped his desire higher. She was perfect for him in every way. She met him stroke for stroke, touch for touch, and feeling for feeling, or at least he hoped so because he was losing the battle to keep his heart out of the mix with her.

* * * *

The hard slide of his cock pushed her closer and closer to the edge of insanity. She wanted him to fuck her harder, but then again, she didn't. The slow glide of his pace brought her to the brink without pushing her over. It was driving her crazy!

"Jason, please."

"Please what, darlin'?"

"Fuck!"

"Yeah, that's what we're doin'."

"You're killing me."

"I'm loving you."

"God, please. Fuck me harder. I need you so bad." With his finger nudging her clit, she exploded on a climactic high she'd never experienced before. "Oh God! Yes, yes, yes," she panted with each penetration. He grabbed her hips, slamming his pelvis against hers with each thrust, but he wasn't hitting quite the right spot for her to come again. She wanted that elusive G spot orgasm, but the angle wasn't right. "Wait!"

His movements came to a screeching halt. "What?"

"Something isn't right."

"Feels right to me."

"No, the angle. It's not right. You aren't hitting the right spot."

"What can I do?"

"Up against the wall. That worked last time, with my legs over your arms."

"Right, baby."

She wrapped her legs around his hips as he swung them both around. "Shower. Wall."

"Okay." He walked the few steps down the hall it took to get to the bathroom.

At least this way if she squirted all over, it wouldn't get on anything but the shower. She wanted to experience that for the first time and she thought if he could hit her G spot, she might get there. The minute her back hit the tile wall, she sucked in a ragged breath waiting for him to start to move.

"Better?" he asked, bringing her legs up over his forearms like before.

"Yeah." He moved his hips and she moaned low in her throat as he hit the right spot. "Oh hell yeah. Right there."

He slowly slid his cock in and out.

"Please."

"Harder?"

"Yes, please, I need—" He slammed into her with several pumps of his hips, sending her skyrocketing into a soul-shattering climax. "Jason!"

She no more came down from one as he said, "You can come again, darlin'. Play with your clit."

"I can't." She panted, feeling boneless as he continued to piston into her. Her body came alive even though she thought for sure she couldn't come again. With each of his thrusts hitting her G spot, her pussy clamped down like she wanted to.

"Yes you can. Play with your clit, baby. Come for me again."

"God, Jason."

"Come on, darlin'. You can do it."

He continued to drive her mad with want as he slowed his thrusts. She reached down between them to spread wetness around her clit and finger the tiny nub of nerves. She couldn't believe it, but she wanted to come so badly, she hurt. "You're driving me insane."

"Good. I don't want to be there by myself when my world implodes."

"Come with me."

"I'm right there. Are you?"

"Yeah, just a little—fuck!" Her climax hit her like a boulder rolling down a mountain to hit a brick wall. "God!"

Jason moaned in her ear as he shuddered to his own completion at the same time. His body shook beneath her fingers as he slipped out of her. After he let her legs fall to the floor, she smoothed her hands down his chest.

"We should shower."

"I would love to shower with you and then I can finish making us dinner. Dessert kind of came before the main course." He reached over and turned on the warm water for a minute before he flipped the showerhead on.

She grabbed the soap and began lathering it in her hands before slicking them over his pecs and abdomen. The soap bubbles slithered down between his legs. She scooped up some, rubbing the slippery substance around his flaccid cock.

"Keep that up and we'll be having more dessert before dinner."

"You going to be up for more so soon?" she asked, rubbing the soap around his balls and the base of his cock, fascinated by the hardening flesh.

"Babe, I'm perpetually horny around you, but we need to eat before we do anything else." One of his sexy eyebrows went up over his eye. "Besides, I have more things I want to do to you."

"Oh?"

"Ever had anal sex?"

"No."

"Would you like to try it?"

She shrugged as she palmed his cock. "As long as there isn't soap involved, I'm game to experience new things."

He tipped his head back on his shoulders as a groan rumbled low in his chest. "I would love to show you all kinds of new things, but if you don't stop that, I'm going to blow again."

"Already?"

"Okay, stop." He pushed her hand away before he stepped under the spray of water to wash the soap off. "Your turn." With a palm full of soap, he washed her from neck to toes, spending a little more time than necessary on her breasts and pussy. "I need to make sure they are clean inside and out so I can feast on your willing flesh after dinner." He guided her under the water to wash all the suds away and then turned off the spigot. After he grabbed two towels to dry off, he pushed her with a hand on her butt toward the door.

"I think my clothes are in living room."

"That's okay. We can eat naked, or you can anyway."

"What if your family comes by?" she asked, with a giggle. "I'm sure you don't want to show off my assets to them."

He wrapped her up in his arms as he kissed her on the nose. "Hell no. I'm not sharing. I'm a pretty possessive guy when I like what I have."

"And do you like what you have?"

"You *are* mine."

"Am I? That sounded pretty possessive to me. I thought we weren't doing a relationship."

"I thought we were dating?"

He headed for the kitchen with just a towel around his hips, enticing her to tear the cotton material off and suck him dry. "Dating, yeah. Exclusive?"

With a glance over his shoulder, he said, "I don't share well." He opened the door on the oven to check whatever was inside. Apparently the food had been cooking on low while they were busy having wild sex.

"You've never been this way with any other woman, why me?"

"I like the way we are. I want it to continue."

"This sounds an awful lot like a relationship, Jason."

He grabbed a knife and began chopping some vegetables to put into a salad bowl. "So it's a relationship."

She popped one of the pieces of celery into her mouth. "I thought we weren't doing a relationship?"

"What's the problem?" he asked, pointing the knife in her direction. "I'm okay with this being what it is, but now you aren't?"

"I wasn't before. I know your reputation. This doesn't sound like you."

"So I'm evolving with what's going on between us. Isn't that okay? I thought things could change between two people."

He continued to chop, but his movements told her she was agitating him beyond words. "I'm sorry. I don't mean to question your motives, but you have to understand where I'm coming from. I've seen nothing from you up to this point, to indicate you were looking for something serious. Now you are changing your tune completely?"

When his movements paused, he turned to face her for a moment to say, "I don't know what I'm looking for, Peyton. All I know is I'm not letting you go if I don't have to. We're good together and I want it to continue until we decide otherwise."

She exhaled sharply as she headed back into the living room to put on her clothes. He might feel comfortable running around in nothing but a towel around his tempting hips, but she needed clothing.

Once she had everything on, she returned to the kitchen to find dinner almost ready and Jason dressed in a low slung pair of jeans. "What are we having?"

"Roasted chicken with mashed potatoes, salad and vegetables."

"Sounds good. Do you like to cook?"

"Yeah. I loved being in the kitchen with my mom while we were growing up. Not having any girls was hard on her, but I enjoyed helping her."

"Smells wonderful."

"Thanks. If you take a seat, I'll get it on the table in the dining room in a second. Everything is done." The apparent agitation he was feeling earlier must have resolved. He was back to his charming self as he placed the food on the table. "Help yourself. Would you like beer, wine, milk, water or what to drink?"

"I'll take a glass of wine."

"Red or white?"

"Aren't you supposed to have white with chicken?"

"I guess. I'm not a wine drinker. White it is." He returned a few minutes later with a glass half full of white wine and set it near the top of her plate. "Chardonnay?"

"Perfect. See? You know more about it than you think." She put her napkin on her lap and proceeded to cut into the chicken. The meat melted like butter on a hot sidewalk, on her tongue. "Wow. This is fabulous. I've never had chicken this tender and juicy before." His lips curved up in that sexy smile she'd come to think of as reserved for her.

"Thanks."

"How did you make it?"

"Several herbs, but the trick is to cook the chicken slowly on low heat so it doesn't dry out."

"Oh my gosh! This is absolutely amazing," she said around bites of the meat and potatoes. The man could really cook. "You'll have to cook for me all the time now that you've spoiled me on your cooking."

"Anytime, darlin'. I love someone who appreciates my *talents* in the kitchen."

She tilted her head slightly to the left and smiled. Oh she would definitely appreciate his talents in the kitchen over and over before the night was through, if she had her way about it.

Chapter Eleven

The conversation during dinner veered away from anything too serious. They talked about the ranch and his duties, his plans for his own herd as well as the bulls he was breeding for the PBR. Her plans for school coming up in the fall, although she didn't go into detail about why she wanted to be an abuse counselor. She didn't feel ready to tell him about Charles.

"When did you get your first piercing?"

"Do you mean besides my earlobes like every other little girl?"

"Yeah." He shoved his plate away and leaned back in his chair. "You have what, your tongue, your ears, belly button which is totally hot, by the way, your eyebrow. What else?"

"Nothing. That's it. Isn't it enough?"

"I guess. Which was your first besides your ears?"

"I did several holes in my ears before I did anything else. The rest came after."

"After what?"

She bit her lower lip as she tried to think of something to say that wouldn't go into the emotional abuse of her past. "After my belly button. I got that one next."

"Oh. Interesting. Is there a reason for each piercing?"

Fear slithered down her spine. She didn't want Jason to know of the emotional scars she still held deep in her soul. Charles certainly had done a number on her not only emotionally, but physically in the way she got the piercings to make her body fit into the picture perfect woman for him. Charles was a big burly man and although he never got physically abusive with her, the emotional toll was enough to send her into a tailspin. She could never please him—from sexual intercourse to cooking dinner—nothing was ever good enough for him. He belittled her constantly and when she'd try to stand up for herself, he'd deny there was a problem. She wanted to go to counseling then, but he refused, insisting there wasn't anything wrong with their relationship. Now that she knew more about emotional abuse, she understood the problem his constant verbal and emotional manipulation took on her. She didn't trust easily and that cumulated in her relationship with men.

"What do you mean?"

"Some people get tats to commemorate a loved one or something. I wasn't sure if the same thing applied to piercings."

For me, yes. I got each one in hopes of making myself beautiful for Charles. "No. I just felt like getting them." *I was never good enough for him.*

"Did they hurt? I mean tats kind of sting depending on where you get them, of course, but I've never had a piercing."

"Not really. They ache a little afterward for a while and you have to take good care of them, but otherwise, no they don't hurt much."

"Are you okay? You seemed kind of lost in thought while we were talking about this."

"I'm fine. I just don't like talking about them."

"Why?"

She jumped to her feet, rubbing her arms to calm the goose bumps flittering across her skin. "I just don't, okay? Please, just let it go."

He moved to her side, took her in his arms and rubbed his hands up and down her back. "It's okay, Peyton. We don't have to discuss them anymore, if you don't want to."

"Thank you," she whispered, snaking her arms around his waist to hold him closer. The solid wall of his chest gave her comfort where she never had any before. Talking about this always made her antsy even with the therapist. *I thought I was over this. Apparently not. I need to make an appointment with Jamie to talk. It's been a couple of weeks.* She pulled him in tighter to chase away the self-doubts. Jason liked her just the way she was. She didn't have to pretend to be anything with him, but the woman.

"Do you want to help me with dishes?"

She sniffed to hide the well of tears sure to break loose if he so much as kissed her right now. This man made everything in her life seem like it wasn't too bad after all. "Sure."

While they cleaned the kitchen, she didn't say much although she kept feeling Jason's gaze on her several times. "What?"

"Nothing. I'm just amazed you're here with me."

"Why?"

"Because you're a very beautiful woman. You could probably have any guy you wanted and you're here with me."

"Oh please. You're the playboy. You've got three quarters of the women over the age of eighteen all twittering like a bunch of thirteen year olds every time you come around. I've seen you at the bar, don't forget."

"You've been paying attention?"

"Yeah, for several months now."

"Interesting." He wrapped the towel he was using on the dishes, around her waist, dragging her into his embrace.

"What's so interesting?"

"You've been watching me."

"Why is that so thought-provoking?"

"Because I've been watching you. The way your hair shines beneath the lights of the bar. The way you grip a glass to pour a beer. How your hair caresses your cheek sometimes when it gets flipped in the front to rest on your breast." He punctuated each sentence with a kiss somewhere, her lips, her eyes, the shell of her ear, the slope of her neck, and the swell of her breast. "I've been dying to touch you for months now."

"You have?" She couldn't believe one of the most gorgeous men in Bandera had been interested in her for months while she panted after him like a lost puppy trying to find her master.

"Yeah."

He nipped at her bottom lip before he plunged his tongue between her parted lips to tangle with her own. *God, I love kissing this man.*

A knock sounded on the door and he groaned as he broke the kiss. "I'm going to kill whoever that is."

She giggled as she pushed him back by the shoulders. "We have all night."

"But I was just getting into kissing you."

"Me too."

The knock sounded again as he heard Jeff's voice outside the door. "Jason? Open up. There's a problem."

Jason sighed as he tipped his head back on his shoulders. "All right. I'm coming."

When he opened the door, Jeff pushed his way inside giving her a perfunctory glance as he turned to face his brother. "There's been an accident."

"What? Who?"

"Joel. Nothing serious, I don't think, but he's been taken to the hospital in San Antonio by ambulance. You coming?"

He raked his fingers through his hair. "Uh, yeah. Let me throw some clothes on."

Jeff glanced back at her, tipped his hat and headed back out the door. "I'll see you there."

"Yeah. I'll be right behind you." He stopped his frantic search for his clothes for a moment to take her in his arms. "I'm sorry."

"Don't be. You're family needs you. Go."

"You'll be here when I get back?"

"I don't think so."

With her hands clasped in his, he said, "Then go with me. I need you."

"Are you sure? I'll just be in the way."

"No you won't. Please?"

"All right. Let me put my boots on and comb my hair. I wouldn't want to show up at the hospital with sex hair." She shoved her fingers through the messy strands in an attempt to tame the wild mass.

He kissed her palms before he shoved a curl behind her ear. "I think you look damned sexy with it all mussed like that."

"That's your opinion, mister. Somehow I think your family is going to know what we were doing before Jeff got here."

He shrugged and stepped back. "Who cares. I don't."

She rolled her eyes as she moved to grab her boots from near the door and shoved her feet inside. Her purse lay on the bench so she grabbed it to find her brush. After running it through her hair a few times, she announced she was ready to go.

"We'll take my truck," he said, returning from putting his shirt and socks on that they'd discarded in the living room before their romp in the kitchen.

"You dressed pretty fast."

"I'm quick when I need to be."

"Not during sex, I hope."

He looked aghast as she laughed. "Never during sex."

They walked out to his truck, avoiding the dog who lounged on the porch, barely lifting his head when they walked around him. The night's inky black sky reflected a thousand stars twinkling overhead. No moon shone tonight to light their way, but she didn't care. She was with a guy she quickly realized her feelings went a lot deeper for than she wanted to admit. Her heart wasn't listening to her head and she was afraid her heart might win the argument.

* * * *

"What the hell did you do to yourself, Trip?" Jason asked Joel as they walked into emergency room at the local hospital. His nickname for his triplet siblings coming through loud and clear. He called Joel, Trip for triplet and Joshua, Doub for double. Jason's nickname from the family had always been One because he was the eldest of the three of them, then Joshua and last came Joel.

"Hit a damned deer with my truck." Joel glanced at his wife sitting next to him holding his hand. "Broke my leg in the process."

"You're lucky you didn't break your head open, you dumbshit."

"Like I had control, you asshole. I didn't plan on hitting a deer. It jumped out in front of me. I didn't have a chance to even stop before it was on my hood and half through my windshield. I'm just glad Mesa wasn't in the truck with me. The deer went into the passenger side seat practically." Joel kissed her fingertips. "I wouldn't want you hurt for anything."

Joshua gagged from his place in the corner. The bed had been completely surrounded by Young family members.

"It'll be your turn soon enough," Nina said, glancing at Jason's hand joined with Peyton's as they stood next to the bed with everyone else. "I'm glad this wasn't worse than it is. A broken leg can be managed although you won't be able to ride for a bit. Maybe you can take over doing some of the office stuff for me."

Joel blanched as Mesa laughed. "Yeah, I can see that. Joel behind a desk?"

"Well, what else is he going to do while he's in a cast for six to eight weeks?" Nina moved to where she stood near the head of Joel's bed. "You'll have to suck it up, buttercup."

The entire family laughed until the doctor came in through the curtains with a soft, "Whoa. Okay. I didn't realize the whole family would be here."

"He's one of ours, so yeah, you get all of us," Jeff replied from his spot near the sink. Terri must have stayed home with the boys since their little one wasn't very old yet.

Jason also noticed Paige wasn't there either, but then again with her twin pregnancy moving along at a rapid pace, she probably didn't need to be out here either. *Since when did I become such a mother hen with the women of our family?* He tucked Peyton's hand into the crook of his arm. "How are you feeling, bro?"

"Hurts like hell, but they've given me pain medicine."

"That's right and we'll be taking him to surgery soon," the doctor added, looking at the chart in his hand. "He'll need a plate or two to stabilize the break. It's a pretty bad fracture since the dashboard was shoved up into his lap. I'm surprised both legs aren't broken."

"Surgery?" Mesa asked, her grip tightening on Joel's hand.

"Yes. It's a must."

"Don't worry, baby. I'll be fine."

"You'd better be. We have some planning to do."

"I know, darlin'."

"Planning?" Nina asked, hope shining in her eyes.

"We didn't want to announce it this way, but we are expecting a baby in about eight months."

"Another grandchild!" Nina clapped before she bent over Joel, kissing him on the head and then doing the same with Mesa. "It's about time. You two have been together for a while."

"It's hasn't been that long, Mom."

"Long enough to expect a grandchild."

Joel and Mesa both laughed as they shook their heads.

Jason shook his brother's hand excitedly. He wasn't sure he wanted kids of his own, certainly not yet, but he was happy for his brother who he knew wanted several children. Mesa had been such a good thing for Joel when they'd gotten together even though when the whole thing started, Jason wasn't sure she was the right girl. The day they'd been married was a joyful occasion at the ranch and one he wouldn't forget.

"Well since everything is fine here, I'm going to head back home."

"You aren't staying for the surgery," James asked from his spot near the wall.

"Do I need to?"

"Had plans, did you?" Joel asked, eyeing Peyton as she stood near his right side. "Sorry I interrupted things."

"It's fine now that I know you're going to be okay. I couldn't have my brother coming to the hospital and me not seeing how you are even if it's nothing major."

"It could have been," Jeff said.

"I know, Jeff. That's why I came. He's still family even though he's my squirt of a younger brother."

"By fifteen minutes, for God's sake!"

"Still younger."

"Asshole."

"You'll be fine if you're cussing me out."

The nurse came through the curtain. "Everyone is going to have to clear out. I need to prep him for surgery, get another IV started and draw more blood."

"Damn woman. You already took two tubes."

"Suck it up. I need five more before they take you to surgery, plus the anesthesiologist will be coming in soon to talk to you."

"We're gone then," Jason said, moving toward the curtain. "Are they going to keep him for a couple of days afterward?"

"At least tomorrow, yes."

"I'll be back by in the morning then."

"Thanks for coming, Jason. I know you were busy with Peyton. I didn't mean to ruin your plans."

"It's okay. No problem. We were done with dinner already anyway so we're going to, ahem, watch a movie."

Joel's eyebrow shot up over his eye. "Movie?"

"Yeah, a movie. Right Peyton?"

"What movie?" The whole group laughed as she blushed so hard the roots of her hair turned red too.

"Come on, babe. Let's go home."

Nina grinned as they all walked out of the curtained area and back down the hall toward the waiting room. The rest of the family left, leaving Jason, Peyton and his mother and father. Mesa, of course, stayed at her husband's bedside until they wheeled him out toward the operating room. Then she joined his parents to wait.

"He'll be fine." Jason hugged Mesa. "I know he will."

"I know, but I'm worried. What if something happens? What if he goes into cardiac arrest or what if he has a reaction to the anesthesia?"

"Is there any reason to worry? No. Quit freaking yourself out."

"I know. I'm being silly, but I love him so much and now that there is a baby on the way, I don't know what I'd do without him."

Nina put her arms around Mesa, cradling her almost like a lost child. Jason felt out of touch with the whole scenario even though it was his triplet brother in there. They didn't talk about it much, but the three of them had a bond. When one hurt, the others hurt. When one was sad, the others could feel it and when Joel had fallen hard for Mesa, Jason knew in his heart she was perfect for his brother in the end.

"We are headed out. Call me when he's out of surgery, please, or I won't sleep a wink tonight and I'll be back up here before morning."

"Of course, son," his dad answered before his mother could as she stood there rocking Mesa and whispering to her that Joel would be fine.

Jason put his arm around Peyton as they walked toward the door. "Thanks, Dad. See you at home."

The ride back to his house was made in silence as he contemplated the turn of events for his brother, his triplet. Joel was going to be a daddy himself and man did it make Jason feel old. His younger sibling was married with a baby on the way. Wasn't it time he settled down too? He glanced across the truck at Peyton. Was she the one? Should he give up his wandering ways for the love of one woman? What if she didn't love him? What if she cheated on him? What if she didn't want anything more than sex like they'd talked about in the beginning? Did he want more now?

"What are you thinking about?" she asked, cocking her head to the side.

"Lots of things."

"Like?"

"What if I asked you to marry me?"

"What? Are you nuts?"

"Maybe am I. I'm thinking about my future and I think you'd be a good fit."

"I'm not marrying you, Jason."

"Why not?"

"We've been dating for what? Two weeks and you want me to marry you? You're crazy."

"No I'm not. My brother did it. He seems happy. I want that too."

"Not with me, you don't."

"Sure I do. You'd be as good as any, I'm thinking."

She punched him in the shoulder. "As good as any? You ask me to marry you without even professing to love me and I'm as good as any? Why don't you just go to The Dusty Boot, grab the first woman who walks through the door and ask her? It'd be about as romantic and caring as the proposal I just got."

"Now just wait a minute, Peyton. I mean we get along good. We're good in bed together. We seem to have some things in common. You're pretty enough."

"Thanks, for that, but no. Take your proposal and stuff it up your ass."

They pulled into the driveway in front of his house. The truck hadn't even come to a complete halt and she was out the passenger side door headed for her car.

"What the hell? Where are you going?" he asked, rushing around the front of his truck as the headlights reflected off the porch. He grabbed the door to her car before she could shut it.

"Let go."

"No, let's talk about this."

"There isn't anything to talk about. I'm not marrying you."

"Fine. Then let's keep going the way we are."

"You know, I don't think so. You want something I can't give you apparently. You've changed, Jason. You said you didn't want a wife and I was good with that since I didn't want to be a wife, but now you're asking me to marry you out of the blue."

"Come inside."

"No. I'm going home. I don't want to see you anymore. We obviously want different things in this." She waved her hand back and forth. "Whatever this is."

"Don't go, Peyton."

"We're done, Jason. I'm sorry, but this isn't going to work." She slammed the door shut, started the car and then backed out of his life in a spray of gravel.

Chapter Twelve

Jason twirled the rope he held over his head before tossing it expertly over the horns of the bull he intended to move to the barn. He had some cows he needed to inseminate. The work on a ranch never ended, never took a break nor did it stop for a broken heart.

Broken heart, bah!

Joshua helped herd the bull through the panels to the holding pen Jason had fashioned so he could collect the sperm from the bull. The steer he planned to use to get the bull ready was already in place. Joey stood nearby waiting with the ejaculation kit for when the bull mounted the steer. Joshua threaded another rope through the ring on the bull's nose as Jason dismounted from his horse and removed the one around the animal's neck. "I'll take it from here." He took the ejaculation kit from Joey as the bull jumped to mount the steer. He easily got the false vagina on the bull, capturing the bull's semen. "See. Easy as pie."

"Do you know which of your cattle you're going to inseminate and your schedule?" Joey asked. He usually handled the horses on their parent's place, but today, Jacob manned the horses and took the guests out. Jacob needed to stay close these days as Paige could have the babies at any time.

"Yeah. Got them penned in the other side of the barn already waiting."

"Perfect," Joshua said, releasing the rope on the bull's nose ring so they didn't tear it out by accident. The nose ring helped to control the bull during the ejaculation process.

This bull was Jason's prized possession and his ace in the hole for having prime livestock for the PBR in the coming years ahead.

"How are things with Peyton?" Joey asked, moving the steer they'd use for bait.

"Who?" Jason didn't want to talk about how shit had gone down with her. He didn't want to talk about her, didn't want to think about her and certainly didn't want to tell his brothers he'd fucked up royally by asking her to marry him in a nervous fuck up.

"Peyton? You know. Pretty, nice rack, works at The Dusty Boot? I thought you were fucking her?" The look in Joshua's eyes as he brought up Peyton made Jason want to punch him.

"I was. Drop it."

"Ah." Joshua and Joey exchanged amused glances.

"Quit acting like you two are laughing."

"We aren't laughing at you, Jason. We're laughing with you. I bet she was a great lay."

"Maybe, but it's none of your business anyway."

"If you aren't fucking her anymore, you can tell us." The brothers leaned over the metal fencing with their arms under their chins.

"Yeah, spill it," Joey said, his eyes gleaming with curiosity.

"I don't fuck and gossip."

The two brothers looked at each other and then back at him. "Sure you do. You always have before, what's so special about her?" Joshua asked, putting the toe of his cowboy boot on the bottom rung of the fence in preparation for a longwinded discussion about women.

"I'm not talking to you about Peyton."

"Why not? What's the deal?"

Jason stored the sperm in a container to inseminate the cows in a little while. He needed to take care of the bull and the steer first. He wiped down his hands with disinfectant. "Because I don't. What happened between us is private."

"I don't believe you. You always talk about the women you've been with." Joshua elbowed Joey. "Didn't he talk about, what was her name? Sheila?"

"Oh don't get me started on her. She's trying to say she's pregnant with my child."

"She what?" Joshua asked, shock clearly written on his face. "Didn't you use a condom man?"

"After we'd been together a few times, no. She said she was on birth control."

"And you fell for that shit?" Joey shook his head. "Never fall for that crap. She's a user if I ever saw one."

"I know. Right now I'm not even sure she's really pregnant, much less if it's mine. I know she's been with other guys since me so who knows." Jason grabbed the rope to lead the bull back outside into the holding pen he would be housed in until they'd extracted a few more sperm samples from him.

"What did Peyton say?"

"What the hell does it matter? Peyton and I aren't together anymore so let it go."

"What happened between you two? You seemed happy before, now you're like a bear with a thorn in its paw," Joey said, lifting his hat off his head and wiping his brow from the sweat collecting under the brim.

The heat today was almost unbearable especially in the stuffiness of the barn. Sunlight filtered through the hayloft slats to the floor below, reflecting the dust floating in the air. The bull stomped his feet, stirring up the dirt from beneath his hoofs as Jason got him situated in his pen. "Easy boy. You'll get your treats and feed in a minute."

"Yeah, Jason. Tells us what happened."

He shut the gate behind the bull. "I asked her to marry me."

"What? Seriously?" Joshua slapped him on the back. "I guess since you aren't seeing each other anymore, she said no."

"Not just no, but hell no."

"Why'd you do something so stupid?" Joey stood with his hands on his hips and his legs braced apart like he planned to jump on some bucking bronc to bring him to his knees.

"God love you, little brother. I really hadn't figured out how stupid I was before now."

"Well?"

He shrugged as he coiled the rope he'd been using. "I don't know why I asked her. After what happened with Joel and realizing all of this could be gone in a split second, I thought about having someone permanent in my life instead of fucking anything that moved. I really want that for some unfucking godly reason."

"With Peyton?" Joshua asked, his stunned expression almost hilarious.

Jason laughed as he nodded his head. "Yeah, with Peyton."

Joshua nodded, clapping Jason on the back. "Good for you, brother. I can see you two together. She seems like a nice girl."

"Wait. Did you miss the part where we aren't seeing each other anymore? She turned me down flat right before she sprayed dust and gravel all over my front door in a hurry to get out of my life."

"You'll convince her."

"And just how the hell am I supposed to do that? She won't even talk to me. I've tried. I've sent her text message after text message. I never get a reply."

"Have you lost what little sense Mom and Dad gave you?" Joey asked. "You don't do this kind of shit over text message, you dumbass. Go to her house. Corner her. Fuck her. Talk to her. Whatever. If you really want her, you need to get right in her face and make her listen to you."

"Oh and you're an expert on relationships? You don't even have a girlfriend."

"But if I did, I'd know how to treat her. I would make sure she knew she was the most important thing in my life the whole time we are together. I'd bring her roses. Take her to lunch just because. Buy her special little presents. You know, all those things girls like."

Jason rubbed his chin, the whisker scraping against his palm. He hadn't shaved in a couple of days, hoping he'd have a chance to talk to Peyton. He thought she liked the five o'clock shadow and rough whisker burn on her skin. He knew he liked seeing it on her. "Maybe."

"Maybe? You really need to pull your head out of your ass, brother. Do you want her?"

"Yes."

"No, do you really want her, like as in permanently?"

"I think so. I mean I can't picture my bed or my life without her in it these days."

"Then go to her."

"Okay. I will. After we're done with this shit this afternoon. I'll go to her house and make her listen to me so she'll realize, I was a bit desperate when I asked her to marry me and maybe that is in the cards down the road, but we can go back to what we had before I blurted that out."

"There you go!" Joshua punched him in the arm. "Now you're on the right track."

"I'm not sure I am, but what do I have to lose. She won't talk to me now so it can't hurt anything by going over there unless she's got a shotgun or something."

* * * *

Peyton stared at the television without conscious thought of what actually played in front of her face.

Paige swiped her hand in front of Peyton's eyes. "Where are you?"

"Huh?"

"You are totally not here right now."

"Sorry. I know we are supposed to be having a girl's night out, but I'm not into this." Peyton got to her feet, spilling popcorn from the bowl as she sat it down on the coffee table. "My mind is elsewhere."

"Yeah, we know," Mandy said, picking up the popcorn bowl.

Her phone beeped. Another text message. She knew who it was from without even looking. Jason. He just didn't give up although he didn't bug her at the bar or come by her house, he still sent text message after text message trying to get her to talk to him. At the bar, he watched her, unnerving her to no end with his piercing blue eyes. He always stayed until she closed, never leaving until he knew she was safely in her car. It had kind of become a game to her. See how pissed off she could make him by flirting with guys at the bar, but she never went home with any of them. No, Jason Young had wormed his way into her thoughts, dreams and life inside of a few short weeks. *Damn him.*

Being this hung up on a guy usually turned out bad. Look at her relationship with Charles.

"Honey, what's wrong?" Paige asked, grimacing a little as she shifted on the couch.

"Are you okay?"

"Yeah, my back hurts is all. Nothing new there, but it's been cramping off and on all day."

"Cramping? Are you sure you aren't in labor, Paige?"

Paige cocked her head to the side. "I still have like two weeks before they'll even take them c-section. I can't be in labor."

"Paige, you're having twins. They do whatever the hell they want. I think you should go to the hospital to get checked out."

"Really?"

"Yeah, really."

"I need to call Jacob. Can you drive me? I'm scared."

"Nothing to be scared about. Those babies are well done already. Aren't you like thirty-eight weeks?"

"Yeah, but I thought pregnancy lasted forty weeks?"

"In the perfect world, honey, but with twins, it's not unusual to have them early." Peyton grabbed her tennis shoes and slipped them on in a rush. Who cared if she was in her Hello Kitty pajama bottoms, a T-shirt and shoes with no socks? Her friend needed her. "You can call Jacob from the car. Let's go."

She quickly ushered Paige and Mandy out to her car, got them inside as Paige got on the phone with Jacob, and then went around to the driver's side. It was going to be a long night if Paige was in labor.

"Hi Honey. Yeah, it's me. Listen, Peyton is taking me to the hospital. I've been cramping all day. I know. It's okay. No, my water hasn't broke. It'll be okay, Jacob. I'm in good hands. Just meet us at the hospital in the labor and delivery department. We'll be there in about forty-five minutes depending on how fast Peyton drives." She glanced at Peyton as she nodded. "Yeah, forty-five minutes. Okay. I love you. See you soon."

Peyton took her hand and squeezed her fingers. "You'll be fine."

"I know. I trust you."

"Thanks. We'll get there in plenty of time."

Twenty minutes later, found them on the side of the road changing a tire. "Fuck, fuck, fuck!"

"Is this going to take much longer, Peyton? I think it's definitely labor. My belly is cramping now."

"How far apart?"

"About five minutes."

"Shit. I'll hurry."

"I sure don't want to have these babies in your car."

"I don't want you to either."

Headlights blinded her for a moment as a truck pulled up behind her car before it shut off. "Oh, thank you, Lord. I hope it's someone who can change this damned tire faster or take Paige onto the hospital before it's too late."

"Peyton?"

"Ah, fuck. It had to be Jason," she mumbled under her breath.

"Jacob has half the county searching for you guys. What's the problem?"

"I picked up a nail and got a flat. I can't get these damned lug nuts off. They are too tight."

"Let me try."

He crouched down beside her, bringing the scent of his aftershave with him. That smell on him did wild things to her insides. She inhaled, bringing the scent to her nose as she closed her eyes.

"Are you sniffing me?"

She caught herself leaning toward him with a jerk. "No."

A half crooked smile creased his lips while he wrestled the last of the lug nuts loose. *Damn the man.*

"Grab the spare for me, would you, please? We'll get you ladies on the road here in a minute."

Within minutes, he had the tire changed.

"Can you hurry please?" Paige groaned as another pain hit her. "They are pretty close together."

"We'll be on our way in a second. Hang tight." She glanced at Jason as they both stood and he put the tire back in the trunk. "Thank you."

"You're welcome. Get her to the hospital before she has those babies in your car."

"We aren't far. Five minutes."

"Hit the emergency room when you get there. Jacob has everyone on high alert."

"Will do." She saluted smartly before she walked around to slide inside the car. Jason stood by his truck as she pulled away, watching him in the rearview mirror. She wondered if he'd follow to the hospital since Jacob sent him out looking for them. Sure enough, he pulled out behind them, the lights of his truck reflecting in her eyes as she glanced back, keeping him in sight.

Thirty minutes later, they pulled into the overhang of the emergency room. Two nurses with a wheelchair rushed out and around to the passenger side of the car as Peyton and Mandy got out. "She's having pains about three minutes apart."

"We'll take it from here." As one nurse helped Paige out of the car, water gushed down her legs. "It appears your water just broke. We are taking you straight to the delivery room. We can check you there."

"But they were supposed to be born by c-section, not natural."

"Honey, these babies decide when they're coming and how they're coming, we don't. You'll do fine."

"Where's Jacob?"

"Right here, darlin'," Jacob answered coming around the car. "What happened to you and Peyton? I thought I would go crazy."

"We got a flat. I couldn't get the damned lug nuts off."

"Jacob, I'm scared."

"You'll be fine, baby. Let's get you inside. The doctor is waiting."

"Oh." She held her stomach as she doubled over in pain.

"Get her inside. I have a feeling baby number one will be making his or her debut soon," the nurse said, taking control of the situation as they pushed her inside the double doors.

Peyton stood there, not sure what to do next. Her friend was in good hands, she hoped, and the babies would be born without any complications. She had to believe that.

"Pull your car around to the parking lot and park to the side. You can meet her upstairs," the second nurse said before she went through the double doors behind Paige.

After a few seconds, Peyton got back in the car with Mandy in the front passenger seat and moved her car to an empty spot. She debated for a few moments when she saw one available next to Jason's truck. He wasn't in it. Apparently, he'd already gone inside to let Jacob know they'd arrived. Good. She really didn't want to be near him anymore than she had to. Not that she minded his physical nearness, but being too close to him brought back the memories she'd been trying desperately to forget over the last two weeks. "Marry him. Is he crazy?"

"What'd you'd say? Marry who?"

"Jason."

"What? He asked you to marry him?"

"Yeah, crazy, huh?"

"I would have said yes in a heartbeat."

Peyton opened her door and slammed it shut behind her as Mandy got out on the other side. "Well, I didn't. I told him he was nuts and there would be no way I would marry him now or any time in the near future. We fucked. It was good, but I'm not in love with him."

"I think you protest too much myself. If you really thought about it for more than a few minutes, you'd realize you are at least half in love with the man already." Mandy came around the front of the car.

"You're as crazy as he is, Mandy." Peyton headed for the sliding door to the hospital lobbying. Bah, in love with Jason. No way. She wouldn't give into that silly emotion especially with a cowboy. Yeah, he was good in bed. They connected that way, but really what else did they have in common? He came from a prominent, solid *large* family whereas she came from a nonexistent one.

She had baggage, emotional scars she wasn't sure she could get past with another man. Fucking had been great between them, but she didn't do emotion very well with anyone. Not since Charles raked her through the coals with breaking her down to a needy wreck.

"You need to move on, Peyton. Jason is a good guy."

"Move on from what?"

"I know about Charles."

"How? I never told you."

Mandy put an arm around Peyton's shoulders even though she tried to shake her off. "Yes you did. One night, when you were very drunk, you broke down and told me everything. He did a number on you, I'll give you that, but are you going to let him ruin you for any other man?"

"Butt out."

"I can't. You are my friend. I see how miserable you are. You were happy when you were with Jason, you aren't now. You've been a bitch the last two weeks since you walked out on him."

"I can handle my relationship with Jason."

"You don't have a relationship, remember?"

"I don't want one either."

"You might lie to me. You might lie to Jason, but don't lie to yourself. You're the only one who knows everything about what is going on inside your brain and your heart. He's good for you. Admit it, even if it's only to yourself." Mandy kissed her on the cheek before she walked inside the hospital, leaving Peyton to ponder her words as she watched from outside.

Jason stood with his family in the waiting room. Every Young was there except Joel, Mesa and Terri who probably stayed home with the boys since they wouldn't be allowed in the hospital anyway. It wasn't a good idea to have kids around all those germs. They looked happy awaiting the arrival of the newest additions to the family.

When Mandy walked in, Jason greeted her with a smile. Jealousy zinged through Peyton. Was he flirting with Mandy? Did Mandy flirt back? Was there something going on there between them? Maybe he'd been fucking all of them simultaneously. Her, Mandy, and Sheila.

"No, that's nuts. I would have known."

Would you?

Jason broke off from the crowd and came out the doors toward her. "Hi."

"Hi."

"You okay?" he asked, shoving his hands in the front pocket of his jeans.

"Yeah."

"Why are you standing out here?"

"Just gettin' some air."

"You can come in with the family, you know. You're good friends with Paige. No one will kick you out."

"I didn't think they would, but…"

"But what, Peyton? Is it me?"

"Well, it's kind of awkward, you know, since we were doing the horizontal mambo."

He smiled as he looked down at the toes of his boots. "Sorry."

"It's okay." She frowned.

"What's the frown for?"

"Something Mandy told me before she went inside is bugging me."

"Something you want to talk about?"

"Not with you."

"Is it about me?"

"Yeah. She's wrong, but you know, it's kind of stuck in my brain and I need to work it out."

"I miss you, you know."

"Please don't."

"Why? It's the truth. I still think about your body pressed up against mine, the warmth of your pussy around my cock when we were making love."

"Fucking, Jason. We were fucking."

"Whatever you want to call it to justify everything in your mind, you go right ahead, darlin', but to me, we were making love."

Chapter Thirteen

Jason scuffed the toe of his boot at a rock, dislodging the stone as he sent it across the grass. "I know I sent you into a tailspin with the marriage thing."

"You think so?"

"Yeah, I know so, but listen. I'm sorry. I was kind of thinking weird the day Joel got hurt and realizing how fast things can change. Not that I didn't mean it."

She put up her hand. "Don't, Jason. I'm not marrying you."

"I'm not asking you to. I just want us to date again."

"Why?"

He skimmed a finger down her cheek. "I miss you. I said that already, but it's true."

Her body broke out in goose bumps from her head to her toes as a shiver rolled through her.

"And I think you miss me too."

"Whatever gave you that idea?"

"Your reaction right now. Don't tell me my touch doesn't affect you because I know it does, just like yours affects me."

"I don't know what you're talkin' about."

"Liar," he whispered, his mouth near her ear. "Are you wet? I'm hard as a damned brick just thinking about you all warm around me."

"Jason, please."

"Please what? Please make love to you? Please, kiss you? Please, touch you where you burn for me?"

Joshua popped his head out the door. "Hey, Jase. The babies are here."

"I'll be right there." He stepped back, taking his heat with him. "This isn't over."

With her hand in his, he led her inside to find out about the babies Paige just gave birth to. Peyton's mind whirled with emotions, sensations and confusion. She didn't know how she felt about Jason these days, but she would have to figure things out soon or go mad trying.

When they made it inside, the way Nina's eyebrow shot up over her eye seeing Peyton's hand clasped tightly in Jason's left her nervous. Nina smiled as she nodded so she figured it would be okay to leave it there…for now.

"It's a boy and a girl!" Jacob shouted as he came out of the obstetrics ward where they'd all moved after Jason and Peyton joined them. "They are healthy and screaming their lungs out. Paige is tired, but fine."

"My first granddaughter!" Nina asked, tears rolling down her cheeks as she hugged Jacob to her. "Names?"

"We haven't decided yet, but you'll be the first to know, Mom."

"Congratulations, son." James slapped him on the back. "Go be with your wife and children. We'll take it from here."

Peyton felt tears welling up in her own eyes as she thought about how far Paige and Jacob had come in such a short time. They hadn't been married long after Paige found out about her pregnancy, but they seemed happy together and very much in love.

How do I feel about finding someone to love for the rest of my life?

"You okay?"

"Yeah." She fanned her hands in front of her face, trying desperately to dry the tears. "Just a little teary thinking about those babies' parents. Theirs is such a great love story."

"It sure is. Did you see the first time they met?"

"Yes. I was working the bar that night. Dan tried to get her to stay out of it, but she couldn't. Not Paige. She is always one for the underdog."

"And now they are a happy family with two little ones."

"She's going to make a great mom."

"Jacob will make a great dad too. He's always loved kids."

"What about you? Do you want kids someday?"

"Maybe, but not for quite a while. I'd like to be just a couple for a few years to spend time with my woman." He dropped his arm around her shoulders.

Jacob came back out the doors. "Two can go in at a time to see Paige. The babies are in the nursery getting cleaned up, weighed and measured right at the moment."

"Peyton, why don't you and Jason go in first? I know you all want to get home soon."

"Thanks, Nina."

Peyton walked up and kissed Jacob on the cheek. "Congrats, Daddy."

He grinned so wide, she thought maybe his face would crack as he puffed up his chest and repeated, "Daddy. I like the sound of that."

When the two of them followed him back, they went by the nursery first to take a peek at the babies. Both were wrapped really tightly in a little blue blanket and a little pink blanket with matching knit hats.

"Aren't they gorgeous?" Jacob asked, tapping on the window as the nurse brought the little boy closer. "I haven't any idea what we are going to name them."

"You two didn't discuss names?"

"Oh, we did, but we couldn't agree. I think I want to name them after Paige's parents though since they aren't here to see their grandchildren."

"How sweet of you, Jacob. I'm sure she'd love it."

"We'll see. She's pretty emotional right now."

"Well, duh. She just gave birth. She's going to be emotional for a while."

"Shit. Really? She's been such a mess for so long during this pregnancy, I was hoping it would all magically go away when the babies were born."

"Don't count on it for about six weeks. It'll take that long for her body to get back to some semblance of normal."

"What about sex?"

"Six weeks, buddy," Jason said, grinning.

"I hate you."

"Don't blame me, blame the doctor. Maybe she won't make you wait that long."

"God, I hope not."

Peyton laughed as they walked down the corridor to the room Paige was in. When they pushed open the door and peeked inside, she was lying on the bed dressed in her pretty pajamas she'd packed in her bag, resting.

"Is she asleep?"

"No, she's not asleep," Paige answered, opening her eyes. "Hey. Come in. Did you see the babies?"

"They were taking the little girl for a bath so we didn't get a close look at her, but we saw your son. What a handsome devil he's going to be."

"I know, right?"

"How are you feeling?"

"Like I've been hit by a bus, but thanks for asking."

"I'm sorry things go so screwed up."

Paige squeezed her hand. "We made it. That's all that matters, although we might not have had Jason not found us and changed the tire."

"You look ravishing, Paige." He leaned over to kiss her forehead.

"Oh stop with you and the flattery, brother-in-law. I look like shit dried up in the summer Texas sun, rolled and boiled to a crisp."

They all laughed. "We won't stay long. There is a ton of people out there waiting to see you and those gorgeous babies. I just wanted to say congratulations. I'll come by to visit tomorrow when things calm down. I want my cuddle time with the twins."

"There will be plenty of that to go around although with having the first granddaughter, I think you might be fighting Nina for cuddle time."

"Well, I have to give her first dibs since she is their grandmother, but as their godmother, I get them second." Peyton smiled as she patted Paige's hand. "Rest. I'll see you tomorrow."

"Okay. Thanks again for everything."

"You're welcome."

"Oh, and I'll expect the gossip when you come tomorrow."

"Gossip?"

Paige tilted her head noting Jason standing close to Peyton.

"Nothing to tell."

"Uh-uh." Paige shook her head. "You can't fool me."

Peyton stepped back. "We'll be going now."

"See you tomorrow."

Jason took her hand as they walked out of the room. She glanced back at Paige, noticing how her eyes twinkled when she caught the gesture. There would be no living with her come tomorrow when she visited. She better think of something fast or Paige would have her and Jason married off in the next couple of weeks.

* * * *

Jason walked Peyton out to her car after Mandy had a chance to visit briefly with Paige as well. He knew he couldn't let her go. If he did, he might never see her again and that wasn't acceptable to him. The need for her drove him to distraction. He couldn't think. He couldn't sleep. He couldn't eat. He was a mess all the way around without her and he would just have to convince her she belonged with him until he could come to terms with this need he harbored for her. He stopped with her next to the car.

"Come home with me."

"You can't be serious," she whispered, trying not to let Mandy know what he said. "I'm not going home with you."

"Why not?"

"We aren't seeing each other at the moment."

"But I want you."

"This is crazy, Jason. You can't just take me home."

"I don't understand what the problem is. When we were having sex before, you didn't have a problem with just coming home with me at the bonfire."

"I know, but that was different."

"Different how?"

She exhaled sharply as she rolled her eyes. "Just different. Besides, I have Mandy with me. We were having a girl's night when Paige went into labor."

"Oh."

"Yeah, oh. I can't just dump her off, tell her to go home, and then come over to your place."

"How about tomorrow?"

"I think I need to do some serious deliberating before I decide to sleep with you again. I'm not sure us getting involved is a good idea."

"We need to talk about it."

"You don't talk. You touch, kiss, nibble, bite…"

"I know. It's amazing, huh?"

"You're lack of communication on this matter is increasingly disturbing." She sighed as he brushed his lips over the curve of her neck.

"I'm trying to communicate my need."

"Your *need* is very apparent against my abdomen."

"See. I'm communicating."

"You are, too much."

They both jumped as Mandy honked the horn on the car. "Get it on or let's go. I'm tired of waitin'."

"I'll call you tomorrow since you've been ignoring my text messages."

"I wasn't interested."

"Are you now?"

"Maybe, but I need a couple of days to think things through, Jason."

He brushed his knuckled over the protruding tip of her breast, stopping her breath in her throat. "No thinking. Just feel."

"I'm feeling a little overwhelmed with you right now."

A deep sigh escaped his lips as he stepped back. "All right. I'll leave you alone. But don't think you can ignore me."

"I won't. You're a pretty persistent guy."

He grinned as he noticed how the flood light from the parking lot of the hospital shone on her face. Her eyes sparkled with interest. Her body called to him to throw her up on the hood of her car and fuck the daylights out of her, but not here. He wanted their reunion to be special, soft, inviting, with candles and soft music playing in the background. Maybe a bubble bath for two. He could be romantic when the need arose.

"Let me call you when I've had time to think."

"Two days, Peyton. I'm giving you two days. If I don't hear from you by then, I'm coming after you." He crushed his mouth against hers, tasting her like he'd die if he did get enough of her soon. The last two weeks had been hell on him, wishing for her to be near, wanting her, dreaming of her, and all the while not wanting to rush her. Well to hell with that, he was done giving her space.

Her hands went up around his neck as she pushed her breasts against his chest. Their kiss lasted a lifetime, but wasn't long enough when he finally lifted his head to look deep into her eyes. Yes, she wanted him, but fear mixed with confusion reflected in her gaze.

"I'll talk to you soon."

"Okay. Be safe going home."

"I will. You too."

She slipped inside her car and shut the door before he watched her back up. Red taillights reflected the slow drizzle beginning to wet the pavement. Summer rain. It would wash the dirt, grime and evil out of the air, leaving things fresh and clean. He dipped his head as he headed back inside to say goodbye to his family before heading home.

His parents were inside visiting Paige and the babies so he talked to the brothers standing nearby, told them he'd see them at home and then headed out to his truck. He needed time to plan the re-seduction of Peyton Matthews.

* * * *

Two days had passed and she still wasn't any closer to coming to a conclusion about Jason. She liked him, liked him a lot, but did she want to try some relationship with him? She still didn't know. What about the emotional scars of Charles' reign?

"So how are you feeling these days?" her therapist asked as she sat down in the chair in her office.

"Good. Physically, anyway. Emotionally, I'm not so sure."

"Why? What's going on?"

"There's this guy."

"Isn't there always a guy who is a bane of our problems?"

She laughed, the sound coming from her mouth hollow and without emotion. "Seems so."

"So tell me about this guy."

"He's sweet, gorgeous, about six-four, muscular and a cowboy."

"Not your typical man from what you've told me."

"No, Charles was a suit. Business man. Lawyer. He was always in control, twenty-four seven about everything from his business to his personal life. I think that's part of the reason I let him control me so much. I'm not a strong soul."

"Yes you are, Peyton. You are one of the strongest women I know. You have to believe that about yourself. Charles broke you down with manipulation."

She blew out a long breath. "I know, but I don't trust myself where men are concerned. What if Jason turns out to be like Charles?"

"Do you really think that's true?"

"No, but what if my perception is so skewed that I can't see it?"

"You'll have to learn to trust your perception. Tell me about how Jason treats you."

Peyton glanced out the window to watch a bird flit from tree to tree. "He's kind, considerate, passionate, and he handles me with kid gloves sometimes. Other times he's in my face forcing me to meet my feelings for him head on."

"And what are your feelings for him?"

"I'm not sure." She got to her feet to wander near the doctor's bookcase to look through the volumes on behaviors in adults and children. Recognizing a few of them, she picked one up and flipped through it. Someday, she would be the one on the other side of this conversation, she vowed silently. She wanted that more than anything.

"Are you in love with him?"

"I'm not sure what love feels like. I loved Charles or thought I did and see where that got me?"

"We all are afraid to let another person become our everything, Peyton."

"He's important to me, yes."

"That's a start." The doctor wrote down something on her notepad as Peyton took the seat she'd vacated only moments before. "Do you see your future with him in or out?"

"I'd like to think he'd be in it."

"As what? Partner, lover, husband?"

"Whoa. I'm nowhere near ready for a husband."

"I didn't say you were. I asked how you saw him in your future."

"For now, lover. I'm good with that."

The doctor tapped her pen to her lips. "Somehow I don't think you are. I think you want more from him, but you're afraid to ask for it thinking he'll deny you the way Charles did."

"Jason doesn't want anything permanent, but he did ask me to marry him a couple of weeks ago."

"You didn't tell me this in our last session."

"Sorry. It was spur of the moment. He didn't mean it. I think he was feeling a little old at the time. His brother had been hurt in an auto accident and he realized he might want to think about settling down. He rescinded the offer the other night."

"It all comes down to what you want from him."

"I like having him in my life."

"Then you are wanting something more permanent than you are wanting to admit."

"Maybe." She picked at the fingernail on her right hand. Did she really want more? Something permanent like marriage? Did she love him?

"Our time is up for today. Think about what you want and what he's willing to give. He sounds like the type of guy you could do well with. Someone patient, understanding and willing to be the strong one in the relationship when it's needed, but also willing to let you be yourself. You didn't have that with Charles."

"Thanks, Doc. You've been very helpful."

"Of course. See you next week?"

"Same time, same place. I'll be here."

"Oh, how is school signups coming along?"

"Perfect. I'm all registered to take classes in a few months. It's going to be a long haul, but I need to feel like I'm helping. Being a therapist is important to me."

"I know it is." The doctor hugged her and then stepped back. "You have my complete support."

"Thanks again, Doc. You're the best."

"Call me if you need anything."

"I will."

"Good luck with Jason."

Peyton nodded as she walked out of the doctor's office and onto the street. The sun shone bright overhead, blinding her for a moment as she turned to go to her car.

A hand came down on her mouth, firmly blocking any kind of scream as a man hauled her up against his chest. "Thought I'd never find you, didn't you?"

Chapter Fourteen

Charles.

"You fucking cunt. You are the biggest worthless piece of shit I've ever had the pleasure to know."

Then why are you here?

"You're going to pay for leaving me. No one leaves me."

He dragged her to the car next to the curb in front of the doctor's office. *How the hell did he find me?*

With his hand over her throat, he cut off the oxygen to her brain. She struggled against him, realizing she would die if she didn't get away from this crazy maniac. He wouldn't have any qualms about killing her, she realized.

Jason. I never got to see him again.

Her world went dark with his face at the forefront of her mind.

When she awoke several minutes later, she gasped for breath as she tried to bring her hands to her throat, but couldn't. She was tied to a bed in a dingy hotel room. She screamed as long and as loud as she could.

"Ah, you're awake finally." He glanced around the room. "Nice, huh? About your speed I would think. I'm sure you know the place well since it's across from that shithole of a bar you work at."

Fuck. He knows where I work?

"Yes, darling. I know where you work, I know where you live, and I know who your friends are." He studied the fingernails on his left hand. "You shouldn't have run."

"I was tired of the way you were treating me. I'm not your plaything." She yanked on the rope, realizing she wouldn't get anywhere talking to him, but the bindings held tight, chafing the tender skin of her wrists.

"Oh, but you are, my dear. You are everything I want to play with until I get tired of you. You can go when that happens. For now, you're mine until I say otherwise." He watched her struggle against her bonds. "You'll only hurt yourself by doing that, Peyton."

"Let me go, Charles, and I won't press charges for kidnapping."

"I don't think anyone will miss you anytime soon. Your friends think you're headed to your fuck buddy's house tonight, do they not?"

"How?"

"You have a very active telephone line."

"You tapped my phone?"

"I have ways of listening, yes."

"You bastard! Why can't you just leave me alone? You've done enough damage already with your abuse. Find someone else to fuck up!"

He shot up out of the chair. With him looming over her, he pulled back his hand and smacked her across the right cheek. "Shut the hell up! I'm not an abuser. You just can't handle criticism at all. You never could do anything right." Her cheek stung where his ring cut into the flesh below her cheekbone. Maybe she should just keep her mouth shut and hope to get free when he left to use the bathroom or something.

He cupped her cheek with his hand as he ran his thumb across her lips. "Now see what you made me do? I don't want to hurt you, Peyton. You're everything I wanted in a woman, but you have to realize I love you and I want you to come home with me of your own freewill."

"I'll never go anywhere with you."

He sighed, moving his hand away. "So be it." He grabbed a bag off the table and pulled out a syringe. "I didn't want to have to do this, but if I have to, I will. You see, you're mine. No way around it, but you have to realize that I will take you home one way or another." He drew up whatever was in the vile into the syringe, pushing the air out the top of the needle once he withdrew it. "I'll keep you anyway I must." As he came closer, a knock sounded on the door. "Who is it?"

"The manager. I've had a complaint about noise."

Charles sighed and set the syringe down on the table, eye level with her. "I can't open the door right now, I'm not dressed, but we'll keep it down." He chuckled. "My lady friend and I just got a little carried away."

"Help me! He's keeping me hostage. Please!"

Charles slapped his hand over her mouth to muffle her cries.

"Is everything all right in there?"

"Yes, sir. My fiancé and I are playing a game of capture, is all. Nothing to be concerned about. We are into a little kinky stuff, but thank you for being concerned. It is much appreciated."

"All right. Just keep it down."

"Yes, sir."

Charles grabbed a roll of duct tape off the table, slapping a piece over her mouth before she could even take a breath to scream again.

"No more fighting me, Peyton." He tilted his head to the side. "I like the piercings and the tats. They are kind of hot."

She shot daggers at him with her gaze.

"I know. I'm such a bastard, but once I get you in the car and we're headed back to Austin, everything will be better. I can guarantee you that." He grabbed the needle from the table. "You'll sleep soundly until we reach Austin and I can take care of you. You'll love the set up I have for you, Peyton. It's private, sound proof and no one knows it's mine because I rented it. It won't be traceable at all. By the time your friends realize you're gone, I'll have you safely ensconced in our private playground where I can use you until my heart is content." After he stuck the needle deep into her thigh, he slowly pushed the medication into her. "Something to help you sleep while we travel. I know how much you hate car rides for longer than an hour." He tsked several times with his tongue. "You can be so needy."

For the second time, her world rocked on its axis as her thoughts shifted to Jason. Would she ever see him again? Would she see her friends? She never did get to go see the babies. Would anyone even miss her at all? As her thoughts jumbled, she thought she heard Jason say he loved her, but that couldn't be. Jason wasn't there.

* * * *

Jason sat in the corner of The Dusty Boot waiting for Peyton to show up for work. He'd made plans to whisk her away after her shift finished, for a fun night of debauchery, but as he glanced at his watch, he realized she was very late. He'd never known her to be late for work before. He signaled Dan at the other end of the bar. When the man moved closer, he asked if the owner knew where Peyton might be.

"Nope. She didn't show for work, which isn't like her at all. I even tried calling her phone and all I got was voicemail. Have you seen her today?"

"No. I had plans this afternoon and didn't get to talk to her."

"Have you called Mandy? Maybe she knows where she might be."

Jason snapped his fingers. "Good thought. I'll give her a call." He grabbed his cell phone from his pocket and dialed Mandy's number from his address book. He had it from before he and Peyton started seeing each other, not that he'd dated Mandy, but she'd been his contact at the feed store for getting much needed information on the equipment he needed for inseminating and storing the sperm from his bulls for use later.

The phone rang several times before she picked it up. "Hey, Jason. What's up?"

"Have you seen Peyton today?"

"I had lunch with her this afternoon and then she had an appointment at three. Why?"

"She didn't show up for work."

"What? Shit."

"What's wrong?"

"There was a creepy guy hanging around my apartment earlier just watching things. I didn't think anything of it at the time, but now I don't know. He really creeped me out. He had on a black business suit, spit shined shoes, slicked back hair. You know the type."

"Yeah, but why would that concern you?"

"She hasn't told you about Charles, has she?"

"No. Who's Charles?"

"Where are you?"

"At The Dusty Boot."

"I'll be there in twenty minutes. We need to talk."

He hung up the phone as trepidation rippled down his back. Something was wrong. He could feel it.

Several minutes later, Mandy came through the door at a dead run. "You haven't heard from her all day?"

"No, why?"

"She said she planned to call you this afternoon after her appointment."

"Who did she have an appointment with?" he asked, taking a sip from his soda on the bar. He wasn't drinking. He needed his wits about him for Peyton's sake.

"Her psychiatrist. She hasn't been seeing her that long, maybe six months?"

"She's seeing a psychiatrist? Why?"

"I have to tell you about Charles for you to understand about her seeing someone. She was with Charles for three years. She thought he was the best thing since sliced bread. Tall, rich, lawyer, and good looking to boot. She thought he would marry her and they would be this little happy family."

Jason growled.

"I'm glad you don't like the thought of that. It tells me you are in love with her as much as she is in love with you."

"She is?"

Mandy nodded as she took a sip of Jason's soda. "She is, although she doesn't want to admit it, but back to Charles. He fucked with her brain. Emotional abuse is what they call it. It's the reason she has the piercings and tats except for the one on her breast for her mother. The others she did for him because everything she did wasn't good enough. He broke down her self-esteem so bad, she wouldn't know love if it smacked her in the face. He belittled her, called her stupid and made her feel like she wasn't good enough for anyone, not even him, but then he would build her back up only to tear her down again. She left him two years ago to move here hoping the obscure remote town would fool him enough he would eventually just leave her alone. Like I said, she's been seeing the therapist for the abuse about six months now. That's who she had an appointment with this afternoon." She grabbed her phone to scroll through the numbers. "I think I have her emergency number here." She stopped, hit the button and put the phone up to her ear. After the phone clicked, she held up her finger and said, "Doctor Nash? Hi. I'm a friend of Peyton's. I know she had an appointment with you this afternoon, but have you talked to her since? No? A couple of us are concerned. She didn't show up for work. Yeah. Huh. Her car was outside your office when you left at five? That's weird. Okay. We are coming over there to check out her car and see if we can find some clues as to her whereabouts. Yeah, I know about Charles. He's a bad dude and I hope he didn't find her. Okay. Thank you." She shut the phone as she looked at Jason. "She hasn't seen her or talked to her since Peyton left her office at about three."

"Something happened to her. I just feel it. What about this Charles? Do you know anything more about him?"

"I did some digging after Peyton spilled her past to me. He practices in Austin as a criminal defense attorney."

"Figures. Do you know his last name and address? I'd like to look him up and punch the shit out of him."

"Yep. Naples is his last name and don't think I won't help you. If he hurt her, I'll kill him myself. I got an address from the internet."

Jason cracked his knuckles. "You'll be standing in line behind me, Mandy. I've already got my sights set on beating him to a pulp for what he did to her."

"Let's go check out her car so we can let the police here know what's up. She has a restraining order against the creep, but I know that doesn't mean a whole lot these days."

He followed Mandy out the door. The doctor's office wasn't far like everything in Bandera. When they reached the office, sure enough, Peyton's car sat in the parking lot beside the building. "Hmm. I don't like the looks of this. I'll call the police station. I know one of the deputies on duty tonight. Saw him checking out the patrons of the bar earlier." Jason dialed the non-emergency line at the sheriff's department.

"Bandera Sherriff's department, Officer Kailer speaking. How can I help you?"

"Hey Dillon. It's Jason Young."

"What's up, Jason?"

"My girlfriend is missing. Can you come over to—" He rattled off the address.

"Sure. Be right there."

Jason clicked the phone shut as they waited for the police to arrive. There had to be something, a clue or someone who saw her. He wandered down the block to the front door of the doctor's office looking along the sidewalk for anything he might find. Darkness surrounded the area, making it difficult to see anything out of the ordinary.

The police car pulled up near the curb, reflecting something silver on the ground. Jason bent down to see what it was, instantly recognizing the silver chain with the tiny star clasped to the end. It was Peyton's.

"So what's up, Jason?"

"My girlfriend has not been seen or heard from since this afternoon at about three. She had an appointment here at the doctor's office with her therapist. We've already talked to the doctor and she hasn't heard from her since she left. Her car is around the side of the building and she didn't show up for work tonight at The Dusty Boot."

"Her name?"

"Peyton Matthews. She has a restraining order against an old boyfriend who was abusing her."

"Did someone see her with this old boyfriend?"

"Not that we know of."

"She hasn't been missing for twenty-four hours. There isn't much I can do."

"This is her necklace she always wore." Jason held it up for the officer to see. "I found it on the sidewalk."

"She wouldn't be without it if her life depended on it," Mandy added as she stopped beside Jason. "Her mother gave her that when she knew she was dying of cancer and wouldn't be around. She never takes it off."

"We still don't have much to go on. It could have been broken and she didn't realize it. Have you called her phone?"

"Yes. It goes straight to voicemail."

"Her car hasn't been tampered with?"

"Not that we can tell."

"Sorry, Jason. There isn't much I can do. I'll take a report, but until she's been missing twenty-four hours, I can't file a missing persons report. She could be anywhere."

"Thanks for your help. I wasn't sure what you could do, but we thought we would try."

"What are you going to do from here?"

"I plan to drive to Austin tonight to check out this ex's place to see if he's seen her even if I have to beat it out of him. I need to find her."

"Be careful. You don't want to end up in jail."

"Yeah, I know and the fucker is an attorney so that would be my luck."

He and Mandy watched the officer pull away as he wondered what the hell to do now. "Where do we go from here?"

"Let's talk to the motel here in town. Maybe Charles rented a room if he was here. Wouldn't hurt."

"Okay."

They looked both ways before making their way across the street and the two blocks up to the dingy little motel in town. It was something out of a cockroach movie, but it was the only one in Bandera. If this idiot Charles stayed in town while he tried to catch up with Peyton, he would have had to stay there.

The door on the motel stood open in the summer night air as Jason and Mandy went inside. "Hey! Anyone here?" Jason rapped on the counter with his knuckles, hoping to get someone's attention.

"I'm comin'. What do you want?"

"We are looking for a friend of ours. We think he might have stayed here in town. Describe him, Mandy."

"Um, tall. Slender build. Dark hair, dark eyes. Nice looking. Probably wearing a suit and tie."

"There was a guy and a woman in the end room over yonder up until this afternoon. I saw him carry her out to the car before he drove off about six. When he checked in, he was wearing a suit. I noticed 'cause people here don't wear those expensive suits like that, you know? Not like Houston or Austin kind of highfalutin type."

"That's got to be him!" Jason slapped his hand on the desk. "Which way were they headed?"

"Out of town. He'd paid through the end of the week. Came in a couple of days ago, but he put his suitcase in the back of his car before he left, so I doubt he's coming back."

"Can we look in the room?"

"Sure, I guess. They've been gone a couple of hours." The manager grabbed the key and walked around the counter. "Follow me."

Jason almost bounced on his toes. He felt they were getting closer and closer to finding Peyton. He just hoped they would be in time before the crazy assed bastard hurt his woman in the process.

When the manager opened the door to the room, Jason and Mandy rushed inside, hoping beyond hope to find Peyton. Nothing. The room had been used from the apparent mussed bed. Jason noted the ropes tied to the headboard. This didn't look good for Peyton. What had the man done to her and what would he continue to do until they found her?

"Do you have a credit card number or anything on file in the office?" Jason asked the manager.

"He paid with cash, but he had to fill out the form with his name, address and phone number on it. I'll go get it."

"Thank you."

When the manager left, Jason inspected the ropes noting a small smear of blood on one.

"He must have drugged her."

"Why do you say that?"

Mandy held up a needle and syringe. "She wouldn't go with him willingly. I know that much."

"Is this guy crazy?"

"I think so, Jason. He didn't physically harm her before, but that doesn't mean he's beyond hurting her. I'm sure he's capable of doing anything to her to keep her, even kill her for running away."

The manager returned with the card. "Here. There's an address in Austin."

"We'll start there then," Jason said, taking the card. "Can I have this?"

"Yeah. That's a copy. I hope you find your friend."

"I hope so too."

Jason and Mandy headed back across the street to retrieve his truck. A trip to Austin would take several hours. He just hoped they'd find Peyton soon. No telling what the crazy bastard who'd taken her would do.

Once they were inside his truck, he opened the glove box and took out his .45. No telling whether he'd need it or not, but he wouldn't take the chance if they found Peyton hurt.

"You really do love her, don't you?" Mandy asked, watching him check the clip for bullets.

"Why do you say that?"

"If you didn't, you wouldn't be running off to Austin with a loaded gun to find her. Admit it Jason Young, you've fallen hard for Peyton."

He stopped for a moment as images of their time together flitted across his mind—Peyton with her hair down around her shoulders, smiling up at him, making love to her in the shower, up against the wall in his room, and across the mattress of his bed, watching her serve customers at the bar from his spot in the corner, her smile lighting up the room even from that distance. When her gaze caught his, the feeling of his stomach in his throat wouldn't go away. Yeah, he loved her. How could he not? "Yeah, I guess so."

"The stubborn fall the hardest. She's in your blood, cowboy, and you'll have no one else taking what's yours."

"Nope. He better plan on hiding well because if I have a chance at him, he'll be pushing up daisies."

"Go get 'em, cowboy!"

They drove out of Bandera hell-bent for leather to reach Austin before any harm could come to Peyton at the hands of her ex.

Chapter Fifteen

Peyton slowly opened her gritty eyes as she tried to swallow. Eating dried parchment would probably have produced more saliva. Her dried throat told her something wasn't right, but she couldn't quite put her finger on what. Everything seemed fuzzy and out of focus.

"Ah, I see you're awake finally. You slept for several hours."

Charles.

"Open those pretty little eyes for me, darling, and we'll get started on your punishment."

"Punishment?" she croaked as she tried to move, only to realize she was bound at the wrists and tied to something overhead. Her toes barely reached the floorboards. She glanced down to see he had her completely stripped of her clothing, which now lay in tatters at her feet. "What have I done?"

"You ran away, baby. I've had a terrible time finding you over the last two years. Unfortunately for you, that means my anger has grown exponentially to a rage it's been difficult to control. No one else could satisfy this need in me."

"You're crazy."

He laughed, the sound reverberated off the rafters as she glanced around. A shiver rolled down her back at the maniacal sound. This wasn't the apartment they'd rented together.

"Do you like it?" he asked, his gaze sweeping the room. "It's roomier. I got it especially for you and me to get reacquainted in now that I can release the inner beast I've been holding back. Something I can easily do since I've been planning this for such a long time."

"Inner beast?"

"Darling, darling, darling." He cupped her face with his palm. "You haven't seen anything from me yet. I didn't want to frighten you before by playing with you the way I wanted to, so I spent time with others to sate my desires, but now it'll be all on you."

He reached into a duffle bag sitting on the floor near her feet. A long leather whip unfurled when he pulled it out.

"What are you going to do with that?"

"Mark up your pretty body so you'll know you belong to me. Only my mark will be forever etched into your brain."

"Mark?"

"I've become quite the master at the bullwhip. I can leave nothing more than a small red spot or I can draw blood, depending on your responses."

"Listen, Charles. I'm sorry I ran, but I didn't know what to do. You were so distant. If you let me go, I'll be the perfect lover for you. I'll do anything you want me to do. I won't run again, I promise."

"Tsk, tsk, tsk. I'm sorry, but I don't believe you anymore, Peyton. You've lied to me, ran from me, cheated on me, and disappointed me beyond repair." He placed his hand over his heart. "Now you'll pay for your misdeeds until I say you've had enough."

He stepped behind her, trailing the whip over her back, leaving goose bumps along her flesh.

"You know, your skin will mark nicely. I haven't had a woman who had skin the color of yours. Black women don't mark so well. White woman are beautiful to mark although I wasn't too picky with those I've taken." He shrugged as he continued to trail the whip over her skin.

"Please, Charles. Just let me go. I won't report anything. I won't tell a soul."

"Sorry. I can't do that, Peyton. You need to be punished." He moved behind her, cracking the whip into the air.

She jumped as tears started to roll down her cheeks. He'd never been physical before, but apparently he'd been saving that little piece of information from her for some time. It was only the emotional abuse she'd had to endure. Now it would be physical too.

The first sting of the whip on her skin made her jump, but it didn't hurt too much, not anymore than the needle from a piercing or tattoo. However, there was a difference in this pain. It wasn't self-inflicted. The piercings and tats helped her deal with the self-loathing, low self-esteem and emotional distress the abuse from Charles had inflicted. The burning slash of the whip didn't make her feel better.

"Charles, stop!"

Having him inflict pain that had nothing to do with pleasure, made it abuse, and she wasn't going to tolerate this from him anymore.

"Oh, baby. You have no idea how far I'm willing to take you."

The whip struck again. This time, she could feel the blood seeping from the wound on her shoulder. He was a monster, crazy beyond anything she'd ever dealt with before.

Before long, he was constantly taking the whip to her back as she tried to disconnect her mind from the pain. He laughed as he stopped for a moment to touch one of the wounds. A scream tore from her throat as the salt from his skin penetrated the wound.

The door burst open as her head swam. "Jason?" Her voice came out in a painful whisper.

"Back away slowly."

"Who the hell are you and what are you doing in my house?"

"I've come for Peyton."

"She's mine to do with as I wish. Leave now before I have you arrested for trespassing."

"She's not yours, she's mine, you bastard, and you can't have her."

Charles coiled the whip.

"Jason!" Peyton yelled, seconds too late as the whip struck his wrist, pulling the pistol from his grasp and sending it skidding across the floor. Charles struck again, landing a slice across Jason's cheek.

Jason dove at Charles as Peyton twisted around trying to keep them in her sights. A set of hands worked at the knots at her wrists. "No! I need to make sure Jason is all right. Leave me. Help him."

"Hush. Jason can handle himself."

"Mandy?"

"Easy, honey. I'll have you down in a minute." Mandy grumbled under her breath about Charles being a bastard and she'd cut his balls off should she get the chance.

The two men struggled on the floor, rolling around, knocking over furniture in their struggle to get the upper hand. "I'll kill you for hurting her."

"She's mine, cowboy, and nothing you can do to stop me. She's my wife."

"Wife?"

"Yes. We were married this evening when we reached Austin."

"Peyton?" Mandy asked.

"I don't know, Mandy. It's a blur from when I left the doctor's office. He was drugging me."

Jason climbed to his feet, breathing hard from the struggle with Charles. Unfortunately, now Charles had the gun and the bullwhip.

"Charles, please. Let them go. I'll do whatever you want," she implored with her hands out as she slowly walked toward him.

"I need to kill them, just like the others, so they can't point fingers at me."

"Others?"

"The women. The ones I used before I found you. They had to die. All of them."

Mandy and Jason looked at each other and then back at Peyton. "They won't say anything, Charles, right Jason?"

"Are you crazy? He just admitted he killed God only knows how many people. He needs to go to jail, Peyton."

"But if you don't say anything, he'll let you go, won't you, Charles? It's your word against theirs that you said anything. You're an attorney. You know the evidence is threadbare."

"They have to die."

She stepped closer, hoping she could get the gun out of his hands or keep him from shooting the two people who meant the world to her. "They'll go. Right guys? Just leave. Go back to Bandera."

"I'm not leaving without you, Peyton."

"Me either."

"Stubborn asses! Go!" She got close enough to see the confusion in Charles' eyes. He really was crazy. "Give me the gun, Charles."

"No. I have to kill them."

"Charles, please, let them go and I'll do whatever you want. I'll stay with you forever."

Charles waved the gun toward Jason, pointing at his chest. "I must kill them or they'll find us again."

He took aim at Jason. Just as he pulled the trigger, Peyton swung, hitting the gun in his hand as she prayed Jason hadn't been hit.

"You bitch!" The gun came up in her face as she stared down the barrel of a .45 pointed between her eyes. "You'll die with them!"

A blur rushed into Charles' side as Jason tackled them both. She screamed out in pain as her back hit the wooden floor.

Jason and Charles wrestled for the gun now trapped between their bodies. An explosion cracked the air and Peyton screamed once more.

* * * *

Jason wrestled with Charles across the floor. The gun trapped between their bodies. This wouldn't turn out well, one way or another, but if it meant Peyton would be safe, then so be it. He would give his life to keep her out of this maniac's hands.

Peyton screamed as the gun went off.

Jason waited for the burn of the bullet as it penetrated his body, but it never came.

He looked down in Charles' wide eyes.

The other man didn't move, his gaze fixed to the ceiling above them in death's blank stare.

"Jason!"

"I'm okay," he said as he moved back, taking the gun from the dead man's hands.

Blood seeped across Charles' chest, spreading over the entire front of his shirt.

"Mandy, call the police," Jason said, stepping back as Peyton threw herself into his arms.

"Already on it," she replied, talking into her cell phone as she gave them the information on where they were located.

"Are you okay?" he asked, pushing her back a little so he could unbutton his shirt.

"You know I love to see your chest, Jason, but really? Is now a good time?"

"Baby, you need something on."

She glanced down at her exposed chest and crossed her arms over her naked breasts. "Oh yeah." He wrapped his shirt around her, helping her to stuff her arms into the sleeves. She hissed as the shirt touched her back.

"You'll be going to the hospital to get those looked at."

"I'm fine." She grabbed him around the waist the moment he finished buttoning up the front of the shirt. "Hold me."

"No problem, darlin'. I'll hold you as long as you want me to."

"Don't ever leave. I need you."

"Honey, you've got me wrapped around your little finger. I'm not goin' anywhere."

Within several minutes, the police arrived with guns drawn. Jason had placed his gun on the bare coffee table across the room and sat with Peyton on the couch trying to calm her shaking as the rush of everything hit her.

"The ambulance is here too."

"He doesn't need one, but she does."

"I'm fine."

"No you aren't, darlin'. You'll let them take a look at your back," he said, holding her as close as he could. He almost lost her and the thought scared the hell out of him. "She's been whipped."

"Let's see so we can evaluate you, ma'am," the paramedic said as she slowly unbuttoned the shirt. "We need to take you in so the doctor can look at those. Some are pretty deep."

She glanced at Jason. "You'll go with me?"

"Of course. I'm not leaving your side if I don't have to."

"Thank you for rescuing me."

"I love you. There is no place I'd rather be."

"You love me?"

"Yes. This isn't the time or place for this conversation, but I do love you and I hope you love me too."

"I do, Jason. I love you so much." She buried her face in his neck and he felt the warm trickle of tears on his skin.

"Ma'am?"

"All right." She wiped the tears from her eyes as she sat back.

Her tears broke his heart. He never wanted to see them again on her pretty face. "There now." He wiped the remaining wetness from her cheeks. "Let's get you fixed up."

"I'll need your statement, sir," one of the officers said, as his partner called the coroner's office. "It appears this is self-defense, but we'll need to get the detectives involved."

"No problem."

"It'll have to be after he gets checked out," the paramedic replied, indicating the small amount of blood on his left side. "It appears you've been shot, sir."

"It's just a flesh wound."

"What? You were shot? Let me see." Peyton turned him so she could inspect the trench dug through his flesh. "Jason, you need to get checked too. This could be serious."

"He missed."

"Not entirely."

"Fine. We'll go together."

"We'll get your statement at the hospital then, sir."

Mandy stepped forward toward the officer. "I'm a witness to what happened. I'll stay and give you a statement too."

The paramedics ushered the two of them out to the waiting ambulance and into the back. Jason insisted they put Peyton on the stretcher on her side so she could relax and he would sit in the front.

He called his parents on the way to the hospital to fill them in on what was happening. "No Mom, I'm fine. It's a flesh wound, but I'm going to have the doctor look at it to make sure it doesn't need anything besides a bandage. Peyton's wounds need to be looked at too. We'll probably stay here in Austin for a couple of days because the police will want to talk to us, I'm sure. No, we'll be okay. You don't need to come. Just do me a favor, call Dan at The Dusty Boot and let him know what is going on so he doesn't get more worried than he is. Have someone check my animals please. Thanks Mom. I love you too and yes, I'll hug Peyton for you. Bye."

Shortly after the sun broke over the horizon, they drove into the ambulance bay at the hospital, the paramedics ushered them both inside into separate rooms, but only sectioned off by a curtain. He asked them to leave it open and even though the nurse seemed reluctant, she did what he asked.

Peyton's wounds weren't too deep, but the doctor had to stitch a few closed. The others would heal on their own. She would have scars to match the wounded soul he now knew lie within. Mandy had told him about the hell she'd went through living with this guy. He knew he would spend the rest of his life making sure she knew she was the most beautiful woman inside and out, he'd ever seen.

"You okay over there?" he asked from across the room.

"Yeah," she replied, her voice small and broken.

He got off the gurney so he could move to her side. "Baby, don't. Don't let him win. He was totally wrong about you."

"I can't help it, Jason. I spent years listening to him tell me how worthless I am. How ugly things were between us. How I couldn't satisfy him in bed…"

"Baby, you're gorgeous. You have a wonderful life. You are going to school in the fall to help people in situations just like yours. You are the most amazing woman I've ever had in my bed. I'll hear no more about all of this. He's gone. He's dead. He can't hurt you anymore and believe me when I say I will spend the rest of my life making sure you know how much you mean to me."

"Did you really mean it when you said you loved me?"

"Of course, I meant it. The minute I get the chance, we're going to get married."

"Married? You want to marry me?"

"Yeah. I want you with me forever."

"Married," she whispered, tears making her eyes sparkle like golden topaz. "I never thought I'd hear those words from you again after you said it before. You aren't the marrying kind, remember?"

"I am now—with you." He leaned in and kissed her. Not a quick peck, but a full onslaught of desire waiting to explode between them at the merest touch. "I love you."

"I love you too."

The doctor cleared his throat as he came into the room. "You two can leave as soon as I get the nurse to dress the wounds."

"Thanks, Doc."

"You're welcome. I hope the guy who did this to her won't be hurting anyone else?"

"No sir, he won't."

"Good and I don't care who hears me say it either."

While they were waiting for their discharge papers, the police came in and told them they would have to come to the station tomorrow morning to make their statements.

"That's fine, officer. We don't plan to leave town for a couple of days if you need us to be here."

"We aren't going home?"

"No, I told my mom to have the guys keep an eye on my cattle and horses for me. We'll stay here a couple of days."

Mandy came through the doorway with a smile. "Everything is good. I'm going to take the bus on home to leave you two some time to get reacquainted."

"Thanks, Mandy, for everything," Peyton said as she hugged her.

"Can you take my truck to the store a few blocks away and get her something to wear besides my shirt, before you go? We'll take you to the bus stop after they release us."

"Okay."

Mandy took his keys, whistling happily as she twirled the key ring around her finger. "I'll be back."

"Don't wreck my truck."

"I won't, cowboy. I like big things." She laughed as she skipped down the hallway.

He took the seat next to the gurney to await their discharge papers. "You can move in with me when we get back."

"But your house isn't even finished yet."

"I know, but you'll be able to decorate it however you want. I'd love to have your help on how certain things should be in the house since it'll be your house now too."

"I like the sound of that."

"You plan to continue your therapy, right? I think you need to so you can work through what happened last night and yesterday."

"Yes, I will. This has all taken me back a step in my recovery, but with you by my side, I can overcome anything."

"That's right. I'll be there for you every step of the way."

"You know I love you, right?"

"I'm glad to hear you say it because you mean everything to me, Peyton. You've become someone very important in my life. I'll do everything I need to do to help you. You own my heart."

"Are you two ready to go?" the nurse asked as she came into the room. "I have your discharge papers here."

"Good."

Once the nurse went through the instructions with each of them after she dressed their wounds, she had them sign the papers and then escorted them out to the waiting room.

"A friend has gone to get her some clothes."

"Just hand the scrubs back to the receptionist before you leave."

"We will. Thank you." He shook the nurse's hand. "We appreciate everything you've done."

"No problem. That's what we are here for."

A few minutes later, Mandy came through the door with a couple of bags of clothes. "I didn't get anything fancy. Just a shirt, jeans. I grabbed your shoes from the house. He didn't ruin those."

"Thanks, Mandy. You're the best." Peyton hugged her quickly and then took the clothes into the nearby bathroom while they waited.

"How's she really doing?" Mandy asked.

"Broken. She needs to talk to her therapist right away. That asshole brought back way too much stuff buried inside her soul."

"So when's the wedding?" Mandy asked, rubbing her hands together in glee.

Jason smiled and shook his head. "Soon, I hope."

Mandy threw her arms around his neck and hugged him tight. "I knew you two were good for each other."

"Thanks."

"Hey, that's my fiancé you are hanging all over." Peyton stopped at their side with her fresh new tank top, jeans, and tennis shoes.

"I know! I think it's totally cool you two are planning to get married. Jason won't tell me when the wedding is, but I better be a maid of honor."

"Of course you will be. We can't give you a date because he just asked me like ten minutes ago."

"Well, I'll leave you two alone. I'm taking a cab to the bus station."

"I told you we'd take you."

"No problem. You two go on and have fun. Be careful with her, she's been through a lot," Mandy scolded as she shook her finger at him

"I will. No hanky panky. I just plan to hold her very tight."

"Good. I'll see you two in a couple of days."

"Thanks again. For everything," Peyton said, hugging her friend for a moment as tears sparkled on her eyelashes. Mandy only hugged her shoulders as she tried not to touch her back. He began to love her even more for her care. "I don't know what I would have done had you and Jason not come to find me."

"Stop. You'll make me cry too." Mandy stepped back, shooing Peyton into his arms. "I love you both." Mandy disappeared out the doors, leaving he and Peyton standing alone.

"Shall we go find a hotel room?"

One eyebrow shot up over Peyton's eye. "Can we have sex?"

"Baby, I don't think that's a good idea with your back."

"You're probably right." She shivered next to him. "We should probably get something to eat before we find a hotel. I'm starving."

"Considering it's about noon, I'm not surprised. I saw a burger joint not far from here."

"Sounds good." She grabbed his hand as they headed outside to his truck.

He knew having sex with her could be bad for her physically, but emotionally, he wasn't sure. He didn't do emotions very well. He wasn't sure if his own could handle a breakdown from her if it occurred, but he would tough it out. She would need him tonight. Her emotions would be fragile with the torture her ex dealt out. Holding her close might help when things came to a head.

Chapter Sixteen

They made the short trip to the burger joint and ordered what they wanted. As they waited for their food to come, he took her hands between his. A kiss to each fingertip made his cock stand up to take notice. *Down boy.* "How are you feeling?"

"Sore."

"What about what's going on in that brain of yours?"

"I'm not sure I know what you mean."

"Baby, you just went through something that would fuck up someone's emotions even on their best day. I know what happened had to have brought back a lot of memories."

She grasped his hands like a lifeline as her knuckles turned white. "Charles didn't abuse me physically before. Apparently, he was holding back that little bit of information from me when he was fucking with my head. Yes, it's hard for me to wrap my brain around it right now because I didn't see this coming. I should have. Many times when someone abuses on an emotional level, the physical is there too, but he didn't, at least not in the past."

He gently rubbed his thumb over the back of her hand until her death grip eased.

"Easy, baby. I will never let anyone hurt you again. He's gone. Dead. He can't hurt you anymore." Why he brought this up here, he wasn't sure. He shouldn't have. "I'm sorry. We can talk about this later when we are alone."

"Okay. I'm going to need to talk, Jason. I've got to let these emotions out and I don't want to do it here in the restaurant."

"It's fine." The waitress brought their food, easing the plates onto the table in front of them. Peyton took a deep breath and dove into her food like a starving woman. Jason squirted some ketchup on his plate for his fries as he kept an eye on his woman. She needed him to be strong for her and he would be. "Let's talk about something else for now. We can get into the emotional turmoil when we get to the hotel. When would you like to get married?"

"Are you sure you want to marry me?"

"I love you, Peyton. Of course, I want to marry you."

"How is your family going to feel about you taking on such a project?"

"My family will love you. My mother already does from what she's told me even though she will want to get to know you better."

"What are they going to say? We haven't really known each other very long."

"Long enough to know I want you in my life. When I found your car at the doctor's office and didn't know where to find you, my heart settled in my stomach. I knew then I loved you because I couldn't think of my life without you in it. If I'd lost you, I would've gone nuts. You are the most important person to me."

"Have I told you I love you?"

"Yes, but I like hearing it. Up to a few months ago, I thought finding the perfect person for me was impossible. I told myself I would stop using women for my own pleasure. You were a test of my abilities because you wanted to have casual sex. I gave into that mentality even though it went against what I'd vowed to change, because I wanted you so badly, I would have done anything to have you." He smiled as her eyes widened. "I've been watching you for several months while you worked the bar, trying to figure out a way to get closer to you. When you showed up at the muddin' party with Aaron, I wanted to rip his throat out."

She laughed. "You did?"

"Yeah, because I thought for sure you were going home with him and he would be getting what I wanted."

"You only wanted me for sex?"

"No, well yeah. Sort of." He popped the last of his hamburger into his mouth. While he chewed, he tried to decide how to tell her at first he wanted sex, but after he'd gotten to know her, it had turned into more. "You see, all I've ever known with a woman is sex. I hadn't wanted anything more until you, but when I thought of you with Aaron, I wanted to be him. I wanted what he was going to have. I didn't know what type of relationship you had with him and it bugged me. When you got into the fight with him and turned to me, it was like my entire world lit up. This is why I resisted so hard when we first started talking that night. I realized I wanted a little more from you than just sex. I wanted to hold you, touch you and love on you all night. I wanted to wake up next to you in the morning so I could see the sunlight touch your hair. I wanted your eyes to light up when you saw me like they do now. You are my world now, Peyton."

A tear rolled down her cheek and he reach across the table to wipe it away. "Sorry."

"Why are you crying?"

"Because I never thought I'd find a love like yours, especially with a cowboy. You've tempted me beyond reason to let love find us. I never thought I would fall for a cowboy." She laughed as she wiped another tear with her napkin, smearing ketchup across her cheek.

"Why not? You don't like cowboys, but you live in Texas?" he asked, laughing with her as he reached over with his own napkin to wipe the red from her face.

"I've certainly learned to love one cowboy—you."

"Good, because I love you so much, I can't think of anyone else anymore." He pushed his plate away. "All finished?"

"Yes." She bit her lip as a frown settled across her brow.

"What's wrong?"

"What about Sheila?"

"What about her?"

"She said she's pregnant with your child."

"I found out from her the other day, she's only two months along or so she says. There is no way she's pregnant with my child. We weren't together in the right time frame."

"Thank God."

"Ready to settle in for the night?"

"Yeah."

"Let's go find us a room then. I want to hold you."

After they finished paying the check, they walked back out to his truck and he opened the door for her. As soon as she was settled in, he went back around the front to the driver's side. They would have a nice room. No dive dump for them tonight. If he could swing the softest bed in the city, he would. "Where do you want to stay?"

"Nothing too expensive, Jason. You need to save your money."

"We'll have a nice room for the days we are here and I'll hear no more about it. You deserve something nice. Maybe a Jacuzzi tub?"

She smiled and he got the impression she liked the idea of a whirlpool tub in their room. He kind of did too. Maybe she'd let him fuck her in it.

He pulled out his phone to check on some hotels nearby. He loved a smart phone. He found a Marriott nearby so he headed in that direction. They were usually a good bet for nice rooms even though they might not have the jetted tub. "We'll go here first and see if they have something."

"Are you sure? Those are expensive."

"Nothing is too good for my girl."

"I think you're going to spoil me something terrible." A smile eased up the corners of her mouth.

He loved to make her smile, moan, groan or scream. Man was he in trouble. This not having sex with her would kill him slowly. "I get to. You're my woman now."

They pulled into the hotel and he looked up at the high-rise. *This should be perfect.*

When they walked through the lobby, he saw all the marble accents and wondered briefly if his wallet could afford a room here for a couple of days, but decided it didn't matter. She was worth every penny. "Do you have rooms with whirlpool tubs in them?"

"Yes, sir."

"I need one for two nights, please," he told the man behind the desk. He swore his credit card groaned as they swiped it for the charges.

"Are you sure about this, Jason? That's a lot of money."

"Very sure."

"You are in twenty-four forty-five. It's a suite on twenty-fourth floor."

"Thank you," Jason said, as he took the key card.

"Do you have luggage?"

"No."

The clerk's eyebrow rose. "I see."

"This was an unexpected trip. We'll be doing some shopping in the morning."

"Very good, sir."

They headed for the elevator to go to their room. "I feel so cheap. That guy thinks this is a hook up."

"Don't worry about him, baby. We'll get some clothes for both of us and a suitcase. It doesn't matter what he thinks, it only matters what we know." He grinned as he slipped his arm around her waist, trying not to touch the sores on her back. "We can do some engagement ring shopping too."

"I can't believe we're going to get married."

He lifted her hand to his lips and kissed her palm. "Believe it. I love you with all my heart."

"I love you too."

The door opened to the twenty-fourth floor. As they walked down the carpeted hallway, he was in awe. There were only three doors along the whole thing. The deskman had said it was a suite, but holy shit! He found their door, then swiped the key before he pushed it open. "Wow."

They walked inside and let the door close behind them as they stood with their mouths open at the grandeur of the room. "Oh my God, Jason. This is gorgeous!" She walked around touching the marble with her fingers, the crystal on the lamps and the cherry wood tables. "Look at this view!" A large bank of windows looked out over the city. "I've never seen Austin like this."

"Me either, but I can imagine you against these windows with your hands braced against the glass as I fuck you from behind."

"If you aren't going to do it, don't tease me like that."

"But just think, tomorrow it'll be better with the anticipation."

"Asshole." She laughed as she spun around and wrapped her arms around his neck. "I love you."

"I love you too. Shall we get some sleep?"

"Yeah. I find I'm really tired now that things are calm."

"Good. I hope you can rest without nightmares or anything."

"If you hold me, I should be fine."

He eased the tank top over her head, revealing her bare breasts. "Did she get some sexy-ass underwear?"

"Yes," she whispered, her breath coming out in short, panting bursts of air. "I want you."

"I want you too, but for now and tonight, I'm just going hold you."

"But…"

"No, buts, darlin'. You need to ease into this again. You had a rough time."

"I know what I want, Jason."

"I know, but we just rest tonight. I have a feeling you're going have a rough night." He stripped off his shirt and T-shirt. She touched his chest, earning herself a moan from his lips. He loved when she let her fingers walk along his skin. He grabbed her hands to stop the motion.

"I only want to touch."

"I know, but your skin on mine is something I can't handle too much of. Holding you without lovin' you is going to be hard enough."

"Party pooper." She pouted with her lip stuck out.

"It's for your own good, darlin'," he said, tapping the end of her nose with his fingertip.

"Okay." She stripped off her jeans, leaving her in nothing but her lacy panties. "I'll sleep in my underwear, but since you are declaring this no sex night, you'll have to suck it up, cowboy."

When she turned to pull down the blankets, the stark whiteness of the bandages on her back made him want to kill the son of a bitch all over again.

They both crawled beneath the covers and he dragged her into his embrace with an arm around her shoulders so he wouldn't touch her back. He wanted to feel her next to him like he needed his next breath.

Within minutes, her breathing slowed to a rhythmic rate indicating she slept. When he thought about what that asshole did to her, rage swept through him. He would die protecting her for the rest of his life.

The feel of her against his side lulled him into a half sleepy state. He knew the night would be rough on her so he slept lightly waiting for the storm of nightmares he felt sure would assault her soon.

He came upright in the bed as she screamed out in her sleep. "Baby, wake up."

"No! Don't hurt me!"

"Peyton, it's me. I'll never hurt you, sweetheart. Wake up."

She jumped out of the bed with her fists clenched and her eyes wide. "Jason?"

"Yeah, baby. It's me. Come back to bed. He can't hurt you anymore."

"Oh God." She scrambled onto the bed, practically jumping into his arms.

"Easy." He swept his hands down her arms, rubbing the warmth back into her limbs. "I love you." Once he pulled her into his embrace, she settled against his side. Her body still shook from the nightmare. "Why don't you tell me about your dream?"

"I was back in that room. He cut off my clothes with a knife, slicing my skin as he did it. The pain was too much, but as I cried, he'd just laugh." She shuddered. "His laughter was crazy. Then he started whipping me so hard, I screamed. That's when I woke up."

"It's over, baby. He's dead."

She pulled him closer. "I know, but I think these nightmares will continue for a bit."

"Probably."

"I know you don't want to make love, but I need you, Jason. I need you to wipe out the memory of what I've been through. We can go easy. I'll be on top or whatever."

"If you think you can handle it."

"I do. I need you to replace all these terrible thoughts with your love. Please?"

"Oh, baby, I'll love you so well, you won't remember what his face looks like." He shifted, leaving her on her side so he could reach her breasts. *Lordy, I so love her breasts.* "These are perfect, you know."

"Are they?"

"Yep. I love how they fit perfectly in my palms." He cupped the two mounds as he licked first the right, then the left. "And your nipples are so sensitive."

She moaned as she closed her eyes. He loved that look of ecstasy on her face as she let the feelings envelope her in sensation.

He let his hand wander down her abdomen as she spread her thighs allowing him touch her. He loved feeling her pussy clench around his fingers when he slipped two inside her. She felt so good, he wanted to taste her.

He moved down her body with little nips on her skin until he reached the juncture of her thighs. He lifted one leg over his shoulder so he could reach her center. The smell of her arousal drove him crazy. One swipe of his tongue over her clit made her groan out loud.

"Please."

He flicked his tongue over the hardened little button of flesh, coaxing it from its hiding place until she squirmed against his mouth seeking a little more pressure so she could come. The soft whimpers and hearty moans told him she was close. To let her come or not, was the question.

Nope. He wanted to be buried deep inside her pussy when she flew apart in his arms.

He lifted his head, ignoring her protests.

"I have an idea. Up you go." With her hand in his, he pulled her to the bank of windows overlooking the city of Austin. "I'm gonna fuck you against the windows."

"But people will see us."

"Do you care? Besides, being dark inside our room, they won't be able to see anything, but what if they do?" He pushed her against the glass, her back to his front although he didn't touch her open wounds. "Your beautiful breasts squashed against the windowpane, the nipples hard from the cooler surface." He ran his tongue down her neck and across her shoulder before he bit the flesh. "Your gorgeous thighs spread for my use, my cock pushed up inside you so deep, you moan with pleasure." He licked across the flesh of her shoulder. "Do you want me, Peyton? Do you want me to fuck you here where everyone could possibly see us?"

"Yes, damn you."

"Ah, such a naughty little girl." He pressed two fingers into her pussy from behind as she spread her thighs. "You're horny just thinking about someone across the way being able to see you getting fucked like this."

"Give it to me."

"In a minute." He finger fucked her for several minutes as she pressed herself against the glass. "I want to make sure you're good and ready for me."

She moaned. "I'm ready. Trust me."

"Feel that cold glass against your breasts. Are your nipples hard from it?"

"Yes."

"Are you wet?"

"Hell yes. Please, Jason."

He dropped his pants and stepped out of the jeans and underwear, then pressed his aching cock against her backside. "Do you want me?"

"Oh yeah."

"Spread your thighs, baby, I'm coming home." He pressed closer, careful to keep his chest away from her wounds as he nudged at her opening from behind. "God, you're going to feel amazing." He pushed his cock into her pussy very slowly. "Fuck yeah."

The heat from her scorched his cock, driving his need higher than he'd ever felt before. They probably should have used a condom, but since they were getting married anyway, he didn't really care if she got pregnant and he knew they were both clean from their conversation before. "Did the hospital ask about rape?"

"Yes, but he didn't," she whispered. "I think he planned on it after he beat me senseless, but you saved me before that happened."

"God, you feel amazing." He shuddered, absorbing the intenseness of being deep inside her. He slowly made love to her against the glass, giving her the security he felt she needed that he loved her and would always protect her from her demons. "I love you. I will always love you. You are everything to me." He slipped inside her, holding himself still until she squirmed with need. "Do you want control?"

"Yes."

He picked her up as he backed toward the bed to lie down. "Reverse cowgirl, baby. Take what you want. You're in control." She slid herself back over his cock, moaning softly as she impaled herself with his entire length. Bracing herself on his thighs, she began a torturous slow glide of his cock in and out of her amazingly hot pussy. "You're going to kill me, darlin'."

"But what a way to go."

She did a slow grind of her pussy against him, driving him insane with lust. "Fuck me, baby."

"Oh I plan to."

With a shift of her hips, she rocked back and forth on him, letting his cock slide in and out of her pussy in the most insanely erotic dance of his life. She started working her clit with her fingertip as she kept up a steady pace with her hips.

When he couldn't stand it anymore, he flipped her over onto her stomach over the edge of the bed and slammed into her with enough force to bang the headboard against the wall.

"I wondered when you would take over, cowboy. I figured it wouldn't take long. You don't like not being in control."

"I'm going to fuck you into next week."

"Do it!"

He slammed his pelvis against her and felt her pussy squeeze his cock almost in two. His rhythm became disjointed as he continued to push his cock into her heated flesh in a rapid pace. He couldn't hold out much longer, but she needed to come along for the ride.

Knowing she needed a little more stimulation, he wrapped his hand around her hip so he could reach her clit. When he touched the hard little button, she growled in satisfaction. He smiled even though he knew she couldn't see the satisfied grin on his face.

"Right there."

"Oh yeah."

With two fingers, he pinched her clit and she came apart on a scream of his name. Her pussy clamped down on him so hard, it almost hurt, but felt amazing at the same time as he lost his load deep inside her.

He collapsed on the bed in a heap, allowing his cock to slide from her depths. "That was fantastic."

"Thank you."

"Can we do it again?"

He laughed as he reached down to kiss her shoulder. "Give me a little bit to recover and we'll love the night away."

"You are my forever."

"And you are mine."

Epilogue

The early spring morning was perfect for a wedding. Peyton just hoped the rain would hold off since the sky looked a bit threatening at times.

Jason had been her everything from the day he'd found her at the hands of Charles, giving her time, space and love. She couldn't have asked for a better husband or lover. He was so patient and understanding with her nightmares and mood swings, but the weekly visits to the therapist had the nightmares down to only infrequently now.

Nina stood next to her as they fluffed her veil, settling it around her shoulders in preparation for her to walk down the aisle. "You look beautiful."

She hugged Jason's mother close as tears threatened to smear her makeup.

"No tears or you'll ruin my makeup job!" Mandy exclaimed, pushing her into the chair so she could finish with the veil.

"Thank you all for everything. I'm sorry my own mother isn't here to see this day, but you all have made me feel so welcomed into the family, I can't thank you enough."

Nina sniffed as she wiped a tear from the corner of her eye. "You are perfect for my son and I'm glad I could help make this day the most special day for you two."

Mesa sat beside her in one of the wing back chairs in the room they were using for the wedding party at the ranch. She almost didn't make the wedding since she was very pregnant with her and Joel's first child.

"Are you okay?" Peyton asked Mesa as she rubbed her bulging stomach.

"I'm fine, just tired. I wish this little one would hurry up and make its appearance. I'm already overdue."

"Only a few days, Mesa," Nina added. "I was two weeks overdue with Jeff. First babies are very difficult to judge."

"Well, I'm ready anytime."

The girls laughed, knowing she was really getting tired of being pregnant. "You'll be a great mom, Mesa," Paige said, as she stood in the corner to look out the window.

Peyton loved having her friends with her on this very important day. "I'm not sure if Jason and I will have children."

"Do you want them?" Nina asked.

"I think so, but with all the trauma in my life, I'm not sure if I could handle them."

"No hurry. You and Jason are still young enough to decide later and with all of my new grandbabies, I can wait a little while for more."

They all laughed.

There was a soft knock on the door. Nina moved toward it to see who it was. The ceremony would be starting soon so she thought it might be Jason's father. She'd asked him to give her away since her own father wasn't in the picture.

James came through the door, looking dapper in his tuxedo shirt, black jacket and tie along with his black jeans and black boots. He wore the same outfit her husband would when they took their vows in a few short minutes.

Her stomach lurched. Was she ready for this?

Nina and James came to stand behind her. "He loves you, Peyton. You love him. You'll be very happy together." Nina glanced at James. "Just like we are as well as the others are. You'll fit in perfectly." She squeezed her fingers. "Welcome to the family."

"Are you ready? It's about time to start," James said taking her hand in his. "Your fingers are like ice."

"I'm a little nervous."

"Perfectly normal for your wedding day. You look beautiful."

"Thank you for standing in to give me away."

"It's my pleasure."

He looped her hand through the crook of his arm as she stood and faced her wedding party. Her bridesmaids looked beautiful in their teal off the shoulder dresses. Mandy wore the same style but in a deep burgundy red.

Everything was perfect.

"Ready?" James asked as he led her toward the door to follow the other women down the stairs.

"Yes."

When the wedding march started several minutes later, she swallowed, took in a deep breath and prepared to meet the man of her dreams in front of the fireplace at Thunder Ridge Ranch.

As they reached the bottom of the stairs, she took in the entire main lodge decorated for her wedding. Her wedding to Jason. The thought scared her and excited her at the same time.

As the crowd parted, she got her first look at her future husband in his finery. He took her breath away, but the one thing that made her heart stop was the look in his eyes as their gazes met across the room.

The love shining in his eyes almost brought her to her knees, causing her to stumble slightly.

"You okay?" James whispered as they made their way toward Jason.

"Yeah."

When they reached Jason's side and his father gave her over to him, she couldn't help but thank God above for tempting her with this cowboy and bringing them together for all eternity.

"I love you."

"I love you too."

"Ready to get married?"

"I've never been more ready for anything in my life."

The End

FOREVER KIND OF COWBOY
Cowboy Dreamin' 5

Sandy Sullivan

Chapter One

Callinda Marie Lewis glanced out the big bay doors of the gas station when Jeremiah Young pulled his truck up to the gas pump. Absent-mindedly, she swiped at the beads of sweat trickling down her neck heading for her shoulder blade and dropped her wrench from her wet palm in the process. The wrench hitting the cement under her feet made a loud clang. *Damn, it's hot today.* Or was it the man standing at the pump causing her to perspire?

As she picked up the tool, she noticed the jacked-up silver dually didn't fit Jeremiah's style from what she knew of the man. Ever since high school, he'd been the quiet Young brother, not too assuming and not one to draw attention, letting his brothers be the rowdy bunch. He crunched numbers on a daily basis. A whiz at math, he'd tutored her for a short time in algebra, but it hadn't lasted long enough for her. By then she'd been smitten.

Her heart thumped loudly in her chest as she tried to go back to work, denying the way she reacted to him. He always did this to her every time she saw him. From the moment he'd called her darlin' one day in high school, she couldn't think straight with him around. Her hands shook when she tried to ignore him standing at the pump in his Wranglers, cowboy hat, dusty boots, and button-down western shirt. "Why does he do this to me?"

"Callie?"

"Sorry, Dad. I'm just talking to myself."

Her father glanced out the bay doors and said, "Ah. I see." He set the carburetor down he'd been working on.

"It's nothin'."

"You've been tied up in knots about that boy for longer than I can remember." He patted her on the shoulder. "I understand, honey. I know what love feels like."

"It's not love, Dad. It's infatuation. That's all. He doesn't know I'm alive." Callie reached up to the bottom of the vehicle on the garage lift and pulled the plug to drain the oil from the engine, paying no mind to her dad moving to the other side of the car. She didn't want to see the look on his face. Ignoring the charismatic man outside was like forcing herself to stop breathing for minutes on end. It didn't happen without her feeling lightheaded.

"Why don't you go out there and see if he needs anything else besides gas?"

She wiped her hands on the rag she pulled from the back pocket of her coveralls. "I just might do that," she said, not taking her eyes off the well-built man standing near the pumps tapping his fingers on the bed of his truck.

Before she knew it, she stood next to him as he swung around, giving her a blinding smile. "Hey, darlin'."

Her toes curled in her steel-toed boots. "Hey, Jeremiah." She stuffed her hands in her pockets. "I thought I'd check to see if you needed anything else besides gas today? I could check your fluids, or somethin'."

"I think I'm good." Jeremiah reached up and wiped a smudge from her cheek. "You've been workin' hard today, huh?"

Her stomach knotted at the touch of his fingers on her face. God, she wished he'd touch her with passion, burying his hands in her long hair, pull it a little and crush his mouth to hers. "Uh, just changing old man Daniels' oil."

"Pretty girls shouldn't have grease smeared on their cheek." The pump made a clunking sound as it turned off. He turned to remove it from the gas tank on his truck and return it to the side of the pump.

"You sure I can't check your fluids for you?" *Wow, that sounded really desperate, you dummy.*

"Maybe next time. I have an appointment so I need to git, but I'll see you around."

"Sure. Thanks for coming in. We appreciate the business."

"Anytime, darlin'." He grasped the brim of his hat between his fingers, tipping it slightly as cowboys do. "I'll see you later." A soft whistling sound escaped his lips after he grinned and winked.

Several minutes later, he pulled out of the gas station, squealing his tires a little on the smooth pavement.

Her heart rate slowed as he went down the road then pulled into the diner his aunt owned. When he jumped out of his truck again, she couldn't help but sigh the second he swept Lydia Wiley up in his arms in a twirling hug. After her feet hit the ground, he brushed his lips against the girl's, earning himself an unseen frown from Callie. She didn't realize he was seeing Lydia, but then again, when wasn't he seeing someone?

Callie turned her back on the scene to walk into the garage. She'd seen enough to know she'd never have a chance with Jeremiah Young in this lifetime. Her type didn't get the gorgeous hunk of a man. That only happened in fairy tales and her life wasn't a fairy tale by any means.

Losing her mom at a young age didn't help. Her dad did the best he could. But being the only child raised by a man had her dressing and acting like a boy while enjoying things like dirt bikes, working on cars, and doing general tomboy stuff. She tied her hair back in a low ponytail just to keep it off her face. Dresses didn't do anything for her. Although once in a while, she broke down and wore something feminine to feel like a woman.

She wished she knew more about how things were supposed to work between two people when she'd given her virginity to David Burger in high school. The experience sucked. Never mind it had happened in the bed of his truck with very little foreplay involved. Somehow she knew things would be different with a man she cared about or one who knew how to handle a woman.

A sigh escaped her in a rush. She just knew someday things would be different. They had to be. She didn't want to spend the rest of her life alone.

* * * *

Jeremiah Young stared out the window of the diner as Lydia prattled on about something or another. Why did woman talk nonstop sometimes? Was it just to hear themselves yap about one thing only to change subjects and go on about something totally different?

"Are you even listening to me, Jeremiah?"

"Yeah," he answered automatically while his gaze fixed on the garage across the street. Callie Lewis moved through the double bay doors in her overalls and boots. Nothing specific to indicate she was a woman in any sense of the word except when she took her hair down and shook it out before putting it back up in the ever-present low ponytail. He'd known her since high school when he'd tutored her in algebra. They'd been in the same classes most of their lives including phys ed. He'd noticed her right away although she wasn't the type he normally took a second glance at. She didn't have huge tits nor was she particularly thin. Curvy would be the word he used for her. Nice curves, but she hid them under long T-shirts, baggy jeans and work boots most of the time. Once in a great while, he would see her in woman's clothes, something pretty like when she went to church on Sundays. The garage was closed those days while she spent the day with her dad. They would go out for Sunday supper at his aunt's diner. He always seemed to be driving by when they went in, not that he'd been looking or anything.

His cell phone beeped indicating an incoming message. He smiled as he checked his phone. As the financial planner of his parents' ranch, he had to keep his pulse on the bank accounts, investments, and inner workings of the ranch at all times. One of the stocks he'd invested heavily in with his own money had doubled today on the market. Good. He would make a tidy profit if it kept increasing before he sold it off.

Investments had been one of his past times since he could remember. He'd started running numbers in his own stocks from the time he'd turned eighteen, then he was careful with the family fortune when he chose to broaden the horizons on their behalf. His parents' trust in his ability to keep them afloat came with a heavy load. If he lost it all, they would be out on a limb, but he'd been lucky. So far, everything he'd put their money into had done well on the market. His own little nest egg seemed to be growing quite well. At this rate, he'd be able to retire soon.

Not that he didn't love his family or the ranch he'd grown up on, but he wanted to be financially stable enough to do his own thing rather than riding rough stock for the rest of his life.

Lydia jabbered on about something to do with her dress, or shoes, so he focused his gaze back out the window.

The town of Bandera, Texas wasn't much to look at, but it was home. His family moved there before he was born. They proceeded to run a cattle ranch as each of his eight brothers came into the world. His parents never had the daughter his mother craved. She made do with the ever-growing number of daughters-in-law and grandchildren as each of his brothers found their life mate. He wasn't sure what the hoopla was all about. One girl for the rest of his life? He wasn't into that quite yet. He had too much living to do. He wanted to see the world a little at a time. Go to Paris, live on the east coast somewhere, see Los Angeles, Seattle, San Francisco, Florida, and maybe even New York. He thought it would be totally cool to see the New York Stock Exchange one day since he dabbled so much in stocks now. Plus, someday he wanted a fancy sports car to zip around in. A Ferrari, or maybe a Lamborghini. What the hell he would do with it in Bandera, Texas he wasn't sure, but having one might be fun. To have so much money he'd never have to work again seemed to always be at the forefront of his mind.

"And this thong was so cute, Jeremiah. You would have loved it on me." Lydia's voice dropped to a whisper. "Or off."

"I'm sure."

She continued to talk as she stirred her Coke with the straw. Her voice faded out when he saw Callie walk across the main road of town headed for the diner. *Must be lunchtime.*

The bell over the door dinged when Callie walked in. Jeremiah kept her in view the whole time as she approached the counter to place her order. Her voice soothed the grating of Lydia's on his nerves. The sing-song lilt sounded so good to his ears.

"Jeremiah?"

"Sorry. What did you say?"

"I knew you weren't listening. What did I say last then?"

"Something about a thong."

"I said that ten minutes ago." Lydia glanced over her shoulder, catching the direction of his gaze. "Really?"

"What?"

"You're looking at Callinda Lewis?" She snorted—actually snorted.

He thought it was funnier than hell. Laughter burst from his lips, earning him a frown from Lydia.

Callie turned toward him for a moment, stuffing her hands in her pockets as she hunched her shoulders.

"She's really not your type, you know. She doesn't even own a dress from what I hear, and makeup? Forget it."

"She doesn't need it."

"Yes, she does. A woman doesn't go out of the house without makeup. It's just not womanly. The mere thought is as hideous as those clothes are." She leaned back in her chair, sipping on her drink a minute before she continued. "She works in her father's garage, for God's sake. A woman doesn't work on cars, dress in overalls, drink beer or cuss like a sailor."

"What about her bugs you, Lydia?" He rapped his knuckles on the table. "That men actually look at her while you're in the room?"

"Look at her? Really, Jeremiah. She's nothing to look at."

"I think she is. She's got something you don't have."

"What's that?"

"A personality beyond everything revolving around her. She doesn't care if she's all decked out in a pretty dress. She cares about the people around her. She's not all about herself, like you are."

Lydia jumped to her feet. "Then go out with her!"

Jeremiah smiled. "I'm glad you give your permission although it's not needed, but thank you anyway. I'll do that." He got to his feet and walked toward Callie as she stood there openmouthed. "I could kiss you right now." Her blue eyes were wide as her mouth hung open like she was ready to catch flies with it, so he put a finger under her chin to push it closed. "Easy, darlin'. I won't. Not yet at least."

"Wha…what?"

"I think you'd be a bit shocked if I did, so how about this? Will you go out to dinner and a movie with me on Friday?" he asked, smirking a little as he glanced back at Lydia.

Lydia jammed her hands on her hips as she glared. "You're a bastard, Jeremiah. No wonder no woman will have you for long," she yelled before she stormed out of the diner.

Jeremiah turned his attention back to Callie. "So what do you say?"

"To?"

"Going out with me on Friday?"

"You weren't serious, were you?"

"Of course, I am. So what do you say?"

"Uh, okay."

"I'll pick you up at your dad's house at six?"

"Sounds fine to me."

"Great." He tipped his hat and said, "I'd invite you to have lunch with me, but I need to get on back to the ranch. I'll see you Friday." He slipped his aunt a ten dollar bill for the hassle before he stepped out into the sunshine of the day, whistling softly as he headed for his truck.

The drive back to the home place went by rather quickly as he let his thoughts wander to Callie. He'd wanted to ask her out for some time, but for some reason he'd never found the opportunity. Well, that wasn't really true. He stopped into the gas station at least once a week whether he needed gas or not, just to see her.

She was a total enigma to him. Real, not made up to be something she wasn't. Liked the same things he liked, fishing, hunting, cars, four-wheeling, and beer, which made her even more fascinating.

Every Friday night, she met with a few of her friends at The Dusty Boot, got a little drunk and then went home. She didn't go home with anyone from what he'd seen of her escapades. Maybe she went to San Antonio for her fun. *Hell, maybe she's a virgin.* The thought brought a frown to his lips. He didn't do virgins. Things got messy with a woman who didn't like sex the way he did. Not that he was weird about sex. Well, maybe a little. He did like variety.

The ranch came into view a few minutes later as he pulled up the gravel drive to the gate. Once he punched in the numbers, the wrought iron gate slowly opened, allowing him entrance onto the property.

Longhorn cattle grazed in the distance to his left when he drove up the long, winding drive to approach the main lodge. The multi-story building was half stone, half wood with three big dormer windows in the front looking out over the yard. A huge porch graced the area with several rockers and benches for guests to sit and enjoy the sunset if they wish.

Jeremiah did a double-take as he noticed the old cowboy sitting in one of the rockers for a second before he disappeared into thin air. The ghosts around the property gave him the shivers sometimes when they made noise or appeared out of nowhere, but most of the time he tried to ignore them.

As he approached the front of the lodge and pushed open the door, he was met by one of the kitchen workers coming out to ring the lunch bell. The guests on the ranch were summoned to meals by the ringing of the steel bell hanging on the hook outside the door.

"Oh hey, Jeremiah," Mandy said as she reached up to grab the rope hanging from the end of the bell.

"Hi, Mandy."

Mandy had been a friend of Paige and Peyton's who now worked on the ranch serving the meals three times a day. She also helped Paige with the twins who were born almost a year ago. Wow, time sure did fly these days. Getting old sucked.

"I thought you were in town?" She clanged the bell three times.

Several people came out of their little cabins and headed toward them. Meals were a very social event at the ranch, one he enjoyed a lot. The different people who came to stay there always made for interesting conversations. Many times, he would sit at a table with some of tourists so he could talk with them. He liked learning about different places. It gave him a mental list of the sights he'd like to see someday. "I was, but I'm home now."

"Are you going to be working this afternoon?"

"Yeah. I guess. I hadn't planned on it, but since my day is messed up, I might as well. Why?"

"Do you think you could help me? I've got some college algebra to do and I just don't get it."

"Sure. Come by my office between the meals when you have some time and I'll help you."

"Thanks. You're a doll."

He leaned in to hug her quickly before the crowd made it to the steps. "Don't tell the ladies. I won't be able to beat them off with a stick I keep behind the door."

"You are too much."

He grinned as he stepped back to allow the guests to enter the lodge for the noon meal. "When are you going to wrangle one of my brothers into marryin' you?"

She laughed as she punched him in the arm. "I'm workin' on it."

He liked Mandy, not the way one would like a girl they were interested in, but like a sister. She'd been an instrumental part of Peyton getting away from her crazy ex and finding her way to being in love with his brother, Jason. He liked that his brothers were pairing up with some really great gals. Maybe it was time for him to settle down too after all.

"I need to get back to work before your mom fires my ass."

Jeremiah chuckled. "Like that's going to happen. You're good for this place."

"Well thank you, kind sir. I love my job and hanging out with you all. It's like a home away from home." She walked with him toward the serving tables. "I'll talk to you after the meal is served and we get the dishes done."

"Okay. Find me in my office." The family table had to be divided into two tables with the addition of all the women in the house.

He noticed an empty spot on the end where Joshua normally sat. He glanced around to find his brother sitting with a pretty, blonde woman at one of the other tables. Maybe the lone, unattached triplet was finding one of his own? He hoped so.

Jeremiah took the empty chair, turning it backward and straddling it with his thighs much to the chagrin of his mother, who frowned from across the table.

"We sit like adults at this table, Jeremiah."

He stood up to turn the chair the right way before he eased his large frame into the seat. Leave it his mother to make him feel like an eight-year-old again. He loved her to pieces, but sometimes she drove him nuts. "Sorry, Mom." His cell phone beeped again. After he removed it from the holster at his hip, he checked the message to see the final stock report for the day. He smiled. Things were looking up.

"No phone at the table, Jeremiah."

"Yes, Mom. Sorry. I had to check on my stock report."

"You know the rules."

"I'll go put it in my office. Be right back." *Damn.* Chastised by his mother at the table, but Nina Young ruled the house with an iron fist and her sons knew it. He should have ignored the urge to immediately answer the beep. Most of the time he could get away with leaving his phone in the holster, but checking it at the table was a no-no.

He opened his office door and flipped on the computer screen for a second as he laid his phone on the desk. The stock report came up immediately when the monitor turned on. A grin spread across his face as his portfolio just took a huge jump with the purchase of the climbing stocks. If he sold in the next couple of days, he would be able to retire on his gains. He pumped his fist into the air a couple of times.

"You coming back to the table?" Jeff asked as he walked by the door.

"Yeah. Be right there."

"You're in a good mood."

"Yep. Financial stability will do that for you."

"That's awesome, Jeremiah. Now if you'd find a good woman to settle down with, you'd be all set."

"Don't put the cart before the horse there, brother." He slapped Jeff on the back as they walked back out toward the dining room together. "We all can't be as happy as you are. How's Terri feeling?"

"A lot better with this pregnancy than the last, although I wish we hadn't added to the family so soon."

"It'll be okay. James is two."

"I know. I just hope it's a girl this time."

"Having boy problems?"

"Ben is getting very mouthy lately. He starts school this fall and I'm afraid the teachers are going to have lots of problems with his back talking."

"He'll be fine. He's his daddy's son."

"That's what I'm afraid of.

Chapter Two

Friday evening rolled around, bringing with it tension and apprehension for Callie. Her shoulders bunched with anxiety, her hands were sweating, her heart raced around her chest like a horse running the Kentucky Derby, and her whole body shuddered with nerves. What the hell was she thinking agreeing to a date with Jeremiah?

"Easy, girl." Her stomach flipped. Yeah, she'd been on dates before, but not with the man she'd lusted after for several years. *Lusted after. That was one way to put it.* She wouldn't agree with her heart when the stubborn organ whispered she was in love with him. She couldn't be. He hardly knew she existed. Besides, she definitely wasn't his type. He went out with skinny, model-thin women, not the rather rounded, plump-figured girls like her. Her boobs were too small, her waist too thick, her legs too rounded and her butt? Wow, don't get her started on her butt. So why did he ask her out? "Just to piss off Lydia, I'm sure."

Like Lydia would care.

Callie glanced at the clock before looking down at the slinky red number she wore. It hugged her curves to perfection, showing off her hourglass figure. This would show off everything she owned. She didn't even know where they were going or what they were going to do, but she felt the need to knock his socks off with her dress. If tart was what he wanted, tart would be what he got. She smoothed her hands over the skirt, looking down at the red high heels on her feet. Her toes looked hideous peeking out of the ends of the shoes, but at least she'd done the girlie thing painting them a bright red to go with her dress. Maybe she should have had a pedicure done. She snorted as she covered her mouth with her hand. Yeah, right. She *had* put on a little makeup and curled her hair. The main attraction was the dress though. She planned to knock him dead with this outfit.

The doorbell rang precisely on time for Jeremiah's arrival.

"I'll get it," her father called from the living room. "Hi, Jeremiah. How are you tonight?"

Voices carried through her partially closed bedroom door. She was ready, but she felt the need to gather her courage a bit before she went into the front room. Not having a mother past her third birthday didn't bode well for being all that feminine, but her aunt had tried raising her up right with all the girly things. Callie didn't care much for it growing up though. She liked working with her dad, going fishing, going hunting, riding dirt bikes, and four-wheelers. All the things girls weren't supposed to enjoy. Tonight she would be the woman Jeremiah went tongue-tied over.

"She'll be out in a minute, son. Have a seat. Can I get you something to drink?"

The rumble of Jeremiah's voice sent shivers racing across her arms. "No, sir. I'm fine. Thank you."

"How are things at your parent's place?"

"Keeping us hopping, although the season is coming to an end."

"True, true. How is the cattle business treating you all?"

"We manage to stay afloat. The guest ranch keeps things moving. We are booked solid through most of the winter even though the weather doesn't give them much to do on a ranch. They still come for the good old-fashioned hospitality, home-cooking, and southern charm."

"I hear you are making yourself a name on the stock market with your trading."

"That right?"

"Yep."

"Do you trade?"

"I dabble. Nothing like you, I'm afraid."

"It's all in the numbers."

"I'm sure. You'll have to let me in on a few you've got going. I'd love to be able to make sure Callie doesn't have to work at the station for the rest of her life to have a home."

"Sure, Mr. Lewis. We can talk more about it tomorrow if you'd like to meet me for lunch?"

"Certainly, Jeremiah. Thanks."

Callie took it as her cue to come out of her room even though she really didn't want to. She was afraid to meet Jeremiah's gaze as she rounded the end of the couch and came into his view, but she shouldn't have been. The appreciation shining in his gaze, as he got to his feet, warmed her soul.

His jaw dropped as she wobbled slightly on the four-inch heels. "Well?"

"Wow. You look fabulous."

"Thanks." She smoothed the tight skirt a little around her thighs. "It's nothing special, but I wasn't sure where we were going, so I didn't know how to dress."

"It's perfect." He took her hand and brought it to his mouth to kiss the back of her fingers.

Holy hell, I'm in trouble.

"You two kids have fun. Be home before midnight."

"Dad!"

Her father laughed as her face flushed red.

"I'm kidding."

"Let me grab my bag. Oh, and my phone."

"Sure."

She rushed back into her bedroom to grab a few things. In a hurried thought, she grabbed two condoms from her nightstand drawer, shoving them into the zippered pocket of her purse before she headed back out to meet Jeremiah in the living room. *I can hope, can't I?*

Jeremiah slid her hand into his as they walked toward the door of her dad's house and then out to his truck. Again, she was struck by how the vehicle didn't suit him although he was a cowboy to the bone with his Wranglers, western shirt, boots, and cowboy hat, she thought there had to be more to him than met the eye.

"What?" he asked as he opened the door for her.

"I always thought you would be more comfortable in a sports car than a truck like your brothers."

He shut the door on her side before walking around the front to get into the driver's side. "You know, one of my dreams is to own a foreign sports car."

She laughed as she turned in the seat to face him. "Why am I not surprised at all. Let me guess. Ferrari."

"That's one of them, yep."

"I can just see you zipping around the back roads of Bandera in your car."

He cranked the engine of his truck over with a twist of the key. The diesel rumbled to life, sending a little thrill through her body. She had a thing for engines in general, but a diesel always ramped her up. Over the years, her dad had taught her to work on all kinds of cars at the garage. There wasn't an engine he couldn't fix, although with the newer cars, it had become more and more difficult for him to make any money at the garage. She hoped things got better soon. Otherwise, they might lose the station.

"Where are we going?"

"I thought we'd get some Tex-Mex at the River Walk in San Antonio and then hit a nice little club I know."

"Okay."

"You do like Mexican food, right?"

"Love it. One of my favorites."

"Good." He glanced across the cab of the truck as they pulled onto the highway headed for the city. "Did I tell you how gorgeous you look tonight?"

"Sort of, but thank you."

"I've never seen you in a dress like that, I think. You usually are more conservative like what you were wearing last Sunday."

"Last Sunday?"

"Yeah, I usually see you with your dad going to Sunday brunch at the diner after church."

"You do?"

"Yes. You look real nice."

She bit the inside of her cheek so she wouldn't ask why he noticed her on Sundays going into the diner. Surely he wasn't that interested in her, right?

"You smell right nice too."

Boy, is he doling out the compliments tonight. What gives? "It's okay, Jeremiah. I know you only asked me out to piss off Lydia, so you might as well take me back home right now rather than go through with this date thing. I'm not the kind of woman you normally go out with and I'm sure taking me in San Antonio is just so you don't have to show up with me at the diner of somewhere else where we might be seen. This is ridic—"

Jeremiah slammed on the breaks, pulling the truck over to the side of the road. When he jammed the gearshift on the truck into park, she pushed her back against the door, a little afraid of what he might do. Fury and frustration made his face look like granite. His eyebrows drew down, making them look slashed above angry grey eyes. She'd never seen Jeremiah Young pissed off before. She wasn't sure she wanted to again.

"Enough. I did not ask you out because I wanted to piss Lydia off. I don't care what she thinks. All I care about is what you think. Whether you believe me or not, I wanted to take you out. I have for a long time. I just didn't have the guts to ask. You're a very beautiful woman and I like you the way you are."

"You wanted to ask me out?"

"Yes. We've known each other a long time, Callie. You aren't the type of woman I usually go out with. You're more of a permanent relationship type girl. I'm not sure I'm ready for that kind of thing. You aren't the type to fuck and walk away from. That scares the hell out of me, which is why I never asked you out before."

"I'm not?" She shook her head. "I mean, no I'm not, but I could be if that's what you wanted." Desperation riddled her subconscious. She wanted him on any terms she could get him even if it was only for one night.

"You would become something you aren't for me?"

"Yes." She blew out a long breath. "I've wanted you for a long time, Jeremiah. I can be whatever you want me to be for however long you want me. No hearts or feelings will get into the mix. I promise."

He swallowed rather hard, his Adam's apple bobbing a couple of times before he spoke again. "Are you propositioning me for a one-nighter?"

"Yes."

"And the rules of this fling?"

"We have one great night, no feelings get involved. We part as friends."

He tapped his fingers on the steering wheel for a minute before he pushed his hat back on his head and turned to look at her. "One night?"

The grey of his eyes turned stormy in the fading light of the evening. Labor Day would be on them soon. The summer would be coming to a close. Winter in Bandera always seemed long and lonely to her. She wished for more than one night, but if that's all there was, then so be it. "Yes. I'm game for one night of hot sex with you."

"You really want to do this?"

"Yep. What do you say?"

A rough exhale pierced the silence of the cab. "Let's have dinner. We can decide for sure at the end of the evening. Who knows, maybe we aren't even compatible."

Like hell. Judging from how I react to your touch, if we aren't compatible, I'll eat my shoe. "Sounds good to me."

He nodded once, put the truck into gear and pulled out into traffic as Callie contemplated what she'd just done. A deal with the devil, no doubt, and she was sure she'd get burned in the process. One night of mind-blowing sex with Jeremiah Young. What could go wrong?

* * * *

Jeremiah parked the truck along the narrow road near the San Antonio River Walk so they could take a stroll down the sidewalk to the restaurant he wanted to take Callie to. He wasn't sure if she'd ever been to this particular restaurant, but it was one of his favorites and they even had a mariachi band that played while the diners ate.

The evening breeze blew softly through the area, cooling things down from the heat of the afternoon sun. Lights bathed each restaurant in a soft glow as they approached the one he'd made reservations for.

"Young, party of two."

"Ah, yes sir. One moment please and I'll have your table ready."

"Thank you."

They stood side by side, not touching, but shifting from foot to foot as they waited for the hostess to seat them. He hadn't said anything more about her crazy scheme on the ride into the city as he continued to roll it over in his mind. It was the perfect scenario, but somehow he just knew things would go wrong in the end. However, he'd never had trouble walking away from a woman before, so he shouldn't with Callie, right? Of course not. His heart and his head hadn't interfered in the past. They would have some great sex and get the urge out of their systems, he hoped. Still being able to see other people when things were said and done seemed like a great idea to him.

"Right this way, please."

He laid the palm of his hand at the small of her back as they followed the hostess through the tables toward the patio area up on the second floor.

"Will this be all right, sir?"

"Perfect. Thank you." Callie rubbed her arms as if chilled, so he took off the suit jacket he wore to drape it over her shoulders. "Can't have you getting chilled with your shoulders bare."

"Thank you."

"You're welcome." He held out her chair while he waited for her to sit before taking his own across from her. He wanted to be able to look into her gorgeous blue eyes while they sipped margaritas and ate chips.

"You're such a gentleman."

"My mother would be proud to hear you say so. She raised us boys right, I guess."

"I would say so." Callie laid the napkin on her lap before she picked up the menu. "Hmm. What sounds good besides having you for supper?"

He wasn't sure he heard her right. "Would you like a margarita?"

"I suppose, although something a bit stronger would certainly loosen things up in the nether regions."

Jeremiah ordered her one and a Jack and Coke for himself when the waitress stopped at their table.

"I'll have one of what he's having instead of the margarita."

"Of course. I'll be right back with your drinks," the waitress said, sliding the tortilla chips and salsa onto the table between them.

He must have had a startled look on his face because she said, "What?"

"I figured you for one of those fruity drink kind of gals."

"I'm feeling right adventurous tonight."

"Apparently." As he perused the menu, he kept glancing over the top to look at the woman across the table from him. He couldn't believe this was the same sweet girl he'd tutored in math in high school. Sure, he'd talked to her, saw her, and watched her off and on since they graduated several years ago, but he hadn't seen her like this.

"Is there something on my nose?" she asked, setting her menu down on the table to her left before she grabbed a chip, dipped it into the salsa and then popped it between those tempting as hell lips.

"No. Why?"

"You're staring."

"Sorry. I'm trying to figure out what happened to the Callinda Lewis I know, because I think you left her back at your house. I don't know this girl at all."

"What's wrong with me being different than the girl you grew up with?"

"Nothing, but I like Callie too. Is this Callie or Callinda?"

"It's me, Jeremiah. I'm not any different than the girl you've known your whole life, but you haven't been out with me on a date. This is how I am."

"Somehow I don't think so. Don't put on a different persona for me. I liked you the way you were."

"You don't like this me?"

"It's not that. I think this you is hotter than holding a firecracker, but the sweet Callie is nice too."

The waitress brought their drinks and then took their order for food. The evening darkness had started to surround them as the sun went down. Candles were lit on the tabletops covered with brightly colored tablecloths. The light flickering from the small candle made her eyes sparkle like sapphires. He hadn't noticed their deep blue color before or how kissable her lips were.

"I'm not a virgin, you know. I've been around a bit. Dabbled in some bondage. Nipple clamps, rope work, dildos…that kind of thing."

He choked on the sip of his drink he'd just swallowed. "Oh?"

Her lips bowed into a teasing little smile. "No. I lost it in high school so you don't have to worry about my inexperience."

After a couple of coughs, he said in a gravelly voice laced with the whiskey he'd practically choked on, "I really hadn't thought about it."

"Well I have. I wish it had been you."

"Callie—"

"Am I making you uncomfortable?"

"A little. I'm not used to you being this bold."

"You don't like bold women?" she asked, sipping her own drink with a wide-eyed expression that made her look all the more innocent except the dark eyeliner she rimmed her eyes with.

This Callie had him stumped. He wasn't sure what to make of the changes in her and he wasn't sure he liked it at all. Of course, he liked bold women to an extent, but this didn't fit the Callie he knew. "I do."

"So what's the problem?"

Their food arrived, saving him from trying to explain his thoughts to her. Was she trying to impress him? Make him want her over Lydia? Didn't she realize he'd much rather go out with her than Lydia?

They ate for several minutes in silence as he tried to think of how to approach this. He didn't want to put Callie off, but he wanted the old Callie, not this new throw herself in your face girl sitting across the table from him.

"You aren't eating. Aren't you hungry?"

He looked down at this plate and true, he'd been shoving his food around with his fork more than he'd been eating his enchilada. Placing the fork to the side, he tented his fingers so he could watch her. "I guess not so much."

A blush spread across her cheeks as she glanced down at her own plate. "The food is wonderful. I'm glad you brought me here. I haven't been to this one before, although I've been down on the River Walk thousands of times."

"This one is my favorite restaurant. I come here as much as I can when I'm in town."

The mariachi band strolled by their table to ask if they wanted them to play a song. After Jeremiah gave them a tip, they played a soft Mexican ballad meant for lovers. A moment later, he felt her foot slide along his inner thigh, heading for his crotch. *Holy hell!* "Listen, Callie." He shoved her foot down. "This is moving a bit fast for me."

"What's wrong?" She swallowed hard, looking like she was about to cry. "I'm coming on too strong, aren't I? I'm sorry. I'm totally embarrassed now."

"It's okay. This just isn't the girl I know. I'm sorry, but I'm not sure I like her very much."

"Wow."

"I'm finished if you want me to take you home." He signaled the waitress for the check as he pulled his wallet out of his pants pocket.

"I guess so."

The moment he paid for their tab, he stood to escort her back to his truck. This whole date had turned into a disaster and he wasn't sure what to think about it. Obviously, he didn't know her as well as he thought he did because man, this Callie wasn't for him. She made Lydia look like a saint. That was hard to do since Lydia was a bitch.

Silence stretched between them on the ride home. They didn't talk at all and he thought he heard her sniffle several times like she might be crying, but he didn't know what to do. If he played it like it was okay, he'd feel like a heel because he'd led her on. He didn't want the girl she'd been at dinner. He wanted the sweet Callie he'd known all his life. He wasn't sure how to find the real girl.

Chapter Three

I'm such an idiot! Callie felt like shit. She'd totally screwed up this date with Jeremiah. She probably wouldn't get a chance with him again and didn't know how to fix this. Trying to be the woman she thought he liked turned out to be the last thing he wanted. What to do? "Jeremiah, I'm sorry."

"For what?"

"Acting like a prima donna or whatever you want to call it. I thought you like those kind of women."

"No. Yes." He raked his fingers through his hair as they pulled up to the curb in front of her house. "I'm not sure what I like at this point, Callie, but I know the woman you were at dinner tonight wasn't what I wanted. I liked you the way you were. Sweet, innocent, tomboyish. It's nice to be with a woman who isn't all about the hair and makeup. You work on cars. You like to go fishing and four-wheelin'. Those are the things I like about you." He shut the truck off before he turned to face her. "I don't need to jump into bed with you on the first date either. Not that I wouldn't mind, but it's not what this is about. I want to get to know you as the girl I went to high school with who has turned into this hottie."

"Hottie?" she asked, blushing to the roots of her hair. He thought she was hot? *Wow.*

"Yeah." He took her hand and threaded his fingers through hers. "I like you the way you are. Don't change."

"Okay." She loved the feeling of her hand in his. Warmth spread up her arm, making her heart flutter in her chest. She had it bad for this man, always had. "Can we start over?"

"Sure."

She captured her bottom lip between her teeth as she tried to think of how to start this whole night again without the act. Once she unbuckled her seatbelt, she turned to face him. "How was your day today?"

His lips lifted in a half grin as he began telling her all about what he did at the ranch, how his stocks were doing, and everything about his life as the Young brother in charge of the finances. Her heart warmed as she relayed everything about her day. They almost sounded like an old married couple as they talked. She told him about working on the transmission she'd been having trouble with at the garage, how the same customers came in every week for gas, including him, and how she enjoyed spending Sundays with her dad going to church before they went out for Sunday dinner at his aunt's diner.

"She enjoys having you for supper, I'm sure."

"It's just me and Dad time, so it's fun. We talk about all kinds of things." She scooted closer. "Tell me what it was like growing up with such a huge family."

"I forgot you were an only child."

"Yeah. When Mom left us, Dad had to do what he could. He didn't know how to raise a girl."

"He did a damn good job. I don't know many women out there who can do what you do. It's a great trait to have." He brought her hand to his lips, brushing the back lightly. "You are an amazing woman, Callie."

She smiled at the compliment, absorbing everything about being with Jeremiah she could. Talking to him about little things made this the best date ever. "Would you like to come in?" She glanced at the front of the house, watching as her dad's light in his bedroom went out. "Dad went to bed so we can sit and watch a movie here since we didn't hit the theater."

"Okay. Do you have some popcorn?"

She gave him her best *are you crazy* look and said, "What is a movie without popcorn?"

With a tip of his head, he pushed open the driver's side door before slamming it shut. She waited for him to come around to open her door and help her out of the truck, knowing it was what men like Jeremiah did.

When they stopped at the door of the house for her to open it, he rested his hand at the small of her back. The warmth emanating from his skin sent goose bumps down her legs. She knew he probably only did it because he was raised to be a gentleman, but she loved having him touch her. "Let me check in with Dad for a minute. There are movies on television or you can pick one of the discs we have in the entertainment center."

"Okay."

She headed down the hall to tap on her father's door. Since he'd seen the light go off only a few minutes before, she figured she should at least let him know she was home. "Dad?"

"Come in."

"We're back."

He glanced at the clock on the bedside table. "It's early."

"I know. We decided to watch a movie here instead of going out."

"All right. You two kids have fun."

"We will. I love you, Daddy."

"I love you too, doll baby. Be good."

She laughed. "I'll try." After she closed the door behind her, she walked down the long hall toward the kitchen to make the popcorn and get them something to drink.

Jeremiah was still looking through the discs when she glanced across the island. "What would you like to drink?"

"Anything cold is fine."

"I have Coke?"

He looked back at her with a grin on his perfect lips. "Perfect!"

She poured him a glass with some ice in it as she kicked off the heels on her feet. With a heavy sigh, she leaned on the bar with her elbow.

"You okay?"

"Yeah, but those heels were killing me."

He set the discs he was looking at down and walked around the island. "You didn't have to do all of this for me."

"I thought you liked those kinds of women."

"Sometimes, but like I said, I like the Callie I already knew. I just want to get to know her better." His gaze raked down her body, causing her nipples to pull into tight little nubs under her dress. "Although you look killer in that dress."

Her cheeks heated with a blush as she set the can down on the counter. "Thanks."

He leaned in to kiss her on the forehead. "Why don't you change into something more comfortable like sweats and a T-shirt?"

Her whole body shivered from the touch of his lips. She really wanted them on hers. Once would be enough, right? Yeah, probably not, but she could live for the moment. "Really?"

"Yes. I like seeing your curves in that clingy little number, but I know it can't be very comfortable."

He'd noticed her curves, wow. "It's not."

He swatted her on the butt as she started to walk toward her room. "Then go change, woman, and I'll get the popcorn in the microwave."

The moment she had a second for herself, she leaned against the closed door and sighed. He'd kissed her even if it was just on the forehead—she'd had Jeremiah's lips on her skin. Why did he have to be the one to turn her upside down like this? Why did it have to be one of the Young brothers? Why not someone easy to love? Not them. They all were bachelors to the core. Well, until they met the right woman. A few of the boys had settled down recently, but all of them were women from somewhere besides here. Bandera, Texas residents weren't what the boys looked for when they contemplated a mate, or at least it appeared so. "They're attracted to a different woman, not some down-home country girl like me." Oh well. She'd take what she could get. For tonight, Jeremiah Young was all hers.

After she quickly changed into a pair of shorts and a T-shirt, she did a quick swipe of a makeup cloth to get the majority of the goop off her face. She'd done herself up with dark eyeliner, lipstick and all, thinking he liked women all dolled up. It turns out he didn't want it at all. Who knew? If she compared herself to Lydia, she came up lacking. She didn't do her hair on a regular basis, she didn't wear makeup all that much, and she didn't dress fancy. With a glance in the mirror behind her door, she screwed up her mouth in a twist of a sarcastic smile before she opened the door so she could head back into the living room.

"Now there's the girl I know and love."

Love?

Jeremiah patted the couch next to him as he settled the full bowl of popcorn on his thigh. "You look like what I picture you always wearing. I bet you're more comfortable too."

"Yeah, I am. This is what I wear most of the time during the summer."

He looked at her legs with a crooked grin as he tossed a couple of kernels of popcorn into his mouth. "Nice legs."

"What? These old things?" She plopped down on the couch beside him, almost spilling the popcorn.

"Easy, woman! The popcorn!"

The peal of his laughter made her smile. She loved his laugh. Hell, she loved everything about him.

"Sorry." She grabbed a few pieces for herself as she asked, "What did you pick out?"

"*Die Hard.*"

"Of course."

"Hey, it's an action flick, but it has the mushy stuff too. I mean, you know how he hollers his wife's name and everything."

She rolled her eyes. "It's so not a woman's kind of movie. *Love Actually*, *You've Got Mail*, those kinds of movies are chick flicks."

"I'm the guest, so I guess that means we watch my movie."

"First, then it'll be my turn."

"Deal."

She grabbed the remote and flipped on the disc player. The movie began to play the opening scenes as she settled in next to Jeremiah on the couch. Being here with him like this was surreal. She never thought this would ever happen to her. Sitting next to the guy she'd been in love with since tenth grade didn't happen to girls like her. *Well, they do now.*

"Are you enjoying the movie?" he asked as their hands brushed together in the midst of the popcorn bowl.

"Yeah. I like Bruce Willis."

"He's a pretty good actor."

"I'd say so. These action flicks are exciting."

"I thought you didn't like action flicks?"

"I never said that. I just said I figured you'd pick one rather than a chick flick. I happen to like movies with car crashes, shootings, and explosions." She turned to face him. "You know I almost went to school to be in stunts."

"Really?"

"Yep. I wanted to be one of those people who flew through the air and landed on one of those big airbags. It looked so fun when I visited Los Angeles and went to Universal Studios."

"Why didn't you?"

"Because Dad needed me here to take over the garage when he can't work on cars anymore. Being the only child sucks sometimes, but I love him."

"You have no idea how lost you get being part of a huge family like mine. Middle kid syndrome jumps on a lot of people when you have a family of nine kids."

"I can imagine it would be hard not to get lost in the shuffle, but you seem to do pretty well for yourself."

"It's even worse now with the extra women in the picture. Mom and Dad are all about the daughters-in-law and the grandkids these days."

"You make sure they're financially secure though, right? I mean, you are the reason they stay in business out there because you keep their finances straight."

"True, but it's not simple to stand out in the crowd gathering out there."

"Have you thought about getting married yourself?"

He laughed as he grabbed her hand. "Are you askin'?"

Her breath stopped in her throat. "Well no, but I wondered since you are getting close to thirty. Shouldn't it be about time?"

"You are too, you know. Are you feeling the itch to be married?"

"A little. My dad is hinting at marriage and grandkids although without a steady guy, it seems unlikely for the time being. With no boyfriend in the mix, it's hard to think about a future and a wedding, not to mention babies."

"We should just get married and put them all out of their misery."

She choked on the popcorn kernel in her mouth. "You can't be serious?"

"Of course not, silly. I'm kidding!"

"Oh, thank God! I mean, we don't really know each other. I could snore or something that you hate. I mean you were mad at me earlier for trying to be what you wanted, remember?" She took a breath to continue only to have him put his hand over her mouth.

"Easy girl. Lighten up, would you?" He tipped his head to the side as a grin spread across his lips. "I'm not about to get married to someone I don't know and am not hopelessly in love with, so calm down."

She blew out a forced exhale. "Good. Me either. I want to be madly in love with the man I marry someday."

"I hope you find him soon. You're a beautiful woman and being out there on the market can be hectic."

"You're teasing me now."

"Yes, I am. Stop being so serious. We're two friends having a nice evening watching a movie with popcorn." He held up a piece to feed her. "Nothing more."

For the next few hours, they joked, threw popcorn at each other and generally had a good time. It was something she'd needed. The stress of the garage, not having a dating life or a steady boyfriend had gotten to her.

"So what kind of girl *do* you like?"

"Well, let's see. Someone who is confident, real, likes kids, is close to her family, not so much into being the eye candy on my arm, but who likes to dress up once in a while and hit the town so every man in the room can't take his eyes off her."

He flipped off the movie since the credits were rolling at the end of *City of Angels*.

She dabbed at her eyes with a tissue from the box next to her on the table. That movie always made her cry. "Sorry."

"For what?"

"For blubbering. You probably didn't need to see me with traces of mascara running down my face."

He took the tissue from her hand as he turned her face toward his. She sucked in a breath as he gently wiped the smudge from beneath her eye. He was so close she could feel his breath on her lips. A shiver raced down her back when he stopped and looked down into her eyes. He leaned in like he planned to kiss her, or wanted to at least, and she closed her eyes in anticipation.

A bang in the hallway startled them both into a quick separation. "Sorry, kids."

"It's fine, Dad. Did you need something?"

"Just getting a glass of milk. Heartburn is killing me tonight."

"Are you sure you're okay?"

"I'm fine, honey. You two just keep doing what you were doing," he said with a wave of his hand.

The refrigerator door opened before the sounds of something being poured into a glass reached her on the couch. She glanced at Jeremiah who seemed to be contemplating something as he studied the picture on the wall above the fireplace with a hell of an intense look in his eyes. *What is he thinking? I feel really stupid now, hoping he would lean in and kiss me. It shouldn't be like that between us. We're friends. Nothing more, right? He doesn't want anything but friendship from me.* She wondered why he looked like he was going to kiss her then.

"I probably should get on home," Jeremiah said, climbing to his feet. "It was a great evening. We'll have to do it again sometime."

"How about tomorrow?"

"Tomorrow?"

"Yeah, are you busy?"

"No." He shoved his hand into his front pocket to retrieve his keys. "We could go to The Dusty Boot to shoot some pool or throw darts."

"Sounds like fun."

"Okay. I'll pick you up about seven unless you want to get some dinner beforehand. Maybe Aunt Anne's diner?"

"Sure. Sounds like fun."

"Great." He shuffled his feet for a second. "I guess I'll see you tomorrow then. Since we are doing dinner, I'll pick you up at six."

She got to her feet to walk him to his car. Dare she hope he would try to kiss her goodnight? A girl could always dream, right? "I'll walk you out."

As they walked to the door, she turned to glance at her father who stood holding up the kitchen island as if his life depended on it while he sipped his glass of milk with a smirk. *Jerk.* He knew how she felt about Jeremiah since she never kept anything from her dad.

The cooler night air hit her in the face as they walked outside toward Jeremiah's truck. "Thanks for tonight. It was a lot of fun even though things started rather badly." She rubbed her arms to ward off the chill.

"We discussed that. Be yourself. I like the Callie I know from the garage."

"Okay."

"I like the fancy dressed Callie too, but don't make yourself up to be something you aren't. I think you just like dressing up sometimes to be all girly."

"Sometimes. It's nice to be a woman occasionally."

"Tell you what, put on a pretty blouse or tank top tomorrow night with some jeans meant to show off your curves and you'll be just right."

She smiled at the thought of the perfect jeans for what she had in mind. "I can do that."

"Good. I'll be interested to see how your ass looks."

"You like my ass?"

"You have a very pretty one. Mind you, I'm an ass man."

"You don't say?"

"Yep. I love me some pretty, curvy butt in a nice, tight pair of jeans."

"I'll see what I can do then." The smile curving his lips made her want to kiss him all the more, but she figured it wasn't the right time.

"I'll see you tomorrow."

He leaned in and kissed her on the forehead. *Damn it! A little lower, please.*

"Thanks, Jeremiah."

He climbed into his truck, started the engine and pulled away from the curb.

She stood near the edge of the lawn, watching as he drove down her street. With a heavy sigh, she headed back into the house and her lonely bed.

"How'd things go?" her dad asked as she shut the front door behind her.

"Fine."

"Did he kiss you?"

"It's not like that between us, Daddy. He's just a friend and I think that's all he'll ever be to me. I want more, but he doesn't see me as girlfriend material."

"Well maybe you need to make him see you as the woman of his dreams."

"Maybe." She shrugged before she poured herself a glass of milk from the refrigerator as well. "I don't think we're very compatible on the romance level though."

"Why do you think so?"

Cold milk felt good on her throat, spreading through her chest. "I don't know. He doesn't act like he's interested in me as a girlfriend." She leaned against the counter, sipping on the white liquid in her glass as she contemplated exactly what to do about Jeremiah Young. Could she convince him she was everything he wanted and needed in a woman? She wasn't sure. Confidence wasn't one of her strong points, especially when she compared herself to the women in town like Lydia. "I'm not his type, Dad. He's always been seen with girly girls, not someone who works on cars."

Her father wrapped an arm around her shoulders, pulling her into a hug. "You have to understand one thing about men, Callie. They don't always know what they need until it slaps them in the face. There is a reason that boy hasn't settled down with a girly girl. Maybe he wants something different, like you."

"One can hope."

"Bide your time, sweetie. He'll come around."

Callie finished off her glass of milk, kissed her dad goodnight and headed to her room to try to sleep. She wasn't sure she'd be able to with the way tonight went or maybe she would dream of Jeremiah kissing her. That would be cool. Not like she didn't dream of him often anyway, at least now she knew the look in his eyes when he was about to kiss her, making the visual more potent.

Chapter Four

Jeremiah pulled up his chair in front of his desk at the ranch before he opened his desktop to his bank account. He pursed his lips as he nodded. He was almost there. Almost to the point where he could leave the ranch as a hand or financial advisor or whatever you wanted to call him. He'd made his first million two years ago. Now he was closing in on ten.

Birds chirped out the window of his office as he glanced outside. Fall in Bandera took on a burnished hue as the weather had started to turn cooler in the evenings, but the days could still be rather hot. For some reason, he felt the need to visit the barn, soak up the atmosphere, the smells, and the general cowboy way of life today. Maybe he'd talk to his brother Jeff for a bit. It seemed they hadn't talked in forever.

Jeff had his own life going with his girlfriend, Terri, and their kids. They seemed happy although he figured Jeff would have married her by now. Poor guy was so gun-shy over marriage he wouldn't do the deed and put a ring on the girl's finger. Terri seemed happy with the way things were, but Jeremiah figured deep down she wanted what every woman wanted, a happy marriage.

How did he feel about matrimony? He wanted a wife someday, someone to come home to, someone to help raise their children together. The picture of Callinda Lewis popped into his head as he stared out the window. Why her? Why now? Surely he didn't feel anything besides friendship for her, although he had been about to kiss her the night before when her dad interrupted them. What would that kiss have been like? She said she wasn't a virgin, that kind of made him mad, but he didn't quite understand why. Maybe it was the fact that some kid had taken advantage of her in high school. He wouldn't have, would he?

Hard to say, he was all about getting laid back then, just like any other high schooler, but Callie was different. Good girls didn't do those kinds of things.

Had it been at prom for her? He thought about asking her. Maybe not. It really wasn't any of his business anyway. But who had she given her virginity to?

His had been some years before that. An older woman at the ranch had cornered him in the barn when he was sixteen. She'd been all about teaching him how to please her and boy did he ever! He used the skills she'd taught him over her two-week stay to learn all he could about making love to a woman. The women he'd been with since seemed to like his prowess. He smiled and then frowned. Could he take Callie to bed?

"What the hell? Why am I even thinking about getting her onto any old flat surface?"

Not that he didn't want a hot partner in the sack, but Callie? Well maybe. She sure looked gorgeous in that red dress she'd worn the night before. He pulled off his hat before wiping the sweat from his forehead. His jeans felt a bit tighter when he thought about how well she'd filled out that material. She was just a friend, right? He shouldn't be thinking about her all dirty like, but man, he'd wanted to kiss her when her dad interrupted. Her lips had looked so tempting, he'd almost lost himself in her mouth for a minute. Good thing her dad had stopped that nonsense. He couldn't afford to get tied up with a good girl. He'd always played the field and that's how he liked it, at least for now.

Later he would think about a wife, not now. He needed to get the family on an even keel with their money so they wouldn't have to worry for the long haul. His parents kept a pretty good eye on the bank account so he kept a different account for what investing he'd been doing. If they ever found out about him hiding their money, they'd kill him. He tapped a few keys on the keyboard, pulling up the account information for the ranch. He'd been investing pretty heavily for them for the last year. The sum had a few more zeros than there had been when he'd started. He was proud to say the ranch now had at least enough to cover them for awhile should things go south.

His mom stopped in the doorway to his office just as he clicked off the page. "Jeremiah?"

"Hi, Mom."

"What are you up to this morning? You don't usually work on the weekends."

"Not computer work anyway. I was checking on things from the stock's closing yesterday to see where things were."

"You've become quite the financial wizard, son."

He smiled as his mom put her hand on his shoulder to peek over at the computer screen. "Yeah. Things are going well."

"When are you going to let your dad and me in on the buying and selling of stock so we can invest for our retirement?"

"Soon."

"Good. I'd like to sit down with you to talk numbers. You know I have a degree in mathematics."

"I know. It's probably where I got my love of numbers."

She leaned in to kiss him on the cheek. "Probably." She turned to go out of the office, but stopped for a second. "Oh, how was your date with Callinda Lewis last night?"

"It wasn't really a date, Mom. We were just hanging out as friends."

"You know you could do a lot worse than her. She's a nice girl."

"I know."

"You should think about her on the girlfriend level. She'd be good for you. Nice, down-to-earth kind of girl to go with my wild son."

"I'm not wild. I'm tame compared to some of my brothers."

"True, but you aren't the settling down forever kind of cowboy right now and I think you should be."

"Why? I'm not that old yet."

"You're getting there, son. Just like your brothers, you don't want to think about being with one woman. I've heard about your escapades with the women of Bandera and San Antonio. I think you need to find a nice girl. I think Callinda Lewis is just what you need." She pressed her palm to his cheek before she turned back toward the door to leave. "Think about it."

Great. That's all I need is to have Mom on the Callie Lewis bandwagon. Once she sets her mind on someone for one of her sons, there's no stopping her meddling.

He didn't need to think about it since he'd already been doing a lot of it about that particular woman since last night. *Damn it!* He was a forever kind of guy, right?

With a flick of the switch, he turned off the monitor on his computer. He climbed to his feet as he scraped his fingers over the stubble on his chin. He'd have to shower and shave for his date with Callie.

Shit. Even he was thinking of their meeting tonight as a date when he shouldn't be. He didn't need the complication of a permanent woman in his life until he was ready to move on from being a cowboy. He might get there sometime, but he sure wasn't ready yet.

It was still early in the day. Not yet noon. He might just take a group of riders out on the next excursion, just for the hell of it. He hadn't done a ride along in forever it seemed. He might be out of practice a bit, but being a cowboy since he could walk, the whole thing came naturally to him. You get right back on when you fall off.

Lunch would be served soon so he'd get with Jeff then so they could talk business with his dad too. He needed to get their take on the expenses for the coming month before the guest population died off at the end of September. After Labor Day, things were slower around the ranch for guests, but the cattle business never took a break.

He adjusted his hat on his head to settle it low on his brow as he glanced down at his work clothes. Dusty boots, Wrangler jeans, standard cowboy hat and western style shirt. He sure looked the part anyway. With a wiry twist of his lips and a shrug, he walked out before shutting the door behind him. Not that anyone would mess with his computer, but he didn't want to take the chance. He wasn't ready to reveal just how well things were going with his own finances, much less the ranch.

The lunch bell clanged in the distance, signaling food was served although the guests ate first and then the family. The ranch had a few empty beds the last week or so, but there were still several people hanging out for those last few days of summer before things wound down. He knew of a few single ladies who were checking out the cowboys on the ranch this week. They'd given him the eye yesterday before supper. He knew his mom's rule of getting together with the guests, but he wondered if it might be a good idea to check out one. He had an itch that hadn't been scratched lately.

What about Callie?

There she was in the forefront of his mind again. He didn't need to think of her when he thought of bedding a lady, but there she was making herself a present part of his thoughts without regard to the fact that he wanted to keep things strictly friends with her. Did he? His thoughts strayed to how she'd looked in her slinky little red dress last night, bringing randy images of her to the front of his brain. Maybe she would be interested in taking their relationship to a friends with benefits status?

Hmm.

When he rounded the corner of the stairs to walk into the dining room, he was struck by the group of people milling about. With a family of nine boys, his own group made up a large portion of the people in the room and with the addition of some of the boys and their significant others, made for an even bigger group.

The single women he'd been eyeing yesterday had already sat down to eat at the back end of the dining room tables. "Jeremiah? Come sit with us."

He tipped his hat before he got in line to get his plate. Nothing like a little female company to make the hours go by faster.

Once he got his plate of food, he stopped by the family table to tell Jeff he needed to talk to him after lunch before he headed toward the ladies at the back of the room. "Ladies."

A petite brunette scooted to one side. "Sit by me."

He took the seat and laid his hat on the bench between them. "Are you ladies having a good time?" The woman next to him, what was her name. Oh yeah, Brenda. "How about you, Brenda?"

"Well, yes. I mean there are all kinds of things to do on a place this size, but we wanted to get to know the cowboys *a lot* better than we have, if you know what I mean." She squeezed his thigh as she batted her eyelashes at him.

He glanced over at her, raising his eyebrow in question. Nope, he wasn't mistaken. Desire was written all over her face. He might take her up on that offer after a ride this afternoon. Maybe he'd take her for a private little outing down by the creek where two people could get to know each other a little bit. "How would you like to go for a ride with me this evening?"

"I would love to."

"I'll meet you here about six. After supper."

She smiled as her friends gasped and sighed. They finished lunch with the conversation floating around him of typical female proportions. He couldn't keep it all straight since he wasn't up on the latest fashions in New York, Broadway musicals, what the celebs were doing in Los Angeles, or even what the latest weather forecast was if it wasn't for their area. Yeah, he kept up on financial news, but women didn't care about that sort of thing.

When he finished his meal, he excused himself with work to be done never ending on a ranch and left the ladies to gossip amongst themselves.

He dumped his plate into the wash basin for the dishes with a smile toward Mandy who had just come out to grab the dirty plates. "What are your plans for tonight, Jeremiah?"

"Oh, I have a late night ride with a lady who is a guest here. I'm supposed to meet her at seven."

"That'll be great. I'm sure she'll enjoy your company."

Mandy grabbed the dishpan right before she disappeared through the double doors leading to the kitchen.

He pulled off his hat and rake his fingers through his hair. Why did he get the feeling he was forgetting something? He shrugged. Apparently, it wasn't important.

His mom walked up behind him as Mandy left through the doors. "I thought you were going out with Callie tonight?"

"Shit. I'd forgotten about that."

"Well you can't be in two places at once."

"No. I'll cancel with Callie."

"Why?"

"It'll be better that way. I don't want her to get the wrong idea, Mom. Two dates in two days? If she thinks there is something going to happen between us, she's mistaken."

"Jeremiah, you are being an ass."

"Sorry, but this is for the best."

"You're going out with a guest on the ranch?"

"Just going for a late evening ride."

"Uh-huh."

"Nothing else."

"Don't forget to call Callie. You'll really be in hot water if you do."

The family had finished up their food as well so he motioned for Jeff and his dad to join him in his office to go over the figures for the month on the supplies.

* * * *

Callie finished dressing in her tight-fitting jeans, white tank top with a sheer blouse she wanted to wear over the top lying on the bed, and her cowboy boots. She planned to be the epitome of what Jeremiah wanted in a woman if it killed her. With a glance at the clock, she realized he should be here any minute so she finished with the light bit of makeup before she clipped her hair back in a barrette. Nothing like being the girl next door and still trying to be a woman a cowboy would be interested in dating on a regular basis. "What if he kisses me tonight?" She closed her eyes as she imagined the look he had on his face when he bent his head to kiss her. He'd been about to, she just knew it, and man did she want him to.

"Callie?"

"Yeah, Dad?"

"Are you about ready? Jeremiah should be here any time."

"Yes. I'll be out in a minute if he comes to the door. I need to put on my blouse."

"All right. I'll man the door."

Fifteen minutes later, she paced in front of the fireplace as she glanced at her watch. Six-fifteen. She'd never known Jeremiah to be late for anything. Maybe she should call him. She had his number from when he'd tutored her so many years ago. She'd never erased it from her phone, always hoping someday he would call her. Well, now he should have and hadn't.

"Why don't you call him? Maybe something happened. He might have forgotten or he got in an accident or whatever."

"I should, huh?"

"Yes, you should."

"Okay." She exhaled forcibly, picked up her phone from the coffee table and scrolled through the numbers to find his. When she had his name highlighted, she hit talk so it would dial his number.

The phone rang several times before it he finally picked up with a breathless hello.

"Jeremiah?"

"Callie?"

"Uh, I thought I'd check with you since you're late. I thought you said six?"

"Oh, shit. God."

A female voice in the background said, "Hey, baby. Where are you going? We're just getting started, cowboy."

"Callie, I'm sorry. I was going to call you. Something came up and..."

"Something came up? Why do I hear a woman in the background?"

"She's a guest at the ranch."

"And the water in the background too?"

"She's in the restroom."

"Why don't I believe you, Jeremiah? If you didn't want to go out tonight, you could have at least called me."

"I meant to."

"You meant to cancel our date because you wanted to go out with a guest at the ranch?"

"Yes, I mean no. Shit."

"Never mind. I understand. I'll talk to you some other time."

"Callie?"

"What?"

"I'm sorry. I'll make it up to you. I promise."

"Fuck you, Jeremiah Young. Do your guest. Get your fucking rocks off because you aren't worth my time, you asshole." Too bad they didn't have a land line. It just wasn't the same forcibly hitting end on a cell phone.

Tears rolled down her cheeks. She should have known. All men were the same. They didn't give a shit about how things were supposed to work. He was supposed to be different. He was supposed to care about her even a little bit, but he didn't apparently. He was more interested in doing one of the guests at the ranch. *Fucker.*

"Aw, baby, I'm sorry."

She hiccupped as she pressed her fist to her mouth and bit down to try to relieve some of the pain she felt. "He's with someone at the ranch, Daddy. He couldn't even take the time to call me and cancel before he took off for parts unknown with some sleazeball guest who wants to fuck a cowboy."

"I know, honey. He's not worth your tears if he's that kind of man."

"God help me."

"It's okay. You should go out tonight anyway. Find yourself a nice young man to hang out with at the bar. Get a little crazy."

She wiped the tears from her face with a tissue from the coffee table. "I think I will, Daddy. Who knows? Maybe I'll meet the man of my dreams, the one who will take the place of Jeremiah Young and shred the thoughts of him right from my mind with one smile."

"I hope so, baby."

"I'm going to touch up my makeup before I head over to The Dusty Boot."

"You do that."

She hugged her dad, and then headed back down the hall to her bedroom to fix her face. When she glanced in the mirror of her bathroom, she saw the red rimmed eyes and blotchy face staring back. "He's not worth the tears. Asshole. I can't believe he did that." A fresh tear slid down her cheek, but she wiped it away angrily. "He's not worth my tears. I thought he was different. Apparently not. If it means a piece of ass, he's all about the most readily available women around. Well, to hell with him. He could have gotten it from me, but no. Asshole wanted some chick on the ranch. Probably a blonde bimbo with big boobs or something." She wiped the mascara that had bled under her eyes so she could refresh the look she'd perfected before.

She'd teach him and his wandering ways. She'd find herself a cowboy to fuck for the night so she could totally forget all about Jeremiah Young. If she was lucky, she might run into her forever cowboy and it wouldn't be him.

Several minutes later, she found herself standing at the open doorway of The Dusty Boot. Music blared through the speakers next to the band playing country music with a two-step beat to it. She wanted a drink. Something strong. Whiskey and Coke maybe.

She found an empty stool at the bar between two men she didn't know. Right up her alley.

Peyton Young made her way toward her to take her drink order and she had to bite her lip to keep from saying something about Jeremiah to his sister-in-law. Of course, it wasn't her fault or Jason's Jeremiah turned out to be an ass. "Hi there." She tilted her head to the side and smiled. "Callie, isn't it?"

"Yes. Hi, Peyton."

"What'll ya have, doll?"

"Jack and Coke, please."

"Coming right up."

As Peyton mixed the drink for her not far from where she sat, she glanced to her left to take in the man next to her. Nope, not her type. Older guy with a beer gut, large belt buckle and cowboy hat probably covering a half-bald head. She looked to her right. Now there was a possibility. The guy sitting next to her was cute. Dark hair peeked out beneath a straw cowboy hat, western style button-down shirt, nice jeans and dirty boots. He apparently worked for a living if he wore dirty boots to the bar.

"Hey."

He looked her way as he brought the beer bottle to his lips. When he finished the sip, he said, "Hi, pretty lady."

She blushed at the compliment as she held out her hand. "My name is Callie."

He took her hand. "Nice to meet you, Callie. I'm Matt."

"Do you live around here? I don't remember seeing you before."

"Nope. Live in San Antonio, but I heard this was a great bar to come to on Saturday night so here I am." He turned to check out the dance floor. "Seems to be a great place."

"Yeah."

"You live around here?"

"Yeah. My dad owns the garage up the road."

"Cool."

He tapped his foot to the beat of the music coming from the band as Peyton slid her drink to her on a napkin. "Six-fifty."

"Can I run a tab? I think I might be drinking a bit tonight."

"Sure. Just give me your card and I'll run it."

"Thanks."

She sipped the drink a let out a small cough.

"Strong?" he asked, one eyebrow shot up over his left eye.

"Yeah, a little. I'm not quite used to it being that strong, I guess."

"They make some pretty mean drinks here, I heard."

"They are pretty generous with the booze, that's for sure."

"Hey, want to dance?"

"Let me finish this drink first and I'd love to."

"How old are you, Callie?"

"Twenty-eight. Why?"

"Just checkin'. You look young, but the bartender didn't card you so I figured you were over twenty-one anyway."

"I know her. She knows me. In fact, most everyone in this bar probably knows me." She looked around the room noting several people she'd went to high school with, a group of the single Young brothers in the corner playing pool, another group of women she knew from around town and there was Lydia hanging all over a good-looking cowboy who worked on one of the other ranches in the area. Boy, she didn't take long finding another hunk. "Yep. I know most everyone in here."

"Maybe I should have you introduce me around. I could use some work."

"Are you a cowboy?"

He tipped his hat. "As cowboy as they come. Been wranglin' for a while now, but the ranch I've been working on sold out recently to a big conglomerate so they won't be running cattle anymore."

"I'm sorry."

"What do you do?"

"I work at my dad's garage."

"Oh, like running the cash register or something?"

"No, I'm a mechanic."

"Really. You work on cars, huh? Not a typical job for a woman."

"No, it's not, but I enjoy doing it and since I'm my dad's only child, I got to learn his trade." She set her empty glass on the bar. "Shall we dance now?"

"Sure."

He took her hand in his and led her to the dance floor. His touch didn't do what Jeremiah's did. She didn't tingle or shiver from the brush of his fingers. She hoped she could get past that because she really did want to like this guy. However, when he wrapped a hand behind her head, he almost punched him. She didn't like being manhandled.

She took his hand and put it on her waist.

"Sorry."

"No problem. I don't like a guy's hand up there is all. It's more comfortable on my waist."

"Okay."

They danced a two-step while she kept looking around the bar. Her vision caught on the other Young brothers playing pool in the corner and her thoughts strayed to Jeremiah. What was he doing? Was he doing the guest from the ranch? Where were they? She'd heard water running in the background, but that could've meant anything. Jeremiah shared half of one of the cabins with one of his brothers, but he could have taken her there. They might have been sharing a bath when he answered the phone or maybe in her room?

"Bastard."

"Excuse me?"

"Sorry. I didn't mean you. I was thinking about someone else."

He placed his hand on his chest. "Ouch. You're dancing with me and thinking about another guy?"

"I'm sorry. I didn't mean to insult you."

"Did you have a fight with your boyfriend tonight? Is that why you're at the bar prowling?"

"I'm not prowling. You make it sound like I'm some slut looking to get laid because my boyfriend cheated on me." They stopped dancing as she jammed her hands on her hips. "I'll have you know I don't have a boyfriend and we didn't have a fight. I'm not here looking to get laid, I'm just here to have a few drinks and unwind, so you can kiss my ass, Matt." She spun on her heel to head back for the bar to get another drink. Strike one.

"Wait a damned minute here. You're the one who muttered bastard I'm asking what's the issue here. I need to know where I stand because it's Saturday and I don't want to go home alone."

"Well if you're looking to get laid, find another girl. I know of several here who are into that kind of thing."

"And you aren't?"

She pulled back her hand and slapped him hard across the cheek. "No, I'm not. Get lost before I deck your ass."

He grabbed her hand and pulled her in, squashing her breasts against his chest. "Like it rough, do you?"

"The lady said get lost, buddy."

Without glancing over Matt's shoulder, she knew who stood a few feet away. Jeremiah.

"Find your own. This one is mine."

"She said no, now let her go before I haul your ass outside for the beating you deserve for manhandling a lady."

Matt pushed her back and raised his hands. "No harm done."

She finally glanced behind Matt to meet Jeremiah's gaze. He looked furious. Well, to hell with him. She had every right to be pissed at him, not him with her. She hadn't done anything wrong. "Jeremiah."

"Callie," he said, his voice turning soft.

Don't fall for it. He's not worth it. He can grovel all he wants, but he was the one who couldn't even take the time out to call you and cancel your date before he went off to fuck some cowboy groupie from the ranch.

"I'm sorry."

"You're sorry? You should be."

He held out his hand. She almost reached for him, but kept her arms across her chest where she'd folded them the minute Matt let her go.

"Let me make it up to you."

"How do you propose to do that, Jeremiah? I'm not falling for your cowboy charm, good looks, and easy way with women. You couldn't even take the time to call me—"

The band started playing again cutting off her words so she couldn't even hear herself think.

"Let's go outside," he said next to her ear so she could hear him. The sensation of his breath on her neck drove her crazy. Goose bumps broke out on her skin, zipping down and back up to settle right between her legs.

"Damn him."

"What?"

"Nothing. Fine. Let's go outside."

He placed his hand at the small of her back as he led her out through the front door into the cooler night air. "My truck is over there."

With a roll of her eyes, she walked toward the big silver dually sitting to the left of the doors. She wasn't going to let him off so easy. He'd hurt her even if there wasn't anything between them except friendship. Standing her up without even a phone call was inexcusable in her book.

"What can I do, Callie?"

"Nothing."

"There has to be something, darlin'."

She stomped her foot. Yeah, it made her look like a five-year-old, but it let off some of the anger she'd been holding in since he interrupted her exchange with Matt. "Don't you darlin' me, mister. I'm so pissed at you right now I could punch you."

"I screwed up. I know that now."

"Now? It didn't cross your mind when you made the date with the chick from the ranch that you had already made a date with me."

"Ours wasn't a date. We were going out as friends."

"Whatever, Jeremiah. I considered it a date whether it was between a guy and his girl or two friends. You fucked up."

"I know." He rubbed his hand up and down her arm. "I realize I shouldn't have even made the date with the other girl since I already had plans with you."

"Why did you?"

"She was available." He shrugged. "I haven't gotten laid in months." He raked his fingers through his hair before putting his hat back on his head. "I don't know, Callie."

"I didn't even cross your mind when you made the date with her, huh?"

"At first no. I remembered after she'd already left. I promise, I planned to call you and cancel, but it slipped my mind."

"So you would have rather went out with her than me."

"I was guaranteed to get laid with her. I wasn't with you."

"I told you last night I would be up for a one-night stand."

"True, but it felt like I would be using you."

"If sex is what you want, Jeremiah, I'm game, but I won't be used. I'm worth more than that. Every woman is worth more than that even if they don't think so. Men aren't on this planet to get laid every time their dick twitches, but they sure as hell think so. As for me, you can find someone else to hang out with, do the dirty deed with or whatever. My value is too high for your bank account, baby. You don't have enough money to buy me."

His lips twitched with a grin he couldn't hide. She wanted to smack him.

"I said I'm sorry. What more can I do to make it up to you?"

"You know what, there isn't anything you can do. I'm so over you, it's not funny. I'm tired of wanting you. I'm tired of loving you from afar. I'm done." She spun on her heels to head back into the bar, but before she got too far, he grabbed her arm and spun her around.

"What did you say?"

She jerked her arm out of his hold. "Nothing. Fuck off." Without a backward glance, she yanked open the door on the bar and strolled back inside. She planned to get really drunk so she could forget all about Jeremiah Young.

* * * *

"That girl is going to get herself into trouble in there with the rowdy bunch here tonight." Jeremiah shook his head as he followed Callie back into the bar. *I'll just stay to keep an eye on her so she doesn't do something stupid like go home with one of those cowboys.* He headed for a corner booth and slid in behind the table. The waitress rolled her hips in a come-and-get-me fashion as she walked up to his table to take his order. "Beer, please."

"Coming right up, Jeremiah." She leaned in close. "I get off at ten if you want to hook up."

"No thanks."

She straightened up and huffed loudly as she spun on her heels to head back to the bar.

Callie rapped her knuckles on the mahogany to get Peyton's attention. "Peyton, give me a shot of tequila and a Corona."

"Shit. She's drinkin' hard from the get-go. I'd better watch her closely." He moved in close so he could keep a good eye on her, but also so he could hear what they were saying. Callie couldn't see him sitting close from where he took up a spot a few stools down from her.

Peyton's eyebrow shot up. "Patrón?"

"That'll do."

"Coming right up."

Peyton moved down the bar and leaned in toward her friend Mandy. "Hey, keep an eye on her, would you? Make friends. She could use one, I think."

"Sure," Mandy replied, grabbing her beer and moving closer. "Hey. I'm Mandy. I'm a good friend of Peyton's. You look like you could use a friend."

"If you want to get stinking drunk with me, then I'll be your best buddy."

"Sounds like a plan to me. I hate drinking alone."

"Name's Callie."

"Nice to meet you. Who are you trying to forget tonight?"

"One of those pain in the ass Young brothers."

Jeremiah's heart thumped in his chest. Was she trying to forget him? He hoped she wasn't so tied up in him he'd hurt her. He didn't want to do that to her.

"Sounds like you and I will be best friends. I could get used to forgetting one myself."

Peyton slid the drink toward her. "I'm shooting tequila. You with me?"

"You got it, babe." Mandy nodded for Peyton to hand her one too as Callie waited for her so they could down the potent liquid together.

The minute they both had a shot glass in their hands, they sprinkled salt on the back of their fist, downed the shot with toss of their heads, quickly bit into the lime wedge on the Corona bottle, then downed a swallow of the beer. "Oh my God, that's nasty."

"You going again?"

"Hell yeah!" Mandy's eyes narrowed as she glanced behind Callie and locked gazes with him.

He wondered which of his brothers she wanted to forget. Obviously she had it bad for one of them and wasn't getting the attention she wanted. Mandy seemed like a nice girl from what he knew about her. Maybe he could help her out a little if he knew which brother caught her interest. Right now he had to keep an eye on Callie though. At the rate she was going, she'd be shit-faced inside of fifteen minutes.

For the next few hours, he watched her closely as she downed shot after shot of tequila with the Corona shooter. The two women got giggly, laughing at everything. She was kind of cute when she got like this, he had to admit.

Then she started inviting men to do body shots. He growled low in his throat at each one in turn as they approached. They didn't heed his warning look and there wasn't much he could do really. She wasn't his girlfriend. At this point she wasn't even his friend according to her, but he still watched out for her.

The men would lick the salt off her neck and then shoot the tequila. His stomach knotted with each jerk who took a shot at her.

Unable to take anymore, he finally grabbed her arm and turned her to face him. "What the hell do you think you're doing? These men are all over you."

She just shot back with, "This is my party and I'll do body shots if I want to. You didn't want what I offered, well maybe one of these other guys does."

He didn't reply to her shot across the bow. She was pretty drunk and it wouldn't do much good to argue with her. *Damn her.* Lusting after her wasn't the hard part, realizing she wanted him too was difficult for him to fathom. She'd been a friend for so long, it was hard for him to think of her beyond friendship, but lately he definitely wanted more from her. Friends with benefits, maybe. He could do something along those lines without a problem.

For now, he would sit back in the corner he'd taken up residence in after she'd told him off, and glower at anyone who got too friendly with her. She wasn't going to let him get between her and her little pity party or whatever it was. She didn't want him around so he'd watch her from afar making sure she didn't get into too much trouble. Yeah, he'd screwed up by forgetting to call her, but the really screwed up part was after he'd gone out riding with the guest from the ranch, he didn't want to be with the woman anymore. When she'd basically thrown herself at him while they'd stopped to water the horses at the pool, he'd had to practically push her off him. All he could think about was Callie, especially after her phone call. How messed up was it to want to be with her when he had a perfectly willing woman right there?

As soon as Callie had hung up, he'd taken the woman back to the ranch, stabled the horses and drove into town. He had a feeling she would go out without him to The Dusty Boot. Sure enough, he'd found her not long after he'd arrived. He'd tried to talk some sense into her and get her to forgive him, but no. Stupid girl. Didn't she know he'd do anything for her?

Chapter Five

Sunlight poured through the curtains of her bedroom, blinding her with its intensity and making her head feel like it wanted to split wide open. "Oh God. What the hell did I do last night?"

At least I'm not waking up in a strange motel room with something worse like a guy I don't know or maybe even worse, a guy I do know...unless it happened to be Jeremiah. I would hope to have remembered sleeping with him.

Her mouth felt like cotton dried up every bit of saliva she had. She remembered shooting tequila with some women she knew from town who seemed to be hell-bent on forgetting a man or two. Peyton's friend Mandy had been there. They'd become fast friends over several shots of tequila. It seemed they both wanted to forget a Young brother. Mandy had her sights set on one of them and kept getting the cold shoulder. Callie, well she knew what hell she was going through without regard to Jeremiah. *The asshole.*

Rolling over, she let a moan escape as her stomach revolted against the movement. She jumped up from her bed and rushed for the bathroom only to hug the toilet as dry heaves wracked her body. *Jesus, please let me die right here. I promise, I'll be good in heaven. I can't handle this.*

Her cell phone jingled on her nightstand in the other room, but there was no way in hell she would be able to answer it hugging the commode.

Her father grabbed the phone. "Hello? Oh hi, Jeremiah. No, she's not up to talking right now."

"I don't want to talk to that asshole. Tell him to bug off."

"She's hugging the toilet at the moment."

"Fuck him!" She heaved again, coughing like her lungs would burst from her chest. They burned like they were on fire as her stomach rebelled against any thoughts of contents.

"I'll tell her to call you when she's feeling better."

"I'm not calling him. He can go to hell."

"All right. Talk to you later then. Bye."

"Why didn't you tell him to go to hell?"

"Because we don't talk like that in this house, especially on Sunday."

"Sorry, but he deserves it."

Her father placed a cool washcloth on her head. "I'm sure he does."

"Oh lordy, that feels like heaven."

"How did you get home? Your car isn't in the drive."

"I took a cab, I guess."

"Got a bit drunk?"

"Yeah, just a little. Mandy is my new best friend."

"Mandy?"

"Yeah, she's a friend of the bartender who is married to one of the Young boys. Mandy is her friend, but she's my new best friend too. We were doing shots of tequila."

"Oh, boy."

"With beer shooters."

"No wonder you're sick. I'll get you some Alka-Seltzer. I'm sure I have some in my bathroom."

"I love you, Dad."

"I'm sure you do, honey. I've been where you are a few times in my life so I know what it feels like to be hung over." Her dad disappeared out the door, but was back in a few minutes with a glass of water with something fizzing in it. "This will either cure what ails you or make you throw up."

"I'm already throwing up."

"It'll help calm your stomach, sweetie. Trust me."

With a dubious glance at her father, she took the glass and sipped at the fizzling liquid.

"Shoot it."

She made a face, plugged her nose and swallowed the entire glass in a matter of a few gulps. "Good God, that's nasty." Her stomach heaved a few times, but nothing came up as she rested her forehead on the cool porcelain. She'd never leave the bathroom again.

Her father took her hand to bring her to her feet. "Now up you go."

"I can't."

"Sure you can. You need some ibuprofen and a few more hours of sleep. You'll be good as new." He helped her to her feet and slowly walked her to her bed. "Lie down."

Once he placed the cool cloth over her eyes and she'd taken the ibuprofen, he told her to sleep. He'd hold off the hoards of admirers until she felt better. She wasn't sure what the hell he meant, but right now she didn't care. Her head hurt, her stomach felt a little better for now, and she wanted to close her gritty eyelids to rest. A little sleep would do her wonders.

Several hours later, she groaned as she rolled over in her bed to the chirping of her cell phone indicating she had a text message. When she picked up the phone so she could press the button, her eyes widened to see twenty-five messages that weren't all from the same guy. "What the hell?"

"Apparently you were pretty free last night with your phone number and address. I've had at least ten men here today wanting to talk to you while you slept. Your phone has been chirping like a bird in heat for the last few hours."

"Shit."

"Callinda."

"Sorry, Dad. I wish I could remember what I did."

"You might ask Peyton since she was probably one of the few people there who weren't drunk last night."

"But that would mean going out to the Young ranch. I don't have her number."

"I still think you should find out before your popularity gets my lawn messed up with the cars and trucks going across it."

"Maybe Mandy will remember. I think I have her number." She pushed her hand into her jeans pocket only to come out with a wad of papers. "What the heck is this?" She spread them on her bed before opening one to find a guy's name and number. "Holy crap!" She opened two more. "These are all phone numbers."

"You've become one very popular young lady."

"I need to call Mandy." She grabbed her cell phone off the nightstand and flipped through the numbers until she found what she was looking for. After she pushed the button to call Mandy, she waited until her new friend picked up with a groggy reply. "Mandy?"

"Yeah. Who is this?"

"Callie."

"Oh, hey, sister in crime. How are you feeling today?"

"Better right now after my dad plied me with home remedies for hangovers, but I still need to get some food in my stomach."

"Don't mention food. I'm so sick my eyes are crossed."

"Listen, I need you to tell me what the heck happened last night."

"Why? You don't remember?"

"No. My phone is about to blow up from text messages, my dad said there have been at least ten guys at my door today, and I have a pocket full of phone numbers."

"I tell you what, let me rouse myself out of bed to get a shower. I'll meet you at Anne's diner for some coffee and food. We'll talk, because honey, you need to be better prepared. You made a lot of friends last night."

"Crap. Okay. I'll meet you there in half an hour."

"Sounds good. See you in a few. Oh, and you're gonna love what you said to Jeremiah when he tried to break up your little party."

With a swipe of the button, she hung up with Mandy as she tipped her head back on her shoulders, wondering what kind of mess she'd gotten herself into this time.

When she walked into the diner a half an hour later, she kept her sunglasses on and took a table in the back. She didn't want anyone to see her in case she was recognized from her escapades at The Dusty Boot last night.

Anne moved to her table and asked, "Coffee?"

"Definitely, two cups. I'm meeting someone in a few minutes. I think she'll want some too."

"Callinda?"

"Shh." She put up her hand to shush Anne. "I don't want anyone to see me."

"Why? You usually come in here every Sunday with your dad anyway. Most people would expect you to be here." She tapped her fingernail on the table. "Where is your father, by the way?" She tilted her head to the side. "And why are you wearing those dark glasses?"

"I'm hung over. My head is beginning to pound again so please keep your voice down."

"Hung over from what? Did you party too hard?"

"You could say that."

Mandy came through the door and Callie waved her over to the booth she'd secured.

"The two of you must have really got into trouble last night," Anne said as she poured the second cup of coffee for Mandy.

"You are a saint, Anne."

"Just being me."

Mandy sipped the strong brew while she cradled the cup between her hands. "Thank you, God. You have no idea how much I needed this."

"I've been there a few times myself, girls. I know how it feels. What you need is some breakfast."

"But you don't serve breakfast this late in the day," Mandy said.

"I'll whip something up for you two. Be right back."

"She's such a great lady." Mandy sipped the coffee again before she braced her elbows on the table. "So, what do you remember?"

"Not a damned thing."

"From what point on?"

She slowly lowered her sunglasses, then laid them on the table. "Not much after my argument with Jeremiah outside."

"He watched you all night, you know."

"He did?"

Mandy nodded, sipping the coffee. "He sat in the corner, but kept an eagle eye on you even though you had every single man watching you. You were dancing on top of the bar."

"Oh, hell."

"Yes, ma'am. You took off that clingy little blouse you had on and tucked your tank top into your bra. When the guys started lining up to do belly shots off you, he growled."

"Growled?"

"Yep, but it didn't stop the guys from licking the salt from your neck before they took the shots. You even let one guy do one from between your boobs."

"Oh, God. I'm so screwed."

"Honey, you are one of the most popular women in this town right now. You shouldn't have any problems getting a date for a long time to come."

She pushed her hair off her forehead. "But Mandy, that's not me. It was the alcohol."

"Live it up while you've got it, babe. Jeremiah can wait."

"You said something about me telling him off when he tried to stop my party?"

"Oh, yeah." Mandy laughed before she groaned as she rubbed her temples for a second. "God, my head is killing me."

Callie laid a hand on Mandy's arm. "Alka-Seltzer and ibuprofen. Does wonders."

The look Mandy gave her said she wished she could curl into a ball and just die. "Your dad's recipe?"

"Worked for me. I feel okay now. Not perfect, but okay." Callie tapped her fingernail on the table. "So spill. Tell me what I said to Jeremiah."

"What's going on with you two anyway?"

"Nothing."

With her head tilted to the side like she didn't believe her, Mandy said, "Nothing my ass. The man doesn't growl, for God's sake, when some guy wants to do body shots from between your boobs without a reason."

Callie smiled. *Jeremiah growled?* "So tell me. What did I say?"

"You said, 'This is my party and I'll do body shots if I want to. You didn't want what I offered, well maybe one of these other guys does.'"

"What did he say?"

"He didn't say anything, just moved back to his corner and watched you for the rest of the night, although he did make sure you got home. I'm pretty sure he drove you there himself. The last I saw you, he was putting you in the front of his truck. Since you made it home okay, I assume he took you there."

"He took me home?"

"Yeah. You were waving to all the other men who saw you outside, but he was the one who poured you into his vehicle to make sure you got home all right and didn't get taken advantage of in your drunken state."

Anne brought two plates heaping with scrambled eggs, bacon, hash browns and toast to their table. "Eat up, girls."

"Oh, Lord. I don't think I can eat this greasy food," Mandy replied, holding her hand over her mouth.

"Here are two ibuprofen and some Alka-Seltzer for your stomach."

"What's with you old people and your remedies? That's what my dad gave me this morning."

"It works, don't it?"

"Yes, ma'am."

"Then hush." She handed Mandy the glass. "Drink up. Quickly. You'll feel better in about five minutes. You need to eat."

"Okay." Mandy downed the entire glass, shuddering with the last gulp. "Oh, my God. That's nasty shit."

"Yeah, but you'll feel better."

"I hope so. I hate hangovers."

"I've never had one before, but I didn't care for mine either," Callie replied. "I hit the toilet first thing this morning as soon as I opened my eyes."

"Your phone call woke me up from mine."

Callie took Mandy's hand to squeeze her fingers in shared misery. "Sorry."

A small smile spread across Mandy's lips. "It was totally worth it. I actually got a few phone numbers myself."

Callie started eating the food in front of her, talking in between bites. "So tell me what else Jeremiah did."

"Not much of anything. He glowered most of the night as he watched you spreading yourself kind of thin around the men in the bar. You had them hanging all over you, especially when you were doing body shots. He didn't like seeing you doing that at all was my guess."

"Well, tough shit."

"My thoughts exactly." Mandy sipped at her coffee, simply sighing after she swallowed. "I love coffee and I actually think I might be able to eat some of this food now." After a couple of tentative bites, she started eating with gusto. "This is really good."

"I need my jolt of java every morning before I go to the station, otherwise I'm a bear."

"So, tell me what's the deal with you two anyway?"

"Nothing much. We were friends, or so I thought. You know, acquaintances or whatever you want to call it. He asked me out Friday."

"Like a date?"

"I'm not sure what the hell it was. We went out to dinner, then went back to my house and watched movies. It wasn't a big deal, but he did ask if I wanted to go out Saturday too after I suggested another date, to hang out at the bar, play pool. That kind of thing. He stood me up for some guest at the ranch who wanted to ride a cowboy. I told him off before he apparently showed up at the bar when I came alone. You know the rest better than I do."

"He acted jealous last night."

"Jealous? Not in this lifetime. He doesn't care about me other than being friends."

"I don't know. The way things went down last night sure doesn't make me think he doesn't care."

"Well, he doesn't. If he did, he wouldn't have stood me up in the first place."

"Maybe he's scared? I know how those Young boys tend to run from feelings too deep. Just asked Peyton, Paige, Mesa, and Terri."

"Scared? I doubt it. I don't think anything frightens Jeremiah. He's tough as nails."

Mandy finished her food and pushed her plate away. "Except when it comes to women, especially one he cares about more than he wants to admit."

"Enough about me and Jeremiah. Who are you trying to forget?"

"Jonathan."

"Why?"

"He doesn't know I exist. I'm right in his face most of the time being at the ranch, but he seems to be so focused on the stuff going on with the ranch's websites, he doesn't even notice I'm there. I think I'm becoming one of those creepy stalker chicks because I watch him all the time. He's not like the others. I mean, yeah, he's a cowboy and all, but he's not in-your-face macho like Jackson or Joey. He's sweet, kind, and gorgeous."

"Oh, you've got it bad."

Mandy sighed. "You think so? What the hell am I going to do?"

"We'll figure out something. Maybe my dad's right, he needs to be knocked upside the head to realize what a catch you are."

"Maybe."

"A smack would do the man good."

"I like how you think." She tapped her fingers on her lips for a moment. "I could seduce him."

"That's not going to get you a long-term relationship with the guy. They get those kinds of offers all the time. You need to be all he wants in a woman, but play it hard to get too."

"Will you help me?"

"Of course. We're sisters in this!" Callie had finished her own food some time before, so she pushed her plate to the side as they shook hands. "Those Young boys don't stand a chance!"

"But I thought you didn't want to give into your feelings for Jeremiah?"

"I love the man. What can I say? He's had me tied up in knots since I was a freshman in high school and I just can't seem to get away from him even if I wanted to."

"So you want him?"

"Hell yeah, I want him, hogtied to my bed would be a good start, but I have to convince him I can be the woman he wants for the rest of his life. I'm not quite sure how to go about doing that, but I think me not giving in to his sorry ass last night went a long way to convincing him he might want to see where things will lead with us."

"How about we kidnap him?"

"Who? Jeremiah or Jonathan?"

"Both?"

Callie laughed, feeling better every second she talked with Mandy. "Sounds about right to me."

"What are you two conspiring about over here? Those smiles tell me you are up to no good and if it has anything to do with my nephews, I want to hear it."

"Will you warn them?"

She leaned on the table edge with her hands under her chin and a gleam in her eye. "Hell no! I'd love to see every one of those Young boys tied to the woman they were meant to be with. It means doing a little on my part, I'm all there."

"I can't believe we're doing this."

The twinkle in Mandy's eyes told the whole story. She was into corralling herself a Young brother, whatever it took. Callie had to admit, she wanted Jeremiah something fierce, but was she ready to do the necessary thing to convince him he might just want to spend the rest of his life with her? Was she ready for that kind of commitment with him herself? Love did funny things to people's hearts and she was about to find out what it meant to truly love someone.

Chapter Six

Callie sighed as she hung up the phone for the third time in less than an hour. Every guy in Bandera seemed to have her number. She couldn't even begin to understand why all of a sudden she'd become one popular lady, but she had. Just to show Jeremiah she wasn't going to wait for his ass, she'd taken a couple of dates over the last several weeks. Unfortunately, they all turned out to be jerks wanting to get into her pants. *I wish I could remember more about that night at The Dusty Boot.* She must have really been wild. To think Jeremiah took her home so nothing bad would happen to her. She really needed to thank him for protecting her because if the few dates she'd had were any indicator, she dodged a bullet that night.

Her cell phone jingled and she rolled her eyes, hoping it wasn't another guy calling to try get laid.

"Hello?"

"Callie?"

"Jeremiah?"

"Yeah."

"How are you?"

"Okay. I've been working a lot at the ranch, but I wanted to see if you were still mad at me."

"Of course I am, but you're a guy. I shouldn't have been surprised by your actions."

"I really am sorry I didn't at least call you."

"So am I."

The line echoed from the silence for several uncomfortable moments. The background noise was hard to distinguish, but it almost sounded like he was at Anne's diner. She smiled thinking Anne might have put him up to this phone call.

"How've you been? I haven't even seen you at the garage in the last few weeks."

"I've been there, but I've been really busy. I've taken time off."

"Busy how?"

"My phone has been ringing nonstop. I've been out on a few dates. You know. Nothing special." She looked down at her nails for a moment. "Except one." *I am so going to hell for lying.*

"Dates as in plural?"

"Yeah. I had a pocket full of phone numbers the next morning and apparently I gave my number to several guys at the bar."

"I think you did too, but I made sure none of them took you home. You were pretty wasted doing tequila shots."

"I know." She shifted the phone from her left ear to her right. "Um, I should thank you for the lift, I suppose."

"It's okay. It wasn't anything special. I wanted to make sure you made it home okay."

"I appreciate it anyway."

"You're welcome."

Another long pause in the conversation where she wasn't sure what else to say followed until an idea sent off sparks in her brain. "Well, I should go. I have a date tonight. I need to make myself beautiful."

"You do?"

"Yeah. This is our third date over the last couple of weeks." She shrugged even though he couldn't see it. "Who knows? He might get lucky tonight."

A strangled cough echoed through the phone line, making her smile. She was getting to him. *Good.*

"Wait, Callie. You shouldn't be havin' sex with someone you hardly know. It's probably not a good idea."

"Oh, you're one to talk, mister. Besides, who are you to judge?"

"Well, I mean, you hardly know the guy, right? Not like us. We've known each other for a long time."

"And we aren't having sex."

"No, we aren't, but at least you would have known me longer than three weeks."

"It'll be fine, Jeremiah. It's not like I'll be comparing you two." She sighed. "I really should go. He's going to pick me up in like thirty minutes. I haven't even showered yet. I'll talk to you later. Thank you again for helping me. You're a great friend."

After she hung up the phone, she stared at the thing for a minute trying to figure out what the hell she was going to do now. She didn't really have a date for tonight, but now she'd better find one and fast. She looked through the stack of numbers sitting on her nightstand, picking out a name she knew. Brad Smithson, football player from high school. He'd do. He was a big guy, not bad-looking, nice body, and dumb as a bag of hammers.

With a few touches of her fingers, she dialed his number and waited for him to pick up.

"Hello?"

"Hey, Brad. It's Callinda Lewis."

"Well, hey, Callinda. How are you, darlin'?"

She cringed as the endearment rolled over her. Everyone in Texas called everybody else darlin', but she wanted it to only be Jeremiah. Only if he cared. "I'm doin' fine. Listen, I know we haven't talked since the night at The Dusty Boot, but I was looking for someone to do a few body shots with tonight. I wanted to know if you were game?"

"Oh hell yeah, baby. I'll be game to suck on you any time of the day or night. What time shall I pick you up?"

With a shudder, she said, "Why don't we meet at the bar? I need to have my own car there."

"I can take care of you, honey."

"I'm sure you can, Brad, but I have a friend who might be there too and if she gets into trouble, I need to be able to take her home. You remember Mandy from that night, right?"

"Yeah. Pretty blonde with the pink stripe in her hair."

Callie laughed. "That's her."

"Okay. No problem. I'll meet you there at seven?"

"Perfect. See you in a few."

She hung up the phone with a smile on her face. Jeremiah needed a little dose of his own medicine. Brad would do nicely for what she had planned.

When she pulled into the bar about an hour later, she noticed there weren't too many vehicles around. Of course, for a Tuesday night this seemed pretty busy. Tonight she didn't have any plans on getting shit-faced drunk, but she did plan on giving Jeremiah something to think about. Not knowing whether he would be there, she had to hope Jeremiah actually cared enough to come to the bar or at least find out what she was up to. *Please God, let him care enough.*

She climbed out of her car and headed toward the bar hoping she'd meet Brad by the door. If Jeremiah was there, she wanted to be coming in with Brad, not meeting him there.

Off to her right, she grinned as she noticed a big silver dually pickup sitting near the back of the parking lot. Jeremiah. He'd come. Maybe he did care, even just a little.

Good. She was going to give him a show he'd never forget. Hopefully jar him into making a move toward something they might be able to work on together.

Brad came across the street where he'd parked his truck. "Hey, Callie. Right on time."

"Hi, Brad."

He leaned in to kiss her, but she turned her face so he grazed her cheek with his lips. "You look great!"

"Thanks. Nothing special."

"You still look hot. Did I tell you that before because you do. I mean, when you were here a few weeks ago, you were like totally hot. I didn't get my turn to do body shots off you, and man, did I want to. Maybe tonight?"

"Maybe." She took a couple of steps away from him. "Let's go inside. I could use a drink."

She pulled open the door, letting the cool darkness wash over her before the blinding stage lights hit her in the face.

"Sure thing, babe."

They stopped inside the door to let their eyes adjust. The bar sat off to the right with barstools lining the mahogany expanse for the patrons. Several tables took up the left side with the pool tables and dart boards near the back. There was a large dance floor where a few couples two-stepped their way around the divided area.

No sign of Jeremiah.

"Let's find a table."

"Sure, babe."

She blew out a breath on a heavy sigh. This was going to be a long night at this rate.

When they found an empty table, she waited for Brad to pull out her chair, but he took the other one, flipped it around and straddled it. She shook her head as she grabbed the chair for herself.

"What'll ya have?" the waitress asked, giving Brad an eyeful as she bent over allowing her tank top to gap open around her breasts.

"I'll have a beer. Bud Light in the bottle, please."

"I'll take a shot of Jack."

"Comin' right up." The waitress sauntered back toward the bar where Peyton was working one end while Dan worked the other.

Peyton waved at Callie before she glanced at her date, frowned and tipped her head to the right. Callie wondered how much Mandy had told Peyton of their plans to corral a couple of Young boys. She hoped Mandy hadn't told her much. After all, she was married to one of them and might be a little more apt to be on their side, right? Except Peyton might want to see her brothers-in-law with wives of their own. What better than to have two of her friends hook up with them?

Callie glanced to the right. Ah, there he was sitting back in one of the dark corners, brooding with a beer. Well, too bad. She had plans for tonight and they included going home with one hot cowboy, preferably Jeremiah Young.

* * * *

Jeremiah sat with his hat pulled down hoping Callie wouldn't see him as he nursed his beer, bringing it to his lips for a small sip. He needed to see who she was going out with so seriously they had three dates in the last couple of weeks. Not knowing why, he had a morbid curiosity to see the man she had the hots for, or so he thought.

"Fucking Brad Smithson, really?" The guy had barely enough brains to fill a thimble. "The man couldn't even pass basic math."

Jeremiah squinted as he watched the couple take a seat at a table near the middle of the room. He scoffed when Brad didn't pull out Callie's chair for her. *Figures. He's got no manners at all. My mom would box my ears for not pulling out a lady's chair.* After they ordered drinks, Callie tried to start a conversation with Brad while he watched every other female coming through the door. *Dickhead.*

Thoughts of walking over there, jerking her to her feet, tossing her over his shoulder and spiriting her away to his room crossed his mind. But he couldn't do any such thing. Could he?

More people walked into the bar with waves and hearty hellos to the bartenders as they passed. Most found a table as the waitresses worked the room. Some danced. Some played pool and some worked the dart boards like they wanted to stab someone in the eye.

The entire time Jeremiah's gaze rarely left Callie. She'd dressed to kill in a tight s kirt and silky-looking loose tank top with a gauzy looking sweater over the top. She'd put her hair up in a little updo that made him want to take it down to run his fingers through the silky strands. Her blonde hair normally hung to the middle of her back the few times he'd seen it loose. He liked to watch the curls flowing behind her.

Her lips parted softly in a smile as she appeared to be shyly taking in whatever Brad had to say. Brad grabbed the back of her chair, scooting it closer so he could wrap an arm around Callie's shoulders.

Jeremiah wanted to hit someone or break something when she leaned into Brad's embrace. With fists clenched, he punched his thigh to relieve some of the pressure.

Joshua and Joey slid into the booth next to him.

"What's up, Jeremiah?" Joshua said.

"Nothin'."

"You look pissed enough to bite someone's head off."

"I am."

"Why?" Joey asked, taking a sip of the beer he'd set on the table until he followed Jeremiah's gaze. "Ah. Callie hooked up with someone else?"

"I don't care."

"Sure you do, that's why you are about to chew the end of your beer bottle off every time you take a sip," Joshua added. "Easy, cowboy. She's workin' you."

"She's here with that bozo."

"And playin' you like a fiddle, brother."

"How?"

"You can see how she's not really into what she's doing. We can. We've been watching this whole thing unfold from the pool table area while we played."

"What are you talkin' about?"

"We've been here almost every time she's been here. She's never once shown up with Brad, but she's acting like she's all into him. She's not comfortable. When he leans in, she's not meeting him halfway, she's pulling back."

Jeremiah watched a little closer, taking in the whole scene in front of him. Brad paid more attention to the women walking by, checking out their asses rather than paying attention to the woman he was with. Callie touched his arm, although her hand shook a little when she did, like she was totally out of her league. "She knows I'm here."

"Hell, yeah, she knows you're here, sulking in the corner like some loser."

"I'm not a loser."

"Then take control of the woman you want instead of sitting over here."

"She's out with another guy."

"One she doesn't want to be with, clearly," Joey piped in, putting in his two cents worth of advice to his older brother.

"Like you two are experts in the love department."

"Love, hell! You want to get in that girl's pants, don't ya?" Joshua asked, punching him in the shoulder.

"Yeah."

"Then go over there, pick her up, throw her over your shoulder and take her home. It's what she wants, I'm telling you."

"How do you know?"

"Mandy."

"Mandy?"

"Yep. She's had a few beers. She's been talkin' about you two a lot since she's been hanging out with us by the pool tables."

"Are you sure?"

"I'm sure, bro. Take control of the woman you want. Otherwise, you're gonna lose your chance."

"Move." Jeremiah shoved Joey out of the way so he could get up. He was done pussyfootin' around with Callie. He definitely wanted to screw with her, literally. The crowd between him and Callie's table parted as he made his way to her. Without a word, he took her arm, brought her to her feet, shoved his shoulder into her stomach and hefted her over his shoulder.

"What the hell are you doing?"

He didn't answer, just smacked her ass after he trapped her legs against his chest. Take control. Oh, yeah. He planned to have her hogtied to his bed inside of about fifteen minutes.

"Ouch. You asshole!"

She started hitting his back with the palm of her hand, although she wasn't hitting hard enough to do any damage.

"Jeremiah, put me down."

The crowd clapped as he made his way outside to his truck. "Are you gonna behave?"

"Behave? I'm not the one acting like a caveman. Put me down."

"Not until you promise not to take off. Otherwise, I'll hogtie you with my belt and don't think I can't do it. Remember, I'm a cowboy to the core." She huffed a few times while he waited next to the door of his truck. "Callie?"

"Fine. I won't run."

"Promise?"

"I promise."

He set her inside the cab of his truck on the seat once he had the door open.

"Where are we going?"

"My place."

"Why?"

"We need to talk and I don't want an audience."

"I was on a date, Jeremiah. How dare you manhandle me. This behavior isn't becoming of the gentleman I thought you were."

"I'm not gentleman around you anymore. You want it rough, baby, you got it." He slammed the door before he went around to the driver's side of the truck. When he glanced through the windshield, he thought he saw a little smile curving her tempting lips.

She wanted the roughneck. Well, she got him.

She was quiet on the way to his place. He glanced over at her side of the truck on several occasions to see her sitting with her arms crossed over her ample chest as she tapped her foot on the floorboard of the vehicle. *What is she thinking?*

"Are you going to talk to me?"

"What do you want me to say? I wanted you to manhandle me out of the bar, showing off my ass to the entire town? No, I didn't."

"Why were you there with Brad?"

"I told you, we had a date."

"You made it sound like you'd being seeing him for several weeks."

"Yeah."

"I know for a fact you haven't. Was tonight the first night you'd been out with him?" He tapped his fingers on the steering wheel. "And don't lie to me, Callinda. I know the truth."

"Then why ask me?"

"Because I want to hear from your lips why you felt the need to lie to me in the first place."

"You made me feel like shit, Jeremiah. I wasn't worth your time to even call me to tell me you made other plans."

"Are you still holding a grudge about our date?"

She sighed as she shook her head. "Not really." She turned in the seat to face him. "Do you want to be with me?"

"What do you mean be with you?"

"Do you want to hang out with me? Do you want to be more than friends? Do you want to have sex with me?"

He choked on his own saliva. "Why do you ask that?"

"Because those are the things I want from you, but I'm getting mixed signals."

"Things between us have been messed up from the get-go, Callie. We were friends or acquaintances or whatever you want to call it. I don't know what we are now."

"Well if you don't know, then I don't know either." She sighed as she twisted back around in the seat. "Why did you throw me over your shoulder and haul me out of the bar?"

"I didn't like seeing you with Brad."

"You were jealous."

"No." He pushed his hat off his head as he raked his fingers through his hair. "Yes. Hell, I don't know. I'm confused where you are concerned."

"Do you want to kiss me?"

He hesitated for a moment before he replied, "Yes."

"Do you want to date me?"

"I'm not sure dating is the right word."

"What would you say is the right word?"

His knuckles turned white on the steering wheel as he fought for control. The hesitation lasted longer this time until he finally sighed. "I want to fuck you until you scream my name as you come around my cock."

"Well then."

"Have I shocked you?"

"No."

"Really?"

She tilted her head to the side, giving him a condescending look out of the corner of her eye, he wasn't sure he appreciated coming from her. Funny, it made her all the more desirable because she didn't take his crap. She stood up to him and gave as good as she got.

"Jeremiah, you are the smartest guy I know, but you can be really dumb sometimes."

"What's that supposed to mean?"

"You can do things with numbers I can't even fathom on any level. You are so smart, you scare me sometimes, but really? When it comes to women, you can be really stupid."

"It's normal for a guy not to understand women. Ask my eight brothers."

She laughed, a hilarious, gut-rolling laugh that made him smile even though their conversation was kind of serious. "You crack me up."

"Thanks."

"Okay. Let's get something straight. We've known each other for a long time. If you aren't into serious, I get that. Those kinds of relationships come with time. Time I have on my hands so it's fine, but I'm not necessarily looking for a serious relationship either. If it happens, it happens."

They reached the front of his cabin and he turned off his truck. He wasn't sure where he wanted to go with this conversation. He wouldn't mind seeing how they were in bed together. He had the normal libido of a guy in his twenties. He liked sex, liked it a lot, and if he could find a girl he could have great sex with who didn't get all serious and shit, he'd have it made until he was ready for any kind of relationship. "I'm not ready for serious either. I have too many things to do with my life. I want a girl I can have fun with, maybe get in some great sex. You know, see where we go from there."

She pushed open the door on her side of the truck, stepping out into the gravel before she shut it behind her.

After he stepped out and closed his own door, he went around to the front of the truck to stand in front of her. "This is my place."

"Nice."

"Come on. I'll show you in the inside." He motioned to the other side of the duplex type cabin. "Jackson shares the other side with me, but he's not home right now."

"I saw him at The Dusty Boot."

"He goes there a lot to hang out. He likes the atmosphere, I think. You know. Lots of unpaired women."

"Isn't he a real player?"

"He can be. He's kind of quiet, but very rugged like a cowboy should be. Not like me." After he unlocked the door, he pushed it open to reveal the inside of his space. It was more of a one room place. A desk sat in the corner to the left. His king sized bed took up one whole wall to the right with a deep blue comforter spread over the expanse. He had a small kitchenette type thing back against the wall in center where he could heat up things with the microwave or cook a small meal if he wanted to entertain a woman here. His large television took up the wall just inside the door with his PlayStation game system and two leather recliners. Overall, he loved his space even if it was kind of small. One day he would build a huge house for lots of kids and a wife, but not yet. He had his special piece of property picked out on the ranch at the top of the back hill where his house would overlook the valley below. He'd go up there sometimes to sit while he dreamed of his future.

"You're a cowboy."

"Yeah, but I'm not an in your face kind. I ride and rope. You know, the normal cowboy stuff, but I like the behind the scenes kind of thing more."

She glanced around his space with a look of awe. "Wow. This is cool."

"Thanks. It's not much since it's one room, but I like it."

"You've done great with it." She walked to the kitchenette and ran her hand over the small countertop. "You have your own space. That is awesome."

"The house you have with your dad is great. I like it."

"Yeah, but it's Dad's, not mine. I'm an interloper, so to speak."

"You've lived there since you were born. How can you say you're an interloper?"

She shrugged as she checked out the model cars on his shelf. "It's not mine. I want my own house someday. A big house. Lots of kids, you know?"

The image of Callie sitting on a long porch with a couple of rocking chairs struck him hard. She looked peaceful there with a baby on her lap and a couple more running around playing cowboy in the yard. He could see her, clear as day. The image kind of shocked him since he'd hadn't really thought of her beyond their friendship, but she had him thinking more and more about things outside their immediate situation. "You see yourself as a mom?"

She turned the car over, looking at every minute detail of the model before setting it back on the shelf carefully. "Oh, definitely. I want at least four. Of course, it depends on their father. You came from a big family, but I didn't. I want that for my kids."

"Boys or girls?"

"I don't really care." She walked closer and put her hand on his chest. "I'd love to talk to your mom sometime. I bet it was interesting raising nine boys."

"Including a set of triplets."

"Yeah." Her lips parted as she looked up.

His brain went haywire at the thought of his lips on hers. He wanted it more than anything. "I want to kiss you."

Chapter Seven

"I want that too," she whispered, leaning toward him. "Take what you want, Jeremiah."

Unable to hold himself back any longer, he crushed his mouth to hers in a lip-bruising kiss meant to steal her will to resist. Not that he expected her to after the way she talked, but he didn't want to give her the chance either.

He wrapped his arms around her, pulling her in so her breasts brushed his chest. The kiss deepened as she moaned softly and opened her lips to his seeking tongue. The first touch of their battling tongues sent a rush of desire straight to his groin. He couldn't help it. He craved her with everything inside him. He wanted to lay her across his bed and eat her pussy until she screamed for him. The thought of burying his cock in her sweet heat drove his desire higher still. His cock ached. His balls felt like they were on fire.

As their lips parted, she whispered, "Wow."

"Yeah." Drawing his finger along the scooped neckline of her tank top in a sensual caress, he walked her backward until the back of her knees hit the edge of his bed. "I want you, Callie. I want to fuck you every way but up and then do it again."

"Yes."

"Are you on birth control?" he asked, slowly sliding the strap of her top down her arm.

"Yeah. Have been for a long time."

"Good. I have condoms to protect us both."

"Good thinking, cowboy."

He ran his tongue along the underside of her chin, across her jawline to the shell of her ear. "I'm always prepared to have a gorgeous woman in my bed."

"Had a few women here?"

"Not here."

She leaned back so she could look into his eyes. "What do you mean, not here?"

With a nimble toss, his hat landed on the dresser against the wall. "I don't bring women here. You're the first to see the inside of this room."

"Why me?"

"Because you're special."

"I am?"

"Yes. You aren't just a pussy for me to fuck. You're a friend too. That's special to me."

"Aw, you're such a gentleman, Jeremiah."

Her sarcastic tone was lost on him. He figured she should feel lucky to be with him. After all, he'd given her a compliment, right? He grinned and then leaned in to kiss her again. He liked the feel of her lips under his. The soft curve fit his perfectly. When he pushed to take the kiss deeper, she wrapped her arms around his shoulders, crushing her breasts against his chest. *Dear God.* He wanted her, needed her with every pump of his heart, craved her like he needed his next breath.

The clothes needed to go. The feel of her skin under his hands had his whole body humming with desire as his cock strained against the front of his jeans.

He brought her hands back down to her sides. "Let's get you out of these clothes. I want to see you."

With his fingers hooked in the straps of her top, he slowly slid them down her arms, bringing her shirt with it to bare her breasts. *Wow.* The rose-colored nipples stood up, as if begging for the touch of his fingers.

He cupped both breasts in his hands, sliding his thumb across the nipples until she tossed her head back. A soft moan escaped her lips. "These are gorgeous. I can't wait to taste them."

"Let me get my top off," she said, reaching for the edge of the shirt to bring it over the head. "There. That's better. Now you can play all you want." She toed off her shoes and reached for the button on her jeans.

"I'll get to that in a minute. I want to play with these beauties for a bit first." He pushed her back so she lay across his bed. He wanted to take his time to relish the feel of her skin beneath his fingers. *So soft.* He ran his tongue from the edge of her pants, up her abdomen, smiling against her skin as it jumped from the touch, up to the bottom edge of her breast. She wanted the touch of his mouth. He could tell from the squirming movements, begging sighs and arching of her back. Well, he'd give it to her because he wanted it too. He grabbed both of her hands in his to put them above her head. "Leave them there."

With one breast in each hand, he lowered his mouth to the left one, slowly sliding his tongue over the tip. She sucked in a ragged breath, holding it for several seconds before exhaling in a rush.

"So good."

He flattened his tongue, running it around the areola, slowly circling but not quite touching her nipple.

"You're killing me."

"What a way to die."

"Jeremiah, please."

"Please what?"

"Touch it, suck it, do something. I'm gonna die here." He wrapped his lips around the tip, sucking the hardened nub as she arched her back. "Yes!"

Her nipples were like ripe little berries, sweet and ready for his mouth. He nipped at one to see what she'd do.

"Fuck yeah."

So she liked a little pain with her sex. Good to know.

He sucked the nub into his mouth, flicking it with the tip of his tongue as he rolled her other nipple between his finger and thumb. She moved her hands to his hair, pressing his head harder against her chest.

"More."

He released her breasts much to her moan of protest. "Put your hands back above your head or I'll tie you to the bed."

"Okay." Her hands fisted as she returned them to the spot above her. "I want to touch you."

"You'll get your chance. For now, it's my turn to explore." He stood, positioning himself near her knees as he worked the button on her jeans loose. "Lift up." Her jeans came off with a tug at her hips, leaving only her socks on her feet. He toed off his own boots, and then unbuttoned his shirt.

"I wanted to do that."

"Next time."

"Will there be a next time?"

"I hope to God there is, because I'm totally enjoying myself here." A sigh escaped his lips as he glanced down at her neatly trimmed pubic hair. "You are simply gorgeous." He ran his hands from her knees, up the inside of her thighs, parting them as he went to give him access to the sweet spot he wanted so badly, he could almost come from the smell of her arousal. "I'm going to eat you up."

"Please do," she said, parting her thighs more to give him room to work.

"You like it when a guy eats you out?"

"It doesn't happen very often, but yeah. I love it."

"Good. I plan on doing that very thing until you come all over my face."

"Such a sweet talker."

He growled as he shoved his hands under her butt to bring her closer to his mouth while he knelt on the floor next to the bed. "Spread yourself for me."

With two fingers each on her pussy, she opened the outer lips showing him the little nub already slick and waiting for him.

He took in her scent with a swift inhale right before he took the tip of his tongue and swirled the hardened flesh with it. Her soft moans and arched back told him she enjoyed what he was doing as he licked every bit of flesh under his mouth.

It didn't take long for her moans to turn to cries of ecstasy as he ate at her with fervor. He wanted to taste the sweetness of her cum on his tongue. The need drove his own desire higher than he'd ever felt before.

When she held his head to her center and cried out his name, he knew his life wouldn't be the same after this.

* * * *

Her legs shook, her pussy throbbed, and her whole body hummed as she cried out, "Oh God, Jeremiah!" She'd never had a man go down on her like that, eating at her like he was starving. Jeremiah didn't do anything half-assed, apparently. "Holy shit. That was amazing."

He wiped his face on the comforter right before he stood to strip off his jeans. "Glad you liked it."

"I did. I mean, wow." Her breathing slowed and her heart quit hammering against her breast as she relaxed against the softness of the bed, watching Jeremiah strip off his jeans. "Holy hell! Damn, you're built."

"Thank you." His brow wrinkled. "I think."

She sat up to run her hand from the fur on his chest, down his rock hard abdomen to the cock nestled in the springy curls at the juncture of his thighs. When she wrapped her hand around his cock, he moaned low in his throat.

"I love how you touch me."

"Good." She leaned in to take his cock in her mouth, just enough to envelop the head between her lips.

"Don't tease me."

She slid to the floor on her knees. "Oh, I plan to tease you mercilessly, Jeremiah. I want to suck this, lick it, swirl my tongue around it, and get you so hard you think your balls are going to explode."

"Damn woman."

"Yep."

She sucked his cock between her lips again, rolling her tongue around the head, and then ran it down the length of the shaft. His thighs quivered as he fisted her hair in his hands. His hips pistoned, driving his cock in and out of her mouth in a steady rhythm she knew would bring him to completion before she wanted him to. She let his cock fall from her mouth in a wet slide as she licked down to his balls. "Easy, baby."

"You're going to kill me."

"What a slow, pleasurable death it would be."

"I want you."

"You can have me. Where are your condoms?"

"In the drawer." His breathing seesawed in and out, billowing his chest as he fought for control.

She grabbed one out, ripped it open with her teeth and then rolled the slick latex down his engorged cock. "I can't wait to have this deep inside me."

"Me either, baby. Me either." He lifted her to her feet and spun her around before pushing her down face first into the comforter. "This first time is going to be hard and fast. I can't hold back much longer. Your mouth did a number on me."

She braced herself on her forearms as she spread her legs, waiting for the first penetration of his cock. Good grief, she'd wanted this forever. Now she was finally at the beginning of a relationship with the man she's longed for since she was a teenager on the bud of womanhood. "Fuck me hard,

Jeremiah." With a snap of his hips, he buried his cock to the hilt deep inside her. A groan escaped at the first feeling of having him inside her. The size of his cock stretched her to the max. Her body adjusted surprisingly fast since she hadn't been with a man in quite a while. "That's it. Do it."

"God, you feel good."

"Faster," she begged at the slow glide of his movements. "Please."

He smacked her on the right butt cheek. "Shush, woman. I'm enjoying myself here." Wrapping his fist in her hair, he pulled back enough to cause a sting on her scalp as he whispered, "What's my name?"

"Jeremiah."

"That's right, baby. I want you to know who's fucking you."

He continued his slow glide for what seemed like forever.

"You can enjoy yourself next time. I need you to fuck me, damn it."

"Only because I can't hold back."

He began hammering into her like tomorrow didn't exist for them, like this was the first and the last time they would be together. Not if she had anything to say about it. Usually once you got a man in bed, he was there to stay, right? God, she hoped he didn't love 'em and leave 'em. "That's it. Hard."

He reached around her hip to pinch her clit with two fingers, sending her into a spasmodic orgasm she felt clear to her toes. Her pussy clenched around his cock as he continued to slam into her, taking her into a second orgasm before the first one had completely died down. Never in her life had she thought she could orgasm so close together, but there it was. Jeremiah had done it for her, taken her where no man had before.

God, do I love this man.

He shivered when he came apart, pushing against her with an uncoordinated rhythm before he slumped over her back, pushing them both to the bed. "Wow."

"Yeah." She sighed. "Can you get off me? I can't breathe very well with you on me."

He pushed himself up on his hands and rolled to his back beside her. "Sorry."

With his arm slung over his eyes and his body splayed out like a god sunning himself on a rock, she wanted to run her tongue all over him, from his luscious mouth to his cock anyway.

"I'll be ready for round two in a minute, or maybe we should watch television for a bit."

His cock bobbed against his stomach like it had a mind of its own.

"Would I mind having sex again? Hell no."

He moved his arm slightly to peer at her with those gorgeous stormy grey eyes. "You are insatiable, woman."

She giggled as she rolled to her side next to him before tracing a finger through the curls on his chest. "I try."

"Let me get rid of this condom so I can put some clothes on."

"If we're going to make love again, why are you putting clothes on?"

He got to his feet and headed for the bathroom. "I thought we might get something to munch on, watch a little television, and see where the evening leads."

She shrugged as she sat up and pushed the hair out of her face. "Sounds good to me." After she managed to get into her clothes, she padded on bare feet to the small couch in front of his television. "What do you want to watch?"

"Oh, I don't know. There are movies there or whatever is on TV is fine."

She watched as he walked back toward her in all his naked glory. No doubt about it, the man was fine. Sculpted chest with just the right amount of chest hair, six pack abs, lean legs, strong calves, and his cock was impressive even in its flaccid state.

"You keep looking at me like that we'll be back to testin' the bedsprings sooner rather than later."

"I'm game." She looked him up one side and down the other. "I could use another roll in the hay."

He didn't look happy or content even after just having mind-blowing sex. Something was up.

"We should talk."

"Oh great. The 'we should talk' thing." She crossed her arms over her chest while she watched him pull his jeans over his hips.

"I don't want you reading too much into this, that's all."

"I think we fit pretty good together."

"Me too, but I'm not ready to settle into a relationship, Callie. I'm still working on my future."

"What about dating?"

"We can date."

"Why do I hear a but in there?"

He slid a T-shirt over his head, slipping his arms through the sleeves. "I don't think we should be exclusive or anything. You know. If you want to date other guys to see if things are *the real deal* with someone else, then I'll go along with it."

"You didn't like me out with Brad tonight. What about that?"

After buttoning his jeans, he took the seat next to her on the couch. "Brad is an idiot."

"So?"

"You can do better."

"Better than what?"

"Better than him or me or any other guy in Bandera. You should date some guy from San Antonio or something."

"Why are you trying to get rid of me?"

"I'm not. I just don't want you putting your hopes and dreams on us when I'm not ready. I don't know if I'll be ready for a long time."

"I'm not asking for a relationship, Jeremiah. I don't know if I'm ready either." *You are such a liar!* "But thank you for thinking of me. If you're okay with me seeing other people, then I will."

His eyes narrowed like he contemplated what she said and it left a sour taste in his mouth.

Good. I don't want to date anyone else, but if that's what I have to do to get him to see we should be together, then so be it.

"I think it's the best option. I don't want to be tied down."

"Me either." She nodded. "Good plan, Jeremiah." She stood and walked to the edge of the bed to slip on her shoes. "I think you should take me back to the bar."

"Why? I thought we were going to hang out?"

"Well if I'm going to date other people, I might as well get started. Pickings around Bandera can be scarce. I'm thinking I'll start hanging out in a few bars in San Antonio."

He climbed to his feet and walked toward her. When he tangled his hand in her hair, she almost lost her battle to give into making love again. *No, it's not making love, at least not to Jeremiah. To him, I'm a fuck buddy.*

"I thought we could still see each other. You know, sometimes."

"Sure," she whispered, loving the feel of his hand in her hair. Her breathing sped up. Her heart hammered in her chest.

"Are you going to be fucking other guys?"

"Well." She glanced down until he tugged on her scalp to bring her gaze back to his. "We aren't exclusive, so yeah." Not like she really would. She only wanted him, but he didn't need to know she didn't care to be with anyone else. She almost cried when he let her go.

"All right."

That's not what I wanted to hear. "I appreciate the ride."

He sat on the side of the bed to pull on his socks and boots. "No problem." After a moment, he slipped on a T-shirt over his head, hiding his chest from her view.

This wasn't turning out like she'd hoped when he'd thrown her over his shoulder to take her out of the bar, but what the hell. She'd get him to realize they were meant to be together somehow. *Damn stubborn cowboy.*

Several minutes later, he pulled up next to her car in the parking lot of The Dusty Boot. Several cars had already gone, leaving hers solemnly sitting by itself in the back corner. When he shut the engine off on his truck and popped open the door, she figured their night was over. Not that she didn't want it to continue, she really did, but apparently he got what he wanted and was done with her.

She felt like shit.

"Thanks for the evening, Jeremiah. I appreciate—" Her words were cut off by his mouth on hers as he cupped her face.

"I'm not done with you. Remember that when you're seeing someone else."

"But you said you weren't ready for anything but friends with benefits or whatever."

"I know what I said."

"You're confusing me."

"Me too. You do what you have to do." He stepped back, leaving her cold.

She watched him climb back into his truck and drive away without a backward glance. After she exhaled forcibly, she pulled the car keys out of her bag, unlocked the door and slid behind the wheel.

Why did men have to be so damned difficult?

Chapter Eight

Jeremiah sat in the corner of the bar watching Callie as she flirted, danced, played pool, and generally had a good time…without him. He took a sip of his beer barely hearing the woman sitting next to him chatter on about shoes or some shit he didn't care about.

This whole situation with Callie seemed to be slowly driving him nuts. He wanted her so why the hell was she there at the bar without him?

Callie threw back her head and laughed at something the guy next to her said before she leaned over to shoot another ball. She stood up abruptly when the guy ran his hand over her hip, and then across her right butt cheek. The shy little look she gave the guy pissed Jeremiah off. He knew she was no inexperienced virgin. The woman knew how to wind a man up to explosive with her perfect little mouth. He could attest to her prowess in the bedroom.

When she leaned in and kissed the guy on the mouth, Jeremiah about lost his mind. The mouth that was supposed to be wrapped around his cock, not some jerk's she picked up at the bar.

He knew just exactly how many men she'd been out with since their little split and how many times he'd asked her to come over for a bit of a romp. She'd always been too busy going out with someone else when he'd asked.

Damn her.

"Are you even listening to me, Jeremiah?"

He cranked his head around to look at the brunette next to him. What was her name again? Didn't really matter. "Yeah, I'm listening."

"Then what did I say?"

"Something about shoes."

"I was telling you about a particularly cute pair of pumps I bought today at the mall. You should pay more attention."

"Okay."

Her voice melded with the music being played as he glanced back at Callie. She'd wrapped her arm around the cowboy she was playing pool with and kissed him full on the mouth. His gut knotted. She wasn't supposed to be kissing anyone but him, right?

He didn't know anymore. She'd done tied him up in knots with this dating other people thing. It had gone on long enough, he figured.

"Excuse me."

"Where are you going?"

"I need to talk to someone. I'll be back."

"Wha—" The girl sputtered next to him as he slid out of the booth and headed toward Callie.

When he got close he heard her laugh again. The sound went right through him, curling his toes in his boots only to center in his balls seconds later. "I need to talk to you."

"Oh hey, Jeremiah. I didn't realize you were here," she said as the guy next to her stood behind her, kissing her exposed neck.

"Can we talk?"

"Um." She giggled when the guy licked her ear. "I'm kind of busy."

"I see that."

"Maybe later?"

"Now." He grabbed her hand, dragging her across the bar to a dark corner.

"What the hell? I thought we had this manhandling thing taken care of. I mean really." She jerked her hand out of his grasp. "The caveman behavior isn't becoming of you. I thought you were more sophisticated than this."

"What are you doing?"

"I'm not doing anything."

"You're letting some guy climb all over you."

She threw up her hands before settling them on her hips as she gave him a glare. "What do you care? Remember, 'let's date other people,' you said. That's what I'm doing, dating other people."

"He's treating you like a whore."

"I'm not a whore, Jeremiah."

"I didn't say you were." He paced a few steps away from her, and then back toward her. "How many guys have you been out with this week?"

"What difference does it make to you? You didn't want to be exclusive, remember? Your words, not mine."

"How many?"

"Six."

"Six different men this week. How many have you slept with? And don't lie to me, I'll know. You aren't a very good liar, Callie."

She pressed her lips together, dropping her gaze to the floor. "None."

"None?"

"None."

"What is going on here then?"

Her head snapped back up. "I'm doing what you wanted, dating other guys. You are dating other women. I know. I saw you with Melissa at the table in the corner."

"That's her name?"

Her mouth fell open before snapping shut. "You don't even know her name?"

"She probably told me, but I forgot."

"You're a jerk, you know that?"

"What?"

"Exactly what is your problem? You drag me over here away from my date, who by the way I do know his name. It's Craig. We were having a good time, and yeah, I might let him have some tonight if it's okay with you, but really I don't give a damn if it is or not because we," she moved her finger between the two of them, "are not a couple!"

"We should be."

"You started this shit. I'm doing what you wanted so back off, Jeremiah. I'm done playing your games. You don't want me. I get it. Well, other guys do, so I'm going with that."

She spun on her booted heel and headed back toward where her date stood leaning against the pool table waiting for her. *If I was her guy, I would have decked whoever dragged her away from me.* "Well, guess what? You aren't her guy."

He glanced back at the table where he'd left the girl he had a date with tonight. What was her name? Oh yeah, Melissa. The table stood empty. *Maybe she went to the bathroom.* He walked over and took his seat as he waited to see if she came back. Nope. He saw her talking to some other guy halfway across the room. Oh well.

His beer had grown warm, but he didn't care, he needed the alcohol. He signaled for the waitress to bring him another. Maybe he'd go home with someone tonight. Ah, who the hell was he kidding? He tried that on a few occasions in the last several weeks without success. The one woman he wanted was dating other guys at his request. The beer went down his throat with a sour aftertaste. Warm beer sucked.

"Here you go, Jeremiah."

"Thanks, uh…"

"Allison."

"Allison. Thank you." He looked her up one side and down the other with an appreciative eye. "How late do you work tonight?"

"Midnight."

"Wanna go home with me?"

"Are you asking me to sleep with you?"

"Yeah."

She pulled back her hand and slapped him hard across the cheek. "I'm not a slut. The least you could do is buy me dinner before fucking me." She dumped the beer in his lap. "I'll find you another waitress."

"Well, shit." He stood up as beer soaked through his jeans. "Damn it to hell!" Several people around him laughed while he fished the keys to his truck out of his pocket and headed for the door. "Screw it. I'm going home."

"Hey, Jeremiah!" Peyton motioned him to the bar. "You okay?"

"Yeah. Just a little wet and not the good kind."

"I see that. I'll have Dan talk to the waitress."

"No biggie. My fault. I approached her all wrong."

"Seems you've had a problem with that a lot lately."

"Yeah, I guess so." He glanced down at the front of his wet jeans. "I'll see you later."

"Be careful."

"I will."

He pushed out the doors and walked to his truck. Tonight would be a long, lonely night because the woman he wanted was laying it on pretty thick with some other guy in the bar right now.

When he slid behind the wheel of his vehicle, he stopped for a moment to watch the front doors. He could go back in there and demand she come home with him, but no, he couldn't do something so caveman-like. Well he could, and he had, but it wouldn't get him anywhere with her now. She'd already made things pretty clear.

What was it about her that made him want her so much? She wasn't beautiful in a model sort of way. Her beauty came from within. She had a heart of gold. He'd seen it on a few occasions when she'd volunteered over Christmas to be Santa's helper at the elementary school. The chance to observe her good deeds only came once in a while, but he knew she volunteered a lot at the nursing home in town too.

It took a lot to keep her dad's shop running as well. She did that. She worked on cars when she didn't have to. She had the brains to do anything she wanted with her life, but she chose to help her dad keep his garage open. That took guts, determination, and a soul of a woman, the kind of woman he'd like to get to know a whole lot better. How though? She wasn't the pushover type. She didn't go for his lines or his smooth words. She wanted something out of life. What did she really want from him?

She said she didn't want a relationship. Neither did he, right?

He wasn't so sure anymore. He wanted to be stable financially before he got serious with a girl and started a family. Did several million in the bank make him stable enough? His family needed to be there too, although they didn't have as much as he did, they were doing pretty well.

He needed to talk to his parents. Maybe by letting them in on what he'd done with their money, it would make the whole thing seem less significant.

Maybe Mom and Dad will have some words of wisdom for me.

He nodded to himself, started his truck, and pulled out onto the road back to the ranch. A discussion seemed to be the right thing to do in a situation like this.

The ride home left him time to think about Callie. Maybe his mom could give him some insight to his situation with her as well. He didn't know what to do anymore.

Several minutes later, the gates of Thunder Ridge Ranch came into view. The large double wrought iron gates were home and had been since he was born. His parents had bought the place when his older brothers were little. He loved living on the ranch, watching the sun come up over the horizon from the front porch while he sipped hot coffee. Dreams of his future always plagued him though. He had plans, big plans, but the illusiveness of who would share those plans eluded him. Callie's face seemed to be taking the place of those illusive dreams more and more.

The numbers came easy as did the money, but was it enough? Would it ever be enough?

He rubbed the fingers of his left hand. The numbness had returned much to his annoyance.

The lights of the main lodge came in to view as he pulled up into his parking spot in front of his cabin. His place only sat a few hundred yards from the big building housing the dining facilities of the ranch, the huge gathering hall with the pool table, dart boards, massive fireplace, and big leather couches. The comforting feelings of home always calmed his restless soul, well, most days. Today, he wasn't so sure.

He turned the truck off, popped open the door then slammed it shut behind him before he headed up the cement walkway to his cabin. He needed to shower and change clothes before he talked to his parents. He glanced up at the inky black, cloudless sky, wondering what Callie was doing right now. *I can't think about her. It'll drive me crazy.*

Off in the distance he heard giggling children. The ghosts of the kids were out wandering the ranch tonight. He'd never thought about why they were trapped at Thunder Ridge before, but there had to be a story there somewhere. He opened the door to his cabin as the giggling faded into the night.

Darkness surrounded him. Not even a small light in his room to illuminate the black space. Just how he liked it. When the sun rose in the morning, it would drag him from his dreams like it did every day. He enjoyed the quiet time on the porch sipping coffee as the ranch came alive around him.

With two fingers on the lamp, he twisted the knob until the light came on. Scenes of the night with Callie came rushing back. She'd been there, teasing him, coaxing him, and loving him for a short time. He hadn't been able to forget that night for more than a few moments since it happened. Her body cradling him as he drove her to heights of ecstasy, haunted him day and night. His cock stirred to life. This he didn't need when he planned to talk to his parents about money, but it was there nonetheless.

After he stripped off his T-shirt, toed off his boots, and pulled down his jeans, he headed for the bathroom off to the back of his room. A nice hot shower would do him good even if he'd taken one this morning. Hot, sticky sweat clung to his body. The sour smell of beer crinkled his nose as he turned on the water in the shower.

Once he had it the right temperature, he dropped his boxers to step under the spray. The hot water cascaded down his chest, abdomen, and groin washing away the sweat of the day, not to mention the beer dumped in his lap earlier. He grabbed the shampoo from the shelf to wash his hair.

Thoughts traveled precariously to Callie on her knees in front of him like she'd been when she sucked his cock. *Damn, I don't need this right now.*

But he couldn't shake the image this time so he let it take him. He grabbed the soap from the dish to scrub his body, letting his imagination run wild with the picture of Callie doing wonderful things to his cock using her mouth.

He wrapped his hand around his cock, stroking it up and down with a firm grip.

Her mouth wrapped around the head as she ran a fingernail around his balls. It felt like heaven and hell at the same time. She sucked lightly, drawing his balls up tight. Moaning deep in his throat, the warmth of her mouth scalded him with heat he could hardly stand to feel. When she licked the length of him, his body shuddered with need. As she went all the way down his length, pulling the entire thing into her mouth, he lost control of his desire, squirting cum down her throat in hot spurts.

A groan escaped him as he slumped against the cool tile wall of the shower, trying desperately to slow his heart rate as the water washed cum from his abdomen. Shivers rolled down his back and his legs trembled with weakness. It had been a long time since he'd had to jack off to get relief from his own desire. Another thing to chalk up to his need for Callie Lewis.

He shut the water off before he grabbed a towel from the rack to dry himself. With it wrapped around his hips, he headed over to put some clean clothes on so he could talk to his parents.

Letting out a long sigh, he shrugged on a clean pair of jeans. He really needed to get Callie out of his thoughts if he planned to do anything but fuck her. She'd taken up residence in his dreams now, driving him to distraction time and time again. *Maybe if I fuck her a few more times, this insatiable need to have her pussy will leave me alone?*

"Yeah, brilliant thought, genius. If it was that easy, I'd have done it already," he said out loud while he pulled on a shirt, socks, and boots.

With a shake of his head to loosen the thoughts of the disturbing woman, he headed out to talk with his parents, hoping it would go well and they didn't get too upset with him for keeping the finances of the ranch a secret.

The walk across the ranch yard didn't take long. A few lights from the other cabins reflected off the cement walkway leading to the big house. Guests were settling in for the night, watching television, playing board games or doing family things. He wanted that someday.

He shrugged before he pushed open the side door leading into the massive dining room where they took their meals. The large living room sat to the left with the big, comfy leather couches in the front of the fireplace. He'd spent many a night in this room growing up, doing homework, wrestling with his brothers, or hanging out talking about girls. He smiled. The memories were good ones.

"Mom?" he called as he headed down the long hallway that led to his parents' private quarters. "Dad?"

"Back here," his dad answered from their small living area. "In the den."

When he came around the corner, he saw his dad sitting in one of the recliners and his mom at the desk typing away on the computer. "Don't you do enough work during the day, Mom? You shouldn't be on the computer after you leave the office."

"But I had one more reservation to look at. Then I'm done. I swear."

His dad raised an eyebrow as he shook his head. "She'll be there for another hour at least, doing one thing or another."

"I need you to take a break for a minute, Mom. I need to talk to you two about something."

"Okay." She shut down the computer screen and turned her chair around. "Have a seat, Jeremiah."

He wiped his sweaty palms on the thighs of his jeans as he took a chair, turning it around so he could straddle it.

"What's up, son?" his dad asked.

"I have something to tell you." He glanced up at the ceiling before facing his parents again. "I've been investing for the ranch."

"Investing?" Nina asked.

"Yes. Stocks, bonds, oil. Those kinds of things."

"We trust you to do what is best for the ranch, Jeremiah. That's why you are in charge of the finances."

He blew out the breath he wasn't aware he'd been holding until then.

"Exactly what are you saying?"

"There is enough money in the ranch account for you to close down and retire if you wanted to."

"Just how much are we talking about?" James tapped his foot on the floor, a sure sign of concentration on his part.

"There is five million in the ranch account."

"Five million?" Nina's shocked face almost made him laugh. What would she say when she found out how much he'd amassed in his own account?

"You said five million, Jeremiah?" His father stopped tapping.

"Yes."

"You've invested enough of our money to make five million for the ranch and you think we'd be mad? My God, son, that's fantastic!" James jumped to his feet and dragged Jeremiah to his feet for a hug. He slapped him on the back with a laugh. "You've done well, son."

"I shouldn't tell you how much I have in my own account."

"More than what is in ours?" his mother asked, surprise written in her eyes.

"Yes. My account has double that amount."

"Why the hell are you still working for us then? Not that I want to lose you as our financial person especially knowing you've managed to make us rich, but you could do so much with your own. Your future is secure."

"I know, but I don't know if it's enough."

"Why not?" Nina dabbed at her eyes as a lone tear trickled down her face.

Why was she crying? He hoped she was happy for all of them, but he couldn't be sure. Nina didn't cry much. He could remember a handful of times during his entire life. "What's wrong, Mom?"

Sobs shook her shoulders. "I'm so happy. I worry about this place from month to month. You've taken a huge load off our shoulders, Jeremiah. You have no idea how relieved I am." She wiped at her face. "Now back to why you don't think you have enough money."

"I think I do, but then I want so many things to be perfect before I worry about taking on a wife and kids. You know?"

"Is there someone specific you are thinking about marrying?"

"No, but I think about it a lot. When I find the right girl, I want to be able to provide for her and our children for the rest of their lives." He held up his hand when his mother went to say something else. "Not that I had a bad childhood. You and Dad provided for us more than we ever wanted, but I want my kids to be able to go to college and not have to pay for it. I want to be able to help them start a business if they want to. I want my wife to not have to work if she doesn't want to. That kind of stuff is important to me."

"Son, if you've found someone you want to marry, what you are holding out for won't be so important."

"I don't think so, Mom." He wiped his hands on his jeans again.

"Is there something else?"

"I feel kind of stupid."

"Why?"

"You know I took Callie Lewis out."

"Yes. I trust you had a good time?"

"Well, not so much. She tried acting all weird. Like some of the other girls I'd been out with. It wasn't right. I told her she needed to be herself. We spent the evening watching movies and eating popcorn."

"Sounds like a nice date."

"It was. Then we were supposed to have a date the following evening, but I screwed up. You remember telling me to call her?"

"Yes."

"Well, I forgot. She was pissed I stood her up."

"I don't blame her."

He raked his fingers through his hair before putting his hat back on his head. "I don't either. I went to the bar to apologize, but she shut me down."

"Again, I don't blame her."

"I know. I fucked up. I wanted to make amends. She got pretty wasted that night. Did some things I'm sure she wasn't proud of. Anyway, she said she was dating someone. I checked it out when they met at the bar. I did something stupid again."

"And?"

"I hauled her over my shoulder, brought her back here and we had sex."

His father's eyebrow shot up, but his dad didn't say a word.

"I know. Not good, but it happened. Anyway, we kind of argued about what I wanted in life. How I wasn't ready for a relationship. We agreed to start dating other people, but the plan has backfired on me."

"Oh?"

"Yeah. She's having a blast while I'm miserable. I've tried dating other women, but they aren't measuring up to her."

"Sounds like you have an infatuation with Callie Lewis," his father replied, coming into the conversation for the first time. "Are you sure you aren't halfway in love with her?"

"No way, Dad. I can't be."

"Why not? You've known her for a long time. You've been friends for a long while and now you're lovers or were anyway. How is it hard to come around to being in love with her?"

Jeremiah jumped to his feet, pacing back and forth a couple of times in front of his parents. This was crazy. He couldn't be in love with Callie. In lust, yes, but in love, no. Not possible. *Why not?* It can't happen like this. He liked her a lot and they were pretty good in bed together, but in love? "I like her."

"I'm sure you do."

"We were pretty good in bed together."

"You've had that before, though. You've had a pretty active sex life for quite a while."

He didn't like talking sex with his parents, but yeah, they were right. Good together in bed didn't make for a healthy relationship.

"What is it about Callie that makes her so different to you?"

"I'm not sure. She gets me. She knows me. She's not afraid of the angry me, the me who kids around, or the me who shows off."

"Does she know about your money in the bank?"

"No."

"Then you know she's not after you for your money."

"She's not after me at all, Mom. She seems indifferent to being with me now, much to the detriment of my ego." He raked his fingers through his hair before putting his hat back on his head. "Fuck."

"Is it the fact she doesn't act like she wants you that has you attracted to her? You know, the want what you can't have scenario?"

"I don't think so. I mean, I like her. She's funny, smart, kind, gorgeous, good with kids, helpful to other people even if it means she loses something in the end."

"Well, I think you should continue to stay away from her. Clearly, she's not the girl for you." The smirk on his mother's face told him she was kidding, but the thought of not seeing her made him sick to his stomach. "Oh, and watch your language, mister. We don't talk with such dirty mouths around here."

"Sorry. I'm upset right now and my mouth gets away from me."

"Well, see that you curb it a bit."
"Yes, ma'am."

Chapter Nine

Callie watched Jeremiah leave with a heavy heart as Craig continued to kiss her neck from behind. The disinterest she felt in having the other man even touch her crowded her heart. She didn't want Craig. She didn't want any other man but Jeremiah. He was driving her nuts with his behavior though. First he didn't want her, then he got pissed because she was with someone else, then he did want her. *What the hell?*

"Yo, Callie?"

"Sorry."

"It's been a long time since I've been with a girl who didn't want to be with me."

"It's not that."

He tipped his head in the direction of the door. "Jeremiah?" he asked, moving around so he could look into her eyes.

"Yeah." She dropped her gaze to the tips of his boots. Disappointment raced through her. She didn't use people, but this felt like she'd been using the men she'd been out with since Jeremiah's statement about dating other people. She didn't want anyone but him. How in the heck did she convince him they belong together? "I'm sorry. I've been a really bad person this week. I don't normally do this kind of thing, but…"

"It's okay. We can be friends."

"Thanks, Craig."

"Sure." He trailed his fingers down her cheek. "Do you want another beer?"

"That would be great. Thanks."

She watched him walk toward the bar, stopping every few feet to talk to someone or another. Craig was a pretty popular guy in Bandera, a great catch, so why couldn't she get into someone like him and not the guy who didn't want her?

"You know he wants you as much as you want him, right?" Joey whispered in her ear from behind.

Startled, she swung around, almost hitting his shoulder with her nose. "Sorry. What did you say?"

"Jeremiah. He's being stubborn, but he wants you as much as you want him."

"How do you know?" she asked, leaning on the pool table.

"I've seen the way he watches you. When he took you out of the bar a few weeks ago, he almost had steam coming out of his ears watching you with Brad."

"Then why doesn't he just give in?"

"Because he's a Young. We don't do anything the easy way. And love? That's the worst one of all for us to admit."

"You're one to talk, Joey. You don't have a girlfriend either."

"No, but I'm always looking. I'm a little young to be settling down yet."

"No, you aren't. You aren't that much younger than me."

"Maybe I'll be *your* boyfriend." He waggled his eyebrows. "You know, I'm better than Jeremiah in the sack."

She laughed and shook her head. "Joey, you are so full of shit, your eyes are brown."

"Why, yes they are." He laughed along with her as he drew her into a hug. "He'll come around."

With her arms wrapped around him, she hugged him tight, hoping he was right. "I hope so, Joey. I wish I knew what to do to make him see me as the woman for him."

"He will."

Craig brought her back her beer finally. "Are you makin' a move on my girl, Young?"

"Nope, but she ain't your girl."

"She is tonight."

"She belongs to my brother."

"Well, he hasn't figured out what the hell he's missing yet, so for tonight she's mine."

Joey's eyes narrowed and Callie thought the two men would fight if she didn't do something quickly. She stepped between them, putting a hand on each of their chests. Joey and Craig were close to the same height, but towered over her by at least several inches. She didn't care. She wouldn't have them fighting over something that wasn't their concern. "Easy, boys. This isn't your fight. You're both right, but tonight I'm here with Craig. He's being a perfect gentleman, Joey, so calm down. Nothing worth fightin' over here."

"But—"

"Nothing, Joe." She stepped in front of him and put both hands on his shoulders. "Stop and listen to me. What's between me and Jeremiah is just that, between the two of us. I know you love your brother and want to see him happy. I get that, but fighting other men over me isn't going to change the situation."

"You should be with him."

"I know that. So does Craig, but he also saw Jeremiah walk out of here without a backward glance."

"I saw your conversation with Jeremiah. Neither of you looked happy."

"We weren't. He was trying to tell me who I could see and who I couldn't after he told me to date other people. I'm doing what he asked. I'm sorry if he doesn't like it."

"He's being an idiot."

"I know this and so do you. So does a lot of people in this bar, but he has to come to the same conclusion before he'll change the way things are. For now, we live with what he has decreed."

"You are too good for him."

"Thank you." She put a hand on his cheek. "You'd make a great brother-in-law."

"When he finally figures out what he's missing, maybe, until then I'm on your side of this fight. I'll do what I have to so you two can be together."

"I appreciate your support. Really." She stood on her tiptoes and kissed him on the cheek. "Now what do we have to do to find you a girl?"

"No, no. Not me."

"Oh, yes." She glanced around the bar, but didn't see anyone she thought would fit the tough as nails cowboy in front of her. The man rode horses for a living, bucking and kicking horses. She was amazed he still seemed to be in one piece.

"Forget it, Callie. I don't need one woman. I need a few."

"Well, I don't see anyone here good enough for you. I'll keep my eye out though." When she glanced back to the bar, she saw a dark-haired woman talking with her hands to some guy sitting on a bar stool. *Wow. I wonder what that's all about?*

"I'll leave you to your *date*, but I'll keep an eye out for you too."

"Thanks." She watched Joey walk toward the bar and take a seat next to the woman she'd seen a little bit ago and then turned to talk to Jackson who had one hand wrapped around the waist of some leggy blonde. Leave it to the Young brothers to have women hanging all over them. "I'm sorry about that, Craig. You know how those guys are."

"Yeah, I know. I've had a run-in with one or two of them before." He picked up the pool cue. "Shall we play another game or two while we waste a few hours here at the good old Dusty Boot?"

For the next few hours she drank, laughed, shot pool, threw some darts and generally had a good time. She didn't think of Jeremiah more than a million times during the time period, or so she thought.

She found she really liked Craig as a friend. If she hadn't been in love with Jeremiah, things would have been a lot easier, but alas, she was, and she would have to deal with it.

* * * *

Jeremiah stared at the computer screen in his cabin. He did his own trading with stocks on his own computer so he didn't mix business with personal stuff. Soft country music played in the background while he watched the numbers change and blur. He squeezed his eyes shut, rubbing them with his fingers to try to bring everything back into focus. He really needed to see an eye doctor, he figured. These episodes of blurry vision were getting more frequent. Not that anyone in his family had vision problems, but there was always one.

Two fingers on his right hand tingled like they were going to sleep. He rubbed them with his left to bring the feeling back into them. Things like this had been happening more and more, he noticed recently. He probably needed to see the family doctor. After all, it had been several years since he'd had a physical, probably the last year of high school so he could run track. Cross country running was the only sport he'd done in high school. Running long distance gave him time to think, lots of time to think.

The numbers are the screen came back into focus. He was doing well. His bank account was steadily increasing as well as the family finances. Complaining at all didn't seem right. He smiled as he flipped off the computer to head to bed. It was midnight and he had to be up early for cowboy call as he named it. He had wrangler duties tomorrow and Joey wanted his help breaking a new mare he'd recently purchased. The duties on a ranch never ceased.

After his talk with his parents, he'd headed back out to his cabin for some me time. He didn't get enough of it with a large family. Tonight he wanted to veg out in front of the television and *not* think about Callie Lewis.

He shook his head to dislodge the thoughts of her, but it was difficult since he'd fucked her hard over the side of his bed. Those images wouldn't leave him alone.

A sigh escaped his lips as he climbed to his feet. Dizziness swamped his head for a moment as he grabbed the back of his chair for balance. These symptoms were coming more frequently. A doctor's visit needed to happen soon. This wasn't normal for a twenty-eight-year-old guy. He'd make an appointment tomorrow, well, today when he woke up.

After checking the time again, he decided to hit the bed. His duties required him to be up by seven in the morning for breakfast and rides, then working with Joey on the horse. Maybe he'd throw some hay tomorrow or something to work off some of this frustration he felt. Couldn't hurt, right?

He stripped off his jeans, tossed his T-shirt over the back of the chair and then climbed under the cool sheets. Lucky for them, they had air-conditioning in all the cabins. He'd die in the summer heat without it even though fall was in the air. He liked to sleep with a very cold room. The moment his head hit the pillow, he drifted off to sleep as dreams clouded his thoughts, dreams of Callie.

She walked in through the door of his cabin wearing a silky blouse and short shorts. Her tanned legs went on forever as she strolled toward him with a smile on her lips. "Jeremiah."

"Callie. What are you doing here?"

"I came because I want you."

"Want me?"

"Bad, cowboy."

"Come closer."

She straddled his legs, bringing her pussy into warm contact with his bulging erection. Lord, he wanted her too. More than his next breath. More than food or water. More than anything.

He trailed his fingers down her cheek until he reached her red lips. She nipped at the pads of his fingers with her teeth, sending shivers down his spine. His cock throbbed behind the fly of his jeans. She knew what to do to drive him crazy.

With a tug on the hem of his T-shirt, she pulled it over his head, dropping the soft cotton to the floor beside the chair. Her fingernails raked across his chest until she reached his nipples. The sting of her sharp nails made his skin bust out in goose bumps.

"Do you like a little pain with your pleasure, Jeremiah?"

"Maybe."

She scooted back on his knees enough where she could reach his chest with her mouth. Her teeth sank into the right nipple, sending pain and pleasure shooting straight to his balls. When she sucked it between her lips, he almost came in his jeans. God, she was good.

"I'm going to suck you dry, cowboy."

She shimmied off his lap before she grabbed his belt buckle to undo it. His jeans came next with a tug of her hands at his hips. He raised his ass high enough she could work the stiff material down his thighs to the tops of his boots. She didn't worry about getting them completely off as she dove into giving him pleasure with her mouth. The slick feeling of her tongue as it danced down his cock pulled a deep growl from his throat. He didn't know how she got so good with her wicked tongue, but he loved it. Her fingers worked his balls into a frenzy as she continued to lick, suck and deep throat his cock.

As his balls drew up in the impending climax of his desire, he pulled her off his cock, pushed her shorts to the floor and forced her to straddle his lap. When he sank balls deep into her pussy, his whole world narrowed to the feel of being deep inside her.

Hot wetness surrounded him. The ridges of her vagina caressed him as she slowly rode him.

"Fuck me, baby."

"Oh I plan to, cowboy. I'm gonna ride you into tomorrow."

The slow crawl of her movements had him panting in moments. He couldn't hold back. He needed to come more than his next breath, but he couldn't, not without making sure she had an orgasm along with him. "You need to come along for the ultimate ride."

Her movements sped up. She rocked her hips back and forth, drawing his own orgasm to the tip of his cock before she moaned softly. "I'm right there. Help me."

He reached down between their bodies, rubbing her clit with his finger faster and faster as she continued to rock. His own climax was held in check *as he gritted his teeth until he felt her quiver around him. "Come with me, Callie."*

"Fuck!" she screamed as her climax broke.

He released the steely hold he had on his own the moment he felt her squeeze him like a vice.

Jeremiah woke up with a start to find cum across his abdomen. *Damn, I haven't had a wet dream since I was a teenager.* He tossed his legs over the side of the bed and struggled to his feet to go to the bathroom to clean up. *Wow. That was intense. It has to be from my forced celibacy the last several weeks.*

Once he cleaned off, he strolled over to his nightstand to check the time on his phone. He wondered if Callie was asleep or out partying at the bar. No, the bar would be closed by now. Was she alone or with Craig?

He crawled back into his bed and lay staring at the ceiling wondering what he should do. Talking to her didn't seem to get him anywhere, but he really needed to try.

That's it. Tomorrow we are going to sit down and have a nice long chat to get all of this out in the open. I'm tired of the way things are so something has to change. Either we are a couple or we aren't. No more beating around the bush, playing Mr. Nice Guy and letting her date whomever she wants. She's mine, damn it! It's about time she realized it.

The jingle of his cell phone startled him. Who the hell would be calling at this time of night? He reached over to grab it, realizing his fingers were numb again. *Damn it!*

The caller ID said Jeff. "What the hell are you doing calling me at this time of night?"

"It's Mom. Joey just called. There's been a bad accident. Get your ass dressed and meet me at the main lodge."

"I'll be right there."

He jumped out of the bed, hopping around on one foot as he tried to put his legs into his jeans. This didn't sound good. Accidents on the back roads of Bandera were bad. After he threw a shirt on, he slipped on his socks and boots before he made a beeline for the door to the lodge. His heart clenched. His mom had to be okay. She just had to be.

The minute he went through the doors, he came to a sliding stop next to the crowd of his brothers to get the scoop. "What's happened?"

"Hang on. We are waiting for Joel and Mesa."

A moment later, the last brother came through the doors. "Tell us."

"Joey called a few minutes ago. Mom was hit head-on by a drunk driver. Right now, she's on her way to the hospital in San Antonio by ambulance. She's not conscious. They don't know the extent of her injuries."

"What hospital?" Jeff rattled off the name of one of the biggest hospitals in the area. "I'm going," Jeremiah said, spinning on his heels to rush to his truck.

"Slow down, Jeremiah. I'm sure we all want to be there, but having the entire Young clan bombard their emergency room isn't what is best for Mom."

"I said I'm going."

"All right, but I think it's best if only a few of us go." The boys all spoke up at once until Jeff raised his hand. "I know you all want to be there, but I think only three of us should go. Dad is already on his way behind the ambulance and Joey, so that would make four. I'll stay here with Terri to make sure the ranch doesn't fall apart. Jeremiah, you go." He pointed to two other brothers. "Jackson, you and Jason go too. The rest of us will stay here. Make sure you call frequently with updates."

"Will do," Jeremiah said, turning to the other two who would be going with him. "We should probably ride together so we don't have all of our vehicles at the hospital."

"Sounds good to me," Jackson replied.

A moment or two later, the three men climbed into Jeremiah's truck to head to San Antonio. It would be a long ass drive without knowing what the hell was going on with their mother. How badly was she hurt? Jeff said she was unconscious. That wasn't a good sign. He'd keep that thought to himself though. Talk amongst the three of them was sobering. They didn't say much, watching the streetlights and empty buildings go by until they hit the interstate to take them into the big city. Luckily the hospital wasn't that far and they made it there in record time as they pulled up into the emergency room parking lot.

Jeremiah quickly called Jeff to let them know they'd made it safely. "Let's hope Joey or Dad are out in the waiting room. I doubt they'll let us back there."

"Right," Jackson answered as they walked in through the double sliding doors.

Joey stood off to the side with his back to the door, waiting.

"Joey?" Jeremiah touched him on the shoulder.

"Oh. Hey."

"How's Mom?"

"I don't know. They haven't told me anything. All I know is she regained consciousness for a few minutes when they put her in the ambulance, but Dad came out and told me she'd slipped back under by the time they got her here."

"Is Dad back there with her?"

"Yeah." Joey pulled his hat off and raked his fingers through his hair.

He wasn't the type to get upset normally, but this had hit them all in the gut. Their mother was the rock of the family. Having her hurt meant someone should die. "Where is the guy who hit her?"

"He's in jail."

"I would hope so."

"I should have stopped him, guys. He was drunk at The Dusty Boot. Drinking hard. I should have taken his keys or something." Joey paced back and forth in front of the door.

"Was it someone we know?"

"I don't think so. I didn't know him before tonight."

"Tonight?"

Joey shoved his hands into the front pockets of his jeans as he exhaled forcibly. "His sister was at the bar trying to get him to go home. He'd had a few beers. Not too many, but we don't know how much he was drinking before she got there." He rocked back on his heels. "I danced with her. In the meantime, he took off. She and I went to find him if we could. We saw the fire trucks take off from the station and followed them. Came up on the scene to realize it was a Thunder Ridge truck. I didn't know Mom was behind the wheel. When they cut her out, she was breathing but not conscious. She regained consciousness while we were there. Asked a few questions and said her leg hurt. When they put her in the ambulance she was awake, but apparently on the way to the hospital, she lost consciousness again according to Dad. They are doing some tests now to see what's wrong."

Jeremiah clapped Joey on the shoulder. "This isn't your fault, Joe. You couldn't have known he would hit someone. You did what you could do to get him off the road."

"It wasn't enough, Jeremiah. What if Mom dies?"

"She's not going to die!" Jackson spoke up for the first time. "Do you hear me? She's not going to die!"

"Easy, Jackson," Jeremiah said as he placed his hands on Jackson's shoulders. "She'll be okay. She has to be."

Their father came through the double doors, walking toward them.

"Any news?" Joey asked.

"She's regained consciousness, but doesn't remember anything. They're taking her back for a CAT scan now to see what's up. She has a concussion at least, but they don't know the extent of it right now. They're concerned with bleeding on the brain. Her leg is broken at the femur so she'll be laid up for a while. They'll probably be keeping her here for a few days. She may need surgery on her leg. They're more concerned with her head at the moment." A tear rolled down their dad's cheek. "I can't lose her, boys."

"She isn't going anywhere, Dad. Trust in God. He has her in His hands now." Jeremiah hugged his dad and then stepped back to see tears rolling down his cheeks. It was difficult to see his dad so broken. They would all be in a world of hurt should anything happen to their mom.

"I know, but it's hard to see her like this. She's so confused."

"Does she know who you are?"

"Yes."

"Then she isn't that confused."

James smiled. "After being together for forty years, I would hope she knew who I was."

The sad look in his dad's eyes hurt Jeremiah's heart. He knew how much in love his parents were. Someday, he wanted the same kind of love, a lifetime wouldn't be long enough.

Chapter Ten

The doctor came out of the double doors. "Mr. Young?"

"Yes?" his father answered.

"We need to discuss your wife's care."

"What's wrong?"

"She has some bleeding on the brain from the accident. Her brain is swelling inside her head."

"What does that mean?"

"She'll need to be admitted into intensive care so we can watch her closely. We're hoping the swelling will reduce on its own, but for now there isn't much we can do. If the swelling gets too bad, we'll have to do surgery."

"Holy shit." Jeremiah's breaths came out short and choppy through his nose and out through his mouth as he tried to control it. Panicking wouldn't help the situation. "Surgery?"

The doctor shoved his hands into the pocket of his lab coat. "Only if it gets bad. If the bleeding stops and the swelling goes down on its own, she'll be fine. Right now, we're monitoring her closely. We'll keep her sedated to let her brain heal. We've put a breathing tube down her throat to make sure she has enough oxygen and to keep her sedated."

The boys gasped.

"It's only precautionary at this point. She could breathe on her own, but we want to make sure the swelling goes down. This will protect her airway while we do that. So far, everything looks good. The bleeding is in some small vessels so they will likely resolve on their own."

"What about her leg?"

"She'll need surgery on it for a repair. We've stabilized it, but we don't want to do surgery until the issue with the bleeding is controlled. A couple of days with the break won't hurt anything. We've contacted our orthopedic surgeon to take a look at her x-rays. He's in complete agreement."

Jeremiah felt like his world had crumbled around him. His mother was hurt. His father was a mess. What else could go wrong?

"If you don't have any further questions, I'll leave you alone. We'll be transferring her to intensive care in a few moments. Then let you know what room shortly." The doctor put his hand on James' shoulder. "She'll be okay, Mr. Young. Have faith."

"Thank you, Doctor."

When the doctor left them alone, the three boys each took turns hugging their father. "She'll be okay, Dad. The doctor said so."

"God, I hope so. I can't lose her, Jeremiah. She's my life."

"I know." His cell phone jingled in his pocket. When he pulled it out, he saw it was Jeff. "Hey."

"What's up with Mom? You didn't call."

"We just talked to the doctor, Jeff. Geez, give me a minute." He told his brothers and his father he would fill Jeff in as he walked away so he could hear. After he gave his brother the report of what the doctor said, he closed the phone and moved back to be with his father. When the nurse came out to tell them what room they had moved his mother to, his father excused himself to go to the intensive care unit as they wouldn't let them all in at once. He told them he would come back out as soon as he talked to the nurse to check on Nina.

The boys took seats in the waiting room as they waited for news.

"She'll be fine. She has to be." Joey leaned forward with his elbows on his knees. "I want to kill the guy who did this. It's a good thing he's in jail."

"Me too," Jackson replied. "I don't see how you didn't kill him right there at the accident scene."

"Trust me. If the cops hadn't already had him in handcuffs, I would have. He was belligerent and self-righteous even though he was being arrested for drunk driving. I feel bad for his sister."

"Was it the same girl who got dumped on the floor?" Jackson asked.

"Yeah. The one I was talking to at The Dusty Boot."

"When you two left, I left too. I took a cab home since I'd had a bit to drink. I must have been right in front of the accident on the road."

"Probably. We hit a couple of other bars looking for him before the fire truck peeled out of the fire house headed for the accident."

"I was in my room when Jeff called," Jeremiah added. "I'd just gone to bed not too long before that."

"I wonder if we should go on home. There isn't much we can do here." Jason adjusted his hat on his head after he'd raked his fingers through his hair.

"I want to see Mom first," Jeremiah answered, with a resounding yeah from the rest of the group. "I hope Dad comes back out soon."

With each brother lost in their own thoughts, Jeremiah couldn't help but compare the four of them. They all had their hang-ups and trials as life went on around them.

Jason had Peyton now. They seemed happy. They hadn't been together long. He hoped his brother enjoyed married life. He'd been kind of against it for a while.

Jackson didn't have a girl and didn't seem to be worried about finding anyone. He did his part on the ranch, but he seemed really interested in the history of the land more so than the rest of them. Jeremiah knew he'd been doing a lot of digging into the past lately.

Joey did his own thing with the horses. He was kind of tied up with the neighbor girl, although at eighteen she seemed kind of young for him. He'd been hot for her for a few years. Jeremiah hoped he didn't get into trouble with hanging around her. Her daddy seemed kind of crazy.

And then there were his issues with Callie lately. He needed to talk to her, but his mom came first. It would have to wait until Nina was better. He just hoped he'd have the time to straighten things out before all hell broke loose or she found someone else. He couldn't handle that if she did.

"Hey, Jeremiah. I saw Callie with Craig tonight at the bar." Joey sat back in the chair with his legs crossed at the ankle.

"And?"

"She didn't seem happy."

"No?"

"When are you going to go after that girl?"

"What the hell is it to you?"

"Because if you don't pull your head out of your ass, you're gonna lose her."

"I plan on talking to her."

"Talking isn't going to get shit done with her. She needs a man to take control."

He narrowed his gaze on his brother, thinking about the conversation at hand. "How would you know?"

"I talked to her. She wants you, not Craig."

"I talked to her tonight too. She basically told me to eat shit and die."

"She was just mad. She's upset because you've been giving her the cold shoulder treatment, or so she thinks."

"No I haven't! I've been trying to tell her she belongs to me."

"Somehow I don't think Callie is the type of woman to be told what to do," Jason added his two cents. "She seems pretty strong-willed. She reminds me a lot of Peyton."

"Yeah, she does," Jeremiah replied. "She doesn't like me giving her orders."

"Have you had sex with her already?"

"Yeah."

"And?"

"It was mind-blowing. We're good together, but I have to make her see we need each other, we complement each other in our personalities. She's a great woman." Jeremiah sat forward. "Did you know she volunteers a lot at the nursing home?"

"Really?"

"So what is the problem here?" Joey asked. "As I see it, you tell her you want her, she drops everything to be with you. Done deal."

Jeremiah laughed so hard, he hurt as he doubled over. "Yeah, somehow that isn't going to work with Callie."

"It didn't work with Peyton either. She's very headstrong."

"Did you know she's become good friends with Mandy?" Jeremiah asked. "In turn I would think that makes her pretty good friends with Peyton. Could be bad news if they got into too much trouble together."

"I'll talk to Peyton."

"Yeah, you do that, bro." Joey laughed. "If I know Peyton at all, she'll tell you to stick it up your ass."

The boys shared a laugh at Jason's expense as he glanced at his phone. "I'm going to call my wife."

Jeremiah thought about it for a moment before he asked, "Did Callie leave with Craig?"

"No."

"She didn't, huh?" He smiled. Maybe things were looking up for him after all. Jeremiah rubbed the fingers on his right hand, hoping to bring some feeling back into them. He was getting kind of worried that they kept going numb on him at odd times. Maybe had a pinched nerve or something. "I should call her."

"No, you should talk to her, but not by phone. This needs to be a face-to-face conversation," Jackson said. "She's important to you, yes?"

"Yeah."

"Then you need to make it a personal talk."

"You're right."

Their father came out several minutes later. "The nurse said you can each go in one at a time. Don't stay more than a few minutes."

"I'm assuming you are staying here, Dad?" Joey asked, getting to his feet.

"Of course. I won't leave her side if I don't have to."

"We'll hold down the ranch." Jackson stood as well. "We should make this fast so Dad can go back in there."

"I knew I could count on you boys."

They each filed in one after the other until only Jeremiah was left. He wanted to see her, but then again, he didn't. He wasn't one for hospitals, and to see his mother with a tube down her throat on a breathing machine messed with his brain. She'd been too lively and giving just a few short hours ago. What was she doing on the road at that late hour anyway? He'd have to ask his father when he had a chance.

The moment he walked in, his heart sank. Tubes and wires strung to the box above her head monitored several things at once. He didn't know what they meant. It frightened him a little. As long as they weren't making loud beeping noises, he figured everything was okay. "Mom?"

The nurse came in behind him. "Talk to her. She might be able to hear you even though she's sedated." She checked a few things, and then turned to leave. "You can stay five minutes."

"Thank you."

"You're welcome."

He picked up his mother's limp hand. "I'm sorry you are here, Mom. When we talked earlier, I never thought you'd be in this shape a few short hours later. You'll be okay though. The doctor said you should be okay." A tear rolled down his cheek, but he wiped it away angrily. "We'll get the guy who did this to you. I promise. He'll pay for hurting you."

Her fingers moved slightly.

"Mom?"

No more movement followed and he realized it was probably an involuntary reflex. It made him feel better though, hoping she could hear him so she would know they were all there for her no matter what it took to make her better.

He squeezed her hand before he walked slowly back toward the door. After several peeks over his shoulder, he finally wandered out to the waiting room where his brothers stood talking softly. "Are we ready to go?"

"Yeah," Joey said. "You have your truck, Dad, so you should be good."

"I'll be sleeping in the waiting room since they won't let me stay in her room. If one of you could bring me some clean clothes at some point, I would appreciate it." He glanced down at the mud on his boots. "I've been wearing these since this morning."

"Will do, Dad," Jackson answered. "We'll see you in a few hours. Some of the other boys might come in rather than us. I'm sure they'll want to see Mom too."

"That's fine. Just tell them what to expect so they aren't shocked when they see your mother. I can't imagine walking in on that without knowing. I don't know if you told them about the tubes?"

"Yeah, I did, so they should be prepared."

"Good. Make sure to tell them they can't stay long."

"We will." Jeremiah hugged his dad before he stepped back. "Tell her we love her and we'll see her later."

"Thanks boys, for being here. You don't know how much this means to me and your mother."

"We're family. It's what families do," Jeremiah answered.

"I know, but you never know how people are going to react when things like this happen. We love you boys."

"We love you too, Dad." The other three murmured in agreement to Jeremiah's statement. He knew his dad was having a hard time in this situation, but their love was strong. They would make it through. "Let's go before it gets too much later. I have early duty."

When they walked into the main lodge three hours after they'd left, none of the brothers had gone to bed. They wanted a full report which between him, Joey, Jason, and Jackson, they got every bit of information the four of them had received.

"I'm going to bed, guys. I have to be up in like three hours," Jeremiah said, stifling a yawn with his hand.

"I think we should all go on to bed," Jeff replied. "There isn't anything else we can do tonight. Dad will call me if Mom's condition changes. We have a ranch to run."

All of the boys agreed, finally filing off to their respective bedrooms and abodes leaving Jeremiah to check the room one last time before he went to bed. When he finally got to crawl under the sheets, he drifted off into dreamless sleep.

Morning came early for Jeremiah as he rolled over with a groan and smacked his alarm to silence the screech. If the guests wanted a cheerful, smiling cowboy this morning they wouldn't get one, he was afraid. He rolled over to his side and wearily sat up. When he climbed to his feet, his left leg felt numb and tingling, like he'd sat on it and put it to sleep. *This is nuts.* He stumbled a few steps before he regained his coordination and could head for the bathroom. He needed a shower this morning more than he needed anything. He had to wake up somehow and coffee alone wouldn't do it. It was going to be a long day.

After his shower, he walked across the room with a towel slung low over his hips to retrieve some clean jeans and shirt.

A timid knock sounded at his door.

"Just a minute." He glanced out the window to find the woman he stood Callie up for, waiting on his stoop. After he threw on his jeans, he didn't bother with a shirt as she knocked again. "Well hello, Brenda, isn't it?"

She stepped inside his cabin and shut the door.

"Can I help you with something?"

"Yes. I'm a horny guest. You need to take care of your guest."

"Listen, Brenda, I don't think that is such a good idea."

"Why not? You were going to the other night until you got that phone call and then dumped me back at the ranch like yesterday's garbage. I didn't appreciate your treatment of me, Jeremiah."

"I'm sorry, but my mother has a strict policy against us messing with those staying at the ranch. I was following her rules."

"I call bullshit. You had every intention of fucking me out there on our ride."

"Can I be truthful with you?"

She walked him backward until his back hit the wall with a thud. Her hands found his chest with both palms resting flat on his skin. "I wish you would."

"I have a girlfriend."

"Is that who called you?"

"Yeah."

"You were going to cheat on your girlfriend?" She slapped him hard across the cheek. "You lowlife scumbag! I can't believe you were going to cheat on her without any regard to her feelings at all."

"But you—"

"Never mind what I was going to do. I didn't realize you had a girlfriend." She spun on her heels and disappeared through the door with a hearty slam.

"Well, shit."

He rubbed his cheek where she'd slapped him before grabbing a shirt, slipping it on and then going to find his socks and boots. If that didn't wake him up, nothing would.

When he went through the main lodge door several minutes later, he found most of the people who were staying on the ranch already eating. His brothers had already got their food so he went through the line to get his own plate and sit down next to Jackson. "Any word from Dad this morning?"

"No, nothing or Jeff hasn't mentioned anything so I would think he hasn't heard anything." Jackson glanced over at him. "You look like shit, bro, and why do you have a nice hand print on your cheek?"

"Brenda paid me a visit this morning."

"Brenda?"

"The guest I took out riding the other day. I think she planned on a morning romp. I told her I had a girlfriend and she slapped me."

"You don't have a girlfriend."

"Not yet, but I hope to by the end of today. I want to have a nice talk with Callie after all my chores are done."

"I hope you two get things straightened out."

"Oh, I plan to. Otherwise, I might have to kidnap her until she listens to me." He shoveled eggs into his mouth, then sipped the hot coffee he'd retrieved before he'd sat down. "Heaven."

"I think we are all feeling the effects of our late night."

"Yeah, but we had to be there for Dad and each other."

"Tragedy always brings people together."

"We are family. It's what we do."

"You got it, bro."

Jeremiah quietly finished his breakfast as he listened to the conversation going around the family dining room table. The guests seemed subdued today even though he didn't think any of them knew what had happened the night before.

The moment he was finished, he stood, took his plate to the wash bin and headed out to the stable to take his first round of guests on the ride over the hills of their home. The boys all traded off doing rides to give each other a break or to do other things around the ranch, but today he could use the time to think. He had plans to make to woo Callie and let her know she was the girl for him.

The sun had begun to set in the sky when Jeremiah emerged from the barn. He'd done his cowboy duty for the day, but now he needed to check on things with the ranch finances.

Joey walked out of the barn behind him, clapping him on the shoulder as they walked toward the main lodge. "Thanks for the help with the mare."

"No problem. I don't get to do enough of this stuff working in an office most of the time."

"I know." Joey laughed. "You need to spend more time in the sun." He compared the tan lines on their arms. "You're lookin' might pale there, bro."

Jeremiah shook his head as he smiled. It felt good to smile for a change with everything going on in his life. He needed that. The break had done him good. "I know what you mean."

Jeff joined them at the door of the lodge. "I heard from Dad. The bleeding has stopped and the pressure is reducing in Mom's brain. They still have her on the breathing machine as a precaution, but they plan to remove it tomorrow."

"Did some of the other brothers go into town today to see her?"

"Yeah. They been going in shifts so they don't overwhelm the poor nurses with our sheer numbers."

"Probably a good idea."

Mandy came out to ring the dinner bell. "Hey guys. How's your mom?"

Jeff gave her a report as soon as she got the guests heading to the dining room for dinner.

"Good. Sounds like things are looking up."

"Yes, they are. We're fortunate she wasn't hurt worse. She is going to need some physical therapy for her leg, but otherwise the doctors think everything else is resolving well."

"That's awesome. She's a nice lady," Mandy replied, stepping behind the serving trays.

The boys headed toward the family table to wait their turn while the guests filled their plates high with food. Jeremiah smiled. Callie would fit in well with the family. *Whoa! I'm thinking long-term here?* He glanced outside and realized yeah, he was thinking long-term relationship with Callie and it felt good. He hoped he could get her on board with the plan.

Chapter Eleven

Callie sat on the couch in the front room flipping through channels on the television without even seeing what might be on. Her mind dwelled on Jeremiah. She'd heard about his mother's accident the other night and wondered how she was doing. She wanted to be there for him, but she didn't know how to go about doing that.

Talk gets around in a small town. It hadn't taken long for everyone to know about it. She felt bad. Nina was a great lady.

The doorbell rang. "I'll get it, Dad."

She climbed to her feet and walked toward the front door. Her life had been pretty busy since her and Mandy's body shots escapades at the bar. She'd been on several dates, following Jeremiah's demand to date other people, but none of those guys were him. None came close to creating the electric impulses he caused in her every time he touched her. Didn't he know they were meant to be together? *Apparently he's too damned stubborn to realize it.*

The bell rang again. "I'm coming."

She pulled open the door and her jaw dropped open. Jeremiah stood on the stoop with a dozen red roses in his hands, dressed to the nines in pressed jeans, brushed clean boots, shiny belt buckle, white dress shirt, suit jacket and his dress black Stetson on his head.

"Hi."

"Hi."

"I'm here to officially ask you on a date. Get dressed."

She jammed her hands on her hips as she frowned. "What the hell, Jeremiah? You can't just show up at my door, ordering me to get dressed up for you. This is bullshit! I'm not at your beck and—"

He leaned in to kiss her full on the mouth before his tongue swept along the seam of her lips and she melted against his chest. When they parted she was breathless and tingly all over.

"I'm here to wine and dine you. Please? Put something pretty on. I want to spend the evening with you."

A breathless sigh escaped her. "Okay."

He grinned when she stepped back to do exactly what he told her. *I'm a terribly weak woman where he is concerned.*

She headed down the hall to her room to shower and change. He'd just have to wait while she got ready since he'd shown up without calling first. She frowned now that she had her wits about her. How does he get off showing up without calling? What if she had a date with someone else?

Her anger exploded through her as she got into the shower, washed her hair and her body and then grabbed a towel to dry off. Yes, she wanted him. She'd do about anything to have him, but this ordering her around shit was for the birds. *I'll show him!* She pulled out the slinky red dress she'd worn before, high heeled shoes and silky stockings. *He's going to know exactly what he's missing when I'm done with him tonight.*

After putting on makeup and blow drying her hair to a pretty upswept hairdo, she slid into her shoes and pronounced herself ready to the reflection in mirror. "Eat your heart out, Jeremiah."

When she walked back down the corridor to find him standing in front of the picture window looking out over the front yard, she stopped to wonder if she was doing the right thing. He was here to take her out. Maybe he'd already realized he wanted to be with her and this was his way of showing her?

"Jeremiah?"

The look on his face made it totally worth the trouble she'd taken to make herself beautiful. His eyes widened as his jaw hung open in appreciation. "You look fabulous."

"Thank you." She glanced down at her dress, tugging on the hem just a little since it only reached mid-thigh when she stood. "I didn't know where we were going, but since you are dressed pretty fancy, I figured I'd better too."

"I'm taking you somewhere special. We need to have a serious conversation about us, but this is going to be a beginning."

Confusion clouded her thoughts. "Beginning?"

"Yes, but I won't say more until we have some alone time." He ran his fingers over her bare shoulder. "You'll need a wrap of some kind. It's chilly out there."

"Let me grab something out of the closet." When she turned around, she noticed he'd found a vase somewhere in one of the cupboards to put the flowers in. "Thank you for the flowers. They're beautiful."

"They don't compare to you."

"You're being such a sweet-talker tonight. What's up?"

"This is me. I hope you don't mind."

"Not at all," she said, grabbing a wrap from the closet and draping it over her shoulders. "Will this be heavy enough? It's wool."

"Should be. The restaurant is indoors so it shouldn't be too bad." His gazed wandered down her frame from head to toe. "Did I tell you how beautiful you are?"

"Yes, but you can say it again. I don't mind."

"How about if I change it up a bit? You are gorgeous." He leaned in to brush her lips lightly with his own. "I can't wait to get you alone."

Wetness coated her panties at the look in his eyes. Desire. Need. Even something she wasn't sure she wanted to name, reflected in his steely grey gaze. *Just maybe?*

He held out his hand for her to take and she slipped hers into his grasp. Her other hand held a small clutch purse with her cell phone, keys and wallet. One always had to be prepared for a night to go completely wrong when on a date. Not that it would with Jeremiah, but one never knew when they might need to get a cab home.

"Shall we?"

She swallowed, trying to wet her parched throat. She wasn't sure what to expect tonight and the thought scared the crap out of her. "Daddy? I'm going out with Jeremiah. Don't wait up."

"Have fun," her father called from his bedroom.

As they walked out to his truck, she got the feeling tonight was going to be a game changer in their relationship. Something had changed his mind about her, although she didn't know what, she wanted to shout to the heavens in thanks.

Jeremiah opened her door for her before she stepped up to slide inside the cab. He shut the door and then walked around the front of the vehicle to get into the other side. Her appreciative sigh echoed in the silence surrounding her. *Boy, was he sharp all dressed up and looking good.*

After he slid inside and started the truck, she snuck a glance in his direction. The jacket molded to his chest, the white shirt was open at the throat, and the jeans were pressed to sharpness. The ultimate cowboy. "You look really nice tonight."

"Thanks. I wanted to dress up for you."

"Are we going to talk now?"

"No. Let's wait until we are sitting at a nice table with a glass of wine or whatever. I want your undivided attention."

"You have it now."

He laughed. "Good, but I want to be able to look into your pretty blue eyes when we talk."

"Sounds serious."

"It is."

"Won't you at least—"

"Nope. You'll have to wait until we get the restaurant."

She crossed her arms over her chest in a silent pout. She didn't want to wait. It would kill her! Okay, maybe not, but the little grin on Jeremiah's face made her wonder what the heck he might be up to.

When they arrived at the restaurant forty-five minutes later, she realized it was one of the swanky places on the riverfront in San Antonio. She'd never been to this particular restaurant before either, but she knew it was expensive and you had to have reservations to get in.

As they approached the podium, Jeremiah's warm hand rested at her back. "Young. We had reservations for seven."

"Ah, yes, sir. Just one moment. Let me check to see if your table is ready."

As they stood waiting, she leaned into Jeremiah's body a little to absorb his warmth and he surrounded her with his arms. It was a nice feeling.

A few minutes later, the guy returned. "Right this way."

He escorted them to a dimly light corner of the restaurant completely situated off by itself. The table had rose petals sprinkled on it with more on the chairs and even some on the floor. It was gorgeous.

"You did this?"

"Yes."

Tears burned her eyes as she tried desperately not to cry. "It's beautiful." He held her chair as she slid into her spot at the table before she spread a napkin on her lap.

The waiter arrived a moment later with a bottle of wine, showed it to Jeremiah, then poured two glasses when Jeremiah gave him a nod of approval. The whole scene was surreal to her. Why was he doing this she didn't know, but she liked it.

She took a sip of the wine and rolled it around on her tongue before she swallowed. "Very tasty, although I'm not a wine connoisseur."

"Neither am I, but it sounded good when I set this up."

She smiled and looked down at her hands folded on the tabletop. "Nice."

He reached over to take her hand in his. "Shall we talk now or wait until after we eat?"

"Now would be good, but we might want to wait until after dinner. Depending on how this goes, I might not have an appetite."

"I think you'll like how this goes, Callie."

"Okay."

He inhaled like he was trying to steady his nerves before taking a leap into a very deep pool of water. "I think I'm in love with you."

"You think?" she asked, tipping her head to the side.

"Well since I've never been in love before, I'm not certain, but after talking to my parents and brothers, I'm pretty sure, yeah, I'm in love with you." He intertwined their fingers, then rubbed the pad of his finger over the knuckle on her thumb. "I've been miserable without you. After we made love that one time, I haven't been able to get you out of my mind. It's been driving me nuts." He dropped his gaze to the table. "Believe me, I tried. I didn't want to fall in love right now, but alas, here I am. I want you in my life. I need you in my bed and I think you feel the same way."

"Jeremiah, I've been in love with you since ninth grade." She smiled as his head snapped up and her gaze met his.

"You have?"

"Yes. I couldn't figure out a way to get you to see me as a woman who might complete you instead of Callie, your friend at the garage."

"You've always been my friend."

"I know, but I wanted to be more."

"I guess I was too blind to see you in a different light than what I'd seen you in forever. After you started hanging out with other men in front of me, I didn't like how it made me feel. I wanted to tear you from their side and drag you away like some caveman."

She laughed. "So that's where the behavior came from."

He grinned. "You have to admit you kinda like that about me."

"Yeah, I guess I do."

The waiter arrived to take their order, but the moment he left, Jeremiah took her hand again. "We need to decide on where we go from here."

"I know I want to be with you and only you so I think we should date exclusively."

"I agree. I don't want anyone else." His gaze was intense as he said the words. He meant everything, including the I love you. "I love you, Callie."

"I love you too, Jeremiah."

"We should get married." His eyes brightened as a smile spread across his lips.

She pulled her hand out of his grasp and held it up. "Whoa! Take a step back. You're going kind of fast for me."

"Fast? I thought when two people loved each other, they got married."

"Yeah, maybe eventually, but we just started this journey. Let's date for a while before we jump on the marriage bandwagon."

He tilted his head to the side. "Why are you so gun-shy now?"

"I'm not. I just think we should take this kind of slow."

"Okay. I'm with you then. We'll date, go on picnics, go out for dinner, go to movies, you know, all those couple things."

"What changed your mind about me?"

He grasped her hand again. "My mom's accident. I talked to them before it happened about you and me."

"You did?"

"Yeah. She told me to stay away from you."

Frustration and anger zipped through her. *Told him to stay away from her, did she?* "Wow. Really?"

"Yep, but telling a Young to stay away from a woman is like throwing meat on the grill at a barbeque and then telling all the people there they can't have it."

"Okay, blonde moment here, I don't understand. Why did she tell you to stay away from me?"

"Not because she didn't want us together, Callie. My mom knew exactly how I would react to the statement. She knew I'd do the opposite so she was playing a little reverse psychology thing on me. She wants us together, trust me on this."

"Are you sure?"

"Positive." He brought her fingers to his lips, kissing the backs before he continued. "She loves you and would welcome you into the family in a heartbeat, baby."

"Okay."

Their dinner arrived as two steamy plates. Hers was steak and lobster tail where his was a huge ribeye. As they ate in silence, Callie contemplated all Jeremiah had said before dinner. He loved her? Why was she not quite convinced he'd changed his mind too quickly. It seemed too easy to her. Jeremiah rubbed the fingers of his right hand, shaking them like they'd gone to sleep. "What's wrong?"

"My fingers have been going numb. I'm going to make a doctor appointment this week. I've had some other things I'd like to talk to him about to see what I should do."

"Like what?"

"Blurry vision but the numbness mostly." He smiled. "Nothing to worry about. It's a pinched nerve probably. I got bucked off a horse about a month ago."

She frowned. "You could have been seriously hurt, Jeremiah. You should have gone to the doctor when it happened. Please call to make an appointment tomorrow. I'm worried now."

"That's sweet. I like you worried about me."

"I'm serious." She wanted to hit him with her plate. *Stubborn man.*

"Me too. I'll call in the morning. I'll be fine."

She exhaled before picking up her wine glass with a shaky hand to drain the remainder. This scared her more than anything. The blurry vision and numbness could be anything, but since they admitted their love for each other, it meant a whole lot more.

When dinner concluded, they walked out to the truck with their arms around each other as she soaked up being close to him like this.

"Come back to my place. I want to love on you."

"Okay, but I can't stay all night. I have to open the garage tomorrow for Dad. He has a doctor's appointment in the morning."

The frown on his face made her smile. He looked like a lost little boy who'd just had someone take his favorite toy away.

"You'll be fine."

"I want you with me all the time."

"We need to take this relationship slowly. We haven't been a couple until now. This is all new."

"I know, but I want to show you off, be with you, sleep with you, wake up next to you. You know, all the things lovers do." He opened her door, lifted her by the waist, and deposited her on the seat, buckled her seatbelt for her and then leaned in to kiss her on the lips. He shut the door before going around to the driver's side.

As they drove back to Bandera, he held her hand over the center of the truck's console the entire trip. She liked this new relationship they had. It was different and special. She'd always known they would be good for each other. It took him some time to figure it out, but now that he had, everything should be fantastic.

"How is your mom doing?" She frowned. "What happened anyway?"

"She's doing better. A drunk driver hit her on the back road to our ranch the other night, head-on. She had some bleeding on the brain so they put a tube down her throat so they could keep her asleep and make sure she has enough oxygen to her brain. They needed the swelling to go down and the bleeding would hopefully stop on its own. It has and they are going to take out the tube tomorrow. I plan to go in to see her sometime in the afternoon. Do you want to come?"

"I don't think that would be a good idea, Jeremiah. I mean, I'm not family."

"You will be eventually."

"But I'm not right now and don't put the cart before the horse. We might find we can't stand each other once we get to know one another better."

He kissed her fingers. "Not going to happen, sweetheart. I love you."

"You have no idea how much I like hearing you say those words."

"You'll hear them a lot more in the coming years."

"I hope so, but no, you go on and see her. I'll wait until she comes home and gets some rest before I stop by."

"She'll have to have rehab for a bit. She broke her leg too."

"Wow. It's a wonder she wasn't killed."

"The guy would have been a dead man if she had."

"I'm sorry. I don't mean to be morbid. I'm glad she wasn't hurt worse."

He shuddered as he squeezed her fingers. "Me too."

Several minutes later, they pulled up the gate of Thunder Ridge and she waited while he punched in the code to open the gate.

"I love this place."

"Me too."

"I hear there are ghosts on the property."

"Yep. A cowboy, a couple upstairs in the main lodge, and a group of children who play in the yard."

"Have you ever done any research on who they are to maybe find out why they're trapped here?"

"No, but I've thought about it. I hear the children the most since I'm out in the cabin area."

"Do you hear them a lot?"

"Yeah. If it's real quiet you can hear them almost every night, especially if I'm coming in late or something."

"That would kind of freak me out, I think." She shivered at the thought.

"Don't worry. I'll protect you. Besides, they're children."

"I know, but ghosts are ghosts."

They pulled up in front of his cabin. When he shut the engine off, he waited for a minute before coming around to open hers. *Gentleman to the core.*

"You're safe. I don't hear them right now."

"Good."

He swept her up into his arms, carrying her toward the door of his cabin after he pushed the truck door closed with his foot.

"You shouldn't be carrying me."

"Why not? I want to hold you."

"Yeah, but if your back is messed up or something is pinched, you could be hurting yourself more by carrying me."

"I'll take my chances." He reached over to kiss her on the lips before she could say another word. "Reach in my shirt pocket for my keys and open the door."

"Okay."

Once the door was opened, he carried her inside to deposit her on the bed. "Stay there."

She kicked off her heels and tucked her legs beneath her as she watched him shut the door and flip on the light.

His space was so much like him, western décor, wrought iron headboard and footboard, wooden nightstands and a huge computer desk, never mind the big-ass television with a top of the line gaming system. He liked his toys apparently.

"Why are you still dressed?"

"Because I thought you might like the honors of peeling this dress off me."

"Oh, yeah. I could do that."

She stood at the side of the bed as he sauntered closer. "You look so awesome tonight in your dressy gear, but I like the rugged cowboy too."

"You do, huh?"

"Yeah." She watched as he peeled off his jacket and hung it on the back of a chair before he toed off his boots and walked over to stand in front of her in his white shirt, pressed jeans, and socks.

He smoothed his hands over her bare shoulders. "You look hot in that dress, but I want you out of it more."

"Take it off then."

Chapter Twelve

With one hand on the zipper at the back of her dress, he slowly peeled it down until the material stopped right at the curve of her butt. The bodice gapped open at her chest, the only thing holding it up were her arms at her sides. He hooked a finger at the bodice on each side and peeled it down her body until the whole thing fell into a pool at her feet. The strapless bra she wore left little to the imagination as he skimmed his fingertips over the swell of her breast.

"I like these."

"My boobs or my bra?"

"Boobs. They are so pretty." He reached behind her to unhook her bra, letting it fall to the floor too. "I love how the little nipples are standing straight up for me." He cupped her right breast in his palm. "They want me."

"Yes, they do." Her voice came out in a breathless sigh. Wanting him this badly made her hot and cold at the same time. Shivers rolled through her whole body, leaving goose bumps on her skin in their wake.

"Are you cold?"

"No. Excited, yes." She splayed her hands on his chest. "I want you out of these clothes."

"In a minute. I want to worship you."

"Such a sweet talker."

"You know it, darlin'."

"There is my favorite word coming from a cowboy."

"What?"

"Darlin' in that little southern drawl. Makes me so horny."

His hands did a slow crawl from her shoulders to her fingertips before each one cupped a breast again. "You weren't horny already?"

"Oh, hell yes I was, but it makes it worse."

"I'll call you darlin' anytime you want me to."

His lips skimmed over her jawline on their way to the shell of her ear. "I'll remember that." This man knew exactly what to do to ramp her up. He did it so well, she almost wondered where he learned all the little tricks he did with his hands and mouth. She might have to ask him one day so she could thank the woman who had taught him to make love. When he laid her back on the bed, she lifted her arms over her head. She remembered how he liked it when she didn't move while he skimmed her body with his mouth or fingers. Pleasing Jeremiah was her utmost concern.

He hooked two fingers in the waistband of her nylons and panties and shimmied them down her legs until he could peel them off her feet. "Open for me." She spread her legs, giving him an unadulterated view of her pussy. "So wet." He dipped one finger inside her, making her eyes roll back in her head. "Uh-uh. Eyes on me."

Their gazes held as he slowly slid between her thighs and then licked her pussy from slit to clit.

"Ah, God!"

"Mmm."

The vibration of his lips on her clit almost threw her into a climax, but she tamped the need down. She didn't want to come yet. She wanted to hold out as long as possible for the ultimate release. He wasn't having any of her holding back though. He went in for the kill, licking, sucking, and doing little figure eights on her clit in a rapid fashion.

"Jeremiah!" She threw her head back on the comforter as her whole body vibrated and the force of her climax bowed her back.

He seemed pleased with himself as he licked his way up her body until he reached her mouth. The smile on his lips was infectious.

"Good."

"Better than good. Amazing."

"Oh, I like amazing. Shall we try for two?"

"Mmm. Only if it's from you inside me. I want to feel you deep."

"I can handle that." He reached over into the nightstand drawer for a condom, tore it open with his teeth and rolled it on with one hand.

"You are pretty good at that."

"I've had some practice."

"I bet."

A soft moan escaped her lips when his cock found the entrance to her pussy and slowly slid inside. "So good."

"You feel fantastic. I've been waiting weeks for this."

"Only weeks?"

"Since the last time, so yeah, it's been weeks."

She looked up into his soft, pewter-colored eyes. "You haven't been with anyone since we were together?"

"No. I couldn't. I only wanted you."

"Me too."

"I love you, Callie."

"I love you too, Jeremiah. You are my life."

He slowly started to move as she wrapped her thighs around his hips. He softly kissed her nose and her cheeks, taking the wetness of the tears from her face.

"Why are you crying?"

"Because I never thought we'd be here like this. I never thought I'd hear you say those words to me. I've waited so long for you."

"I'm sorry it took me this long to see you for the woman of my dreams."

As he continued his slow assault on her senses, she lost the ability to think of anything beyond Jeremiah and what he was doing to her body. Her nipples pebbled into hard little nubs when he sucked first one before the other, between his lips. His tongue worshipped her body, moving from her lips to her breasts and back again as he slowly pumped his hips, driving his cock in and out of her body.

"Uh, Jeremiah?"

"Yeah?"

"Can you speed it up a bit? You're killing me." He pushed up so he was standing between her thighs, shoved his hands under her hips and slammed his pelvis against hers. Heaven on a hill, he was fantastic when he made love.

"This is fucking." He slowed his pace to a crawl again. "This is making love." He moved a little faster. "I like both. Which do you prefer?"

"I want you to shut up and fuck me."

"Your wish is my command, darlin'." He shoved against her so hard, he had to hold her in place with his hands. "I'm going to fuck you until you scream for me."

"I already did once."

"Do it again."

"Oh, oh, oh." Each thrust hit just the right spot inside her to drive her up the side of the cliff, leaving her hanging on by her fingernails. "A little bit…yes!" Her scream echoed off the walls of his cabin as she hit her climax a second time.

A few uncoordinated thrusts later, Jeremiah groaned as he came apart as well, slumping against her chest in a heap of boneless mass meant to squash her into the bed. She grunted at the weight on her chest. He had to weigh two hundred pounds at least. "I can't breathe."

"Sorry." He slowly slid out of her with a groan before he walked toward the bathroom to dispose of the condom. When he returned, he had a warm wash cloth in his hands to clean her up with.

"You don't have to do that."

"I want to." Before he wiped her off though, he took one finger, dipped it inside her pussy and then smeared the wetness around her back hole. "I want you here too."

"You do?"

"I want you every way possible, darlin'. This is one more fantasy of mine."

"Okay."

"Do you like anal?"

"I love it, actually. It's one of my favorite positions."

He smiled as he wiped her pussy from top to bottom. "Good. Next time."

"And when will there be a next time?"

"Soon. I need you with me always, so yeah, soon."

She pushed herself up on the pillow. "Come here. I want some cuddling."

The minute he sat back against the headboard, she laid her head on his chest and sighed in contentment. This is what she wanted. Just him. Forever. "I hope your mom will be okay."

"I'm sure she will. They said things were going better."

"It must have been terrible to see her in such a state." She shuddered until his hand made some soothing circles, rubbing up and down her arm. "I would hate to see my dad like that."

"You know, I don't think I ever heard what happened to your mom. I just knew she wasn't around."

"She left us when I was three. I don't remember her much. She's only a few faded pictures and memories to me."

"I'm sorry, darlin'."

"It's not a big deal. She contacted me several years ago wanting to be a part of my life, but I wouldn't. I found out she had a drug problem and wanted money. She figured if she got all cozy with me, I would give her some, I guess. I have my dad. That's all I need."

"Well, I'm sure my mother will become the mother you didn't have. She's like that."

Her fingers swirled in the hair on his chest, entwining them together like their hearts belong there. "I'd be more than happy to have your mom become a surrogate mother for me. I love your mom."

"I do too. She's great and now that they are financially secure, their life will get so much better, I think."

"Financially secure?"

"Yeah. I've been investing for them. They have quite a bit of money in the bank now so they don't have to work anymore if they don't want to, but I can't see them doing that. They love this ranch more than any of us. It's their life."

"I bet, but I'm glad they are doing so well." She sifted her fingers through the hair on his chest. "You should be investing for yourself too, since you are so good at it." He grinned, but didn't reply, making her wonder what he might be hiding. She studied his expression for a moment before sitting up on the bed. "I hate to fuck and run, but I should be getting home. I have to work in the morning."

"All right."

He moved to grab his clothes as she stood by the side of the bed to locate her own. After she slipped on her dress without her bra, and nylons, she shoved her feet into her shoes and proclaimed herself ready to go as she grabbed her wrap off the chair where it had landed when they stumbled inside the cabin.

Once he managed to shove his feet into his boots, he grabbed his keys and hat. "Let's get you home then."

* * * *

The next morning Jeremiah peeled open his gritty eyelids to the early sunrise. He had some work to do on the finances this morning before he went into San Antonio to see his mom. Hopefully by the time he got there they would have removed the breathing tube so she could sit up and talk to him. He didn't want to see her like she'd been a few nights ago.

When he threw his legs over the side of the bed and stood, he stumbled, leaning to the left. He grabbed the bedpost to steady himself. His left leg felt numb from the hip down like he'd slept on it. "Okay, this is getting crazy. I really need to call the doctor."

He shook out his leg until the feeling came back and he could walk on it again without falling. *This isn't normal. People my age don't have these kinds of things happen. It's probably a pinched nerve or something.*

After he managed to get dressed, he heard the breakfast bell ring as he grabbed his wallet, hat and truck keys from his nightstand. He glanced back at the bed with a smile, remembering the night before. Callie took his breath away, spread out like a virgin for the offering. *Damn, I have it bad for her and I like it.*

Tugging on the handle, he opened the door. A small group of people were headed to the main lodge for breakfast from the cabin just up the way. A couple of little kids were laughing and pushing each other like he and his brothers used to do when they were young.

"Hey mister, are you a real cowboy?"

"Yes, sir."

"Do you ride horses?"

"All the time. I've even ridden a few who weren't very tame."

"Really?"

"Yep."

"I want to ride a horse."

"Well, tell your mom and dad we have horses available for everyone to ride. My brother Joey will take good care of you if you want to learn to ride. He's a great cowboy."

"How many brothers do you have?" the boy asked as they opened the door to the lodge.

"Eight."

"Wow. I only have one and he's a pain in the ass."

"Aaron Jefferson. I will not have you talking like that!" his mother yelled and Jeremiah smiled.

"Sorry, Mom." The kid grinned at Jeremiah and then took his place in line for food as Jeremiah headed for the coffee in the corner.

Jeff came around the corner with Terri and their boys. He left Terri at the table to grab some coffee himself. "Did you hear from Dad this morning? Have they taken the tube out?"

"He hasn't called. I figured nothing has changed yet."

"I plan to go into town to see her later. I'm hoping she's awake and talking."

Jeff leaned in to talk softly. "Dad told me what you've done with the finances."

"Oh?"

"Yeah." He glanced at Terri as he smiled. "Can you help me do some investing?"

"Sure."

After a minute, he whispered, "Are there really millions in the bank?"

"Yes."

"Wow. How the hell did you do that?"

"Smart investments."

"I would say so." He clapped Jeremiah on the shoulder before he headed to the table to sit next to his girl and their boys.

Jeremiah was glad his brother trusted him enough to ask for financial advice. It meant a lot to him to have a close relationship to his family.

After breakfast, he went into his office to go over the bills and income from the last month at the ranch to see how much more he could safely take to put into investments for his parents. He didn't want to bleed the ranch dry.

The computer screen blurred, making him rub his eyes to bring it back into focus. *That's it. I'm calling the doctor.* He grabbed the office phone from the receiver, pulled out the rolodex of cards he kept and then dialed Dr. Evans' number.

"Dr. Evans' office. How may I help you?"

"Hi. This is Jeremiah Young. I need to make an appointment with Dr. Evans."

"Can I ask what this is concerning?"

"I'm not sick or I don't think so, but I've been having some blurry vision, numbness and tingling in my hands and legs. I fell off a horse about two weeks ago and I want to make sure I didn't pinch a nerve or something in my back since I landed pretty hard."

Once the receptionist made him an appointment for two days later, he hung up the phone so he could go back to work on the financials. He had to get the bills straight this afternoon before leaving to visit his mom.

When he walked into the hospital room several hours later, he was delighted to see his mother sitting up in bed eating some Jello. "You look a lot better than when I saw you a few days ago." He leaned in a kissed her on the cheek. "How do you feel?"

"Like I've been kicked by a horse."

"I'm sure." He took a seat in a chair near the side of the bed. "Are they going to move you to a regular room soon?"

"Yes, later today. I have to have surgery on the leg tomorrow."

"Well, that sucks."

"How are things at home?"

"They are fine, Mom. Don't worry. We've got it."

She patted his hand and then squeezed his fingers. "I know you do, Jeremiah. I'm not worried."

He raised an eyebrow.

"Okay, just a little, but you know me. I can't not worry."

"Jeff is handling the daily things. The rest of us are doing what needs to be done. You just get better."

"Have you heard anything about the man who hit me?"

"Other than he's still in jail, no. He'll be charged with drunk driving at least, but that doesn't carry a lot of weight anymore. He'll probably get probation or some shit." She looked at him with that *mom look*. "Sorry." He squeezed her fingers. "Where is Dad?"

"Out flirting with the nurses, I'm sure. They all know him by name and wave every time he comes into my room."

"He's a personable guy."

"He's a flirt, but I love him anyway." She took another bite of her food before she set the spoon down. "What's happening between you and Callie? Something good, I hope."

"We've come to an understanding that we love each other."

"Fantastic, Jeremiah! I'm so happy for you. You two will be very good for each other, I think."

"I think so too." He rubbed his hand where the fingers had gone numb again.

"What's wrong?"

"I've been having some numbness and tingling in my hands and legs as well as some blurry vision."

"Didn't you fall off a horse a few weeks ago?"

"Yeah." He held up his hand. "Don't say it. I've already made an appointment with the doctor for in a couple of days. I'm sure it's nothing."

"Well, to be safe you need to get checked out."

"I know." He glanced at his watch. "I should go," he said, climbing to his feet. "I know they only allow you five minutes in here."

"So soon?"

"Yeah. I want to drop by Callie's and let her know how you are doing. She was worried."

"Tell her hello for me." She kissed him on the cheek as he leaned in to kiss her. "I love you, Jeremiah."

"I love you too, Mom. I'm sure everything will be fine with the surgery. We'll get you home in a couple of days with some physical therapy and you'll be good as new in a few weeks."

"Grr," she grumbled. "I hate being laid up."

"I know, but at least you're alive."

"Yes. Thank God for watching out for me."

"I'll try to come by again in a couple of days if they haven't let you out by then to give my brothers a chance to visit."

"The nurses have been doing a complete double take with each of you. I think they aren't going to let me leave just because they want the man candy that keeps coming in to see me."

He laughed. "I'll tell everyone to behave themselves."

"You do that."

"See you soon."

"Love you!"

"Love you too."

He drove back to Bandera with lots of things on his mind—from the problems with his visions to his love for Callie. He couldn't wait to bring her into the family even though she seemed reluctant to do it just yet. Fear and uncertainty probably had something to do with it. Really, this had all happened rather quickly so he couldn't blame her at all.

When he pulled into the garage, he parked his truck next to the building and then went around to the open bays where they worked on cars. "Hey, babe!"

"Jeremiah?"

"Yeah, who else calls you babe?"

She laughed as she came out from under the hood of an old Chrysler. "No one, but you I would hope." She gave him a smooch on the lips. "Did you visit your mom?"

"Yes. She's looking a lot better. They'll be doing surgery on her leg tomorrow and she'll have to stay in the hospital a couple of more days, but then she'll be home with rehab, I'm sure."

"Sounds awesome. I'm so glad she's doing better."

"Me too." He leaned in as she twisted a wrench on something under the hood. "Do you want to get some dinner?"

"I can't tonight. I promised my dad I would be home. He hasn't been feeling well."

"Okay." He moved around behind her, kissing her neck before he ran his tongue around her ear. "I'm going to miss you."

She shivered, but tipped her head to the side so he could do more. "I'll miss you too."

"How about tomorrow? We can have dinner and maybe do a movie in town?"

"I can't. I have plans with Mandy, Peyton and Paige. We planned a girl's night out."

"All right, day after tomorrow."

"Sounds good." She turned around in his arms and looped hers around his neck. "Did you make a doctor appointment?"

"Yeah. Day after tomorrow, so we'll go out after my appointment."

"Good. It's important for you to find out what's wrong."

"I know." He moved around to kiss her on the lips. "I'm fine. Don't worry."

"I love you. I'm going to worry."

"Then I'll have to kiss you until you forget to worry." He ran his tongue along the seam of her lips until she opened for him on a moan. As their tongues tangled, he lost himself in her kiss, totally forgetting where they were until someone honked from outside. "Sorry."

She giggled, actually giggled. He thought it was cute. "I'd better get back to work."

With a smack on her butt, he said he'd see her later and headed to his truck.

Man, I love that girl.

Chapter Thirteen

Jeremiah didn't like the look on the doctor's face. He seemed worried. When the doctor worried, he needed to worry too. "We'll need to do some x-rays and tests, Jeremiah. I'm not sure what's going on with you, but I don't think it's a pinched nerve."

"What could it be?"

"There are several things I won't go into right now because I don't want you getting on Google to look up the different diseases. I won't know until next week after we get a CAT scan of your head, do some nerve tests, and get some x-rays of your back just to make sure you don't have a disc out or something. I don't think that's what it is because you don't have pain in your back. You've told me your vision blurs. Those kinds of symptoms along with the numbness and tingling are something we need to look at more closely."

"Thanks, Doc, but you're scaring the hell out of me."

"I'm sorry, but until I know more, I can't give you any more information on things." He patted him on the shoulder. "You'll be okay until we get the tests done. You can get the CAT scan today at the hospital in San Antonio. I've already called to schedule you an appointment. They had a cancellation, so they could get to you in about an hour if you can get there."

"I'll get there, besides, I want to check on my mom. They were supposed to be releasing her today. I haven't heard from my dad."

"I'm glad she wasn't hurt too badly. A broken leg heals. Other more terrifying injuries don't."

"I know what you mean. She was lucky."

"Yes, she was." Jeremiah stood. "Now, go get the CAT scan, make an appointment for the other tests and get those done, then make an appointment to see me next week so we can go over them."

"Thanks, Doc."

"You're welcome, my boy. Tell your family hello for me. Remind them to get their checkups. I know how you boys are about coming in to see me."

"Yeah, only for broken bones and such."

After he thanked the doctor again, he paid his tab before he headed out to his truck. He didn't like thinking about this for another week, but he didn't have a choice, he guessed. At least tonight he could lose himself in Callie for a few hours.

* * * *

When he pulled up to her house two hours and forty-five minutes later, he smiled. Spending the evening with her would erase all the bad thoughts from his mind and heart, leaving only her to fill the void. He climbed out and walked up to the door.

With a quick rap of his knuckles, he heard Callie call out that she'd get it before she opened the door. *Damn.* She looked pretty even in something as simple as a sweater and jeans. "Hi."

"Hi." She pushed open the screen for him as she stepped back. "Come in."

"Thanks." He shut the door behind him before he slipped an arm around her waist and dragged her in for a quick kiss. "You taste amazing."

"It's dinner. I thought I'd cook."

"What'd you make?"

"Lasagna with French bread and salad." She stepped back. "Are you hungry?"

"Starving."

"Good. How about a beer? I have some in the fridge."

"Sounds good to me." He checked out her butt in those jeans as she walked back into the kitchen. *What a nice ass!* She returned a few minutes later with a bottle of beer and a kiss before she went back into the kitchen to finish getting dinner ready.

"How did the doctor go?"

"He didn't tell me much. Just scheduled some tests."

"Like what?" she asked, setting the table with plates.

"CAT scan, blood work, x-rays. You know, the normal stuff."

"Did he say what he thought might be the problem?"

"Not really. He wouldn't tell me his thoughts." He took a sip of the beer in his hand. "He didn't want me looking stuff up on the web and self-diagnosing."

"Smart man."

He chuckled and took another sip. "Yeah. He knows our family well."

Her father came out of the bedroom, limping slightly on his left foot.

"Are you okay, Daddy?"

"Yeah, just my MS acting up again."

"MS?" Jeremiah asked, not sure what that was.

"Multiple Sclerosis. I've had it for years. Makes my limbs go numb so I have to walk with a cane sometimes. It's a bitch of a disease, but I get by."

Jeremiah startled when her father described his symptoms. It sounded just like what he'd been going through. "When were you diagnosed?"

"About fifteen years ago. I take a medication daily to keep the symptoms at bay, but it's hard to manage some days. Today was one of those days." He smiled at Callie. "Thank God for Callie at the garage. She handles the stuff I can't on bad days."

"Wait. Don't you have some of the numbness stuff too, Jeremiah?"

"Yeah, but don't you go telling me I have Multiple Sclerosis. I can't be laid up in a wheelchair or something for the rest of my life. Besides, the doctor didn't mention that. I'm sure if he thought it might be some disease, he would have said something."

She put both her hands on his cheeks. "Just stop. You fell from a horse. We know how that can mess with a person. Don't jump to conclusions just because my dad has some of the same symptoms you've been experiencing." She kissed him and then stepped back but not far enough he'd lose touch with her body. "I love you. It doesn't matter what it is. We'll deal with whatever it turns out to be."

He took several deep breaths to calm his racing heart. He couldn't be sick. He didn't feel sick. He felt fine except for the symptoms. "What if it is?"

"Don't, Jeremiah. Don't freak yourself out." He put her arms around his waist, burying her face in his neck. "I love you."

"I love you too."

"Are you two getting married?"

She shook her head before she reached up and gave Jeremiah a quick kiss on the lips. "No, Dad. This is all new. We are dating for now."

Her father sank down onto one of the dining room chairs, propping his cane up on the table. "Well I'm glad to see you together. You two are cute."

She stepped back from Jeremiah and went back into the kitchen to take the food out of the oven. His mind whirled with questions. He wouldn't drag her into an uncertain future if he had some kind of terrible disease like Multiple Sclerosis. He couldn't. That wouldn't be fair to her. She already had to deal with her dad having it, he wouldn't subject her to a life with a cripple for a husband.

Dinner was a hushed time as Jeremiah reflected on the dire straits of his possible diagnosis. He absolutely refused to tie her down to a man who wasn't a hundred percent healthy, one who could take care of her, not the other way around, one who would be there for her and their children in their time of need, not a shell of a man who couldn't wipe his own ass.

Once dinner was over, he excused himself to leave. He needed to think. Thinking meant alone time even though he wanted nothing more than to kiss her, touch her, hold her, and make love to her.

As he walked out to his truck to go home, she stopped him with a hand on his arm. "Jeremiah, don't leave."

"I need to, Callie. I need some time alone."

"Don't shut me out."

"I'm not."

"Yes, you are. You're thinking way too much about this. Don't. Wait until the doctor tells you what is wrong before you start planning your future. You have no idea what the diagnosis will be and you are doing exactly what he told you not to do. Self-diagnosis is a bad thing. Please? I love you."

"I love you too, but I can't be with you right now."

"Please, don't leave. Don't do this, Jeremiah."

"I'm sorry, but I have to." He leaned in to kiss her lightly on the lips before climbing into his truck and leaving her standing in the driveway.

* * * *

Over the next few days, she called constantly to check on him. Sometimes he answered, other times he let her call go to voicemail. He couldn't face her right now, not until he talked to the doctor, which was today. Hopefully they would have some answers for him so he could move on with his life in whatever capacity that entailed.

He sat nervously in the waiting room of the doctor's office for them to call him into the back. He hated this, hated doctors, hated hospitals, and hated what he was doing to Callie, but he felt the need to protect her even if it was from himself.

"Jeremiah? Come on back," the nurse said.

He climbed to his feet and then she put him in one of those small little waiting rooms to go crazy in. They needed to make the things padded or something.

Lucky for him, the doctor didn't wait too long before coming in to take a seat on one of those little rolling stools.

"We have you test results in, Jeremiah."

"And?"

"I'm afraid it isn't good news. It's not a pinched nerve. I feared the worst and it's not that, so you have to be thankful for the small concession. At first I thought it might be a brain tumor with the symptoms, but it's not. You have something called Multiple Sclerosis. It's a disease process affecting the nerve cells in your brain. It's an auto-immune disease where your immune system attacks the brain cells by mistake, damaging the myelin sheath of your brain, spinal cord, and eyes. When these nerve endings get damaged, it affects your movement and your eyesight."

"Is there a cure?"

"No. I'm sorry, there isn't."

"Fuck."

"There are medications to handle the symptoms. You can even go into remission where you won't have symptoms at all for a long time."

"So I have to be on some medicine for the rest of my life?"

"Yes."

"What is the eventual outcome of this?"

"Everything in our life leads to death, Jeremiah. Some people are completely disabled from this. We won't know what type of MS you have until we've sent you to a neurologist who can study your symptoms and decide the best course of action."

"This isn't fair, you know. I just found the girl of my dreams. My future is set. Now this."

He put a hand on Jeremiah's shoulder. "I know, son. You're in the prime of your life. Don't get too worked up about it yet until you see the neurologist in San Antonio. The guy I'm sending you to is fantastic in this field. He knows his stuff. He'll help you manage things so you'll have the best quality of life."

Dread hit him in the chest like a brick. *What am I going to do about Callie?*

"If you have any general questions I can help you with, don't hesitate to call me. I would suggest making a list of things you would like to ask the specialist before you go so you can make an informed decision about your care. This isn't the end of the world, son. You can lead a normal life for the most part as long as you stay on the medications the doctor prescribes for you. You can still marry, have children, and be the young man you should be right now."

"Thanks, Doc."

"You're welcome. I'll have my nurse make you an appointment with the neurologist. You stay here while she does."

The doctor walked out as a tear slid down his cheek. He couldn't ask Callie to marry him now. He wouldn't make her deal with this. Better he cut it off right now and save her the pain.

The nurse came in a few minutes later as he angrily wiped the wetness from his face. Men didn't cry and he wasn't going to let himself break down again.

"Here is your appointment card with the neurologist. It's set for Monday."

"That's fine. Thank you."

"You can stay in here as long as you like. Gather your thoughts, but just remember, this isn't the end of the world. People are diagnosed with this disease all the time. They go on to live happy, healthy, and productive lives. You're still young. You can handle this." She smiled softly and walked back out the door, leaving him alone.

He sat in his truck for several long minutes as his mind raced from one subject to another and back. Callie was at the forefront of his thoughts though while he tried to decide what to do. He'd already pushed her away, trying to save her the heartache of living with a man who wasn't whole, but he would have to tell her the diagnosis and live with her anger as he shut her out of his life for good.

* * * *

Callie waited for Jeremiah at Anne's diner. He'd called her on his way home from the doctor's office to say he wanted to see her. She was surprised he'd picked here, somewhere in public. They should be alone for this, she figured, but apparently he didn't think so.

When she saw him walked through the door, she smiled. *Damn, he looked good, tall, broad-shouldered, and tough.* Whatever this was wouldn't tear them apart. She wouldn't let it.

He slid into the booth seat across from her and took her hand in his. He closed his eyes as his lips brushed her palm. Her heart did a little staccato rhythm at the touch of his mouth. He could totally turn her inside out with nothing more than a look or a touch.

"Hi."

"Hey."

"Why did you want to meet here?"

"I figured it was best."

"Best for whom?"

"Us."

"Why?"

"Hey, kids. Can I get you anything?" Anne stopped at their table with a bright smile.

"I'll take a Coke," Callie replied as Jeremiah shook his head.

"Be right back."

After Anne brought her drink and Callie retrieved her hand reluctantly from Jeremiah's grasp, she sat back in the seat waiting for his words to start flowing.

"We need to break this off."

"Break what off?"

"Our relationship. I don't want to see you anymore."

"What the fuck, Jeremiah? You can't just shut me down like this."

"I can and I will to protect you."

"Protect me from what? You aren't making sense." Trepidation ripped through her at the look in his eyes. He wasn't kidding. The seriousness of his expression made her angry. *Stubborn man!* "I won't let you do this. Whatever it is—"

"It's MS, Callie."

"So?"

"I can't." He shook his head. "I won't let you live your life with a man who can't be a hundred percent for you. You already have to deal with your father having this terrible disease and now your future husband?"

"You will *not* make that decision for me. I've lived with my dad's disease for the last several years. I've seen what it can do and I'm not afraid of it." She grabbed his hand, but he pulled it back out of her reach. "I love you, Jeremiah. Why can't you understand that? Why can't you see it doesn't matter to me? You are my life."

"I refuse to strap you to a man who won't be able to take care of you."

She slapped her hand on the table causing him to jump. "I don't care, you stubborn jackass! But if you want to turn your back on our love because you're afraid, then so be it, but don't use the excuse you don't want to strap me with a crippled man because that isn't going to fly. Loving you means we are together forever no matter what. Obviously you don't love me enough to want to be with me." She leaned in with her elbows on the table. "What if I had MS? Would you turn your back on me?"

He shook his head and refused to look her in the eye. "No. I would be there for you."

"Then why are you pushing me away?" she asked, fear making her all the more angry because he wouldn't face that they were meant to be together. "We can fix this. Don't let us die. The love of a lifetime is worth at least a million tries. What we've got is too good for good-bye."

When he looked back up, she could see the terror, loneliness, and desperation in his gaze. "Don't you see? I'm supposed to be the one taking care of you, not the other way around."

"Listen to yourself. You can justify it all you want to in your head, but it's not going to work. One-sided love isn't for me. If you love me, you'd see this is crazy talk, Jeremiah. Please, don't shut me out."

"I'm sorry, Callie. I refuse to put you through this." He got out of the booth and walked out without another word.

Tears welled up in her eyes as she watched him leave. *How can he do this? How can he turn his back on me? I thought he loved me.*

Anne came over and sat down next to her, wrapping her in a one-armed hug as she cried ugly, sobbing tears into her shoulder.

"He'll come around, honey. He's a Young. They do this kind of thing."

"What am I going to do?"

"Give him time. He's in shock, I'd imagine. I also know Jeremiah is one of most stubborn of the boys, and that is saying a lot because the whole lot of them are stubborn. He's about the most like his momma out of all of the boys. She's got the stubborn streak down to a science. Trust me." She patted Callie's shoulder as she reached for a napkin to dry her tears.

"Thanks, Anne."

"You're welcome, honey. If you want to talk, you call me."

"I will, but right now I think I need to talk to Peyton and Paige. They are married to two of the brothers. They might know more about how to handle this than anyone."

"I'm sure they can help, but remember, I'm here for you."

Callie dug out her phone to call her friends to meet her at her house in an hour. Peyton, Paige and Mandy all converged on her living room with wine, chocolate, chips, and cookies to discuss this new development.

"I need you all to promise not to tell your husbands about this. I don't know if Jeremiah has told his brothers what's going on or not. I don't want to break his confidence. This concerns me and him right now."

Peyton nodded as Paige replied, "Okay."

"Jeremiah has been diagnosed with Multiple Sclerosis." She went on to tell them what she knew about the disease, how her father had it as well, and how things progressed if left unchecked by medication. She explained all she knew about the disease before she went on to tell them about her conversation with Jeremiah at the diner. "I don't know what to do. He's shut me out."

Mandy sat forward on the chair, resting her elbows on her knees. "I didn't realize you two were even serious, but he's being a typical Young from what I know about the family."

"True," Peyton added. "It sounds very much like what my husband would do."

"Mine too." Paige put in her opinion, which is exactly what Callie thought they would say.

"What am I going to do?"

"Give him time," Peyton said. "He needs to come to grips with the diagnosis first. Let him talk to the neurologist and find out his life isn't over because of this disease. He'll come around."

"God, I hope so. I wanted to punch him."

They all laughed as Paige replied, "I bet you did. He's worse than some of the other brothers in his stubbornness. I think it comes from handling all the family finances. He has to be such a hard-ass to be able to tell them no they can't buy a new horse or purchase a new fifty thousand dollar tractor."

She swiped at the tears on her cheeks, sniffing to clear her plugged nose. "Thanks everyone. I knew I could count on you three to help me."

"Honey, you know we are here for you no matter what. We all know what dealing with those boys is like," Mandy said even though she didn't have a brother herself yet.

"Shall we watch some sappy movie tonight?" She looked at Paige. "What did you do with the twins tonight?"

"Daddy is watching them for a change."

"Wow, I bet that is interesting."

"He does pretty well with them. They're getting so big, they're two little terrors on the loose, but he's such a sucker for their little smiles and cuteness."

"What's he going to do when Hannah starts dating?"

"He won't even talk about that right now."

"How are you and Jason doing? Any baby news yet?"

"Oh, hell no. We are waiting for a bit before we start trying for a little one."

"I bet Grandma isn't happy about that."

"She already has enough grandchildren for now. She can wait a few more years."

"How is she taking being laid up at home with the broken leg?"

"Not well. She wants to be up and doing this and that, although we have managed to get her into her office so she can handle some stuff even with a broken leg. She's doing well with the rehab though. The physical therapist is coming out three times a week to work with her."

"That's great. I was so worried when I heard about her accident."

"As we all were."

The rest of the evening passed with the girls getting pretty drunk, laughing at their men, and just spending quality time with each other. Callie needed this, needed the companionable silence as they watched *The Notebook* on television and cried big, ugly tears. The cleansing feeling of being with like-minded women, helped her to understand Jeremiah's feelings and let him go to find his own way, so he could find his way back to her.

Chapter Fourteen

Callie decided to confront Jeremiah after his neurologist appointment on his own turf with his brothers watching. She managed to get Peyton and Paige to gather the brothers as well as his mother and father in one of the lodge's main rooms. He hadn't told them about the disease yet that the girls could fathom so she wanted them to confront him with that fact too.

As she drove to the ranch, fear gripped her. What if this backfired? What if he got angry with her for doing this?

When she'd made this plan, she really hadn't thought of the consequences of her actions, but what could it hurt? He'd pushed her out of his life anyway, so pressing him more couldn't hurt any worse.

When she pulled into the front of the lodge, Peyton stood outside waiting for her.

"Ready?"

"As I'll ever be, I guess."

"The boys are all in the main room. We've put a sign on the door to keep the visitors out until this is over. Jeremiah is in his cabin. Jeff went to get him." She put her arm around Callie. "I did tell him what was going on so he knew why the secrecy and the meeting. He's pissed that Jeremiah didn't tell them, but he understands. He's on your side."

"Good."

When they walked into the lodge, every eye turned toward her. She could see the questions on their faces and in their eyes, but she had to wait to confront Jeremiah.

Jeff practically dragged him into the room several minutes later.

"What the hell is this all about?"

"Why don't you tell us, Jeremiah?"

"I don't know what you are talking about."

"You went to the doctor. Tell us what is going on so we can help you."

Jeremiah's gaze swung to her as she stood in the corner waiting for him to speak. "It's nothing."

"Bullshit. Spill it."

Jeremiah inhaled before he forcibly exhaled. "I have Multiple Sclerosis."

"What is that?" Jackson asked.

"It's an auto-immune disease affecting the nerves in my brain. I went to the neurologist today. He started me on a medication which is supposed to dull the symptoms and make it easier to deal with. Basically, it makes my limbs go numb at times and messes with my vision. For now, those are the symptoms, but eventually it could put me in a wheelchair."

Jeff put his arm around him. "We are here for you, Jeremiah. No matter what. You know that."

The other brothers did the same as they all got together in a group to give him the support he needed. It brought tears to Callie's eyes. She knew they would react this way. Now only if she could convince Jeremiah they belonged together. "I need to say something, please, and I hope you all will bear with me for interrupting your family time, but I feel this is important to say in front of you so you can beat him over the head in my defense." She stepped toward the group. "Jeremiah and I have been seeing each other. We have professed our love for one another a couple of weeks ago, but when he got the diagnosis of this disease, he shut me out claiming he didn't want to burden me with a cripple for a mate. My father has this disease as well. I've been living with it for several years. I know what it can do. I've done the research and I want him to realize it doesn't matter to me. He's my life. Please help me convince him we belong together no matter what life brings."

"What's this all about, Jeremiah?" his mother asked from her wheelchair off to the side of the group.

"I don't want to stick Callie with a cripple for a husband, Mom. I refuse to do that to her."

"She loves you and you love her, right?"

"Yes."

"Then quit being a dumbass and ask that girl to marry you."

"But—"

"But nothing. Life is short. We never know when we'll leave our loved ones behind. I've learned this myself the last several weeks as I saw your father and you boys deal with my accident. I could have been killed. I know it would have left you all devastated, but it's not something we can control. If you love her, then cherish the time you have together by being together and loving each other like your life depends on it."

Callie watched as Jeremiah turned back toward her. His grey eyes reflected love and acceptance as the words from his mother finally sank in.

Jeremiah stepped out of the circle of his brothers to approach her, taking her hand in his as he stopped in front of her. "I'm sorry, Callie. I do love you, but I'm scared."

"I know, Jeremiah. I am too. I don't want to lose you. I don't want to have to deal with your disease, but I'm a strong woman who knows how to handle adversity no matter how much you want to protect me. I love you."

"I love you too. I'm so sorry I put you through this." With tears shining in his eyes, he got down on one knee. "I don't have a ring for you right this minute, but will you marry me?"

She got down on the ground so they were face to face. She grasped his cheeks in her hands as she whispered a exuberant, "Yes!" She threw herself into his embrace, kissing him all over his face while he laughed.

His brothers slapped him on the back in congratulations until she managed to get him down on the floor, lying across his chest.

"This is a precarious position, darlin'. Not that I mind, you see, but I don't think you are into exhibitionism, are you?"

"Jeremiah!"

He laughed as he rolled her under him and kissed her full on the mouth. When they came up for air, the room had cleared of his family. He threaded his fingers in her hair, bringing one small bunch around to tickle her lips. "I love you."

"I love you too. When do you want to get married?"

"I don't care. I want something small though. Only a few friends and family."

"Sounds good to me." A twinkle in his eyes told her he was up to something. "Ever been to Hawaii?"

"Nope."

"Let's get married there. I can fly everyone out there. We'll have a wedding on the beach."

"I love that idea, but how can you afford to fly everyone out there? Won't it be really expensive?"

"We need to talk about finances, darlin', but don't worry, I can afford it and then some."

"If you say so. I'll leave that to you."

"Trust me when I say you won't have to worry about money for the rest of your life."

"Are you rich?"

"Let's say comfortable." He kissed her full on the mouth, letting his tongue slide along the seam of her lips in an erotic dance until she opened for him on a groan.

When they parted, she said, "We are going to have to find somewhere else to live. Although I love your little cabin, there isn't room for both of us."

"I'm already planning on a house on the hill overlooking the valley. I'll show you the plans after we make love."

"Oh, I like the sound of that."

"Good." He climbed to his feet and held out a hand to her, dragging her up before he tossed her over his shoulder to head to his room.

"Jeremiah?"

"Yeah."

"This caveman behavior is perfect."

He laughed all the way to the cabin as her hair hung down his back and her hand had a firm grip on his buttocks.

Epilogue

Orange and red streaked the sky, making the sunset spectacular as they sat on the lounge near their cabana on Maui.

Jeremiah kissed her forehead when she snuggled down into his embrace, admiring the rock on her left hand. She couldn't believe they were actually married.

The ceremony had been beautiful. He'd been dressed in a pure white pair of pants, white shirt, white cowboy hat with no shoes as she approached him in her off-the-shoulder white gown and bare feet. Clutched in her shaking hands was a bouquet of roses, lilies and baby's breath tied with a deep blue ribbon.

His family and her father had stood by as she stopped next to him to take his hand in hers.

When all was said and done, she whispered her new name in awe, not quite believing she'd actually married her Jeremiah.

"What are you thinking about?"

"You. The ceremony. Everything. It's hard for me to believe we are actually here in Hawaii and married. I've waited so long for this."

"I love you, Callie."

"I love you too." She sighed as she ran her fingers through the hair on his chest. "When is the house getting started?"

"Next week. They're breaking ground for the foundation while we're here. Dad is keeping an eye on them after he and mom get back from here."

"It was so great to have our families here for this. It was perfect."

"I only want what my wife wants." She sat up and gave him the most dubious look she could muster. "What?"

"Somehow I doubt that."

"Why would you say something like that? I only want what you want."

"Because I know how stubborn you can be, Jeremiah. Somehow I don't think I'll be getting away with much of anything."

He wrapped an arm around her and pulled her back down to his chest. "You have me wrapped around your little finger, Mrs. Young. Don't think any different."

"What happens when we have kids?"

"They'll have me wrapped around their fingers too, I'm sure, just like their mother."

"Especially if we have little girls."

"Oh, definitely."

"How soon do you want children?" His fingers did a slow crawl down her arm, sending shivers racing in their wake.

"I'm not in any hurry. Are you?"

"Not really. I want to have some time, just the two of us, before we jump into having a family."

"How many kids do you want?"

"I want a big family. Lots of kids, like six. I was lonesome as a child. I don't want our kids to be like that."

"Sounds good to me."

"Are you going to ever tell me exactly how much money is in the bank?"

"Are you curious?"

"Yeah, but that's not the reason I married you. You can handle all the bills and money. As long as I have an allowance to buy groceries, I'm good."

"Honey, you can buy the entire store and it won't hurt our finances."

"How much, Jeremiah?"

He laughed as she ran her fingernail around his nipple. "Current balance or in general?"

"General figure is fine."

"We have over ten million in the bank."

She choked on her saliva as she muttered, "Ten million?"

"Yeah, and it's growing every day."

"Holy shit."

"So when we get back, if you want to close your dad's garage, you can. I'd rather like not having you work."

"But I like working at the garage."

"I know you do, baby, that's why I wouldn't ask you to, unless you wanted to."

"I'll talk to my dad to see what he says. I'd like to set him up so he wouldn't have to worry about anything ever again. He could have someone come in to help him since I won't be there anymore on a regular basis."

"Done."

"I love you, Jeremiah. You are so good to me."

"You are the best wife a man could ask for." He pushed her onto her back and ran his tongue from her shoulder to her ear. "Wanna make love?"

"I thought you'd never ask."

The End

KISS ME, COWBOY
Cowboy Dreamin' 6

Sandy Sullivan

Chapter One

Joshua Young brought the bottle of beer to his lips, to wash away the grime from a day in the saddle on his family ranch. *Damn, I'm beat.* A couple of his friends played pool in the corner as he watched with disinterest. He didn't care much for getting rambunctious tonight. The feeling of restlessness had him in its grip without showing signs of letting up. Maybe a raunchy night of sex would take care of his problem.

He glanced around the bar. A couple of his brothers sat with their girls in a corner booth. It was the first time his triplet, Joel, had been able to get Mesa out of the house since the birth of their little girl a few months before. He was happy for the brothers who'd hooked up with a woman recently. He actually felt it might be time for him to settle down. Jeff had his girl Terri, Joel had Mesa, Jeremiah had a special girl named Callinda, Jacob had Paige and now his other triplet Jason had hooked up with Peyton, one of the bartenders at The Dusty Boot. All of his brothers seemed to be pairing off…Okay, well not all of them. Jackson didn't have a steady girl, neither did Joey or Jonathan, but he started to think he'd be the last to find a woman of his own. He wasn't necessarily looking, but if he found her, then so be it. His plans were at the forefront of his thoughts.

Little did his family know, but he had a plan to make a lot of money to start his own business. He knew his parents would help him if he asked, but he wanted to do this on his own. Of course, he'd never been anything but a cowboy which meant it had to be something along those lines. His specialty was working with leather. With that, he planned to start his own saddlery.

He grabbed his beer and headed for the bar, tipping the bottle to his lips to empty the last dregs of the brew. Another one sounded good tonight, even though he didn't usually drink a ton. Tomorrow came early, so he should probably limit it to two.

Just as he reached the bar, someone bumped into him, dumping cold liquid down his back. "Shit!" He spun around to see who spilled beer, probably, on him and found a woman, who barely reached his shoulder. She had the prettiest green eyes he'd ever seen. They seemed almost a little sad, or maybe lonely would be a better word, before shock at what she'd done had registered.

"Oh my God. I'm so sorry. Someone bumped into me. Are you all right?"

"I'm fine. A little beer never hurt anyone."

"It's really crowded in here."

"Yeah, this is a typical Friday night at The Dusty Boot though." Intrigued, he tilted his head to the side to get a better look at her. "You new here?"

"Sort of." She pressed her lips together, drawing his gaze to the peach colored gloss on the pouty surfaces. "I'm really sorry," she shouted as the band started playing again.

"What?"

She leaned in close enough to be heard, bringing the scent of something fresh to his nose. "I said I'm really sorry for the beer down your shirt."

"Oh. It's okay. I needed a beer bath tonight."

She laughed, a little giggling sound, as she pressed her fingertips to her lips.

"I'm Joshua."

"I'm Candace."

She held out her hand for him. When he grasped it in his, her hold was firm and strong, not like most women he knew with a wimpy handshake. A tingle shot up his arm to warm something in his chest. "Nice name."

"Thank you. Yours too."

"You don't live around here."

"No. Actually, I live in California. I'm here visiting a friend who lives here."

"Welcome to Texas."

She smiled, showing off straight, white teeth and a small dimple in her left cheek. "Thank you."

"Can I buy you another beer?" he asked, stuffing his hand in his front right pocket to pull out some money.

"Um, sure."

He turned around to signal for Peyton to bring him two more beers as the little lady stepped up beside him to let someone pass behind her. "If you want something else, let me know."

"No, beer is fine. I usually don't drink much, but I'm here on vacation, so I want to experience everything Texas has to offer."

"Everything, huh?"

Her gaze slid down his frame from the top of his black Stetson to the tip of his dirty cowboy boots. "Yep."

It just might be his lucky night after all if this pretty little thing wanted to experience his kind of Texas rodeo.

"Six bucks, Joshua," Peyton said over the twang of the guitar on stage. One eyebrow shot up when he handed one to Candace. "New friend?"

"Yeah, sort of."

"I'm Peyton." She held out her hand across the bar to Candace. "I'm his sister-in-law."

"Nice to meet you. Candace."

"You're new here."

Candace laughed. "Is it that obvious?"

"You don't have the Texas twang to your speech, plus I know just about everyone who comes in here regularly. You I haven't seen before."

"I'm visiting a friend."

"Nice." Peyton tapped the bar with her knuckle. "Welcome. Holler if you want another one."

Peyton moved off down the bar to help other patrons while Joshua turned left to face Candace. "You can have the stool if you like."

"Thanks." She glanced down at her feet, showing him the tips of typical cowboy boots. "My feet are killing me in these."

He laughed as she shrugged and slid her cute little bottom up on the stool with an audible sigh. "Better?"

"Oh, much."

With one elbow on the bar, he leaned a little closer to inhale the scent clinging to her hair. But she was a sweet thing. He told himself it was because he wanted to hear her, but in reality, he loved the way she smelled. "Where in California do you live?"

"Do you know California at all?"

"Just the major towns like Los Angeles, San Francisco, you know."

"I live on the outskirts of Los Angeles in a small town called Anaheim."

"Isn't Disneyland there?"

Her lips tilted up at the corners. "Yes."

"Who are you visiting here? I probably know them."

"Arnold Beesman."

Joshua frowned. He knew Arnold from school, tough guy who turned into a pretty mean S.O.B. if he knew right. At least, that's what the rumor was. The guy had been married once, and supposedly, he beat his wife. "Yeah, I know him."

"He was married to my sister."

"Your sister is Mary?"

"Yeah. Did you know her?"

"Not personally, but I'd seen her around town a time or two. She seemed like a nice girl."

"She was."

"What happened to her? I thought they divorced."

"They did. She moved home and died six months later."

"How did she die if you don't mind me askin'?"

"She committed suicide."

"I'm sorry. I didn't mean to bring up bad stuff."

"No, it's okay. She didn't want the divorce. Neither of them did. She thought he'd been cheating on her and left. She found out, after she moved home, all about his infidelity when the woman he'd apparently been with called to laugh at her because she'd broken up their marriage. Mary loved him something fierce, and he loved her."

"So why didn't they get back together if they didn't want the divorce in the first place?"

"By then, he'd married the bitch who broke them up because she said she was pregnant when she wasn't."

"I'm sorry."

"Thanks."

"Would you like to dance?"

"And lose my prime seat?" She laughed as she hopped down. "I'd love to."

She put her beer next to his on the bar top while he tapped the guy next to him. "Save our seat, would you?"

"Sure, Joshua."

"Someone you know?" she asked as he led her to the dance floor with her hand in his.

"I don't think there's anyone in here I don't know, grew up with, or hung out with on Saturday nights at the ranch."

"You own a ranch?"

He swung around to face her. The look in her eyes gave him pause, catching his breath in his throat when he reached for her. Her long red hair hung around her shoulders like a cloud. Her eyes sparkled like emeralds he'd seen once in a jewelry store window. She had a white blouse on, tied under her breasts, leaving her flat abdomen showing as her little denim skirt rode low on her hips. The blush on her cheeks gave her a rosy glow. He couldn't believe his luck in finding such a rose in amongst a bunch of daisies. Not that the women of Bandera were bad looking. He'd been with several over the years, but Candace definitely stood out. He'd have to keep her close to his side if he wanted to see where the night might lead.

"I don't personally. My family has a cattle ranch slash guest ranch on the outskirts of town," he replied when they reached an empty spot on the hardwood. "Did you come with Arnold?" He slipped his hand onto her waist and took her left hand in his right as they started swaying to the music.

"Yeah. He's shooting pool with some guys near the back."

"You aren't into watching guys play pool?"

"Not really. I was enjoying the music when I dumped the beer down your back."

"Do you know how to two-step?"

"No."

"Follow me. Slide, shuffle, slide, slide. It's easy." She looked down at her feet as she tried to follow his steps. "Relax. I don't bite…hard."

Her head snapped up as she grinned. "Do you like sex?"

He stumbled with his steps.

"Gotcha."

He liked her. She had spunk and seemed a little crazy to boot. "I sure do. How about you?"

"Love it. Something about a man going down on me just revs my engine."

"Does it now?"

"Yep." One eyebrow shot up over her left eye. "Do you like going down on a woman?"

"I can't believe we are havin' this conversation."

"Shy?"

"No, but I'm not used to a woman being quite so bold about her sex life."

Leaning in, she tipped her head back to look up into his face. "I like bold men."

"How long you here for?" A man could drown in her eyes if he let himself. Her mouth would reach his should he so chose to bring their lips together.

"A month." She ran her tongue up under his chin until he gave into the temptation and brought his down so their mouths hovered bare inches apart. "Why?"

"I can see us havin' one hell of a good time while you're here. What do you say?"

She shook her hand free of his, sliding both up his chest to wrap around his neck. "Oh, I'd like that."

Her tangy breath whispered over his lips, bringing the thought of them wrapped around his cock tight enough to make him explode. "A bit wild, aren't you?"

"I'm here to have a good time, and by all that's holy, I'm going to have one." She glanced up at him through her lashes. "Now, it can be with you, cowboy, or someone else in this bar."

He felt sweat bead up on his upper lip. This girl was hotter than a branding iron ready to burn through cowhide, but he was ready to jump into this fire with both balls dangling over the hot poker. "Babe, I'm all ready for a wild ride with you."

"Good. We're on the same page then."

"When?"

"Let's dance a bit first. I'll let you know when." She pushed herself up against his chest as he settled his hands on her hips.

When her hips swayed from side to side, he about came in his pants. She kept rubbing herself against his now straining cock. If they walked off the dance floor, everyone would see how fucking horny he was.

"A little horny, cowboy?"

"A lot horny, babe. You've got me wound tighter than the springs on my truck." He rubbed his lips against her neck. "If we don't leave soon, I'm going to lose it right here on the dance floor."

"Ah, poor baby."

Joshua felt his arm almost ripped from the socket as Arnold shoved him back. "What the hell do you think you're doing?"

"Stop it, Arnold."

"You keep your pretty little ass away from him."

"I can dance with whomever I want to. You aren't my father."

"No, but I'm as close to a brother you've got here, Candace. These boys aren't your type."

She backed up and threw up her hands in disgust. "What's my type? You don't even know. I'm here visiting. It doesn't mean you can tell me who I can or cannot fuck."

"You ain't fuckin' nobody. I promised your sister to take care of you if you ever came out here and by damn, I plan to." Arnold moved toward her. "Candy, honey, getting hooked up with one of the Young boys is a bad idea all the way around."

"Look, Arnold. I'm not trying to just get in her pants. I'd like to get to know her," Joshua said, glancing around at the group beginning to form around them. He didn't like scenes, but this was turning into one fast. He needed to defuse the situation or he would be cock-blocked before the end of the evening. He could just feel the whole thing slipping out of his fingers.

Candace jammed her hands on her hips. "I want your cock, cowboy, not your heart."

A few people behind her snickered. It wasn't like the Young brothers to not have a woman to go home with. She wanted him. He wanted her. What the hell was the problem?

"You need to stop with this talk, Candy. Watch your mouth, young lady."

"I'm twenty-three years old, Arnold. I can talk how I want to, I can fuck who I want to, and I can live my life how I want to. If this is going to be a problem for you, then I'll just go back to Los Angeles now and forget this visit."

"No. I don't want you to go home. You're all I have left of Mary."

"Then stop trying to be a big brother."

"I can't."

"Then we have nothing more to talk about. I'll be on the first plane out of San Antonio tomorrow." The crowd parted like the red sea as she spun on her heels, heading for the front door.

Intending to go with her, Joshua stepped toward where she'd disappeared.

"Let her go, Young. She's too good for you," Arnold snapped, following in her wake.

Joshua stopped, turned and headed toward a stool and that long mahogany bar that would bring him some relief from his pent up frustrations with a whole lot of alcohol. He hadn't originally planned to get drunk tonight, but things changed when the little piece of fluff twisted his balls into a knot and left him hanging for the evening. Bitch of it was, he didn't want anyone else.

He needed another beer. His cock ached from need, and now that the woman who had him turned inside out had left for the night, he needed something to soothe his frazzled nerves before he headed home. Tonight would be a blue balls night for sure. None of the women in Bandera stacked up to the beauty who just walked out of his life.

* * * *

"Candy, wait."

"I'm done with this, Arnold. Leave me alone," she said, stopping next to her car to unlock it. "I didn't come here so you could run my life for me. I came to visit. Out of guilt or whatever, I don't know, but I wanted to see how you were. I can see you're just fine. I'm going home."

"Stay please? You mean the world to me, Candy. I don't want you to walk out of my life. I need you to remind me what an ass I am for letting Mary leave me."

With both hands braced on the top edge of her car, she said, "You aren't an ass for letting her leave, Arnold. You're an ass for cheating on her in the first damn place. No use wailing over it. You divorced and remarried. She committed suicide because she couldn't have you anymore and that pushed her over the edge. Why she took things to that extreme, I don't know, but she did. It's over."

"I need to protect you. For her. For Mary."

"No, you don't. I'm a big girl. I can take care of myself, especially where men are concerned. If I want to fuck the entire bar, then so be it. You have nothing to say about it."

He spread his hands out to his sides, imploring her to forgive him for his stupidity. "All right. I'm sorry. I shouldn't have butted in, but you don't want to hook up with one of the Young boys."

"And why not? He seemed like a nice guy. Built. Rugged. Good looking. Just the type I needed tonight."

"He'll use you."

She threw up her hands as she started to pace near the side of her car. "I want to use him. Backward. Forward. Doggie-style. Up the ass. Hell, I don't care, Arnold. Don't you understand? It's a quick fling. Nothing more. I don't need the complication of a man in my life. I just wanted to fuck a guy."

"Don't talk like that, Candy. You're innocent and good. You shouldn't be having sex."

"I'm old enough to know what I want. I'm not a damned virgin, Arnold. Trust me."

"You should be then."

"Stop acting the fool. I just want some down and dirty sex for the evening."

"Fine! Do what you want, but I won't help you pick up a man, and stay away from Joshua Young."

"Whatever. I'm done for tonight. The mystique is gone. I don't want anything to do with a man now. I just want sleep. The plane ride from Los Angeles was a long one. Let's just go home."

"Good. I'm glad you're thinking straight now." He opened his own truck sitting next to her car as she climbed inside hers and slammed the door.

Frustrating fucking man! I want a little cock, not a boyfriend for God's sake!

She cranked the car's engine until it turned over with a rumble. The rental car wasn't anything fancy. It would do in a pinch, unlike her nice little sports car sitting in the airport parking lot at home. One thing she didn't have to worry about was money. Her mother's side of the family name came with old money. Her granddaddy built his fortune from the railroad industry a long time ago, but they didn't flaunt their millions. The whole family worked for what they had.

The family fortune was an issue between Arnold and Mary for a long time. He hated the fact that she could just whip out her credit card and pay for anything. She didn't though. They lived on his income from working on cars. Mary had loved her life with her husband, until the day she'd found out he cheated.

Sure, all the kids got a lump sum when they turned thirty, never mind the fact Candace had a degree in business and ran her own company working with computer programs. This month-long vacation was her chance to cut loose, find a cowboy for the short go around, and live her life before she settled back into the everyday grind at her office. *Is there something wrong with just wanting sex? I don't think so, but maybe I'm wrong. What if something were to happen? What if I got pregnant or caught some disease?* "Stupid, Candace. He was a nice guy. Cute too."

She put the car into drive and followed Arnold out of the bar parking lot. *Oh well, my chance at Joshua Young is gone. If I don't give up and go back to Los Angeles tomorrow, I'd probably never see him again anyway.*

Chapter Two

As predicted, morning came bright and early on the ranch, no matter how much Joshua had drank the night before.

He groaned as he rolled over in bed when his alarm went off. It was his turn to take the guests out on their ride through the hills and valleys of Thunder Ridge Ranch. Most of the time, he loved having the guests here, but this morning wasn't one of them.

After the woman of his fantasies walked out of the bar the night before, he'd drank himself into a stupor. He didn't want to think about going home without getting laid, and no one else in the bar piqued his libido like the red-haired beauty he'd had the chance to hold for way too short of a time. He wanted more, much more, but she'd left without returning to take care of his problem. *Damn bad luck!*

The minute he sat up on the side of the bed, his stomach began to lurch. It wouldn't do any good to be sick. Jeff wouldn't care. Besides, his brother had seen him stagger into the main lodge as he checked the buildings before retiring, so Jeff would know he was drunk off his ass when he'd come in.

"Joshua?"

"Yeah, Dad?"

"Are you up? You have a group waiting at the barn."

"Yeah. I'll be there in a minute."

"I'll tell them."

He heard the front door on the lodge bang shut a few minutes later as the sounds of a couple arguing reached him through the wall. He strained to hear the voices, but they were muffled to his ears. He shrugged and bent over to grab his jeans from the floor. Hearing voices in the main part of the house wasn't unusual. The ghost couple they had living near his rooms in the upstairs part of the lodge kept him awake sometimes until they would finally quiet down and fade into the night. It was strange to hear them in the early morning hours though. They didn't make a lot of noise during the day, just at night.

With the clean T-shirt in his hands that he'd found in a dresser drawer moments earlier, he shrugged into the sweet-smelling, cotton material. He needed to get his ass moving. He might not even have time for a cup of coffee before he had to deal with tourists. His own fault, he knew.

The front door of the lodge banged shut again. "Joshua?"

Jeff.

"I'm coming. Be down in a minute. I'm putting my boots on right now."

What a pain in the ass this was turning into. This living at the main lodge sucked. Maybe it was time for him to get a place of his own.

As soon as he shoved his feet into his boots, he grabbed his straw cowboy hat from the end of his bed and opened the door. The faint odor of flowers drifted to his nose, telling him one of the female ghosts was nearby. "Go on now. I have work to do." He felt the brush of fingertips down his arm for a second before the scent disappeared. He knew one of the female ghosts liked him. She touched him often, but today wasn't a day for lollygagging. He had a lot of work to get done and a woman to forget about.

He grabbed a to-go cup of coffee from the table the minute he reached the downstairs lobby area. They always had some strong brew going from the early morning hours until late at night. Thank goodness for the cowboy way.

When he reached the barn, he was surprised to see such a large group of riders ready to go out this early in the morning. Joey would have to accompany him on this ride since the group had more than ten riders. "Joey?"

"Yeah?"

"I need you to go this morning."

"All right. Let me get Jeremiah to come out and tend the remaining horses while we're gone." Joey disappeared into the house a few minutes later in order for his other brother to be pulled from the work he was doing in one of the offices.

Several minutes later, the two of them returned to the barn. "We've got fifteen riders."

"Should I grab Jonathan?" Joshua asked, adjusting his hat on his head.

"No, we should be fine with us. The group doesn't have any new riders. They all have experience."

"Good. Let's get this over with. I need to get busy doing other chores."

"You okay?" Joey asked when they stepped into the corral with Jeremiah on their heels.

"Yeah, you look kinda green, brother." Jeremiah laughed because he knew Joshua was still hung over from the night before. He'd been watching from his seat next to Callie at the table where all the brothers with girlfriends had taken up residence.

"Kiss my ass, Jeremiah. You know damned well what went down last night."

"A distinctive case of blue balls, I think."

"Fuck you," he growled under his breath to keep the guests from hearing him as they approached. "Who needs help mounting?"

The rest of the morning was spent taking several groups out for hourly rides, grooming the horses, feeding, watering, and just general ranch work. It kept his mind off Candace even though he wished he knew if he'd see her again. *Maybe I can get Arnold's number from the phone book and call there. Nah, too forward.*

He contemplated the idea off and on all day long until the sun finally started to go down. The day had been completed. He could finally take some Tylenol and hit his bed early even though it was a Saturday night. His usual bar hopping would have to wait until his stomach settled down or he died, one or the other.

Car lights came up the driveway, heading for the main lodge.

He really didn't want to deal with guests tonight, so he walked toward the house hoping to avoid the newest arrivals. Just as he got to the door, his mother pushed it open, balancing on her crutches. "Oh Joshua, can you see to the new guest's luggage? She's arriving late and just wanted to settle into her room for the night."

"Uh, sure, Mom." He grumbled to himself as he turned back toward the waiting car. "God, *please* just let me die. I knew I shouldn't have hit those shots of tequila after I drank six beers, but I just needed to forget the ache in my—"

"Joshua?"

"Candace?"

* * * *

"What are you doing here?"

"I asked around town about you, and this is where they pointed me to."

"I thought you were going back to Los Angeles today?"

"I gave Arnold a choice. Stay out of my business or else."

Joshua laughed, the sound rumbling deep in his chest as he came closer. She liked it. The hearty, low laughter fit him perfectly. Those crystal clear, blue eyes reflected the light coming from the house. His hair hung a little longer than she normally liked on a guy, but the little scruff of five o'clock shadow had her humming her appreciation. She liked a man with muscles. Boy, did he have some all over. His biceps bulged from long days wrestling cattle. His chest looked sculpted and hard from throwing hay or some such cowboy thing. She just knew he was the real thing when someone mentioned cowboy.

"I'm glad you came to find me."

"I'm glad too."

"Are you staying at the ranch?" he asked, stuffing his hands in his front pockets.

"For a couple of days. I needed to get away from Arnold if you and I were going to…you know."

"Fuck?"

"Yeah," she replied, heat flaming her cheeks. How could she be embarrassed now after the bold way she talked the night before? It had been the alcohol talking. She probably shouldn't have had those two shots of whiskey between the beers. It was a good thing she hadn't been stopped on the short trip back to Arnold's, otherwise she'd probably have been arrested for DUI.

"What's wrong?"

She lowered her eyes. "Nothing."

He stepped in front of her and brought her chin up with a finger beneath it. "You're embarrassed by crass talk? You weren't last night."

"I had a bit too much to drink last night."

He pulled his hat off and pushed his fingers through his hair. "Yeah, me too. I'm a bit hung over today."

"Me too."

"How about we save the fucking for when we both feel better?"

"I'd like that."

He wrapped an arm around her shoulder in a hug, pulling her into his chest for a minute. "Good. I would too." After he stepped back, he moved around to the back of her car. "Pop the trunk, and I'll get your bag so we can get you registered."

Once she got the back of the car open, she stuffed the keys in her bag before she shut the trunk. "Thank you."

She fell into step beside him as they took the gravel walkway toward the front of the huge main building. A soft, warm glow illuminated the front walk of the house and the rockers set along the front porch. Several antique items graced the long expanse as well, including an old wringer washing machine, an antique ice box and what looked like a piece of an old plow. The whole building looked like something out of an old western movie. She loved it.

"No problem. My mom is waiting for you inside. I'm assuming you were her last minute guest she sent me out to help."

"Your mom?"

"Yeah. You'll love her. She's a great lady."

When Joshua pulled open the door, they ran smack into Jason and Peyton walking out. "Oh hey, bro."

Her mouth fell open in a soft oh as she looked at Jason and back to Joshua.

Joshua explained, "We're two of a set of identical triplets. You'll meet Joel at some point too."

"Triplets?"

"Yes."

"Wow."

"Yeah, a lot of people say that." He pointed to his brother and said, "This is Jason and his wife, Peyton. You met her at the bar last night."

"Oh yeah. Nice to see you again. It's Candace, right?"

"Yes."

"A friend of Arnold's?"

"Right again. He's my ex brother-in-law."

"Mary is your sister?" Jason asked, sliding an arm around Peyton's shoulder. "I remember her. Nice lady."

"Yes, she was."

"Was?"

"She committed suicide about a year ago."

"Oh my. I'm so sorry," Peyton said, squeezing her fingers. "If you want to talk while you're here, I'd be glad to listen."

"Peyton's is finishing up her degree in counseling," Jason said.

"That's awesome." Candace shuffled her feet a little as she glanced down. She wasn't really comfortable talking about her sister and what happened outside of telling people she committed suicide. The whole thing still left a bitter taste in her mouth.

"It's okay if you don't want to. I just thought I'd offer since I've been there myself."

"You have?"

"There were times I thought of suicide, yes. During the emotional abuse I suffered, there were plenty of times I wanted to end it all with a bullet or something, but I couldn't bring myself to do it. I knew there was something better for me out there." She leaned into her husband's embrace. "And I found it right under my nose at The Dusty Boot."

"I love you."

"I love you too, Jason. You're my life."

"Okay. Enough. Gag. Sputter. Spit."

"Oh hush, Joshua. You'll be there someday. Just wait."

Jason and Peyton laughed as they headed out the door. "You two have fun."

"We will," Joshua answered when the door closed behind them, and he ushered Candace through what appeared to be a large dining room. Several large picnic tables lined the walls. A long serving buffet sat off to one side where they served the meals. A huge coffee pot sat on a table between two openings that led into the main room of the ranch. "This is where we take meals. There will be a bell rung when it's time to eat. Breakfast is at eight. Lunch at noon and dinner at six."

They approached an office set back in the corner of the large room. To her left, out of the corner of her eye, she saw a cowboy sitting on one of the long leather couches near the fireplace. When she turned to get a better look, there wasn't anyone there. *Weird.*

A strikingly beautiful woman hobbled out on crutches as they approached, with her hand extended. Her long dark hair hung to the middle of her back in an inky cloud. Her features where close to Joshua's although Candace assumed he shared some other striking resemblance to his father. "You must be Candace. I'm Nina. My husband James and I are the parents of this brood of men."

"Ah. It's nice to meet you."

"You too. I have your room all ready. It's here in the main lodge. Joshua can show you up there. I just need your credit card."

"Sure." Shaking her head, Candace pulled out her wallet to hand Nina the card.

"Something wrong?"

"No. I guess not." She extended her arm toward Nina with her credit card between her fingers. "I just thought I saw someone sitting on the couch over there, but now there isn't anyone there."

"Oh. That's one of our resident ghosts. He's here a lot. Pay him no mind."

Nina went inside the office to run her credit card while Candace glanced at Joshua. "Ghost?"

"Yeah. We have a few. Him. A couple who hangs out upstairs and some kids who make noise in the yard."

"And I'm staying upstairs where these hang out?"

"I can have Mom give you one of the cabin rooms. They're usually quieter."

"No. I'm okay." She shivered a little at the thought of ghosts running around the property willy-nilly. "I think."

"You'll be just down the hall from Joshua's room in two-eleven."

"Great."

"I'll show you where it is so I can take your bag up there."

"I appreciate it."

"Did he tell you when breakfast is?"

"Yes, ma'am."

"Good. Thanks, Joshua," Nina said, closing the office door behind her as she got ready to leave for the night, hobbling on her crutches a few feet. "Coffee is always on down here if you find yourself an early riser or need a cup before bed. There is water for tea too."

She smiled, thinking how lovely this family turned out to be. Joshua had a great home life, it sounded like. "Thank you. You've been such a gracious hostess."

"Oh, you're welcome, dear. Just make sure to lock your door when you retire and ignore any sounds you hear up there during the night. Sometimes they get a little rowdy."

"I will. I have an iPod. I can play some soft music to drown out the sounds if I need to."

"If you hear arguing, that's them. They usually quiet down before midnight though. Did Joshua tell you this used to be a brothel?"

"A brothel? Wow. No, he didn't tell me."

"I was going to give you the tour tomorrow since I'm off."

"That would be fantastic. I'd love to get the whole cowboy feel."

"We have a pool, some horseshoe pits and lots of other things for guests to do. Make sure he shows you everything."

"Oh, I plan to."

"Night, kids." Nina waved as she moved slowly toward the long hall that lead to their personal quarters.

"Come on. I'll show you to your room."

"Will you join me?"

"I thought we agreed not tonight?"

She shrugged as she glanced at the floor. "I wouldn't mind just having you hold me. Being single really sucks sometimes for that one and one feel, you know."

He stopped her with a hand on her arm. "Listen, Candace. Girlfriends are great, but you don't live here. It's not like anything can come of a relationship between us."

With a sigh, she glanced up at him, realizing just how tall he stood compared to her five-something frame. "I'm not looking for a relationship, Joshua. Living in Los Angeles would be conducive to any kind of relationship anyway, even if I wanted one. I don't plan on moving. I have a life there. A business. My family."

"Okay. I just want to make sure we're on the same page, darlin'. If you want to have a good time for the timeframe you're here, I'm all for that."

"Sounds good to me."

They walked up the wooden stairs to the first landing. "There are rooms down this hall, but yours is on the next level."

"Where do the ghosts hang out?"

"On the second floor and third floor landing usually."

"Oh, goody."

"I can change your room if you like. Mom wouldn't mind."

"No, it's fine, but I might end up in your room for the night just so I can sleep. I'm not real fond of ghosts."

He smiled. "They don't hurt anything. It's a residual thing. They argue, you hear some crashing glass and then it stops usually. It only goes on once or twice a night."

"Great." She rolled her eyes as they reached the second floor.

"Your room is at the end of the hall."

"Where is yours?"

"Two doors down from yours."

Tilting her head to the side, she looked him up and down. She really wanted him in her bed tonight, but it probably wasn't a good idea since they both felt like shit. She could really use some sex though. She might just have to dig out B.O.B.

"What are you thinking?" he asked, opening her door and putting her suitcase on the bed.

"How much I want you in my bed."

"How much?"

"A lot, cowboy."

"Good because I want to be there too." He pushed his fingers into the hair at her temple as he lowered his head.

"Do you masturbate?"

Her question snapped his head back in shock.

He choked a bit before he answered, "Sometimes."

She thought the red stain on his cheeks was cute. He really did blush. "Me too, and baby, I plan to masturbate to the look in your eyes when you look at me. You want me. Bad."

"You really are kind of bold, aren't you?"

She raked a fingernail down his chest before she fiddled with a button on the front of his shirt, debating on whether to undo it and lick the skin beneath. "When I know what I want, I go after it. I want you. Right now."

He took her hand in his, stopping her movement. "Tomorrow night. It's a date." He leaned in and kissed her on the nose. "Sleep well."

"Party pooper."

The grin he flashed her curled her toes. The man truly had it all. Tall, dark, handsome, big blue eyes, hair peeking out from under the cowboy hat, tight western shirt across his broad chest and Wrangler jeans just tight enough to make her mouth water. She wondered what the scruff on his face would feel like on the sensitive skin of her inner thighs. She hoped tomorrow, she'd find out.

"You'll survive the night, darlin', and then tomorrow evenin', I'll rock your world."

"Is that a promise?"

"You bet."

"I'm holding you to it."

"I'll see you in the mornin'."

"Night, cowboy."

"Goodnight."

Chapter Three

Used to being up at the crack of dawn, Joshua rolled out of bed at daybreak even though he'd had a rough night. Horny didn't adequately describe his state of affairs after Candace ran her fingernails down his chest. The shivers that had raced down his body mystified him. He'd never reacted to a woman so strongly before, not anyone around Bandera anyway. He'd been to bed with a few of the single ladies in town, but they didn't trip his trigger the way Candace did with merely a touch.

Oh well. He'd play it for what it was worth. She wasn't a local girl. Worrying about her getting all tied up in him the way some women around here played it wouldn't be a problem. Many of them wanted the Young name and what they thought was a lucrative business in their ranch. Little did they know, the place wasn't making millions. They did okay and managed to survive from year to year, but as the boys kept adding to the family herd, things got tighter and tighter.

A moment later, he stood in front of the bathroom mirror in his jeans, tilting his head from left to right, examining the five o'clock shadow on his chin and cheeks. He really hated shaving most mornings. It seemed to be the bane of his existence with the dark hair. Dark chest hair sprinkled across his pecs while a thin line trailed toward his groin. Some women liked that little happy trail. He shrugged. He wondered if Candace liked to go down on a man.

Eating pussy was one of his favorite past times, so he couldn't quite understand when a man didn't want to do that for a woman. They sure seemed to like it when he did it. A chuckle escaped him as he ran his right hand over his cheek. He slathered shaving cream across the surface in preparation to shave the stubble from his face. Whisker burn on a creamy white surface made him smile as he lost himself in thoughts of Candace with her pretty thighs wrapped around his head.

When he'd finished raking the razor over his face, he smoothed his hand over the surface to check for residual stubble left behind. He'd probably have to shave again before their resounding bout of sex tonight so he wouldn't scrape her up with it, but he'd leave that for later. He had plans to wine and dine her today with a picnic, horseback riding, and lots of making out before tonight. He wanted her hot and ready for him when they got around to making the bedsprings squeak.

A small knock on the door spun him around. Who could be there this time of morning? It wasn't even breakfast time yet.

He opened the door a moment later to find Candace dressed in a form fitting pair of jeans, white blouse and cowboy boots.

"I'm glad you're up. How about a sunrise horseback ride?" she asked, leaning against the door frame with her arms crossed under her impressive breasts.

The thought of burying his face between them and licking her pert little nipples had him hard in a flash. Horseback riding would be interesting with a hard-on. "Sure. Have you had coffee yet?"

"Yep. I've been downstairs, drank a cup, did some work on my laptop, and fed the donkeys."

"Wow. Are you always an early riser? I didn't think you'd be up yet."

"I'm usually at work by six in the morning at home. Running your own business is a twenty-four hour job."

"I imagine," he said, slipping on his shirt while she watched. He really did like the look in her eyes when she ran her gaze over his frame. "For us it is. We have guests arriving all hours of the night. Entertaining some of the guests is a big job."

"Does each of you have a specific one to do around the place?"

"Not so much. A few of us do, like Joey handles the new horses. Jeff acts as the foreman of the ranch. Jonathan handles the website and marketing stuff. Jeremiah is the financial planner. He handles our investments and whatnot." He sat on the bed for a moment to slip on his boots. Nothing compared to a well-made pair of cowboy boots, in his mind. Comfort and fit made all the difference in the world. He glanced down at the boots on her feet. They looked brand new. "Did you buy boots in town before you came out here?"

Pink stained her cheeks when she blushed. The tips of the boots bounced up and down slightly as she wiggled her toes in them. "Does it show that much?"

"They look new is all."

"Not like yours."

"I wear mine every day so yeah, there is a difference between my worn ones and your new ones."

"I needed to be the quintessential cowgirl when I came out here. I figured you liked that kind of woman."

He brushed his fingertips across her cheek. "I like you just the way you are. Cowgirls are great, but I don't have to have one to be happy."

"What kind of woman do you like?"

"Your kind."

The smile spreading across her lips lit up the room. It obviously didn't take a lot to make her happy. He frowned, wondering what kind of life she led that the smallest compliment would light up her world.

"Shall we get some coffee?"

She laughed. "I've already had some."

"Would you like another cup? I can't function without having a cup of java before I start the day." He pulled the door shut behind him before they headed down the hall to the stairs. "I hope the ghosts didn't keep you up last night. I don't hear them much anymore since I'm used to it now."

"I heard them for a little bit, but like your mother said, they quieted down before midnight. I worked on some stuff on my laptop. When I heard the noises, I listened for a bit, then went to bed."

"Hear anything interesting?"

"Nothing more than you told me. They argued a bit. I heard something break, and then they stopped." They reached the landing at the bottom of the stairs and headed toward the coffee pot. "It wasn't too bad. It's interesting to hear it though. I couldn't make out the words, just murmuring of an argument."

"You heard the majority of it then."

"Have you ever done more research on the place to see if you could find out who they are?"

"Not really. We know the place was a working cattle ranch way back when and later a brothel when the family lost the ranch to the bank. We think the kids were from the ranch heyday. The cowboy too, but we figure the couple was one of the call girls who worked here when it was a brothel."

"They could be the ranch owner and his wife too."

He nodded in acceptance of her thought. "True."

"It would be interesting to know the background."

"We take the ghosts with a grain of salt. They are here and don't interact much, except the cowboy."

"He does?"

Joshua put his cup beneath the spout on the coffee pot to pour the pungent brew. Coffee was his life's blood sometimes when he'd had a hard night. "Yeah. He answers good mornin' when you say it to him or tips his hat when he's seen, but nothing much more than that." Interesting how she'd taken to wanting to know more about the history of the place than even his parents.

"I think it would make a great documentary. You know how people like ghost stories, and if we caught it on video, that would be something. It would make your place famous."

"We don't want the weirdo ghost people out here sniffing around. We just like to do our thing and leave them to theirs."

Excitement surrounded her. "But you all could be rich. Don't you want more money than you could possibly spend?"

"Not really, no."

"I don't understand."

"Do you come from money, Candace?"

"Well, yeah, I guess you could say that. I grew up not wanting for anything, and I have a trust fund I'll get when I turn thirty."

He pushed his hat back on his head. "How much?"

"What?"

"How much is your trust fund?"

"Ten, but I don't see—"

"Ten what? Million, billion, thousand?"

"Million."

"I'm lucky to have twenty bucks in my pocket to party on during a Saturday night binge at The Dusty Boot. My parents raised us nine boys on this ranch without a silver spoon in our mouths. You don't know what it's like to have to work for your money."

"Yes I do, Joshua. I have my own company. I work from six in the morning to midnight most nights. I work my ass off for what I have."

He sipped his coffee, contemplating how to say what was on his mind without pissing her off. "But you have a trust fund to fall back on. I'm not knocking your way of life, but don't assume we all want what you have, darlin', because we don't. I like the simple life, my horses, the cattle, the sunsets, and sunrises over the hills of our ranch. This is my existence, and I like it this way."

She put her hand on his arm. "I can see how that kind of life would be appealing, but what about nice cars, boats, vacations?"

"I have everything I need right here."

"Let's just agree to disagree on this since I can't seem to convince you that having money isn't all that bad."

"I'm not sayin' it is, but you have to realize everything isn't about money. Love of family is an important part of my life, and I wouldn't change it."

"I love my family too."

"I'm sure you do."

"Why do I get the feeling you're patronizing me?" she asked, her hand on her hip although a smile played on her kissable lips.

She'd matched him word for word during their little disagreement. Her personality definitely said she was intelligent, spunky, and wouldn't back down in a fight. He wondered what the business she mentioned entailed. "I'm not patronizing you at all, darlin'." He brought the cup to his lips for a sip of the coffee as she did the same. "What type of business do you have?"

"I run a computer programming firm."

"So you know computers?"

She laughed. "I've known a few, yeah."

"You'll have great conversations with Jonathan then. He's our computer genius around here."

"Great. I'd like to talk shop with him while I'm here."

The workers started filing in to get breakfast ready which would be in about an hour. "Would you like to wait until after breakfast for our ride?"

"If you want to show me some other stuff around the ranch and then ride, that's fine with me."

"I want to give you the most for your money of the cowboy experience. Ridin', ropin', swimmin', four-wheelin', muddin'—"

She giggled. "What the hell is muddin'?"

"It's where we take our trucks through the huge mud puddle, throwing mud everywhere. It's a great time."

"Mud everywhere?"

"Yep."

"Sounds like fun."

"We usually have a bunch of people from town come out, have a bonfire, roast marshmallows. You know."

"Why don't you show me around the ranch while we wait for breakfast?"

"Sounds good." He tossed the dregs of his coffee into the trashcan as she did the same. He grasped her hand in his, wondering at the zing of spark shooting up his arm from her touch. Women weren't hard to come by when you were a cowboy to the bone. He was used to women coming onto him, but this one was a nice mixture of bold and shy at the same time. "What do you want to see first?"

"Whatever you want to show me."

They wandered around the ranch, checked out the gardens, the barns, walked up the trails a bit, went by the swimming pool, and then stopped at the rocking chairs on the front porch while the donkeys pestered them for goodies, until they heard the clang of the breakfast bell. "Shall we get some breakfast?"

"Yeah, I'm starving."

"Good. A girl who likes to eat. It bugs me when girls only eat a salad or some shit when I'm eating steak."

"Not me, buddy. I like my food."

He laughed as he held out a hand to help her to her feet and escorted her into the dining room. They crossed the main lodge meeting room, through the arched entry way into the dining room while the rest of the guests began filing in for food. He stopped at the family table to tell them he would be eating with Candace.

Once they grabbed their food, she found them a corner spot where they could sit and talk quietly. He knew the noise got to be pretty loud in there when they had big groups. Right now, it was off season so things were a bit slower. They still had a couple of families with some rambunctious kids.

He took the seat across from her to be able to look into her eyes. She had pretty eyes. The green almost reminded him of the junipers on the mountain, a deep forest green. They sparkled with mischief as he put a forkful of eggs into his mouth. "What?"

"You. I never thought I'd be spending time with a real cowboy on this trip. I figured I'd be stuck in Arnold's house watching television the whole time while he worked or something." She looked down at her plate before catching his gaze again. "Thank you."

"I haven't done anything yet, darlin'."

One perfectly arched eyebrow went up over her left eye. "Oh but you will, cowboy, you will."

* * * *

Candace couldn't believe how bold she was being with Joshua. She never acted this way, well almost never. She was usually the bookworm, nerdy type girl, who spent most of her time in the library in college, rather than partying with the girls who couldn't seem to go more than three months without sleeping with someone. Not her. She'd only had one serious boyfriend in her past, and she'd dumped him not too long ago. The creep had been using her for her money and name. She'd kicked him out when she caught him screwing one of her employees on a desk at work. They'd been dating for three years, and she thought she'd loved him. Apparently, he didn't love her though. She hadn't realized it until after she'd caught him cheating, that he'd been pulling away from her the minute he found out she didn't get her trust fund until she was thirty. He couldn't wait that long to start spending her money. She should have known though. The signs had been there, everything from making her buy dinner when they went out to not paying his half of the rent for the last several months. She'd been used heartily. She wouldn't be used again. She planned to be the user in whatever situation now. "Are you up for the rodeo, cowboy?"

"Whatever you say, honey."

The minute they finished their meal, Joshua grabbed both their plates and took them to the dirty dish bin, while she finished her orange juice and walked the glass to the bin herself. "So what's first?" she asked, shoving her hands into her back pockets.

He swiped the hat from his head to brush some of the hair back before replacing it. "I thought we'd go for a ride up in the hills. I can show you the scenery while I check on the fences."

"I thought you were off today?"

"We never really have a day off, it seems. One day is a little less busy than the others is all." He glanced at her face and arms. "Do you have a hat?"

"No."

"Come on. Mom has some in the store you can purchase. You need one to protect your fair complexion in this Texas sun."

"I live in California. I'm in the sun all the time." She looked at her arms and the slight tan she sported. "I'll be okay."

"Trust me on this. You go pick out a hat while I get us a couple of bottles of water to take along. Even though it doesn't seem that hot right now, it could get pretty warm, even this late in the season."

A sharp exhale rushed from her mouth. "All right. I'll bow to your expertise on this since you live here and I don't."

"Good girl." He swatted her butt as she walked back into the main room and to the right to check out the assortment of cowboy hats in the small store.

There were tons of little knick-knacks, cowboy hats, decorations, cowboy things, and T-shirts. She found herself browsing through the selection of hats on the rack, trying on first one and then another before Joshua came in to find her. "Which one looks better? The one with the feathers down the back or the one with the gold hat band?"

"The feathers look more like something you would wear."

"This coming from the cowboy who noticed my brand new boots."

He smiled. "I'm very observant."

"You are, huh?"

"Yes, ma'am. I notice how you lick your lips when I get close, like this." He stepped near her, leaning in so his mouth was only a few inches from hers. "I see your eyes dilate. I can tell your nipples pebble the closer I get."

His breath fanned over her lips, making them ache for the touch of his.

"Your fingers are curled tight around the brim of that hat as the need to reach for me overwhelms you."

His scent surrounded her. Musk and male mixed with a woodsy smell reached her nose as her breathing increased tenfold.

He didn't touch her. He didn't have to. Her body went on high alert for this man the minute he'd turned around in the bar. She needed him, wanted him, would kill to have him kiss her right here, right now in the middle of his mom's shop. "Kiss me."

"Nope." He backed up, taking the hat from her hands and putting it on her head. "Two horses await us, ma'am, and anticipation is half the fun."

He pushed her out the door and around the corner so she could tell his mom to put the hat on her tab before they went outside to find the horses in the stable.

"Have you been on horseback before?"

"Once or twice. Nothing recently."

"I'll make sure to rub your sore spots then." They walked through the big doorway into the cooler interior of the tack room before he escorted her out the back door to where the horses were tied. Black, brown, spotted, gold colored, big ones, smaller ones and one huge red colored horse stood tied to the fences with water buckets near their feet. Each had a heavy leather saddle across their backs with a bulky blanket underneath. Some had metal bits in their mouths with one piece of leather over their ears while others only had what she remembered were called halters.

"Do you want a gentle horse?"

"That would probably be a good idea, although not a glue factory ready-made one, please."

His laughter burst from his lips in a gut-rolling explosion of guffaws. She liked his laugh and his smile. Hell, she liked him…a lot.

A moment later, he brought over a beautiful sorrel mare with a white blaze down her nose. "She's gorgeous!"

"Her name is Pearl."

The hair on the mare's nose felt soft when Candace ran her palm across the surface. "How are you, pretty girl?"

The horse nickered softly as if she answered in kind.

"Do you think you can mount or would you like to use the mounting block?"

"I think I could swing my big butt up there."

He waggled his eyebrows. "I could give you a boost."

"That would be mighty kind of you, sir." She did a little bobbing curtsy, sweeping her imaginary gown to the side. When he picked her up by the waist to plop her in the saddle, she let out a little squeal. "Thank you, kind sir."

He tipped his hat in that adorable cowboy way. "You're mighty welcome, ma'am."

The horse did a little sidestep, jostling her as she stared too hard. The view of Joshua hoisting himself into the saddle on another horse got her blood pumping. *Damn, he had a fine ass in those jeans. Wranglers. Country folks called them Wranglers and by damn I'm going to be country for the month I'm here.*

As Joshua led the way out of the corral, her horse voluntarily followed behind close enough she could see the breadth of his shoulders in his western style shirt, the strength of his hands when he grasped the reins in a relaxed grip and the bulge of his arms as he guided the horse around boulders in their path.

"Where are we going?" she asked, talking loudly in case he couldn't hear her from back where she followed behind.

He twisted around in the saddle a bit to talk to her. "To a little spot I know. You'll love it. There's a nice little pool where the stream comes down the mountain. The water is kind of cold, but you can dip your pretty little toes in it, so you can enjoy the bubbling stream."

"Sounds like heaven."

"It's a little piece of heaven here on Thunder Ridge. Us boys used to go down there in the summer and swim all the time."

"How far is it?"

"Not far. It'll take about half an hour to get there."

"What are all these trees?"

"Juniper."

"Isn't Texas known for bluebonnets?"

"Yes, but they come out in the spring. It's right pretty that time of year around here."

"I bet." They rode in silence for a bit. Her thighs had begun to hurt already from riding. She hoped they got to the pond soon otherwise her pussy wouldn't be up to having sex tonight with the hunky cowboy riding in front of her. "Are we almost there?"

"You're as bad as a kid asking are we there yet." He laughed.

The sound sent shivers down her arms. "Sorry. I haven't been on a horse in a long time."

"We haven't been riding that long."

"I'm still going to be walking bowlegged at this rate."

He chuckled again while they rounded a huge boulder. The scene before her took her breath away. A large pond surrounded by boulders spread out like a smorgasbord with flowers, junipers, and rocks scattered about. Water poured over the large rocks in a beautiful waterfall. "Wow."

"I knew you'd like it."

"This is gorgeous, Joshua. I can see why you wanted to come here."

"We don't get to visit it as much as we did when I was a kid, but I do try to come out here about once a week just to think. It's quiet."

He swung down from his saddle in the smoothest motion she could have imagined. She sighed when he tied his horse to a low hanging branch before he walked toward her in a natural cowboy swagger.

"Let me help you."

She got her leg over the saddle horn before he reached up with his big hands, wrapped them around her waist and swung her around. She slid down his torso. The fire burning in his gaze set her insides into an inferno of need. *Lordy*. She wanted to experience this man's touch more than her next breath. "Joshua," she whispered, holding a death grip on his biceps, afraid he would let her go, and she'd toppled into a heap on the ground at his feet, not that she would mind worshipping him like the god he was.

When her boots finally touched the ground, she realized just how much taller than her five-foot five-inch frame he stood. He had to be at least six foot three, she guessed when she looked up into the beautiful blue of his gaze. *What gorgeous eyes.*

"You are a beautiful woman."

"Uh, thanks."

"I could eat you up." He stepped back. "But I won't right now."

"Why the hell not?"

"It's not the right time." He chuckled again as he moved toward the pool to their right. "Anticipation."

"I'm anticipating throttling you if you don't touch me soon."

He glanced back over his shoulder with a crooked grin while he struggled to take one of his boots off. "You comin'?"

Chapter Four

"Not yet, cowboy."

The cocky grin returned. He got the other boot off, pulled off his socks and then rolled up his pant legs. "The water feels great. Come on."

She sighed heavily before moving to his side. She wanted to push his ass into the water or jump in herself to cool the burning in her pussy. The level of desire this man had her simmering at went beyond anything she'd experienced before. Heat boiled just below the surface of her skin.

"You okay? Your face is flush."

"I'm fine," she gritted out. She plopped down on the rock next to him, clenching her fists while she tried to keep from jumping him right there next to the pool.

"You don't look fine." He touched her cheeks with his palms. "You aren't hot."

"I'm not?"

"Well, you are in one sense of the word, but feverish, no." He reached over and pulled off her boots before her socks. "Put your feet in. It's really a nice temperature."

The cool water soothed her frazzled nerves. Jumping him seemed like a reckless thing to do, but man did she want him badly. "Thanks."

"For what?"

"Helping with my boots. The water does feel fabulous." He smiled that crooked little grin of his, tempting her to taste him from the gorgeous mouth to wherever she ended up last. "What are we going to do from here?"

"Fishing is out since we didn't bring poles." He tapped his fingers against his chin while he concentrated. "We have a lot more land you haven't seen. How about we ride some fence while we're out?"

"Okay." She didn't sound convinced even to herself.

"You wanted to experience everything cowboy, right?"

"Yeah, but I was thinking of other experiences."

"I plan to take you from city to country girl in the space of the month you're here. You will have everything country from the food, to ridin' horses, to muddin', to four-wheelin'."

"Sounds perfect."

He leaned back on the rock with his hands behind his head. His hat shaded his eyes from the sun, keeping her from seeing the gorgeous blue of his gaze. *Those eyes make me all gooey inside.* She wanted nothing more than to snuggle up to his side, rest her head on his tempting chest, and tick away the afternoon without a care in the world. It sounded like a little piece of heaven to her. Instead, she swished her feet around in the water, loving the feel of the cool wetness on her toes.

"Are those the things everyone likes to do for fun around here?"

He turned toward her, pushing his hat back so he could look at her. "Yep. Drinkin', dancin'. You know. All those kinds of thing. What do you city folk do for fun?"

She leaned back on her hands as she watched a bird flit from tree branch to tree branch across the pond. The sunlight reflected off the water, making it sparkle like diamonds in the sunlight. "We go out to the beach to listen to the water lap against the shoreline. Drive out to the mountains to go skiing. Go to the lake to water ski. Maybe go out to dinner at a nice restaurant, all dressed up in our best clothes. Have dinner parties at the house where everyone sits around drinking wine, talking, and laughing."

"Sounds kind of boring."

"No, not really. It's what we do."

"I think you'll like doing all the physical stuff we do our here. You look like a physical kind of girl."

"I do like to go hiking and swimming."

"Did you bring a bathing suit?"

"Of course."

"Are you wearing it now?"

"No." She glanced his way, wondering what he might be getting at.

"Too bad. I'd take you into the pond. It's deep enough to swim, but shallow enough to stand."

A thought crossed her mind and she giggled as she stood up. "Sounds good to me." She drew her T-shirt over her head and tossed it onto the rock next to him. Her bra came next, then her pants and underwear. "Last one in has to ride home in wet clothes." She jumped in, coming up for air in the center.

"Oh no you don't."

He quickly stripped out of his clothing, leaving nothing to her imagination. The man was gorgeous. His broad chest sprinkled with chest hair, took her breath away. The trim waist showed off a body the gods would weep for. A sexy little happy trail wound down his abdomen, showing off his six-pack abs to perfection. His biceps bulged with each movement while he worked his jeans off his legs. His long, thick cock bobbed against his stomach. Even partially aroused, the man had it going on in more ways than one.

"Wow," she whispered as she watched him slide into the pool of water.

He came up for air near where she stood in the middle of the pond. "This feels good. The heat seems to be climbing today."

"Yeah."

"Are you okay?"

"I'm great," she said breathlessly, not sure if it was because he was standing in front of her buck-ass naked or because of the cool water.

His fingers did a slow crawl up her arm to her shoulder, leaving goose bumps in their wake. "Are you sure you're okay? You look, I don't know, a little flustered."

"I am."

"Why," he whispered, leaning in to the point where his lips were almost touching hers.

She wanted him to kiss her. She needed him to touch her somewhere, anywhere. "Kiss me."

"My pleasure."

He softly brushed his lips against hers, a mere touch like butterfly wings softly whispering over her mouth. Everything tingled from the roots of her hair to her toes. She wanted more.

His tongue danced along the seam of her lips, asking her to allow him in. Should she? *What the hell.* She opened her mouth, giving him the access he wanted, letting him take this encounter to the next level. He pushed his tongue deep into her mouth with a soft moan. She titled her head to the side, allowing him to deepen the kiss to mind-blowing. Her hands settled on his shoulders while his snaked around her body, bringing her into full chest to breast contact.

The hair on his skin tickled the swell of her breast, pulling her nipples into tight, tingling nubs of pleasure. Her pussy throbbed with need to have him inside her, but he held back, only kissing her until she couldn't breathe without him surrounding her senses.

When his mouth left hers to slide from her lips to her ear, she sighed in contentment. She wrapped her arms around his neck, guiding his mouth lower.

The water lapped at her breasts just above her nipple line, giving him full access to her neck, shoulder and upper breast. His mouth skimmed over the surface, causing her to shiver in the wake of his assault on her skin. He nipped at her ear, the skin of her neck, then her shoulder while he made his way lower still.

His fingers made their way down her abdomen to dive between her parted thighs.

Yes!

One finger scraped along her clit, driving her up on her toes as his mouth closed over her left nipple to suck strongly.

A heavy moan escaped her lips. She wanted this, needed this. It had been a long time since she'd had sex, and never had a man driven her to distraction the way Joshua had.

"Please."

"Please what?" he asked around the flesh of her breast. "Please suck harder? Please finger-fuck me? Please touch me? You need to be more specific, Candace."

"All of the above?" She squirmed when the tip of his finger penetrated her pussy, giving her just a teasing of what was to come.

He took her nipple into his mouth, sucking hard enough he brought the tip to the roof and rubbed it with his tongue.

"Ah!" When his fingers pushed all the way inside her, the threadbare control with which she held onto her sanity slipped. "God, Joshua. I can't stand it. Make me come, please."

He lifted her into his arms and strolled toward the bank where their clothes lay. The rocks dug into her back when he laid her down on the sandy shoreline, but she didn't care. She wanted this more than anything.

"I'm not going to make love to you."

"What? Why the hell not?"

"Because I want to savor that moment in time with everything inside me. For now, I will worship your body with my mouth."

His lips skimmed over her breast, licking and nipping as he went farther down, across her abdomen until he was positioned between her thighs with her legs over his shoulders. At the first touch of his tongue to her aching clit, she almost came off the sand like a bottle rocket whizzing across the sky. Her body hummed with need so strong, she lost her mind when he shoved two fingers into her pussy again, sucking her clit between his lips not a second later.

When he curled his fingers up behind her pubic bone to hit that special spot, she flew apart on a cry of ecstasy with his name on her lips.

Her body slowly returned to a pre-orgasmic state as her heart rate decelerated and her breathing went back to normal. He crawled up beside her and wrapped her in his embrace as he laid back in the sand.

His cock lay hard against her hip. "I should help you out even if we aren't going to make love. You are hurting, I'm sure."

"Baby, it's okay. I'm good until we can find a bed, some cool sheets and a condom."

"You don't have one on you?"

He propped himself up on his elbow, his free hand skimmed from one breast to the other in a slow motion.

"No. I didn't plan on making love to you out here although it's pretty sexy how you came apart a minute ago."

He circled the nipple of her left breast with his fingers, curling her toes in the process. "Bummer."

"We have plenty of time."

"We should probably get dressed. What if one of your brothers comes out here?"

"They won't unless they are looking for me. I told Joey we were headed out here."

She ran a fingernail down his chest, swirling it in the hair lying there for a moment before she traveled farther down to his cock. "This is rather nice."

"I'm glad you like it."

"What kinds of things do you like when a woman goes down on you?"

"Let's see. Swirling her tongue around the head. Using her fingers to caress my balls while she's sucking. The whole warmth of her mouth around the shaft really does it for me, but it's the feeling of her fingers on my balls at the same time that will shoot me through the ceiling."

"I'll keep that in mind when I have a chance to wrap my mouth around your luscious cock."

His breath caught in his throat for a moment before he released it in a heavy sigh. "Sounds like a little piece of heaven to me."

"Oh, you'll think so before I'm done with you."

"How about we get dressed, head back to the ranch and get some lunch."

"Already?"

He picked up his watch from the pile of clothes. "Yep. It's almost eleven-thirty and by the time we dress and ride back, it'll be lunch time."

He raked his gaze down her body, heating her up with nothing more than the look in his eyes.

"After lunch we can find something else to do. Maybe four-wheelin'."

"Sounds good." She managed to sit up for a second before he pulled her back down for another toe-curling kiss.

"I needed that before we got dressed."

"Mmm. Me too."

The look in his eyes while he watched her put her clothes back on, told her he wanted her badly. When he shoved his still engorged cock into his jeans and zipped them up, her mouth watered to taste him, smell him and see where the afternoon would lead right there on the sandy shoreline. Alas, he didn't bring a condom, and she hadn't either. Love making would have to wait. No matter, she knew they would get there eventually. Anticipation might kill her before they did, but she could handle it if she had to. Right now, she had to.

As she sat on the rock to slip on her boots, she watched him do the same. It would be an uncomfortable ride back for him, she was sure. She shrugged. She'd offered to take care of his problem with or without a condom, but he wouldn't budge. He was careful. Too careful almost, making her consider what might've made him that way. Did he have a past love who'd wronged him? Maybe some women had given him some kind of disease. Or maybe gotten pregnant when he didn't want a child?

She really didn't know much about him. She probably should do some questioning before this went any further.

* * * *

They rode back toward the main lodge house almost in silence. Joshua had to wonder what she was thinking as they made their way around boulders and junipers. His cock throbbed behind the fly of his jeans. What the hell was he thinking not bringing a condom?

His horse stumbled, but regained his footing on the rocking ground. The gelding had pretty good footing most of the time. He would have to check and make sure the horse hadn't thrown a shoe while they'd ridden to the pond. "You're awful quiet back there."

"I'm thinking."

"About?"

"You. What makes you tick?"

"I'm just a simple cowboy."

"Did you always want to be a cowboy?"

"What else would I do with a family owning a ranch?"

"Surely there are other things in your life besides riding, roping, herding cattle, throwing hay, breaking horses, et cetera?"

He shrugged as he picked his way around another boulder. "Maybe."

"So what other things do you like to do?" she asked, sounding like she really wanted to know more about him.

"I work with leather."

"Doing what?"

"Making things like customized bridles and saddles."

"Wow. So you like to work with your hands, huh?"

"Yep."

"What else?"

"I like to drink beer, throw darts, and play pool."

"Well that's seems typical behavior for someone who hangs out at The Dusty Boot."

"I don't go there a lot. I usually spend my weekends working on my leather."

Silence enveloped them for a moment before she asked, "Ever had a serious relationship?"

"What do you mean by serious?"

"Have you been in love before?"

He paused, wondering how much to reveal. He hadn't really told anyone about *her*. "Yeah. Once. It was a girl I met in high school."

"What happened?"

"She found someone else more appealing."

"Seriously?"

"I don't like to talk about it."

"I can understand that. I mean really, how could someone think they could find someone more appealing than you?"

"You're good for my ego."

"Just speaking the truth. You're one sexy dude."

"You aren't just saying that because I gave you an orgasm, are you?" He laughed, letting her know he didn't think that was the case, but when his former love left because of a job, his ego had taken a beating. He wasn't sure when he would find the woman who would make all of the others disappear from his mind, but when he did, he would hold on with both hands. He glanced at Candace before he shook his head. Nope. She didn't live here. A relationship with her wouldn't work even if he thought she was pretty spectacular.

"No, I'm not saying that because you gave me an orgasm. I want to sample all your charms, Joshua, not just how wicked your tongue is."

They rode into the ranch corral with her last words reaching his ears and those of Joey and Jackson who stood nearby. *Damn.*

Jackson's eyebrow went up as a smile spread across his lips. Joey just laughed, taking the reins of her horse in his hand enabling her to dismount.

"Wicked tongue, Joshua?" Jackson asked, stepping up to his side.

Joshua wanted to punch him. "Back off, Jackson."

"What? I think it's cute. You have a wicked tongue, brother."

After he dismounted his horse, he got right in Jackson's face. "I said back off and shut your trap. There is a lady present."

"Lady? Not if she let you do what I think she did. She's probably not—"

Joshua pulled back his fist, punching Jackson in the mouth. "Take it back."

"Fuck you!" he yelled, charging his brother, taking them both to the ground in a cloud of dust.

"Stop it!" Candace shouted, trying to pull them apart only to be grabbed around the waist by Joey and pulled aside.

"Let them duke it out. You can't stop this. It's the way it is with brothers."

"You fucking idiot! Get off me!" Jackson pulled back, punching Joshua in the jaw hard enough to knock him backward.

"Enough!" James pulled Joshua by the arm. "Knock it off you two. This is ridiculous."

"He started it. He punched me first." Jackson dabbed at his nose trying to stop the flow of blood.

"He was saying Candace wasn't a lady. He doesn't even know her, and she's more of a lady than any bitch you've been with lately, Jackson."

"Wait a damned minute."

"Don't go there."

"I said enough, you two. Is this how you treat a woman, Joshua? Fighting in front of her?"

"I'm sorry. He just pissed me off. I was fighting for her honor."

Candace stepped in front of him, placing her hand on the front of his shirt. "And I appreciate it. Thank you for being gallant."

"You're a lady, and I won't have that asshole calling you anything but a lady. What happened between us is just that, between us." He touched his swelling lip with the tips of his fingers and winced at the pain shooting across his face. "Fucker."

"You want more of me, buddy? Come on. I'll beat the shit out of you."

"I don't fucking think so, asswipe. You couldn't punch your way out of a paper bag."

James held his arm, preventing the two of them from fighting more. "Take your girl and go on up to the house. Lunch will be ready soon. Jackson and Joey can take care of the animals."

"What did I do?" Jackson asked, holding his side where Joshua had punched him.

"We'll talk about your rude behavior after Joshua and his girl leave."

His girl. I kind of like that. "Come on, Candace."

The lunch bell clanged as he took her hand and walked her through the tack room. He wouldn't take the time to admire his own handy work in the room, but it was there. Rows and rows of his customized bridles, a couple of saddles he'd made and many more small pieces he'd forged out of the pieces of leather he'd worked on. He loved it, loved working with leather, getting the patterns just right with his tools, bringing out the beautiful design before putting the entire saddle together. These things made him happy.

As they approached the main lodge for lunch, he slipped his hand to the small of her back. "I'm sorry about that back there."

"I'm flattered you beat up your brother for me. I've never had a guy do something like that before. It's chivalrous. Makes me smile even though I'm upset that you got hit." She reached up to touch his face. "Thank you."

"It's nothin'."

"Sure it is. You've got a fat lip because of me."

He leaned in to kiss her lightly. "I'd do it again in a heartbeat." She smiled even though he winced at the pain in his lip. "Ouch."

"Poor baby."

"You can kiss me all over later to make me feel better." He stuck out his puffy lip in a little pout.

"I'll do that."

He smiled, and then frowned. *Damn lip hurts.* "Let's get some grub. I want to show you around the ranch more after lunch."

"Sounds good to me."

As they made their way inside toward the family table, his mother stopped him. "What happened to you?"

"I ran into Jackson's fist."

"Figures. Where are your brothers?"

"Dad is at the stable with Jackson and Joey."

His mother hobbled around on crutches now after her accident a few months prior. She'd been in physical therapy for a while, but she still couldn't walk on it, and plaster remained in place around her leg. "Damn thing."

"You shouldn't be up on it."

"I can't sit in a wheelchair the whole time." She put herself in a chair with a groan. "Joshua, would you get me some tea, please?"

"Sure, Mom." He poured some sweet tea into a glass before bringing it to her spot at the table. "Do you need me to get your plate?"

"No, Jeff is getting it, but thank you."

He glanced at the crowd in the dining room. It wasn't much since it was getting onto the downtime for the ranch. October always proved to be slower than September. They would all be heading out to Hawaii soon for Jeremiah and Callie's wedding. They had one of his uncles coming in to manage the place while they went. It would be fun. He'd never been to Hawaii before. They wouldn't stay long though. They were needed on the ranch. "Would you like to sit at the one of the empty tables or we can sit here at the family table."

"I don't want to take up someone's spot. Why don't we sit at the other table over there?"

"No problem." He led her to a table in the back and they took a seat. "You can go get your plate if you wish."

"Aren't you eating?"

"We have to wait until the guests are served. Mom's rules."

She patted the bench for him to sit beside her. "I'll wait then until you get yours. I'm sure there is plenty of food."

"Oh yeah. There always is," he replied straddling the bench seat in order to face her. "What other things do you want to experience while you're here?"

"Everything."

He laughed, regretting it immediately when his mouth started to throb again.

"I'm sorry. I didn't mean to make you laugh." She leaned in and kissed his fat lip. "There. It should feel better now."

"Of course. Kisses always make me feel better." He waggled his eyebrows at her, making her laugh in turn.

"Such a ham. Not the least bit modest, are you."

"Nope."

He glanced at the group and noticed his family getting up to get their food, so he directed her toward the line.

Jeff and Terri stood in front of them with Ben while Grandma kept an eye on James.

"When is the baby due?" Candace asked.

"Soon." Terri skimmed her hand down her abdomen. "I wish he or she would hurry up. I've been ready for a while now."

"You don't know what it is?"

"No. We wanted to be surprised," she said, leaning into Jeff's embrace.

"You two won't be going to Hawaii then, huh?" Joshua added.

"No. We'll stay here and help Uncle Nathan with the ranch. I wish we could be there, but Terri can't fly. It's too late in the pregnancy."

"It's better this way." Terri rubbed her lower back with her hand as she rested the other one on her abdomen.

"Are you okay, babe?" Jeff asked, worry making his eyebrows scrunch together.

"Yeah, just some back pain."

"You were cramping last night too. Don't you think we should go to the hospital?"

"Maybe, but it's too early. The baby isn't due for another two weeks."

"You went early with James too though."

"True."

"Let's go. Better now that you haven't had breakfast or lunch. You know they don't want you to eat anything."

"I'm not that hungry anyway." They stepped out of line. "See you later, Joshua."

"Take care, Terri. I hope it's time, for your sake."

"Me too. I'm really uncomfortable. He or she is going to be a big baby." She waved to both him and Candace while they moved toward the food.

After a minute or two of talking to Nina, they headed outside the doors of the main lodge in what he assumed to be a mad dash to the hospital in San Antonio. Joshua hoped things went okay for his brother and soon-to-be sister-in-law. He frowned as he twisted up his mouth. It was about time Jeff put a ring on that girl's finger.

"They seem like a great couple."

"It was hard going with them when they first met. Terri is an architect, and she was working with land developers to put in a housing project on some adjacent land. She found a rare bird on the property that stopped them doing anything with it. They weren't happy, but she saved us a major problem."

They moved forward a few steps, picking up empty plates to fill with food.

"They seem very much in love."

"It wasn't that way at first. Jeff hated her." He put a hamburger bun on his plate as he reached the meat and Mandy slid a patty onto his bun. "Well Jeff was married before. Ben is his with his first wife. It was a bad breakup, but he got custody of his son. We found out later his mother was doing drugs. She overdosed a few years ago."

"How sad."

"Yeah, but Terri more than makes up for the mother she wasn't. She's great with the kids."

"How many of your brothers are paired up now? There are nine of you, right?"

"Yes, nine of us. Five out of nine of us have significant others. Jeff and Terri are the only ones not married and I think he'll be taking care of that issue soon. At least I hope so, but he's really gun-shy."

"It sounds like he had a right to be."

They finished grabbing their food and headed back to the table they had secured before to eat. "You don't know the half of it." Joshua squirted some ketchup onto his hamburger and squished down the bun on top before he took a healthy bite. "His first wife cheated on their wedding night with the local sheriff."

Candace picked up a French fry, dipped it in the pool of ketchup she had on her plate before she popped it into her mouth. "Seriously?"

"Yep."

"What a bitch."

"We thought so. It was a special day when Jeff finally saw the light." He chuckled. "He's crazy about the girl he's with now."

"They have a couple kids, right?"

"This pregnancy is their second together and they have Ben. He's a great kid. Growing like a weed. He'll be tall like all the Youngs."

"You are tall."

"Six foot four and a half. I'm one of the tallest of us boys."

"Wow."

She took a healthy bite of her hamburger, leaving a small bit of ketchup on her lips. The swipe of her tongue across the surface had his cock rising to meet the occasion, and he hoped they'd be able to take care of his problem soon. Otherwise, he might just explode with merely a touch.

"How was it growing up with such a big family?"

"Fun and hard. We get along for the most part. Better now that we're all older and a little more mature." One of her eyebrows rose in a questioning quirk. "For the most part. Do you have a big family?"

"Not as big as yours." She took another bite of her hamburger before she went on, "I have two sisters and a brother."

"Where are you in the pecking order?"

"The baby."

"Ah, the spoiled one."

"No, I'm not!"

"Yeah, Joey doesn't think he is either, but he was always the favorite."

She released a sound that came across as a choking gurgle. It didn't sound very sexy at all, but it sure matched the frown on her face. "I'm not the favorite by a long shot. My brother is by far."

"I'm sure your siblings wouldn't agree."

"I don't know. I've never asked them."

He liked teasing her. "Should I call them and ask?" He pulled out his cell. "Give me the number and I'll...,"

She swiped the phone from his hand. "No." A moment later, she started pushing buttons on the screen. "Shall we see how many female phone numbers you have in here?"

"I'll take that back now." He grabbed for the phone, but she kept it out of reach across the table.

"What, Joshua? You don't want me to know how many girlfriends you've had?"

"I have only had one girlfriend. I told you that."

"Well now. I see several female names here. Cindy. Trish. Melanie." She thumbed through more of his contact list. "Theresa. Sharon. Oh look! One with stars next to it. What does that mean, Joshua?"

"Nothing."

"Really? Why don't I believe you?"

He jumped to his feet, grabbing the phone out of her hand. "It's none of your business."

"Well now, why didn't you say so in the beginning?"

Her innocent little smile didn't fool him. Why did she want to know how many women he'd been with? He would satisfy her needs. That's all she needed to know. "I'll take care of you when the time comes."

"I'm jealous. You don't have me in your contact list."

"I don't have your number."

"Well then. Let me give it to you." She held out her hand for his phone. When he handed it to her, she punched in her number into his contact list although she probably scrolled through the numbers too. "Now you have it."

She gave him a saucy wink and returned to eating her hamburger like nothing happened. When he slowly took his seat, he had wondered what she was up to. Did she only want a short term thing for the time she was here or did she have other plans in mind? Maybe she would find herself more attracted to one of his brothers?

Liking her was the easy part. He liked her a lot, but could he trust her? Probably not. She was all woman, and he found most of them lacking in the trust department.

Chapter Five

Candace held on tight when Joshua took them over several bumps in the road. Holding on to his waist or wrapping her arms around his middle did funny things to her insides, even though she tried to concentrate on keeping herself on the four-wheeler. They were already covered in mud from the helmets on their heads to the boots on their feet. Good thing she had a face mask on her helmet or she'd have mud in her teeth. A shower would be a priority before dinner.

Joshua pulled over to the side of the dirty road. "Do you want to drive? We can go back and get one of the other four-wheelers. That way you can have your own."

"No. I'm good. I like holding on to you."

"Do you want to make a trip through the mud again?" He removed his goggles for a moment, leaving the shape of them around his eyes.

Laughter bubbled in her chest. He looked hilarious with mud spattered on his clothes and face. "Sure. The mud sounds fun. Maybe tomorrow we can take two and I'll drive."

"Of course, although I like you sitting behind me." He wiped a bit of mud clinging to her neck. "You look cute all dressed in mud."

He slid back onto the four-wheeler in the front before she grabbed his waist to hold on. Mud sprayed in all different directions as he revved the engine and rushed the mud pit. Jonathan and Jackson did the same from the other direction, effectively spraying them with a large wave of brown. She was certain she would drown in all this watered down dirt.

She had to admit, seeing him interact with his brothers without fighting, was something she enjoyed. They had the camaraderie of a close family even though Jackson had fought with Joshua earlier. They seemed to have forgotten the argument as they gunned the machines back through the mud again. "You do this in your truck too?"

"Yeah. It's even more fun in the truck." Joshua unwrapped the tight Velcro around his wrist to check the time. "We need to get back. Dinner will be happening soon, and I'm sure you want to take a shower before you eat."

"Yes, I do. I have mud in places I didn't know mud could go."

"I can help you wash certain places." He waggled his eyebrows which was hilarious because they were caked in mud.

She giggled at the face he was making. "You are incorrigible, you know that?"

"Yep." Joshua signaled for his brothers to join him. "We're going back. It's almost supper time."

"Okay," Jonathan replied as Jackson nodded. "I need a shower anyway."

"Yeah, us too."

With Jackson in the front of the pack, Jonathan in the middle and Joshua in the rear, they headed back toward the lodge house.

Today had been one of the best days of her life. This cowboy thing was pretty cool. She liked the peaceful atmosphere of the ranch. She couldn't wait to experience more of Joshua's lifestyle. She wanted the experience of living with such a large family. She wanted to see a baby horse born. She liked getting up at dawn to take in the rising sun over the mountains and feeding the donkeys. She could almost get used to living like this. There were no honking cars, no hustling people from place to place like little ants trying to stay ahead, and people out here didn't hurt each other. They didn't shoot at each other over stupid things. Yeah, she thought she might be getting attached to this way of life.

They pulled the four-wheelers next to the equipment barn to hose them off before putting them away. She excused herself as Joshua started spraying the four-wheeler they used, to take a shower and get ready for dinner.

When she crested the second floor landing, she smelled a flowery perfume right before she felt a sharp sting, like something scratched her across the arm. She glanced down to find three angry red welts across her forearm. "What the hell?"

She shoved the key into the lock, quickly went inside and shut the door. "That was weird."

After she calmed her stuttering heart, she strip off her muddy clothes and tossed them into the bathroom tub so they wouldn't get the whole room dirty. She would wash them out before she took a shower.

She washed her hands and forearms in the sink before she grabbed some clean underwear from her suitcase to take a shower. She managed to get most of the mud washed out of the clothes before she put them in the sink. "I think they have a washer I can use."

Hot water sprayed from the overhead rain showerhead, soaking her hair and washing more mud down the drain. She hoped all the dirt didn't clog the tub. She should have had Joshua spray her off before she came upstairs. *Oh well. Too late now.*

Minutes later, with her shower completed, she grabbed a big fluffy towel off the rack, tied her hair up in one, and then draped another around her body. She glanced down at the marks on her arm wondering where they came from. She hadn't bumped into the doorframe or anything like that. *Huh.* She shrugged as she stepped back into the bedroom part of her room to get some clean clothes. A tank top and a pair of jeans should do. She had slip on sandals she could wear since her boots were now covered in mud.

She couldn't help but smile. Four-wheeling had been so much fun, she knew they would have to do it again before her time on the ranch concluded.

And mudding with the trucks. She had to experience that too. Everything cowboy sounded like a hell of a lot of fun.

As she slipped on her clothes, she heard the dinner bell ring from outside. She'd heard what she assumed was Joshua coming up the stairs right before she went into the shower. What would it be like making love with him under the hot spray of the water? The vision of him standing in all his glory at the pond came back in a rush, making her wish they could just lock themselves away for the night. She could slowly lick every inch of his body, from the top to the bottom without missing an inch.

With a long drawn out sigh, she finished slipping on her sandals in order to go downstairs for supper. They ate a lot of food here, she would probably gain twenty pounds before she went home. *Ah well, a little more time at the gym wouldn't hurt anyway.* She wasn't skinny by any means, but she did have a nice curvy figure, and she wanted to make sure she kept the love handles at bay.

When she opened the door, she almost ran smack dab into Joshua. "Wow, you're quick."

"I didn't take a long one. Just washed the mud off." He did a slow glance from her hair to her feet. "You look refreshed."

"I feel it too. I probably washed a ton of mud down the drain between washing out my clothes and taking a shower."

"It's fine. We do it all the time. Mom and Dad have it down pat on the dirt part. We have a muddin' party about once a month anyway until it gets too cool."

"Good. I won't feel guilty about the pound of dirt then." She wrapped her hand and forearm into the crook of his elbow.

"What happened to your arm?"

"I'm not sure. I didn't notice it before I came upstairs, but I must have caught it on a branch while we were out on the four-wheelers. It started to sting when I reached my door." She turned her arm so she could see it better. It looked like fingernail marks. "Weird, huh?"

"Yeah. Just be careful. We don't want you hurt while you're here."

"Oh, I will."

They headed downstairs to eat, making small talk as they walked. "What's for dinner?"

"It's steak night. They grill New York strip steaks once a week."

"Yum. I love steak."

Once they made it to the bottom of the stairs, she noticed the family already serving themselves. They wandered over to get in line. "We can eat at another table or sit with the family?"

"Have you heard anything on Jeff and Terri?"

"She's in labor and they expect the new baby soon. Mom and Dad are at the hospital already. There are plenty of seats left at the family table."

"Sure. Let's do that." After they filled their plates of food, he asked her what she wanted to drink as they made their way to the family table. "Tea is fine. No, make that lemonade."

"Great. If you take my plate, I'll get the drinks."

She took his plate from his hand and headed to the table, trying to decide where to sit. The family had grown so large with the additions of women for the guys and their children, there were two family tables these days.

"You can sit here, Candace." Jonathan offered the two chairs next to his that were empty.

"I don't want to take anyone's seat."

"You aren't. This is where Jeff and Terri usually sit. Since they aren't here, they're free."

"Great!" She took the seat next to Jonathan, sitting Joshua's plate next to hers. "I would love to sit and talk websites with you. I've looked at the ranch site, and I could make some suggestions, if you don't mind."

"Do you do website design?"

"Some. I'm a programmer, but I do some designing on the site as well. There are a couple of things I could help you with."

"That would be awesome. I haven't been formally trained. I learned everything on my own."

"Really? That's fabulous! I went through four years of college to learn web design and programming. I'm returning in the fall for my master's degree." She glanced back at Joshua, noting the frown on his face. "Something wrong?"

"No."

He looked down at where she placed her hand on Jonathan's arm. Okay, obviously he doesn't like her touching his brother. *Hmm.* "Sorry. I'm a touchy feely kind of person."

"You can touch me all you want." Joshua shoved a forkful of potato salad into his mouth.

"Just don't touch your brothers?"

"You're mine."

"I am?"

"For now anyway."

"I'm not a cheater, Joshua. If you want exclusive while I'm here, I'm good with that."

The tension in his shoulder eased as the frown pulling his eyebrows down did too. Jealousy. Interesting concept. He didn't like her being too friendly with his brothers. Apparently, he'd been cheated on at one point too. Maybe the one love of his life had not only chosen someone else over him, but cheated too?

"I can do exclusive."

"Good. I'm all for that. I want you all to myself anyway." Jonathan snorted and rolled his eyes. "Someday you'll be there too, Jonathan, so be quiet over there."

"I'm not looking for a girlfriend."

"That's usually when you find her."

The rest of the meal she listened to the conversations around the table. Some speculation went on about whether Jeff and Terri would have a girl or a boy, then discussion about some work around the ranch came up. The women broke off at some point to talk amongst themselves. It appeared Paige and Peyton were pretty good friends while Callie chatted with Mesa about things going on in town. The boys did their own huddles, bantering about one thing or another. *Wouldn't it be great to be a part of this family?* Whoa!

She shook her head. *Nope. Not going there.*

"Are you okay?"

"Yeah, just thinking."

"About?"

"Getting you between the sheets."

"How about shooting a game of pool?" he asked, steering the conversation back to safer ground around his family, she guessed.

She'd noticed a pool table in the main part of the lodge when she checked in, but tonight she wasn't into playing pool. She wanted hot, kinky, sweaty sex. "Nah. We could take a swim though."

"The pool isn't heated."

"I could use a cool down because," she leaned in close to his ear, "I'm really horny."

"Me too." He glanced at her half eaten plate. "Are you finished?"

"Nope. I'm going to eat this entire steak." She giggled, skimming her hand over his erection. "You'll have to suffer for a little longer." She cut another small piece off her steak and stuck it into her mouth, humming her appreciation for the taste of the meat. Making him suffer a little in his state of arousal seemed kind of mean, but then again, she had to suffer too. Her pussy throbbed with each beat of her heart, reminding her of the need he made her feel just being around him, never mind his kisses.

Conversation swirled around them as she picked at the rest of the food on her plate. The meal was fantastic, the meat cooked to perfection, the potatoes were smooth and fluffy and the vegetables were crisp. Every meal at the ranch reminded her of cookouts at home with her family, and she was sure that's the persona they were going for with the ranch. It fit.

* * * *

Joshua watched Candace take another bite of her food and chew. *God, she has sexy lips.* The way she wrapped them around the tines of her fork made him want to jerk her from her chair and haul her ass up the stairs to his room. If he had to wait one more minute, he might die because his balls were about to explode.

"Aren't you hungry?" she asked, her eyes twinkling with mirth.

She knew exactly what she was doing to him. "I find myself wanting something else to eat."

"Oh? Dessert looks great too. I could get you some if you'd like."

"I want another kind of dessert."

"Really? Like what?"

He leaned in and pressed his lips to her ear. "Pussy." She choked a little on her last bite of food as he let the warmth of his breath caress the side of her neck. "I'm going to lick you all over from the tips of your gorgeous breasts to your clit. I know how much you enjoy my tongue."

She shivered under the touch of his tongue along her neck.

"All right, you two. Enough with the hands on at the dinner table. You know Mom would have a fit to see you acting this way, Joshua," Jeremiah scolded as he draped an arm around Callie's shoulders.

"When is the wedding?" Candace sounded breathless as a sigh escaped her lips. "I heard you were all flying to Hawaii?"

"Yes," Callie answered. "We want to get married on the beach with just our families around. Very small, private ceremony."

"Awesome. Sounds like a really romantic little interlude."

"Have you been to Hawaii?" Callie asked, pushing her plate away.

"Yes, several times actually. Living in California, it's not too expensive to go."

"I lived in California before Joel and I got together," Mesa added. "Where do you live?"

"Anaheim."

"Very nice. I lived outside of Pasadena before I moved out here."

"Do you like it here?"

"I love it. It's quiet. I can write and soak up the cowboy atmosphere all I want."

"You're a writer?"

"Yes. I write romance novels, contemporary western romance novels."

"Oh cool. I read a lot. I could never write. You must be very talented."

Joel laughed as he tugged on a curl hanging from the back of the bun on Mesa's head. "She's sells more now than ever. I wouldn't have to work if I didn't want to. She got a sizable advance from her publisher with her last book."

"What's the titles to a couple? I might have read you."

"I write under Mesa West."

Excitement lit up her face. Apparently, Candace was a big fan of Mesa's books although he didn't see the big hullabaloo where Mesa was concerned.

"Oh wow! I love your cowboy romances. I've read everything you put out. This is awesome! I've never met a real live author before."

Mesa blushed. "Thank you. I love talking to my fans."

Candace bounced a little in the chair. "I'm thrilled!" She frowned. "I wish I had some of my paperbacks with me. I would have you sign them." Everyone at the table was smiling as she gushed over Mesa. "You don't understand. She's Mesa West."

"Yeah, we know." Joel laughed before he reached over and kissed her on the cheek. Their infant daughter began to fuss. Mesa stood and excused herself from the table.

"Your baby is as cute as a button."

"She takes after her momma," Joel gushed a little watching Mesa take the baby from her chair before she went around the corner to take care of her.

"What's her name?"

"Elizabeth Marie after my grandmother and Mesa's mother."

"What a beautiful name."

"We thought so."

"Is she a good baby? I don't think I've heard her cry much."

"Oh yeah. She's already sleeping well into the night. She only gets up once for a feeding."

"How precious."

"Thank you."

"How many grandkids are there now?"

"Jeff and Terri are on their third. Mesa and I have one and Paige and Jacob have boy girl twins."

"Twins? Holy moly."

"Yeah, it keeps us busy," Jacob added, nodding to the two in high chairs in the corner.

She swiveled around to look at the twins. She really had very expressive eyes.

"How cute they are. I bet they are a handful. What are they, about a year?"

Jacob and Paige beamed with pride. "Fourteen months. They're walking and getting into everything."

"I bet."

"Do you want kids?"

"Someday. I have three siblings, but it's not near as crazy busy as having nine kids like your family."

"We hope to have a big family too," Paige answered, glancing at her daughter while she fed herself fingers foods. "We want six at least."

"We do?" Jacob added with a bit of a frown.

"Yes we do. We discussed this, Jacob."

Jacob laughed as he slipped his arm around his wife. "Call me when these two are out of diapers, and we'll discuss having more." Paige leaned over and kissed him soundly on the mouth. "Practice makes perfect."

"I love practicing with you."

"I know you do."

"When are you planning to settle down?" Jacob focused his gaze on Joshua's face.

He cocked an eyebrow, shooting his brother a butt out look. "Someday. I'm not in a hurry."

Jacob glanced her way, giving her the once over before he glanced back his way.

Candace held up her hands. "Don't look at me. I don't even live here. I'm just hanging out for a few weeks, soaking up the cowboy thing."

"I see."

"Good. Matchmaking needs to be out of the picture here."

"Stay away from our mother then. She loves hooking us up with a girl she thinks is perfect for us. Right, honey?" Jacob asked Paige.

"Oh yeah. She's great for meddling." Paige smiled. "I love her to death, but she loves matchmaking."

"I'll avoid her like the plague then."

They laughed in unison making him wonder if they didn't have plans already in the works. He hoped they stayed out of his business, but he had to be careful. His mother loved to get in the middle of relationships. She'd done it with all his brothers. He frowned. Maybe she had something there. After a moment, he glanced at Candace. She would do, although like she said, she didn't live here. He shrugged. She'd be good for a few weeks of some fun, but he should probably look closer to home if he wanted to find the woman he could maybe spend his life with. Long distance relationships didn't work very well.

His thoughts drifted to the past, to Loren. He'd been in love with her a few years ago. In love enough to want to marry her, but she'd been offered a job in New York with a prestigious advertising firm. She'd packed up her stuff and left without so much as a long goodbye. His heart hadn't been the same since. Giving it to someone else didn't seem possible, but he could find someone compatible to spend his life with. Didn't mean his heart had to get involved though.

The conversation moved onto other things besides his lack of relationship status, for which he was mighty thankful. He didn't need his brothers or his mother focusing on him. When the time was right, he'd find someone to settle down with. It didn't mean it had to be now.

Joshua watched Candace while she continued to eat. He wanted to feel the long, silky strands of her hair through his fingers. Right now, she hand it pulled back in a low ponytail to keep it off her neck, he figured, but he really wanted to have it around her shoulders while she rode him into next week.

His cock stiffened painfully behind the fly of his jeans. Yeah, he wanted her, needed her with every breath in his body. He hoped they'd get to that part tonight after the bonfire he planned to take her to. Sex with her would be totally worth the wait. After he cleared his throat and shifted on the chair to try to relieve some of the pressure, he finished his food by shoveling the last few bites into his mouth. "What do you want to do after dinner?"

"I'm not sure."

"I should probably do a little work in the barn, oiling up the leather. You can either help me with that or you can brush down the horses if you like."

"Sounds like a plan."

They both stood, grabbed their plates and headed for the dirty dish bin.

"Hey, Joshua."

"Oh hey, Mandy."

"Are we still on for later?"

"Later?" he asked, confusion rushing through him. Had he made a date with Mandy he'd forgotten? Not that he was interested in her that way, but he didn't want to disappoint a friend.

"You know? You were going to show me how to braid the leather for something for my mom for her birthday coming up."

"Oh that. Yeah, I can show you. I'll be out in the stable oiling up the bridles and saddles. Come and find me."

"Okay." She smiled, a bright spread her lips in a wide arch, smile.

She really was a nice girl and kind of pretty too, although he knew she had the hots for one of the unattached brothers, not him.

"I'll catch you after we get the dinner dishes done."

Candace stepped up and held out her hand. "Hi. I'm Candace. One of the guests for now. I just wanted to say the food is delicious."

"I'll pass it onto the cook. She'll be pleased. I'm glad you like it."

"Definitely, especially the desserts. They are to die for."

"I know what you mean. The chocolate mousse is fabulous. I think I've gained twenty pounds since I started working here from eating the desserts. It all went straight to my butt."

"No way. You look great."

"Well, thank you." Mandy cocked her head and looked at him. "You need to keep her around. She's good for my ego, Joshua."

"Mine too. She kind of likes me."

"I'm sure you'd be a fabulous catch."

He puffed out his chest as he adjusted the hat on his head. "Of course I would." The two women laughed when he smiled. "Let's head out to the barn, Candace, and I'll show you were everything is."

With his hand at the small of her back, he guided her out the door of the lodge, toward the stables and barn. He loved the smell of leather, horses, hay, and everything in the big red structure. It always seemed to calm him when he would get upset as a child. Working with leather pieces gave him peace from the stresses of growing up in such a big family.

"What are you working on now?"

"A custom saddle for my dad for his birthday."

"Wow. Can I see it?"

"Sure. It's been a bitch to keep it hidden from him, but it'll be worth it in the end. I think he's going to love it." He opened the small workshop door on the right side of the barn where he kept his supplies. It had taken several months of hand working the leather to get it just right. It was almost finished. The chocolate colored carved leather gleamed in the light of the room.

"Oh my." Her hand slipped over the carvings of the horses in the leather. "You did this?"

"Yep."

"This is magnificent, Joshua. You're really good."

"Thanks."

"I can't imagine how long this must have taken you to carve."

"Not too long, but it was very precise. I couldn't mess up at all."

"It's beautiful." Her voice came out in a whisper of awe.

The pleasure on her face made him feel like a million bucks. He'd never had anyone exclaim over his work before like she was.

She turned back toward him to put her hand on his chest as she stepped closer. "Would you make me something to remember you by?"

"Like what?"

"How about a cowgirl belt? I could get one of those silver belt buckles to remind me of my time here on the ranch." She frowned a little as she stepped back. "I don't want you to take away from getting your dad's present done though."

He got closer, wanting to feel her hand on his chest again. He liked her hands on him, touching, exploring. The thoughts drove him a little crazy since they hadn't had a chance to do anything related to actual sex except the little oral he'd given her at the pond. With a sigh of expectation, he said, "A belt wouldn't take long at all."

"I would love that."

Her breath flittered across his lips, making them tingle in anticipation. "I'm going to kiss you."

"I wish you would."

With her back pressed against the wood siding, he leaned in and pressed his lips against hers. She felt wonderful, all soft like a fluffy blanket. Closing his eyes, he relished the feel of her lips against his own. She groaned and leaned into his body, wrapping her arms around his neck as she pressed her breasts into his chest. His hands settled on her hips before sliding around her back to bring her closer still. He wouldn't want to fuck her in his office, but man did he want her.

He lifted her, planting her butt on the edge of his desk, pushing the carving tools and template off to the back.

"I want you, Joshua." She trailed kiss across his chin and down his neck, stopping at the opening of his shirt while she began working the buttons loose.

"I want you too. I need to feel your heat around me, but I don't want to do this here."

Her lips blazed a trail down the center of his chest while she got each shirt button undone. Her hands scalded him as she parted the material, pulling the tails from his jeans.

"Do you have a condom?"

"Yeah, in my wallet in my pants."

"Lock the door."

"Are you sure?"

She tossed her shirt to the side after she pulled it over her head, leaving her in nothing but her frilly, pink bra. He wondered if her underwear matched as he stepped back to lock the door.

"Hell yeah. What a better place than surrounded by the smell of leather. It turns me on."

God, she's gorgeous.

She reached behind her back to unhook her bra, when he turned to secure the door. The last thing he wanted was one of his brothers to walk in on this.

Her breasts were perfect, nicely rounded with pert little nipples begging for the touch of his tongue.

She leaned back on her elbows, thrusting her breasts in his direction as she begged with her eyes and her lips. "Lick them."

With his hands on either side of her hips, braced against the metal desk top, he leaned in and took the left nipple between his lips. It was either his imagination running wild or something, but he thought for sure it tasted like a ripe little berry on his tongue.

She grabbed his hat from his head and tossed it on top of the file cabinet in the corner before she speared her fingers through his hair. He loved having her fingers threaded through his hair, cradling his head against her chest.

"Mmmm."

A low purr escaped her mouth, making him smile against her breast. He switched to the other breast to give it some attention while he palmed the left one, rolling the nipple between his thumb and finger. She had beautiful breasts. Just right to fit in his hand.

She worked the belt buckle at his waist until it was loose and hanging front his pants. "I need to touch you."

"Go ahead," he said, jerking the shirt from his shoulders while she unbuttoned and unzipped the catch on his jeans.

When her warm hand found his cock through his boxers, he hissed low in his throat at the shock her touch caused.

"You're a pretty big guy."

"Not really."

"Bigger than anyone I've had before."

"Is that going to be a problem?"

"I don't think so. I can't wait to feel all of this inside me."

He unfastened her jeans before grabbing them at the waist to work them off her hips. When he had them down around her ankles, he pushed them all the way off leaving her totally naked on his desk with her legs spread, ready for his touch.

His desk chair sat nearby. He grabbed it and sat down. He wanted to be at the right angle to pleasure her before he fucked her silly. The plan was to keep her on the brink until she begged him to fuck her hard.

He grabbed her hips and pulled her close. She braced her heels on the edge of the desk.

When he buried his face between her gorgeous thighs, he heard her sigh. Her pussy lips glistened with his saliva and her juices as he licked, sucked, and worshipped her flesh with his tongue. He slipped two fingers into her pussy, feeling the grip of her excitement on his digits. She was amazingly responsive to his touch. He wanted it to go on and on.

"Joshua, please, make me come."

"I'd love to." He sucked her clit into his mouth, rubbing first one side, and then the other. She squirmed on the desk top trying to get closer.

The little whimpers and mewls escaping from her mouth drove him crazy.

"Oh God." She exhaled on a rush. Her pussy gripped him in a vice-like hold when she came apart on a cry of ecstasy. "Joshua."

His name on her lips had him as hard as a brick, ready for the scalding heat of her pussy to envelope his flesh in her tight grip.

He wiped his face with the back of his hand, grinning like a damned fool. "Better?"

"For now." She reached out to take hold of his cock. "I want this now."

Swiping his wallet from the back pocket of his jeans, he groaned as she palmed him. "Easy, darlin'. It's loaded."

"I'm glad."

He pushed his jeans to the floor, taking his boxers along with them until he stood in front of her, bare and raring to go. After he quickly rolled the latex condom over his cock, his positioned it at her opening and slowly penetrated her.

A low moan escaped her lips as she closed her eyes and leaned back on her hands. "Oh my God. That's perfect."

When he was fully inside her, he stopped his movements to catch his breath. If he didn't slow this down, he would come way before he was ready to. He wanted to savor this first moment with her, feel every ripple of her sweet cunt around his dick, and remember this time for the rest of his life. She was one hot babe, hot enough to burn through the wall around his heart if he wasn't careful.

"Move please. I'm dying here."

He eased himself in and out, very slowly while she tossed her head from side to side, balling her hands into fists on the desk top.

"You're killing me."

"I want this to last. I'm so primed, I'll blow too fast."

"Don't worry, we can do it again later. For now, fuck me hard, Joshua. Please!"

Bracketing her hips with his hands, he began to fuck her in earnest, shoving his aching flesh into her hot core fast enough he banged the desk against the wall, rattling the bridles and leather he had hanging there.

"Yes, yes, yes!"

He captured her lips in a devastating kiss when he felt his balls draw up tight against his groin. If he didn't bring her along, he would hate himself in the end. He snaked his hand between them, grabbing her clit in a sharp pinch as he continued to pound into her.

She exploded on a high cry of ecstasy while he lost his control of his own climax, shooting his load into the latex reservoir.

As they slowly came down from their volatile climax, he cradled her head against his chest, loving the feel of her warm breath on his skin.

"That was…"

"I know."

"You okay?"

"I'm fabulous."

He slowly withdrew from her while they both groaned from the lack of intimacy. He loved being inside her, around her, feeling her gripping his cock like a vice.

She was one hot number, and he planned to use her well in the time she was with him.

Yep, he had plans all right, if he could just keep his head on straight in the process.

Chapter Six

The glow she felt from her evening with Joshua wouldn't leave her as she sat staring into the bonfire's light. He sure rocked her world with his love making in his office, and she wasn't quite sure what to make of it.

With her hand in his, they sat listening to the conversations of the other guests around the fire while the kids roasted marshmallows. She'd always loved S'mores when she was a kid, and she wondered if there was one she could convince to let her borrow their stick.

"Here." Joshua handed her a long piece of metal with a fork at the end.

"How did you know?"

"You were eyeing the S'mores the kids were eating, so I figured you wanted one. There are supplies on the table over there. It's something we always have when we do bonfires for the guests. It wouldn't be a campfire without S'mores."

She giggled while he stuck two marshmallows on the end of her roaster. "You roast those nice and melty, and I'll get the chocolate and graham crackers."

He wandered to the table being manned by his mother to retrieve the makings of their S'mores, while she admired the cut of his jeans across his butt and the way his shirt molded to his shoulders. *Damn, the man is built like nothing I've ever seen.* He reminded her of the romance novels Mesa wrote, thinking she might have shaped some of her cowboys after the sexy inspiration she had on the ranch. Why the hell not? She definitely had the goods to back up her fantasies here.

Candace watched as he smiled and exchanged a few words with his mother. They seemed like such a close family, it reminded her of her family back in California. Her dad worked a lot and her mother was a stay at home mom who did everything with the kids when they were growing up. She wished her dad had spent a little more time with them when they were children, but he loved them. This she knew, and she also knew he worked so much because he wanted them to have things he didn't have as a child.

He'd grown up very poor, with an absentee father and without much of a home life. He'd made his first million by the time he'd turned twenty-five, investing in computers when they first got to be the *in* thing. Yes, she and siblings had grown up with money, but they had to work for anything special, doing paper routes or working at the local fast food place. Her mom and dad agreed on teaching their kids the morals of a hard day's work, even with the trust fund left to her mother by her granddaddy.

As Joshua came back toward her, he smiled with a little tilt of his lips meant only for her. Her toes curled when she remembered those lips on hers, his tongue on her most private places, and how he'd brought her to such delight, she'd cried out in her ecstasy.

"You look like the cat who ate the canary," Mandy said, sitting down on the bench next to her.

"Who me?"

"Yeah."

Joshua sat on her other side, holding the chocolate and graham crackers until the marshmallows were done. She'd been admiring him too much to roast them until he returned.

"Why would you say that?"

"Oh, I don't know."

She grinned a little Cheshire cat spread of the lips, making Candace wonder exactly what she's was up to.

"I came by the office, Joshua, but I think you were a little busy."

"Huh?"

"You know, so you could show me how to braid that leather, but when I went to knock, some awfully strange sounds were coming from your office. I figured I'd wait until tomorrow."

"Oh shit." Candace felt her face flush hot. Mandy must have heard them having sex in his office.

"Sorry. I forgot you were coming by."

"No problem. I didn't want to disturb you."

"I'm sorry." Candace turned to apologize to Mandy, losing the marshmallows is the process from the end of the stick. "Crap."

"It's okay. There are more."

"But," she leaned toward him whispering, "she heard us."

"So?"

"But…"

"It's okay." He leaned in and kissed her on the lips. "No one else heard anything."

"I did!" Joey raised his hand from across the fire.

Her face turned red again.

"Me too." Jackson waved from their left. "Way to go, Joshua!"

Jeff raised his hand, as well as Jeremiah, Joel, and Jacob.

"Shit." She wanted to hide. "I'm so embarrassed."

"That's enough, boys. The poor girl is terrified now, I'm sure, and I know damned well most of you didn't hear anything because you were in the house with me," their mother answered, giving Candace a reprieve to believe the majority of them were giving her shit.

"Thank you."

"You're welcome and believe me, sweetie, around here, if the whole place hasn't heard one or another of these boys and their women, I would be surprised. Our barn gets a workout most of the time. With several of them paired off, sometimes they are hard pressed for alone time other than at their own homes. These are randy men. It comes with the territory of being a Texan."

Somehow that didn't make Candace feel all that much better. She couldn't look any of them in the face knowing they might have heard her and Joshua in the barn even though, as his mother said, they'd all been caught at one time or another. That brought her thoughts around to how many other women he'd brought out to the ranch and made love with. She really didn't want to know. He certainly knew his way around a woman's body. Experience wasn't in short supply where he was concerned.

"Well, we know Joshua is no virgin."

Jackson snorted a few feet away, but she wasn't sure who actually said the remark.

"None of you were virgins much past your thirtieth birthday, I don't believe," their mother replied.

"Mom!"

"Well you weren't and if you thought your father and I didn't know, you are in for a shock."

Candace glanced around, thankful to see the regular guests had all taken their leave sometime before. She hoped it was long before this conversation had begun.

The S'mores lay forgotten when the boys started bantering back and forth about their love lives as their wives and girlfriends just shook their heads at the chaos.

She really didn't know if this was normal behavior for the men, but it sure seemed to be as the women around the fire began having their own conversations that had nothing to do with the men or their conquests.

Mesa walked over, took her hand and drew her to their little corner of the campfire. "Come on. You can sit with us. They'll be at this a while. Trust me." Mesa's little girl slept soundly in her carrier at the women's feet. Little tuffs of dark hair graced the baby's head. Little chubby cheeks moved slightly while the baby sucked in her sleep, her little mouth moving ever so slightly.

"She's such a little doll."

"Thank you." Mesa smoothed her hand over the baby's head. "She's a good baby."

Jacob and Paige's twins played in a portable playpen nearby, with a couple of stuffed animals.

Terri was still in the hospital with the newest addition to the Young household, a little baby girl.

Candace was kind of surprised Jeff was at the bonfire when his woman was still in the hospital, but their mother mentioned earlier that Terri had chased him out so she could get some sleep before the baby and she came home to the rambunctiousness of two boys. Jeff had spread the pictures on his phone around to everyone already though and after Grandma and

Grandpa showed their pictures, they proclaimed her to be a beautiful little girl with her daddy's eyes.

"Are you okay, Candace?" Paige asked.

"Yeah, I'm fine. I'm just not used to all this. I don't have this big of a family and it's not all boys."

"You'll get used to it the longer you stick around."

"Well, I'm only here for a few weeks."

"Yeah, that's what a couple of us said too," Mesa added with a wicked little smile.

"No, really. I can't stay. I have a business to run."

"Uh-huh. I'll warn you now, once one of these boys gets you wrapped around their finger, it's impossible to let go. I know. I tried," Peyton said, licking marshmallow off her fingers after she stuffed the last of a S'more in her mouth.

"But you all are in love with your brother, I'm not in love with Joshua."

"Give it time."

Nina grinned from the fringes of their conversation, making Candace feel like she was in so much trouble, she should run back to Los Angeles right now. But when she glanced over at Joshua, she realized she didn't want to run anywhere, at least not for a bit yet. She still had some cowboying stuff to do and it included a lot more raunchy sex with a certain cowboy.

* * * *

Joshua walked her to her door on the second floor of the main lodge with an arm around her waist. He didn't want to say goodnight to her quite yet, so he stalled a bit when she leaned against the wall by putting his hands on either side of her head and leaning in. "Sorry about all the talk at the bonfire."

"It's okay. The girls kept me busy while you boys were doing your thing."

He grinned. "It's just the way we are around each other. The girls have kind of gotten used to it, I guess. They just let us be."

She fingered the button on his shirt. "Yeah, I got that much."

"Would you like to watch some television? It's still kind of early to turn in."

"What are we going to do tomorrow?"

"I figured we go ride fences again for a while. One of the horses went into labor tonight so you might want to see that if the foal comes."

"Oh, that would be fabulous! Do they come fast or slow? Can I touch the momma? What's it like?"

He laughed. "Whoa. Slow down, darlin'. You can watch, but not touch. The mare won't like it too much if there are lots of people involved."

"Okay." She bounced on her toes. "If she gets close tonight, can you wake me? I want to see this."

"I'll have my dad wake me, and then I'll come get you. Okay?"

"Deal." She clapped her hands in excitement. "This is going to be totally awesome!"

"You might not think so if it's at three in the morning."

"Oh, I will. I can sleep in tomorrow if nothing else."

"All right. It's a deal."

She glanced up through her lashes with a sneaky little grin on her lips, the same lips he's been dreaming about since they'd parted this afternoon.

"What do you want to watch on television?"

"I don't know. We have lots of movies in the main lodge. We can go down there, pop some popcorn, watch a chick flick and cuddle on the couch."

"Oh, I like the way you think, cowboy."

"Good." He looked down her body, and then back up. "Do you want to change into something a little more comfortable? If you have pajama pants or something, it would be a little better than stiff jeans."

"You just want me out of my clothes."

"Well that too, but I figured we could make love again after everyone is asleep for the night."

"Who all uses the main lodge for their bedroom?"

"My parents mostly, although Jonathan is the only other one with a room in the main lodge. Joey has a bunkroom in the stable, Jackson has one of the cabins out in the yard and all the guys already paired up have their own places except for Jeremiah and Callie. They're having their place built while they're getting married and on their honeymoon."

"Aren't you going to Hawaii too?"

"Yes, but it's not for another month."

"I'll be gone back to California then." She frowned, smoothing her hand over his chest, but didn't meet his eyes.

He wondered what she was thinking when she looked back up and smiled a sad little smile. Would she miss him just a little? He kind of hoped she would because he sure would miss her smile, her touch, her laugh, and everything else about her. He'd kind of grown fond of her in the few days she'd been with him. How would he feel when her time was over?

It wouldn't matter. He needed to get anything permanent out of his head right now. She lived in California. That was almost as far as New York where Loren took off to, and he sure didn't want to go through that again. No siree. Not in this lifetime.

"What's the frown for?"

"Huh? Oh nothing. I was just thinking about how we have all this time left to get you your cowboy experience."

"It'll be gone before you know it."

"Yeah, probably, but you'll have the experience of a lifetime."

"True and I can't wait to experience more of this life. It's kind of growing on me."

"It is?"

"Yeah, the simplicity of it, the laid back way of life just makes me want to embrace it all the more."

He sighed, tucking a loose curl behind her ear. "I'll meet you downstairs in fifteen minutes. I'd like to take a shower."

"You sure you don't want me to join you? I kinda like shower sex."

She ran her tongue up his neck to his lips, flicking it against the edge in a torturous, tantalizing movement meant to drive him crazy. "Hmm. Maybe tomorrow. I'd like our next go round to be in a bed."

"Party pooper." She pouted a little bit before she turned toward the door and slipped her key into the lock.

As she pushed the door open, he felt fingers along his arm. The ghost was making her displeasure known when he felt a scratch and noticed a red welt coming up on his right forearm.

"What the hell?" Candace touched his arm where the welt had turned a bright red.

"It's nothing."

"Nothing? That's an angry looking scratch. Is there a loose piece on the doorframe or something?"

"No."

"Where did you scratch your arm? I didn't see it before."

He blew out a ragged breath as he felt fingers on his neck, brushing them off absently with his hand. "It's one of the ghosts. There is a female who has attached herself to me."

Her eyes widened as her mouth opened and closed a couple of time. "What?"

"Yeah. I feel her fingertips a lot especially out here in the hall."

"Is she here now?"

"Yes."

"You can feel her?"

"Yeah." He inhaled, taking in the sweet smell he was very familiar with. "Can you smell the perfume?"

"Yes."

"That's her. It's always the same smell and touch." He turned around and looked down the hall. "You need to leave me alone now. I'm here with Candace, so stop this nonsense." The perfume smell faded away on the breeze they felt from the window at the end of the hall, left open slightly to the night breeze.

"That's weird. It's gone now."

"Yep. She'll be back though, probably tomorrow."

"Is this a daily occurrence?"

"Every day."

"Wow," she whispered backing through her doorway and rubbing her arms. "That's kind of creepy. Does your family know about this?"

"A few of them. I don't talk about it much. She doesn't seem to bug anyone, but me so I just deal with it." Candace bit her lip, her eyes wide and nervous. "She won't hurt you."

"Sorry." She ran her hands up and down her forearms. "It makes me nervous is all."

"Do you want to sleep with me?"

"Can I?"

"Sure." He pushed her back into her room. "Go ahead and change. I'll meet you downstairs in a few, and we'll watch a movie." He smiled before running his fingertips down her cheek. "I won't even make it a scary one. We can watch some chick flick."

"That would be good."

"Okay. See you down there."

She backed into her room, slowly closing the door as she peeked out through the slit until the door clicked with the latch.

He shook his head. This ghost might be a problem if she got physical with him over his being with Candace. He might have to talk to his mother about it and see what they could do to bring in a medium or something. They needed to nip this in the bud. It hadn't bothered him before, but he wouldn't let the entity harm Candace.

After a moment, he headed down the hallway toward his own bedroom to take a shower. He smelled like horses, leather, hay and fire from being out near the bonfire tonight. He smiled. He kind of liked how embarrassed Candace got when his brother said he'd heard them, not that he really believed him because that's just how they rolled. They loved to harass each other over women, sex, trucks, and everything cowboy. The women in their lives had to get used to it, and he was glad Mesa, Paige, Peyton, Mandy, and Callinda had taken her under their wings and let her into their little circle of friends. It made him feel better about her being near his family.

What would it be like having her here all the time?

Whoa! Where the hell did that thought come from. No permanent things here. Nope. Not going to happen. Yeah, he wanted a wife someday, and Candace kind of fit the bill, but he couldn't think of her like that since she would be leaving soon.

Oh well.

He pushed open the door on his room, and then shut it behind him. A shower would feel good to wash away the grime and smells of the day so he could cuddle with one gorgeous woman for a few hours while they watched a movie, and then maybe he could get his dick wet before they slept for the night.

A cowboy could dream, couldn't he?

Chapter Seven

Candace felt a chill run down her spine. She wasn't sure why, but the whole ghost thing gave her the willies. To think it could affect its surroundings made her a little creeped out with everything.

After she grabbed her soft pajama pants, she stripped off her boot and jeans, dropping them to the floor, and slipped the fuzzy pants over legs, then tied them at the waist. The tank top came off next, she threw it across the bed, and took off her bra before putting an oversized T-shirt over her head. She left her socks on to keep her feet warm although the weather was humid. A fire in the fireplace would be romantic, but the weather wouldn't permit it right now.

Her imagination went to a big Christmas tree in the corner with a roaring fire. It would be grand to be here for Christmas. Too bad it didn't snow in Bandera. She liked snow covered hills, big trees and a warm body to curl up to. Well, she'd have the warm body this evening anyway.

She moved toward the bathroom to brush her teeth and comb out her hair before she went down to meet Joshua. Since he was taking a shower, it would be a minute or two.

Her reflection stared back from the mirror above the porcelain sink. Big green eyes with light colored eyelashes looked bright and sparkly in the light overhead. A pert little nose with freckles across the bridge was petite enough, she figured. Lips bowed into a small smile as she thought about the evening in Joshua's office. She'd never had sex on a desk before, so that was kind of interesting, but she couldn't wait to actually get him in a bed later on.

With her brush in hand, she ran it through the long, red hair, getting it shiny and soft in the process. *Leave it down or put it up?* Leaving it down sounded good. Maybe Joshua would run his fingers through it. She liked when he touched her hair.

Feeling sexy and bold, she dabbed a bit of perfume behind her ears and down her cleavage before she headed for the door to meet her cowboy. *Her cowboy. I kind of like that sentiment although I shouldn't get too attached.*

Taking the wooden steps down one at a time, she then tiptoed through the quiet lodge until she walked into the main room. The leather couches and chairs gave a homey, comfortable feel to the space. The huge rock fireplace along the back wall would allow roaring fires to heat the room to toasty in the wintertime. Bookcases flanked the fireplace with hundreds of books for the patrons to choose from if they wished to sit and read a good story. Several DVDs lined one shelf so she figured she'd check out the collection and pick something before Joshua came down.

The wind howled outside like a storm was brewing. Thunderstorms were common in Texas, she knew, but she shivered in response anyway. She loved the roll of thunder and lightning across the plains, lighting up the sky with its brightness when the rumble of thunder cracked overhead.

She glanced outside just as a crack of lightning lit up the front yard, seeing a man in a slouched cowboy hat standing on the front lawn. She hoped one of the boys wasn't out in this storm. That couldn't be a good thing. She moved closer to the window and peered out when another clap of thunder rolled across the sky. She couldn't see a thing in the pitch darkness outside.

"You okay?"

She jumped and screamed when Joshua's voice came from right behind her. "God, you scared the crap out of me."

"Sorry. I thought you heard me come down the stairs."

"No. The storm is getting loud."

"This is nothing. A small summer storm is all."

"I love summer storms. We don't get them much in California."

"I like them too." He slipped his hands around her waist, pulling her into his embrace with her back against his chest. "It's cool to stand on the porch out front and watch the rain."

"Sounds great."

"If it starts raining, we'll go out and watch the storm." He put his head on her shoulder. "What movie did you pick out?" She held up the front for him to see. "Dirty Dancing, huh? Good movie."

"Yep. I love Patrick Swayze."

Lightning flashed outside again. She could see their reflection in the window with the light behind them illuminating the main lodge room. They went together perfectly. He was quite a bit taller than her smaller frame, but she liked tall guys. It made her feel safe.

"We look pretty good together, huh?"

"Yeah. I think so too."

He rubbed his hands up and down her arms before turning her to face him. He leaned in a kissed her softly on the mouth, fitting their lips together like two puzzle pieces made for each other. It scared the hell out of her.

"I love the way you mold yourself to me when I kiss you."

"You feel good."

He smiled and brushed his lips against hers again. His tongue darted out to lick the corners of her mouth as she sighed at the touch. He knew exactly what to do to bring her to the heights of sensation with every little touch.

"I like kissing you."

"I like it too."

"Good." After another brush of his mouth over hers, he stepped back, took her hand and led her to the long leather couch facing the big screen television. "You sit. I'll put the movie in."

She watched as he approached the entertainment center housing the DVD player, game consoles, television, and stereo system. Checkered pajama bottoms molded to his nice ass just right, enhancing the visceral experience she had just looking at Joshua. She shifted on the couch trying to relieve some of the pressure in her pussy without success. She needed him to fuck her hard, but now wasn't the time or place. Soon though.

He opened the plastic container with the disc in it before pushing it into the player on the bottom. With the remote in hand, he turned to face her. His cock stood at full attention, tenting the front of his pants in the most provocative way she could ever imagine. He wanted her. Good. She wasn't alone in her needs then because good Lord she wanted him too.

"A little horny, cowboy?"

"A lot horny, little miss, but I'll keep my horny self calm until I can make love to you in a couple of hours."

"How about we skip the movie and get right to the making love part?"

He shook his head as a smile graced his lips. "Anticipation is half the fun. I know I'm anticipating lots of fun to come."

"Well, damn."

He sat next to her on the couch, wrapped an arm around her shoulders and hit play on the remote in his hand. The opening credits to the movie exploded from the speakers loud enough to wake the dead.

"Your parents are going to wake up as well as the entire household with that sound."

He pushed the button to turn the sound down to a tolerable level when the movie started to play.

For the next couple of hours, they watched one of her favorite movies and listened to the dry rumblings of the thunder and lightning outside the window. Small pings against the glass pane signaled the rain had started just as the movie was ending and her desire had reached its max with him running his fingers down her arm, playing with her hair and burying his nose in her neck. He ran soft little kisses over the surface of her shoulder in between all the other touching he was doing.

"Let's go watch the rain."

"Okay."

The ending credits continued to run on the screen while they got to their feet and walked hand in hand outside to stand on the porch. Water sluiced down the gutters, gushing out the ends into the yard. The rain sheeted sideways, pelting the concrete at their feet in huge drops. Thunder rumbled and lightning cracked in an awesome display of power no man could deny.

"Wow."

"We have some pretty spectacular storms around here."

"This is awesome."

"It is pretty cool." He stood with his back against the side of the house, cradling her in his arms in front of him so she could watch everything around her. "One of your brothers was out here earlier."

"Was he?"

"Well, I saw a cowboy standing out here. That's what I was looking at when you scared me before."

"Ah."

"It was one of your brothers, right?"

"I don't know. It could have been Cowboy Joe."

"Cowboy Joe?"

"That's what we call the cowboy who hangs around the main house. He's the ghost of a cowboy who used to live here, we figured." He shrugged his shoulders. "Someday, one of us will find out who he is I guess."

"You really should bring a medium in to see if you can cleanse the house."

"Why? We kind of like having them here. Well, except for the one starting to get a bit aggressive with me now. I might have someone see if they can do something about her. I can't have her scaring off all of my girlfriends."

"Girlfriends, as in many?"

He laughed. "Jealous?"

"Yeah. I'm your current lover. I would hope you wouldn't compare me or bring other *girlfriends* into the mix. I don't share well."

"Good." He kissed her shoulder. "Me either. I'm not a good sharer." He turned her in his arms even with the rain continuing to pound the ground in a staccato rhythm that almost sounded like drums in the faint distance. "How about we retire to upstairs? I want to make love to you properly in a real bed."

"I'd love that."

He took her hand as he pushed open the door to the lodge and moved inside. The pounding of the rain dimmed to a hum on the metal roof over their heads. He reached for the remote, and turned off the television before they headed for the stairs. Tonight would be something dreams were made of. Everything inside her told her she'd better hold on tight. This man was about to rock her world.

Joshua led her up the stairs, past her room and to the door two down from hers. When he turned the knob and pushed open the door, her breath caught in her throat. Even though they'd already had sex once before, this seemed new—different, like the first time without the raw explosiveness that this afternoon entailed. This almost brought tears to her eyes as she glanced around his space.

Typical guy's room. Dark furniture. Sturdy bedframe with a big headboard. Antique lamps gracing the nightstands. A heavy dresser against one wall with a large mirror over it reflecting back the two of them standing at the edge of his bed after he'd shut the door. They were alone in his room.

She waited with bated breath for him to touch her. His hands slowly reached out to wrap around the back of her neck and tug her to him.

"I want you."

"I'm glad because I'm on fire here."

With his hands twisted in her hair, he drew her closer until his mouth touched hers. He tasted good, like chocolate or some other decadent morsel she could totally get into. His tongue slid along her lips until they parted, waiting for the first touch, wanting him so badly, she hurt.

He brought his other hand up to cup her jaw while he devoured her mouth with soft licks, bold strokes, and devastating to her body, spearing. Her nipples stood at attention, reacting to the friction from his chest.

When he lifted his mouth, he tugged her shirt over her head, baring her breasts to his touch. "You are so beautiful, you take my breath away."

"You are good for my ego."

"I only speak the truth," he whispered, touching his forehead to hers. "I could look at you all day."

"Love on me for now. Look later."

He smiled that crooked little grin she loved. "Okay."

The touch of his lips on her breast brought her up on her toes as she cradled his head in her hands. She loved the feel of his hair through her fingers and freshly washed made it that much better. The strands were silky soft to the touch.

He'd shaved the five o'clock shadow from his cheeks for her too. She could feel the softness of his chin and cheeks on her skin as he moved from one breast to the other.

"Mmm."

"You're purring."

"I like what you are doing. Is there a problem with me purring?"

"Oh hell no. I love the sounds you make when I touch you."

His fingers worked at the tie on her pajama pants, getting it undone in record time before he pushed the material down her legs to pool at her feet. She stepped out, kicking them across the room, leaving her in nothing but a smile. Her body hummed as he stroked his hands up and down her thighs while he walked her backward until her legs touched the bed behind her.

She sat on the edge of the mattress, reaching for the waistband of his pants to free his cock from the tented material. The feel of him in her hands made her palms tingle to touch.

"Uh-uh." He pushed her hands away. "Not yet."

"I want to touch you."

"In a minute. I need to taste you first." He pushed her shoulder until she reclined on the bed. "Spread those gorgeous thighs for me, babe. I can smell you from here. I want your essence on my tongue."

She leaned back until she rested on her elbows, and spread her thighs as he crouched down on the floor between them.

The first brush of his fingers on her flesh had her moaning softly. She loved his skin against hers. He knew exactly what to do, exactly how to touch her. It was amazing how in tune he was to her body.

His nose brushed the inside of her right thigh as he kissed his way from her knee to the crease between her thigh and her pussy. He inhaled her scent like he savored everything about her for a memory later on. Would he remember her? She wondered if he would hold these hours they spent together as a beautiful thought for the years to come. It made her frown.

"What's wrong?"

"Nothing, why?"

"You're frowning. I'm down here eating you out. Frowns are not permitted."

She giggled. "Sorry. I wasn't frowning because you aren't doing everything perfectly, I just had a random thought."

"Care to share?"

"No. It's not important."

He licked her from her opening to her clit in one long stroke. She growled low in her throat at the sensation before she fully reclined on the bed and let herself enjoy the moment without thinking too hard.

When his tongue danced over the hard nub of her clit, she almost lost the hold she had on her desire. She needed this, needed him more than she ever could fathom in the darkest recesses of her mind when she's stumbled on him in the bar.

Each stroke of his tongue over her flesh brought her higher and higher until she floated amongst the clouds of her mind, envisioning spending each day doing this again and again.

He pushed both of his hands under her butt. Bringing her closer to his mouth, he flicked her clit with his tongue, ate at her flesh like a starving man, and made her explode in a kaleidoscope of colors. Ecstasy broke over her body in a mind numbing, body tingling burst of sensation she wasn't prepared for.

"Joshua!"

He brought her back down slowly with small licks and tongue flicks that had her shivering from head to toe. "Okay, stop. I can't take anymore."

"You will though. We're only getting started."

He reached over to the nightstand, pulled open the drawer and grabbed a condom. After rolling the latex down his shaft, he positioned himself between her thighs with the head of his cock at her entrance. "Are you ready for me?"

"Oh hell yeah."

He slowly pushed his hard cock into her opening, earning a deep groan from her. She loved the feel of him inside her. Every inch of his cock brought her more ecstasy than any man she'd been with before.

When he was fully inside her, he stopped, letting her adjust to the full length of him.

"Oh my God. You feel so warm, wet, and beautiful."

"I love how you fill me."

He shivered, his whole body rolling with the sensation as she wrapped her legs around his waist to bring him in even more.

When he slowly began to move inside her, the feeling drove her absolutely to the brink of insanity. His cock moved with such precision inside her flesh, he fit perfectly, too perfectly. *Lord, I need to get those thoughts out of my head.* Yes, he was good. Yes, she loved how it felt to make love with him, but good God, she couldn't think of anything past that. It wouldn't work.

He picked up his pace, driving any thoughts from her brain but how it felt to have him fuck her as he pounded into her pussy with enough force he had to hold her hips to keep her from sliding across the bed.

"Yes, yes, yes," she cried with each thrust. "Fuck me."

"Oh God," he whispered as his paced rhythm became ragged and disjointed.

She knew he was close. "I'm there. Do it."

The slapping of flesh on flesh threw her over the brink of sanity into the world where only she and Joshua resided. He slowed his pace bringing them both gradually back to reality, a reality she wasn't sure she was ready to face.

* * * *

"Are you okay?"

"I'm perfect." Her voice sounded like the satisfied purr of a kitten.

He smiled. He liked that sound coming from her. Hell, he liked her an awful lot. "That was amazing."

"You're amazing."

"Well thank you, darlin'."

"I love when you call me, darlin'."

"How about sweetheart, babe, or dear?"

"I could go for those too."

"I like little endearments on you. They go very well." He slowly withdrew his now flaccid cock so he could dispose of the condom in the trashcan near the bed. Her sated body lying across his bed looked mighty good. He liked having her there. "How about you stand up? I'll get the covers back and we can cuddle."

"Do you like to cuddle? I mean I don't want you doing it just because you think women like it."

"I'm a cuddler from way back."

She smiled as he tugged the covers back on the bed. *Man, I really like her smile.* He loved hearing her giggle. He just plain liked her a whole lot in general, but if he didn't get his heart out of the mix, he would be in trouble when she left to go home in a couple of weeks. *Heart? What the fuck?* He didn't need that kind of complication in his life, especially with another woman and long distance. That kind of crap only led to heartache. He knew this for certain since he'd already been there, done that.

When she crawled in to the other side of his bed, she made herself comfortable on his pillow as she held out her hand for him to join her. *This could be bad.*

"Are you all right?"

"Yeah, why?"

"You look like you've got something on your mind."

"Just you."

"That's a good thing. I like being on your mind after we've made love."

Made love. Shit, when did it become making love and not having sex? "No, I'm good."

"Good. Then come in here with me. I want to run my hands all over you."

"That might lead to other things."

"Are you complaining? Because if you don't want to love on me again, just say it."

He crawled under the sheet before drawing her into his embrace, letting her rest her head on his chest. "Anytime, darlin', anytime."

"I'm glad."

He grabbed the remote to the television sitting at the end of his bed, and flipped the TV on to the news. Now that they were cuddled down beneath the sheets, warm, and satisfied sexually, he felt sleepy.

Several minutes later, he heard the soft snores of the woman in his arms as she slept soundly on his chest. He smiled while he ran his fingers up and down her arm in a soft, soothing rhythm. He liked the way she felt there. She fit nicely in his embrace, unlike any other woman he'd ever held like this.

Thoughts like this were driving him nuts. He didn't want to fall for this little bit of a woman. He couldn't. Things wouldn't work out between them, he knew from experience, but he couldn't seem to stop himself. She got under his skin more and more every day he knew her.

He might have to have a talk with his mom. She'd know what to do. She always did.

His eyelids began to get heavy, so he flipped off the television, put the remote on the nightstand and snuggled down into the bed with the gorgeous woman in his arms. He knew he'd have to distance himself soon, otherwise, he'd find himself in deeper than he ever wanted to be with another woman in his life.

Dreams haunted him while he wrestled with himself over his growing feelings for Candace. Watching Loren leave on the plane from somewhere she couldn't see him at the airport, turned into Candace before his very eyes.

He'd watched with a heavy heart as she looked over her shoulder one last time before boarding the plane back to Los Angeles. She was looking for him. Why didn't he stop her? Why would his feet not move to take her in his arms and ask her to stay? Because he couldn't, no, more like he wouldn't. She had a life in Anaheim, one he wasn't a part of, one he couldn't fathom from his experiences in life.

The traffic would drive him crazy. The people would drive him crazier. He needed his life in Bandera, the closeness of his family, the quiet of the ranch life—it was all a part of him, one he wouldn't give up for a woman—any woman.

He settled down into restless sleep for the remainder of the night even though the woman in his arms curled herself around his heart, tighter and tighter.

Morning found him spooning her back, with her leg through his and his hand resting on her breast as he slowly opened his eyes. Her hair smelled like a soft hint of the perfume still clinging to her neck near his nose. He liked the smell on her. He liked her way too much if his dream had anything to do with what was in his heart. He didn't want her to leave. He wanted to explore more with her, teach her about ranch life and the cowboy way, everything his life stood for.

"You awake?" he asked inhaling softly to bring her scent through his head.

"Mmm. Yeah." She rolled over onto her back. "I smell coffee."

"Yeah, me too.

"Are you ready for breakfast?"

His stomach growled. "I think so."

"Me too. I need to stop at my room and shower though. I'll meet you down there in fifteen?"

"Sure. I'll have the coffee waiting. How do you take yours?"

"Cream and sugar."

"Okay. I'll find us a table. They might already be serving. If they are, I'll grab you a plate."

"Perfect." She leaned up and kissed him on the mouth softly before jumping up and tossing her clothes on. "Be there in a few," she said, opening his door.

She swept out like a whirlwind, closing it behind her as he leaned back in the bed with his hands behind his head. What was he going to do about his growing feelings for her? He didn't need this complication in their relationship. It was supposed to be a fun few weeks, not anything serious.

"I'm just going to play it by ear. There isn't anything I can do at this point anyway. If things work out, they work out. If she leaves and I never hear from her again, I'll make it through just like I did with Loren."

After all, the two women were the same in what they wanted, right? His heart didn't figure into the equation of their lives.

Man, I'm so screwed.

Chapter Eight

I love this! Mud splashed the bottom of her jeans, spraying everywhere as one of Joshua's brothers raced through the mud hole with his truck. Nothing like a good mudding party from what Joshua told her, to set her heart free.

He said this was what they did on a Saturday afternoon or evening before they went to the bar, got liquored up and went home at the wee hours of the morning. Tonight, she would spend the night in his arms again, loving him until the early morning, she decided.

She was slowly becoming a little too addicted to the kind of man Joshua Young represented. Right now, she couldn't even remember what men in California looked like.

Her cell phone jingled on her hip, bringing her thoughts back to the work she needed to do. Her vice president of sales called her earlier in the day to tell her they had a problem with one of the computer programs she'd written recently, and she had to deal with it—today.

Putting off work while on vacation, what a concept. *Damn, I don't want to deal with this. Why in hell couldn't he?*

"What?" she barked into the phone.

"Sorry, boss. I needed to tell you we need you to write the patch for the program by tomorrow, so we can get it out to the buyers. This is bad."

She began pacing back and forth, her feet squishing in the mud under her boots without caring what it did to her pant legs. "I said I'll take care of it and I will. I'm on vacation, remember?"

"Yeah, I know."

She tipped her head back on her shoulders, swearing under her breath. "Why can't you handle this?"

"It's your program, Candace. I don't have the coding memorized like you do. It would take me days to write the patch where it will take you a couple of hours."

Sighing, she rolled her eyes and glanced at the gorgeous man across the mud hole from her getting ready to jump into his truck for his next turn at the hole. She liked watching from outside more than she liked sitting in the cab or driving. She'd done both. Joshua had actually let her drive his truck! Shock, she knew. Cowboys didn't let *anyone* drive their truck. "Fine. I'll get it done by tomorrow. You'll have it in your email in the morning."

"Perfect. Thanks."

"Just take care of the office, Aaron. I need your expertise in other areas. I'll handle the coding."

“Have fun on your vacation.”

“I would if you would quit calling me with this shit.”

“I love you too, Candace.”

“It’s a good thing you are my brother, asshole.”

“Smooches, babe. Enjoy your cowboy.”

“How’d you know I’d hooked up with a cowboy?”

“Because I know my little sister like the back of my hand. You can’t handle being around all that testosterone without falling for one. Just don’t bring one home, will you?”

“No problem.”

“Have you seen much of our ex-brother-in-law?”

“Not much. I spent the first few days with him, and I’ll see him this evening for dinner before I hit the bar, but other than that, no.”

“I thought you were there to visit Arnold?”

“Yeah, well, plans have changed.”

“Hmm.”

“Back off, Aaron. I’m living my life, and I intend to have fun while doing it.”

“Good. You were in too much of a funk before you went out there. Just don’t fall in love with one of those Wrangler wearing, cowboy hat types.”

“Me?”

“Yeah, you. I know how you are.”

“Maybe.”

“Look. I’m all for you finding someone to spend the rest of your life with, but a cowboy? Really?”

“I like cowboys.”

“I know you do or do now.”

“Well, no worries. The one here doesn’t want a permanent relationship and long distance ones don’t work.”

“True.”

“Dude, I’m a California girl from the top of my head to the tips of my sandals. I’m not giving up my life there, no matter how gorgeous the guy is.”

“Good to know.”

“I’ll talk to you later. I’m in the middle of a mud bath at the moment.”

“Mud bath?”

“Yeah, the family has taken me out to go muddin’.”

“What the hell is muddin’?”

“I’ll tell you about it when I get home. It’s great fun. Lots of big trucks, mud, water and dirt. You would enjoy it.”

“Somehow, I don’t think so.”

“Yeah, probably not with your Armani suit and spit-shined shoes.”

“Yeah, I don’t like to get dirty.”

“I didn’t think I did either, until now.”

“Well, have fun, and I’ll see you in a week.”

“Wow. Have I been here two weeks already?”

"Yes ma'am, you have, and I, for one, can't wait until you get back."

"See you soon."

"Bye."

She hung up her phone as Joshua spun through the mud hole, sloshing more mud on her jeans. She laughed at the grin on his face when he waved from the driver's seat. Men and their toys. Why did it seem like he was having more fun than she was standing out there with mud to her ankles. Yes, she needed to write the code for the patch, but for now, she planned to have a little more fun before supper.

Joshua parked his mud covered truck off to the side as she watched his other brothers do the same run he'd done a few minutes ago.

When he sauntered closer, he smiled that lip-tilting smile of his that made her panties soaked. She'd spent the better part of the past two weeks in bed, in the barn, at the pond, at the bar and wherever else they could think of loving and living his lifestyle. No, she wasn't ready to go home.

They sat out on the porch rocking chairs just talking like an old married couple, laughing at stories of their childhood, sharing events of their lives, and just soaking up being together.

She sure would miss him when she had to go home in a week, but for now, she would enjoy being with him before her time on the ranch came to a close.

Tonight, they would drink, dance, and love the night away.

He grabbed her around the waist, hefting her into his arms and then strolling toward the mud hole.

"What are you doing?"

"Getting you thoroughly into the party."

"I'm already muddy."

"Not sufficiently. You need a mud bath."

"Joshua, put me down."

"Nope."

"Baby, I don't need mud in my underwear, I need you."

"But it'll be fun cleaning out those spots later in the shower we share. We haven't had shower sex yet."

"Joshua, please." She screeched as he strode right into the mud hole to his knees, and then took her down with him in a splash of water and dirt, sending her under the brown goop. She came back up with brown water streaming down her cheeks after she brushed her wet, dirty hair out of her face. "Oh my God! I don't believe you did that."

He laughed before he leaned in and kissed her full on the mouth. "You look fabulous!"

Not one to be bested, she climbed to her feet and dove at him, knocking him back into the mud until he was covered from head to toe thoroughly as well. His hat floated by. Good thing it was straw and could easily be cleaned, otherwise, she figured he'd have been pissed. *Oh well, he started it.*

She laughed as he came up sputtering. A glob of goop stuck to the top of his head until she took pity on him, reached over and brushed it off. "You look fabulous too!"

Thank goodness he was a good sport, even though he was the one who shoved her into the mud first.

When he climbed to his feet, water and mud sloshed off his tall frame to splash around him. "I'm ready for a shower, some sex, supper, and a beer, not necessarily in that order."

"Good, me too."

He tossed her over his shoulder and headed toward his truck.

"Put me down!"

"Nope. I am going to take advantage of the shower with you."

"But you'll get your truck seats all muddy."

"They're leather. They'll wash."

After he opened the door, he put her on the seat, kissed her on the mouth, and then shut the door. She couldn't help but admire the gorgeous man he was as he walked around the front of the vehicle to climb into the driver's side.

"You're grinning."

"I like the way you look even covered in mud. Is that a crime to grin about?"

His grin matched the one she knew lifted the corners of her mouth. "Nope. Otherwise, they'd be hauling me off too, because I like the way you look too."

"I can't wait to get you in the shower. I hope it's a big stall because I plan on rinsing you clean and then sucking you dry."

"Damn, woman."

"Just thought I'd let you know my plan."

"Good plan."

"I like it."

He kicked up dry dust and dirt as he sped back to the house in record time, bouncing and bumping along the rutted road. It was a good thing she had her seatbelt on, otherwise, she'd have a headache from hitting her head on the ceiling of his truck.

"In a hurry, big boy?"

"You bet. My girl said she was going to suck me dry. I'm in a damn big hurry."

She laughed out loud, snorting in her guffaws of laughter as she covered her nose and mouth.

The moment they hit the parking lot at the main lodge, he had the truck off, the door open and ran around to the passenger side to get to her. She giggled hysterically when he pulled her door open, threw her over his shoulder and ran for the house.

"Gang way! Woman in my arms," he shouted as he ran for the stairs.

Laughing, she bounced against his shoulder, her hair in a stringy mess down his back with her butt in the air. She didn't even think he shut the driver's or passenger's door on his truck in his haste to get her naked.

The minute he had her in his room, he slammed the door and started working on her clothes.

"Easy, cowboy. I can get it."

"But I can do it better," he said, whipping the shirt over her head and then shoving her pants down her legs. "See?"

"You need to be naked too."

"Okay. I can handle that." In seconds, he stood in front of her, naked as the day he was born.

"Nice." She wrapped her hand around his straining cock. "Shower?"

"Yep." He swung her up in his arms and headed for the bathroom at a quick pace.

The shower stall was something out of a home improvement shop. It was bigger than the one in her room and made of solid glass. She loved how the showerheads came out in several directions, soaking a body and massaging it at the same time. "I love your shower."

"Since I've been living in this room for several years, I had Mom and Dad customize it for me."

"Didn't you ever want a room out in one of the cabins?"

"Sometimes, but I like this one the best."

He set her down on her feet before he reached in and turned the spigot on. Water shot out from several directions when she stepped into the glass enclosure, humming her appreciation. Warmth cascaded over her hair and shoulders, washing the mud and grime from her body as Joshua stood at the back of the stall admiring the view, from what she could tell. "What?"

"I like watching you. You're gorgeous."

"Thanks, cowboy."

"No problem, darlin'."

She reached over and grabbed some shampoo to soap her hair, lathering her scalp until it tingled.

"Can I help?"

"Sure." She turned around so he could scrub her hair before she turned back around to rinse.

The water flowed down her body, washing away the mud, but not completely. A moment later, she felt his hands on her breasts, soaping and scrubbing her nipples until they were squeaky clean. "I think those are clean enough."

"I'll be the judge of that."

His mouth found her left nipple, sucking it between his lips until she came up on her toes. "So good." When he lifted his head, he soaped the rest of her body with the aloe scented soap until every spot was more than clean. "Your turn," she said, taking some soap between her hands and lathering it up well while he rinsed the mud from his body under the water spray. She ran her hands down his chest, across his six-pack abs and down to his cock. The hard flesh stood proud and waiting as she ran her soapy hands around and around.

"You're gonna kill me."

"Yep."

She bent down, running her hands down his thighs, around his calves, across his ankles to between his toes. He chuckled when she soaped each toe clean before working her way back up the back of his calves, thighs and buttocks. God, she loved his butt. In or out of Wranglers, she didn't care. He had a nice ass.

After she thoroughly soaped his butt, she ran her hands over the straining muscles of his back, rubbing and pushing her hands into the hard flesh. He groaned, dropping his head forward to his chest as she kneaded every ridge and plain of his back.

"You have a magnificent body."

"Thanks, darlin'."

He turned back around to face her, his eyes bright with desire. "I want you."

"You'll have me, but first I promised to suck you dry." She dropped back to her knees. Taking his cock in her hand, she bent forward to encircle his cockhead with her mouth.

"Oh fuck."

She licked around the underside of the head before pushing the entire length of him into her mouth and humming her appreciation. It wasn't easy, but she inhaled through her nose until she could take all of him into her mouth.

The musky smell of his groin made her throbbing pussy wetter as she slid closer so she could lick and suck until he came in her mouth.

He fisted her hair in his hands as she bobbed her head up and down, slipping and sliding his cock in and out of her mouth while she massaged his balls with her other hand.

"I'm gonna come."

"Mmm." She grabbed both of his butt cheeks in her hands to keep him close as his hips pumped several more times before hot, salty cum shot down her throat.

"Fuck." He stumbled back, taking his cock from between her lips, and slumped against the cold tile of the shower. "That was amazing."

"Told you I'd suck you dry."

"And you did, darlin'. I haven't had such a great blow job in, oh, I don't know, ever?"

She stood, dragging her tongue up his abdomen, across his pecs, up his neck to his waiting mouth.

He wrapped his hands in her wet hair, fisting it until it stung her scalp. "You are…I can't even think of the word."

"That's good enough for me."

"Are we done in here?"

"No. I want you to fuck my ass."

"Seriously?"

"Yeah."

"I don't have any lube in here, and I think a dry run would hurt like a bitch."

"Okay, we'll wait until we get in the bedroom. I don't want to use soap."

"No, that would hurt too."

"You'll do this for me?"

"Oh hell yeah. I love ass sex."

"Good. Me too."

He shut the shower off, grabbed a towel from the rack and dried her from head to toe with soft, tantalizing strokes across her breasts, down between her legs and across her butt. It didn't matter. She was already ready to explode with a mere touch of his hands on her skin, but she didn't. She wanted to feel his cock in her ass.

After he dried himself off, he wrapped the towel around his waist and led her into the bedroom. She didn't know why he bothered with the towel until she realized they might need something to clean up with after all was said and done.

He spread the towel on the bed. "Bend over the bed on your stomach."

"Will you eat me out first?"

"Sure, darlin'. I love your taste."

"Good grief, you make me so wet." She glanced down at his cock as it started to get hard again. He sure didn't need much time to recuperate. "Are you horny again?"

"I'm forever horny around you."

She laid back on the bed, reclining against the pillows so it lifted her back up enough she could watch him between her legs. The sight was amazing to see with his dark curls buried there. It made her pussy throb just to think about it.

At the first touch of his tongue on her clit, she moaned softly. The bristle of his whiskers against her pussy lips scraped deliciously on her skin, enhancing the feel of his mouth on her. She loved when he did this.

After several minutes of licking, sucking, and biting her clit and pussy, he shoved two fingers deep inside her, throwing her into a screaming, color-exploding orgasm meant to rock her world. It did. He did.

"Now," he said, sitting up and leaning over to pull open the nightstand drawer. He pulled out a tube of lubrication and a condom as he got ready to prepare her for his penetration. "You've done this before, I take it."

"Oh yeah."

"Do you enjoy anal?"

"It's one of my favorites."

"Good. Mine too, and I'll love having you squeeze me so tight when you come, I'll explode myself."

She turned over onto her stomach, resting her head on her arms, waiting for him to spread the lube around her anus. When his slick fingers penetrated her ass, she sucked in a ragged breath and blew it out. Even though she loved anal sex, it had been awhile since she trusted a man enough to let him at that dark hole.

"Easy."

"Sorry. It stings a bit."

"Been awhile?"

"Yeah. I haven't been with anyone I trusted enough to do this."

"Thank you."

"For?"

"Trusting me."

"You mean a lot to me, Joshua."

"You mean a lot to me too."

It was the best she could do at this point. She didn't want to admit anything more because it would mean leaving it behind when she went home in a week, and that would break her heart.

Several minutes later, he'd rubbed enough lube into her ass to make her slick to his touch. He'd also did some slow fingering of her clit and pussy to bring her back to the brink of climax until he was ready to ride her ass. As he got behind her and his cock nudged at her back hole, she widened her knees and pushed back against him. The slow glide of his cock into her had her moaning at a high pitch until his groin met her ass cheeks.

"Ah, hell yeah."

"You feel fantastic."

She panted hard trying to keep her climax at bay until he started to move. *Holy hell, it felt amazing having him there.* "Move please. I'm going to die if you don't fuck me."

He began a slow glide in and out, in and out. Her pussy throbbed with her racing heart as her body climbed higher on that plain of ecstasy she craved with her next breath. When he picked up the pace, she teetered on the edge of insanity while she pushed back against his thrusting hips to get every inch of length he could give her.

"Joshua!" She knew she screamed loud enough the entire house had to hear her, but she didn't care right at the moment. She just hoped they were all out and about on the ranch somewhere rather than in their rooms.

"Oh God. Oh God." His panting chant echoed in her ear while he continued to thrust in an uncoordinated rhythm until he groaned with his own climax a few moments later. "Wow."

"Yeah, wow."

He slowly withdrew from her before heading into the bathroom to clean up. She collapsed on the bed in a boneless heap until he returned a couple of minutes later, chuckling to himself. "You look well satisfied."

"Oh, I am. Thank you."

"You're welcome." She felt a warm washcloth caress her folds as he clean her up from front to back.

"You didn't have to do that. I could have managed."

"I wanted to."

"You are one amazing man, Joshua Young."

Chapter Nine

Music poured from the bar as they drove into a parking spot at The Dusty Boot later that evening. She wanted to spend as much time as possible with Joshua before she had to leave, and dancing with the gorgeous cowboy fit right into those plans. Making love with him had been the highlight of her trip to Bandera, but getting to know him on a personal level made the trip worthwhile.

"Is Arnold going to be here tonight? I know you talked to him earlier."

"Yeah, he said he would stop by. He wants to check on me." She dropped her gaze to her lap. "I feel bad. I was supposed to be here visiting him, and all I've done is spend time with you."

"Maybe you should spend the next week at his place."

"Maybe, but then I wouldn't see you."

"No, you wouldn't."

She didn't like that idea at all. Caring for this rugged cowboy had become part of her, and she wasn't sure what to do about it. She wouldn't call it love. Nope, it couldn't be that because she couldn't handle falling in love with him and leaving him behind when she went back to California and to her boring life.

He brought her hand to his mouth, kissing the back before letting her go so he could open her door. *Man, I love the chivalry of the southern gentleman. They have this shit down pat.* He opened her door and took her hand to help her down since she'd worn a short little jean skirt with her cowboy boots just like the other women in Texas. Impressively, she'd even broken her boots in during her stay in the state. How would her staff like it if she started wearing them to the office every day? They were really comfortable once she got them broke in.

Joshua slipped his arm around her shoulders after he shut the truck door to escort her into the bar. It was busy, but then again, she figured it would be on a Saturday night. "Are your brothers here?"

"Some of them. You can't have a bar on Saturday without at least one Young brother in it in Bandera."

She smiled knowing he spoke the truth. She'd learned that about his family over the course of her time on the ranch. They loved each other with a fierceness unsurpassed in any family she'd had the privilege to know in her lifetime, and she envied them that closeness even though she had a great family of her own. They did for one another. They had a bond that she couldn't quite fathom on her own, but one she hoped someday to experience for herself with a man she'd chosen to spend the rest of her life with.

They walked through the double doors to be enveloped in the crowd of people milling and moving about. The dance floor was packed while the band played a quick two-step number. Luckily, Joshua was tall so he could see over most of the crowd to find the table his brothers had secured in the back corner.

"There they are. Let's go."

With her hand in his, he led them through the throngs of people until the crowd parted near the back and she could see Jackson, Joey, Jonathan, Joel, Mesa, Jason, Paige, Jeremiah, Callinda, Jacob, and Peyton in the huge booth. The only brother missing was Jeff, and he was at home with Terri and the new baby. "Wow. What a crowd."

They'd pushed several tables together to seat them all.

Candace glanced around the bar. A sea of cowboy hats could be seen between her and the door to the outside. The place was definitely hopping tonight. The band rocked it on stage while a group of people did the two-step in a wave around the dance floor. She tapped her foot to the music as she watched with a little envy.

"Care to dance?"

"I'd love to." Joshua led her out to the dance floor where they found a small spot to get into the group of dancers, then he pulled her close. "I think there is supposed to be a little more room between us when we two-step."

"Not in my book."

She laughed while he led her around the floor. "You're a good dancer."

"One cannot be a cowboy and not know how to at least two-step. Not in Texas anyway."

"Tis true."

They shuffled around the floor several times as the beat of the music pounded so hard, it felt like her heart would beat out of her chest to the rhythm they were keeping. The band was wonderful. Some of the best sound she'd heard in several years.

As the two-step song came to an end, they wound down into a slow beat. Joshua tugged her in until she rested her head against his chest. She didn't realize the differences in their height until he pulled her in. He was a tall man compared to her smaller frame. Being only five-foot-five, he towered over her, his six foot plus size frame making her feel tiny beside him.

"What are you thinking about?"

"You."

"Are you now?"

"Yep."

"And what are you thinking about me?"

"How much I want to spread you out on my bed, kiss you from head to toe, and make love to you more than anything in this world."

"We just did that earlier."

"Yeah, but I want to do it again and again."

"I'm game, cowboy."

He inhaled through his nose and exhaled on a rush. "I'm not going to take you to bed again tonight. We are going to enjoy ourselves with friends and family, dance, drink, have a good time, get a little wild, and whatever else you want to do. How about a little star gazin'?"

"Sounds romantic." She ran a fingernail down his chest until it reached his belt buckle. "Are you a romantic guy?"

"I like to think so."

She glanced up through her lashes, giving him a smile she hoped came across as a little flirty and a whole lot sexy. "Well for now, how about we end this song, get a beer, tequila, whiskey…whatever and shoot the shit with your family?"

"Sounds like a plan."

"I may even let you do body shots off me."

One eyebrow rose as he looked down at her. "I like the sound of that." His gaze rested on her cleavage. Her nipples pebbled at the heat in his eyes. "I really, really like the sound of that."

"I bet you do, cowboy." She ran a finger from her ear to a sensitive spot between her breasts. "Lick a little salt off my neck, then down the shot of tequila resting between my breasts?" She sighed, thinking about his tongue on her skin.

"I'm gettin' hard thinkin' about all of that lovely flesh beneath my tongue."

"Mmm. I'm wet thinking about you all over me." She pulled his head down so she could whisper in his ear. "How your cock felt riding my ass."

"Keep this up, babe, and we won't be doin' much socializing. I'll take you home and ride you again."

"Promise?"

"Oh yeah, but we said we were going to have a good time tonight."

"Riding me isn't a good time?"

"Hell yeah, it is, but I want more from you than just fuckin'."

"But I like fuckin'."

"Me too, especially with you. You wanted to experience everything cowboy. I aim to provide you with as much experience as you can get crammed into your time here in Bandera. This includes two-steppin', drinkin' beer, and living the cowboy lifestyle which means The Dusty Boot on the weekends."

"Party pooper." She stuck her lip out in a little pout as he laughed.

"We'll get to the other soon enough, darlin'."

"Promise?"

"Oh, yeah."

The song came to an end, slowly drifting off on a long, mournful pluck of the strings on the steel guitar. She wasn't sure, but she thought her heart skipped a beat when she glanced up into Joshua's eyes. His face turned serious for a moment. He almost looked melancholy.

"We should get a drink."

"Okay," she said as he took her hand to lead her off the dance floor.

They came around the corner of the divider right into the arms of a petite brunette. "Joshua."

"Loren."

The woman looked Candace up one side and down the other. "It's nice to see you."

"Yeah."

She could feel the chill from across the room. Was this the someone Joshua referred to as a girlfriend? Did she want to find out? "Hi. I'm Candace."

"Loren."

"What are you doing here? I thought you were in New York."

"I came home."

"Came home?"

"Yeah, as in moved back to Bandera."

"Why?"

"I missed my family."

"Oh yeah?"

"And you."

Candace felt Joshua go totally stiff. So, this was the *girlfriend* he mentioned, and she totally wanted back into his life if she was any judge of people.

"Can we talk somewhere?"

"No."

"You won't even talk to me, Joshua, after all we meant to each other?"

"I never meant shit to you. Not enough to give up New York. We were over a long time ago, Loren, get over it."

"Are you over it?"

"Yeah, I am."

Loren stepped closer, edging out Candace for the spot next to Joshua. Candace's neck hair rose to stand on end. *Oh no, she didn't just push me out of the way!*

"I don't think you are."

Candace rose to her full height, stepping between Loren and Joshua. "Okay, listen bitch. He said he's done. Back off. He's with me tonight. You two can figure this out at a later time. Right now, this is me time."

"Who the fuck are you?"

"His new girlfriend, and trust me, you don't want to mess with me."

"You aren't from around here."

"Nope. I'm from Los Angeles, and I know how to take down puny girls like you."

Loren stepped back. "Joshua?"

"I'm with Candace. I don't have time for you and your games anymore, Loren. Go break someone else's heart. You won't get mine again." He wrapped his arm around her shoulder and walked them back to where his family sat in the corner. The whole group sat silently watching the exchange between their brother and his ex. "Who's buying? I need some salt and a tequila shot to take off my hot date. She promised."

She knew she'd do anything to make him forget the little brunette bimbo who stood nearby watching him with hot eyes. "Yes, I did. Bring it on, cowboy."

Jacob signaled for the waitress who hurried over within minutes. He ordered drinks for everyone including the tequila for her and Joshua. She couldn't wait to get his tongue on her skin.

When the waitress arrived with their drinks, Joshua ordered another round immediately, to keep them in liquor.

She got the impression it would be a hug the commode kind of night.

* * * *

Joshua didn't like the way his gaze kept wandering back to where Loren stood against the wall watching him with Candace. He didn't want to focus on her or the way she looked tonight. His date was with Candace. The waitress brought another shot of tequila. He'd lost count of how many he'd drank, but as far as he was concerned, it wasn't enough.

"Are you okay?" she asked, touching his cheek.

"Yeah. I'm just not drunk enough yet."

She reached up and kissed him on the lips before wiping her lipstick from his mouth. "Don't let her get to you."

"It's not easy."

"I know."

"You've been there?"

"Sort of. I had a fiancé once. I caught him with his secretary doing it on his desk in my own office. We worked together at my company. I found out he was only after the money and name."

"I'm sorry." He felt bad. She'd been through her own kind of hell with a man, and here he was dumping his problem with Loren on her shoulders. She didn't need that. It wasn't fair to her to be second best at any time, but especially tonight. His focus should be on her, not how his ex dumped him like a hot rock the moment the bright lights of New York blinded her to his love.

She shrugged as she fingered the buttons on the front of his shirt. "It's okay. It was a while ago, but it still hurts sometimes, and it sure makes it hard to trust anyone again."

"It sure does."

She sprinkled some salt on her neck, bent her head to the side. "Lick away, cowboy."

"You know. I don't usually drink tequila."

"You're doing pretty fabulous with it tonight."

"I'm a beer kind of cowboy."

"Would you rather I put a beer bottle between my breasts?"

"I'd take anything between your gorgeous tits."

"Use me."

"What?"

She grabbed him behind the head and brought his lips to hers. "I want you to take me out to your truck, fuck me under the stars and use me to get over her. She's not for you. If she was willing to leave you like that, she's not the woman you need to be with. You need to find someone who will love you for yourself, everything you are, and whatever life brings you. Find someone who will be your everything."

"Will you?"

"I can't promise forever. You know that."

"I don't need forever right now, but I need you."

"You have me for however long you need me, Joshua."

He leaned in, bringing their mouths together in a hot kiss. All thoughts of Loren seeped from his mind at the touch of Candace's mouth. He knew her. He wanted her. She was his…for now.

When he finally came up for air, her eyes were bright with desire as they met his. "Shall we go outside? I want to show you the stars."

"Sounds like a plan to me."

He turned to his brothers, said their goodbyes and then headed for the door. The sea of people parted before them without much preamble.

The cooler air of the evening hit him in the face as he opened the door to The Dusty Boot, leaving Loren and her gaze behind. He was done thinking about her and what she'd done to his heart. Moving on became his mantra. He'd start with giving into his desires and need for Candace.

With her hand in his, he led her to the truck, opened the door and then lifted her inside with a hand on each side of her waist. He loved the feel of her body under his touch. She was perfect, at least for him anyway.

"Where are we going?"

"Out to do a little stargazin'."

Smiling, she settled herself into the leather seats of his truck, her booted feet tapped out a rhythm to the song on the radio.

Why he liked her, he wasn't sure. She wasn't his type of woman, really. She didn't do the cowboy thing very well, but she tried, and she seemed to be enjoying everything he was showing her. She cleaned up real nice with her cowboy gear. The short little jean skirt showed off her assets nicely.

They drove in silence down the darkened streets of Bandera, down the paved road leading out to their ranch. He had the perfect spot to show her. It was a hill on their property where you could see for miles. The sleeping bag in the back of his truck would support their bodies and cushion the soft spots from the hard bed. Four wheel drive on his truck would be required to get there, but he didn't mind.

"Is this a special spot?"

"Yep."

"So I'm kinda special?"

He took her hand and brought it to his lips for a kiss on her fingers. "You sure are, darlin'."

A half sliver of moon reflected silver beams off everything around them as they bounced up the gravel road toward the top of the hill. Little did she know, but this was his favorite spot on the ranch. It might be because it was all his. He owned this little track of land given to him by his parents when he turned eighteen. He hoped someday to put his permanent house up here so he could look out over the hills around his family home and dream about his future.

As they rounded a bend in the road, the scenery was revealed. Junipers, rocks, and scrub brush stretched for miles. In the spring, bluebonnets bloomed in masses up here. Below, to the left was a pasture area where he would build his barn. His house, of course, would go on the hill. The plans were already in his head. A long porch to put a couple of rocking chairs on, a big kitchen for his wife to cook in, a giant master bedroom for their huge bed, a wonderful bathroom with a great soaking tub and a shower immense enough for them to take intimate showers together.

One thing he couldn't figure out though. Why did all of his plans now include Candace? She wasn't for him, right? She had her life in California. She'd already made it clear there wasn't anything for them on a long-term basis, but he sure had it bad for her even in the short time she'd been around. How would he feel in a few weeks?

He parked his truck and turned to face her. "What do you think?"

Her mouth hung open in awe. "Oh my. This is absolutely gorgeous, Joshua." She slowly opened the door before sliding out and closing it behind her.

He came around the front of the truck a minute later to stand beside her on the knoll overlooking the back part of Thunder Ridge.

"The stars look close enough to touch."

"I love it up here. I plan to build my house on this very hill, someday."

"This is yours?"

"Yeah. Our parents gave us each a chunk of land when we turned eighteen. This is mine."

"I could totally see you sitting up here with your family running around or when you're old in your rocking chair, a grandkid on your knee."

"I have the same picture in my head."

"It bet it's a big, beautiful house. Log with a great big fireplace in the living room for the chilly winters." She spun around with her arms wide. "The stars above shining through a big skylight in the bedroom so you can see them every night." Her spinning stopped as she wobbled a little. "Now I'm dizzy."

"Here. Sit on this rock with me." He pulled her into his arms, sitting her on his left knee while he rested on the rock he sat on every time he came up here to dream about his future. He thought it kind of poignant that he'd never brought another woman up here.

The smell of her perfume drifted to him, making him want to bury his nose in her neck. She smelled fantastic. The scent subtle, but intoxicating to his senses. He skimmed his fingers down her arm in a slow motion meant to soothe, although it was driving him sexually insane at the same time.

"Better?

"Yeah. I guess I shouldn't have done that with alcohol in me. Not good for my head."

"Let's grab the sleeping bags out of the back of my truck, spread them out on the bed and we'll watch the stars."

"Cool."

Once they had the stuff out of the rear part of the cab of his truck, they spread them out in the bed, threw the pillows near the top and climbed in. He leaned back against the pillows before bringing her into his arms to rest her head in the crook of his shoulder. *Now this is the life.*

"This is perfect," she whispered as she put her hand on his chest.

"You wanted everything cowboy. This is one of my favorite pastimes."

"How many women have you brought up here?"

"None."

She sat straight up in shock, cocking her head to the side. "What? None?"

"Just you."

"Seriously?"

"Yeah."

"Why?"

"Why what?"

"Why me?"

"I like you."

She curled back into his arms as she said, "I'm sure you've liked others. What about that woman at the bar? Loren?"

"I never brought her up here."

"Why not? You loved her, right?"

"Yeah. At least, I thought I did. I'm beginning to wonder if that's the emotion that was involved though."

"I don't understand."

His fingers did a slow crawl on her arm, as he loved the feeling of her skin under his touch. She had such soft skin. "Seeing her tonight hurt, but I'm not sure it was pain from her walking away from me when I thought we were in love or just jealousy because she chose to move without even talking to me about it."

"She didn't even tell you about it?"

"Not until the day before she was supposed to be in New York. I found out from one of my brothers. She wasn't even going to tell me, she said."

"Wow."

"Yeah."

"I would never do that to a guy I loved."

"I don't think you would. You seem to be a straight shooting kind of girl."

"I try."

A shooting star zipped across the sky. "Did you make a wish on the star?"

"Yeah."

"Me too."

"What was your wish?"

"I can't tell you. It won't come true that way."

"Oh." She sat up and looked into his eyes. "I wished this night would go on forever, but since it's impossible, I figured I could tell you."

He pushed his hand into the hair at her temple, bringing her mouth down to his. He couldn't tell her, he'd wished for the same thing.

Chapter Ten

The rise and fall of his chest beneath her cheek and the slow thudding of his heartbeat in her ear, made her sigh.

She couldn't help it. She was falling deeply for this man, and it was all wrong. Love with a cowboy didn't fit in her lifestyle. Texas didn't work for her. She had her family and her business in California. Besides, she didn't think he cared for her in a permanent sort of way. He was still hooked on Loren, from what she could tell, and she wasn't one to play second fiddle to anyone.

His lips brushed across her forehead, sending tingles down her arms. He seemed to care for her, a little anyway, but one couldn't make a relationship work long distance and only based on liking. Love had to be shared to work. She'd found that out the hard way with her ex.

Catching him with his secretary hurt. When she realized he was only after her money and name, that hurt worse than his infidelity. The leggy blonde he'd been doing on his desk, didn't surprise her really. Their love life had taken a stagnant turn. She wanted a little more adventure in their sex, he wanted missionary. She wanted toys, he wanted wham bam thank you ma'am, nothing like making love with Joshua. Her cowboy worshipped her body with his lips and tongue when they'd come together. *My cowboy? Well, yeah, I guess so.* She could think of him as her cowboy if she wanted to while she was here. After all, he did belong to her for the time being.

She slipped two buttons free on the front of his shirt, before sliding her hand between the parted material. His warm skin made her girly parts come alive with a rush of blood. She wanted him more than anything in the world. Would he make love under the stars? Could she give him something to remember her by while she was here? She hoped so, she didn't want him to forget her easily.

Tipping her head back on his bicep, she could see his profile in the moonlight. Strong jaw, full lips, whiskered cheek with the shadow of his unshaven jaw, straight nose, a wisp of dark hair falling across his brow…he almost looked like a young boy until he turned toward her, and the heated gaze met hers.

"I said we weren't going to make love tonight, but I want you out here under the stars."

"I want that too," she whispered, bringing their lips within a hairsbreadth of each other. "Make love to me, Joshua. I need to feel you inside me."

He slowly undressed her, his hands like silk upon her skin.

When she was finally lying beneath him completely naked, she reached her hands up to encircle his neck as he slowly brought their bodies together. The feel of him inside her, made her squirm. She needed to feel everything, every slide of his cock, every touch of his fingers, and every brush of his lips on hers. I love you tingled on her lips while tears gathered in her eyes.

"Why are you crying? I'm not hurting you, am I?"

Unable to answer without bursting into tears, she shook her head no and buried her face in his neck. He didn't love her. She knew that. Cowboys didn't fall in love with city girls.

"God, you feel amazing."

She wrapped her legs around his waist, taking every inch of him into her body. The slow slide of his cock in and out had her moaning softly.

When he slipped his hands beneath her shoulders and brought her into an upright position, she wasn't sure what he planned until his cock went deeper. "Fuck."

"Oh yeah. Ride me, Candace."

The rocking of her hips brought them to the brink of an explosive climax within minutes. He growled in her ear how good she felt, how much he wanted her, and how he wished this moment could go on forever. She wished it too, as she rode herself into an earth shattering climax. The cry of his name on her lips and his answering moan of hers coming from his mouth, made her smile is satisfaction. She'd given that to him.

"You're perfect."

"Thank you. You are pretty special yourself, cowboy."

"Oh shit."

"What?"

"We forgot the condom."

"No worries. I'm on the pill."

His sigh of relief had her wondering if he thought she would try to trap him into a relationship with a baby. The last thing she needed right now would be a pregnancy to complicate things.

"I'm clean."

"Me too."

"Thank the Lord."

She leaned back in his arms so she could look into his gaze. "I would never try to trap you into a relationship, Joshua. I don't want babies yet."

"I didn't think you would, but it is always a concern."

"Why?"

"I'm not sure I even want kids, but definitely not now."

"Then we are on the same page."

"Yeah, I guess we are."

She rose up on her knees, forcing his softening cock to slide out of her body. This conversation bothered her, and she wasn't quite sure why. Nothing prepared her for his immediate response to the no condom thing. She kind of liked the feel of his bare cock inside her pussy and hoped they could do it again, but if his opinion of her was so low he thought she would manipulate him, he didn't know her very well.

"What's wrong?" he asked, sliding his pants back on over his hips. "Whatever I did, I'm sorry."

She resnapped her bra behind her back before slipping on her shirt. "I'm upset you would even think that low of me."

"I don't."

"Then why the big sigh? Has someone tried to trap you before with a pregnancy?"

"No, but Jeff kind of was with his first wife, and then she screwed around on him the night of their wedding. He really loved her, and she treated him like shit."

"I'm not her."

"I know you aren't, but really, I don't know you all that well. We've known each other for only a short time. I'm not saying you would do anything that underhanded."

Great, he thinks I'm a lying, conniving slut! "I appreciate your words. Really, I do."

"Why are you mad?"

"Because deep down you don't trust women."

"No, I don't. Not really. Every woman I've known, outside of my mother, has tried getting to one of us through manipulation in one form or another."

She stomped her foot back into her right boot. "What about your sisters-in-law? Surely you don't think they are manipulating your brothers?"

"Well no. They are great women."

"Then what is your explanation for not trusting women again?" she asked, shoving her fingers through her bedhead hair, trying to straighten it out.

"I told you about Loren."

"Yeah, so?"

"It's difficult trusting someone with your heart when you've been stepped on like that. I see the way my parents are with each other, and I want a relationship like that. I want to be with my special someone for the rest of my life. I want what my brothers have. I want to come home to my wife every night after work, kiss her on the lips and have her melt in my arms the way my mother does when Dad kisses her. They've been married a long time, and they still can't get enough of each other." He grabbed her by the upper arms. "Don't you want it too?"

"Yes." *With you.*

"Then don't settle for less with anyone."

"I don't plan on it."

He leaned in, bringing their mouths close but not touching. "Why do I get the feeling when you walk away in a couple of weeks, I'll be losing something special?"

"Because you will be." She brushed her mouth against his in a tender kiss. "It's not the right time for us though. We both have too much going on to give up our lives as they are on the whim that this might be love."

"Might be?"

"Do you love me, Joshua?"

"I don't know."

"If you did, you'd know."

* * * *

He didn't like the look in her eyes. The sadness hurt his heart. Did he love her? He wasn't sure, and if anything she said was true, she might have feelings for him too. Could one fall in love in a few weeks? "I didn't mean anything by it."

"It's fine, Joshua. Things wouldn't work between us on a long-term basis. We've already come to this conclusion, so no worries." She smoothed her hands down her skirt. "I think we should get back to the house."

"Okay."

She didn't wait for him to open the door before she slid inside the cab of his truck, slamming the door behind her. He exhaled on a rush. He'd pissed her off, he figured by her attitude, although he wasn't sure what he'd done. Women. They sure were difficult creatures to deal with, and to love one seemed like insanity. Something kept him from falling for one, at least he figured he still was safe from the malady his brothers had. For now.

About twenty minutes later, he pulled into an empty spot in front of the big lodge house. The lights were on as usual, but something caught his attention through the dormer windows on the upper floor. A shadow passed in front of one, nothing solid, but something told him tonight would be a weird night from everything he'd experienced before.

"Listen. I think I'm going to take tomorrow for myself. You know, go shopping, read, or something."

"Okay." He frowned as he glanced up at the window again although nothing moved. "If you're sure. I need to get some things done around the ranch too. I have a saddle to finish for Terri's birthday. Jeff commissioned me to make it for her, and her birthday is in two weeks." He lifted her fingers to his lips for a quick kiss. "Come find me in my office if you want to go riding or something."

"I will." She pulled her hand back in a slow, reluctant stretch. "I'm sorry about tonight."

"Nothing for you to be sorry for. I screwed up."

"So we're both sorry, and we can move on from this discussion?"

"Sure."

"Good." She didn't move for a moment as she stared out into the darkness surrounding them. "How about if I get the kitchen to pack us a lunch and we go out by the pond tomorrow?"

"Sounds good. I should be able to take a break by then."

"Okay. I'll see you tomorrow at lunch then." She slid out of his truck and shut the door.

He watched her glance back for a second before she went inside and closed the door behind her. Why did he feel like shit giving her such a line of crap out in the woods? Yeah, he didn't trust women much, but he really did want a relationship with someone who would be his everything and his forever. He pressed his lips together as he looked at the steering wheel on his truck. He'd begun to think his feelings for Loren hadn't been real love. Yeah, he'd been hurt when she walked away from him to head off to New York, but it didn't compare to the feelings he was strongly beginning to think were love for Candace. Time wasn't something they had.

Anyway, tonight might be a good night for reflection and some deep thinking.

He pushed open the door on his truck, listening for any strange sounds before he shut the door behind him.

Children giggled in the distance. The ghosts were alive tonight with the full moon. They always seemed more active on the nights where the moon was the brightest.

Several minutes later, he walked up the stairs to his room. He paused a moment as he walked past Candace's door, wondering if he should knock. She'd become something special to him in the short time she'd been in Bandera, but he didn't think declaring his growing feelings would be the best move right now.

He twisted the keys to his truck around his fingers while he contemplated talking to her again this evening. Maybe giving her some space was a good thing. It seemed they both probably needed it after their love making tonight. He'd been balls deep inside her pussy, feeling like his heart would beat out of his chest. *I love you* hung on the tip of his tongue, but he swallowed it without uttering the words. He didn't want to be in love with her. She'd already told him Texas wasn't her thing. She had family and a business in California she would go back to in a week. He had to understand her life there came before him in any capacity.

With a heavy heart, he turned and headed for his room. The door stood open a crack as he approached, making him frown. *Who the hell has been in my room?* He walked inside and looked around. Nothing seemed out of place. His video games still sat in the entertainment center along with the console. His television still sat on top. His bed was made up neatly indicating his mother probably had been the one invading his space. She looked in his rooms sometimes, complaining at his lack of cleanliness.

The sweet smell of perfume reached his nose. His ghost lady was back.

He felt a soft touch on his arm as he turned toward the bathroom. A faint outline of a woman stood in the doorway. He'd never seen her before. This was new. Normally, he only felt her touch on his arm, his cheek or his chest and smelled her perfume.

"Joshua."

"You can't be here."

"I love you."

"You need to move on. You are dead."

"No."

"Yes."

A soft knock sounded on his door, and he watched as the ghost turned her head toward the sound.

"Joshua?"

A high pitched screech almost hurt his ears before the ghost quickly faded into the night.

"Joshua? Are you still up?"

"Yeah, hang on a minute." He moved toward the door and opened it to find his mother on the other side, leaning heavily on her crutches. "Mom? You shouldn't be doing the stairs on those. You'll hurt yourself."

"Hi." She frowned. "I know, but I needed to talk to you. What the hell was that sound?"

"I think we have a ghost problem."

"No shit."

"No really. There was a woman in my room by the bathroom. She was talking to me."

"Really?"

"Yeah. I think she's kind of hung up on me, and I'm not real comfortable with that."

"I bet. I can talk to the medium I know and see what her suggestion is. Sounds like we might need to see if we can get rid of her. Who is she?"

"I don't know. I think she might be a girl from the bordello days. Her outfit looked like a dancehall girl."

"I'll call my friend in the morning."

"Is there something else you needed, Mom?"

"I wanted to talk to you about a gift for your father for Christmas. How are you coming with the saddle you are making for him?"

"Good. It should be done in plenty of time." He glanced over her shoulder to where Candace's door stood closed.

"Are you okay, son?"

"Yeah."

"You seem preoccupied."

"I am a little, I guess."

She looked over her shoulder to where his gaze had landed. "Candace?"

"Yeah."

"She's a special young lady."

"That she is."

"Have you told her you love her yet?"

"What? No. I don't love her."

One eyebrow shot up over her left eye. "You could have fooled me."

"I can't love her, Mom. We haven't known each other very long."

"Love sometimes works like that, Joshua. Ask your brothers. Joel didn't know Mesa long. Jeff and Terri only knew each other a few short weeks. I could go on."

"I know, but I'm not like them."

She scoffed at that with a snorted laughter. "You think so?"

"What makes you think I love her?"

"The look in your eyes when you glanced over my shoulder to stare at her door. Does she love you?"

"She hasn't said she does."

"Women don't always say what is in their heart, son. Your brothers learned that the hard way."

"How did you know you were in love with Dad?"

She hobbled inside before he shut the door behind her. After he flipped on the light, he sat on the side of the bed to await his mother's words of wisdom.

"I just knew."

"That's it? Surely there is more to it than that."

"Nope."

"Well hells bells."

She laughed as she patted his knee. "You'll know, Joshua. If you can't think without her invading your thoughts, you're in love. If you want to be with her all the time and are miserable without her, you're in love. Do I think you can fall in love with someone in a few weeks? Sure, you can. You forget. You two have been together almost nonstop since you met. That has to mean something. Do you like her?"

"A lot."

"Have you two had sex?"

"Yeah."

"How was it?"

"Do I really want to have this conversation with my mother?"

"How was it?"

He hesitated a moment before he lowered his gaze to his knees. "She blew my mind."

"But that doesn't always mean love, now does it?"

"No. I've had good sex before, but this was different. It's like she touched my soul."

"Then I think you've got some serious thinking to do before she heads back to California."

"But she doesn't want to live here, Mom, and I can't see me living anywhere else. How do we overcome that kind of obstacle?"

"I'm not sure, honey. If she loves you and you love her, you'll work it out somehow. In the meantime, you should probably stay away from her. You know, so you two don't get more wrapped up in each other."

She kissed him on the cheek and left without another word.

His thoughts tumbled through his mind. Did he really love her? Yeah, maybe, he guessed. He raked his fingers through his hair, wishing he knew what he was supposed to think. This love thing sucked donkey balls. He didn't think he liked it very much. *Decisions, decisions. Now what the hell am I supposed to do?*

He flopped back on his head, staring at the ceiling. Love Candace. Okay. So he'd come to the conclusion that he might be in love with her, but what could he do about it? She didn't love him. He figured that much because she only wanted to experience everything cowboy.

Damn it! Why do I get myself in these messes? First Loren and now Candace?

Chapter Eleven

Morning sunlight came through the gauzy curtains on her window, blinding her to the room around her for a moment as she peeled her gritty eyelids open. She'd cried herself to sleep the night before, thinking about Joshua.

She'd stopped herself several times from going to his room, throwing herself into his arms and confessing her love for him. *Bad idea.*

After her tears had cleansed her soul, she'd drifted off to sleep with the taste of his kiss on her lips and the feel of his skin touching hers, if only in her dreams. She couldn't have him. She knew this. Their lives were too different and too far apart to come together even for love.

She'd decided to just enjoy the time they had together, never revealing the love growing in her soul for the cowboy in her life.

They would come together to enjoy her last week here, make love several more times, ride horses, go mudding again, and enjoy the stars and each other's company until she got on the plane for home, leaving her cowboy lover behind.

With a heavy sigh, she flipped the covers off her body, threw her legs over the side of the bed and sat up. She needed a shower to wipe away Joshua's love making from the night before so she could move on with her day. They would probably end up making love again out by the pond, but for now, she needed a clean slate to get this day started.

She'd found one of Mesa's books on the shelf downstairs a couple of days ago, and she wanted to read it before she went home. She might even go buy a copy at the bookstore in San Antonio to have her sign before she left.

She tapped her fingernails to her lips. San Antonio. Maybe she should make a trip into town this morning, do a little shopping, and get back before her lunch date with Joshua. Sounded like a plan to her. *I could buy some sexy little number to knock his socks off. Hmm.* Maybe one of the girls would go with her. She could always ask. Mesa? Paige? Peyton? She snapped her fingers. Mandy. She didn't have a brother she was hooked up with yet. She'd ask her after breakfast.

Smiling to herself, she grabbed some clean clothes and headed for the hot water of a shower.

Several minutes later, she whistled softly as she headed down the stairs to get some breakfast and ask Mandy to head into town with her.

When she rounded the bottom of the stairs, she almost ran headlong into Nina. "Oh, I'm sorry."

"I didn't see you." Nina hobbled back on her crutches, glancing over her thoroughly before she met her gaze again. "Don't you look gorgeous this morning?"

Candace looked at her attire, not really seeing what Nina referred to, but pleased all the same. "Thank you. It's nothing special."

"Maybe it's the twinkle in your eyes. You look beautiful."

"I appreciate you saying so. How are you today?"

"Wonderful! It's a beautiful day here on Thunder Ridge." She leaned in to whisper, "I have it on good authority, one of my boys is expecting a baby. I'm going to be a grandma again."

"Oh?"

"Yes, ma'am, but I've been sworn to secrecy. His spouse hasn't told him yet, so I have to keep it quiet." The smile on her face was big enough, Candace was afraid she was going to start giggling.

"Congrats," Candace whispered in conspiracy.

"Thank you."

She glanced over at the group sitting at the table as they laughed together. No one seemed worse for wear after their night at the bar. Her gaze went around the table to each of the women wondering who was pregnant this time, but she couldn't decide. No one looked anymore sickly or glowing or whatever the newest thing was to tell if a woman was pregnant. Maybe it was still very early, and she wasn't showing the signs yet. It would give her something to think about besides Joshua. "I'm heading into San Antonio this morning for a little shopping. Is there anything I can pick up for you?"

"No, but thank you for asking. I'll be making a trip myself in a couple of days for baby shopping. I do love it when my kids are having new babies." She grinned again, looking over her shoulder at her sons and daughters, but Candace couldn't tell who she was looking at.

"I believe I'll ask Mandy to go with me, if you don't mind."

"Oh no. I'm sure it would be fine, but she'll need to check with the head cook to find out if it's okay. I don't get involved in time off things."

"I'll have her ask then."

"Good." Nina turned her toward the breakfast serving area. "Go eat before you waste away."

"Not likely to happen in this lifetime."

"Oh psh."

Candace laughed. She really loved Joshua's mother a lot, and she hoped someday she would get another great daughter-in-law like the others she had. The thought of Joshua with another woman didn't sit well with Candace at all. She didn't want to wish him years of loneliness, but she sure as hell didn't want him with anyone else either.

When she walked toward the serving tables, she could feel a gaze on her. She hadn't seen Joshua at the table, but he was near. Wanting to give him something to think about while he worked, she swished her hips slightly as she walked. He like her butt, she knew that from their romping anal sex.

Holding out her plate for the servers to give her eggs, bacon, hash browns and a biscuit, she looked at Mandy and said, "Would you like to run into San Antonio with me today? Can you get off work?"

"Let me ask after we are done serving, and I'll let you know."

"Okay." She reached the end of the serving line, grabbed an orange juice and headed for a table at the end of the room. She fully expected Joshua to join her, but he didn't. She brought a forkful of eggs to her mouth, slipping the tines between her lips as she locked her gaze on him, sitting by himself at a side table away from the family.

One eyebrow shot up over his left eye while a small smile played on his lips, tilting the right edge up slightly in a cocking little grin.

We're playing like that, are we?

Once she swallowed, she slowly parted her lips, running her tongue over the bottom one in what she hoped was a sexy little move meant to drive him nuts. Seeing him shift in his chair, she wondered why he didn't come over.

While she continued to eat her breakfast, he stared, hardly blinking, his crystal, blue gaze fixated on her. Her nipples pebbled behind her bra, rubbing enticingly against the material, reminding her of his tongue rasping over the surface. Her pussy throbbed to the beat of her heart, nearly driving her insane with lust.

How could he wind her up like this without even touching her? The man had her so tightly wound, she could easily follow him out to his office, jump his on his desk, and never think twice about it.

She blinked when Mandy stepped between them, breaking their fixation on each other.

"I got the day off so we can go to San Antonio."

"Great."

"Are you okay? You look flush."

"I'm fine. Just a little warm is all."

Mandy glanced behind her to where Joshua sat grinning like a Cheshire cat who got the cream.

Bastard. For that, I'm not going to tell him I'm switching our ride to dinner time. Make him wonder until he finds the note I'm going to leave in his office.

"I'll be ready to go in a few minutes. I need to do something first."

"Okay. I'll help the kitchen do up a few dishes while I wait for you."

"Awesome. I'll meet you here in like ten minutes."

"I've got your plate. You go on and do your errand."

"Thanks, Mandy." Candace blew Joshua a kiss before the door banged shut behind her as she headed to his office. She wanted to get there and leave him a note about their outing.

She pushed open the office door, breathing in the scent of leather and man. The intoxicating smell made her want him all the more. After a moment, she shook her head to jar the titillating thoughts from her mind. *Focus, Candace.*

She found a pen and some paper on the desk to write a quick, sexy note.

> *Joshua-*
> *Sorry to change our lunch plans, but I thought this would be more fun.*
> *Meet me here at 8 p.m. dressed for a midnight ride with your fantasy cowgirl.*
> *~ Candace*

She pressed a lipstick kiss to the paper, giggling softly for a moment before she laid the sheet on the desk where he could find it.

Now to get Mandy's help with the cowgirl thing.

Smiling as she thought of Joshua finding the note, she snuck around the side of the barn when she spotted him across the yard heading toward his office. She hoped he had a hard-on all day long because she knew she was horny for him and would be until they met later that evening.

The moment he went inside, she dashed toward the main lodge to find Mandy.

Several minutes later found the two of them laughing as they drove down the driveway toward the wrought iron gates of Thunder Ridge, headed for San Antonio and a girl's day out.

The first store they hit was Ranch at the Rim, a western wear store with a huge selection of boots, dresses and things for the cowgirl in all of us. She found the perfect short black dress with long flowing sleeves and a silver concho belt to go with it. She already had new boots, but she found a solid black pair with inlaid turquoise and silver accents. They would go perfect with her dress and the turquoise jewelry she found at another western store. The earrings would dangle enticingly against her neck, drawing his gaze, making him want to nibble on the long expanse. The chunky necklace dangled a large group of turquoise beads near her breasts, with silver feathers and hearts going up the sides to clasp at the back of her neck.

She stood in front of the mirror at the final store with the entire outfit on.

"Wow. You look like a red-haired Indian princess," Mandy said, standing behind her. "Joshua won't know what to do with you. How are you going to ride in that though?"

"With it up around my waist, silly. And no underwear." She laughed.

"Ouch. I think that would chafe."

"I'll bring something to put on the saddle so it doesn't."

"Are you planning on seducing him right out of his tight Wranglers?"

"Hell yeah."

Mandy sighed happily.

"Who are you hung up on?"

"I'm not."

"Oh please. I can tell by the way you glance constantly at the family table, but I can't tell which one of those sexy guys has your attention."

"It doesn't matter. He doesn't know I exist."

"Who?"

Mandy glanced around for a minute before answering, "Jonathan."

Candace met her gaze in the mirror. "Oh, the website guy."

"Yeah."

"He's not your typical Young brother cowboy."

Mandy picked at her fingernails, not meeting Candace's gaze any longer. "No, he's not, but yeah, that's why I want him, I think. The other guys are gorgeous, don't get me wrong, but there is something about him that trips my trigger."

"What do we need to do to get him to notice you?"

"I don't know. I'm tired of chasing his ass."

"Sounds like love to me." She laughed a little as she thought about how her relationship with Joshua had gone in the few weeks she'd been at the ranch. Who had done the chasing? She wasn't sure anymore. It seemed mutual to her. Joshua hadn't chased her really. The accident with the beer had started the whole thing. Of course, he'd been happy to oblige, she was sure. He hadn't turned down her advances. Typical guy, really.

The dress swished around her thighs when she turned from side to side, admiring the way it clung to her curved waist and breasts. She liked the look and feel of the clingy material against her body. It made her feel sexy.

"You look great," Mandy said, admiring the reflection. "The dress looks fabulous on you. He'll be totally blown away."

"And the boots?"

"They are perfect for that dress too. You look like the quintessential cowgirl. Now all you need is a black hat. I'm sure this store has a few of those." Mandy laughed as they both looked at the rows and rows of cowboy hats lining the area to the right of the dressing room.

Different brands with everything from snakeskin headbands to feathers hanging down the back, lined the walls. She could have her pick. "I'm sure I can find one that looks good. Although I'm not sure if black looks better on me or brown with my red hair."

"The black looks fabulous on you. Your hair isn't a bright red, it's more of a strawberry blonde, so the black is perfect."

"Okay. Black it is then."

"Good choice."

"What shall we do for lunch?"

"There are some great little shops near the Alamo, and the River Walk is right there. They have some fantastic restaurants with everything from Tex-Mex to steak."

"Joshua hasn't really taken me anywhere except the ranch and The Dusty Boot."

"Well, he needs to then. These restaurants are really romantic. Some even have Mariachi bands that'll play for you specifically. For a price, of course."

"Of course."

Candace went back inside the dressing room to put on her jeans and blouse so they could head down to get some lunch. She wanted to shop for something special to give Joshua. She wanted him to remember her when she went back home. *Something special, but what?* What do you buy for a man who has everything or seems to?

After she redressed, she stepped out into the main area of the western store only to run smack into Loren. "I'm sorry. I didn't mean to bump into you."

"Oh. It's fine." Loren glanced up at her from her small stature. "You're the woman who was with Joshua the other night."

"Loren, right?"

"Yes." Loren gave her an attempted intimidating look. "You realize he's mine, right? He'll never love anyone the way he loved me and still does."

Candace placed her hands on her hips. "If I understand correctly, you left him to run off to New York. What makes you think he'd take you back?"

"Because he still loves me, you idiot."

"Really, because I'm not getting that vibe from him. I think he's over you, and you don't like it because he's moved on with someone who will treat him like he's everything to them."

"And that's you?"

She hesitated a moment, realizing she wanted him to be her everything, but she couldn't. She had a life in Los Angeles, her family, and her business. "Whether it's me or not is none of your business. Obviously, it isn't you since you walked away from him without a backward glance. Why are you back in Bandera? Did your glamorous life in New York not work out?"

"You're a bitch."

"And you're one to talk. It takes one to know one, and by that I mean, yes, you are a bitch too. At least Joshua's feelings mean something to me. They apparently didn't to you when you walked away from him."

"I asked him to come with me."

"Did you? I doubt that, but anyway, how could you ask him to give up his life here? He's a cowboy. He would shrivel up and die in a place like New York." *Or Los Angeles.* She frowned.

"He didn't give a shit about my wants or needs either. My career took me to New York. If he loved me, he would have dropped everything to go with me."

"If you loved him, you wouldn't have asked."

"Well anyway, you can just go back to where you came from and leave him to me. I'm back in Bandera to stay. He'll be mine again soon."

"I doubt that."

"I don't. I saw the way he looked at me at the bar."

"Old feelings die a slow death, but give up, Loren, his feelings for you are dead."

"We'll see about that."

With a flip of her hair, Loren walked out of the store as Mandy and Candace looked at each other.

"Well that was entertaining." Mandy raised an eyebrow and smiled.

Candace laughed although her heart was heavy. The realization she was falling in love with Joshua hit hard, right between the eyes. She'd realized it before, but right now she could totally see him going back to Loren. It bothered her, a lot. Walking away from him came with a price. The price would be a broken heart. A heavy sigh escaped her lips as she headed to the checkout with her purchases. She would live for the moments they had together so she'd have something to hold onto when she went home. Her life in California came before what her heart wanted. Her head said walk away, you still have a life there with your family, friends, and business. He's just another guy. Her heart said no, he was the one. Stay and work it out, but she didn't know how to do that.

Lunch was a quiet affair after all their bantering back and forth in the western store. Mandy seemed quiet too. Thoughtful might be a better word. "Are you okay?"

"Yeah, why?"

"You're pretty quiet."

"Just thinking."

"About what?"

"What else. The Young brother who I can't seem to corner long enough to talk to me."

"We should brainstorm ideas on how to get you two together."

Mandy sighed as she plopped another chip dripping with salsa into her mouth. The moment she finished chewing, she said, "Trust me, it doesn't work. I've tried that with Peyton, Paige, Mesa, Terri and Callinda. They all have their men, but mine doesn't seem to notice anything outside of HTML codes and graphics."

"He's a Young brother, is he not? What about sex?"

"If I thought that would jingle his bells, I would be all over him. I'm beginning to think he might be gay, but I've seen him with a woman or two before, so I know that's not the case either. It's got to be me. He doesn't like blondes? My boobs are too big or too small? I'm too fat? Hell, I wish I knew."

"You are not too fat. You're curvy and just the right size for your height."

She blew out a breath, puffing her cheeks out in a heavy sigh. "Maybe that's it. Maybe I'm too short for him." The straw made a swishing sound when she stirred her margarita with it.

"Oh, stop."

"You can say that. You have a Young brother to yourself."

"Temporarily. We aren't anything permanent, you know. I have to go back to California next week."

"Why?"

"Why what?"

"What's in California that is so important to give up Joshua?"

Candace thought to herself for a moment before she said, "My family."

"They can come visit."

"My apartment."

"You could find something here. There are cheap apartments all over Bandera."

"My business."

"Sell it. Didn't you say your brother was your vice president? I bet he'd buy it in a heartbeat."

"What if I don't want to sell it?"

"Ever hear of relocating your business here? San Antonio is a hubbub of new business starting up all the time. Web design is huge here."

"I don't think Joshua is on the permanent relationship trail. We are having a good time together, but he hasn't said anything about making this a long-term relationship."

"Do you love him?"

Now it was her turn to stir her drink as she contemplated how to answer Mandy's question. Telling her the truth would bring about a flurry of Mandy trying to convince her to stay in Bandera. Her heart wanted her to, but her head said no. How could she possibly pull up her life and move here when she didn't even know if Joshua felt anything for her? Yeah, they were good in bed together, but a couple needed more than that to make a life together, and what happened if they didn't make it? What if she pulled up stakes, moved everything here, and then they broke up somewhere down the line? No, she would be better going back to California and forgetting the man ever existed. It was best. "I have feelings for him, yes, but I can't uproot my life when I don't know if there is anything there for him."

"Have you told him?"

"Hell no. Do I look stupid to you?"

"No, you don't. I think you're trying to protect your heart, and I can really understand that. I can, but if you don't take the chance, you will never know if there is a chance you could make a go of it."

"What if he laughs in my face?"

"I doubt Joshua would do that, but if you are that afraid, wait until you have him buck naked, take his clothes and don't give them back until he professes his love for you."

The laughter coming from her mouth burst out is a loud bubble of giggles and snorts until she covered her mouth and nose, afraid the drink of margarita she'd just taken might spew forth in a shot of alcohol across the table, hitting Mandy square in the face.

"I'm glad I could make you laugh. This conversation was getting a bit too serious." Mandy giggled in return.

"I needed that. Thank you."

"You're welcome." Mandy sobered. "Now, you need to tell him tonight when you have him alone under the stars. See what he says. What can it hurt?"

"I might lose my soul."

"Yeah, but what a way to go!"

"You're a nut!"

Mandy raised her hands as she shook them over her head. "Yep, that's me, nutty Mandy."

Their lunch arrived bringing their conversation to a halt while they dug into their respective plates. Candace enjoyed the tang of Mexican food on her tongue as she savored the spices blended together in her Texas Red Enchilada. While she ate, her thoughts wandered to Joshua as she debated on what to do about him. Yes, her feelings for him were growing stronger every day she was around him, but he never gave any indication her feelings might be returned. What if they were? Could she really pack up and leave her life in California for the love of a man who had trust issues? Would he ever be able to fully trust her after what Loren did to him?

"What are you thinking about?"

"Joshua."

"Big surprise." Mandy took the last bite of her taco salad before pushing her plate away. "Any conclusion?"

"Nope."

"I say play it by ear. If those three little words are on the tip of your tongue tonight as they dance along his cock, then say them. See what happens."

"You are such a bitch."

"I know." Mandy grinned before she swallowed the last of her drink and then leaned back in her chair. "Lordy, I ate too much."

"Me too," Candace replied, pushing her unfinished plate away. "We have more shopping to do though."

"Oh?"

"Yeah, I want to get something special for Joshua."

"Do you know what you are looking for?"

"No, not really. I'll know it when I see it though."

After they paid their bill, they headed out to check out the shops along the River Walk. She'd heard they had specialty shops there that carried all sorts of things a cowboy might want. It needed to be something special, something he couldn't get just anywhere.

When she was about to give up and buy him a hat, they walked down one more street of shops where a small leather tanner and craftsman's shop sat in the back in a tiny area with a glass front. The man had saddles, belts, hat bands, and several other things he'd worked some beautiful patterns into the leather with. She could imagine Joshua doing this full time. He would love it!

As she browsed around the shop for something special to give him, the gentleman looked up from his work and smiled. "Howdy."

"Good afternoon. Are you the owner of this shop?"

"Yes ma'am. Name is Michael West. What's yours?"

"Candace."

He glanced around his shop with a twinkle in his eyes. "Is there somethin' I can show you?"

"I'm not sure. I'm looking for something special to give a man I know. He does this kind of work too."

"Oh?"

"Yes. His name is Joshua Young."

He slapped his knee and laughed. "I know Joshua well. I taught him everything I knows."

"You do?"

"Yes ma'am. Nice boy. He's talented, that one. He's got some great stuff." Michael scratched his bearded cheek. "I haven't seen that boy in a long time. How's he doin'?"

"Wonderful. He's doing great."

"How can I help you?"

"I want to give him something special. Something he can't get anywhere else, but I don't know what. Most of this kind of thing, he can make for himself, you know what I mean?"

"Yes ma'am." He pushed his cowboy hat back on his head before staring her down with quizzical eyes. "I have just the thing."

"You do?"

"Yes'm." He moved to his desk to the right of where they stood and reached into a drawer. When he returned to her side, he held a leather bound square zippered pouched with JY on the cover. "I meant to give this to him a long time ago, but I haven't had the chance to get out to his place."

"What is it?"

"My old leather tooling kit, but I put it in a special case for him."

"Oh my. I couldn't possibly take this."

"I want you to give it to him. It'll be something he surely doesn't have, and it would be a special gift from you and me, if you don't mind me piggyback ridin' your gift."

"Not at all, but are you sure?"

Michael took his hat off, scratching his head for a second before replacing the worn straw hat on his head. "Most assuredly, ma'am. This would mean the world to me if you would give it to him with my special thank you."

"If you're sure."

"I would appreciate it a whole lot. You must be a special girl to Joshua to want to give him a gift like this."

Her face turned a bright red as she felt the heat crawl up her neck and splash across her cheeks. "I don't know how special, but we've been spending a lot of time together over the last few weeks, and he's come to mean a lot to me."

"I'm sure you mean a lot to him too, missy."

"Thank you, Michael. What do I owe you for this? I should pay you something."

"If you just pay for the leather case, we'll call it even. It's twenty dollars."

"No, it has to be more than that. I'll give you a hundred."

"No, ma'am. Twenty is all."

"Twenty it is then." She handed him the twenty, fully intending to drop another hundred on the floor as she left so he would find it under his desk another time. When Michael turned to put the tool case in a bag for her, she slipped a hundred dollar bill into his desk drawer and turned back to face him. "Thank you, Michael. I'm sure he'll be thrilled with it."

"I'm sure he will. Tell him hello for me when you see him."

"I certainly will." She leaned in and gave him a smooch on the cheek. "Thank you again, and I hope to see you soon."

"Me too, sweetie."

Leaving the shop with Mandy, Candace held the bag close to her chest knowing what a special gift it was for Michael to give Joshua his tooling kit. It would mean the world to him to have his mentor's tools to work the leather with.

Evening fast approached. She wanted to take a shower, curl her hair, and put on her little black dress with her boots and jewelry before she met Joshua in his office and gave him his gift. Tonight would be special. She just knew it in her heart. Would she tell him she loved him? She wasn't sure, but for everything it was worth, she did love him. She just wasn't sure she could walk away from her life before Joshua to the possibility of life with Joshua.

Chapter Twelve

Joshua whistled softly as he worked with the belt he was making for Candace. He'd tooled her name into the back band of the leather, hoping she would like what he'd done with the flowers and such along the leather. He glanced down at the tool in his hand. *I need to get some new ones or sharpen these badly. They are pretty worn.* He shook his head when he remembered his mentor, Michael West. The man was a genius with leather, and Joshua only hoped one day to be able to work the designs that man could do in his sleep.

"Are you here?" Candace knocked on the closed door, calling through the panel.

He looked down at this watch before he shoved the belt into the desk drawer. "Yeah, hang on a minute, babe. I'll be right there." He didn't want her to see the belt before he was done with it, and he had a few more things to do to it before he gave it to her. Good thing she wasn't leaving until next week.

"Hi," he said, pulling open the door. His jaw about hit the floor at the picture she made. "Wow."

She twirled in a little circle, billowing out the edge of the dress that barely came to mid-thigh. "You like?"

"You look fabulous. Where did you get that dress and those boots?"

"Shopping today with Mandy. I had to have the perfect outfit for out little rendezvous tonight." She held out something in her palm.

"What's this?"

"A gift."

"You didn't have to get me anything, but that is very sweet of you." He unwrapped the leather binding and gasped. "A tool kit?"

"Yes."

"Where did you get this?" He ran his fingers over the initials on the back of the leather.

"A gentleman who had a shop in San Antonio. He said he knew you well. Michael West?"

"Seriously? He's my mentor. He taught me everything about tooling leather. You met him? What did he say?"

"Slow down, cowboy." She laughed. "He said you were one of the most talented people he knew, he enjoyed teaching you about leather, and how to work with it. When I told him I wanted to buy you a gift, he insisted on giving me this to give to you."

"Wow," he whispered. This meant more to him than anything in the world. "Thank you." He leaned in a kissed her. "You have no idea how much this means to me."

"I hope you like it."

"I love it! I'll probably spend all day tomorrow sharpening them."

She laughed as he turned to lay the kit on his desk, before he turned back around to take her in. She was definitely something special. When he stepped closer again, he slipped a hand up her thigh under the edge of her dress until he reached where her panties should have rested on her hip. "No underwear?"

"Nope. All yours."

"Holy shit," he whispered in awe of her boldness to go horseback riding with no underwear and bare legs. "Are you sure you want to ride like that?"

"I brought a towel to put on the saddle to keep the chafing down. I don't want to be rubbed raw before we get to the fun stuff."

He adjusted his cock in his jeans before groaning softly. "Me either, baby girl. Of course, it's going to be a bitch riding with the hard-on I have already seeing you like this." He watched her nipples bead under the soft fabric of the dress. "No bra either?"

"Nope."

"Damn," he whispered in awe. "Shall we? I've already saddled the horses unless you would rather ride double. My gelding can handle the weight if you'd rather ride across my lap."

"Now, that sounds like fun."

"Good." He pulled the door shut behind him and led her out into the walkway of the barn where the two horses stood. He quickly unsaddled the mare he'd prepared for her to ride, leading the horse back into an empty stall as soon as he finished.

He couldn't help but smile at her attire. The little black dress had long, flowing sleeves that hung to her wrists, with a square bodice and clingy material that hugged every curve of her body. There were small ruffles at the hem that went all the way around, but the most amazing thing to him was her legs. She had gorgeous, long legs he hoped to have wrapped around his waist before the end of the night. The boots on her feet were cute. Pointed toes with turquoise blue coloring woven into the design of the black boots were perfect for her outfit. The necklace around her throat showed off her long, slender neck to perfection, making his mouth water to taste her skin and drink in the beautiful woman she was, with everything inside him.

When he walked back to her side, he leaned in, capturing her mouth in a passionate kiss.

"What was that for?"

"Because you look gorgeous, and I couldn't keep myself from kissing you."

"Well, thank you, sir."

"You are most welcome, darlin'." She rubbed her arms. "Cold?"

"No. You call me darlin', and it gives me goose bumps."

He nuzzled her ear as he whispered, "Good. I like giving you goose bumps." After he stepped back a few inches, he positioned the towel she'd brought over the pommel before he grabbed her around the waist and deposited her into the saddle sideways so her legs hung off the left side of the horse. A moment later, he grabbed the saddle horn, stuck his foot into the stirrup and swung his leg over the back of the horse to settle himself comfortably into the saddle with her sitting across his lap. He made sure he sat back a bit in the saddle giving her a little room between him and the pommel. "Comfortable?"

"Yeah, actually, surprisingly enough, this isn't too bad."

"You'd better wait to make your decision. It might not be too comfortable when we start moving, but then again, you can always straddle me." *Stupid idea. Then her bare pussy would be riding my groin.*

"Oh, straddling you sounds awesome. I like that idea."

Kicking himself mentally, he lifted her by the waist until she swung one leg to his left and the other to his right, leaving her hot little pussy right against his dick. "Fuck."

"Uh-huh. Maybe I'll unzip you."

"I'm already going to die doing this. I need to keep my dick in my pants, little lady."

She stuck out her bottom lip in a little pout that he wanted to bite so badly, he hurt, or was it caused by her pussy scorching him through his pants? He might just die before they even got out of the barn.

With a blanket tucked behind him on the saddle, they were ready for their moonlight ride out to the pond. Good thing it wasn't too far away, and he wouldn't have to wait very long to be inside her. At least, he hoped not. At this rate, he didn't know if his legs would even hold him when he had the chance to stand again.

Moonlight streamed through the trees as they rode through some clearings toward the gurgling sound of the stream running through Thunder Ridge property. He loved coming down here. It had always been a special place for him, and now it would be a special place for them. A place they could look back on and remember fondly about how they spent the evening making love under the stars, with the moonlight shining down on them in a curtain of silver. Tonight was the back half of the full moon from the night before. Something special. He just knew it in his heart.

They reached the pond with the babbling brook running over the rocks, producing the soothing gurgling sound they'd been hearing for the last several minutes.

He groaned softly as he disengaged himself from Candace's lips where she'd been kissing, licking, and sucking on his neck for half the ride.

"Oh. Are we here?"

"Yeah."

"Good, but I was having fun."

"I know you were. You were torturing me beyond belief while I had to keep the horse on the damned trail."

"Poor cowboy." She trailed her fingers down his erection. "A little hard, are we?"

"A lot hard, babe." After he disengaged her legs from around his waist, he swung his leg over the saddle and stood on shaky legs when his booted foot hit the ground. "My legs feel like I haven't ridden in a years."

He put his hands around her waist and helped her to stand beside him. With her hands on his shoulders, she brought their lips together in a heart stopping kiss meant to melt him into a puddle, he was sure.

"Mmm. I can't wait to get these jeans off you, cowboy."

"I brought some dessert in the saddle bags along with a blanket."

"Good thinking. Chocolate, I hope?"

"Yeah, chocolate cake from dinner. I hope it's in one piece."

"Licking the crumbs from your chest would be fun. Too bad we don't have chocolate syrup."

He reached into the bag and pulled out a bottle.

"Awesome! You think of everything, don't you?"

"I try." He grabbed the blanket and handed it to her. "Why don't you find a nice grassy spot while I hobble the horse? I'll join you in a minute."

He watched as she walked over to the stream, found the perfect spot, rolled out the blanket and sat down. Mesmerizing was the word that came to mind before he shook his head to dispel the kinky thoughts running through his brain so he could tie the horse. He wanted her with every breath in his body, every ache in his dick, and every droplet of sweat pouring down his back on the ride over here. The perfection that was Candace wound its way around his soul. *I am so screwed.*

* * * *

Candace sat on the blanket and removed her boots. With her toes now free, she wiggled them a bit to get the cramps out of them from the pointed toe boots. She loved how they looked on her feet, but being comfortable in them wasn't great. Maybe she needed to stretch them out some before she wore them again. She loved that Joshua liked her outfit though. She'd done everything for him.

A few moments later, he slid down beside her on the blanket, half his face in the shadows from the moonlight and the other half lit brightly by the silver lighting. She could still see the twinkle of desire in his eyes, and boy howdy, she couldn't wait to get him naked. She had plans for his body tonight, some she hoped he wouldn't mind because she wanted to ride his hips into next week. "Are you going to take your boots off?"

"Yep. I see you've already got comfortable."

"Yeah. I love the boots, but they pinch my toes a little."

"You need to stretch them out. You should probably take them to a cobbler and have them stretched for you a little, but just wearing them a lot will help."

She smiled at his ever helpful attitude. He always wanted to help someone. It was his nature. "Thanks."

After he yanked his boots and socks off, he put them to the side of the blanket and lay back with his hands behind his head. All she wanted to do was curl up next to him, lay her head on his chest and stay that way forever. Tonight would have to do.

She curled up next to him, put her head on his chest and tucked into his body. "This is nice."

"I like holding you like this."

"It's perfect."

Quiet surrounded them except for the crickets, frogs, birds, and other nighttime animals making their sounds. She didn't mind though. It almost sounded like a chorus of noise meant to soothe someone. She laughed as she thought about how noisy it really was.

"What's so funny?"

"The noises. It would almost be quiet if not for all the sounds."

A laugh rumbled in his chest, reverberating in her ear. "I know what you mean. It gets pretty noisy with all the animals."

She lifted her head, looking up into his eyes. "Kiss me, cowboy."

"My pleasure, darlin'."

He lifted up, rolled her onto her back, leaned in and took her lips. His right hand wandered down to cup her breast while he devoured her mouth with his. *Good God.* She loved kissing this man more than anything on earth. Well, maybe not anything. She liked making love with him more.

His right hand inched down from her breast to the ruffled edge of her dress to slowly pull it up until she left the warm summer breeze against her wet pussy. Why she was surprised she was wet for him already, she wasn't sure. Being around this man had her wound up tighter than a spring from the moment they'd met.

He kissed his way from her lips to her ear, tonguing the lobe for a moment before he captured it between his teeth. The sensation sent goose bumps flittering across her skin from her head to her toes.

"I love the way you smell, all subtle right here behind your ear, along your neck, and down between your breasts."

His lips followed the path he described until he reached the edge of her dress that lay along her breasts. The tip of his tongue traced little swirls along her skin. Her nipples pebbled when he pushed the material farther down, but not quite low enough to reach the peaking flesh. His hand snaked up her thigh until he could skim it across her abdomen. Her belly jumped at his touch.

"Your skin is amazingly soft."

She moaned as his fingers danced along her lower belly, barely touching. "Touch me. I need you."

"Oh, I plan to."

"You're teasing me."

"Yep. Anticipation is half the fun."

He worked the top of her dress down over one breast, taking the stiff peak between his lips in a strong suck. She arched her back, pushing the flesh deeper into his mouth. After she tossed his hat the side, she threaded her fingers through his hair, holding his head against her breast.

Her thigh spread of their own accord, in a silent beg for him to touch her. His hand strayed down between her thighs. She sighed when his fingers finally pushed between her pussy lips to glance across her clit.

"Yes."

He released her breast, kissing his way to the other one as he pushed a finger into her pussy. "You are so wet."

"Only for you. I've never been this wet before with anyone else."

"Ah, flattery will get you anything you want, darlin'."

"Anything?" She took a deep breath and blurted out, "Your heart?"

His movements stopped when he paused in mid-stroke.

"Sorry. I didn't really mean it the way it sounded."

He lifted his head, staring down into her face. His face was bathed in silver light from the moon overhead, his eyes glittering with something she wasn't sure she wanted to name. Without saying a word, he returned to his assault on her senses. She released a pent up breath. She didn't want him to say anything, really, afraid he would either deny her growing feelings or affirm them in a way she wasn't ready for. *Damn traitorous heart anyway.*

After several minutes of getting her worked up enough, she was ready to beg for him to make love to her. He sat up and removed his jeans and shirt, revealing the magnificent form of Joshua Young to her gaze. The springy hair on his chest tickled her breasts when he came back to lay over her form.

"Do I need a condom?"

"No."

He slowly pushed all of his hard flesh between her pussy lips until he was fully inside her body. With her legs wrapped around his hips, holding his pelvis against hers, she hoped to keep him close for just a few minutes longer.

"I've got to move, darlin'. I'm about to explode being inside you like this."

"No eight second ride, please."

"Not on your life, but I'm not sure how long I'll last. You are burning me alive with your hot pussy."

"Fuck me, Joshua. Give it all to me. I want to feel every inch of you inside me."

"You got it, babe."

He slowly started their mutual climb to explosive satisfaction with his measured movements. Her body sang with each stroke. Her pussy quivered with need, hovering on the edge of insanity as she reached the pinnacle of a climax and held there waiting for him.

"Come with me, Candy. I need your sweetness."

It was the first time he'd called her by her nickname. Her body reacted to his deep thrust by pushing her into the most explosive climax she'd ever had. Her world detonated into a kaleidoscope of color behind her eyelids as she screamed his name at the top of her lungs. Bird flew from the trees around them. Frogs stopped croaking. The only sound was his harsh breathing in her ear and the gurgling of the water nearby.

After several minutes, he shifted his weight onto his elbows and looked down into her face. "You okay?"

"Perfect."

He smiled, his teeth flashing white in the moonlight. "Glad I could take care of you."

"You always do."

"I try."

"You succeeded beautifully."

He brushed his lips over her eyelids before reaching her mouth for a drugging kiss. "We should probably head back."

She wrapped her hands around his back, holding him close. "Not yet."

"I could stay like this forever."

"Me too."

They both groaned as he removed his softening cock from her core so he could shift over to her side. Lying beside him like this was a dream come true. He stroked her hair back from her face as he gazed down into her eyes. She couldn't read him though. "What are you thinking about?"

"You and how beautiful you are lying here in the moonlight."

She smiled as a little harsh laugh escaped her mouth. "No, really?"

"Really."

"Hmm."

"What about you? What are you thinking about?"

"How sticky my legs feel."

He laughed as he sat up and reached for his shirt. "I suppose we should be gettin' back to the house."

"Yeah, I guess."

She sat up, pulling her dress back into place to cover her nakedness as she shook her head. In the rush to copulate, they missed the cake and chocolate syrup all together. What does that say about her? Embarrassment flooded her cheeks. Thankful for the darkness of the night, she put her boots on before heading to where the horse stood hobbled.

"Are you all right? You're awfully quiet."

"Yeah, I'm fine."

"You don't sound fine."

She bit her bottom lip and fixed her gaze on the tips of her boots. He put two fingers under her chin to raise her gaze back to his.

"What is it?"

"I feel like such a slut."

"A slut? Why?"

"We didn't even get my dress off before fucking on the ground. What does that say about me?"

"You aren't a slut, Candace. We wanted each other. There is nothing wrong with that."

"Yes, I understand the need part, Joshua, but couldn't we have at least got my dress all the way off?"

He pushed his hands into her hair, cradling her head with his palms. "I thought it was sexy how you couldn't wait for me to pleasure you."

"Really?"

"Yes, really. It says you are a woman who takes what she wants and doesn't worry about what others think. You are sexy as hell, and I couldn't wait to have you." He kissed her lips lightly before continuing. "In fact, every time we've been together, I haven't been able to wait to have you. It says you are something special to me. I've enjoyed this time with you, and I wouldn't trade it for anything."

"Me either," she whispered, choking a little on the sentiment he'd just shared.

"I'm going to miss you when you go home."

"I'll miss you too. Maybe you can come visit me in Anaheim sometime."

"Maybe."

She sniffed a little and stepped back. "We should be getting back."

"Yeah." He stepped around her to cinch the saddle tight again while she grabbed the blanket to fold up.

Within a few minutes, they were both in the saddle, picking their way back toward the house. Conversation was minimal between them as she lost herself in thought. She would be going home soon, a few short days away after being there for a few weeks. Her whole world had changed with one spill of a beer down the back of his shirt. How would she function without him around when she went home? She wasn't sure, but she would have to. Yes, she wanted to be more than a mere roll in the hay to him. She didn't think that was possible. He might care for her a little, she guessed. Not enough to build a relationship on and really, she wasn't prepared to leave her life in California for Texas.

The cowgirl way of life seemed fun to play at for a while, but she missed her office, her employees, her family, and the milder weather of California. Hot, steamy Texas didn't suit her needs at all. Besides, what really would she have here?

It's not like Joshua had professed his love for her with a ring and a proposal.

Chapter Thirteen

Last night, after they'd went to their own rooms, Candace had spent a lot of time thinking about what she wanted from her relationship with Joshua. She wanted him more than anything, so she decided to talk to him about her feelings and see where they might lead.

The more she'd thought about it, the more she'd decided she might be willing to see how things went. They could try a long distance relationship. It wasn't like she couldn't afford to fly out here every few months to see him and maybe pay for him to fly out to Los Angeles to see her. Surely, he could take some time off at the ranch to be with her too, right?

She walked into the barn headed for his office to see if he wanted to spend some time talking, just the two of them.

He meant a lot to her, but she wasn't sure it was love. Was it? She didn't know. She'd thought she'd loved before and things didn't work out very well with her ex. Was this love? Did she really love Joshua or did she just love the cowboy thing a little too much.

After a moment of knocking, she grabbed the handle to push open the door. He wasn't around that she could tell and hadn't been there this morning apparently. Stuff lay scattered on his desk, seemingly out of sorts with the person she thought he was.

Those familiar smells surrounded her. Leather, musk and Joshua swarmed her senses as she glanced from project to project around his space. She loved having this time to absorb him without him really being there. It gave her a sense of finding out more about him without him knowing.

She touched a few pieces of leather he'd been working on, hoping to bring a little of him into her soul while she contemplated how to handle their budding relationship.

A note of paper on the desk and the pen sitting on top of it didn't catch her eye, but the writing on the sheet did. It was her name in his expressive scrawl. Tears welled up in her eyes when she saw what he'd attached to it.

He'd written *Candace Young*.

Her heart tripped over itself in a hard gallop around her chest. *What the hell does that mean? Marriage? I thought he wasn't ready for that, and I know I'm not.*

Panic set in, bone chilling, mind numbing panic. She wasn't ready for this. He wasn't ready for this. He'd only barely gotten over Loren, right? He wasn't ready for marriage. She wasn't ready for marriage. She liked him, yeah, a lot, but this?

She needed to leave. She couldn't stay here any longer. If she broke his heart, she would never forgive herself, but living in Texas wasn't in her plans for her future and neither was a cowboy in a forever kind of basis. Yeah, she'd come to the realization she was in love with him, but it would never work. He needed to find his kind of woman, a cowgirl, who knew her way around horses, cattle, ranch work, and Texas. That wasn't her. She needed her parties, slinky black dress, high heels, and hairdressers, not cowboy boots, jeans, ponytails and no makeup.

After leaving his office in a rush, she headed to the house, but not before dashing behind a bush as Joshua came out, walking swiftly her way. *When had things gotten completely out of control? Shit. This is bad.*

The moment he was out of sight, she ran for the door. Home. She needed to go home and forget about all this cowboy stuff, this way of life and Joshua. Yeah, she needed to forget all about Joshua.

After a quick dash up the stairs, she rushed around her room throwing her clothes in the suitcase. She didn't even care if they charged her for the remaining days she was supposed to be there, she just knew she had to go and go now before things got worse.

With her suitcase in hand, she stopped at Nina's office. "Hey, Nina. Listen, I have family emergency in Los Angeles. I have to catch the next plane back, so I'm checking out."

"Is everything okay? You look worried."

"I am. It's my father, I mean my sister. Yeah, she's been in a car accident, and I need to be there for my parents."

"Oh, my. Of course, honey. You should go home to be with your family." Nina hugged her for a moment and then stepped back. The cast on her leg had been replaced by a walking cast so she wouldn't have to hobble around on crutches anymore. "Have you talked to Joshua?"

"No, I don't have time. The next plane leaves in three hours from San Antonio, and I have to return my car and everything. Can you tell him I'm sorry?" A tear slipped down her cheek as she wiped it away angrily. She didn't have time to cry. She could do that in the privacy of the car on the way to the airport, on the plane to Los Angeles or when she got home. Now, wasn't the time. "I'm so sorry, but he needs to find the right girl, and I'm not her."

"Are you sure you don't want to talk to him before you rush off? I know he's in the barn. I can go get him." Nina stepped around her, but stopped when Candace grabbed her hard with a cry of no.

"I'm sorry, but no. Thank you. You're always so worried about your boys, aren't you?"

"Of course, I am. I want to see them happy."

"Me too, Nina. That's all I want for him is for him to be happy."

"Why are you really running away, Candace?" Nina took her hands, forcing her to sit in the chair. "Are you in love with my son?"

"Yes, but I'm not the girl for him. He needs a girl from here. A cowgirl. A Texas girl, not me."

"I think he's in love with you, Candace. Why don't you give him a chance?"

"I need to go. Please, just let me go."

"Okay, honey. I don't want to pressure you. You have to come to terms with your love for Joshua by yourself and realize you two are meant to be together here in Texas."

She shook her head as tears streamed down her cheeks. "I can't. I won't give up my life for any man." She jumped to her feet before rushing out to her car, as she frantically pushed the button to unlock the door. If Joshua saw her or if she saw him, it would be all over but the singing.

* * * *

Joshua came out of the barn just as Candace was getting in her car with her suitcase. *What the hell?* "Candace?"

She shook her head, not meeting his gaze through the windshield. He walked toward her, but she jammed the car into reverse, spraying gravel and dust everywhere when she gunned the car.

He stood in stunned silence while she sped toward the iron gates of the ranch, punched the button to get out, and then squealed tires, trying to get away.

With his hands on his hips, he dropped his gaze to his boots. Somehow, he knew he would never see her again. It was over. Whatever they had, that is. Hell, he didn't know what they had, but apparently it scared the shit out of her so much, she ran, heading back home without a backward glance in his direction.

A moment later, he felt his mother's arms go around his waist as she put her head on his shoulder. "I'm sorry, Joshua."

"Me too, Mom. I only wish I knew what caused her to run?"

"I don't know either. I tried talking to her inside, but she wouldn't listen. She kept saying she wasn't the right girl for you."

"I think she is."

"So do I, honey, but until she comes to the same conclusion, it's a waste of time to pressure her. She needs space and going back to Anaheim will give her that space."

He sighed in a dejected exhalation. Loving a woman who didn't love you in return seemed to be the way his life would be forever. First Loren, now Candace. Would he never learn? "I'm done with women."

"You don't mean that, Joshua. Candace is scared, honey. Give her some time."

"Nope. I'm done. Getting laid is all I'm about anymore."

"You're hurt. I understand, but don't do something silly."

"I'm not. I'm living my life."

He walked back to his office with more purpose than he'd had in some time. He would live his life as a bachelor, sleeping with random women when he had the itch and never get involved with another one again.

When he stopped at his desk, he saw the pen and paper sitting there with his handwriting all over it. Why had he thought Candace might be different? What made him think she might love him in return and want to stay in Texas with him? With the tip of his finger, he traced where he'd written Candace Young. *Stupid.* He crumpled the paper in a wad and threw it across his office, bouncing it off the wall where the belt he'd been making for her hung by the fancy silver belt buckle he'd bought. He'd been almost finished with it, and he'd planned to give it to her today when they would go out for lunch. He moved toward it, taking the leather in his hands as he traced where he'd carved her name in the back of the belt. *What a fool I am to fall in love with a city girl.*

His cell phone jingled. When he picked it up, he realized he'd hoped it was her, but when Loren popped up on the caller ID, he debated on whether to answer it or not. She'd been decent in bed. Maybe he could get together with her for a quick fling and be done with her too.

"Yeah?" he answered the phone on the fourth ring.

"Joshua?"

"Yeah, Loren. It's me. What do you want?"

"I thought we could get together for coffee or something. You know, for old times' sake."

"Sure. When?"

"This afternoon at your aunt's diner?"

"How about in say fifteen minutes?"

"Sounds fine. I'll see you there."

* * * *

A short time later, he drove through town, headed toward his aunt's diner to meet Loren. He didn't really want to have anything to do with her, he'd concluded, but he had to do something to get over this sense of loss with Candace running away. He still couldn't believe she'd taken off without even talking to him. Why? He didn't know, and he'd tried to convince himself he didn't care. The hole in his heart told him different.

Why am I meeting Loren then?

He pulled into an empty space in front of the diner, shut the truck off and waited for a moment. Maybe he needed this to be able to really walk away from Loren, more than he needed it to come to some conclusion about Candace.

With a heavy sigh, he pushed open the door to the truck and then slammed it shut behind him. It was now or never. He needed to get this over with.

He walked inside the cooler interior of the diner, the door jingling behind him. The place was mostly empty except for Loren, sitting in a corner booth with a glass of Coke in front of her. He moved toward her as her gaze ricocheted up to meet his.

"Hi."

"Hi, Loren." He slipped into the booth on the opposite side from her.

"What can I get you, Joshua," his Aunt Anne asked, coming to the table.

"Coffee, please."

"Sure. Are you two planning on eating?" she asked, curiosity reflecting in her gaze bouncing back and forth between them.

"No. Just talking."

"Okay. Be right back."

He didn't start the conversation until after Anne had put the coffee in front of him and he'd doctored it the way he liked it. He needed to gather his thoughts before he told Loren to leave him alone. The spoon clanged as he stirred his coffee. He knew it irritated Loren to no end. He did it anyway.

She grabbed his hand to stop his movements. "Joshua, please. You know that bothers me."

"Yeah, I do." He set the spoon down on the table, took a sip of his coffee and then returned the cup to the table. "Why did you want to meet me, Loren?"

"I heard your little plaything took off back to Los Angeles this afternoon."

"News travels fast."

"I wanted you to know I'm here for you. You know I still love you, right?"

"No you don't, Loren. You want me because you can't have me. There is a name for that, you know. It's called being selfish. I realized while you were gone, you've always been that way. Whenever we were supposed to go somewhere, it had to be where you wanted to go. The food we ate had to be whatever you wanted to eat. The clothes I wore had to be what you wanted me to wear. I realized recently I didn't want to be in a relationship like that anymore, so I'm glad you decided to bail on us. Again, selfish on your part. It was all about what you wanted, not what we wanted as a couple."

"I'm not that person anymore, Joshua."

"It doesn't matter." He huffed out a laugh. "Something else I realized while I was with Candace. She liked me for me. She didn't try to change me and believe it or not, I love her." He looked around before coming back to face Loren again. "Yeah, I love her and by damn, I'm going after her because I love her, and I want her to love me in return. If she doesn't, that's okay because I can love her enough for both of us until she realizes she wants me too. I need her in my life, and I'm willing to go to whatever lengths it requires for her to be in my life."

He downed the coffee in his cup before pushing it away and getting to his feet. "Thank you for making me realize I needed to step up to the plate here and take what I want because it's the right thing to do." He grabbed a couple of dollars out of his pocket and tossed them on the table. "I hope you find what you are looking for, Loren. Just stay away from me from now on."

The door opened with a push of his hand. He had a woman to find and by damn, he planned to find her before she got on that plane.

After rushing home, he found his mom in the office and asked her what she knew about Candace's travel plans. His mom said she mentioned a plane leaving in three hours from the time she left the ranch. He glanced at his watch. That didn't give him much time. "Do you know which airline?"

His mom punched in a few things into the computer. "Yeah. Southwest is who she came in on. We require that information on the reservations for us, so I'm assuming she's going home on the same airline." She spun back around in her chair. "What are you going to do?"

"Bring her home."

Nina grinned as she shooed him out the door. "Don't forget flowers and a ring if you can."

"I don't have time for the ring, Mom, but flowers I can do."

A moment later, he sent gravel flying behind him as he took off for San Antonio airport to stop the woman he loved from leaving him for good.

Driving up to the airport parking area, he glanced at the clock. He didn't have much time to find her and stop her from getting on that plane. He'd taken a few minutes to stop at a local vendor for flowers before hitting the airport. What he'd told him mom was the truth. He needed a ring, but he didn't have time to buy one. Candace would have to agree to go shopping with him on the way home. Letting her leave on that plane to Los Angeles wasn't an option as far as he was concerned. He loved her. She had to love him too.

He skidded to a halt at the large sign announcing the departures. He would have to figure out how to get through security to get to the gate. Her plane was leaving in thirty minutes. She was probably already through security.

Coming up with a plan, he ran to the ticket counter. Luckily, there was no line.

"Can I help you?"

"Yes, ma'am. I need to talk to a passenger on your Los Angeles flight. Can you page her to come to the ticket counter?"

"I can't do that, sir."

"Please?"

"It's against policy. Can you tell me what this is about?"

He went into a quick rundown of what was going on and a smile spread across the woman's face.

"How romantic."

"Thank you, but I really need you to help me out here. Maybe page her to tell her she left something at the ticket counter and she needs to return to claim it?"

"That might work, sir." The woman picked up the paging phone and spoke into the receiver. "Attention in the concourse, Los Angeles passenger Candace Alexander please return to the ticket counter to claim a lost item."

"Thank you. You have no idea how much this means to me."

"Just making her say yes to those beautiful flowers will be thank you enough." She shooed him with her hands. "If you stand in the corner over there, she won't see you until I direct her toward you."

Grinning, he nodded. "Thank you again."

"You're welcome."

The wait drug on until he finally saw her come rushing around the corner. She didn't seem to notice him approaching from his hidden spot either.

"I was paged to return to the ticket counter?"

"I'm sorry, ma'am, but we didn't page you."

"I heard it. It said there was a lost item here I needed to claim. I swear. I'm not lying."

"Candace?" He stood behind her with the flowers in hand.

She spun around, her eyes wide. "Joshua. What are you doing here?"

"I'm the lost item."

"Huh?"

"You need to claim me, darlin'. I can't live without you. I love you, Candace. Don't go back to Anaheim or if you have to, take me with you."

"I don't understand," she whispered in awe.

"I love you." He handed her the flowers and got down on one knee. The crowd around them hushed and the world seemed to stop spinning. "Marry me."

"You want to marry me?"

"Yeah, say yes."

"But, what about my life, my family, my business?"

"If you want to live in California, we will. I'll go with you. Just say you'll stay with me and love me forever. I don't want to be without you."

Tears streamed down her cheeks. "You love me enough to leave everything behind here in Texas and go with me to California?"

"Yes."

She pressed her fingers to her lips. "I love you too."

"Say you'll marry me."

"Yes. Yes, I'll marry you."

The crowd erupted in cheers as he stood and wrapped his arms around her. Lifting her, he twirled her around in circles, and enthusiastic applause broke out. They laughed together before he kissed her with all the pent up desire he couldn't express.

"You'll come home with me?"

"For now. We'll have to work out the arrangements somehow. All that matters is we love each other. The rest will work itself out."

"Perfect."

Once the airline managed to retrieve her bag before it was sent off to Los Angeles on the plane, he picked her up and carried her out to where his truck sat crooked between three parking spots. He hadn't had time to park correctly in the mad rush to get to her.

After she opened the door to his truck, he set her on the seat and kissed her directly on the mouth. "I love you."

"I love you too."

"Mom is going to be happy you said yes."

"You talked to Nina?"

"Yeah, she told me which airline to look for. Sorry for making you come back to the ticket counter. I couldn't think of any other way to get to you. The counter agent was a gem in her help."

"I couldn't think of what the heck I'd left at the ticket counter, but it was you. I was leaving you behind, and I realized I wasn't okay with that. You mean the world to me, Joshua." She frowned as she touched his face lightly. "What about Loren?"

"I'm done with her. We talked at the diner a little while ago, and she's the one who made me realize I couldn't let you go no matter what."

"Really?"

"Yeah. I knew my relationship with her wasn't a healthy one, but with you, it was so different. You get me. We're good together and you mean a hundred times more to me than she ever did." He rubbed his finger for her left ring finger. "We'll stop here at the mall and get you a ring, if you want to. I want everyone to know you're mine."

"If you'd like. I'm not in a rush. I know I'm yours. No one else matters."

"True." He kissed her again. "We'll wait then so you can pick out the perfect one."

"I need to call my parents."

"Okay. You can call them while we're driving back to the ranch. You'll be sleeping in my bed tonight."

One eyebrow rose. "Yeah?"

"You don't have a room anymore, and the inn is full." She grinned as he waggled his eyebrows at her.

"I can't wait."

"Me either." He shut the door on the truck before going around to the driver's side. "When do you want to get married?"

"I don't know. Give me a bit to absorb this. My parents are going to flip."

"Why? Won't they like me?"

"They'll love you, but it's going to be a shock. I wasn't even dating anyone before I left." She took his hand in hers. "I love you. That's all that matters."

"I'll never get tired of hearing that."

"Me either, so you better say it often, cowboy."

"Every day at least once."

"Good."

The one-sided conversation seemed to go well while he drove back to the ranch. She smiled a lot and seemed to be talking very happily with her parents on the phone. One frown did pop up on her face. He wasn't sure what they asked, but he figured it had something to do with money. He didn't have a lot of money like Jeremiah, but he had a nice savings account himself. They didn't have to worry. He didn't care how much money she had or didn't have. Money didn't mean much to him as long as they were happy.

"No, Daddy. I love him very much, and we're going to get married." She paused. "You'll get to meet him soon. I'm sure we'll come up there in the next few weeks so you can meet him."

He pulled her hand in for a kiss to the back.

"Okay. Two weeks from today? I'll make plane reservations when I get back to the ranch." She tipped her head to him with a silent okay?

He nodded as nervousness rushed through him. Meeting her parents gave him a stomachache. He hoped they wouldn't be difficult about the money thing. They would have to have a nice little chat after she was off the phone with them. He wanted to make sure she knew her money didn't mean anything to him.

"I love you, Daddy. Tell Mom bye. We'll see you in a couple of weeks. I'll text you our arrival time. Bye." She finally pressed end with a heavy sigh. "That went well."

"It didn't sound like it."

"They're worried, Joshua. I mean this kind of sprang up without warning, you know? We've only known each other for a few weeks and here we are getting married?"

"Are you having second thoughts about your feelings for me?"

"No. I know what I want. It's you, but you know how parents are. They tend to be cautious and mine are overly so. They know about my ex wanting me for the name and money. I'm sure they are thinking you are the same since we haven't known each other long."

"I don't care about your money, Candy. I have some of my own, although it isn't as much as your trust fund. You can keep your money. I'll sign a prenup if they want me to. I don't mind. Your money means nothing to me."

She unhooked her seatbelt before sliding over to rebuckle herself into the center seat. "Good to know, Joshua. I'm not worried."

"I have enough for us. If you want to work, you can. If you don't, that's okay too. I can get Jeremiah to help me invest so I can build my savings more. I wanted to do that anyway. He's a wiz at the financial stuff. He's managed to make a pretty little nest egg for my parents and himself. I'm sure he'd be happy to help us."

They pulled into the driveway at Thunder Ridge. While they waited for the gates to open, she turned to him and captured his mouth in a toe-curling kiss. "I love you. I don't care how much money you have or don't have. My money is our money." She kissed him again. "I've been thinking about selling my business anyway. I think my brother would buy it from me. Then my parents can't say anything because it's my money."

He pushed his hands into her hair. "Baby, it doesn't matter. It would be your money. We wouldn't have to touch it. We can live on my salary at the ranch and my savings. What's mine is yours."

"And what's mine is yours, Joshua."

They drove down the long driveway to be met by his mother standing on the walk waiting for them. "So?" she asked when they stepped out of the truck. "I'll assume this is good since she came back with you?"

"She's agreed to marry me."

Nina squealed as she hugged Candace in a big hug. "Welcome to the family!"

Epilogue

Joshua stood at the bottom of the stairs, looking over the group at the table. "Are you coming, Jackson?"

"Chill. I'm almost done. I'll meet you two outside."

"Fine, but we need to get moving. The concert starts in three hours. It's an hour drive to San Antonio."

"I know how far it is, asswipe. I've lived here as long as you have, plus I've driven there plenty of times. We'll be fine."

"But we have backstage passes to meet her, and Candace wants to get there in plenty of time."

"We have lots of time. Ease up, man."

They were headed to a benefit concert Candace had helped plan for a local children's hospital in San Antonio. She loved doing charity work. Since she was working on selling her business to her brother, she needed something to do with her time.

Samantha Harris was a huge country music artist. She'd agreed to do the benefit with the urging of Candace and her contacts in the music industry. She'd done a lot of computer security systems for Samantha, as well as others in the country music business. When Candy called her to do the concert, she jumped at the chance. Since Jackson liked country music, the two of them were dragging him to the concert so he could help with security for Samantha.

Joshua sighed when he thought about the meeting with Candy's parents and how well it had gone. They'd spent a couple of weeks closing up her apartment in Anaheim and getting a moving truck to bring her stuff to Bandera. Where they would put it all, he didn't know, but they'd figure it out once it all got there. She had a lot of stuff. Plenty to put a whole house together, and he hadn't even made plans to start building their house yet.

He glanced up the stairs when his fiancé descended to meet him at the bottom. He still couldn't believe how much he loved her or how lucky he'd been to find her when he'd been about as low as a human being could be when it came to love. "You look fabulous." Leaning in, he kissed her on the lips.

"It's nothing special. Just my cowgirl outfit."

He nudged her neck near her ear before dropping a well-placed kiss on that special spot he knew she liked so well. "I remember that outfit and the pond very well, thank you."

"Me too, cowboy." She left a little kiss on his cheek. "Are we ready?"

"Yeah, we're just waiting for Jackson, Mr. Head of Security."

"I'm coming, Geez!" Jackson got up from the table, placed his hat on his head and swept his hand wide, motioning for them to hurry up now.

Joshua and Candace followed him out to the truck. "I'm taking my own," Jackson announced. "I want to have my own vehicle."

"Fine. Do you know how to get there?"

"Of course, I do."

"Great. We'll see you there."

An hour later, they pulled into the Alamodome back parking lot where security was told to park. He and Candace stepped out of their truck while Jackson took up a spot next to them.

"Can I help you?" One of the security personnel, standing near two huge semi-tractor trailers with Samantha Harris' picture all over them, asked in a clipped tone.

"I'm Candace Alexander, this is my fiancé Joshua Young and his brother Jackson Young."

"Ah, yes. Ms. Harris told me you would be arriving soon. The command post for security has been set up to the left. Ms. Harris is on her bus near the back there. She said to send you right over, Ms. Alexander."

"Thank you. Jackson, I guess you need to check in with security so they can tell you where you need to be. I told them you were to be near Samantha at all times."

"Right." He saluted smartly before wandering over to the tent with his hands in his pockets.

"Shall we?" she asked Joshua as she looped her hand through the crook of his elbow and ushered him toward Samantha's bus. When they got the door, she knocked and they heard a loud, "Come in." Joshua pulled on the handle to open the door on the bus as Jackson approached from the rear.

"I guess I'm supposed to hang out right here until she goes on stage."

"Sounds good."

They walked inside only to be awed by the glamour and glitz of the massive coach. "Wow."

"You like?"

A tall, leggy blonde stepped out of the back dressed to the nines. She has skin tight jeans, a flowing red blouse, red cowboy boots, and a white cowboy hat sitting on top of her long tresses. "Hey, girl. How are you?"

The two women hugged briefly. "This is my fiancé, Joshua. Joshua, meet Samantha Harris."

"Nice to meet you, ma'am."

"Wow. A real one, eh?"

"Real, ma'am?"

"Cowboy. I don't see too many of those these days. Most are wannabes. Drives me nuts."

"Yes, ma'am. About as real as they come."

"Do you ride rodeo?"

"No ma'am. Too busy on my family's ranch outside Bandera to ride rodeo."

She glanced at Candace with a grin. "Definitely a real one. How'd you find him?"

"It's a long story. One we'll have to talk about some other time."

"Is everything set up?"

"Yep. You'll be on stage at nine for an hour. The opening bands will go before you."

"Good. I have some time then. I don't like to have to rush to be ready."

"Aren't you ready now?"

"Mostly, but I have to psych myself up before I go out there."

"Wow, really?"

"Yeah. I still get stage fright."

Candace grinned. "I suppose I should introduce you to your security guard. He's outside."

"Oh?"

"Yeah, he's also one of eight of Joshua's brothers."

"Eight?"

"Yes, ma'am. We have a big family."

"Apparently." She swept her hand to indicate they should proceed her. "Let's meet this security guy you've got to look out for me."

As they walked outside the bus, Samantha bolted around them to head to the back. "Who the hell are you and what are you doing loitering around my bus? Speak up, cowboy, I don't have all day!"

"Ma'am?"

"Don't ma'am me, cowboy. If you don't have any business being back here, get lost."

"I'm Jackson, ma'am."

"Jackson?"

"Samantha Harris, meet Jackson Young, your security detail."

The End

A COWBOY AND
A COUNTRY SONG

Cowboy Dreamin' 7

Sandy Sullivan

Chapter One

Joshua stood at the bottom of the stairs, looking over the group at the table as Jackson continued to eat. "Are you coming, Jackson?"

"Chill. I'm almost done. I'll meet you two outside."

"Fine, but we need to get moving. The concert starts in three hours. It's an hour drive to San Antonio."

Jackson pushed his plate away and stood. "I know how far it is, asswipe. I've lived here as long as you have, plus I've driven there plenty of times. We'll be fine."

"But we have backstage passes to meet her, and Candace wants to get there in plenty of time."

"We have lots of time. Ease up, man."

They were headed to a benefit concert Candace had helped plan for a local children's hospital in San Antonio. He'd volunteered to do security for a country music star during this benefit concert although he wasn't sure why. Yeah, he knew who Samantha Harris was. Even he could admit she was one hot number, but he didn't know about being her bodyguard for the night. Oh well, he didn't have anything better to do. He might as well follow around the leggy blonde and keep the overzealous fans at bay. He couldn't do worse, he figured. At least he'd be where the action was.

Joshua met Candace at the bottom of the stairs with a kiss to her lips.

"Are we ready?"

"Yeah, we are just waiting for Jackson, Mr. Head of Security."

"I'm coming, jeez!" Jackson got up from the table, placed his hat on his head and swept his hand wide, motioning for them to hurry up now.

Joshua and Candace followed him out to the truck. "I'm taking my own," Jackson announced. "I want to have my own vehicle."

"Fine. Do you know how to get there?"

"Of course, I do."

"Great. We'll see you there."

An hour later, they pulled into the Alamodome back parking lot where security was told to park. He and Candace stepped out of their truck with Jackson parked next to them.

"Can I help you?" One of the security personnel standing near two huge semi-tractor trailers with Samantha Harris' picture all over them asked in a clipped tone.

"I'm Candace Alexander, this is my fiancé, Joshua Young, and his brother, Jackson Young."

"Ah, yes. Ms. Harris told me you would be arriving soon. The command post for security has been set up to the left. Ms. Harris is on her bus near the back there. She said to send you right over, Ms. Alexander."

"Thank you. Jackson, I guess you need to check in with security so they can tell you where you need to be. I told them you were to be near Samantha at all times."

"Right." He saluted smartly before wandering over to the tent with his hands in his pockets. As he walked near, the other guys all stood around with radio pieces in their ear talking to each other. "I'm Jackson Young. I'm supposed to report to you guys?"

"Hi. I'm Trevor. I'm head of security for Ms. Harris. You'll be guarding her one on one throughout the night according to Ms. Alexander. Since you're dressed like everyone else here, you should blend in well. I will give you an earpiece though, so we can talk, and you can let me know if there are any issues. Sound good?"

"Yep." Trevor handed him an earpiece and a transmitter for his back pocket. After he placed the piece in his ear, he tested the microphone clipped to his shirt. Trevor gave him the thumbs up.

"You are to be with her at all times. Right now, she's in her bus so just hang out around the door until she needs you to escort her to the backstage area. She'll be doing meet and greets after the show in the back. Keep her secure at all times."

"Got it." He wandered back toward the big brown bus with a huge scrolling SH on the side. Her personal bus. *Hmm.* He wondered what it was like on the inside. Pretty fancy, he imagined. She didn't seem to be the type of girl who went without her comforts of home as much as she was on the road. Not that he paid a lot of attention to her tour schedule or anything, but he knew where she'd be the next six weeks. Okay, yeah, he had a bit of a fascination with Samantha Harris. Who wouldn't? She was a pretty hot woman. He definitely wouldn't mind being her personal roadie for a few nights.

The door flew open on the bus. Joshua, Candace and Samantha came down the stairs. In a heartbeat Samantha bolted around them to head to the back. "Who the hell are you and what are you doing loitering around my bus? Speak up, cowboy, I don't have all day!"

Samantha got right up in his face, giving him his first up close and personal look at the leggy blonde. She wasn't wearing her customary black Stetson. The black short-sleeved blouse emphasized her gorgeous breasts for his enjoyment. The jeans she wore hugged her hips, showing off her legs to perfection. Long blonde hair hung to the middle of her back in a long, straight braid. He wanted to undo it so he could run his fingers through the soft strands. What drew him the most were her eyes. The blue orbs spit fire, right at that moment. "Ma'am?"

"Don't ma'am me, mister. If you don't have any business being back here, get lost."

"I'm Jackson, ma'am."

"Jackson?"

Candace introduced him, indicating he had reason to be there. "Samantha Harris, meet Jackson Young, your security detail. He is Joshua's older brother."

"Security detail?"

"Yeah, Sam. Jackson is your personal bodyguard for the night."

"Well, shit on a stick. Sorry. I didn't mean to go off on you so hard, but I'm always finding people hanging around my bus who shouldn't be."

"That's what I'm here for, ma'am. There won't be any loitering tonight. Unless they have a pass, they won't be allowed near you, and if you give me the nod to get rid of them, I'll handle it."

Sam gave him a saucy wink. "Good. I need a decent man to guard my ass."

"I'd be right honored to guard it for you, ma'am."

Samantha's eyebrow shot up as she smiled, planting her hands on her hips. "I like you. We'll get along just fine." She swung around to face Candace and Joshua. "What do you want to do? Have you two eaten?"

"Yeah. We ate before we came."

"We could get some good alcohol so we can party on my bus before the concert. I don't go on for a while."

"Sound good to me," Candace replied. "I haven't had a good drunk on in some time." She wrapped her arm around Joshua's waist. "Since I have my personal guy here, I can get drunk if I want. He can carry me home."

"Anytime, babe."

Candace stood on her tiptoes to kiss him on the lips. "I love you."

"I love you too."

"You two are too cute. Someday, I'll have that, but for now I sing."

"You're good at it too."

"Thanks, doll." Samantha glanced his direction, giving him the once over from the top of his hat to the tips of his boots. He wondered if she liked what she saw. "You might as well come too, cowboy, if you are to be my bodyguard. I never know when someone will get a little too crazy."

"My pleasure, ma'am."

"And quit calling me ma'am. I feel like I'm forty or something."

"You can't be over twenty-five."

She tossed back her head on her shoulders and laughed, a full gut rolling, belly laugh that sounded full. "I love you already!" She linked her arm with his, leading their group through the maze of buses, big rigs, and people, giving them the complete tour as they walked. Her descriptions of everything that went on in putting together a tour the size of hers, baffled him. "I have over a one hundred people at each stop putting together the stages, getting the lights set up, putting together the sound equipment, and handling the details. It's a major production."

He liked having her on his arm. He didn't like the looks he was getting from the other people in the security detail. It wasn't his fault she'd taken a liking to him, right?

"How long have you been in this business, Samantha?" Joshua asked.

"Ten years, give or take. I've been headlining my own shows for about five years now. Let me tell you, they are a pain in the ass to do. If I would have really understood all the work involved in being the headliner, I would have stayed as an opener for someone else and let them worry about all the crap."

"You are a very popular country music artist though. Wouldn't that seem weird?" Candace's voice got a little louder as some of the bands who would be opening for Samantha started their sound checks.

"Yeah, I guess so. I was kind of pushed into doing it when I got a little more popular than the closing artist. Hitting several number ones in a row helped."

"I can imagine."

"Do you listen to country music, Jackson?"

"Yes."

"Who is your favorite artist?"

"You."

She laughed. "You're saying that because you are guarding me tonight, but I love you for it anyway."

Little did she realize, he was telling the truth. She was one of his favorite artists in country music these days, but she didn't need to know that right now. He didn't want her to get all weirded out by his little infatuation with her. She might think he was some kind of a stalker or something.

At one point they sat in the stands and listened to the other bands warm up. Most of them were pretty good, but he knew Samantha would blow them out of the water, she was that good.

They continued on their little tour, finally ending up back at her bus about an hour later.

"I need to start getting ready." She tipped her head toward Candace. "You guys have front row seats. Talk to the guy at the ticket booth. They are in there for you under your name."

"Thanks, Samantha." Candace rocked back on her booted heels.

Joshua still hadn't been able to get the girl into a regular pair of cowboy boots. She still wore her high heeled, pointed toe boots. Jackson grinned to himself. He really liked Candace. She was the perfect girl for his brother.

When Samantha spoke again, his attention zeroed in on her lips.

"You're welcome. I figured it's the least I can do since you went to all the work to put this thing together for the children's hospital." She glanced his way. "If you would just guard the bus while I'm inside, that would be great."

"My pleasure."

A pretty smile lifted the corners of her mouth and he had the insane urge to lean in and press his lips to hers. *Yeah, not a good idea.* Her gorgeous eyes sparkled with pleasure as she studied his face.

Candace and Joshua waved to him as they walked back toward the barricade between the fans and her bus. There was already a crowd gathering, waving signs, shouting, and making a general ruckus.

"Samantha, baby, I love you!" a tall guy in a black hat hollered.

Samantha laughed as she waved to the guy. "Don't worry about them unless one breaks through the barricade."

"Gotcha."

"Thanks." She waited for a minute or so before she smiled again and disappeared inside her bus, closing the door tightly behind her.

"Hey, dude!"

Jackson turned toward the guy who shouted over the noise of the crowd. He hesitated before he took several steps in the guy's direction.

"What?"

"Are you like her personal bodyguard?"

"Yeah."

"I just want to talk to her. Can you get me in?"

"Nope."

"Come on, man. A hundred bucks. Right here. In my hand." The guy flashed a hundred dollar bill. "I would love to get close to her. I think she would totally dig me, man. If I could just fuck her one time, I'd be in total heaven. I wouldn't hurt her or nothing. I mean I would totally bang her into tomorrow."

Jackson didn't even hesitate. He wanted to deck the guy for even thinking about Samantha, much less trying to bribe him to let the dude get near her. Wasn't happening. Not today, not ever. Jackson signaled for one of his fellow security people. When the guy got close, he tipped his head. "The guy in the black Stetson needs to go. He's talking about getting too close to Miss Harris."

"I'll take care of it." The burly guy stepped up to the man, talking in low tones. When the guy took a swing at the security detail, three more guys jumped on him.

Jackson smiled as he went back to his post standing guard at her door. His own thoughts went haywire as his imagination drifted to what she might be doing in there, as she got ready for her concert. Changing clothes? Doing her hair? Her makeup? She looked fabulous when he'd seen her before, so he couldn't think of what she needed to do to get ready.

He hoped she left her long blonde hair hanging loose. He loved her hair down and straight although she tended to curl it for shows, from what he'd noticed as he'd followed her career. She usually sported a black cowboy hat, jeans, boots, and a pretty, fitted blouse. Damn, she always looked good enough to eat.

The vision of her standing naked in front of him flashed before his eyes. He cleared his throat as he turned so he wasn't facing the crowd behind the barricade. The last thing he needed was for them to see his hard-on. After several deep breaths and thoughts about branding a calf including the wrestle, the sights, the smell, and the possibility of getting kicked in the junk, he managed to calm his erection to a manageable level.

He heard the crowd before he saw them swarm the seating area. *Wow.* Thousands of people pushed each other as they scrambled for the best seats in the front area of the opening seating. Thank God, Joshua and Candace had reserved seats so they didn't have to fight the crowd.

Once everyone got inside, the DJ from the local radio station roused them up again.

"How is everyone tonight?"

The crowd erupted.

"What a group. Are you all ready for some rowdy country music?"

The crowd went wild with cheers.

"We are here tonight to welcome you all to the rowdiest country music festival to grace San Antonio in a decade, but let's not forget the real reason we are here tonight, folks. This is a benefit show put on by some of country's *hottest* acts for the benefit of San Antonio's premiere children's hospital. We are raising money for families who might be facing medical bills they can't pay. There are barrels all over the grounds for you to donate in. Please be generous for the kids. Now, it is my great pleasure to introduce you to one of the best upcoming acts in the business today."

For the next two hours, he heard some great music while he stood guarding Samantha's door. Not once did she pop her head out during that time and he had to wonder what the hell she was doing in there by herself.

* * * *

Samantha Harris watched the crowd from behind the curtain on her bus as her stomach knotted into a ball of nerves. She loved singing, but she never thought of herself as good enough for all the hype everyone said about her. Not like she was Carrie Underwood or someone like her. That girl had talent. She was only a small town girl from Iowa who liked to sing in the church choir and happened to be discovered one night singing karaoke at a local country bar a few years ago.

She blew out a nervous breath before taking a sip of the whiskey in her hand. The alcohol helped, it always eased the nerves before a show. She just had to be careful not to indulge too much or she would mess up on stage. She glanced at the bottle sitting on the counter. *Half a bottle wasn't too much, right?*

Things seemed to be going well lately, multi-million dollar recording contract, busy multi-venue tour, and screaming fans by the thousands. Why did she feel like shit all the time? Why the nerves?

What about finding the man of her dreams?

This life didn't lend well to finding someone who wasn't after her money or her fame. She knew that already. It had happened twice so far and she didn't think she could go through it again. Was it so hard to find someone nice who wasn't trying to further his own career by hooking up and riding piggyback on hers? All she wanted was a nice cowboy who didn't see her as Samantha Harris the country music star, but Samantha Harris the girl from Iowa.

She smiled as the first band came out blazing. They were good, although they hadn't been around long. She liked them a lot. Their music was great, their lead singer had talent and they had a fantastic sound. They would go far in this business.

Her cell phone jingled a familiar tune from its spot on the table across from her. "Hey Daddy."

"Hey, baby girl."

"What's up? There isn't anything wrong, is there?"

"No, honey. Everything is fine. Your mama and I are doing well. I just knew you were doing a big benefit concert tonight, and I wanted to wish you luck. Are you doing all right?"

"Yeah, just nervous."

"There is no reason for you to be nervous, baby. You are one hell of a singer."

"Thanks, Dad."

"Are you being careful? There are some real crazy nut jobs out there who would love to get close to you."

"I'm careful. I have a great security team. I even have my own personal bodyguard this time. He's the brother of the coordinator. Real cowboy from what I can tell."

"You know what they say."

She laughed. "No, what?"

"A real cowboy can protect what's his with one shot, a well-placed fist, or a bunch of friends."

A giggle burst from her lips. "I love you, Dad."

"I love you too, honey. Break a leg and I don't mean literally. Tell that cowboy your dad said to watch out for you with an eagle eye, and I'll pay him double what you are paying him."

"Stop it, now. I'm sure he can take good care of me without your extra incentive."

"I love you, baby. Be safe and we'll talk to you later this week."

"Bye, Daddy."

She hung up the phone with a little tear in her eye. She missed her parents, missed the farm they owned, missed the horses, donkeys, cows, chickens, and all the other animals she grew up with. Now she never had time for anything for herself. It was always work, always recording, writing new songs, listening to new material, doing publicity shots, more and more, and more. Some days she wanted to quit, go back to her life in Iowa to forget this craziness had ever been, but she couldn't. The multi-record deal with her record company said so. They called the shots as much as she hated to admit it.

"Sam. You're on in thirty minutes."

"Thanks, Darryl," she called. She quickly downed the remainder of the whiskey in her glass before refilling it with three fingers more worth of the brown, potent liquid.

She glanced out the window. The cowboy paced back and forth in front of her door. Jackson Young. She had to think about it a minute before she could remember, not that she didn't think he was hotter than a firecracker on the Fourth of July, but the whiskey had blurred her memory a bit. She really should quit before the show. No matter. The guys in the band would take care of her, they always did.

When he moved back in front of the door, she could see the breadth of his shoulders stretched the nice shirt he wore. The hat on his head wasn't a cheap one either. *I wonder what he normally does for a living. Surely he doesn't do private security all the time. He looks like a real-deal cowboy from the top of his head to the boots on his feet.* "Hmm." She brought the glass to her lips, but didn't sip. The vapor from the whiskey burned her nose a little, forcing her to set the glass back on the table next to her. Thoughts about Jackson floated through her mind as she wondered more about him. Does he ride? Is he good with animals? Maybe he does rodeo. She kind of liked men who rode horses, roped, busted broncs, did normal cowboy stuff. After all, she was a cowgirl herself from way back, born and bred by a father who had the belt buckle of a champion calf-roper himself.

Jackson's hair brushed the collar of his shirt, making her fingers tingle to feel if the strands were as soft as they looked. He had his arms crossed over his chest as he stood guard over the door to her bus. She felt silly having someone specifically there to watch over her, but it was needed since she had a stalker these days. They didn't know who he was, only that he sent messages to her through security or someone else close to her. It was kind of scary to think the person could get that close.

Jackson knocked on the door. "Are you ready, Ms. Harris?"

She blew out a breath, downed the rest of the whiskey in her glass, and then stood. Her head swam a bit, but she was used to that. The alcohol would calm her enough she could perform without being terrified of singing in front of thousands of people. She'd become a pretty good actress when it came to acting sober. She checked her appearance in the mirror over the sink. Curls, check. Lipstick, check, black cowboy hat…she grabbed it from the sofa. Check. She was as ready as she'd ever be.

The knock sounded again. "I'm coming."

When she pushed open the door, Jackson held out his hand to help her down from the high step of the bus. Her boot heel hooked on the bottom step as she pitched forward right into his arms.

"Whoa there."

She glanced up into his face, drowning in the grey of his eyes. Her lips parted as she sighed.

"Are you all right?"

"Uh, yeah. Fine."

His brow furrowed as he frowned while he helped her back onto her feet. She stepped out of his arms reluctantly. She liked being in his arms. They made her feel safe, unlike anyone else she'd ever been near. *That's odd. I don't even know this guy.*

"Why don't you take my arm and I'll escort you to the stage. You're on in fifteen minutes."

"That would be great. I hope I'm not coming down with something. I feel kind of woozy." She put her hand to her head. "I took some cold medicine before I came out here."

"Are you sick?"

"I think so. My nose has been stuffy all day. I think I'm coming down with a cold. I hope my voice holds up. Viruses can be hell on a singer."

He looped her hand through the crook in his arm to escort her toward the stairs leading up to the stage. The third of the opening bands had almost finished their set so she would be up next. "I can imagine."

The crowd went wild as the last band finished their set. They had to know her set came next.

"Thank you all for coming tonight," the DJ said as the band took their leave. "We want to tell you all how much we appreciate the donations you are leaving in the barrels for the kids. This means the world to all of us involved in this. Right now I want to introduce our headliner for this evening's festivities."

The crowd screamed as Jackson escorted her up the stairs to just behind the black curtain. She lowered her head to pray for strength, guidance and a whole lot of love from God. She would need it to get through the next ninety minutes of songs.

"Samantha Harris is a five time CMA winner in several categories. She's had eight number one hit records in the last five years. She is a multi-platinum recording artist and this year is up for Entertainer of the Year for the second year running, winning it last year over some of countries hottest superstars. Please help me make welcome our very own, Samantha Harris."

"Go get 'em, tiger."

She glanced at the man next to her with a small smile on her mouth. She really did like him even though she didn't know him very well. "Thanks." She leaned in, kissed him on the cheek before stepping out to greet the crowd.

Chapter Two

Jackson stood behind the curtain as he listened to Samantha do number after number. She really could sing. She hit every note perfectly in pitch and tone. The voice of an angel, some said. Right now, he could believe it.

He closed his eyes as he let the song drift through him. It was one of his favorites on her current album. He could almost believe she did it just for him.

"How ya'll doing tonight?"

The crowd erupted in shouts.

"I hope you are being generous with your dollars for the kids and their families. This concert is for them." She walked to the edge of the stage. "I have to thank my good friend, Candace Alexander for settin' this up. She's down front here with her fiancé, Joshua. Don't they make a cute couple?"

The television camera broadcasting to the big screen, panned down to where Joshua and Candace stood. Jackson could almost see the blush on Candace's cheeks from the attention. She was a computer geek from way back. He could tell she didn't like the hubbub of the camera on her face.

"I think they should get married up here on the stage. What do you think?"

The crowd shouted their approval as Candace and Joshua shook their heads no.

"Ah, come on you two. You're in love, right?"

Jackson could see Candace's face pale as she turned to face Joshua, shaking her head.

"Oh, you two are no fun. Fine then, how about if I get married tonight?"

The crowd fell silent.

"No really. There is this really cute cowboy who is my security detail. He's Joshua's brother. His name is Jackson. Come on out here, Jackson. I want everyone to see you."

He held back by the curtain. *What the hell is she up to?*

"Hey, camera dude and lighting dude, follow me." She headed toward where he stood.

As the bright white light followed her across the stage, his stomach clenched. He wasn't the type to like the limelight and here she was, bringing it to him.

She held out her hand. "Come here."

Not knowing what else to do, he took her hand in his grasp so she could pull him into the bright lighting.

"Isn't he gorgeous?"

The women erupted into wolf whistles and shouts of encouragement. "Now if there were a preacher around, I'd have him marry us."

"Ms. Harris, this isn't funny."

"I'm serious."

"You don't even know me."

"But I like you." She leaned in. "I think you are cute and I could sure use some time ridin' those hips."

"Why don't you sing some more."

She sighed as she brought herself flush against him, turned her head to the audience and said, "Excuse me a minute."

When she lowered the microphone, he wasn't sure what to expect, but her grabbing the back of his head and slamming her mouth down on his, wasn't it.

This certainly wasn't the way he wanted their first kiss to be.

The feel of her mouth against his threw his heart rate through the ceiling, his libido straight out the end of his dick.

Shouts and catcalls finally brought his brain back to the present as he slowly peeled her off his chest.

"We'll continue this later, cowboy." She stepped back, brought the microphone to her mouth, and began the full out rendition of her current single as she left him in the shadows when the spotlight moved with her across the stage.

He wasn't sure whether to shout out loud because she'd kiss him, turn her over his knee for teasing him like that, or slink back into the shadows as she totally forgot about him in the next second.

For now he would blend back into the backdrop to watch her. The taste of her on his mouth made him frown. If he wasn't mistaken, there was alcohol on her breath, not just from cold medicine either. She hadn't sounded stuffed up earlier when they'd been walking around. He hoped his thoughts were wrong, but he had a feeling they weren't.

He glanced at his watch. She still had several more songs to do before she finished.

With a quick look toward the stage, he turned on his heels to head down the steps. The security detail was otherwise occupied, so he opened the door to her bus and walked up the small set of stairs.

The bus's interior stretched out before him. Its gold and white décor reflected Samantha's style. A smooth leather couch lined one wall with a small table to the left. Opposite them sat a white bench seat. The closed door beyond the kitchen had to be her bedroom. His gaze fell upon the dove guitar in a stand near the kitchenette. She didn't use the beautiful instrument onstage, but he knew she wrote a lot of her own music.

Lavender invaded his nose as he walked slowly toward her door. He wanted to see her personal space, but it wasn't his place. He searched from left to right before he found what he was looking for. A three quarter empty bottle of whiskey, Jack Daniel's to be exact. *I knew it!*

He'd been through hell with Jacob a few times to see the signs. She had an alcohol problem.

"Thank you everyone. You are the best. See you on the road!"

Shit.

He scrambled outside, slamming the door before running for the stage to meet her. He managed to skid to a stop at the bottom of the small set of stairs just as she reached the top. Holding his hand out, he helped her down the metal plates until she reached the bottom.

Sweat poured from her temples when she removed her hat. "Wow. What a crowd."

"You did great."

"Thanks."

She wobbled a little as she headed toward her bus while the crowd behind them filed out. Several people had already found their way to the security barricade near her bus. They shouted as they waited for her, hoping she would stop near them, take a few pictures and sign some autographs.

"Man, I need a shower."

"Are you going to greet your fans?"

"Yeah, I need to."

"Are you up to it?"

"It's part of the process, so yeah."

He walked her to the steel gates keeping her fans from trampling her. For the next hour, she greeted fans, signed autographs, took pictures, gave kisses to a few rowdy men although never on the mouth, and did her best to be the star she was.

"I'm done. Let's go."

"That's it folks. Thanks for coming, but Ms. Harris is done for tonight," Jackson said, taking her hand in his to lead her back to her bus.

"I'm beat."

"I bet." He opened the bus door for her, watching as she put her foot on the first step before she glanced back at him.

"Would you join me for a bit? I'd like to talk to you about something."

"Uh, sure, but aren't you afraid of what your fans will think?"

"I guess. Wait a few minutes then and come on in after the majority of them have left. You probably want to say something to your brother and Candace before they leave."

"Yeah."

"Did you bring your own vehicle?"

"Yes."

"Good." She smiled sadly as she pulled the door to the bus closed behind her.

He turned toward the crowd by the gates, noticing Joshua and Candace standing off to the side. When he got to where they stood, he escorted them around the steel barricade and back toward the vehicles sitting toward the rear.

"What the hell was that all about up there?" Joshua asked. "I could have done without the whole 'let's get married' thing."

"Me too." Candace wrapped her arm around Joshua's waist. "I don't know what she was thinking."

"Fuck if I know." He glanced sideways at Candace. "How much do you know about Samantha Harris?"

"Not a lot, why? I mean she's a friend, I guess, but I haven't been around her very much. Mostly just what I know about her is from media."

"I think she might have a drinking problem. She was pretty drunk on stage."

"Drunk?"

"Yeah. I found a three quarter empty bottle of Jack on her table. She tried to pass it off as cold medicine on her breath."

"Wow." Candace bit her lip before saying, "Are you sure?"

"I dealt with Jacob enough on his binges to know someone with an alcohol problem. I seriously think she does. I'm not sure why though. She's talented as all get out."

"Yeah, Jacob was a mess before he got sober."

"She wants to talk to me after the majority of the fans have left." He looked behind Joshua. "Looks like that's now."

Joshua nodded toward the way out. "We're headed home. You be careful."

"I will. I want to talk to her to see if I can find out what's up. Why the drinking before shows. I mean, I know the pressure is hell on performers, but she shouldn't have to drink to the point of getting drunk." With his hands in his pockets, he rocked back on his boot heels.

"Take it easy on her, buddy. She's a pretty nice girl. I don't think she's going to take you butting into her life very easily," Joshua replied.

"I will. I'm not all about getting up in her business. It's not my place, but if she wants to talk, I'll listen."

"We'll catch you later then."

"Be careful going home."

"We will."

He watched as Joshua and Candace headed back for the barricade. Joshua nodded to the security guy when they moved past. The few fans still standing at the gates didn't even seem to notice. They continued to wave signs as they called Samantha's name.

A deep sigh escaped his lips. He wasn't sure how this night might end, but in bed with Samantha wasn't a bad thought. *Jerk. She doesn't need a romping night of sex right now. She needs sympathy, understanding, and a man who will listen.* "Yeah, I can be that for her for the night."

His steps took him back to the bus doors a moment later. A soft knock was answered by a quick come in. He opened the door before taking the first step into her bus, softly closing the door behind him.

"Hi."

"Hey."

He noticed a glass of what looked like soda on the table next to her.

"Can I get you something to drink?"

"What are you having?"

"Coke."

"Sounds good."

She got to her feet before heading to the small kitchen area and the refrigerator. He looked down to realize she was barefoot. Red glossy nail polish graced her toenails. He had to smile. The girlieness seemed completely natural for her. When she bent over to retrieve the can from the shelf, he got a nice view of her round ass in her jeans. He had to admit, she had curves in all the right places.

When she returned to his side, she handed him the soda can before returning to her spot on the opposite side of the coach. Her posture looked relaxed. "I hope security wasn't a big deal for you tonight."

"Nope. Not a problem."

"Good."

"Your performance sounded fantastic."

"Thanks. I always get really nervous before I perform."

"Why? You seem like a natural."

She set her glass of soda on the table before grabbing her hair and pulling it over her shoulder. "I don't know how much you know about me or how I came to be singing for a living, but several years ago if someone told me I'd be standing in front of thousands of people, I would have told them they were crazy."

He took a sip of his Coke. "I'm not sure I understand."

"I got discovered doing karaoke in a bar."

"Wow."

"Yeah. My whole life changed inside of about a week. The record producer offered me a contract and *bam!* The next thing I knew, I was in Nashville, recording a CD, had an agent, and a booking company, fans screaming when they saw me on the street, and the hate of every other country music artist out there because I didn't pay my dues. I never wanted to be a superstar."

"Then why did you allow it to happen? You could have told the producer no."

"I know. Many times I wish I had." She glanced at the Jack Daniel's bottle sitting on the counter. "You know I didn't have cold medicine before the show."

"Yeah, I know."

"I'm sorry I lied to you."

"Don't let it happen again."

She grinned, shook her head and glanced down to where her hands lay in her lap. "You are a hardass, aren't you?"

"Not really. I just know what it's like. I have a sibling who had a drinking problem, so I've dealt with it before."

She jumped to her feet, more pissed off that a wet cat. "I don't have a drinking problem. I have a little alcohol before I go on stage to calm my nerves, but I do *not* have an alcohol problem. I can handle the booze I drink. I mean did I once appear drunk to you?"

"A little."

"I wasn't drunk."

"What was with all the getting married stuff?"

"I thought it would be funny." She spun around to pace from the front to the back of the bus. "Are you saying you wouldn't marry me, given the chance?"

"I don't know you, Ms. Harris."

She stopped her journey when she stood in front of him. "Quit calling me Ms. Harris. That's my mother. I'm Samantha or Sam if you prefer."

"All right, Samantha. No, I wouldn't marry you right now if you wanted me to. I don't take those kinds of things lightly. I don't even know why you would ask since we just met three hours ago."

Deflated, she plopped back down on the couch. "I'm scared, Jackson."

"Scared of what?"

"This whole life, but especially of this person who is stalking me. They have photos of me near my parent's house, on my bus, at truck stops, and the most terrifying thing of all, they know I don't have a steady guy in my life. I don't know if it's a woman or a man, but whoever it is knows way too much about me. I thought if I had a man, they would leave me alone." She shrugged before taking a drink of her soda. "You are as good a choice as any."

"Thanks, I think."

"I didn't mean it as an insult. I'm trying to think of what I can do to discourage this weirdo."

He scraped his hand over the beard covering his face. He liked having whiskers along the bottom of his cheeks, and a mustache framing his mouth meeting with the whiskers along his chin. Women seemed to like how it felt on their skin. The extra scruff also made him stand out a little amongst his brothers who were all clean-shaven. "No insult taken. I'm just trying to figure out where I would fit into the scheme of things."

She bit her lower lip, pulling the plumpness in between her teeth as she concentrated a minute.

He wanted to take it between his teeth and drag it into his mouth to see what she tasted like.

"Maybe we could pretend to be a couple."

"Pretend?"

"Well, that's kind of up to you. I wouldn't mind spending some time with you. You're a gorgeous guy, nice, a cowboy, and you seem to have a good head on your shoulders, but I wouldn't be up for any kind of relationship until we got to know each other. We could pretend to be getting married or something. No one would be able to know about it being fake though. Just you and me."

"What about parents, siblings, etc? Joshua and Candace wouldn't buy this and neither would the rest of my family. They know me better than that."

"I'm afraid they would let the information we weren't really a couple slip."

He looked across the expanse of the bus to where she fiddled with her Coke. "You know you've totally changed the subject."

"Changed the subject from what?"

"Your drinking."

"I already told you, it's not an issue, but this stalker thing is."

He wasn't sure what to do. True, he liked her a lot, but pretending to get married? Nope. Being a couple might have possibilities. He wondered what her plan was. "So, how would this work? I mean your band and everyone here tonight knows I only arrived this evening. They aren't going to buy this either."

"I'll just tell them you've been away on business and arrived only tonight to meet with me. You can go on tour with me. Stay in my bus."

"Wait a minute. We aren't sleeping together are we?"

"Not in the biblical sense of the word, Jackson. I don't know you well enough to spread my legs for you, but there are bunks in this bus behind the door." She pointed to the door closed at the end of the hall. "Down farther is my bedroom which is closed off from the other bunks."

"You want me to move in with you while you are on tour?"

"Yes."

"What about my life on my parent's ranch? I do have a life, you know, outside of obsessing about you, that is."

"You obsess about me?" She grinned as one eyebrow arched over her right eye. "Really?"

"I'm kidding. But I do have a life I can't just walk away from." He thought to himself what exactly his life consisted of on the ranch. Day in and day out, he spent his time doing chores, wrangling cattle, mowing yard, cleaning the pool, taking guests out riding…what else? *Hmm*. It didn't seem so important when you broke things down. "What would your parents say?"

She tucked her feet under her, getting comfortable in the seat like she wasn't going anywhere for a while. Really, where did she have to go? Her next gig?

"Mine are very open-minded. I've already told them you were my security detail, so if you were going to accompany me to protect me, they would be totally cool with the whole thing." She absently braided, then unbraided her hair while she watched him for a reaction, he guessed. The entire process looked like a preoccupied thing she did without realizing she was doing it.

This whole situation sounded crazy. He didn't mind crazy though. It sounded kind of fun and something different than his boring life at Thunder Ridge with all of his siblings pairing off. As one of the remaining single men on the place, he was bombarded with female attention on a daily basis. He didn't mind really, but it got old fending off advances at every turn.

"Mine might be a little weirded out by the situation, but my mom would think it was funny me being tied up with a woman for a couple of months." He tipped his head to the side. "Just how long are we talking about?"

"I don't know. It depends on how long it takes to flush out the weirdo stalking me. You would be my personal bodyguard the whole time. We would be almost inseparable, you know?"

"Sounds like it."

"What do you say, Jackson? Are you game for a little adventure?"

Chapter Three

The next thing he knew, they were bumping along the road from the gates of Thunder Ridge with her bus following behind his truck. Samantha sat in the passenger seat holding onto the oh-shit handle, rocking along with the bumps. He told her they could park her bus behind the main lodge until they could find somewhere in town to park it, not that Bandera had a lot of places to hide a forty-five foot long bus. Good thing Thunder Ridge spanned several thousand acres.

He'd called his mom before they headed out toward the ranch to tell her what was going on or at least to let her know he had Samantha Harris in his truck with her bus traveling behind him. Samantha told him she didn't have anywhere to be for a couple of weeks, so they could spend time building their ruse before they took it on the road. He didn't mind getting to know her a bit before this whole thing started.

His mom booked Samantha a room and said to park the bus around back. He'd already given directions to the driver before they left the concert area. They would keep her privacy as much as possible, but they already had several guests at the ranch for the next week. He would do the best he could to protect her from overzealous guests, but he did have his own chores to do.

They pulled up in front of the block wall keeping the parking lot separate from the grass and walkways to the main lodge.

"Wow. What a great place."

"Thanks."

"I love the big house. It's perfect."

"It's the main lodge where meals are taken. We have a pool table, big fireplace, leather couches to just chill out or whatever. The front porch goes all the way along the side of the house. It has several rocking chairs and old antique things sitting out there, where you can relax, watch the sunsets, feed the donkeys…you know, that kind of stuff."

"You have donkeys?"

"Yeah, three to be exact. They are the biggest babies on the ranch. They wander around all the time, bugging the guests for treats or pats."

"I love animals."

"Where did you grow up?"

"Iowa. My parents own a few hundred acres where they breed horses, run a few cattle, and grow corn."

"Doesn't everyone grow corn in Iowa?" He smiled as he shut the truck off.

"Pretty much." She glanced out the windshield, her expression curious as she took it all in. "So this is where you grew up?"

"Yeah. My parents moved here when my oldest brother was still young and I was a baby. They've been running it ever since."

"And you have eight brothers. Wow. I really need to meet your mother."

"You will. She's the glue holding this place together."

"I can imagine. What I can't imagine is raising nine boys."

"Three of those are triplets."

"Holy shit." She turned to face him on the seat. "Are they identical?"

"Yeah. Some people can tell them apart, but others who don't know them very well, can't. You met Joshua. He's one of the triplets along with Joel and Jason."

"Your parents named you all with J names? I bet that's confusing at times."

"Not for us, but yeah, I imagine it gets a little weird. Mom wanted us all named similar to my father. His name is James." He pushed open the door to the truck. "Come on. I'll introduce you to whoever is around."

He met her around the front of the truck, taking her hand in his to lead her up the walkway. Darkness surrounded them even though white solar lights lined the concrete path, brightening the way to the house. Shadows stretched across the yard as clouds moved over the moon in strange patterns. He loved nights like this. October was one of his favorite months of the year even though the weather didn't really turn cooler until later. The evenings tended to drop in temperature as the year wound down toward Christmas. The fall weather always made him think of home and family for some reason.

"Does all of the family live on the ranch?"

"Yeah, but some of my brothers who have paired off have their own places around the property. My parents gifted us all a chunk of land when we turned eighteen. Some of them have built their homes on their piece."

"Where do you live?"

"In the small cabin over there. I shared half of it with Jeremiah until he and Callie got together. They live in town with her father at the moment, until they can get their house built. They just got married a few weeks ago and are on their honeymoon right now."

"How cool."

"Yeah, they got married in Hawaii. Most of us went and stayed for a week or so. It's pretty cool over there. Have you been there?"

"That's one place I haven't been, I think. These tours have me going just about everywhere, including Europe."

"Europe would be fun. I've never been there. I sure would like to see England, Ireland, and a few other countries."

"Maybe I'll take you there someday."

He grinned, but realized this new relationship, if you could call it that, wouldn't be lasting long enough for her to take him anywhere outside of a few states in the U.S. while she did shows. He imagined her schedule was pretty hectic with one show after the other.

They reached the side door of the main lodge, taking the steps quickly. The heavy wood door pushed open with ease as he laid his palm on the panel. Bright lights illuminated the space where they all took meals, almost blinding him as his eyes adjusted. He didn't normally take notice of the things surrounding the room because he went there all the time, but for a moment he took in the western décor. The scorched brand of their place on the walls, the pictures of different people who had graced the ranch with their presence, and the large wood posts that frame the doorway leading into the main lodge area made this place home.

"We take meals in here. Breakfast is at eight, lunch at twelve-thirty and dinner at five-thirty. They will clang a dinner bell outside to call you when meals are being served."

"Sound good."

"I hope there aren't too many people on the ranch to bother you while you're here. If we would have had a little more notice, we might have been able to accommodate your privacy more."

"It's fine, Jackson. I don't mind, really."

"You say so now, but if you're mobbed, it will be a whole different story."

She smiled as she skimmed her palm across his jaw. "Everything will be fine. We just have to work on convincing everyone we are a couple so we can get this ruse out on the road."

"Do we need to hire security for the ranch while you're here?"

"I don't think so. I'm sure you and your brothers can handle whatever comes."

"Probably."

She blew out a breath. "I just wish I knew who this psycho was so I could get on with my life. It's so hard not knowing who to be afraid of."

"I can imagine, but you're safe here."

"Thanks. I appreciate your family doing this for me. You especially."

"I haven't done anything yet."

"But you will."

"I want to help."

"I know." She leaned in to kiss him on the cheek.

Nina walked through the doorway leading back to her office. "Oh, there you are! I was beginning to wonder about you."

"Sorry, Mom. I didn't mean to make you stay up so late."

"It's fine. I haven't been sleeping well lately anyway. Too much going on." She extended her hand. "You must be Samantha Harris. I'm Nina Young. It's nice to meet you."

Samantha stepped away from him and took his mother's hand. "And you. I want to thank you for doing this for me. I can't imagine how much of a pain this will be for you all."

"Oh, no problem at all. We've had a few celebrities here over the years. I wish we would have had a little more notice. I could have provided you with more security."

"It's fine. I doubt anyone will even notice me."

"I doubt it. You are a very popular young lady."

"Thank you."

"Jackson can show you where your room is. I thought you might be more comfortable in one of cabins so you'll have the privacy. I blocked the room next to yours so we don't rent it out to a family with rambunctious kids or something."

"You didn't have to do that. I love kids."

Nina glanced at him, making him blush. He could see the wheels turning in his mother's brain without even looking. "Great. We do have a few around here with all these boys marrying and having babies. It's great to have so many of my grandkids close."

"I bet you love it."

"Oh definitely." His mother glanced sideways at him as he shook his head. "Anyway, let me get your credit card and I'll retrieve the keys for your cabin."

"That would be great." Samantha retrieved her card from the purse on her shoulder before handing it to his mother.

"Follow me. We'll get you settled in a jiffy."

Jackson shook his head as he followed Samantha and his mother toward the office. If he knew his mother, she had plans already running through her mind. He would have to put a stop to that right away. *I can't. We need to convince the family we are a couple so I can get this crazy nutcase off Samantha's trail. Which will totally play right into Mom's hands. Damn it.*

Several moments later, Samantha was all set with her room key in hand.

"Jackson can show you where it is."

"Thanks. He already directed my bus driver to where to park the bus."

"Great." Nina rocked back on her boot heels as she stuffed her hands in the front pocket of her jeans. "Well, I will bid you two goodnight. Things start up early around here." She pointed at Jackson. "Don't forget, you have ride duty in the morning."

"Thanks for the reminder. I'd forgotten I had early horseback rides."

"There is a group going in the morning too. About nine, I believe, with some new riders."

"Is Joey around?"

"He'll be out there to help you. He already knows the drill."

"Thanks, Mom." He watched as his mother waved before she retreated down the hall to his parents' private quarters. "Shall we?" he asked, tipping his head to the side to indicated heading back out the doors to show her where her cabin stood.

"Sure."

He took her hand in his again, leading her through the lodge and back out the door. "This way."

"Oh, I need to grab some things from my bus."

"Okay." He detoured to the left, between the hitching posts not in use anymore, to the spot around the back where the bus had been parked. The driver stood leaning against the side.

"I need a ride back to town, Sam."

"Sure, Mark. I'm sure we can get a taxi out here to pick you up."

"Not this late at night," Jackson responded. "I'll take him back to town as soon as you are settled."

"Thanks, Jackson," she replied.

"I have a flight out in the morning for home, Sam. I'll fly back in when you're ready to roll again or before, if you need me."

His pointed look in Jackson's direction made the hair rise on his arms. Was the man thinking he would get in between Jackson and Samantha? Was he Sam's stalker? It would make sense since the man was close to her all the time driving the bus. "Problem, Mark?"

"Nope. Just letting her know I'm here for her should she need me. We've known each other a long time, you know."

"I can imagine."

"Stop this pissing contest, you two. Nothing will come of it." She laid her hand on Mark's arm as he turned to face her. "I'm fine. I'll be staying here with Jackson and his family for a couple of weeks. You go on home. I'll call you when I need you to fly back."

"Sure, Sam. Be careful, huh? I wouldn't want you to get hurt."

"I won't, but thanks."

Samantha opened the door to the bus before she climbed the three stairs into the interior. Jackson hesitated a minute, giving Mark a look he hoped said back off as he followed her inside and shut the door behind them.

"I'll just grab a few things. Be out in a minute."

"Okay." Jackson took a seat on the couch to the left as he waited for Samantha to return. He could hear the banging of drawers coming from the back of the bus. *Women. They were so needy sometimes.*

About thirty minutes later, she opened the door to the back part of the bus, rolling three suitcases with her. "Jesus, woman. What the hell do you have in there? Not like you couldn't come back in here anytime to retrieve more stuff."

"I know, but I didn't want to forget anything. One is my hair stuff, makeup, shampoo and all that jazz, one has my shoes, and the other one has my clothes."

"You have one suitcase for just shoes?"

"Oh yeah. I have to have sandals, heels, boots, flip-flops, high-heeled boots, low-heeled boots, high-heel dress shoes, low-heel dress shoes. A woman can never have enough shoes."

"Apparently." He shook his head as he reached for one of the cases to carry it down the stairs. The damn thing weighed about a hundred pounds.

When he had her and her suitcases on the ground, he grabbed one in each hand and headed for the cabin in the distance. He was kind of glad his mother put her near his. It would make getting this whole charade started much easier. *I'm not sure how much of a charade it is since I totally want to get her into my bed.* "Follow me."

"Right." She grabbed the smallest of the three and waved to Mark, before following him the several yards to the front of her cabin.

He liked this particular set of rooms on the property out of all the cabins set aside for guests. It had a small porch running across the front where guests could sit outside, sip coffee or something and watch the sunrise. Big wooden posts held up the porch, providing a railing should you want to hitch a horse to one of them. Two rocking chairs made out of cedar sat near each other with a small table between them. The doors on the cabins were made of solid oak and were very heavy to move. The inside had a large, king size bed with a handmade quilt over the top, hand-sewn curtains on the windows to match the pattern on the quilt, pictures of several different kinds of flowers gracing the walls, and beautiful throw rugs gracing the wooden floors.

"I think you'll like these rooms. There is a door between the two in case you have someone come out who you might want to use the other room."

"I don't know who would do that."

"Maybe you could invite your parents out. I think that would be cool."

She tapped her fingers on her lips as she took in the space around them. "What a great idea. My mom and dad could sure use a vacation away. My sisters can tend the animals for a few days." She gave him a beautiful smile. "Thanks, Jackson."

"No problem." He shoved his hands in his pockets to keep from reaching for her. He wanted to touch her, stroke her skin, run his fingers through her hair to see if he could get her to make sweet little noises as he brought her to the peak of ecstasy.

To keep himself from actually doing what he wanted to do, he let his thoughts drift to other things like if she was an early riser. He figured probably not since she always had to be up late performing. It would be interesting to find out little tidbits about her while she took the two weeks off on the ranch with him. "Well, I should get going so I can take Mark back to San Antonio, plus I have rides to run in the morning."

"Do you all have a gym on site?"

"Yeah, upstairs in the main lodge there is equipment. Take the stairs to the back of the dining room to the second floor, turn left. It's in the back. There is a treadmill, elliptical, weights, and a couple exercise balls."

"Sounds perfect."

"I guess I'll see you tomorrow at breakfast."

"Goodnight."

"Night, Jackson. Sleep well."

* * * *

Samantha slowly closed the door behind Jackson, watching him for several minutes before she got the panel completely closed. She really did like him, a lot. He had the sexy thing down, gorgeous, and those arms, wow. She'd give just about anything to be held in those arms. The muscles of his biceps bulged nicely every time he moved. His chest was something she could get lost in if he hugged her tight. Hugs were the best if they were from the right guy. She really liked how he wore his facial hair. Trimmed nicely, he wore it framing his face along his jawline, a mustache above his lips, and down in almost a goatee style, but only on the edge of his chin. It looked great on him.

She sighed heavily as she backed away from the door, almost tripping over the suitcases left next to the bed. The room screamed country chic with its homey décor, pretty coverlet on the bed, and the nice dried flowers sitting on the nightstand. She could get used to this.

After glancing at the clock and realizing how late it had become, she tossed the biggest suitcase on the bed. She needed something to sleep in.

The roar of Jackson's truck drew her to the window looking out over the front lawn. She watched as he backed out and slowly drove down the gravel driveway to take Mark back to town. Jackson really was a great guy, the kind she could definitely like for longer than a few days.

"Well, bed it is." She returned to the bed, opened the suitcase and pulled out a pair of shorts and a tank top. When she got changed, she put the suitcase on the floor at the bottom of the bed. She needed her smaller one with her toiletries in it so she could brush her teeth and comb out her hair before braiding it for bed. If she didn't tie it back, a wild mess would greet her come morning.

When she had everything in place, she slid beneath the fresh sheets on the bed, and leaned over to flip off the light before she snuggled down under the covers. The bed seemed comfortable and plenty big enough for two. She sighed as she closed her eyes, waiting for sleep to claim her. Her thoughts drifted to Jackson and their conversation on the bus. Was she really an alcoholic? She didn't think so at all. Yeah, she had a few drinks before she performed, sometimes a little vodka in her coffee or a drink before bed, but she could go without the booze anytime she wanted to. *Nah.* She would show him. She wouldn't drink at all while she stayed on his family's ranch. Alcohol didn't mean that much to her. She only used it to calm her nerves at various times during the day when she felt stressed out. Nothing big, right? Right.

She exhaled on a rush, pulling covers up to her ears. As she drifted off to sleep, her dreams filled with thoughts of Jackson and what he could do to bring her to the heights of ecstasy.

He stood at her door in nothing but his jeans, his boots, and his cowboy hat.

"Can I come in?"

"Of course."

He stepped across the threshold and swept her up in his arms, crushing his mouth against hers. His tongue danced along the seam of her lips using small licks, until she opened to his probing. Her body tingled as their tongues dueled from her mouth to his and back. His hands swept down her back, instantly cupping her ass in both of his palms and dragging her up against his chest. His mouth left hers to skim over her cheek, nipping at her jawline as he went, before he reached her ear to slip the lobe between his teeth too. God, she loved a man with a talented mouth.

"I want you, Samantha."

"Oh yeah."

"You are everything a man wants in a woman, bold, sexy, daring, and gorgeous beyond words. I want to eat you until you scream my name. Then I'm going to fuck you so hard, you'll have to brace yourself for the onslaught of feelings racing through you with every thrust of my hips."

"Yes."

He bent down and swept her up in his arms before he moved toward the bed to deposit her in the middle. Two fingers hooked in her underwear, slowly peeled them down her legs and tossed them over his shoulder to somewhere on the floor. She laid there in nothing but one of his dress shirts buttoned up the front. "I'll get to those gorgeous nipples in a minute. Right now, I need to taste you."

Seconds later, his head disappeared between her thighs. The first swipe of his tongue almost brought her out of her skin. "Oh, God."

She tossed his hat across the comforter on the bed. Winding her hands into the hair on the top of his head, she held him tight against her pussy. Good grief, he had a talented tongue. Each swipe, each lick, each nibble brought her higher until she couldn't help tossing her head as he ate at her like a starving man. The whiskers on his chin scraped her flesh, abrading it deliciously as he continued to suck at her clit.

"Come for me, Samantha."

The sharp sting of a bite on her clit threw her into the most amazing orgasm she'd ever had. Lights danced behind her closed eyelids as she screamed his name when he drove two fingers into her pussy, throwing her over the climatic abyss again.

Samantha bolted upright in the bed. Her heart pounded so hard against her chest, she thought she might be having a heart attack. Her breath came out in a ragged seesaw of sounds until realization hit. The whole thing had all been a dream. Jackson wasn't with her making her come so hard she thought she might die.

"Holy shit."

Her pussy ached with a need she couldn't fulfill in the way she wanted to more than anything on this earth at the moment.

"I need a shower. I'd better make it a cold one."

She whipped the covers back, sliding her legs over the edge of the bed before she stood up. Moonlight drifted through the curtains at the front of the cabin, lighting her way to the unfamiliar bathroom. When she flipped on the light, she blinked several times to bring the room into focus. The space sparkled. There were subway titles in black lining all the walls including the fully enclosed shower. Silver accents accompanied everything. A silver framed mirror hung over the white sink with old-fashioned porcelain handles to turn on the hot and cold water. The only other color in the room was the royal blue rugs on the floor and a shower curtain with royal blue flowers. *Breathtaking.*

She turned on the shower before stripping off her clothes and standing beneath the spray. The water cascaded over her shoulders, working away the knots her dream had placed there, with its warmth.

This isn't going to cut it. I need to get off.

She lifted her foot onto the bench seat along the back wall of the shower, sliding her fingers through the curls at the apex of her thighs. Her clit was still slick with her juices from her all too vivid dream of Jackson eating her out.

Her whole body hummed from not being satisfied like she craved.

She quickly began working her clit with her fingertips, rubbing first one side, then the other, hovering on the brink of coming. She let herself get lost in the memory of the dream again. As sensory overload took over, her body bowed tight and she came on a rush. Too bad the self-satisfaction paled in comparison to her dream

Feeling almost unsatisfied to the point of exhaustion, she turned the water off before grabbing a towel to dry her body. She stepped out of the shower, and then padded softly across the wooden floor in her bare feet.

She's almost reached the bed when she heard a soft knock on the door.

Frozen in fear, she wasn't sure whether she should answer or not until she heard a voice she recognized calling her name through the panel.

Chapter Four

"Samantha, are you okay?" Jackson tapped on the door when he saw the light on in her cabin after he'd returned from taking her bus driver back to San Antonio. He wanted to make sure she didn't need anything.

When she opened the door, he almost swallowed his tongue. She stood in front of him in nothing more than a large towel wrapped around her gorgeous frame.

"I'm fine, Jackson." She tossed her hair over her shoulder as she tugged the towel a little closer around her body. "I just took a shower before bed, is all."

"Okay. I saw your light on. I wanted to make sure you didn't need anything." *Like me needing to run my tongue all over your body, licking up every little droplet of water I see.* He swallowed hard. His cock slowly began to fill, pressing on the zipper of his jeans.

She glanced down, and then back up to meet his gaze. One eyebrow rose over her right eye.

"You're standing here in nothing, but a towel. What did you expect to happen?"

She moved a little closer, close enough he could smell the scent of her body wash on her skin. "Do you want to come in?"

"Hell yes, I do, but I don't think that's such a good idea."

"Why?"

"Because you are standing there in nothing but a towel."

"Yeah, I know."

The lump in his throat felt like it would choke him if he swallowed again, but the saliva pooling in his mouth didn't give him much choice in the matter. He stepped forward, bringing her so her breasts brushed his chest. "This is a bad idea."

"I don't think so."

"I do. My mom has a rule against the boys messing with guests."

"I'm not a guest."

"You're not?"

"Well, technically, yes, but we are supposed to be getting to the point where we can convince your family and everyone else, we are a couple."

"And?"

"What if we really are?"

"Do you want to be?"

"I don't know." Her gaze swept over him from head to the toes of his boots. "You're kind of cute with all your cowboyness."

The towel slipped a hair, gaping open in the front around her breasts. Water glistened on her skin, making him wonder if she was cold standing there in the cooler evening air. Maybe he should walk her backward into the room, you know, just for propriety sake. "You make it sound like a disease or something."

"Not at all. If you hadn't noticed, I like cowboys."

"I hadn't noticed."

She laughed as she adjusted the towel.

"Aren't you cold?"

"Yeah, a little."

"I'll leave you to get ready for bed then."

Her bottom lip came out in a pout. "I hoped you'd help me, you know, get dressed or undressed as the case may be."

He would be in hell come morning for lying to her about wanting her right now. "I think it would be better if we waited on that score."

"You don't want to have sex with me?"

"I didn't say I didn't want to have sex with you."

"What's the problem then?"

"Why don't we leave that for when we know each other a bit better?"

She took a step back, readjusting the towel to cover a little more. "Wow. I've never had a guy turn down sex before. This is a first."

"I think it would be a whole lot better if we knew each other a little more beforehand, that's all. I think you're a real nice gal, but I think I'd like to know you a bit before we had sex." He adjusted himself in his jeans. "Not that I don't want you, because yeah, I do. You're a beautiful woman with all the assets I like, but I think it would make things a little awkward should we have sex now, and then try to convince everyone we are having sex, when we might not be in the future." He raked his fingers through his hair, before adjusting his hat back on his head. "Does anything I just said make any sense at all?"

"Sure, Jackson."

She shrugged although the look on her face told him she didn't really understand how he could turn her down.

"I'll see you in the morning at breakfast."

"Of course, thanks for checking on me. I appreciate it."

"You're welcome." She moved to shut the door as he stepped back off the porch. "Night."

"Goodnight."

* * * *

Morning came too damned early for Jackson as he rolled over to punch his pillow for umpteenth time since he'd went to bed. He'd spent the night rolling from one side of the bed to the other because of one blonde beauty who had wound his dick tight enough to shoot the eye out of a cow with his cum should he have let go. Now, his balls ached with need and he'd shut her down to the point where he didn't know if he'd get any or not.

A rousting knock sounded on his door.

"Jackson?"

Samantha. His dick hadn't softened all damned night long, but it was straight up and begging at the sound of her voice.

"I'll be right there."

He jumped out of bed, hitting his toe on the footboard. "Fucking son of a bitch!"

"Are you all right?"

"Yeah. I hit my toe. I'll be there in a second. I need to put some clothes on."

"Don't get dressed on my account."

He needed a shower, cold one preferably, but he didn't have time.

The bell clanged for breakfast.

Late again.

His toe throbbed with every beat of his heart as he limped to his dresser to retrieve some clean clothes. His boots were going to kill him to put on, plus he had to take the group out this morning on the horses. Maybe he could get Joey to take his ride. He hoped he hadn't broken his toe. It hurt like the devil.

Once he had his clothes on, he opened the door to find Samantha decked out in a sexy pair of jeans and a long-sleeved blouse that button down the front in a pretty, solid pink fabric with embroidered flowers on the shoulders. A straw cowboy hat graced her head, covering her blonde hair except for the long straight strands cascading down her back. He wanted nothing more than to touch the silky looking mane.

"You look fresh and rested this morning."

She gave him a once over from his head to his boots. "You look like shit."

"Thanks."

"You're welcome." She bounced on her booted toes, shuffling her feet a little in her haste to be gone. "I thought you could walk me to breakfast. We need to start this little facade of ours sooner rather than later."

"I know, but I'd better warn you about my mother and her matchmaking skills."

"Matchmaking?"

"She'll have us paired whether we want to be or not before the end of the day. She's done that with all of my brothers so far. She's done a pretty good job of picking out their mate for them even if it took them a while to figure things out, but I don't want her to get her hopes up about us. This isn't real or at least not from my end."

She stepped back as he shut the door behind him.

"I know it's not real, Jackson. We are playing a role. It's like acting in a movie or something. We are playing a couple so we can catch this crazy person who is stalking me. We do have to make everything look convincing though.”

“I don’t want my family hurt in this ruse.”

“They won’t be.”

“I’m not so sure.”

She made a cross over her heart. “I promise to do my best not to hurt your family in this.”

“What about your family?”

“Unless for some reason we make a trip to Iowa, they don’t even need to know about us.”

“What if the news reporters pick up on this charade and broadcast it all over the country music news? They’ll see it then.”

She tapped her fingers to her lips for a moment. “Well, we’ll have to make up some kind of excuse why we broke up. Thing like this happen in this business all the time. It won’t be a surprise to anyone.”

“You aren’t taking this very seriously.”

“I’m dead serious, Jackson. I need to get this psycho away from me. I’m afraid, terrified really, and it would make me feel a lot better having you around.”

She definitely knew how to play on his emotions about women in general. Yeah, he liked to fuck them from here to tomorrow, but let one be in trouble, and he would be right there to help. Damn chivalry. “Let’s get some breakfast, shall we? We’ll worry about the other later.”

She fell into step beside him as they made their way toward the main lodge. “What kind of food to do you like?”

“Everything.”

“Like?”

“I’m a meat and potatoes kind of guy, I guess, but one of my weaknesses is cookies.”

“What kind of cookies?”

“Chocolate chip specifically, but I love oatmeal with raisins too.”

As their hands brushed together during their walk, she grabbed his in hers, holding on tightly as she laced their fingers together. When he shot her a look, she just smiled as she snuggled closer to his side. This façade of a relationship was going to kill him sooner rather than later if he didn’t die from blue balls or guilt first.

When they walked through the doors of the big house, he directed her toward the line of people getting their food. “Go ahead and get your plate. The family always waits until everyone else is served.”

“I’ll wait for you.”

“Do you want to sit over here near the door?”

“Where do you usually sit?” she asked, leaning into his arm so her breasts pressed against him.

“With my family at those two long tables near the stairs.”

The whole table of people turned to stare as he and Samantha made their way inside the room. Was it that unusual for him to have a woman by his side? No, but it was different for him to bring one home, so to speak. He didn't do the girlfriend thing and he didn't think Samantha did the simpering female thing either, so she better knock this shit off.

He slowly disengaged his arm from her grasp. The pout on her lips made him want to kiss her, which seemed to be her reasoning behind it so he resisted with everything inside him. As they approached the table, the family fell silent. "Everyone, this is Samantha Harris for those of you who don't know her. Ya'll probably saw her bus out back. She's staying for a couple of weeks in one of the cabins to relax before she hits the road." He went around the table introducing everyone present, skipping those who already knew her, before he found them two seats at the end of the table to the next to Joshua and Candace.

Samantha gave him a blinding smile over her shoulder, as he held out her chair for her. "Thank you."

"You're welcome." He gripped the seatback of the chair next to her. "Can I get you some coffee or juice?"

"Coffee would be great."

"Be right back." His brothers all stared as he made his way toward the large coffee pot sitting to the left in the corner. He knew they had to play this up for everything it was worth, but he wasn't sure exactly how to go about it. How did one treat a girlfriend verses a one-night stand? He wasn't sure. He'd never had a girlfriend per se except in high school and you couldn't really call that a girlfriend. *Okay, be cool. Do things for her like get her plate, hold her chair, open the door, all the things Ma taught us as boys in how to be a gentleman. Good start.*

The conversation from the table drifted to his ears as he poured two cups of coffee, added cream and sugar to his before gathering some for Samantha.

"Are you really Samantha Harris the country music star?" Paige asked.

"Yes."

"I love your music."

"Thank you. I'm thrilled to hear that. I love meeting fans."

"I'm a huge one."

"You can say that again," Jacob added. "She has all your stuff on her iPod."

"I appreciate the support."

"Do you travel a lot?" This came from Mesa.

"Yeah. When we are on tour, we are gone for several weeks without much of a break."

"I bet it's hard being gone all the time."

"Yes, although I'm used to it by now. The bus has all the amenities. It's like living in a small apartment."

"Nice."

"Do you play an instrument like an acoustic guitar?" Joey's voice carried to Jackson's ears from the end of the table.

"Some. I rely a lot on the guys in the band to carry the music. I do write some of my own songs though, so I do have to play a little to be able to do that."

"She plays beautifully. Don't let her fool you," Candace added before she took a sip of her juice. "I've heard her play many times."

It was Samantha's turn to ask a question. "Did any of you come out for the benefit concert last night?"

Several of his brothers nodded affirmatively as well as voiced their pleasure at her performance, but Jeff replied, "You did awesome, Samantha."

When Jackson returned to the table, he noticed the blush on her cheeks. She really didn't know how to handle her fame very well if she turned red at the smallest compliments. He set the cup down in front of her with the cream and sugar, loving how she glanced up as a pretty smile spread across her lips.

Thoughts of leaning in to give her a quick kiss raced across his mind until Jeff started talking about guests coming in, how many they had on the place now, horses needing to be broke, rides needing guides, and more ranch stuff.

Jackson took the seat next to Samantha, sipping the steaming hot liquid in his cup slowly so he didn't burn his mouth, until time for them to get their own plates of food. Samantha got quiet while the rest of the group picked up the slack in the conversations going around the table. "You okay?"

"Yes, why?"

"I don't want you to be overwhelmed with my family. They can be a bit rough on newcomers to the group."

"They are great. I wish I had a big family. I really would love to sit down to talk to your mother about raising all of you. I bet she has some great stories."

"I'm sure."

"Where are you in the pecking order?"

"Second to the eldest. Jeff is the eldest, then me, Jacob, Jason, Joel, Joshua are the triplets, Jonathan, Jeremiah and last is Joey."

"And the only ones not paired off?"

"Me, Jonathan and Joey. Everyone else has a steady girl, married or getting married soon as in Candace and Joshua's case." The group surged to their feet in a large wave as his mother gave the signal for them to get their own plates. "We can eat now."

"Is it always like this?"

"Like what?" he asked, pulling out her chair for her.

"A huge wave of people heading to the food line." She giggled and fell into step beside him as they headed toward the back of the line.

"Yep."

Those of his brothers paired off, who already had children to care for, usually fixed their spouse's plates for them while the women managed the various highchairs hanging around the room. Jacob and Paige had twins, Jeff and Terri had three kids now, Joel and Mesa had their daughter, and the news had broken around the family in the last couple of weeks that they were expecting again. The family had grown exponentially over the last few years with the addition of the women and children. He smiled when he thought about it. His mom was in heaven with all these grandkids and women around after raising nine boys, plus the newest addition coming soon to Joel and Mesa.

"What are you smiling about?"

"Just thinking about my mom with all of her grandkids and daughters-in-law around her. After having nothing but boys, she's ecstatic now and totally in her element."

Samantha glanced over her shoulder as Nina snuggled one of her grandkids on her hip, making the child giggle hysterically. Lucky for all of them, Nina had recovered fully from her car accident a few months ago, that had left her with a broken leg. Time had stood still for all of them that night as they wondered if she would be okay in the long run. Not only had she broke her leg, but she'd had a bleed on her brain when some guy had hit her head on when she was headed to town in one of the ranch trucks.

He really did love his family even though they got on his nerves sometimes.

Nina shot a look his way with a little chin tip in Samantha's direction as a grin graced her lips. His mother was playing matchmaker already. He knew the signs. He hoped she didn't get hurt in this scam they were playing.

As the two of them approached the serving containers, he saw Mandy across the table from him. "Hey, Mandy. This is—"

"Samantha Harris," Mandy gushed a little. "I absolutely love your music. I'm glad you came to the ranch to chill out. I promise I won't bug you."

Samantha laughed. "It's nice to meet you."

"Oh my gosh. You too." Mandy put some eggs on Samantha's plate along with a couple of pieces of bacon. "I hope you enjoy your stay here."

"I'm sure I will."

Mandy motioned with the tongs. "Are you and Jackson like, you know, a couple?"

"Sort of." Samantha grinned in his direction. "We are at the 'get to know you phase'."

"Awesome. He's a great guy. All of the boys are."

"Especially Jonathan." Jackson loved teasing her about her crush on his brother. Jonathan seemed to be the only one who didn't know about her true feelings.

"Yeah, him too."

Samantha frowned as they continued through the line. "Jonathan?"

"Yeah. Mandy has a serious crush going on with him, but he seems to be oblivious to her feelings."

"Well that sucks."

"Yeah."

With their plates now full, they headed back to their seats at the table. He'd have to watch his manners around Samantha. She probably had that kind of thing down pat and he didn't want to look like a heathen shoveling food into his mouth. When he started to care about it, he wasn't sure, but yeah, it seemed the thing to do.

The conversations flowed around them as the table occupants ate, laughed, and sipped their coffee before chores began for the day.

"Jackson, you're on escort duty this morning."

"Yeah, I know."

"There are seven riders unless Samantha wants to go. You can take the group by yourself. I don't think you need a second. Everyone riding is experienced, the new riders backed out earlier."

"No, I think I'll work on a new song I've been kicking around for the last week or so."

"Okay. I will be gone a little over an hour."

Samantha nodded before taking a sip of her coffee. "I'll be here checking out the property or something."

"Sounds good."

Jeff went around the table making sure everyone had their assignments for the day or at least those of the boys who did the physical labor around the ranch. Jeremiah did the financial stuff and Jonathan concentrated on the computer graphics as well as the website marketing.

"Grandma is babysitting all the munchkins while the girls go out to the spa today," Mesa added with a grin.

"I'm game," was the chorus of female agreement around the table as Nina held up her hands and shook her head with an emphatic no way.

"Well damn." Mesa laughed. "I thought for sure we could slip our plans by you, Grandma."

Nina laughed. "I have my own work to do, girls. You'll have to hire babysitters if you want a day at the spa."

"I'm lucky enough Elizabeth still takes naps."

"Yeah, not me with these two," Paige added as she glanced at her two in the corner making a huge mess on the floor with their food. They were working on their fine motor skills with the utensils, but they were still learning. Paige took the spoon and turned it around in Hannah's hand. "It's faster that way, Hannah." Hannah just giggled as she banged the spoon on the highchair. In turn, Josiah did the same thing. "No, Hannah. No Josiah," Paige scolded.

Jackson shook his head as he sipped his coffee. He didn't want kids, at least not yet anyway. He was perfectly fine being a bachelor although he had to admit his clock ticked relentlessly. *How old is Samantha?* He wasn't sure, but he thought she might be in her mid to late twenties, which made her quite a bit younger than his own age. Didn't matter. She was one hell of a pretty woman any way you sliced it.

He glanced at his watch. It was close enough to nine, he needed to get out to the barn to get ready for the group going out this morning. After he drained his cup, he stood. "I'll catch you later, Sam. I need to get out to the barn."

"Sure. I'll hang out here for a bit or whatever. I'm sure there is plenty to do around a working ranch. I don't expect you to take time off to entertain me. I can handle myself just fine."

"Good. See you after while."

"Have fun."

He headed for the door with her gaze fixed on his back. He could feel her look without even glancing behind him. They were attracted to each other, no doubt about that, but what would come of the attraction, he didn't know. Did he want to make this ruse real? Maybe. He sure would like to fuck her. What would it be like living with her on her bus for several weeks, making love to her on a regular basis as they traveled around the country waiting for her stalker to make a move?

As he made his way outside, the thought became more and more intriguing. This might be just the distraction he needed in his life.

Chapter Five

Samantha watched as Jackson headed out the door. *Damn, he's got a nice ass in those jeans.* Not one to ignore or under-appreciate a man's assets, she couldn't help but notice he sported quite the package in the front too. *Maybe thoughts like those aren't very nice to have sitting at the table with his family.*

"What are your plans, Sam," Nina asked.

"I'm not sure. I have some work I can be doing on my bus like writing on this song I have playing over and over in my head. I can check in with my agent. I can clean the mess on the bus. But what I'd really like to do is make some cookies."

"Make cookies?"

"Yeah. Jackson said his favorite was chocolate chip. Do you mind if I make him some?"

The whole family grinned as a few of them laughed. "Not at all. In fact, I believe we have everything in the kitchen to make them, but check with the cook. We haven't had homemade chocolate chip cookies around here in a while. He will really appreciate them, I'm sure. He's a sucker for desserts."

Samantha smiled. The way to get to the man was through his stomach, eh? Well, that's one thing her momma taught her, to cook up a storm, and desserts were her favorite too. She drank the last bit of her coffee, and then stood. "I'm going to do some things on my bus for a bit before I tackle the cookies. That should give them time to clean up from breakfast before I destroy their kitchen again."

The family laughed. It was a good feeling to be around. She missed her parents and her sisters. They were all a bit younger than she was by a few years even though they all had their own lives these days.

When she'd hit it big, she'd paid off her parents' farm, given her sisters some money so they could go to school or whatever they wanted to do, then sat on the rest. She did give to several charities over the years including many who took care of children. She loved kids although she didn't want any of her own for now. Her biological clock had started ticking at a pretty fast pace these days as her own age pushed thirty. She nodded to the group before walking toward the door. Her bus sat around back of the main lodge where Mark had parked it when they came in last night.

Cleaning wasn't her forte, but she realized she needed to straighten up the bus a bit from her frantic throwing together a bag after they'd arrived at the ranch. Even though it was close and she could grab what she wanted, she didn't want to spend a lot of time on the bus. She already spent way too much time on there while traveling. Being on the ranch with Jackson meant relaxation at its finest, and she meant to do exactly that, relax.

When she reached the front of the huge monstrosity she called home most days, she opened the door before taking the few steps up to reach the living space. She took in the clothes strewn across the couch, her customary cowboy hat sitting on the back of the sofa, her boots on the floor, her makeup bag with the majority of her cosmetics on the counter, and the overall appearance of the space. "What a pigsty." She grabbed the clothes and boots before walking back toward her bedroom to toss the offending garments in the dirty clothes bin. She would have to throw some things in the washer since the basket almost overflowed. Washing clothes was one of the tolerable chores she had to do.

A few minutes later, she returned to the front of the bus, spotting the half-empty whiskey bottle sitting on the counter in the kitchen. Nine in the morning wasn't too early for a little drink. It would relax her so she could clean and not notice the work involved. She unscrewed the top on the bottle to pour enough to fill the tumbler half full. Next, she grabbed her iPod, plugged in the headphones, clipped it on her belt and began to clean.

After over an hour of straightening up her bus, she sat down with her guitar, the sheet of paper she'd been writing the new song on and plucked out a few chords. The words started to flow from her mind to her fingers as the song took shape. What she'd written impressed her. The song sounded good. She knew that, but she still had doubts, always doubts.

She glanced over to the bottle on the counter, realizing the entire thing had disappeared when she went to pour another glass. *When did that happen? Oh well. I feel fine.* She stood and her head swam. *Wow. Maybe I'm a little drunk.* She glanced at the clock on the microwave. Eleven in the morning. She'd still have time to make Jackson's cookies before they started preparing for lunch, if she hurried.

Taking the steps quickly as she could without falling, she rushed toward the main lodge. She made it through the door without too much trouble. "Hey," she said, noticing Mandy wiping down tables and preparing the room for lunch.

"Hey."

"I got tied up cleaning and song writing on the bus. Can I still make cookies?"

"Um, I guess. Check with the cook though. She's pretty possessive about her kitchen. It might be better after lunch since we have a little more time between dinner and supper." Mandy wrinkled her nose as Samantha stepped closer.

"Oh, that's sounds like a great plan. I'm sure for me to do enough for everyone, it will take a few hours to bake them all."

"Yeah, I'm sure it will."

"I will check with the cook." Samantha slowly made her way toward the double swinging doors leading into the kitchen. Her boots seemed like they were wet or something, making it hard to lift her feet. It took two tries for her to get through the doorway into the back part of the kitchen where the cook, Millie, stood over the countertop making patties out of raw hamburger. "Hi, Millie?"

Millie turned toward her with a smile on her lips and a twinkle in her eyes. "Yes, ma'am?"

"Nina said I could talk to you about making some chocolate chips cookies for everyone, but especially Jackson."

"That boy does like his dessert."

She laughed. "So I hear."

Millie's eyebrows drew down as her lips formed a frown. Samantha wondered why the cook's demeanor changed. "It's getting too close to lunch to do it now."

"Mandy mentioned after lunch."

"I suppose it would be okay. I can be here to supervise."

"Oh, no need for that. I love to cook, and I'm great in the kitchen."

"Really?"

"Yes, ma'am."

Millie gave her a look like she didn't believe her. "I'd still feel much better if I were here with you. I can show you where everything is and so on."

"I'd much rather cook alone."

"I will check with Ms. Nina, but if that is your wish, so be it."

"Thank you. I'll be back right after lunch is over to get started. Thank you."

Samantha spun on her heels to return to the front of the dining area, wobbling slightly as she walked. *I need some coffee or something. I sure didn't realize I'd drank half a bottle. That's even a bit much for me.*

She waved at Mandy as she made her way back out toward her bus. She had about ninety minutes before lunch from what Jackson said, so she'd just get a little more work done on her song.

When she sat down again with her guitar, she plucked a few strings but it didn't sound right. Something seemed off, but she wasn't sure what. She glanced at the empty bottle again. *A little more wouldn't hurt anything. I seemed to be writing better with a little alcohol in me.* After she searched the cupboards above the sink, she found another full bottle of Jack Daniel's. With a smile on her lips, she poured half a tumbler, sat down with her guitar and the glass in her hand, trying to get comfortable.

The words and chords came much easier as she sipped the brown liquid.

Before she knew it, the lunch bell clanged, jarring her from her thoughts. She grabbed the glass on the table, downed the rest of the alcohol and then stood, setting her guitar on the couch near where she'd been sitting.

Her lips and mouth were as dry as the dessert. She needed water to wet her parched mouth and take away the pasty feeling.

She ran her fingers through her long tresses, trying to straighten out the strands to make herself presentable for lunch. Her stomach grumbled. Food sounded awfully good right now even though it really hadn't been that long since breakfast.

What had Jackson been doing all morning after his ride? She giggled as she pressed her fingertips to her lips. *I'd like to ride him into next week.* "Maybe later if I can get him to cooperate a little."

She blew out a breath, realizing she needed to brush her teeth quickly.

Several minutes later, she stumbled through the door to the main lodge, drawing all eyes to her entrance. Heat flushed her cheeks. She hated making a scene, but that's exactly what she'd done.

Jackson quickly moved to her side. "Are you okay? You didn't trip over the stoop or anything we need to check, did you?"

"No, I'm fine. I tripped over my own two feet is all."

Jackson's eyes narrowed. "Have you been drinking, Sam?"

"No. I was cleaning and writing all morning. Why?"

"You smell like alcohol."

"It's probably the rubbing alcohol I used to clean my makeup brushes."

"On your breath?"

She pushed out of his reach. "I'm not drunk, Jackson."

"I didn't say you were."

"Then stop acting like my keeper. I'm a grown adult. I can do what I want." She moved toward the serving line, not waiting for him or his family. *To hell with him and his judgmental ass.* She would get her food and eat alone. Not like she hadn't been alone before.

Once she filled her plate, she grabbed a Coke from the ice bin, before taking a seat near the door. While she lifted a forkful of potato salad to her lips, she watched Jackson retrieve his own plate of food from the serving line. She wished she knew why she liked him so much or why she was so attracted to his condescending ass.

He reached the end of the line, grabbed a soda from the bin, and then turned to walk in her direction. "Mind if I join you?"

"Yeah, but it's a free country. Sit wherever you want."

He took the bench seat across from her, setting his plate down on the table. "I'm sorry."

"You should be."

"Sam, I am not judging you."

"You already did." She continued to eat, ignoring him as much as she could with his grey gaze studying her so hard. "Will you stop looking at me like that? Why don't you eat with your family since you're all high and mighty and don't do a damned thing wrong."

"I'm sorry. I don't think I'm better than you. I've had my problems. My family has had its problems. We aren't perfect by a long shot."

"Then why are you trying to make me sound like a drunk? I only drink when I need it, which isn't very often."

"Did you drink this morning?"

"None of your business."

"If I'm supposed to be your boyfriend, I'm making it my business."

"Too fucking bad, Jackson, because what I do on my own time is my own. I don't need a keeper. If you think that's what this whole facade is about, then forget it. I'll find someone else to be my pretend boyfriend so I can find this crazy person stalking me. I don't need you."

He grabbed her hand as she tried to stand. "Yes, you do, Samantha. You need me a hell of a lot more than I need you, but that's beside the point. I'm going to help you whether you want me to or not."

She slowly slid back down in her seat. "You're right. I do need you."

"I know you do, and I'm going to help you."

"What do we do?"

"First we have to establish ourselves as a couple, which means spending a lot of time together. I do mean a lot."

She smiled. "I'm game."

"Not like that. Not yet."

She raked her fingernails down his arm in a slow caress. "What did you have in mind?"

"You can help me with chores around here. We always need someone to help shovel shit, groom the animals, toss hay bales, clean tack, and do paperwork."

She wrinkled her nose in disgust. After all, she was a big country music star. They don't shovel shit. "But what about my music?"

"Your music is on the backburner. For now, you are nothing more than the farm girl you were before you started making music."

She blew out a frustrated breath. "Okay."

"Good. We'll start this afternoon."

"Uh, I already have plans this afternoon."

"Doing what?"

"It's a surprise for you."

One eyebrow rose over his left eye. "A surprise?"

"Yes, and I'm not telling you what it is."

His hand still held her fingers. "Fine. We'll start first thing in the morning. I'm usually up at six. I'll expect you to be up by then too. Have you ridden horses?"

"I used to do rodeo when I was in high school."

"What event?"

"Barrels and pole bending."

"Good. You can go with me on guest rides. You can pull up the back of the herd as we go out over the mountains. It should give you plenty of time to think."

"Six?"

"Yep. I help Joey with the horses first thing in the morning. We have stalls to clean, groom the horses, and make sure they are fed before it's time to take the first group out in the morning after breakfast."

"Fine," she grumbled, using a few choice words under her breath for the taskmaster he'd become in the last few minutes. This wasn't going to be a very fun two weeks, and even worse, she made plans to take his ass on the road with her.

What the hell was I thinking?

As soon as they had finished their meal and put their plates in the dirty dishes bin, Jackson disappeared to do some chores around the ranch as she prepared to make his cookies. She pushed through the double doors into the kitchen to find Millie rushing about with two other helpers including Mandy, cleaning up the kitchen from lunch.

"You can use the space over there for your cookie making. I've already put out all the ingredients you'll need. Do you need a recipe?" Milly asked, with her hands on her ample hips.

The woman obviously loved to eat as much as she liked to cook from the size of her. She couldn't stand much above five foot with broad shoulders, round body and short legs. She had rounded cheeks flushed from the heat of the cook stoves in the kitchen. Her greying hair pulled back into a bun at the base of her head reminded Samantha of her grandmother.

"If you have one, that would be great. I know the ingredients but I don't remember all the exact measurements for each thing."

"I have one sitting on the counter near the flour bag for you. I've already preheated the oven. There is a cooking stone to your right you can lay them out on to bake. There is also a timer on the counter for each batch. We should be done with lunch clean up by the time you've got everything measured out and ready for the first batch."

"Thank you, Millie."

The woman wiped her hands on the apron around her middle. "You're welcome. Don't make a big mess, and make sure you clean up after yourself."

"I will."

"All right then. We'll leave you to your baking."

Samantha mixed the ingredients one by one into the bowl until it came to mixing in the chocolate chips. A few made it into her mouth before she poured the entire bag into the mixture. The dough got stiffer as she stirred.

Cooking was one of her favorite pastimes in the world. She'd always loved to cook at home, making dinners and such for her family during her childhood years. If she was upset about boys or something, she'd bake cookies, cakes, pies, rolls, muffins, cupcakes, or whatever her sweet tooth desired.

If her parents were fighting, she would make food. Whenever discord hit the family, she would cook. It was her way of dealing with the bad energy around her, she figured, but this time wasn't about baking because she was upset. Well, maybe it was a little. She didn't like fighting with Jackson. That had upset her. She could make more, but she didn't feel it was her place to take over the ranch's kitchen to assuage her nervous energy. Of course, she could always get some supplies and cook on her bus even though the kitchen wasn't very big.

Humming softly as she spooned the cookie mixture onto the baking stone Millie had provided, Samantha wondered how one of these worked. She'd never used one before, but she seen them and heard they were great for making cookies perfectly. *Hmm.* She should have asked how long to cook them for on one of these. Oh well. It should be about the same.

After she slid the stone into the preheated oven, she shut the door and put her hands on her hips. What to do for the few minutes it would take to make each batch. Maybe she should grab her guitar from the bus so she could jot down a few chords of the new song she was working on. It was really good, if she did say so herself. Being on the ranch seemed to bring out the creative side of her character.

She slipped out the double doors to head to her bus. The first batch of cookies should be ready about the time she returned as long as she didn't get sidetracked. She laughed as she imagined feeding Jackson some of the cookies. One piece at a time as the yummy morsel melted on his tongue. *What a tongue it is too.* She couldn't wait to find out how it felt on her body. It had definitely been awhile since she'd been with a man on an intimate level. Stardom had its drawbacks, definitely.

A few minutes later, she returned to the kitchen with her guitar and paper in hand. The song was almost done. It just needed something special to tweak it a hair. She wasn't quite sure what though.

The timer dinged for the cookies. When she set aside her guitar to retrieve them, she carefully put it to the right on the counter. The guitar was her favorite. It was the first one she'd bought after she got her recording contract. The white dove on the faceplate of the guitar reminded her of the one George Straight used in the movie Pure Country. She felt like him sometimes, just wanting to walk away from the whole thing without a backward glance, but she couldn't. Her family was so proud of her, she couldn't disappoint them.

With a spatula in hand, she scooped each of the cookies off the stone before putting them on the cooling plate to her left. They looked perfect, each one brown, round and gooey. As each batch took their nine minutes to cook, she wrote on the song. The soft melody and haunting chords reminded her she needed someone in her life, someone to help her with this crazy business, someone to love her for who she was, not the money she could provide for him.

So far she didn't think she'd found him, but she hadn't given Jackson a chance to prove himself yet. He seemed like a great guy with a fantastic family. They certainly didn't need her money to provide for the ranch. It looked to be a thriving business for the family with the cattle they raised, the guests they provided for, and the overall atmosphere of the ranch itself. It felt like home.

"I smell cookies."

She hopped off the barstool she'd been using to sit on. "You weren't supposed to come in here."

"How could I not. I smelled my favorite cookies. I needed to find out who loved me enough to make them today."

"Well, I don't know about love you, but I wanted to apologize for my behavior earlier so I asked the cook if I could take over the kitchen to make you chocolate chip cookies." He moved close enough she could almost drown in the grey of his eyes. When he leaned in, licking the corner of her mouth, she almost lost the ability to stand.

His breath warmed the side of her face as he skimmed his tongue from her mouth to her ear. "You had some chocolate on the corner of your mouth."

She cleared her throat nervously. "I, um." The timer dinged as she exhaled forcible. "I need to get the next batch out of the oven," she whispered. She reluctantly stepped back to turn toward the oven. With the oven mitt on her hand, she reached inside to grab the sheet and pulled them out. "Have you been a good boy?"

"Of course."

"Then I'll let you have a warm one, just one though, and only if you do something for me."

"Anything for a cookie."

"Kiss me."

Chapter Six

Jackson's stomach flip-flopped at her whispered words. "Kiss you?" He'd wanted to do nothing more than kiss the daylights out of her since he'd met her yesterday. "I think I can handle such a small task, I mean for a warm cookie and all."

He took her by the arm, slowly turning her to face him. He framed her face with his hands. The wisps of hair caressing her cheek tickled his fingers as he slipped his hands into the hair at her temples. Her head firmly in his grasp, he tipped it back, and leaned in. He stopped a hairsbreadth away from her lips to look into the blue of her gaze. Did she want him as much as he wanted her? "Do you want me?"

"Hell yeah." Her breath whispered over his lips.

He frowned. He could still smell the alcohol mixed with toothpaste. Jacob used to be the king of masking the scent. *Benefit of the doubt is only fair.* Besides, he wanted to kiss her more than anything on this earth.

The first moment their lips touched, he could feel the heat from her mouth. She parted her lips and her tongue flicked out, licking the seam of his lips to encourage him to spar with her. He stepped closer. He needed to feel her body against his, brushing his, touching his. His dick sprang to life as he opened his mouth, drawing her deeper into the experience of their first kiss. He could drown in this experience.

Her hands wandered over his back, up and down, around to his sides where they rested on his hips. The touch of her fingers on his waist drew him further into their embrace. The experience of her mouth on his burst through his resistance to be careful with her. He couldn't help it. After all, she was Samantha Harris, the one woman he thought he'd never have.

The double doors banged against the counter. "Oh, excuse me."

He slowly lifted his head, kissing her on the nose, and then stepped back. "No problem."

"I was, uh, just finishing up the cookies. I have about one more batch to go."

"I needed to get supper started," Millie said as she stepped into the room. "Jackson, are you helping our guest make cookies?"

He swiped one of the warm ones and plopped it into his mouth. "Of course."

"I can tell." Millie moved to the huge refrigerator in the corner and began pulling out potatoes to peel. "If you really want to help, I could use a set of hands on these potatoes?"

"I, uh, have some stalls to clean."

Millie smiled as she turned to snap him with a dishtowel. "I'm sure you do."

"Ouch!" He leaned in a kissed her on the cheek. "I love you, Millie."

"I'm sure you do. Just like your brothers."

Samantha put the last batch of cookie dough into the oven. "I'll come out to help you as soon as these are done."

"Have you been writing?" he asked, noticing her guitar on the counter and the paper next to it.

"Yes, some."

"You'll have to play it for me later."

"It's not finished."

"Just a few chords. I would love to hear it."

She looked down at the tips of her boots as red rushed into her cheeks. "Maybe. We'll see."

He gave her another quick kiss on the lips before he turned on his heels and headed for the door. "I'll be in the barn."

The doors banged against the wall in the dining room as he left.

He whistled softly as he made his way out to the big structure in the distance. He loved the smell of hay and horses. Something about the scents soothed his soul. Of course, being raised on a ranch probably had something to do with it.

The cooler temperature of the barn caressed his bare forearms as he stepped inside and grabbed the shovel from the corner to the left where they kept all the shovels, rakes, wheelbarrow, and so forth for cleaning the stalls. Country music from the radio played softly in the background. He recognized that voice. The song was Samantha's newest release called Country Boy. It was one of his favorites.

The hard physical labor would do him good, help get the testosterone out of his system from kissing Samantha. Damn, she had soft lips. He hadn't really had the chance to enjoy the one she bestowed on him when they were on stage together so this one was awesome in its own right. She definitely knew how to kiss.

As he took the wheelbarrow and shovel to the first stall, his thoughts drifted to what her experience with men might be. She seemed almost shy in some circumstances, but in others, she knew how to please a man. That wasn't something one typically asked a girl though. He wasn't stupid enough to bring up the subject with her either.

Scoop after scoop of horse shit made it into the wheelbarrow as he worked silently to rid himself of the boner he sported. The physical work didn't seem to be doing much since all he had to do was remember the feel of her lips on his and it came back with a vengeance.

"Jackson?"

"In here."

A moment later, the girl stood in the doorway of the stall he was working on. "Where's another shovel?"

"Near the door to the right as you are facing outside."

"Be right back."

"Are you sure you want to do this? Isn't it hard on your hands?"

"Like playing the guitar isn't? I have calluses on my calluses."

He laughed. "I guess so. I hadn't really thought about it, but yeah, guitar strings are hard on the fingers."

"Have you ever played?"

"I've dinked around some. I can play a little."

"I'll give you the sheet music for one of my songs. We can play together."

"I'm not good enough to play with you."

"Jackson, I'm self-taught on the guitar just enough to write. I don't play on stage for a reason. That's the band's job."

"Oh, right."

She stood with another shovel and wheelbarrow at the opening to the stall. "Where to, captain?"

"The stall next to this one needs to be done."

"I'm on it."

They worked in silence for several minutes before she said, "Jackson?"

"Yeah."

"How many women have you been with?"

Oh, we are going there, are we? "A few."

"Like how many?"

"Probably fifteen. Why?"

"I'm just wondering how experienced you are in comparison to me."

"How many guys have you been with?"

"Two."

"Really?"

"Yep. It's hard being on the road all the time. I never know who is around me to be with me or to latch onto the money they think is there."

"I can imagine."

"It's very frustrating."

They worked for a few more minutes. "Have you had a steady boyfriend at all?"

"In high school, but not since I started touring. I have to be so careful."

"I bet."

"How about you? Any girl broke your heart?"

"Nope. I've had a couple of girls I've been with for a few months, but never anyone seriously."

"I don't understand why. You are a cute guy, rugged, probably great in bed, very adventurous to be okay with going on the road with me, what's the problem?"

"I haven't found anyone I wanted to be around for a long period of time, I guess." He shrugged as he dug into the pile of manure in the stall.

"You do realize we will have sex before this is all said and done, right?"

"We will?"

"Yes."

"You're sure."

"Yep."

"How can you tell?"

"Because the kiss in the kitchen almost made me want to fuck you right there on the counter. Good thing we didn't. I'm sure Millie would have been completely embarrassed to find us in a precarious situation like that."

He could hear the shovel making contact with the ground as she worked. She never missed a beat, even with the sexy conversation they were having.

She knew they would have sex, huh? Good thing he was completely on board with the idea. He almost wished they could sneak up to the loft to fuck like bunnies right now, but he kind of wanted their first time to be in a bed with soft sheets and fluffy pillows. "I'm sure she's seen a lot of things over the years in the main lodge. After all, six out of nine of us are paired up. It's hard for some of them to get alone time anywhere on this place."

"I'm sure."

"Do you want to see a bit more of the barn?"

"Of course. It's a great structure. I don't think I've seen one this big in a long time. Is there a big loft?"

"Yep and it's seen a lot of action too."

"What hasn't on this ranch?"

He laughed. "Very true."

"I'm almost done with this stall. Are there shavings to put down?"

"Yeah. There is a huge pile outside to the right. The pile farther back is for the manure."

"Got it." She moved past him with the wheelbarrow as he finished the stall he'd been working on.

He'd been distracted. That had to be the reason she finished before he did or there was less shit in the stall she'd been working in. It couldn't be because she scooped the whole time they talked while he leaned on the handle of the shovel, right?

She returned to the barn as he was wheeling his own load outside. "I can do another one if you want? I'm sure there are tons more to do. You guys have a lot of horses."

"Sure, if you want or we can get back to it after we tour the barn."

"It's big, but I don't think it will take very long."

"It depends on how much you distract me."

"Me?"

"Yep. You are definitely a big distraction with those lips, that body, and those hands."

"My hands. How do you figure?"

"When you touch me, it makes everything go haywire."

"Oh, I like that. I'm glad I'm not alone then because you kind of make my body do some weird tingling things too."

"Oh yeah?"

"Yes, sir."

"I like the sound of that."

"Do you now?"

"Hmm. Let me get rid of this and we'll see where this goes when I get back."

"Hurry."

"I will."

He practically ran around the backside of the barn to dump the load of shit into the pile, load up his wheelbarrow with shavings and run back.

She hadn't moved, but the smile on her lips told him she knew exactly what she was doing to him as she teased him mercilessly with her body, lips, and eyes. *Lord, I want her bad.* A tight pair of jeans encased her long legs. She wore a little tank top with spaghetti straps across her shoulders, leaving them open for his mouth. The boots on her feet looked fairly new, although he knew she probably only had her dress boots to wear so they all were new. Her hair was back in a braid now, which she must have done after she finished the cookies to keep it out of her face while she shoveled.

He hope she wasn't cold wearing that skimpy little top, but he knew exactly how to warm her up. His fingers tingled with the need to touch her, run them through her hair, skim them over her body, and find each and every spot that made her sigh. "Put the shovel down for now. I want to show you the tack room."

She leaned the shovel on the wall to her right. "I love the smell of leather."

"Me too." He left his wheelbarrow and shovel near the next stall. "Come on. We'll see if no one is in there."

"Ever fucked in the tack room?"

"I haven't."

"Want to?"

"Samantha."

"What?"

"I kind of want our first time to be in a bed."

She gave him a quick kiss on the mouth. "Such a traditionalist. You are kind of an old fashioned guy, huh."

"Yeah, I would say so."

"I could give you a blow job."

His body went flush with excitement. "I wouldn't say no."

"All right, then." She grabbed his hand and started pulling him toward the doors. "Let's find the tack room."

"Which one?"

"There is more than one?"

"Yeah, let's see the one in the back of the barn first. It's usually free of traffic as long as Joshua isn't in there working on his saddles and stuff."

"We won't be disturbed?"

"I can't guarantee that."

"Sounds like fun."

They reversed direction toward the dim rear of the barn where a large door stood closed. Jackson worked the lock on the door before swinging it open. The scent of leather met his nose when he inhaled a deep breath. He got a hard-on just thinking about fucking her in the tack room. Maybe he would change his mind about it, but then again, he'd been in a constant state of hard since their kiss in the kitchen. If she went down on him? *Holy hell.* He would be in heaven and probably blow his load in record time.

When he walked inside and turned around, she pulled the door shut, and flipped the latch before she turned around to give him the sexiest smile he'd ever seen on a woman. She sauntered toward him as he backed up to find the stool sitting in the corner. With a toss of her braid, she moved in closer.

She parted her lips as she leaned in toward him. The clink of his belt buckle sounded loud in the quiet room. She slowly unzipped his jeans before grabbing his hard cock in her hand as she pulled him free. "Holy shit. You have a Prince Albert?"

"Yeah."

"Wow. I've never seen one. Can I touch it?" she asked, her hand hovering over the tip of his cock.

"Of course." He wanted her touching him any way he could get her. Hand, mouth, breasts, he didn't care and if she wanted to play with the ball in his cock, so be it. He'd love to have her tongue wrapped around the head right now, but her fascination with his piercing was doing it for him at the moment.

"Did it hurt when they pierced through there?"

"A little."

"How does it feel having sex?"

"You'll find out soon enough."

Her hand moved over his cockhead, drawing a deep moan from his mouth.

"You're a big guy."

"Thanks."

"But I think I can take you." She stroked his cock up and down. "I can't wait to see what your piercing feels like in my pussy."

"Me either." He wrapped his hand around the back of her head. "But right now, I want your mouth on me."

"My pleasure, cowboy." She dropped to her knees and slowly licked his cock like an ice cream cone. "We need these jeans off."

"Down, just down. In case I have to pull them up quickly."

"Whatever. I want access to those nuggets waiting for me below. I want to suck them, lick them, and roll them in my mouth."

"You are such a dirty girl for only having been with two guys." He shoved his jeans off his hip so they rested around his knees.

"They taught me a lot about pleasing a man."

"Thank God," he growled low in his throat as she took the head of his cock into her mouth.

She flicked the piercing with her tongue several times. "This is fun."

"Suck. God, please suck."

She went down on his cock, taking almost the whole thing in her mouth. The head of his dick bumped the back of her throat as she breathed through her nose to accommodate his size. He knew most women gagged, but she was good, very good. Her fingers caressed his balls, dragging a groan from deep in his throat as he leaned back against the wall.

While she worked his cock with her tongue and his balls with her fingers, he tried to put his mind on something, anything that would forestall the explosion of cum from his dick into her waiting mouth. Her movements tore his concentration to shreds in a matter of minutes.

"I'm going to come."

"Please do." She licked one side, then the other before working her mouth over the end of his cock again.

She wanted him to come in her mouth, he would accommodate her wishes. His balls drew up taut and aching toward his groin. A moan surfaced to his lips while he shot his load down her throat in long spurts of cum.

As his cock softened, she slowly licked him clean before stuffing him back in his pants. "Thank you."

"For what?"

"For the blow job. It was magnificent."

She smiled as one perfectly arched eyebrow rose over her right eye. "I'm glad you liked it."

A knock sounded on the door. "Jackson?" It was Jeff.

"Yeah?"

"I thought you were cleaning stalls?"

"We were. I'm showing Samantha the tack room."

"Uh, okay."

"Did you need something?"

"Nope. Carry on."

"Wow. Does that happen a lot?"

"Yeah. I told you this barn gets a lot of use."

"The tack room too?"

"Yes, ma'am. I'm sure we've all used this room a time or two over the years."

Her bottom lip stuck out in a pout. "You mean I'm not the first girl to blow you in the tack room?"

"Sorry, but no. You were the best though, so far."

Indignation rushed across her features, pulling the corners of her mouth down in a frown. "So far?"

"Well, you never know where we are going, Samantha. I can't say you'll be the last to have her way with me in the barn either, just like I can't say I'm the last guy who will fuck you in the bed on your bus."

Her mouth screwed up in a twisted kind of grin. "True."

"See."

"Okay. I'll forgive you for your words."

He rolled his eyes as he rebuckled his belt. "We should get back to work."

"Fuck and run. I see how you are."

"I told you. I want our first actual sex session to be in a bed. Mine, yours or otherwise wouldn't bother me."

She leaned in and brought their mouths together in a deep kiss. "I want you to fuck me every way you can think of."

"I want that too."

"It's a date. In my room later tonight?"

"I'll be there."

"Good." She kissed him again. "I can't wait."

"Me either."

Chapter Seven

Blackness surrounded the cabin as Jackson made his way to the one Samantha was occupying with stealthy feet so he could keep their rendezvous secret from his family. He didn't want them all to know they were having sex, though they probably already figured as much.

The light burned in the window of her cabin when he stepped up on the porch to knock. She didn't give him the chance. The door flung open. She grabbed his hand and dragged him inside the room before slamming the door shut behind him. "I'm glad you're here," she said breathlessly. "I've been imagining this all afternoon."

"You too?"

"Yeah. Are you excited?" She glanced down at his straining cock. "I guess you are."

"I've been replaying our little rendezvous over and over in my mind since you sucked me off in the barn."

She grabbed for his belt. "I can't wait to get you out of these pants."

"You say the sexiest things."

He took ahold of her top at the edges near her stomach so he could lift it over her head and toss it to the side. He wanted to see her, all of her. When her breasts were free from the confines of her top, he stopped to admire the round globes with their dusky pink nipples. They were perfect, just like her. "Beautiful."

With both hands, he took the flesh in his palms and rubbed his fingers over her already hard nipples. She leaned into his touch, begging for more with her gaze. "Lick them."

"Oh, I plan to lick, suck, and anything else I can think of to do to them. Maybe even fuck them." He walked her backward until the backs of her knees hit the bed and she fell to the mattress. Her blonde hair encircled her head like a halo. He knew she was an angel when she sang, but man, he hadn't figured she'd fallen from heaven to torture him like this. He unbuttoned her jeans at the waist, and then pulled them along with her skimpy little thong, down her legs, leaving her naked on the bed. "You are gorgeous."

"Thanks, but I'd really like it if you wouldn't stare."

"I can't help looking at you. Realizing I'm going to get to make love to this beautiful woman has me almost dizzy with excitement."

"You're making me blush."

"Red looks good on you." He ran his hands from her feet, up her calves, and over her thighs until he reached the juncture where her treasures lie. "I'm going to eat you until you scream my name."

"Oh, God, yes." She spread her thighs laying everything open to his gaze.

Her pussy was magnificent as well. She didn't go completely bare but she only left a small thatch of hair on her pussy. The rest had been shaved clean. The pink petals of her labia glistened with juices, waiting for the first thrust of his hips. He needed to taste her first though. He'd been dreaming about this for a long time.

With both hands under her butt, he pulled her to the edge of the bed, went down on his knees, and breathed in her scent. Peaches and cream if he knew anything. She smelled wonderful. He couldn't wait to taste her.

Her hips bucked at the touch of his tongue against her outer lips. The moment he grazed her clit, she moaned, tossing her head from side to side, relishing in the sensations he gave her. He wanted to bombard her with everything he knew how to do. This was the ultimate test of his manhood. Could he please his perfect woman?

"Please."

He loved when she pleaded. The thought of her begging him several times to let her come, almost had him coming in his own pants before he had a chance to fuck her. That wouldn't do. He wanted to be inside her more than his next breath. The tip of his tongue touched her clit again, moving the little button of nerve endings back and forth until she almost sobbed in her need. Her hands clutched at the bed covering.

"God, Jackson. Please. Make me come. I'm dying here." He pushed two fingers into her pussy, bringing her hips off the bed. "Yes."

Her pussy grasped his fingers, sucking on the digits, trying desperately to keep them inside her. She was tight, so tight.

He could feel her quiver around his fingers as he continued his assault on her clit and finger fucking her until she exploded with her climax in a rush of liquid over his hand.

"Jackson!"

He brought her down slowly with soft licks and easy strokes. Her breathing slowed to almost normal.

"God, that was fantastic."

"I'm glad you enjoyed it."

"I can't wait for the rest."

He sat back on his haunches. "I have to ask. Are you on the pill?"

She leaned up on her elbows. "Yes. I take it for my periods even though I haven't been sexually active in quite a while."

"I'll still use a condom since we don't know each other very well."

"I haven't been with anyone in months."

"Me either, but I'd rather be safe than sorry later on for either of us."

"I'm okay with you going bare."

"I'm not. Not that I don't want to experience everything with you, but I'd feel better if I wore one."

"Whichever is good for you. I don't want to ruin the mood because, cowboy, I'm ready for you to be as deep as you can be."

"Hmm." He looked around the room debating on how he wanted to do this to make it good for her, missionary on the bed, modified cowgirl, anal? Of course he didn't know if she'd ever had anal before so that one was probably out for now, but he could get real creative from behind. "Okay, roll on your stomach."

Her eyes lit up as she bit her lip and slowly rolled onto her stomach. "What do you have in mind?"

"I'm going to take you from behind so I can play while I fuck you."

She glanced over her shoulder. "You could play anyway, cowboy. I like your hands on different body parts."

"Yeah, but this way I have your braid to hold onto."

"Ride 'em cowboy."

"Yee haw!"

She spread her legs, giving him a great view of her glistening pussy and her pert little asshole. He so wanted to take her there. Someday, he hoped to if they were together long enough. Up on his feet, he was a little tall to get to her readily, so he shoved two pillows under her hips to bring her assets a little closer to his height.

"There we go."

"Hurry. I'm dying here."

He scraped his finger through her folds before slowly penetrating her with two fingers. Damn, she was wet and ready for his cock. A shiver rolled through him at the sight of her juices on his fingers. Her taste had been like an aphrodisiac to his mouth when she'd come all over his face, now he wanted to see the same liquid coating his cock.

He grabbed for his pants on the floor beside him, reached into his wallet, and pulled out a condom. After he rolled the slippery latex down on his cock, he positioned himself at her opening and slowly pushed inside her. Man, she was tight. Obviously, she hadn't been with anyone in quite a while. It was like slipping his hand into a mink lined glove. Goose bumps broke out on his skin.

She wiggled her hips.

He gritted his teeth trying to hold back the orgasm hovering on the edges of his sanity. He couldn't come yet. *Train wrecks. Lots of train wrecks. Gory images should help me concentrate.*

"Jackson," she pleaded, pushing her cute little ass back, impaling her pussy further on his cock.

"Easy. You feel so fucking fantastic, I won't be able to hold back if you move."

She groaned as he slipped farther inside her. "God, that piercing feels awesome scraping along my vagina. Holy crap."

Once he managed to get his cock as deep as he could, he closed his eyes and bit his lip. Pain would keep him focused, right? It had to, otherwise he would blow his load in nothing flat. Her pussy felt so good, he couldn't stand the feelings bombarding his body.

He pulled back, and then shoved in again.

Her high-pitched moan bounced off the walls. "Fuck. Do that again."

The idea of hitting her G spot beckoned as he pulled out. Pushing in with a snap of his hips, he hit the elusive little spot behind her pelvic bone.

"Oh my God. What the hell did you hit with that ball? That's fantastic."

"Your G spot."

"Holy hell, that's fabulous. I've never had anyone hit it before." Her whole body broke out in one big shiver. "Keep it up, cowboy, and I'll be coming soon."

"Good because I don't know how long I can last. Your pussy feels amazing."

"Fuck me hard, Jackson. Give me everything you got."

He didn't need any more encouragement as he began rocking against her ass, shoving his cock so deep inside her. Within minutes, they were both hovering on the edges of climax. He grasped her braid in his hand and wrapped the hair around his fist so he could pull her head back.

"Hell yeah."

Their mutual climax broke over them like a wave breaking against a jetty's ragged rocks, throwing water against the peaks in a crashing sound loud enough to hurt your ears.

Cum trickled down between them as she squirted around his full cock. Her responsiveness didn't surprise him. She seemed the type to give everything to whatever she was doing at the time and having sex seemed to be no different.

As their bodies cooled and his cock softened, he leaned in to bite her on the shoulder, then sucked her delicate white skin into his mouth, leaving a small purple mark on her back. At least for now, she was his.

* * * *

She curled into his body like she'd been made to be there. His chest made a great pillow as she sifted her fingers through the hair curling around his nipples. The small ring on his right nipple tantalized her, so she flicked it with her fingernail.

"Having fun?"

"Yes. I've never been with a man who has piercings before."

"You don't mind them, do you?"

"Hell no!" She propped herself up on her elbow so she could look him in the face. "I think they are sexier than anything and the tat running from your shoulder to your forearm is cool. You are just a very surprising man, is all. I would never expect a downhome country boy like you to have piercings and tats." She ran her hand from nipple to nipple and then down his abdomen, tracing each ridge with her fingertips. When she curled her fingers around his cock, he started getting hard in her hand. "Again?"

"Sure."

"Maybe this time won't be quite so fast."

"Are you complaining? You had two orgasms that I counted, correct me if I'm wrong."

"I'm selfish. I want more of this magnificent body."

She scooted down on the bed to position herself between his legs. The piercing in his cock fascinated her as she ran her tongue around the ball on the tip. The smaller one on the underside of his cockhead slid along her tongue as she took the head of his cock in her mouth. Both balls together had felt fantastic inside her pussy. The one on the head scraped along her G spot while the other one rubbed along her vagina in the most amazing dance of pleasure her nerve endings had ever experienced. Anticipation of having him inside her again had her pussy soaking wet.

As she slowly slid her tongue up and down the length of his cock, she could make out the faint trace of leather on his skin from his time in the saddle today. God, it turned her on to have such a sexy scent on him. The smell just did something inside her whenever she had a chance to be around it for any length of time.

His deep moan brought her thoughts back to the man. He was perfect in every way. Strong, loyal, faithful, sexy, and about the best thing she'd ever had walk into her life. She wanted to keep him for a good long while, but convincing him to be her boy toy might be a little difficult since he was such a strong-minded individual. Money usually worked well in situations like this. Yeah, she'd offer him a sum he couldn't refuse to stay with her. They hadn't really worked out the details of him going on the road with her, but now that they were having sex, surely he would want to stay with her, right?

"You're killing me, darlin'."

"I'm trying, cowboy."

"You have such a sexy mouth."

"Glad you like it."

"Both here," he touched his lips, "and there." His hips pushed up toward her as he moaned deep in his chest.

She had him right where she wanted him, ready to beg for an orgasm. "Jackson?"

"Yeah?"

"You do have another condom, right?"

"Yes, in my pants."

"Thank God." She grabbed his jeans from the floor, pulled the condom out of the front right pocket, opened it with her teeth, and then slowly rolled it down his length.

By the time she had him gloved, he was groaning, pulling her up his chest. She straddled his hips and positioned his cock, so she could do a slow glide down its thick length.

"Ride me, cowgirl."

"My pleasure, babe."

By the time she had him fully inside her, she'd lost her train of thought. The damned little ball on the tip of his dick rubbed her special little spot so enticingly she couldn't hold back the moan escaping her lips. Bracing herself on his chest, Samantha leisurely moved up and down his cock and shivered from head to her toes. Each thrust of his hips drove the ball right against her spot, driving her absolutely crazy with need.

"You know what?"

"What?" she asked, her concentration ebbing and flowing with the thrust of his hips.

"You feel amazing."

"You do too."

He braced his feet on the bed, giving him more leverage to thrust his hips up, shoving his cock deeper than the time before. She felt like she was about to implode from everything bombarding her.

When he lowered his legs again, she leaned back with her hands on his thighs and thrust her pussy forward. The little ball changed positions inside her body, giving her a whole new myriad of sensations to handle. She whimpered with need. She wanted to come so badly, she ached with it.

"Jackson, please."

"Tell me what you want."

"I don't know. God, help me."

He had one hand on her right hip as the other reached down between her legs to rub her clit. After a minute, he sucked his finger into his mouth, wetting the callused surfaced just enough so it would slide over the hard little nub.

Yes, that's it, right there.

Desire tightened her abdomen as she continued to ride his cock, gyrating and wiggling until she got just the right angle. With his finger rubbing her clit, she exploded in a burst of desire so hot, she felt scorched from the inside out.

"Jackson!"

Cum spilled over his cock, wetting both of them.

"Wow, you're a wet one, lady."

Her breath came out in small little pants as she tried to bring her breathing back to normal. "You make me that way." His hips began a slow rhythm of thrusting. "Shit, you didn't come yet?"

"Nope."

"I'm sorry. Want to switch positions or something?"

"I'm good with this, but lean over my chest. I'll thrust from below."

"Okay." She splayed herself over his chest, burying her nose in his neck. He smelled good enough to eat.

He kneaded her ass with his hands as he slowly built his thrust to where he pounded into her body in a steady rhythm. Her own need began to build again as he rammed himself inside her, filling her to capacity. The fullness of having him there, made her feel whole.

When she climaxed again, it shocked her. It wasn't the explosive climax of earlier, but a small, pleasant experience as she milked his cock while he enjoyed his own orgasm. She didn't have to have a mind-blowing orgasm every time, right? The small ones were great in their own way.

As she lay on his chest, breathing in his scent, she realized she liked him…a lot, more than anyone she'd ever been with before. That was saying a whole bunch because she was around men all the time who wanted her attention.

Now she just had to figure out how to keep his attention, keep him in her bed and hogtie him to her life for a good long while.

"What was it you wanted to ask me before things got moving along in other directions?"

She sat up on his chest and leaned on her elbow. "Well, I was thinking. We hadn't discussed payment for you being on the road with me while we figure out who this stalker is."

"Payment?"

"Yeah. I mean you'll be riding with me on the bus, living with me basically, having sex with me on a regular basis I would guess, so we need to discuss payment."

"What the fuck?" He sat up to abruptly, she fell off to the side of him on the bed before he sprang to his feet, turning to face her. "You can seriously mean to pay me for my services?"

"Well, yeah. I mean I wouldn't expect you to do all it for free."

"Do you hear yourself?"

"What?"

"I'm not a fucking prostitute, Samantha."

"I didn't say you were."

"Well, you sure as hell are acting like I'm one wanting to pay me for services rendered. What? Are you going to start sticking dollar bills in my underwear now?"

"Seriously, Jackson, this is nuts."

"No it's not. I didn't make love to you so you could pay me. I don't need nor do I want your money."

"Everyone wants money."

"I have my own, thank you very much. I don't need yours."

"But I have way more than I could ever spend. I want to give you some."

He threw up his hands and dropped them to his sides in frustration. Carefully, he pulled the condom off his cock before tossing it into the trashcan near the bed.

"Where are you going?"

"Back to my room. Obviously, you have some weird sense of something, I'm not sure what. Entitlement maybe? Who the hell have you been hanging around anyway? If all of your so-called friends want money from you, you need new friends. Friends don't act like that and lovers don't want your money either unless that's all they're in it for. I'm not."

"What are you in this for, Jackson?" she asked, sitting up on the side of the bed. Hurt clouded her mind. She'd apparently done something wrong and she needed to figure out how to fix the situation.

"All I wanted was to spend time with you, get to know you. Samantha Harris the Iowa farm girl, not Samantha Harris the big country star."

"Don't go. I'm sorry. I didn't mean to insult you."

"You did."

"I said I'm sorry. What more do you want?"

"I think I need some space. I just don't want to be around you right now."

"Please, don't leave."

He shoved his legs into his jeans before throwing his T-shirt over his head. "I'm sorry, Sam."

She drew her legs up to her chest, holding in the hurt. She would cry when he walked out, but she wouldn't while he was there. Giving a man that kind of power over you was a bad thing, something she wouldn't think about right now. She wouldn't give him that power.

When he finally pulled open the door to leave, he glanced back over his shoulder. "I'll see you tomorrow. We can talk after I've had time to think."

"I'm sorry," she whispered, tears choking her words as the door slowly closed behind him.

Chapter Eight

After spending a restless night flopping from one side of the bed to the other, Jackson finally got up at daybreak to start his chores. *Why the hell did she do that? Way to make me feel like a loser.*

He grabbed his jeans out of the dresser to slip them over his hips. Today should be an interesting day. He couldn't wait to see what Samantha came up with. She really had a weird sense of right or wrong. He shook his head before pulling a clean T-shirt over his head. By the time he'd stomped his feet into his boots, he was ready to face whatever the day brought, including Samantha Harris.

When he walked past her cabin, he hesitated, not sure whether he should try to talk to her this morning. He glanced at his watch. Six in the morning. Too early even though she was going to get up and do some chores with him, he figured he'd let her sleep. He'd catch her at breakfast maybe and see if they could work out the crazy thought process she had. Right now, he needed coffee.

As he approached the main lodge, the heavy wooden door opened and then closed without anyone going in or out. The ghost of the old cowboy was active this morning apparently.

Jackson pushed open the door and headed for the coffee urn to the left side. Luckily, someone was already up and had started it. He needed the fortification after his rough night.

Once he'd poured a cup, he doctored it with the normal offerings before heading into the main lodge area where the three big leather couches, tables, pool table and small gift shop sat. In here, a couple of weddings had taken place and many Christmases were celebrated, along with lots of birthday parties over the years.

He wandered outside to the front porch, taking a seat in the rocker to the right of the door. What the hell was he going to do about Samantha? Did she really think paying him was the way to get him to stay with her? Did she have no self-esteem or did she really think he was the type of guy she could pay off?

He sipped his coffee as rain began to drizzle off the roof. Great. What a shitty day this turned out to be.

For over two hours, he turned the situation with her over in his brain until his head began to hurt. *Maybe talking to Mom will shed some light on the subject, but then if I do that, she'll have to be in on the ruse.*

The door opened beside him, revealing the woman he thought hung the moon.

"Hey, son."

"Hey, Mom."

"You look lost in thought."

"I am kind of."

"Did you have a fight with Samantha?"

"Sort of."

"Do you want to talk about it?"

"If I do, I'm going to have to let you in on a secret."

"You know I can keep one if you need me to."

"I know." He set his empty coffee cup on the table next to his chair. "Sam and I aren't really a couple."

"Could have fooled me."

"I know and that was the plan. She has someone stalking her. She asked me to pretend to be her boyfriend for the next several months or until we can catch whoever is doing this."

"Okay." She took a drink of her own coffee. "I understand."

"Well, things kind of changed last night."

"Oh?"

"Yeah. We had sex."

"I would think it kind of means the ruse of a relationship is no longer a ruse."

"You know it takes more than sex to make a relationship."

"Very true. Do you think of your situation as a relationship?"

"I'm not sure."

"Tell me the rest. What did you fight over?"

"She basically wants to pay me for pretending to be her boyfriend, which includes us having sex on a regular basis."

"Hmm."

"Yeah. I totally feel like a prostitute here. She wants to pay me for sex."

"No. She wants to pay you for pretending to be her boyfriend."

"Which includes having sex."

"That's a benefit of the situation, I'm assuming."

"I'm sure it would be."

She took another sip of her coffee. "Think of it this way, Jackson. She's a young woman surrounded by people who want to be near her for whatever reason. They want her attention. They want her money. They want her fame. She doesn't know who to trust. She obviously trusts you to some extent, but she's not used to having someone do something for her just because they want to help. It is who you are."

"I do want to help her."

"Then make her understand that, honey. Having someone around without an agenda is new to her."

"Do you really think talking to her would fix the situation?"

"Yes."

The bell clanged for breakfast. They both stood and he leaned in to kiss his mom on the cheek. "Thanks, Mom. You always know what to say."

"I'm a listener. She's a complicated young lady, but one who, I think, will give you a good run for your money if you let her."

"Stop matchmaking. I don't want a long-term relationship with her. Helping her doesn't require that."

"You never know where things might lead, though, Jackson."

"I know, but I certainly am not looking for it right now."

"You should be. You aren't getting any younger, mister." She pushed her still coal black hair over her shoulder. "Neither am I."

"You look fabulous, Mom, and you know it. You don't look a day over thirty-five."

She pushed against his shoulder. "Get out. I certainly do not look thirty-five, forty-five maybe."

They laughed as he pushed open the door to the lodge to head in for breakfast. When they reached the dining room, he glanced around, but didn't see Samantha. *Oh well. Maybe she slept in this morning.* She certainly deserved some relaxation and he'd do everything he could do give it to her.

Plus, he had chores to do to keep him occupied today. They were bringing some of the cattle down from the north pasture to get them ready to take to market. It was their last run before spring. He could be riding herd all day even though they would be back in for lunch and then back out again afterward.

After breakfast, he managed to sneak a few leftover chocolate chip cookies before he headed to the barn to saddle his horse. The rain would put a hamper on their work, but rain or shine didn't matter, work needed to be done anyway.

He pulled his hat low on his forehead before dashing across the yard, dodging as many raindrops as he possibly could. His mad dash into the shaded interior of the barn stopped the moment he crossed through the double doorway. His horse stood in the stall three down from the end. The big bay gelding was his special friend. He'd owned the horse since he was twelve and bought it himself with the money he'd saved shoveling out stalls for the neighbors one summer. Hot, backbreaking work, but he was proud to say he owned one of the best cutting horses in the county.

"Hey, boy."

The horse knickered softly as Jackson approached to stroke his nose.

"We have a lot of work to do today." The horse nudged his shoulder. "Let me get your tack and we'll get a move on."

A few minutes later, found him mounting his horse, tapping him with his booted heels and making their way out of the barn. *Today is going to suck donkey balls if this rain doesn't stop.* He glanced back at Samantha's cabin, noting the curtains still pulled tightly shut and shrugged. She'd missed breakfast, but she probably had stuff on her bus she could eat if she got up between now and lunch. She's a big girl, he figured she could handle missing breakfast.

He met his brothers at the back of the corral where they all lined up to head out to the pasture. It would be a long day at this rate.

When he returned right before lunch, he noticed the curtains still drawn shut on Samantha's cabin. He wondered if she'd make an appearance for the noon meal. Maybe she was avoiding him after their blowup last night. She might still be pissed at him, although her face last night said she was more hurt than pissed. If she didn't show for lunch, he would get the spare key and check on her. He was getting a bit worried about her.

The bell clanged to signal lunch as he tied his horse to the hitching post inside the barn with some water and feed. The horse could rest out of the weather while he ate.

As the meal progressed without a sign of Samantha, the worry became more prominent. He hadn't left that late the night before.

Everything is all right. It has to be.

When the meal concluded and she never arrived, he found his mom in her office. "Mom, can I have the key to Samantha's cabin?"

"Why?"

"I haven't seen her all day. She hasn't taken any meals. She doesn't have a car to go anywhere else and I've already checked her bus. She's not there. I'm worried."

"Sure, baby." Nina grabbed the key off the board on the wall. "Let me know what's up."

He took the key in his hand and quickly headed through the lodge toward the door. Trepidation surrounded his heart. Something was wrong. He knew it in his gut. When he approached the door, he decided to knock first just to make sure she wasn't sulking her day away in her cabin after their fight.

"Samantha?" He knocked several times without an answer. He leaned his ear against the door. Was that a moan? "Samantha!" He shoved the key into the lock and turned it. He called her name again as he pushed open the door. Daylight spilled into the dark room, but he could see a figure under the blankets on the bed. "Samantha?"

He walked slowly toward the bed, fearing the worst. With the toe of his boot, he kicked something glass against the wall. The room stunk like alcohol.

"Samantha, wake up."

She moaned softly, but didn't arouse.

The sheet had pulled down over her breasts revealing she was at least naked on the top as her rosy nipples peeked out from the edge. He swallowed hard when his cock jumped to life at the sight.

He touched her arm. "Samantha, wake up," he said again, shaking her slightly.

She didn't even moan this time.

The light on the lamp flicked on with a twist of his fingers. An empty bottle of Jack Daniel's lay against the wall where he'd kicked it, with another half-empty bottle sitting on the nightstand.

"How much fucking whiskey did she drink? Holy shit!" He lifted her eyelid, peering at her pupils. They were dilated and the whites of her eyes were bloodshot red. Her breathing was deep and unlabored. He shook her hard enough to wake the dead as he called her name again. She didn't stir.

He pulled out his cell phone and called 911, giving them the address to the ranch, her condition, and an idea of how much she drank. "Hurry. She's unresponsive." After he hung up, he called his mother. "Mom, she's in bad shape. I don't know how much she had to drink, but she won't wake up at all. I've called an ambulance so they can check her out."

"Okay, honey. I hope she's all right."

"I don't know, Mom. This is serious."

"Sounds like it. Are you okay?"

"I'm fine, but I'll go to the hospital with her to give them her information and whatnot as best I can."

"I'll be out there in a second so you can go on her bus to find her information. Does she have a purse there?"

He glanced around the room. "Not that I can see. It might be on the bus."

"I'll be right there."

"Thanks, Mom." He hung up his cell and moved to the side of the bed to cover her naked body.

He didn't know what else to do to help her. This drinking thing would kill her if she didn't get help, but she wouldn't until something slapped her in the face to wake her up to the facts of life. Jacob had to go through the same thing. Maybe he could talk to Samantha and help her realize her destructive behavior would be the death of her. "Lady, I wish I knew what was causing you to do this so I could help you."

Jackson could hear the sirens coming up the street about the same time his mother appeared in the doorway of the cabin.

"It sounds like the ambulance is here."

"Yeah."

"You go find her purse."

"Thanks."

"I'll tell them all I can. Still no idea how much she had?"

"No, not really. There is an empty fifth on the floor by the wall that I kicked when I came in and another half-empty bottle on the table there."

"Wow," his mom whispered.

"I know."

"Does she normally drink like this?"

"I'm beginning to wonder. We'll talk more when I've had a chance to confront her about this, but I'm betting she's got a bit of an alcohol problem.

Her behavior is very telling and reminds me a lot of Jacob before he met Paige."

"I hope we can help her."

"Me too." He walked to the door. "The ambulance is pulling up now. I'll go see if I can find her purse in the bus while they check her."

"Okay."

The paramedics hurried up the walkway with their gurney. "Where is the patient?"

"In her bed. My mother will give you the details we know. I'm going to find her personal information, if I can, so you have it."

"Thanks."

As they rushed inside to treat Samantha, Jackson ran toward the back where her bus sat parked. The door opened with ease as he pulled on the handle. *Best check her bedroom.* Yep, her purse was sitting on the bed. He grabbed it by the handles, but stopped for a moment as he thought about going through her personal things. It wasn't kosher to do that to someone. *She gave up the right to be indignant about it when she drank herself unconscious.* He opened her wallet and glanced at her driver's license with her birthdate and address. She was twenty-nine this past March, so almost thirty. He wouldn't have guessed. Her tall, willowy form was something people wished for with her long legs, lean torso, nice sized breasts and flat abdomen. Of course, he would guess she'd never had kids or anything and she probably worked out frequently to keep her shape.

Shaking his head, he shoved her wallet back into her purse. He walked down the stairs of the bus and out to the waiting ambulance just as they wheeled her out on the gurney.

"I'm coming with you guys."

"You'll have to follow since you aren't family. We can only take the patient in the ambulance."

"That's fine. I'll follow then. I have her purse with her personal information like her birthdate, age, address, and so forth."

"They'll need the information at the hospital. We are taking her into San Antonio to University Hospital."

"Great. I'll meet you there."

His stomach clenched when they loaded her into the ambulance. Worry furrowed his brow. He hoped she'd be okay. He didn't wish this kind of thing on her, but hopefully she would learn from this experience and lay off the alcohol.

Forty-five minutes later, the ambulance pulled into the emergency entrance of the hospital while he parked his truck off to the side, grabbed her purse and headed in through the double doors.

"Can I help you?"

"Yes, they just brought in my…um a friend of mine through emergency. You will need her information to register her. She's unresponsive."

"What's her name?"

"Samantha Harris."

The clerk's head jerked up at the mention of Samantha's name. "Okay."

"I have her purse here with her address and everything on it. I don't know whether she has insurance or anything like that."

The clerk clicked the mouse and began filling in Samantha's information into the computer as he read off everything he could find on her driver's license.

"Do you know her medical history?"

"No, ma'am."

"All right. Have a seat. The doctor will be out to talk to you when they have her stable."

"Thank you."

He pulled out his cell to call Jeff and have him take care of his gelding since he'd forgotten at the house. "Hey."

"How's Samantha?"

"I don't know yet. I just got here. Can you take care of Scout for me?"

"Already done, bro."

"Thanks."

"No problem. Hey, keep us updated when you hear something. She's a nice girl, but it sounds like she might have some issues."

"Yeah, I think so too. I just hope I can help her with them."

"Aren't you getting in a little deep, Jackson? You just met her."

"I know, but there is something about her that's special. I can't put my finger on it."

"Easy, cowboy. She's got a lot on her plate to be taking on."

"Thanks, brother."

"Anytime."

He hung up the phone, preparing to wait. He knew how hospitals worked, slow and slower. Waiting wasn't in his genes. Unfortunately, this was going to be a long wait and an even harder confrontation when the time came.

Over an hour later, the doctor came through the door. "Uh, is there anyone here with Samantha Harris?"

Jackson stood. "I am."

"Follow me so we can talk in private."

"No problem."

The doctor led him back through a locked door, down a long hall and into a curtained off exam room. Samantha lay on the bed clothed in a hospital gown to her neck, with a sheet to her waist. Wires and tubes stuck out everywhere. He could see the monitor above her head beeping in a steady rhythm. Her breathing seemed deep with a slight snore. Her long blonde hair framed her head in almost a halo, giving her an ethereal look.

"We can talk here. There isn't anything I'm going to tell you outside of general details."

"Okay."

"She drank too much alcohol and is bordering on the upper level of alcohol poisoning. Her blood alcohol level is toxic. We are giving her fluids to keep her hydrated, monitoring her blood sugar levels, vitamin levels, and alcohol levels. We have to make sure she doesn't have seizures. We might have to pump her stomach."

Jackson blew out a breath as he took off his hat and raked his fingers through his hair. "How does this happen?"

"She drank a lot in a short period of time. When was the last time you saw her?"

"Last night about eleven. She didn't come in for breakfast or lunch today. When I went to check on her, this is how I found her."

"Did she appear to have vomited?"

"I don't think so. I found her in bed, but there wasn't any on the bed or pillow."

"Good. We are always concerned about aspiration with this kind of thing."

"I guess you are going to put her in the hospital?"

"Yes, for a couple of days to get her alcohol level down. She won't be released until it's zero."

"Good. Can you get her some counseling?"

"Does she have a drinking problem?"

"I believe so."

"Without her consent, no. She has to ask for help."

"Damn."

"I'm sorry. I wish I could do more."

"How long will she be out?"

"It's hard to say. It depends on how much she regularly drinks. This is most likely caused by rapid ingestion rather than her drinking over a period of time."

"Thanks, Doc."

"My pleasure." The two men shook hands. "We will be moving her to a room in the next hour or so. You'll be allowed to stay with her in the room upstairs if you wish."

"Okay." He sighed. "She doesn't have family here."

"I know who she is. She's got a beautiful voice and is very talented. Too bad this is the result of a quick rise to fame, probably."

"Yeah, I think so too."

"I've heard of it a lot with people in the music industry. I hope she lets you help her. You seem like a great guy."

"Thanks. I hope she lets me in. Right now, I think she's still in denial." He set her purse on the edge of the bed. "I'm going to see if I can get in touch with her parents to let them know what's going on."

"Good idea." The doctor laid his hand on Jackson's shoulder. "I think you'd be good for her."

The doctor walked out as Jackson opened her purse to see if she had a cell phone with her parent's number in it. This wasn't going to be an easy task.

Chapter Nine

"Samantha?"

"Hi, um, no. My name is Jackson Young. I'm a friend of your daughter's."

"Where's Samantha, and why are you calling from her cell phone?"

"Is this her dad?"

"Yes, this is Michael Harris."

"I'm currently at University Hospital in San Antonio with Samantha."

"What? What happened?"

"I'm not exactly sure, sir. I was with Samantha last night. We had a little fight. I left her in her room at my family's ranch to go to bed. When I checked on her this afternoon, she was unresponsive in her bed. She was breathing and everything, but she wouldn't wake up."

"Holy hell. Is she going to be okay?"

"I believe so. She's in the emergency room right now. They're giving her fluids, monitoring her. She'll be here for a couple of days to flush the alcohol out of her system."

"Wait, alcohol?"

"Yes, sir. It appears she drank a lot of whiskey in a very short period of time last night or early this morning. The doctors are saying she's got alcohol poisoning."

"Oh my God. I told her to stop with the drinking or she would hurt herself, but she wouldn't listen. She's stubborn like that."

"I can imagine, sir."

"Who did you say you were again, son?"

"My name is Jackson Young. My brother's fiancé is the one who booked her to play the benefit concert in Bandera the other night. She's been staying at my family's guest ranch for the last couple of days."

"Oh yes. She mentioned you when I talked to her yesterday for a short time. Said you two were dating."

"Yes, sir."

"My wife and I will book a flight out tomorrow morning for San Antonio so we can be there to bring her home. She'll need to get some help with this problem."

"I understand, sir, but I don't think she'll go. She doesn't believe she has a problem."

"Well, son, with this episode, I think she does."

"I'm right there with you, but she won't get help until she comes to terms with it being a problem. Trust me on this. I had a brother who went through the same thing."

"She needs to be home with her family so we can take care of her."

"I'm sorry, sir, but I don't agree with you."

"I don't care what you agree with, young man. Her mother and I believe she needs to be in Iowa."

"What kind of treatment facilities are there for her? She probably needs inpatient treatment."

"We live in a small town. There isn't much here except corn and farms."

"I understand that, sir, but there is a top of the line treatment facility here in Texas where she can get the best treatment there is, if she'll allow it. Convincing her is the first step. She needs a firm hand, not someone who will buckle under her batting her eyes and giving you a little pouty lip."

"Are you saying we aren't hard enough on her?"

"Maybe. I don't know you and your wife or your family. I don't know Samantha that well, but we are trying to get to know each other in this weird little situation. I think she needs someone a little farther removed from her than family to be tough with her."

"What do you suggest we do?"

"Stay in Iowa. I'll keep her at the ranch with me and try to get her help here. She doesn't have to be on the road for a little bit longer so I'm hoping I can convince her to talk to someone at least."

"All right. Make sure to have her call us as soon as she is able."

"Of course."

"Thank you for calling, Jackson. You sound like a good guy. I hope you and Samantha become better acquainted. I think you'll be good for her."

"You're welcome, sir, and I hope to get to talk to you under better circumstances sometime soon."

"Take care of our girl."

"I will."

He hung up the phone and went to sit beside her bed. He brushed the hair back off her forehead and leaned in to kiss her there. She was something special, but damn if he knew what to do with her now. If she reacted this way every time they had a fight, he wasn't sure he could handle being with her even on a temporary basis. If he could get her off the alcohol and sober her up, she would be a handful he could really get into having with him daily. He took the chair next to the bed to watch her sleep.

They transferred her to a room upstairs about thirty minutes later, but she didn't stir much at all except to moan when they shifted her from the gurney to the regular bed in her room. Jackson got comfortable in the chair close by. It would be a long night at this rate.

About two hours later, she rolled her head toward him and cracked her eyes open slightly.

"Where am I?"

"At the hospital."

"Jackson?"

"Yeah."

She licked her dry lips. "What am I doing at the hospital?" She lifted her hand to her head. "Oh my God, I have such a headache. I feel like I've been kicked by a mule."

"I found you unresponsive in your bed at the ranch about three hours ago after you didn't come out for breakfast or lunch."

"What time is it?"

He glanced at his watch. "About five o'clock in the evening."

"What day?"

"You don't even know what day it is?"

She turned away from him. "No."

"We fought last night in your cabin so it's Monday."

"Shit," she whispered, turning back to face him. "I'm sorry."

"Do you want to tell me what's going on?"

"Nothing really."

He shoved his hands through his hair, wanting to do nothing more than pull it from his scalp in frustration. She didn't get it, apparently. "Nothing? I find you passed out in your bed with one completely empty bottle of whiskey on the floor and another half empty on your nightstand. The doctors are saying you had alcohol poisoning. You don't get that from leisurely drinking, Samantha. You get that from binge drinking. I've been reading up on it since you've been out cold, plus I dealt with this a lot with my brother."

"I'm sorry." Tears choked her words.

"Sorry isn't enough. You need help."

"I know."

"You know?" It would be incredible if she made things that easy to convince her, but he didn't think so.

She sat up farther in the bed, holding out a hand toward him. "I'll stop. I promise. No more alcohol. That's it. I'm done."

"I've heard those words before." He didn't believe her. This was the same trick Jacob had pulled when he'd confronted him on several occasions about his drinking. He hadn't binged on alcohol, but he'd drank until he was too drunk to walk many times. The night Paige had found him, he'd been so drunk, he'd puked in the hall at the Dusty Boot.

"Not from me."

"No, from my brother who didn't stop until he'd gotten his ass kicked in a bar fight and had to be rescued by a woman."

"I swear. I'll stop. It shouldn't be that hard, right? I mean I don't drink a lot normally."

"You were drunk when you came to breakfast yesterday."

"No I wasn't." Her hand shook as she held it out for him to take. "All right, yes, I'd had a few before I came to breakfast. It helps me when I'm writing songs. I makes the creative juices flow better from my brain to the paper, but I wasn't drunk."

"I could smell it on your breath."

"I know. I'd had a few, but I wasn't drunk."

"Did you have trouble walking? Were you having trouble concentrating on getting into the building?"

"I was a little wobbly."

He gave her an incredulous look. She really didn't believe she wasn't drunk and he couldn't fathom that. If she couldn't walk a straight line and had trouble with the smallest of tasks, yeah, she was probably well on her way to being three sheets to the wind.

"But I don't drink that much, Jackson, just a few to calm my nerves."

"Calming your nerves had nothing to do with last night. Did you get drunk because we fought?"

"You walked out on me."

"You practically called me a prostitute, Samantha. You offered to pay me for my services."

"I didn't mean for it to sound like I was paying you for your services. You jumped to the wrong conclusion. All I meant was to pay you for being my bodyguard and helping me catch this stalker." She nervously folded the sheet around her abdomen. "I never meant to insult you."

"Well you did, but my mother kind of made me see where you were coming from. It just didn't sound right the way you put it." He picked up her hand from where it lay on the white sheet. "I'm sorry I jumped to conclusions."

"I'm sorry I made it sound like I expected you to sell yourself to me."

He leaned in a kissed her on the lips. "How about we put this all behind us?"

"Sounds good. Can we start over?"

"Kind of hard to do since we've already had sex, but I'm game."

"Me too."

He looked over her face. She was pale and drawn. Her skin looked kind of sallow, too, and he expected it was all from the alcohol she drank. Her liver was still trying to process everything though. "I'm sorry I didn't ask this before. How are you feeling?"

"Like shit. Hung over would be a good term."

"I can imagine."

She glanced at the bag of fluid hanging from the pole next to the bed. "What are they giving me?"

"Fluids to help flush out the alcohol from your system faster. You'll be here until at least tomorrow. They won't let you go until your blood alcohol level is zero."

She exhaled as she closed her eyes. A tear escaped from the corner.

He felt like shit watching her cry, but he wasn't sure what to do. She needed to talk to someone and he didn't think he was qualified to deal with whatever stuff caused her to drink like she did.

"I think you need to talk to someone."

"Maybe."

"Jacob might be able to help or even Peyton. She's almost done with her degree in counseling and she's been in some tough situations before herself."

She wiped the errant tear from her cheek. "I could talk to them, I suppose, but I really don't believe I'm an alcoholic, Jackson. I can quit anytime I want to."

"I'm here to help you any way I can."

"And I appreciate that you are willing to do that."

The nurse came in a few minutes later. "My name is Camille. I'm the nurse who will be taking care of you for a few more hours. We change shift at seven. How are you feeling?"

"Like shit. Can I get something for a headache?"

"I'm sorry, but I can't even give you Tylenol because your liver is trying to process the alcohol in your system. You did a pretty good number on your body. Is there something you need to talk to a counselor about?"

"No."

"I have to ask this now that you are awake and aware. Were you trying to hurt yourself in any way?"

"Hell no! I wasn't trying to kill myself. Are you nuts?"

"Sorry. I had to ask with the way you came into the emergency room."

"What a thing to ask someone."

"It's protocol." She checked the needle in Samantha's arm, took her temperature, blood pressure before checking her heart and lungs. "Everything looks good. We will be drawing blood quite frequently during the night to check your levels and make sure your liver is functioning well."

The woman glanced at him, lowered her eyes, and smiled like she was flirting with him right in front of Samantha. *Wow.* The whole scene took him aback.

"Will you being staying the night with your girlfriend?"

He wanted to tell the nurse Samantha wasn't his girlfriend, but he figured if they were trying to pull off this ruse, he'd better play the part. "I can't. I have to work."

She smiled again. "We'll make her as comfortable as possible." The woman licked her lips before tilting her head to the side. "Are you a real cowboy?"

"As real as they get, I reckon. I live on a ranch with my family out in Bandera."

"Very nice." Camille gave him a once over from the top of his cowboy hat to his duty boots.

Thinking he could discourage the woman, he pulled Samantha's hand to his mouth and kissed her fingers. "We'll go shopping for a ring after you get out of here. Okay, babe?"

"Really? Wow. I love you, Jackson."

"I love you too, Sam."

The nurse frowned and took a couple of steps back. "Uh, I'll check on you later."

"Thank you."

As soon as the door closed behind her, Samantha pulled her hand from Jackson's grasp. "It wasn't just me, right? She was ready to jump you right here in front of me."

"Yeah, I think so."

"Does that happen often?"

"Not as much as you apparently think."

"You're a good looking guy. I would think it happens a lot."

"Nope."

Samantha laughed. "You're just being shy."

"Not really." He shrugged as he tugged at the thighs of his jeans to pull them down a bit. "My brothers get more attention than I do, especially the triplets. I think they've even been propositioned for a threesome."

"Now that I could believe."

"What is it with you women and sharing? I don't share."

"A little possessive are you?"

"A lot possessive of the woman I'm in love with, other than that, not so much."

"You would let a woman you were dating, date someone else at the same time?"

"I didn't say that, but if she was really into wanting sex with two guys…" He shrugged, letting the sentence die.

She sat farther up in the bed. Apparently, the thought intrigued her. "Really? You'd do a ménage?"

"As long as I didn't have to have sex with the other guy, sure. Why not?" He pointed a finger at her. "But not if we are in a serious relationship. If we were casually dating, then there wouldn't be any feelings involved."

"Oh, so you're saying if you love her, then you won't share, but if you don't, all bets are off."

He gave her a one-shoulder shrug. "Sure, I guess, although I haven't been faced with the situation, so I'm not sure how I would react to tell you the truth."

"What if I said I wanted you and Joey?"

His heart thumped loudly in his chest. Joey was his brother. Could he share a woman with him? Could he share Samantha with him? "I don't think that would be a good idea."

"What if it was a guy you'd never met?"

He still didn't like the way his gut clenched at the thought of watching Samantha with another guy. Not that they were exclusive or anything, but for now, she belonged to him. Nope, he decided he wouldn't share well.

"No."

"So you have a little double standard there?"

"Not really." He got to his feet and moved toward the window. He didn't like where this conversation was heading at all. She didn't need to be dating or having sex with anyone but him. *What if she really wanted to though? It's not like we are really a couple or anything, right?*

"I think you do, Jackson. What if I said I wanted a ménage?"

"Without me?"

"With or without. It depends on if you are game or not?"

He spun around on his boot heels so quick, the room spun. "Who else are you having sex with?"

"I'm not. It's hypothetical, cowboy. Get your jeans out of your ass." She raised her hand and held it out to him. "I'm not having sex with anyone else. I don't want to. You brought up the question, not me."

He moved closer to take her palm in his. "Good. I don't like the thought of sharing you with anyone else."

"A little contradictory there?"

"Maybe. I can't see me sharing you."

"Good. I don't want to share either."

"You don't?"

"No. If you were to ask to bring another woman into the mix, I'd turn you down flat and that would be the end of any kind of relationship."

"Are we in a relationship?" he asked, taking the chair again as he continued to cradle her hand in his.

"Sort of, I guess. For what it's worth."

"Then we are discussing your drinking, for what it's worth."

She sighed heavily as she titled her head back against the pillow. "I do not have a drinking problem, Jackson."

"I believe you do."

"I told you. I'm quitting. I won't drink again unless it's casually and with you around. Okay?"

He didn't really believe her, but what else could he do? Until she realized she had a problem, he couldn't help her. He needed help with this. He needed his family's support behind him when he went through her bus and found her stash of alcohol because he had a gut feeling there was one there. Otherwise, how had she retrieved two bottles of Jack to drink last night?

"Where did you get the Jack Daniel's you drank last night?"

"I had it on my bus."

"Do you always carry such a large quantity of alcohol on the bus?"

"Sometimes. It depends on how far between gigs we will be traveling. I told you. I drink before shows to calm my nerves, but not that much. Maybe three or four glasses."

"Three or four?"

"Yeah, but they aren't full glasses. They are tumblers."

"Straight whiskey?"

"I put a little ice in it, but yeah, usually straight."

He coughed. *Holy shit!*

"What do you drink when you drink?"

"A couple of beers."

"Beer doesn't do anything for me. I don't like the taste."

He leaned back in the chair, folding his arms across his chest. This conversation just got real. "Yeah, I guess it wouldn't."

"What's that supposed to mean?"

"Samantha, three or four glasses of whiskey straight is a lot of alcohol. When did you start drinking?"

"When I was in high school, but only on weekends at parties and stuff."

"You've been drinking like this for twelve years or so?"

She laughed. "No, silly. I used to drink wine back then. Nothing strong. I started drinking whiskey when I got my record deal."

"Did you used to have to drink when you sang karaoke?"

"No, I was singing in front of friends mostly, so it didn't bother me. They'd already heard me sing lots of times. When I had to start singing in front of hundreds or thousands of people, I couldn't get the words out. The first couple of concerts were terrible. I sounded really bad. In fact, they made me lip-sync for a few shows. After that, I drank a little and things got better."

"Do you hear yourself?"

"What?"

"You are drinking at every show and from what I've seen while you've been on the ranch, you are drinking daily."

Her brow wrinkled as a frown pulled down the edges of her lips. "No. I don't think so."

"I do."

She shook her head. "It doesn't matter. I told you I would stop, and I will. I'm done with it. I'll figure out some other way to deal with my anxiety about getting in front of people to perform."

"Good."

"You do realize we need to hit the road like next week, right?"

"Next week?"

"Yeah. My next show is in California and it will take a bit to get there. I need to text the band and Mark to get them ready to roll."

"You have two buses, right?"

"Yeah. One for the band and one for me."

"Good. I really didn't want to explain my existence to them right away when most of them haven't seen me before the other day at the show."

"No worries. I'll take care of it."

"Is there anyone in the band or road crew that you feel could be the stalker?"

She bit her lip as she stared straight into his gaze. Her blue eyes were serious with the change of subject matter. He could tell she was really frightened by the thought of someone so close being the person who wanted to get to her.

"I don't think so, but it's hard to tell. Most of the guys have been with me for a long time, but we do switch our roadies frequently. We take on new people at each stop for security and whatnot." He could see her body shudder. She really was terrified. "What if we never find him or her?"

"We will."

"What if we don't? I will have to watch my back forever. I don't think I can do that, Jackson."

"I'll be there to protect you for however long you need me to."

She swung her legs around in the bed so she was sitting on the side with her knees between his. "I could really fall in love with you very easily, you know that? You are one special guy."

Chapter Ten

The next day, Samantha waited for Jackson to pick her up from the hospital to bring her back to the ranch. The nurses had already removed the needle from her arm and she'd sat in her hospital gown waiting from him to bring her clothes since she was naked when they brought her into emergency room. She felt like a kid waiting for her parent. Was that what he was turning into, her father?

Ewww. That thought disgusted her. She didn't need another parent. Hers had been strict enough on her and her sisters growing up. She held out her hand, watching as tremors made it shake uncontrollably. Her head pounded as her stomach rolled. Sweat poured down her back. God, she hoped this wouldn't last long. Quitting the booze wasn't going to be as easy as she thought it would when she told Jackson she was done.

She licked her parched lips. A little sip would calm her if only she had the flask she kept in her purse handy. She stood to walk to the long, thin closet tucked into the wall to see if her purse might be in there. *The flask should be in hidden inside.* One sip wouldn't hurt anything. She opened the door, grabbed her purse, and moved back to sit on the side of the bed. The gown bunched up around her butt, leaving it exposed to the air in the room. Disgusted by the feel of the bare sheet on her ass, she stood, yanked the offending garment around her butt, and sat back down. "Stupid things."

With her purse in her lap, she opened the zipper and began to dig around in the contents. Wallet. Keys. Checkbook. Makeup. Pens. Notebook. She flipped through the contents one piece at a time. *Surely my flask is in here.* After she had everything on the bed, she smiled as she finally pulled out the silver flask with the small plastic top. *One sip, that's all I need.* She unscrewed the cap and tipped the flask to her lips.

The door to the room opened, surprising her. Jackson strolled inside with a large bouquet of flowers in his hands. "What the hell are you doing?"

She hid the flask behind her back. "Nothing."

He tossed the flowers on the bed, grabbed the flask from her hand, took it to the sink, and dumped the small amount of contents down the drain.

"That's mine!"

"Not anymore. You said you quit, remember?"

"I just needed a sip, Jackson. I'm so shaky. I have a terrible headache, and I'm really thirsty."

He tossed the empty flask to her. "Drink water."

"One sip wouldn't hurt."

"Yes, it will. You said you could quit anytime."

"I can."

"We'll see. No more, Samantha. That's it. If I catch you with anymore, I won't stick around."

"But I need you."

"No, you think you need the booze." He tossed her clothes on the bed. "Get dressed. We are going back to the ranch and you are going to talk to Jacob and Peyton." He cupped her face with his palms as he looked deep into her eyes. "Honey, I'm trying to help you."

"You aren't helping me by taking it away like this."

"Yes I am." He stepped back. "You need to see a doctor. I think there is medication they can give you to help you through the withdrawal symptoms. Jacob took something right after he quit."

"I don't need medicine to help me. I can do this. I promise, I can do this."

"You can't do it alone, and yes, you do need the medicine. It's not good for you to go cold turkey as you can see by your symptoms."

A lump formed in her throat, forcing her to swallow hard. "I'm sorry. I thought one little sip wouldn't hurt me and it would help me get through this."

"It's okay, darlin'. We'll do this together."

"You are so good for me."

"My family will help too. We've been through some rough things as a group."

"I don't want them to know."

"They already do. I couldn't help but tell them what was going on when they took you away in an ambulance the other day."

"Well shit."

"It'll be okay. We tend to gather people to us when there is trouble, and baby, you are full of trouble right now."

"Thanks, cowboy."

He smiled as he brushed the hair back from her forehead. "You're welcome. Anytime, darlin'." He picked up the clothes and handed them to her gently. "I'll let you get dressed. I think the nurse was waiting for me to show up to boot your ass out of here."

"Yeah. She's already given me discharge papers."

"Okay. I'll step out."

She raked her gaze from the top of his head to his feet. "Not like you haven't seen it all before." He flushed red and she had to giggle a little. "Did I embarrass you?"

"Just get dressed. I'll be out in the hall."

She shook her head as she stripped off the gown. The pink lacy bra sitting on the bed gave her pause. She wondered if he picked it out himself or he had his mother grab her some clothes from her suitcases in the cabin. Probably his mom, she figured. Not that they hadn't already been intimate, but she thought it kind of funny how flustered he got with the threat of seeing her naked. Surely they would be doing the horizontal mambo again soon. She certainly wanted to experience the nice little ball he carried around on the end of his dick. It sure had felt good.

After she finally got dressed, she grabbed her purse, stuffed everything back inside, and then opened the door to find him leaning against the wall nearby. He sure was one sexy-ass man, she had to admit. She was really glad they were a couple, well sort of. Their relationship had a weird bit of a twist to it.

"Ready?"

"Yeah."

The nurse arrived with a wheelchair. "Sit, please."

"I can walk." She eyed the wheelchair with disgust. There wasn't any reason why she couldn't walk down to his truck.

The nurse pointed to the chair, indicating Samantha needed to sit. "It's protocol. We have to take you down in a wheelchair for your own safety." She glanced at Jackson. "Where are you parked?"

"Out front."

"You can go down and pull around to the loading zone near the doors. We'll follow you down."

"All right." He headed down the hall with them following close behind.

Samantha sniffed the flowers in her hands. They really were beautiful. She couldn't believe he'd actually bought her flowers. Guys didn't do this kind of thing anymore, did they? Well, he apparently did. She kind of got the feeling he was one of those gentlemanly types who liked to hold your door, give you flowers or give you their coat when you were cold. *His ass looks mighty nice in those jeans too.*

He really was the down to earth kind of man she'd always wanted when she thought of settling down. She wasn't sure he'd be the type to settle down with her though.

* * * *

The trip back to the ranch was made in silence. He wondered what she thought the whole time they drove, but he didn't want to ask. Hopefully, she was thinking about how she was going to quit the alcohol because she needed to.

His thoughts turned to when he'd walked into the room and found her about to drink from the flask. He didn't know what she was going for, but he knew he had to stop her. One sip would set her back days in her recovery.

He glanced at her hands clasped in her lap. He could see the trembling from his side of the truck. This wasn't going to be easy, he knew, but he was determined to help her get through this.

As they pulled through the gates of Thunder Ridge, she sighed.

"You okay?"

"Yeah."

"What's wrong?"

"This is going to be tough facing your family. I wish you hadn't told them."

"I didn't have a choice."

"I'm surprised it hasn't hit the tabloids yet."

"Uh, it has."

"Shit." She grabbed her purse and pulled out her cell phone. "The battery is dead."

"I'm not surprised."

"My manager is probably freaking out."

"He's called the ranch, but due to privacy issues, we couldn't tell him anything."

She rolled her head around on her shoulders like she was trying to pop her neck. "I'll call him as soon as I can plug this thing in. He'll need to issue a statement to the press."

"I think he already has according to the papers. He protected your privacy though and didn't tell them anything other than you were in the hospital being treated for an unknown ailment and would be discharged soon."

"That's good."

"Yeah. We haven't had the press out here yet. I don't think they knew you were staying with us."

"No, we kept that on the down-low."

"Good."

When they pulled up to the parking spaces, she glanced at the little cabin she called home for now. She wondered if Jackson would be joining her later this evening for a little fun or not. *Maybe not. My head is pounding and I feel like shit.*

"I already have it set up for you to talk to Jacob and Peyton."

"Now?"

"Yes. The sooner the better. I've also arranged for the doctor Jacob saw to make a house call. He'll be here in an hour to talk to you and get you some medicine."

"I guess."

"You have to start right away, Samantha. You can't do this alone."

"I know. I'm not feeling up to talking to anyone right now, but I'll do it for you."

"Do it for yourself, not for me."

"Okay."

He stepped out of the truck and moved around to her side to open her door. "Let's drop the flowers in your room before we head to the lodge."

"I have to do this talk at the lodge?"

"Yeah. Someplace open would be best for everyone involved. Jacob and Peyton will talk to you together."

"Great. Way to gang up on me."

"You'll see. It'll be fine."

Once they put the flowers in her cabin, he strolled back across the yard with her, cradling her hand in his. He knew this wouldn't be easy for her, but she had to start right now. Jacob and Peyton sat at one of the long tables as they walked into the large room. The rest of the place was empty, thank goodness. He didn't think she would do this if there were anyone else around.

"Peyton, Jacob, you both know Samantha."

"Hi Samantha. It's nice to see you again," Peyton replied. "Sit down. We don't bite."

"Hi. I'm not sure you remember me from the large gathering at breakfast the other day. I'm Jacob."

"Yes, I remember you and you as well, Peyton. Thank you for talking with me tonight and taking time away from your families."

"As long as you are with Jackson, you are family," Jacob replied. "Please, sit."

"Let's get started, shall we?" Peyton asked. "Are you staying, Jackson?"

"If Samantha wants me to."

"Yes!" She grabbed at his hand, drawing him down on the bench with her.

"I'll stay then."

Peyton drew out a pad of paper to jot some notes down on. "Why don't you tell us when you first started drinking?"

"In high school. I used to drink at parties."

"Do you know why you started drinking so early?"

"I wanted to fit in. Everyone drank."

She squeezed his hand like a lifeline.

"You can do this."

"Let me tell you a bit about myself, Samantha." Peyton set the pen down on the pad. "I was in an abusive relationship with an ex of mine. He physically, emotionally, and sexually abused me for years. When I finally decided I'd had enough, I took what I could before moving here hoping to stay hidden. I work as a bartender at the Dusty Boot so I see this kind of alcohol abuse all the time." She glanced at Jacob and smiled. "I used to watch Jacob come in time after time and get shitfaced although I didn't know the reasons behind it, I wanted to help. Fortunately, Paige found him, helped him, and he's been clean for a while now."

"But staying away from the alcohol is a never ending process. Most people, not all, but most people can't drink casually without going back into the same binge drinking that you and I suffer from." Jacob steepled his hands in front of his face as he regarded Samantha from across the table.

"Samantha thinks she can stop cold turkey." Jackson leaned in a kissed her on the head. "I've told her about the medication you took, Jacob, that helped with the symptoms of withdrawal."

"Yeah. The doctor will be here in a little while to help you with those things, but you have to take them regularly." Jacob picked up Samantha's hand, holding it between his. "You have tremors. I can feel them in your hand. I bet you have a headache, feel nauseated, and are anxious too."

"Yes."

"These are all symptoms of withdrawal." Jacob laid her hand back down. "How long have you been drinking heavily?"

"What do you mean by heavily?"

"Jackson said you drank an entire bottle of whiskey and half of another the other night. That's heavy drinking."

"I drink some before I go on stage."

"How much?"

"Three or four glasses. Straight."

Jacob didn't bat an eyelash, making Jackson wonder how much his brother had really drank over the years.

"I understand. I really do. Let me tell you a bit about my situation. I got a girl pregnant a few years ago. I knew about the baby. I asked her to marry me. She refused. She talked about abortion. I begged her not to. She did it anyway without my knowledge until a few days later when she told me. The guilt killed me. She killed my child and it wasn't something I could get over easily. I started drinking heavily. I was drunk at work, drunk at home, drunk at the bar, and driving drunk. I was lucky. I never hurt anyone, but one night I got into a huge bar fight with three big, burly guys over a pool game. I was betting and losing. They didn't want to take my money anymore and were prepared to walk away. I got in one guy's face. He hit me hard enough to scoot me across the floor on my ass. Paige stepped between us to save me. She's trained in martial arts so it wasn't much to her to protect me, but she did. When I remembered what happened later, I was so embarrassed by what she'd done, I quit drinking cold turkey."

"Did you go through withdrawals?"

"You could say that. It was bad. I basically stayed in bed for three days solid, not eating, not drinking, just shaking, vomiting, and so on."

"Wow."

"Yeah. I didn't see anyone but my mom for those three days. She finally got the same doctor who is coming out today, to come out here for me. He prescribed me some medication to help, but you can't drink with them. There are a lot of things you need to watch for. Seizures is one. DT's can kill you. They don't suggest you go cold turkey, but you can have the same symptoms and everything even if you just cut down dramatically from what you were drinking before."

"Basically, what Jackson wants us to do for you is to make you realize you aren't alone in this. We've both been in situations where we needed something. The abuse I suffered through made me want to end my life on several occasions."

"I don't want to kill myself. I have too much to live for."

"Great, but you must realize you need to seek counseling with a professional substance abuse counselor."

"I thought you were."

"I'm in school for it, but I'm not done yet. You need to talk to someone who is experienced although I would love to talk to you anytime you want to. I'm sure Jacob would too."

"Of course I would. I'll be your sponsor if you want."

"I'd like that."

Jacob asked for a piece of paper from Peyton. "Here is my cell number. You call me anytime, day or night. I'll warn Paige so she won't freak when there is a phone call at three in the morning."

"I won't call at three."

"If you need me, you call. I don't care what time it is or where you are. If you feel like you are going to drink because you are depressed, anxious or whatever, you call me. Right, Jackson? I know he will be traveling with you in the coming weeks, but you call me if you need me."

A tear slid down her cheek. "I don't know how to thank you." She leaned into Jackson's embrace. "All of you. You've been so good to me and I've only know you people a few days."

"We care about you."

She shook her head as she wiped the tears from her face. "Thank you," she whispered.

He kissed the top of her head, holding her close while Peyton and Jacob stood. "Anytime, Samantha."

The doctor came through the door a few minutes later and found them still sitting in the same spot. "Jackson."

"Hey, Doc."

"I guess this is Samantha Harris." The grey hair man held out his hand. "I'm Dr. King."

"It's nice to meet you."

The doctor took a seat across from her. "I'm a specialist in substance abuse. If you want me to, I can see you throughout your treatment regimen no matter where you are. I understand you are a performer?"

"Yes, sir."

"Good. I'm assuming you travel extensively."

"Yes, sir."

"We will keep you in medication for your symptoms then and you will be able to refill them anywhere you are should you run out."

"I appreciate that." She glanced at Jackson. "This medicine will help with the tremors, nausea, headaches, and other stuff?"

"Yes, they will, but the big thing is you can't drink with them. It is important to understand the dangers in taking that path. Just like with any other medication, alcohol is a bad mixture."

"I won't. I promise."

The doctor glanced at him. "I understand you and Jackson are in a relationship?"

"Yes, sir."

"You will be monitoring her quite closely, right, son?"

"Yes. If I can prevent her from drinking at all, that's my plan."

"Good. She's going to need all the support she can get, which means everyone around her."

"Understood."

"Well then, I will leave you two to your privacy. I've called in the prescription to the local pharmacy here in Bandera for you to pick up." He stood and held out his hand.

Samantha stood as well, taking the man's hand in hers to shake. "Thank you for coming, Doctor King. I appreciate it tremendously."

"You're welcome, my dear. I hope to see you in my office in a couple of weeks if you can make it just to check up. Call me anytime though." He handed her some brochures out of his briefcase. "Here are some treatment facilities that you might look into. Even if you can't do inpatient treatment, I would suggest AA. Jacob can direct you to a local chapter although I don't know how long you'll be here before you have to travel on."

"Not long."

"I figured as much." He shot a look at Jackson. "There are AA chapters everywhere. I suggest you look up some in the areas she'll be in. She's going to need the support even if she has a sponsor here."

"Jacob agreed to be her sponsor."

"Good. He'll be a fantastic sponsor and he's been through this himself. He knows what you're going through." The man stepped around the table. "I'll take my leave. You two take care of each other. It's going to be a long hard road."

"Thank you."

As the doctor left, Jackson turned her to face him. "Are you okay?"

"Yes," she whispered. "I don't know if I can do this, Jackson."

"Sure you can, babe. I'll be there for you every step of the way."

"You keep this up, and I'm going to fall in love with you."

Chapter Eleven

The love word scared the crap out of him. He didn't need to fall in love with anyone nor did he need someone falling in love with him. His life seemed just fine the way it was. "You shouldn't talk like that, Samantha. Your life is too much of a rollercoaster right now to be fallin' in love with anyone."

"No worries, cowboy. I'm kind of a loner."

He pushed a piece of hair back behind her ear, loving the feel of the silky strands in his fingers. "Good. I'm not sure if we would be good for each other or not anyway. I'm kind of a bossy guy."

"I don't take orders well."

"See. We totally wouldn't get along on a long-term basis." He brushed his lips against hers. "How about we go to bed?"

One of her eyebrows went up over her eye. "Bed?"

"Yeah. I mean we are pretty good together when we have sex."

"True."

"How 'bout it? I mean if you feel up to it."

"I do have a bit of a headache."

"Why don't we run into town, pick up your prescription and see how you feel later? It's still early."

"Okay."

"We could grab a bite to eat at the diner if you want, something a little more intimate than dealing with my entire family for the supper meal."

"Sounds good to me." She brushed her lipstick off his bottom lip. "I'd like to have you to myself for a bit."

"Great." He wrapped an arm around her shoulders to lead her toward the door to the outside. "My aunt will love you. I think she's a fan."

"Your aunt?"

"Yep. She owns the diner."

"Sounds great. Let me grab a couple CDs and I'll sign them for her."

"That would be fantastic. I'm sure she'll love you even more if you did."

"Let's get them from the bus. I always keep a stash on there."

"Sure."

She popped the door of the bus open a few minutes later, and took the steps up into the interior of the big motor coach. He was always struck by the clean lines of the interior of her space. It was like her, beautiful and simply designed. She wasn't really a complicated individual from what he knew of her, which granted wasn't much more than what he knew from the media. Maybe they should have that talk during supper.

Once she had several CDs in her hands, they walked back down the stairs, locked the door, and headed out to his truck to drive into town. "We'll have to hit the pharmacy first. I think they close fairly early."

"No problem."

The drive into Bandera only took about ten minutes, not long enough to really get into a conversation. He wanted to suggest going to the Dusty Boot, but he felt it wasn't a good idea with her going through withdrawals right now. The alcohol would be flowing, tempting her to throw her first chance at sobriety to the wind and drink again. He wouldn't do something so cruel to her.

He glanced at her across the truck as the bar came into view. They had to drive past it to get his aunt's diner. She licked her lips and watched closely as they drove by.

"Is that the local bar?"

"Yeah. It's where Peyton works."

"Looks busy."

"It usually is. It's really the only place to hang out in Bandera so it's hopping most of the time." He took her hand in his as he pulled into an empty spot in front of the diner. "Are you okay?"

"Yeah. It's hard, you know?"

"I can imagine."

"You are such a strong person, Jackson. I can't imagine you being weak to anything."

"I have my issues too, Samantha. I tend to be hardnosed sometimes, not giving people the benefit of the doubt in some situations." He kissed her fingers. "We can talk more inside. I'm kind of hungry."

"Me too. The food wasn't very good at the hospital."

"I can imagine." He pushed open his door and rushed around the front of the truck to open hers for her once he slammed his own shut. "My lady."

"Such a gallant gentleman. Your mother would be proud." She smiled a little crooked half grin as she palmed his cheek. "You are one of the good guys, Jackson. Any woman would be happy to call you their own."

"Someday, maybe. I'm not in a hurry."

He opened the door, holding it for her to enter as the little bell tinkled announcing their arrival. The diner was kind of slow tonight from what it looked like, but that was okay with him. Having a quiet dinner, just the two of them sounded good.

There was a long bar to the left with old fashioned round stools for the patrons to sit on who might be dining alone with several booths and tables scattered around the room, giving the diner an old fashioned feel. His Aunt Ann had run the place for as long as he could remember.

"Jackson! How the heck are you? I haven't seen you in here in a while, son." Ann hugged him with one arm as she held a coffee pot with the other. "Who's the beautiful girl?"

"Ann, this is Samantha Harris."

"Oh my!" Ann put her hand to her chest. "*The* Samantha Harris? I didn't recognize you without your hat. I'm a huge fan of yours."

"So I heard, and thank you. You are more than kind."

"Honey, you have the voice of an angel. I just love your songs. I could listen to you for hours. I have all of your CDs."

"I guess you wouldn't be interested in them signed, then huh?"

"Signed. Oh hell yeah, I would! That would be fantastic!" Ann set the coffee pot down on the counter and hugged Samantha. "I love you. You…"

Jackson thought it was kind of funny how Samantha hugged her back kind of awkwardly as she glanced over Ann's shoulder.

"What the heck are you doing here with this rascal?"

"It's a long story."

"You'll have to tell me sometime, but for now, get yourselves a booth. What would you like to drink?"

"Coke is fine for me."

"Sprite would be great if you have it."

"Certainly." Ann giggled like a total fangirl. "Samantha Harris, in my diner. Wow."

She waddled off to get their drinks as he and Samantha took a seat in one of the booths. He handed Sam a menu from behind the salt and pepper shakers. As he looked over the menu he knew by heart, a small girl with bright red hair stopped at the edge of their table.

"Are you really Samantha Harris the country singer?"

"Yes, honey, I am."

The little girl twisted a napkin in her palm. "Can I get your autograph? I love your songs."

"Sure, baby." Samantha smiled at the little girl. "Do you want it on the napkin?"

The little girl handed it over to Sam. "Uh. Yeah. Sorry. It's kind of wrinkled."

"That's okay. How about if I grab one out of our holder to sign?"

The little girl nodded so fast, her curls bounced.

"What's your name?"

"Abby."

He watched as Samantha signed it with a marker he didn't realize she had, asked the little girl to take a picture with her, and chatted with her for a few minutes. She really did love her fans from what he could tell.

"Oh." Samantha pulled out a CD from her purse. "Here is a CD for you too, since you are such a big fan."

"Wow," Abby whispered. A second later, she practically leapt into Samantha's arms as she hugged her tightly before she rushed back to her mother's side. The woman had tears in her eyes as she mouthed, thank you over Abby's head.

"You are a sucker for fans, huh?"

"Yeah. I love meeting them and talking with them."

"You made that little girl's whole year probably."

"You think so?"

"Yeah." He grasped her hands in his. "You are a beautiful person inside and out."

She flushed red. "You're embarrassing me."

"You are easily embarrassed, but it's the truth."

"Thank you."

He reluctantly pulled his hand back to grab his menu again. Not that he needed to read it. The thing hadn't changed in twenty years, but he really needed to keep his hands busy, otherwise he might do something really stupid like grab her and kiss her right there in the diner.

Ann came to their table a minute later with their drinks. "Sorry. I didn't mean to take so long, but I didn't want to interrupt your time with Abby. She's a sweet girl for everything she's going through."

"Oh?" Samantha asked, putting her menu down.

"Yeah. She was diagnosed with Leukemia about a month ago. She's getting ready to start treatments this coming week."

"Oh my. How sad."

"Honey, you are the reason that little girl is smiling right now. Don't be sad for her. She's got a fighting spirit and great chances for remission. I bet she'll play that CD until it's plum wore out."

"Thanks, Ann, but I didn't do anything."

"Hush. Yes you did. You made that little girl's day a little brighter with your kindness. It takes a special person to be good to others. You've got it, whatever it is." Ann pulled out her pen and pad. "What are you having for supper?"

After they ordered, he sipped his Coke while he watched Samantha across the table. What Ann said was right. There was something special about this woman and he aimed to find out what it was before they were through, even if it took him the whole six weeks they would be together to figure things out.

"What?"

"Nothing, why?"

"You're staring."

"Sorry. You are a beautiful woman. I'm lucky to be sitting here with you." He set his Coke back down. "Why don't we get to know each other a little better?"

"Okay."

"What's your favorite color?"

"Green. Yours?"

"Red. Favorite flower?"

"Um, Lilies."

"Favorite song?"

"Not one of mine?" she asked, taking a sip from her drink.

"Nope."

"Stay from Little Big Town."

"Favorite movie?"

"Ghost. That one is my all-time favorites. I love Patrick Swayze." She took another drink before setting the glass back down. "Your turn. Favorite movie?"

"Remember the Titians."

"Favorite sport?"

"Hockey, but I like baseball and football too."

"Not rodeo?"

"No. I watch bull riding on television sometimes, but I think those boys are crazy." Ann came by the table with their food. Everything looked fabulous, as usual. "Thanks, Ann."

"You're welcome." She wiped her hands on the apron around her middle. "You two enjoy."

They dug into their food with gusto, enjoying the homemade food of a good cook.

"This is fabulous!"

"Ann is one of the best cooks in the area. Her diner does well through the seasons where most places would have a hard time. She's got the local crowd coming here multiple times during the week."

As Samantha shoved a forkful of potato into her mouth, she hummed her appreciation. His dick jumped at the sound, hoping she would make the same one when she sucked his cock later. It hadn't been more than a couple of days, but he wanted her with a fervor he didn't know he possessed.

"You're looking at me funny."

"I can't wait to get you back to the cabin so I can fuck you properly," he whispered. He didn't need the whole place knowing his dick was about to explode.

She slowly licked the tinges of the fork before putting them into her mouth and leisurely pulling it back out. A small piece of potato clung on her lip, making him want to lick it off with everything inside him. Her eyes twinkled with mirth as she slowly, methodically tortured him to death right there in the middle of the diner.

"So? How was supper?" Ann asked, dragging him back from his erotic thoughts.

"Fantastic as usual."

"Good. I wanted to make sure you enjoyed it."

"The food was to die for, Ann." She turned sideways in the chair to dig into her purse. "Here are the CDs I promised you. They're all signed for your collection or whatever."

"Thank you!"

"You're welcome. I hope you can come out to a show soon. I would love for you to come backstage with me and Jackson."

"I would love to. I'm not sure if you'll be around here coming up or not."

"I'd have to check my schedule. I think we are doing a show in Houston, but that might be too far for you to come."

"For you, honey, I'd go to Florida."

Samantha laughed as she leaned back in her chair. "I would love to see you."

Ann glanced back and forth between them for a minute before she grinned from ear to ear. He knew that look. His mother had a knack for matchmaking, but her sister was good at it too. "You two are cute together. I hope to see more of this."

"Hold your horses, Ann. We are getting to know each other." Though he had a sneaky suspicion he was falling in love with Samantha.

"That's the first step!" Ann grabbed their now empty plates. "Can I get you two some pie?"

"You have to have a piece of pie, Samantha. Her apple and cherry are the best."

"Okay. Apple it is."

"Two?" Ann glanced at him with a questioning look.

"Of course. I can't pass up your pie. With ice cream, please."

Samantha nodded quickly. "Oh yeah, me too. Ice cream, definitely."

"Be right back."

Samantha reached across the table and picked up his hand before bringing his fingers to her mouth.

"What are you doing?"

"Seeing if you have anything on your fingers." She licked around the end of his pinky. "Nope. Not on that one." She tried the next, and then the next.

My cock is so hard, it hurts to breathe. "You're killing me."

"I know. Don't you love it?"

"You'll pay for this when we get back. I'm going to torture the hell out of you."

"I hope so."

Ann returned with their pie, setting one plate down in front of each of them. "Enjoy."

Sam turned on the torture during the pie eating by licking the fork and moaning softly with each bite. She sounded like she might orgasm right there from eating pie, but the joke was on him.

With each little moan, pre-cum leaked from the end of his dick. His balls ached, and his breath came out in ragged pants.

Worst thing of all, he didn't taste one bite of his pie and ice cream.

* * * *

The ride home after they'd picked they'd eaten was torturous for Samantha. Her nipples hurt from being so tight she could key a car with them, to her pussy throbbing with each beat of her heart. Good grief, she wanted to rip his damned clothes off right there in the truck and fuck him every which way but up. She wanted to feel the fun little knob on the end of his cock, rubbing the sweet little spot inside her. She needed to have him eat her pussy until she creamed all over his face. The desire she felt for this man, scared her a little. She didn't need someone like this, this badly. *What happens when he walks away at the end of our journey?* She didn't want to think about that right now. For the immediate future, she needed to concentrate on staying sober, living her life, and finding out who the stalker was so she could move on.

When they pulled up in front of her cabin, she turned to face him on the seat. "Are you going to join me?"

"Hell yeah, I am." He frowned and then adjusted his hat on his head. "Unless you don't want me to."

"Of course I want you to, silly. I've been thinking about this all afternoon. Well, in between headaches and bouts of nausea."

"If you aren't feeling up to this, we can postpone it."

"No way. I'm hornier than a cow in heat." She laughed. "That wasn't a very sexy euphemism, was it?"

He wrinkled his nose. "Not really."

"Anyway, yes I want you to stay the night and no, I won't call you a prostitute this time."

"Good. We are okay on the money thing, right?"

"I still think you should be paid for being my bodyguard or whatever you want to call it, but no, I'm not paying you for having sex with me. That's a bonus."

"Bonus?"

"Yeah, bonus for me having your sexy-ass body all to myself for however long you are on the road with me. Score!"

He shook his head as he rolled his eyes. She knew she was being silly, but it was kind of fun to cut loose and not worry about all the business of being a singer, just for one night. Tonight, she planned to enjoy Jackson Young to the fullest of her abilities and love every minute of it.

When he came around to her side of the truck, he opened the door, and swept her up in his arms before pushing the truck door closed with his boot. A quick kiss revealed the longing in him as he walked quickly toward her cabin.

"Where's the key?"

"In my pants pocket."

"Can you reach it?"

She unlooped her hands from around his neck. The key was in her front left pocket. "Yes," she said, pulling it from the confines.

He leaned in so she could open the door. It was kind of sexy how he carried her across the threshold of the cabin before dropping her in the middle of the bed.

After he went back to shut the door, he stripped off his shirt and then went to undo his belt buckle. She licked her suddenly dry lips as he slowly peeled his jeans down to reveal his cock to her gaze. The man had it going on. His cock sprang up from the curly black hair at the base, to rest against his abdomen. The piercing fascinated her with its simplicity. The stud went through the cock itself, leaving a ball at the head of his cock and one on the underside of the head. She remembered how the thing felt against her G spot, tantalizing and rubbing the special little spot into the most amazing orgasm she'd ever felt. She knew she'd never had an orgasm from there before.

He moved close enough for her to touch without reaching out too far. "I want your mouth. I've been dreaming of those lips around my cock all day."

"Come closer." He moved next to the bed as she brought her hand to his balls, massaging the rounded nuts with her hand while the other grasped his cock at the base. "This is incredible."

"I'm glad you like it."

"And the piercing is to die for. I love it." She took him in her mouth just far enough to drag a moan from his. She flicked the little ball with her tongue, rolling it around and around until his hips rocked toward her. She knew what he wanted, but she would make him wait a little longer to get his full on blowjob. Licking and swirling, she teased her tongue up and down the shaft.

He grabbed a fistful of her hair, pulling until her scalp burned slightly. "You're killing me. Suck."

She hummed around his cock as she continued her assault on his senses. *Torture is too good for him.* She wanted him to suffer a little before she gave him what he wanted so badly. "Oh no, not yet, cowboy."

"You will so pay for this."

"I'm counting on it."

She continued to bring him to the brink of insanity, dragging out her assault, before backing him off slowly.

"God, woman. Finish it."

"All right. Since you asked so nicely."

She deep throated his cock until he bumped the back of her throat, sucking him on the way back up. Up and down she sucked, stopping every few minutes to nibble on the end of his dick.

His hips rocked into her face as he held her head in place with his hands twisted in her hair.

She loved every tug, every pull, to the point she wanted to reach down and finger her own clit to bring some relief to the pounding of her blood. She was so horny, she hurt.

A moment later, hot cum spurted out the end of his dick deep into her throat. She swallowed every drop of the sticky liquid until nothing remained.

First, his knees hit the bed beside her, before he fell face first onto the mattress.

"You okay?" she asked, running her hands down his back and right arm. She liked the tattoo scrolled over his shoulder, almost as much as she loved the piercing in his dick and the one in his nipple. "I hope you aren't done for the night?"

"Give me a minute."

"Of course." She sat up on the side of the bed before stripping off her clothes and boots. Once she had everything off, she climbed back onto the mattress, spread her legs, and began to slowly finger her clit.

He turned toward her and opened his eyes. "Damn woman."

"What?"

"That is about the sexiest thing I've ever seen."

She brought her fingers to her mouth, wet the surface and then returned to her clit. "You've never seen a woman masturbate?"

"A time or two. I love to watch you anyway I can though."

"I hope you plan on eating me, because I *really* like when you do that."

He rolled onto his side and propped himself up on his elbow. She glanced down at his cock, amazed it had begun to get hard again.

"You do have some stamina for an old guy."

"Old?"

"You're what? Like thirty-five, right?"

"Yeah, so?"

"Women are in there prime during their thirties and forties. Men are usually on the downhill slide at your age."

"I'll show you downhill slide."

He jumped toward her so fast, she squealed, laughing hilariously as she tried to get away. He quickly tackled her on to the bed with his body weight, pinning her arms near her sides.

His lips did a slow crawl from her mouth to her ear. "I've got more than you can handle, babe."

"I'm hoping so. I want you to fuck me so hard, we break the bed."

"Break the bed, huh?"

"I'll buy a new one if you do."

"Sounds like a plan to me."

He scooted down her body, dragging his lips along her chest until he reached her right nipple. The jutting tip stood taut, waiting for his mouth to close over it. He ran his teeth over the end, dragging a moan from her mouth that sounded like something dragged from deep inside her chest.

"Oh God."

"Master will do."

"Yeah, no."

"Party pooper." He raked his teeth over the other nipple. "I can do this all night."

"I hope so. Good God, I hope so."

He continued to trail his mouth down her abdomen until he reached the juncture of her thighs. The first touch of his tongue on her clit, drove her hips straight up until he pressed them back to the bed with his hands on her hip bones. "Easy, darlin."

She loved when he called her that.

The man has a wicked tongue totally meant to pleasure a woman, not just any woman, me specifically.

Pleasure darted through her as he worked her clit, flicking it, sucking it, and moving it back and forth. He definitely knew his way around a woman's body.

His fingers rolled her right nipple, shooting desire straight to her pussy. Her heart raced, beating wildly inside her chest. Her nipples burned, pulling into tight little nubs. The muscles of her abdomen quivered as the soft touch of his fingers tickled the skin.

Her body went on high alert as he pushed two fingers into her pussy, slowly pumping them in and out. He licked her clit, rolling the tiny nub with his tongue.

"Ever had a man in your ass?"

"Mmm. Yes." Her breathing seesawed in a rapid rhythm as she whispered the words. "One of my favorite positions."

He slipped a third finger into her back hole.

"Good. I love the position too."

Her whole body hurt from the need to come. "Please, Jackson. Make me come."

"I plan to. In a minute or twenty."

"I can't stand it!" The slow lick of his tongue on her clit held her on the edge of a climax.

"It'll be that much more powerful when you do."

"You're such a tease."

"Yep." He moved back. "Roll over."

She flipped around so her ass was in the air. Good Lord, she needed this more than anything to take the edge off. Her life seemed to have done a nosedive in the last couple of days. Relief in the way of a mind-blowing orgasm would help tremendously. "Do it."

"Give me a second. I need a condom and some lube."

"Lube is in the drawer. Hurry. I'm dying here."

Seconds later, she felt the head of his cock bump against the puckered hole of her ass as cold liquid dribbled down her crack. She knew the burn would be painful, but she didn't care. She needed this, needed the pain to reset her brain from the rapid firing thoughts bouncing around in there.

The first slide of his penetration made her suck in her breath.

"Relax."

"I'm trying."

With one palm on each butt cheek, he worked her ass farther apart as he moved past the ring of muscles.

“Oh yeah.”

“I’m almost in.”

“Give me all of it. I need this. I need you.”

He pushed steadily until he was all the way in and she felt the brush of his hair against her butt.

“Yes.”

“I feel so full. You’re a big guy.”

“Feels fantastic.”

“Move, please.” The deliberate, slow in and out rhythm of his thrusts would drive her to climax in seconds if he kept it up much longer. “Faster.”

“I don’t want to hurt you. You’re very tight.”

“Please.”

He increased his pace until he was slamming against her ass in a body jarring motion, however, the minute he reached around and fingered her clit, she exploded into shards of herself as her world centered on what he was doing to her body. Her mind floated out and around them, bringing her into a peaceful, drifting feeling.

Several minutes later, he shouted his own release as he pushed against her ass in a jagged tempo. They both went down on the bed as he collapsed on her back.

Chapter Twelve

The next several days were spent making love, finding out more about Jackson and his family, and general relaxation. She knew they would be back to the crazy schedule of the road soon. She wasn't looking forward to it anymore. Yeah, it would be great to have Jackson with her, but the daily grind of moving from one place to the other every couple of days just didn't appeal anymore. Maybe it was time to hang up her microphone. Her manager, agent, and record label would have a fit. She needed to do what she needed to do for her sanity though.

She licked her lips. The days had went by fairly quick even without the alcohol to numb her brain. She actually felt pretty good on the medication when she needed it, which wasn't really all that often. Occasionally, she would have an anxiety attack, freak out a little, and need her pill, but Jackson knew how to bring her down from those episodes.

This morning she sat on her bus plucking out a few new lyrics and chords to a song she was writing. She really liked where this one seemed to be headed. It fit her life at the moment, even though it was a love song.

Love song.

She tapped the pencil to her lips. What the hell to do about Jackson Young. He had become more important to her life as the days went by. What would happen when they spent several weeks in close contact on her bus? Lots of love making, she hoped, but was afraid that would be detrimental to her heart.

If she admitted it to herself, she was already half in love with the cowboy. This wouldn't do. She didn't want to drag someone into this crazy life with her. She knew she could trust him though, and she knew he wasn't after her money or fame. He had his own life. Did it include her, she wondered as she went back to doodling on the paper. When she looked down, she realized she'd written Jackson's name along with her own, several times.

She blew out a breath as she put the pencil down. Getting into a relationship with him wasn't really a good idea, but she couldn't seem to help herself. Relationship, real or fake, it didn't matter, they were in it now whether she wanted to believe it or not.

A knock sounded on the door.

"Come in."

The door opened and Jacob peeked inside the bus. "How are you doing?"

"I'm good. Come on up."

Jacob climbed the stairs in quick secession. "Wow. Nice."

"Thanks."

"Is this what you travel in all the time?"

"Yeah. I need my comforts, I guess. It has to be home for several weeks at a time." She motioned to the couch across from her. "Have a seat and tell me what brings you to my humble abode."

He took a seat on the white leather couch, pulling at the thighs of his jeans. She could definitely tell Jacob and Jackson were brothers. They both had the dark hair, sexy face, and penetrating stare, not that they both were amazing to look at. Jackson wore facial hair where most of his brothers didn't. Plus, he had that awesome tribal tattoo from his shoulder to his wrist swirling around his arm.

"I wanted to check on you. I know it's been a few days since you had your last drink. It's usually the roughest the first few days, but it can also last for several weeks."

"I'm doing okay. I've had a few anxiety episodes. The medication helps." She set the guitar next to her on the floor. "I think the big test will be when we get on the road."

"You are still taking Jackson, right?"

"Yes, if he wants to. I won't force him, of course."

Jacob laughed. "I don't think you could force him to do anything he didn't want to do. He's about the most stubborn of all of us, although I'm not sure my mother would agree."

She laughed a little as she glanced down at her hands. "I do appreciate you asking about me. You don't have to keep such a close eye on me though. I think I've got this handled."

One eyebrow shot up over his eye. "You think so?"

"Yep. I've been clean and sober for a week. I've got this." She nodded, confident she could handle her life without booze or pills.

He frowned. "There will be a time you'll be tested on that theory. Just remember, I'm here, Peyton is here, and Jackson too. We are all here to help you get past this." He dangled his hands between his knees. "Have you contacted an AA group or went to one of their meetings?"

"No. I don't need those people. Besides, I have to be careful this doesn't get out into the media. It could kill my career if they knew I had an alcohol problem."

"Have, Samantha. You have an alcohol problem. You have to think of this as an ongoing issue. I haven't had a drink since Paige rescued me at the bar. I still have an alcohol problem. It isn't something that goes away with time. It will always be a problem in your life and something you have to battle constantly. Are there days I want a drink? Yep, and it's something I fight daily."

"Really?"

"Yes. Please don't think this is an issue you can just stop without realizing it will always be with you. You'll fail if you do. That's the last thing I want for you."

She bit the left side of the inside of her mouth as she looked at the paper she'd been writing on. "You've given me a lot to think about. I hope I can make all of you proud of me, but I didn't think of this in that way. I thought once I quit, I wouldn't have the problem anymore. That it was done, but it sounds like that's not the case."

"You have to understand. It is a difficult journey to go through and it definitely is something you will require help with. You will feel weak. You will want a drink. You will possibly fail, but you have to get back up and try again."

"I'm ready, Jacob. I really am. I need to get over this fear of performing to realize I am talented, I am a good person, and I can entertain people. I have to get past people being jealous of my success. They want me to fail, but I won't. I'm better than that."

"Yes, you are. You're a great performer. Your fans love you." He slowly climbed to his feet. "I will leave to you write. I know you are working on some new material."

"I am." She turned the paper over, not wanting him to see her doodles on the sheet. "It's kind of private though."

He smiled. She had a feeling he'd already seen her drawings. "I won't ask you how your relationship with Jackson is going. I know he can be kind of an ass."

"He's great, actually. Things are progressing, and I'm sure we'll have a great time on the road. I think he'll be right in his element guarding me. He seems to be the type to like to take charge."

"That he is, definitely." He walked toward the stairs. "If you need me, call. You have my number."

"Yes, I do. Thank you."

He tipped his hat and headed out of the bus, leaving her wondering. Did she really think this whole thing would blow over? Did she believe she had a drinking problem or not? If not, then she was going about this all wrong. She shrugged and turned over the paper she'd been writing the song on, going over it one more time. It was finished other than the intro chords to lead up to the words.

After she finished this, she needed to get the bus ready. They were leaving to head to California first thing in the morning. Mark would be flying back into San Antonio today and Jackson was on his way to pick him up at the airport. The band's bus had been parked at a storage lot in San Antonio and she'd already sent the guys' driver to get it ready to leave in the morning. He could sleep on the bus until he picked the guys up at the airport. They were all to meet at a central rendezvous point outside of town to head out. They would hit the road together. The first show had been scheduled in San Francisco, which was a good twenty-five hours on a good day, with buses it would take longer. The big trucks would make their way there from Nashville, where she'd sent them to go through the equipment and make sure everything was set for this tour. They would be doing a couple of shows a week for the next six weeks with only travel time between each venue. Luckily, they had booked them so it wouldn't be too hard to get from one to the other on a short time schedule.

A knock on the door brought her attention back to the task at hand. "Come in."

Jackson and Mark climbed the stairs.

"Hey, darlin'."

Her toes curled. "Hey, how was the trip? Not too much traffic, I hope."

"No, not much. Mark was already waiting when I got to the baggage claim, so it was a quick pick up and back on the road."

"Mark, I've already booked you a room in the main lodge for tonight so we'll be ready to roll out in the morning."

"Thanks."

"How was your break?"

"Good. I did a little fishin', some huntin', and a lot of relaxing. I'm ready to punch out this tour. You?"

"I'm doing better. I've quit drinking."

Mark looked surprised. "Really? I didn't think you were drinking that much."

"Well, I was. I landed in the hospital for a couple of days for it. Jackson here, helped me turn things around."

Mark glanced at Jackson with a bit of a frown on his face. "He did, huh?"

"Yep. With the help of him and his family, I've been sober for over a week. No more drinking. In fact, if you see me with anything alcoholic, stop me, please."

"Sure." His glance moved between her and Jackson several time before shooting back to her. "Does that mean the band and I have to stay clean too?"

"No, but I would appreciate it if you didn't drink around me. This is going to be hard enough."

"Sure, doll."

"What are you working on?" Jackson asked, taking the seat beside her.

"Nothing much. A new song," she said, turning the paper over quickly.

"Can I see it?"

"No."

"Why not? I'm one of your biggest fans, remember?"

"I know, but I don't like people seeing what I've got going until I'm done and it's been polished."

"Polished as in adding all the strings, horns, and other various instruments so it's ready to be recorded?"

"Something like that, yeah." She stuffed the paper at the bottom of her guitar case, put the guitar inside, and closed the lid. "You'll hear it when it's done."

"Have you been rehearsing?"

"Yeah, some. I have all the songs down I want to do at the show this weekend, but I'll go over them again while we are on the road." She took a sip of the Coke sitting on the table. "Can I get you guys something to drink?"

"I'm good," Mark replied. "I'm going to do a quick walk around on the bus and make sure everything looks okay. We don't want to break down anywhere."

"Good idea," Jackson said as Mark took the steps down to the exterior or the bus.

"Was he this talkative on the road back from the airport?"

"Yeah, pretty much. I don't think he said two words to me."

She pressed her lips together. "He's never been this quiet before. He usually runs off at the mouth a lot while we are driving, telling me stories, making me laugh, and keeping me company."

"You sound pretty close."

"Well, most of the time it's just the two of us on the bus since the guys in the band have their own." She shrugged as she looked out the front window. "I guess. He's like a brother to me."

"Good to know."

"No worries, Jackson. You are my guy."

"At least for now."

"For now."

The bell clanged for supper. "You ready to eat?"

"Yeah. I've been working for a while. I'm kind of hungry."

He took her hand and brought it to his lips for a kiss to the back. "Let's go get some food then. We'll grab Mark on the way out."

After dinner, she sat next to Jackson on the couch in the front room of the lodge, sipping a cup of coffee, and watching the flames dance in the fireplace. She probably shouldn't have been drinking it because the caffeine would keep her awake when it was bedtime, but she wanted to finish the song she'd been working earlier. The words drifted back to her mind, bringing a smile to her lips.

"What's the smile for?"

"I'm thinking about the song I was working on earlier."

"That good?"

"I think so. I really believe it will be a hit on my next CD."

"When do you start recording it?"

"After this next six weeks is up. I have some time booked in the studio to work on it."

"How long does it take to record a CD?"

"About a year or year and a half. It depends on how fast I find the songs I want to record, how easy they are to get, and how well the recording goes."

She took another drink of her coffee, before putting it on the coffee table. *This being sober thing is going pretty well. I haven't even really wanted a drink in a day or two. I think I've got this licked.*

Jackson's fingers did a slow crawl across the back of her neck, sending shivers down her arms. Had it really only been since last night since they'd had sex? She was becoming addicted to his brand of loving. She really liked the wicked things his tongue did to her clit.

"What am I going to need to do for you while we are on the road?"

"Make sure no one gets near me that's not supposed to."

"Kind of like what I did at the charity concert?"

"Yeah, although you'll have full access to my bus, the band's bus, and the rigs with the equipment, but the main thing is guarding me."

"That I can do." He nuzzled her neck near her ear.

"Are you ready for bed?"

"Always with you."

"Shall we head here then?"

"Um, I really need to get this song done."

"Are you turning me down for sex?"

She cringed as she said, "Yes, and no. Later?"

He laughed as he kissed her ear. "Later is fine. I know you want to work on the song you're writing."

"Thank you. You are a very special guy."

"No thanks needed. I can work on some stuff in my room. I need to pack anyway so we can leave first thing in the morning."

"I need to do that too. I've got stuff strung all over the cabin."

"Looks like a typical woman's room to me every time I see it."

She drank the last dregs of her coffee before she stood. Jackson climbed to his feet beside her. They dropped their coffee cups in the dirty dish bin on their way to the door. As they went their separate ways in the dark, she wondered how on earth she'd managed to find such a great guy.

Several hours later, she tapped her booted foot as she strummed the guitar, humming the melody to herself as she closed her eyes, letting the music flow through her. She had it. The final version of the song was completed. It was perfect and she knew her manager, her agent, her records producer, and most of all Jackson would love it. Excitement skittered through her. She wanted to play it for him now, but then again, she didn't. She wanted to let the musicians do their thing before she let him hear it, kind of as a surprise.

She glanced down at the paper at the last lyric.

I love you.

Did she? Did she really fall in love with Jackson Young in ten days? Wasn't that kind of strange? She wasn't sure and she really wished she had someone she could call and talk to about it, but it was one in the morning now and everyone she knew had already long gone to bed. She quickly glanced out the front window of the bus, noticing Jackson's light still burned.

Depression set in as she saw the light go out moments later. She didn't want to disturb him now that he'd gone onto bed, but she really needed him tonight. Nerves had begun to shake her when she thought about performing in a few days' time. How would she be able to get on that stage, rock the house, and play it well for the fans without having a little liquid courage ahead of time?

She chewed her lip as she thought about having a drink. She really needed one right now to calm things down, but she wouldn't. *Go onto bed and sleep it off.* That's what she'd do. She was stronger than they thought she was. Handling this alcohol thing wasn't easy, but she could do it, she knew she could.

After playing through the song one more time, she allowed a tear to slip down her cheek. Yep, she'd gone and fallen in love with the cowboy and now she had to figure out how to turn their relationship into something real.

The question tonight was whether to slip into his room, ravish his naked body, and leave him with a smile on his lips until morning or let him sleep.

Her pussy creamed at the thought of silently stroking his cock to hardness, taking him into her mouth as she tongued the wicked little piercing, and then riding his hips until he came so hard, he saw stars. Sounded like a plan to her.

I hope he left his door unlocked.

She laughed as she set the guitar aside before climbing to her feet. By the time she'd made it outside to the ground, she was grinning like a Cheshire cat who'd swallowed a canary. The winter evening had turned colder. She rubbed her arms to ward off the chill.

With her key, she locked the bus, before heading in the direction of his cabin. She silently tiptoed onto the wooden porch, careful not to make a sound. The doorknob easily turned under her hand as she sent up a thankful prayer, glad he'd left it unlocked.

Moonlight streamed through the window over his head, illuminating his body on the bed. He had one arm draped over his eyes, the sheet pulled down to expose his naked chest, and the rest of it bunch around his hips. She would easily be able to slowly peel it off him without waking him.

She silently closed the door, being careful not to wake him. After she quickly toed off her boots, she moved on stocking feet to the side of the bed.

His leg moved and she held her breath. A soft snore reached her ears. She smiled thinking about what would go through his mind when he awoke to her mouth on his cock.

She slipped off her clothes as quietly as possible, and then moved toward the bed. The sheet looked bunched around his hips, but loose enough she should be able to free his cock to her touch. Giving it a little tug, she managed to free his hips from the sheet, thankful he slept nude.

His cock was semi-hard, lying against his stomach. The ball on the end near the slit glistened in the moonlight. Her fingers itched to touch him all over. She wanted to run her hands from his pierced nipple to his cock, smoothing her palms over his contours and valleys. Tonight, she would do that even if it meant tying his hands to the headboard. Touching him gave her such pleasure and now that she'd given into her feelings by admitting to herself she was in love with him, it took on a whole new meaning.

She smoothed her fingertip over the end of his cock. He didn't stir although his dick twitched. She smiled.

Bent over at the waist, she licked around the metal ball before flicking her tongue over the head of his cock. He moaned softly.

Taking his balls in her palm, she worked them with her fingers as she took the head of his cock in her mouth and sucked.

"You are a little witch coming in here like this after leaving me hanging until early morning."

"You love it," she whispered against his now fully erect dick. "I wanted to take advantage of you in your sleep."

"You did."

She deep throated his cock, allowing the ball to bump the back of her throat. A deep hum vibrated the skin on his cock as she went up and down on the hard shaft. Sucking his cock really did it for her in the most primal way. It was her way of giving him pleasure beyond the norm before she received her own pleasure from him. She wanted to take care of him, love him, and make him see her as something besides a woman needing him to take care of her.

"I wanted to give you something for everything you're doing for me. I'm going to suck you until you almost come, then I'm going to ride you until you explode inside me."

"Sounds like a plan." He wound his hands in her loose hair, guiding her mouth as she continued to suck and play with his cock.

His soft moans echoed in the quiet room. His little words of encouragement and endearments made her heart sing. Maybe he did feel something for her after all even if it wasn't love, yet.

"Okay, enough. I can't take it. I need to be inside you."

"Condom?"

"In the drawer."

She grabbed one out of the drawer next to the bed, grabbed his cock, and then rolled the slippery latex down over his impressive erection.

The moment she had him sheathed, she straddled his hip, and positioned his cock before slowly sliding his length inside her. The feeling was incredible. He fit so perfectly, she couldn't help but wonder if they were made for each other. Surely so. Everything about him did it for her, his kindness, his caring, the way he made love, the way he took care of his family, the way he did for others, and mostly the way he took care of her. He'd done so much for her since they had met, it was no wonder she'd fallen in love with him.

"Ride me, darlin'."

As she began to move her hips, the glide of his cock felt absolutely wonderful. The little ball hit something inside her, sending her senses into overdrive, her pussy into spasms on the verge of climax, and her nipples to throbbing with every beat of her heart. She gasped as he palmed both her breasts in his hands, massaging the globes as she threw back her head. Her nipples burned for his touch. "Roll them. Pluck them. I need the pain."

"My pleasure. I love your boobs."

She moaned as she leaned back to brace her hands on his thighs while she continued to ride his cock like a bucking-bronc rider in the rodeo.

"You feel fantastic. Squeeze me," he said, rolling her nipples between his thumb and first finger.

She did a few Kegel maneuvers.

"Oh yeah, that's perfect. Do it again."

Desire skittered down her back. Need ripped through her groin, making her clit throb more as she continued to ride him. His left hand skimmed down her front to settle between her legs.

The next thing she felt was his thumb rubbing her clit in rhythm to her movements. It was an amazing feeling. All the emotions she'd kept bottle up burst forth. A gut wrenching sob bubbled from her lips as she shifted forward to lean over his chest.

"Are you okay? I didn't hurt you, did I?"

"No."

"What's wrong, baby?"

"Nothing. I just…"

"Tell me."

She hesitated for several minutes. Could she tell him the truth and risk him leaving? Should she lie about what was in her heart, hoping he would chose to love her sometime in the future? Unable to hold it in any longer, she blurted, "I love you, Jackson. I know it's not the time or place for this, but I can't hold it in anymore. I need you in my life. I want you to be with me always. It's okay if you don't feel the same way. In time maybe—"

"Darlin', you've come to mean more to me than life itself over the days we've spent together. I never, ever thought I would find someone I could spend the rest of my life with or even wanted to spend more than a month with, but you're it. I've realized that I need you. You are everything to me and something I never thought I'd say to any women is I love you too."

She sighed heavily as her heart lifted. He loved her too. Wow. This was more than she ever imagined when she came to San Antonio for the benefit concert. Never in her life did she think she'd find the man of her dreams here.

"Better?"

She sniffed as she wiped her face. "Yeah."

"Good. I'm dyin' here."

"Sorry. I kind of lost it there for a minute."

"I'm sure you didn't get yours either so if you don't mind, ride me until we both get to come."

"Yes, sir." She pushed herself up on his chest, scooting her knees a little closer to his hips, and lifted herself up until his cock barely stayed inside her. "How do you want it?"

"Any way you wanna give it me."

She squeezed her muscles as she slowly took him insider her body. God, she loved his cock almost as much as she loved him. Wouldn't it be great to have him all the time? What a life they'd have. They can travel to her shows together, buy a big place in Nashville or somewhere and have a fantastic life together.

He wouldn't mind moving from Thunder Ridge. She just knew it. It would be perfect.

Chapter Thirteen

The next morning found them on the bus with Mark at the wheel, Jackson relaxing on the white leather sofa, and Samantha picking away at her guitar.

They had only been on the road a few hours and he was bored beyond bored as he watched her pick out chords before jotting something down on the paper.

Yeah, he loved her. He would have to get used to this kind of thing, he guessed. Life with her wouldn't be boring, that's for sure. Well, maybe except for this traveling shit. He would have to take up some kind of hobby, otherwise he'd go crazy. Maybe they could hook up a horse trailer to the back of her bus and take his horse along so he'd have something to do.

An instrument?

He could always take up playing something, although he was kind of old to be learning to play. He'd had a guitar once years ago. It didn't amount to much, but if he remember right, he'd been pretty good at Mary Had a Little Lamb.

"What are you smiling about?" she asked as she glanced up.

"Nothing."

"There has to be something behind your little grin."

"I was thinking about taking up the guitar again. I had one when I was a kid, but I didn't do much with it. I played a mean Mary Had a Little Lamb."

She laughed. "It's not hard. I didn't start playing until I got my record deal."

"Yeah, but you are musically inclined. I'm not."

"We could write songs together."

"I could do lyrics while you do the melody. I'm pretty good at poetry."

"Really? That's fabulous!"

"Why don't you give me what you already have down, and I can see what I can come up with."

For the next couple of hours, they bounced ideas on lyrics off each other as the miles rolled by. It was actually a lot of fun for him. It definitely wasn't something he thought he would be doing. You know, writing songs wasn't really up his alley, but apparently it was.

"Wow. That's awesome. We totally have the song lyrics down in a couple of hours."

"I had a blast working the words out with you."

"You are pretty good at lyrics, you know? You could make a living at writing them for songs while others create the music."

"Nah. It's okay to do it for you, but I don't think it's for me on a regular basis for someone else."

"It's okay. I'll keep you to myself."

During their little writing session, he'd moved over to sit next to Samantha so they could share the paper she'd been writing music on as she hummed a melody. Now, he glanced at Mark who met his gaze in the rearview mirror over his head. Mark had a deep frown on his face and Jackson wondered why. The other man bugged him, if he was honest with himself. Nothing specific triggered the feelings that he could think of, but Mark just rubbed him wrong.

"Are you friends with any artist who plays country music?"

"A few, but a lot of them feel I didn't pay my dues before making it big, so they shun me in public."

"Well, that sucks. Who are you friends with?"

"Jason Aldean, Kellie Pickler, and a few others. Most of the big names don't want to have anything to do with me."

"Their loss."

She put her hand on his cheek. "You are too sweet. No wonder, I love you."

"I love you too." He leaned in a kissed her on the lips, before glancing back at the mirror again. Mark looked up and frowned again. *What the hell is his problem?*

"Hey, wanna go in the back and mess around?"

"Sure. The rocking of the bus should make for an interesting thrusting motion."

She set her guitar aside before grabbing his hand as she jumped to her feet. "Let's go."

For the next few hours they lost themselves in each other as they cuddled, kissed, made love, and enjoyed cocooning themselves in their own private little bedroom in the back of the bus. The world faded away as Jackson held her against his side, stroking her soft skin as she slept soundly next to him.

He knew she didn't sleep well even with the anxiety meds she had. With her brain always working, he figured it was difficult for her to rest. The alcohol had helped her so much since her career took off, the time it would take for her to get past the cravings would be a long haul. Now, he would be here for her for the rest of his life.

A smile crept across his lips. He never thought he would fall in love with anyone, much less Samantha Harris. She was perfect for him though. They had a lot in common, they loved helping people, they enjoyed the same things, and he couldn't picture his life without her. Was marriage on the horizon? He figure eventually, yeah, he would ask her to marry him, but he wanted her to get past all this shit with her alcohol problem and her nervousness of getting up in front of people to sing without the booze on board. She had a long road to go yet.

She stirred in her sleep as she rolled to her other side. He spooned in behind her as he felt the bus slow. They must be stopping for something. She opened her eyes as she rolled back toward him. "We're stopping."

"Yeah. I'll check with Mark to see what's up. Someone probably has to take a piss or something."

She pushed her hair out of her face. "It's almost dinner time anyway. We should get food. I didn't get a chance to grocery shop and stock the bus."

He was already up putting his pants on. "I'll radio the others and see what they want to do. You don't have to get up yet."

Before the words were out of his mouth, she sat up in the bed with the sheet clutched to her breasts. "I'm awake now."

"Okay." He opened the door to the bedroom as the bus rolled to a stop. With it firmly shut behind him, he walked toward the front as Mark hopped out of the driver's seat. "Where are we?"

"At a rest stop, slugger." He glanced at Jackson's lack of shirt and bare feet. "The driver of one of the rigs needed to stop."

Jackson crossed his arms over his chest. "Samantha wants to get supper. Talk to the guys and we can stop in the next town for something to eat."

"No problem." Mark didn't move.

"Is there something you want to say?"

"What's going on with you and Samantha?"

"What's it look like? We are a couple, have been since the charity benefit concert a few weeks ago."

Mark raised an eyebrow. "Let me get something off my chest. I don't like you. I think you are after her money, and you are nothing but a low-down, no good cowboy looking for a quick bit of fun. I'm keeping my eye on you, cowboy. Don't hurt her."

"Or what?"

"You'll answer to me. I've been with her for a long time. She's special to me, if you know what I mean."

"I think so."

"Then do what I tell you and no one will get hurt."

"Are you threatening me?"

"It's a promise, cowboy, not a threat." Mark spun on his heels and went down the stairs.

The bus door slammed behind him a minute later.

"What was that all about?" Samantha asked, coming out of the back in a robe.

"Nothing."

"It didn't sound like nothing."

"Do you always walk around in a bathrobe?"

"No, but I heard the door slam so I thought I should check it out."

"Do you have anything on under there?"

"Yeah, bra and panties. Is there a problem?"

"I don't think you should be walking around in a bathrobe in front of Mark."

"Mark is like a brother to me. I told you before. Besides, he's not even in here."

"He was."

"He's not now. I knew he left before I came out. Get off your high horse, Jackson. It's fine."

"It's not fine."

"What's really bugging you?"

"Nothing."

She put her hand on his face. "Nothing? It doesn't sound like it. I love you. It doesn't matter what anyone else sees, hears, or does. I'm yours."

"We still have a stalker to worry about, Samantha. It could be anyone, including Mark."

"That's crazy. Mark wouldn't think of me as anything more than an annoying sister."

"We need to start watching everyone, checking on everyone, that means all your band, your roadies, drivers, anyone else who is close to you. It could even be a fan, which would make it that much harder to track."

"Wow. I hadn't even though of those people."

"Have you done background checks on everybody?" He slipped his hands around her waist to take her into his embrace.

"No. Most came as recommended from someone else on the crew. It can't be one of my crew guys. They're all friends."

"It could be anyone."

She kissed his lips briefly and then stepped back. "I'm going to get dressed."

"I already told Mark you wanted to get some food. One of the rig drivers needed to stop so they are having a cigarette or something out there behind the buses. I'll put a shirt and my boots on so I can make sure they all know we are stopping for food."

"Good idea." She smiled. "Don't worry. We'll catch whoever it is."

"I hope so. It worries me that you are so vulnerable."

"I'm not with you around."

"I'm only one man."

"But you are my man. I love you."

"I love you too."

* * * *

The whole situation got on his nerves. He wanted to protect her and he was doing the best he could, but they still didn't know who the stalker might be. His gut told him it was someone on her team, but he hadn't been able to nail down the culprit yet.

His gaze swept the back around where they set up camp for the show in San Francisco. They had arrived earlier in the day, parked all the vehicles and got security ready to roll. Samantha had a sound check to do in the next thirty minutes while he stood guard outside her bus to make sure no one went in there without his permission.

It had been a steady stream of visitors since they arrived. Everyone from the coordinator of the show, to promotions, to the bands members needing her time, which shoved him to the outside looking in. He didn't like it, but it was something he would have to get used to. Right now the band was on the bus going through the playlist from what he could gather as he paced from the back to the front.

Darryl met him at the door after his next pass.

"Can you tell Sam and the guys we need them to sound check in a few minutes?"

"Sure." Jackson glanced at the twenty-something guy. "How long have you been one of Sam's roadies?"

"For a while now. She's so talented. I just love to listen to her sing." The kid gave him a once over. "Hey, aren't you the guy who did security for her at the charity concert a few weeks ago?"

"Yeah. I'm her permanent personal bodyguard now."

The kid frowned. "I didn't think she needed a personal bodyguard. Is there a problem?"

"Maybe. It seems there is someone who wants to get a little too close to her. My job is to keep them at bay."

"Hmm." Darryl shrugged. "She's a nice person. I'm sure whoever it is doesn't want to hurt her or anything. He might just want to have a little one-on-one with her, if you know what I mean. Nothing wrong with that, right?"

Jackson took a little closer notice of the kid. He couldn't be more than five-foot-five, skinny as a rail, with nerdy type glasses perched on his nose. "What exactly do you do for Sam?"

"I keep everything straight during set up and make sure she's on stage on time. She's late all the time if I don't stay on top of her."

"Oh?"

"Yeah. It's my job to remind her when it's time to go on and make sure she gets out there ready to perform. I'm an important part of her life, you know?"

"I can see that." Jackson frowned. He didn't like the way this kid made it sound like he was indispensable to Samantha. "I'll tell her and make sure she's out there in a few minutes."

"Thanks, man." The kid waved as he walked away. "Nice talking to you."

"You too."

Jackson knocked on the bus door, listening for her soft command to come in. When he took the stairs up, he was surprised to see the large group of people in the small space. He didn't think they could fit that many in there, but apparently, they did. "You need to do your sound check in a few."

"Thanks, baby." She smiled as she set her guitar down. "We'll be right out. Right guys?"

A chorus of affirmatives followed her statement as the men began to rise and shuffle toward the door.

Jackson stepped back as the group of men filed out, leaving Samantha standing alone in the middle of the bus. "Are you ready for this?"

"Yeah. The sound checks are okay. I don't know about the actual concert though."

He wrapped his arms around her, tucking her head under his chin. "You'll do great, darlin'. You are very talented."

"Thanks."

"You're welcome." He stepped back. "Now go get your sound check done so you can relax for a few hours before the concert begins. I have some security stuff to check on."

"Sure, baby, and thank you for having my back."

"I'll always have your back, your front, and both sides."

"I love you."

"I love you too."

She walked down the stairs and out the front of the bus as he watched her head toward the stage. He knew she would be fine, but she didn't, and he really hoped he could get her through this first concert.

Jackson took a seat at the laptop on the table and started typing in some names. He wanted to know as much about Mark Rogers and Darryl Minsky as he could find.

After about an hour of doing some research on the two men, he hadn't come up with much. Neither had a criminal background and both had references that checked out before they had come to work for Samantha. There wasn't anything he could pin his feelings on, but he knew in his gut one of the two men was involved in this stalker thing, but which one?

Samantha returned to the bus several minutes later. "That was fantastic! The sound is awesome in this place. Acoustics are fabulous."

"Great, honey."

She twirled in a circle with her arms out. "You don't understand, Jackson. I haven't played anywhere this nice before. There will be at least ten-thousand people in attendance at this concert and they are here to see me!"

"I know."

She flopped down on the couch with her arms resting on the back, letting out a huge sigh. "I should call my parents."

"Why?"

"I always talk to them before a show, you know, kind of a pep talk sort of thing."

"Then by all means, call them. I need to do security rounds so I'll be back, but if I'm not back before you go on, I love you. You'll do great."

"I love you too, Jackson. You are everything to me."

He kissed her long and hot. Man, he really did love this woman. He couldn't wait to see how tonight's show went. He had a feeling she was going to knock 'em dead.

Time came for the concert to start and he was stuck watching the back of the stage when it was Samantha's turn to go on. The lights went low. The fog machine started blowing smoke from the back of the stage toward the front. The crowd went wild with cheers.

He saw her walk half way up the stairs toward the back and then stop. He could see her waiver but knew she had to do this herself as much as he wanted to go to her side, hold her tight and encourage her. He'd done all he could do.

She finally took the last two stairs up to the top of the platform. She smiled back in his direction before she walked out onto the stage to the roar of the crowd.

"How is everyone tonight?"

The crowd went wild.

"Sounds like ya'll are ready to par-tay?" She turned toward the band. "Let's rock the house!"

He watched her perform from the rear of the stage, making sure no one on the floor climbed up. Security had her back with several guys stationed on the floor, two big bouncers off the side of the stage, and him. If the need arose, he would grab her and protect her with his life.

She was on the last few songs of her set when all hell broke loose.

Her boot caught on an exposed plank sending her careening off the front of the stage down into the pit area. Jackson flew past everyone, dove feet first off the platform and was near her side in a heartbeat. "Honey, are you hurt?"

She was out cold. He looked her over from head to toe, noting the funny angle of her right ankle. *Shit, it's probably broken.* "Call an ambulance. Now!" He glanced at security. "Get these people out of here. Concert is over."

One of the band got on the mic and made an announcement that the concert was over and everyone needed to file out. He told them Samantha would be okay, but they were calling an ambulance to make sure.

Jackson touched her neck to check her pulse, and leaned in to feel her breath on his face. The distinctive scent of whiskey met his nose. *Fucking son of a bitch. She's been drinking.*

"Samantha?"

She moaned softly as she moved her head from side to side, but didn't wake up fully.

She probably has a concussion on top of a broken ankle.

The band and security made a wide circle around her.

Someone asked, "Is she okay?"

"I'm not sure. I'm not a paramedic, but I think her ankle is broken, plus she's not waking up right away so she might have a concussion."

Her eyes fluttered open. "What's going on?" Her hand went to the back of her head and came away with blood. "Fuck."

"Lay still, darlin'. You fell off the stage. We've got paramedics on the way." As the words left his mouth, he heard sirens in the distance. "Sounds like they are close."

"What happened?"

"You must have hooked your boot on something. You tumbled off the stage."

"My ankle hurts."

"I think it's broken, baby. Don't move."

Tears smeared her mascara. "God, Jackson. What the hell have I done?"

"It was an accident. You'll be okay although you're going to be hurting for a while with a cast or boot on."

"Let us by, please." The paramedics brought a gurney and their equipment.

Jackson held her hand until they made him move, but he took up a spot near her head. "She's bleeding from the back of her head."

The paramedics checked her over, wrapped a bandage around her head, stabilized her ankle and moved her to the gurney. "We'll be taking her to Saint Luke's."

"I'll be there as soon as I can. I need to get a cab."

"I've already got a call into one, Jackson," Darryl said. "They'll be here in fifteen minutes."

"Thanks, Darryl."

"You can find her at the emergency room when you get there," the paramedic said as they moved her toward the ambulance.

"Jackson?"

"I'll be there shortly, baby. Hang in there."

"I love you," she shouted as they put her inside the ambulance.

"I love you too, honey."

He watched with a heavy heart as the ambulance drove away with her in the back.

The cab pulled up a few minutes later. When he wrenched open the door and hopped in the back, he told the driver where to go as he pulled out his cell phone to call her dad.

"Hey, Mr. Harris? This is Jackson Young."

"Hi, Jackson. What has Samantha done now?"

"She fell off the stage and it appears she's probably broken her ankle. I believe she has a concussion too, but we won't know anything for a bit. I'm on the way to the hospital to see what's up."

"Thanks for calling. Let me know when you know something about her condition."

"I certainly will, sir."

"Thank you for being there with her. You are a godsend, son."

"You're welcome. I love her so I wouldn't be anywhere else."

"That's nice to hear, Jackson. I hope she loves you too."

"She says she does, but after this I'm going to kick her ass. She's been drinking again."

"Oh man."

"Yeah, I could smell it on her breath after the fall."

"Lord have mercy."

"She's going to need it when I get done reaming her for this. She should have never been performing after she drank, but anyway, I'm at the hospital, so I'll call you after while."

"Thank you. Talk to you soon."

Jackson paid the cab driver and climbed out of the car. When he got his hands on his girl, he wouldn't be nice. This was way beyond something he would tolerate. She hadn't talked to him. He would bet good money, she didn't call Jacob either.

He stopped at the desk and asked for her room.

"She's being triaged in the emergency room. If you'll have a seat, the doctor will be out to get you soon."

Hadn't he just done this not two weeks ago with her? What the hell was she thinking?

He noticed a coffee pot sitting off to the side of the entrance. The liquid had probably gone stale, but it was better than nothing. He had a feeling tonight would be a long night.

Chapter Fourteen

Jackson stood as the doctor came through the door and asked for whoever was with Samantha Harris.

"That would be me."

"Are you family?"

"Sort of. I'm her boyfriend."

"Well then, come with me. We'll talk on the way to her room."

"Thanks."

He led Jackson through the double doors as they headed down a long hall. "You are probably aware, she has a concussion and a broken ankle. We've stabilized the ankle, but she'll have to have surgery on it in the next day or two. It's shattered when she fell so she'll need plates and screws to hold it together. I've already consulted the orthopedic surgeon. He's planning on taking her to surgery tomorrow sometime depending on how her confusion is resolving."

"Confusion?"

"Yes. Typical of a concussion, she's repeating her questions and not sure where she is. She keeps asking for you, which is why you are coming back here so you can help calm her down. We don't want to give her any medication with her blood alcohol level." The doctor glanced at him, and then back down the hall. "Were you aware she'd been drinking?"

"Not until after she fell off the stage at the concert. She's an alcoholic and she's been recovering for the last week to ten days. Apparently, she started drinking again this evening before the concert."

"Her blood alcohol level is very high. Do you know what she drank?"

"My guess is whiskey. It's her drink of choice."

"She must have had half a bottle or so."

"She had a bout of blood alcohol poisoning about ten days ago, thus trying to get sober. Obviously, it didn't work too well."

"I'm sure you are aware it is a process and a long one for someone to recover from alcoholism."

"Yes, I know. My brother is her sponsor."

They reached a door to the right. "She's in here."

"Jackson!" She moaned. "Where's Jackson?"

"He'll be here in just a minute. The doctor went to get him."

"Don't be hard on her for now. The concussion wasn't severe, but it was enough to cause the confusion. Will you be staying with her tonight?"

"I will if they need me to. No problem."

"It would probably the best. The rooms upstairs have chairs that fold out into a cot. I've slept on them myself. They aren't too bad." The doctor held out his hand. "I hope you get her the help she needs."

"I hope so too."

"They'll be in to transfer her upstairs soon."

"Thanks, Doctor."

"You're welcome." He laid a hand on Jackson's shoulder before he turned and walked to the desk.

Jackson took a deep breath then pushed open the door.

"Jackson!"

"I'm right here, Samantha."

"Oh, thank God. Where have you been? I've been here for hours and they wouldn't tell me what's going on."

"You have a concussion and a broken ankle. You'll have to have surgery tomorrow to fix it."

She sat up higher on the gurney. "Surgery? Holy shit. I did a bang up job, huh?"

"Yeah, you did."

"What happened?"

"You tripped on something on the stage and fell off the front. You wacked your head and broke your ankle."

"Wow. I did a bang up job, huh?"

"Yes, you did."

"I'm repeating myself, aren't I?"

"Yes, but that's from your concussion."

"Sorry."

"They'll be transferring you upstairs before too long."

"How is everything at the venue?"

"I'm sure it's fine. The guys know their jobs. They'll take care of things. You'll probably have to cancel the next couple of shows until you're able to put some weight on your ankle or whatever they recommend. You might not be able to move around except on crutches for a while."

"This is going to put a real cramp in the show schedule. I had another one this week and one next week. The next six weeks were going to be very busy."

"I know, Sam. I know your schedule pretty well."

"Yeah, I guess you probably do."

Silence filled the room as she looked from him to the door and back like she was looking for an escape. That wouldn't happen with her injuries, but she definitely didn't want to look him in the eye for some reason.

A tear slid down her cheek. "I'm sorry," she whispered as her gaze came back to his. "I screwed up."

He didn't respond, figuring it was best for her to talk this out, but he did take her hand in his, rubbing his thumb over the knuckles to reassure her she could tell him anything.

"I couldn't stop, Jackson. I drank half a bottle before the show. I didn't do what I was supposed to. I didn't call Jacob when I had the urge to drink, I just downed that bottle like it was water."

"I know."

"You know?"

"I could smell it on your breath when I reached your side after you fell. The doctor also said your blood alcohol level is very high."

"I don't know what to do anymore."

"You need help."

"I know. I thought I was getting help and doing okay. I hadn't had a drink in ten days, but the minute things got crazy, I went right back to the whiskey." She grabbed the sheet lying over her to wipe the tears from her face. "What am I going to do, Jackson?"

He leaned back in the chair knowing he needed to be tough with her. This was important. "You need to talk to Jacob and to your doctor. Did you take your anxiety meds?"

"No. The bottle sounded better. I guess I should have taken it instead."

"Yeah."

"How was the show?"

"It was a good one. The crowd loved you."

"I don't remember it."

"That could be from the concussion or the alcohol."

She bit her lip for a moment before she said, "You know what's bad?"

"What?"

"I don't remember a lot of the shows I've done over the years."

"I'm not surprised."

"It's gotten better though. I guess my tolerance for the whiskey has cleared my memory some. Problem is, I just have to keep drinking more and more to get the same feeling."

"That's why they call it alcoholism, Sam."

"I'll try to do better. No more alcohol. I promise."

"You said that before."

"This time I mean it. I won't drink again. Ever."

"I hope you are willing to go that extra mile. You didn't seem to want to admit you really have a problem before."

She grasped his hand in hers, bringing it to her lips. "I do now, Jackson, honest I do. I know I have a drinking problem. I know I need help with it. You are here for me. I love you and I want us to be together for a long time to come."

"So do I."

"We'll be moving her upstairs now," the nurse said after she peeked through the doorway. "Give me a minute to get her paperwork together."

"Sure."

They made small talk for several minutes as they waited for the nurse to move her upstairs.

"I called your dad."

She blew out a heavy sigh. "Great. What did he say?"

"He's really worried about you."

"Did you tell him about the alcohol?"

"Yeah."

"Crap. I'll never hear the end of this now."

"You are lucky he's not flying out here to drag your ass back to Iowa and whup some sense into your head."

She laughed and he couldn't help but smile. "He would too."

"You're damned right he would. I'm tempted to take the situation under my own control and beat your ass myself."

"I might like it."

"You probably would."

The nurse came through the door, dropped her paperwork on the gurney and popped the break. "Are you coming up with us?" she asked him.

"Yes, ma'am."

"Follow me then."

Fifteen minutes later, they had her settled in a bed with her foot propped up on pillows as he sank down in the chair near the window.

"Are you staying the night with me?"

"I might as well. It's either here or on your bus and the doctor was worried about your confusion with the concussion."

"I think I'm better now though. I can remember some things but not others, and I'm not repeating myself."

"True, but it might be better for me to stay."

She glanced around the room. "I'd love for you to climb in this bed with me. I really don't think the nurses would like it much."

"No, the doctor said these chairs fold out into a bed. As long as they give me a pillow, I can crash here. I'm used to sleeping in much worse spots."

"I can imagine so."

He flipped on the television before asking her if there was anything particular she wanted to watch.

"No, not really. I'm kind of sleepy from the pain meds they gave me, so why don't you find something. I think I'll just get some shuteye."

"Okay. You let me know if you need anything during the night. They'll probably be waking you up regularly during the night anyway."

"Probably." She turned toward him. "Can you kiss me before I go to sleep?"

"Of course, darlin'." He got to his feet and walked toward the side of the bed. She really was cute with her hair in a braid down her back, her stage makeup was kind of smeared under her eyes, and her lipstick messy, but he loved her anyway. He leaned in and pressed his lips over hers. "I love you."

"I love you too, Jackson. Don't ever forget that okay? I know I'm kind of a mess, but you mean everything to me."

Her eyes drifted shut before he even had a chance to reply. It was going to be a long haul with this drinking thing. If she was really willing to stop, he would stand by her.

* * * *

Samantha woke in the night confused as to where she was. The dark room frightened her in her state of mind until she turned her head to realize Jackson snored softly on the chair across the room. She knew he would never let anything bad happen to her.

Memories flooded back. Falling off the stage. Drinking before the concert even though she knew she shouldn't. It all came rushing in, bringing tears to her eyes. The call of the alcohol couldn't be shut off as easily as she'd thought when she talked to Jacob and her doctor at the ranch.

A choking sob rocked her body as she wrapped her arms around herself trying to hold everything in as her world came apart. If she lost Jackson because of this, she wouldn't be able to go on.

"Are you in pain, darlin'?"

"No."

"What can I do to help you?"

"Hold me."

He scooted up on the side of the bed as she moved over to make room. When he wrapped her in his arms, the world righted itself again instead of careening out of control. She knew he would always do this for her. She just had to figure out how to keep him around forever to be able to right everything for her.

"Better?"

"Yeah. Thank you."

"Anytime, honey. You know that, I hope."

"What am I going to do, Jackson?"

"What do you mean?"

"I'm afraid. I'm terrified, really, that I can't sing in front of the crowd without the alcohol in me. I'm not strong enough to overcome that."

He kissed the top of her head before snuggling her in closer. "Yes you are, Samantha. You have a beautiful voice. You are a very talented lady. You have to find some way to get past your fear. Maybe talking to a therapist would help."

"I have to do something or my career is over."

"You are a strong lady. You can overcome this. No problem."

"But what if I can't? What if my life as a country singer is over because I can't get up in front of people and sing anymore?"

He tipped her chin up with his finger. "You can handle this."

"What happens to us?"

"What do you mean?"

"What if I can't handle this? What happens to us?"

"Samantha, I'm not with you because you're a country star and have a bunch of money or whatever. I'm with you because I love you. Yes, at first I was in awe of you being Samantha Harris and that you were attracted enough to me to want to have sex with me, but it's not what made me love you. You are what made me love you. The way you are with everyone, the way you take care of people and everything. That's what's important. If your career was over tomorrow, it wouldn't change the way I feel about you. I will always love you, no matter what happens." He brushed his lips over hers, sweeping his tongue along the seam to encourage her to open for him.

This is what she needed—him. "I want you to make love to me."

"I can't. Not here." He kissed her forehead. "Besides, honey, your ankle is going to make things difficult for a bit. You're going to be in a lot of pain."

"I don't hurt right now."

"You have quite a bit of pain killer in you." He moved to the chair sitting beside the bed. "You need to sleep. You are having surgery tomorrow, remember?"

"Yeah. I hate being without food or water. My mouth is so dry."

"I'm sure having your blood alcohol coming down is doing that. I can see if you can wet your mouth, but you can't swallow any of the water." He climbed to his feet. "Let me ask the nurse."

"I'll hit the call button."

"Okay."

After the nurse came in and gave her some swabs to wet her mouth with, she settled back on the bed and closed her eyes. She needed to sleep so this whole ordeal would be over soon. The disappointment in Jackson's eyes hurt. It was a look she never wanted to see again, and by George, she would make it happen one way or another.

The next morning, they got her ready for surgery while Jackson waited in the chair in her room. She knew he would be there when she awoke, but she was still scared. She didn't like the feelings of coming out of anesthesia any more than she liked being hung over from drinking too much. It didn't happen often, but once in a while, she overdid and she would feel like shit the next morning.

She gingerly transferred herself to the gurney by scooting over as the nurse and the attendant managed her immobilized ankle. They had given her pain medicine earlier in the morning to numb it when they did this and she knew they would take care of her after surgery, but for now, she was too hyped up on adrenaline to care. "You'll be here when I get back?"

"Of course, darlin'. I'm not going anywhere."

"Thank you."

"For what?"

"For being here for me."

"I wouldn't be anywhere else. I love you."

"I love you too." The nurse tucked the blanket around her hips. "I'll see you in a bit."

"Yes, ma'am." He grinned before leaning down to kiss her. "You'll do fine, darlin'."

They wheeled her out and down the hall. She shivered under the blanket, from nerves mostly, she supposed, but the thought of going into a deep sleep terrified her.

"Are you all right? You look pretty pale," the nurse asked.

"I'm scared is all."

"It'll be okay. We have one of the best orthopedic doctors on staff. He'll get you fixed up and back on the road to recovery. You'll probably have to be in a boot for about six weeks depending on the damage, but he'll come talk to you and your boyfriend after all is said and done to give you the information you need."

"Thanks."

"Would you like another blanket?"

"That would be great."

She stopped the gurney next to a door. "Let me grab a warm one. Those are always fabulous when you are shivering like you are."

"Sweet."

After she had the warm blanket over her, she closed her eyes and relaxed on the gurney for the short trip to the operating room. She didn't remember much after that since they quickly moved her to the operating table, and put her to sleep.

She woke up several hours later, back in her own room with Jackson sitting at the side of her bed.

"Easy, darlin'. Are you in pain?"

"A little," she croaked. "Is it over?"

"Yes. A long time ago. It's seven-thirty in the evening now. You had surgery at ten this morning."

"Wow. I've slept all day?"

"Yep. I guess you needed the rest. I don't think you slept well last night. You moaned a lot in your sleep."

"I'm sorry."

"For what?" he asked, grasping her hand in his to rub his thumb over her knuckles.

"For being such a pain in the ass."

"I want to be a pain in your ass soon, but we have to wait a while."

"Oh, sounds like fun." She shifted on the bed. "I can't wait." Her body was on high alert from lack of sex. She knew this and she was sure Jackson knew it too, poor guy. Not that it had been a particularly long time since they had made love, but two healthy, active thirty year olds needed a raucous sex life, right?

"You need to heal first."

"Party pooper."

He pushed the button to call the nurse. "We can talk about the details of your surgery in a minute. First you need to eat something and probably get something for pain before it gets out of control."

"Good idea. I'm starving."

The nurse came in to see what they needed. "I'll get you a tray from the kitchen and be back in a jiff with some pain meds."

"Thank you."

The nurse gave Jackson a sexy little smile. "My pleasure."

After she left, Samantha sighed.

"What's wrong, darlin'?"

"Do they all have to flirt with you with me sitting right here?"

"She wasn't flirting."

"Yes, she was. Didn't you see that little smile she gave you? She wasn't looking at me like that."

"I don't know what you want me to do, babe. I can't help them talking to me."

"I'll use it to my advantage. You can ask them for stuff. They'll give it to you before they give it to me."

He laughed and shook his head. "Whatever you say, babe."

After she got some food and pain meds, she settled in to talk to him about the surgery and what would be required for her ankle to heal properly.

"The doctor said you'll be on crutches for a few weeks with a cast, but you might be able to graduate to a boot so you can walk around with it. Either way, you'll be in something for six to eight weeks."

"Great," she grumbled. "What about sex?"

"What about it?"

"When can we have it again?"

"I didn't ask."

"You didn't? Why the hell not?"

"I figured when you aren't in pain and we can maneuver your ankle so it doesn't hurt during, we would be good to go." He kissed her briefly, certainly not long enough for her taste. "Besides, you can ask him when you do a follow-up appointment with him in a couple of weeks."

"We can't stay here for two weeks. I have shows to do."

"Honey, I've already talked to your manager. We've cancelled the shows coming up for the next two weeks."

"You can't do that!"

"The hell I can't. Your health comes first and Billy agreed with me when I talked to him. We will reschedule when you are better. Your fans will understand."

She crossed her arms over her chest and glared at him. "Don't you ever get in the middle of my career again."

Chapter Fifteen

"Excuse me?" The tone of her voice pissed him off. He was doing the best for her and her career and she was going to get pissy about him stepping in to rearrange her schedule?

"You will not get in the middle of me and my career. I will do the rearranging if things need to be rearranged. I will talk with my manager. I will talk with my record label execs. You will not."

"Now listen, Samantha. I did what was best for you while you were unconscious. I didn't think it was a big deal."

"It is a big deal. I will handle my career. I don't need you getting in the middle of it."

"If we're in a relationship, that means I'm in the middle of it. Get off your high horse and take a chill pill. We are in this together."

"You know nothing about my music career. You work on a ranch riding horses, herding cattle, and taking care of guests for a living. I've had to run this business on my own since I started. I know what I'm doing, you don't."

"What the fuck is your problem?"

"What's yours? Why are you trying to take over my career?"

"I'm not!" He threw up his hands as he began pacing from the window back to her bed. "I'm trying to help you, damn it! All I did was agree with Billy when he said you should cancel the next two weeks shows until you can get on the damn stage. You won't be able to climb stairs safely until you are in a boot. Stop being stubborn!" *What the hell?* He jerked off his hat, raked his fingers through his hair, and then shoved it back low on his forehead. "Listen, Samantha. I'm not trying to run this for you. You're right. I don't know the first thing about running a music career and I'm not trying to learn on a shoestring. I love you. I'm trying to be there for you and help you, not run things for you."

She glared for a full minute, he figured, before she lowered her gaze from his. "I'm sorry," she whispered. "You're right. I'm glad you cancelled the shows."

"I don't frickin' believe you. You jump my shit about making any kind of decision for you, and now you think you can make this all better by apologizing sweetly?"

"I can't?"

Frustration zipped through him. He rolled his neck a little to relieve the tension building there so he wasn't tempted to strangle her. "I need to take a walk." He headed for the door. "I'll be back." He slammed out before heading for the elevator. Coffee, soda, or something. He wasn't sure what he needed, but he would head to the cafeteria and take a break from her. Just for a few minutes anyway. The short ride down in the elevator did nothing to assuage his anger. He couldn't believe how she'd ripped him a new asshole about cancelling her shows and then turned on the charm to calm him down. How manipulative could someone get? Did she do that shit all the time with her producers, managers, agents, and so forth? He would have to watch her behavior a little more closely.

Oh, who was he kidding? He loved her. She could bat her eyelashes at him and he would be kissing her damned painted toes inside of seconds. Still, he needed to get away from her for a few minutes to calm down. She could still get his blood pressure up with her attitude some times.

As the doors slid open, he stepped out into the hallway, following the smells of food. His stomach grumbled. He probably needed to eat a sandwich or something since he hadn't eaten for quite a while. Breakfast, actually, come to think of it. He found the end of the line to the food, grabbed a sandwich, a Coke, and a small cup of some vegetable soup before he paid for his meal, and then went to find a table.

While he ate, he watched the crowds. Families with small children, men looking worn out, women with tears in their eyes, they all looked sad and forlorn making him wonder what their stories were. Obviously, they had family members here going through some kind of medical necessity, but his mind often ran with a scenario for each one building something out of nothing but a look on their faces.

He chuckled to himself as he finished his food. *I wonder if this is what Mesa goes through when she's thinking of new stories to write. Maybe I should sit down and chitchat with her sometime.* His mind always seemed to whirl with ideas about people he'd seen or talked to while he made up some kind of life for them out of his own thoughts.

He did see a gentleman with a large bouquet of flowers rushing through the lobby. Maybe a man with a new baby? Wouldn't that be fun, he decided. Sure, someday he wanted kids.

He frowned a moment when he thought about Samantha. Did she want kids? What kind of life would they have if she was on the road all the time? Where would they live if she was back and forth to Nashville all the time? These were things they needed to work out, he supposed, if they were to build a life together.

A life together. Was he really thinking along marriage lines? Yeah, he loved her, but did he really want to commit to a lifetime with her? A smile spread across his face. Yes, he did. He wanted to marry her.

With a gleeful lightness to his heart, he tossed his trash into the receptacle as he headed back to Samantha's room. He wouldn't ask her to marry him just yet. Something special would be in order for that moment, something he needed to think on for a bit. Besides, he needed to ask her dad for his permission anyway, which might be a little sticky since they really hadn't known each other all that long. He would have to buy a ring, something simple, but elegant like her. She always came across to him as someone who appreciated the smaller things in life rather than the fancy cars, big house, and servants kind of thing. Growing up a small town Iowa girl made her a lot like him.

When he approached her door, he drew in a deep breath hoping things had calmed down. He felt better for having taken the break, but they really needed to talk about her attitude. Now was probably not a good time. He pushed through the door to find the room dark. *She must have gone to sleep.*

He moved toward the chair in the corner and unfolded it into a bed so he could lie down and rest. Sleep would probably come hard tonight since he had so much whirling through his brain.

"Jackson?"

"Yeah?"

"I really am sorry."

"I know, darlin'."

"Are you still mad at me?"

"We'll talk tomorrow, but no, I'm not still mad."

"Good." Silence reigned for a minute. "I love you."

"I love you too. Now, go to sleep. We have to get you checked out of here tomorrow and back on the bus before we find somewhere to wait out the next two weeks."

* * * *

Two weeks. Two fucking weeks they'd been on the bus sitting in a small campground while the other band members went home for an unscheduled break. The other bus and rigs were parked at a storage place until she got the all clear for a boot so she could walk on her foot.

She hadn't been out of this can since she left the hospital and she was about to go out of her mind. Her appointment with the doctor was tomorrow, thank goodness, because if she didn't get out of here soon, she would kill someone, namely Jackson.

For a person who's normal routine included being outside on horseback working with his hands, he was surprisingly content to be on the bus tapping away at the laptop most of the time. She had no idea what he did all day while she rested and healed, but she'd had enough. If she didn't get a break soon, she'd go bat-shit crazy.

Jackson sat at the table tapping away at the keyboard beneath his fingers. The sounds grated on her nerves like nails on a chalkboard. Normally, it didn't bother her, but since she'd heard nothing else for two weeks, she was totally over it. "Can you please stop whatever it is you're doing?"

"I'm chatting."

"With who?"

"Jonathan."

"Jonathan?"

"My brother at the ranch. I'm asking how things are going and all that. I haven't really talked to any of them since your accident."

"Oh."

"Are you hurting?"

"No."

"Are you sure you don't need a pain pill? It's been quite a while since you've had one."

"No! I don't need a pain pill. I need to get the fuck out of this bus before I go stir crazy."

He turned in his chair to look at her. His eyes sparkled with mirth.

She wanted to throw something at him.

"Please, Jackson. I need out of here. I need to breathe some fresh air, go outside, go to the store, go to a movie, something. I'm about to go crazy."

"We can watch a movie."

"At a theatre?"

"I guess. I can carry you inside, put you in the seat and then carry you back out. We would need to call a cab since moving the bus is a silly idea."

She sat up straighter in her chair. Writing songs had become a chore like everything else since she'd been hurt so that wouldn't help matters, but getting out of here would. Anything to see outside again. "I can walk on my crutches as long as you are spotting me."

"Okay." He turned back toward the laptop. "Let's find a theatre around here and we'll go see something."

She bounced in her chair excitedly. "Thank you!"

After he managed to find somewhere they could go to see a movie, he helped her pull on a coat. She couldn't make it off the bus without him carrying her because of the width of the stairs. Of course, she didn't mind being in his arms and if she managed to lick his neck, bite his ear, and generally make him horny in the process. Well. Her job was complete.

"You'll pay for teasing me later, you know. I'm going to drive you insane before I let you come."

"Promises, promises."

"Definitely a promise," he said as he helped her maneuver into the cab. "After all, I let you pick the movie so that's another reason to torture you later since you are making me watch a chick flick."

"I need a good cry."

"Why?"

She wrapped her hand around his bicep and leaned into his side. "Because being cooped up has pissed me off. You're lucky you still have a head, but since you were nice enough to take me out, you'll live to see another day."

"Hopefully, the doctor will put you in a boot tomorrow and you can get around again, do your shows, and be a normal human being." He kissed her on the nose. "You should have been writing songs the last two weeks, but you haven't been."

"I didn't feel like it. I've been too grumpy to write."

"Too keyed up?"

"That too although the sex has helped a lot."

"I'm glad I could be of service to you, milady."

"Aw, aren't you such a handsome devil. I think I'll keep you around for a bit."

"So nice of you to say so. Besides, you can't get rid of me that easy."

"I hope not. I like having you here."

"I like being here."

"Good."

They pulled up to the theatre a minute later. He paid the driver before he got out and went around to her side of the cab. She scooted her butt around on the seat when he opened the door, then slid her cast out to rest on the ground before he helped her put the crutches under her arms. They managed to get inside without too much trouble, pay for their tickets and then hobble her inside the specific room where the show they would be seeing played.

"Do you want me to get popcorn and Coke?"

"Of course. What is a movie without popcorn?"

"I'll be right back then."

While he was gone, she let her mind wander to Jackson. She really did love him more than she could ever show him. He'd been there for her, helped her in every way, and supported her like no other had ever done in her life. Yes, she loved him with all her heart. She hoped he loved her as much. They would work out the details of where they would live soon, she hoped. She had a lot of ideas she wanted to bounce off him.

He returned several minutes later with a huge tub of popcorn and the biggest cup of something cold she'd see in a long time.

She wet her lips thinking about the Coke in that glass. What she wouldn't give to put a little whiskey in with it right now. This being clean and sober sucked pretty badly when all she wanted was a little alcohol to take the edge off. She would feel so much better if she had some, but it wasn't to be, at least for now. Darryl wasn't around to get it for her at the moment.

"You okay?"

"Yeah, why?"

"You're quiet."

"You're supposed to be quiet in a theatre."

"Not until the movie starts."

"I suppose."

"Are you thinking about getting back to singing?"

"A little. I'm nervous about it."

"You shouldn't be. I've told you before, you are very talented and you've got a great show."

She tilted her head to the side. "You aren't just saying that because you love me, are you?"

He leaned in and kissed her on the lips. "No."

"Okay." She reached over to grab a handful of popcorn. "Thanks."

The movie made her cry, big, blubbery girlie sobs she couldn't hold in if she tried. She needed the cry though. She'd had so much pent up frustration, anger, and just general bullshit tied up inside her, she had to let go somehow. Now, she could move on.

They waited for the crowd to disburse after the movie before she hobbled out on her crutches to the lobby.

"I'll call the cab company. We might have to wait a few minutes though."

"No problem." She sipped the last of the Coke, making the contents gurgle in the bottom of the cup. "We can sit here and chill until they get here."

A young woman about seventeen shyly walked up to them. "Are you Samantha Harris the country music singer?"

"Yes I am. Do you like country music?"

The girl gushed. "Oh yeah. You are my absolute favorite singer. Can I get a picture and an autograph?"

"Sure, doll."

She should have known. The moment it got around the movie theatre she was there, she had a line of people wanting autographs and pictures. This she didn't mind. She actually loved being with her fans, talking, taking pictures, and all of the stuff that went with being a popular singer even though most days she didn't feel like it.

Jackson asked the cab company to come back in thirty minutes so she could take care of her fans.

God, she loved him.

She sighed and closed her eyes for a moment. "Tired?"

"Yeah."

"Want me to cut this off?"

"Yeah, I think so."

"Folks, I'm sorry but as you can see Samantha hurt herself a few weeks ago and tonight is the first time she's been out since the accident. She's really tired and needs to go rest. She'll be doing another show in the area in the next couple of months, so please make sure you check it out, get tickets, and come by. She would love to see you."

He grabbed her crutches, scooped her up in his arms, much to the sighs of some of the ladies in the crowd, and carried her out to the cab.

The ride back to the bus was made in silence as she rested her head on his shoulder.

Tomorrow would be a busy day. She hoped the doctor would put her in a boot and she could start performing again. Her stomach knotted. She needed to get over this before the next show.

When they reached the bus, he helped her out so she could hobble to the stairwell before he swept her up in his arms again to carry her inside. *Such a gentleman.* "Are we going to make love now?"

"If you want to. You seem really tired. I figured we could wait."

"I am tired, but not too tired for you."

He let her hobble into the back bedroom before she sank down on the end of their bed. Everything in the bus belonged to him too, these days. He'd certainly made himself at home when he moved into her space to live. His shaving cream and toothbrush took up space in the bathroom, his underwear and socks had their own drawers in her dresser, his jeans hung in the closet along with his western shirts. Yep, he'd moved in and taken over her life. She didn't mind at all.

She slipped off the T-shirt she'd worn to the movies, tossing it to the pile in the corner of dirty clothes. Her bra came next, leaving her completely bare to his gaze. His eyes sparkled with lust as his gaze slid over her. "Do you want me?" she asked, her voice barely coming out in a whisper.

"Hell yeah, I want you."

"Take me then." She laid back on the bed so he could help her take her pants off over her cast. They'd been really creative with the sex since her accident, but tonight she didn't want creative, she wanted down and dirty, hot and sweaty sex. "Fuck me."

"I'd plan to torture for a while, but I don't think I can wait. I want you too bad." He quickly stripped off his clothes. "Can you turn over?"

"Yeah." She flipped on to her stomach, then shuffled back so her butt was on the edge of the bed. "What's your pleasure, cowboy? Back or front?"

"I want your hot little pussy first, then I'm going to take your ass."

She shivered. Lord, she loved making love with him and to have him take her this way was the best. His cock bumped at her opening, the piercing sliding enticingly along her vaginal walls as he slowly pushed inside her. "Holy fuck."

"You are so tight."

"I love how you feel inside me. Go hard."

He slammed his pelvis against her butt, as they both moaned. The quick thrust of his hips brought her to the brink of an explosive orgasm within minutes as he pounded into her from behind. She loved hot, dirty sex and Jackson was the master of it from the experiences she'd had with him. His hand went around to between her legs and he rubbed her clit with a rapid you-will-come-now rhythm. She exploded in an earth-shattering climax as lights danced behind her closed eyelids. "Oh God."

He panted behind her. She could almost feel him gritting his teeth to hold back his own climax. "You okay for me to go up the back?"

"Hell yeah."

"Okay." He pulled his cock from her pussy, smearing cum along with it up the crack of her ass. She was so hot and slick, they wouldn't need any lube this time. "Deep breath, sweetheart."

He pushed his dick slowly through the puckered hole at her ass, past the ring of muscles and stopped until she felt her whole body relax with his penetration. "Oh yeah. Perfect."

His hips began the slow thrusting motion meant to keep his own climax at the surface, but not allow him to fall over, she knew from experience, but it would bring her to another climax shortly if she knew her own body very well at all. She felt her pussy throb with each beat of her racing heart. Sweat slicked her skin. Goosebumps rose from the cooler air hitting her. She needed this more than he knew.

"Please, Jackson. Harder. Faster."

"I want this to last."

"I'm there, baby. I swear. Fuck me."

He growled low in his throat as his thrusts became uncoordinated, hurried and rough. Her body shattered on a high-scream climax she knew would stay with her for a long time to come.

Chapter Sixteen

Apprehension slid down her back. This was the first show since the accident. Jackson was out doing his rounds before the show began. She knew she wouldn't see him until after the whole thing was over.

Her stomach knotted.

She'd already taken two Xanax to calm her nerves. It hadn't done anything. She took three more just a few minutes ago.

A knock sounded on the door.

"Come in."

Darryl climbed the stairs a minute later, the brown package in his hands, her lifesaver.

"Are you sure you want to do this, Samantha?"

"I have to, Darryl."

He handed her the paper bag. She blew out a breath as she opened the bottle and took a long swig of the whiskey. She could feel her body relax that quickly. Her life is what it is. She couldn't do this without the whiskey, she just couldn't.

"I'll leave you to it then. You're on in thirty."

"Thanks, Darryl. You are very important to me, you know."

"I'm your supplier, Sam. I don't like it."

"But—"

"Nothing. Jackson is going to kill me, but I can't say no to you." He walked out without a backward glance.

For the next thirty minutes, she drank. Big swigs, little sips, it didn't matter, she needed the alcohol.

She sat back against the cushion of the couch as she let the alcohol take effect. Her eyelids felt heavy. Maybe a little nap would be a good idea, but didn't she need to be somewhere? She couldn't remember. Oh well, Jackson would take care of her. The couch cushion looked so soft. She would just close her eyes for a few minutes and then she would feel a lot better.

* * * *

Jackson knocked on the door of the bus. Samantha was supposed to have been on stage five minutes ago and he hadn't seen hide nor hair of her. *She must be messing with her makeup or something.* He got no answer.

He opened the door and bound up the stairs, worry rushing through him. It wasn't like Samantha to not answer the door.

Holy fuck!

He rushed to her side when he spotted the three quarter empty bottle of whiskey on the table along with her bottle of medication for anxiety. "Samantha?" He shook her shoulder. She didn't even moan. He peeled back her eyelids. Her pupils were pinpoint. "Samantha?" She started to throw up so he rolled her on her side and held her there as he screamed for some help. Darryl came rushing up the steps.

"What's going on?"

"Call an ambulance. Now!"

Darryl's hand shook as he dialed 911.

Jackson prayed and prayed hard. *God, please let her be okay so I can beat her ever lovin' ass for this.*

"Samantha?" He rolled her onto her back, pushing her hair out of her face. "God, Sam, please, don't die."

"She's going to die?" Tears ran down Darryl's face.

"No, damn it! She's not going to die, but you need to get yourself together. Go out and tell Mark what is going on so he can direct the ambulance. The band needs to cancel the show. We will reschedule it for another time, but for now, get these people out of here."

"Okay."

"Darryl?"

"Yeah?"

"Do you know where she got the booze?"

"I gave it to her." The smaller man shook from head to toe. "I'm sorry, Jackson. She asked me to get it for her and I did. I know she drinks too much, but I figure she'd only drink a little so she could get on the stage, not like this."

"You do realize this is bad. I don't know what the hell is going on here, but it's bad."

"I know. God, I'm sorry."

"You should be, now go do what I told you."

Darryl practically ran down the stairs and out the door. Mark came in a minute later. Jackson gave him a run down. "I don't know if she took some of her medication or not with the alcohol. Right now, she's breathing but very shallow. This could kill her."

"The ambulance should be here in a minute."

"Okay. Get them up here immediately. I'll carry her down to them so they can work on her."

"All right."

He held her hand watching her chest rise and fall. *Keep breathing, baby, keep breathing.*

The ambulance arrived as he scooped her up in his arms and rushed down the steps to their waiting gurney. "All I know is she probably drank three quarters of a bottle of whiskey and possibly took some Xanax. They are prescribed, although she's not supposed to have the alcohol. She's vomited as you can tell by her shirt. She won't respond to her name." He raked his fingers through his hair, not even sure where his hat ended up. "God, help her, guys, please."

As the paramedics went to work on her, getting her vital signs and putting a needle in her arm, he paced. *She has to be okay. She just has to be.*

They decided to put a tube down her throat to make sure she didn't breathe in any vomit and to help her respiration since it was so shallow.

"We are taking her to Mission Hospital. Will you be following?"

"I'll be right behind you."

Someone called a cab while all hell had broken loose, thank goodness. He didn't know what he would do without the group he had around him. They were great people and cared about Samantha a lot. Unfortunately, they'd been through something similar with her twice now so they knew what to do. He would let them handle the show, breaking it down and getting everyone situated.

He followed the ambulance to the hospital praying the whole time. He didn't know what else to do in this case. No one close to him had ever been in this situation before. He wasn't sure how to handle it other than doing what he'd done when she had alcohol poisoning. He would talk to the doctors and go from there.

This hospital shit was for the birds. He'd done it way too often with her in the short time they'd known each other now, but by God damn, he'd had enough with her. She was going to find some inpatient rehab or something because he couldn't keep going on like this.

He found a cup of coffee after he let the receptionist know who he was there with and began to pace. He needed to call her dad…again, and he really could use a shoulder right now. Maybe he'd call his mom or no, Jacob. Jacob would know how to handle this.

Grabbing his cell phone, he pulled up his brother's number and hit talk.

"Jackson, what's wrong. You never call me."

"It's Sam."

"What happened?"

"I'm not sure other than I think she drank most of a bottle of whiskey. I think she took some Xanax, too, but I don't know for sure until I talk to the doctor."

"Do you think she was trying to commit suicide?"

"Hell no! Why would you say that?"

"The combination of those two could kill her."

"I know that, Jacob, but I don't think suicide was what she was going for. This was her first show after her accident. You know how terrified she is about getting up there. I think she couldn't handle it without the alcohol. Darryl got it for her. He's been supplying her apparently."

"He needs to find a new job."

"Yeah, I know."

"Who is here with Samantha Harris?" the nurse called as she came out the doors.

He raised his hand as he walked toward her. "Me. Listen, I need to go, Jacob, prayers would be good."

"No problem, brother. Call me later."

"Okay."

He followed the nurse through the doors and down the hall to a curtained off area to the right. The doctor was at Samantha's bedside. "Are you with her?"

"I'm her boyfriend, yes."

"Do you know what happened tonight?"

"From what I saw, she must have drunk three quarters of a fifth of whiskey. There was also a bottle of Xanax on her table near where I found her."

"That doesn't surprise me. We found benzodiazepines in her system when we did the toxicology screening. Her blood alcohol is very high. I'm glad the paramedics intubated her. She's not out of the woods yet, but she's stable. We will be transferring her to the Intensive Care Unit until we can take the tube out of her mouth, which may be a couple of days. It's going to take at least twelve hours for her to come around." The man's face got serious. "You don't think she was trying to commit suicide, do you?"

"No, sir. I talked to her earlier. She was fine. She's never had a problem with depression or anything like that, but she does have an alcohol problem we've been working on. Not very successfully from what it appears."

"What's up with the boot?"

"She broke her ankle falling off the stage three weeks ago after another bout with the alcohol."

"Sounds like you've got your hands full."

"Yes, sir, I do."

"The nurse will let you know when they are ready to transfer her. You won't be able to stay with her in the ICU, but there is a family waiting room outside you can stay in unless you are going home."

"Home is her bus at the moment, sir."

"I see. Is she some kind of performer?"

"Yes. She was supposed to do a show at the amphitheater tonight. She's a popular country music artist."

"Okay. Well, I will leave you to sit with her. You can talk to her if you like. We don't know how much a person who is sedated or in a coma can hear, but it doesn't hurt to talk."

"Thank you."

"You're welcome. I hope you can help her. She seems to have some rough stuff going on."

"Very true."

Jackson took a seat next to her bed. He picked up her limp hand in his, wrapping his fingers around hers in a grip he knew would probably bother

her if she was awake. He needed something to hold onto. She was completely out of control and he wasn't sure he was strong enough to help her anymore. Inpatient rehab would be something he would have to bring up when she got over this. She wouldn't like it, he knew, but what else could he suggest? Doing it on her own obviously wasn't working.

He listened to the sounds of the machine breathing for her. It scared him. All of this scared him out of his mind. "Honey, I hope you can hear me. I'm right here for you. I know you didn't do this on purpose, baby, but we have to talk about this as if you did something you knew would hurt you. God, what am I going to do with you, Samantha? You can't keep doing this to yourself. I know you're terrified to get on that stage. It is just something you're going to have to get over some other way than with alcohol and drugs."

A tear slid down his cheek.

"I don't think I'm strong enough to help you through this. I thought I was, but I don't think so anymore. You need someone to be there who is a professional, someone who knows how to deal with this kind of addiction.

What the hell am I going to do?

He didn't say anymore to her even after she woke up and they took the tube out of her mouth. He couldn't bring himself to talk rehab to her until she was strong enough to answer some questions for him. The answers from her would tell him how to proceed.

"Can I go home today?" she asked, three days after she'd arrive at the hospital.

"Yes. The doctors will be in to release you this morning."

She looked like hell. Dark circles rimmed her eyes, her skin was pale and translucent, and her demeanor seemed timid at best. This wasn't the woman he'd grown to love. She was a shadow of the girl he knew.

He didn't know what to say to her anymore so their conversations were strained.

When they finally made it back to her bus a few hours later, he decided it was time for them to get this out in the open so he could make some decisions about their lives…his life.

* * * *

Samantha struggled up the steps on the bus. She just wanted to get back to normal with Jackson. The last three days had been hell on both of them and she wasn't sure how to fix it. They needed to talk, she knew that, but where to begin.

After she got settled on the couch, she leaned back, propped her booted foot on the coffee table and got comfortable. This was going to be a long talk.

"Talk to me, Jackson. I can't stand these stilted conversations between us. We haven't really talked in three days. Hell, you haven't even kissed me since I woke up for being intubated."

"I know. We need to talk, but I'm not sure where to start."

"From the beginning?"

He threw up his hands before they settle back at his sides balled into fists. "God damn it, Sam. You could have died!"

At least he was talking to her. Not that she liked the way this was starting, but it had to start somewhere. "I know, Jackson. I'm sorry. I don't know what you want me to say."

He tossed his hat on the couch before raking his fingers through his hair. "You don't have a clue, do you?"

Deep in her heart, she didn't know what to do, what to say to fix this. He meant everything to her. "I guess I don't. Tell me what to do. I'll do anything to make this better."

"I can't, baby. If you don't know, I can't help you. You have to want help."

"Help me, Jackson."

"You don't even know what you are asking for help with."

"No, I don't, but if it is something you understand that I don't, make me understand. Help me understand what it is that is so shattered inside of me."

"That's just it. You don't know." He paced from one side of the small enclosure to the other with his hands fisted at his sides like he was trying desperately not to reach for her.

She wanted him to hold her, touch her, make love to her, but if he did, it wouldn't mend the broken fences. His grey eyes looked sad as he fought with some demon she couldn't fathom. If he'd only tell her, she would do anything for him.

"I'm done, Sam."

"Done?"

He stopped pacing, facing her with hurt and anger in his gaze. "I can't do this anymore."

"Please, Jackson, don't say that. I need you."

"No. You need the alcohol and the pills, you don't need me."

"Is that what this is all about? I'll quit. I can do it. No problem. I don't need them, really I don't."

"I've heard those words several times, Sam, but you keep going back to them every time things get stressful. We've had this conversation. You said you'd stop the drinking. You didn't, you just hid it from me. When it came down to it, the habit put you in the hospital and almost killed you. I can't sit back and watch you destroy yourself, I won't."

"I love you. Please." She held out her hands, hoping he'd take them like he'd done so many times before in the last several weeks. She needed him. She couldn't do this without him. Tears clouded her vision.

He didn't budge. He grabbed his hat from the couch, placing it on his head before adjusting it to sit low on his forehead. "I'm sorry, Sam."

Her cowboy. He was walking out on her.

He slowly turned, walked to the three steps that lead out of her door, never looking back once.

The door popped into place as she slid to her knees in the middle of the floor of her bus. The tears were coming in streams now, running down her cheeks as sobs wracked her body. Her body shook from the emotions running through her. *What the hell am I going to do now?*

* * * *

Jackson called a cab to head for the airport. He hadn't even packed his shit. It didn't matter. He was going home, back to Thunder Ridge. Until Samantha Harris figured out how to beat this problem, he couldn't be with her. She had to do it on her own or had to figure out how to get the help she so desperately needed to beat this addiction.

Lucky for him, a flight would be leaving in two hours for San Antonio. He'd already texted Jacob to meet him at the airport so his ride was in place to be home in his own bed within a few hours. The flight home wouldn't take long.

By the time his butt hit the seat, he leaned back, closed his eyes and tried to relax. He hadn't slept much the last three days with Samantha in the hospital.

It was going to be difficult explaining everything to his family.

He turned his head and looked out the window as the lights of California faded into the night sky. The roar of the engine lulled him a little. Really, he had too much on his mind to be able to sleep anyway.

The tears in Samantha's eyes almost broke his resolve. He had to stay strong. His thought on the matter was if she loved him enough, she would get the help she needed. He hoped it worked because he didn't know what else to do. Tough love. If it didn't work, he would have to learn to live without her for the rest of his life.

As he stepped out of the baggage claim area to find Jacob, he sighed wondering what Sam was doing now. She'd probably flipped out after he left. What if she went on a drinking binge again and there was no one there to call an ambulance? What if she died this time? How would he ever forgive himself?

Maybe I should call her.

"No. She needs to figure this out and being strong for her is the only way. Besides, Mark is with her. He'll take her wherever she needs to go and hopefully, that's home."

When he saw Jacob's truck, he opened the door and slid inside.

"Hey."

"Hey."

They pulled out into traffic headed for the airport's exit. The signs flew by as he stared out the window, lost in his own thoughts.

"You okay?"

"No. I just left the woman I love to struggle through this on her own, Jacob. Did I do the right thing?"

"Man, I wish I knew. I hope she calls me, but I don't know if she will. She needs help, Jackson, professional help."

"I know."

"So what exactly happened the last few days?"

After he relayed the entire story to Jacob, his brother whistled softly.

"Wow."

"Yeah."

"So what's the plan?"

"I'm home. That's it."

"Nothing else?"

"I'm hoping the tough love thing will work and she'll seek out some professional help as in inpatient rehab. She needs it for like a few months."

"I agree."

The rest of the ride was made in silence as he lost himself in the terrible feeling he had in the pit of his stomach. If he didn't do the right thing, he could have just pushed her right over the edge into something he didn't want to acknowledge. She might actually try suicide.

Chapter Seventeen

Three damned months. He hadn't heard hide nor hair about her in three damned months. He'd talked to her manager, but got nothing but vague answers from Billy. He got more info from the media, which said she cancelled all her shows indefinitely without really saying why.

His life had become a living hell without her. He couldn't sleep, couldn't eat, couldn't work without messing shit up, and he certainly couldn't fuck another woman.

A month after her incident, Darryl had been arrested for stalking. Apparently, the young man went to her bus after he'd left, confessed his love for Samantha and professed his adoration would find no end if she would just love him in return.

The mission had worked. The stalker had been revealed and her supplier was now in jail so hopefully she would get the help she needed.

Where is she? What is going on with her and why haven't I heard anything? Nothing new in the media, nothing from her parents, nothing from her, her manager won't talk to me and the guys in the band are silent as well. This shit sucks!

He walked out of the barn headed for the main lodge. He wanted to talk to his mother to find out what he should do because this living without Samantha wasn't working.

A black sedan caught his attention as he walked past the cabins, up the gravel area, and past the old hitching posts stationed strategically throughout the property.

Nice car. It wasn't really his type, but the shiny black exterior was definitely sharp in the early spring afternoon.

He took the steps two at a time to reach the big wooden door to the inside of the lodge. The dining room was quiet this time of day as lunch had been served an hour or so ago and supper wouldn't be out for several hours. The guests usually took this time to go for afternoon rides, play horseshoes, go swimming or just hang out around the ranch.

When he made his way through the large living space, he thought he heard Samantha's voice coming from the back of the room. He shook his head. She couldn't be here. Imagining her showing up to tell him everything would be okay, that she'd spent the last three months in rehab getting clean, wouldn't lend him any favors.

He rounded the corner of the table and came to a stop. Someone was in his mom's office.

The woman turned at the noise he made with his boots on the floor.

It was Samantha.

She climbed to her feet before turning toward him. "Hi."

"Hey."

"I was talking with your mom a little before I came to find you."

"I see that."

"Can we talk somewhere private?"

"My cabin is free."

"Sounds good." She turned toward Nina. "Thank you for your advice. I appreciate it and I'm sure everything will work out like it should."

"You're welcome, Samantha. Let me know if you need anything else."

"I will."

She followed him out and across the yard to his place. Nerves racked his body. What was she doing here? Where the hell had she been? She seemed sober, but then again, she didn't always drink during the day. She had the problem with it before shows.

After he opened the door and waved her in, he shut it behind them as she took a seat on one of the chairs near the window.

"How have you been?" he asked as he sat in the chair across from her.

"Fine."

Silence. God, he hated the silence, but he needed to let her tell him why she was here.

"Uh, I've missed you."

"I've missed you too."

She sighed and looked down at her hands. "I guess I should start with what I've been doing the last three months since you left."

"That would be good."

"I cancelled all my shows."

"I heard that much."

"I found a great rehab facility in Nashville. I've been there drying out. I haven't had a drink since the incident at the concert with the alcohol and the Xanax." She sat forward in her chair. "I need you to know something, Jackson. I never intended to hurt myself. I took the Xanax to calm down for the show. I forgotten I'd taken some, so I guess I took more based on what the labs results showed in my system. There was way more there than the one or two pills should have been. Darryl brought me the whiskey. I downed half the bottle. I couldn't face going out there without it."

"You've been in rehab?"

"Yes. I've been sober for three months. I feel really good. I'm seeing a therapist and I think I've got my shit together now."

"That's great."

"I don't know if you can forgive me or not, but I had to tell you what's been going on. I don't expect you to want back in my life after everything you've been through with me. I needed you to know something. I love you. That hasn't changed one bit since you walked out, which by the way, thank you. Knowing you weren't going to put up with my drinking anymore kicked me in the ass. I needed the smack upside my head."

"I'm glad I could help."

"If you don't want me in your life, I understand."

He dropped to his knees in front of her, taking her hands in his. "I love you, Samantha. That hasn't changed. I've been miserable without you, but I knew you had to do this on your own. You needed to make the decision to get help, otherwise, it would never work. I'm glad you've been sober for three months. I hope it continues."

"It will. I'm done with the alcohol. I've even been writing some and singing. I've done a couple of shows, small ones, but shows nonetheless where I haven't needed the booze to bolster my self-esteem. They've been fabulous and I've even made some new friends in the recording business. Some of the artists who've had problems too, have come forward to help me get my confidence back to sing again. I've also found out all of the animosity I felt from them was self-perceived. They did like me, but they thought I was aloof and hard to approach so they kept their distance."

"That's fantastic."

"So do you think we can start over and be boyfriend and girlfriend again?"

"I'd like to very much."

"Me too."

He put both of his hands on her face, bringing her closer so he could kiss her. God, he missed her more than anything in this world, and he wasn't going to let her go again, not in this lifetime.

Epilogue

Christmas found them gathered around the huge tree in the main lodge of the family's guest ranch. They had been splitting their time with her touring, recording, and doing the fan stuff with spending time on the ranch with his family.

Life had been almost boring without the frequent trips to the emergency rooms in various states where they traveled.

Her career had taken off again after she came clean with the media about her drinking problem. She had a new CD coming out in the next month and her new single was already climbing the charts.

"Where are you two headed next?" Nina asked from her seat on the couch as the grandkids ran around the lodge.

"Back east. I have a couple of shows in the south and two up in the northeast." Samantha took a bite of sugar cookie. "These are fantastic."

"Wow. This time of year is bad for travel," James added.

"Yeah, but her bus driver is one of the best and so are the rig drivers. They can handle it."

"When is the new CD coming out?" Mesa asked.

"Next month, but don't you dare go buy it."

"Why is that?"

"You'll have two then, but I'm not saying anything else."

Jackson stood near the mantle with his arm resting on the wood as he drank his Coke. They never had alcohol in their home anymore, not even for him, which was fine. He didn't need it anyway. She'd been doing great so far and he didn't want to give her any reason to backslide. He would protect her with his life.

Tonight was special. They hadn't really talked marriage yet, but he was ready. The ring was burning a hole in his pocket as they sat around making small talk with his family. He just needed the right moment.

Everyone settled down and quiet descended on the group.

Now would be great.

"Samantha, can you come up here with me for a minute."

"Sure, babe."

She got to her feet and weaved her way through the kids on the floor as they waited for the grandparents to say it was time to open presents.

"I wanted to do this with my family present and on such a great holiday as Christmas." He got down on one knee as he took her hand in his and pulled out the marque cut diamond solitaire. "Will you marry me?"

Tears rolled down her cheeks as she whispered a soft, "Yes."

He got to his feet and wrapped her in a warm hug before kissing her on the lips.

"Ew!"

They laughed as they separated.

"When's the wedding?"

"Oh my! I have a wedding to plan now."

"Don't worry. We are all old pros at it. We'll help," Mesa volunteered as she held her eight month old little boy on her lap. "Right ladies?"

Peyton, Paige, Callie, Candace, Terri, and Nina all agreed.

"I would love for all of you to help. I've never done this before so I'm kind of lost."

"No worries. We've got you covered," Paige said as she grabbed Hannah when she ran by.

The entire group shouted at the same time, "Welcome to the family!"

The End

A COWBOY OF MY OWN
Cowboy Dreamin' 8

Sandy Sullivan

Chapter One

Jonathan Young glanced through his lashes at the blonde woman serving breakfast behind the counter. The pink streak in her hair always captivated him, as did her blue eyes, curvy body, and bold attitude. He liked her a lot, but what the hell to do about it.

The form fitting tank top she wore showed off her breasts to perfection but didn't give too much away. She wore low-slung jeans that hugged her hips, making his fingers tingle to touch her everywhere.

Being the shy Young brother didn't bode well for finding women. Of course, he could always take advantage of his brothers' castoffs. He didn't like to at all, but he wasn't the in your face kind of cowboy either. He did the website, advertising, and marketing for the ranch so he sat behind his computer all day messing with codes.

He sipped his coffee while he watched her interact with the guests. She'd been working in the ranch's kitchen for a couple of years now besides being good friends with several of his brothers' wives.

Mandy.

Even her name rolled off his tongue like a caress.

Laughter burst from her lips causing a shiver to skitter down his back. He wanted her. No doubt about it.

Maybe he should ask one of his brothers what to do about his attraction for the leggy blonde. Nah. Not a good idea. They would razz him beyond a tolerable level if he even thought about mentioning his fascination with her.

She captured her bottom lip between her teeth. *Damn.* He wanted to suck that pouty little piece of flesh.

When her gaze locked with his, he looked quickly at his coffee cup. He couldn't let her catch him watching her. That wouldn't do at all. She couldn't know about his desire for her, otherwise he wouldn't be able to function. He already knew she wanted him. It wasn't a secret around the ranch, but he just didn't have the balls to approach her and take things to the next level.

Damn this shyness. It was almost debilitating to him. He didn't know what to do about it. He wasn't shy around his family, just in social situations and with women. Good Lord, was he shy around women.

He'd had a few girlfriends in his life, but not many. After the one terrible breakup in high school, he tended to avoid situations where he would have to prove his manhood to anyone.

He hadn't had sex in a long time, too long. After Melissa had laughed when he tried to get her to have sex with him in high school, he'd avoided those types of situations like the plague. What he needed was to get laid.

When he looked back up, Mandy's gaze had moved on to one of the guests in front of her as she smiled.

Wow, her smile twisted his guts into knots.

This shit is for the birds. I need to stop this and just talk to her.

"Jonathan?"

"Sorry. What did you say, Mom?"

"How is the new marketing campaign coming?"

"Really good. Our website traffic has increased by over a thousand hits per month. I'm pushing for more, but it's a start."

"That's great."

"Yes and if it translates to bookings, that's even better."

His mother signaled for the family to get their plates from the serving line. As the group got to their feet to file over for breakfast, the noise of the room rose exponentially. There was a large group of romance writers at the ranch this weekend, who were friends or acquaintances of each other and the conversations going on around the room seemed to be really loud.

Mesa sat with one of the groups at another table since she knew a large portion of the attendees. Joel managed their two children while she did her best to entertain the group of writers.

It seemed most of them wrote westerns, which made it kind of amusing but expected with them being on the ranch. They said it was for research as they followed his brothers around while they did their chores. Luckily, most of them left him alone since he didn't fit their idea of the cowboy persona.

Cowboy. Why couldn't he be more like his brothers in that way? They all seemed to be naturals at the cowboy thing. Him? Not so much. Yeah, he knew how to ride, rope, handle the animals, and do all the other things cowboys did, but he would rather leave it to Joey. The youngest of the Young clan did all the wrangling with the horses, although they all took their turns with ranch work during calving season.

As he moved in front of Mandy in the serving line, he tipped his hat as she said, "Morning."

"Mornin'."

"Are you busy later?" she asked, her blue eyes taking in his entire frame in one sweep of her gaze.

"Not really."

"Okay. I wanted to ask you some questions if you have time."

"Um, sure." He dropped his gaze to his plate as he moved down the line. His stomach knotted. He would be alone with her. Damn.

He grabbed silverware from the containers on the serving counter before walking back to the family table. Eating might be a bit difficult after he'd actually had a conversation with her over the eggs and now had an *appointment* to spend at least a few minutes with her this afternoon. What she wanted to ask him, he didn't know, although she was in school for marketing and advertising from what he'd heard. Maybe it was something to do with that and not about him at all. What if he was blowing this whole thing out of proportion for no reason?

He put a bite of his eggs in his mouth as he glanced across the room to where she served the last few people before getting her own.

A little smile played on her lips as she winked.

Fuck.

The eggs lodged in his throat, throwing him into a coughing fit. Jackson pounded him between the shoulder blades.

"You okay, bro?"

"Yeah," he croaked as he coughed a couple more times. "Thanks."

"No problem." Jackson glanced to his left, leaned in, and kissed Samantha.

It was a rare time for them to be at the ranch since they hooked up. The two of them were gone a lot traveling while Samantha did her singing gigs. It had been almost a year since they'd gotten together and their wedding was planned for December.

Jonathan glanced around the table, noting all of his brothers paired up with their significant other. Jackson and Samantha would be getting married soon. Joey didn't have a steady girl at the moment, but he was always on the prowl.

Jacob had Paige, Joel had Mesa. Joshua had Candace, Jeremiah had Callie. Jason had Peyton, and Jeff had Terri and their kids. They weren't married yet. Jonathan knew it would be soon. Jeff had finally realized how important his woman was to him when she had to leave for two weeks back in the spring for a job. Jeff had been home taking care of the kids without her and realized just what the hell his life would be like if she ever left. Ben had come down with chicken pox, giving it to his siblings in the process. Even though their mother had helped him with the kids, he'd been so frazzled by the time Terri came back, he'd popped the question to his longtime girlfriend on a beautiful spring day near the pond. Of course, she said yes and there was a wedding planned for June. Jeff wasn't wasting any time getting her to the altar. Jonathan had never laughed so hard in his life when Jeff had come up to the house dragging an itching Ben, trying to figure out what the heck was up with his son.

He really loved his family, but it wasn't easy being a Young from Thunder Ridge and one of the last single ones in the county. Good Lord! Everyone from Aunt Ann to his mother had been trying to hook him up with a woman. He already had one in mind.

After he finished his breakfast, he got to his feet and put his plate in the dirty dish bin before heading to his office to get some work done. He needed to get his new plan for marketing up to speed to get the bookings up at the ranch. Not that his parents required more money since Jeremiah had hooked them up and made them financially secure for the rest of their lives with his investments, but his goal was to make them the premiere guest ranch in the area. They had added spa services in the last year, focusing on massages and things for the ladies. They also catered weddings, were planning a rodeo this summer, and he wanted to make some more notes on what other things they could bring to the ranch to take them a step above the rest.

He sat down at this desk with a cup of coffee at his elbow and began typing away. Today, he was revamping the website for the ranch. The website coding page pulled up easily under his experienced fingers.

Tap, tap, tap.

He cocked his head to side listening for the foreign sound. There were so many ghosts inhabiting the ranch, he could hardly keep up with the goings on. The one that fascinated him the most was the old cowboy who hung out in the main ranch house and near the barns. They saw him often, but had no idea who he was. No one had really done much research on the old guy or the other ghosts on the place. When his family had bought the ranch many years ago, the ghosts had become part of the atmosphere and embraced by everyone at Thunder Ridge.

He wanted to do the research. He wanted to find out who they were. The whole thing fascinated him to the point where he went ghost hunting several times. He'd caught some sounds on recording devices and some images on camera, but nothing he could pin down. So far, he hadn't found much on the owners of the ranch previous to those his parents had bought the place from some thirty years ago.

They often heard giggling of children out in the ranch yard, the arguing of a couple upstairs in the mail lodge, and saw the cowboy hanging out on the front porch and in the big room of the house.

The sound came again. He climbed to his feet, walked to the door of his office, and glanced down the hall. No one was about. He shrugged and went back to his desk. Redesigning the website would take some time.

He cocked his head to the side when he heard the voice of the woman who took up a lot of time in his thoughts. His office wasn't far from the kitchen where she worked so he could hear her clearly. His fingers froze on the keys of his computer as he listened.

"I don't know what to do. He won't even acknowledge me."

"I know, honey. He seems indifferent to you completely," Peyton replied. "I wish I knew what to do to help you. It's been a couple of years now and you aren't any further in this relationship that you were at the beginning."

"Tell me about it."

"He doesn't talk much about himself even in a group setting with the family. He's the quiet one," Paige added.

"Maybe he's extremely shy or something? I mean, with as how in your face as the other boys are, it's must be hard being one of them."

He nodded in answer to the question she posed even though Mandy didn't know he heard every word they said.

"I can totally imagine that," Peyton said. "But come on. It's not like you've been secretive about your attraction for the guy."

"I know."

He heard the clanging of dishes as they loaded the pots and pans into the sink.

"What are you going to do about it?"

"For right this minute, nothing. I plan to go into town this evening, get rip-roaring drunk, and sleep my days off away."

"Sounds like a plan. We can get the girls together and join you. I'm sure Mesa, Terri, Callie, Candace, and Samantha could use a night out as well. These boys can get to be a bit too much to handle at times," Paige said. "We'll meet at the main house and take a couple of cars. Someone will have to be the designated drivers otherwise we'll have to get a cab."

"I'm so ready to get shitfaced drunk. I need to do something to get past this. He's driving me batshit crazy with his indifference."

Their voices faded as they moved to a different section of the kitchen. He felt like shit for putting her through this ridiculous thing. Why he couldn't just talk to her and get it over with, he didn't know.

He got up, shut the door to his office, and then sank down in his chair. He had work to do and thinking about Mandy Jenkins wasn't helping him get it done. Maybe he would find himself at The Dusty Boot later on tonight. After all, someone had to look out for the ladies of Thunder Ridge, right?

* * * *

Mandy studied herself in the bathroom mirror as she finished outlining her eyes with her makeup pencil. She wanted to look good tonight for some reason. Maybe she would get over her infatuation with Jonathan Young with another good-looking cowboy even if only for the night. Damn it, she was horny. She needed to get laid. It had been so long, she'd worn out the batteries on her dildo. Almost a year was a long time.

Her cell phone rang.

"Hello?"

"Hey," Peyton answered. "You almost ready?"

"Yeah, but since I'm already in town, why don't I meet you all at The Dusty Boot?" She fluffed her hair as she sprayed a little hairspray on it to give it more volume.

"Sounds good."

"Are the guys coming?"

"Nope. We are leaving them home with the kids, animals, and so on."

"I so need this night out. You have no idea."

"I had a feeling you were getting a bit uptight."

"I'm wound so tight, I squeak."

Peyton laughed on the other end of the line. "Get some alcohol in you and you'll loosen right up, girlfriend."

"God, I hope so." Blush brightened her cheekbones as she slid the bristles against her skin.

"See you in about half an hour at The Boot?"

"Yep, with bells on."

Thirty minutes later, she pulled her little car up to the curb of The Dusty Boot. A neon light flickered off and on over the door pointing the way to the entrance. The huge sign above the bar itself reflected the bar's logo in bright lights. The place seemed to be hopping for a Friday night, but then again, it was the best place in town to hook up, get a beer, do some dancing, and just hang out with friends. They had pool tables, dartboards, a dance floor, a band most nights, and lots of alcohol.

One of her best friends usually tended bar, but not tonight. She would be with the other ladies of Thunder Ridge drinking and having a good time. Peyton had hooked up with Jason Young some time ago, finding love in the most unexpected place with the rugged cowboy. The two of them were opposites to the core, but they made it work as one of the luckiest couples in Bandera. All the boys had lucked out with their respective women, finding love in the most unexpected place. The only two boys left unattached were Jonathan and Joey.

She'd sure hoped by now Jonathan would be hers. Lusting after the shy cowboy for a couple of years had been hard on her heart. Maybe it was time to give up and move on. A Young brother wasn't in the cards for her, she guessed.

A tear gathered in her eye before she dabbed it away. She wouldn't cry over him. After she squared her shoulders, she brushed some lipstick over her mouth as she glanced in the mirror behind her visor. Tonight was about her. She planned to get shitfaced drunk, have a good time, dance, and maybe find someone to go home with.

The visor popped back into place with a push of her fingers before she gathered her purse and opened the door.

Wolf whistles sounded behind her as she shut it.

She glanced over her shoulder. A group of cowboys stood near a jacked up Chevy.

"Hey, baby."

"Hey."

"You free tonight?"

"Maybe."

"I'll find you inside. I would love to see what's inside them jeans."

She rolled her eyes as she headed inside. Typical guy. All about the sex. Tonight, she might be onboard with that notion though.

She opened the big, heavy wooden door with a push against the panel. Country music washed over her in a heavy blanket as she glanced around the room trying to locate the group of women from Thunder Ridge. A moment later, Paige came rushing up to her, grabbed her hand, and dragged her toward the back of the bar. The girls had taken over a large, half-circular booth. Six of the women had drinks in front of them. Samantha would be their designated driver tonight since she didn't drink anymore.

"There you are!" Mesa took a drink from her glass. "I thought maybe you had backed out."

"Hell no. I'm ready to par-tay!" She slid in behind Paige as the waitress came up to the table. "Whiskey on the rocks."

"Damn girl. Hitting it hard right away?" Callie asked.

"Yep. I'm prepared to get rip-roaring drunk." She glanced at Samantha. "You're driving, right?"

"Yes. I brought the ranch van so I can take everyone home."

"Are you going to be okay?" Peyton asked her. "I mean with all this alcohol around?"

"I'm good. I'll be drinking Coke plain and if things get rough, I have my sponsor to call."

"Love my baby." Paige preened a little as they brought up her husband. "He's home with the kids, but he'll be right here if you need him, Samantha."

"I know, Paige. He's a great guy and I couldn't do this without his help."

"Jackson was okay with you coming out with us?" Mesa asked.

"He was fine with it. I'll call him if I need him, but it'll be okay, ladies. I promise. I'm fine."

"Okay," the women chorused together.

The waitress brought Mandy her whiskey. She took a couple of sips before setting it down. "I was propositioned already."

"When?" Candace asked.

"In the parking lot. A group of cowboys were whistling and carrying on. I told one of them to come find me."

"Wow." Candace took a sip of her drink.

"What? I'm the only single one here. The whole town knows you all are hooked up with a Young brother. The cowboys in this bar aren't going to touch any of you tonight."

"Some of Joel's friends are here. They'll dance with me if I want them to," Mesa added. "They know they are safe as long as they don't get too friendly."

"Where did you get your hair done, Mandy?" Candace curled a piece of her hair around her finger. "I want a streak like that."

"In San Antonio at a place on the square. They were really good and reasonable." She took another sip of her drink, already feeling the warmth spreading through her. "What color are you going to get?"

"Blue, I think. Something a little tamer than yours. I don't think Joshua would let me get hot pink."

Mandy touched the pink strip of hair she sported as she shrugged. She liked being bold and outgoing although it didn't get her much these days. Her gaze shifted around the bar, making the rounds of the tables as she swallowed the last of her whiskey until her gaze connected with the one man she didn't want to see tonight.

Jonathan Young nursed a beer at the bar and when he turned to face her, their gazes connected, sending a shockwave through her with enough heat, her nipples pulled tight under her tank top.

Chapter Two

Jonathan turned on the barstool to face the group of women in the corner as he sipped his beer. He was painfully aware of when Mandy walked into the bar to meet her friends. His whole body went on high alert the moment she'd stepped through the door. When she slid into the booth with the other women of Thunder Ridge, he'd received an eyeful of her ass as she sat down. The jeans she wore did nothing to hide the fact that her thong peeped out of the waistband as well as the purple butterfly on her lower back.

His cock hardened painfully behind the fly of his jeans. It had been way too long since he'd gotten laid.

His gaze locked with her blue one, across the bar. Boldly, he held up his beer in salute as he leaned his elbows on the bar behind him. He wouldn't let her nearness chase him out of the bar tonight. He was going to play the good Samaritan if it killed him. Tonight, he was there to make sure his sisters-in-law didn't get into any trouble and if that included Mandy, then so be it.

He might even break down and ask her to dance.

A big cowboy came in through the door and made a beeline for the table. Jonathan sat up on his barstool, prepared to jump in if need be. The guy stopped near Mandy and bent down to speak into her ear.

She glanced over the guy's shoulder to catch his gaze before she smiled, nodded, and then stood. The guy took her hand and led her out onto the dance floor.

Jonathan watched as the guy wrapped his arms around Mandy, firmly placing his hands on her jean-clad ass. Rage ripped through him. *She's mine, damn it.* No one should be handling her like that, but him. He couldn't move. He didn't want to make a scene, but watching it happen was getting him more and more pissed off.

A warm hand touched him on the shoulder. His gaze broke from Mandy as he focused on Candace. "Easy, cowboy."

"Hey, Candace."

"You know she's all about you, right?"

He turned around on the stool. "Is she? It sure doesn't look like it from here."

"Jonathan, she is so tied up in you, she can't see straight. But, honey, you are blowing it here. You can only play hard to get so long before she'll walk."

"I'm not playing hard to get."

"Could have fooled me." When the guy behind her moved, she took the stool next to him. "What's really going on?"

"I can't talk to her. You know how I am. Hell, I couldn't talk to you for a few weeks when you first came to the ranch. I just can't talk to women, especially her." He sipped his beer, looking back to where Mandy and the guy swayed to the music.

"Do you want me to help you?"

"I don't know."

"I can, you know. What if you asked her to dance?"

"I can't."

"Don't you want to be wrapped up in those arms, rather than him? Don't you want your hands on her ass?"

"Hell yeah."

"Then do it."

He shook his head and downed the rest of his beer. "I'm just here to make sure you girls are okay."

"Taking care of your brothers' women?"

"Yeah, something like that." He raised his hand to signal for another beer. He wouldn't drink more than a couple in case he needed to get into a brawl or something.

The song ended as he turned back around to watch Mandy kiss the guy before walking back to the table.

His stomach knotted. He'd bet his next paycheck she would go home with the guy. When she met his gaze across the bar, a little smirk lifted her lips. She knew he had watched, and she was playing it for all it was worth, the little minx.

He lifted his beer in silent salute before tipping the rim of the bottle to his lips and taking a long draw.

"I don't know about you two. You're all about torturing each other, I think," Candace said. "Are you into being a sadist or a masochist?"

"No, why?"

"Because you're all about the pain of keeping apart, from what I see."

"She wants a Young brother, and I'm not sure I'm the one for her."

"Why not? She likes you. She wants you."

"I'm not like my brothers. She sees what they are, how they act so bold and out there. I'm not like that at all. I'm the computer nerd."

"You are still a Young. Those genes run through your veins, brother-in-law. You can't deny your heritage."

He shrugged as he turned back toward the bar, contemplating the liquid in the brown bottle in front of him.

"You know, if you showed her half an ounce of encouragement, you would be surprised at what would come of it."

"I get tongue-tied around her. I haven't been able to say two words to her since she came to work at the ranch."

"You talked to her at breakfast."

"That was about work, not about personal stuff."

The group in the corner started to get loud. "I guess I'd better get over there. They're getting rambunctious, and I'm missing all the fun." She leaned in with her arm around his shoulders. "Relax, Jonathan. You'll be fine if you chill out and not make such a big deal of this. She's a woman who has a huge crush on you. Work with it."

"I'll try."

Candace kissed him on the cheek before shuffling back to the table. The girls were halfway to being drunk already. He could tell by how loud they were getting, laughing and shouting inappropriate things at the cowboys passing the table. Not that any of them would do anything since *everyone* in Bandera knew they belonged to the Young brothers and unless you wanted nine badass cowboys pissed off at you, you didn't mess with their women.

He glanced back over his shoulder to see Mandy sipping what looked like a glass of whiskey or something in a tumbler. *So, she's a hard liquor drinker, eh?* She laughed at something one of the other girls said, tossing back her blonde curls over her shoulder. He liked that she was individual enough to put that pink streak in her hair from root to tip. He turned back to his beer, thinking everything was okay for the moment.

"All of you are high and mighty bitches. You think you own the damned place because you've snagged a Young brother. Well, let me tell you this, you are nothing but pathetic losers willing to spread your legs for one of those boys to snag a ring on your finger."

Jonathan spun around to see who was making a ruckus loud enough he heard the words over the band. A brunette was standing toe-to-toe with Mandy.

Mandy shoved the girl by the shoulder. "You're a bitch!"

The women got right back in her face. "Look who stood up for the group and she doesn't even have a Young brother between her legs."

Mandy swung, hitting the girl in the eye, dropping her to the floor. "Take it back, bitch."

"Fuck you."

Mandy straddled the girl's hips and punched her again. "Take it back."

"Never."

After she landed another punch and the girl was out cold, the bouncers finally arrived to pull Mandy away. "You're leaving."

"She started it."

"You swung first."

Mandy held up her hands, her knuckles bleeding slightly from the brawl. "I'm here with my friends. I promise, I won't cause any more problems."

The next thing he knew, he was standing next to the bouncer's shoulder. "I'll vouch for her. She's usually not a troublemaker."

"See? And he's a Young, so you better do what he says."

He grabbed her arm and moved her behind him. "Shut up, Mandy."

With both hands on his shoulders, she leaned to the right to look at the bouncers in front of him. "He'll protect me."

He glanced over his shoulder. "I said, shut up before your mouth gets you into major trouble." When he turned back to the bouncers, the biggest one nodded.

"We'll leave her be for now, but keep an eye on her, Jonathan. If she stirs trouble again, out she goes."

"Got it." The bouncers left with the girl she'd punched under their arms, as he spun around to face her. "What got into you?" He took her hand to examine her scraped knuckles. "You shouldn't fistfight. Ladies, don't fistfight."

"This one does when it's to protect my girls."

"They weren't in any danger. Besides, I would have gotten involved should there been a need to intervene."

"I'm sorry."

"You should be." He ran his finger over the back of her hand, before glancing back up and getting trapped by her blue eyes.

"Do you realize this is the most you've talked to me in three years?" she asked, smiling like the cat who ate the canary.

I'm so screwed. His gaze dropped to her hand, and he automatically jerked his away like it burned. It did, burn that is. Her skin scorched his, bringing to mind thoughts of hot, sweaty bodies writhing on clean white sheets.

She dipped down to look into his eyes. "It's okay. You can talk to me anytime you want to."

"I'm going back to the bar."

"No. Stay. Dance with me."

"I…uh."

"You do know how to dance, right?"

"Yes."

"Two-step? You can two-step, I bet." She took his hand, dragging him out toward the dance floor.

How he ended up with her hand in his, his hand on her hip and hers on his shoulder, he wasn't sure, but there he was dancing with the woman who turned him inside out. He let the natural rhythm lead his booted feet as he tried his damnedest to unstick his tongue from the roof of his mouth.

He couldn't think of what to say that sounded witty, cool, or anything other than stupid to his ears.

"I never got into your office to talk to you today."

"No."

"Can we make some time tomorrow maybe or Monday?"

"Okay."

"You aren't very talkative, are you?"

"No."

"Why?"

He shrugged, dropping his gaze to her chest. Bad idea. She had on a tank top that showed off her curves to perfection, including the swell of her breasts. The freckled skin made his fingers itch to touch. He wanted to stroke his fingertips along the edge of her tank top to see if it was as soft as it looked.

"Jonathan?"

His gaze shot back to her face. "I don't know."

"Maybe you should have some more alcohol. That always loosens my tongue."

"I'm driving."

"Oh, right."

The song came to an end as Mandy slowly stepped back from his embrace. "Thank you for the dance."

"Sure." She didn't lean in and kiss him like she did the other guy she'd danced with.

"You should join us at the table since you are here to watch out for us."

"No, thanks. The bar is okay."

"Whatever you want to do is fine."

They separated near the table with him returning to his seat at the bar and her sitting back down with the girls.

He signaled for another drink, ordering Coke this time since he'd already had two beers. With a heavy sigh, he willed his heart rate back to normal from the pounding rhythm it had taken up the moment she put her hands on him. The moment the bartender returned with his drink, he downed about half in several gulps. His palms were slick with sweat and his brain had turned to mush while they danced. It was a wonder he didn't step on her toes. *That would have been just dandy.*

His cell phone rang. Jeff.

He answered as he moved toward the back of the bar so he could hear. "Hello?"

"Where are you?"

"At The Dusty Boot watching your women."

"Are they getting into trouble?"

"Not yet, but they're working on it. There's enough alcohol flowing to shut down some livers."

"Damn."

"They're fine, Jeff. I'll make sure they don't get into trouble."

"I hope one of them isn't drinking so they can get home safely."

"I doubt Samantha is. She's been doing so well, I don't think she'll fall off the wagon for a girls' night out." He shifted the phone to his other ear. "Although Mandy got into a fistfight already."

"Shit."

"It's okay. I handled it. It was some big mouth chick talking trash. Mandy punched her."

"That's handling it?"

"Easy, brother. Mandy doesn't belong to any of us so she can do what she wants. She was just standing up for the girls."

"If they get out of hand, call me. I'll come down."

"You take care of the kids. I got this."

"Okay. Thanks, Jonathan."

"No problem." He saw the waitress bring a round of shot glasses to their table. "I better go. They're doing shots now."

"Call me if you need me."

"I will."

"Bye."

* * * *

Mandy glanced to where Jonathan stood talking on the phone. "I need some hunky cowboy to do body shots off of." She signaled to the waitress. "Bring us a round of Patrón." The group cheered with a couple of them pounding on the table. She loved these women like they were the sisters she didn't have. She'd grown so close to them, she didn't miss not having her family close by anymore. She'd been through hell with a couple of them, and they meant the world to her.

When the waitress brought the shot glasses, each of those drinking took one. Mandy raised hers. "To all of us. May we each love our men hard, long, and with our entire soul."

"Here, here!"

They all slammed back the tequila, turning their glass upside down on the table as the potent liquid burned its way down their throats.

"You got your dance on with Jonathan there for a minute," Peyton said.

"Yes, yes, I did and it was awesome, even though he hardly said two words to me."

"He's not a talkative guy," Candace said.

"Why?"

"He's very shy, the total opposite of his brothers."

"He talks to you all the time."

"I know, but it took a lot for us to get to that point. We have something in common, websites and computer stuff."

Mandy frowned. Truth be known, she didn't have much in common with Jonathan other than she thought he was the hottest Young brother in the county and she wanted nothing more than to ride his hips into tomorrow, reverse cowgirl preferably. She needed more alcohol. With a raised hand, she signaled for more Patrón from the waitress.

"Are you sure that is such a good idea?" Samantha asked, sipping her Coke.

"I need alcohol. If ya'll don't want to join me, that's fine," Mandy replied. "Fortification is required if I'm going to trap me a Young brother tonight."

"Well, since there are only two not tied up already, I can imagine which one we are discussing here." Mesa giggled, already a little tipsy from the last shot.

Mandy glanced across the room, only to catch Joel's gaze narrowing on his wife and the group. *Well shit. We've been had.* Her gaze took in the rest of the Young brothers sipping beers as they watched their wives and girlfriends. They were all there except Jeff. Jacob, Jason, Jackson, Joel, Joshua, and Jeremiah kept an eye on the girls. She glanced to the right to catch Jonathan watching her from the bar. She knew he was there to keep an eye on all of them, but apparently his brothers wanted to make sure they were all safe and sound themselves.

Jonathan's gaze followed hers across the room to where the brothers sat in a booth.

"Damn." Paige shook her head. "We've been had. They're all here, aren't they?"

"Yep," Mandy replied. "Seems so."

"Well, I say we show them we can have a good time whether they're here or not." Paige held up her hand to the waitress. "Bring us more tequila."

"That's right!" Peyton shouted. "I'll be damned if Jason is going to keep me from having a good time with my friends. I haven't been out of the house, except for work, in a month or more."

Callie agreed and so did Candace.

Samantha shook her head. "You all are going to be so sorry tomorrow when you have hangovers from hell. Trust me, I've been there."

"Right now, I don't care if I'm puking on Jeremiah's cowboy boots on the way in the house. I'm having a good time tonight." Callie took the shot the waitress just dropped off on the table, brought it to her lips and threw the contents to the back of her throat. Her eyes watered and she coughed a couple of times before she wiped her mouth with the back of her hand, slammed the shot glass upside down on the table, and dared the rest of them to do the same with theirs. "Drink up, ladies!"

Mandy sprinkled some salt on her hand before licking it off, tossing back the shot, and then biting into a lemon wedge. She shuddered from the burn of the alcohol going down her throat. *Damn the stubborn-ass cowboy. If he doesn't want me, I'll find someone who does! There is a whole bar full of cowboys just waiting for someone like me to sidle up to for the night.* "Holy shit, that's potent."

Samantha rolled her eyes, as she looked across the bar toward where the men were sitting. She shook her head and shrugged as Mandy glanced over there too to catch the silent communication between her and Jackson. He raised his beer bottle in silent salute when she sipped her Coke. Mandy thought she had it going on. How the woman had beat alcohol and managed to salvage her career was amazing. Samantha had a pretty bad problem there for a while, from what she'd heard, but here she was hanging out with a group of women hell-bent on getting shitfaced. Kudos to her.

The two of them were so cute together. With their wedding coming up in a few months, things were a bit hectic around the ranch. The media had been camped out on the road outside the ranch for a few days now, anticipating the wedding because no one was leaking when it was supposed to be. Stupid reporters. The wedding wasn't until December. They planned it for Christmas so they could get married in front of the huge tree the Young's had in the main lodge every year. The reporters would have a long wait. Ah, the joys of being famous, she guessed. In fact, she'd bet a hundred bucks there were a few reporters hanging out in the bar tonight, hoping for Samantha to lose her battle with the bottle. Her friend was stronger than that though.

Mandy struggled to her feet. "I'm finding me a cowboy."

"You go, girl!" Every single one of the women in the group high-fived her before she stumbled slightly as she headed for a group of cowboys standing off to the left of the dance floor. She recognized a few of them as guys that worked the local ranches. She'd be damned if she'd go home alone tonight. Being the only single woman in the group from Thunder Ridge, she planned to find her a cowboy if it took her all night, more alcohol, and less clothes.

"Hey," she said, coming to stand at the left of one tall drink of water.

"Hi there."

"I'm Mandy."

"Noah." His gaze raked her from the top of her head to the tips of her cowboy boots. Appreciation reflected brightly in his eyes when they met hers again.

She stepped in front of him and put her hands on his chest, before sliding them up around his neck. "Well, Noah. How about a dance?"

"Sure, pretty lady." He glanced over her shoulder. "You aren't here with anyone?"

She shrugged her left shoulder. "A group of female friends, yes, but I'm not here with anything that looks like you, handsome."

"All right then. Let's dance." He placed his hands on her hips and began backing them toward the edge of the dance floor. "You sure are pretty."

"Thanks." He stepped on her toe. *Okay, so he's not the most graceful thing here.* "You work around here?"

"Not at the moment. Work seems to be scare."

Great. "What kind of work do you normally do?"

"Oh, this and that."

Well, shit. A dead-beat. "You got a girlfriend, Noah?"

"Uh, no."

She grabbed his left hand and brought it around to her gaze. *Fuck. A wedding ring.* "Sorry, buddy. I don't fuck with guys who belong to other women." She stepped back, turned on her heels, and headed back for the table. *What a waste of time.*

"What happened?" Peyton asked.

"Married."

"Shit."

"Yeah." She glanced back at the bar to see a dark-haired woman talking to Jonathan. *What the fuck? He can't talk to me, but he can chat it up with another woman?* "He fucking can't talk to me, but he can flirt with someone else?"

Candace laid her hand on top of Mandy's. "He can't talk to you because he's interested in you, silly. He gets tongue-tied around you."

She blew out a long breath. "What can I do to get this moving along?"

"You might have to take control."

"I need another drink." She glanced at the bar realizing the waitress was tied up serving others.

"That's it. Take control, Mandy. He needs a big nudge," Paige replied.

Mandy focused her gaze on her prey. She just might do that, take control that is. Seducing him sounded like a really good idea right now. When she climbed to her feet again, the room spun. She probably shouldn't have drunk the last round of tequila, but what the hell. Caring at this point, didn't cross her mind. She needed a man and by damn, she had the perfect one in mind. With a slow deep breath, she began to weave her way toward him and the women trying to get his attention. As she got closer, she realized the woman was talking, but Jonathan wasn't. He continued to sip his drink without really replying or focusing on the woman. "Jonathan."

His gaze focused on her. "Yes?"

"I want you to take me home."

"Home?"

"Yeah, I'm too drunk to drive."

"Uh, okay." He climbed to his feet, pushing the other woman off to the side.

"Well, I never."

"Yeah and you won't with him, babe. He's mine." She wrapped her hand through his arm and started for the door.

"Shouldn't you tell the others you're leaving?"

She shook her head. "I'm sure they've figured it out. Besides, their men will be corralling them soon to take them home, fuck the hell out of them, and be as happy as little piggys in shit."

The group yelled, hooped, and hollered as she got to the door with Jonathan on her arm. *I'm sure they understand what I'm going for here without giving them the details. Getting Jonathan between my thighs has been something I've been working on for three damned years now.* "Where are you parked?"

"Uh, to the side of the building, but let me tell my brothers I'm leaving so they keep an eye on their women."

"Sure."

Swaying with her support no longer there, she tilted her head to the side as she watched him walk toward where his brothers sat. *Damn, he's got a fine ass in those jeans.* Tight denim formed to his butt cheeks in a perfect caress of flesh. His western style, long-sleeved shirt stretched across his shoulders, making her hands tingle with the need to smooth the material across the width of his skin. The black hat on his head almost blended with his hair peeping out under the rim. The brown cowboy boots on his feet looked worn even though she knew he didn't do a lot of work around the ranch outside. He still rode a horse on occasion, shoveled shit, tossed hay, and helped with breaking the new horses sometimes. Even if he sat in front of the computer most of the day, he was still a cowboy at heart.

He returned a few moments later. "Okay, let's go." He wrapped an arm around her waist, snuggling her close to his side, and she sighed.

This is right where she wanted to be.

Chapter Three

Jonathan rested his hand on the shoulder of the pretty woman with her head on his thigh. She'd promptly given him her address to plug into his GPS before she'd dozed off. Soft snores met his ear as he smiled. When the evening had started, he sure didn't think he'd be ending it with her head in his lap, and her sound asleep.

What to do about her. Yes, the physical need for her had him tied up in knots. Candace said just go for it, but how? Easier said than done, he figured with how little they'd interacted in the past.

She was an enigma to him, and he didn't know how to change their relationship from acquaintances to lovers or whatever. Hell, he didn't even know what he truly wanted from her at this very moment. Lovers? Yes, at least that, but what else?

He pulled into the driveway at her apartment building and over to the side. As much as he didn't want to have to wake her, he didn't know which building was hers. Having her in his arms, even for a moment, was heaven. "Mandy? Darlin', wake up."

"Hmm." She rubbed her face on his thigh.

His cock jumped at the close contact of her mouth to his straining shaft. He exhaled on a rush.

"Baby, wake up. We are at your place, but I don't know which building is yours."

"Around to the right in the back. Building C," she mumbled before she put her hand on his thigh, using it to push herself upright.

He swallowed *hard*. Letting his foot off the brake, he drove around to the back of the apartments, and pulled into an unmarked spot. "Which apartment?"

"Two-forty-one. Second floor."

She started breathing through her nose in a rough and rapid fashion. "Oh God. I think I'm going to be sick."

"Hang tight. Let me open the door."

She dry heaved a couple of times before he could pop open the door and race around to open hers. The minute the door was open, puke sprayed the pavement, catching the tips of his boots in the process.

"I'm sorry, Jonathan."

"It's okay. Tequila will do that." He helped her out, moved her toward the grass, and held her hair back from her face as she threw up again. The stench of alcohol permeated the air around them, making his stomach roll too. He didn't do puke very well. He swallowed several times, willing the nausea bombarding him to settle down, as she continued to throw up everything in her stomach. "Honey, we need to get you inside," he said, after a few minutes of silence.

"Okay. My purse is in the truck. My keys are in there."

"Stay here." He grabbed her purse from the floor board, before pushing the doors shut and locking the truck. "Let's go." With her keys in hand, he helped her stand up so they could head for her place. He managed to find what looked like a house key as they approached the stairs going up to her landing. "Do you think you can climb the stairs?"

"Maybe."

Shaking his head, he handed her the purse. "Hold this." He bent down, swung her up in his arms, and started up the flight of stairs, his booted heels clicking on the concrete.

"Wow. I've never been carried like this."

"Well, it was the easiest solution."

She wrapped her arms around his neck and snuggled her head into the crook between his chin and his chest with a soft hum.

He could get used to this.

"I'm sorry I puked on your boots."

"It's okay."

When they reached the door, he slipped the key into the lock, turned the handle, and pushed it open with his boot.

She reached over and flipped the light on with her right hand.

"Thanks."

"Yep."

"Where's your bedroom?"

"Down the hall. First door on the right."

He pushed the door closed with his foot before heading down the hall to her room. He didn't have time to look over her space except to notice the cleanliness of the apartment. Everything in its place seemed to be her motto.

A soft meow met his ears as he moved into her bedroom where she'd left a soft glowing light on the bedside table. The big queen sized bed with the white comforter was home to a black, purring feline. The cat stretched out its front paws while it lifted his butt in the air and yawned.

Jonathan slowly lowered Mandy onto the bed as the cat sniffed the air before moving over to the other side and jumping down. "You need to get out of those clothes. I think you have puke on them."

"I probably do." She swung her legs over the side of the bed and sat up. "Whoa. The room is spinning."

"Too much tequila?"

"Yeah," she said, holding her head. "Can you help me?"

Oh shit. "Uh…"

"Please? I have a t-shirt I sleep in on the dresser over there." She pointed to the large dresser in the corner with the huge mirror behind it.

He could hand her the t-shirt. That wouldn't be a problem.

When he turned back around, he almost choked on his spit. She'd taken her shirt off, leaving her in nothing but a pink bra cupping her beautiful breasts. A groan escaped his lips as she climbed to her feet, unbuttoned her skirt and then shimmied out of it. Her little dance revealed a matching pink thong.

"Much better."

His heart hammered in his chest, leaving him breathless, or was that the gorgeous woman standing in front of him half-naked? Probably the latter. "Mandy?"

"What?"

"Uh…" He handed her the shirt. "Here."

"Thanks." She reached around behind her, unsnapped her bra, and let it fall to the floor. "Jonathan?"

"Yeah?"

"How come you don't like me?"

"I do. Holy shit, but I do."

"Then why don't you talk to me very much?" she asked, sliding the t-shirt over her head.

With the soft cotton material in place, he could almost breathe, almost. "I'm not really a talkative kind of guy."

"Would you do me a favor?"

"What?"

"Kiss me?"

"I don't think that's such a good idea."

"Oh, right. I have puke on my breath. Not good for kissing." She spun around, grabbed her head, and swayed a little before she caught her balance and headed for what he assumed was the bathroom to the left. "Let me brush my teeth and then we will get to the kissing part."

He was so screwed.

* * * *

The mint toothpaste tasted awful in her mouth, but it was better than the taste of throw up. Jonathan wouldn't kiss her if she tasted like puke. She really wanted to kiss him. Embarrassment at her behavior had her skin turning pink as she glanced at her reflection in the mirror above the sink. Black rimmed her eyes and her hair stuck out in several different directions. *Damn, I look like hell.* After she rinsed the toothpaste from her mouth, she grabbed a washcloth from the drawer beneath the sink, got it wet, and washed the black from her eyes. *No makeup will have to do. He'll have to think I'm gorgeous without it.*

A tapping sound reached her ears through the door. "Are you okay in there?"

"Yeah, just finishing up. I'll be right out."

She finished washing her face with a little soap and water before she shut the water off and hung up the washcloth on the rack. *Man, I look like shit.* She sighed heavily and pulled open the door to find him leaning against the doorjamb with his arms over his chest.

"Better?"

"Yeah. Sorry about that."

"It's okay." He straightened up. "You should probably go to bed."

"I know." She didn't move. The urge to thread her fingers through the hair at the base of his neck made her fingers tingle. "I hope the girls got home okay."

"I'm sure my brothers took good care of them."

"I'm sure they did." She wiped her damp face on the sleeve of her shirt. "You know, this is the most you've ever said to me."

"I know."

"Why don't you talk to me like ever?"

"Because I like you and it's hard for me to talk to women I like." He spun on his heels, heading for the door. "I should go."

"No, don't."

"I should. It's a bad idea for me to be here with you like this."

"Why?"

He turned back around to face her at the doorway. His lips were pressed in a tight line, a mere slash across his gorgeous mouth.

"Jonathan?"

"Because I want to kiss you and bury myself inside you so badly, I hurt, Mandy, and that's not good. We aren't in that kind of a relationship and being here with you is killing me."

"We could be."

"No, no we can't."

"Why not? I want you, you want me. I don't see what the problem is." She threw up her hands as she moved toward him. "Damn it! I've been chasing your ass for three years. What the hell can I do to make you see we could be good together?"

"You aren't the girl for me."

"What?"

"I'm not the right guy for you. You need someone like Joey. Yeah, maybe you should try to go out with Joey."

"I don't want Joey, I want you." She stood toe-to-toe with him. "I've wanted you from the moment I set eyes on you and that's not going to change until I get you out of my blood, however I go about doing that." She grabbed the back of his head, pulling him down so their mouths were mere inches apart as she knocked his hat to the floor behind him. "I want to taste your kiss. I want you to make love to me until we are both breathless. I want to feel you hard and pulsating inside me."

Their first kiss was meant to be magical, not hungry and passionate, but it was all about making him see that he was the perfect guy for her at the moment. Except he took possession of the kiss, and she lost all coherent thought. His hungry mouth and grasping hands came at her all at once, like he was starved for her. He forced her to accept his invading tongue as his hands wrapped around behind her, pulling her to him until her breasts were crushed to his chest. His cock strained the front of his pants as he cradled her. He was all around her.

This was a man voracious in his appetite for her body. This wasn't the Jonathan she expected.

She needed to slow things down.

She twisted her mouth from his, gasping as she dragged air into her lungs after the explosive kiss.

His lips trailed down her throat. His teeth nipped at the flesh of her neck, biting in little stinging pinches. He would devour her if she didn't stop this, but God she didn't want to stop this. She wanted this with everything inside her. "Jonathan?"

He growled.

"We need to slow down."

He halted his assault on her senses, panting hard against her flesh. After a minute or two, he stepped back, raking his fingers through his hair. "I'm sorry. That was uncalled for."

"No, no it wasn't. I forced you into that."

"I'm the man. I need to control my urges better."

"Fuck that. I want those urges. I want you to consume me, but, baby, we need to take things a little slower."

"Do you want me to make love to you or not?"

"More than anything in the world, but since I'm still half-drunk, it's probably not a good idea." *What the fuck am I saying? Back peddle here, Mandy girl.* "Don't get me wrong, I want you to fuck me good and hard, but I want to remember it and relish it. Right now, I don't think I can."

His eyes blazed with need. She could see his pulse pounding in the hollow of his throat. He wiped his hands on the thighs of his jeans as if his palms itched to touch her. His cock strained at the fly of his jeans. She could only imagine how painful it would be to drive home and try to sleep like that. She knew what going to bed horny was like. She'd been that way for three years now, waiting and wanting this man with everything she had, but now wasn't the time. God, help her, she wanted it to be special the first time they made love.

"I, uh, I'm going to go."

"Okay." She placed her hand on his arm as he turned back toward the door. "Jonathan, this is just starting between us. Don't shut me out, okay?"

"Yeah, we'll see what happens from here."

"I'll see you tomorrow?" She glanced at the clock on the bedside table. "I guess it's today now."

"Yeah. In the morning." He reached out to touch her face. "You're a beautiful woman, Mandy."

"I'll see you at the ranch."

He walked out of her door, closing it softly behind him. A minute later, she heard the front door to her apartment close behind him.

"Tomorrow. You can bet your ass there will a tomorrow, a next day, and a next day, buddy. We aren't done by a long shot."

* * * *

Mandy groaned as she opened her eyes to the sunlight pouring through the curtains on her window. Memories flooded back as she rolled over and punched her pillow to soften the rock hard lumps irritating her pounding head. Comfortable again, she stared up at the ceiling, picturing the night before with more clarity than she thought she would possess this morning.

Their first kiss.

His hands on her body.

Her putting a stop to his touch.

"God, what a fucking idiot I am! He would have made love to me last night, but I pushed him away!"

Petra jumped up on the bed, planting herself in the middle of Mandy's chest, purring softly.

"Hi, kitty." Mandy stroked the cat's soft fur for several minutes, her thoughts in a complete jumble. *What am I going to do now? What if he won't talk to me again? What if he doesn't want anything to do with me now?*

First things first, she needed to check on her friends after their night at the bar.

She tossed the covers back on her bed and gingerly rose to a sitting position. That's when it hit her. His smell still lingered in the room. She inhaled a deep breath, taking the scent into her lungs like a drowning man going down for the last time. Something spicy with a little hint of musk. God, she loved it.

After a moment, she realized his cologne clung to the shirt she wore. She brought the material to her nose, taking in everything about the scent she could.

Her cell rang in her purse lying on the dresser.

"Hello?"

"Hey."

"Hey, Samantha. How are the girls today?"

"Most of them are hung over and nursing headaches. The guys weren't happy when they drug them out of the bar last night shortly after you left. Most of them were so drunk, they couldn't walk. A couple of the guys just flung them over their shoulders and strolled out."

"I suppose I'm in trouble for stirring the pot?"

"Nope. They know the girls were responsible for their own behavior. I think the guys will forgive them, eventually, without too much fuss, but they'll play it for all it's worth until then. How are you doing this morning?"

"I'm okay. I need some home remedies for a hangover myself. Got anything for me from your bag of tricks?"

"Nope. Hydration is the big thing. Drink lots of water. Alka Seltzer is a good thing. It's your friend even if it tastes like shit."

"Thanks. I think I have some in the bathroom cabinet, although I'm not sure how old it is."

"Are you coming into the ranch today?"

"Yeah, I have a cowboy to corral."

"He took you home last night, didn't he?"

"Yep, and I proceeded to puke on his boots."

"Oh, not good."

"I know, but I think we made some progress last night. He actually talked to me more than yes, no, okay, and nope."

"That's a step in the right direction then."

"I agree."

"So you didn't do anything last night?"

"As far as?"

"You know, down and dirty."

"No, although he would have, I think, if I hadn't put a stop to it."

"You stopped it? What the hell for?"

"I don't know actually. I'm thinking I lost my marbles somewhere between the bar and my house before I threw up in the parking lot of my apartment complex." She shook her head, moaning softly when it hurt to move. "I want our first time to be special, I guess, and I didn't want to be half-drunk when it happened."

"Smart girl."

"Do you think so? Because I'm really questioning my sanity this morning. What the hell am I going to do if we go back to the way it was? You know, with him avoiding me and not talking to me?"

"I don't think it will. I think you made some great progress with him last night. Now that you two are over the hump, things will progress into whatever type of relationship you want."

"And what type of relationship is that?"

"Lovers, friends, fuck buddies, or whatever. You decide."

She let that sink in. What exactly did she want from Jonathan anyway? She'd been chasing his ass for so long, she'd lost track of what exactly she did want past at least one night in his arms. "I may need to take some time to figure that out."

"So be it. There isn't any rush now."

"There might be if he takes a huge step back."

"He'll come around. He wants you too."

"How do you know?"

"I've seen the way he watches you at the ranch when you aren't looking. He avoids eye contact with you whenever he can, but he watches you, nonetheless. I think it's rather cute."

"Frustrating."

"I imagine so."

"I've been waiting on that man for three years. Three fucking years!"

"Have you had sex in that time frame?"

"Yes, but not in the last year and not with anyone I wanted a repeat performance with."

"Holy shit, girl. You must be wound tighter than a spring."

"Ya think?"

"I hope you have at least a toy to take the edge off."

"Yeah, but it's not doing the trick much anymore. Every time I get close to him, I want to rip his clothes off. The bad part, now my room and my sleep shirt smell like him."

"How did that happen?"

"After I puked on his boots, he carried me to my room and laid me on my bed. He helped me get my nightshirt on and before he left when I told him we needed to slow things down, he'd been all over me."

"You are torturing yourself, you know."

"Yeah, I know, but somehow I think pushing him away last night will make it better in the long run. God, I hope so."

"I think it will." There was a pause on the line. "Listen, I need to go. Jackson walked in a second ago, and we need to talk about some scheduling stuff with concerts coming up."

"Okay. I'll talk to you later."

"Take care, honey, and don't worry. I think you did the right thing."

"Thanks, Samantha."

Once her friend hung up, Mandy grabbed some clothes and headed for the bathroom. She needed to shower before she went out to the ranch, and she hoped her day turned out the way she wanted, with Jonathan begging to make love to her before the night was through.

Chapter Four

Jonathan pushed himself away from his desk in his office, his thoughts not on work at all after the night before. After he'd pulled into the driveway of Thunder Ridge, he'd found his way to his small cabin only to be torn from the quiet of his room.

Restlessness tormented him to the point he found himself staring at his computer screen throughout the night rather than going to his lonely bed.

What the hell had happened?

He raked his fingers through his hair before tipping his head back on his shoulders to stare at the ceiling above his head. Memories of the night before tortured him with visions of Mandy as he kissed her, touched her, and fought with himself about making love to her like he wanted to. She wanted him, he knew that, but after she put the brakes on what they were about to do, he realized she was right. The first time they made love needed to be special, candlelight, soft music, everything perfect. He wanted that with her.

"Jonathan?"

"Hey, Mom."

"You're up early."

"I haven't been to bed."

"Why not?"

"I wasn't tired, I guess. I've been sitting here all night, trying to get some work done."

"Honey, you look like hell. It's Sunday. Go get some rest."

"I will after a while. Right now, I'm too restless." He climbed to his feet. "In fact, I might go ride the fences or throw some hay this morning. I can't concentrate on marketing today."

"Whatever you want to do is fine, you know that."

"I know." His mother stared at him for what seemed like a long time. "What?"

"Did something happen at the bar last night?"

"No, why?"

"The others came dragging their women home, most of them very drunk, but you didn't come home right away. I heard you drive in."

"I took Mandy home. She was too drunk to drive."

"Ah."

His mother didn't elaborate on her exclamation.

"Ah?"

"Nothing."

"Nothing happened, Mom."

"I didn't say it did."

"She was too drunk anyway. In fact, she puked on my boots."

"I hope you helped her to her apartment and all that."

"I did. She was in her room and ready for bed when I left."

His mother stepped closer. "Why does your shirt smell like her perfume?"

"I had to carry her up to her apartment. She couldn't walk up the stairs."

"Such a gentleman. I'm glad you boys were raised right."

"Thanks to you and Dad."

"Honey, that's born and bred country boy right there. That is part of who you are."

"Anyway, nothing happened."

"Nothing?"

He glanced down at his boots, glad he'd washed them off with the hose when he'd gotten home last night, to at least get the puke off. "I kissed her."

"And?"

"She wanted me to make love to her. I almost did and then she stopped things. She said she didn't want to do that kind of thing being half-drunk. I left her standing in her room, in her night clothes, drove home, and wished I'd taken a cold shower."

"I'm sure you two will work things out in the end, but for now, you should probably stay away from her."

He shook his head in disbelief. He couldn't fight the small smile playing on his mouth at his mother's words. "Don't pull that on me, Mom. You did that with several of my brothers and look where they ended up, married or in a serious relationship with the one you said to stay away from."

She grinned. "True enough, but you aren't in love with her and she's not in love with you. There is a difference in your relationship with Mandy that wasn't there with your brothers."

He thought about that for a moment. What she said was true. He wasn't in any kind of relationship with Mandy, at the moment, and he wasn't sure if that's what he wanted or not. He liked her, yeah, but did he want a future with her?

"You haven't made up your mind about her yet. I understand that."

"No, I haven't. I don't even really know her."

"Then get to know her, Jonathan. She's a nice girl, otherwise she wouldn't have been working here on the ranch for the last few years, and she wouldn't be good friends with your sisters-in-law."

"I know."

"Well then, don't give into your baser instincts yet. Date her. Take her out. Woo her before you break down and slide between the sheets with her."

He thought about his mother's words as she quietly left him in the office alone to think. He loved his mother. She gave good advice, but did she really know Mandy well enough to be able to judge her and what she wanted from a relationship?

He had some thinking to do and the best way to think was to get some physical work done. *Throwing hay it is.* They'd gotten a load in yesterday that needed to be stacked in the barn. Sounded like a good place to start. A little sweat and a lot of thinking before breakfast might clear his mind of these confusing thoughts he had about the woman. He'd lusted after her for so long, he'd begun to think his dick might fall off.

Dust floated in the sunlight dancing through the slats in the barn, when he walked through the big double doors. The smell of hay, horses, grain, and cattle reached his nose, bringing his worry and stress down several notches. Even though he didn't get out and do a lot of the physical work much, he still loved the smells and sounds of a working ranch. It was in his blood.

He took in the scents with a deep breath as he stood just inside the doors. Horses stuck their heads out of the stalls with soft nickers in greeting.

"Hey, sweetheart," he said, stopping to run his hand down the nose of one of the mares who had recently foaled. The gorgeous sorrel foal stood near his mother. He'd make a fine stud for some of their mares in a few years.

The moment he stripped off his shirt and begun moving the hay bales from point A to point B, he'd felt better. Sweat dribbled down from his temples to drip onto his chest. Muscles strained from the exertion.

After an hour of straining, backbreaking work, his mind was clearer, and his thoughts were more focused.

The moment she walked into the barn, his brain hay-wired again.

"Hey." The sweet, soft sound of her greeting sent him into a tailspin.

"Hi."

"You don't usually do this kind of work."

"No, but I needed to clear my head. Physical work does that for me." He grabbed his shirt, wiping the sweat from his neck and chest.

Her gaze followed his movements before ricocheting back to his face. "Well, um. I figured we needed to talk."

"Yeah, I think we do."

"Can you take a break?"

"Sure. Let me put my shirt on."

"Don't do that on my account. I kind of like the sweaty cowboy look on you. It's nice."

He grinned as he adjusted his cowboy hat, but slipped his shirt back on anyway before he took a seat on one of the hay bales. "Have a seat." Mandy sat down next to him, bringing her clean, sweet scent with her. He loved her smell. "So?"

"I wanted to apologize again for last night. Things kind of got out of hand."

"It's okay."

"No, no it's not, but I'm glad we are talking still and you aren't running away from me anymore."

"I'm sorry it seemed that way to you. It takes a lot for me to talk to women, any women, but when it's someone I'm attracted to, it's worse. I'm not bold, like my brothers."

"I get that. Candace told me."

"She did?"

"Yeah. It kind of pissed me off because you would talk to her just fine, but you wouldn't talk to me."

"It took a lot for me to talk to her too. We had common ground in the computer stuff and websites, though. I didn't talk to her much when she first got here because she belonged to Joshua, and I didn't want to step on toes or piss him off."

"I get that now."

"Good." He wiped his sweaty palms on his jeans. He seemed to do that a lot around her. He got to his feet, facing the stalls for a second so he could gather his thoughts. "Um. Would you like to have dinner with me tonight? You know, we could go to the diner and then maybe a movie in San Antonio?"

"Are you asking me on a date?"

He spun around quickly to face her, his face hot with the blush he knew stained his cheeks. "Yeah, I guess so. My mom said I should try to get to know you better, rather than jumping into the sack with you." He held out his hands, imploring her to understand what he meant. "Not that I don't want that too, but that's not all I want. I mean, it is, but it isn't." He yanked off his hat and ran his fingers through his sweaty hair. "I'm not doing a very good job of this." The smile on her lips made him want to kiss her senseless.

"I know what you mean, cowboy. I'd love to have dinner with you and go see a movie."

The grin he felt on his lips, made him smile bigger. He liked her. He really did. "Okay, then. Um, how about I pick you up about six? We'll go to dinner on the Riverwalk before we find a movie to see. Or you can pick a movie today some time and we can find a theater to go to?"

"Sounds good." She climbed to her feet, taking a step toward him before she framed his face with her hands and leaned in.

The brush of her lips on his sent his desire spiraling. The need to have her beneath him was almost overwhelming. He pushed his hands into her hair, cradling her head, and tilted her so he could sample her mouth better.

Last night's kiss was an awakening of passion. This one was a sampling of awareness to the feelings building between them.

Her lips softened under his as she leaned into him. A soft hum escaped her lips. He felt the touch of her tongue on his lips, begging for entrance into his mouth. When he opened his lips and touched her tongue with his, his world narrowed to only her and what she felt like in his arms. He let his hands wander down over her shoulders, down her sides, and to her hips where he let his hands cradle her, bringing her in tighter to his embrace.

The clearing of a throat brought them apart slowly. He didn't want to give up what they'd experienced in each other's arms.

When he glanced up, he saw a smile playing on his father's lips and a twinkle in his eyes. "Sorry. I didn't mean to disturb you. I was headed out to feed the horses this morning. Joey isn't feeling well."

He stepped back from Mandy as she dropped her hands back to her sides. "I need to go anyway. I want to check on the girls."

"See you tonight?"

"Yes. Six o'clock."

"Right."

He watched her turn and walk through the opening of the barn doors with a sexy sway to her hips. *She's perfect.*

"You okay, Jonathan?" his dad asked, walking toward him. "I'm sorry I interrupted."

He could feel his face flush red with embarrassment. "It's fine. It kind of happened out of the blue so, yeah." He grabbed another bale of hay and tossed it to the pile he'd made to the left, his thoughts completely on the woman who'd left him hard and wanting with nothing more than a kiss.

"I'm glad to see you and Mandy getting along. It's been a long time coming."

"Yeah?"

"Yes. She's been hot on your tail for quite a while, son, if you hadn't noticed."

"I noticed."

"They why were you waiting?"

"I guess I wasn't sure about her, you know? She's bold, brash sometimes and very pretty. Not my usual type of woman."

"Do you have a usual type? Because, I haven't seen you with very many women over the years."

"Thanks, Dad."

"Observation, son. You keep to yourself a lot. I've been worried about you." His dad dropped his gaze to the floor before it came back to meet his. "I even thought for a bit there, you might be gay."

"Me, gay? No. I like women. It just takes a lot for me to talk to them."

"You weren't having any problem communicating with Mandy when I walked in." His dad smiled knowingly. "You seemed to be very into her there."

Jonathan felt his mouth lift in a grin. "Yeah. You could say that." He turned back to the hay to move another bale. "She's a good kisser."

"I'm glad you two are hitting it off finally."

"Me too. She's been an interest of mine for quite a while."

His dad grabbed a bale of hay to toss into the stall of the horse Jonathan had stopped to pet. "So, you two are going on a date?"

"Yep. I asked her to dinner and a movie."

"Great start."

He tossed two more bales. "I thought so. I want to go slow with her. Get to know her some."

"Sounds like a good plan."

"Mom told me to stay away from her."

"Your mother has this reverse psychology thing working on you boys. She's all about daughters and grandbabies."

"I know."

James grabbed the water hose and began filling a bucket. "Works though."

"Yeah, kind of. The minute she said I should stay away from Mandy, I wanted nothing more than to find her, lay her out on one of these hay bales, and make love to her."

"Hay bales are scratchy on delicate skin."

"True, but you would know this how?"

"We didn't have nine boys without knowing how hay feels a few times, son."

"TMI, Dad."

His dad laughed as he shut the water off. "Come on now. You know how babies are made."

"True, but I don't need to know that my parents are having raunchy sex in the barn."

"Not anymore. I'll leave that to you boys and don't tell me you and your brothers haven't made use of the loft a few times over the years."

Jonathan sheepishly dropped his gaze to his boot tips. He hadn't used the loft himself but he knew his brothers had—several times even recently. "Well, that's not for me to comment on."

After he stacked the last bale, he walked toward where his dad was grabbing a shovel to clean out the stall. "I'm headed back inside to work on some marketing stuff. I'll talk to you later."

"Sure, son. Have fun tonight."

"I'm sure we will. Thanks for the talk, Dad."

"You're welcome."

Jonathan buttoned his shirt as he walked toward the main lodge, passing a group of older women sitting in some lawn chairs outside their room. "Mornin', ladies."

"Mornin'."

The bell clanged for breakfast a moment later. "Breakfast is served."

"We'll be right there, handsome. Save us a seat?"

"Certainly."

The women giggled like schoolgirls, and he had to smile. He loved talking to the older women. They always seemed to treat him like one of their own children. He tipped his cowboy hat at them before heading to the main lodge.

He detoured to his cabin to change his shirt. He couldn't go into breakfast smelling like sweat, hay, horse shit, and leather. A shower would feel wonderful right now, but he didn't have time if he wanted breakfast. Oh well, a clean shirt it was.

He pushed open his door and stopped.

A child's giggle drifted to him on the wind. The sound made him smile. He wanted kids someday, but with the right girl. Children were important to him.

He made his way inside his cabin, shutting the door behind him before he walked to the dresser by the wall. His bed took up the entire other wall in the room to accommodate his six-foot-six-inch frame. He needed every inch to be able to sleep comfortably since he was one of the tallest of the Young brothers.

When he reached into his dresser drawer, he pulled out a t-shirt, and slipped it over his head, the cotton material smooth and soft against his skin.

Before he tossed his sweaty shirt into the dirty clothes hamper, he brought it to his nose to see if he could still smell Mandy's perfume on the material. The faint scent made him smile. Even through the stench of the barn, he could still smell her. He closed his eyes, feeling the taste of her kiss on his lips. The lip-lock when they were in the barn, played over in his mind like a slow motion movie.

He slowly opened his eyes, hoping beyond hope that she was standing there in front of him, but alas, she wasn't. The whole thing was in his head. Soon. Soon he would have her in his arms again. Maybe tonight even.

* * * *

Mandy fluffed her hair as she stared at herself in the mirror. She'd taken her time to shower again for the second time today, splash some nice perfume in appropriate places, and dabbed on some light makeup to freshen up her appearance. Looking like a hussy wouldn't do. Jonathan was a down-home cowboy and she would be the wannabe cowgirl he needed if it killed her. Most girls who were real cowgirls didn't put on the thick makeup, so it was light foundation, a little blush to the cheekbones, thin eyeliner, and a nice rose colored lipstick. Her long blonde hair was curled in big ringlets, emphasizing the pink streak that ran from root to tip. Her blue eyes sparkled in the light over the sink as a smile spread across her lips. She definitely had plans for one Jonathan Young tonight and for several nights to come.

Her cell phone jingled on her nightstand. She had told the girls she had a date with Jonathan, so she wondered who it was. When she picked it up, she saw the name Peyton.

"Hey."

"Hi."

"Are you getting ready for your date?"

"Yeah."

"Where are you going?"

"Just out for dinner and a movie, I think. Nothing special."

"I hope you have a good time. Did you buy condoms?"

"Now why would I need condoms?"

Peyton laughed on the other end of the phone. "Honey, you are going out with a Young brother. If you aren't prepared, you'd better be."

Mandy rolled her eyes even though her friend couldn't see her. "You know, all of you are a bad influence on me."

"Us?"

"Yeah. You all think because you have one of the Young boys in your back pocket, we all should. What if he doesn't like me enough to want to go to bed with me?"

"Seriously? You can't really think he would turn down a good fuck if you offered, do you?"

"You make me sound so sleazy."

"I'm just saying, take advantage of the evening if the opportunity arises."

"We'll see. No promises."

"Okay. Call me when everything is said and done. I want deets."

"Yes, Mother."

Peyton made kissing sounds on the phone and then hung up. Mandy smiled as she thought about how her relationship with Peyton had evolved from the time they met.

She'd been friends with Peyton ever since her friend had shown up in Bandera sporting bruises to her body and avoiding eye contact with everyone in town. After several probing questions during a drunken binge, Mandy found out that Peyton was hiding from an abusive ex who'd beaten her over several years of their relationship. When she and Jason had been dating, her crazy ex had found her, beaten the shit out of her with a bullwhip, and almost got away with killing all three of them before Jason managed to shoot him in self-defense.

Even though she was close with all the girls at Thunder Ridge, Peyton was her best friend in the whole world and the only one to know her secret, the secret she carried in her heart hoping no one else would ever find out.

Mandy dabbed at her eyes, hoping the lone tear wouldn't ruin her makeup. She didn't need to feel pity this evening. Tonight was the beginning of something special between her and Jonathan, she hoped.

She slipped on a cute little tank top, a slimming pair of jeans, socks, and cowboy boots. A bit of hairspray and a fluff of the bangs lying across her forehead and she declared herself ready for anything that might happen with Jonathan.

The doorbell rang and then a soft knock echoed.

With a fortifying breath, she walked toward the front door to answer it. Butterflies fluttered in her stomach, her palms were sweaty, and her throat was dry. Why was she reacting this way? It wasn't like she didn't know Jonathan, but this would be their first official date. She was scared to death.

When she finally turned the knob, she was surprised to see Jonathan on the landing holding a bouquet of flowers.

"Hi."

"Hi."

He extended his hand, pushing the flowers into her chest. "These are for you."

"Thank you. They are beautiful," she said, stepping back so he could come inside the apartment while she put the flowers in some water. "Let me get a vase for these."

"Okay."

She heard the door click shut behind them as she walked into the small kitchen off to the left. It wasn't much to look at, but it was all hers and something she'd worked her ass off to keep while going to school full-time. Working at the local feed store for the last several years paid the rent, but it didn't leave much for anything else. Thank God for student loans and grants or she would never have been able to go. Graduating this year was the highlight of her life. She couldn't wait to get hired somewhere to work on websites and do marketing for all types of different businesses.

Once she got the flowers in some water and set them on the dining room table, she turned to face him, taking in his gorgeous self for a moment while he wasn't looking. Jonathan stood taller than the rest of his brothers, at probably six-foot-five or so, with broad shoulders, biceps that strained the material of his shirt, long, slim legs that looked powerful in his jeans, and black, shiny boots on his feet that matched the cowboy hat on his head. His hair curled slightly at his collar, making her fingers itch to run through it.

His gaze moved back to her face while his brown eyes narrowed slightly. "What?"

"Nothin'."

"You were staring."

"I like to look at you. You are one nice looking man, Jonathan."

A blush stole across his cheeks. "If you say so."

"I do. You can turn a few heads in this town, you know, including mine."

He dropped his gaze to the floor at their feet as he shoved his hands inside the front pockets of his jeans. "Thanks."

"Shall we go?"

"Sure," he said, coming toward her to place his hand at the small of her back and guide her toward the door.

She liked the gentlemanly behavior all the Young brothers seemed to have, but this was special since it was aimed at her. "Thank you."

"For what?" he asked as they shut the door, locked it, and walked out toward where his truck was parked.

"Being such a gentleman."

"You might not think I'm such a gentleman after the night is over."

"One can hope. A gentleman is nice, but I like a little bad boy mixed in there too, you know."

They stopped at the passenger side of his truck, and he turned her so her back was pressed against the door. The twinkle in his eyes mesmerized her as he leaned in, tilted his head, and nipped at the tender flesh of her neck where it met her collarbone.

Holy shit!

Her body erupted in goose bumps when he continued to rub his lips up the side of her neck.

"Bad boy, I can do, if that's what you want."

"Oh yeah." Her words came out in an urgent sigh. Her hands shook as she settled them on his shoulders, leaning into his body. He pressed her harder against the door, her back digging into the metal. Wetness coated her underwear, making her very aware of the magnetism of the man currently nipping at her flesh. God, she wanted him more than anything on the planet.

"We should get some food." His words were puffs of warm air against her flesh.

"Yeah, food."

With a sigh, he stepped back, taking his warmth with him. She took a couple of steps to the left so he could open her door.

When she was settled in the passenger seat of the truck, he buckled her seatbelt for her, brushed a quick kiss against her lips, and then shut the door behind him. As she watched him walk around the front of the vehicle, her heart hammered like a trapped bird inside a cage. Tonight would be *the* night. She was sure of it.

Chapter Five

Jonathan watched the gorgeous woman across from him as he picked at his food. He really wasn't all that hungry, he just wanted to watch her. This was his favorite restaurant on the River Walk of San Antonio, but everything tasted like sawdust in his mouth.

The edges of the fork disappeared between her red lips as she ate. His cock jumped behind the fly of his jeans, wishing they were wrapped around his straining flesh. He wanted that from her. Good Lord, he wanted her. The scent of her skin still lingered in his nose. The tang of her flesh still tingled on his tongue. The feel of her body beneath his hands made his fingers itch to touch her again.

He was such a goner for this girl.

"Jonathan?"

"Yeah?"

"Are you okay? You seem really quiet."

"You'll realize that's kind of the way I am, if you're around me much."

"I gathered that, but I feel like I'm talking your ear off. You don't want to hear all about me."

"Yes, I do. I want to learn all there is about you, all your secrets, your desires, your plans for the future—all of it."

She dropped her gaze to her plate and moved her chicken around with her fork.

He tilted his head slightly while he watched her. She seemed like she wanted to talk but was afraid of telling him something that might scare him off. There wasn't anything in the world she could say that would frighten him. Well murder, maybe, but yeah, nothing else he could think of. "Mandy?"

"Sorry. I was formulating what I wanted to say. I'm kind of an analytical person so I have to work things through my brain before I speak." She shoved a piece of enchilada into her mouth and chewed thoughtfully as she sat back in her chair. When her mouth was clear, she glanced at the boat going down the river for a moment, watching it slowly sluice by. "Let's see. I'm twenty-five. I've been in the area, San Antonio/Bandera for about ten years. My parents moved us here when I was fifteen. It sucked. I hated moving in high school. I didn't have a ton of friends."

"Where did you move from?"

"Minnesota."

"Wow. Minnesota to Texas. That's a switch in climate."

"Yeah. The heat killed me the first few years, but I liked not having to trek to the bus in snow that was waist deep during the winter."

"I can imagine."

"Anyway, my stepdad got a job here in San Antonio, so we moved. Being fifteen, a girl, and moving at that time in your life really was bad. I got into trouble a lot, hated my parents, hated the area, hated my life, so I rebelled. I started smoking pot, running around, sneaking out of the house, and generally being a pain in the ass to my parents in an attempt to force them to move back. It didn't work." She took another bite of her food, chewing thoughtfully before she continued. "Finally, I got into horses. They were my saving grace. I started riding barrels in the local rodeos. Got pretty good too, I would say, although never made championship material. I did place several times."

"That's great!"

She smiled. His heart stopped beating for a moment, before slamming against his ribs as it restarted with a thump.

"That was my senior year in high school. I finally adapted to the life here, and it's been pretty boring ever since. I didn't go to college right away, as I'm sure you guessed. Spent a few years working different jobs like the feed store. Working part-time there and the ranch and going to school has been tough."

"The Arlington family is an old family in these parts. They've owned that store ever since I can remember."

"They are great. I love them like they are my own family. They've bought me gifts for birthdays and Christmas over the years. I'll be sad to not work there anymore once I get my degree."

"What do you plan to do with your degree?"

"Well, it's in information technology and graphic design so I hope to build websites, working on computers, do marketing. Heck, I'm not quite sure." She pushed her plate away before sipping on her margarita. "How did you get so good at web design and marketing?"

"I went to San Antonio Art and Design school. I've always been one of those with a pencil and a piece of paper in my hands, drawing things I saw. When we started taking on guests at the ranch, I jumped right into building the website. Marketing the cowboy experience of Thunder Ridge was my way of contributing."

"How old are you?"

"I'm going on thirty now."

"Where are you in the pecking order of the boys?"

"Third to the youngest, so a middle child if there ever was one."

She laughed, the tinkling sound of her giggle made him smile. He liked when she laughed.

"I don't think of you as having middle child syndrome. You are too quiet and reserved to be wild and forcing your parents to pay attention to you."

"It's hard being just another Young brother."

After another sip of her drink, she said, "I can imagine so."

"So, do you have siblings?"

"Yes, two sisters and a brother. I'm the baby of the family. They were already gone when we moved here, so I was like an only child."

"That must have been lonely."

"I was, terribly so, which is one of the reasons I hated it here."

"Do you hate it now?"

"Not at all. I love Texas, and I love the Hill Country. Working at the ranch has been great. Being around you all, the girls, the animals, and the guests is fantastic, and I wouldn't trade it for anything in the world. I'm so glad your mom brought me into the fold."

"She's kind of like that. Taking in strays is in her blood, I think."

The look she shot him across the table screamed of contemplation. "Do you really think of me as a stray?"

He shook his head, afraid he'd insulted her with his musings. "Not at all. I'm not surprised my mother took you under her wing. That's what she does. You were part of the family before anyway, because of your association with Peyton. With you helping to find her and save her, my mother took you in as one of her daughters. She always wanted daughters anyway."

Her lips tilted up in a smile. "That she does."

"So what else is there to know about you? Are you close to your parents?"

"Sort of, I guess. I don't talk to them as much as I should."

"Do they still live in San Antonio?"

"Yes. They have a small house on the outskirts of town with a little acreage."

"A ranch?"

"No, nothing like Thunder Ridge. They have a few acres for horses and goats they raise. I think it's only about ten acres."

"That's a good start though."

"Yeah, right. How big is Thunder Ridge?"

"Several hundred acres."

"See?"

"See what?"

"You all have one of the biggest ranches in the area."

"Ranching is hard work, though, and having Thunder Ridge as a guest ranch makes even more work."

She leaned in, put her elbows on the table, and propped her chin on her hand. "What about the ghosts?"

"Ghosts?"

She tapped her fingers against his forearm a couple of times. "You know what I mean. I've seen the old cowboy a time or two, heard the kids giggling in the yard, and heard the fighting upstairs when I've filled in to clean a couple of the guest rooms after check-out. You've been there since you were born. Don't tell me you don't believe in them."

"I've seen and heard them too. The kids make me smile even though I'm sad they are trapped there."

"Why?"

"Because someday I want lots of kids. A big family like my parents did."

Her smile faded as a cloud of sadness came over her face. Her gaze reflected bitterness when she raised her eyes to his again.

"Something I said?"

"No." Her face brightened again. "We should go ghost hunting."

"Ghost hunting?"

"Yeah, you know, hang around the ranch and see what we see or hear. I would love to do some research on the place to find out who these people are. Has anyone in the family done that?"

"Not that I know of," he said, taking a sip of his beer for the first time all night. He'd totally neglected his food and drink indifference to staring at her.

Her blonde hair reflected the moonlight overhead, the pink streak giving her an air of defiance to the world around her. Her blue eyes were clear and sparkling when they looked at him. She had pink lipstick on that made him want to smudge it with his mouth. Her white gauzy top with the white tank top underneath emphasized her pert, little breasts. He was totally an ass man, so yeah, her breast size was okay with him. She wasn't a big breasts type woman, but they looked like they would fit nicely in his palms. She wasn't a thin girl. Her curves made him want to pull her in, cuddle her close, and find out where all the spots were that made her sigh with pleasure.

Soon. Real soon.

"What are you thinking about?"

"Nothing specific, why?"

"You had a little smile on your lips and you were staring at me." She bit her lower lip, taking it in between her teeth and nibbling on the pink flesh.

"All right. I confess. I was thinking about you."

"Me?" Her lips tipped up at the corners in a little smile. "What were you thinking about me?"

"How your hair shines in the moonlight. How your lips are just the right kind of kissable. How your eyes sparkle with laughter and then darken with sadness when you think about something that makes you uncomfortable." He leaned closer. "How your breasts would fit perfectly in my palms. How I want to—" He glanced from side to side for a moment. "Fuck the hell out of you."

"You do?"

"Yes, ma'am. More than anything in the world."

"Shall we skip the movie and go back to my place?" One of her eyebrows quirked up. "I mean, if you want to, that is."

"I would like nothing more than to go back to your place with you or my place. Either one."

"It might be a little embarrassing for me to be seen with you on the ranch."

"Why? It's not like we haven't been dancing around each other for the last three years."

"True, but I'd feel more comfortable at my place."

"I don't remember exactly. Do you have a four-poster bed?"

"Yeah, why?"

"No reason." His heart beat double-time in his chest thinking about all the ways he could tie her up. Spread eagle would be awesome. *Damn, I didn't bring rope. No matter, this first time should be sweet, sexy, and mind blowing.*

"Shall we go?"

He grabbed the check, slipped his credit card into the sleeve, and they both finished their drinks while they waited on the waitress. The moment she returned with the receipt and his card, he put everything away, grabbed Mandy's hand, and practically dragged her back toward the truck.

"What's your hurry, cowboy? We've got all night."

"I know. I don't know about you, but I'm really, really horny."

"Me too. It's been a bit for me. You'll have to take your time—not too much time though. I might burst into flames or something."

He slowed his walk. There was no reason to make this a hit and run. He didn't want that with her, he wanted slow, sexy, and explosive. He tucked her hand into the crook of his arm, bringing her in close contact with his side. Everything tingled where they touched. His whole body went on alert, not like it hadn't already been buzzing with sensation up until now. "I'm sorry. I'm a little excited about the prospect of making love to you."

"Me too, cowboy."

When they reached the side of his truck, he opened the passenger side door, and helped her in before shutting it behind her. As he walked around the front of the truck, he glanced to his left to catch her watching him. She ran her tongue over her lips slowly. Blood pounded in his ears and his steps faltered.

Tonight was going to be one hell of a night if he had anything to say about it.

* * * *

They drove through the night in silence back to her apartment. Her blood sang in her veins as she thought about actually making love with Jonathan tonight. She's waited so long for this, she could hardly believe it was really about to happen, in her apartment, in her bed. It would be something she could hold tight to for a long time to come, no matter what happened between them. If tonight was to be the only time they fucked, then so be it. The memory would sustain her, it might have to.

"You okay?" he asked as he pulled into her parking lot and found an empty, unmarked spot.

"Yes. Just nervously excited." She wiped her sweaty palms down the thigh of the jeans she wore. They were one of her favorite pairs since they showed off her ass to perfection.

"Me too." He shut off the truck. "Shall we?"

"Yeah," she said, reaching to open her door.

"Let me. I can be the gentleman here and get your door."

"Thanks."

He opened his side and shut the door before walking around the front of the truck to open hers. He held out his hand, palm side up waiting for her to place her trust in him that he wouldn't hurt her. God help her, she was afraid he would. He easily could as much as she wanted him, but she wouldn't think of that now. Tonight was for connecting, not thinking about what the future might hold. Tonight, she would feel without reading anything into the situation outside of two people wanting to take comfort in each other's arms.

She placed her palm in his, letting him help her from the vehicle. The warmth of his hand reassured her this was what he wanted. He wanted her. She wanted him. They would let the rest work itself out.

When he shut the door behind him, the bang of the metal door made her jump. The sound vibrated through her with finality. It was now or never. If they didn't make love tonight, they might never get around to it.

"Ready?"

"Yeah."

"Nervous?"

"Hell yeah."

"Me too."

"You are?"

"Yeah. I've wanted this for so long, I can't believe we are here, ready to take this step in our relationship."

She frowned. "Relationship?"

"Yeah. You know, like boyfriend and girlfriend kind of thing."

"Let's not jump the gun here, Jonathan. It's sex, that's it, right?"

His brows formed a weird little wrinkle between them as his mouth pulled down in a frown. "I suppose. I mean, I thought we could date at least. I'm not really into one-night stands, Mandy. Are you?"

"I don't think of this as a one-night stand either, but I didn't think we were on the verge of getting serious or anything. We only started dating tonight. It's been one date."

"I got that part, but I thought we might see where things go, you know?"

"I'm fine with seeing what lies ahead, but I'm not ready to call it a relationship."

He held up his hands. "Okay, my mistake. Sorry. I won't call it a relationship ever again. You can drive this bus."

She nodded as she slipped the key into the door. "Good."

As she pushed open the door with her right hand, she felt around with her left until she touched the light switch. With a flick of her fingers, she illuminated the small apartment.

Jonathan stepped in behind her and shut the door. She could feel the warmth of his body against her back as he moved her hair to the side and brushed his lips against her neck. Goose bumps exploded along her arms. Her body began to hum from excitement. It really was going to happen. They were actually going to make love for the first time, and she couldn't wait to feel him over her and inside of her.

"You are a very beautiful woman."

"Thanks."

"I can't wait to feel every inch of you around me, all warm, slick, and wet."

She exhaled sharply.

He took her shoulders, turning her so she faced him. He was so tall and so big, she wasn't sure how things were going to work. She barely came to his shoulder.

"You're so tall."

"Six-six."

"I'm only five-five."

"We'll make it work. Promise." His fingers reached for the front of her button down top, releasing each one slowly, to expose her skin to his touch.

When the material parted with a push of his fingers, her breath caught in her throat. The tips of his fingers brushed against her skin, causing her whole body to tingle from the touch.

"You have very soft skin." He buried his nose in the little crook behind her ear. "You smell fantastic. Flowers."

"Sweet pea."

"I love it on your skin."

"Jonathan," she breathed.

"Right here, darlin'."

The soft brush of his lips against her neck threw her into a fit of giggles. "Sorry. I'm ticklish there."

"Hmm. I'll keep that in mind."

She swept the cowboy hat off his head, tossing it onto the couch behind them. This gave her full access to his thick, dark curls. It had been a fantasy of hers for a long time, to bury her fingers in his hair and hold his head to her as he ate at her pussy like a starving man. *Soon.*

His lips danced from her collarbone in a downward motion toward her breast. She wanted to feel his mouth on there more than anything right at the moment.

He pushed her top from her shoulders and she let it drop to the floor at their feet. She'd worn a tank top beneath her blouse, but right now, she wished she hadn't. Too many clothes made for a frustrating scenario.

As he kissed his way across her chest, he worked the straps of her tank top down her arms, freeing her breasts from the confines of the top, leaving her in just her bra.

"We should take this in the bedroom."

"I want you naked."

"You're doing a pretty good job of it, cowboy, but with our height difference, this would be easier in there where we can lie down."

He bent at the waist, scooped her up in his arms, bringing her high against his chest. She let out a little squeak of surprise and then giggled as he strolled down the hall.

He pushed open the door with his booted foot and then closed it behind them the same way, before laying her softly on the queen-size bed.

The look in his eyes told her how much he wanted her. Fire blazed from the depths, igniting her body in an inferno of need. The desire she felt for this man went beyond what should be happening, but she didn't care. She'd been chasing his ass for a long time, and it was about time for him to pay up on the debt.

"You are very beautiful. Lord knows I want to bury myself deep inside your hot center."

"Sounds like a plan to me, cowboy."

He quickly shucked his clothes, leaving them in a pile on the floor before joining her on the bed. "Do you want me?" he asked, propping himself up on his elbow as his gaze raked over her.

She took in his form as he got comfortable next to her. His chest was sprinkled with dark chest hair with a nice little happy trail from his navel to the nest of curls at his groin. His cock stood long and thick against his abdomen. Her mouth watered to taste. "Hell yes."

He leaned in, raining kisses from her nose to her lips, down her chest to her left nipple before encircling the straining nub with his tongue. She pressed her breast against his mouth, loving the sensation of his lips on her aching flesh. "God, Jonathan."

The suction of his lips on the tip drove her need higher. She wanted him buried inside her. She wanted all he had to give and then some.

His hand wandered down her abdomen, skimming across the surface of her skin, headed toward the center of her need. "Please, touch me."

"We need to get rid of these clothes." He sat up, worked the fancy, bespangled belt loose from her waist and then worked on the button at the waistband of her jeans. Next came her boots and socks. The moment he had those off, he grabbed her pants at the waist, jerking them down and off her legs before tossing them across the room along with her panties. "Nice." He brought her foot up to his mouth, kissing his way up the inside of her foot and then running his tongue along the surface of her calf.

Her breath caught in her throat as he continued his journey by kissing his way toward where she needed him most. She spread her thighs, anticipating his mouth on her center, eating her pussy like a starving man.

When his mouth finally settled on her pussy, she exhaled on a rush. "Oh, God."

"Mmmm."

The vibration of his hum against her flesh was like a little bullet vibrator on her clit. If he did it again, she'd come for sure.

She could feel liquid seeping from her pussy as he lapped, sucked, and licked her flesh. Her body shook from the feelings he was evoking while he worked to bring her to a climax with his mouth. She wanted that orgasm, she needed that orgasm more than anything. It had been a long damned time since she'd had sex, too long, way too long.

"Jonathan?"

"Hmm?"

"Make me come."

"My pleasure."

He worked her pussy like a madman, until she was shaking so hard from holding back her orgasm, she thought her head would explode. Shivers raced up and down her spine.

The moment her climax hit, she felt a rush of sensation from her toes that settled in her pelvis. Her moan of satisfaction echoed in the small room as he licked and sucked the fluid gushing from her center. She'd never come so hard in her life. "Oh my God."

He pushed himself up on his arms, skimming his lips up her body in a slow crawl to reach her mouth. After he kissed her thoroughly, he moved off the bed for a moment, grabbing his pants from the floor. At her questioning look, he held up a condom from his pocket between his fingers.

"Good thinking."

"Yeah, I thought it was a good idea."

"Anticipating this happening tonight, were you?"

"No, but ever hopeful."

She could feel the silly grin spreading across her lips as she watched him climb back into the bed with her, the condom left on the bed beside him. "Should we get under the covers?"

"I'm good. I kind of want you bent over the side of the bed so I can go deep from behind."

"Sounds fun." She skimmed her hand down his chest, loving the feeling of his chest hair under her palm. The softness of the springy curls tickled a little as she continued her path down his abdomen. The trail of hair from his navel to his cock intrigued her. She's never been with a dark-haired man, much less one who had one of these.

His belly jumped from her touch, tempting her further to explore the hardness beneath her fingers. Her fingers continued their journey until she reached his hard cock lying against his belly. She encircled the head with just the tip of her finger, spreading the glistening drop of pre-cum from the little slit in the top. Her breath came out in little pants of air as she licked her lips, wanting that salty taste on her tongue.

He groaned softly, encouraging her touch.

She wrapped her hand around his length, slowly gliding her hand up and down the hard shaft. The softness of the skin against her palm felt wonderful.

"That's it, touch me. I want your hands all over me."

She laid her hand on his chest and pushed. When he sprawled back on the bed, she began kissing him from his tempting lips, over his jaw, across his chest, and then down his abdomen, following the happy little trail of hair until it reached his groin. She pushed her nose into the space between his ball sack and the base of his cock, inhaling the musty scent of his sex. The smell was intoxicating.

She ran her tongue around his balls, licking each in turn until he moaned and arched his back.

His hand fisted in her hair, guiding her mouth to where he wanted her most. The tortured groan that escaped from his lips when she took the head of his cock in her mouth, made her wet and ready.

She licked her way from the tip of his cock, down the front, flicking the veins she found with the tip of her tongue, until she reached the base. She relished the sounds coming from his throat. Every one of them made her smile against his flesh.

His hips came off the bed when she returned to take his entire length into her mouth, sucking as she went down and then running her teeth up the shaft as she came back up.

"God woman. You're gonna kill me."

"Sweet heavens, what a way to die." She continued to suck his cock until he was groaning incoherently, muttering her name in a growl that came from deep in his throat. The sound had her shivering as she moved up his chest, licking his skin as she went, until she reached his mouth.

Grabbing the condom from the bed, she tore it open with her teeth and then rolled the slippery latex over his cock, before she straddled his hips. She positioned his cock at her opening and slowly took him inside her body, loving the feel of him stretching her with his length. "Oh fuck."

"Ride me, Mandy."

She shifted her hips so she could slide his cock in and out of her body slowly. The tortured groans spilling from his lips brought a smile to hers. "So good."

He grabbed her hips in a powerful grip, lifting her, and guiding her movements in the best way to bring them both pleasure.

"Uh-uh. I control this." She clamped down on his cock with her vaginal muscles.

"Holy shit."

A giggle escaped her mouth as she placed his hands around the metal rungs of the headboard. "Keep them there. This is my party for the moment. You can have control in a minute."

His eyes glittered, reflecting the light above her head as he glanced up and caught her gaze with his own. He wanted this as much as she did, maybe more. The thought made her heart sing. She'd been lusting after him for so long, she'd almost forgotten how to be with anyone else. Now, she had him right where she wanted him, balls deep inside her pussy while she rode his hips into tomorrow.

She lifted her hips up and down, riding his length as she tossed back her head. The feel of him inside her was everything she'd hoped it be and more. Each push down, he met her halfway, thrusting up with his own pelvis at the same time, driving his cock that much deeper. "Damn, that feels good. Just right."

"You're tight."

"It's been a while since I've had sex."

"Feels like a soft glove wrapped around me, squeezing me while I slide in and out of you."

"Such a poet."

His hands slid up her abdomen until he cupped a breast in his each palm. He rubbed his thumb over her nipples, bringing them to achy little points of desire. "Ride me, cowgirl."

She spread her thighs a bit more, leaned forward, rested her hands on his chest, and began to rock her hips frontward, sliding his cock in and out of her pussy. The position brought everything into sharp focus, his cock, her pussy, the way he rubbed her nipples, and the spot he was hitting with the head of his cock deep inside her. "Fuck yeah."

"Can you come like this?"

"Almost there. Need a little more." Jonathan braced his feet on the bed and used the leverage to piston his cock with growing speed until she hung on the edge of an explosive orgasm. "Yeah, that's it. Fuck me." She exploded in a mind-numbing orgasm that had little points of light igniting behind her eyelids as she tossed her head back and screamed his name at the top of her lungs. "Jonathan!"

She collapsed on his chest, her breath coming out in rapid pants of air as she tried desperately to bring her heart rate and her breathing back to normal.

His hand stroke the back of her head, following the length of her hair down her back where it rested almost to her hips.

"Wow."

He kissed the top of her head as he continued to stroke her back.

That's when she realized, he was still hard inside of her.

"You didn't come?"

"No."

"I'm sorry." She sat up and moved to the side of his body. "Tell me what you want me to do."

"It's okay."

"No it isn't. This was for both of us, not just me." She leaned over and kissed him on the mouth, stroking his tongue with her own until he groaned softly. When she sat up again, she repeated. "Tell me what you want me to do?"

"Lean over the side of the bed on your stomach. That way our height difference shouldn't be so much of a problem."

He scooted off the bed and stood, looking around for something although she wasn't sure what. When he grabbed a pillow and threw it on the floor, she began to get some idea of what he planned.

As she positioned herself on her belly across the edge of the bed with her feet on the floor, cream dribbled from her pussy, sliding down her inner thigh. She spread her legs waiting for the moment he would plunge his entire length deep into her.

She couldn't see him behind her, but certainly felt it the moment the head of his cock pushed through her opening. "Oh God."

"Easy, girl."

His hand stroked her hair before sliding down her spine and then resting on her hip.

He pushed deeper until his entire length was buried inside her. The fullness was almost too much.

"Breathe."

She exhaled softly, ruffling the fringes of the bangs resting on her forehead as she grasped the bedspread in her tight fists.

He didn't move for a moment, waiting for her to adjust to him being so deep.

"Relax, Mandy. I won't hurt you."

"I know. It just feels so weird having you so deep. It's almost painful." She laughed a little. "You aren't a small man by any stretch of the imagination, Jonathan."

"You took me the other way, you can handle this."

"I know. I need a moment to adjust, is all."

"I won't move until you say it's okay."

She breathed in through her mouth and out through her nose, waiting for her body to adjust. *It shouldn't be this hard. He was just inside me, but this different position makes him feel huge.* She spread her thighs a little bit farther apart and titled her pelvis down into the bed.

He moaned deep from inside his chest.

Her pussy felt like it softened or something, to allow him in. The sensation was extraordinarily fabulous when he moved slightly, pushing his cock inside her a little bit farther. "Okay. I'm good."

"Thank you, God," he whispered, slowly sliding his cock out of her pussy and then back in. "You feel fantastic. Tight and wet."

"More. Faster."

He picked up the pace a little, giving her more and more of his fabulous cock with each plunge.

Soon he was pounding into her at a pace that had her pressed hard against the edge of the mattress. Her pussy quivered, taking every inch of him inside her, riding out the pleasure he created, until she was about to detonate in an explosion of sensation. "Oh God. Oh God. Oh God."

"Come for me, sweetheart. I want to feel you orgasm so hard, you almost lose consciousness."

Her orgasm rolled over her like a wave on the shore, completely out of her control, tossing her to and fro until she was so spent, she melted into the bedspread.

Jonathan roared his completion behind her, saying her name in a reverent whisper as he collapsed across her back, his nose buried in her hair.

They didn't move for several moments, until she grunted at the weight of his body and shifted. "You're kind of heavy, Jonathan."

He slid to her side and collapsed on the bed with his arm over his eyes. "Sorry."

"It's fine. I didn't need to breathe anyway and the bedspread smells pretty good from the laundry detergent I used the last time I washed it."

After a second, he laughed, a deep rumbling that came from deep in his chest before bursting to the surface of his lips. "You always make me crack up."

She moved her head so she could see him lying next to her in all his naked glory. Her gaze shifted down his chest, following his chest hair across the wide expanse to the happy trail in the sexy little line that went from his navel to his cock. When she got to that impressive length, she was surprised to see it wasn't as huge as it felt inside her in its softened state.

He peeked at her from beneath his arm. "I guess we need to get cleaned up, and I should find a trashcan for this condom."

"In the bathroom."

He rose to his feet, removed the condom from his flaccid cock before tying the end, and walked into the bathroom across the hall from her bedroom. She heard the water run for a moment or two as she lay there on the bed reliving the last few moments of their love making in her mind.

She'd never felt anything like what he'd made her body do. Her orgasms had been exceptionally explosive, so much so that she thought her head might explode with the sensations running through her. Her pussy was hot and throbbing from his lovemaking, and her heart hammered in such a rapid beat, she thought it might burst from her chest.

After a moment, she decided she needed to move, get dressed, or do something, otherwise, it might get a bit awkward when he came back into the room. She pushed herself up and turned to sit on the side of the bed while she brushed her hair out of her face. Her clothes lay in a pile on the floor with her pink underwear lying on top. With her toe, she picked up the elastic band and brought them up to her lap as she decided how they would proceed with this newfound thing going on between them.

Relationship?

She wasn't sure. Maybe.

She slipped her underwear on and grabbed her bra from the floor. *Clothing first, then think about the heavy stuff.* Keeping an eye and ear open to the sounds coming from the bathroom, she tugged her bra on and snapped it in the back. "You okay in there?"

"Yeah. I'll be right out. Just washing up a little."

"You can use the shower if you want."

"I'm good."

"You certainly are," she whispered.

"What did you say?"

"Nothing. Just talking to myself."

He laughed for a second before she heard the water turn off and he strolled through her doorway in all his naked glory. *Holy shit!* She had to touch her lips to make sure there wasn't drool rolling out of her mouth.

"What's wrong?"

"N-nothing. Why?"

"Your mouth is hanging open." He swiped his hand down his chest. "Did I leave some soap on me or something?"

"No. I'm admiring the scenery is all."

"You look pretty hot yourself, you know, sitting there in nothing but your bra and panties." He moved a step closer and cocked his head to the side. "I probably should get going."

Her gaze shot back to his. "Why?"

"I don't know. I guess I could stick around for a bit. Do you want to watch a movie or something?" He pushed his hand through his hair. "This after sex thing is a little awkward."

She dropped her gaze to the floor by his feet, not sure where to look when he was standing in front of her naked as the day he was born. "I know what you mean."

"Uh, let me put some clothes on and then we can figure out what we want to do." He moved toward where his clothing lay in a pile on the floor.

"Yeah, me too." She climbed to her feet, retrieved her pants and shirt from the floor before she slid past him into the bathroom, shutting the door behind her. With her back against the wooden panel, she inhaled a big gulp of air and then pushed it out in a sigh. *What the hell am I going to do now?*

Chapter Six

The aftershock of being with Mandy had totally turned him upside down. After she'd come out of the bathroom completely dressed, he'd felt stupid and inadequate. He'd mumbled something about needing to go home and grabbed his wallet and keys before ducking out of her door with his tail between his legs.

Today, he sat in front of his computer not really seeing anything on the screen. He hadn't eaten breakfast this morning, taking the chance to avoid meeting her gaze across the dining room. He'd felt like a teenager after his first sexual encounter with a girl he'd been lusting after. Now, he was back to not being able to talk to her.

"Damn it!"

"Jonathan?"

"In here, Mom."

Nina poked her head through the doorway. "I didn't see you at breakfast." She took a seat in the wooden chair across from his desk as she gave him a concerned look. "Are you okay, son?"

"Yeah, why?"

"Didn't you have a date with Mandy last night?"

"Yes."

She cocked her head to the side as her gaze moved over his face. He couldn't continue to meet her stare without revealing everything that happened the night before. No, he wasn't a virgin, but he felt kind of off this morning after having made love with Mandy. Why was he being so shy now? They'd had a rousing bout of sex that was off the charts, but today he felt stupid and awkward. Why couldn't he have the self-esteem his brothers had around women?

"Honey, don't worry. You are an exceptional man and any woman would be thrilled to be with you, including Mandy."

"But I'm not as outgoing and self-assured as my brothers."

"No, but you have your own attributes that are exceptional."

"Like what?" he asked, shoving back away from the desk and turning his chair to face his mother.

"You are kind, intelligent, careful with others feelings, very good looking, a gentleman if there ever was one, and you have the most amazing personality."

"Everything a mother would say."

"Why don't you ask Mandy why she is attracted to you and not your brothers?"

"For one, everyone except Joey is taken."

"Not true three years ago when she came to work here and found you. Some of the boys were not attached, yet she's always been focused on you."

"She might not be now."

"Why would you say that? Just because you probably had sex with her last night?"

"How'd you know?"

"A woman can tell these things. Besides, she's glowing rather prettily today. The kind of glow only comes from a woman well satisfied."

"This is kind of a strange conversation for me to have with my mother."

She smiled and shook her head. "I don't see why. I've raised you boys to be open and honest with me and your father. You can tell me anything, Jonathan. I hope you know that."

"I know, Mom, but it's kind of hard to talk about my sex life with you."

"Do you think I don't know about sex? You boys weren't born from a chicken, you know." She laughed and sat forward in the chair. "Your dad and I have a very active sex life even at our age and I know you boys were active pretty early in your teen years. The barn saw a lot of action for quite a while. How many times do you think I went out there only to turn around and go back into the house because of the noises coming from the hayloft?"

Heat flushed his face when he thought about the one time he'd been caught with a girl from high school in the hayloft by his father. She'd been his first experience with sex. Wild and experimenting at the tender age of fifteen, he'd taken her to the hayloft and found out just how scratchy hay can be on tender skin. It's not as romantic as people think.

"I didn't mean to embarrass you, Jonathan. I just wanted you to know you can talk to me about anything including what happened between you and Mandy. You don't have to give me details, but I get the impression you are avoiding her today."

"I am."

"Why? Was the sex not good between you?"

"It was fantastic, off the wall amazing."

"Then what might be the issue?"

"I feel awkward and stupid today. I don't know what to say to her. I kind of left in a hurry last night, and I'm afraid I've made her really mad at me."

Nina took his hand in her grasp. "Honey, she's not mad at you, but she is confused because you are avoiding her."

"I know. I'm sorry."

"Tell her that. She could stand to see one of your smiles right now. She's feeling pretty used."

"Ah hell. I didn't want that to happen."

She brought him to his feet, turned him toward the door, and pushed him out in the hall. "Go talk to her."

"Is everyone gone?"

"Yes. The guests have dispersed elsewhere and your brothers and their families have headed off to do their own thing. I'm going to work on reservations for the coming week."

She turned the opposite direction he was headed and disappeared into her office, leaving him standing in the hall with his hands in his pockets unsure of what to do or what to say. He took a couple of steps forward, feeling resolve stiffen his spine. He needed to apologize if nothing else.

When he turned the corner of the hall that led out into the dining room area, he saw her cleaning off one of the tables. With hesitant steps, he made his way toward her. "Mandy?"

She spun around, her eyes wide. "Oh. You scared me."

"Sorry. I didn't mean to startle you." He dropped his gaze to the floor. "I wanted to apologize."

"For what?"

"For taking off so quickly last night. I shouldn't have done that. I'm sure it made you feel kind of used and that was not my intention."

She took a seat on the bench across the table while he slid onto the other one. "It's fine. I know you were feeling kind of weirded out by the whole thing."

"Yeah, but that's not why I left."

"Why did you then?"

"You were backpedaling on the relationship thing earlier so I was afraid I'd moved too fast."

She dropped her gaze to her hands clasped around the towel she'd been using to wipe the tables with. "Listen, I'm not sure about a relationship between us. We can take things slow though, and see where they go, if that's okay with you?"

"Sure. I guess."

"I just don't know where my life is going at the moment, and I'm afraid to become too attached to someone. What if, after I graduate from my college courses, I get a job in Houston? I might have to move. I don't want to pressure someone I care about to move with me and give up everything they've ever known."

"I see."

She reached across the table and laid her hand on his. "Not that what happened last night wasn't great, because it was. Fantastic even, but I need to take this slow, Jonathan. Can you understand that?"

"I'm at a bit of a loss here, Mandy. You've been chasing me for years and now you want to slow down?"

"I'm afraid."

"Of what?"

"I'm not sure, but I think I'm a bit scared that this relationship won't live up to the fantasies and expectations of what I've dreamed about this whole time. Does that make sense?"

He shoved his fingers through his hair before settling his hat back on his head. He didn't know what to do with her confession. Wanting her wasn't a problem. He'd been doing that for a long time now, but what if it was like she said and didn't live up to the expectations they had placed on it? They were good together in bed. That much he knew from the night before. A sigh escaped his lips as he tipped his head back and stared at the wooden beams above him. When he gathered his thoughts a bit, he caught her gaze with his. "Okay. Let's take this slow. We'll date, spend time together, and do everything couples do, but we won't talk about the future or what that might hold. We'll see how things play out."

The smile spreading across her lips made his heart skip a beat. She really was the prettiest thing he'd seen in a long time and he couldn't wait to taste her again.

"Deal."

* * * *

Mandy scrubbed the pot beneath the water as her mind wandered to Jonathan. He seemed so sad earlier when she talked about slowing things down between them. Her stomach cramped at the thought of walking away from him. She sure didn't want to, but what if he didn't understand her secret? She wasn't sure she could tell him now or ever and with all the Young family having kids, she felt left out.

Peyton came in through the double doors into the kitchen. "Hey."

"Hi."

"You okay?"

"Yeah, why?"

"You were very quiet at lunch and dinner too. It's not like you."

"Sorry. I've got some stuff on my mind."

"Jonathan?" Peyton asked, stealing a cookie from the dish on the counter then popping it into her mouth.

"Yep." She continue to scrub the same dish until she realized she'd better pull her shit together or she would be there all night washing supper dishes. After she slipped the plate under the cool water to rinse it, she put it in the drying rack on the opposite countertop.

"What happened last night with your date?"

"Not much."

"I find that hard to believe. You had the look of a very satisfied woman this morning at breakfast. Did you have sex?"

"Yeah, and it was pretty awesome."

Peyton took another bite of her cookie as she scooted her butt up on the countertop. "So what's the problem?"

"I told him earlier that I wanted to slow things down."

"That doesn't sound like you after the way you've been trying to get his attention for so long."

"I know." She grabbed a pot from the counter and dunked it in the water. "What if he finds out my secret?"

"If you care about him, you'll have to tell him eventually, Mandy."

"I can't. He wants kids, lots of kids." She turned toward Peyton, her hands full of suds. "He wouldn't understand."

"Honey, it wasn't your fault. You were only fifteen."

"What if we fall in love? What if he wants to marry me? What then? How will I explain that I had a baby at fifteen, gave her up for adoption, and the pregnancy did so much damage to my insides that I can't have anymore? How the hell do I tell a man like him I can't have any more children?"

"There is always adoption."

"How ironic would that be? I gave up the only biological child I can ever have and then end up adopting someone else's child." Tears pricked her eyes as she fought not to cry. He wouldn't understand. His family wouldn't understand. Nina wanted lots of grandchildren. She talked so lovingly about the ones she had now that she would never accept Mandy into the fold if she knew she wouldn't be able to give her more.

Peyton hopped down and folded Mandy into an embrace. "Don't cry. You don't know how Jonathan would react to your news."

"Yes, I do. He already told me he wanted lots of kids like his parents."

"Don't judge him before he has a chance, Mandy. That's not fair to him."

"I should just cut this off right now. Walk away before I get any more attached or God forbid he falls in love with me."

"Mandy, listen to yourself. You're willing to walk away from one of the best things to ever happen to you because of some idea you have in your brain? Jonathan isn't that shallow. If he falls in love with you, then he'll be in love with you, not your ability to have children or not. Do you think Jason would walk away from me if for some reason I couldn't conceive?"

"Are you trying?"

"Maybe."

"You need a baby, Peyton."

"I haven't decided yet if I'm going to go along with the idea of having one right now. We're still newlyweds."

"Newlyweds, hell. You've been married for a few years now. It's time to start a family."

"I like having him all to myself, you know." She glanced away.

"What is it, Peyton?" Mandy asked, not liking the look in her friend's eyes. She took Peyton's hand in hers. "You can tell me."

"Jason wants a baby. I'm not sure if I do."

"You don't want children?"

Peyton shrugged as she dropped her gaze to the floor.

"Talk to me. We've been friends a long time. You know I won't say anything to anyone if you don't want me to."

Peyton walked to the opposite countertop and began to fiddle with the spices in the rack. Mandy let her keep her silence for now. She didn't want to push Peyton, but she had a feeling her friend needed to talk.

"I love Jason with all my heart."

"But?"

"I don't know if I want children."

"None at all?"

"No."

"Have you talked to him?"

"Yeah." She shrugged. "Well sort of."

"What do you mean?"

"We've talked. He wants kids."

"You two didn't discuss this before you got married?"

"We did or I thought we did, but I guess not." She cringed. "After everything with my ex and what happened, I knew I loved Jason and would do anything for him. Now that we've been together for a few years, I'm thinking there are some differences in our relationship we should have explored before we said I do."

Mandy drew Peyton into a big hug. "Oh Peyton. You need to have a heart-to-heart talk with your husband."

"I know, but I'm scared I'll lose him if I tell him I don't want kids."

"Are you sure you don't want any at all or just not right now?"

"I don't want any, Mandy."

"Oh honey. I'm sorry." She hugged Peyton to her, realizing her problem was probably a lot less of an issue than Peyton's. With the Young brothers, you just didn't tell one of them you didn't want to have children. "Things will work out. You'll see."

"I hope so. I can't lose him. My life would be over if I did."

"Aren't we a pair?"

"Right?" Peyton let out a dry laugh and stepped back. "You want kids and can't have anymore, and I don't want any and probably wouldn't have any trouble having one."

"It'll be okay. We'll get through this."

"I know. Thanks for listening. This isn't why I came in here. I wanted to help you and in the meantime you helped me."

"That's what I'm here for, sister dear."

"You are like a sister to me too. I don't know what I would do without you."

"You'd be miserable." Mandy laughed as she walked back to the sink. "Now let me get my work done so I can go home, get a pint of ice cream, and sit in front of the television to watch some lame program on it."

"Okay. See you tomorrow?"

"Yep. I'll be here."

"Night, Mandy."

"Night, Peyton." Mandy watched as Peyton went through the double doors out into the main dining area. The door swung shut behind her, leaving Mandy alone in the kitchen with her thoughts.

The night before flashed back to her in sharp clarity. Making love with Jonathan had been like a dream come true, one she'd fantasized about for the last few years, and it had been even better in person than in her dreams.

They had come to an agreement to take things slow earlier. It felt weird to think that after all she'd been through to get his attention. Why was she so terrified to think of them having a future together? Her past would haunt her for the rest of her life, but she couldn't let that stop her from finding love with the man of her dreams, right? Maybe she should talk to Nina and see what her take is on a daughter who couldn't have any children. Of course, it wouldn't matter what Nina wanted if Jonathan was determined to have a bunch of kids.

Their relationship, or whatever you wanted to call it, was too new to worry about these things. If things were meant to be between her and Jonathan, then they would work out just fine and he wouldn't leave her in the dust when he found out she couldn't give him biological children.

She exhaled sharply as determination stiffened her spine.

Enough.

Things would work out as they were meant to. She had to believe that and go forward with everything, otherwise she would probably spend the rest of her life alone. That wasn't a very good option in her opinion.

She finished the dishes, putting everything in its place for the morning. After a quick sweep of the room to make sure she hadn't forgotten anything, she grabbed her purse from the desk in the corner, flipped off the light switch plunging everything into darkness, and headed toward the main lodge.

A few guests were sitting chatting quietly on the leather sofas near the dark fireplace.

"Can I get you anything else before I leave?"

The two turned to the sound of her voice, smiling as they replied, "No, thank you. You all have been very gracious with your time and energy. We'll be fine tonight." The woman raised her wine glass, showing off the deep burgundy of the liquid. "We are going to finish this glass of wine and head off to bed. We have a ride scheduled for early in the morning, so we need to be up with the sun. We are planning to watch the sunrise over the hills."

"Sounds beautiful. The sunrises are gorgeous here this time of year." Mandy slung her purse over her shoulder and headed for the door. "Enjoy your evening, and I will see you at breakfast."

"Thank you. See you then."

Mandy walked through the heavy wood door, letting it bang softly behind her as she walked through the pitch-blackness toward where she'd left her car. Small external lights lit the walkway, but other than that, there was nothing to mar the beauty of the night. Stars twinkled above her as she glanced up. The moon reflected brightly to her right, lighting her walk.

When she reached her car, she heard the faint giggles of children on the breeze. A smile lifted the corners of her mouth. The children in the yard always made her feel better.

One day she hoped to find her biological daughter again and let her know it wasn't that she didn't love her and want her when she was born, it was the fact that she couldn't take care of a baby at fifteen. Her parents had forced her to give the child up for adoption at birth. They were pretty strict Christians and didn't believe in abortion. Not that she would have chosen to take care of her situation like that anyway, but when the day had come for her to give birth, they never even let her hold her daughter, just took her away, gave her to her new parents, and never spoke of it again.

Someday, baby girl, I will find you.

Chapter Seven

Jonathan let out a sharp exhale as he stared at the apartment complex where Mandy lived. The building itself wasn't much to look at, two stories with stairs that ran up the middle and then split off to each apartment. The whole thing was a dull brown color without very much in the way of shrubbery. If it was his, he would have flowering bushes, green shrubs, and perennial flowering plants all over. Something to brighten up the place would have been nice. It wasn't very homey.

He worried his lips with his teeth, unsure of himself now. He contemplated going home, but that would make him an asshole. He might be shy and introverted, but those traits didn't make him an asshole unless he pulled something stupid. After a moment, he popped the door of his truck open so he could walk up to her place. When he'd asked Mandy this morning if she wanted to go out to dinner and a movie tonight, she'd said yes. She even smiled, which was good. He'd been afraid he'd totally fucked everything up with his behavior the other night. When she'd said she wanted to slow things down, his stomach had knotted something fierce.

A light shown in her apartment, indicating that she was indeed home. Good. Well, sort of good. That meant she really did want to go with him somewhere, at least that's what he hoped it meant.

He stopped in front of her door with his hand raised to knock, hesitating a moment as he listened to the sounds coming from behind the door. She had some country music turned up pretty loud, and he had to smile when he recognized Jackson's wife Samantha's voice as Mandy sang along. Mandy couldn't sing very well. He gave her points for trying, though. He couldn't really say anything since he couldn't sing worth beans either. Now, give him a good two-stepping song and he'd be all over that shit.

The plan for tonight would include dancing after they had dinner. He would love to hold her in his arms as they slow danced to a good tune.

A quick rap on the door with his knuckles brought the music back down to a low hum. She opened the door decked out in a really pretty pink dress with something sparkly on the material. Her shoulders wear bare as the material of the dress clung to her breasts in some sort of silky wrap around her body. The hem reached mid-thigh as his gaze wandered down her body. *Holy shit, that's sexy.* The heels she had on her feet were open-toed and she'd painted her toenails bright pink to match her dress.

"You like?"

"Very much so. You look gorgeous."

"Thank you, kind sir." She stepped closer bringing their bodies to where they almost touched as she went up on her toes and left a brief kiss on his lips. "I'm glad you approve."

Her scent sent him reeling straight into a raging hard-on. His hands automatically reached for her shoulders to bring her in closer, but she stepped back out of his reach with a saucy little smile on her lips, one that made him want to toss her over his shoulder and head straight into her bedroom.

"Uh-uh. We have reservations somewhere, right?"

"Yeah."

"Let me grab my wrap then and we'll go."

"Tease."

"You bet, cowboy."

Her curls bounced on her shoulders as she walked into the other room. He enjoyed the view of her going almost as much as the one of her coming back toward him. "Ready?"

He cleared his throat as a small squeak came out from between his lips. "Yeah. Let's go before I do something I might regret later."

"No regrets, Jonathan."

"You say that now, but if I slammed the door and took you right there on your table, you'd probably regret it."

"Oh, hell no, I wouldn't, but we do already have plans." She touched his lips with her fingertip. "Keep that in mind for later." She turned the lock on the doorknob and walked out in front of him. "Pull that shut, would you, please?"

"Sure."

Her cute little butt swished back and forth in her tight dress, giving him a nice view as they walked down the walkway toward his truck. He reached for the door latch to open it for her, and then helped her up into the cab with a hand on her butt.

She turned and gave him a raised eyebrow look.

"What?"

"Thanks for the boost up."

"You're welcome." He grinned thinking he liked how her soft butt cheek fit nicely in his palm. He had to adjust his cock behind his fly as he walked around the front of the truck to get in on the driver's side. It was going to be one uncomfortable night.

As they pulled out of the parking lot, he wondered about her. She apparently liked country music, which was a plus since it was his favorite too. Mexican food seemed to be something she enjoyed. What about steak, seafood, or Italian? Did she ride horses? Did she want kids? Was she a bed hog with the covers at night?

"What are you thinking about?" she asked as she turned toward him on the seat.

When he glanced her way, he could see her eyes sparkling in the dim light inside the cab. The color of her eyes fascinated him. He wasn't quite sure if they were blue or gray. They seemed to change with her moods, he noticed. "You. Why?"

"Me?"

"Yup."

"What about me?"

"I'm realizing I don't know that much about you even though you've been on the ranch for a couple of years. I know you are close to Peyton."

"Yeah. She and I are best friends, but I like all the girls on the ranch. I've become friends with all your brother's wives since they have hooked up with a Young brother."

"You seem to be protective of them, I noticed. At the bar the other night, you were ready to take on anyone and everyone who said anything bad about them."

"I would. They are like sisters to me."

"A little spitfire, I see."

She shrugged one shoulder as she glanced back out the front windshield. "Those girls have my back and I have theirs. I don't like people who talk with marbles in their mouths."

He laughed out loud. "I've never heard that saying before."

"No?" She smiled. "My dad used to say it all the time about people who talk about others when they don't know what they are talking about. You know how it sounds all garbled and stuff."

"Yeah, I get the picture."

"Don't your mom and dad have weird sayings like that?"

"I suppose. I never thought about it."

"I love your mom and dad. They are great people. They've raised some awesome kids."

"I'll pass it along."

She smacked him on the arm. "I'm not being facetious. I'm being truthful. All of you boys are thoughtful with others, kind, real gentlemen, and possibly the perfect cowboy."

"I don't believe that."

"I do. I've seen how your brothers are with their women. They love them without boundaries. They accept the little insecurities all women have and make them seem like the best thing in the world. You all are some of the best guys in the area, which is why so many women are after the two remaining Young brothers in the pool."

"I don't have women chasing me."

"Yes, you do. Haven't you seen the looks you get when you're at the diner or when you're interacting with guests? Those women would sell their soul to be with a real gentleman cowboy."

"Would you?" A slight smile played on her lips when he turned to glance her way.

"Yes, sir, I certainly would."

He shook his head as he grinned a little. He knew she was bold and outspoken most of the time. It was one of the things he liked about her. Actually, there were several things he liked about her, come to think of it. "I'll keep that in mind."

"I hope you do."

They pulled up to the restaurant on the outskirts of San Antonio. McGregor's Inn was known for their steaks. Juicy, thick, and cooked exactly how you wanted it had made their reputation for the best steakhouse in the state of Texas, which was an awesome feat in itself in the state where beef was prime. The inn looked like an old western bunkhouse. Two stories with huge barn doors that graced the front, opened to the wide dining area. There were stairs that led up to a large seating area at the top of the building where you could look down on the diners seated in the bottom. They prepared the steaks on an open grilling stand with mesquite wood, giving it a smoky flavor that would make your mouth water. They served baked potatoes with it, corn on the cob, salad, and hot rolls. Old tack, pictures, plows, and a huge fireplace decorated the area giving it that old farmhouse feel.

"Wow."

"You've never been here?"

"Nope. I love it. It's gorgeous in here," she said as they approached the hostess.

"Can I help you?"

"Yes, ma'am. We have reservations under the name Jonathan Young."

"Yes, sir. Your table will be ready in a moment. If you would like to take a seat, I'll tell the server you're here."

"Thank you." He placed his hand at the small of Mandy's back, guiding her to the seat near the door. The evening had turned brisk with a slight chill to the air. "Are you cold?"

"No. I'm good with my wrap."

"Okay." He'd done his best to make this a special night for them. It was the start of something wonderful, he hoped, so he'd dressed in his finest attire with his best black jeans, a sport coat, white long sleeved shirt open at the neck, and his finest black Stetson on his head.

Her gaze slipped over him from the top of his cowboy hat to the boots on his feet. "Did I tell you how nice you looked?"

"No."

"Well, you do. I love the dressed up cowboy look."

He studied her, his gaze sliding over her form. "I like your dress too. It's really nice on you."

"Thank you." She tilted her head to the side for a moment as she pursed her lips. "I think we look mighty good together."

"I do too."

"Mr. Young?"

Jonathan climbed to his feet. "Yes?"

"Right this way, sir. Your table is ready."

"Thank you." He splayed his hand at the small of her back again, to guide her along. He liked touching her way too much, but he couldn't help himself. Her lithe body fit well with his—in spite of her being a tiny little thing even in heels—in comparison to his six-foot-six frame.

He held out her chair as she whispered a soft thank you. The gesture wasn't something he did with any thought, it was the way he was raised. You take care of your woman by holding the door, holding her chair, walking on the busy side of the street to keep her safe, and you do everything you can to make her happy. Without much thought, he leaned down and kissed her shoulder. Her skin beneath his lips was soft and smelled like flowers. He liked her scent a whole lot.

Once he took his seat across from her, he found the view of her most enjoyable. Her cheeks were rosy and her eyes sparkled in the small flickering lamplight bouncing behind the globe on the table. Her lips looked kissable as he thought about how they felt under his when they'd made love the other night. Thinking about it as fucking, wasn't for him.

The waitress handed them their menus and as she opened hers to peruse the selections, he watched her over the top of his own. Having been to this particular restaurant many times, he already knew what he wanted, but it gave him a chance to study her. She didn't wear a lot of makeup, just a hint of color on her eyelids with a little mascara on her lashes, and a little swipe of tint to her lips. Her hair hung in long curls around her shoulders. The pink stripe from the top of her head to the ends of hair fascinated him. He often wondered why the bit of color.

She glanced over her menu and caught him staring. "What?"

"Nothing, why?"

"You're staring at me."

"I'm admiring the view."

Red crept up her neck, before fading across her face in a pretty pink color. She pressed a hand to her cheek. "You're embarrassing me."

"Why? You're a beautiful woman."

"No I'm not. I'm plain. There isn't anything special about me."

"Sure there is. You're a good friend, you are nice to people who come to the ranch as guests, and you make a special place for kids when they come. I've seen you around them."

She dropped her gaze to the tabletop as she set aside her menu. "I want to make them feel welcome, that's all."

"You do more than that. You are always playing with them, reading to them, and showing them a good time, all above and beyond your duties in the kitchen."

Her pretty bare shoulders lifted in a shrug. "It's nothing."

"Yes it is. You would be a great mom." She looked up at him and her face paled. "Did I say something wrong?"

"N-no."

"You look like you are about to be sick. Are you okay?"

Her throat visibly moved as she swallowed hard. "Yes. I'm fine."

"Did I say something wrong?"

"No. It's okay. I'm just a little warm."

"Do you need to go outside and get some air?"

She set aside her napkin and rose to her feet. "I'm going to run to the ladies room. I'll be right back."

She disappeared so fast, Jonathan thought she'd break a leg on those heels as she dashed through the throng of diners, heading for the bathroom.

What the hell did I say?

The waitress returned to get their drink orders, but he didn't know what Mandy might want. He'd order a bottle of wine, but he wasn't even sure she liked wine. "I'll wait until my date gets back."

"Very good, sir."

He tapped his fingers on the tabletop as he waited trying to figure out what he said that sent her to the bathroom in such a rush. When he looked around him, he noticed several other diners watching him as they sipped their wine, ate their food, or peeked over their menus. He considered going to the women's restroom to make sure she was okay, after she hadn't returned in several minutes. *She seemed rather pale. Maybe she is sick to her stomach or something.*

A moment later, he saw her come around the corner from where the restrooms were. "Are you all right?" he asked as he got up to pull out her chair.

"Yes. Sorry I took off like that."

"It's okay. I was worried about you though."

"Don't be. I'm fine. I, um, just got a little lightheaded is all."

"You aren't coming down with something are you?"

"I don't think so."

"You still look a little pale. Are you sure you don't want to go home?"

"No!" She sobered as she looked around and lowered her voice. "No. I don't want to ruin our evening. It's okay. I'm fine now."

He blew out a breath as the waitress approached their table. "Would you like some wine, Mandy? I would have ordered some, but I didn't know if you drank wine."

"Uh, sure, that's fine. Something red and sweet would be good."

He ordered a Merlot for them before he glanced her way again. "Are you sure you're all right?"

"I'm fine, Jonathan." She put her napkin in her lap. "Can we talk about something else?"

"Okay, like what?"

"What are your plans for the website for the ranch? I think you mentioned redoing the layout recently."

He took a minute to look at her closely before he decided to let the incident lie and began to explain what his plans were for the ranch. She would understand everything he said since her degree would be in graphic design, website management, and layout.

When the waitress returned a few moments later with their wine, she poured a small amount in his glass for him to taste and approve before giving Mandy hers. Mandy took a healthy gulp of the sweet liquid before setting her glass back down. For some reason, he got the impression the incident from earlier had her more rattled than she let on. Something bothered her so much, she'd got deathly pale and bolted for the bathroom, and by God he was determined to find out what it was so he could fix it for her if necessary.

* * * *

Mandy's stomach hurt from being in knots throughout dinner. Jonathan made a great dinner partner, but his personal questions made her uncomfortable. She shouldn't be though. He only wanted to get to know her, right?

After they'd finished their food, they had a dessert they shared over the candlelit table. He'd even fed her small bites of the chocolate cake from his spoon. Good grief, he was something special, and she really needed to let herself be with him and hope for the best.

As they drove down the interstate back toward Bandera, she watched him under the fan of her lashes. His hands were large with long tapered fingers, his arms were fit, and his chest was broad and well-muscled. His hair brushed against his collar with some of the curl showing beneath his cowboy hat. She liked it like that, but he probably thought he needed a haircut. His nose was straight and regal above his full lips. She knew he had a small dimple in his cheek when he smiled, which he did often when he was at home. She should know since she'd been watching him for so long.

When they had made love, he'd been a considerate lover, making sure her pleasure came before his own. Not many men did that these days.

He said he was shy, but she didn't see that in him even though he tended to be the quiet Young brother.

The cowboy thing was part of them like breathing. He couldn't get away from his upbringing no matter what he tried to do being the office hermit. He still rode horses, he still branded cattle when branding season came around, and he still liked the ranch life as a whole from what she could tell.

"Jonathan?"

"Yes?"

"I'm sorry for taking off earlier like that."

"It's okay. You obviously weren't feeling well or something."

"It wasn't that. I needed to take a minute is all."

"Was it something I said?"

"No." She looked out the windshield as she gathered her thoughts. How did you tell someone you were attracted to, that you were raped as a fifteen-year-old by someone close to you? She couldn't right now, maybe not ever.

Her life had taken a bad turn back then and because of her upbringing, her parents wouldn't let her abort the child. She was glad she hadn't now because the family that had adopted her daughter had seemed very loving, and she figured they had given her little girl a good home. Someday, she hoped to be able to tell her daughter the real reason she hadn't kept her and raised her, but how do you explain to someone that she'd been conceived during a terrible act such as rape?

Mandy shivered as she rubbed her arms in an attempt to warm her soul. Even though it had been over ten years ago, she still vividly remembered the night it had happened. Her stepfather's brother had come to visit one Christmas. He hadn't visited often, but when he had before, he'd been her favorite uncle. He would spend time with her, listen to her talk about problems she was having as a teenager, and be the best friend she'd wished she had.

Christmas night, they had opened gifts. Hers from him had been a gorgeous butterfly necklace in solid silver with pretty multi-colored wings. When he'd placed it around her neck, she'd beamed. She loved it and loved him. "Thank you, Uncle Matt. It's perfect. I will wear it always."

"Fantastic. I'm glad you like it. Now give me a hug." He'd hugged her tight, pulling her onto his lap.

She hadn't thought anything about it at the time when he'd rubbed her back before bringing his hands around to her budding breasts, cupping them, and then pushing her back. "Shouldn't you be getting ready for bed? Santa will be coming soon."

"Oh come on, Uncle Matt. I don't believe in Santa."

He scolded her. "You should. He is going to be bringing you a wonderful present this year."

"Really?"

"Yes."

"All right then." She glanced at the clock on the wall, realizing it was getting late. "I'm going up to my room then. I will see you all in the morning."

"Good night," her parents had chimed in together.

"Sleep well, sweetie," Uncle Matt had said, giving her a wink before he took another sip of his drink.

She hadn't realized it at the time, but he'd been several sheets to the wind by the time she'd gone to bed.

Two hours later, she'd awoken to his hands on her hair. "Uncle Matt?" She rubbed her eyes.

"Sshh, sweetie. I just need to touch you."

"O-okay."

His hands had gone farther, brushing down her shoulders and across her breasts. "You are so pretty, filling out so nicely all over. Your breasts are very nice and your hips are perfect."

His hands had crept lower. "Please don't."

"It's okay, sweetheart. I won't hurt you," he said as he pulled her underwear down off her hips and legs.

But he had. He'd forced himself on her, telling her if she told anyone, they wouldn't believe her. She was nothing but a teenage girl and he was a man. Men could do what they wanted. Men were perfect.

She told her parents two weeks later when her period hadn't come.

They didn't believe her. They had assumed she'd been sleeping with someone in school and forced her to give the baby up.

It had been the worst ten months of her life. She'd been an outcast at school being a teenage mother, her grades had suffered, and her life had never been the same.

A tear slipped down her cheek, but she brushed it away before the man next to her could see.

She would never be taken advantage of again, not now, not ever.

Chapter Eight

Jonathan watched Mandy as she opened the door to her apartment. She'd been really quiet on the ride home, watching out the window without saying much of anything. Something was bothering her, and he wished she'd talk to him so he could help her.

She laid her wrap on the arm of the couch and turned to face him. Her eyes were sad.

"Tell me what's bothering you, Mandy. I want to help."

She smiled a pitiful smile as she touched his face. "I wish you could help me, Jonathan. No one can."

He pulled her into a tight hug, kissing her hair before resting his chin on her head.

She clung tightly to him, like she never wanted him to leave. "Make love to me."

"Are you sure you want that?"

"Yeah. I need you to help me erase some bad memories."

He pulled back to look into her eyes. The sadness in the depths broke his heart. If she wanted him to make love to her, then he would. He'd pour everything he had into making her smile again.

With both hands buried in her hair, he tipped her head to the side and brought his mouth down to hers. The sounds she made as he asked for permission to slip his tongue inside made him as hard as a damn rock. The soft whimpers and cute little sighs were almost too much for his libido to handle.

Her lips were soft enough to drown in as he pushed his tongue into her mouth to duel with hers. He loved kissing her. The feeling was something he hadn't been able to name, but he'd do his best to make sure she wasn't sorry she gave him her body.

Her hands fisted in his shirt, pulling him close enough that her breasts were crushed against him. The tips of her nipples poked him deliciously as she rubbed them all over his chest.

"Jonathan, please."

"Tell me what you want, Mandy."

"Love me."

He lifted her high into his arms as he headed down the hall to her bedroom. If she needed him to erase something from her mind, he'd do his best.

When he laid her on the bed, she sat up on her elbows to watch him undress. His jacket and shirt were disposed of before he quickly toed off his boots as her gaze moved over him. An appreciative smile curved her lips when he pushed his jeans down off his hips and over his legs.

"You are so nice to look at."

"Are you going to get undressed?"

"In a minute. I'm enjoying the scenery that is you, cowboy."

He moved to her side to take her lips. She wrapped her arms around his neck and pressed herself against him as he laid her back on the bed. He'd get to her clothes in a minute, right now he needed to taste her. He took her mouth in a soul-stopping kiss meant to take everything out of her mind but him. When he moved from her mouth to her cheek, and then her neck, she sighed as he nibbled at the flesh there. The shell of her ear would make a tasty morsel too, he decided.

Her legs started to move as she pressed her hips against his groin and shifted back and forth.

His cock ached with the need to be inside her. He wouldn't push the issue yet. There were things he wanted to do to her.

He lifted his mouth from her flesh. "Do you have any scarves?"

Her eyes were wide as she answered, "Yeah, in the drawer over there. Why?"

"Do you have anything wrong with your shoulders or arms?"

"No."

"Good." He got up and moved to her dresser to find what he searched for. When he returned to her side with several silky pieces of material in his hands, her eyes were wide with wonder.

"What are you going to do with those?"

"You'll see." His gaze moved over her body. "Sit up a minute." She followed instruction, and he reached for the zipper at the back of her dress. The bodice of her pink dress dipped forward revealing her perky, coral nipples. "Gorgeous." He ran his tongue along the edge of where her dress gapped. Her wispy sighs were his undoing.

He slipped a scarf over her wrist before tying it to the rungs of her headboard. After he secured the other, leaving her open to his mouth, he pulled the dress down over her hips, and then off her feet. "Oh hell." She'd gone commando. No underwear to be found and the lacy garter thing sent his thoughts spiraling out of control. "Those sexy heels and stockings are going to stay." He ran a finger around the edge of where they encircled her thigh and attached to the garter belt around her waist.

She shivered as she closed her eyes and arched her back.

A woman under his hands this responsive was a dream come true. He knew his tastes were a little out there, so finding this one was a treasure he would forever cherish.

He couldn't wait to get his cock buried in her sweet heat. For now, he would bring her up until she was ready to blow before he brought her back down.

The tips of her sexy breasts pulled into tight little nubs had his mouth watering. He couldn't help himself when he encircled one with the tip of his tongue.

She whimpered when he flicked it.

"I will leave your ankles unbound if you open for me and don't move."

Her breathes came out in small gasps as she spread her thighs. Her pussy glistened with juices. He wanted nothing more than to lick her clean and keep licking until she came in his mouth.

When he made room for his shoulders between her thighs, she sighed as she waited for him to do something. He smiled to himself knowing the anticipation was half the fun.

He blew a warm breath across her clit.

Her hips came up off the bed.

"Don't move." He'd leave the repercussions for her movement to her imagination.

Goose bumps broke out on her legs.

He licked the inside of her right thigh as he worked his way closer and closer to her pussy. She shivered when he ran his tongue up the crease between her thigh and her pussy lips.

One small swipe over her clit had more cream spilling from her.

"Such a sweet pussy."

When he glanced up from his position between her legs, he could see her straining against the bindings at her wrists as her chest rose and fell in a rapid pattern of need. Her heartbeat fluttered at her throat. Her mouth was open in a silent plea or a sigh, he wasn't sure which, but he could tell she was excited enough it wouldn't take much to throw her over the threshold into a mind-numbing orgasm.

He centered himself over her clit again, taking a few swipes of her juice on his tongue before he went to work bringing her to that orgasm she clung to by a thread.

She tossed her head back and forth on the pillow while she moaned louder with each pass of his tongue. "God, Jonathan, please, I need to come so badly."

A moment later, he pressed two fingers into her grasping cunt before he pushed his tongue against her clit and flicked it quickly. The second he pulled her clit into his mouth and bit down, she exploded into a screaming orgasm, his name a whisper on the wind.

Sweat clung to her body as he moved up over her abdomen, skimming his tongue along her flesh. She tasted sweet and salty at the same time. Her breasts quivered when he reached them, her nipples still pulled into hard points. A sigh escaped her lips when he brushed his tongue against the tip of one.

He moved between her parted thighs and pushed his cock into her heat. The feeling was something he'd never been able to put words to. All warm, wet, and silky and...*fuck*. He'd forgotten the condom.

Gritting his teeth, he pulled out, and rolled to his side. His cock and balls ached to be back inside her, but he had to protect them both. Children were something for the future, not right now.

"Jonathan?"

"Just a second. I have to get a condom before we continue this." The sensations running through his body had him strung tighter than a banjo string. If he didn't lose it the moment he got back inside her, it would be a miracle.

"Untie me."

He reached up and grabbed the end of the scarves to release her. She rolled to her other side, grabbed something out of the nightstand drawer, and then rolled back toward him. With a sexy little grin on her lips, she opened the package with her teeth before she slipped in over the head of his cock and then down the shaft.

"As hot as that was, I want to ride you, cowboy." In the next second, she was straddling his hips and taking his cock inside her in one push of her pussy. "Now that's perfect."

"Fuck yeah." White-hot need speared through him like a lightning bolt hitting the ground. His balls drew up against his groin, aching with pleasure almost to the point of pain.

"Dirty talker. I love it."

She lifted her hips before pushing them back down on his cock. Her pussy gripped him in a tight fist of warmth as she began to move. Her hands were braced on his chest while his gripped her hips, helping her move in just the right rhythm. His head felt like it was about to blow off when she increase her movements, bringing him to the edge of orgasm. He gritted his teeth trying to keep it from happening so soon. He wanted her to come for him too.

When she tipped her pelvis forward, dragging her clit over his pelvis, he knew she was close. The small whimpers and increasing sighs told him as much.

"Come for me, darlin'."

"Oh God."

The excited sigh from her lips as he felt the warm liquid dribble from her pussy brought on his own orgasm as he shouted his pleasure to the ceiling.

She draped herself over his chest, tucking her head beneath his chin as she wrapped herself around him.

"Mmm. That was perfect."

"I agree," he said, running his hands down her back. He loved the feeling of her skin beneath his hands. The softness reminded him that she was all woman and one he could totally see himself with for the long haul. Did that mean he wanted something more permanent with her? He wasn't so sure, but he definitely wanted to see how far this thing would go, if she would be willing.

They lay like that for several minutes while he listened to her soft breathing and felt her heart slow in the aftermath of their explosive lovemaking.

"Will you stay?" she asked quietly.

"If you want me to."

"I would love to wake up with you next to me. I'll make breakfast."

"Now, how could I possibly refuse that offer?"

She giggled a little as she moved to the side of his body and rolled off the bed. After she shoved her hair out of her face, she slipped off her heels so she was walking around in her sexy stockings. The sight of her naked ass did wonderful things to him.

He propped himself up on his elbow as he watched her putter around her room, grabbing his clothes and laying them across the chair in the corner before she grabbed his dress shirt and put it on.

"How come you get clothes and I'm laying here buck naked?"

"Because I like you buck naked."

"Listen, baby girl. We need to have a discussion on who is in charge here."

"Oh?"

"Yes, ma'am."

When she turned to look at him, her eyes sparkled with a bit of a challenge. *So that's how it's gonna be, huh?* He crooked his finger in her direction.

She only raised an eyebrow as she placed her hands on her hips.

A brat. He loved a dare.

Before she could react, he vaulted off the bed, catching her around the waist.

She screamed as he tossed her over his shoulder.

A tiny fist hit him mid-back.

In retaliation, he brought his hand down on her ass cheek, swift and hard.

"Ouch! You didn't just spank me?"

"That was a warning."

"Or what?"

He took a seat on the bed and brought her over his knees with a hand on her back, her head down toward the floor and her ass high in the air. He yanked the shirt up, baring her ass before one hand came down swiftly on her right butt cheek, leaving a nice red handprint.

"Son of a bitch!"

"I warned you."

"What the hell?"

His hand came down again in three rapid swats to her left butt cheek.

She wiggled to get free, but he put a hand on the spot he knew stung from his spanking.

"Lie still and take your punishment for being a brat."

After a momentary hiss, she quit moving as he delivered another six quick slaps to her behind, alternating between the right and the left. When he was finished, he pulled her back up, bringing her up to his lap.

Her makeup had run where she'd silently wept from the stinging spanking, so he wiped it from her cheeks. Somehow, he'd been given the impression she probably needed the release tears would bring. Maybe it was the sadness in her eyes that had drawn him to spank her or the challenge in her stance, but whatever it was, he'd been pulled into spanking her for her own good.

"Why did you spank me?"

"I won't tolerate disrespect."

"I'm sorry," she whispered, even though her eyes were clearer and brighter now.

If she reacted this way to punishment, she might fit very nicely into his life. "You're forgiven. It's over now. We won't talk about it again."

"Jonathan?"

"Yes?"

"I like when you tied me up."

"I liked it too."

"Can we do that again?"

He smiled. Things were looking up if she was open to experimenting with his little fetishes. He could really get into doing more with her in the future.

"Yes, darlin', we can."

* * * *

The next day as Mandy worked on preparing the food for lunch at the ranch, she winced as her butt stung from the spanking she'd received from Jonathan the night before. It was strange to think about the weight that had been lifted from her shoulders after she'd cried. She'd felt lighter and freer than she had in years.

After she'd fixed him breakfast, he'd kissed her softly, grabbed his hat, and left for home. Something had changed with their relationship in those moments they'd bonded over her stinging ass cheeks. He'd become the man she needed in her life, the one who would understand her, forgive her, and would hopefully love her until they were both old and gray.

God, she sounded like such a sap, but her happy heart wouldn't be quiet today.

Peyton came through the double doors of the kitchen and grabbed a lemon bar from the cooling rack. "You look gorgeous today. What did you do different?"

"Nothing. Why?"

"Your cheeks are a pretty pink and your eyes are sparkling." Peyton tipped her head to the side and grinned. "You look like a girl in love."

Mandy put her hand over Peyton's mouth and shushed her. "Be quiet. Don't be saying that too loudly. Nina will be planning a wedding before the weekend if she hears you."

Peyton moved her hand and whispered, "You are in love. I knew it!" She took another bite of her lemon bar. "Nice night with Jonathan?"

A heated blush crept up her face as she went back to slicing tomato. "Yeah. It was pretty special."

"I can tell. I think I heard him sneaking in this morning."

She glanced over her shoulder at Peyton and said, "Keep it close to your chest, please. I don't need gossip running rampant through the guest ranch."

"Sure, honey. I won't say a word."

The gleam in Peyton's eyes didn't bode well for Mandy, she knew. Her friend had a tendency of sticking her nose in where it didn't belong sometimes. "Are we having a girl's night out again soon?"

"I don't know. Have you talked to the others?"

"No, but I think we should. At least once a month is a good idea to get everyone away from the house and their kids."

"I'm sure the others would enjoy it. They had fun the last time."

"Oh, Candace told me she was putting together a bachelor auction for the children's hospital she helps raise money for. You know the one that Samantha did the benefit concert for?"

"Yeah. That sounds like fun."

"I thought so too, although I wouldn't be able to buy anyone. We could still get really drunk and set you up with some hunky cowboy. Jonathan wouldn't have to know."

"I couldn't do that to him."

"Maybe Candace can get him to go up there."

"Jonathan? Yeah, right. He's way too shy."

"I bet he would do it for her. They are like this." She crossed her fingers and held them up.

"I know."

"Does that bother you?"

"A little, but I know they are just friends. Candace is his sister-in-law. He would never do anything to hurt Joshua."

"Besides, he's all tied up in you."

Tied up. Now there's a thought. I wonder if he would let me tie him to the bed like he did me? "I should talk to Candace about this auction. If Jonathan got up there, I could bid on him and have him at my mercy for however long I want."

"Now you're talkin'!"

Mandy grinned, thinking of the possibilities. They were endless.

She arranged the tomatoes on a plate to put in the service area so those who wanted them could take them or not before she got the salad mix out and put some in the large bowl. Tongs went in next for serving along with bottles of dressing and thick slices of French bread. For lunch today, lasagna.

Soon, it was time to put lunch out for the guests. Mandy and the other kitchen workers got the food out on the hot table as Peyton went to ring the bell, letting the guests know it was time to eat.

There were a few families staying on the ranch right now with several small children. The weather was still warm for October in Texas, which meant most of them spent the day in the pool area, riding, hiking, or hanging out with the animals.

Mandy smiled as she watched everyone file in for lunch. The family always sat at two large tables at the front of the room and the guests had several picnic type tables to choose from. The family always waited until the guests were served before they got their own plates, which always made Mandy proud to know them. The guests came first in everything at Thunder Ridge.

She turned to see Jonathan come around the corner of the stairs. His office sat back behind them in the corner near where his parents had their private quarters. She'd been in his office a time or two and knew he kept it quite tidy. Everything in its place. His desk was a large oak monstrosity that took up most of the space. It suited him though since he was such a big guy.

His gaze fixed on her the moment he realized she was there. The stare burned with something she wasn't sure she wanted to put a name to. His brown eyes took in everything about her from the top of her head down, stopping to focus on her breasts for a moment before a crooked little grin creased his face, showing the dimple in his cheek.

Mandy had to shift her stance in a vain attempt to relieve the pressure that look caused between her thighs. The man could send her into a combustible state with nothing more than a glance. Damn him.

Jonathan took a seat at the table as they waited for the guests to be served, but he never once stopped his ogling of her. The heat from his scrutiny seared her skin, burning her clear through. She blew her hair off her forehead in an attempt to cool herself off.

His smile widened.

He knew what he did to her, the rat bastard.

She cleared her throat as she pulled her attention back to the guest in front of her ready to serve up some lasagna, garlic bread, and green beans. "There is salad to your left, sir."

"Thank you."

"You're welcome."

The man's attention focused on her breasts where they pressed against her tank top. "Is there something else I can help you with?"

"That depends."

"On?"

"What time do you get off work?"

"Seven."

"Would you like to have a drink with me?"

She glanced at the growing line behind him before focusing back on his leering face. Something about him reminded her of the man who raped her. She shuddered before she pulled back her shoulders and said, "No, sir."

The man frowned as his disgusting look ricocheted back to her face. "Aren't you supposed to make the guests happy?"

"What I do on my own time is my own business."

"Problem?" Jonathan appeared at her elbow.

"Yeah. I thought the employees were supposed to take care of the guests."

"They are, sir."

"Well then tell blondie here she needs to go out with me tonight."

"No, sir. I will not."

"What?"

"Mandy is an employee here, yes, but she's also her own person. If she doesn't want to go out with you, she is more than capable of making that decision herself. We do not force our employees to do anything."

"That's fucking bullshit!"

"What's your name, sir?"

"Leon Ornado."

"Mr. Ornado. Your bill will be credited for the days remaining on your stay. You will leave the ranch now. Pack your belongings and be gone within the hour."

"I'm not leaving."

"Yes you are."

"Who the hell are you to tell me to leave?"

In the next moment the entire clan of Young men stood around him. "I am one of the owners of this piece of property, and my family will back my decision to insist that you leave…now."

"Fuck you! Fuck you all!" The man threw down his plate on the serving bar, turned on his heels, and disappeared out the main lodge doors.

"I'll make sure he's gone," Jeff said, as he nodded to his family before following the man outside.

Mandy's whole body quivered with the adrenaline pumping through her. The family stood beside her as Jonathan took her in his arms, running soothing strokes down her back.

"Ssh. It's okay. He's gone."

"Thank you."

"You are part of this family, Mandy. We stand beside those who are ours."

She held on tight for a moment before stepping back. "I need to finish serving lunch."

"Go into the kitchen and take a minute to gather yourself. I'll handle serving for now."

"You'd do that?"

"Of course. I wield a mean spoon." Jonathan grinned as he shooed her through the double doors and took up his place behind the hot table.

She paused for a moment in the doorway as she watched him charm the pants off the guests with his quick wit, charming smile, and cowboy way.

God, she loved him.

Chapter Nine

Mandy made her way across the darkened ground toward the big barn in the distance. After supper, she'd asked where he'd gotten off to since he'd disappeared right after he'd eaten. "Jonathan?"

"In the tack room."

She smiled as she made her way down the well-lit center aisle of the huge structure. The barn was two story and big enough to house most of their horses in individual stalls should they find the need like during a storm or something. It also housed a huge indoor arena for working the horses if they wanted to do so in an enclosed area. Joey took care of the horses on the place, but each of the boys had their own mount.

As she came around the corner, she found him sitting in a chair at the desk with a bridle in his hands working soap into the leather. "Whatcha doin'?"

He looked up, smiled, and then let his gaze roam down her frame. "Cleaning some tack."

"I thought that was Joey's job."

"We all help out on occasion, besides it's kind of soothing to do. You can do a lot of thinking while you are working the soap into the piece." He leaned toward her and pushed out another chair. "Have a seat."

She took the chair, turned it around, and straddled it. His eyebrow rose over his left eye as his grin widened.

"Done in the kitchen for the day?"

"Yep."

"What brings you out here?"

"You. I had to ask where you disappeared to after supper."

He shrugged as he went back to his work. "I figured you'd be busy for a bit and this stuff is filthy."

She saw the dirt-caked towel across his knee as well as the one in his hands. "Wow. Yeah, it really is."

"It can rub the animal raw if it doesn't get cleaned regularly."

"Where's Joey?"

"Off running around town somewhere, I guess. He's been hanging out a lot with one of the neighbor girls. I think he's going to get himself into trouble with her, but he won't listen. I hope he finds a nice girl to settle down with soon."

"Doesn't he ride rodeo?"

"Yeah, sometimes. Bronc mostly."

"Cool."

"Why all of the interest in Joey suddenly?"

"I'm not *interested* if that's what you mean. I already have one Young brother to keep up with. Two would be too much."

"Remember that."

"Jealous?"

"Yep, even if he is my brother. I like having you under me."

"Or on top of you."

"That too."

He set the bridle aside on the desk before he turned back toward her and crooked his finger. She rose to her feet, sauntering closer as she wondered what he had in mind. There were a lot of things he could use to make this a very enjoyable encounter, right there under his hands. Saddles, bridles, leather straps, blankets, latigo, and more, were at his disposal.

When she got close enough, his fingers began to work the buttons on the front of her blouse as she worked herself between his parted thighs. As each inch of skin was exposed, he followed the path with his mouth, licking and sucking bits of flesh until she tingled all over. She buried her hands in his thick hair, knocking his hat to the floor behind the chair.

The scent of leather was one of her favorites, making her hot and needy from the moment she'd stepped into the room surrounding herself with all the tack.

The second her blouse was completely open, he pulled it from the waistband of her jeans before pushing it off her shoulders, leaving her in nothing but a soft pink bra with lacy edges

With a grasp on the straps at her shoulders, he pulled each one down over her arms until her bra gapped at the front. He slowly peeled the material down until her breasts were free to be devoured by his mouth.

She moaned the moment he took the right nipple between his lips. "We should probably shut the door."

He shook his head, but didn't lose his suction on her breasts.

"What if we get caught?"

He tongued the tip for a moment before he finally released her and looked up. "What if we do?"

Her body flushed as she thought about someone walking in on them having sex in the tack room surrounded by the tangy scent of leather.

"The thought excites you, doesn't it."

It wasn't a question. It was a statement and one she couldn't deny. She'd never had the chance to be anything close to an exhibitionist, but the thought of people watching them fuck made her hotter than a comet.

He watched her face as he unbutton her jeans, grasped them along with her panties at the waist and slowly peeled them down her body. Standing in front of him naked except for the jeans around her ankles, with the cool night air caressing her back from the open door, had cream dribbling from her pussy.

"I can smell your arousal."

Her breath hitched.

One finger spread her juices from her clit to her ass before he nudged the tip of his finger inside her.

"Oh God."

"Like that do you?"

Her answer came out as a soft moan as she tipped her head back on her shoulders and shivered.

"You are so beautiful."

He removed his hand from between her legs, much to her dismay, but when he grabbed a fistful of her hair, forced her to straddle his thigh, and then took her mouth in a soul-shattering kiss, she couldn't help but lose herself to his touch. His mouth and tongue took possession of her in a way she'd never imagined would turn her on. It did.

The friction of his jean-clad thigh along her clit had her hurting with the need to come. She rubbed herself along his thigh, bringing herself to the peak of pleasure until his hand came down in a hard slap to her butt cheek.

"No cheating."

"Please, Jonathan."

"Nope. You'll come when I say you can." He pushed her back, forcing her to stand on shaking legs as he came to his feet in front of her. "Remove your boots and jeans." He watched her through dark intense eyes as she finished stripping off her clothing. "There is a saddle there on that stand. I want your ass on the seat sideways, legs spread."

Excitement sizzled along her nerves as she moved toward where the saddle stood. She didn't know what he had planned, but God, help her, she wanted everything he had to give. When she put her butt on the hard, cold seat, she hissed at the sensations the friction caused on her heated skin.

He pushed a long, wood toolbox closer to her, indicating she should brace her feet on the edges as he sat down between her spread thighs.

"Gorgeous," he whispered reverently as he spread her labia with his fingers and blew a soft puff of air over her wet pussy.

The moment his tongue flicked against her clit, she almost lost control of her orgasm.

"Don't come until I tell you."

"I'm going to die."

"No you won't. Be the good girl I know you can be."

For him, she would. She would do anything he wanted her to do as long as he continued to torture her poor flesh with his mouth and tongue.

She whimpered softly as he pressed his nose into the crease between her pussy and her thigh, ran his tongue up the crack, and then hummed his appreciation over her clit.

Her hands fisted in his hair, trying desperately to push his head against her to give her more and more of the tormenting pleasure.

As he began to rapidly flick her clit with his tongue, she could feel her orgasm creeping up her legs in a warm rush that would soon burst through her pelvis.

Then he did the most torturous thing he could do, he started to slowly lick her clit in soft, small strokes. He gripped her butt in his hands and held her to his mouth, making little humming noises as he feasted on her flesh.

The minute he sucked her clit into his mouth and bit down, she couldn't stop the rush of climax that broke over her in a tingling wave meant to leave her mindless. She came apart with his name on her lips in a high cry of satisfaction that bounced off the rafters over their heads.

He continued to lick softly as she came down from her high and her heart rate slowed to a slow gallop. "I'm sorry."

He lifted his head, her juices still clinging to his lips as he swiped his tongue over the surface of his mouth. "You came without permission."

"I know. I need to be punished." She flushed hot just thinking about his hand on her ass, swiftly smacking until it burned.

"I think you like that too much."

"But…"

He smiled and leaned down to kiss her with long, slow movements of his mouth on her lips. His hands began a smooth journey over her breasts, bringing the nipples back to achy points. When he pinched the tip between his thumb and first finger, she almost came off her perch. The sensation was incredibly painful, but pleasurable at the same time.

Unable to contain herself any longer, she grasped at his belt buckle in wild desperation to part the metal from the leather. "Son of a bitch. I can't get it loose."

"Easy, little filly." He unbuckled it himself, before parting his jeans to free his cock from the confines.

She worked her hand into his jeans to grasp his cock in her shaking hands. "I need this. I need you."

"In a minute. No rush."

"Yes there is. I'm so fucking horny, my head feels like it is about to explode."

"You just had an orgasm. Are you telling me it wasn't enough?"

She grabbed his face between her hands and brought his mouth close to hers. "That was the tip of the iceberg. I hurt from wanting you. You've been driving me crazy all day with sexy looks, little winks, and those dimpled smiles of yours. Every time I looked your way, I could feel my pussy getting hot and throbbing. Don't torture me anymore, please." She pushed his jeans down past his hips before she grabbed his cock in her palm again. "I want this."

He didn't even bother to take his pants all the way off before he grabbed a condom from his back pocket, slipped it on, and eased himself into her.

Her cunt quivered around him as he pushed inside. Her heart hammered against her ribs as he began a slow, hip-grinding thrust.

"When we're done fucking like this, I aim to take your ass."

Holy mother of God.

"For now, I'm going to fuck you slow and easy until you are squirming on my cock."

Heat flushed her skin a bright red as he did what he said, slow and easy. It didn't take long for her to realize what a sadist he was, but what did that make her? She never thought of herself as a masochist. However, the pain he'd dished out with his hand on her ass left an enjoyable impression. The notion might be something they would need to explore further. For now, she needed to focus on the feel of him deep inside her. The hardness spreading her wide, made her want to whimper and moan while he eased in and then out.

She leaned back on her hands as she gripped the pommel of the saddle in one hand and the cantle in the other. Her toes cramped from where she had her feet up on the edges of the toolbox he'd been sitting on when he'd ate her like a starving man. In this position, she could see his cock penetrating her with the slow rocking of his hips. The sight brought more wetness between her legs. "Good God, that's hot."

"You like watching me fuck you?"

"Yes. I've never seen anything so sexy in my life."

"Do you want to come again before I take you from behind?"

"I've never had a man there so I'm not sure how to answer that question."

He kept talking as he continued to push his cock into her pussy. "I love the thought of being your first anal experience."

"You won't hurt me?"

His movements stopped as he looked down into her eyes. "God no. I would never hurt you. You can stop things any time you want. I want it to be a pleasurable experience for you too." She moaned when he pulled his cock from her center. "Roll over on the saddle with your butt in the air, your feet on the toolbox and spread your cheeks for me."

She shivered as she followed his instructions, not sure what the sounds were he was making behind her as he opened and closed a couple of drawers on the desk. When she felt a dollop of cold liquid hit her hot ass, she hissed between her teeth.

Anticipation crawled over her skin in a wave of desire she couldn't control. Fear made her breathing coming out fast and hard. She'd heard anal sex hurt, but she trusted Jonathan with her heart and soul, knowing he would never intentionally hurt her.

As she reached back to spread herself for him, she felt the hard head of his cock at her back hole.

"I'm going to go very slow. I want you to tell me everything you are feeling whether it be pleasure or pain. All right?"

"Okay," she whispered as he eased himself in.

The first sensation she experienced was a burn, a sweet burn. "It burns a little."

He stopped moving. "Are you okay?"

"Yes. It's a good feeling. I like the little bite of pain."

He pushed a slight bit forward again.

"Oh, oh, oh."

"Talk to me, Mandy."

"It's good. Holy hell, it's good. The pressure makes me feel full in a good way." She felt her pussy cream. "God, that's hot."

He continued to push forward inch by inch until she felt the hair on his pelvis brush against her ass. "I'm all the way in. Tell me what you're feeling."

"Oh my God. It's fantastic. I don't know how to describe it." She shivered. "What now?"

"I'm going to start to move. I'll go slow."

As he started pulling his cock out before shoving it back in, she thought her head would explode from the emotions screaming through her body. She felt hot and needy, desperate to come in a climax that would surpass anything she'd felt in the past. "I need to come, Jonathan. God, please, let me come."

His pace picked up in quick, hard thrusts, shoving her hard against the saddle under her. His breathing echoed in the small room. She could hear him grinding his teeth together in a vain attempt to hold back his own orgasm.

"I need, oh God, I need to come."

"Come for me, Mandy."

Lights exploded behind her eyelids as her whole body shivered in response to his command. Her pussy throbbed and spilled cum on the floor beneath them as she lost all coherent thought for the entire time it took her body to absorb the climax she'd just had.

She slumped over the saddle beneath her, exhausted from their sexcapades, as he eased himself from her ass and disposed of the condom.

"You okay?"

"I'm better than okay. I can't move."

"Do I need to help you?"

"You mean you can think coherently right now because I certainly can't." He laid a sharp slap on her naked butt, bringing her up straight. "That wasn't very nice."

"I thought it was. You have a very nice ass. I enjoyed fucking it tremendously."

She couldn't help the smile that spread across her face at his offhanded compliment. "Thank you for easing me into that."

He reached out, touching her cheek with his palm. "Baby, I would do anything for you. I hope you know that."

Her happy heart sang with delight as his words filled the emptiness in her soul. This thing between them might just work out. *God, I hope so, otherwise he could really hurt me.*

* * * *

Jonathan shook his head as he tried to focus on the screen in front of him so he could get some work done. It had become harder and harder to get anything accomplished in his office since he kept thinking about Mandy and how things had went from casual to serious in such a short time. If he wasn't careful, he would find himself ass deep in love with her.

Sorry buddy, but I think you're there already.

"Aw, hell."

He pushed back his chair, tossed his pen on the desk, and jumped to his feet. He needed some air and fast.

Quick steps took him through the main lodge and out the side door as he headed for the barn. Riding always helped to clear his mind when he was a kid, maybe it would do the trick this time. Sure couldn't hurt, he figured.

As he reached the cooler interior of the barn and let his eyes adjust to the darkness, he caught a glimpse of Joey working with one of the new horses in the arena. He didn't want to answer any questions from his nosey brothers, so he quietly retrieved his horse from the paddock to the right, tied him to the post in the barn, and got his tack from the tack room.

A light shown through the office doorway as he passed. He looked inside and saw Jeff sitting at the desk doing some work. "I'm going riding. I need to think."

"You okay?" Jeff asked, looking up from his paperwork. "Need to talk?"

"Yeah, I'm okay. I'm headed to the pond. I'll be back in a bit."

"Okay."

The moment he had everything in place, he unhooked his gelding and walked him out the back, which led to the corral. The back entrance where they brought the guests in and out from their rides stood empty. No one was around except the horses waiting tied to their spots, happily munching on hay.

He gathered the reins in his left hand, stuck his foot in the stirrup and hoisted himself up into the saddle. His horse sidestepped a moment, anxious for a run. The appaloosa was one of the different animals on the ranch. Most of the horses they had were quarter horses because of their stamina on the ride, but he'd always preferred the eager to please attitude and great disposition of this breed.

A light tap of his heels to the animal's side, and the horse took off like a shot.

He ate up the ground under his pounding hooves like his ass was on fire. Maybe it was.

Wind whipped by him as the junipers became a blur. He leaned over the horse's neck, urging him on to more speed. They flew over the rocky ground, headed for where, he wasn't sure. He needed this solitude, this quiet moment to gather his thoughts.

The mud pit the family enjoyed going mudding in didn't stop him, although good memories assaulted him with the glance at the terrain.

A small tree branch smacked him in the leg as he sped down the trail.

He could see the neighbor's houses from the top of the hill where he finally stopped to rest his winded horse. The animal's side billowed in and out while he tried to catch his breath. "Sorry, boy." The horse tossed his head for a moment as he pawed at the ground. Jonathan smiled. His horse still wanted to run, but Jonathan knew he needed to give him a little break. "Easy, boy. We will go slower."

Jonathan tapped him with his heels while keeping a tight grip on the reins so the horse knew he wanted him to walk for a bit.

The air seemed crisper today. October could go either way in Hill Country. This year, fall seemed to have a colder tinge to the air.

The horse picked his way along the path, avoiding tree branches, huge rocks, and areas where the footing might not be so safe. This animal was well trained for trail riding.

Quiet surrounded him. Not even the sound of an insect broke the solitude he'd craved when his butt hit the saddle this morning.

The reins were gripped loosely in his left hand, not that he really needed to guide the appaloosa. The saddle creaked under him, soothing his soul like nothing else could. The trees, the bushes, the silence, the animal beneath him, and the sun on his shoulders would do more for his spirit than anything, which seemed funny because he normally worked in the office from sunup until sundown on the websites and marketing.

I guess I really am a cowboy at heart.

Jonathan headed to the pond. It had always been one of his favorite spots on the ranch and today, he wanted to sit and think.

As the horse approached the area, he saw a deer standing at the edge of the water, silently sipping the cool, clear liquid until its thirst had been sated. The animals in the area used this lot for watering, so it wasn't unusual to see wildlife here. He pulled his horse to a stop as he waited for the skittish deer to finish. When the doe lifted her head, she spotted him across the water, turned to the left and spirited off at a quick run.

The moment the deer disappeared through the brush, his horse walked to the edge of the pond and put his head down to drink. Jonathan dismounted and ground tied the animal knowing he wouldn't wander too far.

His boots crunched the rock beneath his feet as he moved toward the big rocks at the top of the pond where the water trickled down from the stream above. It was the perfect perch to watch the area and to think.

He sat down on the biggest rock, hooking one boot on a smaller rock below him and one on a rock to his left. He glanced up at the blue skies over his head, realizing it was very close to the color of Mandy's eyes, that pure sky blue.

Images of their relationship over the last few weeks sped across his mind. Things had been going good. They were communicating, enjoying each other on an intimate level and it was something he hadn't experienced with anyone else. It was kind of nice. Their time together had been special. She'd definitely had a good time when they had made love. Talks between them were open, honest, and great, but he still felt she was holding something back. What though? Surely there wasn't anything in her past that would be an issue. He didn't care if she'd been into drugs and stuff during her teenage years. Hell, they had all experimented at one time or another.

Nothing during their times making love seemed out of sorts. She'd enjoyed being tied up from what she'd said. Anal sex hadn't bothered her even though she'd never experienced it before.

"Am I really falling in love with her?" he asked the nothingness around him looking for the answer without having to delve too far into his soul.

His heart whispered back an affirmative yes.

He couldn't really picture his life without her in it. She'd been such a part of Thunder Ridge for the last few years that she'd seemed part of the family even though she hadn't been dating any of his brothers. He couldn't picture her with any of them though. He knew her body and he knew she'd become something special to him, even if he'd only been seeing her for a few weeks. Their bond had grown to the point where he wanted her in his life on a permanent basis. Did that mean marriage? Maybe. Right now, he needed to see where her heart was in the scheme of things. If she couldn't see herself with him for the long haul, he wasn't sure what he'd do. It would be difficult for him to be around her all the time and not want her.

The crunch of hooves alerted him to someone approaching. He knew his brothers came here often too, so it didn't surprise him when Jeff rode into the clearing. *Right on time.*

"Hey. I thought I'd join you. You sounded like you might need someone to talk to."

"Yeah, maybe."

"So. What's up?"

"My relationship with Mandy."

Jeff dismounted and ground tied his horse near Jonathan's appaloosa. "Do you want to talk about it?"

Jonathan sighed. He was close to all of his brothers, but Jeff was the eldest and held a bit of big brother attitude on his shoulders. He wanted to be able to fix everyone's problems all the time. His efforts didn't usually work out very well, but it might not hurt to get his opinion.

"I think I'm falling in love with her."

"What makes you think so?"

"Well, I can't seem to get her off my mind. Sex has been great between us and she really seems to be into me too."

"True. She's been chasing you for three years now."

"I know and we are getting along great."

"Why do you think you're in love with her though? What makes her any more special than anyone else you've dated?"

"She gets me. We understand each other. We have a lot in common, and she's open to my particular brand of sexual tendencies."

"So she would make a good pet?"

"If you mean pet as in submissive, maybe, but if you mean pet like in dog, no. She's independent, not a doormat."

"I didn't realize you were looking for a dominant/submissive type relationship."

"I didn't either until she came along. I mean, I'm not twenty-four seven BDSM, but I do like a little spice to my sex life and she was open to experimenting so I guess that's good."

"Yeah, it's better than finding out she's grossed out by it."

Jonathan glanced sideways at his brother. Jeff had grown older in the last few years, but he seemed very happy in his relationship with his live-in girlfriend and their children. A wedding was being planned for next June and it made Jonathan happy to see his brother finally come to his senses. It was about time. "How's the wedding planning coming?"

"It's been hell." Jeff sighed as he shifted on the rock he'd taken a seat on.

"Why?"

"Terri is driving me nuts with all the details and it's still several months off. I'll be glad when it's over."

"You're happy though?"

Jeff smiled as he tipped his hat back on his head with a finger to the brim. "Yeah. I can't believe I didn't marry her before. I don't know what I was thinking."

"You were thinking about how your ex hurt you and you were afraid Terri would too."

"Maybe, but she's proven to me that she's here to stay, so I'll be happy to put a ring on her finger."

"I'm glad you two are together. She's good for you. She doesn't put up with your shit."

Jeff punched him in the shoulder. "And you do?"

"Hell no. I've got your number, big brother."

"You and Joey are the only two unattached Young brothers left. Are you getting lots of attention because of it? I know the local women are becoming a lot bolder in their pursuit."

"I don't really see it. Maybe Joey is, but I don't get that kind of attention. Not that I'm aware of anyway."

"I see the way they look at you two when you are around the bar with us. You aren't paying much attention because you are kind of shy."

"Yeah, I guess, but I'm really thinking it's time to find that special lady."

"Well, then you need to settle down with someone and take yourself off the market. Leave the pursuing to Joey. He's up for the challenge."

They laughed in unison knowing their youngest sibling could totally handle more than one woman pursuing him.

"So what are you going to do about Mandy?"

"I'm not sure. I came out here because I'm confused about my feelings for her. I like her a lot and I think we are good together, but something is telling me she's not being completely honest with me."

"Have you talked to Peyton? Maybe she could give you some insight."

"No. That might be a good idea. Mandy and Peyton have been friends for quite a long time. She might be able to tell me what's going on in Mandy's head."

"I suggest you talk to her then."

"Okay. I will. Tonight. After supper."

They both stood and walked back to where their horses had stopped to munch on some grass. After they had both mounted, they turned toward home, riding in silence, lost in their own thoughts, until the main lodge came into view.

Jonathan loved the old house with its wraparound porches and antique pieces on the front area next to the rocking chairs. He loved to go out there with his coffee in the mornings and just think. It was peaceful.

"What the hell?"

"What?"

Jeff jerked his head to the side, indicating the front of the main lodge. "Look."

Chapter Ten

Terri stood in front of the porch in a long white gown, holding a bouquet of flowers. Her family and his stood beside her as she stepped forward to meet them.

Jonathan grinned. He'd been in on the surprise for his eldest brother. Thank God Jeff had taken the bait and come after him when he'd stopped at the office to tell him where he would be. His eldest brother couldn't stay out of other people's business if his life depended on it, so Jonathan knew if he told him he needed to think, his brother would follow.

"What's going on, Terri?" he asked as he dismounted from his horse.

"I know I've been driving you nuts with wedding planning, and I know we were going to wait until next year, but I decided I didn't want to wait anymore. I've waited on your ass long enough, Jeff Young. Will you marry me right here, right now in front of your family and mine?"

Jeff glanced around him as a slow smile lifted the corners of his mouth. "You bet!" He swept her off her feet and carried her to where the preacher stood waiting at the end of the walkway. When he set her on her feet and turned expectantly toward the preacher, every one of his family laughed. "Sorry I'm not in my finery."

"You look like the cowboy I fell in love with."

The families took their places standing behind the couple as the preacher went through the wedding ceremony.

Jeff frowned as he turned toward his family. "I don't have a ring. I haven't had a chance to go shopping."

Nina stepped forward holding out her first wedding set in her hands. "I would be honored if you would wear mine, Terri. Jeff is my eldest, and as such, is entitled to the first wedding set James ever bought for me."

"Thank you, Mom." Terri kissed her on the cheek as Jeff took the rings in his hand.

"I love you, Mom," Jeff said, as he turned back toward Terri and repeated the vows as he slipped the beautiful rings onto her finger. "You're mine now, woman. No running off on me. You're stuck."

"Like glue, baby, like glue." Terri reached up, wrapped her hand behind Jeff's head, and crushed their mouths together while the rest of the family cheered.

Jonathan looked across the group, and his gaze caught on Mandy. There were tears swimming in her eyes as she watched Terri and Jeff greet everyone in the group. She fit, that's all there was to it. She had become part of this family over the last few years, and he couldn't see her not being here for things like this, Christmases, birthdays, anniversaries, births, and everything else families did.

When she looked his way, he smiled when she automatically started toward him. Surely it was a sign, something that told him they belong together.

"Hey," she said, stopping in front of him.

She looked gorgeous in her pink off the shoulder dress and pink toenails. She wasn't wearing any shoes. The smile on her lips made her eyes sparkle. Happiness radiated from her. Maybe she was ready for them to become more.

"Hey," he replied, reaching out to touch the curl lying on her shoulder. "You look beautiful."

"Thanks. You look pretty handsome yourself."

He glanced down, taking in his dirty jeans, button down western shirt, and dusty boots before he looked back up into her eyes. "Not really. It's just my riding gear. I couldn't let on to Jeff anything was up, otherwise he wouldn't have been surprised."

She tipped her head to the side a little and smiled. "It did go off brilliantly, didn't it?"

"Yep."

"He didn't have a clue?"

"Nope." He took her hand in his and led her to a bench sitting on the porch as the party atmosphere around them escalated. Several of the guests on the ranch had been included in the festivities, so it was getting rather crowded and loud as the party got started with the cake and food. His mom and sisters-in-law had done a fantastic job getting everything ready in such a short time without Jeff being the wiser. Leave it to a bunch of women to pull something like this off without the man of the hour knowing anything about it.

Jonathan held Mandy's hand as they rocked in the double rocker. He loved being here like this with her, together without any expectations or anything going on. She watched the proceedings going on around them as he watched her form the corner of his eye. The little smile playing on her lips seemed so like her, he was taken aback by how his heart expanded at the thought of having her in his life. "Do you want to get married?"

"Excuse me?" she said, turning to face him.

"I don't mean right now, but someday, do you want to marry someone?"

She exhaled as the grin reappeared. "Well, yes. I mean, someday, when I know I've found the right guy, I do."

"I know what you mean. I think marriage is in my future too…someday."

She leaned into his shoulder, snuggling a little closer. "This was nice. I'm glad we managed to pull it off."

"You did a fabulous job."

A blush crept up her cheeks. "I didn't do much."

"You helped with the food and cake."

"True, but you kept him occupied and away from the ranch long enough for us to get everything ready."

"All I could do was hope he fell for it. He's a smart man. If he would have guessed something was up, he would have hightailed it out of here."

"You know, I don't think so. He wanted to marry Terri. It's obvious how much in love they are, but he's been burned. His skittishness made him all the more desirable to her, I think. She fell in love with him and wanted him to spend the rest of his life with her. Marriage terrified him, though."

"Yep, but he's in this hook, line, and sinker now."

Someone started up some country music from the stereo in the lodge. One of his favorite artists came on singing about love and how you had to work at it to make it forever. Jonathan climbed to his feet bringing Mandy up with him. "Dance with me, please."

"Of course."

He led her out to the middle of the lawn where they came together perfectly. He liked holding her way too much, he decided, but what the hell. He tucked her into his arms where her head barely reached his shoulder. Her perfume surrounded him as he took a deep breath. He loved how she smelled. The scent drove him to distraction, past the point of reason. "What kind of perfume are you wearing?"

"Nothing special. Just a new perfume I bought recently. Do you like it?"

"I want you to put it in the crease of your thighs next time we make love. I want it surrounding me as I eat your pussy until you scream my name."

"When might this occur, sir?"

"I love when you call me that." He bent his head so he could whisper in her ear. "As soon as we can get away from here."

She shivered in his arms as she tipped her head a little to the side and sighed. God, he loved when she sighed for him. It made him feel powerful and wanted more than anything else in the entire world.

"Will you tie me to the bed again?"

"Maybe. Remember who is in charge here, pet."

"Yes, sir."

He ran his hands up and down her back, soothing her with his touch. Sometimes she acted a bit skittish when they came together, which worried him.

With a glance across the lawn, he caught Peyton's gaze on them. She smiled before winking in his direction. Apparently, his sister-in-law approved of him and Mandy. Good to know, but he still wanted to talk to her, and it probably should be before he and Mandy made love again.

He leaned back in her embrace so he could look into her eyes. "Listen, I need to get a little work done before I cut out for the weekend. How about I meet you at your place in a couple of hours?"

"Should I be wearing something special?"

"Skin, baby, only skin."

A wicked gleam in her eyes promised things he could only imagine as she stepped back, bit her lips, and then licked the bright red surface. His imagination went wild as he thought about those ruby red lips enclosed on his cock as she went down on him.

"Naughty girl."

"Only for you."

"I can't wait."

"I'll see you in a bit then. Don't work too hard."

"I won't."

She raked a fingernail down his chest until she reached the belt buckle at his waist. When the single digit dipped below his waistband, he sucked in a ragged breath and closed his eyes.

The moment the sensation disappeared, he opened his eyes again to see her smiling before she turned and walked away, her hips swaying slightly.

He exhaled on a rush, willing his now hard cock to soften otherwise he would totally embarrass himself as he walked back into the main lodge. *Maybe I should wait a few minutes to talk to Peyton, so she doesn't think I'm some kind of weirdo.*

Too late.

Peyton made her way to his side before he could disappear into the house.

"Hey, cowboy."

"What's up, Peyton?"

"Where did Mandy go?"

"Uh, home, I guess. Why?"

"Well, you two looked pretty chummy. I thought maybe you were going to leave together."

"Why would you think that?"

"I know you're sleeping together, Jonathan. She doesn't keep those kinds of secrets from me."

"So?"

"I'm disappointed is all, I guess."

"We are meeting later. Does that help?"

She grinned a sly, evil little grin. "Yep."

"Uh, can I talk to you a minute in private?"

Now she looked worried. "Yeah. I guess."

She followed him into the house and to his office before he shut the door and turned to face her. "I need to ask you some questions about Mandy." He sat down in his chair, indicating with his hand she should sit in the one opposite him. "You're her best friend so I figured you know her better than anyone."

"I probably do." She folded her hands together in her lap, clutching her fingers tightly. "I don't know whether I can help you though."

"Well, I'm getting the impression she's hiding something. I don't know what and it's bugging me."

"How serious are you about her?"

"I think I'm falling in love with her." He pulled his hat off and raked his fingers through his hair before he put it back on. "I can't get her out of my head. We are great together in bed and she's becoming very special to me, but I fear she's holding back for some reason."

Peyton bit her lip.

"What aren't you telling me, Peyton?"

"I can't talk about it, Jonathan. It's not my place. You need to talk to Mandy."

"Great. Just fucking great."

"Give her time. She's had a rough life."

"What made it so rough? I thought she had a good childhood from what she's told me. She's fairly close to her parents. She got a little wild as a teenager, but nothing major. I don't understand."

"Ask her to be honest with you. Tell her how you feel, Jonathan. If she's feeling the same way, she'll need to explain everything to you. You won't be able to be a couple if she doesn't tell you because it will become a problem at a later date."

"You're being very cryptic."

"I know, but I can't break her confidence." Peyton got to her feet. "I'm sorry. You know I love you. You are family, but she's my best friend."

Peyton disappeared out the door, leaving him to stew in his own thoughts. *Now what the hell am I going to do? What if she won't tell me? What if it's something that could be detrimental to our relationship?*

Jonathan sat in his office until the sun went down, turning the small space dark. The party outside had long ago dispersed, leaving the place in an eerie quiet that made him uncomfortable. Mandy had called several times. Not sure what to think about the conversation he'd had with Peyton, he'd ignored her calls, choosing to think things through before he talked to her.

An Internet search of her name had led to some disturbing information.

He couldn't quite wrap his head around her being arrested for prostitution when she was eighteen. It didn't fit her personality at all. Of course, she probably had been able to pull herself out of that downward spiral of a life. She'd admitted to using drugs when she was younger, but she'd never told him she'd been busted for heroin either. The new picture emerging had him scratching his head. What happened to her in her childhood that led to prostitution and drugs?

A drink sounded really good right now.

He sat in the dark for what seemed like hours as he went over and over in his mind, the information he'd found. A glance at the clock revealed the time. Two am.

His phone rang again. Mandy. His hand hovered over the button, debating on whether to answer and outright ask her about what he'd found, or let it go to voicemail until he could gather his thoughts. He needed to let her explain. It was only fair.

When he picked up his phone and listened to her last message, he really felt like shit.

"Jonathan, it's Mandy again. Please call me when you get this. I'm scared right now and my imagination is running wild with terrifying thoughts. I wanted this to be a special night for us, but now you aren't even talking to me for some reason. Please. God, please, call me. I need you to hold me right now more than anything in the world and tell me we are going to be okay."

She'd hung up after that, leaving him with this hollow feeling in his soul.

Forgiveness was a virtue. What really did he have to forgive her for? It wasn't like this all had happened recently. It had been several years ago, during her wild teenage years, and in all reality, it wasn't fair for him to judge her by her past mistakes. He wasn't perfect by any means, so where did he get off judging her?

His mother tapped on the door as she called out his name. "Jonathan?"

"Come in, Mom."

After she opened the door, she said, "Why are you sitting in the dark at two in the morning, son?"

"I'm thinking. I do it better in the dark."

"About what?"

He sighed heavily as his mother took the seat Peyton had been in several hours before. "I found out some things and I'm not sure how to handle the information."

"What things?"

"Mom, Mandy was arrested at eighteen for prostitution and drugs, heroin to be exact."

"Oh, honey."

"I know. Shocking, right?"

"Not really."

"Why not really?"

"Jonathan, I knew about Mandy's record a long time ago. When she first started, she told me about it because you know we do a background check on everyone who works here. She explained the circumstances of her arrest then. I understand why she did what she did."

"Explain it to me, Mom, because I sure don't get it."

"I can't, son. She needs to tell you herself."

He jumped to his feet, sending his chair crashing to the floor behind him. "What the fuck?"

"Don't talk to me like that."

"Sorry, but I don't understand why everyone is keeping stuff from me. How can I think about being in love with her if no one will tell me what is going on?"

Nina got to her feet and took her son in a big hug. "Jonathan, it's her place to tell you. Have you told her you love her?"

"No."

"Then that's the first step. If she loves you too, then she'll tell you about her past. It's not my place to break her confidence."

Nina silently walked out of his office, shutting the door behind her.

Jonathan paced the floor several times before he grabbed his keys, his wallet, and his hat, and walked out.

Within minutes, he was headed down the road toward Bandera. He was going to get some answers to his questions if it was the last thing he did. If their relationship survived the night, they would probably survive anything.

* * * *

Mandy stared at her phone after her last call to Jonathan. Her heart hurt as she wrapped her arms around her middle and sank down on the couch. She didn't know what to think anymore. He'd been so loving earlier at Terri and Jeff's wedding when they had danced, but now he wasn't taking her calls.

She pressed her lips together to hold back the tears. Falling in love with him, deeper than anything she'd ever felt before, hurt really bad. She didn't understand why he'd turned his back on her, but he apparently had.

A soft knock brought her to her feet as she wiped away the trickle of a tear on her face. She sniffed a couple of times, trying desperately to clear her nose before she looked to see who had dropped by. She peeked out the peephole, surprised to find Jonathan in front of her door.

Not sure what to expect, she unlocked the top lock and then the bottom one before she opened it.

"Hey."

"Hi."

"Can I come in?"

"Uh, yeah, I guess so." She stepped back, allowing his big frame to step around her. After she shut the door, she turned to face him as she rubbed her bare arms to calm the chills. "You were supposed to come over several hours ago."

"I know."

"How come you didn't answer my calls?" she asked, as she took a seat across from him. Right now it didn't seem like a good idea to sit next to him. "I called several times."

"I know, and I'm sorry."

He looked nervous, edgy, and uncomfortable. Why, she wondered. "Jonathan, what's going on? You seem so distant right now when you weren't earlier. What have I done to displease you?"

"I need to ask you some questions, and I'm trying to think of how to word them without pissing you off."

She got a sinking feeling in the pit of her stomach. Something wasn't right here, and the thought of what he was getting at terrified her. "Okay."

"Will you tell me the truth?"

Somehow, that made her suspicion worse. "If I can, but there are things in my past I won't discuss, even with you."

"That doesn't make me feel better, Mandy."

"I'm sorry. I can't talk about them." She rubbed her arms again. "There are some things better left buried."

He took his hat off, sitting it on the arm of the chair before he faced her again. "I did an Internet search on you and I found something out that's bothering me."

"You did what?"

"An Internet search. You know. It brings up past records and things like that."

She jumped to her feet, rage rolling through her at his audacity. "You son of a bitch! What's in my past is in my past. You didn't even ask me, you just went on the fucking web and searched. How dare you!"

"I had to. I knew you were hiding something from me. Will you tell me why you were arrested for prostitution and heroin possession? I need to understand, Mandy."

"Get out! I don't want to see you again. Do you hear me? Never. Don't talk to me, don't call me, don't touch me!"

He stood and reached out his hand, but she slapped it away. "I said don't touch me. I hate you! Do you hear me? I hate everything about your fucking perfect life. You've never done a damned thing wrong, I'm sure, and it shows. You and your perfect family. No one is good enough for you. Go find some good little girl who's never done a damned thing wrong, never been in a situation where she had to do something to survive."

He came closer, trying to draw her into his arms. "Mandy, talked to me. Don't shut me out."

She pushed him away with her hands on his chest, ignoring the way her palms and fingers tingled from the contact. "I said go." Tears streamed down her cheeks now, but she was unable to stop them, even for him. "Just go," she whispered, broken, body and soul.

The soft snick of the door echoed in the small apartment as she sank to the floor.

Chapter Eleven

Days went by, turning into weeks, and then months. Christmas came and went including the beautiful wedding of Jackson and Samantha.

Jonathan had tried to contact her on several occasions, but she'd let his calls go to voicemail. She couldn't see them together anymore, not with her past. Moving on seemed the best option.

Mandy didn't attend even though it hurt her not to. Samantha was her friend.

She'd quit the ranch right after the blow up with Jonathan. When she'd talked to Nina and told her what happened, she'd understood even though she suggested telling him the truth about her past. Mandy couldn't. Her whole messed up life was her fault, she knew. The rape, the drug possession, and the prostitution arrest. Everything was her fault, exactly how her parents had told her all those years ago.

Summer would be here soon. After graduating from her courses in June, she could move on to somewhere else outside of Bandera.

The girls on the ranch didn't understand either since she wouldn't tell them what happened between her and Jonathan, only that they had a disagreement, and no, they weren't seeing each other anymore. Only Peyton and Nina knew the truth.

She looked in the mirror as she put on her makeup to cover up the dark circles under her eyes. Sleep eluded her most nights these days, except for the reoccurring nightmare of reliving the rape in her dreams. Nothing seemed to erase those feelings of helplessness anymore, not even talking to Peyton.

Maybe professional help would make it easier for her to deal with this. She could try, she guessed. It wouldn't hurt.

As soon as she'd finished putting on her makeup, she grabbed her purse and keys before she headed toward the door to go to class. At least that kept her occupied for a few hours each day. The rest of the time, she couldn't concentrate on anything besides the feelings of loneliness and worthlessness that were a constant blanket of guilt.

A guy in one of her classes approached her as she sat outside trying to study for their upcoming exam.

"Hi there."

She glanced up, catching the reflection off his sunglasses. She shielded her eyes from the glare. "Hi." She'd seen him in a few of her classes, they'd exchanged greetings a few times, but weren't friends by any stretch of the imagination.

"Can I join you?"

"Uh, sure. I guess."

"You're Mandy, right?"

"Yes, and you are?"

"Brandon."

"Nice to meet you."

"You too."

The silence stretched for a moment while she tried to figure out why he'd come over in the first place. It wasn't like she'd talked to him before or even really noticed him, for that matter. He was kind of cute in a boyish kind of way, but not the rugged type she enjoyed. "Is there something I can help you with?"

"Yeah. I think so. How about a cup of coffee?"

"You know, I don't think that's such a good idea."

"Why not? Are you seeing someone?"

Despair threatened to choke her as she thought about Jonathan. "No, not really."

"Then you should be free for coffee, right?"

"Why are you being so persistent about this?"

"I think you're cute. I've watched you during class."

Okay, that's kind of weird.

"Come on. It's just coffee. Please?"

What the hell. It's just coffee, right? "All right."

"Fantastic. There's a shop around the corner." Brandon stood and held out his hand to help her to her feet. "Maybe we can brainstorm a bit about this exam coming up. I'm kind of lost on the subject matter."

She laughed a little, and it was a good feeling. It wasn't something she'd done much of over the last few months. "I know what you mean." She grabbed her backpack from the table, slipping her book in through the zippered pouch before closing it and slinging it over her shoulder.

They walked side-by-side down the concrete walkway to the edge of the street and turned left. The coffee shop sat one block down. She'd been there frequently over the last few years of attending classes at the college, so she knew the owners and most of the employees by first name.

The bell dinged when they went through the door to find a table. The only empty one in the whole place sat near the back. The red upholstered seats were cool to the back of her thighs where her bare skin touched when she slid into the booth. Fifties music played on the overhead speaker system. It reminded her of an old diner like they had during the run on Happy Days on television.

The waitress stopped at their table, taking a pen from behind her ear to write down their order. "What can I get'cha?"

"Coffee please. Cream and sugar?"

"You, sir?"

"Same."

"Be right back."

When the woman left them, Mandy glanced across the table right into the green eyes of the man who had asked her for coffee. "I'm sorry. What did you say your name was?"

"Brandon. Brandon Gilliand."

Her world went dark. *What the fuck?* "Uh, where did you say you're from?"

"Minnesota. Why?" He grabbed her hand from across the table. "Are you okay? You're very pale."

"Yeah," she squeaked. "I, uh—" *Oh God. He can't be related. Surely he's not related to that motherfucker I would kill if I could get my hands on him.*

"Mandy?"

She took several deeps breaths to calm her racing heart. No way could he have found her, right? It's just coincidence. She cleared her throat. "Sorry. You remind me of someone, that's all."

"Obviously someone you aren't fond of by the look on your face."

No way could she explain how now that she looked at him, really looked at him, he reminded her of Matt Gilliand, the man who'd rape her as a fifteen-year-old child. "Not really, no."

"Care to explain?" His cell phone rang in his pocket. "Let me grab this. It's my dad, and it might be important." He punched the screen on his phone. "Hey, Dad. What's up?"

The voice on the other end of the phone had memories rushing back in a spiraling kaleidoscope of colors making her stomach roll with nausea.

It's okay for me to touch you, Mandy. You are a special girl to me. I won't hurt you. You'll like it, I promise.

She jumped to her feet, sprinting for the door. The moment she hit the edge of the sidewalk, she threw up into the gutter. Her body shook as she tried breathing through her nose to calm her stomach. Her world tilted sideways.

Strong hands gripped her shoulders, pulling her hair out of her face. "It's okay, baby. I'm here."

"Jonathan?" she asked, her gaze swimming with tears as she looked up into the familiar eyes of the man she loved. Where had he come from? Was he following her? "What are you doing here?" She quickly wiped her face with her hand. He handed her a handkerchief. "Thank you."

"You're welcome. You okay?"

"Yes." She shook her head as the tears returned. "No."

He pulled her into his arms as she broke down in gut-wrenching sobs that rocked her entire frame. "Ssh. It's okay. I won't let anything hurt you." With his arm around her shoulders, he led her to his truck parked a few feet down the road.

The guy she'd been about to have coffee with came up behind them carrying the backpack she'd left in the booth and handed it to her. "Mandy? Are you okay?"

"I'm fine, Brandon. I'm sorry, but I won't be able to have coffee with you." She noticed he took a long look at Jonathan before he nodded and turned away.

"New boyfriend?"

"No. He's in one of my classes. He asked me out for coffee."

"And that made you throw up in the gutter?"

She pressed her lips together as his image swam in front of her.

"Mandy, honey, I can't help you if you won't tell me what's going on." With a gentle hand, he pushed her hair off her forehead and pressed a kiss there.

"I can't. You'll hate me. Everyone will blame me, just like my parents did. It was all my fault. Everything was my fault." Hiccups wracked her body as he opened the door on the truck and lifted her like a child into the seat before he shut the door. Her body shuddered as she pressed her hands between her knees.

When he got into the driver's seat, he turned the ignition key, the engine roaring to life. They pulled away from the curb and drove down the street, headed for where, she didn't know. Right now, she didn't care.

Why had he been in San Antonio near the college? Was he following her? What if he knew about her past and now he hated her enough to hurt her? She shook her head. Jonathan would never do anything to harm her, not in a million years. But that still left the unanswered question of why he was there?

Her voice came out in a whisper. "Where are we going?"

"Some place where we can talk."

Crap. Now he wants answers again.

Scenery went by in a blur as they drove out of town back toward Bandera. It didn't surprise her that he would take her back toward home. It was what he knew and was comfortable with.

Silence enveloped them during the forty-five minute ride.

Terror gripped her. What the hell would she tell him as to why she'd lost it outside the coffee shop? She couldn't possibly tell him the truth. He would never understand and he would blame her just like her parents had, for everything.

When they drove on past Thunder Ridge's gate, she got confused. Even though she'd been on the ranch for several years, she'd never really ventured down the road past the gates. The road turned from blacktop to gravel as he continued on. Fences still lined the road, telling her there were ranches even down this far.

Soon, he turned off on a side road that went up and over the hill toward the right. Deer sprang out of the bushes, crossing in front of the bumper of the truck. Jonathan never said a word.

They crested a hill before he pulled off near a metal gate with a huge lock to keep anyone from roaming onto the property without permission.

When he got out and unlocked the gate, she figured it was probably Thunder Ridge property and he was taking her somewhere private.

Good. If she lost him to the memories bombarding her, it wouldn't be in front of his family.

He locked the gate back up as soon as they pulled through and then jumped back inside the truck to continue on until they were at the top of one of the hills overlooking the area. Bluebonnets blanketed the landscape this time of year, giving the hillside a bright blue splash of color.

"How beautiful."

"Yes, you are."

She glanced his way and blushed. "Not me, silly, the hillside."

"You put the landscape to shame."

"You're a charmer."

"Stating the truth, darlin'."

She pulled the visor down in front of her face, to check how badly her makeup had smeared when she puked in the gutter. "Wow. Yeah, I'm beautiful with all this mascara under my eyes." She searched in his glove box for a tissue or napkin she could wipe her face with. "Ah. Found one." She wiped the black from beneath her eyes until she was satisfied that she no longer looked like a raccoon. "Better."

"Do you want to tell me what that was all about back there?"

"I wish I could."

In a complete bout of rage not like him at all, he punch his fist against the dashboard of his truck, breaking the skin on his knuckles.

"Jesus, Jonathan." She grabbed for his hand to wipe the blood from his skin. "Are you nuts?"

"No, I'm fucking frustrated as all hell, Mandy. I've been going crazy trying to figure out what the hell happened between us."

She dabbed at the skin until the blood was gone. She shrugged when he pulled his hand back. "We broke up."

"No, you shut me out."

She closed her eyes for a moment before opening them again to meet his gaze. "Yeah, I guess I did."

"Why?"

"Because there are things in my past you are better off not knowing, and when you snooped into my police record to find out some things, it pissed me off. I wanted to be the perfect girl for you like your family wants and like you want, but I can't be that."

"I don't want a Barbie doll, Mandy. I wanted you. I still do."

"How, Jonathan? How can you say that?"

"Because I love you, you crazy woman. I haven't been able to get you out of my mind no matter how hard I try. You are a part of my heart that can't be replaced, no matter how far you go or how much you shut me out."

"You love me?"

He scooted to the center of the seat, unbuckled her seat belt, and took her face in his hands. "Yes, I love you."

Fresh tears streamed down her cheeks. She had no idea how someone so perfect could be in love with her, but she wasn't going to question his feelings or her own anymore. She had to tell him the truth about her past. It wasn't a matter of him turning his back on her now. If he did, it would hurt like nothing she'd ever felt before, but maybe, just maybe, he would understand.

"I love you too."

He grasped her to his chest and whispered, "Thank you, God."

When he moved back so she could see his face, she was surprised to see tears in his own eyes.

"You mean everything to me."

"I hope you'll continue to love me when I tell you about my past."

"Honey, it doesn't matter. What's in the past is just that, in the past."

"I still have to tell you for my own piece of mind. There can be no more secrets between us."

"I'm glad to hear you say that."

She closed her eyes as she bent her head. "I had a baby at fifteen. I gave her up for adoption because my parents wouldn't let me keep her. I don't know where she is, but I would like to find her someday."

"I'm sure it was something you regret every day."

"It is, but there is more. I was raped. It resulted in my pregnancy. My parents didn't believe me when I told them about it because it was my stepfather's brother. He was twenty years older than me at the time and visiting us for Christmas. He came into my room and forced himself on me. He mocked me, said if I told anyone they wouldn't believe me, but I still told my parents. He was right. They thought I was lying to cover up sleeping with someone in my class. When the pregnancy was discovered, they forced me to have her and give her up."

"Oh, baby. I'm so sorry you've had to deal with this for all this time." He grasped her face in his hands, forcing her to look into his eyes. "Listen to me, Mandy. You were fifteen. It wasn't your fault."

"But he said I made him do it. He said I was pretty, and he couldn't help himself."

"Mandy, he was the adult. He is responsible, not you. You did nothing wrong, honey. In fact, I will help you if you want to bring charges against him."

"I…I don't know if I can."

"It's up to you, but I hope you think about it for yourself and your daughter. You need closure."

"There's more."

"Go ahead."

"Yes, I was arrested for prostitution and drugs when I was eighteen. I left home in a hurry when I finished high school and had to live on the streets for a while since I had no job and no money. I got in with the wrong crowd. I ended up having sex for money and getting busted for drugs. I didn't take them, but I had heroin in my possession when they arrested me on the streets. I was dealing at the same time I was prostituting myself." She exhaled and tipped her head back on her shoulders. "God, I feel like such a fool."

"You were a kid trying to make it on your own. We all make mistakes."

"Not you, not the perfect Young family."

"Mandy, you have no idea the things some of my brothers and I have gotten into over the years. We've barely managed to keep ourselves out of jail on plenty of occasions."

"Really?"

"Yes. Ask my mother. She'll tell you all about it."

Mandy couldn't help but smile a little thinking about the nine of them getting into trouble with their parents. Obviously, it hadn't been that bad or they would have a record. Of course, she had no idea if any of them did or not, but it was nice to know they weren't perfect either.

"I need to tell you one more thing because it might change how you feel about me."

"Nothing will change the way I feel."

"Don't say that until you've heard this."

"Okay. Go ahead."

"I can't have children."

"Why?"

"The pregnancy and birth did so much damage to my insides that I can't carry a baby to term anymore. There is way too much scar tissue in my uterus."

"It's okay."

"No, it's not, Jonathan. You want children. You told me as much. You want a big family like your parents had, and I can't give that to you."

"Mandy, listen to me. I would like children, yes, but that doesn't mean I wouldn't love any child we had together whether we are the biological parents or not. We can adopt or look into other options."

"You'd do that?"

"Yes, ma'am. There are plenty of kids out there who need parents that don't have any. I wouldn't have any trouble loving a child like that."

"How did I get so lucky to find you?"

"You corralled me a long time ago, sweetheart. The moment I saw you with Peyton, I knew you were someone special. It just took me a few years to figure out how special."

"I love you, Jonathan."

"I love you too, baby."

He slowly lowered his head so he could take her mouth in a soft, soul-stealing kiss. The moment he lifted his head, she knew this was it. He was the one she'd been destined to find, the one who could heal her tattered heart, hold it in the palm of his hand, and forever be the cowboy she could call her own.

Chapter Twelve

Darkness fell around them as they laid in the bed of his truck looking up at the stars over their heads.

After their talk, they climbed into the back, spread out the blanket he produced from behind the seats, and she'd laid her head on his chest.

His heartbeat steady and strong, something she knew she would forever hold in her heart. He loved her. It was something that would take a lifetime for her to comprehend, but he did love her.

His fingers did a slow crawl up and down her arm, leaving goose bumps in their wake. Tingles spread from where he touched her to every part of her body. From the moment he'd laid his hands on her, she'd been putty in his grasp.

"I love you," he whispered against her hair, before he kissed the top of her head.

"I love you and just for the record, I will never get tired of hearing that so you can say it all you want."

A rumble of laughter echoed beneath her ear. "Good to know, baby girl."

A coyote howled in the distance. Leaves rustled in the night breeze over their heads as the temperature began to drop.

She shivered.

"Are you cold?"

"A little."

"Want me to warm you up?"

"How do you plan to go about doing that, cowboy?"

"I have my ways, little lady." He moved so he was now over her as he began to kiss his way from her forehead, down over her eyelids, across her cheek, until he reached her right ear. "I'm going to make you come so hard, you'll see stars."

"Promises, promises."

"Remember that when you are begging me to let you come."

His teeth nipped at her earlobe, bringing awareness to her whole body as he continued his journey down her neck, nibbling as he went.

"Sit up," he said moving so she could rise. Her t-shirt whipped over her head, leaving her in her lacy pink bra. "I do love your undergarments. They are so sexy." He ran his tongue along the each cup of her bra where they laid against her breasts.

Her nipples pulled into tight nubs, rubbing against the fabric of her bra in the most erotic way she could ever have imagined.

He avoided moving the cups out of his way as he continued down her abdomen until he reached the waist of her jeans. "Lie back now."

She got comfortable on her back as he worked the button loose on her pants and removed them along with her underwear in one swish of fabric. Cool night air wafted over her skin, making her shiver or was it the anticipation of his touch? She wasn't sure anymore. "Touch me."

"I will. In a minute, but for right now, I want to look."

She could almost feel his gaze on her skin.

"You are magnificent. All soft, glowing, and ready for me."

His hands were rough on her flesh, the calluses erotically abrasive. He took her foot in his hand and brought it to his mouth, kissing and nipping as he moved up the inside of her leg. Her pussy wept with the need to have him touch her there, with his tongue, with his mouth, with his fingers. Hell, she didn't care. She just needed him to do something besides this erotic, slow seduction he was hell-bent on performing. "Jonathan, please."

"Oh, I love when you beg, my beautiful woman."

His mouth moved to the other foot as she sighed in frustration. He would be the death of her before the night was over if he didn't hurry up.

When she felt the warm puff of air on her clit, she almost came straight up off the bed of the truck. "Yes."

He brushed his mouth against her inner thigh, and she almost smacked him in the head for avoiding the point where she ached for him. But when he returned to lick her clit once, then twice, she opened her thighs farther and scrunched her eyes closed as she waited with bated breath. Her climax would be fast and furious when it broke over her.

He licked slowly, bringing her up a miniscule degree at a time. Her legs began to shake as she hovered on the edge of climax for several moments, waiting for him to tell her it was okay for her to come. She held her breath, afraid to breathe until he whispered the words.

Finally, he whispered, "Come for me, Mandy."

Her world exploded in a shower of flashing lights as she screamed his name to the wind. "Jonathan!"

He continued to slowly lick her as her heart and breathing returned to a semi-normal rate and she began to shiver from the chill in the air, or her body ramping up again, she wasn't sure.

"I'll be right back. There is another blanket in the truck."

When he returned moments later, he carried a wool blanket in his hands as he hopped back up in the bed of the truck. He covered her body with it, letting her catch her breath and warm herself up before things progressed to the next step. "I wish it was a little warmer. I would spread you out on that bed of grass over there, make you come several more times, and then fuck you into tomorrow."

"We'll save that for something to do in a couple of months." She giggled as he moved up beside her.

"I'm glad you are thinking of a future for us."

"I love you. I want to be with you."

He twisted a strand of her hair around his finger before bringing it to his lips and rubbing it across the surface. "I love you too."

His eyes darkened in the cab light over their heads. "What's wrong?"

"I'm hard and achy for you, but there are a couple of things we need to get out in the open."

Her stomach knotted as she tried to think of what he might be talking about. She'd been honest with him, telling about the rape, her daughter, and the arrests. What else could he want to talk about? "Make love to me, Jonathan. We can talk afterward."

"No. We need to talk now before things go any further."

She waited not so patiently as he continued to run his gaze over her face.

"What happened earlier when I found you outside the coffee shop? Why were you throwing up in the gutter?"

"I told you there was a guy from my class who asked me out for coffee. It turns out he is the son of the man who raped me."

"Oh shit."

She tucked the blanket around her and sat up, determined to clear the air now that she knew he loved her and wouldn't leave her alone. "Yeah. I'm terrified that he's found me. I didn't even know he had children. That makes the whole thing really gross, not that it wasn't before. He has a son that is about the same age I am."

"You don't have to worry, honey. I won't let him hurt you ever again."

"I know you won't." She leaned back against the bed of the truck as she gazed into the eyes of the man she loved. They'd come a long way in a short time, learning to love each other and accept the differences between them, but loving each other through whatever came would be the trick of a lifetime. "Why were you near the coffee shop anyway?"

"I came to find you. I got your class schedule from Peyton. I figured it was time we talked and cleared the air. You are important to me."

He moved to her side and pulled her into his embrace, her head on his chest. She could feel the steady beat of his heart beneath her cheek. The slow rise and fall of his chest when he breathed made her feel calm and safe. He did that for her without even trying. "You are the best thing that's ever happened to me, and I'm trying to figure out why I deserve you."

"Because you're a special woman. You're always doing things for other people. You care about others more than yourself and it shows. We are good together, you and I."

She grasped the button at the top of his shirt, slowing going down each one in turn until she could push the material aside. His chest was sprinkled with dark chair that she loved to bury her fingers in. She let her hand smooth over the muscles of his pecs before she ran a fingernail over his left nipple.

He shuddered in response to her touch.

When she let her hand wander down his abdomen to the belt buckle at his waist, she slowly undid it, leaving it hanging loose as she reached for his button. His breath hitched as she parted the material, letting his cock spring free. He was commando.

"No underwear? You naughty boy."

He groaned as she ran her fingernail down his bulging cock.

She sat up, letting the blanket hang loose as she moved down and grasped his jeans at the hips to pull them off. She wanted to taste him, breathe in his scent, and bring him pleasure beyond what he'd ever felt before.

After she got his jeans down around his ankles, she licked her way up his thigh until she could bury her nose in the crease between his balls and his leg. His scent drove her wild with need. It was somewhere between musk and man.

She ran her tongue around the base of his balls. His moan of satisfaction made her smile against his skin. The little sounds he made when they made love, made her heart sing with joy. She did that for him, only her.

The moment she licked from his balls to the tip of his cock, he lifted his hips in silent invitation to take him in her mouth. She circled the head, once, twice, before she slipped him between her lips. The small amount of suction she applied to the head pulled a guttural sound from deep in his throat.

He fisted her hair, guiding her to what he wanted.

With her mouth encircling his cock, she pushed downward until she felt the head bump against the back of her throat, and her nose was buried in the hair at the base of his cock. She worked her throat a couple of times, bringing a primitive noise from his mouth she'd never heard before.

She loved to make him loose control and this blow job was doing the trick.

Jonathan pulled at her hair, forcing her to release his cock from her mouth. "Stop, Mandy, or I'll come in your mouth when I want to be buried in your pussy." He pulled her up his chest and rolled her over onto her back. "Do I need to continue to use a condom?"

"I don't think so. We are exclusive, right?"

"Yes, ma'am."

"Then no. I think we're good. I haven't been with anyone but you in quite a while."

"I've been celibate myself for about eighteen months before we had sex."

The head of his cock bumped against her pussy lips, slowly parting her so he could bury himself to the hilt. Giving him a blow job had ramped up her own desire to almost explosive, doing almost as much for her as it did for him.

When he slowly pushed inside her pussy, she wet her finger in her mouth before she reached down to encircle her clit.

"Watching you masturbate is really hot." He looked down to where their bodies met. "Make yourself really wet for me." He continued to slowly sink inside her until he was fully buried. He shuddered as he closed his eyes.

The view was perfection. He'd braced himself on his hands so as not to put too much weight on her chest. His arms bulged from the strain of holding himself still while he unhurriedly rocked his hips. His head was tipped back on his shoulders, his face intense with concentration. She could tell he was absorbing every slick slide of his cock inside her, feeling each ripple of her pussy around him, and enjoying every sensation going through his body.

The sight of him loosing himself to her, made her need spiral out of control. Her orgasm hovered on the edge of her consciousness as she worked her clit with her fingers. The need to come overwhelmed her to the point where she had to grit her teeth to keep it under control. She pinched herself with her left hand to stop the oncoming tide of pleasure, making it recede back slightly so she wouldn't come before he told her she could.

"You feel fantastic. So wet. So tight." He thrust several more times. "I could fuck you all night."

"Jonathan?"

"Yeah?"

"I'm hurting. I need to come so badly, I ache."

"Only when I say you can, not before."

She groaned as she closed her eyes and tried to think of something, anything that would forestall the roll of the orgasm. She whimpered, the sound a high cry of need she couldn't control.

His thrusts began to increase in intensity and speed. Her head felt like it was about to detonate from the tight rein she held on her climax.

His breathing became ragged. His thrusting rhythm became disjointed as he continued to bury himself inside her.

"I'm so there, Jonathan. Please, let me come."

He opened his eyes and looked down into her face. The love shining in his gaze brought tears to her eyes. She'd never seen something so precious and beautiful in her life.

"Come for me, Mandy. Milk me dry."

Her climax washed over her like waves breaking on the shores, exploding in shards of color so brilliant, she couldn't see beyond the rainbow. She cried out his name as she wrapped her legs around his hips and brought them tighter together.

He shuddered as he came inside her, his own climax enough to cause him to collapse on her chest, his nose buried in her hair. His breath came out in harsh pants, hot against her ear.

She wrapped her arms around his back, holding him close to her heart. He'd earned every piece, heart, body, and soul. There was no way she could deny her feelings for him. He was a part of her now, forever.

$*\ *\ *\ *$

Jonathan peeked into the window of the jewelry shop in downtown San Antonio, checking out the sparkling diamonds in the pretty settings. He had in mind what he wanted for Mandy, but he hadn't been able to find it yet. It needed to be special, like her, but not gaudy. He decided to go inside and see what they might have in the case before he moved onto the next shop.

It had been several weeks now since he'd told her he loved her and she returned his feelings tenfold. They spent many a night making love, talking, laughing, and loving each other beyond anything he'd ever felt, and he knew it was time to make things official. He wanted to ask her to marry him.

Graduation was a week off for her. She would finally have her degree and then she needed to figure out what to do from there. He'd told her if she wanted to move to Houston, he would move with her. He could do the marketing and website remotely for Thunder Ridge if need be. Maybe come back to the ranch once a month or something to catch up on things that needed to be done or to meet with his parents about new items requiring addition to the plan. It would work, he knew it would. It all depended on where she wanted to go to get a job. He'd follow her anywhere, even if it meant leaving Thunder Ridge.

After all, he was an adult and needed to find his own way in life with her by his side.

"May I help you?"

"Yes, sir. I'm looking for an engagement ring for my girlfriend."

"Very good, sir. I have a whole case of settings over here that you might be interested in looking at. Of course, if you would like to design your own, that's an option too. We can set any diamond in whatever you might come up with."

"I hadn't thought of designing my own. Thank you for bringing that up, but I would still like to see what you have."

"Of course." The white haired man moved down to a case to Jonathan's right. "These are the settings we have. Take your time. Look over each one. If there is something you would like to see more closely, let me know."

"Thank you."

The man moved back down to the other cases, shifting things around to show them better to the customers as Jonathan looked over the pieces in the case. There were several he liked, but nothing seemed to be exactly right.

One caught his attention as he leaned closer to see inside the case better. It was a square cut diamond in a simple band with smaller diamonds surrounding it as well as along the band itself. The gold swirled up and around the center diamond, reminding him of something he'd seen in her apartment, a painting of horses running along a stream and the swirl of dandelions as the horses moved past. The white puffs of the flowers were spotted all over the painting making it almost look like snow. "May I see that one?"

"Certainly, sir." The man unlocked the case, brought the ring box out, and handed it to Jonathan. "It's a two carat center diamond with the smaller round cut diamonds on the band. Total weight on the ring itself is three carats. It was a special design for a lady here in town by her fiancé, but they broke up before he gave it to her."

"It's gorgeous."

"It is beautiful, yes, and very special. There isn't another one like it."

"How much?" Jonathan about choked when he was told the total, but after he thought about it for a minute, he knew Mandy was worth every penny. "I'll take it."

"Very good, sir. Do you know your ladies ring size? I can have it sized accordingly and have it ready by Friday."

"I don't at the moment, but give me a minute and I'll find out." He pulled out his cell phone and hit Peyton's number.

"Hey, you."

"Hi, Peyton. Listen, I have a question for you, but you can't let on that you know anything, all right?"

"Sure. What's up?"

"I'm buying Mandy a ring, but I don't know her size. Do you?"

"Yep. I bought her a ring last year for Christmas. She wears a seven."

He smiled and nodded to the gentleman across the counter. "Perfect. Thank you."

"You bet. I hope it's gorgeous. She's a special lady."

"Don't I know it. Thanks again." He hung up his phone, grabbed his wallet, and handed over his credit card. Yes, she was worth every penny and then some.

That evening while he laid in bed holding her to his side as she slept on his chest, he ran his hands down her arm, loving the feel of her skin beneath his fingers. She smelled like flowers and woman, the woman he loved, and he couldn't help the smile that played on his lips. Everything about her fit him so perfectly he was almost scared to wonder what their life would be like together.

She rolled away from him, tucking the pillow under her face. The curve of her bare back was beautiful. He couldn't help but reach out to run his fingers down her spine until he reached the swell of her buttocks. They'd made love already tonight, but he wanted her again. When his hand reached her butt cheek, he smoothed his palm over the surface. She moaned softly in her sleep but didn't awaken.

Her legs were parted slightly, with one knee in front of the other, leaving her pussy open to his touch. He slowly penetrated her pussy with one finger, feeling her wetness on his hand. She widened her legs a little, giving him more access even though her breathing told him she still slept.

Good God, she's wet and ready for me.

He pushed two fingers into her, slowly pumping them in and out, as her hips began to move with his rhythm. He trailed his lips up her back to the nape of her neck, nipping at the skin of her shoulder.

"Are you going to tease me forever or are you going to fuck me?"

He smiled against her skin. "Do you want me to fuck you?"

"Hell yea, you silly man." He pulled his fingers out as she rolled back toward him. "You were giving me a really nice dream, but now that I'm awake, I want the real thing."

"You looked so sexy lying there with your back to me. Your ass is just begging to be fucked."

"Is that a promise?"

"You bet, sweetheart, but I'm going to eat you out first, until you're crying out wanting to come."

"You can be a real bastard, you know that?"

"Yep." He smiled as he settled himself between her thighs, and began a slow, thorough job of bringing her to the brink of insanity. He licked around her clit and then down the slit before he wriggled his tongue inside her pussy as she moaned softly. "You taste good."

"Quit talking and lick me."

"Demanding woman." He laughed a little before he did his best to give her what she wanted without actually giving her an orgasm. He would torture her a little and then give her the pleasure she sought with his cock. She'd climaxed before with him in her ass, but he'd brought a surprise to the table tonight she hadn't seen yet. A nice little clit bullet waited in the bedside table, for just this moment.

When she was to the point her hips, legs, and abdomen quivered with the need to come, he sat up, rolled her over, and grabbed the bullet vibrator as well as the lube from the nightstand drawer. He dribbled the slick, wet substance down the crack of her ass, slicking her and himself up so it wouldn't be uncomfortable for her. "I have a surprise for you."

"Oh?"

"Yep. Here." He flipped on the vibrator and handed it to her. "Put it on your clit."

She reached between her legs, placing it right on her clit. "Oh fuck."

"Nice, eh?"

"Holy hell, that's good."

He pushed the head of his cock through the tight muscles of her ass, shuddering at the sensations bombarding him from all sides. The slick channel hugged him like a glove on a cold winter day, making it almost impossible for him not to push farther faster. He could feel the vibrator as he slowly pushed deeper. The vibrations zipped along his cock, before settling in his balls, and then sizzling along his spine. He knew he wouldn't last long at this rate, but the sounds she was making below him told him she wouldn't last long either.

"Oh God, oh God, oh God."

She spread her thighs farther apart, taking him even deeper.

"I can't hold on."

"I'm right there. Push harder. Faster. I'll go off like a rocket."

He picked up his pace, fucking her with increasing speed and thrust. The bed bounced hard against the wall as they fucked like bunnies.

Snap!

"What the hell?"

A burse of laughter echoed in the small room as the bed frame split, sending them crashing down onto the floor, him still buried in her ass. "Shit. We broke the bed."

He couldn't help himself from joining her as they laughed so loud, Joey banged on the wall beside them.

"You two want to keep in down in there? Good God!"

They continued to laugh until he sobered enough to remove his now soft cock from her backside. He walked into the bathroom, coming back with a warm washcloth to clean her up.

She hadn't moved, but continued to giggle as she buried her face in the pillow.

He wiped her pussy and ass free of the lube, before tossing the wet cloth onto the dresser.

"I guess I can truly say you are the man for me. You broke a bed for me."

With a shake of his head, rolled her over, and helped her get to her feet. "Where are we going to sleep now?"

"My place, I guess."

"We need to talk about that."

"Talk about what?"

"Where you are going to live. Of course, now that you've broken my bed, we will have to sleep on yours until we can get another one, a nice one, a bigger one."

"I don't care where we sleep, as long as you are beside me."

"Good answer." He kissed her nose. "I love you, Mandy."

"I love you too."

He pulled on his jeans and then slipped on a t-shirt as she gathered up her clothes and began to put them on. "Are you hungry?"

"Yeah, a little."

"How about we go into town and grab a burger?"

"Sounds good."

A few minutes later, they were bouncing along the dirt road toward the gate of Thunder Ridge. Miller's Burger Shack in Bandera was the perfect place to get a burger this late at night. The bar crowd and the high school kids usually hung out there every weekend, but since it was Tuesday, there shouldn't be too many people around.

When they pulled up in front of the place, Mandy sighed. "I love this place."

"Me too. I used to hang out here a lot after school."

She smiled and winked. "Did you buy some pretty girl milkshakes?"

He brought her hand to his mouth, kissing her fingers one by one until she was breathless. "Nope. The woman I wanted wasn't here yet."

"You are such a gentleman."

"I try."

They climbed out of the truck, meeting in the front as they clasped hands and headed for the door. He loved the thought of being with her forever. She was the perfect fit to his other half.

After they went through the door, she stopped dead in her tracks, her face sheet white.

"Mandy?"

"It's him."

Chapter Thirteen

"Who?"

She shivered as she tried to get closer to Jonathan. *How did he find me?* "The man who raped me."

"Are you sure?" Jonathan asked, as he wrapped his arm around her and pulled her closer to his side.

"I'll never forget his face, Jonathan, or his voice telling me he wouldn't hurt me and it would be okay for him to touch me."

"Do you want to leave?"

She closed her eyes and tried to focus. The man had no control over her anymore and it was time for her to face her fear of him. She wasn't the one at fault for what he'd done, he was. She had been a child, a young girl coming into her own, when he'd stolen her innocence away from her. "No." She pulled in a deep breath and opened her eyes. Brandon sat across the booth from him. "I'm not going to let him hurt me anymore."

"Good girl."

They walked forward, moving past the booth where they sat, so they could take a seat farther down. She could feel his gaze on her, but she refused to acknowledge his existence. He was nothing to her.

"Mandy?" Brandon called to her as they sat down. "Hey."

"Hi, Brandon."

"Uh, it's nice to see you. Do you live here in Bandera?"

"Yes."

Brandon turned toward his father. "Dad, I want you to meet Mandy. She's in one of my classes at the college."

The cold gray eyes of her rapist met hers from across the room. "Nice to meet you, Mandy."

So, he's going to play it like that, is he? Well, fuck you! I refuse to let you be in control of this. "Matt."

Brandon looked confused as his gaze went back and forth between her and his father. "Do you two know each other?"

"You could say that," she replied, taking Jonathan's hand in her own for strength. She needed his presence to keep her centered. "My mother is married to his brother."

"He's your uncle by marriage? Really. Wow. I never knew that." Brandon turned toward his father. "Uncle Roland is her stepfather?"

"Yes."

"Apparently, he didn't share a lot of things with you, Brandon." She laughed a dry, brittle sound. "He used to spend Christmases with us."

"That must have been when I was living with mom."

The man never took his gaze off her. Her skin crawled with revulsion. "I imagine so, Brandon." She wanted to shout to the heavens about how he'd forced himself on her and raped her in her own bedroom, but for some reason she kept quiet. Maybe she wanted him to acknowledge what he'd done to her, but she figured he never would. As far as he was concerned, he hadn't done anything wrong.

Matt lowered his gaze to the table, leaving her curious and apprehensive.

"I'm sorry, Mandy."

Her heart stopped beating. He hadn't just apologized, had he? No, it was a trick, an illusion. He wasn't sorry. He was repentant. He was the bastard who had taken everything from her and left her a hollow and broken person, someone who'd turned to drugs and prostitution to make herself feel like someone cared. Should she acknowledge his apology?

She looked at Jonathan.

Understanding swam in his gaze as he nodded without saying a word. He was leaving it up to her to decide what she should do, but he would support her in whatever that decision might be. She swallowed hard, the accusations hanging on the tip of her tongue.

When she glanced back at Matt, she saw something different. He was old and harried. Maybe what he'd done played hard on his soul. She hoped so, but she had to come to terms with either pressing charges against him for something that happened ten years ago or moving on with her life. Her life needed to revolve around finding her daughter, living with the man who had her heart in the palm of his hands, and who would keep her safe and love her no matter what.

"Jonathan, let's go."

"Are you sure, darlin'?"

"Yeah. I'm suddenly hungry for Mexican food rather than a burger."

"Whatever you want, honey."

They scooted out of the booth, leaving the two men to watch them leave never knowing how hard it was for her to walk away from her past and move on with her future.

When they reached the side of his truck on the passenger side, Jonathan leaned down and kissed her soundly on the mouth. "You did well, Mandy. I hope you know I will support you no matter what you decide to do. Personally, I would kick the man's ass for you, but it's your decision on how to handle things."

"I know, and I love you all the more for it. You're my rock, baby, and I will love you forever."

He helped her up inside the truck, buckled her seatbelt for her, and then shut the door behind him. Stopping in front of the vehicle, he turned toward where the two men were still watching through the windows. She saw him turn his right hip toward them, making sure they were aware of the pistol he carried in the holster. Matt went pale before turning back toward his son.

Jonathan went around to the driver's side, opened the door, and hopped in.

Once he'd started the truck, she took his hand in hers, lacing their fingers together before she brought it to her lips and kissed him on the back of the hand. "I love you."

He smiled at her before he checked around the truck and then backed out of the spot.

After they were seated at the Mexican restaurant, he asked, "Are you okay?"

"Yeah. Actually, I'm better than I've ever been. I have some closure now, and I'm ready to move on with my life. The situation is in my past, and I refuse to let it control me anymore."

"You probably should still get some counseling."

"I know and I will. I'll ask Peyton who she trusts and recommends." She brought their hands together on the tabletop. "I want you to know though that it's over. I'm a better person now, and I'm ready to make my life with you."

"I'm ready for us to build a life together."

"Me too."

He kissed her fingers as the waitress brought their menus. "What can I get you two to drink?"

"Coke for me."

"Me too."

"Coming right up."

When he finally let go of her hands, she opened her menu to decide what she wanted to eat. Enchiladas sounded really good, she decided, realizing her shoulders felt lighter now that she'd gotten rid of the weight she'd been carrying for such a long time. "Will you help me find my daughter?"

"Of course, honey. I know how important that is for you, but be prepared, she may not want anything to do with you."

"I know and that's something I'll have to deal with, but I want to tell her that I didn't give her up because I wanted to, I was forced to, and she's a part of me even if she chooses not to be a part of my life."

"We will start first thing in the morning. It might take a while to find her."

"It's okay. However long it takes."

"You should make a list of everything you know. Who the agency was you went through, her birthdate, what hospital she was born in, the doctor who delivered her, and so on. The more information you have, the easier it will be to get answers."

She smiled across the table at the man she loved. Leave it to him to prioritize everything so quickly and efficiently. They would find her. She just knew they would.

Epilogue

Mandy vibrated with excitement as they stood near the park bench at Concepcion Park. Jonathan stood next to her with his arm around her shoulders, holding her in one spot so she wouldn't float away on the cloud of happiness surrounding her.

She glanced down at the ring on her left hand sparkling in the summer sunshine. He'd given it to her the week after they had run into her rapist at the burger shop in Bandera, when he'd asked her to marry him. The wedding was planned for the fall at Thunder Ridge.

Today, she stood waiting for her daughter to arrive at the park so she could see her for the first time.

Miraculously enough, they had managed to track her down to where she lived with her parents in Houston, within two months of starting their search.

Thank God, for social media.

Mandy had contacted the attorney who'd worked with her parents on the adoption. He said he couldn't help her without contacting the parents who had adopted her daughter to make sure it was okay with them that he put her in touch with them. Luckily for her, they had agreed. The attorney had given Mandy their name and address, telling her they wanted her to write to them first before they agreed to tell her daughter about her.

Their first priority was the girl.

Mandy agreed. She didn't want to do anything that would hurt her daughter in any shape or form. If it was better for the girl to not know her, then so be it.

When the return letter had come back to her, she'd stared at it for two hours before she'd allowed herself to open it. Jonathan had been by her side, a rock in the storm of her life, while she fought with herself over whether this was the right thing to do.

After she'd finally tore it open and began to read, tears streamed down her face when she looked up and caught Jonathan's loving gaze with hers. "She wants to meet me."

"That's fantastic, darlin'."

She dropped the letter on the table and shook so hard, he had to take her in his arms to calm her down. "She wants to meet me, Jonathan. Oh my God! What will I say to her?"

"Tell her the truth, honey. You were only fifteen at the time and your parents didn't give you a choice."

"I know, but I'm afraid she'll hate me."

"I doubt she hates you, baby. She's coming from Houston to meet you. Are her parents coming too?"

"Yes. I think so."

Now, she stood here waiting with bated breath.

A black Chevrolet Capri pulled up to the curb near where they stood. No one moved.

Finally, the door opened and a beautiful young woman with bright red hair stepped out of the passenger side of the car, followed shortly by a nice looking man out of the driver's side. "Mandy?"

"Yes, ma'am."

"I'm Patricia Moore. This is my husband, Greg."

"It's nice to meet you."

"Gabrielle is in the car. I told her to get out when she was ready."

"I appreciate you bringing her here."

"We were surprised by your correspondence with the attorney. We were not aware of the circumstances of her adoption until now. I'm very sorry about how things happened."

"It's okay. It wasn't your fault in any way. You wanted a child."

"Yes, we did, so very much, and she's been the bright spot in our lives for ten years."

Mandy held her breath as the door of the car slowly opened. A young girl with bright blonde hair stepped out, shutting the door behind her, before she slowly moved to her mother's side. At first she didn't even meet Mandy's gaze, but as she raised her head and looked at Mandy, Mandy's heart stopped in her chest. The same exact blue eyes that stared back at her in the mirror every day were gracing her daughter's face.

"Hi." Mandy stepped forward, but the little girl stepped back. "It's okay. I know you don't know me. My name is Mandy."

The little girl peeked around her mother's back, taking a long look at her before her gaze ricocheted to Jonathan. Mandy knew he could be intimidating with his size. "That's my fiancé. He won't hurt you, baby. His name is Jonathan."

"Are you really my mother?"

"I gave birth to you, yes, but Patricia is your mother. She's been with you since you were born."

Gabrielle's brows crinkled as she looked up at Patricia and then back at Mandy. "I don't understand."

"It's hard to explain, sweetie." Mandy held out her hand. "Can we sit down for a minute so I can explain?"

Gabrielle moved around Patricia and walked toward her although she didn't take Mandy's hand. She took a seat on the bench, her feet swinging back and forth.

"You see, when I had you in my stomach, I was only fifteen, and I couldn't take care of you like you deserved to be taken care of." Mandy wasn't about to go into the circumstances of how she got pregnant or why her parents made her give the little girl up, but she did want to explain as best she could. "Patricia and Greg wanted a child. When you were born, I let them take you so you could have a wonderful life with loving parents, a beautiful home, and be loved."

"Didn't you love me?"

"Oh, honey, more than anything in the world, but since I was so young myself, I couldn't take care of you even though I loved you so much, it made my heart hurt to let you go."

"Do you have other kids?"

"No."

"Why not?"

"Unfortunately, sweetie, I can't have any more babies."

Her face scrunched up as she looked at Mandy. "What do you want from me?"

"I just wanted to know you are happy and healthy. I wanted you to know I loved you then and I love you now, but I know you have your own life and I won't try to stick my nose into it. I will leave you alone now, but if you ever decide you want to be a part of my life, you are more than welcome to." Mandy turned toward Jonathan, taking his hand in her own as she smiled up into his gorgeous face. "Let's go home."

As she took a couple of steps away from the little girl she might not ever know, she heard a small little voice behind her say, "Can I call you and talk to you whenever I want?"

Mandy turned back toward Gabrielle. "Honey, you can call me anytime. I would love to hear about school, your friends, and what you've been doing. I promise, I'm not trying to take your mom's place. I just want to get to know you."

Gabrielle stepped forward and wrapped her arms around Mandy's waist.

Tears blurred her vision as she hugged her daughter closer and whispered a quick thank you to God for bringing her little girl to her.

When she glanced at Jonathan, she could have sworn there were tears in his eyes too as he kissed her on the forehead. "I love you."

"I love you too," she whispered back.

Her life was now complete. She would get to know her daughter, marry the man of her dreams in a few short months, and together they would live happily ever after, just like in the storybooks.

The End

A COWBOY'S PROMISE
Cowboy Dreamin' 9

Sandy Sullivan

Chapter One

"I'm gonna shoot your ass, Joseph Young! Don't you come around Jessie no more! You hear me."

Joey ran across the field toward his truck in his bare feet, hopping every couple of steps when he stepped on a rock. *Damn it!* His shirt hung down his back, covering the top of his naked ass as his belt buckle clinked every few steps. He carried his boots and his cowboy hat in one hand while he tried to get in his pants pocket for his keys with the other.

Ping. Ping.

Buckshot hit the back of his tailgate. "Crazy fuckin' old man."

Ping. Ping.

"I'm leavin', damn it! Quit shootin' at me!"

"Get your ass off my property. If you show up here again, this won't be buckshot, boy."

"Stop it, Daddy!" Jessica Marshall yelled from the front porch.

"Get back in the house, Jessica."

"Joey? Are you all right?"

He could see her standing in her bare feet, jeans, and a tank top.

Boy, she'd dressed fast after her father caught them in her room in a state of semi-undress. "I'm fine. Go on in the house, Jess. I'll see you later."

"No you won't!"

Ping. Ping.

"Daddy, quit shooting at him."

"I'll teach his ass to come sniffing around my baby girl."

"I'm a grown woman. Stop acting like a fool."

"You're still my baby. You won't be hookin' up with one of them Young boys. They're all just lookin' to get in bed with a young lady like you, Jess. Think about it."

"I have, Daddy. This is crazy. Joey isn't like that."

"I know boys. They're all the same."

Ping. Ping.

He ducked as he reached the side of his truck, fumbling with the latch on the door. *Duh, locked.* Once he finally got his keys in his hands, he unlocked the door, and tossed the things he had in his hand inside the cab.

He had to admit, the one thing he wanted from her was her body when this whole thing started, but he'd thought about her a lot lately and he really liked Jessica. Her daddy was probably right though. He didn't have a lot to offer a woman. He worked on his parent's ranch with the horses, caring for them, breaking them and occasionally riding a few bucking broncs when there was a rodeo close enough to San Antonio.

A drink sounded good right about now after the evening had left him with blue balls. Maybe he'd head home to see if one of his brothers would go into town to The Dusty Boot for a beer. It was early, right?

Every one of his brothers now had a woman of their own. He wouldn't be finding any of them ready to go out for the night. It sucked being the baby of the family even at his age.

That didn't make him too old for Jessica, right? Twenty-two to thirty-one wasn't a bad spread even if he'd had an eye on her since she was sixteen. She was legal and he aimed to take advantage of the fact even if her daddy didn't like him much.

He drove up to the gates of Thunder Ridge, punching in the code to open the gates. It appeared the group was having a bonfire outside the main lodge of the guest ranch he helped run with his family—all nine, plus these days eight of his brothers had found either wives or girlfriends in the last couple of years.

As for himself, he wasn't ready to settle down. Not yet. Not him. All of his older brothers had, but he was having too much fun being the bachelor he was.

Once he drove up to the house, he shut off his truck and wiggled around so he could make himself presentable. Luckily, it wasn't far from Jessica's to his parent's place, but he still drove without his boots so now he had to put them back on his feet.

Tap, tap, tap. He jerked his head around to find his mother standing next to the truck, staring hard at him through the window.

"What are you up to, young man?" his mother asked with a raised eyebrow. Even in her mid-sixties, she was a beautiful woman with her long dark hair pulled back in a braid down her back, straw cowboy hat adorning her head, and her brown eyes sparkling in mischief.

"Nothing, Mom."

"Why are you getting dressed in your truck? Were you over bugging Jessica again?"

"I was at her place, yeah."

"It appears her daddy didn't like you sniffin' around his daughter. Your truck is full of dings."

"I know," he said, pushing open the door. He'd have to check his truck when he could see better. "Where is everyone?" With a slam, he shut the door so he could face his mother.

She pointed behind her. "Down by the bonfire. Most of them are enjoying a nice evening with the guests."

"Are you loosening up your 'no messin' with the guests' policy, because I'm sure I could find me a pretty lady down there."

Her hands on her hips stance made him feel like a kid again, like when he'd got into trouble and got grounded for it.

"No, but I can't very well enforce it when you don't seem to care what I say about it."

He shoved his hands in his pockets as he rocked back on the heels of his boots. "I care, Mom. It's just when the women come onto me, it's real hard to resist."

"I'm sure it is." She tapped the brim of his cowboy hat. "Go on."

"Thanks. I'm gonna see if any of them will go into town with me and shoot some pool or somethin'. It's too early to turn in."

"One of them might. Take Chris, that young wrangler we just hired." She leaned in on her tiptoes to kiss his cheek. Even though she wasn't short, by any means, all of the boys towered over her by several inches. "You boys be careful."

"We will."

He finished tucking in his shirt as he approached the fire where several guests sat around talking to each other, while his brothers chimed in every once in a while with a remark. Chris sat on one of the benches between two pretty girls he'd seen check-in the day before. Joey rolled his eyes. "Chris!"

"What?" the new kid yelled back without taking his gaze off the pretty brunette next to him.

"Let's go to town."

"Why?"

"I need a drink," Joey said, stopping directly in front of Chris and the two women.

"Take one of your brothers. I'm off work."

"No, you. Come on."

Chris's gaze shifted to land on him. "Fine." He stood, bowing to the two women. "I'll see you ladies tomorrow on the ride at nine in the mornin'."

"We can't wait." The blonde grinned a nice pearly white smile. "Have fun."

"Oh, we will." Joey grabbed his arm. "I'll drive."

As they headed back to his truck, Chris said, "We could have taken them with us, you know."

"They're guests. You know my mom's rule about messin' with the guests."

"Yeah, but it's not like I'm going to sleep with either of them. I was talking to them, that's all." Chris popped open the passenger side door and slid inside. "I thought you were over at Jessica Marshall's house?"

"I was until her daddy caught us."

"Well that blows."

"Yeah." Joey started the truck and backed out of the spot before he headed down the long driveway back toward the front gates of the guest ranch. The wrought iron blocking the road coming onto the ranch slid open to allow them to drive out.

"What are you gonna do now?"

"I don't know. I like her, but a piece of ass ain't worth gettin' shot at."

"He shot at you?"

"With buckshot, yeah. Good thing he didn't hit me, but I'm sure my truck looks like shit now."

"You need to find a girl who will be an occasional roll between the sheets. You're too young to worry about settlin' down."

"Who said anything about settlin' down? All I wanted from her was a good lay." He pushed his hat back on his head. "I don't know. There's somethin' about her. I mean she pretty, got a nice rack, kisses like she ain't no virgin, yet when we were together tonight, she seemed shy. Like she didn't know the first thing about havin' sex."

"She's barely twenty-two, man. Find yourself a lady who knows how to treat a man."

"I guess."

"Trust me, bro. I bet you can find some pretty thing at the bar."

"I certainly have a case of blue balls right now."

"Been that long?"

"A few months, yeah." He glanced over at his friend and then back to the road. "What about you?"

"I could get laid. It's been a while for me too." Chris tapped his fingers on his thigh for a moment. "There are some pretty women at the bar, but maybe it's not such a good idea to hook up with one for one night."

"Yet you want me to?" Joey asked as they drove down the main street of Bandera.

The Dusty Boot sat to the right of the street with several trucks in various makes and models, in their parking lot. The sign above the western motif of the building depicted a boot with a spur dangling from the back. It was the Young brothers' home away from home on any given night of the week. The place looked busy for a Tuesday night. *Good. I need to unwind.*

"Sure. It's right up your alley, Joey. Find some hot babe, get your rocks off, and then worry about your future."

Once he found a parking spot next to the dumpster, they both crawled out of his truck, slamming the doors with a bang.

Music from the bar flowed through the doors as people moved in and out. Joey really liked the band they had here. They were pretty talented. They'd even played a barbeque Paige's family had put on at their church a couple of years ago.

Summer tourist season was upon them now, which made the ranch busier than ever. More and more people came to their ranch every summer and this one was no exception. His mother said the other day, they were booked solid for this month, with a waiting list for some weekends. Not that he minded. The business of keeping the horses everyday made for a demanding job since he was in charge of the animals—breaking, feeding, trail rides and the like. There was also a rodeo this weekend in San Antonio he wanted to do. He got his adrenaline rush from riding bucking horses. He didn't do too bad at it either.

Chris slapped him on the back as they walk through the double doors of the building. *Man, the place is crowded tonight.* He glanced around for a place to sit, noting two stools at the far end of the bar. "Let's go."

His friend brought up the rear as they made their way through the crowd hoping the stools would be there when they finally finished bobbing and weaving amongst the tight pack of bodies. Rhinestones and tight jeans in the sea of cowboy hats seemed to be the flavor of the evening. He knew it had been a good idea to come here.

They got to the two seats, taking the ones at the end of the bar. Lily Richards was serving this end of the group. He really did think she was kind of pretty with her black hair brushing the edge of her waist as the thick braid fell down her back. Unfortunately, for him, she wasn't his type. He wasn't into the kind of woman who tended bar. Give him a nice little cowgirl and he'd be happy as a pig in shit.

"Whatcha drinkin', boys?" Lily asked stopping in front of them.

"Couple of beers, please," Chris answered. "How's it hanging, Lily?"

"Just fine, Chris. Busier than a bull during matin' season here tonight, but then again, it's always busy here during the summer." She poured two beers and set them down in front of them. "You boys hanging out tonight?"

"Yeah. Joey got his ass shot at by old man Marshall so we're hookin' him up."

"Shut up, Chris."

Lily laughed. "Why am I not surprised by that statement?" She tapped the bar with her knuckle. "I'll check on you two in a bit. If you need another, holler."

Joey turned on the stool to take in the crowd around them. He recognized several women in a group near the back. A few he'd even been with. One waved. He tipped his hat. She excused herself from the group to head in their direction. "Ah, shit."

"What?" Chris asked as he spun around.

"She's comin' over here."

Chris laughed. "You asked for it, I'm sure."

"I was bein' friendly."

"A little too friendly."

"Hi, Joey."

"Jennifer."

"You here alone?" she asked, looking from side to side.

"No. I'm here with Chris."

"You know what I mean. You gotta a girl with you?" She stepped close enough to brush her thigh against his knee.

"Nope."

Chris elbowed him.

"I mean yeah." He noticed a pretty little thing nursing a glass of wine next to him. "I'm with her."

Joey placed his hand on the woman's shoulder. When she looked up at him, he was startled to realize he knew her from somewhere, although he couldn't place her at the moment. "Hey, babe. Do you need another glass of wine?"

"Uh, no."

"How about a dance?"

"Uh, no. I'm here to unwind, nothing more."

He turned his stool to face her. "Since we came together, I figure we should dance or something."

The woman glanced over his shoulder at Jennifer, and then met his gaze again. He tried communicating to her what he wanted. Her eyes widened when he shifted his gaze from her to Jennifer and back.

"Oh, of course. Let me finish my glass and we'll dance."

"Sure, honey."

He swung back toward Jennifer for a moment. Her eyes had become slits of indignation before she turned on her heels and stomped back toward the group at the back table. When he faced the woman sitting next to him at the bar again, he said, "Thank you for going along with me."

She took a sip of her drink. "Not someone you wanted to hang with tonight?"

"Not really. I dated her several months ago and she got real possessive."

"Ah."

He held out his hand for her to shake. "My name is Joseph Young."

"Nice to meet you, Joseph. I'm Clarissa."

"I am assuming you are here alone?"

"Yes, but as I said, I'm only here to unwind from work before I go home—alone."

He nodded and smiled. "I understand. So what do you do, Clarissa, that you need to unwind from?"

"I'm a trauma nurse."

"Wow. That must be really hard."

"It is. Some days it's very rewarding, but other days, it's very difficult to separate yourself from all the hurt, death, and crap that people do to themselves and to others." She took another sip of her wine and placed the glass back on the bar. "Tonight, I need the noisy atmosphere of this bar to take my mind off of what I saw today."

"I'm sorry to hear that."

She shrugged as she flashed him a little smile. "It's okay." She looked across the bar, and then back at him. "What are you drinking?"

"Just beer."

"Cowboy's choice of beverages, huh?"

"Yeah." He smiled as he reached out and touched her bare arm. "It's a guy thing."

She glanced down to where he touched her and then back up at him. "Sorry, Joey, but I'm not looking for a hook up. I have a boyfriend."

He removed his hand as he nodded in understanding. "Hands off. Got it."

"I don't mind sitting here shooting the shit with you though, that is unless you were really here to pick someone up for the night."

"Not really." He looked over her shoulder for a second. "Well, yeah, kind of. I had a problem with an old man, a shot gun, and his twenty-two-year-old daughter earlier. I've got a good case of blue balls, right now."

She tossed back her head and laughed. The sound was cute. A little snort and a giggle was the only way he could describe it. "Poor baby."

"I know. It's terrible, right?"

"Yes, yes it is, but I'm sure you will survive."

"I don't know. There's this nurse I know, who kind of put me off. She wouldn't treat my injury."

A grin played on her lips as she shook her head. "This nurse knows you won't die from a case of blue balls."

"I don't know. It's awful painful."

"I'm sure it is."

He took a drag off his beer, swallowing the malty liquid in a cool wash of goodness running down his throat. Yeah, beer was definitely a guy thing, although he knew lots of women who drank beer. "So, are you from around here?"

"Not really. I moved to the area a few years back."

"Do you live in Bandera?"

"Yeah. I work in San Antonio at one of the hospitals, but I rent a small house here. I like the quiet. San Antonio is very noisy. I do the craziness at the hospital. This gives me the quiet to contemplate things." She brought her glass of wine to her lips to take a long drink. "What about you?"

"My family owns a guest ranch a few miles outside of town. I help run things there with my eight brothers and their wives."

"Eight brothers? Holy shit. Your mom must have been one busy woman."

"Yes, she was and still is. It's great to have a big family."

"Where are you in the pecking order?"

"The youngest."

She tilted her head to the side and smiled. "Ah, the baby of the family."

One shoulder lifted in a shrug. "I guess."

"What do you do on the ranch?"

"I'm the head wrangler. I handle the horses for the guests to ride, break new ones we buy, and that kind of thing."

"A real cowboy then."

"As real as they come."

She glanced down to the floor. "So those dusty boots are for real."

"Yep."

"Nice."

"Where is your family?"

"Back east. Philadelphia to be exact."

"You moved here from Pennsylvania?"

"Yes. I like Texas. I love the weather and I love the animals. There just wasn't enough space for me back East. I needed room to stretch out."

"Texas has that for sure."

Her glass sat empty on the bar. "Do you want another? I'm buying since you saved me."

"No, thank you. I really need to get home. My boyfriend will be wondering where I am since it's going on ten now and I'm usually home by eight-thirty. I'm surprised he hasn't called my cell yet."

"He sounds kind of possessive."

"Sometimes, yes, but only in the best way." She gave him a wink and got to her feet.

"Thank you for the chat, Joseph. You seem like a really nice guy. I hope you have some luck tonight and manage to take care of your problem."

"Thank you for helping me out, Clarissa. I hope to see you again soon."

"See you around."

He tipped his hat as she moved around him and headed for the door.

The rest of the night he managed to keep himself away from the overzealous women of Bandera. He probably shouldn't have since the point to being here was to get laid, but after talking with Clarissa, he realized not everything came down to getting your rocks off. Chris managed to find a woman and disappeared right before closing time. He figured his friend and fellow ranch worker could find his own way home.

Joey crawled into his truck about two a.m., turned the key and headed back for Thunder Ridge.

Friday night had been a bust for him all the way around. Nothing seemed to have worked in his favor, not Jessica, and certainly not Clarissa. Oh well. It wasn't like he hadn't been in this situation before or wouldn't be in it again before his bachelor days were through.

Tomorrow would come with the rising of the sun. Work would be his top priority since he needed to get to the feed store by the end of the day to get some supplies for the horses. They'd run low on grain this week and he figured he'd hit Milligan's after the rush in the afternoon. Most local ranchers did their shopping first thing in the morning. His parents wouldn't mind if he slept in a little since he didn't have first ride outs and that little buckskin mare he'd purchased last weekend needed to be worked.

Headlights came at him from the direction of home. He wondered who in the hell was out headed for town at this time of the night. Probably one of his brothers on a middle of the night pregnancy craving run. Callie and Candace were both expecting in the coming months. That's one thing he wasn't looking forward to once he did decide to settle down with one girl, the craziness of having kids. He liked kids, sure, but they were a lot of work, and he just didn't have that itch right now.

The vehicle slowed as they met in the roadway.

When the driver's side window went down, he wasn't surprised to see Jeremiah at the wheel.

"Headed out for a midnight snack?"

Jeremiah rolled his eyes. "Yeah. Callie woke up with a craving for moose tracks ice cream. We don't have any at the house so I'm headed into town to see if the local corner market is open and has some, otherwise, I'll be driving into San Antonio."

"That sucks."

"Oh well. It's my life for the moment. She won't be pregnant forever, thank goodness." He tipped his chin like guys always do. "Coming back from The Dusty Boot?"

"Yep."

"Alone?"

"Yep."

"Rough night?"

"Yep."

"You are full of answers tonight."

"Nothing to tell."

"I heard you got shot at my Jessica Marshall's old man earlier."

"Mom has a big mouth."

"Get caught with your pants down?"

He shook his head and smiled a little. "You could say that."

"You really need to stay away from that girl. Her dad is crazy."

"Don't I know it."

Jeremiah's cell phone jingled. "I better go. I'll see you tomorrow."

"I'll be around."

"Be careful, there were several deer on the side of the road up ahead."

"Thanks."

"Later." He heard Jeremiah pick up the call just as he was driving away. "Yes, baby. I'll be home as soon as I can. I might have to go into San Antonio."

Joey laughed at how pussy-whipped his brother was by his wife. Callie was a sweet girl most of the time, but since getting pregnant she was growly and grumpy. Luckily for all of them, she only had six more months to go.

As he pulled up to the gate and punched in the numbers to open it, he looked out over the land they all shared. Each of the boys was given a lot of land on the home place, for their own, when they'd turned eighteen. He hadn't done much with his spot yet since he worked so close to the main lodge most days. But he had his own cabin near the back of the main compound. It was cozy, warm, and all his. He didn't have to put up with shit from his family for coming and going at all hours of the night. He especially liked it that way.

His other home away from home was a small office off the back of the barn. He used it for keeping track of the horses—their bloodlines, where they were in their training, the cost to purchase and price sold if they ever got rid of one. Of course, he also had to put up with his brothers using the barn for their little getaway place from time to time. Their old barn had seen its share of raunchy sex.

Moonlight lit the way to the barn as he parked his truck and got out. Leaves rustled overhead in the evening breeze. He really did love the old place. It had such character. The big main lodge housed several rooms they rented out to guests, but it was also where his parents had their rooms. Two of his brothers had once had rooms upstairs, but now that they were married, they'd built their own homes on their piece of land. None of them lived near the main lodge anymore. It made it kind of lonely actually, but quiet and peaceful too.

When he started walking down the path from the parking lot to the barn, he felt eyes on him. It was a strange feeling, but not unusual around there since they did have some resident ghosts on the place.

The barn loomed in the darkness ahead of him. Someone had left the main lights on in the building, illuminating the dirt path that led to the tack room and his apartment. A horse stomped its foot. *Bang. Bang. Bang.* One the horses were apparently disgruntled with being inside on such a pretty night. He smiled. Most people would have attributed that to the ghosts. He knew it was one of the animals kicking at their stall.

He opened the door to his office, flipped on the lights, and then turned off the lights to the barn, plunging the place into darkness before he shut the door to his place.

He had a little work to do on the files before he called it a night. One of the mares was getting ready to foal and he wanted to make sure his paperwork on her was up-to-date, but he also had a new animal he was getting ready to break in the next few days. *My exciting life.* He chuckled as he sat down in his office chair and flipped on the computer.

"Settle down, hell. I'm too young. I don't need a wife and a bunch of kids yet."

He glanced at the ceiling and prayed God wasn't laughing at him. The old adage was tell God about your plans and watch what happens when he laughs. God has his own plans for your future and it usually didn't look anything like what you had in mind.

Chapter Two

The afternoon heat left Joey breathless as he drove down the road toward town. The air conditioning in his truck didn't work at the moment, and he was about to die from the ninety plus heat index. Normal temperatures for this area were ninety or better, so he should be thankful it wasn't hotter today. The run to the feed store had to be done, but he wished now he would have done it in the cooler morning temps. He would survive though. The pool at the ranch sounded really good right about now.

He rounded the corner on the road only to be met with a nasty scene. A motorcyclist had hit a deer, unusual in itself because deer didn't usually move around much in the heat of the afternoon.

He parked his truck on the side of the road and got out. Obviously, the accident had happened in the last few moments because no one else was anywhere close. The motorcycle was torn into several pieces as he stopped near the shattered bike. He glanced left and then right, looking for the rider and/or anybody else who might have been on the bike with the rider. The deer lay twitching on the side of the road. He took out the pistol on his waist and shot the deer in the head. No use making the animal suffer.

"Help. God, please help me."

Joey ran several yards up the road and across the ditch on the side to find a man with his helmet off, bleeding from a gash in his head. His right leg was turned at an odd angle.

"Are you hurt badly?"

"Fuck. I don't know. I can't move my leg."

Joey heard another car coming up the road. "Hang tight. I hear another car. I'll call for emergency and we will see what we can do until they get here. Don't move."

"Hurry."

Joey sprinted back toward the road and noticed a blue four door sedan slowing down. He moved toward the car to see if the person had an emergency kit. He'd taken his out the other day and had forgotten to replace it.

He knocked on the window and was shocked when the driver rolled it down. "Clarissa?"

"Joseph. What's going on?" she asked, opening her door. "What can I do to help?"

"Do you have a blanket or something? A motorcyclist hit a deer. He's pretty messed up over there on the ground. He's bleeding badly from his head and his leg looks like it might be broken."

"I'll grab my stuff from the trunk and see to him. You call 911 and get an ambulance out here."

"Right." Joey grabbed his cell phone from his belt holder and dialed emergency assistance. He told them all he could about the condition of the guy and what had happened, which wasn't much, but as least they were on the way. He headed back to where he'd left the guy only to find Clarissa holding pressure on a wound inside his shirt. "Emergency is on the way. Should be here within a couple of minutes." Blood coated her hands. "Is he going to be okay?"

"I don't know. He's got a bad head wound, a broken leg more than likely, and an abdominal wound that's open and bleeding. It's the worst of his injuries, so I'm holding pressure on it as best as I can."

"I'm glad you came by."

"Me too. I hope he makes it." She glanced down. "He's unconscious now. He's lost a lot of blood."

"They'll fly him out if they need to."

"They probably will have to. He's hurt pretty badly." Clarissa pushed her hair back with her shoulder.

Within a few short minutes, he could hear sirens wailing as they came up the road. "I'll go flag them down and direct them."

"Good idea."

He jumped over the ditch and stopped at the edge of the gravel, waving his hands in the air. A firetruck and ambulance came to a screeching halt, spraying gravel around them as they stopped.

"Where is the patient?"

"Over there in the pasture. You'll have to go through the fencing. It's barbed wire."

"Got it."

"There is a trauma nurse with him. She was on the road and stopped."

"Thank you."

"You're welcome." Joey stood back as he watched the paramedics and fireman go across the ditch, work their way through the fencing, and disappear over the rise where the guy was laying. He hoped the guy was okay. He didn't like seeing anyone hurt like that. Unfortunately, it was a concern out here on the back roads, especially for a motorcyclist.

It wasn't too long before they came dragging the guy out, strapped to the stretcher with something holding his head in place, one paramedic holding pressure on the guys belly, and Clarissa bringing up the rear. Her clothes had dirt streaks on the thighs of her jeans, her hair had come out of the ponytail she had at the back of her head, and her blouse had a tear in it from where she must have snagged it on the fence when she went through.

As they loaded the guy into the ambulance, Clarissa moved to his side, removed the gloves she'd put on her hands, and tossed them into the truck of her car. "Not the way I wanted to spend my day off."

"I bet."

She smoothed back her hair, fixed her ponytail, and then let her arms drop to her sides as she sighed. "I could use something to drink. I guess I'll drive back into town."

"Hey, how about having lunch with me?"

"I don't know, Joseph."

"No pressure. Just lunch between friends." He nodded to the ambulance as it flipped a u-turn in the road, and went screaming back toward town. "You probably saved that guy's life back there. It deserves someone buying you lunch."

"All in a day's work."

"Not on your day off, though." He touched her shoulder. "Come on. Let me buy you lunch at the diner. Besides, I get a family discount there." He grinned as she smiled.

"All right. I have a spare scrub top in my trunk. I'll change at the diner."

"I'll meet you there."

When he pulled up to the diner about fifteen minutes later, he was surprised that there weren't too many people there. In fact, there only seemed to be one or two cars in front.

After he got out of his truck, he shut the door with a bang, and stepped up on the curb. Clarissa pulled her car into the spot next to him.

"You know, I've never eaten here," she said, when she reached his side.

"Really? You are in for a treat then."

"Is this owned by your family?" she asked as he opened the door for her and followed her inside.

"Sort of. It belongs to my aunt on my mother's side."

"Joey!" Anne called from behind the counter. "What brings you in?"

"A friend and I are here to get some food and a cold drink."

Anne nodded as she smiled. "Sit anywhere, honey, and I'll bring you some menus."

He placed his hand at the small of Clarissa's back, guiding her toward a booth to the right. He loved Anne's diner. It was decorated in the fifties style with chrome everywhere, red seats, and white tables. She hadn't changed a thing since she opened it back in the sixties when they'd first moved to Bandera.

He slid into one side of the booth while Clarissa stayed standing at the table. "I need to go wash up, change my shirt and comb my hair."

"Sure. The restrooms are to the back and around that corner."

"I'll be right back."

She disappeared as Anne approached the table and put two menus down. "Do you know what your friend wants to drink?"

"No."

"I'll come back in a second then."

When Clarissa returned, Anne took their drink order while they decided on what to eat.

The bacon cheeseburger sounded good to him. It was his favorite anyway, and he figured after the afternoon they'd had, he deserved a juicy, greasy hamburger with cheese, lettuce, tomato, bacon, and onion with fries on the side. He set his menu down, glancing around the diner while Clarissa made up her mind what she wanted to eat. He could see the two of them becoming good friends.

As his gaze did a thorough sweep of the place, he noticed a red-haired woman sitting alone at one of the tables by the window. She appeared to be writing or drawing something on a large pad of paper. *Odd for this area.* He'd never seen her around here before. She was different enough that he would have noticed her should she be a local. Since he'd lived here all his life, he would know her if she was.

She glanced out the window, then would run the pencil over the paper before looking outside again. He figured she must be drawing something that had caught her attention in their quaint little town.

Clarissa put her menu down. "I think I'll have a French dip. I love those things."

"Anne makes good ones, too, with lots of roast beef."

"Wonderful."

He looked at Clarissa for a moment before his gaze was drawn back to the redhead. Curiosity got the better of him as Anne came back to the table to take their order. When she'd written down what they wanted, he asked, "Who's the woman by the window?"

"I don't know. She came in a few hours ago, ate lunch, and has been sketching ever since. Nice girl, from what I can tell, but she's not from around here."

"I gathered that since I don't know her, and I pretty much know everyone in Bandera."

"You didn't know me, Joseph, when we met at The Dusty Boot last night."

"True. If she just moved here, I probably wouldn't know her then." He looked across the diner again, noticing her gaze fixed outside. "Do you know what she's sketching?"

"No. She hides it every time I get close."

"Hmm. Interesting."

Anne disappeared back behind the counter as he sipped on his Coke.

Clarissa tried bringing up conversation as they sat in the booth waiting for their food, but for some reason, his attention wouldn't stay off the redhead for long.

When she turned and their eyes met, he felt like he'd been kicked in the chest by a horse. Her eyes were a bright green with long eyelashes curled up away from her eyes, framed by black square glasses that made her eyes look bigger. Her cheeks were brushed with pink that darkened the longer he looked. Her red hair hung to her waist in a riot of curls it appeared she tried to tame with a hair tie. Her lips lifted in a tiny smile before she turned away and concentrated on her pad again.

His breath rushed back into his lungs like he'd been underwater way too long.

What the hell?

He'd never reacted to someone like that before, never.

"Are you okay, Joseph? You look really pale."

He shook his head as he focused back on Clarissa. "I'm okay. I just had a really weird reaction to someone, and I'm kind of at a loss as to how to explain it." *I need to keep my focus on my dining partner, not the mystery woman across the room.*

Anne arrived with their plates, giving him more of a reason to concentrate on the woman with him.

Their food looked wonderful, as always. Joey squirted some ketchup onto his burger, squished the bun down so he could fit it into his mouth, and then picked it up to take a bite. Clarissa laughed as he pushed a huge bite of food between his lips.

"Hungry?" Clarissa asked, fixing her own food to her liking before she scooped up a bit of ketchup on her fry and stuffed it into her mouth.

He chewed for a moment and swallowed. "Yes. I haven't eaten today since I slept in this morning."

"You didn't have to work today?"

"Not in a sense. I did have to make a run to the feed store to get something, but I didn't have rides to do." He stuck a french fry into his mouth. "What are your plans for the rest of the day?"

"I don't know. I thought I might wander a bit. I didn't have to work and felt a bit restless. That's why I was out on the back road." She glanced at her watch. "Wow. I didn't realize it was getting so late in the afternoon. My boyfriend will be home from work soon and if I'm not there, he'll flip."

"You don't have to tell him everywhere you go, do you?"

"Nah, nothing like that. He doesn't mind my need to roam as long as he has an idea of where I am. I'd better go though, we have plans." She scooted out of the booth and got to her feet as she grabbed her wallet. "Besides it looks as if you may have another admirer."

As if that was anything new.

"I got it, Clarissa."

"Are you sure?"

"Yeah. I asked you to lunch so my treat."

She smiled as she leaned in a kissed him on the cheek. "You're sweet. I hope you find a nice girl someday soon."

"Thanks."

She gave him another nod of her head before she disappeared out the door of the diner. He hoped they could continue to be friends. He'd like that.

When he focused back on the inside of the diner and not the girl who'd just walked out the door, he was surprised to find the redhead staring at him.

Her eyes were wide, her lips were parted slightly, and her right hand was posed over her pad. She broke the contact of their gazes as she looked back down at her paper, her hand moving quickly over the pad.

Curiosity got the better of him as he got to his feet and made his way to her side. "Hi."

She jumped as she pressed the pad to her chest. "Hello."

"I noticed you were drawin' on your pad. Can I ask what you're drawin'?"

Her bottom lip disappeared between her teeth for a moment as she glanced around the diner like she was looking for an escape. "I don't usually show people my drawings."

"If you don't want to, that's okay." He grabbed the chair across the table from her, flipped it around and straddled it. "My name is Joseph Young."

"It's nice to meet you. I'm Rose Gilbert."

"You aren't from here. I can tell by your accent." She smiled and his breath truly caught in his throat. Her whole face lit up when she smiled.

"No, I'm not."

"Are you just visitin'? Do you have family here?"

"No, actually I don't. I'm here on business for the company I work for." She glanced behind him before her gaze came back to him. "Did your girlfriend leave?"

"My who?"

"Your girlfriend. I saw you eating with that dark haired woman."

"Oh, Clarissa? She's not my girlfriend. She's just a friend. I met her at The Dusty Boot last night and we kind of ran into each other today."

"The Dusty Boot?"

"It's the local watering hole or cowboy bar. It's where all the cowboys hang out."

"Ah, I see." She looked out the window for a second before her gaze came back to him. "Sounds nice."

That kicked in the chest feeling came back as he forced his breath out in a whoosh. He chuckled as he pushed his hat back on his head. "Not really. It's pretty rowdy on the weekends, but yeah, we all go there for a good time."

The conversation lagged a little before she blurted out, "Are you a real cowboy?"

"Depends on what you mean by real cowboy? If you mean do I ride horses, mend fences, break new horses to ride, and brand cattle, then yeah, I'm about as real as they come."

"Wow," she whispered, her voice almost reverent in its tone. "I've seen several people walking around town with the same clothing on."

He looked out the window himself for a moment, noticing the people of town walking around. Some went across the street to the bank, others went to the grocery store on the corner, and still more drove down the main street in their trucks. He hadn't realized how it might look to someone not from here. "That's how people dress in Texas."

"It's fascinating."

"Where did you say you're from again?"

"New York. I've never been out of the state before this."

"Well, welcome to Texas, darlin'."

* * * *

Rose's toes curled in her shoes when she heard Joseph say darlin'. Holy crap, he had the cowboy thing down to a science, but if he's a real cowboy, that made sense.

She took in everything about him from the top of his worn cowboy hat to the dusty boots on his feet. He was over six feet tall of solid muscle from what she could see. He had dark hair that peeked out under his hat and curled around his neck, making her want to run her fingers through the thickness. The light blue T-shirt he had on stretched tight over the muscles of his chest and strained against the bulging muscles of his arms. He obviously worked hard every day to have a body like that. His brown eyes reminded her of dark chocolate and when they crinkled at the corners, she could tell he laughed a lot and enjoyed life. *Probably a player then.* Players were something she didn't have time for. She had a purpose in Bandera and it didn't include getting tied up with a local cowboy.

Besides, she probably wasn't his type anyway. With her unruly red hair and thick glasses, she was the persona of nerd. Guys like him didn't go for girls like her. He probably liked his women with tight jeans, big boobs, big blonde hair, and blue eyes. She'd seen lots of pictures of women in Texas and she certainly didn't fit in at all.

Her job sent her to this remote area to get soil and water samples to study the microorganisms that grew in this area. Being a microbiologist was really boring for most people, but it fascinated her like nothing else. She loved to get things under her microscope and figure out what bacteria might be growing in a certain environment. Bandera was mostly cattle ranches, and as such, the Environmental Protection Agency was interested in the effects these animals were having on the water and soil.

"So what brings you to our little town?"

"Work."

"What kind of work do you do?"

She blushed when she thought about how boring her job really was to someone like him. For crying out loud, he broke horses for a living. "I'm a microbiologist."

"Really? That's important work."

"Yes, it is." He smiled and her heart stopped before it jumped into beating again. She rubbed her hand over her stomach where it seemed to be fluttering like crazy. "I, uh…"

"How long have you been doing that kind of work?"

"Two years."

"I've never met a scientist before." He glanced down at her sketch pad where she'd absently laid it down on the table. He craned his head a little as he looked at the sketch. "Is that me?"

"Well, uh, yeah."

"Can I see it?"

"I suppose."

He turned it around so he could see the picture better. "Wow. That's a great likeness. You're very talented."

"Thanks. I only draw for my own pleasure and relaxation. It helps me unwind."

"What other stuff were you drawin'?"

One of her shoulders lifted in a shrug as she felt the heat of a blush rush across her cheeks. Ah, the life of a redhead. "People in town. The town itself with the stoplights and things. Nothing special."

His gaze came back to her. "Can I look at those too? I wouldn't want to be out of line by looking if you don't want me to."

Her heart thumped against her chest, fluttering like a butterfly trapped in a cage. "No, it's fine. They aren't very good since it's only a pencil sketch," she said as he flipped to the next picture and then the next.

"Do you paint?"

"Some."

"I don't know a whole lot about art, but these are really good."

She couldn't help but smile at his compliment. He would never be a New York critic or anything, but somehow his pleasure at her drawings meant more than any critic. "Have you ever been to New York?"

"Nope. My travels are limited to Texas mostly with a few trips to Oklahoma." He closed her sketch pad and focused on her face.

Wow. She could hardly breathe. Her palms felt sweaty and her whole body hummed with awareness of the man sitting so close. She'd never had a reaction to another human being like this before. It felt weird and exciting at the same time. It made her anxious in a way that was very new to her. She always thought she would meet and marry some sophisticated banker, lawyer, doctor, or something along those lines. A guy in a worn cowboy hat, dirty boots, and tight jeans wasn't on her radar at all.

She reached up and adjusted her glasses on her face. It was a nervous gesture, but she needed something to do with her hands. "Does all of Texas look like this?"

He laughed. "Not at all. Some of it's flat. You can see for miles. Hill country like this area is hilly."

"What about the weather? I hear it's really hot here in the summer."

"It is, but the winters can be cold, too."

"I see you made a new friend, Joseph."

He tipped his head toward her, and said, "This is Rose, Aunt Anne."

"Your aunt?"

"Yes, ma'am, on my mother's side."

"Wow. That's cool."

Anne smiled at them and Rose could see the resemblance. "Can I get you two something to drink, more coffee or a Coke?"

He looked up at the older woman standing near their table. "I'll take another Coke, please."

"Yeah, I'll take one too."

"Coming right up."

Anne returned a moment later with two fresh glasses of Coke. "Here ya go."

"Thanks, Aunt Anne."

"You're welcome, nephew." She smiled as she walked away from the table.

"Have you lived here your whole life?" she asked Joseph, fascinated by him and the area they lived in. Her parents had always lived in New York, but that was different. They hadn't lived in the same place within the state more than a few years before moving again either closer to the city or farther out when her dad got a hair up his ass about living in the country.

"Yes, ma'am. Been here since I was born. My parents bought a ranch outside of town when my older brothers were little. The rest of us were born here."

"Rest of you?"

"Yep. I have eight older brothers."

"Holy shit." She covered her mouth as she blushed hard. "I'm sorry," she whispered, afraid she'd offended him in some way. When he chuckled, she realized he'd probably heard a lot worse.

"It's okay. I hear worse than that all the time. Remember nine brothers in a predominantly male household."

"Your mother probably has no hair raising all of you."

He smiled, showing off straight white teeth and a dimple in his cheek. "Actually, she's one tough lady. She had to be with all of us, but especially since three of my brothers are triplets."

"I'd love to meet her. I can't even imagine raising triplets much less six other boys in the mixture."

"I can arrange that."

"Really? I would love to see a real working ranch. Sketching horses would be fantastic."

"If you're free this afternoon, I can take you out there."

"Are you sure? I wouldn't want to impose."

"Darlin', it's a working ranch, yes, but it's also a guest ranch. We have folks around almost all the time, who are staying with us."

She slipped her sketch book into her large bag by her feet. "I'm free for you to do with as you wish."

His eyebrows went up to his hairline as a tiny little grin spread across his lips. "Anything?"

Her face flushed with heat. "Well, almost anything."

"I'm game, honey. I'll give you the executive tour." They both climbed to their feet as he threw some money down on the table.

"What are you doing?"

"Buying your lunch or breakfast, whatever it was."

"You can't do that."

"Why not?"

"Well, I—" She hesitated a moment. "You shouldn't, that's all."

"I want to."

"But then I'll be obligated to you."

He tilted his head to the side and said, "For a little thing like buying you a meal?" He shook his head. "You won't owe me anything other than the joy of your company, Rose."

"Are you sure?"

"Yes, ma'am." He picked up her ticket, handed it and the money to Anne, and then moved to her side. "I would be honored to show you Thunder Ridge."

"I can't wait."

Chapter Three

They drove through big wrought iron gates with a huge TR right in the middle, a little bit later. Joseph had convinced her to leave her car at the diner and take his truck out to the ranch. He insisted it wasn't far from Bandera, so it would be no trouble returning her to town when they were finished.

Rose could feel her heart thumping loudly in her chest as they passed onto the land. Junipers and scrub brush lined the gravel driveway they crept along. Pasture land stretched for a long time in both directions, lined by barbed wire fencing. She couldn't believe her eyes when her gaze stopped on the cattle off to the left. "Oh my. Are those longhorn cattle?"

"Yes. We raise them on the ranch, but these that are out here are like pets. We have more up in the hills that we take to market." He stopped the truck and pointed toward one that was white with brown spots. "See that one right there?"

"Yes," she whispered, in awe of the huge animal.

"He's been on the ranch for the longest. He's almost as old as I am."

"Wow. What's his name?"

"Randy."

She giggled as she pressed her fingertips to her lips. "Really? Randy?"

"Yes, ma'am."

When he turned to look at her, her breath stopped in her throat. The pride on his face made it even more handsome. "He's gorgeous."

"He's randy most of the time, even for his age."

She smiled as she thought about that for a moment, wondering how many little cows he'd made. Cows. Hmm. Was that what they called baby cows? She might have to ask Joseph since she didn't know the first thing about ranching, cows, horses or anything closely resembling the cowboy thing. Talk about being out of her comfort zone. "This is fantastic."

The truck moved slowly forward as she watched the cows continue to graze on the lush green grass beneath their feet. *Feet? I have no idea what they are really called.*

As she turned to look out the front windshield, she was shocked to see a huge two story ranch house come into view. It had a solid rock side with a big wooden door. The porch on the front of the building wrapped all the way around two sides with rockers strategically placed to enjoy. Old farming implements took up residence on the lawn. There were several smaller buildings that complimented the main house, but they were more wood cabin like in design, and were situated a few feet away. A huge barn sat in the distance with fenced off areas situated behind it and to the right. Majestic horses in many different colors stood tied to the posts as if waiting for their owners.

"Wow."

Joseph smiled as he pulled his truck into the parking area, put it in park, and hopped out to open her door.

A gentleman who opens your door for you? I must be in some fairytale or something. Dreaming maybe?

"Thank you."

He tipped his hat.

She sighed.

The gravel crunched under her tennis shoes as they walked to the pathway that led to the main house. She was definitely out of her element here in this atmosphere.

When they approached the wooden door on the side of the building, he pulled it open and motioned for her to go inside.

Pandemonium was the only way she could describe the scene before her. There had to be fifty people laughing, eating, and socializing, the huge room an explosion of noise.

Joseph moved to her side, talking close to her ear. The warmth of his breath on the shell of her ear had her body exploding in goose bumps from head to toe. Even her hair tingled from the sensation.

"We probably should have waited to come out here. There's a large group of writers here this weekend, with my sister-in-law. She's a writer."

"Really? What's her name?" she asked, spinning around to face him before turning back around to search the group. Getting to talk to one of her favorite romance writers would be the epitome of cool.

"Mesa West is what she writes under."

"Oh my God! Seriously? I love her stuff."

"Yes." He placed his hand at the small of her back to guide her forward. "We can go into the main room or into one of the suites upstairs if you want something a bit quieter."

"No. This is exciting." She glanced around the room, taking in all the people who were talking in small groups, leaving very little space to walk. "I can't wait to see the rest of the house."

"Well, this is main dining room where all the meals are served to the guests at the ranch. There are rooms upstairs for people to sleep as well as the cabins you saw outside. The big barn out back is for the horses. It's where I spend most of my time."

"Can we see the other room?"

"Sure." He motioned for her to precede him through the arched doorway into the main room.

There was a huge rock fireplace to the left with big bookcases rising almost to the ceiling. Three big leather couches were positioned near the fireplace with several individual lounge chairs scattered around the room. An old piano stood against one wall.

She took in the entire room, absorbing the atmosphere and the ambiance of the lifestyle. The whole thing held her spellbound.

"My mother's office is right there in the corner and the one farther down the hall is my brother Jonathan's. He's the marketing person and website guru."

"What do your other brothers do around here besides ride horses?"

He motioned for her to follow him to another small room where there were a couple of leather loveseats, things for sale, and thankfully, doors that could be closed. As she found a comfortable spot to sit, he pulled the glass sliding door shut, leaving them in blessed silence.

"This is very nice."

"Can I get you something cold? There are Cokes in here as well as some wine if you'd like."

"It's a little early for wine, but a Coke would be great. Thank you."

Joseph reached into the cooler in the corner and pulled out a can of Coke to hand to her. "Here you go."

He took a seat next to her.

After she'd quenched her thirst, she set the can on the small table to her right before she turned to face him again. "So, what's your typical day like?"

"I'm up by six normally. I feed and water the horses, brush them all down, clean their hooves, and saddle them for the day."

"Do they stand around all day in that heavy leather?"

"Yes, but we don't cinch them until we know someone is about to go out for a ride. The saddles are on their backs, but not tight."

"Oh. That's good. I wouldn't want to be standing around in the heat of the summer with those heavy blankets and bulky load on."

"We take very good care of our animals."

"What else do you do?"

"Sometimes I take riders out. We usually go for an hour unless it's a special ride that has been booked in advance to go out longer. I also help maintain the tack for the animals, the saddles, bridles, and such."

"If you hadn't guessed, I know absolutely nothing about horses, what you called tack, or how to take care of a horse."

"Horses are great animals. They are very affectionate with people they know. They love to please. We have several different breeds here including quarter horses, Arabians, Morgans, Mustangs, Paints, Saddlebreds, and so on."

She couldn't help but laugh since she had no idea what any of those types of horses were. Born and raised in New York had its perks and drawbacks, not having a clue about the country lifestyle was one of them.

"What do your brothers do on the place?"

"Jeff is the eldest. He's the foreman around here. Jackson is second in line. He's married to a country singer, so he's not around a lot anymore, but he does some wrangling when he's home. Jacob is third. He helps around the place too. Like most of my brothers, he has his own place now and does his own thing. Jason, Joel, and Joshua are the triplets. Joel is married to Mesa who is the writer. Jason is married to Peyton who is a bartender at The Dusty Boot and Joshua is married to Candace. She does a lot with websites. All three of them have their own houses, but help out around the home place during roundup, branding, and whatever else. Jonathan recently got engaged to one of the women who works here. Her name is Mandy and she's good friends with Peyton, and then there is Jeremiah. He's married to Callie. They were friends in high school, but got together not too long ago. Jeremiah is the financial planner for the ranch. He watches all the money that goes in and out of here."

"Holy crap. Sounds like a very busy place to be."

"Yeah, sometimes it's hard to get alone time around here." He chuckled as he put his arm across the back of the sofa, crossed one leg over the other so his ankle was on the opposite knee, and relaxed against the arm behind him. "So tell me what you do when you aren't hunting bacteria."

She blushed thinking how boring her life sounded in comparison to what went on here. "I study bacteria under a microscope, differentiating the various types, what they do, and how they affect their environment, like water and soil."

"I'm impressed."

"You are?"

"Yeah. I've never really talked to a scientist before. I mean, I took biology in high school, of course, but I've never been to college like some of my brothers. I'm just a cowboy."

She laid her palm on his foot. "That's a very important job, Joseph. You do what you do to make it safe for people to come here, have a good time, and not worry about being hurt."

He shrugged one shoulder. "Most of the time, I feel like I don't matter all that much. Being the baby of the family makes me feel like I'm replaceable, you know?"

"I'm sure you aren't at all. You are a very important part of this operation if you are the only one who is responsible for the animals here. Didn't you say you break the new horses you buy, as well?"

"Yes."

"That's a dangerous thing to do all the time. Have you been hurt before?"

"Yeah. I broke my leg when I was like twelve." He shuddered before focusing back on her face. "It wasn't a pleasant experience. I hate hospitals."

She smiled and dropped her gaze to the coffee table top. It was very unique. Kind of a mosaic top with a wood base that had little spots burnt into it. She'd never seen anything similar in her life. Then again, this whole cowboy thing was new to her.

When she raised her gaze again, there were frown lines between his dark eyebrows. "Yet you continue to do it."

"Well, yeah. It's my job and I haven't been hurt in a long time. I'm very careful when I ride or break in a new horse."

"How does one break in a new horse?"

"It's a slow, meticulous process. We put them in a smaller pen, work with them to gentle them, and break them to halter first."

She shook her head and grinned. "It's like you are talking a foreign language to me. What's a halter?"

He tried showing her with his hands. "It's usually made of nylon. You put it on their nose and then back behind their ears." He laid his hands back down and shrugged. "It would be much easier to just show you."

She jumped to her feet. "Okay!"

"Like right now?"

"Of course. Show me what you do."

He climbed to his feet with a grin on his lips. "All right then. Follow me."

Excitement quickened her steps as she followed him back through the throng of people in the main lodge and dining room, out the side door, and across the lawn to the big red structure toward the back. The smells surrounding her were intriguing. The scent had a sweet aroma to it, from what she wasn't sure. Sweat, dirt, and grass smells assaulted her senses as they approached the big double doors.

When they moved through and down the long dirt hall, she noticed several smaller areas that had short, sliding half doors on them with bars on the tops. "What are those?"

"Stalls. We keep the horses in them at night."

She stopped to look inside, disappointed there were no animals to peek at.

"The horses are all out in the paddock right now."

"Paddock?"

He smiled, showing off a small dimple in his cheek. "I forget that you have no idea what I'm talking about. The lingo to me is natural, but for someone who has never been around horses or farm animals, you are totally lost."

She nodded as she moved back to his side. "You'll have to explain it to me."

"Paddocks are small areas that are designated to hold the horse while they are waiting for riders. Ours is a long, wide area where we tie them."

"They have food and water, right?"

He frowned. "Of course. We don't neglect our animals."

"I didn't say you did. It just occurred to me that they are unable to get water and stuff for themselves if they are tied to a pole or whatever."

"I'm sorry. It bothers me when folks think we don't take care of our horses. They are well fed, brushed daily, bathed regularly, and exercised even if they aren't out on a ride. My brothers and I switch out which animals we ride when we are taking a group out. That way all of them are ridden regularly. We don't want any of them to get ornery with a guest since most of the guests aren't experienced riders."

As they continued down the walkway, she noticed a large covered area off to the side. "What's that for?"

"It's where we work the horses sometimes or when I have to break one, I'll take it in there to work with it so that I can keep it contained. Wild horses can be difficult to break. They aren't used to being around people."

"Do you have a lot of wild horses on your property?"

"No. We buy them from auction most of the time. The only thing roaming our land is our guests, our horses, and our cattle."

"Is that what you call the long-horn one out there in the front?"

"Yes. Cows are referred to as cattle."

"What are baby cows called?"

"Calves."

"Baby horses?"

"Foals until they are a year old. A girl horse is a mare. A boy horse that has been fixed so he can't make babies is a gelding. A boy horse that still is able to make babies is a stud. A baby female horse is a filly and a baby male horse is a colt."

"Wow." She glanced up into the rafters of the barn. "What's up there?"

"Our hayloft. We keep the extra hay we have for the horses, up there."

"I bet it's fun up there."

He shrugged as a small grin appeared on his lips. "It can be."

"Have you ever had sex in the hayloft?"

He choked and coughed as he blushed a deep red. "Well now, I don't go around discussing my sex life with strangers, but it has been used a time or two by those in the family."

She liked that he was a bit embarrassed by discussing his sex life. Most guys were very open and boastful about how many women they'd been with. It was cute.

The scent of leather met her nose. "Where is the leather scent coming from?"

"Our tack room near the back. We keep all our saddles, bridles, bits, and other riding equipment back there."

"Can I see it? I love the smell of leather."

"Sure," he said, leading her to the end of the dirt walkway, past all the stalls to the door that was shut. He knocked loudly for a moment, before entering.

"Why did you knock?"

"My brother, Jeremiah, has his office in there." He looked down at the floor as he scuffed the dirt with the toe of his boot. "He and Callie sometimes go in there to be alone so I always knock."

No sound came from the room.

He slowly turned the door handle and peered inside. "It's safe."

She giggled as she pressed her fingertips to her lips. The thought of bursting in on a couple was almost funny. She could totally imagine how hard it would be to get some alone time in a place like this, with so many people around all the time.

When they stepped into the large room, she noticed wooden things on the wall. Some had saddles on them and some were empty. "What are those?" She pointed to the leather contraption with a metal thing hanging crossways in the middle of it.

"Bridles." He took one off the hook and showed it to her. "This part goes in the horse's mouth, this part goes behind their ears, and these go around their neck so the rider can guide them where they want them to go."

"Sounds complicated."

"Not really." He put it back on the hook before he took down another piece. "This is a halter." He stretched one part open. "This goes over their nose and this part goes behind their ears."

"What is it for?"

"It's to help catch them when they are in an open area. It's not uncomfortable for them or anything, but with a lead rope hooked to the ring under their chin, it makes it easier to lead them where we need them to go."

"I see." She glanced down at the bucket on the floor with several things in it. "What are those for?"

"They are different brushes we use to groom them." He picked up a metal hook. "This is to clean their hooves with."

"Why do you have to do that?"

"We make sure they are in good condition, no sores or that they don't have any rocks that could hurt their hoof after they've gone out on rides. Sores on their feet are really bad for horses. We're constantly checking them to make sure they aren't developing anything within the hoof."

"Caring for them is a lot of work."

"Yes it is." He swept out his hand toward the door. "Let me show you the animals we have out in the paddock."

"I would love to see them." She grinned as she went through the door and then waited for him to shut it behind them before walking in front of her through a doorway a little ways down and off to the right.

When they stepped out into the sunshine, she was partially blinded by the glare. He grabbed a straw cowboy hat from the rack to their left, plopping it on her head. The wide brim of the hat shaded her eyes enough that she could see around her.

He grinned as he tapped the brim of the hat. "You look cute."

"Thanks." She winced. "I guess."

"Now all you need are jeans and boots and you'll look like a regular cowgirl."

"I'll see what I can do."

He showed her the horses, naming each one, telling her how old they were, what type of horse they were, where the family acquired it, and what kind of temperament it had. "Well, that's all of them except those that are pastured right now. We swap out the herd every so often so that they all get exercise, but also get a chance to rest."

"This is fascinating, Joseph."

"I'm glad you like it."

This all felt very strange to her. She'd just met this man, but it seemed like she'd known him for a long time. Her comfort level around him amazed her. She frowned. She shouldn't be feeling this. She was in love with someone else, wasn't she?

Brandt wouldn't like her being friendly with another man.

"What's wrong?"

"Uh, nothing. Thank you for the tour."

"You're welcome." He rocked back on the heels of his boots as he stuffed his hands in his front pockets. "Would you like to stay for supper?"

This is all research, right? I mean, I need the soil and water samples from the area in different places to get a good variable exposure. "Uh, sure. That sounds like fun."

"I'll warn you, my family can be overwhelming."

"That's okay. I like big families."

"You'll definitely get that with mine."

His warm hand at the small of her back felt safe and comfortable as he guided her back through the barn toward the house.

"It'll be a while before we eat, but you'll hear the dinner bell they ring to let everyone know when the meal is served. Would you like to see more of the property while we wait?"

"I would love to."

He took her hand in his and led her to his truck, opened the door, and then helped her inside with his hands on her waist.

Holy shit! Did this guy just step out of a western romance novel or something?

She wiped the drool from her chin as she watched him walk around the front bumper to the driver's side. Men like this didn't exist, did they?

Apparently in Bandera, Texas they did.

Chapter Four

Joey glanced at the pretty redhead across the cab of his truck before looking back out the windshield. She wasn't the typical cowgirl he normally went out with. It was kind of funny how totally out of her element she seemed. She knew nothing about cattle, horses, or ranching. He guessed he'd feel the same way if he went to her neck of the woods. "What would you like to see?"

"Everything."

He laughed. "That's a tall order." After he backed out of the parking spot, he headed around the back of the cabins to the cattle guard across the north pasture area. They would go around the hills, across the streams, and out by the mud pit where they all wet muddin' on occasion during the summer. The rumble of the cattle guard when his tires went over made her giggle and look at him.

His heart skipped a beat at the pure joy she found in something so simple. Her eyes were wide as her hand gripped the door handle to her right while they took the road to the left. Gravel crunched under the tires as they drove along slowly so she could take it all in. Showing her the sights of his home made him feel powerful and important. It was a brand new feeling to him. He liked it, liked it a lot.

They spent the next two hours roaming around the property belonging to Thunder Ridge. He found some of the cattle grazing in one of the back pastures and stopped so she could watch them.

Seeing things through her innocent eyes had him appreciating what he'd taken for granted for so long. The beauty of the hill country in spring, the large long-horned cattle peacefully munching on the tall grass, the blooming Bluebonnets that made the area explode in bright color, and the peacefulness of the pond where he and his brothers swam as children. Even now, he'd be out riding fences and come up on the pond only to hear the soft sighs and low moans of one of his brothers and their girls spending some alone time.

Realizing he wanted that for himself made him stop with a start.

"Is something wrong?"

"N-no. I'm realizing how the whole area looks through your eyes, someone who has never been here before, and it makes me appreciate it all the more." He stopped several yards away from the pond. "Would you like to see a special spot we swam in as kids?"

She nodded enthusiastically as she turned to open the door, but he stopped her with a hand on her arm.

"Let me get it."

The smile on her lips made his breath catch in his throat. He couldn't wait to see her in the sunshine with the sparkling water of the pond behind her. He knew she would love it as much as he did, maybe more.

After he opened her door, he held out his hand to help her out of the cab of the truck. He knew it was kind of high off the ground. Her head came to about the middle of his nose when she stepped out and stood on the ground. That made her about five-foot-eight, he figured.

Her red hair blew wildly in the spring breeze as she rubbed her arms. He should have thought to have her bring a coat. It got cool up here in the spring sometimes. "Wait right here."

He hurried around to the other side, opened the door, and grabbed his jean jacket that he kept behind his seat.

When he held it out for her to place her arms in, she smiled up at him. Her perfect pink lips parted slightly as he lost himself in her green eyes.

She giggled softly, pushed her arms into the jacket, and spun around so she could wrap it around her.

He kicked himself for being such a sap. Yes, she was beautiful, smart, funny, and good company, but he really didn't need a complication in his life right now. He already had too many women to keep track of besides keeping his ass out of trouble. Jessica's father kept trying to shoot him, Clarissa had a boyfriend and didn't need anyone in her life to complicate things, and Rose wasn't here but for a short time to do a job. Being attracted to her was one thing, but he couldn't act on it. "This way," he said, taking two steps in front of her to lead the way. Why he was showing her this special spot, he wasn't sure since he figured it was a bad idea to get involved with her.

A gasp escaped her mouth as they crested the hill that led down to where the pond was. "This is beautiful, Joseph." She walked on past him, down to the pond's edge.

Sparkling in the sunlight, the water appeared bluer than normal as a few fish swam about. She sat on a rock near the edge and took off her tennis shoe and sock, before sticking her toes in. "It's warm!"

"Yes, it's a warm spring. It stays a constant seventy degrees no matter how hot or how cold it is outside."

"This is magnificent! I wish I had brought a swimming suit. I would go in."

He smiled at her enthusiasm. It was contagious. He moved to sit beside her so he could watch her. Her face lit up with excitement at the area around them. The small sandy beach his dad had made for them, the rocks that surrounded the area, keeping it secluded, the blue water, the small fish, and the sunshine sparkling off the still edges all made for a very pretty spot.

"You used to swim here as a child?"

"Yeah, my brothers and I used to come out here all the time, even in the winter."

"I can't imagine getting out of that warm water into the cold air." She shivered and wrapped the coat tighter around her.

Unable to stop himself, he moved to sit behind her and drew her back between his legs so she could rest against his chest and be warm. "There. Better?"

"Yes, much. Thank you."

He tucked her head under his chin and wrapped his arms around her shoulders, pulling her in tight.

"Joseph?"

"Yeah?"

"How old are you?"

"Thirty-one. Why?"

"Curiosity mostly."

"How old are you?"

"Twenty-six."

"And you are a microbiologist?"

"Yes."

"What kind of schooling does that require? I assume you went to college for it."

"Yep. Four years and a bachelor's degree, but I am planning to finish my Ph.D."

"What's that?"

"My doctorate degree."

"Oh." *Wow*. He felt really stupid. He'd never gone to college. He'd never been anywhere except Texas and Oklahoma. He'd never had a steady girl. He'd never done a lot of things, but here was this girl who was younger than he was, who had a degree, lived in New York, knew about stuff he had no idea about like under a microscope and shit, and he was nothing more than a lowly cowboy. She was totally out of his league and he might as well get that through his thick skull before he did something stupid, like kiss her.

He liked the way she felt in his arms though, tucked into his embrace like she was meant to be there.

Where in the hell did that come from?

"Rose?"

"Yeah?"

"How long are you here for?"

"A few weeks is all. Once I collect the samples I need, I'll be heading back to New York."

"How would you like to stay here at the ranch, collect your samples, and be exposed to some real southern hospitality?"

"What are you asking?"

"I'm asking if you would like to stay on the ranch and hang out with me. I can show you Bandera, San Antonio, Houston or wherever you want to go, give you the royal treatment for the time you're here."

She turned in his arms so she faced him even though she was still sideways in his embrace. Her breath warmed his lips as she stared up into his eyes. Her pupils dilated. Her lips parted. Her breathing sped up as they looked at each other without saying a word.

He wanted to kiss her more than anything.

His fingers tangled in her hair, scraping his fingertips over her scalp, as he slowly drew her closer. When he closed his eyes and drifted toward her mouth, he anticipated the taste of her lips, the softness of the surface, and the pleasure he would feel at the first touch of her mouth. He wasn't prepared for the reaction of his body to the brush of her lips against his. Desire rushed through his blood, exploding in a high he'd never felt before. His head spun. Blood rushed in his ears. His heart sped up until it was pounding in his chest like a runaway freight train.

When she placed her hand on his chest, he thought his heart had stopped. He tilted his head to the side to deepen the kiss as his tongue brushed against her lips seeking her permission to enter her mouth.

She parted her lips slightly, letting him in so his tongue slipped along hers. A soft moan escaped her mouth as he lost himself in her kiss.

His cell phone jingled in his pocket, making him jump, which in turn broke the kiss.

She pulled the jacket tighter around herself and stood as he fished the phone out of his pocket and answered it.

"Hello?"

"Joey, it's Jessica."

"Hey."

"Can I see you tonight? My dad is out of town buying cattle."

He looked at Rose who'd wandered a few feet away, his thoughts in turmoil. "I, uh, I can't, Jess. I have company." Rose wasn't a guarantee of getting sex, but then again neither was Jessica. Yeah, Jessica came on like an experienced woman, but Joey didn't know if she was or not. What happened if she backed out at the last minute? What if her dad had someone watching the place for just this type of situation? No, he needed to stick with Rose even if she wasn't a shoo-in for a great night of sex, besides, he liked her. She wasn't the typical Texas woman. She wasn't from here at all, and it was kind of nice to have that difference.

"Seriously? This is the perfect opportunity for us to have some alone time, and you can't because you have company? What the hell, Joey?"

"Sorry, Jess, but yeah. I'm busy tonight and probably for the next couple of weeks. An old family friend will be spending some time at the ranch, and I've been volunteered to show her around."

"Her?"

"Uh, yeah. She's an old family friend. Matronly even. She's like fifty or something."

"Is everything okay, Joseph? Do we need to go back to the house?" Rose said, her voice clearly carrying over the phone.

"She doesn't sound very matronly to me and exactly where are you that you need to go back to the house?"

"Listen, I gotta go, Jess. I'll talk to you later." He quickly hit the end button on his phone before stuffing it back into his front pocket. Talk about cock blocked. "Everything is fine. We don't have to go back unless you want to, Rose."

"Who is Jess? I didn't think you had any sisters."

"I don't. She's, uh, a friend."

"Oh." Rose headed back to where his truck was parked. "I suppose we should get back anyway."

"Didn't you want to get some samples or something? I mean, we don't have to go back yet." After he looked at the watch on his arm, he shoved his hands in his pockets as he followed behind her. "I was enjoying being out here with you."

She smiled as she leaned against the front bumper. "I gathered that, but no, I can't get my samples right now. I don't have my equipment with me."

"We could go hike up over the hill there, so I can show you more of the area."

"I really don't have hiking shoes on." She glanced down as she wiggled her shoe so he could see the flats she wore. "Cowboy boots, hiking boots. Wow. I need to hit a store before I go anywhere else with you."

He grinned as he stopped in front of her. "I guess you do."

"Isn't it about time for supper at the house?"

"Not really, and come to think of it, I would love to take you out some place for supper, if you'd go with me."

"Oh?"

"Yeah. I could show you San Antonio down on the River Walk. They have some great restaurants down there like Tex-Mex, steak, seafood, or whatever. You pick."

* * * *

"I was kind of looking forward to having supper with your family. I think it would be great to get to know them." A frown pulled down the corners of his mouth making her want to smooth it away with her fingers. *He's too cute to frown.* "We could always do San Antonio tomorrow evening." She reached up to caress the side of his face and smooth out the little lines near his mouth. "Don't frown. It gives you wrinkles."

He shook his head as the corners of his mouth now lifted in a smile. "All right. Tomorrow it is, and after supper, we'll hit The Dusty Boot."

"You really are trying to kill my feet, aren't you?"

"Nope, but you will need to get some boots. You sure can't be seen in the best country bar in Bandera in those. There are names for folks like that."

"There are?"

"Yep."

"What's that?"

"Yankees or honkees."

She started to giggle and as it turned into a full-blown, gut rolling laugh, he joined in. His laughter was contagious as his eyes twinkled with mirth. They continued to laugh until they were both holding their stomachs. "You are too much."

"It's the truth."

After she pushed off the bumper of the truck, she walked around to the passenger side. He followed, opening the door for her to climb back up in the cab. His hands on her waist as he helped her up, felt strange but right in some way. "Thank you."

"You're welcome." He tipped his hat before he shut the door.

Her mind spun as she watched him walk around the front of the vehicle to the driver's side. *There is something weird going on here, and I'm not sure what. I have a boyfriend, one I thought I was in love with, but this attraction to Joseph is making me have second thoughts about my relationship with Brandt. How can I be attracted to someone this strongly? I really need to break things off with Brandt if I'm having these second thoughts.*

"You okay?"

"Yes, why?"

"You look lost in thought." He turned the key, bringing the truck to life with a roar of the diesel engine before he faced her. "I'm sorry if I got a little carried away back there with the kiss and all."

"I didn't mind, and I'm not sorry you kissed me."

"Good."

"Good?"

"Yeah, because I really want to do it again. I didn't want to be out of line though, if you weren't okay with it."

She smiled as she lowered her gaze to where her hands were folded in her lap. She liked Joseph, a lot, but she wasn't the type to cheat. Calling Brandt tonight would be a good idea, so she could clear her heart. After supper when she was back in her hotel room, she'd do it, she'd call him and breakup.

They drove back to the lodge in virtual silence other than a comment now and again about the current song on the radio. She hadn't really appreciated the tunes on country radio until she stopped to listen. The lyrics really spoke to her now that she slowed down to really hear them. Her toe tapped to the beat as her fingers did a little strum on her thigh.

"Enjoying the music?"

"Yes. I listen to some country music, but not a ton. We don't have very many good country stations where I live. I do have a couple that are my favorites though."

"What kind of music do you normally listen to?"

She glanced at him across the cab and said, "Opera and classical mostly. I go to the shows on Broadway sometimes."

His lips stretched into a big grin, showing off that sexy little dimple in his cheek.

"You're laughing at me."

"No, I'm not. I'm realizing how different we are, is all."

They pulled up in front of the main lodge. She noticed a large group of women making their way in through the doors for supper or dinner. She couldn't remember what they called it in the South, but she knew there was a difference. There was no way she would ask Joseph. He would laugh at her again. Then again, she didn't mind seeing his smile. He had a really sexy one.

It wouldn't be dark for a while yet, so she hoped they could still explore near the main lodge a bit or she might be able to help him with the horses for the night.

After he parked the truck and walked around to open her door, they walked up toward the house. He took her hand in his, making her shiver with sensation. Why his touch did this to her, she wasn't sure, but she knew she liked it. Brandt's touch had never caused such a reaction in her, leaving her baffled.

"Cold?"

"Uh, no, not really."

He smiled as he pulled her closer to his side and wrapped his arm around her shoulders. "Just in case."

Snuggling with a hot guy, best place to be in the world.

They walked through the door into the mayhem of supper inside Thunder Ridge. It was a good thing she didn't have any social anxiety because there were a ton of people including his family, all of the guests, and the staff.

"Let's head up by the stairs. That's where the family sits."

Several of the people sitting at the table swiveled their heads around as Joseph escorted her to a chair and held it out for her. She smiled slightly, hoping to ease their obvious curiosity at her appearance at their table. Joseph took the chair next to her.

"Joey?"

"Uh. Everyone, this is Rose Gilbert. She's a friend I've invited to supper." He went around the table introducing his entire family. "And that's my mother, Nina, and my father, James."

"It's very nice to meet you all. I'm sorry, but I won't be able to remember all your names."

"It's fine, honey," Nina replied. "I hope you aren't too overwhelmed with this bunch." Nina turned to the family. "You all behave yourselves tonight and don't frighten this poor girl." She smiled at Rose. "Welcome to Thunder Ridge."

"Thank you."

"Where are you from? You have an accent I'm not familiar with."

"I'm from New York."

"Interesting place. I've been there a time or two."

"Oh? Which part?"

"New York City. I've done a little traveling over the years."

"I like it, but I'm realizing how different Texas is from New York."

"That's the God's honest truth, honey. I do hope you will enjoy our hospitality while you're in the area."

"I'm sure I will. Joseph has shown me parts of your property today. The pond is beautiful."

A few snickers could be heard from the other males at the table. She frowned, wondering why the mention of the pond was so funny.

Nina shot them all a motherly glare, quieting them quickly.

Rose looked down the table, taking in the group as a whole. It was apparent they were all brothers, carrying the same coloring and mostly the same facial features, although she noticed the different eye colors the group had. The triplets were another shocker. They were indeed identical and it kind of threw her off a bit. It was weird to see the same face on three different people. She had to wonder if their wives could tell them apart because she was having a hard time of it. The women all sat by their men with their children close by at another table if they were old enough or in high chairs if they needed to be closer to their parents. They appeared to be a very loving group of people the way they all cuddled their spouses, kissed them, hugged them or had an arm around their shoulders. They were all tall even though some were taller than the others.

Joseph's parents were an interesting pair as well. Nina had the dark coloring of the boys with long black hair and dark eyes while James was lighter in coloring. Nina appeared to have Native American blood somewhere in her lineage, evident by her features. Striking was the only word she could think of for Joseph's mother.

"Joseph?" Jeff said, snickering behind his hand. "Did you break that new mare today?"

She turned to see Joseph glare at his brother down the table wondering at the flare of anger in his gaze. "Actually, no. I had to make a run into town to get feed, remember, and then I met Rose at the diner. I never made it to the breaking paddock. I'll do it tomorrow."

"Did you get the feed?"

"No. I came across a motorcycle verses deer this morning before I could make it there. The guy was pretty messed up. I met a friend on the road who stopped as well, and we went to the diner for lunch. That's where I met Rose. We came out here afterwards. I totally forgot about the feed."

"You'll need to go back into town for it then. We need it tonight."

"Fine."

Jeff grinned as he pulled his wife's hand up to place a kiss to the back of it. Rose melted at the scene. These guys sure seemed to have the gentleman thing down pat. They all had a hand or something on their spouse, making her feel like she might be intruding on a special moment for them.

She cleared her throat as she turned to see most of the guests had retrieved their plates and taken their seats. The family as a whole got up from their chairs and she slowly stood as well, unsure of what was going on.

Joseph leaned in and whispered in her ear, "We can eat now. We always wait for the guests to be served and seated before we eat."

"Ah. I see." She followed Joseph to the line near the serving counter, grabbed a plate from the stack, and allowed the servers to fill it. As she neared the salad, she realized the food was already overflowing and she would never be able to eat it all.

Joseph smiled as he urged her on. "You don't have to eat everything."

"Thank God. My stomach hurts just looking at it all."

They returned to their seats at the table as the conversations flowed around her. Talk centered on cattle, horses, ranch work, the pregnancies of the group and their current cravings, how Samantha's tour was going, and how Mesa's newest book was selling. She hadn't realized there were other famous people within the group until someone mentioned Samantha. "You're Samantha Harris-Young?"

Samantha smiled and nodded.

Rose thought her world had just come full circle. One of her favorite country music singers and one of her favorite romance novelists were part of the same family. "Oh my God! I love your songs. I have your new CD. Heck, I have all your CDs."

"Thank you. I appreciate you being a fan."

"Dang it! I don't have them all with me, or I would have you sign them." She frowned as she looked down the table. "If that wouldn't be too weird, you know."

"No, honey. It's fine." Samantha smiled at Jackson and then back at her. "If you send them to the ranch, I will sign them and send them back to you once you get home."

"I would love that!" Rose glanced at Joseph as he sat next to her grinning from ear to ear. "What?"

"You are too cute."

"I'm not embarrassing you, am I? I'm sorry."

"No, darlin'. It's fine. Samantha is used to it, I'm sure, and after supper, I will introduce you to Mesa. She is sitting with her friends tonight. You might even know some of them that are here."

She grasped his hand and squeezed it. "Thank you."

"I haven't done anything."

"You brought me here. You have no idea how much this means to me."

"I'm glad I could do this for you."

She smiled again before she grabbed her fork and dug into her food. The mixture of spices exploded on her tongue as she tasted the combination of the dish they were eating. She wasn't sure what it was, but it sure was interesting to eat. Then again, she wasn't familiar with the different foods they might be eating in Texas.

"Do you like it?" Nina asked before her fork slid between her lips.

"Yes. It's an interesting combination of flavor. May I ask what it is?"

"We call it Texas Chili. It has a lot of different flavors inside including onion, garlic, beer, jalapenos, cilantro, unsweet chocolate, and several other things." Nina nodded to the tortillas on the plate next to her. "Try ripping off a piece of the tortilla to scoop some up and eat it that way."

Rose nodded, tore off a piece of the flour tortilla and dipped the small piece into the bowl before putting it between her lips. Her mouth tingled from the flavors bursting on her tongue as she chewed and then swallowed the savory food. "Oh my, that is fantastic. Thank you for the tip, Nina." She blushed as she bit her lip for a moment. "Or should I call you Mrs. Young?"

"Oh my goodness, no. Nina is fine, honey. I've never been Mrs. Young to anyone except the folks at the bank when we first got married."

The group laughed, including her, making her feel like part of the family. Thinking that way would get her into trouble though, so she'd better remember her place. A guest is all she was and all she would ever be on this ranch.

Chapter Five

Joey walked her out to the truck so he could take her back to her rental car still parked at the diner. He wished the evening wouldn't end, but it was getting late plus he had plans to see her again tomorrow evening for dinner and some dancing at The Dusty Boot. The thought of holding her in his arms as they swayed on the dance floor had him smiling.

"What are you grinning about?"

"I was thinking about tomorrow evening and how I can't wait to hold you while we dance."

A frown pulled down the corners of her mouth and made a cute little wrinkle appear between her eyebrows.

"What's wrong?"

"I, uh. I don't know how to dance."

"I'm sure you've slow danced before, right?"

"Well, yes, but not a lot. High school was probably the last time I did."

He laughed. "It hasn't changed."

She smacked him on the arm. "I didn't think it had, silly. I don't know how to do all those other dances that you do here."

"You mean two-step?"

"That's one of them, yes."

"I'll teach you."

"Are you sure? I mean, what if I step on your toes?"

"You wouldn't be the first, darlin'."

Silence enveloped them for a moment as he continued down the darkened road toward town. Stars winked in the nighttime sky. The moon shone bright outside the front windshield. Thinking about how soft her lips had been under his when he'd kissed her earlier, had him getting uncomfortably hard in his jeans. Her taste had been intoxicating. The way her mouth molded to his made him think of doing other things with her, things he probably shouldn't be thinking about on such a basic level. Her hair had been so soft in his hand, curling around it like it was meant to be there. *Damn it. I need to get laid, but having Rose right now isn't the answer.*

"It really is beautiful out here. The stars are so bright. You can see millions of them."

"Yep."

"In New York, the city lights are so blinding, you can hardly see the stars at night unless you go outside of the city."

"Do you do that? Go outside the city, I mean."

"Yeah. My parents own a place upstate in a small community where we have a house. It's beautiful there in the summer, cool with a lovely lake nearby, and lots of green trees."

"Sounds nice."

"Maybe I'll be able to show it to you someday."

"I'd like that."

"Me too, Joseph."

He pulled up next to her car in the parking lot of the diner and shut off the engine. They sat in the dark truck for what seemed like a long time. The radio played softly in the background. He turned toward her and took her hand in his. "Thank you for spending the day with me."

A smile spread across her lips. "Thank you for taking me. I haven't had that much fun in a long time. I learned a lot about you and your family. They are great people."

"I appreciate you saying that. Even if they do drive me crazy sometimes, I still love them. I wouldn't trade them for anything."

"I imagine."

"You haven't told me about your family. I know you live in New York, but not much else." He let his hand relax, cradling her palm in his as he laced their fingers together. It felt intimate and he wasn't sure why he was doing it. He wasn't much of a hand holder type. He didn't do the small things for the women he dated, but he sure felt like doing it with her—slow, sensuous kisses, holding hands, stroking her arm, touching her face, rubbing a section of her hair between his fingers.

"We probably don't have time to go into my whole life story tonight." She glanced at the dashboard. The clock read ten.

"It's still early."

"Not really. I've been up since five this morning."

"An early riser. Me too." He shrugged. "Of course, my excuse is usually because of work."

"Mine too, but not this morning. I found myself wanting to see the sunrise over the hills when I woke up in the motel."

"Are staying here in town?"

"Yes. There is a small one not far from downtown and right across from the bar you mentioned."

"The Dusty Boot. Yeah, there is. It's not a bad place, although I've never stayed there."

"No, I imagine you haven't."

She licked her lips, tempting him to kiss her again. He wanted to, very badly. Instead, he looked back out the windshield and the deserted street.

"I should get going."

"Yeah, me too. Sunrise comes early."

"Yes it does."

"What time do you want me to pick you up for supper tomorrow?"

"Uh, four? It's about forty-five minutes to an hour back into San Antonio, right?"

"Yes. I'll make reservations for five then."

"Where are we going?"

"It's a surprise."

She smiled again, reminding him of a flower opening to the morning sunshine. "I love surprises."

"Good." He brought her hand to his mouth, brushing the back of it with his lips. She shivered under his touch. The reaction made his heart pound. She was attracted to him too. The thought had his heart thumping in his ears, but he had to slow this down. His short terms plans had room for fun with a green-eyed redhead. What of his long term plans? Those didn't include a woman, did they? He didn't think so.

He let her go as he opened his door so he could help her out on her side.

When she stepped out, he laid his palm at the small of her back to escort her to her car. It wasn't far across the parking lot, in fact it was only a few steps in all, way too short for his taste.

She unlocked the car with a press of the key fob in her hand. The lights flickered as the locks clicked. "Thank you again for taking me out to the ranch. It was a lot of fun."

"You're welcome. I'm glad you enjoyed yourself."

"I did." She pressed her lips together as she dropped her gaze to the ground at their feet.

He stepped closer, bringing her head back up with a finger under her chin. The light from the street lamp illuminated her face. Her eyes sparkled in the light as her lips parted slightly. He couldn't stop himself from kissing her.

Their mouths met in the softest, barest touch. He lost himself in the feel of her lips as they molded to his. She sighed, allowing him access. Her hands were flat on his chest, but he could still feel her touch burning his skin through his shirt. His heart raced, pounding loudly in his ears. He rested his palms on her hips, bringing her closer to his body with a slight tug. He wanted to feel her molded to him as close as he could get.

A car honked as they went by, whistling loudly.

They separated reluctantly, but a smile lingered on her mouth when he looked down.

"Sorry about that."

"The kiss?"

"Oh hell no. The honking car. People are a bit redneck around here."

She giggled as she rested her forehead against his. He loved the way she did that.

"I should go," she whispered.

Her breath was warm against his mouth.

"I need to let you go."

"I wish I didn't have to."

"I know what you mean." He stepped back. "I'll see you tomorrow. Do you want to come out to the ranch in the morning? I know you need samples and stuff. I don't know if you need them specifically from our ground though."

She bit her lip for a moment before she smiled again. "I could use some from there even though I need a few more than just from there. That would be a good place to start. I can get some others from nearby too, while I'm out that way."

"Good. Maybe we could go for a ride."

"On a horse?"

"Well, sure."

"I've never been on a horse before."

"I'll teach you. It's easy. We have some real gentle ones that would be good for you. I've broke most every one of the horses on the ranch myself."

She nodded as she touched his face. He kissed her palm before it dropped to her side. "What time?"

"How about you come out for lunch at around eleven-thirty, and then we'll go out afterwards."

"All right."

He stepped back to give himself a little room to breathe. She tied him up in knots, and he really could use the air right now. "I'll see you tomorrow then."

"Yep."

"Good night, Rose."

"Good night, Joseph."

* * * *

Rose slipped into the driver's side of her rental car as Joseph pushed the door shut, tipped his hat, and then returned to his truck. A wistful sigh escaped her lips while she watched him in her side mirror. She touched the surface of her lips with her fingertips. They still tingled from his kiss.

She started the car, put it in drive, and pulled away from the curb. The hotel wasn't far, a few blocks down the road was all, but it gave her a little thrill to realize Joseph followed her to the hotel to make sure she got there okay.

He honked once before waving and turning around to head back down the road toward the ranch. Gentleman seemed to describe him to a T, and the thought of his little gestures made her heart trip over itself a little.

As she turned off the car and got ready to get out, her cell phone jingled in her purse. She grabbed it from its pocket in the back, turning it over to see who was calling.

Brandt.

She really needed to take his call.

"Hello?"

"Hey, sweetheart. How are things going in Texas?"

"Hi, Brandt." She gathered her thoughts for a moment. "Things are going fine here although I haven't been here long enough to really say much about it."

"I'm sure two days hasn't given you much time to do what you need to do yet."

"No, it hasn't. I've only settled into the hotel, unpacked my things and gotten something to eat." She cleared her throat knowing he was hinting at something. He always did. Now that she thought about it, his constant fishing for compliments and reassurance from her made him seem really annoying and not at all the self-assured man she'd originally thought he was.

"Do you miss me?"

She hesitated, realizing she really didn't miss him, not at all, but she couldn't tell him that. Brandt had been her constant companion for the last few years. They had dated for some time and had naturally gone to the next step with talking marriage. He considered himself her fiancé, although she didn't have a ring and he'd never really proposed. "Yes, of course I do." Her stomach knotted at the lie. She really wasn't an evil, conniving person but her spending time with Joseph felt like she was cheating.

"When will you be home, sweetheart?"

"Uh, I'm not sure, Brandt. It depends on how long it takes me to get the samples I need. I have to take them from several spots around the area, so it could take a week or more."

"How is the weather there?"

"Warm and sunny during the day, but not too hot yet. It's really nice."

"You sound like you are enjoying yourself." He sounded like a pouty five-year-old.

"I am for a change. Most of the time these trips are really boring. I've never been to Texas so it's a nice escape."

"But you love New York."

"I didn't say I didn't, Brandt. I like the area is all."

He went on for another several minutes talking about his work, his family, his apartment, his neighbors, and even his last meal.

"Listen, Brandt, I really need to go. I've been out all day and I'm exhausted. I just got back to my hotel room and I'm going to take a shower before I hit the bed."

"All right, sweetheart. I miss you and I can't wait for you to come home."

"I'll see you soon, I guess."

"I love you."

"Yeah, good night, Brandt." She hung up quickly before he could say another word. After spending the day with Joseph and his family, she realized that she wasn't in love with Brandt at all. Her idea of love was being with someone who could make her body tingle from a look, a touch of a hand that sent her heart to thundering in her chest, or the caress of a pair of lips that made her want to tear clothes off and do naughty things.

She blew out a breath, pushed open her car door, and climbed out.

The night sky was brilliantly lit with stars. Her head back, she stared at the beautiful sight above her head. *They've never looked this bright in New York.*

After a moment, she pulled out her room key, shut the door on the car, and walked to her room. She glanced across the road to where The Dusty Boot sat. Music blared as the doors opened and closed with each patron that moved through them. Men and women alike stood outside, some smoking cigarettes, and some hanging around talking with others. Everyone was dressed in jeans, western shirts, cowboy boots, and hats, even the women. A few men good-naturedly shoved each other as laughter echoed through the night, reaching her on the breeze.

The building itself caught her eye. A huge neon boot blinked over the top of the building. There was even a wooden rail along the sidewalk that reminded her of some old western movie where they tied their horses. Bright beer signs blinked in the windows advertising different types of the malt liquor for the patrons to try.

She smiled when she thought about Joseph taking her there tomorrow night. Shivering in the cooling night air, she wondered if it was from the weather or the anticipation of tomorrow. Her phone beeping brought her back to the present and Brandt's call. She blew out a frustrated breath. Better to deal with these feelings than let herself get any more bitter toward him than she already was.

Things with him hadn't been that great the last few weeks before she left. He'd become needy and clinging. He'd started asking her to do things for him like pick up his dry cleaning, do his grocery shopping, and he'd even asked her to buy his mother an anniversary gift, from him of course.

Lately, she'd even been going over to his house to pick up after him, make his bed, hang up his clothes, clean his apartment, and water his plants.

God forbid, she say anything about their sex life. Not that it had ever been much to talk about. He wasn't inventive in the bedroom and if she suggested anything new, he would say something about where she'd heard of that or had she been talking to her friends about what they did in the bedroom. It was straight missionary for him and most of the time it was over in a matter of minutes, leaving her unsatisfied. She had a feeling sex with Joseph wouldn't be boring in any sense of the word.

With a tired sigh, she headed for her room and slipped the key into the lock. The simple room was clean and simply adorned without much luxury outside of the bed, a dresser with an older television set sitting on top, and a small table with a chair for working on her computer. The clean but faded coverlet on the bed was typical for a hotel room with bright swirls and a paisley design. The curtains on the window were the same pattern. The bathroom was small, but it had a nice tub and shower combination that had a great showerhead in it.

She laid her purse on the table, kicked off her shoes, and sat down on the edge of the bed. She needed to get up, get her comfy PJs on and go to bed, but she felt wound up. Spending the day on the ranch seemed to have done that to her. She didn't really feel all that sleepy even though she really should be exhausted from all the excitement.

She tapped her fingers on her lips as she thought about what she could do to unwind. *Maybe a hot bath would be good or a nice novel to read. I have one of Mesa's books in my carryon that I was reading on the plane.*

With a smile of anticipation on her lips, she stood and grabbed her carryon bag from the floor next to the dresser. She pulled the paperback from the bag and turned it over in her hand to read the back.

What happens when a city girl meets a real hometown cowboy from a small town in Texas?

Sparks fly.

Missy Anderson leaves her comfortable existence in the big city to see what life might hold in Texas where the Bluebonnets bloom, everything is much simpler, summers are hot, and the men are hotter. When she's almost run over by a muddy, jacked up four-by-four and literally knocked on her butt by a handsome cowboy, she isn't prepared for the crystal clear blue eyes staring back. No one told her a cowboy might bowl her over with his gentlemanly behavior, sexy dimpled smile, and gorgeous ass in those jeans.

Dalton Jameson is as cowboy as they come. Born and raised on a small Texas ranch, he'd been breaking horses, riding fences, branding cattle, and living the cowboy dream since the day he'd been old enough to straddle a horse. Life didn't come better than waking up to a beautiful sunrise with a cup of coffee in his left hand and a set of reins in his right. The only thing missing was a cowgirl to call his own. He'd never pictured her as a woman with bright red hair, big green eyes, brand new cowboy boots, tight bespangled jeans, with an equally flashy blouse who he'd landed on when she almost got run over in the middle of town.

Can a woman who is used to catered meals, fancy cars, and diamonds and pearls be interested in a guy who drives a tractor, rides horses, and goes two-steppin' on Saturday nights? Can two such different people find what they are yearning for in the arms of a stranger?

She sighed as she hugged the book to her chest. Mesa's books had touched her in ways she hadn't even been aware of until recently. They made her lose herself in the story, picturing her own hair flying behind her as she rode across hills and valleys beside a gorgeous man on horseback. It didn't matter that she'd never ridden one before. She could still almost feel the soreness between her legs after she'd dismounted.

What about how her heroes made love? Holy shit, she wanted that, wanted it so badly she could almost taste it on her tongue. The excitement of making love with a man who knew what he was doing and cared about her satisfaction would be phenomenal. Brandt had always taken his pleasure, never caring whether she'd had an orgasm or not. In fact, most of the time she had to wait until he went to sleep, and then masturbated herself to one to get anything out of their sexual encounters.

A deep sigh escaped her at understanding how pathetic her relationship with Brandt actually was. He definitely wasn't the man she wanted to spend the rest of her life with anymore.

She licked her lips realizing she could still taste Joseph on them. Her heart did a little happy beat in her chest when she thought about experiencing a little more with him.

A breakup with Brandt was in order before she could give into those fantasies though.

Chapter Six

Joey cracked open his eyelids to the sunshine coming through the window of his room. When he rolled over the clock on the bedside table read six. He groaned softly as he buried his head under the pillow.

Sleep hadn't come easy for him the night before. Fanciful thoughts of one red haired girl had plagued him all night. Dreams of making love to her over and over had made it too uncomfortable to sleep. They kept dissipating the minute he'd be ready to bury himself in her sweet heat, leaving him aching and horny. His cock was already hard this morning.

He groaned as he rolled out from under the covers. Work called, much to his chagrin. He had horses to feed, stalls to clean, and tack to clean. His work day began early and didn't let up until the sun went down, but tonight he had a date, a date with a gorgeous woman that he couldn't seem to get out of his head.

Shower first, then work.

He grabbed a clean set of clothes and headed for the bathroom. It wasn't much since his room was one of the cabins farther away from the main lodge. He liked having his own space even though it didn't consist of a lot. A big room for his personal things like his bed, his dresser, his television, a computer, and a closet for his clothes was all he needed. The bathroom was separate and only had a bath/shower combination, a sink, and a toilet. It was enough for now. He didn't need much since he didn't have a woman and a bunch of kids like his brothers. When it was time for him to build his house, he'd have it on his piece of land his parents gave him on his eighteenth birthday.

The acreage was perfect with its own little pond, a great place for the house, and some land for him to raise horses.

He turned on the shower, letting it run for a few minutes to get some hot water going before he climbed inside. Once he stood underneath the spray, he let the water run over his head, sluicing down his chest in long rivulets. His thoughts drifted off to the beautiful redhead he'd met yesterday and what it would feel like to have her on her knees in the shower with him, sucking his cock like she wanted nothing more than to bring him to a shouting orgasm.

Deciding not to fight the fantasy, he palmed his cock with his right hand as he placed his left on the tile wall. He could picture her so clearly, gazing up at him with those emerald green eyes, her gorgeous long hair trailing down her back in long waves. Her lips parted as she smiled up at him, took him in her hand, and ran her tongue from the base of his cock to the tip. As her mouth engulfed the head of his cock, he groaned deep in his throat. The wet, warm sensations had him on the edge of climax within minutes, but he didn't want to come so soon. He wanted to relish her hot mouth around him. He dropped his head back on his shoulders as she continued to suck him until his legs shook.

Taking his balls in her hands, she rolled the flesh in her palm and continued to run her tongue up and around his cock. His pleasure reaching its climax, he grabbed her hair in his fists, guiding her to what would bring him to the brink of ecstasy.

His balls drew up against his groin as his orgasm hovered right on the precipice.

Seconds later, cum shot out of the end of his dick, painting the tile wall in front of him. A moan escaped his lips as he collapsed against the cold tile. "Fuck."

His breath came out in rapid pants as he tried to get his body under control. It had been a long time since he'd come that hard.

After he recovered, he grabbed the soap, washed the speckles of cum from his abdomen, and scrubbed the rest of his body clean. Shampoo came next as he scrubbed his hair.

He turned the water off after rinsing all the soap away and then grabbed a towel from the rack. Once he was dry, he pulled on his clean clothes, combed out his hair, put on some deodorant, and headed back into the bedroom to tug on his boots.

Coffee would definitely be required this morning. Maybe a bucketful of pure caffeine to keep him functioning.

The table by the door held his keys, his wallet, his cell phone, and his sunglasses in a small bowl. He slid everything into his pockets, except his sunglasses, which went on his face. Grabbing his hat off the rack on the wall, he placed it on his head.

When he opened the door, he was hit by a blast of cooler air. Apparently spring wasn't ready to give way to the warmer temperatures of Texas just yet. *It couldn't be much warmer than about forty degrees today.* Deciding to take his jacket with him, he grabbed it off the hook and slipped it on. The barn would be cold this morning.

He pulled the door shut behind him before he jiggled the handle to make sure it was locked. Even though there wasn't much worry about anyone on the place stealing things, he didn't want to tempt fate. Last summer they'd had a guest steal a few items before he'd been caught by Jason and escorted off the property.

His steps took him across the ground via the relatively long concrete walkway to the main lodge where coffee would be brewing. Those who worked the kitchen would be there already getting things ready for the guests' breakfast. Since they had such a large crowd right now, breakfast would be a big deal. Mesa's romance writer friends would be going home soon, but for now, they were guests and thus treated with every convenience the ranch could muster. It was kind of nice having a large group on the ranch during what was usually a slow period. They'd been really fun to have around these last few days.

Joey rounded the front of the main lodge and stopped dead in his tracks. Sitting in one of the chairs in front of the window was the old cowboy they'd seen over and over on the ranch since they'd lived there. They didn't know who he was but he showed himself sometimes at the oddest times.

The old man nodded, smiled, and then faded away like the morning mist.

Joey had always been fascinated by the stories of the ghosts on the ranch and now that he had a little time, he thought he might do some research on the place. It would be kind of cool if he could find out who the old man was. He knew the place had been a working brothel way back when, but it had also been a working ranch for many years. The old cowboy was probably a ranch hand who loved the place so much, he couldn't leave, even in death.

After a moment, he shook his head and continued on down the front porch to check on the donkeys before he went inside for his coffee. The donkey family they had were great for the guests. They liked being petted and fed when the guests were around, so they were real friendly, but it was his job as the head wrangler to make sure they were clean, trimmed, and in good shape.

He rounded the far corner of the porch to find the donkeys happily munching on some new spring grass. "There you are."

They jerked their heads up, ears forward, and started toward him. They knew who took care of them.

"Come on, Jack, Jenny, and Junior. I need to trim your hooves today so that means going to the barn."

The donkey family happily followed him out around the back of the main lodge, across the parking lot for the guests' cars, and to the barn in the distance. He would get them into a stall with some sweet feed, lock the door, and then get his coffee. It could get interesting rounding those three up in the mornings.

Once he got them locked in a stall, he headed back to the big house to grab his coffee and maybe a muffin to tie him over until breakfast was ready.

He pushed open the side door of the main lodge and moved inside. Scents of baking reached his nose, making his stomach growl in anticipation of a warm blueberry muffin. The coffee pot sat on the table near where the family usually ate their meals, ready and waiting with its luminescent red light on telling him that it was ready and hot. Finding his normal cup sitting in the clean rack, he grabbed it and stuck it under the spout before pulling the handle down to fill the cup. After he doctored it with a little cream and sugar, he sipped on the hot liquid as he groaned in appreciation.

"Mornin', Joey."

He turned to find Jonathan's girl, Mandy, walking toward him with muffins in a basket. "Mornin', Mandy. Are there blueberry in there?"

"Of course. I know how you love those and it's your early day in the barn this morning."

"God love you, woman." He kissed her on the cheek.

"You are such a sweetheart. I hope you find a nice girl soon, and that doesn't mean that little slut next door."

He frowned as he mumbled through the muffin. "Jessie?"

"Yeah, that's her." She nodded. "Be careful of her. She's out to trap her a Young brother and you're the only one left."

"Don't worry, Mandy."

Mandy laid the basket of muffins on the table near the coffee pot. "I think that girl you brought to dinner last night was cute. You met her at the diner?"

"Yes. She was sketching at one of the tables." He shoved another bite of muffin into his mouth. "She's really good."

"She doesn't live here?"

"No. She's from New York."

"What's she doing in Bandera, Texas?"

"She's a microbiologist. She's here to study the water and soil for the company she works for."

Mandy's brow crinkled as she frowned. "Okay."

Joseph laughed. "I don't know much about it either. I'm only a simple cowboy." Mandy punched him in the arm as he faked being hurt while he rubbed his bicep. "Ow!"

"Yeah, whatever, you ass. You have more talent in your pinky than most of the men on this place. You have a way with animals they could only hope to have."

He shrugged, dropping his gaze to the floor. "I ain't nothin' special."

She pushed his hat back. "You are too. You single-handedly run that barn with all those horses for the guests, break new animals that come in, keep the donkey family happy, and most importantly you keep the horses taken care of so they can give the guests the cowboy experience they are here for. You are very special."

"Okay, okay. Thanks for the pep talk."

"You're welcome. Now, I'm sure you have some hungry animals out there to take care of. I can hear the donkeys braying all the way up here."

"Yeah, they weren't happy to be locked in the stall."

"They never are, but they need to be taken care of too. All the crap they get from the dining room can't be good for them."

He leaned in a kissed her on the cheek again. "You are a special woman, Mandy."

They could hear a pair of boots on the hardwood as Jonathan appeared around the corner of the dining room. "You bet she is, brother, now get your hands off my lady."

Joseph grinned as he turned on his booted heels and headed back for the barn. He was glad Jonathan finally came to his senses about Mandy. She'd been a part of the group at Thunder Ridge for a few years now. Her pining over his brother had been apparent to everyone but him. Jonathan had realized if he didn't do something soon, he'd lose his chance with the feisty blonde. They were planning to get married soon.

He frowned as his boots crunched under the gravel of the walkway. All of his brothers were paired off now, leaving him to fend for himself when it came to women. He really didn't think he was ready to settle down yet. He still had a lot of living to do, and besides, he wasn't financially prepared to take on a wife. He didn't have much in savings except for a few thousand he'd managed to squirrel away from riding broncs on the rodeo circuit.

As he passed through the big double doors of the barn, he was surrounded by familiar scents. The mixed aromas of horses, hay, manure, and leather met his nose, making him smile. The smells embraced him as he inhaled a big deep breath. Home.

A soft whistle left his lips as he walked down the dirt center of the barn toward his small office space in the back. He kept his records and such in there, so he knew exactly when each horse was born, broke, died, retired or foaled. It was important for him to know these facts since he was responsible for every animal on the place.

Today meant a trip into town too. He needed to get the feed and get the mare broke he'd forgotten about yesterday, not that he'd minded being distracted. The pretty redhead was quite the distraction.

Excitement rippled down his back when he thought about her. He glanced at his watch. Still too early for her to be here. He'd told her eleven. He snapped his figures. *I'll trim the donkeys, run into town for feed, and be back in time for her to be here for lunch.*

He nodded at his plan as he grabbed his snippers and file before he went back down to the stall he'd locked the donkeys in. Jack kicked the door as he approached. "Easy, boy. I'm comin'."

When he reached the stall, he popped open the door and stepped inside to hook a lead rope to the donkey's halter. He led him out into the middle of the walkway, shutting the door behind him so Jenny and Junior wouldn't come out. They had hooks connected to two of the wooden beams in order to saddle horses, work on them, or whatever they needed to do. Once he had Jack crosstied, he went back down the aisle to where he'd hung his leather chaps. He needed those to keep his legs safe in case something went terribly wrong while he was shoeing or clipping hooves. Lucky for him, he hadn't had a problem in a long time.

The chaps around his hips and legs, he got the nippers out, picked up a hoof and started trimming around it. Jack was a patient animal, always standing perfectly still while he did what he had to do. Jenny wasn't such an easy one to work on and forget Junior. Being so young, the little guy needed some help being comfortable with getting his feet trimmed.

He worked for over an hour on the three donkeys, getting them brushed, feet trimmed and ready to meet their public. He laughed to himself. The donkeys had a fan club even.

By the time he was done, it was almost time for breakfast. He would have to hurry if he was going to get the horses fed, watered and saddled for the nine o'clock trail ride and be inside for his own food. He hated missing breakfast.

Jeff drove up in his truck, parking near the barn. He got out and walked through the double doors. "Need some help?"

"Yeah, a little. I trimmed hooves this morning and got a little behind. If you can get the horses out and fill their water buckets, I'll get the feed. Is anyone else around who might be able to saddle some of them?"

"I think Joel is inside. Let me go see if I can find him."

"Thanks."

"Sure."

Jeff disappeared for several minutes into the main lodge, but when he returned he had Joel and Jason with him. "These two were hanging out near the coffee pot."

Joseph laughed before he started directing everyone to what he needed done. Within thirty minutes, they had all the horses being used that day tied out in their spots in the corral, watered, fed, and saddled. "Thanks, guys."

"You're welcome. Now you don't have to miss breakfast." Joel laughed as he slapped Joey on the back. "I know how irritable you can get without food."

"Asshole."

Joel grinned as they all headed toward the house just as the breakfast bell began to clang, calling everyone in for the meal.

Breakfast was the social event of the hour at the ranch. Most of the guests made it to the first meal of the day before they went on with the other activities available at the ranch. It was still rather cool outside in the mornings, so there wouldn't be anyone swimming, and since the majority of the guests on the ranch at the moment were Mesa's writer friends, much of their time seemed to be spent observing the guys.

The room buzzed with conversation as they headed toward the family table. A couple of women whistled when they walked by. Joel tipped his hat and grinned the patent Young grin, leaving them laughing behind him.

"Mesa, you got so lucky, girl. I want me a cowboy."

Mesa wrapped her arms around Joel's shoulders and kissed him on the mouth. "Well, there is only of the boys not attached. Keep your hands off Joel. He's mine."

"You bet, babe." He swept her up in a hug, twirling her around a couple of times as the women behind them sighed.

"Point out the one that isn't taken."

"Come up here, Joey."

She motioned at him with her hand as he tried to blend into the woodwork. Leave it to Mesa to embarrass the hell of out him. She knew he didn't like to be the center of attention, except in the rodeo arena. He shook his head.

She grabbed his hand and dragged him out in front of everyone. He could feel his face flush beet red.

"This, ladies, is Joseph Young. He's the youngest of the boys. He's the head wrangler on the place. He likes working with his hands, rope, leather, and occasionally rides rodeo. He stands over six feet tall and built solid. Wouldn't you love running your hands over these muscles?"

He was going to kill her even if she was his sister-in-law. "Mesa," he growled.

"He growls too, ladies."

The women twittered behind their hands.

"I'm going to sit down."

Mesa laughed as he turned his back to the group and walked to the family table. "And look at that butt in those jeans!"

He stopped next to Joel. "I'm going to kill your wife."

"She's only havin' fun at your expense."

"I realize that, but I'm still going to kill her because now they won't leave me alone for the rest of the time they're here."

"They might if you bring that pretty redhead back."

"She'll be here for lunch."

Joel grinned and slapped him on the back. "She seems to like you."

"I like her too."

"Better than Jessie?"

He thought about that for a moment and realized yeah, he liked Rose a lot more than he liked Jessica or any other woman he'd known in his past. "Yeah. I guess I do."

"You are a goner, buddy."

A few hours later, after he'd made the run into town for feed and Jeff, Joel, and Jason helped him unload, he paced the walkway from the barn to the back of the cabins as he waited for Rose to appear. The anxiousness sitting in the pit of his stomach worried him. He wasn't used to being this way with a woman, any woman. It wasn't like there could be anything between them anyway. She didn't live here. Hell, she lived at least a couple of thousand miles away.

He stopped in the doorway of the barn and turned to watch the driveway. He took off his hat and ran his fingers through his hair before putting it back on his head. Why he was so nervous about seeing her again, he wasn't sure. Yeah, she was pretty, smart, and all that, but it was something more, something he wasn't sure he wanted to explore.

The gate was too far away to see, but when a cloud of dust appeared, he moved toward the parking lot to await her arrival. He glanced at his watch, right on time. It was unheard of for any woman he knew to be punctual, apparently she was an exception to the rule.

When she stopped the car near the bottom of the hill by the pool, he hurried his steps to reach her side before she had a chance to get out of the car. He pulled open the door, grinning as she let out a startled squeak. "I didn't mean to frighten you."

"Joseph." She sighed. "I didn't expect you to be right here by the car. I'm sure you have work to do, right?"

"True, but I've been waiting for you."

"I'm flattered," she said, stepping out and pushing the door shut behind her. "Have you been busy this morning?"

"Yeah, a little. Nothing too strenuous though. I trimmed the donkeys, got the horses being used today ready to ride, normal stuff." He placed his hand at the small of her back to lead her toward the house. "Lunch should be ready shortly."

She giggled as they walked. "I'm going to get fat with all this food you have around here."

"You? No way. Besides, we have a lot of things you can do around here to work off whatever you eat."

"Oh?"

His thoughts went straight into the toilet as he imagined her spread out on a bale of hay waiting for him with her arms raised above her head, her red hair spread out around her like a halo, and a come-hither smile on her lips. "Yeah." He'd had women in the barn before, on a few occasions, but he couldn't get the thought of Rose in the hayloft with him out of his head. He cleared his throat trying to dispel the image. "I've talked to Mesa, and she would love to meet you."

"Really?"

"Yeah. She likes meeting her fans."

"I wish I had all my books with me. I have several of hers, but I only brought one."

"I'm sure she'd be glad to sign it."

She placed her hand on his arm to stop his steps. "Thank you, Joseph."

When her lips brushed his cheek, he had to keep himself from grabbing her, pulling her into his arms, and devouring her mouth.

As she stepped back, he took her hand, threaded their fingers together, and continued onto the main lodge. "There may be some other authors here that you know. Most of them are western authors from what I understand. I don't know if you read those or not."

"I've read some, yes, but I feel very ignorant when it comes to horses and stuff."

"I think the authors are going home on Monday, so you have a few days if you want to talk to them."

A frown pulled down the corners of her mouth. "I don't want to ruin my time with you either. I think you are a very special person, and I'm enjoying your company."

"I like having you here."

She smiled again as he opened the door for her to go in front of him. When they walked inside, the room was in total chaos as it had been since this group had arrived. They spent every waking moment in the main lodge or outside with his brothers, writing things down, taking pictures, and doing whatever it is writers do. He had to laugh a little because they were a nosy bunch.

One of the authors got up from her seat and came toward them, stopping them in the middle of walkway. "Hi, Joseph."

"Hello."

She ran a finger down his chest. "I could really use some personal, one-on-one time with you. You know, for research."

"Uh, sorry, but I have a friend here today that I'm helping with a project."

The woman glanced at Rose before focusing on him again. "Are you going to be busy all weekend?"

"Probably." *God, I hope so. This woman is at least twenty years older than me.* "I'm sorry. We appreciate you coming to the ranch, but Rose needs my help with gathering some samples from our property. I'm sure it will take until at least Tuesday." He glanced down into Rose's eyes. "Right, Rose?" *I hope she gets my message.*

"Yes, of course. Tuesday will probably be the soonest we are finished."

"I'm sure you understand."

The woman fingered the buttons on the front of his shirt. Apprehension slithered down his spine as he grasped Rose's hand tighter. When the woman looked up, he caught something in her gaze that he wasn't sure he liked. Determination to get what she wanted, stared back.

"All right then. Maybe some other time."

"Sure."

She stepped away and went back to her spot near her friends, but her gaze never left his back as he continued toward the family table with Rose by his side.

"I don't trust her," Rose whispered as he pulled out the chair for her.

"Yeah, me either, but it is what it is. I'll keep a close eye on her."

"Do you always get that kind of attention?"

"More and more these days."

"Why is that? I mean other than you being a very handsome man."

He smiled as he looked down into her eyes. "Thank you, but it's mostly because I'm the only unattached cowboy left of the original nine brothers. It comes with its hazards, I guess." He pulled up the chair next to her and sat down. "We have to be nice to the guests, so it comes with getting attention we might not necessarily want."

"I see."

He took her hand in his, slowly rubbing a spot on the back. He liked the feeling of her skin beneath his. It was very soft to the touch. "I don't worry much about them. They'll be gone soon."

Mesa walked over from where she'd been sitting with a small group at one of the large square tables. "You must be Rose."

"I…yes."

Mesa held out her hand. "I'm Mesa Young or Mesa West is how you might know me."

Rose put her hand to her throat and stuttered out a few words that made no sense to him at all.

"It's okay. I just wanted to stop and say hello. I hear you like my books."

"Yes, ma'am. I love them. I have your latest in my hotel room. I'm reading it right now."

"Thank you, Rose. I appreciate you being a fan, and I hope you are enjoying the book."

"Tremendously." Rose leaned toward Mesa slightly. "Tell me. Are your cowboys based on Joel and his brothers?"

Mesa laughed. "Some, yes, but not always. The boys are great inspiration though." Mesa laid her hand on his shoulder. "In fact, the one I'm currently writing reminds me a lot of Joey."

"Really?"

"Yes, but don't tell him that. He might get a big head or something." She leaned down and kissed him on the cheek. "Love you, Joey."

"Love you too, Mesa, now go back over there and behave or I'll have Joel take a switch to your behind."

Mesa's eyes widened as a grin spread across her lips. "I might like it."

"You just might."

When Mesa walked away, Rose turned to him and whispered under her breath, "Do you like to spank women?"

Chapter Seven

Joseph coughed and sputtered as his eyes widened. "Well, I, uh…"

"I'm kidding, Joseph." She giggled before laying her hand on his thigh. "Whatever you do in the bedroom is your business."

He smiled and touched her nose with his finger.

A sigh escaped her lips when he stood so they could get their lunch since the guests had already retrieved theirs. As she followed him to the line, he pushed her in front of him, giving her the opportunity to get her food first.

"Guests first."

"I'm not a guest."

"Yes, you are. You're my guest."

He put his hands on her hips and turned her so her back was to his chest. Shivers raced down her spine as she felt his warm breath on her neck where she'd tied her hair up in a ponytail today. She wanted his lips there more than anything she could think of. Her feet felt like lead when she took a step toward the food being served. *How fast can this meal be over?*

Her thoughts did a one-eighty when she remembered Brandt. She'd been so inspired by Mesa's book that dealing with the reality of her own relationship slipped her mind this morning. *Well shit. I need to take care of that pronto, otherwise, I can't move forward with Joseph even if it's a temporary thing.*

Do I want to end things with Brandt if this thing with Joseph is only for a few weeks?

Yes.

After lunch I will take a moment and call Brandt to cut things off.

"You okay?" he asked as they took their seats and he set her plate down in front of her.

"I'm fine. I just remembered I need to make a phone call after we are done eating."

"Sure." He glanced down at her and then to the refreshment table. "Tea, lemonade, or water?"

"Lemonade would be great. Thank you."

As the rest of the family returned to the table, conversation flowed around her. She couldn't quite keep up with what everyone was talking about, so she focused on one conversation near her between Jackson and Samantha.

"Babe, we need to work on the tour schedule this afternoon."

"I need to rehearse this afternoon, Jackson. The guys from the band are traveling into San Antonio so we can work on some new material."

"I realize that, but I can't book your dates if I don't know what we already have in the pipeline."

Samantha wiped something from the corner of his mouth. "It will work out, cowboy. It always does." She leaned in a kissed him on the mouth.

Rose sighed as she watched. She wanted that more than anything. She wanted to be able to touch a guy tenderly, stroke his skin, run her fingers through his hair, and be with him every moment without worrying about how uncomfortable that made him feel. Couples shouldn't be uncomfortable around each other like her and Brandt had become. He didn't like when she watched television while he was working on paperwork. He didn't like what she cooked for dinner. He didn't like how she did his laundry. He didn't like how she wanted more from their sex life. *Why haven't I broken up with him before now?*

What appeared to be an argument coming to a head at the end of the table caught her attention.

"No, Jason."

"Now, Peyton, you know you want to."

"No, actually, I don't. We've had this discussion." Peyton glanced around the table, lowering her voice, but not enough that Rose couldn't hear it. "Stop badgering me. I'm not going to change my mind."

"Why? I don't understand."

"We are not having this conversation at the family table, Jason. I've told you where I stand on this subject, we've talked about it, and you said you understood. Are you saying now you don't?"

"Baby, I know you are apprehensive, but it's a natural thing. It's what couples do when they are married and in love."

"This half of this couple doesn't want any."

Nina laid her napkin aside and focused on Peyton. "Is everything all right, Peyton?"

"You know what, no, it's not. Jason and I have had a conversation about having children. I don't want any, period. He's being persistent that I will change my mind once I become pregnant. He said he understood, but now he's driving me nuts with all this talk about babies."

"Jason, why don't you and Peyton take this into the office," Nina suggested as she glanced at the now quiet room.

"Fine." Jason grabbed his wife's hand, pulled her up, and dragged her off down the hall and around the corner until they disappeared from view.

A door slammed in the distance.

Rose swallowed hard as she glanced at Joseph.

Nina rose from her seat to address the group in the dining room. "Sorry. That shouldn't have happened at the table. We try to encourage our children to talk out their problems, but we do hope they won't do it in front of guests. Please accept our apologies and enjoy the rest of your meal."

Lunch continued as a quiet affair and Rose couldn't wait to leave. Couple problems always made her anxious whether they were her own or someone else's.

When they'd finished their meal, Joseph grabbed their plates to put them in the dish bin.

"Ready to go?"

"Yes." She breathed a sigh of relief to be able to go outside into the sunshine and forget the tension in the room.

He held open the door as she passed through it and then placed his palm at the small of her back to guide her toward the barn.

As they moved through the huge doorway into the cooler interior of the barn, her eyes adjusted to the dark and she noticed several horses still in their stalls. She knew Joseph would have already taken several out to have them ready for guests to ride. She couldn't wait to get on the back of a horse. Ever since she was a little girl, she'd wanted a horse.

"Uh, can you give me a few minutes to make that call I mentioned?"

"Sure. You can use Jeremiah's office, if you want. He's still in the house with Callie, so he won't disturb you."

"Thank you. Are we going riding today?"

"If you want, but first I need to teach you a few things about being around horses. After you make your call, we can grab the tack for them. I didn't saddle my horse this morning and the one you would ride isn't saddled either."

"Okay." She loved the smell of the tack room. When they'd been in there before, she pulled all those scents into her lungs and held them. Leather had always turned her on.

They passed through the doorway and Joseph moved toward where the saddles were kept on the wall. She went to the open door to Jeremiah's office and closed it behind her as she pulled out her cell phone.

"Hello?"

"Hi, Brandt."

"Hi, Rose. It's odd for you to be calling me in the middle of the day. Is there something wrong?"

"No. You aren't in a meeting, are you?"

"No. I'm free for about thirty minutes. I have a client coming in for a consultation after lunch."

"Oh. I forgot that Texas is an hour behind New York."

"Is something wrong, honey?"

"Listen, Brandt. I know things have not been great between us for some time. We've been drifting apart for months, you don't like how I do many of the things around our place, and face it, sex between us has gotten to the point where it's boring."

"What are you saying, Rose?"

"I don't want to see you anymore. I will have my father come over and move my personal things out of our apartment tomorrow. The rest of my furniture and bigger items will be taken care of when I get back from Texas in a week or so.”

“What!”

“I’m sorry, Brandt, but I feel this is for the best. I’m not in love with you anymore and I think the best thing for us both is to move on.”

“What the hell, Rose? Are you seeing some hick Texas cowboy or something? Where did this come from? Everything was fine before you left.”

“No, no it wasn’t, Brandt. Things have been bad for me for a while. And no, I’m not seeing some hick Texas cowboy while I’m here. I’ve made a few friends, but that’s it. I’m trying to get my work done so I can come back to New York, but I don’t want to come back to you.”

“You can’t do this! I had plans for us, big plans. I need you by my side when I make partner at the firm. I need your father’s backing.”

“Excuse me?”

“You heard me. I need your father’s backing, his financial support while I’m working on making partner and when I start my political career. You owe me!”

“For one, neither I, nor my father, owe you anything, Brandt. Apparently, you’ve been after my family’s financial backing all this time, and I just wasn’t aware of your motivation. Now that I am, I don’t feel the least bit sorry to be ending this relationship. As I said, I will have my father come over tomorrow to pack my personal items. If they aren’t in pristine condition when he arrives, you will be hearing from my attorney. Since both of our names are on the lease, I will be contacting the landlord to let them know you will be staying, but I’m leaving. We are already past our lease date on this apartment, so me moving out shouldn’t be a problem with them.”

“You can’t do this, Rose! I love you. I need you. Don’t walk out on me, please.”

His whiny voice grated on her nerves as she held the phone away from her ear. “I’m done, Brandt. I’m sorry it has to end this way, but I need to try new things and staying with you isn’t in the cards. Goodbye.” She hit the end button on her cell and exhaled a long, slow breath. *That wasn’t pleasant at all.*

Checking her appearance, she looked down at her blouse tucked into her brand new jeans and saw the dust on the tips of her brand new cowboy boots. At least Joseph couldn’t say she hadn’t dressed the part today. Feeling relieved and a little more lighthearted, she pushed open the door and came face to face with a scowling Joseph Young.

“Joseph? Is there a problem?”

“Why didn’t you tell me you had a boyfriend, Rose? You let me kiss you by the pond.” His hat hit the floor behind him as he raked his fingers through his hair. “What the hell?”

“That’s not it at all.”

"What is it then, Rose? I don't mess with women who belong to someone else." He reached down and picked up his hat before shoving it back on his head.

Irritation radiated off him in waves.

She moved close enough to touch him as she reached up and smoothed the frown lines from his face. "I assume you heard part of my conversation."

"Yeah."

"I did have a boyfriend when I came here. His name is Brandt and he's an attorney."

"Fucking wonderful." He spun on his heel and moved toward one of the stalls.

He pulled back his arm and punched his hand through the board in front of him. When he lifted his hand to his face, his knuckles were bleeding and torn.

She winced as she touched his back, smoothing his shirt over his broad shoulders. "Joseph, I'm sorry. I never meant to hurt you." She put her forehead on his shoulder blade. "When you kissed me the first time, it was like I awoke from a dream. It was so different from anything I'd experienced." He hadn't moved. Hell, she wasn't sure he'd heard her except for the pounding of his heart under her cheek when she laid it flat on his back and encircled his waist with her arms. "I broke up with him on the phone. Things haven't been good between us for a long time. You made me see that. You brought out sensations in me I've never felt with him and it made me realize things with him were bad for a while."

"Maybe you shouldn't have broken up with him. Maybe you should have tried to work things out." He turned to face her and she was taken aback by the look in his eyes. Frustration, anger, and disappointment reflected in his gaze.

She touched his face. "I'm attracted to you, which is why I broke things off with him. I didn't feel it was fair to either of you to be playing like that." After several tense moments, he framed her face with his hands, grimacing when he bent his knuckles. "You should clean that up," she whispered, her gaze stopping on his lips and how close they were to her mouth. She wanted his mouth on hers. She needed to feel his lips brushing hers, his tongue demanding entrance, and his body wrapped around hers. The passion between them could set the barn on fire, if they let it, but he was holding back.

She looked up into his eyes. The brown of his irises looked like dark chocolate. She wanted to drown in him.

"Joseph," she murmured, drawing his gaze to her lips.

"Why do I feel like I'm drowning in your eyes? I can't help myself when I'm around you. I have this desperate need to touch you, kiss you, and see what making love to you would be like." He continued to stare at her face, his gaze running over the surfaces for long moments before he slowly brought their mouths together. The soft meeting of their lips, the feel of his hands framing her face, and the warmth of his body close to hers had her sighing into his mouth. Being kissed like this, so softly and so gently, was something she'd only ever dreamed of. The man knew how to kiss.

Tingling started in her toes and rushed up her legs as if her feet had gone to sleep. Her whole body turned warm and languid, pliable to his hands. The need for something to anchor her had her wrapping her hands around his wrists as her body came alive under his. Her nipples pulled into tight little nubs. Her belly turned into one large knot as she waited for him to do something, anything.

His tongue slipped along the seam of her lips, asking for permission to take the kiss deeper. When she opened her mouth, a growl erupted from him as he tilted his head and devoured her. It was the only word she could think of for the way he ate at her mouth, his tongue sliding over hers in a desperate need to taste her, kiss her, and make her his.

His hands wandered over her shoulders, and down her arms, stopping at her waist. He grasped her hips and pulled her into his embrace so they were touching from lips to hips. His cock lay hard against her belly, clearly outlined by his jeans.

When his lips left hers, he kissed his way across her cheek, nibbling along her jawline with his teeth as she tipped her head back to give him better access to what he desired. One hand came up to cup her breast, rasping his thumb across the already hard nipple.

"God, Joseph."

He growled low in his throat as he snuck his hand up her blouse.

Skin to skin felt amazing. The calluses on his hand rubbed deliciously against her flesh. She wrapped her arms around his shoulders, giving him better access to her breast. When his hand pushed her bra out of the way, she sucked in a ragged breath as a shiver raced down her spine. The callus on his thumb scraped the tip of her nipple, driving a moan from her mouth.

His hand grasped the ponytail holder and pulled it out of her hair, leaving it flowing down around her shoulders. He lifted his head, looking down into her gaze. "I love your hair," he whispered before he buried his hands in the strands, pulling her head back again. "It works so well when I want your neck bared to my touch."

He nipped at her neck as he worked his way from her jaw to her collarbone. The little bites on her flesh drove her wild with desire. Brandt had never taken what he wanted when they made love. She had a feeling Joseph would give her little choice as he played her body until she was strung tighter than a violin string.

His breath came out in rasping pants against her skin as he slowed down, touching her softly before he removed his hands altogether and stepped back.

Fog clouded her brain as she tried to figure out why he stopped. "Joseph?"

"Rose, you are so beautiful, so sexy." He kissed her nose. "God, I want you so bad, I hurt, but I don't want to take something you aren't willing to give me. Your body is something precious. Making love with you would be very special to me, but we haven't known each other very long, only a couple of days, and I don't want to take advantage of you." He turned his back and walked a few steps away from her, lacing his hands behind his head.

She pressed herself against his back. "You won't be taking advantage of me. I want you to make love to me. I want to feel what it's like to be with someone who takes care of my needs. I think you would be that guy."

"You know I can't promise anything beyond right now."

"I don't expect you to, Joseph. We both have separate lives we are living and they don't mesh, not even close. We could have a lot of fun for a few days, learn some things about each other, and ourselves, I think." She turned him back around to face her so she could see the expressions that were clear in his eyes. "I want you. I want to feel you inside me. I have a feeling you could teach me a thing or two about sex. I'm willing to be your student. Someday that might come in handy."

He grinned as he shook his head. "You want me to teach you about sex?"

"Yes, actually, I do. I want to know what it's like to be with someone who knows what they are doing and has a handle on how to make sure a woman is taken care of."

"Not a problem, baby. It would be my pleasure to show you how your body can react to certain sensations, touching, stroking, licking, sucking, and everything your body will crave before actual sex occurs."

She brought his hand to her mouth, taking one finger inside to suck like she would his cock if he gave her the chance. Blowjobs were something she enjoyed doing to the guy she was with, not that she had a lot of experience at it, but she liked making a man lose control. When she released his finger, she smiled as she ran her tongue over her lips. "Where can we go?"

"I have my own room in the back part of the barn. It's quiet and private."

"Perfect."

"You're sure?"

"Definitely sure."

He laced their fingers together as he turned and led her down past the stalls to an uncircumspect door off in the corner of the barn. He glanced around him, over his shoulder, and listened before he pulled out a set of keys, unlocked the door, and swept his hand aside to allow her to precede him.

"We won't get into trouble, will we? I mean, you should be working right now."

He held up on finger and pulled out his cell phone. After a moment, he hit a button and put the phone up to his ear. "Hey, Jeff. I'm going to be tied up for a couple of hours. I, uh, had to run into town for a piece of tack that broke while I was cleaning it the other day."

She smiled. A couple of hours would be grand to spend in his arms. They would have to make sure they were very quiet though. Guests would be walking around in the barn and out in the paddocks as well as his brothers.

"Yeah. I'll be back soon." He glanced at his watch. "Hey, can you take out the two o'clock and three o'clock rides? I was scheduled for those, but I will probably have to go to San Antonio to get this piece so I won't be back." He nodded as he smiled over at her. "Yeah, Joshua or Joel can take one and you can take the other, if that works for you."

She began working the buttons on her blouse loose as he continued his conversation with Jeff on the phone. A small giggle escaped her lips as his eyes widened the closer she got to the bottom of the blouse. Her bra was still pushed up around her neck. When she parted the material, her breasts were partially exposed to his darkening gaze. His pupils were now dilated and his face was flush with desire. He swallowed hard when she wet her index finger of her right hand, pushed the material out of the way, and began to run her wet finger around her nipple.

"Uh, yeah. Listen, I need to go so I can get back." He hit end on the phone, tossed it onto the desk next to the wall and stalked closer. "You left the door open."

She glanced behind her. "I did, didn't I."

"Do you want everyone to see what we are about to do?"

She tilted her head to the side, slowly she snaked her hand down her abdomen to where the button at her waist held her pants together, flicked it open, and pushed her hand under the waistband of her jeans and underwear.

"You're a naughty girl."

"Don't you like naughty girls?"

He pushed the door shut, snicked the lock, and turned back to face her. "I love naughty girls." He leaned back against the door, crossing his feet at the ankles, and got comfortable. "Touch yourself."

"I am."

His words came out on a sigh. "Like you mean it. Like you want me to touch you."

She pulled her bottom lip between her teeth as she pushed her jeans and underwear down around her boots. She slid her fingers down to her pussy, wet them with her juices, and then spread it around her clit. The sensation was something she wasn't prepared for as desire rushed through her veins. Her body pulsed with need. Her head felt like it was about to come off her shoulders, all because of the look in his eyes.

The desire radiating off him was something she'd only dreamt about.

He stalked toward her with measured steps, a slow rolling of his hips. "You are so fucking hot right now."

As he got to within a few steps of her, she stopped pleasuring herself and slowly slid her hand up her abdomen to cup her breast and swirl the wet fingertip around her nipple.

With a quick move, she reached around behind herself, unsnapped her bra and pulled it as well as her top off her arms.

He grasped his T-shirt in his hands, tugging it up and over his head, effectively knocking his hat to the floor.

She toed off her boots and dragged her jeans and underwear off her feet before she took a few steps backwards, landing on his bed. Naked as the day she was born, she watched him unbuckled his belt, unfasten his jeans, and push them all to the floor.

When his cock sprang free of the confinement of his jeans, she sucked in a ragged breath before releasing it on a sigh. His cock was long and thick. The head was purple and glistening with a drop of pre-cum on the tip. He definitely wanted her that was for sure.

He dropped in a small chair to toe off his boots and get rid of his jeans.

"You do have a condom, right?"

"Yeah. In the nightstand drawer. I like to be prepared."

She rolled on her side on the bed, pulled open the drawer and had to stifle a giggle as she pulled out a long string of condoms. "Prepared or wishful thinking?"

He grinned as he stood and moved toward her. "I bought them last night after I dropped you off at your car."

"You didn't answer my question."

"A little of both maybe? I knew what I wanted, Rose. I just wanted to make sure you wanted it too."

"From the moment you kissed me at the pond, I wanted this with you."

He frowned as he took the place next to her on the bed. "You are okay with this, right? I mean, you just broke up with your boyfriend. I have no idea how long you'd been seeing him, but I imagine it wasn't just a casual relationship."

"We'd been together for a while, but that doesn't matter now, he doesn't matter now. I don't love him, and I don't want to be with him anymore. Even if you weren't part of the equation, Joseph, this would have been the outcome for him and I. I'd begun to realize that even before I came to Texas and met you." She skimmed her hand over his chest, letting the curls slide through her fingers. "Now are you going to make love to me or not?"

Chapter Eight

Joseph quickly rolled her over onto her back, hovering over her. "You're damned right I'm going to make love to you, fuck your brains out, give you multiple orgasms, and make you feel like you've never felt before."

"Sounds perfect."

He brought their lips together, relishing the softness of hers under his. She felt perfect, more than perfect, she felt amazing. Her lips fit against his so well he was lost to the sensations.

As he skimmed his hand up her side to the under part of her breast, she sucked in a choppy breath. Her eyes were bright and sparkling in the light of his room. Red hair framed her face in small, wispy curls. She apparently didn't spend much time in the sun with her pale complexion. He wasn't surprised though with her features, she probably had some Irish in her and would burn easily.

"You have beautiful breasts. They are the perfect size for my hands." He cupped the right one, feeling the weight of the flesh in his palm. He bent his head and took the nipple into his mouth, biting the tip with small nips.

A moan escaped her lips as her back arched, pushing the flesh into him. "That feels fantastic."

He leaned up, noticing her head was thrown back on the pillow, her eyes were closed, and her mouth was open in a silent sound of ecstasy. The picture was magnificent.

A stroke of his tongue along the underside of her breast brought a groan to the surface. As he continued to brush his tongue over her skin on his way to the red curls at the apex of her thighs, she wiggled under his mouth until he placed his hands at her hips to still her.

"Joseph?"

"Sshh. I'll make you feel good. I promise." He positioned himself between her thighs, kissing the inside of her legs before he nipped at them playfully, and then brought his nose to the crease between her pussy and her thigh. He loved the faint scent of her perfume and the musky smell of an aroused woman.

Her hands were fisted at her sides until he swiped his tongue from her pussy to her clit.

"Oh, God!"

Her thighs opened wider as he continued his planned seduction of her body in order to give her the most satisfaction he possibly could. He wanted to make sure she remembered him and how he made her feel for a long time to come.

Liquid seeped from her pussy as he continued to lick, suck, and eat at her flesh like a starving man. He loved the taste of her and the feel of her under his hands.

She tried lifting her hips to push her clit harder against his mouth, but he held her hips in place with an arm across her pelvis.

He ramped up her pleasure as he slipped two fingers deep into her pussy while still teasing her with his tongue.

Her moans became more frequent and louder until she pulled the pillow from the other side of the bed over her face.

He almost laughed because he knew she was trying to muffle the sounds of her enjoyment from anyone who might be close enough to hear outside their little sanctuary. Personally, he didn't care if anyone heard them.

The moment her orgasm hit, she stuffed the edge of the pillow into her mouth and screamed as she flooded his mouth with her sweetness. He continued to lap at her clit until her orgasm subsided and she pulled the pillow from her face.

"Better?"

"Holy hell, that was fantastic."

He scooted up her body, centering himself over her on his forearms so she didn't have to bear his weight. "I'm glad you liked it."

"I've never, and I mean never ever, had an orgasm like that."

"Didn't your ex ever eat you out?"

"Only when he had to. He sure didn't relish in doing it."

"There is nothing like a woman sedate from an orgasm right before she is built back up again with a cock in her pussy."

"Hmm. You say that like you mean it."

"I do." He grabbed the condom from where it had landed on the bed, sat up, and rolled it down his cock. "Ready for me?"

"Hell yeah."

Surprised at her language and demeanor, he laughed out loud. "I thought you were some shy, quiet little mouse of a girl when I saw you in the diner. Now I realize how outspoken and daring you are." He smiled as he looked down into her eyes. "I can't wait to feel you around me."

"Me either."

He positioned himself at her opening and slowly pushed inside her hot center as he braced himself on his hands. "Holy fuck, you feel good." She'd spread her legs and wrapped them around his hips, bringing her pussy up higher and more in line with his dick. As she shifted her hips in tune with his slow thrusts, he could feel her rubbing her clit along his pelvic bone. His breathing sped up as his heart hammered. Her heartbeat pounding at the base of her neck caught his attention as she threw her head back. Her pussy squeezed his dick in a pulsating rhythm that he knew would send him into a mind-blowing orgasm shortly. "Touch yourself. Rub your clit."

Her hand snaked down between them until he felt it at the top of her mound.

"That's it."

She scooped up some liquid from their joined bodies and began to rub her clit in a fast, circular motion meant to bring her to orgasm quickly. He didn't mind since he was right there too.

His balls drew up against his groin. "You there?"

"Oh yeah. Fuck yeah."

"Come for me, Rose."

She shouted her completion so loud everything outside the room went silent. Unable to hold back his own, he groaned as he continued to pump his hips until he'd emptied everything he had into the end of the condom.

"Shit,' she whispered. "I'm sure everyone outside heard that."

"Yeah, probably." He grinned as she smacked him on the chest.

"Everyone will know what we were doing in here."

"I'm sure they do."

"You aren't helping matters, Joseph."

He sobered slightly, but not much as he rolled off her and peeled off the condom. "What? Don't you think shit is going to hit the fan when Jeff finds out I lied, that I'm really in my room having sex?"

She got to her feet and looked around.

"The bathroom is behind that door over there."

"Thanks." She went through the doorway and closed the door behind her.

He tied the end of the condom and tossed it into the trashcan by the side of the bed, before he laid back, put his hand behind his head, and stared at the ceiling. Sex with Rose had been phenomenal. He couldn't have asked for better. She was giving, sensuous, expressive, and didn't hold anything back. They'd been fantastic together, and he couldn't wait to do it again.

When she opened the door, he had a clear, unobstructed view of her gorgeous body. Red hair framed her face hanging down in long waves around her shoulders, her eyes sparkled, her body was flushed a pretty shade of pink, and her lips were swollen and red from his kisses. She was the most beautiful woman he'd ever seen.

"What?"

"Nothing. Why?"

"You are staring," she said, coming back to the side of the bed and grabbing her clothes from the floor.

"I'm admiring the view. You are a very beautiful woman."

"Thank you, kind sir." She slipped on her underwear and then her bra. "We should probably go out and see what the damage is. Besides, I do need to get some samples this afternoon."

"Yeah, I suppose so. Plus, I'll have to face my brothers when they realize I didn't go to town. Jeff isn't going to be happy I lied to him."

She flipped her hair back over her shoulder after she'd put her shirt in place. "Oh come on. I'm sure he's had sex in the barn before. What about when he was dating his wife?"

"I'm sure they did, although I wasn't keeping track of where and when they spent time together. Some of my brothers still make use of the barn."

She laughed as she pulled on her pants. "That's fantastic. Cowboys having sex in the barn. Classic." When she slipped the button on her jeans through the hole, he finally sat up and threw his legs over the edge over the bed.

Her hair spread down around her shoulders as she finger-combed the tresses into some semblance of order. He took a moment to admire her body. Even in clothes, she was gorgeous and round in all the rights places.

"All right, mister. Up and at 'em. We've got things to do."

"We could fuck again."

A sexy, spirited grin spread across her lips as she placed her hands on her hips. "Later. Right now, you probably have guests you are supposed to be taking care of, a horse to break, or stalls to clean, and I have samples to obtain."

He climbed to his feet and pulled on his jeans, buttoning them at the waist. After he grabbed a clean T-shirt from the drawer, he tugged it over his head, smoothing it down with his hands. "True. Do you need me to take you out to the pond so you can get samples?"

"Are there other water sources on the ranch, other streams or ponds?"

"There are a couple of other streams, yes, but they originate on other properties around us."

"I need to see those as well."

He grabbed his boots from the floor and tugged them on over the socks he'd managed to retrieve. "All right. Let me get one of the others to do the guests rides and we'll take a couple of horses out."

"Uh, Joseph?"

"Yeah?"

"I told you, I've never been on a horse before."

"Oh, right. Okay." He tapped his finger on his chin. How were they going to do this? There were a few places on the ranch that the only way you could get to them was on horseback. "Can you wait to get your samples?"

"I suppose. Why?"

"I need to give you some riding lessons. Some of the spots where we'll need to go aren't reachable by truck. Of course, we could take the four-wheelers. Have you ever been on one of those?"

"No."

He smiled and laughed. "Wow. You really have been sheltered."

The frown on her face told him he'd probably stepped over the line a bit with that remark.

"I am not sheltered. Just because I haven't ridden a horse or been on a four-wheeler doesn't mean I haven't lived, Joseph. Have you walked in Central Park?"

"No."

"Have you been to the theatre and seen a Broadway play?"

"No."

"Have you been to the beaches on Long Island?"

"No."

"Then don't call me sheltered. Our lives have taken different paths, we've experienced different things, but that doesn't mean we shouldn't be open to new things, learn from each other, and see what life has to offer through each other's eyes."

She whipped open the door and stomped out, her irritation clear in her steps as she headed toward the paddock.

He pulled the door shut behind him as he followed, shaking his head as he tried to understand why she was upset. He didn't mean anything by it. New York was like a foreign country to him, so trying to figure out how her life differed from his seemed to something he would have to work on. He liked Rose and wanted to spend more time with her, but he'd never had to deal with someone who seemed to be very opinionated, well, other than his brothers that is.

"Wait up, Rose."

When she turned back around to face him as they approached the doors that lead outside, her hands were on her hips, her face was flushed, and her hair swirled wildly around her shoulders. She was magnificent.

"Let me take you out there. There are a few of the horses that can be cantankerous to be around if they want to be."

"All right." She lowered her gaze to the ground at their feet. "I'm sorry. I didn't mean to get so defensive back there."

He put his finger under her chin and raised her face so he could see her eyes. 'Honey, it's okay. I realize we've grown up very differently and things that are easy and familiar for you, aren't for me and vice versa. If you are willing to learn from me, I'm willing to learn from you." He leaned in, brushing her lips with his. "By the way, you are gorgeous when you're riled up."

"Thank you. I think."

He kissed her again before he turned her around by the shoulders, took her hand and led her outside into the sunshine.

"Where the hell have you been?" Jason scowled as he cinched one of the saddles tighter. "You should have been here to take the last ride out."

"Sorry. I was busy, besides Jeff said he would get someone to take them out for me."

Jason's gaze moved over Rose's face, hair, and clothing before he glowered and turned his back to work on the next animal. "Apparently."

"What?"

"Nothing." Jason glanced his way. "Get ready. The next group will be here shortly to go out."

"Can't you take them?"

"No. I have some other work to do."

"What about Joel and Joshua?" he asked, stopping at the rear of the horse Jason was working with. "Jeff said they would take my two o'clock and three o'clock rides."

"That's when he thought you were going into town, not fucking around in the barn." Jason turned to face him. "We each have a role to play in the running of this ranch, Joey. Yours is wrangler, which means you are in charge of the horses, guest rides, the barn, and the tack. You can't just take off and not be here when it's your turn to do the rides."

"I told you, I was busy."

"Yeah, I could tell."

Joseph glanced at Rose, noting how flushed her face was from embarrassment. "Back off, Jason. I'm allowed free time too."

"Not during the work day."

"Don't fucking tell me what to do. I know there are plenty of times you fucked off during a work day with Peyton when you were supposed to be working."

"Watch your mouth, brother. She's my wife."

"I don't care. Putting a fucking ring on her finger doesn't make it okay for you to do whatever you want during work hours. Every single one of you has taken time off work to have a little playtime with your significant other. I'm doing nothing different than you."

Jason stepped closer, getting close enough Joey could feel Jason's hot breath on his face. "Fucking around with your latest squeeze in the barn is different than us taking personal time with our wives. You don't have anything permanent going on with this girl. She's your latest lay and that's it."

"Take it back, you asshole. Rose isn't like that."

"I won't. Don't tell me you weren't fucking her in your room just a little bit ago. Everyone heard it."

"I said take it back or I will make you wish you hadn't said anything. Rose is a nice girl."

Jason glanced over his shoulder, raking Rose with his gaze. "What the fuck ever."

Joey took two steps back and turned away from his brother. The look in Rose's eyes tore him up. Tears sparkled on her lashes as she pressed her fingers to her mouth. He couldn't stand the embarrassment and mortification on her face.

He spun back around, took the two steps back to Jason's side, and punched him in the mouth.

Jason flew backwards, landing several feet away, blood on his lip and rage on his face. "You didn't fucking just hit me, you asshole."

"Yes, I did. I never once talked about Peyton in any disrespectful manner while you were dating her. I would appreciate the same in return, otherwise we'll be having another talk like this one." He spun around and moved to Rose's side. "I'm sorry." He took her hand, kissed her fingers, and laced the digits together. "Let's go."

"Where are we going?"

"I don't know. I need to stop at the house for a minute, and then we can go wherever you want to go. I need to get the hell away from here before I kill someone."

Hurried steps took them across the yard toward the main lodge. The door swung open under his hand easily as he headed inside, Rose on his heels. When he got the door of the office, he saw his mother sitting at the desk. "Mom?"

Nina looked up, a smile on her face until she caught the look in his eyes and the posture of his body. "What's wrong, honey?"

"I'm taking the rest of the day off."

"What happened?"

"I punched Jason and left him with a bloody lip. Luckily, he wasn't stupid enough to get up before I left the paddock. He said some really nasty things about Rose, and I'm not going to listen to it anymore this afternoon. Rose and I are going into San Antonio or somewhere so I don't kill him."

Nina walked over to him, reaching for the fists clenched at his sides. "It's fine. I'll take care of Jason. You two go on and have a nice afternoon."

"Thanks, Mom."

"Sure, baby. I know how you boys get. I've been dealing with this for years." She smiled as she touched his cheek. "Go out and have some fun. We'll see you in the morning."

He kissed his mom on the cheek before he turned toward Rose, took her hand again, and led her back out into the common room. He didn't want to face any of his brothers right now, afraid of what he'd do if someone else said something derogatory toward Rose. The protective feelings surging through him were odd, but he wasn't about to question them right now. "Where do you want to go?"

Rose stopped him with a hand on his arm. "Joseph, it's okay, really."

"No it's not, Rose. He had no business saying those things, none of them do. They've all been caught at one time or another, playing hooky, fucking in the barn, and doing stupid shit. I'm not saying I'm a saint, far from it, but this is really twofaced of them, all of them. I'm tired of being the baby of the family and getting shit on."

Rose wrapped her arms around his neck, pulling him into a hug. He wasn't sure how to take it. Should he hug her too? Should be pat her on the back to pacify her? Unable to decide, he leaned in and took solace in her comfort.

"It'll be okay. I'm over it. I don't care what they think of me. All I care about is you."

She felt right in his arms, too right. She fit perfectly against his frame. Her arms around him gave him the comfort to walk away from the rage rushing through him. She shouldn't have to be the buffer between him and his brothers, especially when she was the reason for the fight. "I'm sorry."

"Why?" She pulled back in his embrace and he could clearly see the forgiveness in her eyes. "You have nothing to be sorry for."

"For my asshole brother."

"It's a man thing, Joseph. Don't worry about it. All men think a woman who freely gives her body to another without the benefit of a ring, is loose or out for something."

"What the hell, Rose? Not all men think like that."

"Really? Don't you think that way?"

"Not about you."

"Not about me." She smiled, but he could tell she was humoring him into thinking he was smart about the whole thing. "Okay, what about the girl on the phone yesterday? Jessie?"

"What about her?" he asked, afraid he knew where this was going, and he didn't like it.

"Weren't you using her to have sex?"

"I've never slept with her."

"But you would have, given the chance, right?"

Well, fuck.

Chapter Nine

"Well?"

"All right, yeah, I'd planned to have sex with her."

"And?"

"No, I didn't plan to give her a ring or even really date her. I was in it for the sex. Satisfied?" He moved away from her to stare out over the pasture land of the rolling hills through the big front windows. This whole conversation made him feel like an asshole for the way he'd treated women in the past. Yes, he'd used them to get laid without the benefit of a relationship usually. Did that make him a jerk? Yeah, probably.

Rose touched his shoulder. "I wasn't trying to make you feel bad. I wanted you to see that most men thought of women that way until they were ready for something more. There is a double standard in life. Women can't act that way without being called names like whore or slut, but a man doing the same thing is slapped on the back and made to feel proud."

"I understand."

"Do you?"

"Yes." He turned to face her before he placed his hands on her cheeks. "I can't apologize for men all over the world, but I promise, from now on I will not treat women like they are nothing more than a warm place for me to put my dick."

She giggled as she reached up and kissed him on the lips. "Such a poet."

"You still willing to be seen with me while you're here after all of that?"

"Of course! I'm in it for the sex, Joseph, nothing more. I'll be going home in a couple of weeks or whatever, back to my life in New York, and moving on with whatever life is going to throw my way. I don't need the complications of a relationship with you or anyone."

He wasn't sure he liked being used like a… What were they called? Oh yeah, a gigolo. It all seemed rather uncaring. He frowned as she turned back toward the middle of the room and walked toward the pool table. As she began rolling the balls from one end to the other, he realized she really had a different outlook on this whole situation. Most women were all about the ring and the relationship. Here was Rose giving him an out. Sex was it for her and she apparently wanted to experience it with him. *Well, I'll give her the best damned sex she's ever had!*

A second later, he crept up behind her, pulled her back against his chest, and kissed her neck. A shiver rolled through her, one he could feel as his hands moved down her body. Goose bumps rose on her arms. He liked that the touch of his lips did that for her. It made him feel attractive, sexy, and downright invincible. "Let's go somewhere."

"Where?"

"I don't know. How about we get into my truck and just drive, see where it takes us. I have the next couple of days off here at the ranch. We can go to Houston, Austin, or somewhere else. I can show you what the differences are in the area. We can go out to the gulf and hang out on the beach, go swimming in the warm waters, get drunk, be stupid, or do whatever we want. What do you say?"

She turned to face him and wrapped her arms around his neck. "You are a persuasive man, cowboy."

"Is that a yes?"

"Yes." She kissed him on the lips and then leaned back. "But, I have to get some samples first before we leave the area. It does no good for me to have them from Houston."

"All right. I can take you up the road so you can get some from the neighboring property as well as ours."

"I need some from your faucets too. You are on well water, right?"

"Yeah."

"Then if we get some water samples from your faucets, your pond, and maybe one other water source, that should be sufficient for your property. If we can get a few from some of your neighbors, we can call it good for the water. I would need some soil samples too, but I can get those later this week."

"How many samples do you need?"

"As many as I can get, really. The more I have, the easier it is to get a good report microbiologically for the area."

"Why are you doing these tests anyway?"

"The company I work for is thinking of doing some developing out here."

"Like buying up property?"

She shrugged as she wiped her lipstick from his mouth. "I'm not sure what they are doing actually. I don't get into that part of the corporation. They usually check water for contamination because someone has been reported sick or something like that."

He didn't like the idea of a corporation buying up the property out here to develop it. The family had gone through this kind of situation when Terri first showed up. She'd been in the area to check things out for a development firm who had already bought property and planned to put up a housing project. Luckily, Terri had found the nest of an endangered bird on their property. The bird's habitat made it impossible for them to build houses on it.

"What's wrong?"

He shook his head, filing away this information for later. He needed to alert the family if there was going to be an issue again with developers. "Nothing."

"You're frowning."

He took her hand and headed for the door. "It's nothing, really. Let's get these samples you need so we can pack up and head out of town for a couple of days." When he stopped to open the door, he turned toward her. "You're okay with leaving for a couple of days, right?"

"It should be fine. I'm here for a few weeks, so taking a couple of days off to play around won't be a problem."

"Good."

As they walked through the door and out onto the long concrete porch that ran around the entire front of the house, they were greeted by Jeff.

"Where are you going?"

"Out with Rose."

"Don't you have a mare to break this afternoon?"

"Yeah, but it can wait."

Jeff frowned as he glanced to Joey's left where Rose stood, holding his hand. "We don't blow off work, Joey."

"I've already talked to Mom." He stepped closer to Jeff. He stood as tall as his eldest brother and was bulkier because of the work he did. If Jeff wanted to push the issue, he'd push right back. "I'm taking the afternoon off to help Rose get the water and dirt samples she needs for her work. Then we are leaving for a couple of days."

"What the hell?"

"Get over it, Jeff. I rarely take a day off for myself and, by God, I'm doing it right now. All of you have done it a time or two. Now it's my turn." He tugged Rose along behind him as he swept past his brother, leaving him standing on the porch. *They'll be fine. The mare can wait until I come back.* Rose followed him as they went around the house, heading for the barn. "We'll need to go on horseback if we are going to reach the places you need."

"I, uh." She started to drag her feet. "Remember, I've never been on a horse before."

As they breached the doorway of the barn, enveloping them in the scents of horse, hay, and manure, he stopped and turned toward her. "It'll be okay. I'll give you a quick lesson. You'll be fine. The horses here are well-trained. I've trained every one of them, so I know them like the back of my hand."

"Are you sure?"

With both hands framing her face, he said, "Don't worry. I would never let you get hurt on one of our animals." He couldn't help himself, he had to kiss her. When his lips touched hers, he lost himself in the feel of her mouth.

A soft moan escaped her lips, only to be caught in his, as she opened her mouth and allowed him to push his tongue inside. He loved the taste of her, the feel of her, and the way she responded to him. It was like they were meant to find each other in this moment, to experience this together, even if it was only for a short time.

His heart hammered in his chest as he lifted his head and looked down into her eyes. He noticed her pulse beating wildly at the base of her neck as he traced the spot with his finger. "You are so beautiful," he whispered. He pulled her into a hug so he could bury his nose in her hair. The scent he found was intoxicating to his senses. "We need to go, otherwise I'll grab you up and take you back to my place."

"Mmm. I could go for that."

When he stepped back, he had to stifle a groan. His cock was painfully hard. "If we do, we'll never get anything done." He pressed her palm against his erection. "Of course, it's going to be a bitch riding like this."

"Oh, poor baby." Her eyes glittered in the sunlight streaming through the rafters above their heads. "I could take care of that for you. If you want, that is." She licked her lips before bringing the bottom one between her teeth.

"Shit." He dropped his head back. "I would love for you to, but really, we need to get away from here before another one of my brothers decides to give me shit for taking the afternoon off."

"They really do treat you like the baby of the family, don't they?"

"Yeah. It sucks."

She pressed her palm to his cheek. "It'll be okay. I promise." She tilted her head to the side. "We can take a break while we are out riding too. Bring a blanket and a condom."

He liked the way she thought. "You got it, babe."

When he returned a few minutes later, he found her out in the paddock. "I like this one."

He stood behind her, watching as her hands moved over the mare. "You can ride her. She's very gentle. A good mount for a first timer."

She twisted her head around, wrinkling her nose as she glanced back at him. "I'm not sure I like that metaphor."

He laughed at her expression. "There's a first time for everything." He moved in so he covered her back from shoulders to buttocks. "Ever had anal sex?"

"Mmm. No."

"First time for everything."

She sighed as she rubbed her buttocks against his hard-on. "Maybe."

He buried his nose in the crook of her neck. The natural scent of her skin drove him crazy. "You are hell on my body, lady."

"Good. I like the thought of keeping in you on your toes, cowboy."

She shivered under his touch when he rubbed his whiskered jaw along her neck, abrading the skin to a slight redness. The paleness of her skin showed the abrasion like a brand. He liked the thought of that a little too much.

After he cleared his throat and stepped back, she turned toward him with a little smile curling the corners of her mouth.

"Will you help me up?"

"Sure." He helped her turn, slide her foot into the stirrup, and then boosted her up with a helpful hand to her ass. When she glanced down and gave him a reprimanding look, he grinned and shrugged. "Let's go through some basics of riding now that you are comfortably in the saddle." As he went through how to guide the horse left and right, he couldn't help but admire her seat in the saddle, her ease with the reins, and how well she took instruction. "Now pull back on them to stop her."

A beautiful smile spread across her lips. "I think I got it."

"If you want her to trot, you can press her sides with your knees." He watched her guide the mare around the paddock in a slow trot. She was doing a great job for someone who'd never been on a horse before. When she brought the animal to a stop near him, he gave her an approving nod. "You did fantastic."

"Thank you. Coming from an expert, that means a lot."

"I'm no expert by any means."

"Sure you are. You've trained all these animals to be different levels for different rider abilities. That's a big feat."

He could feel the heat rushing up to his face. Compliments weren't something he was used to, not from strangers anyway. He frowned. She really was a stranger to him if he thought about it. He'd only known her a few days, but it sure seemed like he'd known her a lot longer.

Clearing his throat, he adjusted the hat on his head and moved to where his own mount stood tied to the pole. "Are you ready to go?"

"Uh, one thing. I need my bag from the car. It has my sample kit in it for the water and soil samples I need."

"If you give me your keys, I'll go fetch it for you."

"Sure." She pulled the keys from the front pocket of her jeans, dangling them in front of him as he reached up to grab them. "There is a small duffle type bag in the backseat."

When he returned a few minutes later, he saw Jeremiah talking with her as he stood near the mare's nose.

"Jeremiah."

"Hey, Joey." Jeremiah continued to stroke the horse's nose. "I was talking with your friend, and she said you two were going out riding. I thought you had a mare to break this afternoon."

"I do, but I'm taking the afternoon off."

"Oh?"

"Yeah. Rose needs a guide so she can get the water and dirt samples she needs for her work."

"That's right. I'm here in Bandera to gather samples for the company I work for in New York."

"I see." Jeremiah's eyes narrowed.

Joey knew thoughts were running through his brother's head, the same as his. After running into a similar situation when Terri showed up in Bandera a few years ago, they were all wary of people snooping around the property too much, wanting information. He'd have to do a little more digging on the company she worked for.

"Here you go." He helped secure the small bag to the back of her saddle before moving toward where his gelding stood tied. Once he was mounted, he headed toward the back of the paddock that led out onto the many trails running through Thunder Ridge.

Sunshine beat down on their heads, making sweat trickle down his back between his shoulder blades. He removed his hat, wiping wetness from his forehead and letting the slight breeze ruffle his hair before he put it back on. He turned in his saddle, glancing back at Rose. "You okay?"

"Yes, but I'm going to be really sore, I think."

"Yeah, you will, but I have some great ointment to help with those sore muscles." He grinned as she shifted in the saddle. "I love having my hands all over you."

"I like that too, cowboy."

"We should be there shortly. It's just over the ridge."

"Good. My ass is killing me."

He chuckled as they crested the hill where the small pond sat. An underground stream fed this particular spot and the run trickled down to an area outside the horse's pen at the back of the house. It was a constant source of water for them, even in the heat of the summer.

When he stopped his gelding and dismounted, he ground tied the animal before moving to her side. "Here. Let me help you down."

He reached up his hands as she brought her leg over the pommel, and then slid down into his arms. As her toes hit the ground, he looked down into her bright green eyes. He stood there just drinking her in.

He lowered his head until their lips were a hairsbreadth apart. His breath mingled with hers. Her eyes dilated so the pupils were big and black, almost covering the irises of her eyes. Kissing her seemed like the best thing to do at the moment, and Lord did he love kissing her. Grazing her lips with his, he barely brushed them across hers so it wasn't really a kiss, but a tease of things to come. Her heartbeat hammered at the base of her neck, matching his own erratic rhythm.

He cupped her cheek. The softness of her skin beneath his touch made his palm tingle. He slid his fingers down so he could wrap his hand around her neck, caressing the bounding pulse at the base with his thumb.

Wrapping her braid around his other hand, he pulled her head back, baring her neck to his touch. He grazed his teeth across the silky surface, forcing a moan from her mouth. A little nip along her jawline had her grasping his biceps as she shivered under his touch. *So responsive.*

With one leg now wedged between her parted thighs, he pulled her down so she straddled his thigh. His cock rested against her belly, throbbing behind the fly of his jeans. He wanted to be inside her wet, grasping pussy so badly he could hardly stand to take this slow.

Two fingers flicked the button on her jeans loose before he parted the material to reveal her silky panties. He slipped his hand down the back of her pants, grasping her buttocks in his palm. All he could think about was being in her ass. That would come in time, if she was around long enough.

He pushed back slightly so he could look at her. Her skin glowed, it was so pale. Freckles dotted her exposed flesh, now pink from the sun. He would have to loan her his hat for the trip back.

She gasped as he pulled her pelvis closer to him, letting her ride his leg. "I need you to make love to me, Joseph."

"Soon, sweetheart, very soon."

She wrapped her legs around his waist, leaning into the side of the horse for balance. "Fuck me here, right here."

He forced her legs back down so she stood on the ground. "Let me grab the blanket. We'll go down by the creek. There is a small sandy area where we can take our time and get this right."

A sigh escaped her lips and she brought the bottom one in between her teeth.

He moved back toward his horse to retrieve the blanket and the condoms he brought, before returning to her side, taking her hand, and leading her down by the water.

His balls ached with the need to come. He hadn't been this horny in a long time.

They stopped near the stream, and he turned to face her. He brought her hands up to his mouth, kissing her knuckles before he released her and spread the blanket down on the sand. Once he got it all out and straight, he took her hands, drawing her down with him on the soft makeshift bed.

He brought both hands up to cup her face. "I love how your skin glows. It's so soft to touch, I could skim my fingers over you all day long. Your eyes are so expressive, I can tell what you are feeling every time I look into them. Your body is so responsive to mine, it's incredible. It makes me feel invincible seeing the desire in your gaze."

"I want you."

"I want you too. I need you so bad, I hurt."

She reached for his belt buckle, tugging on it until it was loose and hanging at the waistband of his jeans. Her hand cupped his erection, skimming up and down, making him moan low in his throat and his eyes roll back.

"Easy, darlin'. I want to be inside you when I come."

"Don't worry. I know how far to push you before you explode." She brushed her lips over his, tentatively touching her tongue to his mouth.

He opened for her, allowing her tongue in to duel with his as he buried his hands in her hair. He wished it was loose. He would love to tangle his hands in the strands as he rode her mouth.

As if she heard his thoughts, she urged him to follow her up on her knees while continuing their kiss. After she tore her mouth from his, she worked the buttons out of their holes so his shirt hung off him and she could run her mouth down his chest. She stopped to flick his nipples with her tongue before biting at the tip.

"Fuck."

"Mmm. Yes, we will." Her hands worked at the button on his jeans until she had it open and she could push them down around his thighs.

His cock sprung free, relieving him of a little pressure, but now he strained up and proud, waiting for her mouth.

The moment she encircled the head with her lips, he shivered as he fought to keep from coming so soon. Even though he couldn't wrap his hands in the strands of her hair, he did wind the braid around his fist, guiding her in her task. The heat of her mouth drove his desire to explosive. His thighs ached from holding still.

She fingered the skin between his balls and his ass, sliding them up and down, dragging deep moans from his throat.

He almost came apart when she pressed her finger into his ass. No one had ever done that before. Pulling away, he sat back on his boot heels. "Holy hell, woman. Are you trying to kill me?"

She grinned as she ran her hand around his cock. "You didn't like it?"

"It was awesome, but different. Where did you learn that?"

"Someone in my past used to enjoy it. Not all men do, but I thought I'd see what you thought."

He shakily got to his feet, toed off his boots, and then stripped off his jeans. "Strip." Some time while she was sucking his cock, he'd lost his hat behind him. He didn't care. His cock hurt, he was so hard.

She stood and took her clothes off as quickly as she could. When she stood naked in front of him, he reached out a shaky hand, circling her areola with his fingertip. She leaned into his touch as she dropped her head back. Goose bumps broke out on her skin.

With his fist around his hard flesh, he leaned in and took her nipple between his lips. The nub hardened as he sucked.

She shoved her fingers through his hair, holding his head against her breast. "Oh, yeah." Whimpers escaped her mouth as he sucked and nipped at the flesh. After a few minutes, she sank down on the blanket, drawing him down with her as he kissed her again.

He ran his mouth over her skin from her lips, down her neck, across her breasts, and down her belly until he reached the juncture of her thighs. She spread her legs, giving him the space he needed. The scent of peaches reached his nose. "You smell fantastic."

She giggled. "It's my lotion."

"I don't care. I love the smell." He buried his nose near her mound and inhaled. "It makes me want to eat you all the more."

"Please do. I love having my pussy licked."

He licked her clit once, then twice. She spread her thighs farther apart as her breath came out in panting spurts. Her clit had begun to swell and turn a bright red, just like he wanted. He bit the tip of the bud, driving a deep, throaty moan from her lips.

"God, Joseph, please."

He forced his hands up under her buttocks so he could bring her closer to his mouth. As he continued licking and sucking, the moans he heard thrilled him. She definitely enjoyed this and he couldn't be happier.

When he pushed two fingers into her pussy and licked her clit quickly, she screamed loud and high as her climax rolled over her.

He continued to lick softly against her clit, bringing her down slowly until she sighed and relaxed into the blanket. Brushing a quick kiss to the inside of her right thigh, he reached over to grab his jeans and retrieve the condoms he'd brought.

A giggle escaped her lips when he pulled out the string. "Just how many times are you planning on fucking me while we are out here?"

Embarrassment flushed his cheeks with heat. "Well, I, uh…"

She sat up and put her hand on his face. "It's okay. I'm hoping we can use them all."

"Maybe by the end of the day, but not all at once."

"Are you saying you can't—" She grabbed the strip and counted them out. "Come six times in an hour?"

"Yeah, probably not."

"I'm so disappointed, Joseph." Her grin softened that statement.

"You are in so much trouble, girl."

Her eyes widened in mock fear as she pressed the strip of condoms to her chest. His eyebrow went up as she tore one off with her teeth. When she had it opened, she moved closer, got up on her knees, and rolled it down his cock. She leaned in and brought her mouth close to his. "Is that a promise?"

Damn, she's a sight! He crushed his mouth against hers, taking what he wanted from her willing lips as she caressed his cock with her hand. By the time they were both breathing hard, he let her mouth go so he could get to the fucking. Boy, was he ready for that part. He lay on his back, pulling her with him so she could straddle his hips. She took instruction well as he helped her position herself across his middle. Her hot pussy almost scalded him when he pushed his cock up and just barely inside her. She tossed back her head, braced her hands on his chest, and moaned long and loud.

As she took him inside her body, she rolled her pelvis forward, riding his cock like it was the last time she would ever have sex. He slipped in and out of her, feeling her vagina grip him like a vice. The walls contracted as he felt her quiver around him.

"Fuck, Rose, you are so gorgeous like this. Ride me, honey." He grasped both her breasts in his palms, kneading them with his fingers before he took each nipple between his first finger and his thumb to roll them. The dusky nipples turned a deep rose color as her need skyrocketed.

With her face to the sky, her eyes were closed, her mouth tight with desire, and body flush with need. Lord, she was beautiful as she moved over him.

Her long red hair brushed against his thighs, tickling the skin. The pain in his cock pulled his balls up tight against his groin with the need to come, but he needed to make sure she got her orgasm before he could take pleasure in his.

She continued to rub her clit along his pelvic bone while she rode his cock.

He reached down between them with one hand, took the swollen little nub between his fingers, and pinched it *hard*.

Her orgasm rolled over her in a wave he could see as she cried out her pleasure to the air around them in a long, loud scream.

His own orgasm ripped through him, surging up from his balls before shooting out the end of his cock like a rocket.

When Rose collapsed across his chest, he could feel her rapid breathing against his neck, the sweat clinging to her body as he skimmed his hands down her back, and the softness of her hair against his palm.

She fit against him perfectly.

He wasn't sure where this train of thought was headed, but he sure didn't like it. Nope. Not one bit.

Chapter Ten

The heat from Joseph's gaze rested on her back as she bent down and scooped up some soil from a spot where they'd stopped the horses. She needed several samples of both water and dirt to send back to the company. They'd had a few reports of contaminated water from an anonymous source, but she couldn't see the Young family operating their guest ranch knowing they had contaminated water. They didn't seem to the type of family that took advantage of people like that. She had to be sure though, and the only way to do that was to test for every microorganism they could think of in the lab.

When she stood, she turned to face him, excited by where his gaze rested before coming up to her face. "Joseph?"

"Yeah?"

"I think I have what I need from your ranch, except for getting a few water samples from the house and a couple of the guest cabins."

"All right."

"I do need to see if I can get some from a couple of your neighbors though. Is that a possibility?"

"I'm sure I can talk to some of them."

"A few from some of your direct neighbors would be great."

He frowned.

"Something wrong?"

"No. I guess not."

"You don't sound so convincing."

"Well, one of our neighbors is The Marshalls. They aren't too friendly with us or should I say with me."

"Oh?"

"Yeah. Jessica's Old Man Marshall's daughter."

"*The* Jessica from the phone call?"

"Yep."

"I see." She didn't like the thought of Joseph with another woman. *Easy girl. He's only yours temporarily.* She took a deep breath as she tried to calm the cramp in her stomach. "Maybe if I go there by myself he would be okay with it."

"Maybe. I can show you where to go, but it's probably not a good idea for me to go with you. He'd be more likely to shoot at me than welcome me to his porch."

"Shoot at you? What the hell did you do the last time you were there?"

He dropped his gaze to the tips of his boots, scuffing them in the dirt. "We were both half naked when he found me there the last time. He chased me out to my truck shooting at me with buckshot in his shotgun."

She busted out laughing so hard she snorted and tears rolled down her cheeks. He frowned at her when she took a seat on a large rock because she thought she was about to pee her pants. "Oh my God! That's priceless!" She rolled off the rock onto her hands and knees as she giggled hysterically.

"It really wasn't that funny, Rose. He dented my tailgate something fierce with that shit."

She laughed harder. She could only image him running across this man's lawn holding his jeans up with one hand, his boots in the other, all while trying to avoid getting buckshot in his ass. After she'd calmed down a little, she wiped her face, and looked up at him. "I'm sorry, Joseph, but it's hilarious to think of you running across their lawn in your bare feet, trying to avoid getting shot."

Even though he had a frown on his face, he held out a hand to help her to her feet. "We should be getting back if we are planning to go to Houston tonight. It's a four hour drive."

When she managed to calm her giggles, she replied, "Wow, really?"

"Yeah."

"Are you sure you want to go there? I'm sure we can find stuff to do a little closer."

"It's up to you. You haven't been here before. I want to show you what Texas is all about, so you have some good memories to take home."

Trailing her fingertips down the buttons on his shirt, she glanced up through her lashes and caught him staring at her lips. No matter that they'd had sex less than an hour ago, she still wanted him as need clawed low in her belly. Desire had never had her in its clutches like this with Brandt or anyone else in her past for that matter, and it seemed like it wasn't about to let her go until she'd got this cowboy out of her system. "We could go back to my hotel room."

"That place is a dump. You should take a room at Thunder Ridge. Then you'd be close."

"Close enough for what?"

"I could visit you."

"Would you?"

"Hell yeah. Every chance I got."

Up on her toes, she placed her hands on his shoulders and brushed her lips against his in a very light caress. "I like the sound of that."

"Then let's get you settled in a room."

They mounted their horses and set out back toward the main lodge. She kind of liked the idea of being close to Joseph, but it also gave her a chance to check things out around the ranch and the places nearby.

As she watched his back while they rode, she loved the way his shirt stretched across the surface. It molded nicely to his broad shoulders, giving her a great view of his muscles. His ass fit into the rear of the saddle spectacularly too. There sure was something about a cowboy in a pair of Wranglers.

When they rode into the yard a little while later, the scene made her smile. His brothers were bustling around, taking care of what needed on the ranch. It fascinated her to watch them working, their hands busy with tasks that she'd never even thought of living in New York.

They dismounted in front of the barn, and Joseph took the horses inside to do whatever it was they do, while she stood outside in the sun, stretching her abused muscles. Her ass hurt from riding, and the inside of her thighs screamed from the mistreatment of having sex on the hard ground and being spread around the girth of the horse. She moaned softly, not fully aware of the audience of women nearby.

Mesa walked over, touching her on the shoulder. "Are you okay?"

She glanced up and smiled. "I'm fine, just sore from the ride."

"Have you been on a horse before?"

"No, never."

Mesa laughed. "You'll be a lot more sore tomorrow, I'm afraid. I had the same affliction after I got here."

"How long have you and Joel been married?"

"About six years now."

"That's awesome. I hope someday to say the same thing."

"He's my world outside of our kids. I can't imagine my life without him, this ranch, and our family."

"I can imagine."

Joseph came out of the barn a minute later, carrying her duffle. "Come on. Let's get you a room. I know there should be one available. Mesa's group of friends is leaving this afternoon."

Mesa smiled. "Yes, they are. I'm glad they came. It's been a great week, but I'm ready for some quiet around here for a few days."

"I bet it gets crazy in the summer."

"Yes, it does. We have a crowd every week, it seems."

Rose waved to Mesa as Joseph took her hand and led her inside. Nina met them in the main room. "Well, hello there."

"Mom, Rose needs a room. One of the cabins would be great."

Nina's eyebrow went up. "Let's see what we can find." She turned around to head into the registration office. "I have one near the back of the compound. It's private and not attached to another room."

"That would be good," Joseph replied before Rose had a chance to answer.

"I think Rose can answer for herself, Joseph."

Rose gave him a sideways glance. "Yes, I can, and yes, that would fine."

Once she gave Nina her business credit card and had her key in hand, Joseph walked her back out toward her car. "I can get my stuff from my hotel room and be back in about an hour."

"Want me to go with you?"

"You don't have to, Joseph. I know you have some things to do around here."

"I took the afternoon off, remember?"

"I know, but it sounds like your family is having a problem with you doing that."

He pulled her close to his chest. "Too bad. This is our time."

She fingered the top button on his shirt. "I know, but I don't need to piss off your family for dragging you away from your work."

"They'll get over it." He brushed his lips over hers in a brief kiss. "If you'd rather go by yourself, that's fine."

"I probably should. I need to call the office anyway to check in."

His brow furrowed for a second. "Sure."

"All right. I'll be back in a couple of hours and then we can decide what to do for the rest of the evening."

He stepped back so she could open the door on her car and held it for her. "Be careful."

"I will."

As she started her car to go back into Bandera and get her things, she wondered what the evening would bring. Making love with Joseph was phenomenal, and she couldn't wait to do it again. Did that make her a slut? She shrugged. *Whatever. I'm going to enjoy this and worry about consequences later.*

She only had a few days left here in Texas before she needed to go home. She planned to make the most of it with one hot cowboy.

About an hour later, she'd packed her things and sat down at the table in her room to call her boss at work. They'd already planned a conference call today, so she figured she might as well do it while she had the chance.

As the phone rang, she contemplated what she'd found out on Thunder Ridge. No one knew what the water and soil held until they examined it under a microscope. Even finding tiny particles of contaminates could shut down the ranch. She hoped that didn't happen. The family there would be devastated should something like that be brought to light.

"Rose?"

"Hello, Mr. Albright."

"Hello. How is Texas?"

She took a sip of the can of Coke in her hand. "Interesting place. I've met some of the locals."

"Don't forget, you are there on business."

"I know. I'm enjoying the area on my off time. I'm getting what you need. Don't worry."

"I hope so. We need that information as soon as possible. The investors, uh, I mean the community needs to know whether there are any problems near there."

She frowned. *Investors? What the hell is he talking about?* "I have the samples from Thunder Ridge. I need to get some from the neighbors next door. I'm going over there tomorrow."

"Good, good. You have the FedEx information to send those samples when you have them."

"Yes."

"I'm looking forward to seeing the results."

Odd. He's never taken an active interest in this stuff before. "Anyway, do you want me to call you when I have the other samples?"

"Yes, please. I assume then you'll be on your way back to New York?"

"Yes, sir."

"I'm looking forward to having you back in the office, Rose."

"Thank you, sir. I will talk to you tomorrow or the next day."

"That's fine. Talk to you then."

"Bye." She hung up the phone, frowning at it for a moment as the conversation played over in her head. The company she worked for was a microbiology lab that tested water and soil samples for a variety of reasons, usually involving complaints filed with the county. Something sounded awfully fishy with this. Digging a little deeper into the situation might be in order.

She grabbed her suitcases and opened her motel room door. The sun was shining, the birds were singing, and there were a few locals about on the streets. Trucks zipped by without a care in the world, some blaring country music, some jacked up so high she would need a stepstool to get inside. The light at the center of town turned to red in the distance. Life went on whether she stood on the threshold of something new or not. Right now she wasn't sure, but her whole world seemed like it was about to be turned upside down, and she didn't know how to stop it.

When she arrived back at the ranch about half an hour later, she was caught by surprise to find Joseph waiting for her near the driveway. It made her happy to see him as he stepped up near the car as she stopped. "Well, hello."

"Hi," he replied as she stepped out. He leaned in and kissed her on the mouth.

"What a way to be greeted. You don't meet all the guests like this, do you?"

"Nope. Only you."

"Such a charmer." She shut the door and moved around to the back of the car to grab her suitcase. Joseph took it out of the trunk before she could reach for it. "I can get it."

"A lady doesn't carry her own bags when there is a cowboy around." He jingled the key to her cabin in front of her eyes. "I come bearing the key."

She smiled as she shut the trunk and followed him to her cabin. When he opened the door for her, she got her first look at the interior. A huge king sized bed with a wrought iron headboard and footboard took up most of the room. The coverlet on the bed specifically drew her attention to the beautiful wedding ring pattern in multiple colors. "Wow. This place is gorgeous."

"I'm glad you like it. It's one of my favorite cabins. We use it as a honeymoon suite." He pushed open the door to the right. "The bathroom is in here. It's got a huge soaking tub with jets."

"Oh my. My body will love that a little later. The ride earlier took its toll on my thighs."

He moved to her side, coming up behind her as she turned toward the window to look outside. The hills in the distance captured the dying evening light in shadows of black, purple, and blue.

Joseph put his hands on her shoulders before running his hands up and down her arms. "I promised to help with the soreness in those muscles. After supper I'll give you a good rub down with some special stuff."

"I can't wait," she whispered, tipping her head back on his shoulder.

The bell clanged in the distance signaling supper was ready.

He brushed his lips over her neck, giving her a little nip before he moved away. "Let's go get some food so we can get this party started."

A shivered rolled down her back as the heat from his chest left her cold when he stepped back. "All right."

Supper was an interesting affair. Most of Mesa's group had left, so the main lodge seemed quiet in comparison. The family still took up a big portion of the room at the end, but the guests had thinned out a lot, leaving empty tables.

She listened as conversation went around the table. Jeff brought up things on the ranch requiring attention tomorrow. Nina talked about the bookings for the coming week. Jonathan mentioned some new website stuff he was working on. Jeremiah talked about a new upstart company he wanted to invest some of the family's money in. Rose frowned when he mentioned the name of the company. Something was familiar about it, but she couldn't place it just yet.

"What kind of company is it, Jeremiah?" James asked, before taking a bite of his food.

"It's a development company that I've been talking to about our land."

"What the hell are you talking about?" Jeff asked, his voice hard and sharp.

"Don't get all bent out of shape, Jeff. This would be a good thing for Thunder Ridge."

"How do you figure? If someone wants to come in and take over the area for whatever purpose that can't be good for ranches like ours. We went through that when Terri got here and the development company who bought up the neighbor's ranch wanted to put houses in."

"This company isn't wanting to put in houses. They're here to test for oil."

"Oil?" Nina laid her fork on the table. "As in oil wells?"

"Yes, Mom."

"I don't like the sound of this, Jeremiah. It sounds risky."

"All investments are risky, but if we get in on the ground floor, this could be great for us."

"We don't need the money, son," his father added. "You've already seen to that."

"I understand, Dad, but think about it. If we hit oil on our property, none of us would ever have to work again."

Rose wanted to say something. Being a microbiologist, she knew the signs of possible oil on a property and the changes it would make in the surrounding landscape. Thunder Ridge as a guest ranch would cease to exist once the oil drillers came in. They would level everything to put up the wells. They would tear up the countryside. The cattle wouldn't be able to graze here anymore because of the contamination to the water. She started to shake.

"What's the name of the company, Jeremiah?" James folded his hands on the tabletop as the conversation went on around them.

"Mission Drilling."

Joseph turned toward her, taking her hand in his warm one. "Rose?"

"I, uh, I need to leave, Joseph, please?"

"What's wrong?"

She knew that name. She'd seen it several times on documents at the office where she worked. They were in the market to shut out the small ranchers, farmers, and land owners. They used her company to prove the water was contaminated and the owners of the property couldn't continue to run a business or live on their property, making their land worthless and unusable. The drilling company would buy the land cheap, knowing there were probably deep pockets of rich oil, and then drill, making millions. "Please. Let's just go."

"All right."

Joseph brought her to her feet, bringing all eyes on them. "Rose isn't feeling well. I'm going to take her back to her cabin."

"Are you all right, Rose?" Nina asked climbing to her feet and moving toward them.

"Yes. I'll be fine. I guess I overdid today with the ride and the sun."

"Do you need anything, honey? I can have the cook make you some soup or something."

"No. I'll be fine, Mrs. Young."

"Nina, honey, call me Nina."

"Nina. Thank you. I think I'll go onto bed and rest. I'll be fine tomorrow."

"Good night then. Rest well."

Joseph led her down the center of the main lodge dining room, out the side door to walk her toward her cabin in the distance. Darkness had fallen, but the path was lit by individual lights along the walkway.

They'd left the light on inside the room when they'd left earlier. Now, it was a beacon in the night to her soul. She needed to think.

"Rose?" His voice held a question, one she wasn't sure she could answer.

"I'm okay, Joseph. I need to relax, take a bath, and get some sleep, I think." She touched his cheek as he held her in his arms. She liked how he wanted to take care of her. Leave it to the cowboy to want to help. "I'll be fine in the morning." The disappointment in his eyes hurt her heart. "I'm sorry. I wanted us to be able to spend tonight together."

"It's okay, darlin'. If you aren't feeling well, then I'll take a raincheck."

"Thank you."

He kissed her on the nose and stepped back. "Sleep well, sweetheart."

When he disappeared into the night, she sighed. It was so hard when a person really liked someone but knew it could go nowhere. A few days of happiness, good sex with an amazing man, and the welcoming feeling of family here on the ranch couldn't replace the depression she felt surrounding her heart.

I have a really bad feeling about this.

Chapter Eleven

Rose spent the next morning on the Internet and pooling her resources to find out as much as she could about Mission Drilling. The information wasn't what she wanted to hear. She had a few contacts on the inside of the company since her boss had done business with them before, and she'd been their lead biologist on different projects.

When Joseph had come by the cabin, she'd feigned still not feeling well.

"Is there something I can get you, Rose?"

"No, Joseph. I'm okay. Rest is the best thing for me. Besides, I'm sure you have work to do today since you took yesterday off to take me around."

"Yeah, I do. I really need to work with the mare I need to break, plus we have a load of feed coming in this morning and riders to take out." He touched her cheek and frowned. "You do feel a little warm. Maybe you are coming down with something."

"Maybe. I'll take a couple of Tylenol and sleep for a few hours. I'll see you in the barn later or at lunch. Okay?"

"All right. Rest up and we'll talk later."

She watched as he stepped off her small porch and headed toward the barn. Deceiving him didn't sit well with her, but she had to find out what the hell this Mission Drilling wanted with Thunder Ridge land. She couldn't go riding by herself to check out the area since she didn't do well on horseback, and her car wasn't up to driving over some of the dirt roads around here either. Information is what she needed. Tapping her fingers to her lips as she sat back in the chair in front of her computer, she contemplated how to proceed.

The samples still had to be obtained from the neighbors and Joseph mentioned the Marshalls. If she could get samples from their property, she might be able to prove drilling here wouldn't be a good idea. Then again, if she sent those samples into her boss, they would have the information they needed to declare the area contaminated, thus forcing the locals to move out.

If she could find a local biology lab to run the tests without alerting the company she worked for and got the results she needed, she could forestall the issue.

She would likely lose her job over this if they found out, and possibly her livelihood. A microbiologist with the reputation for bucking against her employer wouldn't be employable anywhere else. Doing the right thing meant more than her job though.

If the family finds out I know more about this than I'm letting on, they won't be happy, I'm sure.

"If I can save their land, it will be worth it."

For the next couple of hours, she found out all she could about oil drilling, water contamination, soil issues, and Mission Drilling.

The company had been around for a number of years, twelve to be exact, and had made millions drilling for oil in Texas on land they'd bought that wasn't inhabitable because of one reason or another. They were owned by two brothers.

When she typed their names into the Internet search, she found an interesting tidbit. Their third cousin by marriage was Walter Albright. "Son of a bitch. My boss is their cousin? Holy hell. No wonder he wants these samples like yesterday. Even if there is no contamination and everything checks out, God knows how he might tamper with them to say this land is unusable. It doesn't matter whether they have been ranching this area for a couple hundred years or not."

She heard a tap on the door and looked at the clock. It was almost noon.

"Rose?"

Joseph. "Just a second." She closed her laptop, shuffled the papers she'd been jotting on into the desk, and straightened her clothes. Her hair was a disaster. She looked down to realize she hadn't even gotten dressed yet. *Oh well, it lends itself to the story of me being ill.* She really hated lying to Joseph, but if it meant helping his family, she'd do whatever it took.

When she opened the door, she was struck by the man again. He really was the epitome of the cowboy with his hat pulled down to shade his eyes from the sun, the western button-down shirt stretched across his chest, the formfitting jeans, and the dusty boots. Her mouth watered to run her tongue over every inch of his skin and listen to him moan.

"You look like hell."

"Thanks, Joseph."

"Do you feel any better?"

"Yeah. I'm okay. I just need to shower."

His lips lifted in a little grin. "I could join you. I'm pretty dirty from working with that mare all mornin'." His gaze traveled down her frame, making her nipples pebble into hard little nubs. "Of course, I don't have any clean clothes with me."

"Did she give you trouble?"

"Some, yeah. She didn't like having me on her back."

"Are you okay?"

"I'm good. Nothing new for me." He stepped across the threshold of her cabin when she moved back to let him inside. "I could go grab some clothes and be back in a second to join you."

"Sounds good to me."

He touched her cheek. "Are you sure you are feeling up to it?"

"I'm fine, Joseph, and I really want you to make love to me." She brushed her mouth against his, taking in the taste of his lips. He was everything she wanted right now.

"I'll be right back then."

When he disappeared out the door in a flash, she couldn't help but smile. She planned to give as good as she got until this whole thing was over, either way.

After she stepped into the bathroom to warm up the shower, she hummed a tune to herself while she stripped off her pajamas and underwear.

A moment later, she heard the door open and then close. *Wow. That didn't take long.* When he didn't appear in the bathroom, she opened the door and peered out. No one was in the room. *Now, that's weird.*

She shivered in the cool air from the bedroom before she shut the door, letting the steam from the shower soothe her. She'd heard there were ghosts on the place and apparently one was paying her a visit.

Joseph returned a few minutes later. "Rose?"

"In the bathroom waiting for you."

When he came through the door, he wasn't wearing a stitch of clothing. The smattering of chest hair tempted her to touch with her fingertips, but his cock was what she really wanted. With her fingers wrapped around his length, she guided him toward her mouth as she knelt on the bath rug.

He wrapped his hands in her hair, fisting her scalp to the point of stinging. She loved feeling him take what he wanted as he fucked her mouth.

A groan rumbled from between his lips. "Holy crap, Rose."

She hummed her satisfaction against his flesh. Having him in her mouth drove her need to explosive. She wouldn't be able to hold back very long when he finally pushed inside her.

After bringing him to the brink of losing all control, she stood, took his hand, and led him into the tiled shower stall.

Soap suds slid down his chest as she smoothed her slick hands over his chest, down his abdomen, and around his cock. She loved the feel of his skin beneath her hands, every plane, and every muscle.

He backed her under the spray to wet her hair before he grabbed the shampoo and scrubbed her scalp. No one had ever washed her hair in the past and to have his hands there felt amazing.

Once her hair was squeaky clean, he soaped her body up, paying close attention to all the hidden spots that had her panting. Around her breasts he moved, weighing each one in his palm before he rinsed it clean and then sucked on the nipple until she squirmed. "God, Joseph. You're driving me crazy."

"I like to give as good as I get."

He pushed her down on the little bench seat in the corner of the stall, dropped to his knees, and then started to lick her pussy like a dying man enjoying his last sip of water. Her body broke out in goose bumps. She rested her legs over his shoulders, loving what he was doing to her body.

Moments later, he slid two fingers into her pussy as he continued to lick and suck at her clit.

Her orgasm crashed over her without much warning, bursting into stars behind her eyelids as she cried out her pleasure with his name on her lips.

Once she came down from her high, he picked her up, wrapped her legs around his waist, and then slid into her in one thrust. The feeling wasn't anything she could remember ever having before.

"Fuck."

"What?"

"I don't have a condom."

"It's fine. I'm clean and on the pill."

His gaze fixed on hers, looking deep into her soul. She could see the debate in his eyes. Did he want to take the chance and go ahead with this or pull out and walk away?

"Joseph?"

"Ah hell." He moved a little before thrusting again. "I can't stop."

"Thank God."

He chuckled before he groaned deep in his throat and pressed his forehead against her. "You feel fantastic, Rose. Going bare with you is amazing. You are so tight, so good."

She couldn't say a word as he continued slowly thrusting his hips, driving his cock deep into her pussy time and time again. Every inch of him touched her, making her want to take him inside her and keep him there forever.

Shit. This is bad.

* * * *

Joseph watched Rose as she talked to his mother at lunch. Something was different, but he couldn't put a finger on what.

Sex in the shower had been fantastic. He couldn't remember when he'd experienced something like that before. He knew he hadn't.

The feeling she was hiding something from him had him on edge though, and he couldn't shake it.

"Rose, didn't you say you were a microbiologist?" Jeremiah asked from his spot two seats down.

"Yes. I'm here taking samples of the water and soil."

"Why?"

She bit the inside of her lip as she glanced down at the table. It appeared she was attempting to formulate a response. When she glanced up, she shot a look at him before she focused on Jeremiah. "The company I work for is a lab. Actually, they had a couple of complaints from the surrounding area about contaminated water. They sent me here to get some samples we can test and know for sure, so we can tell the county."

"We are on well water. Ours doesn't come from the county."

"I understand that, but if there are contaminants in the soil, it might be a problem with your water too. The Bandera County River Authority and Groundwater District is concerned about the area, from what I've been told."

He didn't like the sound of this at all. Why would the county be worried about them if they were on well water?

"I don't know the details. All I know is I am here to get some samples." She shifted her gaze around the table. "I'm not here to hurt anyone or do anything to jeopardize your operation."

"We didn't think you were, honey." His mother patted her hand. "Did we, boys?"

The murmur of agreement went around the table and he saw Rose physically relax.

"Thank you. I appreciate the backing."

The rest of the meal went by without any more confrontations, but he saw Jeff watching Rose very closely. It bothered him that his brother was suspicious of Rose, but then again, he was becoming more wary of her as well.

After they were finished, he walked Rose back to her cabin. "I need to finish up some work with that mare. Will you be okay by yourself until supper?"

She smiled and laid her palm against his cheek. "Yes, Joseph. I have some work I need to do as well. I might go ahead and run over to your neighbor's place to see if I can get the samples I need since they don't care for you. I wouldn't want you to get shot at again."

He frowned as she turned toward the cabin door and unlocked it.

When she turned back to face him, she said, "Oh, something strange happened earlier. After you'd left to get your clothes, I heard my door open and then close. I thought it was you returning already, but when you didn't come into the bathroom I looked out into the bedroom. There wasn't anyone there."

"I don't like you leaving your door unlocked."

"You were coming right back. I didn't think anything of it."

"Make sure you lock it when you're in there by yourself. It is usually safe on the ranch, but there is always the potential for problems. We do have other ranch hands besides my brothers and me."

"Didn't you say you had ghosts on the place?"

"Supposedly, yes."

"Hmm. I'm going to do some digging if you don't mind. I love the thought of ghosts, and I would love to see if I can find out some information."

"That'd be fine. All of us boys have thought about doing some research, but no one has had the time."

"Well, let me see what I can find. I might go into town too. Is there a library there?"

"Yeah. They should have old newspapers or books or something you can look at."

"Great." She reached up and kissed him on the lips, her mouth lingering for a hot second before she stepped back. "I'll see you at supper."

He turned on his heels and headed for the barn. The mare awaited him and he needed to finish getting her broke. It wasn't a simple process. It took weeks to properly train a horse to trail ride, especially getting one gentle enough where an inexperienced rider could be on it. They had a lot of horses on the place, many who were very gentle, but this little mare was kind of special. He'd picked her out himself on a trip to Houston a few months ago. She was a spotted saddle mare and had gorgeous markings. A white blaze ran down her nose and she had chestnut colored spots over most of her body along with lots of white.

The cooler interior felt good against the spring heat of the day. Some of the horses in the barn nickered at him as he made his way to the back and out to the paddock area where the mare had been stabled. He'd left her munching on some hay while he'd gone to eat. She lifted her head and gave him a bored look before going back to the small pile still left on the ground.

First things first. He needed to start with the halter. The one he was going to use hung over the fence post.

He grabbed the polyester rigging and approached her slowly, talking in small words and soothing tones as he moved. "Hey, pretty girl."

The mare eyed him warily.

"Easy, baby."

He held the halter in his right hand while he eased his left hand over the top of her head. She skittered away, side-stepping him as he continued to move closer every time she moved away.

Breaking a horse was a dance of sorts. It took a lot of patience and work.

He glanced to his right, noticing Jacob standing at the fence with his boot on the bottom railing and his arms dangling over the top. *Hmm.*

Without taking his eyes off the mare, he said, "Somethin' I can do for you, Jacob?"

"Nope."

"Don't you have somewhere to be?"

"Nope."

He liked his brothers, all of them, but Jacob was kind of special to him. There had been some hard times for his brother while he dealt with some personal issues. When he'd found his wife Paige, Joey had been the first one there with congratulations. In fact, one night he and a couple of the others had thought it would be a good idea to kidnap Paige and bring her to the ranch. Jacob had been in a particularly bad mood so they thought it would be funny to bring her home for his brother. They had been pretty drunk at the time, but it really had been hilarious when she met them at the top of her stairs with a shotgun, a mean dog, and a threat to blow holes through all of them.

"I'm sure Paige is looking for you right about now."

Jacob pulled his hat down lower on his forehead. "Not really. She's busy with the kids."

"So you decided to come hang out at the paddock with me? I'm touched."

"Actually, I'm curious about you and this redhead you've been hanging with."

"Rose?"

"Yep."

"Why?"

"She seems nice enough."

"But?"

"I'm concerned with her gathering these samples she's talking about."

"And?"

"What if something comes up in them to hurt the ranch? We could all lose our livelihood here. I mean for some of us, this is all we know, like you."

He contemplated that thought a lot longer than he probably needed to, but it bothered him nonetheless. He didn't know anything beyond ranching, horses, and cattle. If this wasn't here anymore, he wouldn't know what to do. College had never appealed to him although he could probably go back for agriculture or something along those lines. "It'll be fine."

"You're sure?"

"Hell no, Jacob! I don't fucking know anything, but I can't think about that. It's out of our hands if there is something here. I don't think Rose is out to hurt us though."

"I don't think so either. I can't help being concerned though, Joey. Do you know who the company is she's working for?"

"No. I haven't known her that long."

Jacob shifted so his other boot was on the rung of the rail. "Can you find out? Maybe we need to do a little digging of our own to find out what is going on."

He managed to get the halter over the mares head and hook it around her ears. He ran his hand over her nose, calming her even though her coat still twitched from nervousness. His palm slid down her side, smoothing the hair while he thought about Rose and what having her on the ranch could mean for the family. As much as he liked her, family came first. "I'll see what I can find out, Jacob. I wish I knew more about what she's talking about with these things."

"I'm sure. It's confusing with all this chemical stuff."

"You aren't kidding." He led the mare toward the fence. "Do you know what Jeremiah was talking about with this company he mentioned?"

"No. You know how he is. He's got his hands in so many different things, I'm not sure he even knows what they all are."

"That's true. He did mention a company by name and Rose got a funny look on her face. She asked to leave right after that."

Jacob ran his hand along his chin. "Where is she now?"

"She went into town. She said she had some work to do, and she needed to go by the Marshall's place to get a sample from there."

"Well, I guess there isn't anything more we can go right now. You do need to see if you can get the name of the company she words for though."

"I'll see what I can do."

"Okay." Jacob stepped back, dropping his booted foot to ground. "I'll see you at supper."

"Yep."

As his brother walked away, Joey wondered how he was going to go about getting the information about Rose's employer. He didn't want to make her suspicious or anything since he had no idea what they would do with the information once they had it.

He probably needed to talk to Jeremiah too. Rose's reaction when he mentioned the company's name was weird. She's gone pale and started to shake before she asked to leave in a hurry.

With the mare following close behind, he took her inside the barn and put her in a stall. He would work with her more tomorrow and see if he could actually get a saddle on her. Right now, he had some digging to do.

Chapter Twelve

Rose closed the newspaper she had opened on the huge table in the middle of the library. After she folded the paper, she sat back in her chair and thought about all she'd learned over the last several hours.

She'd gathered quite a bit of information on Thunder Ridge, its past inhabitants, and some of the colorful history of the area. She found that the ranch had been a working cattle ranch for quite some time, over one hundred years to be exact. After the Civil War, the area became a staging area for the Western Trail bringing along cowboys and settlers alike, including women of the night.

Some of those women took up residence at Thunder Ridge or what Thunder Ridge used to be a long time ago.

She gathered from the information that the main lodge that stood there now used to, in part, be the place where the women would take men upstairs to entertain. The lower level was for gambling and drinking mostly for the local cowboys before they went on long trail rides.

She had names of people who had been killed on the property including a couple of cowboys, a lady of the night, and three women who'd came west with their husbands to help settle the area, with their children. She didn't know all the details of what ghosts were seen or heard out there, but she was definitely intrigued by the stories she'd read in the newspapers at the library.

When a series of floods wiped out a lot of the local area in the early 1900s, the area became almost inaccessible. In the 1930s, the area became known for taking in guests at the local ranches offering camping, rodeos, dance halls, and fun for everyone.

She didn't know when Joseph's family had bought the ranch other than when the two older boys were little. By her calculations, that would have been about thirty years earlier, give or take, fairly recently by Old West standards.

The town itself had been established back in the mid-1850s.

History fascinated her, so this was right up her alley. She loved hearing about how the cattle trails went through, how the ranches were established usually by generations and generations of families, and the landscape had changed over the years.

"I'm sorry, ma'am, but the library is closing."

"Oh. Thank you. I hadn't realized how late it had gotten. I appreciate you letting me look through all these old newspapers."

The elderly woman glanced down at her notes. "You are doing some research on Thunder Ridge?"

"Yes, ma'am. I'm staying out there, and I've become friends with some of the family."

"You know about the ghosts, right?"

"I've heard that, yes. I was researching who lived out there and who might have died out there so I could help them learn something about the spirits they have on the place."

"The only one I know anything about is the old cowboy they've said they have seen. His name is Charlie Wilcom or that's what us locals believe. He'd been a ranch hand on the place when the ranch was built by the original owners. They had a big cattle ranch back then. Several thousand acres. From what I hear, he was trampled during a stampede during one of the rides. The description I've heard from the family fits the small picture we have of some cowboys here in the library."

"Can I see it?"

"Certainly." The woman led her down a long hallway toward the back of the library where several old pictures and artifacts were displayed. "This is a picture of several cowboys from that timeframe in front of the court house." She pointed to one man standing on the edge of the group.

Rose leaned closer to the picture to bring the man's face more into focus. *Interesting looking man.* When she stepped back, the librarian smiled. "I wonder if the family knows this picture is here?"

"You know, I'm not sure."

"I will definitely share this information with them as well as the other things I've learned." She held out her hand to shake the woman's. "I appreciate you helping me with this."

"It's nice to see young people interested in the local history. Not too many are these days." The woman tilted her head to the side. "If you don't mind me asking, where are you from? You don't have a Texas accent."

"I'm from New York. I came down here for work and met a local guy. His family owns the ranch, and I told him I would look into some of the history while I was in town today."

"Ah, yes. The Young family. Nice people." She laughed. "Those boys have been an important part of this town for a long time. They are all grown now and having families of their own."

"Yes, they are."

The clock in the corner bonged loudly on the hour. "Well, time for this old woman to go home. It was very nice talking to you, miss?"

"My name is Rose Gilbert."

"Pretty name."

"Thank you."

"I hope to see you around here again some time."

"I appreciate it, but probably not. I will be going back to New York in a few days."

"Ah." She shook her head. "Pity." A smile lifted the corners of her mouth. "But then again, one of those Young brothers might catch your eye and you'll stay for a while."

Rose couldn't help but smile in return. "Maybe." She moved back to the table to gather her bag. "Thank you again for helping me. I appreciate your time."

"Not a problem, young lady."

"Goodbye."

"Goodbye."

Rose went through the doors as the woman locked it behind her. She glanced first one way and then the other down the streets of Bandera. The town itself seemed quaint, somewhere she would enjoy wiling the day away beneath a nice tree as she sipped something cold. For tonight though, she needed to do some more digging. The information she'd received on Thunder Ridge was intriguing, and she hoped the family would be interested in it.

After she approached her car and slid inside, she took a moment to check her cell phone for messages. She'd had it shut off in the library. Once the cell phone tower connected, she got a beep indicating a message.

When she punched the voicemail button, she heard her boss's voice. "Rose, I need you to call me immediately. The county is pushing for results on those samples. They want them as soon as possible."

The county? Somehow, I don't think it's the county wanting these yesterday.

She started her car to head back out to the ranch. It was almost supper time. Her job was finished. Everything had been collected. *Now what am I going to do? Going home seemed so distant a few days ago, but now that it is looming in the next couple of days, I don't want to go.*

The samples she retrieved from the Marshall's place sat in her bag in the backseat. The old man seemed suspicious of her when she'd approached their door earlier, which was understandable. They probably didn't have too many visitors from New York around this area.

She also got a glimpse of Jessica. The girl was gorgeous with long dark hair, big brown eyes, a nice straight smile, and thin. She could have been a model. Rose didn't like the feelings stirring in her heart when she thought of the girl with Joseph. Not knowing whether the two had ever had sex for sure, all she could imagine was the two of them twisted up in the sheets having wild, passionate sex. Her stomach knotted at the thought.

Barbed wire fences zipped past her window as she drove down the paved road. Out here in Hill Country, there wasn't much other than ranches scattered here and there, junipers, Bluebonnets, cattle, and an occasional sighting of wildlife. Life here would be simple—work hard, love harder, and cherish the little things. In New York, her life was hustle and bustle from the time the sun came up until she went to bed exhausted at the end of the day. You never really had time for yourself.

She pulled into the driveway of the ranch, pressed in the code, and watched as the gate slowly slid open. Longhorn cattle grazed in the distance, periodically bawling to each other.

Sound.

It was something that was part of everyday life in New York.

In Texas silence surrounded a person. Other than the buzz of a bee, rattle of horse tack, or the laughter of a child, the quiet solitude of the ranch enveloped you in the simplicity of ranch life.

When she pulled her car up in front of her little cabin, she pushed the gearshift into park and shut it off. Her gaze focused on the bushes in front of her car. *How in the hell am I going to get out of this with work? I'm afraid they are going to rig the results, causing the ranch to have to close so the drilling company can buy it cheap. If I tell the family the truth, they are going to think I had something to do with this.*

Her phone jiggled and as she looked at the screen, she cussed under her breath. It was her boss. She had to answer it or he would continue to call.

"Hello?"

"Did you get my message earlier, Rose? I need those samples."

"I have them done. I will FedEx them tomorrow. You should have them the day after."

"Excellent. The investors…uh, I mean the county is harping on me for those samples."

Fucker. He's totally in on this. "I understand."

"Good, good. I will talk to you as soon as I have the samples. Plan on being back in the office Monday morning."

"Yes, sir."

He hung up the phone without even a goodbye. *This whole thing just stinks of corruption. But what the hell do I do about it?*

* * * *

Joey watched Rose walk through the door to the main lodge, drinking her in as she came closer. She was a beautiful woman and one he'd been growing fonder of as they spent more time together.

If he really thought about it, he could say she'd become an important part of his life in a very short time, but what to do with that information.

"Joseph."

"Hey, babe." He pulled out the chair next to him for her. "We should be eating soon, but as a guest you can go on up there if you want."

"No, it's okay. I'll wait for you and the family."

"How was your day, Rose?" Nina asked from across the table.

All eyes focused on Rose. "It's was productive. I found out some interesting information on the ranch for you all, concerning the ghosts and the history."

"Oh?" His dad picked up his glass of iced tea and took a drink. "Tell us about it."

"I was going to wait until everyone was served their meal, but I got some great stuff at the library and the librarian even gave me some insight." He retrieved a glass for her, sitting it down by her plate. "Thank you, Joseph."

"You're welcome."

"Anyway, as you probably know, this was a working cattle ranch for over one hundred years. The whole area was part of the Western Trail, and this property was a big contributor to that."

The few guests staying on the ranch had filled their plates and took their seats.

Nina indicated the family could be served now as everyone climbed to their feet to get their food.

Once the group took their places again, Rose continued. "There was also a brothel here, in this very house. The rooms upstairs were used for the ladies of the night while the main rooms were used for gambling, drinking, and so forth." She glanced at him. "Didn't you say you have a cowboy ghost here?"

"Yeah."

"From my research, I got a name and I also saw a picture of him in the library. I haven't seen him myself so I don't know for sure it's the same guy, but the librarian seemed pretty sure. His name is Charlie Wilcom. From what I understand, he was trampled in a stampede during a trail drive. He'd been a ranch hand on the place from the time of the original owners."

"What else did you learn, Rose?" His mom tilted her head to the side as she focused on what Rose was saying.

"There wasn't anything concrete on anyone being killed during the brothel days. I did get some information saying there were three women and some children that had come west to meet up with one's husband who had come earlier. There was apparently a fire here that took their lives in a house that had sat back on the hill behind the cabins. It was a grandmother, mother, and sister along with several children."

"Wow." Jeff had set his fork down and was completely intrigued by the information. "That's more than any of us have been able to find out for quite some time. Good job, Rose."

"Thank you. Actually, it was a lot of fun. I love history and this gave me the opportunity to explore it. I appreciate you all letting me dig into the past of your property." Joey reached under the table, squeezing her fingers to let her know he was proud of her. "I wish I would have been able to learn more."

The conversation changed directions as everyone began eating in earnest.

James cleared his throat. "Joey, did you get that mare broke today?"

"Yes, Dad, I did or partially broke. I got the halter on her. She seems very sweet, and I think she'll make a great addition to the herd."

"Excellent."

Chatter flowed around him as he thought about the ranch, his job, and what the whole thing meant to him. His talk with Jacob earlier had bothered him all day and he hadn't been able to get it out of his thoughts. If something were to happen with this place, his whole life would change. Several of his brothers would have the same problem without a secondary career to fall back on. True, most of the wives in the group had a career that would sustain them for a while, but their long term future would be in jeopardy.

Jeremiah spoke up. "I've done some more digging on the drilling in the area and I think we need to seriously contemplate having our property tested for oil."

James turned to face him. "I'm not sure that is a good idea, Jeremiah. I know it could possibly set the entire family up for life, but it might also be detrimental to our setup."

"I've been in contact with the drilling company. If we give them the okay, they'll be out within days to test."

"This needs to be a family vote, I think," Nina added. "We don't want one person to go off on a tangent that might hurt the family as a whole."

"I agree, sweetheart, but let's leave this discussion for another time when we don't have guests close by. This is a family topic, not something we need to be sharing with the public."

"Of course, James."

Topics turned to the cattle operation, what would be happening for the next week, and guests that would be arriving to stay.

Darkness descended over the ranch as dinner concluded and everyone went their separate ways for the evening. He knew his brothers would be off with their spouses and kids, his parents would retire to their private quarters for the night, and Rose would probably go to her cabin. *Would it be better to follow her in a bit or go with her now?* Thoughts of being with her this evening had been driving him nuts all day. He wanted her, there was no doubt about that, but maybe he should let her be tonight. They had been together almost constantly since they'd met. Some might misconstrue that to be a relationship, which it wasn't. Relationships were for people who lived near each other, could be together all the time, and had thoughts of the future, right?

Right.

"Joseph?"

"Yeah?" She ran her fingernail down the front of his shirt along the row of buttons.

"Are you going to join me tonight in my cabin?"

"Do you want me to?"

Lust sparkled in her gaze. "Of course."

"I thought maybe you might want to have a night to yourself."

"I'd much rather have you."

"I aim to please."

"That you do, cowboy, that you do." She took his hand in hers, guiding him out the door of the lodge, down the path to her cabin, and then through the door after she'd unlocked it.

When she closed it behind them, he pushed her against the dark panel of wood behind her as he brought their mouths close, but not touching. Their breaths mingle as he stared into her eyes. Desire raged in her gaze, dilating her pupils until they almost encompassed her entire iris. Her breasts were crushed against his chest. One knee parted her thighs. Her heat scorched his leg were it rested against her center.

With one wrist in each hand, he kept her pinned to the door. His heart hammered in his chest, pounding against his ribs. He brushed his lips against hers in a slow, tempting taste, barely resisting crushing their mouths together in a frantic meeting.

His hard-on felt like it was drilling a hole in his pants. Desperate need clawed at his insides to be buried inside her sweet heat soon. "I need you, Rose."

"Take me. Make me yours."

Unable to resist her pull, he took what he desired more than anything in the world right at this moment.

He picked her up, so she could wrap her legs around his waist, and moved toward the big bed next to the wall. When he released her from his hold, she slid down his body in an unhurried move that drove him crazy.

Her top came off with a tug of the material over her head, revealing her naked breasts to his gaze. She hadn't worn a bra today under her tank top. Her nipples were already pulled into tight little nubs that just begged for his mouth. He cupped each one in his palms before rubbing his thumbs over the tips.

A groan spilled from her lips as she tilted her head back on her shoulders. "More."

He took the right one in his mouth, sucking hard as she grabbed his head and held it to her breast. The mounds were perfect, pink tipped, and deliciously hard against his tongue.

Her knees gave out as she sank to the bed and laid back. He followed her down, loving how she moaned softly and tossed her head from side to side. *So responsive.*

He moved his left hand to the button at her waist, flicking it open with his fingers so he could touch her. The heat of her pussy scalded him as he slipped his fingers beneath her panties. She was hot enough to sear him.

One finger glanced off her clit, bringing her hips surging up. "God, Joseph. Please touch me."

Gathering a little bit of her juices on his fingers, he rubbed her clit in a circular motion first fast, and then slow. He wanted to drive her wild.

She tossed her head as she moaned deep in her throat, her fists pulling at the bedspread beneath her hands.

He moved around so he could pull off her jeans and panties, exposing her to his gaze. The sight of her open, glistening pussy drove him beyond crazy. The need to taste her had him panting like he'd run a hundred miles at top speed.

Two fingers spread her open for him as she offered herself. Her clit was puffy and pink, peeking out from under the hood. Cream glittered from where it had been smeared on her thighs. The tangy scent of her passion reached his nose as he settled himself between her thighs. He loved the smell of her. With his nose buried in the crease of her thigh, he inhaled, taking it in so he could savor it knowing he put it there.

He flattened his tongue, licking her from slit to clit in one long stroke. The taste of her drove his desire higher.

Her hips bucked against the mattress as she groaned softly. "Yes, please, more."

Using only the tip of his tongue, he flicked the nub of her clit quickly, knowing he would drive her to an explosive climax quickly if he continued.

He slowed the battering of her senses, letting her come down a little before he drove her back up. Over and over he brought her almost to the edge without letting her come.

"Joseph, God please let me come. I hurt so bad," she begged softly.

"Since you asked so nicely, I will give you what you want." He flicked her clit several times as he drove two fingers into her grasping channel. The walls of her vagina clamped down on him as she exploded in a climax, shouting his name loud enough they probably heard her at the main lodge. He didn't care.

He quickly shed his clothes, dropping everything to the floor in a pile after he toed off his boots, and then settled himself between her parted thighs. The head of his cock bumped at her opening before he slowly pushed inside of her hot center. "You feel so good."

"Fuck me, Joseph. Please."

Thrust after thrust, he drove his cock deeper. The heat of her burned him clear to his soul, imprinting her there. He would never be the same after Rose.

Chapter Thirteen

Two days later she stood near her car where it was parked next to her cabin, touching the front of Joseph's shirt with her fingertips. Letting go had never been so hard.

"You'll call me when you get home?" he asked in a whisper.

"Yes, but it will be late this evening."

"It's okay. I'm usually up late."

She leaned her forehead against his chin. The thought of leaving him, this place, was like a hot poker to her chest. Her heart ached with the need to stay, but that wasn't possible. Her life, her job, her family—everything was in New York. "I wish I didn't have to go." She choked back a small sob, trying desperately not to cry.

He kissed her head and pulled her tighter to his chest. "I'm gonna miss you."

"Don't. Please. This is hard enough."

"It's true."

Tears came in earnest as she desperately tried to wipe them away with the back of her hand.

He took over the chore, kissing them away with his lips.

"Maybe I can come and visit sometime."

"Sure. You're welcome anytime. I hope you know that."

"Thank you." She sniffed, wiped her nose, and stepped out of his embrace. "I'd better go. My plane leaves in three hours."

He opened her car door and waited for her to slide inside before shutting it behind her. She rolled the window down so she could touch him one last time. "Thank you for everything."

"No thanks needed."

"Yes, there is. You've made the time here very special for me, Joseph, and I will always treasure it, more than you know."

He cleared his throat before he said, "I've grown rather fond of you, Rose. I hope you know that."

She pressed her lips together as she tried to fight the smile that wanted to break free. It didn't work. "I really like you too, Joseph." *Say it! Tell him you love him!* "You have a special place in my heart."

"You should probably go."

"Yeah, I should."

"Safe travels."

"I'll call you later tonight."

He tapped on the top of her car as she rolled the window back up and waved a little goodbye.

The long driveway out of Thunder Ridge seemed like it took forever, but not long enough as fresh tears scalded her cheeks, blurring her vision as she tried to blink them away. God help her she did love him. *How in the hell can I fall in love with someone in such a short time?* "Easy when it's Joseph."

Her chest ached with the need to go back, to tell him she loved him, and see where things might go from there, but she couldn't. Everything she had was in New York, and walking away from it all for someone she wasn't even sure returned her feelings seemed ludicrous.

"No. Right now, I have things I need to do in New York. I'll keep in touch with him and we'll see what happens. If he cares about me like I care about him, then things will work out. I have to believe that."

The drive to San Antonio dragged on forever, or so it seemed. She returned her rental car, took the bus to the terminal, and then checked-in for her flight. A quick glance at the watch on her wrist told her she had about two hours before flight time. After she went through security, she slowly walked down the long terminal searching for her gate. When she found it, she spied an empty seat next to the wall, opened her phone, and checked her messages.

None.

Her life seemed so empty now without Joseph and his family. What did she have to look forward to? Her parents lived across town from her in New York, Brandt had moved out of their apartment when she'd broken up with him, instead of her needing her father to pick up her stuff, and she didn't have a ton of friends.

Work would be waiting when she got there in the morning. She needed to report first thing to her boss on her trip to Texas. The samples she'd sent should already been through processing, and she wanted to see the reports.

Deciding to try to get her mind off the here and now, she opened Mesa's book she had in her carryon. It was the same one she'd started on the trip out there, but now it seemed so much more real to her. She could see the faces of the cowboys as if they stood in front of her. Funny thing was, they all looked like the Young brothers.

Before she knew it, it was time to board. The flight home would be several hours, including a plane change. She hoped she could sleep. It would help her forget for a short time anyway.

When she took her seat onboard, she really hoped she wouldn't get some talkative older woman next to her. Talking wasn't high on her list right now. She just wanted to be left alone to wallow in her misery.

A woman about seventy asked, "Is this seat taken?"

"No, ma'am."

"Thank you."

"You're welcome." Rose tried to look out the window to discourage talk, but it didn't work.

"What beautiful hair you have."

Rose glanced back at the woman and said, "Thank you."

She smiled before sliding her purse under the seat in front of her. "Are you headed home?"

"Yes, ma'am."

"Did you have a good time in Texas?"

"Yes, I did. I spent the better part of it out in Bandera at a fantastic guest ranch."

"Which one? I live out near Bandera."

"It's called Thunder Ridge."

The older woman clapped her hands. "Oh yes! Nina, James, and the boys. I've been friends with that family for a number of years. My husband used to go with them to auctions all the time."

"Do you own a ranch as well?"

"Oh no. My Bill just loved cattle, horses, and ranching, but we never owned one ourselves. Too much work for us old folks, but James and the boys were very kind to him, letting him go with them for the experience. We had a small piece of property not far from Thunder Ridge. The boys always came over to look in on us. They are such nice boys."

"Yes, they are. Are you headed to New York for vacation?"

"No. I'm going to visit our daughter and her family. My husband died last year and I haven't seen them since the funeral."

"Oh, I'm so sorry."

"Thank you, honey, but its fine." She reached over and patted Rose's hand. "We had sixty-three years together and he lived a long, happy life. He was eighty-nine when he passed."

The plane pushed back from the gate and was in the air before she knew it. "Where does your daughter live?"

"Not far from Central Park on West 77th Street."

"That's amazing. I have a small apartment on 78th Street."

"Really? How fascinating. Such a small world."

"When were you in New York last?"

"It's been several years. Bill wasn't well for quite a while before he died, so we couldn't travel much. My daughter would come to us." The flight attendant came by to ask what they wanted to drink and to hand them peanuts. "So not like it used to be. I can remember when you used to get a full meal on these flights."

Rose smiled. She really liked this woman. "I hope you have a good time with your daughter and family."

"I'm sure I will. It's been pretty quiet at home without my husband and with no other family in the area, I don't get out much. I'm thinking of selling the property and moving to New York to be close to her."

"I'm sure you would be able to sell it easy enough."

"Maybe. It's a nice place with some good pasture land even though it hasn't been ranched for a very long time. Nina's boys would come over and hay it for us every year."

"Sounds nice."

"Listen to me. I've talked your ear off for over thirty minutes and I don't even know your name."

"It's Rose."

"What a beautiful name and it fits you perfectly." Her eyes twinkled as she glanced over at Rose. "Mine is Milly Henderson."

"It's nice to meet you, Milly."

The flight attendant brought their drinks and they settled into their seats to enjoy them.

"So which of the boys were you spending time with while you were at Thunder Ridge? I believe the only one not attached these days is Joseph."

Rose grinned. "It was Joseph."

"I should have guessed, even if he is the only one available these days. He's a sweet boy. Very handsome too."

"Yes, he is."

"Just my observation, but he would be a nice catch for you, Rose."

She chuckled. "I'm sure he would, Milly, but I don't live in the area, remember?"

"Yes, but wouldn't you like to live in Texas? It's a beautiful place."

"It is, that's true."

"I can see you've thought about it."

"I won't lie, yes I have, but there are things that would prevent that from happening. One is my job."

"What do you do?"

"I'm a microbiologist."

"Well now, that's an impressive title."

"Yes it is, but it also makes working outside of a larger area a bit more difficult."

"Tell me what you love about New York?"

"It's great having everything so close by, shops, restaurants, museums, or the park. You can get anywhere pretty quickly by subway. The seasons are seasons with snow in the winter, warm summers, beautiful falls, and green springs. My family is close."

"Now what do you not like about the city?"

"The crime. Too many people. Noise. Close neighbors. Smog. Traffic."

"What was the one thing you noticed about Bandera that made an impression on you?"

"The quiet. I could hear myself think out there." She inhaled a long, deep breath and glanced out the window as she rubbed the spot above her heart. It ached right now, something fierce. When she turned back toward Milly, she could see the woman's piercing gaze on her.

"You left there a few hours ago. What do you miss already about being there?"

With her lips pressed together, she fought the tears burning her eyes before she whispered, "Joseph."

"I think you should tell him when you get home. He probably would like to hear that."

"Maybe." She exhaled a big breath. "I don't think he feels the same."

"I bet he does. I've known those boys a long time, him especially since he's the baby, and I can tell you one thing about him, when he falls, he will fall hard. He loves his family fiercely and when he picks the one girl he wants to spend the rest of his life with, he won't let go."

"Thank you, Milly. I'll think about it. There is something I need to clear up with my employer before I can think to my future, and it might affect things with him on a really bad level."

"I'm sure everything will work out as it should. Keep the faith, Rose. If it is meant to be, it will be."

* * * *

Jeremiah handed Joseph the report they had received from the county that morning. The whole family was gathered in the main lodge to discuss what this meant. He read the words, his heart sinking into the pit of his stomach like a rock.

Conversation buzzed around him like a thousand bees on the trail of pollen in the spring. The one thing that registered in his brain was the mention of Rose.

"She had to know. She's the one who got the samples. They probably told her days ago, even before she left." Jeff paced the room, running his hands through his hair. "I knew we shouldn't have trusted her here."

"Jeff, you can't blame Rose. She was doing her job," Nina said from her spot on the couch.

"Bullshit! I bet they called her the minute they got the results, and she hit the pavement on the run so she wouldn't have to fuckin' face any of us."

Rose had left five days before to return to New York and it had seemed very fast. One minute she was there and the next she had to go back.

All eyes focused on him. "What? I didn't know anything about this."

"You brought her here, Joey."

"She would have come even if I hadn't. It was her job to get the samples. I didn't know about it before she came out, but she would have anyway."

"You were sleepin' with her," Joel replied. "You didn't suspect anything?"

"Like fuckin' her had anything to do with her job, Joel."

James raised his voice so he could be heard above the rapidly rising noise. "Enough, boys. That kind of talk is best not done here in front of the women and children."

"I, for one, want to know what's going on, Dad," Mesa said as she kept a close eye on her kids running around the couches. "This affects all of us."

"She's right." Peyton, Paige, Callie, Candace, Mandy, Samantha, and Terri all nodded in agreement. "We are all in this together, whatever happens."

"James, what exactly does the paper say?" Nina climbed to her feet and approached Joey where he stood still holding the paper tightly in his hands. "Let me see." He watched his mother scan the document before she turned to face the group. "Apparently there was a complaint filed with the county saying our water has been contaminated and they brought in an out-of-state lab to test the samples. The county has been given information on the water and soil samples taken from our property and tested by Reece Labs in New York City." She turned and looked him in the eye. "I'm assuming this is the company that Rose worked for?"

"I guess. I never asked."

She placed her hand on his cheek. "This is not your fault, Joey."

"I know."

She glanced down at the paper again. "This letter says that due to the quality of the water on the property and potential health hazards to the guests and people living on the land, we either have to totally redig the wells to check for contamination, or we have to close the ranch."

The room exploded in a roar of sound. Everyone talked at once, shouting over each other to try to be heard. He didn't understand what this all meant, but he knew it wasn't good. Needing a moment to himself, he turned on his heels, walked through the dining area and went outside. The sun beat down on his head as he walked toward the barn, his solace in the crazy world Thunder Ridge had become.

What the hell would they do if they had to close and move? This was their home, the only home they had ever known. True, his parents had enough money they could move somewhere else, but if the property was uninhabitable they wouldn't be able to sell it for anything.

He approached the stall where they kept the wheelbarrow and shovel for cleaning out the stalls. Hard work never hurt anyone and it would give him a task to do to keep his mind numb. *Mom and Dad will figure this out, they have to.*

After several minutes, he heard boots on the dirt coming toward him. When he turned to see who it was, he wasn't surprised to see Jeremiah. "What's up?"

"I figured this is where you would be."

"I needed to get out of there. It was getting crazy."

"Yeah, I know. It's not much better yet. Jeff is yelling, of course, and everyone else is trying to figure out what we do from here."

"What do we do, Jeremiah? If the water is bad, we won't be able to sell if we have to close."

"No, we won't. I'm in contact with the oil drilling company though. They still want to drill."

"At what cost though? Are they willing to buy the property with bad water?"

"They don't care about water quality, but the big thing is, the property isn't worth near as much in mineral rights this way."

"So we have to sell the rights for a lot less than we would have before? Less money to divide up."

"Yeah."

"This stinks to high heaven."

"I know."

"What do we do for now?"

"We have to close the ranch until we see what our options are. I don't think we have a lot though."

"It doesn't sound like it."

"I'm going to tell everyone that I've set up a meeting with the drilling company for one week from today to see what their offer is. Until then, we can't take guests."

Joey exhaled as he rested on the shovel's handle. Work still needed to be done. Animals still needed to be cared for. The world still went around even if it seemed their lives were about to get turned upside down. "Want me to come back in?"

"Yeah. You need to be there too."

"All right. I'll be there in a sec. Let me dump this load."

"Things will work out. We'll be okay as long as we stick together as a family."

"I know."

"See you in a minute."

Joey watched his brother's slumped shoulders as he headed back toward the main lodge. His gut told him something wasn't right, but he didn't know what and for some reason it had a lot to do with Rose.

All eyes focused on him when he came through the door. Being the center of attention made him uncomfortable on his best day. Today, it felt even worse.

He took a seat at one of the tables as Jeremiah took a spot at the head of the room under where Clyde, Thunder Ridge's first longhorn bull, hung above the fireplace.

"All right. This is what I need to tell you all. Please, hold any questions until I'm done. Mission Drilling has been in contact with me again today. They want to come out to talk with us in a week, to give us some information on an offer for the property, I assume. Knowing what I know, their offer will be significantly less than what it was before for the drilling rights. With the water containments here on the property, we won't be able to sell as a working ranch any longer, if that's what we had thought to do. As it stands, we will have to shut down to guests until we figure out what we are doing. It's probably not even safe for any of us to be on the property."

"I'm not leaving. This is my home." His mom stood straight and tall as she stood by the window with her arms across her chest. "I don't care what they say. I'm not leaving."

Several of the others shouted their agreement.

"Besides, most of us have our own homes on this land. If the water in Thunder Ridge's wells are bad, ours probably are too." Jason had his arm around his wife as Peyton snuggled into his embrace.

"Then I think we are all in this together. We will stay until we can at least talk to the drilling company next week, and then we came make a decision," Jeremiah concluded as he pulled Callie up next to him. "You all know I will do everything I can to secure a future for this family, even if it takes every dime I have in the bank. I will never turn my back on any one of you."

All of them disbursed to take care of the things needing their attention as Joey wandered back to the barn. He wanted to call Rose, but he knew right now she was probably at work. Did she really know about this before she went home? Did she have anything to do with this whole thing? If so, why didn't she warn them?

His thoughts went back to their time spent together on the ranch making love, getting to know each other, and the way she'd wiggled herself into his heart before he'd ever even realized she was there.

For the last several days, they'd talk almost every night. She'd call when she got home from work and she would tell him about her day, how her cat was, what the weather was like in New York. Then she would tell him how much she missed his touch, his kiss, and the way he would make love to her.

He'd even made tentative plans to go out to see her in a couple of months, but now, he didn't know what to do. Had he misplaced his trust in her?

His cell phone jingled in his pocket. When he pulled it out, he saw it was Rose on the phone. Not sure what to say to her at this point in time, he let it go to voicemail, and returned it to his pocket. Maybe later he would call her back. Right now, he didn't know what to think. His heart told him to trust in his feelings for her, but his head said she had something to do with this mess. Love wasn't always the right answer.

Chapter Fourteen

One solid week. She hadn't talk to him in seven days and here she was on a damned plane to Texas.

The reports had come in on Thunder Ridge's samples over a week ago and rather than try to explain anything to the family, she'd tried talking to Joseph. He wouldn't answer her calls. Message after message had been left on his voicemail without one single return call.

This was bad, but good.

After she'd seen the report, she'd taken the last week to run her own tests on the samples. When she'd taken them in the first place, her gut feeling had been to keep a second set of samples in her own gear, and not send them to the lab with the others. Now she had the proof in her hands that the first set of samples had been tampered with.

She'd rerun the second set of tubes several times to check her results and every time they had come back clean, so why did the first ones contain contaminants? The only answer was tampering. The property had to appear so uninhabitable the family would have to sell to the drilling company at rock bottom prices.

The plane touched down in San Antonio minutes later. The second she had her bags in her hands, she was headed to the rental car company. Bandera was an hour drive. It would give her time to formulate her proof to present to the family. They had to believe her, they just had to.

What if they didn't? What if they all turned their backs on her, including Joseph?

I'll have to make sure he knows I love him and that I did what I could to protect him and his family.

Her hands gripped the steering wheel tight enough her knuckles turned white. "They have to understand."

Unable to stand the quiet, she turned on the radio, tapping her fingers along with the tune as she tried to focus on something besides how shit could hit the fan and she would be out on her ass if this didn't go down like she wanted it to. She'd quit her job in New York the instant she was positive the results had been tampered with, given notice at her apartment, and packed a bag to head back to Texas.

God help her if this blew up in her face.

When the gate slid open as she pulled up to it she had to take a deep breath to calm her nerves. She drove down the long driveway and parked her car, still unsure of how to approach this. She wanted to find Joseph first and explain things to him before they got the family together to try to sort this out, but other than the barn, she wasn't sure where he might be.

Deciding to go into the main lodge first since she'd checked the clock on the dash and found it to be almost supper time, she figured they might be there. She really didn't want to barge in on the meal, so she went around to the front of the lodge to go in through the main room.

As she pushed open the door, she heard voices.

"Mr. Young, this is a very lucrative offer we are making you on the drilling rights."

"It's a lot lower than the original offer you had shown Jeremiah."

"Yes it is, but because of the contaminated water, you won't be able to use the property for anything else before, during, or after drilling has ceased. The property is basically worthless without finding oil, which we aren't even positive exists."

Shit, am I too late? She moved inside quietly, not to alert anyone she was there. She wanted to hear what they were saying before she made her presence known.

"We understand that, Mr. Pritchard, but this is our home. This is all we know, and to ask us to basically give it up is not something we are willing to do without a fair price so we can move on and find something else."

"Dad, I think we should have the water and soil tested ourselves," Jonathan suggested.

Mr. Pritchard turned purple. "That would take weeks."

"We aren't in any hurry."

"As you know by the reports provided by Reece Labs out of New York your wells are contaminated with microorganisms that make your property uninhabitable. What we are proposing should make your family very comfortable for the foreseeable future."

Rose couldn't keep quiet any longer. She had the proof in her hands that what they said wasn't true. "Excuse me."

Twenty sets of eyes turned to her.

"Rose?" Joseph came toward her. "What are you doing here?"

Jeff stormed toward her. "Get her the fuck out of here! She doesn't belong on this property."

"Please, let me explain."

"There is nothing to explain." He grabbed her arm to shove her out, but Joseph stepped between them.

"Let her talk."

"I had to come, Joseph. I had to set things straight."

"What are you talking about?"

"The reports. They're wrong. They've been tampered with. There is nothing wrong with your water or soil. It's as clean as it needs to be for your family to continue to operate Thunder Ridge."

"What? How do you know?"

"I reran the tests myself after I saw the report. I've been trying to call you for a week to explain, but you wouldn't answer the phone."

His gaze dropped before coming back to hers. "I'm sorry."

"It's okay. I understand. I'm sure your whole family was upset."

"Yeah."

Mr. Pritchard stopped next to her. "Who the hell are you to question those results?"

"I am or was the lead microbiologist on this project. I suspected tampering so I did the tests myself on a second set of samples I kept on my person until I got them to the lab." She turned to Nina and James. "There is a connection between this drilling company and my former boss, Mr. Albright. He is a cousin of the owners of the drilling company. I believe they've been manipulating not just your family but several others as well so they could buy oil rich property for next to nothing, and make millions drilling it, leaving the land dry before they sell it." She held the report out to James. "As you can see, this shows normal flora in the water and soil. I've filed this new report with the county already, so you should be receiving a new letter from them in the next day or two, showing your property to be fine for habitation by your family and guests."

James stepped forward and took the report from her fingers. After he scanned it for several moments, he turned to their guest. "Mr. Pritchard, I believe you need to leave our property and take your proposal with you. Tell your partners or whoever you represent that Thunder Ridge is not for sale now nor will it ever be to the likes of you."

Rose grinned as the man huffed, grabbed his briefcase, and headed for the door.

Joseph had moved off by himself to her left as the conversation flowed around her. There were several questions from Nina and James as well as Jeremiah on what she'd learned and what they needed to do now to fix this whole thing.

Right now, she just wanted to talk to Joseph.

Nina moved to her side and said, "Rose, I hope you plan to stay here on Thunder Ridge at least for a day or two so we can properly thank you. It sounds as if you gave up your job for us, and for that we need to take care of you for at least a couple of days."

"I would appreciate it, Nina. I don't have a place to stay yet. I flew here as soon as I could in hopes of making things right."

Nina hugged her tight. "You did well, sweetie. I think you need to talk to Joey though. He's been torn about this whole thing."

She nodded as she stepped back. "I will right now."

When she made her way toward him, he wouldn't meet her gaze.

"Joseph?"

He glanced up and she was taken aback by the sadness in his eyes. She didn't know how to respond to that. Why was he sad? Had she hurt him in some way she wasn't aware of?

"Can we talk?"

"I suppose."

Nina shoved a key into her hand. "Here. Go on out to your cabin. It's quiet there."

Rose took his hand in hers and led him out the door. They walked in silence out to the cabin she'd used before, her heart pounding in her chest the whole way there. She wasn't sure what to say or do to fix whatever the problem was.

After she opened the door, she led him inside and shut it behind her before she turned to face him.

He stood in the middle of the room, his hands shoved in his pockets like he didn't know what to do with them. He looked so good to her, she wanted to eat him up, but first she needed him to hold her more than anything.

She took a step toward him. He looked up, meeting her gaze.

"I'm sorry, Joseph."

"You saved my family. You saved the ranch."

She shook her head. "I didn't do anything other than what was right. I should have said something before when I had suspicions. I'd done some research on the drilling company when Jeremiah mentioned them, but I didn't say anything. I found out then there was a connection between my boss and the drilling company."

He took a couple of steps toward her before shoving his hands in the hair by her ears so he could cradle her head. "God, I missed you."

The words were music to her ears. "I missed you too."

"Did you really quit your job?"

"Yes."

"What are you gonna do now?"

"I don't know. I thought I'd stay here for a few weeks. I kind of like being on the ranch."

"What about work? Your family? Your place in New York?"

"My parents are watching my apartment for now. I've already given them notice that I'm moving."

He frowned. "Where are you moving to?"

"I thought I'd find a place in San Antonio or something."

"Here?"

"Yeah, that is if you won't be too upset to have me close by."

"Baby, I'm more than happy to have you here. The closer the better." He pulled her to his chest. "In fact, this isn't quite close enough for me."

His whispered words against her mouth were a balm to her soul. He wanted her.

"Joseph?"

"Yeah?"

She took in a big breath and then said, "I love you."

When he leaned back, she wasn't sure he would answer until a grin spread across his lips. "I love you too."

"You do?"

"Yeah. I've been going crazy without you here. I've been impossible to live with not talking to you this past week. My brothers almost threw me out."

She giggled. "I can totally see them doing that."

"I really do love you."

Unable to wait any longer to have her mouth against his, she reached behind his head and brought his lips closer. "I need you to kiss me, but I want you to know I love you so much, my heart is full. You are everything to me."

He brought their mouths together in a slow, sensuous kiss before he let go of his passion and crushed their mouths together. Need exploded low in her belly. Her body trembled with everything running through her, wanting to be closer to this man. How, why, where she'd fallen in love with him, she didn't know, but she had. It was part of her, he was part of her, and she didn't want it to ever end. He'd become her life.

His hands skimmed down her back, pulling her in closer as he gripped her butt in his palms.

His lips moved along her jaw, nipping at the flesh until he reached her ear. His hot breath scalded her as he whispered, "I love you so much."

Tears pricked behind her eyelids. She never thought she'd hear those words from someone like him.

Milly's comment came back to her with sharp clarity. When he fell, he would fall hard, and love with all his heart. Apparently, he fallen for her, Rose, the strange woman from New York who'd blown into his life one early spring day.

"Why are you crying?" he asked, looking down into her eyes.

"Because I realize that you are a special man and for you to say you love me means everything."

"Darlin', I think I fell in love with you the day I met you. Seeing you sitting at the diner in the sun, your hair burning like it had a life of its own, sketching something as if you were in your own little world, and then you looked up and caught my gaze across the room. My heart literally stopped at that moment before it began to beat again with only a rhythm you and I can hear."

"You weren't alone."

"No, I wasn't, but right then, nothing else seemed to matter except finding out who you were."

"I saw you sitting there with your friend and the first thing I wondered about was if you were a real cowboy. You looked the part, but one never knows. Then when you stopped to talk to me, it was like my world centered."

"Don't we sound like two sappy lovebirds?"

"I know, right?"

His deep, rich laughter sent shivers along her arms.

"What do we do now, Joseph?"

"I'm not sure, darlin'. I've never been in love before."

"Me either, really. I thought I was, but it was nothing like this. These feelings for you are so raw, so powerful, I'm not sure how to handle it. The last week without you has been something I don't want to do again. I couldn't eat, I couldn't sleep, and trying to work seemed impossible."

He ran his fingertips down her cheek. "Stay here with me. We will figure out something. I need you with me."

She glanced down at his chest and then back up. "You know eventually you will have to marry me."

His lips lifted in a small grin. "Oh, I plan to, darlin'. I didn't want to ask without a ring and doin' it up proper."

"Will you make love to me now?"

"Right now?"

"Yeah. I've missed having you surround me."

"It would be my pleasure, darlin'."

She didn't waste any time getting her clothes off so she could feel him, the friction of his skin against hers, the rough rub of the hair on his body over the softer surface of her own, and the ridges of his muscles as she ran her hands over his chest.

He lifted her in his arms, carrying her to the big bed in the corner before laying her down on the wedding-ring quilt. It seemed fitting now.

His clothes fell away from his body as he stripped down to nothing. She'd almost forgotten how magnificent he was to look at, to touch, and to love.

She raised her arms, welcoming him into her embrace.

When his skin finally touched hers, she sighed. She'd come home.

Epilogue

Joseph spread the quilt out on the sand near the pond. The late summer evening seemed the perfect time. They'd been together for several months now and he realized every day how much he loved Rose and wanted her in his life. It had seemed strange at first, how she'd become such a part of him when he hadn't been looking for love at all.

She'd given up her life in New York and moved to Bandera right after the water incident. He'd even gone to New York with her to help her move her stuff. That had been an adventure and a half since he'd never been there. Life there seemed way too fast for a cowboy like him.

"Joseph?" She held out her hand after she placed the picnic basket on the quilt, guiding him to her side. "Are you hungry?"

"I'm starving."

She laughed. "Aren't you always?"

"Probably." He sank down on the quilt as she took out the chicken, potato salad, bottle of wine, and dessert from the basket. "Did you cook this?"

"Yes, sir. I've been taking lessons in Southern cooking from the women in the kitchen."

"It looks great, Rose."

She handed him a plate, holding it back so she could kiss him before he took it. The little sneaky grin on her lips made him wonder what she might be up to. He was the one with the surprise.

They talked during the meal about several things including the ranch, the fantastic number of guests they'd had this year, how the horses were doing in the heat of the summer, and her latest project at her job.

She'd been hired as a research microbiologist for a large lab in San Antonio at a really good salary. "It's a great project. I can't go into details, but I think the outcome will be something very important to the development of some new drugs."

"As long as you enjoy what you're doin', nothing else matters."

"Oh, I do. I'm excited to see where this all goes."

She slid the fork between her lips, making him think about those lips around his cock. Had it only been this morning since they'd made love? He couldn't seem to get enough of her.

"Stop looking at me like that, Joseph."

"Like what?"

"Like you want to eat me alive."

"I do." He set his plate down and crawled toward her. "You have no idea how much I want you."

"Here?"

"Yep. It was one of the first places we made love after we met. Seems kind of fitting, don't you think?"

She glanced around as a smile spread across her lips.

He leaned in and kissed her softly on the lips. He wanted to do something before they made love again. This time they would be bound together for the rest of their lives. "Rose?" He sat back on his heels, taking her hand in his.

A frown turned down the corners of her mouth. "Yes?"

"I need to ask you somethin'. It's important, so if you want to take some time to think about it, that's okay." He reached into the front pocket of his jeans. "I love you with all my heart. You've become the most important thing in my life. I know you've given up a ton to be here with me in Texas, and you have no idea how much that means to me." She gasped as he opened the small box in his hands. "Will you marry me?"

"Oh, Joseph," she whispered. "Of course, I'll marry you. I love you."

He took out the ring he'd spent the last few months saving for and slid it onto her left ring finger. "From my heart and soul this cowboy's promise is to love you forever."

She launched herself into his arms and they fell back against the quilt, laughing. She pelted him with kisses all over his face until she finally reached his mouth. When she paused, he looked up into her gorgeous green eyes and saw what he'd always wanted but never realized it until he'd found it.

Love.

The End

About the Author

Sandy Sullivan is a romance author, who, when not writing, spends her time with her husband Shaun on their farm in middle Tennessee. She loves to ride her horses, play with their dogs and relax on the porch, enjoying the rolling hills of her home south of Nashville. Country music is a passion of hers and she loves to listen to it while she writes.

She is an avid reader of romance novels and enjoys reading Nora Roberts, Jude Deveraux and Susan Wiggs. Finding new authors and delving into something different helps feed the need for literature. A registered nurse by education, she loves to help people and spread the enjoyment of romance to those around her with her novels. She loves cowboys so you'll find many of her novels have sexy men in tight jeans and cowboy boots.

Sandy's website
www.romancestorytime.com

Other books by Sandy
Love Me Once, Love Me Twice (Montana Cowboys 1)
Before the Night is Over (Montana Cowboys 2)
Two for the Price of One (Montana Cowboys 3)
Difficult Choices (Montana Cowboys 4)
Doctor Me Up (Montana Cowboys 5)
Stakin' His Claim
Country Minded Cougar
Meet Me in the Barn
Taming the Cougar
Trouble With a Cowboy
Gotta Love a Cowboy
Make Mine a Cowboy (Cowboy Dreamin' 1)
Healing a Cowboy's Heart (Cowboy Dreamin' 2)
For the Love of a Cowboy (Cowboy Dreamin' 3)
Tempted by the Cowboy (Cowboy Dreamin' 4)
Forever Kind of Cowboy (Cowboy Dreamin' 5)
Kiss Me, Cowboy (Cowboy Dreamin' 6)
A Cowboy and a Country Song (Cowboy Dreamin' 7)
A Cowboy of My Own (Cowboy Dreamin' 8)
Falling Hard (Eight Second Ride Book 1)
Loving Hard (Eight Second Ride Book 2)

www.ingramcontent.com/pod-product-compliance
Lightning Source LLC
Chambersburg PA
CBHW070807190726
48292CB00006B/1915